ROBERT LUDLUM

ROBERT LUDLUM

THE PARSIFAL MOSAIC

THE AQUITAINE PROGRESSION

The Parsifal Mosaic
First published 1982
Copyright © Robert Ludlum 1982

The Aquitaine Progression
First published 1984
Copyright © Robert Ludlum 1984

This omnibus edition first published exclusively for
Marks & Spencer plc in 1988 by Grafton Books,
a Division of the Collins Publishing Group,
8 Grafton Street, London W1X 3LA

ISBN 0 261 10091 2

Typeset by Centracet, Cambridge

Printed by The Bath Press, Bath

CONTENTS

THE PARSIFAL
MOSAIC

For Dolores and Charles Ryducha.
Two of the finest people I've
ever known. From a grateful
brother.

Na Zdrowie!

BOOK I

1

The cold rays of the moon streaked down from the night sky, bouncing off the rolling surf, which burst into suspended sprays of white where isolated waves crashed into the rocks of the shore-line. This stretch of beach between the towering boulders of the Costa Brava was the execution ground. It had to be.

He could see her now. And hear her through the sounds of the sea and the breaking surf. She was running wildly, screaming hysterically: *'Pro Boha Živetto! Proc! Co to Dělás! Prestan! Proc! Proc!'*

Her blonde hair was caught in the moonlight, her racing silhouette given substance by the beam of a powerful light fifty yards behind her. She fell; the gap closed and a staccato burst of gunfire abruptly, insolently, split the night air, bullets exploding the sand and the wild grass all around her. She would be dead in a matter of seconds.

His love would be gone.

They were high on the hill overlooking the Moldau, the boats on the river ploughing the waters north and south, their wakes creating furrows. The curling smoke from the factories below diffused in the bright afternoon sky, obscuring the mountains in the distance; and Michael watched, wondering whether the winds above Prague would blow the smoke away so that he could see the mountains again. His head was on Jenna's lap, his long legs stretched out, touching the wicker basket she had packed with sandwiches and chilled wine. She sat on the grass, her back against the smooth bark of a birch tree, stroking his hair; then her fingers circled his face, gently outlining his lips and cheekbones.

'Mikhail, my darling, I was thinking. Those tweed jackets and dark trousers you wear, and that very proper English which must come from your very proper university, they will never remove the Havlicek from Havelock.'

'I don't think they were meant to. One's a uniform of sorts, and the other you kind of learn in self-defence.' He smiled, touching her hand. 'Besides, that university was a long time ago.'

'So much was a long time ago, wasn't it? Right down there.'

'It happened.'

'You were there, my poor darling.'

'It's history. I survived.'

'Many did not.'

The blonde woman rose, spinning in the sand, pulling at the wild grass, plunging to her right, for several seconds eluding the beam of light. She headed towards the dirt road above the beach, staying in darkness, crouching, lunging, using the cover of night and the patches of tall grass to conceal her body.

It won't do her any good, thought the tall man in the black sweater at his post between two trees above the road, above the terrible violence that was taking place below. He had looked down at her once before, not so very long ago. She had not been panicked then; she had been magnificent.

In the dark office he folded the curtain back slowly, carefully, his back pressed against the wall, his face inching towards the window. He could see her crossing the floodlit courtyard below, the tattoo of her high heels on the cobblestones echoing martially between the surrounding buildings. The guards were recessed in shadows – rigid marionettes in their Soviet style uniforms. Heads turned, directing appreciative glances at the figure striding confidently towards the iron gate in the centre of the iron fence which enclosed the stone compound, the core of Prague's secret police. The thoughts behind the glances were clear: this was no mere secretary working overtime, this was a privileged kurva *who took dictation on a commissar's couch till all hours of the night.* Natsztrzency chlopak!*

But others, too, were watching – from other darkened windows. One break in her confident stride, one instant of hesitation, and a phone would be picked up, detention orders issued to the gate. Embarrassments, of course, were to be avoided where commissars were concerned, but not if there appeared to be substance behind suspicions. Everything was appearance.

There was no break, no hesitation. She was carrying it off . . . carrying it out! They had done it! Suddenly he felt a jolt of pain in his chest, and he knew what it was: fear. Pure, raw, sickening fear. He was remembering – memories within memories. As he watched her, his mind went back to a city of rubble, to the terrible sounds of mass execution. Lidice. And a child – one of many children – scurrying through billowing grey, smoking debris, carrying messages, with pockets full of plastic explosives. One break, one hesitation then . . . history.

She reached the gate. An obsequious guard was permitted to leer. She was magnificent. God, he loved her!

She had reached the shoulder of the road, legs and arms working furiously, digging into the sand and dirt, clawing for survival. With no wild grass to conceal her, the beam of light would find her, and the end would come quickly.

He watched, suspending emotion, erasing pain, a human litmus paper accepting impressions without comment. He had to . . . professionally. He had learned the truth; the stretch of beach on the Costa Brava was confirmation of her guilt, proof of her crimes. The hysterical woman below was a killer, an agent for the infamous *Voennaya Kontr Razvedka*, the savage branch of the Soviet KGB that spawned terrorism everywhere. That was the undeniable truth. He had seen it all, talked to Washington from Madrid. The rendezvous that night had been ordered by Moscow; VKR Field Officer Jenna Karras was to deliver a schedule of assassination to a faction of the Baader Meinhof at an isolated beach, called Montebello, north of the town of Blanes. That was the truth.

The truth bound him to another truth, an obligation of his profession. Those who betrayed the living and brokered death had to die. No matter who, no matter . . . Michael Havelock had made the decision, and it was irrevocable. He had set the last phase of the trap himself, for the death of the woman who briefly had given him more happiness than any other person on earth. His love was a killer; to permit her to live would mean the killing of hundreds, perhaps thousands. Irrevocable.

What Moscow did not know was that Langley had broken the VKR codes. He himself had sent the last transmission to a boat half a mile off the Costa Brava shoreline. *KGB confirmation. Officer contact compromised by US Intelligence. Schedules false. Eliminate.* The codes were virtually unbreakable; elimination was guaranteed.

She was rising now! It was going to *happen*! The woman about to die *was* his love. They had held each other and there had been quiet talk of a lifetime together, of children, of peace and the splendid comfort of being one . . . together. Once he had believed it all but it was not to be.

They were in bed, her head on his chest, her soft blonde hair falling across her face. He brushed it aside, lifting up the strands that concealed her eyes, and laughed.

'You're hiding,' he said.

'It seems we're always hiding.' She smiled sadly. 'Except when we wish to be seen by people who should see us. We do nothing that we simply want to. Everything is calculated, Mikhail. Regimented. We live in a movable prison.'

'It hasn't been that long, and it won't last for ever.'

'I suppose not. One day they'll find they don't need us, don't want us any longer, perhaps. Will they let us go, do you think? Or will we disappear?'

'Washington's not Prague. Or Moscow. We'll walk out of our movable prison, me with a gold watch, you with some kind of silent decoration with your papers.'

'Are you sure? We know a great deal. Too much, perhaps.'

'Our protection lies in what we do know. What I know. They'll always wonder: Did he write it down somewhere? Take care, watch him, be good to him . . . It's not unusual, really. We'll walk out.'

'Always protection,' she said, tracing his eyebrows. 'You never forget, do you? The early days, the terrible days.'

'History. I've forgotten.'

'What will we do?'

'Live. I love you.'

'Do you think we'll have children? Watch them going off to school; hold them, scold them. Go to hockey ball games.'

'Football . . . or baseball. Not hockey ball. Yes, I hope so.'

'What will you do, Mikhail?'

'Teach, I suppose. At a college somewhere. I've a couple of starched degrees that say I'm qualified. We'll be happy, I know that. I'm counting on it.'

'What will you teach?'

He looked at her, touching her face, then his eyes wandered up to the shabby ceiling in the run-down hotel room. 'History,' he said. And then he reached for her, taking her in his arms.

The beam of light swung across the darkness. It caught her, a bird on fire, trying to rise, trapped by the light that was her darkness. The gunshots followed – terrorists' gunfire for a terrorist. The woman arched backwards, the first bullets penetrating the base of her spine, her blonde hair cascading behind her. Three shots then came separately, with finality, a marksman's eye delivering a marksman's score; they entered the back of her neck and her skull, propelling her forward over the mound of dirt and sand, her fingers clawing the earth, her blood-streaked face mercifully concealed. A final spasm, and all movement stopped.

His love was dead – for some part of love was part of whatever they were. He had done what he had to do, just as she had done the same. Each was right, each wrong, ultimately so terribly wrong. He closed his eyes, feeling the unwanted dampness.

What will you do, Mikhail?

Teach, I suppose. At a college somewhere . . .

What will you teach?

History . . .

It was all history now. Remembrances of things too painful. Let it be cold history, as the early days were history. They cannot be a part of me any longer. She cannot be a part of me, if she ever was, even in her pretence. Yet I will keep a promise, not to her now, but to myself. I am finished. I shall disappear into another life, a new life. I shall go somewhere, teach somewhere. Illuminate the lessons of futility.

He heard the voices and opened his eyes. Below, the Baader-Meinhof killers had reached the condemned woman, sprawled in death, clutching the ground that was her execution place . . . geopolitically preordained. Had she really been so magnificent a liar? Yes, she had been, for he had seen the truth. Even in her eyes, he had seen it.

The two executioners bent down to grab the corpse and drag it away, to consign her once-graceful body to fire or the deep. He would not interfere; the evidence would have to be reflected upon later when the trap was revealed, another lesson taught. Futility . . . geopolitically required.

A gust of wind suddenly whipped across the open beach; the killers braced themselves, their feet slipping in the sand. One of them raised a hand in an unsuccessful attempt to keep on his visored fishing cap; it blew away, rolling towards the dune that formed the shoulder of the road. He released his hold on the corpse and ran after it. Havelock watched as he came closer. There was something about him . . . about the face? No, it was the hair, seen clearly in the moonlight. It was wavy and dark, but not completely dark; there was a streak of white above his forehead, a sudden intrusion that could not be missed. He had seen that head of hair, seen that face somewhere before. But where? There were so many memories. Files analysed, photographs studied . . . contacts, sources, enemies. Where was this man from? *KGB?* The dreaded *Voennaya?* A splinter faction paid by Moscow when not drawing contingency funds from a CIA station chief in Lisbon?

It did not matter. The deadly puppets and the vulnerable pawns no longer concerned Michael Havelock . . . nor Mikhail Havlicek, for that matter. He would route a cable to Washington through the embassy in Madrid in the morning. He was finished, he had nothing more to give. Whatever his superiors wanted in the way of debriefing he would permit. Even going to a clinic; he simply did not care. But they would have no more of his life.

That was history. It had ended on an isolated beach called Montebello on the Costa Brava.

2

Time was the true narcotic for pain. Either the pain disappeared when it ran its course or a person learned to live with it. Havelock understood this, knowing that at this moment something of both applied. The pain had not disappeared, but there was less of it; there were periods when the memories were dulled, the scar tissue sensitive only when prodded. And travelling helped; he had forgotten what it was like to cope with the complexities facing the tourist.

'If you'll note, sir, it's printed here on your ticket. "Subject to change without notice".'

'Where?'

'Down here.'

'I can't read it.'

'I can.'

'You've memorized it.'

'I'm familiar with it, sir.'

And the immigration lines. Followed by customs inspections. The intolerable preceded by the impossible; men and women who countered their own boredom by slamming rubber stamps and savagely attacking defenceless zips planned for planned obsolescence.

There was no question about it, he was spoiled. His previous life had its difficulties and its risks, but they had not included the perils that confront the traveller at every turn. In his other life, on the other hand, whenever he got to where he was going, there was the movable prison. No, not exactly. There were appointments to keep, sources to contact, informers to pay. Too often at night, in shadows, far away from seeing or being seen. Now there was none of that. There hadn't been for nearly eight weeks. He walked in daylight, as he was walking now down the Damrak in Amsterdam towards the American Express office. He wondered whether the cable would be there. If it was, it would signify the beginning of something. A concrete beginning.

Employment. A job. Strange how the unexpected was so often connected to the routine. It had been three months since that night on the Costa Brava, two months and five days since the end of his debriefing and formal separation from the government. He had gone up to Washington from the clinic in Virginia where he had spent twelve days under therapy. (Whatever they had expected to find wasn't there; he could have told them that. He didn't care any more; couldn't they understand?) He had emerged from the doors of the State Department at 4 o'clock in the afternoon a free man . . . also an unemployed, unpensioned citizen with resources hardly of a magnitude to be considered an annuity. It had occurred to him as he stood there on the pavement that some time in the future a job had to be found, a job where he could illuminate the lessons of . . . the lessons. But not for a while;

for a while he would do the minimum required of a functioning human being.

He would travel, revisit all those places he had never really visited . . . in the sunlight. He would read . . . reread, actually . . . not codes and schedules and dossiers, but all those books he had not read since university. If he was going to illuminate anything for anybody, he had to relearn so much that he had forgotten.

But if there was one thing on his mind at 4 o'clock that afternoon, it was a fine dinner. After twelve days' treatment, with various chemicals and a restricted diet, he had ached at the thought of a good meal. He had been about to return to his hotel for a shower and a change of clothes when an accommodating taxi drove down C Street, the sun bouncing off its windows, obscuring any occupants. It stopped at the kerb in front of him – at the behest of his signal, Michael had assumed. Instead, a passenger carrying an attaché case stepped out quickly, a harried man late for an appointment, fumbling for his wallet. At first neither Havelock nor the passenger recognized each other; Michael's thoughts were on a restaurant, the other's on paying the driver.

'Havelock?' the passenger had inquired suddenly, adjusting his glasses. 'It *is* you, isn't it, Michael?'

'Harry? Harry Lewis?'

'You've got it. How are you, M.H.?'

Lewis was one of the few people he ever saw – and he rarely saw Harry – who called him by his initials. It was a minor legacy from university – he and Lewis had both been at Princeton. Michael had gone into government, Lewis into academia. Dr Harry Lewis was chairman of the political science department at a small, prestigious university in New England, travelling down to DC now and then for consultation chores at State. They had run into each other several times when both were in Washington.

'Fine. Still picking up *per diems*, Harry?'

'A lot fewer than before. Someone taught you people how to read evaluation reports from our more esoteric graduate schools.'

'Good Christ, I'm being replaced by a beard in blue jeans with funny cigarettes.'

The bespectacled professor was stunned. 'You're kidding. You're *out*? I thought you were in for life!'

'The opposite, Harry. Life began between five and seven minutes ago when I wrote my final signature. And in a couple of hours I'm going to be faced with the first dinner bill in years that I can't take out of contingency funds.'

'What are you going to do, Michael?'

'No thoughts. Don't want any for a while.'

The academician paused, taking his change from the taxi driver, then spoke rapidly. 'Listen, I'm late for upstairs, but I'm in town overnight. Since I'm on *per diem*, let me pay for the dinner. Where are you staying? I may have an idea.'

No government *per diem* in the civilized world could have paid for the dinner that night two months and five days ago, but Harry Lewis did have an idea. They had been friends once; they became friends again, and

Havelock found it easier to talk with a person who was at least vaguely aware of the work he had done for the government rather than with someone who knew nothing about it. It was always difficult to explain that something could not be explained; Lewis understood. One thing led to another, which in turn led to Harry's idea.

'Have you ever given any thought to getting back to a campus?'

Michael smiled. 'How would "constantly" sound?'

'I know, I know,' Lewis pressed, suspecting sarcasm. 'You fellows – "spooks", I assume, is the term – get all kinds of offers from the multinationals at damn good money; I'm aware of that. But, M.H., you were one of the best. Your dissertation was picked up by a dozen university presses; you even had your own seminars. Your academic record coupled with your years at State – most of which I realize you can't go into specifically – could make you very attractive to a university administration. We're always saying: "Let's find someone who's been there, not just a theoretician." Damn it, Michael, I think you're *it*. Now, I know the money's not . . .'

'Harry, you misunderstood. I meant it. I *constantly* think about getting back.'

It was Harry Lewis's turn to smile. 'Then I've got another idea.'

A week later Havelock had flown to Boston and driven from there to the brick-and-ivy-and-white-birch campus on the outskirts of Concord, New Hampshire. He spent four days with Harry Lewis and his wife, wandering around, attending various lectures and seminars, and meeting those of the faculty and administration whose support Harry thought likely to be helpful. Michael's opinions had been sought 'casually' over coffee, drinks and dinners; men and women had looked at him as if they considered him a promising candidate. Lewis had done his missionary work well.

At the end of the fourth day Harry announced at lunch: 'They like you!'

'Why not?' his wife had interrupted. 'He's damned likeable.'

'They're quite excited, actually. It's what I said the other day, M.H. You've *been there*. Sixteen years with the State Department kind of makes you special.'

'And?'

'There's the annual administration-trustees conference coming up in eight weeks. That's when the supply-and-demand quotients are studied. Horseflesh. I think you'll be offered a job. Where can I reach you?'

'I'll be travelling. I'll call you.'

He had called Harry from London two days ago. The conference was still in progress, but Lewis thought there would be an answer any moment.

'Cable me Am Ex, Amsterdam,' Michael had said. 'And thanks, Harry.'

He saw the glass doors of the American Express office swing open just ahead. A couple emerged, the man awkwardly balancing the shoulder straps of two cameras while counting money. Havelock stopped, wondering for a moment whether he really wanted to go inside. If the cable was there it would contain either a rejection or an offer. If a rejection he would simply go on wandering – and there was a certain comfort in that; the floating passivity of not planning had become something of value to him. If an offer, what then? Was he ready for it? Was he prepared to make a decision? Not the kind of decision one made in the field, which had to be instinctive if one was to survive, but rather a decision to commit oneself. Was he capable of a commitment? Where were yesterday's commitments?

He took a deep breath, consciously putting one foot in front of the other, and approached the glass doors.

Position available Visiting Professor of Government for period of two years. Associate status pending mutual acceptance at the end of this time. Initial salary Twenty-seven. Will need your reply within ten days. Don't keep me holding my breath. Ever, Harry.

Michael folded the cable and put it in his jacket pocket; he did not go back to the counter to write out his own cable to Harry Lewis, Concord, New Hampshire, USA. It would come later. It was enough for the moment to be wanted, to know there was a beginning. It would take several days to absorb the knowledge of his own legitimacy, perhaps several days thereafter to come to grips with it. For in the legitimacy was the possibility of commitment; there was no real beginning without it.

He walked out onto the Damrak, breathing the cold air of Amsterdam, feeling the damp chill floating up from the canal. The sun was setting, briefly blocked by a low-flying cloud, it re-emerged, an orange globe hurling its rays through the intercepting vapours. It reminded Havelock of an ocean dawn on the coast of Spain – on the Costa Brava. He had stayed there all night – that night, until the sun had forced itself up over the horizon, firing the mists above the water. He had gone down to the shoulder of the road, to the sand and the dirt . . .

Don't think about it. That was another life.

Two months and five days ago by sheer chance Harry Lewis had stepped out of a taxi and started to change the world for an old friend. Now, two months and five days later, the change was there to be taken. He would take it, Michael knew, but something was missing: change should be shared, and there was no one to share it with, no one to say, *What will you teach?*

The black-coated waiter at the *Dikker en Thijs* ground the lip of the flaming brandy glass into the silver receptacle of sugar; the ingredients would follow for the *café Jamaïque*. It was a ridiculous indulgence, and probably a waste of very good liqueur, but Harry Lewis had insisted they each have one that night in Washington. He would repeat the ritual in Amsterdam.

'Thank you, Harry,' he said silently once the waiter had left, raising his glass to his invisible companion. It was better, after all, not to be completely alone.

He could both feel the approaching presence of a man and see an enlarging darkness in the corner of his eye. A figure dressed in a conservative, pin-striped suit was threading his way through the shadows and the candlelight towards his booth. Havelock angled the glass and raised his eyes to the face. The man's name was George; he was the CIA station chief in Amsterdam. They had worked together before, not always pleasantly, but professionally.

'That's one way to announce your arrival here,' he said, glancing at the waiter's tray table, the silver sugar bowl still on it. 'May I sit down?'

'My pleasure. How are you, George?'

'I've been better,' said the CIA man, sliding across the seat opposite Michael.

'Sorry to hear that. Care for a drink?'

'That depends.'

'On what?'

'Whether I'll stay long enough.'

'Aren't we cryptic,' said Havelock. 'But then you're probably still working.'

'I wasn't aware the hours were that clear cut.'

'No, I guess they're not. Am I the reason, George?'

'At the moment maybe. I'm surprised to see you here. I heard you retired.'

'You heard correctly.'

'Then why are you here?'

'Why not? I'm travelling. I like Amsterdam. You could say I'm spending a lot of accumulated severance pay visiting all those places I rarely got to see in the daytime.'

'You could *say* it, but that doesn't mean I believe it.'

'Believe, George. It's the truth.'

'No screen?' His curious eyes were levelled at Michael. 'I can find out, you know.'

'None at all. I'm out, finished, temporarily unemployed. If you check, that's what you'll learn, but I don't think you have to waste channel time to Langley. I'm sure the centrex codes have been altered where I was concerned, all sources and informers in Amsterdam alerted as to my status. I'm off-limits, George. Anyone dealing with me is asking for a short term payroll and quite possibly an obscure funeral.'

'Those are the *surface* facts,' agreed the CIA man.

'They're the only facts. Don't bother looking for anything else; you won't find it.'

'All right, say I believe you. You're travelling, spending your severance pay.' The agent paused as he leaned forward. 'It's going to run out.'

'What is?'

'The severance pay.'

'Inevitably. At which time I expect I'll find gainful employment. As a matter of fact, this afternoon . . .'

'Why wait? I might be able to help you there.'

'No, you can't, George. I haven't anything to sell.'

'Sure you do. Expertise. A consultant's fee paid out of contingency. No name, no records, untraceable.'

'If you're running a test, you're doing it badly.'

'No test. I'm willing to pay in order to look better than I am. I wouldn't admit that if I were testing you.'

'You might, but you'd be a damn fool. It's third-rate entrapment; it's so awkward you've probably done it for real. None of us wants those contingency funds scrutinized too carefully, do we?'

'I may not be in your league, but I'm not third-rate. I need help. We need help.'

'That's better. You're appealing to my ego. Much better.'

'How about it, Michael? The KGB's all over The Hague. We don't know who they've bought or how far up they go. NATO's compromised.'

'We're all compromised, George, and I *can't* help. Because I don't think it makes any difference. We get to square five, pushing them back to four, so they jump over us to seven. Then we buy our way to eight; they block us at nine, and no one reaches square ten. Everyone nods pensively and starts all over again. In the meantime we lament our losses and extol the body count, never admitting that it doesn't make any difference.'

'That's a crock of shit! We're not going to be buried by *anyone*.'

'Yes, we are, George. All of us. By "children yet unborn and unbegot". Unless they're smarter than we are, which may very well be the case. Christ, I hope so.'

'What the hell are you talking about?'

'"The purple atomic testament of bleeding war."'

'*What!*'

'History, George. Let's have that drink.'

'No, thanks.' The CIA station chief slid back across the seat. 'And I think you've had enough,' he added, standing up.

'Not yet.'

'Go to hell, Havelock.' The intelligence officer started to turn away.

'George.'

'What?'

'You missed. I was about to say something about this afternoon, but you didn't let me finish.'

'So what?'

'So you knew what it was I was going to tell you. When did you intercept the cable? Around noon?'

'Go to hell.'

Michael watched as the CIA man returned to his table across the room. He had been dining alone, but Havelock knew he was not alone. Within three minutes, the judgement was confirmed. George signed his bill – bad form – and walked rapidly through the entrance arch into the lobby. Forty-five seconds later a youngish man from a table on the right side of the room got up to leave, leading a bewildered lady by the elbow. A minute passed and two men who had been in a booth on the left side rose as one and started for the arch. Through the candlelight, Michael focused on the plates in the booth. Both were piled with food. Bad form.

They had been following him, watching him, employing intercepts. Why? Why couldn't they leave him alone?

So much for Amsterdam.

The noonday sun in Paris was a blinding yellow, its quivering rays bouncing off the Seine below the bridge. Havelock reached the mid-point of the Pont Royal, his small hotel only blocks away on the rue du Bac, the route he followed being the most logical one from the Louvre. He knew it was important not to deviate, not to let whoever it was behind him think he suspected his or her presence. He had spotted the taxi, the same taxi, as it made two swift turns in traffic to keep him in sight. Whoever was directing the driver was good; the taxi had stopped for less than two or three seconds at a corner, and then had sped away in the opposite direction. Which meant that whoever was following him was not on foot on the crowded bridge. If contact was the objective, crowds were helpful, and a bridge even more so. People stopped on bridges over the Seine simply to stare absently down at the water; they had been doing so for centuries. Conversations could be had unobtrusively. If contact was the objective, and not surveillance alone.

Michael stopped, leaned against the chest-high stone wall that served as a railing, and lit a cigarette. If anyone were watching him, it would seem as if he were looking at the *bateau mouche* about to pass under the bridge, waving his hand casually at the passengers below. But he was not; pretending to shield his eyes from the sun, he concentrated on the tall figure approaching on his right.

He could distinguish the grey Homburg, the velvet collared overcoat and the glistening black patent leather shoes; they were enough. The man was the essence of Parisian wealth and elegance, his attendance coveted in the salons of the rich all over Europe. His name was Gravet. He was considered the most knowledgeable critic of classical art in Paris, which meant the Continent, and only those who had to knew that he also sold far more than his critical expertise.

He stopped at the railing seven feet to the right of Havelock and adjusted his velvet collar.

'I thought it was you. I've been following you since the rue Barnard.' He spoke just loud enough to be heard.

'I know. What do you want?'

'The question is, What do *you* want? Why are you in Paris? We were given to understand you were no longer active. Quite frankly, you were to be avoided.'

'And reported immediately if I made contact, right?'

'Naturally.'

'But you're reversing the process. You've approached me. That's a little foolish, isn't it?'

'A minor risk worth taking,' said Gravet, standing erect and glancing about. 'We go back a long time, Michael. I don't for a moment believe you're in Paris for your cultural rebirth.'

'Neither do I. Who said I was?'

'You were at the Louvre for exactly twenty-seven minutes. Too short a time to absorb anything, and too long to relieve yourself. But quite plausible for meeting someone inside a dark, crowded exhibition room, say at the far end of the third floor.'

Havelock began to laugh. 'Listen, Gravet – '

'Don't look at me, please! Keep your eyes on the water.'

'I went to the Roman collection on the mezzanine. It was filled with a tour from Provence, so I left.'

'You were always quick, I admired you for it. And now this ominous alarm. "He's no longer active. Avoid him."'

'It happens to be true.'

'Whatever this new cover of yours,' continued Gravet quickly, dusting the elbows of his coat, 'for it to be so radical can only mean you're among very distinguished company. I'm also a broker with a wide range of information. The more distinguished my clients, the better I like it.'

'Sorry, I'm not buying. Avoid me.'

'Don't be preposterous. You don't know what I have to offer. Incredible things are happening everywhere. Allies become enemies, enemies allies. The Persian Gulf is on fire and all Africa moves in contradictory circles; the Warsaw block has lacerations you know nothing about, and Washington pursues a dozen counterproductive strategies matched only by the unbeliev- able stupidity of the Soviets. I could give you chapter and verse on *their* recent follies. Don't dismiss me, Michael. Pay me. You'll climb even higher.'

'Why should I want to climb higher when I've climbed out?'

'Again preposterous. You're a relatively young man; they wouldn't let you go.'

'They can watch me, but they can't hold me. All I had to do was give up a pension somewhere down the road.'

'Too simple. You all have bank accounts in remote but accessible places, everyone knows that. Diverted contingency funds, covert payments made to non-existent sources, fees for sudden departures or suddenly required papers. You had your retirement covered by the time you were thirty-five.'

'You're exaggerating both my talents and my financial security,' said Havelock, smiling.

'Or perhaps a rather lengthy document,' the Frenchman went on, as though Michael had not interrupted, 'detailing certain covert procedures – solutions, you might say – that must, perforce, describe specific events and personnel. Placed beyond reach of those most interested.'

Havelock stopped smiling, but Gravet persisted. 'Naturally, that's not *financial* security, but it adds to a sense of well-being, doesn't it?'

'You're wasting your time, I'm not in the market. If you've got something of value, you'll get your price. You know whom to deal with.'

'They're frightened second-raters. None of them has your direct avenues to the . . . centres of determination, shall we say.'

'I don't have them any more.'

'I don't believe you. You're the only man here in Europe who talks directly with Anthony Matthias.'

'Leave him out of it. And for your information I haven't spoken with him in months.' Suddenly Havelock stood up and turned openly to the French- man. 'Let's find a taxi and go to the embassy. I know some people over there. I'll introduce you to a first-level attaché and tell him you're selling but I don't have either the resources or the interest to get involved. Okay?'

'You know I can't do that! And, *please* – ' Gravet did not have to finish the request.

'All right, all right,' Michael returned to the wall with the river below. 'Then give me a number or a place of contact. I'll phone it in and you can listen.'

'Why are you doing this? Why the charade?'

'Because it's not a charade. As you said, we go back a long time. I'll do you the favour and maybe you'll be convinced. Maybe you'll convince others, if they ask. Even if they don't ask. How about it?'

The Frenchman pivoted his head while leaning over the wall and stared at Havelock. 'No, thank you, Michael. As with all manner of Satans, better a second-rater I've dealt with than one I haven't. For what it's worth, I think I believe you. You would not reveal a source like me, even to a first-level attaché. I'm down too deep, too respectable; you might need me. Yes, I do believe you.'

'Make my life easier. Don't keep it a secret.'

'What about your opposite numbers in the KGB? Will they be convinced?'

'I'm sure of it. Their moles probably got word to Dzerzhinsky Square before I signed the separation papers.'

'They'll suspect a ploy.'

'All the more reason to leave me alone. Why bite into poisoned bait?'

'They have chemicals. You all have chemicals.'

'I can't tell them anything they don't know, and what I do know has already been changed. That's the funny thing: my enemies have nothing to fear from me. The few names they might learn aren't worth the price. There'd be reprisals.'

'You've inflicted a great many wounds. There's pride, vengeance; it's the human condition.'

'Not applicable. In those areas we're even, and again I'm not worth it because there's no practical result. Nobody kills unless there's a reason. None of us wants to be responsible for the fallout. Crazy, isn't it? Almost Victorian. When we're finished, we're out. Maybe we'll all get together in a large black strategy room in hell and have a few drinks, but while we're here, we're out. That's the irony, the futility, Gravet. When we're out we don't care any more. We don't have any reason to hate. Or to kill.'

'Nicely phrased, my friend. You've obviously thought about these things.'

'I've had a lot of time recently.'

'And there are those who are extremely *interested* in your recent observations, your conclusions – your role in life, as it were. But then it's to be expected. They're such a manic-depressive people. Morose, then jubilant; one minute filled with violence, the next with songs of the earth and sadness. And often quite paranoid; the darker aspects of classicism. I think. The slashing diagonals of Delacroix in a multi-racial national psyche, so far-reaching, so contradictory. So suspicious . . . so Soviet.'

Havelock stopped breathing; he returned Gravet's stare. 'Why did you do it?'

'There was no harm. Had I learned otherwise, who knows what I should have told them? But since I *do* believe you, I explain why I had to test you.'

'Moscow thinks I'm still in?'

'I shall render the judgement that you are not. Whether they accept it or not is another matter.'

'Why won't they?' asked Havelock, his eyes on the water below.

'I have no idea. I shall miss you, Michael. You were always civilized. Difficult but civilized. Then again, you're not a native-born American, are you? You're really European.'

'I'm American,' said Havelock quietly. 'Really.'

'You've done well by its cause, I'll say that. If you change your mind – or it's changed for you – get in touch with me. We can always do business.'

'It's not likely, but thanks.'

'That's not an outright rejection, either.'

'I'm being polite.'

'Civilized. *Au 'voir*, Mikhail . . . I prefer the name you were born with.'

Havelock turned his head slowly and watched Gravet walk with studied grace down the pavement of the Pont Royal towards the entrance of the bridge. This elegant Frenchman had accepted a blind interrogation from people he found loathsome; he must have been paid very well. But why?

The CIA was in Amsterdam and the CIA did not believe him. The KGB was in Paris and the KGB did not believe him either. *Why?*

So much for Paris. How far would they go to keep him under a microscope?

The Arethusa Delphi was one of those small hotels near the Syntagma Square in Athens that never let the traveller forget he was in Greece. The rooms were white on white on shimmering white. Walls, furniture and space-dividing ornamental beads were relieved only by garish oil paintings framed in plastic, depicting the antiquities: temples, forums and oracles romanticized by postcard artists. Each room had a pair of narrow double doors that opened onto a miniature balcony – large enough for two small chairs and a Lilliputian table – on which guests could have black morning coffee. Throughout the lobby and in the lifts one never escaped the rhythmic pounding of Greek folk music, strings and cymbals predominant.

Havelock led the olive-skinned woman out of the lift, and as the doors closed, both stood for a moment in mock anticipation. The music was gone; they sighed in relief.

'Zorba took a break.' Michael gestured to the left towards his room.

'The rest of the world must think we are nervous wrecks,' said the woman, laughing, touching her dark hair and smoothing out the long white dress that complemented her skin and accentuated her breasts and tapered body. Her English was heavily accented, cultivated on those Mediterranean islands that were the play-grounds of the Mediterranean rich. She was a high-priced courtesan whose favours were sought after by the princes of commerce and inheritance, a good-natured whore with a decent wit and a quick laugh; a woman who knew her time of pleasure-giving was limited. 'You rescued me,' she said, squeezing Havelock's arm as they walked down the corridor.

'I kidnapped you.'

'Often interchangeable terms,' she replied, laughing again.

It had been a little of both. Michael had run across a man on the Marathonos with whom he had worked in the Thermaïkós sector five years ago. A dinner party was being held that night at a café in Syntagma Square; since it was convenient, Havelock accepted the invitation. The woman was there, escorted by a considerably older, boorish businessman. The ouzo and *bazouki* had done their damage. Havelock and the woman had been seated next to each other; legs and hands touched, they exchanged looks – comparisons were obvious. Michael and the island courtesan had slipped away.

'I think I'm going to face an angry Athenian tomorrow,' said Havelock, opening the door of his room, leading the woman inside.

'Don't be silly,' she protested. 'He's not a gentleman. He's from Epidaurus; there are no gentlemen in Epidaurus. He's an ageing bull of a peasant who made money under the colonels. One of the nastier consequences of their regime.'

'When in Athens,' said Michael, going to the bureau where there was a bottle of prized Scotch and glasses, 'stay away from Epidaurians.' He poured drinks.

'Have you been to Athens often?'

'A few times.'

'What did you do? What line of work?'

'I bought things. Sold things.' Havelock carried the drinks back across the room. What he saw was what he wanted to see, although he had not expected to see it so quickly. The woman had removed her thin silk cape and draped it on a chair. She then proceeded to unbutton her gown from the top, the swelling of her breasts provocative, inviting.

'You didn't buy me,' she said, taking the drink with her free hand. 'I came of my own free will. *Efharistó*, Michael Havelock. Do I say your name right?'

'Very nicely.'

She touched his glass with hers, the sound gentle as she stepped closer. She reached up and placed her fingers on his lips, then his cheek, and finally around the back of his neck, drawing his face to hers. They kissed, her lips parting, the soft swollen flesh and moisture of her mouth arousing him; she pressed her body against his, pulling his left hand to the breast beneath her open gown. She leaned back, breathing deeply.

'Where is your bathroom? I'll get into something – less.'

'Over there.'

'Why don't *you*? Get into something less, that is. We'll meet at the bed. I'm really rather anxious. You're very, *very* attractive, and I'm – very anxious.'

She picked up her cape from the chair and walked casually, sensually towards the door beyond the bed. She went inside, glancing back over her shoulder, her eyes telling him things that probably were not true but were nevertheless exciting for the night. The practised whore, whatever her reasons were, would perform, and he wanted, needed, the release of that performance.

Michael stripped himself down to his pants, carried his drink to the bed and tore away the bedspread and the blanket. He climbed under the sheet and reached for a cigarette, turning his body away from the wall.

'*Dobriy vyecher, priyatyel.*'

At the sound of the deep male voice, Havelock spun round on the bed, instinctively reaching for a weapon – a weapon that was not there. Standing in the frame of the bathroom door was a balding man whose face Michael recognized from dozens of photographs going back years. He was from Moscow, one of the most powerful men in the Soviet KGB. In his hand was a gun, a large, black Graz-Burya automatic. There was a click; the hammer snapped into firing position.

3

'You may leave now,' said the Russian to the woman concealed behind him. She slid past, glancing at Havelock, then rushed to the door and let herself out.

'You're Rostov. Pyotr Rostov. Director of External Strategies. KGB Moscow.'

'Your face and name are also known to me. And your dossier.'

'You went to a lot of trouble, *priyatyel*,' said Michael, using the Russian word for friend, its meaning, however, denied by his cold delivery. He shook his head, trying to clear it of a sickening mist, the effect of the ouzo and Scotch. 'You could have stopped me on the street and invited me for a drink. You wouldn't have learned any more or any less, and very little that's valuable. Unless this is a *nyet gorya*.'

'No execution, Havlicek.'

'Havelock.'

'Son of Havlicek.'

'You'd do well not to remind me.'

'The gun is in my hand, not yours.' Rostov eased the hammer of his automatic back into its recess, the weapon still levelled at Michael's head. 'But that's in the distant past and has no connection with me. Your recent activities, however, are very much my concern. Our concern, if you will.'

'Then your moles aren't earning their money.'

'They file reports with irritating frequency, if only to justify it. But are they accurate?'

'If they told you I was finished, they were accurate.'

'"Finished"? A word with such finality, yet subject to interpretation, no? Finished with what? Finished with one phase, on to another?'

'Finished with anything that might concern you.'

'Out of sanction?' asked the KGB officer, rounding the border of the door frame and leaning against the wall, his Graz-Burya steady, levelled now at Havelock's throat. 'No longer employed by your government in any official capacity? It's difficult to accept. It must have been a blow to your dear friend Anthony Matthias.'

Michael studied the Russian's face, lowering his eyes to the huge gun aimed at him. 'A Frenchman mentioned Matthias the other day. I'll tell you what I told him, although I don't know why I should. You paid him to bring up Matthias's name.'

'Gravet? He despises us. He's civil to us only when he's walking through the galleries of the Kremlin or the Hermitage in Leningrad. He might tell us anything.'

'Why did you use him then?'

'Because he's fond of you. It's far easier to spot a lie when the liar is referring to someone he likes.'

'Then you believed him.'

'Or you convinced him and our people had no choice. Tell *me*. How did the brilliant and charismatic American Secretary of State react to his *krajan*'s resignation?'

'I have no idea, but I assume he understood. It's exactly what I told Gravet. I haven't seen Matthias or spoken to him for months., He's got enough problems; there's no reason why those of an old student should be added.'

'But you were far more than a student. His family knew your family in Prague. You became what you are – '

'*Were*,' interrupted Havelock.

' – because of *Anton* Matthias,' completed the Russian.

'It was a long time ago.'

Rostov was silent; he lowered his weapon slightly, then spoke. 'Very well, a long time ago. What about now? No one's irreplaceable, but you're a valuable man. Knowledgeable, productive.'

'Value and productivity are generally associated with commitment. I don't have it any more. Let's say I lost it.'

'Am I to infer you could be tempted?' The KGB man lowered the weapon farther. 'In the direction of another commitment?'

'You know better than that. Apart from personal revulsions that go back a couple of decades, we've got a mole or two in the Dzerzhinsky. I've no intention of being marked beyond salvage.'

'A hypocritical term. It implies compassion on the part of your executioners.'

'It says it.'

'Not well.' Rostov raised his automatic, thrusting it forward slowly. 'We have no such problems with verbal rationales. A traitor is a traitor. I could take you in, you know.'

'Not easily.' Michael remained still, his eyes locked with the Russian's. 'There are corridors and lifts, lobbies to pass through and streets to cross; there's risk. You could lose. Everything. Because I have nothing to lose but a cell at the Lubyanka.'

'A room, not a cell. We're not barbarians.'

'Sorry. A room. The same kind of room we have reserved in Virginia for someone like you – and we're both wasting money. When people like you and me get out with our heads still on, everything's altered. The Amytals and the Pentothals are invitations to traps.'

'There are still the moles.'

'I don't know who they are any more than you did when you were in the field – for those same reasons, those same rooms. None of us do on either side. We only know the current codes, words that take us where we have to go. Whatever ones I had are meaningless now.'

'In all sincerity, are you trying to persuade me a man of your experience is of no value to us?'

'I didn't say that,' interrupted Havelock. 'I'm simply suggesting that you weigh the risks. Also something else, which, frankly, you pulled off with reasonable success two years ago. We took a man of yours who was finished, ready for a farm in Grasnov. We got him out through Riga into Finland and flew him to a room in Fairfax, Virginia. He was injected with everything from scopolamine to triple Amytal, and we learned a lot. Strategies were aborted, whole networks restructured, confusion the order of the day. Then we learned something else: everything he told us was a lie. His head was programmed like a computer disc; valuable men became useless, time was lost. Supposing you got me to the Lubyanka – which I don't think you could – how do you know I'm not our answer to what you did to us?'

'Because you would not expose the possibility.' Rostov pulled the gun back, but did not lower it.

'Really? It strikes me as a pretty good blanket. I mean, you'd never know, would you? On the other hand, we've developed a serum – which I know nothing about except that it's injected at the base of the skull – that voids the programming. Something to do with neutralizing the *lobus occipitalis*, whatever the hell that is. From now on we can make the distinction.'

'Such an admission astonishes me.'

'Why should it? Perhaps I'm just saving our respective directors a lot of aggravation; that could be my objective. Or maybe none of it's true; maybe there is no serum, no protection, and I'm making it all up. That's also a possibility.'

The Russian smiled. '*Khvatit!* You *are* out! You amuse us both with logic that could serve you. You're on your way to that farm in your own Grasnov.'

'That's what I've been trying to tell you. Am I worth the risk?'

'Let's find out.' Suddenly the Russian flipped his automatic, barrel up; he slapped it back in the palm of his hand and threw it to Havelock on the bed. Michael's had shot up, catching the weapon in mid air.

'What am I supposed to do with this?'

'What do you want to do with it?'

'Nothing. Assuming the first three shells are rubber capsules filled with dye, I'd only soil your clothes.' Havelock pressed the magazine release; the clip dropped to the bed. 'It's not a very good test anyway. Suppose the firing pin works and this thing makes any noise at all, twenty *chruscikis* could break in here and blow me out of the park.'

'The firing pin works and there's no one outside in the hall. The Arethusa Delphi is very much in Washington's camp; it's watched and I'm not so foolish as to parade our personnel. I think you know that. It's why you're here.'

'What are you trying to prove?'

The Russian smiled again and shrugged. 'I'm not really sure. A brief something in the eyes, perhaps. When a man's under a hostile gun and that gun is suddenly his, there is an instant compulsion to eliminate the prior threat . . . assuming the hostility is returned. It's in the eyes; no amount of control can disguise it – if the enmity is active.'

'What was in my eyes?'

'Absolute indifference. Weariness, if you will.'

'I'm not sure you're right, but I admire your courage. It's more than I've got. The firing pin really works?'

'Yes.'

'No capsules?'

The Russian shook his head, his expression conveying quiet amusement.

'No bullets. That is to say, no power in the shells.' Rostov raised his left hand, and with his right pulled back the sleeve of his overcoat. Strapped to the flat of his wrist, extending up towards his elbow, was a thin barrel, the trigger mechanism apparently activated by the bending of his arm. He touched the taut spring-like wires. 'What you call narcotic darts. You would have slept peacefully for the better part of tomorrow, while a doctor insisted that your odd fever must be studied at the hospital. We'd have got you out, flown you up to Salonika and over the Dardanelles into Sevastopol.' The Russian unsnapped a strap above his wrist and removed the weapon.

Havelock studied the KGB man, not a little perplexed. 'You really could have taken me.'

'Until the attempt is made, one never knows. I might have missed the first shot, and you're younger, stronger than me; you could have attacked, broken my neck. But the odds were on my side.'

'I'd say completely. Why didn't you play them?'

'Because you're right. We *don't* want you. The risks *are* too great – not those you spoke of, but others. I simply had to know the truth and I'm now convinced. You are no longer in the service of your government.'

'What risks?'

'They're unknown to us, but they are there. Anything you can't understand in this business is a risk, but I don't have to tell you that.'

'Tell me *something*. I just got a pardon; I'd like to know why.'

'Very well.' The Soviet intelligence officer hesitated; he walked aimlessly towards the double doors that led to the miniature balcony and opened one several inches. Then he closed it and turned to Havelock. 'I should tell you first that I'm not here on orders from Dzerzhinsky Square, or even with its blessings. To be frank, my ageing superiors in the KGB believe I'm in Athens on an unrelated matter. You can either accept that or not.'

'Give me a reason to or not. Someone must know. You *people* don't do anything solo.'

'Specifically, two others. A close associate in Moscow and a dedicated man – a mole, to be sure – out of Washington.'

'You mean Langley?'

The Russian shook his head; he replied softly. 'The White House.'

'I'm impressed. So two ranking *Kantralyors* of the KGB and a Soviet mole within walking distance of the Oval Office decide they want to talk to me, but they don't want to take me. They can fly me into Sevastopol and from there to a room at the Lubyanka, where any talking we did would be far more productive – from their point of view – but they won't do that. Instead, the spokesman for these three – a man I know only from photographs and by reputation – tells me there are risks associated with me that he can't define but knows that they exist and because of them I'm given the option of talking or not – about what I haven't the vaguest idea. Is that a fair reading?'

'You have the Slavic propensity for going right to the core of a subject.'

'I don't see any ancestral connection. It's common sense. You spoke, I listened; that's what you said – or what you're about to say. Basic logic.'

Rostov stepped away from the balcony doors, his expression pensive. 'I'm afraid that's the one factor that's missing. The logic.'

'Now we're talking about something else.'

'Yes, we are.'

'What?'

'You. The Costa Brava.'

Havelock paused. The anger was in his eyes, but it was controlled. 'Go on.'

'The woman. She's why you retired, isn't she?'

'This conversation is terminated,' said Havelock abruptly. 'Get out of here.'

'Please.' The Russian raised both hands, a gesture of truce, perhaps a plea. 'I think you should listen to me.'

'I don't think so. There's nothing you could say that would remotely interest me. The *Voennaya* is to be congratulated; it was a hell of a job. They won, she won. And then she lost. It's finished, and there's nothing further to say about it.'

'There is.'

'Not to me.'

'The VKR are maniacs,' said the Russian quietly, urgently. 'I don't have to tell you that. You and I are enemies and neither would pretend otherwise, but we acknowledge certain rules between us. We're not salivating dogs, we're professionals. There's a fundamental respect each has for the other, perhaps grounded in fear, although not necessarily. Grant me that, *priyatyel*.'

Their eyes were level, penetrating. Havelock nodded. 'I know you from the files, just as you know me. You weren't part of it.'

'Wasted death is still death, still a waste. Unnecessary and provocative death a very dangerous waste. It can be hurled back tenfold in fury at the instigator.'

'Tell that to the *Voennaya*. There was no waste as far as they were concerned. Only necessity.'

'Butchers!' snapped Rostov, his voice guttural. 'Who can tell them anything? They're descendants of the old OGPU slaughter-houses, inheritors of the mad assassin Yagoda. They're also up to their throats in paranoid fantasies going back half a century, when Yagoda gunned down the quieter, more reasonable men, hating their lack of fanaticism, equating that lack with treason against the revolution. Do you *know* the VKR?'

'Enough to stand far back and hope to hell you can control it.'

'I wish I could answer confidently in the affirmative. It's as if a band of your screaming right-wing zealots had been given official status as a subdivision of the Central Intelligence Agency.'

'We have checks and balances – sometimes. If such subdivision came to be – and it could – it would be continuously scrutinized, openly critized. Funds would be watched closely, methods studied, ultimately the group would be thrown out.'

'You've had your lapses, your various un-American activities committees, your McCarthys, the Huston plans, purges in the irresponsible press. Careers have been destroyed, lives degraded. Yes, you've had your share of lapses.'

'Always short-lived. We have no gulags, no "rehabilitation" programmes in the Lubyanka. And that irresponsible press has a way of becoming responsible now and then. It threw out a regime of arrogant hot shots. The Kremlin's wilder ones stay in place.'

'We both have our lapses then. But we're so much younger; youth is allowed mistakes.'

'And there's nothing,' interrupted Michael, 'to compare with the VKR's *paminyatchik* operation. That wouldn't be tolerated or funded by the worst Congress or administration in history.'

'Another paranoid fantasy!' cried the KGB officer, adding derisively, 'The *paminyatchik* travellers! A discredited strategy mounted decades ago! You can't honestly believe it still flourishes.'

'Perhaps less than the *Voennaya* does. Obviously more than you do – if you're not lying.'

'Oh *come*, Havelock! Russian infants sent to the United States, growing up with old-line, no doubt pathetically senile Marxists so as to become entrenched Soviet agents? Insanity! Be reasonable. It's psychologically unsound – if not disastrous – to say nothing of certain inevitable comparisons. We'd lose the majority to blue jeans, rock music and fast cars. We'd be idiots.'

'Now you're lying. They exist. You know it and we know it.'

Rostov shrugged. 'A question of numbers, then. And value, I might add. How many can be left? Fifty, a hundred, two hundred at the outside? Sad, amateurishly conspiratorial creatures wandering around a few cities, meeting in cellars to exchange nonsense, uncertain of their own values, the very reasons for being where they are. Very little credence is given these so-called "travellers", take my word for it.'

'But you haven't pulled them out.'

'Where would we put them? Few even speak the Russian language; they're a large embarrassment. Attrition, *priyatyel*, that's the answer. And dismissing them with lip-service, as you Americans say.'

'The *Voennaya* doesn't dismiss them.'

'I told you, the men of the VKR pursue misguided fantasies.'

'I wonder if you believe that,' said Michael, studying the Russian. 'Not all those families were pathetic and senile, not all the travellers amateurs.'

'If there is currently – or in the recent past – any movement of consequence on the part of the *paminyatchiks*, we are not aware of it,' said Rostov firmly.

'And if there is and you're not aware of it that would be something of consequence, wouldn't it?'

The Russian stood motionless; he spoke, his voice low and pensive. 'The VKR is incredibly secretive. It would be something of consequence.'

'Then maybe I've given you something to think about. Call it a parting gift from a retired enemy.'

'I look for no such gifts,' said Rostov coldly. 'They're as gratuitous as your presence here in Athens.'

'Since you don't approve, go back to Moscow and fight your own fights. Your infrastructure doesn't concern me any longer. And unless you've got another comic book weapon up your other sleeve, I suggest you leave.'

'That's just it, *pyeshka*. Yes, *pyeshka*. *Pawn*. It is as you say . . . an infrastructure. Separate sections, indeed, but one entity. There is first the KGB; all else follows. A man – or a woman – may gravitate to the *Voennaya*, may even excel in its deepest operations, but first he – or she – must have sprung from the KGB. At the very minimum there *has* to be a Dzerzhinsky dossier *somewhere*. With foreign recruits it's, as you would say, a double imperative. Internal protection, of course.'

Havelock sat forward on the bed, confusion joining the anger in his eyes. 'Say what you're trying to say and say it quickly. There's a smell about you, *priyatyel!*'

'I suspect there is about all of us, Mikhail Havlicek. Our nostrils never quite adjust, do they? Perversely, they become sensitive – to variations of that basic odour. Like animals.'

'Say it.'

'There is no listing for a Jenna Karras at the KGB.'

Havelock stared at the Russian, then suddenly spun off the bed, gripping the sheet and whipping it into the air, obscuring the Russian's vision. He lunged forward, hammering Rostov against the wall beyond the balcony doors. He twisted the KGB man clockwise by the wrist and smashed his head into the frame of a cheap oil painting as he whipped his right arm around Rostov's neck in a hammerlock. 'I could kill you for that,' he whispered, breathless, the muscles of his jaw pulsating against Rostov's bald head. 'You said I might break your neck. I could do it right *now!*'

'You could,' rejoined the Russian, choking. 'And you'd be cut down. Either in this room or on the street outside.'

'I thought you didn't have anyone in the hotel!'

'I lied. There are three men, two dressed as waiters in the hall by the lift, one inside the staircase. There's no final protection for you here in Athens. My people are out there – on the street as well – every doorway covered. My instructions are clear: I'm to emerge from a specific exit at a specific time. Any deviations from either will result in your death. The room will be stormed; the cordon around the Arethusa is unbreakable. I'm not an idiot.'

'Maybe not, but as you said, you're an *animal!*' He released the Russian and hurled him across the room. 'Go back to Moscow and tell them the bait's too obvious, the stench too *rotten!* I'm not taking it, *priyatyel*. Get out of here!'

'No bait,' protested Rostov, regaining his balance and holding his throat. 'Your own argument: what could you really tell us that would be worth the risks, or the reprisals, perhaps? *Or* the uncertainties? You're finished. Without programming you could lead us into a hundred traps – a theory that has crossed our minds, incidentally. You talk freely and we act on what you say, but what you tell us is no longer operative. Through you we go after strategies – not simple codes and ciphers, but supposedly long-term vital strategies – that Washington has aborted without telling *you*. In the process we reveal our personnel. Surely you're aware of this. You talk of *logic?* Heed your own words!'

Havelock stared at the Soviet officer, his breathing audible, anger and bewilderment compounding the emotional strain. Even the shadow of a possibility that an error had been made at Costa Brava was more than he could face. But there was no error. A Baader-Meinhof defector had set off the revealing chain of events. The evidence had been sent to Madrid, and he had pored over it, sifting every fragment for a shred to the contrary.

There was nothing; there was everything. Even Anthony Matthias – *Anton* Matthias, friend, mentor, surrogate father – had demanded in-depth verification; it had been returned: positive.

'No! The proof was there! *She* was there! I saw for myself! I said I had to see for myself and they agreed!'

'"They"? Who is "they"?'

'You know as well as I do! Men like you! The inside shell – strategists! You didn't look hard enough. You're *wrong!*'

The Russian moved his head slowly in circles, his left hand massaging his throat; he spoke softly. 'I won't deny the possibility exists – as I said, the VKR is maniacally secretive, *especially* in Moscow – but that possibility is remote. We were astonished. An unusually productive decoy-conduit is led into a terrorist trap by her own people, who then proceed to hold the KGB responsible for her death by claiming she was one of us. The result of this manipulation is the neutering of the woman's constant companion, her lover, a deep-cover, multilingual field agent of exceptional talent. Disillusion and disgust overwhelm him; he takes himself out. We are amazed; we search the dossier vaults, including the most inaccessible. She is *nowhere*. Jenna Karras was never a part of us.' Rostov paused, his eyes conveying his awareness: Michael Havelock was a dangerously provoked panther about to spring, about to strike. The Russian continued, his voice flat. 'We are grateful; we profit by your elimination, but we ask ourselves why? Why was this done? Is it a trick? If so, for what purpose? Who gains? On the surface we do, but again, why? *How?*'

'Ask the VKR!' shouted Michael contemptuously. 'They didn't plan it this way, but that's the way it happened. I'm the bonus! Ask *them!*'

'We did,' said the Russian. 'A section director saner than most, who, because of his relative sanity, is frightened of his peers. He told us that he personally was not familiar with the Karras woman or the details of Costa Brava, but since the field personnel raised no questions, he assumed no questions *should* be raised. As he pointed out, the results were favourable: two vultures shot down, both talented, one exceptional. The *Voennaya* was pleased to take credit.'

'Why shouldn't they? I was out, and she could be justified. A sacrifice by any name is still the same. It's expendable for a purpose. He said it; he acknowledged it.'

'He did not acknowledge it and he was saying something quite different. I told you, he's a frightened man. Only my rank persuaded him to go as far as he did.'

'You're reaching.'

'I listened. As you listened to me a few moments ago. He was telling us that he hadn't the vaguest idea what had happened or why.'

'He *personally* didn't know,' said Havelock angrily. 'The people in the field knew. *She* knew!'

'A tenuous rationalization. His office is responsible for all activities in the south-west Mediterranean sector. The territory includes the Costa Brava. An emergency rendezvous – especially one ostensibly involving the Baader-Meinhof – would certainly be cleared by him.' Rostov paused briefly, then added quietly, 'Under normal circumstances.'

'A not-so-tenuous rationalization?' asked Michael.

'I leave myself the narrowest margin for error. An extremely remote possibility.'

'It's the one I accept!' Havelock shouted again, suddenly disturbed at his own outburst.

'You want to accept it. Perhaps you have to.'

'The VKR more often than not gets its orders directly from the policy rooms of the Kremlin. It's no secret. If you're not lying, you were passed over.'

'To be sure, and the thought frightens me more than I can tell you. But as much as I'm forced to acknowledge your professional accomplishments, *priyatyel*, I do not think the policy makers in the Kremlin are concerned with the likes of you and me. They have more weighty matters, global matters. And, to the point, they have no expertise where we're concerned.'

'They do with Baader-Meinhof! *And* the PLO, *and* the Brigate Rosse, *and* a couple of dozen "red armies" blowing things up all over the goddamn place! *That's* policy!'

'Only for maniacs.'

'Which is exactly what we're talking about! Maniacs!' Michael paused, the obvious striking him. 'We broke the VKR codes. They were authentic; I've seen too many variations not to know. *I* set up the contact. She *responded*. I sent the final transmission to the men in the boat offshore. *They* responded! Explain that!'

'I can't.'

'Then get *out*!'

The KGB officer looked at his watch. 'I must in any event. Time is up.'

'Yes, it is.'

'We're at an impasse,' said the Russian.

'I'm not.'

'No, I don't think you are, and that compounds the risk about you. You know what you know and I know what I know. Impasse, whether you like it or not.'

'Your time's up, remember?'

'I'm not forgetting. I don't care to be caught in the crossfire. I'll leave now.' Rostov went to the door and turned, his hand on the knob. 'Several minutes ago you said the bait was too obvious, the stench too rotten. Tell that to Washington, *priyatyel*. We're not taking it either.'

'Get *out*!'

The door closed and Havelock stood motionless for nearly a minute, picturing the Russian's eyes. They had held too much truth in them. Over the years Michael had learned to discern the truth, especially in his enemies. Rostov had not been lying; he had spoken the truth as he believed it to be. Which meant that this powerful strategist for the KGB was being manipulated by his own people in Moscow. Pyotr Rostov was a blind probe – an influential intelligence officer sent out with information he is convinced his superiors do not have in order to make contact with the enemy and turn an American agent, recruiting him for the Soviets. The higher up the officer, the more credible his story – as long as he spoke the truth as he saw it, truth that was perceived as such by his enemy.

Michael walked to the bedside table where he had left the glass of whisky a half hour ago. He picked it up, drained the Scotch and looked down at the bed. He smiled to himself, thinking how the evening had veered from where it had been heading thirty minutes ago. The whore had performed, but not in any way he might have expected. The sensuous courtesan from the playgrounds of the rich had been part of a well-planned set-up. When were the set-ups going to stop? Amsterdam. Paris. Athens.

Perhaps they would not stop until he did. Perhaps as long as he kept moving the would-be trappers would keep moving with him, watching him, cornering him, waiting for him to commit whatever crimes their imaginations led them to expect. It was in the movement itself that they found the ominous substance for their suspicions. No man wandered aimlessly after a lifetime of wandering under orders. If he kept it up, it must mean he was following other orders, different orders; otherwise he'd stay put. Somewhere.

Perhaps it was time he stopped. Maybe his odyssey of recovery had about run its course; there was a cable to be sent, a commitment to be made. A beginning. A nearly forgotten friend had become a friend again, and that man had offered him a new life, where the old life could be buried, where there were roots to cultivate, relationships to create, things to teach.

What will you teach, Mikhail?

Leave me alone! You are no part of me – you never were!

He would send the cable to Harry Lewis in the morning, then rent a car and drive north-west to catch the ferry for the Ionian port of Kérkira, where he would catch the boat to Brindisi in Italy. He had done it before under God knows what name or with what objective. He would do it now as Michael Havelock, Visiting Professor of Government. From Brindisi he would take the circuitous train routes across Italy into Rome, a city he enjoyed immensely. He would stay in Rome for a week or two; it would be the last stop on his odyssey, the place where he would put to rest all thoughts of a life that was over.

There were things to do in Concord, New Hampshire, USA. He would assume his duties as visiting professor in something less than three months; in the meantime there were practicalities to be dealt with: lectures to be sketched under the guidance of knowledgeable associates, curricula to study and evaluate, determining where his contributions might best be directed. A short stay, perhaps, with Matthias, who would certainly have insights to offer. No matter how pressed for time, Matthias would *make* the time, because, above all men, Anton would be happiest for him. His old student had returned to the campus. It was where it all began.

So many things to do. He needed a place to live: a house, furniture, pots and pans and books, a chair to sit in, a bed to sleep in. Choices. He had not thought about such things ever before. He thought about them now and felt the excitement growing inside him.

He went to the bureau, uncapped the Scotch and poured himself a drink. 'Priyatyel,' he said softly, for no particular reason, as he looked at his face in the mirror. Suddenly he stared at his eyes and, in terror, slammed the glass down with such force that it shattered. Blood spread slowly over his hand. His eyes would not let him go! And he understood. Had they seen the truth that night on the Costa Brava?

'*Stop it!*' he screamed, whether silently or out loud he could not tell.

Dr Harry Lewis sat at his desk in his book-lined study, the cablegram in his hand. He listened for the sound of his wife's voice. It came.

'See you later, dear,' she called from the hall beyond. The front door opened and closed. She was out of the house.

Lewis picked up his telephone and dialled the area code *202*. Washington, DC. The seven digits that followed had been committed to memory, never written down. Nor would they be recorded on a bill, having bypassed the computers electronically.

'Yes? asked the male voice on the other end of the line.

'Birchtree,' said Harry.

'Go ahead, Birchtree. You're being taped.'

'He's accepted. The cable came from Athens.'

'Is there any change in dates?'

'No. He'll be here a month before the trimester starts.'

'Did he say where he was going from Athens?'

'No.'

'We'll watch the airports. Thank you, Birchtree.'

The Rome Havelock had come to visit was not the Rome in which he cared to stay. Strikes were everywhere, the chaos compounded by volatile Italian tempers that erupted on every street corner, every picket line, in the parks and around the fountains. Mail had been strewn in gutters, adding to the uncollected rubbish; taxis were scarce, practically non-existent, and most of the restaurants had been closed for lack of deliveries. The *Poliziotti*, having taken sufficient abuse, had stopped work, snarling further the normal insanity of Rome's traffic; and since the telephones were part of a government's postal service, they functioned on a level below normal, which made them damn near impossible. The city was full of a kind of hysteria, aggravated by yet another stern papal decree – from a foreigner, a *Polacco!* – that was at odds with every progressive step since Vatican II. *Giovanni Ventitre! Dove Sei?*

It was his second night, and Michael had left his *pensione* on the via Due Macelli more than two hours before, walking almost a mile to the via Flaminia in the hope of finding a favourite restaurant open. It was not, and no amount of patience brought forth a taxi to take him back to the Spanish Steps.

Reaching the north end of via Veneto, he headed for the side street by which he could escape the crowds on the gaudy carnival of the busy shopping street, when he saw it: a poster in the lighted window of a travel agency proclaiming the glories of Venice.

Why not? Why the hell not? The floating passivity of not planning included sudden changes of plan. He looked at his watch; it was barely eight-thirty, probably too late to get out to the airport and chance a reservtion on a plane, but if he remembered correctly – and he did – the trains kept running out of Rome until midnight. Why not a train? The lazy, circuitous trip by rail from Brindisi had been startlingly beautiful, passing through countryside that had not changed in centuries. He could pack his single suitcase in minutes, walk to the station in twenty. Surely the money he was willing to pay would buy him accommodation; if not, he could always return to the via Due Macelli. He had paid for a week in advance.

Forty-five mintues later Havelock passed through the huge portals of the massive Ostia Railway Station, built by Mussolini in the halcyon days of trumpets and drums and marching boots and trains that ran on time.

Italian was not Michael's best language, but he could read it well enough. *Biglietto per Venezia. Prima Classe.*

The queue was short and his luck held. The famous *Venezia Ferrovia* was leaving in eight minutes, and if the *signore* wished to pay a premium, he could have the finest accommodation in the shape of his own compartment. He did wish, and, as the clerk stamped his ornate ticket, he was told that the *Ferrovia* was leaving from *Binario trentasei*, a double platform several football fields away.

'Fate presto, signore! Non perdete tempo! Fate in fretta!'

Michael walked rapidly into the mass of rushing humanity, threading his way as fast as possible towards platform 36. As usual – as he recalled from memories past – the giant dome was filled with crowds. Screeching arrivals and wailing departures were joined in counterpoint; screamed epithets punctuated the deafening roar because the porters, too, were obviously on strike. It took nearly five hectic minutes to shoulder a way through the huge stone arch and emerge on the double track platform. It was, if possible, more chaotic than the station itself. A crowded train had arrived from the north as the *Venezia Ferrovia* was about to depart. Freight dollies collided with hordes of embarking and disembarking passengers. It was a scene from a lower circle of Dante, screaming pandemonium.

Suddenly, across the platform, through the milling crowds, he caught sight of the back of a woman's head, the rim of a soft hat shadowing the side of her face. She was stepping out of the incoming train from the north, and had turned to talk to the guard. It had happened before: the same colour or cut of the hair, the shape of the neck. A scarf, or a hat or a raincoat, like those she had worn. It had happened before. Too often.

Then the woman turned, and sharp bolts of pain seared Havelock's eyes and temples, and surged downward – like hot knives into his chest. The face across the platform, seen sporadically through the weaving, colliding crowds, was no illusion. It was *she*.

Their eyes locked. Hers widened in raw fear; her face froze. Then she whipped her head away and plunged into the crowds in front of her.

Michael pressed his eyelids shut, then opened them, trying to rid himself of the pain and the shock and the sudden trembling that immobilized him. He dropped his suitcase. He had to *move*, run, race after this living corpse from the Costa Brava! She was alive! This woman he had loved, this apparition who had betrayed that love and had died for it was *alive*!

Like a crazed animal, he parted the bodies in his path screaming her name, ordering her to stop, commanding the crowds to stop her. He raced up the ramp and through the massive stone archway oblivious to the shrieking, furious passengers he pummelled and left in his wake, unaware of the slaps and punches and body blocks hurled at him, unconscious of the hands that ripped his clothing.

She was nowhere to be seen in the station crowds.

4

With the terrifying impact of a bolt of lightning the sight of Jenna Karras had thrown him back in the shadow world he had left behind. She was alive! He had to keep moving; he had to find her. He ran blindly through the crowds, separating arms and gesturing hands and protesting shoulders. First one exit, then the other; and a third and a fourth. He stopped to question what few police he found, picking the words from a blurred Italian lexicon somewhere in his mind. He shouted her description, ending each distorted phrase with '*Soccorso!*' – only to be met with shrugs and looks of disapproval.

He kept running. A staircase – a door – a lift. He thrust 2000 lire on a woman heading into the ladies room; 5000 to a workman. He pleaded with three guards leaving the station, carrying satchels, on their way home.

Nothing. She was nowhere.

Havelock leaned over a litter bin, the sweat rolling down his face and neck, his hands scraped and bleeding. He thought for a moment that he would vomit into the rubbish; he had passed over the edge of hysteria. He had to pull himself back; he had to get hold of himself.

And the only way to do so was to keep moving, slower and slower, but to keep moving. Let the pounding in his chest decelerate, find a part of his mind so he could think. He vaguely remembered his suitcase; the possibility that it was still there was remote, but looking for it was something to do, somewhere to go at that moment. He started back through the crowds, body aching, perceptions numbed, buffeted by the gesticulating hordes around him as if he were in a dark tunnel filled with shadows and swirling winds. He had no idea how long it took him to pass through the arch and walk down the ramp to the near-deserted platform. The *Ferrovia* had left, and the cleaners were invading the cars of the stationary train from the north . . . the train that had carried Jenna Karras.

There it was, crushed but still intact, straps broken, clothes protruding, yet oddly whole. His suitcase was wedged in the narrow space between the edge of the platform and the filthy, flat side of the third carriage. He knelt down and pulled it out of its jammed recess, sliding up first one side and then the other, hearing the abrasive squeaks of the leather, he lost his balance, falling to the concrete, still holding onto the half-destroyed handle. A man in overalls, pushing a wide broom, approached. Michael got to his feet, awkwardly, aware that the maintenance man had stopped, his broom motionless, his eyes conveying equal parts amusement and disgust. He thought Michael was drunk.

The handle broke; held by a single clasp, the suitcase abruptly tilted downward. Havelock yanked it up and clutched it in his arms; he started down the platform towards the ramp, knowing his walk was trance-like.

How many minutes later, or which particular exit he used, he would never know, but he was out on the street, the suitcase held against his chest, walking unsteadily past a row of lighted shops. He was conscious of the fact that people kept glancing at him, at his torn clothes and the crushed suitcase, its contents spilling out. The swirling mists were beginning to break up, the cold night air diffusing them. He had to find his sanity by concentrating on the little things: he would wash his face, change his clothes, have a cigarette, replace the suitcase.

Emporio Per Viaggiatori. The neon letters glowed impressively in deep red above the wide shop window filled with accessories for the traveller. It was one of those shops near the Ostia Station that catered to the wealthy foreigner and the self-indulgent Italian. The merchandise was expensive, replicas of ordinary objects turned into luxuries by way of sterling silver and polished brass.

Havelock stood for a moment, breathing deeply, holding onto the suitcase as if it were somehow an object that would carry him like a plank in the wild sea. He walked inside; mercifully, it was near closing time, and the shop was devoid of customers.

The manager emerged from behind the middle counter, his expression alarmed. He hesitated, then stepped back as if to retreat quickly. Havelock spoke rapidly in barely passable Italian. 'I was caught in an insane crowd on the platform. I'm afraid I fell. I'll need to buy a few things . . . a number of things, actually. I'm expected at the Hassler fairly soon.'

At the mention of Rome's most exclusive hotel, the manager at once turned sympathetic, even brotherly.

'*Animali!*' he exclaimed, gesturing to his God. 'How perfectly dreadful for you, *signore*! Here, let me help you – '

'I'll need a new piece of luggage. Soft, very good leather, if you have it.'

'*Naturalmente.*'

'I realize it's an imposition, but could I possibly wash somewhere? I'd hate to greet the *Contessa* the way I look now.'

'This way, *signore*! A thousand apologies! I speak for all Rome! This way . . .'

While Michael washed and changed his clothes in the back room, he focused his thoughts – as they came to him – on the brief visits he and Jenna Karras had made to Rome. There had been two. On the first they had passed through for a single night; the second was much longer, very official – three or four days, if he remembered correctly. They had been awaiting orders from Washington, having travelled as a Yugoslav couple through the Balkan countries in order to gather information on the sudden expansion in border defences. There had been a man, an army intelligence officer not easily forgotten; he had been Havelock's DC conduit. What made the man memorable was his cover; he was posing as the only first-level black attaché at the embassy.

Their first conference had not been without humour – black humour. Michael and Jenna were to meet the attaché at an out-of-the-way restaurant west of the Palatine. They had waited in the crowded stand-up bar, preferring to let the conduit select a table, oblivious of the tall black soldier ordering a vodka martini on their right. After several minutes the man smiled, and said,

'I'm jes' Rastus in the *pila di bosco*, Massa Havelock. Do you think we might sit down?'

His name was Lawrence Brown. Lieutenant-Colonel Lawrence B. Brown – the middle initial standing for his real name, Baylor.

'So help me God,' the colonel had told them over after-dinner drinks that night, 'the fellows in G-Two felt there was more "concrete association" – that's what they called it – by using Brown in the cover. It went under the heading of "psy-acceptance", can you believe it? Hell, I suppose it's better than Attaché Coffee-Face.'

Baylor was a man he could talk to . . . if Baylor would agree to talk to him. And where? It would not be anywhere near the embassy; the United States government had several terrible things to explain to a retired field agent.

It took over twenty minutes on the manager's phone – while the manager repacked Michael's clothing in an outrageously priced new suitcase – before Havelock reached the embassy switchboard. Senior Attaché Brown was currently attending a reception on the first floor.

'Tell him it's urgent,' said Michael. 'My name is . . . Baylor.'

Lawrence Baylor was reluctant to the point of turning Havelock down. Anything a retired intelligence officer had to say would best be said at the embassy. For any number of reasons.

'Suppose I told you I just came out of retirement. I may not be on your payroll – or anyone else's – but I'm very much back in. I'd suggest you don't blow this, Colonel.'

'There's a café on the via Pancrazio, *La Ruota del Pavone*. Do you know it?'

'I'll find it.'

'Forty-five minutes.'

'I'll be there. Waiting.'

Havelock watched from a table in the darkest corner of the café as the army officer ordered a carafe of wine from the bar and began walking across the dimly-lit room. Baylor's mahogany face was taut; he was not comfortable, and when he reached the table, he did not offer his hand. He sat down opposite Michael, exhaled slowly and attempted a grim smile.

'Nice to see you,' he said with little conviction.

'Thank you.'

'And unless you've got something to say we want to hear, you're putting me in a pretty rough spot, buddy. I hope you know that.'

'I've got something that'll blow your mind,' said Havelock, his voice involuntarily a whisper. The trembling had returned; he gripped his wrist to control it. 'It's blown mine.'

The colonel studied Michael, his eyes dropping to Havelock's hands. 'You're stretched, I can see that. What is it?'

'She's *alive*. I *saw* her!'

Baylor was silent, immobile. His eyes roamed Michael's face, noting the marks of recent scrapes and bruises on Havelock's skin. It was obvious that he had made the connection. 'Are you referring to the Costa Brava?' he asked finally.

'You know damn well I am!' said Michael angrily. 'My abrupt retirement and the circumstances thereof have been flashed to every goddamned station and post we've got. It's why you just said what you did. "Beware the screwed-up talent," Washington tells you. He might do anything, say anything, think he has scores to settle.'

'It's happened.'

'Not to me. I don't have any scores to think about because I'm not interested in the ballgame. I'm rational. I saw what I saw. And she saw *me*! She acknowledged *me*! She *ran*!'

'Emotional stress is the first cousin to hysteria,' said the colonel quietly. 'A man can see a lot of things that aren't there in that condition. And you had a jolt.'

'Past tense, not currently applicable. I was out. I accepted the fact and the reasons – '

'Come *on*, buddy,' insisted the soldier. 'You don't throw away sixteen years of involvement.'

'*I* did.'

'You were here in Rome with her. Memories get activated, twisted. As I said, it happens.'

'Again, negative. Nothing was activated, nothing twisted. I *saw* – '

'You even called me,' interrupted Baylor sharply. 'The three of us spent a couple of evenings together. A few drinks, a few laughs. Association; you reached me.'

'There was no one else. My cover was D-squared. You were my only contact here in Rome! I can walk into the embassy now, I couldn't then.'

'Then let's go,' said the colonel quickly.

'No way! Besides, it's not the point. *You* are. You fielded orders to me from Washington seven months ago, and now you're going to send an emergency flag back to those same people. Tell them what I've told you, what I saw. You haven't got a choice.'

'I've got an opinion. I'm relaying what a former talent said while in a state of extreme anxiety.'

'Fine! Good! Then try this. Five days ago in Athens I nearly killed a man we both know from the Dzerzhinsky files for telling me Costa Brava wasn't a Soviet exercise. That she wasn't any part of the KGB, much less the VKR. I didn't kill him because I thought it was a probe, a *blind* probe – that man was telling the *truth*, as he knew the truth. I sent a message back to Moscow. The bait was too obvious, the smell too rotten.'

'I suppose that was charitable of you considering your record.'

'Oh, no, the charity started with *him*. You see, he could have taken me. I could have found myself in Sevastopol on my way to Dzerzhinsky Square without even knowing I'd left Athens.'

'He was that good? That well connected?'

'So much so he was self-effacing. But he didn't take me. I wasn't booked on the Dardanelles airlift. He didn't want me.'

'Why not?'

'Because he was convinced *I* was the bait. Pretty fair irony, isn't it? There was no room at the Lubyanka. I was turned out. Instead, he gave me his own message for Washington. Dzerzhinsky wouldn't touch me.' Havelock paused. 'And now *this*.'

The colonel narrowed his eyes pensively, and, with both hands, turned his glass on the table. 'I don't have your expertise, but say you actually did see what you say you saw . . .'

'I did. Accept it.'

'No concessions, but say it's possible – it could still be a lure. They've got you under a glass, know your plans, your itinerary. Their computers pick up a woman reasonably similar in appearance, and with a little cosmetic surgery they've got a double good enough for short distances. "Beware the screwed-up talent." You never know when he thinks he has "scores to settle". Especially if he's given some time to stew, to get worked up.'

'What I saw was in her *eyes*! But even if you won't accept that there's something else; it voids the strategy, and every point can be checked. Two hours ago I didn't know I'd be inside that station; ten minutes before I saw her I didn't know I'd be on that platform and neither could anyone else. I came here yesterday and took a room in a *pensione* on the Due Macelli for a week, paid in advance. At eight-thirty tonight I saw a poster in a window and decided to go to Venice. I didn't speak to anyone.' Michael reached into his pocket, took out his ticket for the *Venezia Ferrovia* and placed it in front of Lawrence Baylor. 'The *Ferrovia* was scheduled to leave at nine-thirty-five. The time of purchase is stamped across the top of this. Read it!'

'Twenty-one, twenty-seven,' said Baylor, reading. 'Twenty-seven past nine. Eight minutes before the train left.'

'All verifiable. Now look at me and tell me I'm lying. And while you're at it, explain how that set-up could have been mounted given the time span *and* the fact that she was on an incoming train!'

'I can't. *If* she –'

'She was talking to a guard seconds before she got off. I'm sure I can find him.'

Baylor was silent again; he stared at Havelock, then spoke softly. 'Don't bother. I'll send the flag.' He paused, adding, 'Along with qualified support. Whatever you saw, you're not lying. Where can I reach you?'

'Sorry. I'll reach you.'

'They'll want to talk to you, probably in a hurry.'

'I'll be in touch.'

'Why the static?'

'Something Rostov said in Athens.'

'*Rostov?* Pyotr Rostov?' The colonel's eyes widened. 'You don't go much higher in the Dzerzhinsky.'

'There's higher.'

'He'll do. What did he say? What did he tell you?'

'That our nostrils never quite adjust. Instead, they develop a kind of sensitivity – to variations of the basic rotten smell. Like animals.'

'I expected something less abtract,' said Baylor, annoyed.

'Really? From where I stand, it sounds concrete as hell. The Costa Brava trap was engineered in Washington, the evidence compiled by the inner shell in one of those white, sterile offices on the top floor of State.'

'I understand you were in control,' interrupted Baylor.

'The last phase. I insisted on it.'

'Then you –'

'I acted on everything that was given to me. And now I want to know *why* it was given to me. Why I saw what I did tonight.'

'*If* you saw –'

'She's *alive*. I want to know why! How!'

'I still don't understand.'

'Costa Brava was meant for *me*. Someone wanted me out. Not dead, but out. Comfortably removed from those temptations that often afflict men like me.'

'Scores to settle?' asked the colonel. 'The Agee syndrome? The Snepp complex? I didn't know you were infected.'

'I've had my quota of shocks, my share of questions. Someone wanted those questions buried and *she* went along. Why?'

'Two assumptions I'm not willing to concede are facts. And if you intended to bear a few shocks not in the national interest, I imagine – and I'm speaking hypothetically in the extreme, of course – there are other methods of . . . burying them.'

'Dispatch? Call me dead?'

'I didn't say we'd kill you. We don't live in that kind of country.' The colonel paused, then added, 'On the other hand, why not?'

'For the same reason others haven't met with odd accidents that pre-arranged pathologists might label something else. Self-protection is ingrained in our job, brother. It's another syndrome; it's called the Nuremberg. Those shocks, instead of being buried, might surface. Sealed depositions to be opened by unnamed attorneys in the event of questionable et ceteras.'

'*Jesus*, you said that? You went that far?'

'Strangely enough, I never did. Not seriously. I simple got angry. The rest was assumed.'

'What kind of world do you people live in?'

'The same one you do – only we've been around a little longer, a little deeper. And that's why I won't tell you where you can reach me. My nostrils have picked up a sickening odour from the Potomac.' Havelock leaned forward, his voice harsh, low, nearly a whisper again. 'I know that girl. For her to do what she did, something must have been done to her, held over her. Something obscene. I want to know what it was and why.'

'Assuming,' Baylor began slowly, 'assuming you're right, and I don't for one instant concede that you are, what makes you think they'll tell you?'

'It was all so sudden,' said Michael, leaning back, his body rigid, his voice now floating as if in a painful dream. 'It was a Tuesday and we were in Barcelona. We'd been there for a week; something was going to happen in the sector, that's all Washington told us. Then word came from Madrid: a Four Zero communication had been flown in by courier, contents restricted to the embassy, Eyes Only. Mine only. There's no Cons Op station in Madrid, no one cleared to relay the information, so I flew in on Wednesday morning, signed for that goddamned steel container, and opened it in a room guarded by three marines. Everything was there, everything she'd done, all the information she'd transmitted – information she could have got only from me. The trap was there, too, myself in control if I so wished – and I so wished. They knew it was the only way I'd be convinced. On Friday I was back in Barcelona, and by Saturday it was over . . . and I *was* convinced. Five days and the walls came tumbling down. No trumpets, just lights and screams and loud ugly noises intruding on the surf. Five days – so sudden, so swift, everything pitched at a crescendo. It was the only way it could have been done.'

'You haven't answered my question,' Baylor interrupted quietly. 'If you're right, what makes you think they'll tell you?'

Havelock levelled his eyes at the soldier. 'Because they're afraid. It comes down to the "why". The questions, the shocks; which one was it?'

'What are you talking about?'

'The decision to remove me wasn't made gradually, Colonel. Something triggered it. They don't force a man out the way I was forced out because of accumulated differences. Talent's expensive; proven field talent too difficult to replace. Accommodations can be made, explanations offered, agreements reached. All these are tried before they let the talent go. But no one tried with me.'

'Can you be more specific?' the officer pressed, again annoyed.

'I wish I could be. It's something I know, or they *think* I know. Something I could have written down. And it's a bomb.'

'Do you,' Baylor asked, coldly, professionally, 'have such a piece of information?'

'I'll find it,' replied Havelock, suddenly moving his chair back, prepared to leave. 'You tell them that. Just as I'll find her, tell them that, too. It won't be easy because she's not with them any more. She got away; she's gone under. I also saw that in her eyes. But I'll find her.'

'Maybe – ' Baylor said urgently, 'maybe if everything you say proves out, they'd be willing to help.'

'They'd better be,' said Michael, getting to his feet and looking down at the soldier-conduit. 'I'll need all the help I can get. In the meantime I want this whole goddamned thing spelled out – chapter and verse, to quote an old source of mine. Because if it isn't, I'm going to start telling tales out of school. When and from where none of you will know, but the words will be there loud and clear. And somewhere among them will be that bomb.'

'Don't do anything stupid!'

'Don't mistake me, I don't want to. But what was done to her, to me – to *us* – just wasn't fair, Colonel. I'm back in. Solo. I'll be in touch.'

Havelock turned and walked swiftly out of the café into the via Pancrazio.

He reached the via Galvani on his way back to the railway station where he had deposited his newly acquired suitcase in a locker. Suddenly, the painful irony struck him. It had been a suitcase in a locker at an airport in Barcelona that had condemned Jenna Karras. The defector from the Baader Meinhof had led them to it – in exchange for the quiet cancellation of a death sentence pronounced *in absentia*. The German terrorist had told Madrid that *die Fräulein Karras* kept secret, updated field records within her reach at all times. It was a *Voennaya* custom dictated by the strange relationship the violent and clandestine branch of Soviet intelligence had with the rest of the KGB. Certain field personnel on long-range deep cover operations had access to their own files in the event of their superiors in Moscow suddenly not being accessible. Self-protection sometimes assumed odd forms; no one had questioned it.

No one had questioned. Not even he.

Someone makes contact with her and gives her a key, stating a location. A room or a locker, even a bank. The material is there, including new objectives as they are developed.

A man had stopped her one afternoon two days before Michael left for Madrid. In a café on the Paseo Isabel. A drunk. He had shaken her hand, then kissed it. Three days later Michael had found a key in Jenna's purse. The next day she was dead.

There had been a key, but whose key was it? He had seen photocopies verified by Langley of every item in that suitcase. But whose suitcase was it? If not hers, how did three sets of fingerprints confirmed to be hers get inside? And if the prints were hers, why did she permit it?

What had they done to her? What had they done to a blonde woman on the Costa Brava who had screamed in Czech and whose spine and neck and head had been pierced with bullets? What kind of people were they who could put human beings on strings and blow them up as calmly as one might explode mannequins in a horror show. That woman had died; he had seen too much death to be mistaken. It was no charade, as the elegant Gravet might have put it.

Yet it was all a charade. They were all puppets. But on what stage and for whose benefit were they performing?

He hurried faster; the via Della Mamorata was in sight. He was only blocks now from the massive railway station; he would begin there. At least, he had an idea; whether it made sense or not the next half-hour would tell.

He passed a garishly lit news-stand where tabloids competed with glossy magazines. Capped teeth and outsized breasts battled for attention with mutilated bodies and graphic descriptions of rape and mayhem. And then he saw the famous face staring up at him from the cover of the international edition of *Time*. The clear eyes behind the horn-rimmed glasses shone as they always did, filled with high intelligence – cold at first glance, yet somehow warmer the longer one looked at them. Softened, perhaps by an understanding few on this earth possessed. There he was, the high cheek-bones and the aquiline nose, the generous lips from which such extraordinary words poured forth.

'A Man for all seasons, all peoples.' That was the simple caption beneath the photograph. No name, no title; none was necessary. The world knew the American Secretary of State, heard his reasoned, deliberate voice and understood. This *was* a man for all; he transcended borders and languages and national insanities. There were those who believed – and Michael was one of them – that either the world would listen to Anthony Matthias or it would be blown to hell in a mushroom cloud.

Anton Matthias. Friend, mentor, surrogate father. Where Costa Brava was concerned, he, too, had been a puppet.

As Havelock put several lire notes down on the counter and picked up the magazine, he remembered vividly the handwritten note Anton had insisted the strategists in Washington include with the Four Zero file flown to Madrid. From their few brief conversations with Havelock in Georgetown, Matthias had grasped the depth of his feelings for the woman assigned to him for the past eight months. At last, perhaps, he was ready to get out and find the peace that had eluded him all these years. The statesman had made gentle fun of the situation; when a fellow Czech past forty and in Michael's line of work decided to concentrate on one woman, Slav tradition and contemporary fiction suffered irreparable blows.

But there had been no such levity in Matthias's note.

Moje Rozmilý Syn

The attached pains my heart as it will yours. You who suffered so much in the early days, and have given of yourself so brilliantly and selflessly to our adopted country in these later ones, must again know pain. I have demanded and received a complete verification of these findings. If you wish to remove yourself from the scene, you may, of course, do so. Do not feel bound by the attached recommendations. There is only so much a nation can ask, and you have given with honour and more. Perhaps now the angers we spoke of years ago, the furies that propelled you into this terrible life, have subsided, permitting you to return to another world that needs the labours of your mind. I pray so.

Milovati, pritel,
Anton M.

Havelock forced the note from his mind; it served only to aggravate the incomprehensible. Verification: *Positive.* He opened the magazine to the article on Matthias. There was nothing new, merely a recap of his more recent accomplishments in the area of arms negotiations. It ended with the observation that the Secretary of State was off for a well-deserved vacation at an unnamed location. Michael smiled; he knew where it was. A cabin in the Shenandoah Valley. It was entirely possible that before the night was over he would use a dozen codes to reach that mountain cabin. But not until he found out what had happened. For Anton Matthias had been touched by it too.

The crowds inside the giant dome of the Ostia had thinned out, the last of the trains leaving Rome having departed or being just about to depart. Havelock pulled his suitcase from the locker and looked around for a sign; it had to be somewhere. It could well be a waste of time, but he did not think so; at least it was a place to start. He had told the intelligence officer–attaché in the café on the via Pancrazio: 'She was talking to a guard seconds before she got off. I'm sure I can find him.'

Surely someone running did not casually strike up a conversation with a guard for the sake of conviviality; too much was on that someone's mind. And in every city there were those sections where men and women who wished to disappear could do so, where cash was the only currency, mouths were kept shut, and hotel registries rarely reflected accurate identities. Jenna Karras might know the names of districts, even streets, but she did not – had not known – Rome itself. A city on strike might just possibly persuade someone running that it was urgent to ask a question or a direction of someone who might have the answer.

* * *

There was the sign on the wall, an arrow pointing to the office complex: *Amministratore della Stazione.*

Thirty-five minutes later, having persuaded a night manager that it was imperative, and in both his and the guard's financial interest that the guard should be found, he had the address of the man assigned to cars *tre, quattro* and *cinque* for the incoming train on *Binario Trentasei* at eight-thirty that evening. As the rail system was a government service, a photograph was attached to the employment sheet. It was the man he had seen talking to Jenna Karras. Among his qualifications was a proficiency in English. *Livello Uno.*

He climbed the worn stone steps of the block of flats to the fifth floor, found the name 'Mascolo' on the door and knocked. The red-faced guard was dressed in loose trousers held up by wide braces over a vest. His breath reeked of cheap wine and his eyes were not entirely focused. Havelock took a 10,000-lire note from his pocket.

'Who can remember one passenger among thousands?' protested the man, seated opposite Michael at the kitchen table.

'I'm sure *you* can,' said Havelock, removing another bill. '*Think.* She was probably one of the last people you spoke to on that train. Slender, medium height, a wide-brimmed hat – you were standing at the door.'

'*Sì! Naturalmente. Una bella ragazza!* I remember!' The guard took the money and drank some wine; he belched and continued. 'She asked me if I knew where she could make connections for Civitavecchia.'

'Civitavecchia? That's a town north of here, isn't it?'

'*Sì.* A port on the Tyrrhenian Sea.'

'Did you know?'

'There are very few trains between Rome and Civitavecchia, *signore*, and certainly not at that hour. It is at best a stop for freight, not passengers.'

'What did you tell her?'

'Just that. She appeared reasonably well dressed so I suggested she negotiate a taxi for a flat rate. If she could find one. Rome is a *manicomio di pazzi!*'

Havelock nodded thanks, placed another note on the table and went to the door. He glanced at his watch; it was twenty past one in the morning. Civitavecchia. A seaport on the Tyrrhenian. Ships heading out to sea on a given day invariably left with the early light. At dawn.

He had roughly three hours to reach Civitavecchia, search the waterfront, find a pier, find a ship – find an unlisted passenger.

5

He raced out of the marble lobby of the hotel in Bernini Circle, rushing blindly up through the winding streets until he reached the via Veneto. The desk clerk at the hotel had not been able to help him but not for lack of trying; spurred on by the thick folds of lire, he futilely punched the telephone bar and screamed numbers at the sleepy switchboard operator. The night clerk's contacts were limited; he could not raise a rented car.

Havelock stopped for breath, studying the lights on the Veneto. Several cafés and the Excelsior Hotel were still illuminated. Someone had to help him – he had to get to Civitavecchia! *He had to find her. He could not lose her.* Not again, not *ever* again! He had to reach her and hold her and tell her that terrible things had been done to them, tell her over and over again until she saw the truth in his eyes and heard that truth in his voice, and saw the love he felt so deeply, and understood the unendurable guilt that never left him – for he had killed that love.

He began running away, first into the Excelsior, where no amount of money interested an arrogant clerk.

'You've got to help me!'

'You are not even a guest, *signore*,' said the man, glancing to his left.

Slowly Michael angled his head. Across the lobby two policemen were watching the scene. They conferred; obviously the night operation at the Excelsior was under open official scrutiny. Pedlars of capsules and pills, white powder and syringes, were working the world-famous street. One of the uniformed men stepped forward. Havelock turned and walked rapidly to the entrance, once again running into the half-deserted street, towards the nearest profusion of light.

The tired *maître d'hôtel* of the Café de Paris told him he was a *capo zuccone*. Who would rent a car to a stranger at this hour? The American manager of a third-rate saloon told him to 'pound sand'.

Again the winding streets, again the sweat drenching his hair-line, rolling down his cheeks. The Hassler – the Villa Medici! He had used the name of the elegant hotel in the luggage shop near the station . . .

The night *concierge* at the Hassler's Villa Medici was accustomed to the vagaries of Rome's wealthiest hotel guests. Arrangements were made for Michael to hire a Fiat, one of the Hassler's staff vehicles. The price was exorbitant, but with it came a map of Rome and its environs, the most direct route to Civitavecchia marked in red.

He reached the port city at three-fifteen, and by three-forty-five he had driven up and down the waterfront, studying it until he had decided where to park.

It was a section common to most waterfronts, where the flood-lights washing the piers remained on all night and activity never stopped; where groupings of dockworkers and deckhands mingled like slow-moving automatons, criss-crossing one another – men and machinery meshed in volatile conflict – loading the cargo holds and preparing the massive boilers and outdated engines of the larger vessels soon to head out into deep water. Where cafés and coffee houses lined the mist-laden alleys, punctuated by the diffused light of the street lamps – places of refuge serving the harshest whisky and the most glutinous food.

To the north and south were the smaller piers, where halyards and masts swayed in silhouette against the moonlight; filthy harbours for the fishing boats and *controllori* trawlers that ventured no more than forty kilometres out to where decades of experience and tradition told the captains the catches were most plentiful. These piers did not begin to stir until early light was closer, when faint sprays of yellowish white inched their way over the south-east horizon, pushing the night sky up. Only then did groaning, dull-eyed men walk down the wooden planks towards oily gunwales and the interminable, blinding day ahead. Jenna Karras would not be here but somewhere in that complex of larger piers, where ships looked to the tides and charts and sailed to other ports, other countries.

She was somewhere in this stretch of the waterfront where swirling pockets of mist rolled off the sea and across the docks, through intersecting pools of floodlights and the hammering tattoo of nocturnal labours. She would be hidden from the *controllori* of the piers, who were paid by the state and the shipping companies to be on the lookout for material and human contraband. Keep her out of sight; the moment would come when she could be taken on board, after a *capo-operaio* had inspected a hold and signed the papers stating the ship in question was legally free to depart. Then she could walk swiftly out of the shadows and down a pier, *controllori* and *operai* themselves out of sight, their duties finished.

Which pier? Which ship? *Where are you, Jenna?*

There were three freighters, all of medium tonnage, berthed alongside one another at three of the four major cargo docks. The fourth housed two smaller vessels – barge class – with conveyor equipment and thick piping machinery transporting and pumping bulk cargo into the open holds. She would be taken aboard one of the freighters; the immediate thing to learn was the departure time of each.

He parked the Fiat on a side street that intersected the *viale* fronting the four piers. He walked across the wide avenue, dodging several vans and trucks, to the first pier on the left, to the gate manned by a uniformed guard, a civil servant of questionable civility. He was unpleasant, and the nuisance of having to piece together Havelock's barely fluent Italian added to his hostility.

'What do you want to know for?' asked the guard, filling the doorway of the gatehouse. 'What's it to you?'

'I'm trying to find someone who may have booked passage,' said Michael, hoping the words he used were close enough to his meaning.

'*Passaggio? Biglietto?* Who buys a ticket on a Portuguese freighter?'

Havelock saw his opening; he leaned closer, glancing about as he spoke. 'This is the ship then. Forgive my poor use of your language, *Signor Controllore*. It's unforgivable. Actually, I'm with the Embassy of Portugal in Rome. In my way an . . . inspector, as you are. We were told there may be certain irregularities with this vessel. Any co-operation from you could be duly conveyed to your superiors.'

The opportunistic human ego was not affected by the lowliness of a civil service rating. The hostile guard was abruptly pleasant, moving aside to admit the *straniero importante*.

'*Scusatemi, signore!* I did not understand. We who patrol these holes of corruption must co-operate with one another, no? And, in truth, a word to my superiors – in Rome, of course.'

'Of course. Not here.'

'Of course. Not here. They are brutes down here. Come in, come in. It must be chilly for you.'

The *Miguel Cristobal* was scheduled to leave port at 5:00 a.m. Its captain was a man named Aliandro, who had been in the wheelhouse of the *Cristobal* for the past twelve years, a skipper who, it was said, knew every island, every shoal in the Western Mediterranean.

The two other freighters were of Italian registry. The guards at the gates were wearily co-operative, perfectly willing to give whatever information the oddly spoken foreigner requested. What he wished to know he could read in any newspaper under *Navi Informazione-Civitavecchia*, the pages of which were usually torn out and tacked to the walls of the various cafés around the waterfront. They helped when crewmen got drunk and forgot their schedules.

The *Isola d'Elba* was leaving at five-thirty, the *Santa Teresa* twenty minutes later at five-fifty.

Havelock started to walk away from the third gate. He looked at his watch; it was eight minutes past four. So little time.

Jenna! Where are you?

He heard the sound of a bell behind him. It was sudden, abrasive, echoing in its own vibrations, an outside bell meant to be heard above the shouts and machinery of the piers. Alarmed, he turned quickly. The guard had stepped inside the glass cubicle that was his gatehouse and was answering the telephone. The verbal flow of attentive *Sìs* emphasized the fact that whoever was on the other end of the line was issuing orders that must be thoroughly understood.

Telephones and guards at checkpoints were sources of concern to Michael. For a moment he was not sure whether or not to run. The answer was given instantly. The guard hung up the phone and stuck his head out of the door.

'You! You want to know so much about this stinking tub, here's something else! The *Teresa* stays put. She doesn't sail until six godforsaken trucks get here from Torino, which could be eight hours from now. The unions will make those bastards pay, let me tell you! Then they'll fine the crew for being drunk! They're *all* bastards!'

The *Teresa* was out of the running, for a while at least. He could concentrate on the *Elba* and the *Cristobal*, and for them he still had only minutes. His approach had to be direct; there was no time for the subtleties of move and countermove, for circling the grounds of inquiry and selecting targets cautiously, being aware of whoever might be watching him. There was time only for money – if takers could be found. Or force.

Havelock walked quickly back to the second gate where the *Isola d'Elba* was berthed, altering his story only slightly for the weary guard. He wished to speak to a few of the vessel's crew, those who might be on shore awaiting the ship's call. Would the co-operative civil servant, having shaken a hand with several thousand lire folded in the palm, know which of the waterfront cafés were favoured by the *Elba*'s crew?

'They stick together, no, *signore*? When fights break out, seamen want their friends around, even those they hate on board. Try *Il Pinguino*. Or perhaps *La Carrozza Mare*. The whisky's cheaper at the first, but the food makes one vomit. It's better at *La Carrozza*.'

The once hostile, now obsequious, guard at the gate of the *Cristobal* was more than co-operative; he was effusively friendly. 'There is a café on the Via Maggio where it is said many things change hands.'

'Would the *Cristobal*'s men be there?'

'Some perhaps. The Portuguese do not mix well, of course. No one trusts them – Not *you, signore*! I refer only to the garbage of the sea. The same everywhere. Not *you*, may God forgive me!'

'The name please?'

'*Il Tritone*.'

It took less than twelve minutes to disqualify *Il Tritone*. Michael walked through the heavy doors, beneath the crude *bas-relief* of a naked creature half-man and half-fish, into the raucous squalor of the waterfront bar. The smoke was thick, the stench of stale whisky thicker. Men shouted between the tables; others lurched about, and not a few were slumped at their tables, their heads resting on folded arms, small pools of alcohol surrounding hands and nostrils and bearded cheeks.

Havelock chose the oldest-looking man behind the bar and approached him first. 'Are there any here from the *Cristobal*?'

'*Portoghesi*?'

'*Sì*.'

'A few . . . over there, I think.'

Michael looked through the smoke and the weaving bodies to a table across the room. There were four men. 'What about the *Isola d'Elba*?' he asked, turning back to the bartender.

'*Maiali*!' replied the man. 'Pigs! They come in here, I throw them out! Scum!'

'They must be something,' said Havelock, scanning the *Tritone*'s clientele, his throat trembling at the thought of Jenna among such men.

'You want crew from the *Elba*, go to *Il Pinguino*. Over there, they don't care.'

Michael took out a ten thousand lire note and placed it in front of the barman. 'Do you speak Portuguese? Enough to be understood?'

'Down here, if one cares to make a living one must be understood in half a dozen tongues.' The man slipped the money into his apron pocket, adding, 'They no doubt speak Italian, probably better than you, *signore*. So let us speak in English. What do you wish me to do?'

'There's an empty table back there,' said Havelock, relieved, changing language, and gesturing with his head towards a rear corner of the café. 'I'm going over to sit down. You go to those men and tell them I want to see them – one at a time. If you think they won't understand me, come over with each and be my interpreter.'

'*Interprete?*'

'*Sì.*'

'*Bene.*'

One by one the four Portuguese sailors came to the table, each bewildered, two proficient in Italian, one in English, one needing the services of the *interprete*. To each, Michael said the same words.

'I'm looking for a woman. It's a minor matter, nothing to be concerned about; call it an affair of the heart. She's an impetuous woman; we've all known them, haven't we? But now she may have gone too far for her own good. I'm told she has a friend on the *Cristobal*. She may have been around the pier, asking questions, looking for transport. She's an attractive woman, average height, blonde hair, probably wearing a raincoat and a wide-brimmed hat. Have you seen anyone like that? If you have, there could be a lot more money in your pocket than there is now.'

And to each man he gave an explanation for his summons that the sailor could take back to his companions, along with five thousand lire.

'Whatever you tell me remains between us. For my good more than yours. When you go back to your table you can say the same thing I'm telling everyone. I want rough sex with someone leaving Civitavecchia, but I'm not going to take it from any son of a bitch who won't leave his papers at a hotel desk. Got it?'

Only with the third man did the barman, who insisted on being present at each interview, caution Havelock firmly. 'This one will leave his papers at a desk,' he said.

'Then he's not my type.'

'*Bene!*'

'*Grazie.*'

'*Prego.*'

Nothing. No such woman had been seen or heard of on the *Cristobal* pier. The four Portuguese crewmen resumed their drinking.

Havelock thanked the perplexed older man beside him and pressed another bill into his apron pocket. 'Which way to *Il Pinguino*?' he asked.

'The *Elba* crew?'

'That's right.'

'I'll go with you,' said the barman, removing his apron and the money in its pocket.

'Why?'

'You sound like a decent man. Also stupid. You walk into *Il Pinguino* asking questions, your money's for everyone. All it takes is one sailor with a quiet knife.'

'I can take care of myself.'

'You are not only stupid, you are *very* stupid. I own *Il Tritone*; they respect me at *Pinguino*. You'll be safer with me. You pass money too quickly.'

'I'm in a hurry.'

'*Presto!* Let's get on with it. It's a bad morning here. Not like the old days when men knew that half a chestful was enough. You taste it in your throat, you know. These assholes mix up comfort with wanting no memory. *Vieni!*'

The café five blocks away brought back memories of a life he had thought was over. He had been in too many such places in that other life; it was a sewer, a place consigned to oblivion. If *Il Tritone* catered to the garbage of humanity, *Il Pinguino* took the dregs and considered it *prima clientela*. The smoke was thicker, the shouting louder; men did not lurch, they lunged at nothing and everything, intent only on the violence in their minds. These were men who found amusement in the sudden exposure of another's weakness – or a semblance of weakness – which they construed as an absence of manhood – and then attacked.

They had nothing else. They challenged the shadows of their own deepest fears.

The owner of *Il Tritone* was greeted by his counterpart within seconds of ushering Havelock through the door. The *Pinguino*'s *proprietario* matched his establishment, having few teeth and arms that hung like huge, hairy cheeses. He was not as large as Michael's new-found friend, but there was a sense of violence about him reminiscent of a boar, that could be quickly stirred to anger.

The greetings between the two men were spoken rapidly, perfunctorily. But there was respect, as *Il Tritone*'s owner said there would be, and the arrangements were made swiftly, with a minimum of explanation.

'The American looks for a woman. It is a *malinteso*, and not our business,' said the owner of *Il Tritone*. 'She may be sailing with the *Elba* and one of these thieves may have seen her. He's willing to pay.'

'He'd better hurry,' replied the sullen boar. 'The oilers left an hour ago; they're sweating piss-green by now. The second mate will be here any minute to gather up the rest of the deck.'

'How many are there?'

'Eight, ten, who knows? I count lire, not faces.'

'Get one of your people to go round and ask quietly, find them, and tell me who they are. Clear a table for my companion. I'll bring each one to him.'

Separately, warily, in varying phases of stupor, the remaining crew of the *Elba* sat down and listened to Havelock, whose Italian increasingly became more fluent as he repeated his question. And with each he studied the man's face, the eyes, looking for a reaction, a glint of recognition, a brief straying of glance that covered a lie. With the sixth man he thought he found it; it was in the lips – a sudden stretching unrelated to the sagging muscle tone induced by whisky, and in the clouded eyes, dulled by an instinctive desire not to listen. The man knew something.

'You've seen her, *haven't* you?' said Michael, losing control, speaking in English.

'*Ascolta*,' broke in the owner of *Il Tritone*. '*In italiano, signore.*'

'Sorry.' Havelock repeated the question, which was more an accusation, in Italian.

The sailor responded with a shrug, shifted his position and started to get up. Michael reached over quickly, clamping his hand on the seaman's arm. The response was now ugly; the sailor squinted his rheumy, red-veined eyes, his mouth like that of an angry dog, lips parted, stained yellow teeth showing. In seconds he would lunge – drunkenly, to be sure – but nevertheless, attack was imminent.

'*Rilassati*,' ordered the owner of *Il Tritone*; then spoke rapidly under his breath in English. 'Show him money. Quickly! This pig will grab your throat, and they'll be all over us and you will learn nothing. You are right. He's seen her.'

Havelock released the man's arm, reached into his pocket and took out the thick pack of awkwardly small lire notes. He separated two bills, placing them in front of the sailor; they totalled 40,000 lire, a day's pay on board ship.

'As you can see,' he said in Italian, 'there's more here. You can't take it from me, but I can give it to you. On the other hand, you can walk away and not tell me anything.' Michael paused, leaned back in the chair, staring at the man, his expression hostile. 'But I can make trouble for you. And I will.'

'*In che modo?*' The crewman was as angry as he was bewildered, his eyes darting between Havelock's face, the money and the owner of *Il Tritone*, who sat impassively, his rigid posture showing that he was aware of the danger in Michael's tactic.

'How?' Havelock leaned forward, his fingers pulling the lire towards him, as though retrieving two vital cards in a game of *baccarat*. 'I'll go over to the *Elba* and find your captain. Whatever I say to him about you he's not going to like.'

'*Che cosa?* What? ... What can you say to him *in riguardo a me* that he would *ascoltare?*' The sailor's sudden use of English words was unexpected. He turned to the owner of *Il Tritone*. 'Perhaps this pig will grab *your* throat, old man. I need no help from others. For you or this *ricco americano*.' The man unzipped his coarse wool jacket; the handle of a knife protruded from a scabbard strapped to his belt; his head swayed from the effects of the whisky. A very thin line was about to be crossed.

Abruptly, Michael settled back in his chair and laughed quietly. It was a genuine laugh, in no way hostile or challenging, further confusing the seaman. '*Bene!*' said Michael, suddenly leaning forward again, removing two more 5,000 lire notes from the loose packet of bills. 'I wanted to find out if you had balls, and you told me. Good! A man without balls doesn't know what he sees. He makes things up because he's afraid, or because he sees money.' Havelock gripped the man's hand at the wrist, forcing the palm open. It was a strong if friendly grip, indicating a strength the sailor had to acknowledge. 'Here! Fifty thousand lire. There's no quarrel between us. Where did you see her?'

The abrupt changes of mood were beyond the man's comprehension. He was reluctant to forgo the challenge, but the combination of the money, the grip and the infectious laugh made him retreat. 'Are you ... go to my captain?' he asked in English, eyes swimming.

'What for? You just told me. It has nothing to do with him. Why bring that *farabutto* into it? Let him earn his own money. Where did you see her?'

'On the street. *Bionda. Bella. Largo cappello.*'

'Blonde, attractive ... wide hat! *Where?* Who was she with? A mate, a ship's officer? *Un ufficiale?*'

'Not the *Elba*. The next ship. *Barca mercantile*.'

'There are only two. The *Cristobal* and the *Teresa*. Which one?'

The man glanced around, head bobbing, eyes only half focused. 'She was talking to two men . . . one a *capitano*.'

'Which *one*?'

'*A destra*,' whispered the sailor, pulling the back of his hand across his wet lips.

'On the right?' asked Michael quickly. 'The *Santa Teresa*?'

The seaman now rubbed his chin and blinked; he was afraid, his eyes suddenly focused to the left of the table. He shrugged, crushing the money in his right hand, as he pushed back his chair. '*Non conosco. Niente. Una prostituta di capitano*.'

'*Mercantile italiana*?' pressed Havelock. 'The Italian freighter? The *Santa Teresa*?'

The sailor stood up, his face white. '*Sì . . . No! Destra . . . sinistra!*' The man's eyes were now riveted somewhere across the room; Michael angled his head unobtrusively. Three men at a table against the wall were watching the crewman from the *Elba*. '*Il capitano. Un marinaio superiore! Il migliore!*' cried the seaman hoarsely. 'I know nothing else, *signore!*' He lurched away, shouldering a path through the bodies gathered at the bar towards the alley door.

'You play dangerously,' commented the owner of the *Il Tritone*. 'It could have gone either way.'

'With a mule – drunk or otherwise – nothing's ever replaced the carrot and the whip,' said Havelock, his head still angled slightly, his concentration still on the three men at the table across the room.

'You could have had blood on your stomach and learned nothing at all.'

'But I *did* learn something.'

'Not a great deal. A freighter on the right, on the left. Which?'

'He said on the right first.'

'Coming off the pier, or going onto it?'

'From his immediate point of view. Going on. *Destra*. The *Santa Teresa*. She'll be put on board the *Teresa*, which means I have time to find her before she's given the signal. She's somewhere within sight of the dock.'

'I'm not so sure,' said *Il Tritone*'s owner, shaking his head. 'Our mule was specific. The captain was *un marinaio superiore. Il migliore*. The best, a great seaman. The captain of the *Teresa* is a tired merchantman. He never sails past Marseilles.'

'Who are those men at the table over there?' asked Michael, his question barely audible through the din. 'Don't turn your head, just shift your eyes. Who are they?'

'I do not know them by name.'

'What does that mean?'

'*Italiano*,' said the owner of *Il Tritone*, his voice flat.

'The *Santa Teresa*,' said Havelock, removing a number of bills and putting the rest of the money back into his pocket. 'You've been a great help,' he said. 'I owe the *proprietario*. The rest is for you.'

'*Grazie*.'

'*Prego*.'

'I will see you down the alley to the waterfront. I still do not like it. We don't know those men are from the *Teresa*. Something is not *in equilibrio*.'

'The percentages say otherwise. It's the *Teresa*. Let's go.'

Outside the loud café the narrow thoroughfare was comparatively silent; naked light bulbs shone weakly, enveloped in mist above intermittent doorways, and centuries-old smooth cobblestones muffled the sound of footsteps. At the end of the alley the wide avenue that fronted the piers could be seen in the glow of the street lamps; until one reached it the alley itself was a gauntlet of shadows. One walked cautiously, alert to the spaces of black silence.

'*Ecco!*' whispered the Italian. 'Someone's in that doorway. On the left. Do you have a weapon?'

'No. I haven't had time . . .'

'Then *quickly!*' The owner of *Il Tritone* suddenly broke into a run, passing the doorway as a figure lurched out – a stocky man with arms raised, hands poised for interception. But there was no gun in those hands, no weapon but the thick hands themselves.

Havelock took several rapid strides towards the prowler, then spun into the shadows on the opposite side of the alley. The man lunged; Michael spun around again and, grabbing his assailant's coat, hammered his right foot up into the man's midsection. He pivoted a third time, now yanking the intruder off the ground, and hurled him into the wall. As the man fell, Havelock sprang downwards, his left knee sinking into the man's stomach, his right hand gripping the face and clawing at the eyes.

'*Deter-se! Favor! Se Deus quizer!*' choked the prowler, holding his groin, saliva dribbling from his mouth.

The language was Portuguese, the man one of the crew of the *Cristobal*. Michael yanked him up against the wall, into the dim light; he was the seaman who had spoken a few words of English at the table in *Il Tritone*.

'If you're going into theft with assault and battery, you're not doing it very well!'

'No, senhor! I wish only to talk, but I cannot be seen! You pay me, I'll tell you things, but not where I can be seen with you!'

'Go on.'

'You pay!'

Havelock clamped the sailor's neck against the brick with his forearm, reached into his pocket and took out his money. Shoving his knee into the man's chest and freeing his hand, he removed two notes. 'Twenty thousand lire,' he said. 'Talk!'

'It's worth more. Much more, senhor! You will see.'

'I can take it back if it's not . . . Thirty thousand, that's it. Go *on!*'

'The woman goes aboard the *Cristobal* . . . *sette* . . . seven *minutos* before we sail. It is arranged. She comes out of the east warehouse door. She is guarded now; you cannot reach her. But she must walk forty metres to the cargo boarding plank.'

Michael released him and added another note to the three in the seaman's hand. 'Get out of here,' he said. 'I never saw you.'

'You must *swear* to it, senhor!' cried the man, scrambling to his feet.

'Sworn. Now get out.'

Suddenly voices were heard at the end of the alley; two men came running out of the light.

'*Americano! Americano!*' It was the owner of *Il Tritone*; he had returned with help. As the Portuguese started to race away, they grabbed him.

'Let him go!' yelled Havelock. 'It's all right! Let him go!'

Sixty seconds later Michael explained to the owner of *Il Tritone*. 'It's not the *Teresa*. It's the *Cristobal*.'

'It's what was missing!' cried the Italian. 'The knowledgeable *capitano*, the great seaman. It was there and I did not see it. Aliandro, Juan Aliandro! The finest captain in the Mediterranean. He could work his ship into any dangerous coastline, dropping off cargo wherever he wished, wherever the rocks and shoals called for no observers on shore. You have found your woman, *signore*.'

He crouched in the shadows of a stationary crane, the open spaces of the machinery allowing him unobstructed sight lines. The freighter's cargo had been loaded, the teams of stevedores dispersed, swearing as they went their various ways across the wide avenue and down the narrow alleys into the cafés. Except for the four-man cast-off crew the pier was deserted, and even they were barely visible, standing motionless by the huge piles, two men to a line, fore and aft.

A hundred yards behind him was the entrance gate, the obsequious guard inside his glass booth, his figure a grey silhouette in the rolling early-morning fog. Diagonally to the left in front of the crane some eighty-odd feet away was the ribbed, weather-beaten gangplank that went up to the *Cristobal*'s forward deck. It was the last physical connection, to be hauled on board the ship before the giant hawsers were slipped off the pilings, freeing the behemoth for the open water.

On the right, no more than sixty feet from the crane, was the door to the pier's warehouse office; it was locked, and all lights were off inside. And beyond that door was Jenna Karras, a fugitive from her own and others' betrayal – his love, who had turned on that love for reasons only she could tell him . . .

A hundred and forty-odd feet was the span she had to cross in order to disappear. Again. Not in death, but in an enigma.

Michael looked at his watch; it was four-fifty-two, the second hand approaching the minute mark – seven minutes before the *Cristobal* was scheduled to blast its bass-toned departure signal, followed by sharper, higher sounds that warned all vessels of its imminent thrust out of its secure haven, the rules of the sea instantly in force. High up on the deck, fore and midships, a few men wandered aimlessly, pinpointed by the erratic glow of their cigarettes. Except for those on the rope winches and the gang-plank detail, there was nothing for them to do but smoke and drink coffee and hope their heads would clear without excessive pain. From inside the massive black hull, the muffled roar of the turbines was heard; behind the fires the coarse, muted meshing of giant gear-wheels signified the approaching command to engage the mammoth screws in third-torque speed. Oily, dark waters churned around the curve of the *Cristobal*'s stern.

The warehouse door opened and the hammering in Havelock's chest became intolerable, the pain in his eyes excruciating; he had to endure both for seconds longer. Once Jenna reached the mid-point of the pier, in sight of the gate and the guard and the alarms he could raise, Michael would intercept her. Not an instant sooner.

She was there! *Now.*

He lunged from behind the crane and raced forward, not caring about the sound of his footsteps, intent only on reaching her.

'Jenna! For God's sake, *Jenna!*'

He grabbed her shoulders; the woman spun around in terror.

His breath exploded from his throat. The face that was turned up to him was an old face, an ugly face, the pockmarked face of a waterfront whore. The eyes that stared at him were the wide, dark eyes of a rodent, outlined with thick, running borders of cheap mascara; the lips were blood-red and cracked, the teeth stained and chipped.

'*Who are you?*' His scream was the scream of a madman. '*Liar! Liar!* Why are you *lying*? Why are you *here*? Why *aren't* you here? *Liar!*'

Mists not of the sea filled his mind, cross-currents of blurred insanity: he was beyond reason, knowing only that his hands had become claws, then fists – scraping, hammering – *kill the rodent, kill the impostor! Kill, kill!*

Other screams, other shouts, commands and counter-commands, filled the roaring caverns of his consciousness. There was no beginning, no end, only a furious core of frenzy.

Then he felt blows, but did not feel pain. Men were all around him, then above him; fists and heavy boots struck him. Repeatedly. Everywhere.

And then the darkness came. And silence.

Above the pier, on the second floor of the warehouse office, a figure stood at the window looking down at the scene of violence below. She breathed deeply, her fingers stretched across her lips, tears welling in her clear brown eyes. Absently Jenna Karras pulled her hand away from her face and pressed it against the side of her head, against the long blonde hair that fell beneath the wide-brimmed hat.

'Why did you do it, Mikhail?' she whispered softly to herself. 'Why do you want to kill me?'

6

He opened his eyes, aware of the sickening stench of cheap whisky, feeling the dampness about his chest and throat – his shirt, jacket and trousers had been drenched. In front of him were gradations of darkness, shadows of grey and black interrupted by tiny, dancing specks of light that bobbed and weaved in the farthest darkness. There was dull pain everywhere, centred in his stomach, rising through his neck to his head, which felt swollen and numb. He had been beaten and dragged to the end of the pier – the far right end, beyond the warehouse, if his blurred orientation was anywhere near accurate – and left to regain consciousness, or conceivably, to roll over the edge into a watery death.

But he had not been killed; that told him something. Slowly, he moved his right hand to his left wrist; his watch was there. He stretched his legs and reached into his pocket; his money, too, was intact. He had not been robbed; that told him something else.

He had spoken with too many men, and too many others had seen him in those strange conversations. They had been his protection. Murder was murder, and regardless of what *Il Tritone*'s owner had said, a 'quiet knife' on the waterfront was a subject for investigation, as was assault and robbery when the victim was a wealthy foreigner. No one wanted too many questions asked on the piers; cool heads had ordered him left as he was, which meant they had been paid to implement other orders, higher orders. Otherwise something would have been stolen – a watch, a few thousand lire; this was the waterfront.

Nothing. An inquisitive, wealthy foreigner had gone berserk, attacking a blonde whore on the pier, and men had protected her. No investigation was called for, as long as the *ricco americano maledetto* had his property intact, if not his senses.

A set-up. A professionally executed snare, the trappers exonerated once the trap had sprung shut. The whole night, the morning, had been a set-up! He rolled over to his left; the south-east ocean was a line of fire beyond the horizon. Dawn had come, and the *Cristobal* was but one of a dozen small silhouettes on the water.

Slowly Havelock got to his knees, pressing them against the wet planks beneath him, pushing himself up painfully with his hands. Once on his feet he turned around, again slowly, testing his legs and ankles, moving his shoulders, arching his neck, then his back. There was nothing broken, but the machine was badly bruised; it would not respond to quick commands, and he hoped he would not have to issue any.

The guard. Had the ego-stroked civil servant been part of the act? Had he been told to confront the foreigner with hostility at first, then turn to obsequiousness, pulling the mark in for the trap? It was effective strategy; he should have seen through it. Neither of the other two guards had been difficult, each perfectly willing to tell him whatever he wanted to know, the man at the gate of the *Teresa*'s pier even going so far as to inform him of the freighter's delayed schedule.

The owner of *Il Tritone*? The sailor from the *Cristobal* in a narrow dark alley? Were they, too, part of it? Had the coincidence of logical progression led him to those men on the waterfront who had been waiting for him? Yet how could they have been waiting? Four hours ago Civitavecchia was a vaguely remembered name on a map; it had held no meaning for him. There had been no reason for him to come to Civitavecchia, no way for an unknown message to be telegraphed. Yet it had been; he had to accept that without knowing how or why. There was so much beyond his understanding, a maddening mosaic with too many pieces missing.

Anything you can't understand in this business is a risk, but I don't have to tell you that. Rostov. Athens.

A decoy had been paraded through the pre-dawn mist to pull him out and force him to act. But *why?* What had they expected him to do? He had made it plain what he intended to do. So what was learned, what clarified? What was the point? Was she trying to kill *him?* Was that what Costa Brava was all about?

Jenna, why are you doing this? What happened to you? To us?

He walked unsteadily, stopping occasionally to brace his legs and regain his balance. Reaching the edge of the warehouse, he propelled himself along the wall past darkened windows and the huge loading doors, until he came to the corner of the building. Beyond was the deserted pier, the wash of intersecting floodlights swollen with pockets of rolling fog. He peered around the steel moulding, squinting to focus on the glass cubicle of the guard's post. As before, the figure inside was barely visible, but he was there; Michael could see the stationary glow of a cigarette in the centre of the middle pane.

The glow moved to the right; the guard was sliding the door of the booth open. A man was walking through the mist towards him, medium-sized, in an overcoat, wearing a hat, the brim angled as a stroller's might be on the Via Veneto. The clothes were not the clothes of the waterfront; they belonged in the city streets. The figure approached the glass booth, stopped by the door and spoke to the guard. Both then looked towards the end of the pier, at the warehouse; the guard gestured and Michael knew they were talking about him. The man nodded, turned and raised his hand; within seconds his summons was obeyed. Two other men came into view, both large, both wearing clothes more suited to the waterfront.

Havelock leaned his head against the edge of steel, a deep, despairing sense of futility mingling with his pain. Exhaustion overwhelmed him. He was no match for such men; he could barely raise his arms, nor his feet. He had no weapons at all.

Where was Jenna? Had she gone aboard the *Cristobal* after the decoy had succeeded? It was a logical – no, it wasn't! The commotion would have centred too much attention on the freighter and would have roused unfriendly or unpaid officials too easily. The ship itself had been a decoy. Jenna was boarding one of the other two!

Michael turned away from the wall and hobbled across the wet planks towards the edge of the pier. He wiped his eyes, staring through the heavy mist. Involuntarily, he gasped, the pain in his stomach acute. The *Elba* was gone. He had been pulled to the wrong pier, duped into an uncontrollable situation while Jenna went on board the *Elba*. Was the captain of the *Elba*, like the skipper of the *Cristobal*, a master navigator? Would he – could he – manoeuvre his awkward ship close enough to an unpatrolled shoreline for a small boat to ferry his contraband to a beach?

One man had the answer. A man in an overcoat and an angled hat, clothes worn on the waterfront by someone who did not haul and fork-lift but, instead, bought and sold. That man would know; he had negotiated Jenna's passage.

Havelock lurched back to the corner of the warehouse wall. He had to reach that man; he had to get by two others coming for him. If only he had a weapon, *any* kind of weapon. He looked around in the faintly lessening darkness. Nothing. Not even a loose board or a slat from a broken crate.

The water. The drop was long but he could manage it. If he could get to the far end of the pier before he was seen, it would be presumed he had plunged over while unconscious. How many seconds did he have? He peered around the moulding into the wash of the floodlights, prepared to push himself away and run.

But the two men were no longer walking towards him. They were standing motionless inside the fenced gate. Why? Why was he being left where he was without further interference?

Suddenly, from out of the impenetrable mist several piers away, came the ear-shattering screech of a ship's siren. Then another, followed by a prolonged, bass chord that vibrated throughout the harbour. It was the *Santa Teresa*! It was his answer! The two men had been summoned not to punish him further, but to restrict him to the first pier. There was no delayed schedule for the *Teresa*; that, too, was part of the set-up. She was sailing on time, and Jenna was *on board*. As the ship's clock ran down, there was only one thing left for the negotiator to do: keep the disabled hunter in place.

Fiercely he told himself he had to get to that pier, stop her, stop the freighter from casting off, for once the giant lines were slipped off the pilings there was nothing he could do, no way to reach her. She would disappear into one of a dozen countries, a hundred cities . . . nothing left, not for him, not any longer. Without her he didn't want to go on!

He wished he knew what the blaring signals meant, how much time he had. He could only estimate. There had been two high pitched blasts from the *Cristobal*; moments later the blonde decoy had emerged from the shadows of the warehouse door. Seven minutes. Did the bass-tone chord signify less or more time? He probed his memory, racing over scores of assignments that had taken him to waterfronts everywhere.

He remembered; more accurately, he *thought* he remembered, as a blurred recent memory tried to surface. The high-pitched shrieks were for ships in the distance, the vibrating lower tones for those nearer by – a rule of thumb for the sea – and the docks. And while he was being beaten, the outer vibrations of a low, grinding chord had fused with his own screams of protest and fury. The bass-toned whistle had followed shortly after the shrieks – prelude to imminent departure. Seven minutes – less one, more likely two, perhaps three.

He had only minutes. Six, five . . . four, no more than that. The *Teresa*'s pier was several hundred yards away; in his condition it would take at least two minutes to get there, and that would happen only if he could get past the two jacketed men who had been called to stop him. Four minutes at the outside, two minimum. Jesus! *How?* He looked around again, trying to control his panic, aware that every second reduced his chances.

A stocky black object was silhouetted between two pilings ten yards away; he had not noticed it before because it was a stationary part of the dock. He studied it now. It was a barrel, an ordinary barrel, undoubtedly punctured during loading or unloading procedures, and now used as a receptacle for coffee cups, rubbish, pre-dawn fires; they were on piers everywhere. He ran to it, gripped it, rocked it. It swung free; he lowered it to its side and rolled it back towards the wall. Time elapsed: thirty, perhaps forty seconds. Time remaining; between one and a half and three-plus minutes. The tactic that came into focus was a desperate one . . . but it was the only one that was possible. He could not get past those men unless they came to him, unless the fog and the translucent, brightening darkness worked for him and against them. There was no time to think about the guard and the man in the overcoat.

He crouched in the shadows, against the wall, both hands on the sides of the filthy barrel. He took a deep breath and screamed as loud as he could, knowing the scream would echo throughout the deserted pier.

'*Soccorso! Presto! Sanguino! Muoio!*'

He stopped, listening. In the distance he heard the shouts; they were questions, then commands. He screamed again.

'*Assistenza! Soccorso!*'

Silence.

Then racing footsteps. Nearer . . . drawing nearer.

Now! He shoved the barrel with all the strength he could muster. It clanked as it rolled laterally over the planks, through the fog, towards the edge of the pier.

The two men rounded the corner of the warehouse in the misty light; the barrel reached the edge of the dock. It struck one of the pilings! Oh, *Christ*! Then it spun and plunged over. The sound of the splash below was loud; the two men shouted at each other and raced to the edge.

Now!

Havelock rose to his feet and ran out of the shadows, his hands extended, shoulders and arms like battering rams. He forced his unsteady legs to respond, each racing step painful, but calculated. He made contact. First the man on the right, pummelling him with both outstretched hands; then the Italian on his left, crashing his shoulder into the small of the man's back.

A deafening blast from the *Teresa*'s funnels covered the screams of the two men as they plummeted into the water below. Michael swung to his left and hobbled back towards the corner of the warehouse; he would go out onto the deserted pier and face the once obsequious guard and the elegantly dressed man. Time elapsed: another minute. Less than three remained at most.

He ran unsteadily out into the vast expanse of the pier with its fog-laden pools of floodlights and immobile machinery. Pitching his voice at the edge of hysteria, he shouted in broken Italian: 'Help me! Help *them*! It's *crazy*! I'm hurt. Two men came to help me. As they drew near there were gunshots! *Three gunshots!* From the next pier. I could hardly hear them because of the freighter but I did! *Gunshots!* Quickly! They're wounded. One dead, I think! Oh, *Christ*, hurry!'

The exchange between the two men was verbal chaos. As Havelock staggered erratically towards the gate he could see that the guard's automatic was drawn, but it was not the same guard; he was shorter, stockier, older. His broad face was full of angry resentment, in contrast to that of the civilian – in his mid-thirties, tanned, suave – which was cold and without expression. He was ordering the guard to investigate; but the guard was shouting that he would not leave his post, not for twenty thousand lire! The *capo-regime* could look after his own garbage; *he* was no frightened *bambino* of the docks. The *capo* could buy a few hours of his time, his disappearance, but no more!

A set-up. From the beginning, a charade.

'*Andate voi stesso!*' yelled the guard.

Swearing, the civilian started towards the warehouse and broke into a run, then abruptly slowed his pace. He cautiously approached the corner of the building.

The guard was now in front of the glass booth, his gun levelled at Michael. 'You! Walk to the fence,' he shouted in Italian. 'Raise your hands above you and grab the wire as high as you can! Do not turn round! I'll fire into your head if you do!'

Barely two minutes left; if it was going to work, it would happen now.

'Oh, *Jesus!*' Havelock screamed as he gripped his chest and fell.

The guard rushed forward; Michael remained motionless in a foetal position, dead weight on the damp, hard surface. 'Get up!' commanded the uniformed man. 'Get to your feet!'

The guard reached down, grabbing Havelock's shoulder. It was the movement Michael had been waiting for. He spun off the ground, clasping the weapon above his head and gripped the wrist at his shoulder, wrenching it clockwise as he rose and hammered his knee into the falling guard's throat. The gun barrel was in his hand; he swung it down, crashing it into the base of the Italian's skull. The man collapsed. Havelock dragged him into the shadows of the booth, then raced out of the open gate, jamming the weapon into his jacket pocket.

A prolonged, belching sound came from the distance, followed by four hysterically pitched screeches. The *Teresa* was about to slip away from its berth! Michael felt a sickening sense of futility sweeping over him as he ran breathlessly down the wide avenue, his legs barely able to carry him, his feet swerving, slapping the pavement. When he reached the *Teresa*'s pier, the guard – the same guard – was inside his glass booth, once again on the telephone, nodding his outsized head, his dull eyes accepting other lies.

There was now a chain stretched across the open gate – only an official hindrance, not a prohibition. Havelock grabbed the hook and yanked it out of its cemented base; the chain curled snake-like into the air and clattered to the ground.

'*Che cosa!? Fermati!*'

Michael raced – his legs in agony – down the long stretch of the pier, through the circular pools of floodlights, past immobile machinery, towards the freighter outlined in the swirling mists at the end of the dock. His right leg collapsed; his hands broke the fall but not the impact, his right shoulder sliding across the moist surface. He grabbed his leg, forcing himself up, and propelled himself along the planks until he could work up the momentum to run again.

Gasping for air as he ran, he finally reached the end of the pier. The futility was complete: the freighter *Santa Teresa* was floating thirty feet beyond the pilings, the giant hawsers slithering over the dark waters, hauled in by men who looked down at him through the shadows.

'Jenna!' he screamed. 'Jenna! *Jenna!*'

He fell to the wet wood of the pier, arms and legs throbbing, chest in spasms, his head splitting as if cracked open with an axe. He . . . had . . . lost her . . . A small boat could drop her off at any of a thousand unpatrolled stretches of coastline in the Mediterranean; she was gone. The only person on earth he cared about was gone for ever. Nothing was his, and he was nothing.

He heard the shouts behind him, then the hammering of racing feet. And as he heard the sounds he was reminded of other sounds, other feet . . . another pier. From where the *Cristobal* had sailed!

There was a man in an overcoat who had ordered other men to come after him; they, too, had run across a deserted pier through shimmering pools of floodlights and the mist. If he could find that man! If he found him, he would peel the suntanned flesh from the face until he was told what he had to know.

He got to his feet and began limping rapidly towards the guard who was running at him, weapon extended.

'*Fermati! Mani in alto.*'

'*Un errore!*' Havelock shouted back, his voice both aggressive and apologetic; he had to get by the man, not be detained. He took several notes from his pocket, holding them in front of him so they could be seen in the spill of the floodlights. 'What can I tell you?' he continued in Italian. 'I made a mistake . . . which benefits *you*, doesn't it? You and I, we spoke before, remember?' He pressed the money into the guard's hand while slapping him on the back. 'Come on, put that thing away. I'm your friend, remember? What harm is there? Except I'm a little poorer and you're a little richer. Also, I've had too much wine.'

'I thought it was you!' said the guard grudgingly, taking the bills and ramming them into his pocket, his eyes darting about. 'You're crazy in the head! You could have been shot. For *what?*'

'You told me the *Teresa* wasn't sailing for hours.'

'It's what *I* was told! They're bastards, *all* bastards! They're crazy too! They don't know what they're doing.'

'They know exactly what they're doing,' said Michael quietly. 'I've got to get along now. Thanks for your help.'

Before the angry guard could answer Havelock started forward rapidly, wincing in pain as he tried to control his throbbing legs and aching chest. *For God's sake, hurry!*

He reached the stretch of fence that enclosed the *Cristobal*'s pier, his hand now in his pocket, grateful for the weapon. The unconscious guard was still on the ground in the lower shadows of the glass booth. He had neither moved nor been moved in the five minutes, perhaps six, that he had lain there. Was the man in the overcoat still on the pier? The odds favoured it; logic dictated that he would have looked for the guard because he did not see him in the booth and, when he found him, would have questioned the fallen man. In doing so, some part of the unconscious body would have been moved; it had not been.

But why would the *capo-regime* remain on the pier for so long? The answer came from the sea through the fog and the wind. Shouts, questions, followed by commands and further questions. The man in the overcoat was still on the pier, his gorillas screaming from the waters below.

Michael clenched his teeth, forcing the pain from his mind. He slid along the side wall of the warehouse, past the door from which the blonde decoy had emerged, to the corner of the building. The morning light was growing brighter, the mists rising, the absence of the freighter permitting the early rays of the sun to spread over the dock. In the distance, on the water, another ship was steaming slowly towards the harbour of Civitavecchia; it might well be heading for the berth recently vacated by the *Cristobal*. If so, there was very little time remaining before the landing crews arrived. He had to move swiftly, act effectively and he was not at all sure he was capable of doing either.

A stretch of unpatrolled coastline. Did the man only yards away from him now know which? He must find out. He had to be capable.

He rounded the corner, holding the weapon against the cloth of his jacket. He could not use it, he understood that; it would serve no purpose because it would only eliminate his source and draw attention to the pier. But the threat had to be conveyed as genuine; his anger had to seem desperate. He was capable of that.

He stared through the rising mist. The man in the overcoat was at the edge of the dock, excitedly barking instructions in a low voice; he too, was obviously afraid of drawing attention from stray crewmen who might be loitering on the adjacent pier. The effect was comic. From what Michael could gather, one of the men below was hanging onto a piling strut, reluctant to let go because apparently he couldn't swim. The negotiator was ordering the second man to support his companion, but he appeared to be refusing, concerned that he might be pulled under by his incompetent associate.

'Don't talk any more!' Havelock said sharply in Italian, his words clear if not precise, his voice commanding, not loud.

The startled man spun round, his right hand reaching under his overcoat.

'If I see a gun,' continued Michael, moving closer, 'you'll be dead and in the water before you can raise it. Move away from there. Walk towards me. Now to your left. Over to the wall. Move! Don't stop!'

The man lurched forward. 'I could have had you killed, *signore*. I did not. Surely that is worth something to you.'

'It is – obviously. I thank you.'

'Nor was anything on your person taken, I assume you are aware of that. My orders were clear.'

'I'm aware. Now tell me why. On both counts.'

'I am neither a killer nor a thief, *signore*.'

'Not good enough. Raise your hands! Lean against the wall and spread your legs!' The Italian complied; it was not the first time such orders had been given him. Havelock came up behind him, kicking the man's right calf as he whipped his hand around the *capo-regime's* waist, pulling the gun from the Italian's belt. He glanced at it, impressed. The weapon was a Spanish automatic, a Llama .38 calibre, with grip and manual safeties. A quality gun, undoubtedly less expensive on the waterfront. He shoved it into his own belt. 'Tell me about the girl. Quickly!'

'I was paid. What more can I tell you?'

'A great deal.' Michael reached up and grabbed the man's left hand; it was soft. The negotiator was not a violent man, the term *capo-regime* which the guard had used was misapplied. This Italian was no part of the Mafia;

a Mafioso at his age would have come up through the ranks and would not have soft hands.

A sudden cacophony of ship's whistles erupted from the harbour. They were joined by panicked shouts from the lone man in the slapping waters below the pier. Taking advantage of the sounds, Michael rammed the pistol into the negotiator's kidney. The man screamed. Then Havelock crashed the handle into the side of the Italin's neck and there was another scream, followed by a gasping and a series of whimpering pleas.

'*Signore . . . signore!* You are American; we speak American! Do not do this to me! I saved your life – my word on it!'

'We'll get to that. The *girl*! Tell me about the girl! Quickly!'

'I do favours around the docks. Everyone knows that! She needed a favour. She paid!'

'To get out of Italy?'

'What else?'

'She paid for a lot more than that! How many did *you* pay? For the set-up.'

'*Cosa dice?* Set . . . up?'

'That show you put on! The pig who walked out of that door over there!' Havelock gripped the Italian by the shoulder and spun him round, slamming him back into the wall. 'Right around that corner,' he added, gesturing. 'What was that all about? Tell me! She paid for that, too. *Why?*'

'As you say, *signore*. She paid. *Spiegazioni* . . . explanations . . . were not required.'

Michael jammed the barrel of the pistol deep into the man's stomach. 'Not good enough. *Tell* me!'

'She said she had to *know*,' the negotiator spat out, doubling over.

'Know what?' Havelock slapped the man's hat off and, grabbing him by the hair, crashed his head into the wall. 'Know *what?*'

'What you would do!'

'How did she know I'd follow her here?'

'She did not!'

'Then why?'

'She said you *might* do so! You were . . . *ingegnoso* . . . a resourceful man. You've hunted other men; you have means at your disposal. Contacts, sources.'

'That's too loose! *How?*' Michael bunched the Italian's hair in his fist, pulling it half out of its roots.

'*Signore* . . . she said she spoke to three drivers on the *piattaforma* before she found a taxi to bring her to Civitavecchia! She was afraid!'

It made sense. It had not occurred to him to look for a taxi ramp at the station; taxis were not in abundant supply in Rome. In truth, he had simply not been thinking, only moving.

'*Per favore! Soccorso! Mio Dio!*' The screams came from the water below.

The ships in the harbour filled the air with whistles and steam. There was so little time left; soon the crews would come, men and machinery crawling all over the pier. He had to learn exactly what the negotiator had sold; he gripped the man's throat with his left hand.

'She's on the *Teresa*, isn't she?'

'*Sì!*'

Havelock recalled the words of *Il Tritone*'s owner: the *Teresa* sailed to Marseilles. 'How is she to be taken off the ship?'

The Italian did not answer; Michael plunged his fingers deeper into the man's throat, choking the windpipe. He went on: 'Understand me, and understand me well.If you don't tell me, I'll kill you now. And if you lie, and she gets past me in Marseilles, I'll come back for you. She was right, I'm resourceful and I've hunted a great many men. I'll find you.'

The negotiator went into a spasm, his mouth gaping as he tried to speak. Havelock reduced the pressure on his neck. The Italian coughed violently, grabbing his throat, and said, 'What's it to me anyway, so I'll tell you. I don't want *afflizione* with the likes of you, *signore*! I should have known better. I should have listened better!'

'Go on.'

'Not Marseilles. San Remo. The *Teresa* stops at San Remo. How or where she is to be brought on shore, I do not know – my word on it! She buys her way to Paris. She's to be taken across the border at Col des Moulinets. When, I do not know – my word! From there to Paris. I swear on the blood of Christ!'

The negotiator did not have to swear. It was clear he was telling the truth. He was being honest out of fear, extraordinary fear. What had Jenna told him? Why hadn't he ordered Michael killed? And why had nothing been stolen? Michael released his grip on the Italian's neck.

He spoke quietly. 'You said you could have had me killed, but you didn't. Now tell me why.'

'No, *signore*, I will not say it,' whispered the man. 'In the name of God, you'll never see me again! I say nothing, know nothing!'

Havelock raised the pistol slowly, resting the point of the barrel on the man's left eye. 'Say it,' he said.

'*Signore*, I have a small, profitable business here, but I have never once – *never* – involved myself with political activities! Or anything remotely connected to such things. I swear on the tears of the Madonna! I thought she was lying, appealing to me with lies! I never once believed her!'

'But I wasn't killed, nothing on my person taken, I think you said.' Michael paused, then shouted, as he jammed the barrel into the Italian's eye. 'Why?'

The man screamed, spitting out the words. 'She said you were an American working with the *comunisti*! With the Soviets. I did not believe her! I know nothing of such things! But caution would naturally be called for . . . caution. In Civitavecchia we are outside such wars. They are too . . . *internazionali* . . . for people like us who make our few unimportant lire on the docks. These things mean nothing to us – my word on it! We wish no trouble from you, any of you! . . . *Signore*, you can *understand*. You attacked a woman – a *prostituta*, to be certain, but a woman – on the pier. Men stopped you, pulled you away, but when I saw, I stopped *them*! I told them we should be cautious. We had to think . . .'

The frightened man continued to babble, but Havelock was not listening. What he had heard stunned him beyond anything he imagined he might hear. *An American working with the Soviets*. Jenna had said this? It was insane!

Had she tried to appeal to the man with a lie, to instil a very real fear in the small-time operator after the fact, *after* the trap? The Italian had not equivocated; he had repeated her story out of fear. He had not lied.

Did she believe it? Was that what he had seen in her eyes on the platform at the Ostia station? Did she really believe it – just as he had believed beyond any doubt in his mind that she was a deep cover officer for the *Voennaya*?

Oh, *Christ*! Each turned against the other with the same manoeuvre! Had the evidence against him been as airtight as the evidence against her? It must have been; that was also in her eyes. Fear, hurt . . . pain. There was no one she could trust, not now, not for a while, perhaps not ever. She could only run – as he had kept running. God! What had they *done*?

Why?

She was on her way to Paris. He would find her in Paris. Or fly to San Remo or Col des Moulinets, and intercept her at one or the other. He had the advantage of fast transport; she was on an old freighter plodding across the water and he would be flying. He had time.

He would use that time. There was an intelligence officer at the embassy in Rome who was about to know the depth of his anger. Lieutenant-Colonel Lawrence Baylor Brown was going to supply answers or all the exposés of Washington's clandestine activities would be mere footnotes compared with what he would reveal; the incompetences, the illegalities, the miscalculations and errors costing the lives of thousands the world over every year.

He would start with a black diplomat in Rome who funnelled secret orders to American agents throughout Italy and the western Mediterranean.

'*Capisce?* You *do* understand, *signore?*' The Italian was pleading, buying time, his eyes glancing furtively to the right. Over on the second pier three men were walking through the early light towards the far pile; two blasts of a ship's whistle told why. The freighter steaming into port was to be tied up at the *Elba*'s berth. In moments, additional crews would arrive. 'We are cautious . . . *naturalmente*, but we know nothing of such things! We are *creature* of the docks, nothing more?'

'I understand,' said Michael, touching the man's shoulder and turning him around. 'Walk to the edge,' he ordered quietly.

'*Signore*, please! I beg you!'

'Just do as I say. *Now*.'

'I swear on the patron saint of mercy Himself! On the blood of Christ, on the tears of the Holy Mother!' The Italian was weeping, his voice rising. 'I am an insignificant merchant, *signore*! I know nothing! Say nothing!'

As they reached the edge of the pier, Havelock said, 'Jump,' and pushed the negotiator over the side.

'*Mio Dio! Assistenza!*' screamed the henchman below as his employer joined him in the water.

Michael turned and hobbled back to the corner of the warehouse wall. The dock was still deserted, but the guard was beginning to move, shaking his head, trying to pull himself up in the shadows of the booth. Havelock slapped open the cylinder of the pistol and shook the bullets out of their tracks; they clattered onto the dock. He hurried towards the gate, and when he reached the door of the glass booth, he threw the weapon inside. He ran as fast as he was capable of running through the gate, towards the rented car.

Rome. There would be answers in Rome.

7

The four men around the table in the white-walled room on the third floor of the State Department building were youngish men by upper-echelon Washington standards. Their ages ranged from the mid-thirties to the late forties, but their lined faces and hollow look made them old beyond their years. Their work entailed sleepless nights and prolonged periods of anxiety, acerbated by their insular existence: none of them could discuss the crises they faced in that room with anyone outside it. These were the strategists of covert operations, the air traffic controllers of clandestine activities; roving vultures could be shot down on their slightest miscalculation. Others above them might request the broad objectives; others below might design the specific assignments. But only these men were aware of every conceivable variation, every likely consequence of a given operation; they were the clearing house. Each was a specialist, each an authority. Only they could give the final nod for the vultures to fly.

Yet they had no radar grids or circling antennae to aid them; they had only the projections of human behaviour to guide them. They had to examine actions and reactions, not simply those of the enemy but those of their own people in the field as well. Evaluation was a never-ending struggle, which was rarely resolved to everyone's satisfaction. The 'what if' probabilities were geometrically compounded with each new twist of events, each human reaction to abruptly-altered circumstances. They were psycho-analysts in an endless labyrinth of abnormality, their patients the products of that disorder. They were specialists in a macabre way of life where the truth was usually a lie and lies too often were the only means of survival. Stress was the factor that frightened them most, for under maximum or prolonged stress both one's enemies and one's own people saw things and did things they might not do otherwise. The totally unpredictable added to the abnormal made dangerous territory.

This was the conclusion the four men had reached regarding the crisis late that night. Lt-Colonel Lawrence Baylor Brown in Rome had sent his cable on priority cipher; its contents required the opening of a dead file so that each strategist could study the facts.

They were beyond dispute. The events at that isolated beach on the Costa Brava had been verified by two on-site confirmations, one of them Foreign Service Officer Havelock himself, the other a man unknown to Havelock named Steven MacKenzie, one of the most experienced undercover opera-tives working in Europe for the Central Intelligence Agency. He had risked his life to bring back proof: torn garments stained with blood. Everything had been microscopically examined, the results positive: Jenna Karras. The reasons for a back-up confirmation had not been made explicit, nor was that necessary. The relationship between Havelock and the Karras woman was known to those who had to know; a man under maximum stress might fall apart, be incapable of carrying out what had to be done. Washington had to know. Agent MacKenzie had been positioned two hundred feet north of Havelock; his view was clear, his confirmation absolute, his proof incontrovertible. The Karras woman had been killed that night. The fact that Steven MacKenzie had died of a heart seizure while sailing in Chesapeake Bay three weeks after he returned from Barcelona, in no way diminished his contribution. The doctor who had been summoned by the Coast Guard patrol was a well-established physician on the Eastern Shore, a surgeon named Randolph with impeccable credentials. A thorough post-mortem was conclusive: MacKenzie's death was from natural causes.

Beyond Costa Brava itself, the evidence against Jenna Karras had been subjected to the most exhaustive scrutiny. Secretary of State Anthony Matthias had demanded it, and the strategists knew why. There was another relationship to take into consideration: one that had existed between Matthias and Michael Havelock for nearly twenty years since student had met teacher at Princeton University. Fellow Czechs by birth, one had established himself as perhaps the most brilliant geopolitical mind in the academic world, while the other, a young, haunted expatriate, was desperately searching for his own identity. The differences were considerable, but the friendship was strong.

Anton Matthias had come to America over forty years ago, the son of a prominent doctor from Prague who had hurried his family out of Czechoslovakia under the shadow of the Nazis and was welcomed by the medical community. Havelock's immigration, on the other hand, was managed covertly as a joint exercise of American and British intelligence; his origins were obscured, initally for the child's own safety. And whereas Matthias's meteoric rise in government followed from a succession of influential political figures who openly sought his counsel and publicly extolled his brilliance, the much younger man from Prague proceeded to establish his own worth through clandestine accomplishments that would never see the light of day. Yet in spite of the dissimilarities of age and reputation, intellect and temperament, there existed a bond between them, held firm by the elder, never taken advantage of by the younger.

Those who confirmed the evidence against the Karras woman understood that there was no room for error, just as the strategists understood now that the cable from Rome had to be studied carefully, handled delicately. Above all, for the time being, it must be kept from Anthony Matthias. For though the media had announced that the extraordinary Secretary of State was off on a well-deserved holiday, the truth was something else. Matthias was ill, some whispered gravely ill, and although through his subordinates he was in constant touch with State, he had not been in Washington for nearly five weeks. Even those perceptive men and women of the press corps who suspected the vacation ploy said nothing and printed nothing. No one really wanted to think about it; the world could not afford it.

And Rome could not become an additional burden for Anthony Matthias.

'He's hallucinating, of course,' said the balding man named Miller, putting his copy of the cable down on the table in front of him. Paul Miller, MD, was a psychiatrist, an authority on diagnosing erratic behaviour.

'Is there anything in his record that might have warned us?' asked a red-haired, stocky man in rumpled suit and an open collar, his tie unknotted. His name was Ogilvie, a former field agent.

'Nothing you would have read,' replied Daniel Stern, the strategist on Miller's left. His title was Director of Consular Operations, which was a euphemism for the section chief of State's clandestine activities.

'Why not?' asked the fourth strategist, a conservatively dressed man who might have stepped out of an advertisement in the *Wall Street Journal* for IBM. He was seated next to Ogilvie. His name was Dawson, a specialist in international law. He pressed his point. 'Are you saying there were – are – omissions in his service file?'

'Yes. A security hangover from years ago. No one ever bothered to reassess, so the file remained incomplete. But the answer to Ogilvie's question might be found there. The warning we missed.'

'How so?' asked Miller, peering over his glasses, his fingers spread across his balding hairline.

'He could be finally burned out. Over the edge.'

'What do you mean?' Ogilvie leaned forward, his expression none too pleasant. 'Evaluation depends on available data, goddamn it.'

'I don't think anyone thought it was necessary. His record's superior. Except for an outburst or two, he's been extremely productive, reasonable under very adverse conditions.'

'Only, now he's seeing dead people in railroad stations,' interrupted Dawson. 'Why?'

'Do you know Havelock?' asked Stern.

'Only from a field personnel interview,' answered the lawyer. 'Eight or nine months ago; he flew back for it. He seemed efficient.'

'He was,' agreed the Director of Cons Op. 'Efficient, productive, reasonable . . . very tough, very cold, very bright. But then he was trained at an early age under rather extraordinary circumstances. Maybe that's what we should have looked at.' Stern paused, picked up a large manilla envelope, and removed a red bordered file folder, sliding out carefully. 'Here's the complete background dossier on Havelock. What we had before was basic and acceptable. A graduate from Princeton with a Ph.D. in European History and a lesser degree in Slavic languages. Home: Greenwich, Connecticut. A war orphan brought over from England and adopted by a couple named Webster, both cleared. What we all looked at,' of course, was the recommendation from Matthias, someone even then to be reckoned with. And what the recruiters here at State saw sixteen years ago was fairly obvious. A highly intelligent graduate willing to work for bureaucratic spit, even willing to perfect his linguistic dialects and go into deep-cover work. But that wasn't necessary – the language part. Czech was his native tongue; he knew it better than we thought he did. That's what's here; it's the rest of his story and could be the reason for the breakdown we're witnessing now.'

'That's a hell of a leap backward,' said Ogilvie. 'Can you sketch it for us? I don't like surprises; retired paranoids we don't need.'

'Apparently we've got one,' interjected Miller, picking up the cable. 'If Brown's judgement means anything – '

'It does,' Stern broke in. 'He's one of the best we've got in Europe.'

'Still, he's Pentagon,' added Dawson. 'Judgement's not a strong point.'

'It is with him,' corrected the Cons Op director. 'He's black and had to be good.'

'As I was about to say,' Miller continued, 'Baylor includes a strong recommendation that we take Havelock seriously. He saw what he saw.'

'Which is impossible,' said Ogilvie. 'Which means we've got a whacko. What's in there, Dan?'

'An ugly early life,' replied Stern, lifting the cover of the file and turning several pages. 'We knew he was Czech, but that's all we knew. There were several thousand Czechoslovakian refugees in England during the war, and that was the explanation given for his being there. But it wasn't true. There were two stories, one real, the other a cover. He wasn't in England during the war, nor were his parents. He spent those years in and around Prague. It was a long nightmare and very real for him. It started when he was old enough to know it, see it. Unfortunately, we can't get inside his head, and that could be vital now.' The director turned to Miller. 'You'll have to advise us here, Paul. He could be extremely dangerous.'

'Then you'd better clarify,' said the doctor. 'How far back do we go? And why?'

'Let's take the "why" first,' said Stern, removing a number of pages from the dossier. 'He's lived with the spectre of betrayal since he was a child. There was a period during adolescence and early adulthood – at school and college – when the pressures were absent, but the memories must have been pretty horrible for him. Then for the next sixteen years – these past sixteen years – he's been back in that same kind of world. Perhaps he's seen too many ghosts.'

'Be specific, Daniel,' pressed the psychiatrist.

'To do that,' said the director, his eyes scanning the top page in his hand, 'we have to go back to June of 1942, the war in Czechoslovakia. You see, his name isn't Havelock, it's Havlicek. Mikhail Havlicek. He was born in Prague some time in the middle 'thirties, the exact date unknown. All the records were destroyed by the Gestapo.'

'*Gestapo?*' The attorney, Dawson, leaned back in his chair; a recollection prodded. 'June 1942 . . . there was something in the Nuremberg trials.'

'It was a sizeable item on the Nuremberg agenda,' agreed Stern. 'On 27 May, Reinhard Heydrich, known as *der Henker* – the hangman of Prague – was killed by Czech partisans. They were led by a professor who'd been dismissed from the Karlova University and worked with British Intelligence. His name was Havlicek and he lived with his wife and son in a village roughly eight miles outside Prague where he organized the partisan cells. The village was Lidice.'

'Oh, Christ,' said Miller slowly, dropping the cable from Rome on the table.

'He wasn't noticeably in evidence,' commented Stern dryly as he shifted the pages in his hand. 'Afraid that he might have been seen at the site of Heydrich's assassination, Havlicek stayed away from his house for nearly two weeks, living in the cellars at the university. *He* hadn't been spotted, but someone else from Lidice had been; the price was set for Heydrich's death: execution for all adult males; for the women, conscription – slave labour for the factories, the more presentable to be sent to the officers' barracks to be *Feldhuren*. The children . . . they would simply "disappear". *Jugendmöglichkeiten*. The adaptable would be adopted, the rest gassed in mobile vans.'

'Efficient bastards, weren't they?' said Ogilvie.

'The orders from Berlin were kept quiet until the morning of 10 June, the day of the mass executions,' continued Stern, reading. 'It was also the day Havlicek decided to go home. When the word went out – the proclamations were nailed to telephone poles and broadcast over the radio – the partisans stopped him. They locked him up, sedated him with drugs; they knew there was nothing he could do, and he was too valuable. Finally, he was told the worst. His wife had been sent to the whore camps – it was later learned that she killed herself the first night, taking a Wehrmacht officer with her – and his son was nowhere to be found.'

'But he hadn't, obviously, been taken with the other children,' said Dawson.

'No. He'd been trapping rabbits and came back in time to see the round-ups, the executions, the corpses thrown in ditches. He went into shock, fled into the woods and, for weeks, lived like an animal. The stories began spreading through the countryside: a child was seen running in the forest, footprints found near barns, leading back into the woods. The father heard them and knew; he had told his son that if the Germans ever came for him he was to escape into the forests. It took over a month, but Havlicek tracked the boy. He had been hiding in caves and trees, terrified to show himself, eating whatever he could steal and scratch from the ground, the nightmare of the massacre never leaving him.'

'A lovely childhood,' said the psychiatrist, making a note on a pad.

'It was only the beginning,' The director of Cons Op reached for another page in the dossier. 'Havlicek and his son remained in the Prague-Boleslav sector and the underground war accelerated, with the father as the partisan leader. A few months later the boy became one of the youngest recruits in the *Děti Brigada*, the Children's Brigade. They were used as couriers, as often as not, carrying nitroglycerin and plastic explosives as messages. One mis-step, one search, one soldier hungry for a small boy, and it was over.'

'His father *let* him?' asked Miller incredulously.

'He couldn't stop him. The boy found out what they'd done to his mother. For three years he lived that lovely childhood you described, Paul. It was uncanny, macabre. During those nights when his father was around, he was given lessons like any other school kid. Then during the days, in the woods and the fields, others taught him how to run and hide, how to lie. How to kill.'

'That was the training you mentioned, wasn't it?' said Ogilvie quietly.

'Yes. He knew what it was like to take lives, see friends' lives taken, before he was ten years old. Grisly.'

'Indelible,' added the psychiatrist. 'Explosives planted over thirty years ago.'

'Could the Costa Brava trigger them thirty years later?' asked the lawyer, looking at the doctor.

'It could. There's a couple of dozen blood-red images floating around, some pretty grim symbols. I'd have to know a hell of a lot more.' Miller turned to Stern, pencil poised above his pad. 'What happened to him then?'

'To all of them,' said Stern. 'Peace finally came – I should say, the formal war was over – but there was no peace in Prague. The Russians had their own plans, and another kind of madness took over. The elder Havlicek was visibly political, jealous of the freedom he and the partisans had fought for. He found himself in another war, as covert as before and just as brutal. With the Russians.' The director turned to another page. 'For him it ended on 10 March 1948, with the assassination of Jan Masaryk and the collapse of the Social Democrats.'

'In what sense?'

'He disappeared. Shipped to a gulag in Siberia or to a nearer grave. His political friends were quick; the Czechs share a proverb with the Russians: "The playful cub is tomorrow's wolf." They hid young Havlicek and reached British M16. Someone's conscience was stirred; the boy was smuggled out of the country, and taken to England.'

'That proverb about the cub turning into tomorrow's wolf,' interjected Ogilvie. 'Proved to be true, didn't it?'

'In ways the Russians could never envision.'

'How did the Websters fit in?' asked Miller. 'They were his sponsors over here, obviously, but the boy was in England.'

'It was chance, actually. Webster had been a reserve colonel in the war, attached to Supreme Command Central. In 'forty-eight he was in London on business, his wife with him, and one night at dinner with wartime friends they heard about the young Czech brought out of Prague, living at an orphanage in Kent. One thing led to another – the Websters had no children, and God knows the boy's story was intriguing, if not incredible – so the two of them drove down to Kent and interviewed him. That's the word here. "Interviewed." Cold, isn't it?'

'They obviously weren't.'

'No. they weren't. Webster went to work. Papers were mocked up, laws bent and a very disturbed child flown over here with a new identity. Havlicek was fortunate; he went from an English orphanage to a comfortable home in a well-to-do American suburb, including one of the better prep schools and Princeton University.'

'And a new name,' said Dawson.

Daniel Stern smiled. 'As long as a cover was deemed necessary, our reserve colonel and his lady apparently felt Anglicization was called for in Greenwich. We all have our foibles.'

'Why not their name?'

'The boy wouldn't go that far. As I said before, the memories must be there. Indelibly, as Paul put it.'

'Are the Websters still alive?'

'No. They'd be almost a hundred if they were. They both died in the early 'sixties when Havelock was at Princeton.'

'Where he met Matthias?' asked Ogilvie, making a statement.

'Yes,' answered the director of Cons Op. 'That softened the blow. Matthias took an interest in him, not only because of Havelock's work, but, perhaps more important, because his family had known the Havliceks in Prague. They were all part of the intellectual community until the Germans blew it apart and the Russians – for all intents and purposes – buried the survivors.'

'Did Matthias know the full story?'

'All of it,' replied Stern.

'That letter in the Costa Brava file makes more sense now,' said the lawyer. 'The note Matthias sent to Havelock.'

'He wanted it included,' explained Stern, 'so there'd be no misunderstanding on our part. If Havelock opted for immediate withdrawal, we were to permit it.'

'I know,' continued Dawson. 'But I assumed when Matthias made a reference to how much Havelock had suffered in . . . "the early days", I think he wrote, he meant simply losing both parents in the war. Nothing like *this*.'

'Now you know. We know.' Stern again turned to the psychiatrist. 'Any guidance, Paul?'

'The obvious,' said Miller. 'Bring him in. Promise him *anything*, but bring him in. And we can't afford any accidents. Get him here alive.'

'I agree that's the optimum,' interrupted the red-haired Ogilvie, 'but I can't see it ruling out every option.'

'You'd better,' said the doctor. 'You even said it yourself. Paranoid. Whacko. Costa Brava was intensely personal to Havelock. Witness to the execution. It could very well have set off those explosives planted thirty years ago. A part of him is back there protecting himself, building a web of defences against persecution, against attack. He's running through the woods after having witnessed the executions in Lidice; he's with the Children's Brigade, nitroglycerin strapped to his body.'

'It's what Baylor mentions in his cable.' Dawson picked it up. 'Here it is. "Sealed depositions", "tales out of school". He could do it all.'

'He could do anything,' continued the psychiatrist. 'There are no rules. Once he's hallucinated, he can slip back and forth between fantasy and reality, each phase serving the dual objective of at once convincing himself of the persecution and at the same time ridding himself of it.'

'What about Rostov in Athens?' asked Stern.

'We don't know that there was any Rostov in Athens,' Miller said. 'It could be part of the fantasy, retroactively recalling a man in the street who looked like him. We *do* know the Karras woman was KGB. Why would a man like Rostov suddenly appear and deny it?'

Ogilvie leaned forward. 'Baylor says Havelock called it a blind probe. Rostov could have taken him, got him out of Greece.'

'Then why *didn't* he?' asked Miller. 'Come on, Red, you were in the field for ten years. Blind probe or no blind probe, if you were Rostov and knew what was back at the Lubyanka, wouldn't you have taken Havelock under the circumstances described in that cable?'

Ogilvie paused, staring at the psychiatrist. 'Yes,' he said finally. 'Because

I could always let him go – if I wanted to – before anyone knew I'd taken him.'

'Exactly. It's inconsistent. Was it Rostov in Athens, or anywhere else? Or was our patient fantasizing, building his own case for persecution and subsequent defence?'

'From what this Colonel Baylor says, he was damned convincing,' interjected the lawyer Dawson.

'A hallucinating schizophrenic – if that's what he is – can be extraordinarily convincing because he believes totally what he's saying.'

'But you can't be sure, Paul,' insisted Daniel Stern.

'No, I can't be. But *we're* sure of one thing – two things, actually. The Karras woman *was* KGB and she was killed on that beach on the Costa Brava. The evidence was irrefutable for the first, and we have two on-site confirmations for the second, including one from Havelock himself.' The psychiatrist looked at the faces of the three men. 'That's all I can base a diagnosis on; that and this new information on one Mikhail Havlicek. I'm in no position to do anything else. You asked for guidance, not absolutes.'

'"Promise him anything . . ."' repeated Ogilvie. 'Like that goddamned commercial.'

'But bring him in,' completed Miller. 'And just as fast as you can. Get him into a clinic, under therapy, but find out what he's done and where he's left those defence mechanisms of his. The "sealed depositions" and "tales out of school".'

'I don't have to remind anyone here,' interrupted Dawson quietly. 'Havelock knows a great deal that could be extremely damaging if revealed. The damage would be as extensive to our own credibility – here and abroad – as in anything the Soviets might learn. Frankly, more so. Ciphers, informers, sources – all these can be changed, the networks warned. We can't go back and rewrite certain incidents where intelligence treaties were violated, the laws of a host country broken by our people.'

'To say nothing of the domestic restrictions placed on us over here,' added Stern. 'I know you included that, I just want to emphasize it. Havelock knows about them; he's negotiated a number of exchanges as a result of them.'

'Whatever we've done was justified,' said Ogilvie curtly. 'If anyone wants proof, there's a couple of hundred files that show what we've accomplished.'

'And a few thousand that don't,' objected the lawyer. 'Besides, there's also the Constitution. I'm playing devil's advocate, of course.'

'Horseshit!' Ogilvie shot back. 'By the time we get court orders and warrants, some poor son of a bitch over here has a wife or a father shipped to one of those gulags over there when someone like Havelock could have made a deal, *if* we could have placed a tap on time, assigned surveillance, and found out what was going on.'

'It's a grey area, Red,' explained Dawson, not unsympathetically. 'When is homicide justified, *really* justified? On balance, there are those who would say our accomplishments don't justify our failures.'

'One man crossing a checkpoint to our side justifies them.' Ogilvie's eyes were rigid, cold. 'One family taken out of a camp in Magya-Orszag or Krakow or Dannenwalde or Liberec justifies them. Because that's where they are, Counsellor, and they shouldn't *be* there. Who the hell gets hurt, *really* hurt? A few screaming freaks with political hatchets and outsize egos. They're not worth it.'

'The law says they are. The Constitution says they are.'

'Then fuck the law, and let's put a couple of holes in the Constitution. I'm sick to death of its being used by loud-mouthed, bushy-haired smart asses who mount any cause they can think of just to tie our hands and draw attention to themselves. I've seen those *rehabilitation* camps, Mr Lawyer. I've *been* there.'

'Which is why you're valuable here,' interceded Stern quickly, putting out the fire. 'Each of us has a value, even when he renders judgements he'd rather avoid. I think the point Dawson's making is that this is no time for a Senate inquiry or the hanging judges of a congressional oversight committee. They could tie our hands far more effectively than any mob from the ageing radical-chic or the bran-and-wheatgerm crowd.'

'Or,' said Dawson, glancing at Ogilvie, his look conveying mutual understanding, 'representatives of half a dozen governments showing up at our embassies and telling us to shut down certain operations. You've been there, too, Red. I don't think you want that.'

'Our patient can make it happen,' interjected Miller. 'And very probably will unless we reach him in time. The longer his hallucinations are allowed to continue without medical attention, the farther he'll slip into fantasy, the rate of acceleration growing faster. The persecutions will multiply until they become unbearable to him and he thinks he has to strike out – strike back. With his own attacks. They're his defence mechanisms.'

'What form might they take, Paul?' asked the director.

'Any of several,' replied the psychiatrist. 'The extreme would be his making contact with men he's known – or known of – in foreign intelligence circles and offering to deliver classified information. That could be the root fantasy of the Rostov "encounter". Or he could write letters – with copies to us – or send cables – easily intercepted by us – that hint at past activities we can't afford to have scrutinized. Whatever he does, he'll be extremely cautious, secretive, the reality of his own expertise protecting his manipulative fantasies. You said it, Daniel; he could be dangerous. He *is* dangerous.'

'"*Offering* to deliver",' said the lawyer, repeating Miller's phrase. 'Hinting . . . not delivering, not giving outright?'

'Not at first. He'll try to force us – blackmail us – into telling him what he wants to hear. That the Karras woman is alive, that there was a conspiracy to retire him.'

'Neither of which we can do convincingly because there's not a damn thing we can offer him as proof,' said Ogilvie. 'Nothing he'll accept. He's a field man. Whatever we send him, he'll filter, chew it around for accuracy and spit it back in the dungheap. So what do we tell him?'

'Don't *tell* him anything,' answered Miller. 'You *promise* to tell him. Put it any way you like. The information's too classified to send by courier, too dangerous to be permitted outside these rooms. Play his game, suck him in. Remember, he desperately wants – needs, if you like – his primary hallucination confirmed. He *saw* a dead woman; he has to believe that. And the confirmation's over here; it could be irresistible to him.'

'Sorry, Headman.' The red-haired former field agent raised the palms of his hands. 'He won't buy it, not that way. His – what did you call it? his "reality" part? – would reject it. That's buying a code in a box of crackers. It just doesn't happen. He'll want something stronger, much stronger.'

'Matthias?' asked Dawson quietly.

'Optimum,' agreed the psychiatrist.

'Not yet,' said Stern. 'Not until we have no other choice. The quiet word is that he's aware of his failing condition; he's conserving his strength for SALT 3. We can't lay this on him now.'

'We may *have* to,' insisted Dawson.

'We may, then again we may not.' The director turned to Ogilvie. 'Why does Havelock have to buy anything concrete, Red?'

'So we can get close enough to grab him.'

'Couldn't a sequence be designed – say, one piece of information leading to another, each more vital than the last – to draw him in, suck him in, as Paul says? He can't get the last unless he shows up?'

'A treasure hunt?' asked Ogilvie, laughing.

'That's what he's on,' said Miller quietly.

'The answer's no.' The red-haired man leaned forward, his elbows on the table. 'A sequence operation depends on credibility, the better the field man the firmer the credibility. It's also a very delicate exercise. The subject, if he's someone like Havelock, will use decoys, blind intermediaries. He'll reverse the process by programming his decoys with information of their own, give his intermediaries questions they want answered on the spot; he'll suck *you* in. He won't expect perfect answers; he'd be suspicious as hell if he got them, but he'll want what we used to call a "stomach consensus". It's not something you can write down on paper and analyse; it's a gut feeling for believability. There aren't that many good men who could fool Havelock in sequence. One substantial misstep and he closes the book and walks away.'

'And sets off the explosions,' said Miller.

'I see,' said Stern.

And it was clear that the men around that table *did* see. It was one of those moments when the unkempt, irascible Ogilvie confirmed his value, as he did so frequently. He had been out in that labyrinth called the 'field', and his conclusions had a peculiar eloquence and sagacity.

'There is a way, however,' continued the former agent. 'I'm not sure there's any other.'

'What is it?' asked the director of Cons Op.

'Me.'

'Out of the question.'

'Think about it,' said Ogilvie quickly. '*I'm* the credibility. Havelock knows me – more important, he knows I sit at this table. To him I'm one of *them*, a half-assed strategist who may not know what he's asking for but sure as hell knows why. And with me there's a difference; a few of them out there might even count on it. I've been where they've been. None of the rest of you have. Apart from Matthias, if there's anyone he'll listen to, anyone he'll meet, it's me.'

'I'm sorry, Red. Even if I agreed with you, and I think I do, I can't permit it. You know the rules. Once you step inside this room, you never go out in the field again.'

'That rule was *made* in this room. It's not a holy writ.'

'It was made for a very good reason,' said the lawyer. 'The same reason our houses are watched around the clock, our cars followed, our telephones tapped with our consent. If any of us was taken by interested parties, from Moscow to Peking to the Persian Gulf, the consequences would be beyond recall.'

'No disrespect, Counsellor, but those safeguards were designed for people like you and the Headman here. Even Daniel. I'm a little different. They wouldn't try to take me because they know they'd wind up with nothing.'

'No one doubts your capabilites,' countered Dawson. 'But I submit – '

'It hasn't anything to do with capabilities,' interrupted Ogilvie, raising his hand to the lapel of his worn tweed jacket; he turned up the flap towards the lawyer next to him. 'Look closely, Counsellor. There's a slight bulge an inch from the tip here.'

Dawson's eyes dropped to the fabric, his expression noncommittal. 'Cyanide?'

'That's right.'

'Sometimes, Red, I find you hard to believe.'

'Don't mistake me,' said Ogilvie simply. 'I don't ever want to use this – or the others I've got conveniently placed. I'm no macho freak trying to shock you. I don't hold my arm over a fire to show how brave I am any more than I want to kill someone or have him try to kill me. I've got these pills because I'm a coward, Mr Lawyer. You say we're being watched, guarded twenty-four hours a day. That's terrific, but I think you're overreacting to something that doesn't exist. I don't think there *is* a file on you in Dzerzhinsky Square; at least not on you or the doctor here. I'm sure there's one on Stern, but grabbing him is like codes in crackers, or our going in and grabbing someone like Rostov. It doesn't happen. But there's a file on me – you can bet your legal ass on that – and I'm not retired. What I know is still very operative, more so than ever since I stepped inside this room. That's why I've got these little bastards. I know how I'd go in and how I'd come out, and they know I know. Strangely enough, these pills are my protection. They know I've got them and they know I'd use them. Because I'm a coward.'

'And you've just spelled out the reasons why you can't go into the field,' said the Director of Consular Operations.

'Have I? Then either you didn't listen or you should be fired for incompetence. For not taking into account what I *didn't* spell out. What do you want, teacher? A note from my doctor? Excusing me from all activity?'

The strategists glanced briefly at one another, looking uncomfortable. 'Come on, Red, cut it out,' said Stern. 'That's not called for.'

'Yes, it is, Dan. It's the sort of thing you consider when making a decision. We all know about it; we just don't talk about it, and I suppose that's another kind of consideration. How long have I got? Three months, maybe four? It's why I'm here, and *that* was an intelligent decision.'

'It was hardly the sole reason,' offered Dawson softly.

'If it didn't weigh heavily in my favour, it should have, Counsellor. You should always pick someone from the field whose longevity – or lack of it – can be counted on.' Ogilvie turned to the balding Miller. 'Our doctor knows, don't you, Paul?'

'I'm not your doctor, Red,' said the psychiatrist quietly.

'You don't have to be; you've read the reports. In five weeks or so the pain will start getting worse . . . then worse after that. I won't feel it, of course, because by then I'll be moved to a hospital room where injections will keep it under control, and all those phoney cheerful voices will tell me I'm actually getting better. Until I can't focus, or hear them, and then they don't have to say anything.' The former field man leaned back in his chair, looking now at Stern. 'We've got here what our learned lawyer might call a confluence of beneficial prerogatives. Chances are that the Russians won't touch me, but if they tried, nothing's lost for me, you can be goddamned sure of that. And I'm the only one around who can pull Havelock out in the open, far enough so we can take him.'

Stern's gaze was steady on the red-haired man who was dying. 'You're persuasive,' he said.

'I'm not only persuasive, I'm right.' Suddenly Ogilvie pushed his chair back and stood up. 'I'm so right I'm going home to pack and grab a cab to Andrews. Get me on a military transport to Italy; there's no point in advertising the trip on a commercial flight. Those KGB turkeys know every passport, every cover I've ever used and there's no time to be inventive. Route me through Brussels into the base at Palombara. Then cable Baylor to expect me . . . Call me Apache.'

'Apache?' asked Dawson.

'Damn good trackers.'

'Assuming Havelock will meet you,' said the psychiatrist, 'what'll you say to him?'

'Not a hell of a lot. Once he's an arm's length away he's mine.'

'He's experienced, Red,' said Stern, studying Ogilvie's face. 'He may not be all there, but he's tough.'

'I'll have equipment,' replied the dying man, heading for the door. 'And I'm experienced, too, which is why I'm a coward. I don't go near anything I can't walk away from. Mostly.' Ogilvie opened the door and left without another word. The exit was clean, swift, the sound of the closing door final.

'We won't see him again,' said Miller.

'I know,' said Stern. 'So does he.'

'Do you think he'll reach Havelock?' asked Dawson.

'I'm sure of it,' replied the director. 'He'll take him, turn him over to Baylor and a couple of resident physicians we've got in Rome, then he'll disappear. He told us. He's not going into that hospital room with all those lying voices. He'll go his own way.'

'He's entitled to that,' said the psychiatrist.

'I suppose so,' agreed the lawyer without conviction, turing to Stern. 'As Red might say, "No disrespect", but I wish to God we could be certain about Havelock. He's *got* to be immobilized. We could be hauled in by authorities all over Europe, fuel for the fanatics of every persuasion. Embassies could be burnt to the ground, networks scattered, time lost, hostages taken and – don't fool yourself – a great many people killed. All because one man fell off balance. We've seen it happen with far less provocation than Havelock could provide.'

'That's why I'm so sure Ogilvie will bring him in,' said Stern. 'I'm not in Paul's line of work, but I think I know what's going through Red's mind. He's offended, deeply offended. He's watched friends die in the field – from Africa to Istanbul – unable to do anything because of his cover. He saw a wife and three children leave him because of his job; he hasn't seen his kids for five years. Now he's got to live with what he's got – die from what he's got. All things considered, if *he* stays on track, what gives Havelock the right, the privilege, to go over the edge? Our Apache's on his last hunt, setting his last trap. He'll see it through because he's angry.'

'That and one other thing,' said the psychiatrist. 'There's nothing else left for him. It's his final justification.'

'For what?' asked the lawyer.

'The pain,' answered Miller. 'His *and* Havelock's. You see, he respected him once. He can't forget that.'

8

The unmarked jet swept down from the skies forty miles due north of the airport at Palombara Sabina. It had flown from Brussels, avoiding all military and commercial air routes, and, soaring over the Alps east of the Lepontine sector, its altitude was so great and its descent so rapid that the probability of observation was practically non-existent. Its blip on defence radar screens was prearranged: it would appear and disappear without comment, without investigation. And when it landed at Palombara, it would bring in a man who had been taken on board secretly at three o'clock in the morning, Brussels time. A man without a reasonable name, referred to only as the Apache. This man, as with many like him, could not risk the formalities of identification at immigration desks or border checkpoints. Appearances might be altered and names changed, but other men watched such places, knowing what to look for, their minds trained to react like memory banks, too often they were successful. For the Apache – as for many like him – the current means of travel was more the norm than otherwise.

The engines were cut back as the pilot – trained in carrier landings – guided his aircraft over the forests in the stretched-out, low approach to the field. It was a mile-long black strip cut out of the woods, with maintenance hangars and traffic towers set back and camouflaged, odd yet barely visible intrusions on the countryside. The plane touched down, and the young pilot turned in his seat as the reverse thrust of the jets echoed throughout the small cabin. He raised his voice to be heard, addressing the red-haired, middle-aged man behind him.

'Here we are Indian. You can take out your bow and arrows.'

'Funny boy,' said Ogilvie, releasing the clamp that held the strap across his chest. He looked at his watch. 'What's the time here? I'm still on a Washington clock.'

'O-five-fifty-seven; you've lost six hours. You're working on midnight, but here it's morning. If you're expected at the office, I hope you got some sleep.'

'Enough. Is transport arranged?'

'Right to the big chief's wigwam on the Via Vittorio.'

'Very cute. The embassy?'

'That's right. You're a special package. Delivery guaranteed straight from Brussels.'

'That's wrong. The embassy's out.'

'We've got our orders.'

'I'm issuing new ones.'

Ogilvie walked into the small office reserved for men like himself in the maintenance building of the unmapped airfield. It was a room devoid of windows, with only basic furniture: there were two telephones, both routed perpetually through electronic scrambler systems. The outside corridor that led to the office was guarded by three men dressed innocuously in overalls. Under the bulging fabric, however, each carried a weapon and, should any unidentified persons interfere with the incoming passenger or the presence of a camera even be suspected, the weapons would be bared, used instantly if necessary. These arrangements were the result of extraordinary conferences between unknown men of both governments whose concerns transcended the stated limits of covert co-operation: quite simply, they were necessary.

Ogilvie walked to the desk, sat down and picked up the telephone on his left; it was black, signifying domestic use. He dialled the number he had committed to memory, and twelve seconds later the sleepy voice of Lieutenant-Colonel Lawrence Brown was on the line.

'Brown. What is it?'

'Baylor Brown?'

'Apache?'

'Yes. I'm at Palombara. Have you heard anything?'

'Not a word. I've got tracers out all over Rome; there's not a line on him.'

'You've got *what*?'

'Tracers. Every source we can pay or who owes us a favour – '

'Goddamn it, call them off! What the hell do you think you're doing?'

'Hey, easy, buddy. I don't think we're going to get along.'

'And I don't give a duck's fuck whether we do or not! You're not dealing with a G-two crossword puzzle; he's a snake, *buddy*. You let him find out you're going after him, he figures you've broken the rules. And he *will* find out; that's when he bites. Jesus, you think he's never been traced before?'

'You think I don't know my tracers?' countered Baylor angrily, defensively.

'I think we'd better talk.'

'Come on in, then,' said the colonel.

'That's another thing,' replied Ogilvie. 'The embassy's out.'

'Why?'

'Among other things, he could be in a window across the street.'

'So?'

'He knows I'd never show up in-territory. KGB cameras operate around the clock, aimed at every entrance.'

'He doesn't even know you're coming,' protested Baylor. 'Or who you are.'

'He will when you tell him.'

'A *name*, please?' said the army officer testily.

'Apache'll do for now.'

'That'll mean something to him?'

'It will.'

'It doesn't to me.'

'It's not supposed to.'

'We're definitely not going to get along.'

'Sorry about that.'

'Since you won't come in, where do we meet?'

'The Borghese. In the gardens. I'll find you.'

'That'll be easier than my finding *you*.'

'You're wrong, Baylor.'

'About *that*?'

'No. I think we will get along.' Ogilvie paused briefly. 'Make it two hours from now. Our target may try to reach you by then.'

'Two hours.'

'And, Baylor?'

'What?'

'Call off those duck-fucking tracers, *buddy*.'

The month of March was not kind to the Borghese. The chill of the Roman winter, mild as the winter was, still lingered, inhibiting the budding of flowers and the full explosion of the gardens that in spring and summer formed rows and circles of dazzling colours. The myriad paths that led through the tall pines towards the great museum seemed just a little dirty, the green of the pine trees tired, dormant. Even the benches that lined the narrow footpaths were layered with dust. A transparent film had descended over the park that was the Villa Borghese; it would disappear with the April rains, but for now the lifelessness of March remained.

Ogilvie stood by the thick trunk of an oak tree on the border of the gardens behind the museum. It was too early for any but a few students and fewer tourists; a scattering of these strolled along the paths waiting for the guards to open the doors that led to the Casino Borghese's treasures. The former field man, now in the field again, looked at his watch, wrinkles of annoyance spreading across his deeply lined face. It was nearly twenty minutes to nine; the army intelligence officer was over half an hour late. Ogilvie's irritation was directed as much at himself as towards Baylor. In his haste to veto his going to the embassy as well as making it clear that he was the control he had chosen a poor rendezvous, and he knew it. So would the colonel, if he thought about it; perhaps he had, perhaps that was why he was late. The Borghese at this hour was too quiet, too remote, with far too many shadowed recesses from which either of them could be observed, visually and electronically. Ogilvie silently swore at himself; it was no way to initiate his authority. The attaché-conduit had probably taken a circuitous, change-of-vehicle route, employing frequency scanners in the hope of exposing and thus losing presumed surveillance. KGB cameras *were* trained on the embassy; the colonel had been put in a difficult situation, thanks to an abrasive source from Washington enigmatically called Apache, a cover from the back of a cereal box.

The enigma was there, but not the foolishness, not the cereal box. Seven years ago in Istanbul two undercover field men, code names Apache and Navajo, nearly lost their lives trying to prevent a KGB assassination on the Mesrutiyet. They had failed, and in the process Navajo had been cornered on the deserted Ataturk Boulevard at 4 o'clock in the morning. KGB killer teams at both ends. It was a total-loss situation until Apache sped across the bridge in a stolen car, screeching to a stop by the pedestrian alley, shouting at his associate to climb in or get his head blown off. Ogilvie had then raced through a fusillade of gunfire, receiving a graze-wound at his temple and two bullets in his right hand while breaking through the thunderous early-morning barricade. The man called Navajo seven years ago would not readily forget Apache. Without him Michael Havelock would have died in Istanbul. Ogilvie counted on that memory.

Snap. Behind him. He turned, a black hand was held up in front of him, the black face beyond the hand immobile, eyes wide and steady staring at him. Baylor shook his head sharply twice, bringing his index finger to his lips. Then slowly, moving closer and pulling both of them behind the tree trunk and the foliage, the army officer gestured towards the south garden, at the rear entrance of the stone museum. About forty yards away a man in a dark suit was glancing about, his expression indecisive, as he moved first in one direction then in another, unable to choose a path. In the distance there were three rapid blasts of a high-pitched horn, followed by the gunning of an engine. The man stopped, then broke into a run towards the direction of the intruding sounds and disappeared beyond the east wall of the Borghese.

'This is a dumb location,' said the colonel, checking his watch.

'That horn was yours?' asked Ogilvie.

'It's parked by the Veneto gates. It was near enough to be heard; that was all that mattered.'

'Sorry,' said the former field man quietly. 'It's been a long time. I don't usually make mistakes like this. The Borghese was always crowded.'

'No sweat. And I'm not sure it was a mistake.'

'Let the needle out. Don't stick me with kindness.'

'You're not reading me. Your feelings aren't any concern of mine. I've never been put under KGB surveillance before – not that I know of. Why now?'

Ogilvie smiled; he was the control after all. 'You put out the tracers. I think I mentioned that.'

The black officer was silent, his dark eyes aware. 'Then I'm finished in Rome,' he said finally.

'Maybe.'

'No maybe. I'm finished, anyway. It's why I'm late.'

'He reached you.' The red-haired agent made the statement softly.

'With full artillery and I'm the first who'll be exposed. He picked up the Karras woman's trail and followed her to the port of Civitavecchia where she got out. He won't say how or on what ship. It was a trap; he waded through and reversed it, targeting the man responsible – a small-time operator on the docks. Havelock broke him, and what he learned – what he *thinks* he learned – has turned him into a stockpile of nitro.'

'What is it?'

'Double programming. Same tactic supposedly employed with him. She was sandbagged against him by us.'

'How?'

'By someone persuading her he'd gone over to the Soviets, that he was going to kill her.'

'That's a crock of shit.'

'I'm only repeating what he said – what he was told. All things considered, it's not without logic. It would explain a lot. The KGB's got some pretty fair actors; they could have put on a performance for her. It's sound strategy. He's out and she's running. A productive team neutralized.'

'I mean the whole *thing's* a crock of shit,' countered Ogilvie. 'There is no Jenna Karras; she died on a beach called Montebello on the Costa Brava. And she *was* KGB – a deep-cover VKR field officer. No mistakes were made, but even that doesn't matter now. The main point is she's dead.'

'He doesn't believe it; when you talk to him you may not, either. I'm not sure I do.'

'Havelock believes what he wants to believe, what he has to believe. I've heard the medical terms and, reduced to our language, he's gone over the edge. He crosses back and forth between what is and what isn't, but fundamentally he's gone.'

'He's damned convincing.'

'Because he's not lying. That's part of it. He saw what he saw.'

'That's what he says.'

'But he couldn't have; that's also part of it. His vision's distorted. When he goes over, he doesn't see with his eyes, only his head, and that's damaged.'

'You're convincing too.'

'Because I'm not lying and my head's not damaged.' Olgivie reached into his pocket for a pack of cigarettes. He extracted one and lit it with an old, tarnished Zippo purchased a quarter of a century ago. 'Those are the facts, Colonel. You can fill in the blank spaces, but the bottom line's firm. Havelock's got to be taken.'

'That won't be so easy. He may be running around in his own foggy tunnels but he's not an amateur. He may not know where he's going but he's survived in the field for sixteen years. He's smart, defensive.'

'We're aware of that. It's the reality part. You told him I was here, didn't you?'

'I told him a man named Apache was here.' The army officer paused.

'Well?'

'He didn't like it. Why you?'

'Why not me?'

'I don't know. Maybe he doesn't like you.'

'He owes me.'

'Maybe that's your answer.'

'What are you, a psychologist? Or a lawyer?'

'A little of both,' said the colonel. 'Constantly. Aren't you?'

'Right now I'm just annoyed. What the hell are you driving at?'

'Havelock's reaction to you was very quick, very vocal. "So they sent the Gunslinger," he said. Is that your other name?'

'Kid stuff. A bad joke.'

'He didn't sound amused. He's going to call at noon with instructions for you.'

'At the embassy?'

'No. I'm to take a room at the Excelsior. You're to be there with me; you're to get on the phone.'

'Son of a bitch!' Ogilvie sucked breath through his teeth.

'That's a problem?'

'He knows where I am but I don't know where he is. He can watch me but I can't watch him.'

'What difference does it make? He's obviously willing to meet you. In order to take him, you've got to meet him.'

'You're the new boy on the block, Colonel, no offence intended. He's forcing my hand at the top.'

'How so?'

'I'll need two men – Italians preferably, as inconspicuous as possible – to follow me when I leave the hotel.'

'Why?'

'Because he could take *me*,' said the former field man reflectively. 'From behind. On any crowded pavement. There isn't a jump he doesn't know . . . A man collapses in the street, a friend helps him to a nearby car. Both Americans, nothing out of the ordinary.'

'That presumes I won't be with you. Still, I'm the conduit. I could make a case for my being there.'

'Definitely the new boy; he'd head for Cairo. And if you tried to keep me in sight, I have an idea he'd spot you. No – '

'Offence intended,' completed the colonel. 'There *are* drawbacks . . . I'll get you your cover.' He paused again, then continued, 'But not two men. I think a couple would be better.'

'That's good. You've got possibilites, Colonel.'

'I've also got a recommendation to make that I'll deny if it's ever ascribed to me. And considering that soubriquet, Gunslinger, I don't think I'd have any difficulty saying I heard it from you.'

'I can't wait to hear it myself.'

'I'm responsible for a large territory in this area of operations. The work I do for the Pentagon and State gets compounded; it's unavoidable. I need a favour, or someone needs one from us, so the circle quietly grows bigger, even if we've never met one another.'

'I hate to repeat myself,' interrupted Ogilvie, 'but what the hell are you driving at now?'

'I have a lot of friends out there. Men and women who trust me, trust my office. If I have to go I'd like the office to remain intact, of course, but there's something more basic. I don't want those friends – known and unknown – to get hurt, and Havelock could hurt them. He's worked Italy, the Adriatic, the Ligurian – from Trieste across the borders, along the northern coast all the way to Gibraltar. He could provoke reprisals. I don't think one messed up retired field man is worth it.'

'Neither do I.'

'Then take him out. Don't just take him, take him *out*.'

'You could have heard that from me.'

'Do I hear it now?'

The man from Washington was silent for a moment, then he replied. 'No.'

'Why not?'

'Because the act could bring about the consequences you don't want.'

'Impossible. He hasn't had time.'

'You don't know that. If this thing's been growing since Costa Brava, there's no way to tell what deposits he's made or where he's made them. He could have left documents in half a dozen countries with specific instructions to release them if scheduled contacts were missed. During the last six weeks he's been in London, Amsterdam, Paris, Athens and Rome. Why? Why those places? With the whole world to choose from, and with money in his pocket, he returns to the cities where he operated extensively under cover. It could be a pattern.'

'Or coincidence. He knew them. He was out; he felt safe.'

'Maybe, maybe not.'

'I don't follow the logic. If you simply take him, he still won't make those contacts.'

'There are ways.'

'The clinics, I assume. Laboratories where doctors inject drugs that loosen tongues and minds.'

'That's right.'

'And I think you're wrong. I don't know whether he saw the Karras woman or not, but whatever he saw – whatever happened – happened during the past twenty-four hours. He hasn't had time to do a *goddamned thing*. He may tell you he has, but he hasn't.'

'Is that an opinion, or are you clairvoyant?'

'Neither. It's fact. I listened to a man in shock. A man who'd just gone through a mind-blowing experience – his phrase, incidentally. It wasn't the result of a festering mental aberration, it had just *happened*. When you talk about what he could have done, the deposits he could have made, you're using the words I gave you because they're the words he said to me. He was speculating on what he *might* do, not what he did. There's a hell of difference, Mr Strategist.'

'And because of it you want him dead?'

'I want a lot of other people to live.'

'So do we. That's why I'm here.'

'So you can take him back alive,' said Baylor sardonically. 'Just like Frank Buck.'

'That'll do.'

'No, it won't. Suppose you miss? Suppose he gets away?'

'It won't happen.'

'Opinion or clairvoyance?'

'Fact.'

'No way. It's conjecture, a probability factor I don't want to count on.'

'You don't have a choice, *soldier*. The chain of command has spoken.'

'Then let me spell it out for you, *civilian*. Don't talk to me about chains of command. I worked my black ass off in this white man's army – white at the top, black at the bottom – until they had to make me a vital cog in the big white wheel. Now you come along with your secret agent act and a code name right out of – '

'The back of a cereal packet?' interjected Ogilvie.

'You got it. A cereal packet. No name I can point to, no identification I can bargain with to get me off the hook, just a balloon from a comic strip. And if you do miss, and Havelock does get away, I'm on the firing line – as the target. Coffee-Face blew it; his network's compromised. Take him out of the big white wheel.'

'You hypocritical bastard,' said the man from Washington in disgust. 'The only thing you're interested in saving is your own skin.'

'For a lot or reasons too benign for you to understand. There're going to be more like me, not less . . . Wherever you go in this town, I'm not far behind. You take him your way, that's fine with me. I'll get you back to Palombara and strap the two of you into a jet myself with a letter of recommendation written in classical Latin. But if you can't bring it off, and he breaks, he goes down my way.'

'That doesn't sound like the man who believed his story, who pleaded his case.'

'I didn't plead his case; I reported it. And it doesn't make any difference whether I believe him or not. He's an active, dangerous threat to me and my function here in Rome and a large part of the network I've cultivated on the orders of my government and at the expense of the American taxpayer.' The colonel stopped; he smiled. 'That's all I have to know to pull a trigger.'

'You could go far.'

'I intend to, I've got points to make.'

Ogilvie stepped away from the tree; he looked past the bordering foliage at the dormant gardens beyond. He spoke quietly, his voice flat, noncommittal. 'I could lose you, you know. Kill you, if I had to.'

'Right on,' agreed the officer. 'So I'll forget about the Excelsior. You take a room in my name and when the call comes from Havelock, you pretend to be me. He expects me to be there, confirm your presence; he knows I've got a stake in this. And by the way, when you talk to him as me, don't make it too nigger. I'm a Rhodes Scholar. Oxford, 'seventy-one.'

The agent turned. 'You're also something else. I can bring you up on charges, a court martial guaranteed. Direct disobedience of a superior in the field.'

'For a conversation that never took place? Or perhaps it did, and I exercised on-the-spot military judgement. The subject found the contact unacceptable; I wanted another man in Rome. How does that grab you, *Gunslinger?*'

Ogilvie did not answer for the better part of a minute. He threw his cigarette on the ground, crushing it underfoot, grinding his shoe into the dirt. 'You're talented, Colonel,' he said finally. 'I need you.'

'You really want him, don't you?'

'Yes.'

'I thought so. It was in your voice on the phone. I wanted that confirmation, Mr Strategist. Just consider me an insurance policy you don't want to carry but your accountant says you must. If I have to pay off, nothing's lost. I can justify the act better than anyone around a DC conference table. I'm the only one who's spoken to him. I know what he's done and what he hasn't done.'

'A very short time could prove you wrong.'

'I'll chance it. That's how sure I am.'

'You won't have to. There'll be no payoff from you because I won't miss, and he won't get away.'

'Glad to hear it. Apart from the couple who'll pick you up when you leave the hotel, what else do you need?'

'Nothing. I brought my equipment with me.'

'What are you going to tell him?'

'Whatever he wants to hear.'

'What are you going to use?'

'Experience. Have you made arrangements for the room?'

'Forty-five minutes ago,' said Baylor. 'Only it's not a room, it's a suite. That way there're two phones. Just in case you're tempted to give me a wrong rendezvous, I'll be listening to everything he says.'

'You're boxing me in, boy.'

'I'll let that pass. Look at it this way. When today's over you'll be heading back to Washington either with him or without him, but with no hooks in you. If you've got him, fine. If not, I'll take the heat. My judgement's respected at the Pentagon; under the circumstances the solution will be "last extremity", and acceptable.'

'You know that book, don't you?'

'Right down to a hundred-odd contradictions. Go back to the good life, Mr Strategist. Be well and happy in the Georgetown circuit. Make your pronouncements from a distance and leave the field to us. You live better that way.'

Ogilvie controlled the wince that was about to crease his face. He could feel the sharp pain shooting up through his rib cage, bolting and clawing at the base of his throat. It was spreading; every day it went a little further, hurt a little more. Signals of the irreversible. 'Thanks for the advice,' he said.

9

The Palatine, one of the seven hills of Rome, rising beyond the Arch of Constantine, its sloping fields dotted with the alabaster ruins of antiquity. It was the rendezvous.

A quarter of a mile north-west of the Gregorio gate was an ancient arbour, with a bust of the Emperor Domitian resting upon a fluted pedestal at the end of a stone path bordered on both sides by the marble remnants of a jagged wall. Branches of wild olive cascaded over the chiselled rock, while vines of brown and green crept underneath, filling crevices and spreading a spidery latticework across the cracked yet ageless marble. At the end of the path, behind the blotched, stern face of Domitian, were the remains of a fountain built into the hill. The arbour abruptly stopped; there was no exit.

This sylvan fragment of another time was the contact ground. Time span: thirty minutes – between three o'clock and half past, when the sun was at midpoint in the western sky. Here two men would meet, each with different objectives, both aware that the differences might cause the death of one or the other, neither wanting that finality. Wariness was the order of the afternoon.

It was twenty minutes before three, the start of the span. Havelock had positioned himself behind a cluster of bushes on the nearest hill overlooking the arbour, several hundred feet above the bust of Domitian. He was concerned, angry, as his eyes roamed over the stone path and the untamed fields beyond the walls below. Half an hour ago from a pavement café across the Via Veneto from the Excelsior, he had seen what he was afraid he might see. Seconds after the red-haired Ogilvie had walked through the glass doors he had been picked up by a man and woman who had emerged casually – too casually, a bit too swiftly – from the jewellery shop next door. The shop had a wide-angled, display-case entrance, affording observers inside a decent range of vision. The man from Washington had veered briefly to his right and stopped before entering the stream of pedestrians heading left. It was a sighting back-up, an unobtrusive movement of a hand or a fleeting glance at the pavement, gestures that marked him in the crowds. There would be no taking the Apache unawares before he reached the Palatine. Ogilvie had anticipated that the attempt might be made and had protected himself. On the phone, the former field man, now a vaunted stategist, had offered only accommodation. He had reasonable – if highly classified – data to deliver; in them would be found the answers Michael sought.

Not to worry, Navajo. We'll talk.

But if the Apache had reasonable explanations to offer, he did not require protection. And why had Ogilvie agreed so readily to the out-of-the-way rendezvous? Why hadn't he simply suggested meeting on the street, or at a café? A man confident of the news he bore did not set up defences, yet the strategist had done just that.

Instead of an explanation, had Washington sent another message?
Dispatch? Call me dead?

I didn't say we'd kill you. We don't live in that kind of country . . . On the other hand, why not? Lt-Colonel Baylor Brown, Intelligence conduit, US Embassy, Rome.

If Washington had reached that conclusion, the planners had sent a qualified assassin. Havelock respected Ogilvie's talents, but he did not admire the man. The former operative was one of those men who justified their violence too glibly, with self-serving scraps of philosophy that implied personal revulsion for committing even necessary acts of violence. Associates in the field knew better. Ogilvie was a killer, driven by some inner compulsion to avenge himself against his own personal furies, which he concealed from all but those who worked closely with him under maximum stress; and those who did know him tried their level best never to work with him again.

After Istanbul, Michael did something he had never thought he would do. He had reached Anthony Matthias and advised him to take Red Ogilvie out of the field. The man was dangerous. Michael had volunteered to appear before a closed hearing with the strategists, but, as always, Matthias had the better, less divisive method. Ogilvie was an expert; few men had his background in covert activities. The Secretary of State had ordered him up the ladder, making Ogilvie a strategist himself.

Matthias was out of Washington these days. It was not a comforting thought. Decisions were often arrived at without accountability for the simple reason that those who should be apprised in depth were not accessible. The urgency of a given crisis was frequently a green light for movement.

That was it, thought Havelock, as his eyes settled on a figure in the distance, in the sloping field beyond the right wall. It was the man who had accompanied the woman out of the jewellery store next to the Excelsior, the one who had picked up Ogilvie. Michael looked to his left; there was the woman. She was standing by the steps of an ancient bath, a sketch pad in her left hand. But there was no sketching pencil in her right which she held under the lapel of her gabardine coat. Havelock returned to the man in the field on the right. He was sitting on the ground now, legs stretched, a book open on his lap – a Roman finding an hour's peace, reading. And by no coincidence his hand, too, was held in place at the upper regions of his coarse tweed jacket. The two were in communication and Michael knew the language. Italian.

Italians. No subordinates from the embassy, no CIA stringers, no Baylor – no Americans in sight. When Ogilvie arrived, he'd be the only one. It fit; remove all US personnel, all avenues of record. Use only local back-ups, men or women themselves beyond salvage. Dispatch.

Why? Why was he a crisis? What had he done or what did he know that made men in Washington want him dead? First they wanted him out by way of Jenna Karras. Now dead. Christ in heaven, what was it?

Besides the couple, were there others? He strained his eyes against the sun, studying every patch of ground, separating the terrain into blocks – an awkward puzzle. The arbour of Domitian was not a prominent site on the

Palatine Hill; it was a minor scrap of antiquity left to decay. The dismal month of March had further reduced the number of trespassers. In the distance, on a hill to the east, a group of children played under the watchful glances of two adults. Teachers, perhaps. Below, to the south, there was an uncut green lawn with marble columns of the early empire standing like upright, bloodless corpses of widely differing heights. Several tourists laden with camera equipment – straps over straps, and bulging cases – were taking photographs, posing one another in front of the fluted remains. But apart from the couple covering both sides of the arbour's entrance, there was no one in the immediate vicinity of Domitian's retreat. If they were competent marksmen, no additional back-ups were necessary. There was only one entrance, and a man climbing a wall was an easy target; it was a gauntlet with a single exit. That, too, fitted the policy of dispatch. Use as few locals as possible, remembering always that they can snap back with extortion.

The irony had come about unconsciously. Michael had wandered over the Palatine that morning, selecting the site for the very advantages that now could be used against him. He looked at his watch: fourteen minutes to three. He had to move quickly, but not until he saw Ogilvie. The Apache was smart; he knew the odds favoured his remaining out of sight as long as possible, riveting his adversary's concentration on his anticipated appearance. Michael understood, so he concentrated on his options: on the woman with a sketch pad in her hand, and the man reclining on the grass.

Suddenly, he was there. At one minute to three the red-haired agent came into view, his head and shoulders seen first as he walked up the path from the Gregorio gate, passing the man in the field without acknowledgement. Something was odd, thought Havelock, something about Ogilvie himself. Perhaps it was his clothes, as usual rumpled, ill-fitting . . . but too large for his stocky frame? Whatever it was, he seemed different; not the face – he was too far away for his face to be seen clearly. It was in his walk, the way he held his shoulders, as if the gentle slope of the hill was far steeper than it was. The Apache had changed since Istanbul; the two years had not been kind.

Ogilvie reached the remnants of the marble arch that was the arbour's entrance; he would remain inside. It was three o'clock; the time span had begun.

Michael crept away from his recess behind the cluster of wild bushes and crawled rapidly through the descending field of high grass, keeping his body close to the ground and making a wide arc north until he came to the base of the hill. He glanced at his watch; it had taken him nearly two minutes.

The woman was now above him, roughly a hundred yards away in the centre of the field below and to the right of Domitian's arbour. He could not see her, but he knew she had not moved. She had chosen her sight lines carefully, a back-up killer's habit. He started up the slope on his hands and knees, separating the blades of grass in front of him, listening for the sounds of unexpected voices. There were none.

He reached the crest. The woman was directly ahead, no more than sixty feet away, still standing on the first rung of curving white steps that led down to the ancient marble bath. She held the sketch pad in front of her, but her eyes were not on it. They were staring at the entrance of the arbour, her concentration absolute, her body primed to move instantly. Then Havelock saw what he had hoped he would see: the heavy-set woman's right hand was no longer on her lapel. It was now concealed under her gabardine coat, without question gripping an automatic she could remove quickly and aim accurately, unencumbered by the awkwardness of a pocket. Michael feared that weapon, but he feared the radio more. In moments it might be an ally; now it was his enemy, as deadly as any gun.

He looked at his watch again, annoyed at the sight of the seconds ticking off; he had to move swiftly. He did so, staying below the crest of the field, working his way around towards the broken stone trench that led to the well of the Roman bath. Huge weeds sprang up from the sides and from the cracks in the trench, covering it and giving it the appearance of an ugly, giant centipede. Havelock parted the moist, filthy overgrowth, slid forward on his stomach and crawled along the jagged marble ditch. Thirty seconds later he emerged from the weeds into the ancient remains of the circular pool that centuries ago had held the oiled, pampered bodies of emperors and courtesans. Seven feet above him – eight decayed steps away – was the woman whose function was to kill him should her current employer be incapable of doing so. Her back was to him, her thick legs planted like those of a sergeant-major commanding a machine-gun squad.

He studied the remains of the marble staircase; it was fragile and was protected by a twelve-inch iron fence on the second rung to prevent onlookers from venturing farther down. The weight of a body on any single step could cause the stone to crack, and the sound would be his undoing. But what if the sound was accompanied by the impact of a severe physical blow? He knew he had to decide quickly, move quickly. Every minute that went by was adding to the growing alarm of the assassin in Domitian's arbour.

Silently he moved his hands about under the tangled weeds, his fingers struck a hard, rough-edged object. It was a fragment of marble, a chiselled part of an artisan's design two thousand years ago. He gripped it in his right hand and, with the other, removed from his belt the Llama automatic he had taken from the would-be mafioso in Civitavecchia. Long ago he had trained himself to fire with his left hand as well as with his right, a basic precaution. The skill would serve him now; it was his own particular back-up. If his tactic failed, he would kill the woman who had been hired to make certain he died on the Palatine Hill. But it was a back-up, merely an option to make sure he stayed alive. He wanted to keep his rendezvous in Domitian's arbour.

He brought his legs slowly into a crouch and, extending one knee, prepared to spring. The woman was less than four feet away, directly above him. He raised his right arm, the heavy, jagged fragment in his hand, and lunged as he hurled the heavy piece of marble at the wide expanse of gabardine between her shoulders, whipping his arm with all the force he could muster.

Sound and instinct. The woman started to turn, but the impact came. The jagged fragment crashed into her neck at the base of her skull, blood matting her dark hair instantly. Havelock rushed up the steps, and, grabbing her coat at the waist, pulled her down over the small iron fence while jamming his forearm against her mouth and choking off the scream. The two of them plunged down into the marble well, Michael twisting the woman's body as they fell. They hit the hard surface; he rammed his knee into her chest between her breasts and thrust the barrel of the Llama deep against her throat.

'You listen to me!' he whispered harshly, knowing that neither the embassy nor Ogilvie would employ a back-up who was not fluent in English and who might misinterpret orders. 'Get on your radio and tell your friend to come over here as fast as he can! Say it's an emergency. Tell him to use the woods below the archway. You don't want the American to see him.'

'*Cosa dici?*'

'You heard me and you understand me! Do as I say! Tell him you think you've both been betrayed. *Prudente! Io parlo Italiano! Capisci?*' added Have-lock, applying further pressure both with his knee and the barrel of the gun. '*Presto!*'

The woman grimaced, sucking her breath between her clenched teeth, her broad, masculine face stretched like that of a striking cobra caught in a snake fork. Haltingly, as Michael removed his knee, she raised her right hand to her lapel and folded it back, revealing a transistorized microphone in the shape of a thick button attached to the cloth. In the centre was a small, flat transmission switch; she pressed it. There was a brief hum, the signal travelling three hundred feet due west on the Palatine Hill; she spoke.

'*Trifoglio, trifoglio,*' she said rapidly for identification. '*Ascolta! Abbiamo un'emergenza . . . !*' She carried out Michael's orders, the whispered urgency of her voice conveying the panic she felt as the Llama was shoved deeper into her throat. The response came in the sound of startled, metallic Italian.

'*Che avete? Quale?*'

'*I – retta!*'

'*Arrivo!*'

Havelock pulled the woman to her knees, ripping her coat apart as he did so. Held in place above her waist by a wide strap was an elongated holster, revealing the handle of a powerful Magnum automatic. The outsized leather case accommodated an appendage attached to the barrel: a perforated cylinder – a silencer, permanently secured and zeroed for accuracy. The woman was, indeed, a professional. Michael quickly removed the weapon and shoved it under his belt. He yanked the woman to her feet and pushed her violently into the curving stairs, forcing her up to the second step so that both of them could see – between the spikes of the small iron fence – over the top of the ancient bath. He was behind her, his body pressed into hers locking her in place, the Llama at her right temple, his left arm around her neck. In seconds he saw her companion, crouching as he raced through the foliage below the arbour; it was all he had to see. Without warning, he snapped his left arm back, choking the breath out of the woman's throat and forcing her head forward into the crushing vice. Her body went limp; she would remain unconscious until dark. He did not want to kill her; he wanted her to tell her story to the patriots who had hired her. He let her slide down the cracked marble to the weed-infested well below, and waited.

The man emerged cautiously on the sloping field, his hand beneath his tweed jacket. Too many minutes; time was passing too swiftly, the span half over. Much longer, and the assassin sent by Washington would become alarmed. If he walked outside the arbour he would know that his guards were not in place, that his control was lost; he would run. It must not happen! The answers Havelock sought were fifty yards away inside a remnant of antiquity. Once the control was shifted – *only* if it was shifted – could those answers be learned. *Make your move, employee*, thought Havelock, as the Italian approached.

'*Trifoglio, trifoglio!*' said Michael in a sharp whisper as he grabbed debris from the steps and threw it over the top of the marble casement to his right, at the opposite end of the circular enclosure.

The man broke into a run towards the sound of the voice repeating the code and the sight of flying dirt. Havelock moved to his left and crouched on the third step, his hand on a spoke of the fence, his feet constantly testing the stone beneath; it *had* to hold him.

It did. Michael lurched over the top as the Italian reached the marble rim, so startling the man that he gasped in shock, his panic immobilizing him. Havelock lunged, swinging the Llama into the Italian's face, shattering bone and teeth, blood burst from his mouth and splattered his shirt and jacket. The man started to collapse; Havelock rushed forward to grab him, then turned and propelled him over the side of the marble bath. The Italian plummeted, arms and legs flailing; at the bottom he lay motionless, sprawled over the body of the woman, his bloody head on her stomach. He, too, would have a story to tell, thought Michael. It was important that the stategists in Washington should hear it, for if the answers were not forthcoming during the next few minutes, the Palatine was only the beginning.

Havelock forced the Llama into the inside pocket of his jacket and felt the uncomfortable pressure of the out-sized Magnum automatic under his belt. He would keep both weapons; the Llama was a short piece and easily concealed, while the Magnum with its permanently attached silencer could be advantageous in other circumstances. Suddenly a cold wind of depression swept through him. Twenty-four hours ago he had thought that he would never again hold a gun in his hand for the rest of his life – his new life. In truth, he loathed weapons; feared and hated them, and for this reason he had learned to master them – so that he could go on living and use them to still other weapons – the guns of his childhood. The early days, the terrible days; in a way they were what his whole life had been about, the life he had thought he had put finally to rest. Root out the abusers, permit life to the living . . . destroy the killers of all Lidices in any form. He had left that life, but the killers were still there, in another form. He buttoned his jacket and started towards the entrance of the arbour, and the man who had come to kill him.

As he approached the decrepit marble archway his eyes instinctively scanned the ground, his feet avoiding stray branches that could snap underfoot, announcing his presence. He reached the jagged wall of the arch and silently sidestepped his way to the opening. Gently he pushed away the cascading vines and looked inside. Ogilvie was at the far end of the stone path by the pedestalled bust of Domitian. He was smoking a cigarette, studying the hill above the arbour to his right, the very hill – the same area with the cluster of wild bushes – where Michael had concealed himself nineteen minutes before. The Apache had made his own assessment, the accuracy of his analysis apparent.

There was a slight chill in the air and Havelock noted that Ogilvie's wrinkled, ill-fitting jacket was buttoned. But he also saw that this did not prevent swift access to a gun. Then Michael focused on the strategist's face; the change was startling. It was paler than Havelock remembered ever having seen it. The lines that had been there before were chiselled deeper now and drawn longer, like the ridges of decay in the faded marble of the ancient arbour. One did not have to be a doctor to know that Ogilvie was a sick man and that his illness was severe. If there was a great deal of strength left in him, it was as concealed as the weapons he carried.

Michael stepped inside, watching intently for any sudden movement on the part of the former field man. 'Hello, Red?' he said.

Ogilvie's head turned only slightly, conveying the fact that he had seen Havelock out of the corner of his eye before the greeting. 'Good to see you, Navajo.'

'Drop the "Navajo". This isn't Istanbul.'

'No, it isn't, but I saved your ass there, didn't I?'

'You saved it after you damn near got me killed. I told you the the bridge was a trap, but you, my so-called superior – a label you overworked, incidentally – insisted otherwise. You came back for me because I told you it was a trap in front of our control in the Mesrutiyet. He would have racked you in his briefing report.'

'Still, I came *back*,' pressed Ogilvie quickly, angrily, colour spreading across his pallid face. Then he checked himself, smiled wanly and shrugged. 'What the hell, it doesn't matter.'

'No, it doesn't. I think you'd risk blowing yourself and all your kids apart to justify yourself, but as you say, you did come back. Thanks for that. It was quicker, if not necessarily safer, than jumping into the Bosporus.'

'You never would have made it.'

'Maybe, maybe not.'

Ogilvie threw his cigarette on the ground, crushed it underfoot and stepped forward. 'Not the kids, Havelock. Me, yes. Not the kids.'

'All right, not the kids.' At the reference to children – his unthinking reference – Michael felt momentary embarrassment. He recalled that Ogilvie's children had been taken away from him. This suddenly old man was alone in his shadow world with his personal furies.

'Let's talk,' said the man from Washington, walking towards a marble bench on the border of the stone path. 'Sit down . . . Michael. Or is it Mike? I don't remember.'

'Whatever you like. I'll stand.'

'I'll sit. I don't mind telling you, I'm beat. It's a long way from DC, a lot of flying time. I don't sleep well on planes.'

'You look tired.'

At the remark, Ogilvie stopped and glanced at Havelock. 'Cute,' he said, and then sat down. 'Tell me something, Michael. Are *you* tired?'

'Yes,' said Havelock. 'Of the whole goddamned lie. Of everything that's happened. To her. To me. To all of you in your sterile white offices, with

your filthy minds – God help me, I was part of you. What did you think you
were doing? Why did you *do* it?'

'That's a large indictment, Navajo.'

'I told you. Drop that fucking name.'

'Like from a cereal packet, huh?'

'Worse. For your enlightenment, the Navajos were related to the Apaches;
but unlike the Apaches, the tribe was essentially peaceful, defensive. The
name didn't fit in Istanbul, and it doesn't fit now.'

'That's interesting; I didn't know that. But then, I suppose it's the sort of
thing someone not born in a country – brought over after a pretty harrowing
childhood somewhere else – would find out about. I mean, studying that
kind of history is a way of saying "Thanks", isn't it?'

'I don't know what you're talking about.'

'Sure you do. A kid lives through wholesale slaughter, sees friends and
neighbours machine-gunned in a field and thrown into ditches, his own
mother sent away to God knows what, knowing he'll never see her again.
This kid is something. He hides in the woods with nothing to eat except
what he can trap or steal, afraid to come out. Then he's found and spends
the next few years running through the streets with explosives strapped to
his back, the enemy everywhere, any one of them his potential executioner.
All this before he's ten years old, and by the time he's twelve, his father's
killed by the Soviets . . . Christ, a kid like that, when he finally gets to a safe
harbour, he's going to learn everything he can about the place. He's really
saying "Thanks for letting me come here." Wouldn't you agree . . . *Havlicek?*'

*So the inviolate was not impenetrable. Of course the strategists knew, he should have
realized that; his own actions had brought it about. The sole guarantee he had been
given was that his true file would be provided only on a need-to-know basis to the highest
levels of personnel screening. Those below would be shown the British M16 addendum.
A Slovak orphan, parents killed in a Brighton bombing raid, cleared for adoption and
immigration. It was all they had to know, all they should know. Before. Not now.*

'It's not pertinent.'

'Well, maybe it is,' said the former field man, shifting his position on the
bench, his hand casually moving towards his jacket pocket.

'Don't do that.'

'What?'

'Your hand. Keep it out of there.'

'Oh, sorry . . . As I was saying, all that early stuff *could* be pertinent. A
man can take just so much over the years; it accumulates, you know what I
mean? Then one day something snaps, and without his realizing it his head
plays tricks on him. He goes back – way back – to when things happened to
him – terrible things – and the years and the motives of people he knew *then*
get mixed up – with the years and the people he knows *now*. He begins to
blame the present for all the lousy things that happened in the past. It
happens a lot to men who live the way you and I have lived. It's not even
unusual.'

'Are you *finished?*' asked Havelock harshly. 'Because if you *are* – '

'Come on back with me, Michael,' interrupted the man from Washington.
'You need help. We can help you.'

'You travelled five thousand miles to tell me *that*?' shouted Havelock. 'That's the *data*, your *explanation*?'

'Take it easy. Cool it.'

'No, *you* take it easy! *You* cool it, because you're going to need every cold nerve you've got! All of you! I'll start here in Rome and work my way up and over, through Switzerland, Germany . . . Prague, Krakow, Warsaw . . . right up into Moscow, if I have to! And the more I talk, the more of a mess you'll be in, every one of you.

'Who the hell are you to explain what or where my head is? I saw that woman. She's *alive*! I followed her to Civitavecchia, where she faded, but I found out what you said to her, what you *did* to her! I'm going after her, but every day it takes will cost you! I'll start the minute I get out of here and you won't be able to stop me. Listen to the news tonight and read the morning papers. There's a conduit here in Rome, a respected first-level attaché, a member of a *minority* – one hell of a screen. Only he's going to lose his value *and* his network before the sun goes down! You *bastards*! Who do you think you *are*?'

'All right, all *right*!' pleaded Ogilvie, both hands in the air, nodding his head in a rapid gesture of conciliation. 'You've got it all, but you can't blame me for trying. Those were the orders. "Get him back so we can tell him over here," that's what they said. "Try anything, but don't *say* anything, not while he's out of the country." I told them it wouldn't work, not with you. I made them give me the disclosure option; they didn't want to, but I hammered it out of them.'

'Then *talk*!'

'Okay, okay, you've got it.' The man from Washington expelled his breath, shaking his head slowly back and forth. 'Jesus, things get screwed up.'

'Unscrew them!'

Ogilvie looked up at Michael, raising his hand to the upper left area of his rumpled jacket. 'A smoke, do you mind?'

'Pull it back.'

The strategist peeled back his lapel, revealing a pack of cigarettes in his shirt pocket. Havelock nodded; Ogilvie took out the cigarettes and a book of matches behind the pack. He shook a cigarette into his right hand and flipped open the matchbook cover; the book was empty. 'Shit,' he muttered. 'Have you got a light?'

Michael reached into his pocket, took out matches and handed them over. 'What you've got to say had better make a great deal of sense – '

Oh, my God! Whether it was the slight movement of the head of red hair below him, or the odd position of Ogilvie's right hand, or the flash of sunlight reflecting off the cigarette pack's cellophane, he would never know, but in that confluence of unexpected factors, he knew the trap had been sprung. He lashed out with his left foot, catching the strategist's right arm and reeling it back; the force of the blow threw Ogilvie off the bench. Suddenly the air was filled with a billowing cloud of mist. He dived to his right, beyond the path, holding his nostrils, closing his eyes, rolling on the ground until he slammed into the remains of the jagged wall, out of range of the gaseous cloud.

The collapsible vial had been concealed in the pack of cigarettes, and the acrid odour that permeated the arbour told him what the vial had contained. It was nerve gas that inhibited all muscular control if a target was caught in the nucleus; its effect lasted no less than an hour, no more than three. It was used almost exclusively for abduction, rarely if ever as a prelude to dispatch.

Havelock opened his eyes and got to his knees, supporting himself on the wall. Beyond the marble bench the man from Washington was thrashing around on the overgrown grass, coughing, struggling to rise, his body in convulsions. He had been caught in the milder periphery of the burst, just enough to make him momentarily lose control.

Michael got to his feet, watching the bluish-grey cloud evaporate in the air above the Palatine, its centre holding until diffused by the breezes. He opened his jacket, feeling the pain of the scrapes and bruises made by the Magnum under his belt as a result of his violent movements. He took out the weapon with the ugly perforated cylinder on the barrel and walked unsteadily across the grass to Ogilvie. The red-haired man was breathing with difficulty, but his eyes were clear; he stopped struggling and stared up at Havelock and then at the weapon in Michael's hand.

'Go ahead, Navajo,' he said, his voice barely above a whisper. 'Save me the trouble.'

'I thought so,' replied Havelock, looking at the former field man's gaunt, lined face that had the chalk-white pallor of death about it.

'Don't think. Shoot.'

'Why should I? Make it easier, I mean. Or harder, for that matter. You didn't come to kill me, you came to take me. And you don't have any answers at all.'

'I gave them to you.'

'When?'

'A couple of minutes ago . . . *Havlicek*. The war. Czechoslovakia, Prague. Your father and mother. Lidice. All those things that aren't pertinent.'

'What the *hell* are you talking about?'

'Your head's damaged, Navajo. I'm not lying about that.'

'*What?*'

'You didn't see the Karras woman. She's dead.'

'She's *alive!*' shouted Michael, crouching beside the man from Washington, grabbing him by the lapel of his rumpled coat. 'Goddamn you, she saw me! She ran from me!'

'No way,' said Ogilvie, shaking his head. 'You weren't the only one at Costa Brava; there was someone else. We have his sighting; he brought back proof . . . fragments of clothing, matching blood, the works. She died on that beach on the Costa Brava.'

'That's a *lie*! I was there all night! I went down to the road, down to the beach. There weren't any pieces of clothing; she was running, she wasn't touched until after she was dead, after the bullets hit her. Whoever she was, her body was carried away intact, nothing torn, nothing left on the beach! How *could* there be? *Why* would there be? That sighting's a lie!'

The strategist lay motionless, his eyes boring up into Havelock's, his breathing steadier now. It was obvious that his mind was racing, filtering truth where he could find the truth. 'It was dark,' he said in a monotone. 'You couldn't tell.'

'When I walked down to the beach, the sun was up.'

Ogilvie winced, forcing his head into his left shoulder, his mouth stretched, a searing pain apparently shooting up through his chest and down his arm. 'The man who made that sighting had a coronary three weeks later,' said the strategist, his voice a strained whisper. 'He died on a goddamned boat in the Chesapeake . . . If you're right, there's a problem back in DC neither you nor I know about. Help me. We've got to get out to Palombara.'

'*You* get out to Palombara. I don't come in without answers. I told you that.'

'You've got to! Because you're not getting out of here without me, and that's Holy Writ.'

'You've lost your touch, Apache. I took this Magnum from that pretty face you hired. Incidentally, her *gumbar* is with her now, both resting at the bottom of a marble bath.'

'Not them! *Him!*' The man from Washington was suddenly alarmed. He pushed himself up on his elbows, his neck craning, his eyes squinting into the sun, scanning the hill above the arbour. 'He's waiting, watching us,' he whispered. 'Put the gun down! Drop the advantage. Hurry up!'

'Who? Why? What for?'

'For Christ's sake, do as I say! Quickly!'

Michael shook his head and got to his feet. 'You're full of little tricks, Red, but you've been away too long. You've got the same stench about you that I can smell all the way from the Potomac – '

'Don't! *No!*' screamed the former field man, his eyes wide, straining, focused on the high point of the hill. Then with an unreasonable reservoir of miraculous strength he lurched off the ground, clutching Havelock and pulling him away from the stone path.

Havelock raised the barrel with the heavy cylinder attached and was about to crash it into Ogilvie's skull, when the snaps came, two muted reports from above. Ogilvie gasped, then exhaled audibly, making a terrible sound like rushing water, and went limp, falling backwards on the grass. His throat was ripped open; he was dead, having stopped the bullet meant for Michael.

Havelock lunged to the wall; three more shots came, exploding marble and dirt all around him. He raced to the end of the jagged wall, the Magnum by his face, and peered between a V-shaped break in the stone.

Silence.

A forearm. A shoulder. Beyond a cluster of wild bushes. Now! He aimed carefully and fired four shots in rapid succession. A bloody hand whipped up in the air, followed by a pivoting shoulder. Then the wounded man lurched out of the foliage and limped rapidly over the crest of the hill. The hair on the hatless figure was close-cropped and black, the skin deep brown. Mahogany. The would-be assassin on the Palatine was Rome's conduit for covert activities in the northern sector of the Mediterranean. Had he squeezed the trigger in anger, or fear, or a combination of both, afraid and furious because his cover and his network would be exposed? Or had he coldly followed orders? Another question, one more shapeless fragment in the mosaic.

Havelock turned and leaned against the wall, exhausted, frightened, feeling as vulnerable as in the early days, the terrible days. He looked down at Red Ogilvie – John Philip Ogilvie, if he remembered correctly. Minutes ago he was a dying man; now he was a dead man. Killed saving the life of another he did not want to see die. The Apache had not come to dispatch the Navajo; he had come to save him. But safety was not found among the strategists in Washington; they had been programmed by liars. Liars were in control.

Why? For what purpose?

No time. He had to get out of Rome, out of Italy. To the border at Col des Moulinets, and if that failed, to Paris.

To Jenna. Always Jenna, now more than ever!

10

The two phone calls took forty-seven minutes to complete from two separate boxes in the crowded Leonardo da Vinci airport. The first was to the office of the *direttore* of Rome's *Amministrazione di Sicurezza*, Italy's watchdog over covert foreign activities. With short, succinct references to authentic clandestine operations going back several years, Havelock was put through without identification to the director's administrative assistant. He held the man on the line for less than a minute, hanging up after saying what he had to say. The second call, from a box at the opposite end of the hall, was placed to the *redattore* of *Il Progresso Giornale*, Rome's highly political, highly opinionated, largely anti-American newspaper. Considering the implied subject matter, the editor was a far less difficult man to reach. And when the journalist interrupted Michael for identification and clarification, Havelock countered with two suggestions; the first, to check with the administrative assistant to the *direttore* of the *Amministrazione di Sicurezza*; the second, to watch the United States embassy during the next seventy-two hours, with particular attention paid to the individual in question.

'*Mezzani!*' fumed the editor.

'*Addio*,' said Michael, replacing the receiver.

Lt-Colonel Lawrence Baylor Brown, diplomatic attaché and a prime example of America's recognition of minorities, was out of a job. The conduit was finished, his network rendered useless; it would take months, possibly a year, to rebuild. And regardless of how seriously he was wounded, the colonel would be flown out of Rome within hours to explain the death of the red-haired man on the Palatine.

The first floodgate had been opened. Others would follow. *Every day it takes will cost you.*

He meant it.

* * *

'I'm glad you got here,' said Daniel Stern, closing the door of the white, windowless room on the fifth floor of the State Department. The two men he addressed were sitting at the conference table: the balding psychiatrist, Dr Paul Miller, going through his notes; the lawyer named Dawson gazing absently at the wall, his hand resting on a yellow legal pad in front of him. 'I've just come from Walter Reed hospital – the Baylor debriefing. It's all confirmed. I heard it myself, questioned him myself. He's one torn apart soldier, physically and emotionally. But he's reining tight; he's a good man.'

'No deviations from the original report?' asked the lawyer.

'Nothing substantive; he was thorough the first time. The capsule was secreted in Ogilvie's cigarettes, a mild diphenylamine compound released through a CO_2 cartridge triggered by pressure.'

'That's what Red meant when he told us he could take Havelock if he got him within arm's reach,' interrupted Miller quietly.

'He nearly did,' said Stern, walking into the room. There was a red telephone on a small table beside his chair; he flipped a switch on the sloping front of the instrument and sat down. 'Hearing Baylor tell it is a lot more vivid than reading a dry report,' said the Director of Consular Operations, and fell silent; the two strategists waited. Stern continued softly. 'He's quiet, almost passive, but you look at his face and you know how deeply he feels. How responsible.'

Dawson leaned forward. 'Did you ask him what tipped Havelock off? It wasn't in the report.'

'It wasn't there because he doesn't know. Until the last second, Havelock didn't appear to suspect anything. Just as the report says, the two of them were talking; Ogilvie took the cigarettes out of his pocket and apparently asked for a light. Havelock reached into his pocket for matches, brought them over to Red and then it happened. He suddenly kicked out, sending Ogilvie reeling off the bench, and the capsule exploded. When the smoke cleared, Red was on the ground and Havelock was standing over him with a gun in his hand.'

'Why didn't Baylor shoot *then*? At that moment?' The lawyer was disturbed; it was in his voice.

'Because of us,' replied Stern. 'Our orders were firm. Havelock was to be brought in alive. Only a "last extremity" judgement could intervene.'

'He could have been,' said Dawson quickly, almost questioningly. 'I've read Brown's – Baylor's – service report. He's a qualified expert in weapons, special emphasis on side arms. There's very little he's not a "qualified expert" in; he's a walking advertisement for the NAACP *and* the officer corps. Rhodes scholar, Special Forces, tactical guerrilla warfare. You name it, he's got it in his file.'

'He's black; he's had to be good. I told you that before. What's your point?'

'He could have wounded Havelock. Legs, shoulders, the pelvic area. Between them, he and Ogilvie *could* have taken him.'

'That's asking for a lot of accuracy from seventy-five to a hundred feet.'

'Twenty-five to thirty yards. Almost the equivalent of a hand-gun firing range, and Havelock was standing still. He wasn't a moving target. Did you question Baylor about that?'

'Frankly, I didn't see any reason to. He's got enough on his mind, including a shot-up hand that may take him out of the army. In my opinion, he acted correctly in a hairy situation. He waited until he saw Havelock point his gun at Ogilvie, until he was convinced Red didn't have a chance. He only fired then, at the precise moment Ogilvie lunged at Havelock, taking the bullet. Everything corresponds with the autopsy in Rome.'

'The delay cost Red his life,' said Dawson, not satisfied.

'Shortened it,' corrected the doctor. 'And not by much.'

'That's also in the autopsy report,' added Stern.

'This may sound pretty cold under the circumstances,' said the lawyer. 'But perhaps it's related. We overestimated him.'

'No,' disagreed the director. 'We underestimated Havelock. What more do you need? It's been three days since the Palatine, and in those three days he's destroyed a conduit, frightened off the locals in Rome – no one wants to work for us now – and collapsed a network. In addition he routed a cable through Switzerland to the chairman of Congressional Oversight, alluding to CIA incompetence and corruption in Amsterdam. And this morning we get a call from the chief of White House security, who doesn't know whether to be panicked or outraged. He, too, received a cable, this one in sixteen-hundred cipher, implying that there was a Soviet mole close to the President.'

'That comes from Havelock's so-called confrontation with Rostov in Athens,' said Dawson, glancing at the yellow legal pad. 'Baylor reported it.'

'And Paul here doubts that it ever took place,' said Stern, looking at Miller.

'Fantasy and reality,' interjected the psychiatrist. 'If all the information we've gathered is accurate, he slips back and forth unable to distinguish which. *If* our data is accurate. In all likelihood, there's a degree of incompetence, perhaps minor corruption, in Amsterdam. However, I'd think it's pretty unlikely that a Soviet mole could break into the presidential circle.'

'We can and do make mistakes *here*,' offered Stern, 'as well as at the Pentagon, and, God knows, in Langley. But over there the chances of that type of error are minuscule. I don't say it can't happen or hasn't happened, but anyone close to the Oval Office has had every year, every month, every week of his life put under the microscope, even the President's closest friends. The bright recruits are studied as if they might be Stalin's heirs; it's been standard procedure since "forty seven".' The director paused again, again not finished. His eyes strayed to the sheaf of loose notes in front of the doctor. He continued slowly, pensively. 'Havelock knows which buttons to press, which people to reach, the right ciphers to use; even old ciphers have impact. He can create panic because he gives his information authentically . . . How far will he go, Paul?'

'No absolutes, Daniel,' said the psychiatrist, shaking his head. 'Whatever I say is barely above guesswork.'

'Trained guesswork,' interrupted the lawyer.

'How would you like to assess a case without access to the client?' asked Miller.

'You've got depositions, statistics, a current on-site briefing and a detailed dossier. It's fair background.'

'Bad analogy. Sorry I brought it up.'

'If we can't find him, how far will he go?' pressed the Director of Cons Op. 'How long have we got before he starts costing lives?'

'He already has,' broke in Dawson.

'Not in a controlled sense,' contradicted Miller. 'It was a direct reaction to a violent attack on his own life. There's a difference.'

'Spell out the difference, Paul.'

'As *I* see it,' said the psychiatrist, picking up his notes and adjusting his glasses. 'And, to use a favourite phrase of Ogilvie's, I don't claim it's Holy Writ. But there are a couple of things that shed a little light, and I'll be honest with you, they disturb me. The key, of course, is in whatever was said between Havelock and Ogilvie; but since we can't know what it was, we can only go by Baylor's detailed description of the scene, the physical movements, the general tone. I've read it over and over again, and until the final moments – the eruption of violence – I was struck by a note I didn't expect to find. The absence of sustained hostility.'

'Sustained hostility?' asked Stern. 'I don't know what that implies in behavioural terms, but I hope it doesn't mean they didn't argue because they did. Baylor makes that clear.'

'Of course they argued; it was a confrontation. There was a prolonged outburst on Havelock's part, restating the threats he's made before, but then the shouting stopped; it had to. Some kind of accommodation was reached. It couldn't have been otherwise in the light of what followed.'

'In the light of what followed?' questioned Stern, bewildered 'What followed was Ogilvie's trap, the diphenylamine, the explosion.'

'I'm sorry, you're wrong, Daniel. There was a retreat before then. Remember, from the moment Havelock showed himself until that instant at the bench when he kicked out, aborting the trap, there was no show of physical violence, no display of weapons. There was talk, *conversation*. Then the cigarettes, the matches. It's too damned reasonable.'

'What do you mean?'

'Put yourself in Havelock's place. Your grievance is enormous, your anger at fever pitch, and a man you consider your enemy asks you for a light. What do you do?'

'It's only a match.'

'That's right, only a match. But you're consumed, your head throbbing with anxiety, your state of mind actually vicious. The man in front of you represents betrayal at its worst, at its most personal, most deeply felt. These are the things a paranoid schizophrenic feels at a time like this, with a man like this. And that man, that enemy – even if he's promised to tell you everything you want to hear – asks you for a light. How do you react?'

'I'd give it to him.'

'*How?*'

'Well, I'd – ' The section chief stopped, his eyes locked with Miller's. Then he completed the answer, speaking quietly. 'I'd throw it to him.'

'Or tell him to forget about it, or shove it, or just to keep on talking. But I don't think you'd take the matches from your pocket and walk over, handing them to that man as though it were a momentary pause in an argument rather than an interruption of a highly charged moment of extreme personal anxiety. No. I don't think you'd do that. I don't think any of us would.'

'We don't know what Ogilvie said to him,' objected Stern. 'He could have – '

'It almost doesn't matter, don't you see?' interrupted the psychiatrist. 'It's the pattern, the goddamned *pattern.*'

'Discerned from a book of *matches?*'

'Yes, because it's symptomatic. Throughout the entire confrontation, with the exception of a single outburst, there was a remarkable absence of aggressiveness on Havelock's part. If Baylor is as accurate as you say – and I suspect that he is because under the circumstances he'd be prone to exaggerate any threatening movements or gestures – Havelock exercised extraordinary control . . . rational behaviour.'

'What does that tell you?' asked Dawson, breaking his silence, watching Miller closely.

'I'm not sure,' said the doctor, returning the lawyer's stare. 'But I know it doesn't fit the portrait of the man we've persuaded ourselves we're dealing with. To twist a phrase, there's too much reason afoot, not enough madness.'

'Even with his slipping in and out of reality?' continued Dawson.

'It's not relevant here. His reality is the product of his whole experience, his everyday living. Not his convictions; they're based largely on his emotions. Under the conditions of the rendezvous, they should have surfaced more, distorting his reality, forcing him into listening less, into a more aggressive posture . . . He listened too much.'

'You know what you're saying, don't you, Paul?' said the lawyer.

'I know what I'm *implying*, based on the data we've all accepted as being totally accurate . . . from the beginning.'

'That the man on the Palatine three days ago doesn't fit the portrait?' suggested Dawson.

'*Might* not fit it. No absolutes, only "trained" guesswork. We don't know what was said, but there was too much rationality in what was described to suit me. Or the portrait.'

'Which was predicated on information we've considered infallible,' concluded the lawyer. 'In your words, "from the beginning". From Costa Brava.'

'Exactly. But suppose it wasn't? Suppose it *isn't?*'

'Impossible!' said the Director of Consular Operations. 'That information was filtered through a dozen sieves, then filtered again through twenty more. There was *no* margin for error. The Karras woman *was* KGB; she *died* at Costa Brava.'

'That's what we've accepted,' agreed the psychiatrist. 'And I hope to God it's accurate, and that my guesswork observations are worthless reactions to an *in*accurately described scene. But if it's not and they're not, if there's the remotest possibility that we're not dealing with a psychopath but with a man who's telling the truth because it *is* the truth, then we're faced with something I don't even want to think about.'

The three men fell silent, each grappling with the enormity of the implication. Finally Dawson spoke. 'We have to think about it.'

'It's appalling even to consider it,' said Stern. 'There was MacKenzie's confirmation, and it *was* a confirmation. The torn clothing, parts of a blouse, a skirt, they *belonged* to her, it was established. And the blood type, A-negative. *Hers.*'

'And Steven MacKenzie died of a coronary three weeks later,' interrupted Miller. 'We looked into it, but it just faded away.'

'Come on, Paul,' objected Stern. 'That doctor in Maryland is one of the most respected on the Eastern Shore. What's his name? . . . Randolph. Matthew Randolph. Johns Hopkins, Mayo Clinic, on the boards of Massachusetts General and New York's Mount Sinai, and with his own medical centre. He was thoroughly interviewed.'

'I'd like to talk to him again,' the doctor said.

'And I remind you,' pressed the director, 'MacKenzie had just about the finest record that ever came out of the Central Intelligence Agency. What you're suggesting is inconceivable.'

'So was the horse in Troy,' said the lawyer. 'When it was conceived.' He turned to Miller, who had removed his glasses. 'Trained guesswork, Paul. Let's take it all the way; we can always scratch it, but say there's substance. What do you think he'll do now?'

'I'll tell you what he won't do – if there's substance. He won't come in, and we can't trick him with ploys because he understands – rationally – that whatever's happened we're either a part of it, or ignorant of it, or it's beyond our control. The attack's been made on him; he'll mount every defence he's learned in the sixteen years he's been in the field. And from now on he'll be ruthless, because he *has* been betrayed. By men he can't see in places where they shouldn't be.' The psychiatrist looked at Stern. 'There's your answer, Daniel, if there's substance. Oddly enough, he's really back in his early days now – the machine-guns, Lidice, betrayal. He's running through the streets wondering who in the crowds might be his executioner.'

A sharp, abrasive hum erupted from the red telephone on the small, low table next to Stern. The director reached down and picked it up, his eyes still on Miller. 'Yes?'

Thirty seconds of silence followed, interrupted only by quiet acknowledgements on Stern's part as he listened, staring across at the psychiatrist's notes, absorbing the information being given him. 'Stay on the line,' he said finally, snapping the switch and looking up at both strategists. 'This is Rome. They've found a man in Civitavecchia; the name of a ship. It may *be* the girl. Or a Soviet hoax; that's entirely possible. It was Baylor's theory and he still holds to it . . . The original order stands. Take Havelock, but not dispatch; he's not to be considered "beyond salvage" . . . Now, I've got to ask you a question – primarily you, Paul, and I know I can't hold you to absolutes.'

'That's the only absolute.'

'We've acted on the assumption that we're dealing with an unbalanced man, with someone whose paranoia may compel him to place documents or statements exposing past operations with third parties, to be released on instructions. Is that right?'

'Basically, yes. It's the sort of manipulation a schizophrenic mentality would indulge in, the satisfaction derived as much from revenge as from the threat itself. Remember, the third parties in question would undoubtedly come from undesirable elements; respectable people would shun such a person, and underneath he knows that. It's a compulsive, involuntary game. He really can't win, only seek vengeance, and there's the danger.'

'Would a sane man play that game?'

The psychiatrist paused, fingering his glasses. 'Not the same way.'

'How do you mean?'

'Would you?'

'*Please*, Paul.'

'No, I'm serious. You'd be more concerned with the threat than with the revenge. You want something; revenge may be down the road, but it's not what's primarily on your mind now. You want answers. Threats might get them for you, but risking exposure of classified information by delivering it to highly suspect brokers defeats the purpose.'

'What would a sane man do?'

'Probably get word to those he's threatening as to the kind of information he intends to reveal. Then he'd proceed to reach qualified third parties – publishers, perhaps, or men and women who head organizations that legitimately, openly, resist the kind of work we do here – and make arrangements with them. That's a sane man's approach, his attack, his ultimate threat.'

'There's no evidence that Havelock's done any of these things.'

'It's only been three days since the Palatine; he hasn't had time. These things take time.'

'Lending credence to the matches. To his sanity.'

'I think so, and I'm biting the bullet. I gave him the label – based on what we had – and now I'm wondering if it should be removed.'

'And if we remove it, we accept the possibility of a sane man's attack. As you said, he'll be ruthless, far more dangerous than a schizophrenic.'

'Yes,' agreed the psychiatrist. 'An unbalanced man can be repudiated, blackmailers dealt with . . . and it's important to realize that since Costa Brava no such extortionists have tried to reach us. But legitimate interests, no matter how misguided, could inflict extraordinary damage.'

'Costing networks, informants, sources, years of work . . .' The director's hand reached down to the telephone, to the switch, 'And lives.'

'Yet *if* he's sane,' interrupted Dawson sharply, once again breaking a silence, 'if it *is* the girl, that presupposes a much deeper problem, doesn't it? Her guilt, her death, everything's in question. All that *infallible* information that was filtered through all those high-level sieves suddenly looks like a massive deception where deception shouldn't *be*. Those are the answers Havelock wants.'

'We know the questions,' replied Stern quietly, his hand still on the telephone switch, 'and we can't *give* him the answers. We can only stop him from inflicting extraordinary damage.' The Director of Cons Op fell silent for a moment, his eyes on the telephone. 'When each of us entered this room, we understood. The only morality here is pragmatic morality, no philosophy but our own brand of utilitarianism. The greatest advantage for the many . . . over the few, over the individual.'

'If you put him "beyond salvage", Daniel,' continued the lawyer softly, emphatically, 'I can't support you. And not from an ethical point of view, but from a very practical one.'

Stern looked up. 'What is it?'

'We need him for tracing the second, deeper problem. If he's sane, there's an approach we haven't tried, an approach he may listen to. As you said, we've acted on the assumption that he was unbalanced; it was the only reasonable assumption we could make. But if he isn't, he may listen to the truth.'

'What truth?'

'That we don't *know*. Let's grant him that he *did* see the Karras woman, that she *is* alive. Then tell him we want the answers as badly as he does. Perhaps more so.'

'Assuming we can get that word to him, suppose he doesn't listen, suppose he demands only the answers we can't give, and considers everything else a trick to take him. Or take him out. What then? We've got the Costa Brava files; they contain the names of everyone involved. What help can he really be? On the other hand, we know the damage he can do, the panic he can create, the lives he can cost.'

'The victim becomes the villain,' said Miller wearily. 'Jesus Christ.'

'We take our problems in order of appearance and priority,' said Stern, 'and in my judgement these are two separate crises. Related but separate now. We go after the first. What else can we do?'

'We can admit we don't know!' answered Dawson urgently,

'Every effort will be made to comply with the original order, to take him alive. But they have to be given the option.'

'By giving it you're telling them he's a traitor. They'll use it on the slightest provocation. They'll kill him. I repeat, I can't support you.'

The director slowly looked up at the lawyer; there were deep creases around his tired eyes, which were filled with doubt. 'If we're this far apart, then it's time,' he said quietly, reluctantly.

'For what?' asked Miller.

'To give this to Matthias's office. They can reach the old man, or not, knowing that time's running out. I'll go up myself and summarize.' Stern flipped the switch on the telephone. 'Rome? Sorry to keep you hanging, and I'm afraid it's going to get worse. Keep the ship under air surveillance, and send your people to Col des Moulinets, their radio frequency on scrambler for instructions. If they don't get their orders by the time they land, they're to reach you every fifteen minutes. You stay by this line and close it down – for your use only. We'll get back to you as soon as we can, either myself or someone upstairs. If it's not me, the code will be . . . "Ambiguity". Have you got that? "Ambiguity". That's all for now, Rome.' The director replaced the phone, snapped the switch, and got up from his chair. 'I hate like hell doing this . . . at a time like this,' he said. 'We're supposed to be the shield with a thousand eyes, all-seeing, all knowing. Others can plan, others execute, but we're the ones who give the word. The lousy decisions are supposed to be made here, that's our *function*, goddamn it.'

'We've needed help before,' said the psychiatrist.

'Only on tactical questions that Ogilvie couldn't answer, never on matters of evaluation. Never for anything like this.'

'Dan, we're not playing corporate chairs in the boardroom,' added Dawson. 'We inherited Costa Brava, we didn't initiate it.'

'I know that,' said Stern, going to the door. 'I suppose it's a consolation.'

'Do you want us to go with you?' asked Miller.

'No, I'll present it fairly.'

'Never doubted it,' interjected the lawyer.

'We're running against a clock in Rome,' continued the director. 'The fewer of us, the fewer questions. It's reduced to one anyway. Sane or insane. "Beyond salvage" or not.' Stern opened the door and left as the two strategists watched, an uneasy sense of relief apparent on both their faces.

'Do you realize,' said Miller, turning in his chair. 'That for the first time in three years the phrase "I can't support you" was used? Not "I don't think so" or "I disagree", but "I can't support you".'

'I couldn't,' said Dawson. 'Daniel's a statistician. He sees numbers – fractions, equations, totals – and they spell out the odds for him. God knows he's brilliant at it; he's saved the lives of hundreds with those statistics. But I'm a lawyer; I see complications, ramifications. Parties of the first part turning on parties of the second part. Prosecutors stymied because a point of law prohibits them from connecting one piece of evidence to another when it should be permitted. Criminals outraged over minor discrepancies of testimony when the only things outrageous were their crimes. I've seen it all, Paul, and there are times when the odds aren't found in numbers. They're found in things you can't perceive at the moment.'

'Strange isn't it? The differences between us, I mean. Daniel sees numbers, you see complications, and I see – full-blown possibilities based on particles.'

'A book of matches?'

'I guess so.' The psychiatrist levelled his eyes at the lawyer. 'I believe in those matches. I believe in what they stand for.'

'So do I. At least in the possibility they represent. That's the complication, "Headman" – as Ogilvie would have said. If there's a possibility that Havelock's sane, then everything he says is true. The girl – false guilt generated in our deepest laboratories – alive, running. Rostov in Athens – bait not taken to the Lubyanka for reasons unknown, a Soviet mole at Sixteen Hundred . . . Complications, Doctor. We need Michael Havelock to help us unravel a melted ball of wax. *If* it's happened – whatever it is – it's frightening.' Dawson abruptly pushed his chair back and stood up. 'I've got to get back to my office. I'll leave a message for Stern; he may want to come over and talk. How about you?'

'What? Oh, no, thanks,' answered Miller, preoccupied. 'I've got a five-thirty session at Bethesda, a marine from Teheran.' He looked up. 'It *is* frightening, isn't it?'

'Yes, Paul. Very.'

'We did the right thing. No one in Matthias's section will put Mikhail Havlicek "beyond salvage".'

'I know. I counted on it.'

* * *

The Director of Consular Operations came out of the office on the fifth floor, L section, of State, closing the door quietly behind him – closing, too, a part of the problem from his mind. It was shared now, the responsibility spread. The man he had shared it with – the man who would reach Rome under the code name 'Ambiguity' and render the judgement – was chosen carefully. He was one of Anthony Matthias's inner circle, someone the Secretary of State trusted implicitly. He would consider all the options before making the decision . . . undoubtedly not alone.

The issue was clear as it could be. If Havelock was sane and telling the truth, he was capable of doing extraordinary damage because he had been betrayed. And if that was the case, there was treason here in Washington in inconceivable places. Related but separate crises. Should he then be placed immediately "beyond salvage", so that his death would prevent the great harm he could inflict on intelligence operations throughout all Europe? Or should the order for his execution be delayed, in the hope that something might happen which would reconcile a man who was an innocent victim to those who would *not* betray him?

The only way was to find the woman in Col des Moulinets, and if it *was* Jenna Karras to bring her to Havelock, let them join forces and together run down the second, potentially greater crisis here in Washington. But if it was *not* Jenna Karras, if it was a Soviet ploy, if she did not exist except as a deadly puppet-hoax to drive a man mad and into treason, what then? Or if she was alive and they could not find her, would Havelock listen? Would Mikhail Havlicek, victim, survivor of Lidice and Soviet Prague, listen? Or would he see betrayal where there was none, and in turn betray his own? Could the delay then be justified? God knew it could not be justified to dismantled networks or to undercover agents who found themselves in the Lubyanka. And if that was the answer there was the possibility – the probability – that a man had to die because he was right.

The only morality here is pragmatic reality, no philosophy but our own brand of utilitarianism: the greatest advantage for the many – over the few, over the individual.

That was the real answer, the statistics proved it. But this was the inner territory of Anthony Matthias's domain. Would they see it here? In all likelihood they would not, Stern realized. Fear would compel the man he had talked with to reach Matthias, and the revered Secretary of State would delay.

And a part of Daniel Stern – not the professional, but the person inside – did not object. A man should not die because he was right, because he was sane. Yet Stern had done his professional best to make the options clear, to justify that death if it came down to it. And he had been fortunate in one respect, he thought, as he approached the door to the outer reception room. He could not have brought the problem to a fairer, more level-headed man. Arthur Pierce's title – like that of so many other young middle-aged men in the Department – was Undersecretary of State, but he was head and shoulders above the many others. There had been about twenty senior personnel still in L Section when Stern reached the fifth floor, but Pierce's name had stood out. To begin with, Pierce was not in Washington every day; he was assigned to the United Nations in New York as chief liaison officer between the ambassador and the State Department, a position decreed by Anthony Matthias who knew what he was doing. Given a respectable amount of time, Arthur Pierce would be made the UN ambassador, and a good man, a decent man, would be rewarded not only for his high intelligence, but for his decency.

And God knew decency was needed now . . . Or was it? wondered Stern, startling himself, his hand reaching for the knob of the reception room door. *The only morality here is pragmatic morality* . . . There was decency in that for hundreds of potential victims in the field.

No matter, it was out of his hands, Stern thought, as he opened the door. The decision to be made and transmitted under the code name Ambiguity was on Pierce's conscience now. Quiet, bright, understanding Arthur Pierce – apart from Mikhail Havlicek the closest to Matthias – would ponder all sides of the question, then bring in others. The decision would be made by committee, if it was to be made. *They* were Ambiguity now.

'Mr Stern?' the receptionist called out as he passed her, making for the lift.

'Yes?'

'Message for you, sir.'

It said: 'Daniel. I'll be at my office for a while. If you're of a mind, come over for a drink. I'll drive you home, chicken.'

Dawson had not signed his name, nor was it necessary. The often aloof, circumspect lawyer always seemed to know when quiet talk was called for; it was his warmer side. The two cold, analytical men every now and then needed the solace of each other's rarely seen lighter traits. The humorous offer to drive him home was a reference to Stern's distaste for Washington traffic. He took taxis everywhere, to the annoyance of his personal surveillance. Well, whatever team was on now, it could take a break and pick him up later at home in Virginia; Dawson's guards could serve them both until then.

Ogilvie had been right, the whole business was foolish, a hangover from the Angleton days in Langley. Stern looked at his watch; it was twenty minutes past seven, but he knew the lawyer would still be at his office, still waiting for the quiet talk.

They talked for over an hour before going down to Dawson's car, analysing and reanalysing the events at Costa Brava, realizing there was no explanation, no answer within their grasp. Each had called his wife; both women were inured to the interminable hours demanded by the State Department, and claimed to understand. Each lied and both husbands understood; the clandestine regions of government placed too much strain on the marriage vows. It would all come to an end one day. There was a far healthier world beyond the Potomac than either man had known for too many years.

'Pierce will go to Matthias, and Matthias won't consider it, you know that, don't you?' said Dawson, turning off the crowded highway into the back country road in Virginia, passing luminous signs that read *Construction Ahead*. 'He'll demand a review.'

'My conference with Pierce was one-to-one,' said Stern, absently glancing at the rear-view mirror outside the window, knowing that a pair of headlights would be there in moments. The watchdogs stayed on their leashes. 'I was balanced but firm; either decision has merit, both have drawbacks. When he talks to his committee they may decide to do without Matthias because of the time factor. I emphasized it. In less than three hours our people will be in Col des Moulinets; so will Havelock. They have to know how to proceed.'

'Whatever comes down, they'll first try to take him alive.'

'That's the priority; no one here wants it otherwise.' Stern looked through the flashing shadows at his companion. 'But I don't kid myself, you were right before. If it comes down "beyond salvage", he's dead. It's a licence to kill someone who'll kill you if he can.'

'Not necessarily. I may have overreacted. If the order's clear – dispatch the last resort – I could be wrong.'

'You're wrong now, I'm afraid. Do you think Havelock will give them a choice? He survived the Palatine; he'll use every trick in his very thick book. No one'll get close enough to take him. But getting him in a rifle sight is another matter. That can be done and no doubt will be.'

'I'm not sure I agree.'

'That's better than not supporting me.'

'It's easier,' said Dawson, smiling briefly. 'But Havelock doesn't know we found the man in Civitavecchia; he doesn't know we're on him in Col des Moulinets.'

'He'll assume it. He told Baylor about the Karras woman getting out, how he's convinced she got out. He'll expect us to follow up. We'll concentrate on her, of course. If it *is* Jenna Karras, she's the answer to everything; we'd be home free without a shot. Then *with* Havelock we can go after the mess here. That's the optimum, and I hope to Christ it happens. But it may not.'

'And then we're left with a man in the cross-hairs of a rifle scope,' said Dawson with an edge to his voice, as he accelerated down the flat stretch of back country road. 'If it is the Karras woman, we've *got* to find her. We *have* to.'

'No matter who it is, we'll do our damnedest,' said Stern, his eyes again straying to the mirror outside the window. There were no headlights. 'That's odd. The watchdogs have strayed, or your foot's outracing them.'

'There was a lot of traffic on the highway. If they got in a slow lane, they could crack their butts breaking out. It's Friday in Virginia, Martini time for the hunt country diplomats. On nights like this, I begin to understand why you don't drive.'

'What team's on tonight, by the way?'

The question was never answered. Instead, an ear-shattering scream exploded from the attorney's throat as the deafening impact came, smashing the windshield into a thousand blades of flying glass, piercing flesh and eyes, severing veins and arteries. Metal shrieked against metal, twisting, breaking, curling, crushing against itself as the left side of the car rose off the ground throwing the bodies into the well of deep red rivulets below.

The steel behemoth of yellow and black, its colours glistening in the reflection of its single front floodlight, vibrated thunderously, the giant treads of its spiked cables rolled through the huge wheel casings, relentlessly pressing the monster forward. This enormous machine that moved earth from mountains and forests now crawled ahead, crushing the demolished vehicle as it sent it over and beyond the road. The lawyer's car plunged down the steep incline of a shallow ravine; the fuel tank exploded and fire spread everywhere, consuming the bodies within the car.

Then the brightly coloured machine, its curved implement of destruction hydraulically raised in triumph, jerked back and forth, its massive gears remeshing, the pitch of the sound higher – an animal proclaiming its kill. And with sporadic but deliberate movements it retreated across the road into its lair at the edge of the woods.

High in the darkness of the cab the unseen driver turned off the engine and raised a hand-held radio to his lips.

'Ambiguity terminated,' he said.

'Get out of there,' was the reply.

The long grey saloon roared off the highway into the small country road. The licence plates indicated that the vehicle was registered in the State of North Carolina, but a persistent investigator could learn that the individual in Raleigh listed as the owner was in reality one of twenty-four men stationed in Washington, DC. They were a unit, each having had extensive experience in military police and counter intelligence; they were assigned to the Department of State. The car now racing down the dark country road in Virginia, was one of a fleet of twelve; they, too, were assigned to State, Division of Consular Operations.

'File a report with the insurance company in Raleigh,' said the man sitting next to the driver, speaking into a microphone attached to a large radio console beneath the dashboard. 'Some clown side-swiped us and we ploughed into a guy from Jersey. There was no damage to us, of course, but he doesn't have much of a trunk left. We wanted to get out there, so we told him –'

'*Graham!*'

'What?'

'Up ahead! The fire!'

'Jesus *Christ*! *Move!*'

The grey car leapt forward, the sound of its powerful engine echoing through the dark Virginia countryside. Nine seconds later it reached the steep incline that fronted the shallow ravine, and tyres screeched as the brakes were applied. Both men leaped out and raced to the edge, the heat of the flames directly below causing both to step back, with their hands shielding their eyes from the fire.

'Oh, my *God*!' cried the driver. 'It's Dawson's car! Maybe we can – '

'*No!*' shouted the man named Graham, stopping his associate from crawling down the flank of the ravine. His eyes were drawn to the yellow-and-black bulldozer standing motionless in its recess on the side of the road. Then . . . 'Miller!' he screamed 'Where's *Miller?*'

'The chart said Bethesda, I think.'

'Find him!' ordered Graham, running across the road, crouching, reaching behind for the weapon in his hip holster. 'Get Bethesda! *Raise* him!'

The head nurse at the reception counter on the sixth floor of the Bethesda Naval Hospital was adamant. Nor did she appreciate the aggressive tone of voice used by the man on the telephone; it was a poor connection to begin with and his shouting only made it worse.

'I repeat, Dr Miller is in psychiatric session and can't be disturbed.'

'You get him on the line and you get him on *now*! This is a Four-Zero emergency, Department of State, Consular Operations. This is a direct order routed and coded through the State Department's switchboard. Confirm, please.'

'Confirmed,' said a third voice flatly. 'This is operator one-seven, State, for your recheck.'

'Very well, operator one-seven, and you may be sure we *will* check.' The nurse jammed her forefinger on the hold button, cutting off further conversation as she got out of her chair and walked around the counter. It was hysterical men like the so-called special agent from Consular Operations that kept the psychiatric wards in full operation, she thought as she proceeded down the white corridor towards the row of therapy rooms. They screamed emergency for the flimsiest reason, more often than not trying to impress everyone with their so-called authority. It would serve special agent Consular-whatever right if the doctor refused to come to the phone. But he would not refuse; the head nurse knew that. Dr Miller's brilliance in no way thwarted his genuine kindness; if he had a fault, it was his excessive generosity. He had checked into T. R. Twenty; she approached it, noting that the red light at the side of the door was on, signifying occupancy, she pressed the intercom button.

'Dr Miller, I hate to interrupt but there's a man from the State Department on the telephone. He says it's an emergency.'

There was no reply; perhaps the intercom was not working. The head nurse pressed the button again, applying more pressure, speaking louder. 'Dr Miller? I realize this is highly irregular, but there's a man on the phone from State. He's most insistent and the operator *did* confirm the status of the call.'

Nothing. Silence. No sound of the knob being turned, no acknowledgement whatsoever. The doctor obviously could not hear her; the intercom was not working. She rapped on the door.

'Dr Miller? Dr *Miller*?'

Really, the man was not deaf. What was he *doing*? His patient was a marine, one of the hostages from Teheran. Not violent; over passive, actually. Had there been a regression? The nurse turned the knob and opened the door of Therapy Room Twenty.

She screamed – again and again.

Crouched in the corner, trembling, was the young marine in his government issue bathrobe. He was staring through the light of the desk lamp, his gaze riveted on the figure sprawled back on the chair. Miller's eyes were open wide, glass-like – dead. In the centre of his forehead was a single bullet hole from which blood poured out, rolling down his face and onto the collar of his white shirt.

The man in Rome looked at his watch. It was a quarter past four in the morning, his men in position in Col des Moulinets, and still no word from Washington. The only other person in the code room was the radio operator.

Bored with the inactivity, he was absently scanning his dials, picking up insignificant traffic signals, from ships mainly. Every now and then he would lean back and flip through the pages of an Italian magazine, mouthing the phrases that had become his third language – the radio was his second.

The light on the telephone preceded the hum. The man picked it up. 'Rome,' he said.

'This is Ambiguity, Rome.' The voice was clear, deliberate. 'That name gives me complete authority regarding all orders issued to your unit at Col des Moulinets. I assume Director Stern made that clear to you.'

'Very clear, sir.'

'Are we on total scrambler?'

'Total.'

'We're not to be taped or logged. Is that understood?'

'Understood. No tape, no log. What's the word?'

'"Beyond Salvage". Complete.'

'That's it, then.'

'Not yet. There's more.'

'What?'

'Clarification. There's been no contact with the freighter, has there?'

'Of course not. Small plane surveillance until it's too dark, then we shift to parallel coast sightings.'

'Good. She'll be put ashore somewhere before San Remo, I'd guess.'

'We're ready.'

'Is the Corsican in charge up there?' asked the voice from Washington.

'The one who came on board three days ago?'

'Yes.'

'He is. He put the unit together and I can tell you we owe him. Our drones over here have dwindled.'

'Good.'

'Speaking of clarification, I assume the colonel's order still holds. We bring the woman in.'

'Inoperative. Whoever she is, she's *not* the Karras woman; she was killed at Costa Brava, we know that.'

'Then what do we do?'

'Let Moscow have her back. This one's Soviet poison, a lure to drive the target out of his head. It worked; he's already talked. He's –'

'"Beyond Salvage",' completed Rome.

'Just get her out of there. We don't want any trail that could lead back to us, no reopened speculations on Costa Brava. The Corsican will know what to do.'

'I've got to say it, I'm not sure I understand.'

'You don't have to. We just want proof of dispatch. *His* dispatch.'

'You'll have it. Our man with the eyes is up there.'

'Have a good day, Rome. A good day with no mistakes.'

'No mistakes, no tape, no log.'

'Out,' said the voice known only as Ambiguity.

The man behind the desk was outlined in silhouette. He was in front of a window overlooking the grounds below the Department of State, the soft glow of faraway streetlamps the only light intruding on the dark office. The man had been facing the window, the telephone held close to his lips. He swivelled in his chair, his features in shadow and as he replaced the phone and leaned forward, resting his forehead on the extended fingers of both hands, the curious streak of white that shot through his dark hair gleamed even in the dim light.

Undersecretary of State Arthur Pierce, born Nicolai Petrovich Malyekov in the village of Ramenskoye, south-east of Moscow, and raised in the State of Iowa, breathed deeply, steadily, imposing calm over himself as he had learned to do throughout the years whenever a crisis called for swift, dangerous decisions; he knew full well the consequences of failure. That, of course, was the strength of men such as he: they were not afraid to fail. They understood that the great accomplishments in history demanded the greatest risks; that, indeed, history itself was shaped by the boldness not only of individual initiative but of collective action. Those who panicked at the thought of failure, who did not act with clarity and determination when the moments of crisis were upon them, deserved the limitations to which their fears committed them.

There had been another decision to make, a decision every bit as dangerous as the one he had transmitted to Rome; but there was no avoiding it. The strategists of Consular Operations had reopened the events of that night on the Costa Brava; they had been peeling away the layers of deceit, about which they knew *nothing*! It all had to be buried – *they* had to be buried. At all costs, at all risk. Costa Brava had to be submerged again, become an obscure deception in a convoluted world of lies. In a few hours word would be sent from Col des Moulinets: *'The order for beyond-salvage has been carried out. Authorization: Code Ambiguity – established and cleared by D. S. Stern, Director of Consular Operations.'*

But only the strategists knew whom Stern had come to with his ambiguous dilemma. In fact, Stern himself had not known whom he would approach until he had emerged on the fifth floor and studied the roster of senior personnel on the premises; he had made that clear. No matter, thought Arthur Pierce in the dark office as he glanced at the inscribed photograph of Anthony Matthias on the wall. All things considered, it would have been unthinkable for him not to have been consulted regarding the crisis. It was simply more convenient for him to have been in his office when Stern and the other strategists had made the decision to bring the insoluble problem upstairs. Had he not been on the floor, he would have been reached, his counsel sought. The result would have been the same: 'beyond salvage'. Only the method would have been different: an unacknowledged consensus by a faceless committee. Everything worked out for the best; the past two hours had been orchestrated properly. Failure had been considered, but not contemplated. Failure had been out of the question. The strategists were dead, all links to code-name Ambiguity severed.

They needed time. Days, a week, a month. They had to find the man who had accomplished the incredible – with *their help*. They would find him, for he was leaving a trail of fear – no, not fear, *terror* – and trails could be tracked. And when they found him, it would not be the meek who inherited the earth. It would be the *Voennaya*.

There were so few of them left on this side of the world. So few, but so strong, so right. They had seen it all, lived it all. The lies, the corruption, the essential rot at the cores of power; they had been part of it for a greater cause. They had not forgotten who they were, or what they were. Or *why* they were. They were the travellers, and there was no higher calling; its concept was based in reality, not in romantic illusions. They were the men and women of the new world, and the old one needed them desperately. They were not many in numbers – less than a hundred, committed beyond life – but they were finely tuned units, prepared to react instantly to any given opportunity or emergency. They had the positions, the right papers, the proper vehicles. The *Voennaya* was generous; they, in turn were loyal to the élite corps of the KGB.

The death of the strategists had been crucial. The resulting vacuum would paralyse the original architects of Costa Brava, stunning them into silence. They would say nothing, cover-up would be paramount. For the man in shadows behind the desk had not lied to Rome: there could be no reopened speculations on Costa Brava. For either side.

Darkness obscuring his movements, Arthur Pierce, the most powerful *paminyatchik* in the Department of State, rose from the desk and walked silently to the armchair against the wall. He sat down and stretched his legs; he would remain there until morning, until the crowds of senior and subordinate personnel began to fill up the fifth floor. Then he would mingle with the others, signing a forgotten roster sheet; his morning presence would be temporary, for he was needed back in New York. He was, after all, Washington's senior aide to the ambassador of the American delegation at the United Nations. In essence, he was the State Department's major voice on the East River; soon he would be the ambassador. That had been Anthony Matthias's design; everyone knew it. It would be yet another significant step in his extraordinary career.

Suddenly Malyekov-Pierce bolted up in the chair. There was a last phone call to be placed to Rome, a last voice to be stilled: a man in a radio room who answered a sterile telephone and took an untaped, unlogged message.

11

'She's not on board, I *swear* it!' protested the harassed captain of the freighter *Santa Teresa*, seated at his desk in the small cabin aft of the wheelhouse. 'Search, if you wish, signore. No one will interfere. We put her ashore three . . . three and a half hours ago. *Madre di Dio!* Such madness!'

'How? *Where?*' demanded Havelock.

'Same as you. A motor launch came out to meet us twelve kilometres south of Arma di Taggia. I swear to you, I knew *nothing*! I'll *kill* that pig in Civitavecchia! Just a political refugee from the Balkans, he said – a woman with a little money and friends in France. There are so many these days. Where is the sin in helping one more?'

Michael leaned over and picked up the outdated diplomatic identification card that gave his status as consular attaché, US Department of State, and said calmly, 'No sin at all, if that's what you believed.'

'It's true, signore! For nearly thirty years I've pushed my old cows through these waters. Soon I leave the sea with a little land, a little money. I grow grapes. Never *narcotici*! Never *contrabbandi*! But people – yes. Now and then *people*, and I am not ashamed. Those who flee places and men you and I know nothing about. I ask you again, where is the sin?'

'In making mistakes.'

'I cannot believe this woman is a criminal.'

'I didn't say that. I said we had to find her.'

The captain nodded his head in resignation. 'Badly enough to report me. I leave the sea for prison. *Grazie, Signore Americano Grande.*'

'I didn't say that, either,' said Michael quietly.

The captain's eyes widened as he looked up, his head motionless. *'Che cosa?'*

'I didn't expect you to be what you seem to be.'

'Quale?'

'Never mind. There are times when embarrassment should be avoided. If you co-operate, nothing may have to be said. *If* you co-operate.'

'In any way you wish! It's a gift I did not expect.'

'Tell me everything she said to you. And do it quickly.'

'There was much that was meaningless – '

'That's not what I want to hear.'

'I understand. She was calm, obviously highly intelligent, but, beneath, a very frightened woman. She stayed in this cabin.'

'Oh?'

'Not with me, I can assure you. I have daughters her age, signore. We had three meals together; there was no other place for her, and my crew is not what I would have my daughters eat with. Also, she carried a great deal of lire on her person. She had to; the transport she purchased did not come cheap . . . She looked forward to much trouble. Tonight.'

'What do you mean?'

'She asked me if I had ever been to the village of Col des Moulinets in the Ligurian mountains.'

'She told you about Col des Moulinets?'

'I think she assumed I knew, that I was merely one part of her journey, aware of the other parts. As it happened, I *have* been to Moulinets several times. The ships they give me are often in need of repair, here in San Remo, or Savona, or Marseilles, which, incidentally, is my farthest port of call. I am not what is known as a *capitano superiore* – '

'*Please.* Go on.'

'We have been dry-docked here in San Remo a few times and I have gone up to the mountains, to Col des Moulinets. It's across the French border west of Monesi, a lovely town filled with mountain streams and . . . how do you say it? *Route a pale?*'

'Paddlewheels. *Moulinets* can also mean paddlewheels in French.'

'*Si*. It's a minor pass in the lower Alps, not used very much. It's difficult to reach, the facilities poor, the transport poorer. And the border guards are the most lax in the Ligurian or Maritime Alps; they barely take the

Gauloises out of their mouths to glance at papers. I tried to assure my frightened refugee that she would have no trouble.'

'You think they'll try to go through a checkpoint?'

'There's only one, a short bridge across a mountain river. Why not? I doubt if it would be necessary even to bribe a guard; one woman among a group of well-dressed people at night – what concern is it of theirs?'

'Men like me.'

The captain paused; he leaned back in his chair appraising the American official, as if in a somewhat different light. 'Then you would have to answer that yourself, signore. Who else knows?' Both men looked at each other, neither speaking. The captain nodded and continued. 'But I tell you this; if they don't use the bridge, they will have to make their way through very dense forest with much steep rock, and don't forget the river.'

'Thanks. That's the kind of information I need. Did she say why she was getting out this way?'

'The usual. The airports were watched; the train stations also, as well as the major roads that cross into France.'

'Watched by whom?'

'Men like you, signore?'

'Is that what she said?'

'She did not have to say anything more than she did, and I did not inquire. That is the truth.'

'I believe you.'

'Will you answer the question then? Do others know?'

'I'm not sure,' said Michael. 'The truth.'

'Because if they do, I am arrested. I leave the sea for prison.'

'Would that mean it's public information?'

'Most certainly. Charges would be brought before a *commissione*.'

'Then I don't think they'll touch you. I have an idea that this incident is the last thing on earth the men I'm involved with want known. If they haven't reached you by now – by radio, or a fast boat, or by helicopter – they either don't know about you, or they don't want to touch you.'

Again the captain paused, looking carefully at Havelock. 'Men you are involved with, signore?' he said, the words suspended. '*Avvolgere, non includere?*'

'I don't understand.'

'Involved but not *of*, is that correct?'

'It's not important.'

'You wish to help this woman, do you not? You are not after her to . . . penalize her.'

'The answer to the first is yes. The second, no.'

'Then I will tell you. She asked me if I knew the airfield near Col des Moulinets. I did not. I never heard of it.'

'An airfield?' Michael understood. It was added information he would not have been given ten seconds ago. 'A bridge over a mountain river, and an airfield. Tonight.'

'That is all I can tell you.'

* * *

The mountain road leading out of Monesi towards the French border was wide enough, but the profusion of rock and boulder and bordering over-growth made it appear narrow, more suited to heavy-wheeled trucks and rugged jeeps than to any normal car. It was the excuse that Michael used to travel the last half mile on foot, to the relief of the taxi driver from Monesi.

He had learned there was a country inn just before the bridge, a watering spot for the Italian and French patrols, where both languages were suf-ficiently understood by the small garrisons on either side, as well as by the few nationals and fewer tourists who occasionally passed back and forth. From what little Havelock had seen and had been told, the captain of the *Santa Teresa* was right. The border checkpoint of Col des Moulinets was at a minor pass in the lower Alps, not easily accessible and poorly staffed, manned no doubt because it was there – had been for decades – and no bureaucratic legislation had bothered to remove it. The general flow of traffic between the two countries used either the wide coast roads of the Mediterranean fifteen miles south or the larger, more accommodating passes in the north, such as Col de Larche or Col du Mont Cenis, west of Turin.

The late afternoon sun was now a fan-shaped arc of deep orange and yellows, spraying up from behind the higher mountains, filling the sky above the Maritimes with receding echoes of light. The shadows on the primitive road were growing longer, sharper; in minutes their outlines would fade and they would become obscure grey shapes, indistinguishable within the dull darkness of early evening. Michael walked along the edge of the woods, prepared to spring into the undergrowth at the first sounds not part of the forest. He knew that every move he made must be prejudged on the assumption that Rome had learned about Col des Moulinets. He had not lied to the captain of the *Santa Teresa*; there could be any number of reasons why those working for the embassy would stay away from a ship in international waters. The slow freighter could be tracked and watched – very likely had been – but it was another matter to board her in a legitimate official capacity. It was a high-risk tactic, inquiries too easily raised with a *commissione*.

Had Rome found the man in Civitavecchia? He could only presume that others could do what he had done; no one was that unique or that lucky. He had in his anger – no, his outrage – shouted the name of the port city into the phone and Baylor Brown had repeated it. If the wounded intelligence officer was capable of functioning after the Palatine, he would order his people to prowl the Civitavecchia waterfront and find a broker of illegal passage.

Yet there were always gaps, spaces that could not be filled. Would the man in Civitavecchia name the specific ship, knowing that if he did so, he'd never again be trusted on the waterfront? Trusted, hell; he could be killed in any one of a dozen mist-filled back streets. Or might he plead ignorance to that phase of the escape – sold by others unknown to him – but reveal Col des Moulinets so as to curry favour with powerful Americans in Rome, who everyone knew could be inordinately generous. 'One more refugee from the Balkans; where was the sin, signore?'

So many gaps, so little was concrete . . . so little time to think, so many inconsistencies. Who would have thought there'd be a tired, ageing captain opposed to trafficking in the profitable world of narcotics and contraband but perfectly willing to smuggle refugees out of Italy – no less a risk, no less a cause for imprisonment?

Or blunt Red Ogilvie, a violent man who never stopped trying to justify violence. There was ambivalence in that strange justification. What had driven John Philip Ogilvie? Why does a man strain all his life to break out of self-imposed chains? Who really was the Apache? The gunslinger. Whoever and whatever, he had died violently at the very moment he had understood a violent truth. The liars were in control in Washington.

Above all, Jenna. His love who had not betrayed that love but, instead, had been betrayed. How could she have believed the liars? What could they have said to her, what irrefutable proof could they have presented that she would accept? Most important of all, *who* were the liars? What were their names and where had they come from?

He was so close now that he could sense it, feel it with every step he took on the darkening mountain road. Before the disappearing sun came up on the other side of the world, he would have the answers, have his love back. If they *had* come from Rome, they were no match for him; he knew that. His belief in himself swelled within him; it was unjustified all too often, but it was necessary. One did not come out of the early days, the terrible days, and survive without it. Each step and he was nearer.

And when he had the answers, and his love, the call would be made to a cabin in another range of mountains thousands of miles away. To the Blue Ridge and the Shenandoah, USA. His mentor, his *pritel*, Anton Matthias would be presented with a conspiracy that reached into the bowels of clandestine operations, its existence incontrovertible, its purpose unknown.

Suddenly he saw a small circle of light up ahead, shining through the foliage on the left-hand side of the road. He crouched and studied it, trying to define it. It did not move; it was merely there, where no light had been before. He crept forward, mesmerized, frightened; what *was* it?

Then he stood up, relieved, breathing again. There was a bend in the road, and in its cradle were the outlines of a building; it was the country inn. Someone had just turned on an outside post lamp; other lights would follow shortly. The darkness had come abruptly, as if the sun had dropped into a chasm; the tall pines and the massive boulders blocked the shafts of orange and yellow that could still be seen in the sky. Light now appeared in windows, three on the nearest side, more in front – how many he could not tell, but at least six, judging from the spill that washed over the grass and gravelled entrance of the building.

Michael stepped into the woods to check the undergrowth and foliage. Both were manageable, so he made his way towards the three lighted windows. There was no point in staying on the road any longer; if there were surprises in store, he did not care to be on the receiving end.

He reached the border of the woods, where the thick trunk of a pine tree stood between him and a deeply rutted driveway of hard mud. The drive extended along the side of the inn and curved behind it into some kind of parking area next to what appeared to be a delivery entrance. The distance to the window directly across was about twenty-five feet; he stepped out from behind the tree.

Instantly he was blinded by headlights. The truck thundered out of the primitive road thirty yards to his right, careening into the narrow driveway of ridged mud. Havelock spun back into the foliage, behind the trunk of the pine, and reached for the Spanish automatic strapped to his chest. The truck bounced past, pitching and rolling over the hardened ruts of the drive like a small barge in choppy water. From inside the van could be heard the angry shouts of men objecting to the discomfort of their ride.

Havelock could not tell whether he had been seen or not; again he crouched for protective cover and watched. The truck lurched to a stop at the entrance of the wide, flat parking area; the driver opened his door and jumped to the ground. Prepared to race into the woods, Michael crept back several feet. It was not necessary; the driver stretched while swearing in Italian, his figure suddenly caught in the spill of a floodlight someone had switched on from inside the building. What the light revealed was bewildering; the driver was in the uniform of the Italian army, but his insignia was that of a border guard. He walked to the back of the truck and opened the large double doors.

'Get out, you bastards!' he shouted in Italian. 'You've got about an hour to fill your kidneys before you go on duty. I'll walk up to the bridge and tell the others we're here.'

'The way you drive, Sergeant,' said a soldier, grimacing as he stepped out, 'they heard you half-way back to Monesi.'

'Up yours!'

Three other men got out in varying stages of contortions, stamping their feet and stretching; all were guards.

The sergeant continued, 'Paolo, you take the new man. Teach him the rules.' As the non-commissioned officer lumbered up the driveway past Havelock, he scratched his groin and pulled down the underwear beneath his trousers – signs of a long, uncomfortable trip.

'You, Ricci!' shouted a soldier at the rear of the truck, looking up into the van. 'Your name's Ricci, right?'

'Yes,' said the voice from inside and a fifth figure emerged from the shadows.

'You've got the best duty you'll find in the army, *paesano*! The quarters are up at the bridge, but we have an arrangement: we damn near live *here*. We don't go up there until we go on. Once you walk in, you sign in, understand?'

'I understand,' said the soldier named Ricci.

But his name was not Ricci, thought Micahel, staring at the blond man slapping his barracks hat against his left hand. Havelock's mind raced back over a dozen photographs; his mind's eye selected one. The man was not a soldier in the Italian army – certainly no border guard. He was a Corsican, a very proficient drone with a rifle or a handgun, a string of wire or a knife. His real name was irrelevant; he used too many to count. He was a 'specialist', used only in 'extreme-prejudice' situations, a reliable executioner who knew his way around the western Mediterranean better than most such men, as much at home in the Balearic Islands as he was in the forests of Sicily. His photograph and a file of his known accomplishments had been provided for Michael several years ago by a CIA agent in a sealed-off room at Palombara. Havelock had tracked a *Brigate Rosse* unit and was moving in for a non-attributable kill; he had rejected the blond man now standing thirty feet away from him in the floodlit driveway. He had not cared to trust him then, but Rome did now.

Rome did now! The embassy had found a man in Civitavecchia, and Rome had sent an executioner – for a non-attributable kill. Something or someone had persuaded the liars in Washington that a former field officer was now a threat only if he lived; so they had put out the word that he was 'beyond salvage', his immediate dispatch the highest priority. Non-attributable, of course.

The liars could not let him reach Jenna Karras, for she was part of their lie, her mock death on the Spanish coast intrinsic to it. Yet Jenna was running too; somehow, some way after Costa Brava she had escaped. Was she now included in the execution order? It was inevitable; the bait could not be permitted to live, and therefore the blond assassin was not the only killer on the bridge at Col des Moulinets. On, or near it.

The four soldiers and the new recruit started towards the rear entrance of the country inn. The door beneath the floodlight was opened, and a heavy-set man spoke in a loud voice. 'If you pigs spent all your money in Monesi, stay the hell out of here!'

'Ah, Gianni, then we'd have to close you up for selling French girls higher than ours!'

'*You* pay!' howled the obese man.

'Ricci, this is Gianni the thief. He owns this dung heap. Be careful what you eat.'

'I want to use the bathroom,' said the new recruit. He had just looked at his watch; it was an odd thing to do.

'Who doesn't?' shouted another soldier, as all five went inside.

The instant the door closed Havelock ran across the drive to the first window. It looked in on a dining-room. The tables were covered with red-checked cloths, with cheap silver and glassware in place, but there were no diners; either it was too early for the kitchen or there were no takers that evening. Beyond, separated only by a wide archway that extended the length of the wall, was the larger central bar. From what he could see there were a number of people seated at small round tables – between ten and fifteen would be his estimate – nearly all men. The two women in his sight lines were in their sixties, one fat, one gaunt, sitting at adjacent tables with mustachioed men: they were both talking and drinking beer. Early evening in the Ligurian Alps. He wondered if there were any other women in that room; he wondered – his chest aching – whether Jenna was huddled at a corner table he could not see. If that was the case, he must be able to watch a door from the rear quarters – from the kitchen, perhaps – from which the five soldiers would emerge into the bar. He *had* to be able to see. The next few minutes could tell him what he needed to know: who among the clientele in that bar would the blond killer recognize, if only with a glance, a twitch of his lips or an almost imperceptible nod?

Michael crouched and ran to the second window along the drive; the angle of vision was still too restricting. He raced to the third, appraised the view and rejected it, then rounded the corner of the building to the first window in front. He could see the door now – Cucina, the lettering said; the five soldiers would walk out of that door any second, but he could not see all the tables. There were two windows remaining that faced the stone path leading to the entrance. The second window was too close to the door for reasonable cover, but he held his breath and crawled swiftly to it, then stood up in the shadow of a spreading pine. He inched his face to the glass, and what he saw allowed him to let out the breath he had held. Jenna Karras was not an ambushed target sitting in a corner. The window was beyond the inside archway; he could see not only the kitchen entrance but every table, every person in the room. Jenna was not there. And then his eyes strayed to the far right wall; there was another door, a narrow door with two separate lines of letters. Uomini and Hommes, the men's room.

The door labelled Cucina swung open and the five soldiers straggled in; Gianni the thief had his head on the shoulder of the blond man whose name was not Ricci. Havelock stared at the killer, stared at the eyes with all his concentration. The owner of the inn gestured to his left – Michael's right – and the assassin started across the room towards the men's room. The eyes. Watch the eyes!

It came! Barely a flicker of the lids, but it was there, the glance was there. Recognition. Havelock followed the blond man's line of sight. *Confirmed.* Two men were at a table in the centre of the room; one had lowered his eyes to his drink while talking, the other – bad form – had actually shifted his legs so as to turn his head away from the path of the killer's movement. Two more members of the unit – but only one of them was active. The other was an observer. The man who had shifted his legs was the agent of record who would confirm the dispatch but in no way participate. He was an American; his mistakes bore it out. His jacket was an expensive Swiss windbreaker, wrong for the scene and out of season; his shoes were soft black leather, and he wore a shiny digital chronometer on his wrist – all so impressive, so irresistible to a swollen paycheque overseas, so much in contrast to the shabby mountain garments of his companion. So American. The agent-of-record – but it was a file no more than six men alive would ever see.

Something else was inconsistent; it was in the numbers. A unit of three with only two active weapons was understaffed, considering the priority of the kill and the background of the foreign service officer who was the primary target. Michael began studying every face in the room isolating each, watching eyes, seeing if any strayed to the oddly matched pair at the centre table. After the faces came the clothes, especially those belonging to the few faces angled away from him. Shoes, trousers and belts where they could be seen; shirts, jackets, hats and whatever jewellery was visible. He kept trying to spot another chronometer or an Alpine windbreaker or soft leather shoes. Inconsistencies. If they were there, he could not find them. With the exception of the two men at the centre table, the drinkers at the inn were a ramshackle collection of mountain people. Farmers, guides, shopkeepers – apparently French from across the bridge – and, of course, the border guards.

'*Ehi! Cosa avete?*' The words were hurled at him, a soldier's challenge. The sergeant from the truck stood, with his hand on his holster, in the semi darkness of the path that led to the entrance of the inn.

'*La mia sposa,*' said Havelock quickly, his voice low, urgent, properly respectful. '*Siamo molto disturbati, signor Maggiore. Ho avuto un affare con una ragazza francese. La mia sposa mi seguira!*'

The soldier grinned and removed his hand from the gun case. He admonished Havelock in barracks Italian: 'So the men of Monesi still go across the border for French ass, eh? If your wife's not in there, she's probably back in your own bedroom being pumped by a Frenchman! Did you ever think of that?'

'The way of the world, Major,' replied Michael obsequiously, shrugging, and wishing to Christ the loud-mouthed dolt would go inside and leave him alone. He had to get back to the window!

'You're not from Monesi,' said the sergeant, suddenly alarmed. 'You don't talk like a man from Monesi.'

'The *Swiss* border, Major. I come from Lugano. I moved here two years ago.'

The soldier was silent for a moment, his eyes squinting. Havelock slowly moved his hand in the shadows towards his waist, where, secured uncomfortably under his belt, was the heavy Magnum with the silencer attached. There could be no sound of gunfire, if it came to that.

Finally, the sergeant threw up his hands, shaking his head in disgust. 'Swiss! *Italian*-Swiss, but more *Swiss* than Italian! All of you! Sneaky bastards. I won't serve in a battalion north of Milan, I swear it. I'll get out of the army first. Go back to your sneaking, *Swiss!*' He turned and stalked into the inn.

Inside, another door – the narrow door to the men's room – was opened. A man walked out, and Michael knew not only that he had found a third weapon in the unit from Rome but that there had to be a fourth. The man was part of a team – two demolition experts who worked together – veteran mercenaries who had spent several years in Africa blowing up everything from dams and airports to grand villas suddenly occupied by inept despots in comic opera regalia. The CIA had found them in Angola, on the wrong side, but the American dollar was healthier then, and persuasive. The two experts had been placed in a single black-bordered file deep in the cabinets of clandestine operations.

And their being at the bridge of Col des Moulinets gave Havelock a vital piece of information: a vehicle or vehicles were anticipated. One of these two demolition specialists could pause for ten seconds by a car and, ten minutes later, it would explode, killing everyone in the immediate vicinity. Jenna Karras was expected to cross the border by car; minutes later she would be dead, a successful, non-attributable kill.

The airfield. Rome had learned about the airfield from the man in Civitavecchia. Somewhere on the road out of Col des Moulinets whatever conveyance she was in would be blown into the night sky.

Michael dropped to the ground behind the pine tree. Through the window he could see the explosives expert walking directly to the front door of the inn; the man glanced at his watch, as the blond killer had done minutes ago. A schedule was in progress, but *what* schedule?

The man emerged, his swarthy face looked even darker in the dim light of the post lamp at the end of the path. He began walking faster, but the acceleration was barely perceptible; this was a professional who knew the value of control. Havelock rose cautiously, prepared to follow; he glanced at the window, then looked again, alarmed. Inside, by the bar, the sergeant was talking to the blond recruit he called Ricci, obviously delivering an unwanted order. The killer seemed to be protesting, raising his beer as if it were much needed medicine and thus an excuse for not obeying. Then he grimaced, drank his drink in several swallows, and started for the door.

The schedule was being adhered to. Through pre-arrangement, someone at the bridge had been instructed to call for the new recruit in advance of the duty hour; he was to be put on duty *before* the shift was over. Procedural methods would be the cover, and no one would argue; but it was not procedure, it was the schedule.

They knew. The unit from Rome knew that Jenna Karras was on her way to the bridge. A motor launch had been picked up in Arma di Taggia and the party had been followed; the vehicle in which she travelled into the Ligurian mountains had now been spotted within minutes of its arrival at the checkpoint of Col des Moulinets. It was so logical: what better time to cross a border than at the end of a shift, when the soldiers were tired, weary of the dull monotony, waiting for relief, more careless than usual?

The door opened, and Michael crouched again, peering to his right through the branches of the pine tree at the road beyond the post lamp. The mercenary had crossed diagonally to the shoulder on the other side, bearing left towards the bridge – an ordinary stroller, a Frenchman perhaps, returning to Col des Moulinets. But in moments he would fade into the woods, taking up a pre-determined position east of the bridge's entrance, from which he could crawl to a car briefly held up by the guards. The blond killer was now half-way to the post lamp; he paused, lighting a cigarette, which gave another reason for his delay. He heard the sound of the door being opened and was satisfied. The 'soldier' continued on his way, as the two men from the centre table – the American agent-of-record and his roughly-dressed companion, the second weapon in the unit from Rome – came out.

Havelock understood now. The trap had been engineered with precision; in a matter of minutes it would be in place. Two expert marksmen would take out the intruder who tried to interfere with the car carrying Jenna Karras – take him out instantly, with a fusillade of bullets the second he came in sight; and two demolition specialists would guarantee that the car waved through would explode somewhere in the streets of Col des Moulinets, or on a road to an unmarked airfield.

Another assumption could be made, beyond the fact that there was a schedule in progress that included a car on its way to the bridge. The unit from Rome knew he was there, knew he would be close enough to the border patrols to observe all those in any vehicle offering passports to the guards. They would examine closely every male figure that came into view, their hands on their weapons as they did so. Their advantage was in their numbers, but he, too, had an advantage and it was considerable: he knew who they were.

The well-dressed American and his employee, the second gun, separated at the road, the agent-of-record turning right in order to remove himself from the execution ground, the killer going left to the bridge. Two small trucks clattered up the road from Monesi, one with only a single headlight, the other with both headlights but no windscreen. Neither the American nor his hired weapon paid any attention; they knew the vehicle they were waiting for, and it was neither of these.

If you know a strategy, you can counter a strategy – his father's words so many years ago. He could recall the tall, erudite man patiently explaining things to a cell of partisans, calming their fears, channelling their angers. Lidice was their cause, the death of Germans their objective. He remembered it all now as he crept back to the driveway and raced across into the woods.

He got his first glimpse of the bridge from three hundred yards, on the edge of the bend in the road that led to the country inn – the curve he had avoided by heading into the woods. From what he could see, it was narrow and not long, which was a blessing for drivers in that two cars crossing at the same time would doubtless have grazed fenders. A dual string of naked bulbs was now lighted; it arched over the central steel span, sagging between the struts; several of the bulbs had been burned out. The checkpoint itself consisted of two opposing structures that served as gatehouses, the windows high and wide, each with a ceiling light fixture; between the two small, square buildings, a hand-winched barrier painted with intense, light-reflecting orange fell across the road. To the right of the winch was a shoulder-high gate that opened onto the pedestrian walk.

Two soldiers in their brown uniforms with the red and green stripes were on either side of the second truck, talking wearily but animatedly with the driver. A third guard was at the rear, his attention not on the truck but on the woods beyond the bridge. He was studying the areas on both sides as a hunter might when stalking a wounded mountain cat: he stood motionless, his eyes roving, his head barely turning. He was the blond assassin. Who would suspect that a lowly soldier at a border checkpoint was a killer whose hunting-ground spanned the Mediterranean?

A fourth man had just been passed through the pedestrian gate. He was trudging slowly up the slight incline towards the midpoint of the bridge. But this man had no intention of crossing to the other side, no intention of greeting the French patrols in Ligurian *patois*, claiming as so many did that the air was different in *la belle France* and thank God for slender women. No, thought Michael, this crudely dressed peasant of the mountains with the drooping trousers and the large, heavy jacket would remain in the centre shadows and, if the light was dark enough, would check his weapon, probably a braced, repeating, rapid fire machine-gun, its stock a steel bar clamped to the shoulders, easily concealed beneath garments. He would release the safety catch and be prepared to race down to the checkpoint at the moment of execution, ready to kill the Italian guards if they interfered, intent on firing into the body of a man coming out of the darkness to reach a woman crossing the border. This man, last seen at a centre table in the country inn, was the back-up support for the blond-haired killer.

It was a gauntlet, at once simple and well manned, using the natural procedure of roadblocks; once the target entered, he was trapped both within and without. Two men waited with explosives and weapons at the mouth of the trap, one at its core and a fourth at its outer rim. Well conceived, very professional.

12

The tiny glow of a cupped cigarette could be seen in the bushes diagonally across the dark road. Bad form. The agent-of-record was an indulgent man denying himself neither chronometers nor cigarettes during the early stages of a kill. He should be replaced; he would be replaced.

Havelock judged the angle of the cigarette, its distance to the ground; the man was crouched or sitting, not standing. Because of the density of the foliage it was impossible for the man to see the road clearly, which meant that he did not expect the car with Jenna Karras for some time yet; he was being too casual for a momentary sighting. The sergeant had said that the soldiers had an hour to fill their kidneys; twenty minutes had passed, leaving forty. Yet not really forty. The final ten minutes of the shift would be avoided because the changing of the guard would require an exchange of information, no matter how inconsequential or proforma. Michael had very little time to do what had to be done, to mount his own counter strategy. First, he had to learn all he could of Rome's.

He side-stepped his way back along the edge of the foliage until the distant spill of light from the bridge was virtually blocked by the trees. He ran across the road and into the undergrowth, turning left, testing every step to ensure the silence that was essential. For a brief, terrible moment he was back in the forests of Prague, the echoes of the guns of Lidice in his ears, the sight of screaming, writhing bodies before his eyes. Then he snapped back to the immediate present, remembering who and where he was. He was the mountain cat, the most meaningful lair of his life soiled, corrupted by liars who were no better than those who commanded the guns at Lidice . . . or others who ordered 'suicides' and gulags when the guns were stilled. He was in his element, in the forest which had befriended him when he had no one to depend on, and no one better understood it.

The agent-of-record was sitting on a rock and, true to his indulgence, was playing with his watch, apparently pushing buttons, controlling time, master of the half-second. Havelock reached into his pocket and took out one of the items he had purchased in Monesi, a four-inch fish-scaling knife encased in a leather scabbard. He parted the branches in front of him, crouched low, then lunged.

'*You!* Jesus *Christ!* . . . *Don't!* What are you doing? Oh, my *God!*'

'You talk above a whisper, you won't have a face!' Michael's knee was rammed into the agent's throat, the razor-sharp, jagged blade pressed against the man's cheek below his left eye. 'This knife cleans fish, you son of a bitch. I'll peel your skin off unless you tell me what I want to know. Right *now*.'

'You're a maniac!'

'And you're the loser, if you believe that. How long have you been here?'

'Twenty-six hours.'

'Who gave the order?'

'How do I know.'

'Because even an asshole like you would cover yourself! It's the first thing we learn in dispatch, isn't it? The *order*! Who gave it?'

'*Ambiguity!* The code was Ambiguity,' cried the agent-of-record, as the scaling edge of the blade dug into his face. 'I swear to Christ, that's all I know! Whoever used it was cleared by Cons Op, DC. It can be traced back *there*! *Jesus*, I only know our orders came from the code! It was our clearance!'

'I'll accept it. Now, give me the step-schedule. *All* of it. You picked her up in Arma di Taggia, and she's been followed ever since. How?'

'Change of vehicles up from the coast.'

'Where is she now? What's the car? When's it expected?'

'A Lancia. The ETA, as of a half-hour ago, barring – '

'Cut it out! *When?*'

'Seven-forty arrival. A bug was planted in the car; they'll be here at twenty to eight.'

'I know you don't have a radio, a radio would be evidence in your case. How were you contacted?'

'The phone at the inn. *Jesus!* Get that thing away from me!'

'Not yet, sane man. The schedule, the steps? Who's on the car now?'

'Two men in a beat-up truck, a quarter of a mile behind. In case you intercept, they'll hear it and be on you.'

'If I don't, then what?'

'We've made arrangements. Starting at seven-thirty everyone crossing the border gets out of his car or truck or whatever. Vehicles are searched – we spread lire – so one way or the other she'll have to show herself.'

'That's when you figured I'd come out?'

'If we . . . *they* . . . don't find you first. They think they'll spot you before she gets here.'

'And if they don't?'

'I don't know! It's *their* plan.'

'It's *your* plan!' Havelock broke the skin on the agent's face; blood streaked down his cheek.

'Christ! Don't, *please*!'

'Tell me!'

'It's made to look as if you attacked. They know you've got a weapon, whether you show it or not. They nail you and pull it out if it's not in your hand. It doesn't matter; it's only for confusion. They'll run; the truck's got a good engine.'

'And the car? What about the *car?*'

'It's shoved through. We just want it out of there. She's not Karras, she's a Soviet lure. We're to let Moscow have her back. The French won't argue, a guard was paid.'

'Liar! Goddamned *liar*!' Michael slid the blade of the fishing knife across the agent's face to the other cheek. 'Liars should be marked! You're going to be *marked, liar*!' He broke the skin with the point. 'Those two nitro clowns, the ones who worked Africa – Tanzania, Mozambique, Angola – they're not here for the mountain air, *liar*!'

'Oh, *Jesus!* You're killing me!'

'Not yet, but it's entirely possible. What's their act?'

'They're just back-ups! Ricci brought them!'

'The Corsican?'

'I don't know . . . Corsican.'

'The blond.'

'*Yes!* Don't cut me! *Please*, don't *cut* me!'

'Back-ups? Like your friend at the table?'

'The *table?* Christ, what *are* you?'

'An observer, and you're stupid. For you, they're only guns?'

'Jesus, *yes!* That's what they *are!*'

So the liars in Washington lied even to their own in Rome. Jenna Karras did not exist. The woman in the car was to be dispatched beyond Rome's cognizance. Liars! Killers!

Why?

'Where are they?'

'I'm bleeding! I've got blood in my mouth!'

'You'll drown in it if you don't tell me. *Where?*'

'One on both sides! Twenty, thirty feet before the gate. *Christ*, I'm *dying*!'

'No, you're not dying, agent-of-record. You're just marked; you're finished. You're not worth surgery.' Havelock switched the knife to his left hand and raised his right, his fingers straight out, taut, the muscles of the palm's underside rigid. He crashed the hand into the man's throat; he would be immobilized for no less than an hour. It would be long enough; it *had* to be.

He crawled through the undergrowth, sure of his footing, at home in the friendly forest.

He found him. The man was on his knees hunched over a canvas bag – a knapsack or small duffle bag; the light from the bridge was just bright enough to outline the figure but too dim to see clearly if one did not know what to look for. Suddenly there was the growing sound of an engine, accompanied by the clatter of a loose tailpipe or a bumper making contact with the rock-filled road. Michael spun around, holding his breath, his hand reaching towards his belt. A broken-down van came into view. A sickening feeling spread through him. Had the agent lied? he wondered. He looked back at the explosives specialist; the man crouched lower, making no other move at all, and Havelock slowly let out his breath.

The van rattled by and stopped at the bridge. The blond killer was standing by a guard; he had obviously been instructed to observe procedure, but instead his eyes were roaming the woods and the road below. Loud voices filled the gate area: a couple in the van was objecting to the unexpected demand to get out; apparently they made the trip daily across the border.

Michael knew the noise was his cover; he crept forward. He was within seven feet of the man when the rear door of the van was opened and the shouted obscenities rose to a crescendo. The door was slammed shut.

Havelock lunged out of the undergrowth, arms extended, with fingers curved for the attack.

'*Di quale . . . ?*'

The specialist had no chance to experience further shock. His head was slammed into soft earth and rock, his neck viced by Michael's right hand; he coughed spastically and went limp. Havelock turned the unconscious body over and, whipping the man's belt out of his trousers, slipped it under the arms and yanked it taut beneath the shoulderblades. He then looped it over, and knotted it. He removed the Llama from his chest holster, and brought the short barrel down on the man's head above the right temple – the expert would remain unconscious that much longer.

Michael tore into the canvas bag. It was a specialist's mobile laboratory, filled with compact blocks of dynamite and soft rolls of plastic explosive. The devices with wires extending from miniaturized clocks with radium dials were detonators, positive and negative poles plugged into one another across the lethal powder, set to emit charges at a given minute by a twist of the fingers. There was also another type of detonating device: small, flat, circular modules, no larger than the face of a man's watch; these were without wires, having only a bar with a luminous numerical read-out and a tiny button on the right with which to set the desired time. Designed specifically for the plastic charges, buried inside, they were accurate to five seconds over a time span of twenty-four hours. Havelock felt the casing of a single *plastique*. On the top surface was a self-sealing lip through which a module was inserted, while the bottom was marked by a flap which had to be peeled away several minutes before placement. The peeling process released an epoxy stronger than a weld; it would adhere to a second surface through earthquake and hurricane. He removed three charges and modules, and put them in his pockets. Then he crawled away, pulling the canvas bag behind him. Ten feet farther into the forest, he shoved it under a fallen pine branch. He looked at his watch. Twelve minutes to go.

The yelling at the bridge had stopped. The angry couple was back in the van, while the guards apologized for the crazy, temporary regulations. *Funzionari burocratici!* The engine was started, a series of metallic groans preceding the full roar of an accelerator pressed to the floor. The headlights were turned back on and the orange barrier raised as the gears ground abrasively and the decrepit vehicle crept onto the bridge. The clatter was louder now, actually deafening as the van rumbled across the surface of the bridge ridged with narrow, open metal struts.

The noise echoed below and above, filling the air with an unrelenting staccato that made one of the guards wince and put both hands to his ears. The clatter, the headlights; the first was diversion, the second, distraction. If he could get into a decent line of sight, he might – just possibly – eliminate his back-up executioner; he would not make the attempt unless the odds were his.

The burly man in the heavy jacket would hug the rail, leaning over perhaps, to be as inconspicuous as possible in the glare of the headlights, a weary pedestrian with too much wine in him. No single shot could be counted on; no man was that accurate at eighty feet or more. But the Magnum was a powerful weapon, the permanently-attached silencer designed for zero sighting as much as any handgun could be. Therefore a marksman firing five or six rounds at a given target would have the probabilities on his side, but only if the bullets were fired in what amounted to a single burst; each instant of separation was a margin for error. It would require a steady arm supported by a solid object, a view undistorted by light and shadow. It would not hurt to get closer, either.

With his concentration split equally between the undergrowth in front of him and the blond assassin, whom he could see through the trees on his left, he made his way as swiftly, as silently as he could, to the edge of the river gorge.

A torch beam shot out behind him. He scrambled behind a huge boulder, sliding partially down the smooth surface and catching his foot on a protruding ridge. His sanctuary was the top of a jagged wall of rock and bush that led to the roiling waters several hundred feet below. His vision at the far side was clear; he stared at the end of the beam of light. Some part of the foliage he had raced through had snapped and the blond killer was standing motionless, the light in his hand. Gradually his attention waned: an animal or a night bird, he judged, there was no human being to be seen.

Above, the clattering truck neared the midpoint of the bridge. There he was! Less than seventy feet away, he leaned over the rail, his head huddled deep in the collar of his heavy jacket. The clanging was thunderous now, the echoes full as the back-up executioner was caught in the glare of the headlights. Havelock spun around on the boulder, steadying his feet on the flanking rocks. There would be no more than a second to make the decision, no more than two or three to fire the Magnum during the short space of time when the rear of the van would block the view from the booths at the entrance. Full of uncertainty, Michael pulled the heavy weapon from his belt and braced his arm against the boulder, his feet anchored by pressure, his left hand gripping his right wrist to steady the barrel that was aimed diagonally above. He had to be *sure*; he could not risk the night and everything the night stood for. But if the odds were his . . .

They *were*. As the bonnet of the van passed the man he stood up, now silhouetted in the back light, a large immobile target. Havelock fired four rounds in rapid succession in concert with the deafening clatter on the bridge. The support killer arched backwards, then sank down into the shadows of the solid steel barricade of the pedestrian walk.

The clanging receded as the van reached the far side of the bridge. There was no orange barrier across the entrance on the French side: francs had been paid; the two guards leaned against a gatehouse wall, smoking their cigarettes. However, another sound intruded; it came from behind, quite far behind, down the road from Monesi. Michael curved his spine into the surface of the rock and slid back into the edge of the woods, crouching instantly, shoving the warm Magnum under his belt. He glanced through the trees at the checkpoint; the two authentic soldiers in the nearest gatehouse on the right could be seen beyond the large glass windows, nodding as if counting something in their hands – lire had reached the second level. The blond impostor was outside, an outsider as far as the current transaction was concerned; he was staring down the road, squinting in the dim light.

He raised his hand to the midpoint of his chest and shook his wrist twice – an innocuous gesture, a man restoring circulation to a forearm strained by carrying too much weight too recently. It was a signal.

The killer brought his hand down to his right hip, and it took no imagination to realize he was releasing the snap on his holster while keeping his concentration on the road below. Havelock crept rapidly through the woods until he reached the unconscious figure of the explosives specialist. The sound of a motor grew louder, joined now by a faint, base-toned hum in the farther distance – a second vehicle steadily increasing its speed. Michael parted the thick branches of an overhanging pine and looked to his left. Several hundred yards down the road the glistening grille of a large car could be seen, reflecting the light from the bridge. It swung into the curve; it was a Lancia. Jenna! Havelock imposed a control over his mind and body he never thought possible. The next few minutes would bring into play everything he had learned – that no one should ever have to learn – since he was a child in Prague, every skill he had absorbed from the shadow world in which he had lived so long.

The Lancia drew nearer, and sharp bolts of pain shot through Michael's chest as he stared at the windscreen. Jenna was not there. Instead, two men could be seen in the wash of the dashboard, the driver smoking, his companion apparently talking garrulously, waving his hands for emphasis. Then the driver turned his head sideways, addressing a remark to someone in the back seat. The Lancia began to slow down; it was within two hundred feet of the checkpoint.

The blond impostor at the orange barrier turned and walked quickly to the gatehouse booth; he knocked on the window, then pointed to the approaching vehicle and then to himself. He was the eager recruit telling his veteran superiors that he could handle the immediate assignment. The two soldiers looked up, annoyed at the intrusion, perhaps wondering whether the intruder had seen money changing hands; they nodded, waving him away.

Instead of leaving immediately, the assassin employed by Rome reached into his pocket and took out an object, while moving unobtrusively towards the closed door of the booth. He reached down and inserted the object into the frame below the window, the movements of his shoulders indicating that he used considerable force. Havelock tried to imagine what it was, what the killer was doing. And then it was clear; the door of the booth was a sliding door, but it would not slide now. The man called Ricci had wedged a thin steel plate with small angled spikes into the space between frame and panel; the door was jammed. The more force that was used to open it, the deeper the tiny spikes would embed themselves until all movement would be impossible. The two soldiers were trapped inside, and as with checkpoints everywhere – no matter how minor – the booth was sturdily constructed with thick glass in the windows. Yet there was a fallacy: a simple call to the barracks somewhere on the other side would bring assistance. Michael peered through the dim light above the gatehouse and saw there was no fallacy. Dangling from the limb of a tree was a heavy-gauge telephone wire; it had been severed. The killers from Rome controlled the checkpoint.

The blond man strode to the metal plank that separated the road from the entrance to the bridge, assumed a military stance – the feet apart, the left hand at his waist, the right held up in the HALT position – and faced the oncoming sedan.

The Lancia came to a stop. The front windows were rolled down and passports were proffered by the two men in the front seat.

The killer walked to the driver's window and spoke quietly – too quietly for Havelock to hear the words – while looking past the driver into the rear seat.

The driver was explaining something and turned to his companion for confirmation. The second man leaned across the seat, nodding his head, then shaking it, as if in sorrow. The false guard stood back and spoke louder, with a soldier's authority.

'Regrets, signori and signora,' he said in Italian. 'Tonight's regulations require that all passengers step out of their cars while they are examined.'

'But we were assured that we could proceed across into Col des Moulinets as rapidly as possible, *Caporale*,' protested the driver, raising his voice. 'The dear woman buried her husband less than two hours ago. She is distraught . . . Here are her papers, her passport. Ours also. Everything is in order, I can assure you. We are expected for an eight o'clock mass. She is from a fine family, a Franco-Italian marriage tragically ended by a dreadful accident. The mayors of both Monesi and Moulinets were at the funeral – '

'Regrets, signore,' repeated the killer. 'Please, step out. There is a truck behind you and it is not right that you should hold up the line.'

Havelock turned his head, looking at the run-down truck with the powerful engine. There was no one inside. Instead, the two men were on opposite shoulders of the road, dressed in mountain clothes, their eyes scanning the country road and the woods, their hands in their pockets. Back-ups for back-ups, support for support. The border belonged to the unit from Rome, secure in its knowledge that no one could pass through without being seen, and if the target was seen, the target would die.

And if he was not seen? Would the secondary order hold? Would the secondary target – the bait – be eliminated in Col des Moulinets because she was no longer feasible bait? The answer was as painful for Michael to admit to himself as it was self-evident. She had to be. She did not exist, her existence was too dangerous for the liars who gave orders to strategists and embassies alike. The unit would return to Rome without its primary kill, the only loser an agent-of-record who had not been apprised of the secondary target.

The tall, slender figure in black climbed out of the car – a woman in mourning, an opaque veil of black lace falling from her wide-brimmed hat and covering her face. Havelock stared: the pain in his chest was almost unbearable. She was no more than twenty feet away, yet the gulf was filled with death, her death to follow shortly whether his came or not.

'My regrets again, signora,' said the killer in uniform. 'It will be necessary for you to remove your hat.'

'Good Lord, *why*?' asked Jenna Karras, her voice low, controlled, but with a trace of a throb, which could be a sign of grief as well as of fear.

'Merely to match your face with the photograph on the passport, signora. Surely you know it's customary.'

Jenna slowly lifted the veil from her face, and then the hat from her head. The skin that was so often bronzed by the sun was chalk white in the dim, eerie light of the bridge, her delicate features taut, the high cheekbones mask-like, chiselled in marble as if the owner belonged to the Palatine, her long blonde hair pulled back and knotted severely. Michael watched, breathing slowly, silently, a part of him wanting to cry out, another desperately, foolishly, placing them back in another time . . . lying together on the grass overlooking the Moldau, walking down the Ringstrasse, holding hands as children might, laughing at the irony of two deep cover agents behaving like human beings. In bed, holding each other, telling themselves they would somehow break out of their movable prison.

'The signora has lovely hair,' said the blond killer, with a smile that denied his rank. 'My mother would approve. We, too, are from the north.'

'Thank you. May I replace my veil, *Caporale*? I am in mourning.'

'In one moment, please,' replied Ricci, holding up the passport but not looking at it. Instead, he was glancing everywhere at once without moving his head, his anger obviously mounting. Jenna's escorts stood motionless by the car, avoiding the soldier's looks.

Behind the Lancia, on either side of the run-down truck, the support assassins were tense, peering into the shadows, then repeatedly looking in the vicinity of the country inn, anticipation on their faces. It was as though they all expected him to materialize out of the darkness, to appear suddenly, walking either casually or resolutely up the path from the inn, or from behind the thick trunk of a pine tree on the edge of the road, calling out to the woman by the car. It was what they expected; these were the moments they had calculated as the crisis span – the target would be found now if he had not been found before. And from their viewpoint, it had to happen. Everything was clean, nothing wrinkled. The target had not crossed over the bridge within the past twenty-six hours – and it would have been stupid to have crossed over prior to minus-twenty-six. There was no way he could know which vehicle carried Jenna Karras or which road it would take through Col des Moulinets. Besides, there was no reason for the man marked for dispatch to know there was a unit from Rome at the checkpoint. It would happen now, or it would not happen.

The tension at the scene was stretched to breaking point. It was compounded by the two soldiers inside the gatehouse booth, who were trying to open the door and shouting through the windows, their voices muted by the thick glass. Nothing was lost on Jenna Karras or her paid escorts; the driver had edged towards the door, his companion towards the border of the road and the woods. A trap was in the making, but for reasons they could not understand it was not a trap for them. If it had been, they would have been summarily taken.

Havelock knew that everything now was timing: the eternal wait until the moment came, and then that instant when instinct told him to move. He could not rearrange the odds to favour him, but he could reduce those against him. Against Jenna.

'*Finira in niente*,' said the uniformed killer, just loud enough to be heard. He brought his hand to his waist and shook his wrist twice as he had done before, giving a signal as he had given it before.

Michael reached into his pocket and took out a packet of plastic explosive and a module. The luminous read-out was at *0000*; he pressed the timer button delicately until he had the figures he wanted, then inserted the module into the self-sealing lip. He had checked and rechecked his position in the darkness; he knew the path least obstructed and used it now. He snaked his way eight feet into the forest, observed the outlines of the branches against the night sky, and threw the packet into the air. The moment it was out of his hand, he scrambled back towards the road, arching to his left, now parallel to the run-down truck, ten feet from the back-up killer dressed in mountain clothes. He had two shells left in the Magnum; it was possible he would have to use both before he cared to, but the muted sounds were preferable to explosions from the Llama automatic. Seconds now.

'Regrets again for the delay, signora and signori,' said the assassin sent by Rome, walking away from the Lancia towards the winch that operated the orange barrier. 'Procedures must be followed. You may return to your vehicle now, all is in order.' The blond man passed the windows of the booth, ignoring the angry shouts of the soldiers inside; he had no time to waste on minor players. A plan had failed, a finely tuned strategy became an exercise in futility; anger and frustration were second only to his professional instincts to get out of the area. There was only one chore left to finish, which an agent-of-record was to know nothing about. He raised the orange barrier and immediately stepped back out into the centre of the entrance, blocking passage. He removed a notebook and a pencil from his pocket – the border guard attending to his last procedure, the numbers of a vehicle's licence. It, too, was a signal.

Only seconds.

Jenna and her two escorts climbed back in the car, the faces of the two men betraying bewilderment and cautious relief. The doors slammed shut, and at the sound a short, stocky man came slowly out of the foliage across the road near the boot of the Lancia. He walked directly to the rear of the vehicle, but his attention was on the woods beyond the road. He raised his right hand to his waist and shook his wrist twice, perplexed at the lack of response to his signal. He stood for a moment, his frown conveying minor alarm but not panic. Men in his business understood the problems of equipment malfunction; they were sudden and deadly, which was why the two specialists travelled as a team. He turned his head quickly towards the checkpoint; the blond assassin was impatient. The man knelt down, took an object out of his left hand, transferring it to his right. He reached under the car, the area directly beneath the fuel tank.

There were no seconds left. The target could not wait.

Havelock had the man in the sights of his Magnum. He fired; the specialist screamed as his body crashed up into the metal of the fender, the packet flying out of his hand as his arm whipped back; the bullet had lodged in his spine and his body arched in searing pain. Though in agony the killer turned towards the source of the explosive spit, pulled an automatic from his pocket and levelled it instantly. Frantically Michael rolled out of the area until the dense undergrowth stopped his movement. The gunshots echoed everywhere, bullets spraying the ground, as Havelock raised the

Magnum and fired its last round. The muffled report was followed by a loud
gasp from the man by the truck as his neck was blown away.

'*Di dove? Dove?*' shouted the blond assassin at the checkpoint, racing
around the Lancia.

The explosion filled the air, the blinding light of the detonated *plastique*
bathing the darkness of the woods, echoing throughout the mountains. The
assassin lunged to the ground and, aiming at nothing, began shooting at
everything. The Lancia's engine roared, its wheels spun and the car surged
onto the bridge. Jenna was *free*.

Seconds more. He had to do it.

Michael got to his feet and raced out of the forest, the empty Magnum in
his belt, the Llama in his hand. The assassin saw him in the light of the
spreading flames in the woods; getting up on his knees, supporting his right
arm with his left, he spun on the ground, pivoting up to his knees, aimed at
Havelock. He fired rapidly, repeatedly; the bullets shrieked in ricochets and
snapped the air above and to the right of Michael as he lurched for the cover
of the truck. But it was no cover; he heard the scraping, then the footsteps
behind him, and he whirled around, his back against the door. At the rear
of the truck the killer-driver came out crouching – the movements of a
professional cornering a quarry at close range – as he raised his weapon and
fired. Havelock dropped to the ground at first sighting and returned two
shots: feeling the ice-like pain in his shoulder, he knew he had been hit, but
not how seriously. The driver rolled spastically off the edge of the road; if he
was not gone, he would be soon.

Suddenly, the earth exploded in front of Michael; the blond assassin was
free to resume firing now that his associate was finished. Havelock dived to
his right, then plunged under the truck, crawling in panic to the other side.
Seconds. Only seconds left. He sprang to his feet and sidestepped his way to the
door. The crowd of frightened people down at the inn were shouting at one
another, running in all directions. There was so little time; men would race
out of barracks, perhaps were racing even now. He reached for the handle
and yanked the door open; he saw what he wanted to see: the keys were in
the ignition as he had dared to think they would be. The unit from Rome
had been in control, and control meant being able to get away from the
execution ground instantly.

He leaped up into the seat, his head low, his fingers working furiously. He
turned the key; the powerful engine caught, and at the first sound, gunfire
came from the road ahead and bullets embedded themselves in metal. There
was a pause, and Michael understood; the assassin was reloading his gun.
These were the crucial seconds. He switched on the headlights – like the motor,
they were powerful, in themselves blinding. Up ahead, the blond man was
crouched off the shoulder of the road, slamming a clip into the base of his
automatic. Havelock jammed the clutch, pulled the gear lever and pressed
the accelerator to the floor.

The heavy truck jolted forward, its tyres screeching over rock and earth.
Michael spun the wheel to his right, and the engine roared with the
gathering speed. Rapid gunshots; the windscreen was punctured and a web
of cracks spread throughout the glass as bullets screamed into the cab.
Havelock raised his head just high enough to see what he had to see; the

killer was centred in the glare of the headlights. Michael kept his course until he felt and heard the impact, accompanied by a scream of fury which was abruptly cut short as the assassin lurched and twisted, but was held in place, his legs crushed under the heavy reinforced tyres of the truck. Havelock spun the wheel again, now to his left, back onto the road proper; he sped past the two gatehouses onto the bridge, noting as he raced by that the two guards were prone on the floor of the booth.

There was chaos on the French side, but no barrier to block his way. Soldiers were running to and from the checkpoint, shouting orders at no one and everyone; inside a lighted booth four guards were huddled together, one screaming into a telephone. The road into Col des Moulinets bore to the left off the bridge, then curved right, heading straight into a silhouetted patchwork of small wood-framed houses, set close together, with sloping roofs typical of a thousand villages in this part of the Alps. He entered a narrow cobblestoned street; several pedestrians jumped onto the narrow pavement, startled as much by the sound as by the sight of the heavy Italian truck.

He saw the red lights . . . the wide, rear lights of the Lancia. It was far in the distance; it turned into a street – God only knew what street, there were so many. Col des Moulinets was one of those villages where every long-ago path and pasture bypass had been paved with stone; some had been converted into streets, others into merely quaint alleyways, barely wide enough for produce carts. But he would know it when he came to it; he *had* to.

The intersecting streets grew wider, the houses and shops set farther back; narrow pavements widened, and more and more villagers were seen strolling past the lighted shops. The Lancia was nowhere; it had disappeared!

'S'il vous plaît! Où est l'aéroport?' he yelled out of the window to an elderly couple about to step off the pavement into the cobblestoned street.

'Airport?' said the old man in French, the word itself pronouced more with an Italian accent than Gallic. 'There is no airport in Col des Moulinets, monsieur. You can take the southern road down to Cap Martin.'

'There *is* an airport near the village, I'm sure of it,' cried Havelock, trying to control his anxiety. 'A friend, a very *good* friend, told me he was flying into Col des Moulinets. I'm to meet him. I'm late.'

'Your friend meant Cap Martin, monsieur.'

'Perhaps not,' called out a younger man, leaning against the doorway of a shop closed for the evening. 'There is no real airport, monsieur, but there is an airfield fifteen, twenty kilometres north on the road to Tende. It's used by the rich who have estates in Roquebillière and Breil.'

'That's it! What's the fastest way?'

'Take the next turning right, then right again back three streets to rue Maritimes. Turn left; it will lead you onto the mountain autoroute. Fifteen, eighteen kilometres north.'

'Thank you.'

Time was a racing montage of light and shadow, filled with peopled streets and leaping figures, small interfering cars and glaring headlights, gradually replaced by fewer buildings, fewer people, fewer streetlamps; he had reached the outskirts of the village. If the police had been alerted by the panicked border guards, he had eluded them by the odds of a small force versus a larger area. Minutes later – how many he would never know – he was tearing through the darkness of the Maritimes countryside, the rolling hills everywhere that were introductions to the mountains beyond, barricades to be negotiated with all the speed the powerful truck could manage. And as the grinding gears strained and the tyres under his screamed to a crescendo, he saw the silhouettes of paddlewheels – like the hills, they were everywhere – slowly turning, a certain majesty in their never-ending movements, alongside houses by mountain streams and rivulets, proof again that time and nature were constant whether attention was paid or not. In a strange way, Michael needed the reaffirmation; he was close to losing his mind.

There were no lights on the autoroute, no red specks in the darkness. The Lancia was nowhere to be seen. Was he even going in the right direction? Or had anxiety warped his senses? So close and yet so terribly far away, one gulf traversed, one more to breach. Traversed? Breach? We said it better in Prague. *Przheyest* said it better.

Milaji vas, maj sladky. We understand these words, Jenna. We do not need the language of liars. We never should have learned it. *Don't listen to the liars! They neutralized us; now they want to kill us. They have to because I know they're there. I know, and so will you.*

A searchlight! Its beam was sweeping the night sky. Beyond the nearest hills, diagonally ahead on the left. Somewhere the road would turn; somewhere minutes away was an airfield and a plane – and Jenna.

The second hill was steep, the other side of it steeper, with curves; he held the wheel with all his strength, careening into each turn. *Lights.* Wide white beams in front, two red dots behind. It was the Lancia! A mile, two miles ahead and below; it was impossible to tell, but the field was there. Parallel lines of yellow ground lights crossed each other at forty-plus degree points; the valley winds had been studied for maximum lift. The airfield was in a valley, sufficiently wide and long for small jets as well as prop aircraft . . . *used by the rich with estates in Roquebillière and Breil.*

Havelock kept the accelerator to the floor, his left foot grazing the brake for those instants when balance was in jeopardy. The road levelled out and became a flat track that circled the fenced-off airfield. Within the enormous compound were the vivid reflections of glistening wings and fuselages; perhaps a dozen stationary planes were moored to the ground in varying positions off the runways – the yachts of yesterday had been replaced by silver tubes that sailed through the skies. The ten-foot high fence was strung with barbed wire across the top and angled an additional four feet inside. The rich of Roquebillière and Breil cared for their airborne possessions. Such a fence – a double mile in length – carried a price of several hundred thousand; and that being the case, would there be a security gate and guards somewhat more attentive than those at a remote French or Italian border post?

There were. He screeched into the entrance roadway. The heavy, ten-foot gate was closing three hundred feet in front of him. Inside, the Lancia was racing across the field. Suddenly, its lights were extinguished; somewhere within the expanse of grass and asphalt its driver had spotted a plane.

Lights would reveal markings and markings were traces; if he could see the Lancia's headlights several miles away in the darkness of the valley, his, too, could be seen. There were only seconds and half-seconds now, each minuscule movement of a clock narrowing the final gulf or widening it.

While gripping the wheel, he jammed the palms of both hands on the rim of the truck's horn, hammering out the only alarm code that came to him. *Mayday, Mayday, Mayday!* He repeated it over and over again as he sped down the entrance drive towards the closing gate.

Two uniformed guards were inside the fence, one pushing the thick metal crossbar of the gate, the other standing by the latch, prepared to receive the sliding bar and insert the clamp. As the gate reached the three-quarter mark, both guards stared through the wire mesh at the powerful truck bearing down, the blaring series of shrieking notes not lost on them. Their terrified faces revealed no intention of staying in the path of the wild vehicle. The guard at the crossbar released it and ran to his left; the gate swung back partially – only partially – when he withdrew his grip. The man by the latch scrambled to his right, diving into the grass and the protection of the extended fence.

The impact came, the truck ripping the gate away, twisting it up off its hinges and smashing it into the small booth, shattering glass and severing an electrical wire that erupted in sparks and static. Michael raced onto the field, his wounded shoulder pitched in pain, the truck careening sharply, narrowly missing two adjacent planes parked in the shadows of a single wide hangar. He spun the wheel to his left, sending the truck in the direction the Lancia had been heading less than a minute ago.

Nothing. Absolutely *nothing*! Where was it? Where *was* it?

A flicker of light. Movement – at the far end of the field, beyond the glowing yellow lines of the north runway, slightly above the farthest row of grounded planes. The cabin of a plane had been opened, an interior light snapped briefly on, then instantly turned off. He whipped the wheel to the right – blood from his wrenched wounded shoulder spreading through his shirt – and raced diagonally across the enormous compound. Heavy, weatherproof bulbs exploded under the tyres as he sped towards the now darkened area where seconds ago there had been the dim flash of light.

There it was! Not a jet, but a twin-engine, single-wing, its propellers suddenly revving furiously, flames belching from its exhausts. It was not on the runway, but instead beyond the glow of the parallel lines of yellow lights: the pilot was about to taxi into the take-off position. But he was not moving now; he was holding!

The Lancia. It was behind and to the right of the plane. Again, a light! Not from the aircraft now, but from the Lancia itself. Doors opened, figures leapt out, dashing for the plane. The cabin door, another light! For an instant Michael considered ramming the fuselage or crashing into the nearest wing, but it could be a tragic error. If he struck a fuel tank the aircraft would blow up in seconds. He swerved the heavy truck to the right, then to the left, screeching to a stop yards in front of the plane.

'Jenna! *Jenna! Poslouchat já! Stát! Listen to me!*'

She was climbing on board, pushed up the steps by the driver of the Lancia, who followed her inside and closed the door. He ran, oblivious to everything but her; he had to *stop* her! The plane spun in place like a grotesque, dark cormorant. Its path was free of the Lancia!

The blow came out of the shadows, muffled and at the same time magnified by the furious winds of the propeller's wash. His head snapped back as his legs buckled, blood matting the hair above his right temple. He was on his knees, supporting himself with his hands, staring up at the plane, at the window of the moving plane, and he could *not move*! The cabin lights remained on for several seconds and he saw her face in the glass, her eyes staring back at him. It was a sight he would remember for as long as he lived . . . if he lived. A second blow with a blunt instrument was delivered to the back of his neck.

He could not think about the terrible sight now, about *her* now! He could hear the sirens screaming across the field, see the glare of searchlights shooting over the runway, catching the glistening metal of the plane as it sped down between the yellow lights. The man who had struck him twice was running towards the Lancia; he had to *move*! He had to move *now*, or he would not be permitted to live, permitted ever to see her again. He struggled to his feet as he pulled the Llama automatic from under his jacket.

He fired twice above the roof of the car; the man leaping into the seat could have killed him moments ago; he would not kill that man now. His hands were too unsteady, the flashing, sweeping lights too bewildering to ensure inflicting only a wound. But he *had* to have the car. He fired again, the bullet ricocheting off the metal as he approached the window.

'Get out or you're dead!' he shouted, gripping the door handle. 'You heard what I said! Get *out*!' Havelock yanked the man by the cloth of his coat and pulled him, propelling him onto the grass. There was no time for a dozen questions he wanted to ask. He had to escape! He slid behind the wheel and slammed the door shut; the engine was running.

For the next forty-five seconds he criss-crossed the airfield at enormous speeds, evading the airfield's security police by weaving in and out of searchlight beams. A dozen times he nearly crashed into stationary aircraft before reaching the demolished gate. He raced through, not seeing the road, functioning only on nerves and instinct.

He could not shut out the terrible sight of Jenna's face in the window of the moving plane. In Rome her face had shown raw fear and confusion. Moments ago there had been something else; it was in her eyes.

Cold, immaculate hatred.

13

He drove south-west to Provence, then due south towards the coast, to the small city of Cagnes-sur-Mer. He had worked the northern Mediterranean for years and knew a doctor between Cagnes and Antibes; he needed help. He had ripped the sleeve of his shirt and tied a knot around the wound in his shoulder, but it did not prevent the loss of blood. His entire chest was soaked, cloth sticking to skin and giving the sweet-acrid odour that he knew only too well. His neck was merely bruised – a paramedical opinion which in no way diminished the pain – but the blow to his head required stitches; the slightest graze would reopen the laceration that was sealed with coagulated blood.

He needed other help, too, and Dr Henri Salanne would provide it. He must reach Matthias; to delay any longer was asinine. Specific identities could be traced from orders, from a code name. Ambiguity; there was enough information. Surface evidence of the massive conspiracy was clear from Jenna's having survived Costa Brava – when she had been officially recorded as dead – and from his own condemnation as 'beyond-salvage'. The first Matthias would accept from his *pritel*, the second could be confirmed from sealed black-bordered directives in the files of Consular Operations. Granted the whys were beyond Havelock's reach, but not the facts – they existed, and Matthias could act on them. And while the Secretary of State acted, Michael had to get to Paris as quickly as possible. It would not be simple; every airport, main road and train station in Provence and the Maritimes would be watched, and Matthias could do nothing about it. Time and communications were on the side of the liars. Issuing covert orders was far easier than rescinding them; they spread like a darkening web of ink on soft paper as the recipients disappeared, each wanting credit for the kill.

Within an hour – if not already – Rome would be apprised of the events at Col des Moulinets. Telephones and little-used radio frequencies would be employed to send out the word: *the man 'beyond salvage' is loose; he can cost us too much that's valuable, including time and our lives. All network personnel are on alert; use every source, every weapon available. Zero-area: Col des Moulinets. Radius: Maximum two hours' travel, reported to be wounded. Last known vehicles: a nondescript farm truck with a powerful engine, and a Lancia saloon. Find him. Kill him.*

No doubt the liars on the Potomac had already reached Salanne, but as with so many in the shadow world there were hidden confidences – things in and of his past – that those who cleared payrolls in Washington or Rome or Paris knew nothing about. Only certain men in the field who had been on a given scene at a given time knew drones such as Dr Henri Salanne; they stored away their names for future personal use should the necessity ever arise. There was even a vague morality about this practice, for more often than not the incriminating information or the events themselves were the result of a temporary crisis or a weakness that did not require that the man or the woman be destroyed . . . or killed.

With Salanne, Havelock had been there when it happened – to be precise, eleven hours after the act took place, time enough to alter the consequences. The doctor had sold out an American agent in Cannes who co-ordinated a small fleet of ocean-going pleasure craft for the purpose of monitoring Russian naval positions in the sector. Salanne had sold him for money to a KGB informant, and Michael had not understood; neither money nor betrayal was a motive that made sense where the doctor was concerned. It took only one, low-keyed confrontation to learn the truth, and it was a truth – or a juxtaposition of truths – as old as the grotesque world in which they all lived. The gentle if somewhat cynical middle-aged doctor was a compulsive gambler; it was the primary reason why years ago a brilliant young surgeon from *L'Hôpital de Paris* had sought out a practice in the Monte Carlo triangle. His credentials and references were honoured in Monaco, which was a good thing, but his losses at the Casino were not.

Enter the American, whose cover was that of a yacht-owning jet setter and who spent the taxpayers' money cautiously but obnoxiously at the tables. His obnoxiousness, however, did not end at chemin de fer; he was a womanizer with a preference for young girls, an image, he rationalized, that did nothing to harm his cover. One of the girls he brought to his busy bed was Salanne's daughter, Claudie, an impressionable child who suffered a severe depression when nothing further came of the relationship.

The Russians were in the market; the doctor's losses could be covered, and a preying *violateur* removed from the scene. *Pourquoi pas?* The act had taken place.

Enter Havelock, who had traced the betrayal, got the American out before the boats were identified, and confronted Henri Salanne. He never reported his findings; there was no point, and the doctor understood the conditions of his 'pardon'. Never again . . . and an obligation was assumed.

Michael found a telephone box at a deserted corner in the centre of Cagnes-sur-Mer. He braced himself and got out of the car with difficulty, clutching his jacket around him as he stood up; he was cold, bleeding still. Inside the *cabine*, he pulled out the Llama from his holster, smashed the overhead light and studied the dial in the shadows. After what seemed like an interminable wait, he was given Salanne's number by Antibes information.

'*Votre fille Claudie, comment va-t-elle?*' he asked quietly.

There was dead silence. Finally the doctor spoke, his use of English deliberate. 'I wondered if I'd hear from you. If it *is* you, they say you may be hurt.'

'I am.'

'How badly?'

'I need cleaning up and a few stitches. That's all, I think.'

'Nothing internal?'

'Not that I can tell.'

'I hope you're right. A hospital would be in questionable taste right now. I suspect all emergency rooms in the area are being watched.'

Michael was suddenly alarmed. 'What about you?'

'There's only so much manpower. They won't waste it on someone they assume would rather see ten patients die on an operating table than be cut off from their generosity.'

'Would you?'

'Let's halve it,' said Salanne, laughing softly. 'In spite of my habits, my conscience couldn't take more than five.' The doctor paused but not long enough for Havelock to speak. 'However, there could be a problem. They say you're driving a medium-sized truck – '

'I'm not.'

'Or possibly a dark grey Lancia,' continued Salanne.

'I am.'

'Get rid of it, or get away from it.'

Michael looked at the large car outside the box. The engine had overheated; steam was escaping from the radiator, vapour rising and diffusing under the light of the street lamp. All this was calling attention to the car. 'I'm not sure how far I can walk,' he said to the doctor.

'Loss of blood?'

'Enough so I can feel it.'

'*Merde!* Where are you?'

Havelock told him. 'I've been here before, but I can't remember much.'

'Disorientation or absence of impressions?'

'What difference does it make?'

'Blood.'

'I feel dizzy, if that's what you mean.'

'It is. I think I know the corner. Is there a *bijouterie* on the other side? Called something-and-son?'

Michael squinted through the glass beyond the Lancia. 'Ariale et Fils?' he said, reading the raised white letters of a sign above a dark shopfront across the street. ' "Fine Jewellery. Watches, Diamonds". Is that it?'

'Ariale, of course. I've had good nights, too, you know. They're much more reasonable than the thieves in the Spélugues. Now then, several shops north of Ariale's is an alley that leads to a small parking area behind. I'll get there as fast as I can, twenty minutes at the outside. I don't want to race through the streets under the circumstances.'

'Please don't.'

'Nor should you. Walk slowly, and if there are cars parked there, crawl under one and lie flat on your back. When you see me arrive, strike a match. As little movement as possible, is that understood?'

'Understood.'

Havelock left the box, but before crossing the street he opened his jacket, pulled the blood-soaked shirt out of his belt and squeezed it until drops of dark red appeared on the pavement. Leaning over, he took a dozen rapid steps straight ahead, past the corner building into the shadows, scuffing the blood with the soles of his shoes, streaking it backwards; anyone studying the Lancia and the immediate area would assume he had run down the intersecting street. He then stopped, awkwardly removed both shoes, and sidestepped carefully to the kerb, pulling his jacket around him. He reversed direction and hobbled across the intersection to the side of the street that housed Ariale et Fils.

He lay on his back, matches in his hand, staring up at the black grease-laden underside of a Peugeot facing the car park wall, keeping his mind alert with an exercise in the improbable. Proposition: the owner returned with a companion, and both got into the car. What should Michael do and how would he do it without being seen? The answer to the first was to roll out – obviously – but on which side?

Twin headlight beams pierced the entrance of the parking area, cutting short his ruminations. The headlights were turned off ten feet inside the unmanned gate; the car stopped, the engine still running. It was Salanne, telling him he had arrived. Havelock crawled to the edge of the Peugeot's chassis and struck a match. Seconds later the doctor was above him, and within minutes they were driving south on the road towards Antibes, Michael in the back seat, angled in the corner, legs stretched, out of sight.

'If you recall,' said Salanne, 'there is a side entrance to my house, reached from the drive. It leads directly to my surgery.'

'I remember. I've used it.'

'I'll go inside first, just to make certain.'

'What are you going to do if there are cars in front?'

'I'd rather not think about it.'

'Maybe you should.'

'Actually, I have. There's a colleague of mine in Villefranche, an elderly man, above reproach. I'd prefer not to involve him, of course.'

'I appreciate what you're doing,' said Havelock, looking at the back of the doctor's head in the coruscating light, noting that the hair touched with grey only a year or so ago was practically white now.

' I appreciate what you did for me,' replied Salanne softly. 'I assumed a debt. I never thought otherwise.'

'I know. That's pretty cold, isn't it?'

'Not at all. You asked how Claudie was, so let me tell you. She is happy and with child and married to a young doctor at the hospital in Nice. Two years ago she nearly took her own life. How much is that worth to me, my friend?'

'I'm glad to hear it.'

'Besides, what they say about you is preposterous.'

'What do they say?'

'That you are insane, a dangerous psychopath who threatens us all with exposure – certain death from roving jackals of the KGB – if you are allowed to live.'

'And that's preposterous to you?'

'Since an hour ago, *mon mauvais ami*. You remember the man in Cannes who was involved with my indiscretion?'

'The KGB informant?'

'Yes.'

'Would you say's he's knowledgeable?'

'As any in the sector,' replied Havelock. 'To the point where we left him alone and tried to feed him disinformation. What about him?'

'When the word came through about you, I rang him up – from a public box, of course. I wanted confirmation of this new, incredible judgement, so I asked him how soft the market was, how flexible in terms of price for the American consular attaché whose origins were in Prague. What he told me was both startling and specific.'

'Which was?' asked Michael, leaning forward in pain.

'There is no market for you, no price – high, low or otherwise. You are a leper and Moscow wants no part of your disease. You are not to be touched, even acknowledged. So who could you expose in this manner?' The doctor shook his head. 'Rome lied, which means that someone in Washington lied to Rome. "Beyond-salvage"? Beyond *belief*.'

'Would you repeat those words to someone?'

'And by doing so, call for my own execution? There are limits to my gratitude.'

'You won't be identified, my word on it.'

'Who would believe you without naming a source he could check?'

'Anthony Matthias.'

'*Matthias?*' cried Salanne, whipping his head to the side, gripping the wheel, his eyes straining to stay on the road. 'Why would *he* . . . ?'

'Because you're with me. Again, my word on it.'

'A man like Matthias is beyond one's well-intentioned word, my friend. He asks and you must tell him.'

'Only if you cleared it.'

'Why would he believe you? Believe *me?*'

'You just said it. The attaché whose origins were in Prague. So were his.'

'I see,' said the doctor pensively, his head turned forward again. 'I never made the connection, never even thought about it.'

'It's complicated, and I don't talk about it. We go back a long time; our families go back.'

'I must think. To deal with such a man puts everything in another perspective, doesn't it? We are ordinary men doing our foolish things; he is not ordinary. He lives on another plane. The Americans have a phrase for what you ask.'

'A different ballgame?'

'It's not. It's the same game, and it's rigged against him. Against all of us.'

There were no strange cars within a four-block radius of Salanne's house, no need to travel to Villefranche and an elderly physician above reproach. Inside the examining room. Havelock's clothes were removed, his body sponged and the wounds sutured, the doctor's petite, somewhat uncommunicative wife assisting Salanne.

'You should rest for several days,' said the Frenchman, after his wife had left, taking Michael's garments to wash out what she could and burn the irrecoverable. 'If there are no ruptures the dressing will last for five, perhaps six days, then it should be changed. But you should rest.'

'I can't,' answered Havelock, grimacing, raising himself into a sitting position on the table, his legs over the edge.

'It hurts to move even those few inches, doesn't it?'

'Only the shoulder, that's all.'

'You've lost blood, you know that.'

'I've lost more; I know that, too.' Michael paused, studying Salanne. 'Do you have a dictating machine in your office?'

'Of course. Letters and reports – medical reports – must be dealt with long after nurses and receptionists have gone home.'

'I want you to show me how to use it, and I want you to listen. It won't take long, and you won't be identified on the tape. Then I want to place an overseas call to the United States.'

'Matthias?'

'Yes. But the circumstances will determine how much I can tell him. Who's with him, how sterile the phone is; he'll know what to do. The point is, after you hear what I've got to say, listen to the tape in your machine, you can decide whether to speak to him or not – if it comes up.'

'You place a burden on me.'

'I'm sorry – there won't be many more. In the morning, I'll need clothes. Everything I had is back in Monesi.'

'No problem. Mine would not fit, but my wife buys for me. Tomorrow, she will buy for you.'

'Speaking of buying, I've got a fair amount of money but I'll need more. I have accounts in Paris; you'll get it back.'

'Now you embarrass me.'

'I don't mean to, but, you see, there's a catch. In order for you to get it back, I have to get to Paris.'

'Surely Matthias can effect swift, safe transportation.'

'I doubt it. You'll understand when you hear what I say in your office. Those who lied to Rome are very high in Washington. I don't know who or where they are, but I know they'll transmit only what they want. His orders will be sidetracked, because *their* orders have gone out and they don't want them voided. And if I say where I am, where I can be reached, they'll send in men after me. In any case, they might succeed, which is why I need the tape. May we do it now, please?'

Thirty-four minutes later, Havelock depressed the switch on the cassette microphone and placed it on the Frenchman's desk. He had told it all, from the screams at Costa Brava to the explosions at Col des Moulinets. He could not refrain from adding a last judgement. The civilized world might well survive the compromising of any sprawling, monolithic intelligence service – regardless of race, creed or national origin – but not when one of the victims was a man that the same civilized world depended on: Anthony Matthias, a statesman respected by geopolitical friends and adversaries everywhere. He had been systematically lied to on a matter to which he had addressed himself in depth. How many more lies had been fed to him?

Salanne sat across the office, deep in a soft leather armchair, his body motionless, his face rigid, his eyes staring at Havelock. He was stunned, speechless. After several moments he shook his head and broke his silence.

'Why?' he asked in a barely audible voice. 'It's all so preposterous, as preposterous as what they say about you. *Why?*'

'I've asked myself that over and over again, and I keep going back to what I said to Baylor in Rome. They think I know something I shouldn't know, something that frightens them.'

'Do you?'

'He asked me that.'

'Who?'

'Baylor. And I was honest with him – perhaps too honest – but the shock of seeing her had blown my mind. I couldn't think straight. Especially after what Rostov had said in Athens.'

'What did you say?'

'The truth. That if I *did* know something, I'd forgotten it, or it had never made much of an impression on me.'

'That's not like you. They say you are a walking data bank, someone who recalls a name, a face, a minor event that took place years ago.'

'Like most such opinions, it's a myth. I was a graduate student for a long time, so I developed certain disciplines, but I'm no computer.'

'I'm aware of that,' said the Frenchman quietly. 'No computer would have done what you did for me.' Salanne paused, leaning forward in the chair. 'Have you gone over the months preceding Costa Brava?'

'Months, weeks, days – everything, every place we were . . . I was. Belgrade, Prague, Krakow, Vienna, Washington, Paris. There was nothing remotely startling, but I suppose that's a comparative term. With the exception of an exercise in Prague where we got some documents out of the *nachlazeni bezpečnost* – the secret police headquarters – everything was pretty routine. Gathering information which damn near any tourist could have done, that's all.'

'Washington?'

'Less than nothing. I flew back for five days. It's an annual event for field men, an evaluation interview which is mostly a waste of time, but I suppose they catch a whack-o now and then.'

'Whack-o?'

'Someone who's crossed over the mental line, thinks he's someone he's not, who's fantasized a basically routine job. Cloak-and-dagger flakes, I suppose you could call them. It comes with the stress, with too often pretending you *are* someone you're not.'

'Interesting,' said the doctor, nodding his head in some abstract recognition. 'Did anything else happen while you were there?'

'Zero. I went to New York for a night to see a couple I knew when I was young. He owns a marina on Long Island, and if he ever had a political thought in his head I've never heard it. Then I spent two days with Matthias, a duty visit, really.'

'You *were* close . . . *are* close.'

'I told you, we go back a long time. He was there when I needed him; he understood.'

'What about those two days?'

'Less than zero. I only saw him during the evenings when we had dinner together, two dinners, actually. Even then, although we were alone, he was constantly interrupted by phone calls and by harried people from State – supplicants, he called them – who insisted on bringing him reports.' Havelock stopped, seeing a sudden tight expression on Salanne's face; he continued quickly. 'No one saw me, if that's what you're thinking. He'd confer with them in his study, and the dining-room's on the other side of the house. Again, he understood; we agreed not to display our friendship. For my benefit, really. No one likes a great man's protégé.'

'It's difficult for me to think of you that way.'

'It'd be impossible if you'd had dinner with us,' said Michael, laughing quietly. 'All we did was rehash papers I'd written for him nearly twenty years ago; he could still punch holes in them. Talk about total recall, he has it.' Havelock smiled, then the smile faded as he said, 'It's time,' and reached for the telephone.

The lodge in the Shenandoah Valley was reached by a sequence of telephone numbers, the first activating a remote mechanism at Matthias's residence in Georgetown, which in turn was electronically patched into a line a hundred and forty miles away in the Blue Ridge mountains, ringing the private telephone of the Secretary of State. If he was not on the premises, that phone was never answered; if he was, only he picked it up. The original number was known to perhaps a dozen people in the nation, among them the President and Vice-President, the Speaker of the House, the Chairman of the Joint Chiefs, the Secretary of Defense, the President of the Security Council of the United Nations, two senior aides at State, and Mikhail Havlicek. The last was a privilege that Matthias had insisted upon for his *krajan*, his *učenec* from the university, whose father in Prague had been a colleague in intellect and spirit, if not in good fortune. Michael had used it twice during the past six years. The first time when he was briefly in Washington for new instructions, Matthias had left word at his hotel that he should do so, and the call was merely social. The second was not pleasant for Havelock to recall. It had concerned a man named Ogilvie who Michael felt strongly should be removed from the field.

The Antibes operator offered to ring him back when the call to Washington, DC was put through, but experience had taught Havelock to stay on the line. Nothing so tested the concentration of an operator as an open circuit; calls were more swiftly completed by remaining connected. And while he listened to the series of high-pitched sounds that signified international transmission, Salanne spoke.

'Why haven't you called him before now?'

'Because nothing made sense, and I wanted it to. I wanted to give him something concrete. A name or names, a position, a title, some kind of identity.'

'But from what I've heard you still can't do that.'

'Yes I can. The authorization for dispatch had a source. Code name, Ambiguity. It could only come from one of three or four offices, the word itself cleared by someone very high at State who was in touch with Rome. Matthias reaches Rome, has the incoming logs checked, talks to the receiver and learns who gave Ambiguity its status. There's another name, too, but I don't know how much good it'll do. There was a second, so-called confirmation at Costa Brava, including torn pieces of blood-stained clothing. It's all a lie; there were no clothes left behind.'

'Then find that man.'

'He's dead. They say he died of a heart attack on a boat three weeks later. But there are things to look for, if they haven't been obscured. Where he came from, who assigned him to Costa Brava . . .'

'And if I may add,' said the Frenchman, 'the doctor who made out the death certificate.'

'You're right.' The sing-song tones disappeared from the line, replaced by two short, steady hums, then a break of silence, followed by a normal ring. The electronic remote control had done its work; the telephone in the Shenandoah lodge was ringing. Michael felt the pounding in his throat and the shortness of breath that came with anxiety. He had so much to say to his *pritel*; he hoped to Christ he could say it and begin the ending of the nightmare. The ringing stopped, the phone was picked up. *Thank God!*

'Yes?' asked the voice over four thousand miles away in the Blue Ridge mountains, a male voice, but not the voice of Anton Matthias. Or was the sound distorted, the single word too short to identify the man?

'Jak se vam daře?'

'What? Who's this?'

It was *not* Matthias. Had the rules been changed? If they had, it did not make sense. This was the emergency line, Matthias's personal phone, which was swept for intercepts daily; only he answered it. After five rings the caller was to hang up, dial the regular telephone number and leave his name and whatever message he cared to, aware that confidentiality was far less secure. Perhaps there was a simple explanation, an off-hand request by Matthias for a friend nearer to the ringing phone to pick it up.

'Secretary of State Matthias, please?' said Havelock.

'Who's calling?'

'The fact that I used this number relieves me of the need to answer that. The Secretary, if you please. This is an emergency *and* confidential.'

'Mr Matthias is in conference at the moment and has asked for all calls to be held. If you'd give me your name – '

'Goddamn it, you're not listening! This is an emergency!'

'He has one, too, sir.'

'You break into that conference and say the following words to him. *Krajan.* . . and *bouře*. Have you got that? Just two words! *Krajan* and *bouře*. Do it now! Because if you don't, he'll have your head and your job when I talk to him! *Do* it!'

'*Krajan*,' said the male voice hesitantly. '*Bouře*.'

The line went silent, the silence interrupted once by the low undercurrent of men talking in the distance. The waiting was agony, and Michael could hear the echoes of his own erratic breathing. Finally the voice came back.

'I'm afraid you'll have to be clearer, sir.'

'*What?*'

'If you'd give me the details of the emergency and a telephone number where you can be reached – '

'Did you give him the message? The *words*! Did you say them?'

'The Secretary is extremely busy and requests that you clarify the nature of your call.'

'Goddamn it, did you *say* them?'

'I'm repeating what the Secretary said, sir. He can't be disturbed now, but if you'll outline the details and leave a number, someone will be in contact with you.'

'*Someone?* What the hell *is* this? Who *are* you? What's your name?'

There was a pause. 'Smith,' said the voice.

'Your name! I want your *name*!'

'I just gave it to you.'

'You get Matthias on this phone – !'

There was a click; the line went dead.

Havelock stared at the instrument in his hand, then closed his eyes. His mentor, his *krajan*, his *pritel*, had cut him off. What had happened?

He had to find out; it made no sense, no sense at all! There was another number in the Blue Ridge Mountains, the home of a man Matthias saw frequently when he was in the Shenandoah, an older man whose love of chess and fine old wine took Anton's mind off his monumental pressures. Michael had met Leon Zelienski a number of times and was always struck by the camaraderie between the two academics; he was happy for Matthias that such a person existed whose roots, though not in Prague, were not so far away, in Warsaw.

Zelienski had been a highly regarded professor of European history brought over to America years ago from the University of Warsaw to teach and lecture at Berkeley. Anton had met Leon during one of his early forays into the campus lecture circuit; additional funds were always welcome to Matthias. A friendship had developed – mostly by way of the mails and over chess – and upon retirement and the death of Zelienski's wife, Anton had persuaded the elderly scholar to come to the Shenandoah.

The Antibes operator took far longer with the second call, but finally Havelock heard the old man's voice.

'Good evening?'

'Leon? Is that you, Leon?'

'Who is this?'

'It's Michael Havelock. Do you remember me, Leon?'

'*Mikhail!* Do I *remember*! No, of course not, and I never touch *kielbasa*, either, you young *dupa*! How are you? Are you visiting our valley? You sound far away.'

'I'm very far away, Leon. I'm also very concerned . . .' Havelock explained his concern; he was unable to reach their beloved mutual friend, and was old Zelienski planning to see Anton while Matthias was in the Shenandoah?

'If he's here, Mikhail, I do not know it. Anton, of course, is a busy man. Sometimes I think the busiest man in this world . . . but he doesn't find time for me these days. I leave messages at the lodge, but I'm afraid he ignores them. Naturally, I understand. He moves with great figures . . . he *is* a great figure, and I am hardly one of them.'

'I'm sorry to hear that . . . that he hasn't been in touch.'

'Oh, men call me to express his regrets, saying that he rarely comes out to our valley these days, but I tell you, our chess games suffer. Incidentally, I must settle for another mutual friend of ours, Mikhail. He was out here frequently several months ago. That fine journalist Raymond Alexander. Alexander the Great, I call him, but as a player he's a far better writer.'

'Raymond Alexander?' said Havelock, barely listening. 'Give him my best. And thank you, Leon.' Havelock replaced the phone and looked over at Salanne. 'He hasn't time for us any more,' he said, bewildered.

14

He had reached Paris by eight o'clock in the morning, made contact with Gravet by nine and, by a quarter past eleven, was walking south amid the crowds on the Boulevard Saint Germain. The fastidious art critic and broker of secrets would approach him somewhere between the rue de Pontoise and the Quai St Bernard. Gravet needed the two hours to seek out as many sources as possible relating to the information Havelock needed. Michael, on the other hand, used the time to move slowly, to rest – leaning upright against walls, never sitting – and to improve his immediate wardrobe.

There had been no time for Salanne's wife to buy him clothes in the morning, no thought but to get to Paris as quickly as he could, for every moment lost widened the distance between Jenna and himself. She had never been to Paris except with him and there were only so many options open to her; he must be there when she narrowed them down.

The doctor had driven for three and a half hours at very high speed to Avignon, where there had been a one o'clock produce train bound for Paris. Michael had caught it, dressed in what could be salvaged fron his own clothes, in addition to a sweater and an ill-fitting gabardine topcoat furnished by Salanne. Now he looked at his reflection in a shop window; the jacket, trousers, open shirt and hat he had purchased off the racks in the Raspail forty-five minutes ago suited his purpose. They were loose and nondescript. A man wearing such clothes would not be singled out, and the brim of the soft hat fell just low enough over his forehead to cast a shadow across his face.

Beyond the window was a narrow pillar of clear glass, part of the merchandise display, a mirror. He was drawn to it, to the face in the shadow of the hat brim. *His* face. It was haggard, with black circles under his eyes and stubble of a dark beard. He had not thought of shaving. Even when shopping in Raspail – there had been mirrors in the store – he had looked only at the clothes, while concentrating his thoughts on the Paris he and Jenna Karras had known together: one or two embassy contacts; several colleagues-in-cover, as they were; a few French friends – government mainly, whose *ministères* brought them into his orbit; and three or four acquaintances they had made at late night cafés having nothing whatsoever to do with the world in which he made his living.

Now in the Boulevard Saint Germain the ashen face he saw reminded him of how tired and racked with pain he was, how much he just wanted to lie down and let his strength come back to him. As Salanne had said, he needed rest badly. He had tried to sleep on the train from Avignon, but the frequent stops at rural halts that were farmers' points of delivery had jolted him awake whenever he dozed. And when awake, his head had throbbed, his mind filled with a profound sense of loss, confusion and anger. The one man on earth to whom he had given his trust and love, the giant who had replaced his father and shaped his life, had cut him loose and he had no idea why. Throughout the years, during the most harrowing and isolated times, he was somehow never alone because the presence of Anton Matthias was always with him. Anton was the spur that drove him to be better than he was, his protection against the memories of the early terrible days, because his *pritel* had given them meaning, perspective. Certainly no justification, but a reason for doing what he was doing, for spending his life in an abnormal world until something inside him told him he could join the normal one. He had fought against the guns of Lidice and the arbiters of gulag termination in whatever form he had found them.

Those guns will always be with you, my pritel. *I wish to Almighty God you could walk away from them, but I don't think you can. So do what lessens the pain, what gives purpose for you, what removes the guilt of having survived. Absolution is not here among the books and argumentative theoreticians; you have no patience with their conceptualism. You have to see practical results . . . One day you will be free, your anger spent and you will return. I hope I am alive to witness it. I intend to be.*

He had come so close to being free, his anger reduced to an abstract sense of futility, his return to a normal world within his grasp and understanding. It had happened twice. Once with the woman he loved, who had given another breadth of meaning to his life . . . and then without her, loving neither her nor the memory of her, believing the lies of liars, betraying his innermost feelings – and her. Oh, *God*!

And now the one man who could fulfil the prophecy he had made years ago to his *krajan*, his student, his son, had thrown him out of his life. The giant was a mortal, after all. And now his enemy.

'*Mon Dieu*, you look like a graduate of Auschwitz!' whispered the tall Frenchman in the velvet-collared overcoat and gleaming black shoes standing several feet to the right of Havelock in front of the window. 'What *happened* to you? . . . No, don't tell me! Not here.'

'Where?'

'On the Quai Bernard, past the university, is a small park, a playground for children mostly,' continued Gravet, admiring his own figure in the glass. 'If the benches are occupied, find a place by the fence and I'll join you. On your way, purchase a bag of sweets and try to look like a father, not a sex deviate.'

'Thanks for the confidence. Did you bring me anything?'

'Let's say you are heavily in my debt. Far more than your impecunious appearance would suggest you could pay.'

'About *her*?'

'I'm still working on that. On her.'

'Then *what*?'

'The Quai Bernard,' said Gravet, adjusting his scarlet tie and tilting his grey Homburg in the reflection of the window. He turned with the grace of a ballet master and walked away.

The small park was chilled by the winds off the Seine, but they did not deter the nurses, nannies and young mothers from bringing their boisterous charges to the playground. Children were everywhere – on the swings, jungle-gyms, seesaws – it was bedlam. Fortunately for Michael's waning strength, there was a vacant bench against the far back wall, away from the more chaotic centre of the riverside part. He sat down, absently picking tiny coloured mints out of a white paper bag while looking at a particularly obnoxious child kicking a tricycle; he hoped that whoever might be observing him would think the youngster was his, reasoning that the small boy's real guardian would stay as far away as possible. The child stopped punishing the three wheels long enough to return his stare with astonishing malevolence.

The elegant Gravet walked through the red-striped entrance and levitated his way around the outside aisle of the playground, nodding pleasantly, benignly to the screaming children in his path, an elder full of kindness towards the young. It was quite a performance, thought Havelock, knowing that the epicene critic loathed the surroundings. Finally he reached the bench and sat down, snapping a newspaper out in front of him.

'Should you see a doctor?' asked the critic, his eyes on the paper.

'I left one only hours ago,' replied Michael, his lips by the edge of the white paper bag. 'I'm all right, just tired.'

'I'm relieved, but I suggest you clean yourself up, including a shave. The two of us in this particular park could bring on the *gendarmes*. The opposite poles of an obscene spectrum, would be the conclusion.'

'I don't feel like being funny, Gravet. What have you got?'

The critic folded the paper, snapping it again, as he spoke. 'A contradiction, if my sources are accurate, and I have every reason to believe they are. A somewhat incredible contradiction, in fact.'

'What is it?'

'The KGB has no interest in you whatsoever. I could deliver you, a willing, garrulous defector snapped from the jaws of imperialists, to their Paris headquarters – an importing firm on the Beaumarchais, but I suspect you know that – and I wouldn't get a *sou*.'

'Why is that a contradiction? I said the same thing to you several weeks ago on the Pont Royal.'

'*That* isn't the contradiction.'

'What is?'

'Someone else is looking for you. He flew in last night because he thinks you're either in Paris now or on your way here. The word is he'll pay a fortune for your corpse. He's not KGB in the usual sense, but make no mistake about it, he's Soviet.'

'Not . . . in the usual sense?' asked Havelock, bewildered, yet sensing the approach of an ominous memory, a recent memory.

'I traced him through a source in the *Etrangers Militaires*. He's from a special branch of Soviet intelligence, an elite corps of . . .'

'*Voennaya Kontr Razvedka*,' Michael broke in harshly.

'If the shortened form is VKR, that's it.'

'It is.'

'He wants you. He'll pay dearly.'

'Maniacs.'

'Mikhail, I should tell you. He flew in from Barcelona.'

'*Costa Brava!*' Across the aisle, the ferocious child screamed. 'Don't look at me! Move to the edge of the bench!'

'Do you know what you just *told* me?'

'You're upset. I must leave.'

'No!. . . All right, all *right*!' Havelock lifted the white paper bag to his face; both his hands were trembling, and he could hardly breathe as the pain in his chest surged up to his temples. 'You know what you've got to deliver now, don't you? You've got it, so give it to me.'

'You're in no condition.'

'I'll be judge of that. *Tell* me!'

'I wonder if I should. Quite apart from the payment I may never see, there's a moral dilemma. You see, I like you, Mikhail. You're a civilized man, perhaps even a good man in a very unsavoury business. You took yourself out; have I the right to put you back in?'

'I *am* back in!'

'The Costa Brava?'

'Yes!'

'Go to your embassy.'

'I *can't*! Don't you understand that?'

Gravet broke his own sacrosanct rule: he lowered the newspaper and looked at Havelock. 'My God, they couldn't,' he said quietly.

'Just tell me.'

'You leave me no choice.'

'*Tell* me! Where is he?'

The critic rose from the bench, folding the paper, as he spoke. 'There's a rundown hotel on the rue Etienne. *La Couronne Nouvelle*. He's on the first floor, Room Twenty-three. It's at the front; he observes everyone who enters.'

The bent-over figure of the tramp was like that of a derelict in any large city. His clothes were ragged but thick enough to ward off the cold in deserted alleyways at night, his shoes cast-off heavy-soled boots, the laces broken and tied in large, awkward knots. On his head was a woollen knitted cap set low on his brow; his eyes focused downward, avoiding the world in which he could not compete, and which in turn found his presence unnerving. But over the tramp's shoulder was his soiled canvas satchel, the oily straps held in a firm grip as if he were proclaiming the dignity of possession: *this is my all, what is left of me, and it is mine*. The man approaching *La Couronne Nouvelle* had no age, he measured time only by what he had lost. He stopped at a wire litter basket and dug through the contents with methodical patience – a pavement archaeologist.

Havelock separated a torn lampshade from a soggy bag of a half-eaten lunch and angled the small tinted mirror between them, his hands concealed by the filthy fabric of the shade. He could see the Russian directly above in the first floor window; the man was leaning against the sill, watching the street, studying the pedestrians, waiting. He would stay by that window for a simple reason: his strike force was deployed; had a counterstrike been mounted? Michael knew him – not by name or reputation, or even from a photograph in a file, but he knew him, knew the set of the face, the look in the eyes. Havelock had been where this man had been – where he was now. The process had been set in motion, the word cautiously put out; word was awaited back at the command post of one. The lethal compromisers had been reached, none having allegiance to anything or anybody except the dollar, the franc, the pound and the Deutschmark. A sliding scale of incentive payments had been circulated, bonuses matching the value of various contributions, the highest, of course, the kill with proof of the kill. Word and method of the target's arrival, sightings at specific locations, alone or with known or unknown associates, a hotel, a café, a *pension*, a rooming house – all had value in terms of immediate payment. A competition had been created among the qualified practitioners of violence, each professional enough to know that one did not lie to the command post. Today's loss was another day's kill.

Sooner or later the man in the window would start getting his responses. A few would be mere speculation based on second-hand information; others would be honest error, which would not be penalized but analysed for what it was, confirmation improbable. Then a single call would come, its authenticity established by a descriptive phrase or a certain reaction – unmistakably the target's – and the command post would have its first breakthrough. A street, a café, a bench perhaps in a children's park on the Seine – the practitioners would have spread out everywhere. The hunt was on, the prize many times a year's income. And when the hunt came to an end, the man in the window would come out of his movable prison. Yes, thought Michael, he had been there. The waiting was the worst part.

He looked at his watch, his hand buried in the refuse. There was a second wire litter basket down the block, on the other side of the hotel's entrance; he wondered if it would be necessary to go to it and continue foraging. He had gone past the hotel twice in a taxi – projecting his movements on foot, calculating his timing – before he had sought out the second-hand clothes shops in Séverin – those and an obscure shop beside the Somme where he had purchased ammunition for the Llama automatic and the Magnum. He had phoned Gravet seven minutes ago and told him the clock was on; the Frenchman would place his call from a booth in the Place Vendôme; the crowds would guarantee his untraceable anonymity. What was holding him up? There were so many possibilities. Occupied booths, out-of-order phones, a talkative acquaintance who insisted on prolonging street corner conversation, all were reasonable assumptions. But whatever the cause of delay, Havelock knew he could not stay where he was any longer. Awkwardly, like an old man in pain – and indeed he was a not-so-young man in pain – he began to push himself up. He would force a deliberately unfocused eye to see what it should not see.

The man in the window whipped his head round. An intrusion had interrupted his concentration on the street; he walked back into the shadows of the room. Gravet had made his call. *Now*.

Michael lifted the satchel off the ground, dropped it into the wire receptacle and rapidly walked diagonally across the pavement towards the short flight of steps that led to the hotel's entrance. With each stride he lessened his stooped posture to return gradually to normal height. As he climbed the concrete steps he placed his hand on the side of his face, his fingers gripping the edge of the woollen cap. No more than eight feet above was the window in which the Soviet VKR officer had been standing only seconds ago, and in seconds he would return. Gravet's call would be brief, professional, in no way could it be construed as a device. There was a possible sighting in the Montparnasse. Was the target injured? Did he walk with a pronounced limp? Whatever answers the Russian gave, the call would be terminated, probably in mid-sentence. If it *was* the target, he was heading for the *Métro*; the hunter would call back.

Inside the dark, musty lobby with the cracked tile floor and the cobwebs spanning the four corners of the ceiling, Havelock took off his cap flattened the lapels of his dishevelled jacket and ripped the already torn cloth that hung from the bottom of his coat. It was not much of an improvement, but in the dim light and with erect bearing, it was not inappropriate to a hotel that catered for drifters and whores. It was not an establishment which scrutinized its clientele, only the legitimacy of their currency.

It had been Michael's intention to project the image of a man painfully coming out of a long drunk, seeking a bed in which to shake through the final ordeal. It was not necessary; an obese *concierge* behind the cracked marble counter was dozing in a chair, his soft, fat hands folded on his protruding stomach. There was one other person in the lobby: a gaunt old man seated on a bench, a cigarette dangling from his lips below an unkempt grey moustache, his head bent forward as he squinted at a newspaper in his hands. He did not look up.

Havelock dropped the cap on the floor, side-kicked it towards the wall and walked to his left, where there was a narrow staircase, the steps worn smooth from decades of use and neglect, the banister broken in several places. He started up the creaking steps and was relieved that the staircase was short. There were no turns, no mid-point landings; the steps led straight from one level to the next. He reached the first floor and stood motionless, listening. There was no sound other than the distant hum of traffic, punctuated by sporadic shrieks of impatient horns. He looked at the door ten feet away, at the faded painted number, *23*. He could discern no vocal undercurrent of a one-sided telephone conversation; the call from Gravet was over and the Soviet VKR officer was back at his window, the elapsed time no more than forty-five seconds. Michael unbuttoned his ragged jacket, reached underneath and gripped the handle of the Magnum. As he pulled the gun out from under his belt, the perforated cylinder caught briefly on the leather; with his thumb he released the safety catch, and started down the dark, narrow hallway towards the door.

A creak in the floorboards, not his, not under him, *behind* him! He spun as the first door on the left beyond the staircase was pulled slowly open. Since it had been left ajar, there had been no sound of a turning knob; the open crack was a line of sight for someone inside. A short, heavy-set man emerged, shoulders and spine against the frame, a weapon in his hand at his side. He raised the gun. Havelock had no time for assessment or appraisal, he could only react. Under different circumstances he might have held up his hand and sharply whispered, a word, a signal, a note of warning to avert a terrible error; instead he fired. The man was blown off his feet, buckling back into the door frame. Michael looked at the gun still gripped in the man's hand. He had been right to shoot; the weapon was a Graz-Burya, the most powerful, accurate automatic produced in Russia. The VKR officer was not alone. And if there was one . . .

A knob was being turned; it was the door directly across from Room Twenty-three. Havelock lurched to the wall to the right of the frame: the door opened and he spun around, the Magnum raised chest high, prepared to fire or deliver a blow – or drop his arm if it should turn out to be an innocent hotel guest. The man was in a crouch, and held a gun. Havelock crashed the barrel of the Magnum on the man's head. The Russian fell back inside the room; Michael followed and gripped the door to prevent it from slamming shut. He held the crack open less than an inch, stood still and waited. There was silence in the hall, except for the far away sounds of traffic. He backed away from the door, the Magnum levelled at it, his eyes scanning the floor for the man's gun. It was several feet behind the prone, unconscious figure; he kicked it forward beside the body, kneeled down and picked it up. It, too, was a Graz-Burya; the detail sent to Paris was equipped with the best. He shoved it into his jacket pocket, reached over and pulled the Russian towards him; the man was limp and would not be conscious for hours.

He got to his feet and left the room. The violent movements had drained him; he leaned against the wall, breathing slowly, deeply, trying to put out of his mind the weakness and pain in his body. He could not stop now. There was the first man in the door beyond the staircase; the door was open. Someone walking past would look inside and have hysterics. Michael pushed himself away from the wall, and silently, on the balls of his thick-soled feet, made his way down the narrow corridor past the staircase. He pulled the door shut and started back towards Room Twenty-three.

He stood facing the barely legible numbers and knew he had to find the strength. There was nothing for it but to depend on the shock of the totally unexpected. He tensed his chest and stepped back from the door, then, leading with his unwounded shoulder, crashed the full weight of his body against the wood. The door splintered and broke open, as the VKR officer pivoted away from the window, his hand reaching for the exposed holster strapped to his belt. He stopped, swiftly thrusting both hands out in front of him, his eyes staring at the huge barrel of the Magnum pointed at his head.

'I believe you were looking for me,' said Havelock.

'It appears I trusted the wrong people,' answered the Russian quietly in well-accented English.

'But not your own people,' interrupted Michael.

'You're special.'

'You lost.'

'I never ordered your death. They might have.'

'Now you're lying, but it doesn't matter. As I said, you lost.'

'You're to be commended,' mumbled the VKR officer, his eyes straying above Havelock's shoulder to the broken door.

'You didn't hear me. You lost. There's a man in the room across the hall; he won't be attending you.'

'I see.'

'And another down the way, beyond the staircase. He's dead.'

'*Nyet! Molniya!*' The Soviet agent blanched: his fingers were stretched, taut, six inches from his belt.

'I speak Russian, if you prefer.'

'It's immaterial,' said the startled man. 'I'm a graduate of the Massachusetts Institute of Technology.'

'Or of the American compound in Novgorod, KGB degree.'

'Cambridge, Massachusetts, not Novgorod,' objected the Russian, disdain in his voice.

'I forgot. The VKR is an élite corps. A degree from the parent organization might be considered an insult. The untutored and unskilled conferring honours upon its in-house superiors.'

'There are no such divisions in the Soviet government.'

'My ass.'

'This is pointless.'

'Yes, it is. What happened at the Costa Brava?'

'I have no idea what you mean.'

'You're VKR, Barcelona! The Costa Brava is in your sector! What happened that night of 4 January?'

'Nothing that concerned us.'

'*Move!*'

'What?'

'Against the wall!'

It was an outside wall, built of mortar and heavy brick, solid for decades, weight pressing against weight, impenetrable. The Russian moved slowly, haltingly in front of it. Havelock continued.

'I'm so special your sector chief in Moscow doesn't know the truth. But you do. It's why you're here in Paris, why you put out a premium call on me.'

'You've been misinformed. It is a crime tantamount to treason to withhold information from our superiors. As to my coming from Barcelona, surely you understand that. It was your last assignment and I was your last counterpart. I had the most up-to-date information on you. Who better to send after you?'

'You're very good. You glide well.'

'I've told you nothing you don't know, nothing you could not learn.'

'You missed something. Why am I special? Your colleagues at KGB haven't the slightest interest in me. On the contrary, they won't touch me; they consider me a bad text. Yet you say I'm special. The *Voennaya* wants me.'

'I won't deny there's a degree of inter-service rivalry, even departmental. Perhaps we learned it from you. You have an abundance of it.'

'You haven't answered my question.'

'We know certain things our comrades are not aware of.'

'Such as?'

'You were placed "beyond salvage" by your own government.'

'Do you know why?'

'The reasons at this juncture are secondary. We offer refuge.'

'The reasons are never secondary,' corrected Michael.

'Very well,' agreed the Soviet officer reluctantly. 'A judgement was made that you were unbalanced.'

'On what basis?'

'Pronounced hostility, accompanied by threats, cables. Delusions, hallucinations.'

'Because of Costa Brava?'

'Yes.'

'Just like that? One day walking around sane, filing reports, honourably retired; the next a cuckoo bird whistling at the moon? Now you're not very good. You're not gliding well at all.'

'I'm telling you what I know!' insisted the Russian. 'I do not make these determinations, I follow instructions. The premium, as you call it, was to be paid for a meeting between us. Why should it be otherwise? If killing you was the objective, it would be far simpler to pay for your whereabouts and telephone your embassy on the Avenue Gabriel, asking for a specific extension; I can assure you we know it. The information would reach the proper personnel and we are not involved, no possibility of errors leading to future repercussions.'

'But by offering me refuge and bringing me in, you take back a trophy your less talented comrades avoided because they thought I was a trap, programmed or otherwise.'

'Basically, yes. May we talk?'

'We're talking.' Havelock studied the man; he was convincing, quite possibly telling his version of the truth. Refuge or a bullet, which was it? Only the exposure of lies would tell. One had to look for the lies, not a subordinate's interpretation of the truth. In his peripheral vision Michael caught the reflection of a dull mirror above a shabby bureau against the wall; he spoke again.

'You'd expect me to deliver information you know I've got.'

'We'd be saving your life. The order for "beyond-salvage" termination will not be rescinded, you know that.'

'You're suggesting I defect.'

'What choice do you have? How long do you think you can keep running? How many days or weeks will it be before their networks and their computers find you?'

'I'm experienced. I have resources. Perhaps I'm willing to take my chances. Men have been known to disappear – not into gulags, but to other places – and live happily ever after. What else can you offer?'

'What are you looking for? Comfort, money, a good life? We offer these. You deserve them.'

'Not in your country. I won't live in the Soviet Union.'

'Oh?'

'Suppose I told you I've picked out a place. It's thousands of miles away in the Pacific, in the Solomon Islands. I've been there; it's civilized but remote, no one would ever find me. Given enough money, I could live well there.'

'Arrangements can be made. I am empowered to guarantee that.'

Lie number one. No defector ever left the Soviet Union and the VKR officer knew it.

'You flew into Paris last night. How did you know I was here?'

'Informants in Rome, how else?'

'How did they learn?'

'One doesn't question informants too closely.'

'The hell one doesn't.'

'*If* they are trusted.'

'You ask for a source. You don't leave a station and fly to a city hundreds of miles away without being pretty damn sure the source can be confirmed.'

'Very well,' said the VKR officer, gliding confidently with the cross-currents again. 'There was an investigation; a man was found in Civitavecchia. He said you were on your way to Paris.'

'When did you get the word?'

'Yesterday, of course,' replied the Russian impatiently.

'When yesterday?'

'Late afternoon. Five-thirty, I believe. Five-thirty-five, to be precise.'

Lie number two, the falsehood found in the precision. The decision to head for Paris was forced on him after Col des Moulinets. Eight o'clock at night.

'You're convinced that what I can divulge about our European intelligence operations is of such value to you that you are willing to accept the retaliations that come with defection at my level?'

'Naturally.'

'That opinion isn't shared by the directors' committee of the KGB.'

'They're fools. Frightened, tired rabbits among the wolves. We'll replace them.'

'You're not troubled that I may be programmed? That whatever I tell you could be poison, useless?'

'Not for a moment. It's why you're "beyond-salvage".'

'Or that I'm paranoid?'

'Never. You're neither paranoid nor hallucinatory. You are what you have always been, a highly intelligent specialist in your field.'

Lie number three. Word of his supposed psychotic condition had been spread. Washington believed it; the dead Ogilvie had confirmed it on the Palatine.

'I see,' said Havelock, grimacing, feigning pain that needed very little pretence. 'I'm so goddamned tired,' he said, lowering the Magnum slightly, turning slightly to his left, his eyes millimetres from making contact with the mirror on the wall. 'I was shot. I haven't had any sleep. As you said, I just keep running, trying to figure it out . . .'

'What more is there?' asked the Russian, his voice now gliding into compassion. 'It's basically an economic, time-saving decision, you know that. Rather than altering codes, networks and sources, they've decided to eliminate the man who knows too much. Sixteen years of service in the field and this is your retirement bonus. "Beyond-salvage".'

Michael lowered the gun further, his head bent down but his eyes now on the mirror. 'I have to think,' he whispered. 'It's all so crazy, so impossible.'

Lie number four – the most telling lie! The Russian went for his gun!

Havelock spun round and fired: the bullet snapped into the wall. The VKR officer grabbed his elbow as blood erupted through his shirt and dripped onto the floor.

'*Levobokec!*' he cried.

'We've only just begun!' said Michael, his voice a roar though still a whisper. He approached the Russian and pushed him against the wall, then removed the exposed weapon from the holster and threw it across the room. 'You're too sure of yourself, comrade, too sure of your facts! Never state them so confidently; leave room for error because there *may* be one. You had several.'

The Russian answered him with silence, his eyes full of both loathing and resignation. Havelock knew those eyes, knew the combination of hatred and the recognition of mortality; they were intrinsic to the nature of certain men, trained for years to hate and die. By any name they were recognizable: *Gestapo. Nippon Kai. Palestinian Liberationists. Voennaya* . . . And by lesser leagues whose amateur status stopped with arrogance and hate, death no part of their childish bargains, screeching fanatics who marched to the drums of sanctimonious loathing.

Michael returned silence for silence, look for look. And then he spoke.

'Don't waste the adrenalin,' he said quietly. 'I'm not going to kill you. You're prepared for that; you've been ready for it for years. Damned if I'm going to accommodate you. Instead, I'm going to blow off both your kneecaps – and then your hands. You're not trained to live with results. No one is, really, especially not your kind. So many routine things'll be beyond you. Simple things. Walking to a door or a locked file cabinet, opening either. Dialling a phone or going to the toilet. Reaching for a gun and pulling a trigger.'

The Russian's face went pale and his lower lip began to tremble. '*Nyet,*' he whispered hoarsely.

'*Da,*' said Havelock. 'There's only one way you can stop me. Tell me what happened at the Costa Brava.'

'I *told* you! *Nothing!*'

Michael lowered the Magnum and fired into the Soviet's thigh; blood splattered against the wall. The Russian started to scream, collapsing on the floor; Havelock gripped his mouth with his left hand.

'I missed the kneecap. I won't miss now. Either one.' He stood up, levelling the weapon downward.

'*No!* Stop!' The VKR officer rolled over, clutching his leg. He was broken; he could accept death, but not what Michael promised him. 'I'll tell you what I know.'

'*I'll* know if you're lying. My finger's on the trigger, the gun pointed at your right hand. If you lie, you won't have it any more.'

'What I told you *is* true. We were not at the Costa Brava that night.'

'Your code was broken. Washington broke it. I saw it. I *sent* it!'

'Washington broke nothing. That code was abandoned seven days before the night of the fourth of January. Even if you sent it and we accepted it, we could not have responded. It would have been physically impossible.'

'Why?'

'We were nowhere near the area, any of us. We were sent out of the sector.' The Russian coughed in pain, his face twisted. 'For the period of time in question, all activities were cancelled. We were prohibited from going within twenty miles of the Montebello beach on the Costa Brava.'

'*Liar!*'

'No,' said the VKR officer, his bleeding leg pulled up under him, his body taut, his eyes staring at Michael. 'No, I am not lying. Those were the orders from Moscow.'

BOOK II

BOOK II

15

It was raining that night in Washington, angry, diagonal sheets of rain
driven by erratic winds, making drivers and pedestrians alike mistrust their
vision; headlights refracted, blinded in suddenly shifting angles. The chauffeur at the wheel of the limousine heading down 14th Street towards the
East Gate of the White House was not immune to the problem. He slammed
on his brakes and swerved to avoid an onrushing small car, whose high
beams gave the illusion of a huge attacking insect. It was in fact well to his
left, on its side of the line, so the manoeuvre proved unnecessary. The
chauffeur wondered whether his very important passengers had noticed the
error.

'Sorry, sirs,' he said, his voice directed at the intercom, his eyes on the
rear view mirror and the glass partition that separated him from them.

Neither man responded. It was as if neither had heard him, yet he knew
both had; the blue intercom light was on, which meant that his voice was
transmitted. The red light, of course, was dark; he could not hear anything
being said in the rear seat. The red light was always off, except when
instructions were being given, and twice every day the system was checked
in the garage before he or any other driver left the premises. It was said that
tiny circuit breakers had been installed that tripped at the slightest tampering with the intercom mechanism.

The men who rode in these limousines had been assigned to them by the
President of the United States, and the chauffeurs who drove them were
continuously subjected to the most stringent security checks. Each of them
was unmarried and without children, and each was a combat veteran –
proven under fire – with extensive experience in guerrilla warfare and
diversionary tactics. The vehicles they drove were designed for maximum
protection. The windows could withstand the impact of .45 calibre bullets,
homing devices were implanted throughout the undersides, and small jets
that released two separate types of gas with a flick of a switch were
positioned at all points of the frame – one gas merely numbed and was used
for riots and unruly protesters, while the other was a near-lethal dioxide
compound, designed for terrorists. The chauffeurs' orders were to guard
their passengers with their lives. For their charges held the secrets of the
nation; they were the President's closest advisers in times of crisis.

The driver glanced at the dashboard clock. It was nine-twenty, nearly
four hours since he had completed his previous assignment, waited for the
electronics check back in the garage and left for the night. Thirty-five
minutes later he had been having a drink at a restaurant on K Street and
was about to order dinner when the jarring one-note signal of his bleeper
erupted from its case on his belt. He had telephoned the unlisted number
for Security Dispatch and been ordered to the garage immediately: *Aquarius
One emergency, Scorpio descending.* Out of context and out of orbit, but the

message was clear. The Oval Office had pushed a button; the senior drivers were now on duty, all previous schedules aborted.

Back in the garage he had been mildy surprised to see that only two vehicles had been prepared for transport. He had expected to find six or seven black-stretch Abrahams wheeled out of their docks and ready to roll; instead, there were just two – one ordered to an address in Berwyn Heights, Maryland, and the second – his – to Andrews Airfield to await the arrival of two men being flown in on Army jets from separate islands in the Caribbean. Times had been coordinated; the ETAs were within fifteen minutes of each other.

The younger of the two old men had arrived first, and the driver recognized him instantly; not everyone would have done so. His name was Halyard, like the line on a sailing boat, but his reputation had been made on land. Lt-General Malcolm Halyard: WWII, Korea, Vietnam. The bald soldier had started off commanding platoons and companies in France and across the Rhone, then battalions in Kaesong and Inchon, and, finally, armies in South-east Asia, where the driver had seen him more than once in Danang. He was something of an odd-ball in the upper ranks of the army; he was never known to have held a press conference, but he had been known to bar photographers – military and civilian alike – from wherever he happened to be. 'Tightrope' Halyard was considerd a brilliant tactician, one of the first to state for the *Congressional Record* that Vietnam was no-win idiocy. He avoided publicity with the same tenacity that he displayed on the battlefield, and his low profile, it was said, appealed to the President.

The retired general had been escorted to the limousine, and after greeting the driver, had waited in the back seat without another word.

The second man had arrived twelve minutes later. He was as far removed from 'Tightrope' Halyard as the eagle is from the lion, but both were superb examples of their species. Addison Brooks had been a lawyer, an international banker, a consultant to statesmen, an ambassador and, finally, an elder statesman himself and adviser to presidents. He was the embodiment of the Eastern Establishment aristocracy, the last of the old-school-tie crowd, the ultimate WASP who tempered the image with a swift wit that could be as gentle and compassionate as it could be devastating. He had survived the political wars by exercising the same agility displayed by Halyard on the battlefield. In essence, both men would compromise with reality, but not with principle. This was not, of course, the driver's own judgement; he had read about it in the *Washington Post*, his interest having been drawn to a political column which had analysed the two advisers because he knew the ambassador and had seen the general in Danang. He had driven the ambassador on a number of occasions, and was always flattered that old Brooks remembered his name and had something a little personal to say to him: 'Damn it, Jack, don't you ever put on weight? My wife makes me drink my gin with some God-awful diet fruit juice.' Which had to be an exaggeration, for the ambassador was a tall, slender man, his silver hair, aquiline features and perfectly-groomed grey moustache making him look more English than American.

Tonight, however, there had been no personal greeting at Andrews Field and no jokes. Instead, Brooks had nodded absently when the driver opened the rear door for him; then he had paused as his eyes made contact with the general inside. At that moment only one word was spoken.

'Parsifal,' the ambassador said, his voice low, sombre; it was the sole greeting.

After Brooks had climbed in beside Halyard, they talked briefly, their faces set, glancing frequently at each other, as if asking questions neither could answer. Then they fell silent, or so it appeared, at least, whenever the driver's eyes strayed to the rear view mirror. The few times he had looked at them, as he was looking at them now, both the diplomat and the soldier had been staring straight ahead, neither speaking. Whatever crisis had brought them to the White House, each from an island in the Caribbean, it was obviously beyond discussion.

The driver's memories were stirred as he turned into the short drive that led to the East Gate guardhouse. Like many collegiate athletes whose ability was somewhat greater on the playing field than in the classroom or laboratory, he had had to take a course in musical appreciation at the instigation of his coaches. He had found much of it beyond him. Still, he remembered . . . Parsifal was an opera by Wagner.

The driver of Abraham Seven turned off the Kenilworth Road into the residential section of Berwyn Heights, Maryland. He had been to the house twice before, which was why he was selected for the route tonight despite his previous request not to be given Undersecretary of State Emory Bradford as an assignment again. When Security Dispatch had asked why, he could only answer that he did not like him.

'That doesn't really concern us, Yahoo,' had been the reply. 'Your likes and dislikes have yet to become policy around here. Just do your job.'

Of course that was the point – the job. If part of the job included protecting Bradford's life at a risk to his own, he was not sure he could comply. Fifteen years ago the cold analytical Emory Bradford had been one of the best and the brightest, the new breed of young pragmatists who skewered adversaries right and left in the pursuit of power. And the tragedy at Dallas had done nothing to slow this pursuit; the mourning had been quickly replaced by adjustment to a changed situation. The nation was in peril and those endowed with the capacity to understand the aggressive nature of factionalized communism had to stand firm and rally the forces of strength. The tight-lipped, unemotional Bradford became an impassioned hawk. A game called dominoes was suddenly a theory on which the survival of freedom was based.

A strapping farm boy from Idaho was caught up in the fever. He answered the call; it was his personal statement against the long-haired freaks who burned flags and draft cards and spat on things that were decent and – *American*. Eight months later the farm boy was in the jungles watching friends getting blown away. He saw Arvin troops running from fire fights and their commanders selling rifles and jeeps and whole consignments of battalion rations. He came to understand what was so obvious to everyone but Washington and Command Saigon. The so-called victims of the so-called atheistic hordes didn't give a doodily shit about anything except their hides and their profits. They were the ones who were spitting and burning everything that could not be traded or sold, and laughing. *Jesus*, were they laughing! At their so-called saviours, the pink-faced, round-eyed suckers who took the fire and the land mines, and lost heads and faces and arms and legs.

And then it happened. The frenzied hawk that was Emory Bradford in Washington saw the light, a different light. In an extraordinary public display of *mea culpa* he appeared before a Senate committee and announced to the nation that something had gone wrong, the brilliant planners – himself included – had erred grievously. He advocated immediate withdrawal; the impassioned hawk became a passionate dove.

He was accorded a standing ovation. While heads and faces and arms and legs were scattered over the jungles, and a farm boy from Idaho was doing his damnedest not to want to die as a prisoner of war. A *standing ovation*, goddam it!

No, Mr Emory Bradford, I will not risk my life for you. I will not die for you – again.

The large three-storeyed colonial house was set back beyond a manicured lawn that promised a pool and a tennis court hidden somewhere. The best and the brightest also frolicked; it was part of their life style, intrinsic to their worth and their image. The farm boy from Idaho wondered how Undersecretary of State Emory Bradford would behave in a river cage infested with water rats in the Mekong Delta. Probably very well, goddamn it.

The driver reached under the dashboard and pulled out the retractable microphone. He pressed the button and spoke.

'Abraham Seven to dispatch.'

'Go ahead, Abraham Seven.'

'Have reached location. Please raise cargo by phone.'

'Will do, Seven. Good timing. You and Abraham Four should reach Aquarius at about the same time.'

'Glad you approve. We try to please.'

The three descended in the lift together, the two older men astonished that the conference was to take place in one of the underground strategy rooms and not in the Oval Office. The Undersecretary of State, briefcase in hand, seemed to understand why. The advantages, of course, were found in the equipment. There were computers and projectors that threw images and information onto a huge wall screen, communications devices that linked the White House to just about anybody anywhere in the world, and data processing machines that isolated facts from volumes of useless scholarship. Yet all the sophisticated equipment in Washington was in itself useless without a breakthrough. Had it happened? wondered the older advisers as each looked questioningly at the other. Had the breakthrough come? If it had, the summons from the President had given no indication of it. Instead, the opposite had been conveyed. 'Scorpio descending' was akin to catastrophe, and each felt the tightening of his stomach muscles as the lower level was reached and the lift door opened onto the pristine white-walled corridor. They emerged and walked in unison down the hallway towards the assigned room and the President of the United States.

President Charles Berquist greeted each man curtly, and each understood. It was not the nature of the stocky Minnesotan to be cold – tough, yes, very tough – but not cold; he was frightened. He gestured impatiently at the raised U-shaped conference table at the end of the room; it faced the wall screen thirty feet away where images would be projected. The three men walked up the two steps with the President and took their places at the table; at each place was a small Tensor lamp angled down on a note pad. Addison Brooks sat on Berquist's right, General Halyard on his left, and the younger Emory Bradford beyond the statesman, one chair removed so that he could address the three. It was a pecking order rooted in logic; most of the questions would be directed at Bradford, as he in turn would ask most of the questions directed at anyone brought in for interrogation. Below the U-shaped table and facing it midway to the screen was another table, smaller, rectangular, with two swivel chairs that enabled whoever sat in them to turn and watch the images projected on the wall.

'You look tired, Mr President,' said Brooks, once all were seated and the lamps adjusted.

'I'm tired,' agreed Berquist. 'I'm also sorry to bring you and Mal back to this rotten weather.'

'Insofar as you saw fit to call us back,' commented Halyard sincerely, 'I'd say the weather is the least of our problems.'

'You're right.' The President pressed a button embedded in the table on his left. 'The first slide, if you please.' The overhead lights were extinguished and only the Tensors remained on; the photographs of four men appeared on a split screen at the end of the room. 'Do you know any of these men?' asked Berquist, then added hastily, 'The question's not for Emory. He does.'

The ambassador and the general glanced at Bradford, then turned to the photographs. Addison Brooks spoke. 'The fellow on the upper right is named Stern. David or Daniel Stern, I believe. He's over at State, isn't he? One of the European specialists, bright, analytical, a good man.'

'Yes,' confirmed Berquist quietly. 'What about you, Mal? Recognize anybody up there?'

'I'm not sure,' said the retired general, squinting at the screen. 'The one below this Stern, lower right. I think I've seen him before.'

'You have,' said Bradford. 'He spent time at the Pentagon.'

'I can't picture the uniform, the rank.'

'He didn't wear one, have one. He's a doctor; he testified before a number of panels on POW trauma. You were seated on two or three, I believe.'

'Yes, of course, I remember now. He's a psychiatrist.'

'One of the leading authorities on stress-behaviour,' said Bradford, watching the two old men.

'What was that?' the ambassador asked urgently. 'Stress-behaviour?'

The words had startled the advisers. The old soldier leaned forward. 'Is there a connection?' he demanded of the Undersecretary.

'To Parsifal?'

'Who the hell else would I mean? *Is* there?'

'There is, but that's not it.'

'What isn't?' asked Brooks apprehensively.

'Miller's specialization. That's his name. Dr Paul Miller. We don't think his link to Parisfal has anything to do with his studies of stress.'

'Thank *God*,' muttered the general.

'Then what *is*?' the elder diplomat pressed impatiently.

'May I, Mr President?' asked Bradford, his eyes on the Commander in Chief. Berquist nodded silently; the Undersecretary turned to the screen and the photographs. 'The two men on the left, top and bottom, respectively, are John Philip Ogilvie, and Victor Alan Dawson.'

'Dawson's a lawyer,' interrupted Addison Brooks. 'I've never met him but I've read a number of his briefs. He's brilliant on international treaty negotiations. He has a gut feeling for foreign legal systems and their nuances.'

'Brilliant,' agreed the President softly.

'The last man,' continued Bradford rapidly, 'was no less an expert in his line of work. He was an undercover agent for nearly twenty years, one of the most knowledgeable tacticians in the field of covert operations.'

The Undersecretary's use of the past tense was not lost on the two advisers. They looked at each other, and then at President Berquist. The Minnesotan nodded.

'They're dead,' said the President, bringing his right hand to his forehead, his fingers nervously massaging his brows. 'All of them. Ogilvie died four days ago in Rome, a misplaced bullet, the circumstances acceptable. The others were not accidents; they were killed here. Dawson and Stern simultaneously, Miller twenty miles away at the same time.'

The ambassador leaned forward, his eyes on the screen. 'Four men,' he said anxiously. 'One an expert in European affairs and policies, another a lawyer whose work was almost exclusively in international law, the third a veteran undercover agent with broad tactical experience, and the fourth a psychiatrist acknowledged to be a leading specialist in stress-behaviour.'

'An odd collection of targets,' concluded the old soldier.

'They're connected, Mal,' said Brooks. 'To each other before Parsifal. Am I correct, Mr President?'

'Let Emory explain,' replied Berquist. 'He has to take the heat, so let him explain.'

Bradford's glance conveyed the fact that the explanation might be his to give but responsibility should be shared. Nevertheless, his slow intake of breath and the quiet delivery of his voice also indicated that he expected the worst.

'These men were the strategists of Consular Operations.'

'Costa Brava!' The name exploded in a whisper from the ambassador's lips.

'They peeled it away and found us,' said Halyard, his eyes filled with a soldier's angry acceptance. 'And they paid for it.'

'Yes,' agreed Bradford, 'but we don't know how it happened.'

'How they were *killed*?' asked the general incredulously.

'We know that,' replied the Undersecretary. 'Very professionally, the decision made quickly.'

'Then what don't you understand?' Brooks was annoyed.

'The connection to Parsifal.'

'But you said there *was* a connection,' insisted the elder statesman. 'Is there or isn't there?'

'There must be. We just can't follow it.'

'I can't follow you,' said the soldier.

'Start from the beginning, Emory,' interrupted the President. 'As you understand the beginning. From Rome.'

Bradford nodded. 'Five days ago the strategists received a priority cable from our conduit in Rome, a Lieutenant-Colonel Baylor – cover-name Brown. He oversees the clandestine activities network.'

'Larry Baylor?'

'Yes, General.'

'One hell of a fine officer. Give me twenty Negroes like him you can throw out the War College.'

'Colonel Baylor's black, Mr Ambassador.'

'Apparently, Mr Undersecretary.'

'For Christ's sake, Emory,' said Berquist.

'Yes, Mr President. To continue, Colonel Baylor's cable referred to a meeting he had with – ' Bradford paused. He delivered the name reluctantly, 'Michael Havelock.'

'Costa Brava,' muttered the soldier quietly.

'Parsifal,' added Brooks, halting briefly, then continuing, his words a protest. 'But Havelock was ruled out. After the clinic and his separation, he was watched, tested, his every moved placed under what I believe is called a microscope. We were assured there was nothing, absolutely *nothing*.'

'Less than nothing.' agreed the man from State. 'Under controlled circumstances he accepted a teaching position – an assistant professorship – at Concord University in New Hampshire. To all intents and purposes, he was completely out and we were back with the original scenario.'

'What changed it?' asked the soldier. 'What changed Havelock's status?'

Again Bradford paused, once more his delivery reluctant. 'The Karras woman,' he said quietly. 'She surfaced; he saw her. In Rome.'

The silence around the table conveyed the shock. The faces of the two old men hardened, both pairs of eyes boring into the Undersecretary, who accepted the looks with granite resignation. Finally, the ambassador spoke. 'When did this happen?'

'Ten days ago.'

'Why weren't we informed, Mr President?' continued Brooks, his eyes still on Bradford.

'Quite simply,' replied the Undersecretary before the President could speak, his eyes locked with the statesman's, 'because *I* wasn't informed.'

'I find that unacceptable.'

'Intolerable,' added the old soldier sharply. 'What the hell are you running over there?'

'An extremely efficient organization that responds to input. In this case, perhaps too efficient, too responsive.'

'Explain that,' ordered Halyard.

'These four men,' said Bradford, gesturing at the projectd photographs of the dead strategists, 'were convinced beyond doubt that the Karras woman was killed at Costa Brava. How could they think otherwise? We played everything out – *carried* everything out – down to the smallest detail. Nothing was left to speculation; her death was witnessed by Havelock, later confirmed by bloodstained clothing. We wanted it accepted and no one questioned it, least of all Havelock himself.'

'But she surfaced,' insisted Halyard. 'You say he *saw* her. I presume that information was in Colonel Baylor's cable.'

'Yes.'

'Then why wasn't it reported immediately?' demanded Brooks.

'Because they didn't believe it,' answered Bradford. 'They thought Havelock was crazy – hallucinating crazy, the real thing. They sent Ogilvie to Rome, which in itself was extraordinary, indicating how serious they considered the situation to be. Baylor confirmed it. He said Ogilvie told him Havelock had gone over the edge, seeing things that weren't there, the hallucinations brought on by deep, latent hostilities and years of pressure. He simply exploded; at least that's what Ogilvie implied.'

'That'd be Miller's judgement,' interrupted the President. 'It's the only one he could have arrived at when you think of it.'

'Havelock's behaviour deteriorated rapidly,' continued the Undersecretary. 'He threatened to expose past and present covert operations, which would have compromised us all over Europe, if he wasn't given answers, explanations. He even sent disrupting cables to show what he could do. The strategists took him very seriously. Ogilvie was in Rome either to bring Havelock back . . . or to kill him.'

'Instead, he was killed himself,' said the soldier. A statement.

'Tragically. Colonel Baylor was covering Ogilvie's meeting with Havelock on the Palatine Hill; it was an isolated area. There was an argument, a premature eruption of nerve gas triggered by Ogilvie and, when the device failed, Havelock went after him with a gun. As Baylor tells it, he waited until he couldn't wait any longer. He fired at the precise moment he believed Havelock was about to kill Ogilvie, and apparently he was right. Ogilvie must have felt the same thing; at that same moment he lunged up and caught the bullet. It's all in Baylor's report, available to you both, of course.'

'Those were the acceptable circumstances, Mr President?' asked Brooks.

'Only in terms of explanation, Addison.'

'Naturally,' said Halyard, nodding, looking at Bradford. 'If those are Larry Baylor's words, I don't need the report. How's he taking it? That buck doesn't like to lose or goof up.'

'He was severely wounded in his right hand. It was shattered and may not come back. Naturally, it'll curtail his activities.'

'Don't wash him out; it'd be a mistake. Put him behind a field desk.'

'I'll recommend that to the Pentagon, General.'

'Let's get back to the Cons Op strategists,' said the statesman. 'It's still not clear to me why they didn't report Colonel Baylor's information, especially the reasons behind Havelock's actions – those "disrupting cables", I believe you called them. Incidentally, how disrupting were they?'

'"Alarming" is a better word; "false-alarming" better still. One message came here – in a recent sixteen-hundred priority cipher – stating that there was a deep-cover Soviet agent in the White House. Another was sent to Congressional Oversight; it claimed there was CIA corruption in Amsterdam. In both instances the use of the cipher and naming names in Amsterdam obviously lent authority to the data.'

'Any substance?' asked the soldier.

'None whatsoever. But the reactions were volatile. The strategists knew they could get worse.'

'All the more reason why they should have reported Havelock's motives,' insisted Brooks.

'They may have,' answered Bradford softly. 'To someone. We'll get to that.'

'Why were they killed? What is their connection to Parsifal?' The general lowered his voice. 'To Costa Brava?'

'There was no "Costa Brava" until we invented it, Mal,' said the President. 'But that, too, has to be told in sequence. It's the only way we can make sense out of it . . . if there *is* any sense.'

'It never should have happened,' interjected the silver-haired statesman. 'We had no right.'

'We had no *choice*, Mr Ambassador,' said Bradford, leaning forward. 'Secretary of State Matthias built the case against the Karras woman; we know that. His objective, as near as we can determine, was to remove Havelock from service, but we could never be certain. Their friendship was strong, going back years, their family ties stronger, reaching back to Prague. Was Havelock part of Matthias's plans or not? Was a willing player following orders, pretending to do what others would call perfectly understandable, or was he the unknowing victim of a terrible manipulation? We had to find out.'

'We *did* find out,' protested Addison Brooks quietly, indignantly. 'At the clinic in Virginia. He was probed with everything doctors and laboratories can probe with; he knew absolutely nothing. As you said, we were back to the original scenario, completely in the dark ourselves. Why did Matthias want him out? It's the unanswered, perhaps now unanswerable, question. When we understood that, we should have told Havelock the truth.'

'We couldn't.' The Undersecretary leaned back in the chair. 'Jenna Karras had disappeared; we had no idea whether she was alive or dead. Under the circumstances Havelock would have raised questions that cannot be raised outside the Oval Office – or a room like this.'

'Questions,' added the President of the United States, 'which, if exposed, would plunge the world into a global nuclear war in a matter of hours. If the Soviet Union or the People's Republic of China knew this government was out of control, ICBMs would be launched from both hemispheres, a thousand submarines poised in both oceans for secondary tactical strikes – obliteration. And we *are* out of control.'

Silence.

'There's someone I'd like you to meet,' said Bradford finally. 'I had him flown in from an Alpine pass called Col des Moulinets. He's from Rome.'

'Nuclear war,' whispered the President as he pressed the button on the huge, curved desk and the screen went dark.

16

Havelock drew two lines through the seventeenth and eighteenth names on the list, hung up the telephone on the wall and left the shabby café in Montmartre. Two calls per phone were all he permitted himself. Sophisticated electronic scanners could pick up a location in a matter of minutes and, should any of those he reached be patched into equipment at the American embassy, it would be no different from his calling the Paris conduit of Cons Op and setting the time for his own execution. Two calls per phone, each phone a minimum of six blocks from the previous one, no conversation lasting more than ninety seconds. He had worked through half the list, but now the rest of the names would have to wait. It was nearly nine o'clock, the gaudy lights of Montmartre were battering the streets with frenzied eruptions of colour that matched the frantic cacophony of the district's night-time revels. And he was to meet Gravet in an alley off the rue Norvins. The art critic had spent the afternoon tracking down anyone and everyone in his peculiar world who might have knowledge of Jenna Karras.

In a way, so had Michael, but his initial work had been cerebral. He had retrieved his clothes from a *Métro* locker, purchased basic toiletries, a note pad and a ballpoint pen and taken a room at a cheap hotel around the corner from *La Couronne Nouvelle*. He reasoned that if the wounded VKR officer raised help, he would not think to send his killers down the street for the target. Havelock had shaved and bathed, and now lay on the decrepit bed, his body enjoying a respite but not his mind. He had gone back in time, disciplining his memory, recalling every moment he and Jenna had shared in Paris. He had approached the exercise academically, as a graduate student might doggedly follow a single development chronologically through a chaotic period in history. He and Jenna, Jenna and he; where they had gone, what they had seen, whom they had spoken with, all in order of sequence. Each place and scene had a location and a reason for their being there; finally, each face that had any meaning had a name, or if not a specific name, the identity of someone who knew him or her.

After two hours and forty minutes of probing, he had sat up, reached for the notepad and pen he had placed on a bedside chair and begun his list. A half hour later it was complete – as complete as his memory permitted – and he relaxed, back on the bed, knowing that much-needed sleep would come, knowing also that the clock in his mind would awaken him when daylight faded. It did. And minutes later he was out in the streets, going from one telephone box to another, one café with a *téléphone* sign in the window to the next, each instrument six blocks away from the last.

He began the conversations quickly but casually, and kept his ears primed to pick up any telltale signs of alarm in the responses. In each case his approach was the same; he was to have met Jenna that noon at the Meurice bar, each having flown into Paris from a different city, but his plane had been hours late. And since Jenna had mentioned the person's name frequently – fondness implied – Michael wondered if she had called him or her, perhaps looking for an afternoon companion in a city she barely knew.

Most were mildly surprised to hear from Havelock, especially so casually, and even more surprised that Jenna Karras would have remembered their names, much less having recalled them with affection; they were by and large only brief acquaintances. However, in no instance was there the slightest hesitation other than the normal caution required when confronted with the unexpected. Eighteen names. Nothing. Where had she gone? What was she doing? She could not go underground in Paris, not without his finding her; she had to know that. *Christ, where are you?*

He reached the rue Ravignan and began the steep ascent up the Montmartre hill, passing the dark, old houses that were once the homes of legends, emerged on the small square that was the Place Clément and started down the rue Norvins. The street was crowded, the revels of would-be Bohemians fuelled by the genuine residents who dressed their roles and later went home to count their profits. The alley Gravet had described was just before the narrow rue des Saules; he could see the break in the row of ancient buildings up ahead and walked faster.

The old brick alleyway was dark and empty. Havelock went in, his right hand instinctively edging towards the break in his jacket and belt where the Magnum was awkwardly in place. Gravet was late, a discourtesy the critic himself found abhorrent. What had happened?

Michael found a shadowed doorway in the dimly lit thoroughfare; he leaned against the brick frame, took out a cigarette and struck a match. As he cupped the flame his mind leaped back to the Palatine Hill, to a book of matches and a man who had tried to save his life, not take it. A dying man who had died only moments later, knowing there was betrayal at the highest levels of his government.

There was a sudden commotion out in the rue Norvins, a brief flare-up of tempers as two men collided. Then a tall, slender man stood momentarily erect, and let forth a stream of invective in French. His much younger, stockier adversary made a sullen comment about the man's ancestry and moved along. The injured party smoothed his lapels, turned to his left and entered the alley. Gravet had arrived, not without his customary *élan*.

'*Merde!*' the critic spat out, seeing Havelock walk out of the shadows into the dim light. 'It's those filthy, ragged field jackets they wear! You just know they dribble when they eat and their teeth are yellow. God knows when they last bathed or spoke civilly. Sorry to be late.'

'It's only a few minutes. I just got here.'

'I'm late. I intended to be in the rue Norvins a half hour ago to make sure you weren't followed.'

'I wasn't.'

'Yes, you'd know that, wouldn't you?'

'I'd know. What kept you?'

'A young man I've cultivated who works in the catacombs of the Quai d'Orsay.'

'You're honest.'

'And you misinterpret.' Gravet moved to the wall, turning his head back and forth, looking at both entrances of the alley; he was satisfied. He clasped his hands below his waist, arms extended, a balletic priest about to issue a priestly admonition. 'Since you called after your business at the *Couronne Nouvelle* – a call, incidentally, I wasn't sure you'd ever make – I've been in touch with every conceivable contact who might know something about a lone woman in Paris looking for sanctuary, or papers, or secret transportation, and no one could help. It was really quite illogical; after all there are only so many sources of illegal machinations, and precious few I'm not aware of. I even checked the Italian districts, thinking her escorts from Col des Moulinets might have provided her with a name or two. Nothing . . . Then it occurred to me. *Illegal* efforts? Perhaps I was searching in the wrong areas. Perhaps, instead, such a woman might seek more legitimate assistance, without necessarily detailing her illegitimate reasons. After all, she was an experienced field operative. She had to know – or know of – certain personnel in allied governments if only through you.'

'The Quai d'Orsay.'

'*Naturellement.* But the undersides, the catacombs, where distinctly unpublicized conveniences had to exist for you.'

'If they did, I'm not aware of them. I crossed paths with a number of people in the ministries but I never heard of the catacombs.'

'London's Foreign Office calls them Clearing Centres. Your own State Department refers to them less subtly. Division of Diplomatic Transfers.'

'Immunity,' said Havelock. 'Did you find something?'

'My young friend spent the last several hours tracing it down. I told him the timing was advantageously narrow. If anything happened, it could only have happened today. So he returned to his little cave after the dinner hour on some pretext or other and riffled through the day's security duplicates. He thinks he may have found it, but he can't be certain and neither can I. However, you might be able to make the connection.'

'What is it?'

'At ten forty-five this morning there was a memorandum from the *Ministère des Affaires Etrangères* ordering an open identity. Subject: white female, early thirties, languages: Czech, Russian, Serbo-Croatian, cover name and statistics requested immediately. Now, I realize there are dozens –'

'What section at the ministry?' interrupted Havelock.

'Four. Section Four.'

'Régine Broussac,' said Havelock. 'Madame Régine Broussac. First Assistant Deputy, Section Four.'

'That's the connection. It's the name and signature on the request.'

'She's twenty-ninth on my list, twenty-ninth out of thirty-one. We saw her – *I* saw her – for less than a minute on the street almost a year ago. I barely introduced Jenna. It doesn't make sense; she hardly knows her, *doesn't* know her.'

'Were the circumstances of your seeing her a year ago notable?'

'I suppose so. One of their people was a double agent at the French embassy in Bonn; he made periodic flights to the East by way of Luckenwalde. We found him on the wrong side of Berlin. At a meeting of the *Nachrichtgeheimdienst*'.

'The Moscow puppet's offspring of the SS. I'd say quite notable.' Gravet paused, unfolding his hands. 'This Broussac. She's an older woman, isn't she? Years ago a heroine of the *Résistance*?'

'She and her husband, yes. He was taken by the Gestapo; what they found of him wasn't pleasant.'

'But she carried on.'

'Yes.'

'Did you, perhaps, tell any of this to your friend?'

Havelock thought back as he drew on the cigarette, then dropped it, crushing it under foot. 'Probably. Régine's not always easy to take; she can be abrupt, caustic, some call her a bitch, but she's not. She *had* to be tough.'

'Then let me ask you another question, the answer to which I vaguely know, but it's based merely on rumour; nothing I've read that pretended to be official.' The critic folded his hands again. 'What prompted your friend to do what she did, to live the sort of life she led with you and, obviously, before you?'

'Nineteen-sixty-eight,' replied Havelock flatly.

'The Warsaw bloc invasion?'

'The *černý den* of August. The black days. Her parents had died, and she was living in Ostrava with her two older brothers, one married. Both were Dubček activists, the younger a student, the older an engineer who was forbidden any meaningful work by the Novotný regime. When the tanks rolled in, the younger brother was killed in the streets, the older one rounded up by advance Soviet troops for "interrogation". He was crippled for life – arms and legs – almost helpless. He blew his brains out and his wife disappeared. Jenna travelled to Prague, where no one knew her, and went underground. She knew whom to reach, what she wanted to do.'

Gravet nodded, his chiselled face drawn in the dim light, the lines deep. 'The people who do what you do, quietly, so efficiently, you all have different stories, yet common themes run through them. Violence, pain . . . loss. And genuine revenge.'

'What did you expect? Only ideologues can afford to shout; we've generally got other things on our minds. It's why we're sent in first. It doesn't take much to make us efficient.'

'Or to recognize one another, I imagine.'

'Under certain circumstances, yes. We don't make too much of it. What's your point?'

'The Broussac woman. Your friend from the Costa Brava would remember her. A husband, brothers, pain, loss . . . a woman alone. Such a woman would remember . . . another woman . . . who carried on.'

'She obviously did, I just wouldn't have thought so.' Havelock nodded silently. 'You're right,' he said quietly. 'Thanks for giving it perspective. Of course she would.'

'Be careful, Michael.'

'Of what?'

'Genuine revenge. There must be a *sympathie* between them. She could turn you over to your own, trap you.'

'I'll be careful; so will she. What else can you tell me about the memorandum? Was a destination mentioned?'

'No, she could be going anywhere. That will be fixed at *Etrangères* and kept quiet.'

'What about her cover? A name?'

'That was processed and beyond my young friend's eyes, at least this evening. Perhaps tomorrow he can pry into files that are locked tonight.'

'Too late. You said the memorandum asked for an immediate response. That passport's been mocked up and issued. She's on her way out of France. I have to move quickly.'

'What's one day? Twelve hours from now perhaps we can find a name. You can call the airlines on an emergency basis and they'll check their manifests. You'll know where she's gone.'

'But not how.'

'*Je ne comprends pas.*'

'Broussac. If she's done this much for Jenna, she'll do more. She wouldn't leave her on her own at an airport somewhere. Arrangements were made. I have to know what they are.'

'And you think she'll tell you?'

'She must.' Havelock buttoned his loose-fitting jacket and pulled the lapels up around his neck. The alley was a tunnel for the damp breezes from below, and there was a chill. 'One way or the other, she has to tell me. Thanks, Gravet, I owe you.'

'Yes, you do.'

'I'll see Broussac tonight and leave in the morning . . . one way or the other. But before I go, there's a bank here in Paris where I've got a safety deposit box; I'll clean it out and leave an envelope for you there. Call it part payment. It's the Banque Germaine on the Avenue Georges Cinq.'

'You're most considerate, but is it wise? In all modesty, I'm something of a public figure and must be careful in my associations. Someone there might know you.'

'Not by any name you've ever heard of.'

'Then what name shall I use?'

'None. Just say the "gentleman from Texas"; he's left an envelope for you. If it makes you feel any better, say you've never met me. I'm negotiating the purchase of a painting for an anonymous buyer in Houston.'

'And if there are complications?'

'There won't be. You know where I'm going tonight, and by extension, tomorrow.'

'At the last, we're professionals, aren't we, Michael?'

'I wouldn't have it any other way. It's cleaner.' Havelock extended his hand. 'Thanks again. You know the help you've been. I won't belabour it.'

'You can forget about the envelope, if you like,' said Gravet, shaking hands, studying Michael's face in the shadows. 'You may need the money, and my expenses were minimal. I can always collect on your next trip to Paris.'

'Don't change the rules, we've lived too long by them. But I appreciate the vote of confidence.'

'You were always civilized, and I don't understand any of this business. Why her? Why you?'

'I wish to God I knew.'

'That's the key, isn't it? Something you *do* know.'

'If it is, I haven't the vaguest idea of what it could be. Goodbye, Gravet.'

'*Au 'voir*. I really don't want the envelope, *Mikhail*. Come back to Paris. You owe me.' The distinguished critic turned and disappeared up the alley.

There was no point in being evasive with Régine Broussac; she would sense the evasion instantly, the coincidence of timing being too unbelievable. On the other hand, to give her the advantage of naming the rendezvous was equally foolish; she would stake out the area with personnel the Quai d'Orsay had no idea were on its payroll. Broussac was tough, knowing when and when not to involve her government, and depending upon what Jenna had told her, she might consider any dealings with an unbalanced retired American field officer more suited to treatment by unofficial methods. There were no checks and balances in those methods; they were dangerous because there was no line of responsibility, only diverted monies that no one cared to acknowledge. Drones by any other names or payments were first cousins to the practitioners of violence – whether employed by Rome in Col des Moulinets or by a VKR officer in a cheap hotel on the rue Etienne. All were essentially lethal, it was merely a question of degree, and all should be avoided unless one was the employer. Havelock understood; he had to get Broussac alone, and to do that, he had to persuade her he was not dangerous – to her – and might even have information that could be extraordinarily valuable.

An odd thought struck him as he descended the endless steps of Montmartre. He was talking to himself about the truth. He would tell her part of it, but not all of it. Liars twisted the truth and she might listen to their version of it, not his.

She was in the Paris telephone book. Rue Losserand.

'. . . I've never given you wrong information and I'm not going to start tonight. But it's out of sanction. Way out. To judge just how far, use someone else's name at the Quai d'Orsay and call the embassy. Ask about my status, directing the inquiry to the senior attaché of Consular Operations. Say I called you from somewhere in the south and wanted to set up a meeting. As an official of a friendly government, request instructions. I'll call you back in ten minutes, not on this phone, of course.'

'Of course. Ten minutes.'

'Régine?'

'Yes?'

'Remember Bonn.'

'Ten minutes.'

Havelock walked south to Berlioz Square, checking his watch frequently, knowing he would add an additional five to seven minutes beyond the stated ten. Stretching a call-back under tension often exposed more than the recipient intended to reveal. There was a *cabine* on the corner, a young woman inside screaming into the phone, gesturing frantically. In a fit of temper, she slammed down the receiver and stalked out of the booth.

'*Vache!*' exclaimed the angry girl as she passed Havelock, furiously adjusting the shoulder strap of her large bag.

He opened the door and walked in; the extended stretch-time had reached nine minutes. He made the call and listened.

'Yes?' Broussac's voice broke off the first ring. She was anxious; she had reached the embassy.

'Did you speak to the attaché?'

'You're late. You said ten minutes.'

'Did you speak to him?'

'Yes. I'll meet you. Come to my flat as soon as you can.'

'Sorry. I'll call you back in a little while.'

'*Havelock!*'

He hung up and walked out of the box, his eyes scanning the street for a vacant taxi.

Twenty-five minutes later he was in another *cabine*, the numbers indistinguishable in the shadows. He struck a match and dialled.

'*Yes!*'

'Take the *Métro* to the Bercy station and walk up into the street. Several blocks down on the right is a row of warehouses. I'll be in the area. Come alone, because I'll know if you don't. And if you don't, I won't show.'

'This is *ridiculous*! A lone woman at night in Bercy!'

'If there's anyone around at this hour, I'll warn him about you.'

'Preposterous! What are you *thinking* of?'

'A year ago in another street,' said Michael. 'Of Bonn.' He lowered the phone into the cradle.

The area was deserted, the row of warehouses dark, the street lights dim, the wattage low by municipal decree. It was a favourable hour and location for a drop that entailed more than a pick up or an exchange of merchandise. A conversation could be held without the din of crowded streets or the jostling of impatient pedestrians, and unlike a café or a city park, there were few places where an unknown observer could conceal himself. The few residents who emerged from the lighted cavern of the *Métro* up the street could be watched, hesitation or sudden disappearance noted; a stray car could be seen blocks away. The complete advantage was found, of course, in being there at the rendezvous before it was established. He was; he left the box and started across the Boulevard de Bercy.

Two trucks were parked, one behind the other at the kerb in front of a loading platform. Their open planked carriers were empty, stationary symbols of an early morning call for the drivers. He would wait between the two vehicles, the sightlines in either direction clear. Régine Broussac would come; the agitated huntress, prodded and provoked, would be unable to resist the unexplained.

Eleven separate times he heard the muted rumble of the underground trains and felt the vibrations in the concrete and earth beneath him. Starting with the sixth, he concentrated on the *Métro*'s entrance; she could not have arrived before it did. However, radio dispatch was commonplace and rapid; only minutes after his final call he had begun to study the street, the infrequent cars, the less frequent bicycles. He saw nothing that alarmed him, and the most insignificant intrusion would have done so.

The twelfth rumble stopped, the faint vibrations still echoing underfoot, and by the time the below-ground thunder commenced again he could see her climbing up out of the steps; her short, broad figure emerging from the brighter light into the dimly lit street. A couple preceded her; Michael watched them carefully. They were elderly, older than Broussac, their pace slow and deliberate; they would be of no value to her. They turned left, around the squared iron latticework of the entrance and away from the trucks and warehouses; they were no part of a night unit. Régine continued forward, with the hesitant stride of an apprehensive older woman aware of her vulnerability, her head turning slowly, reluctantly, at each odd noise, real and imagined. She passed under a street light and Havelock remembered; her skin was as grey as her short-cropped hair, testimony to years of unacknowledged torments, yet her face was softened by wide blue eyes as often expressive as they were clouded. As she passed through the light into the shadows, Gravet's words came back to Havelock: '*Violence, pain, loss*'. Régine Broussac had lived through it all and survived – quiet, wary, silently tough and in no way beaten. She revelled in the secret, unseen powers her government had given her; it helped her get even. Michael understood; after all, she was one of them. A survivor.

She came alongside him on the pavement. He called out softly from between the trucks. 'Régine.'

She stopped, standing motionless, her eyes straight ahead, not looking at him. She said, 'Is it necessary to hold a weapon on me?'

'I have no gun aimed at you. I have a gun, but it's not in my hand.'

'*Bien!*' Broussac spun around, her handbag raised. An explosion blew a hole through the fabric, and the concrete and stone shattered beneath Havelock's feet, fragments of rock and cement piercing his trousers, scraping his flesh. 'For what you did to Jenna *Karras!*' shouted the woman, her grey face contorted. 'Do not move! One step, one gesture, and I will put a hole in your throat!'

'What are you *doing*?'

'What have you *done*? Who do you work for *now*?'

'*Myself*, goddamn you! Myself and *Jenna!*' Havelock raised his hand, an instinctive move, but no less a plea. It was not accepted.

A second explosion came from the shattered bag, the bullet grazing his outer palm, ricocheting off the truck's metal, whining out into the night.

'*Arrêtez!* I'd as soon deliver a corpse as a breathing body. Perhaps more so in your case, *cochon*.'

'Deliver to whom?'

'You said you would call me "in a little while" – were they not your words? Well, in a little while several colleagues of mine will be here, a time span I was willing to risk. In less than thirty minutes you would have felt secure; you would have shown yourself. When they arrive we'll drive to a house out in the countryside where we shall have a session with you. Then we'll give you to the Gabriel. They want you very badly. They called you dangerous, that's all I had to know . . . with what I knew.'

'Not to *you*! I'm dangerous to *them*, not you!'

'What do you take me for? Take *us* for?'

'You saw Jenna. You helped her – '

'I saw her. I listened to her. I heard the truth.'

'As she believes it, not as it *is*! Hear *me*! Listen to *me*!'

'You'll talk under the proper conditions. You know what they are as well as I do.'

'I don't need chemicals, you bitch! You won't hear anything different!'

'We'll follow procedures,' said Broussac, removing her hand and the gun from the ruptured bag. Move out of there,' she continued, gesturing with the weapon. 'You're standing in the shadows. I don't like it.'

Of course she didn't like it, thought Havelock, watching the old woman blink her eyes. As with many ageing people night was no friend to vision. It accounted for her constantly moving head as she walked away from the lighted entrance of the *Métro*; she had been as concerned with the unexpected shadows as with sounds. He had to keep her talking, direct some part of her concentration.

'You think the American embassy will tolerate what you're doing?' said Michael, stepping out of the patterned shadow created by the slats of the open truck and the spill of the street lamps.

'There'll be no international incident; we had no alternative but to sedate you. In their words, you're dangerous.'

'They won't accept that and you know it.'

'They'll have little choice. The Avenue Gabriel has been alerted that a situation of extreme abnormality exists in which a former American intelligence officer – a specialist in clandestine activities – may be attempting to compromise an official of the Quai d'Orsay. The anticipated confrontation will take place twenty miles from Paris, near Argenteuil, and the Americans are requested to have a vehicle with armed personnel in the vicinity. A radio frequency has been established. We shall turn over an American problem to the Americans once we learn the nature of the extortion. We protect the interests of our government. Perfectly acceptable, even generous.'

'Christ, you're thorough.'

'Very. I've known men like you. And women; we used to shave their heads. I despise you.'

'Because of what she told you?'

'Like you, I know when I've heard the truth. She did not lie.'

'I agree. Because she believes it all – just as I did. And I was wrong – *God*, was I wrong – just as she's wrong now. We were used, both of us *used*.'

'By your own people? For what purpose?'

'I don't *know!*'

She was listening, her concentration beginning to split. She could not help herself, the unexplored was too compelling.

'Why do you think I reached you?' he asked. 'For Christ's sake, if I had the leverage to find you, I could have by-passed you! I don't need you, Régine. I could have learned what I wanted to learn without you. I called you because I trusted you!'

Broussac blinked, the grey flesh around her eyes wrinkling in thought. 'You'll have your chance to talk . . . under the proper conditions.'

'Don't do this!' cried Michael, taking a short step forward. She did not fire; she did not move her gun. 'You've set it in motion; you'll have to turn me over! They know it's me and you'll be forced to. Your friends'll insist. They're not going to go down with you, no matter what you hear from me – under proper conditions!'

'Why should we go down?'

'Because the embassy is being lied to. By people way the hell up!'

The old woman's eyes now blinked rapidly as she flinched. She had not fired when he moved only seconds ago.

Now!

Havelock lunged forward, his right arm extended, rigid, as straight as an iron bar, his left hand under his wrist. He made contact with the gun, sweeping it aside as a third explosion broke the silence of the deserted street. With his left hand he grabbed the barrel and ripped it out of her grip, then slammed her against the wall of the warehouse.

'*Cochon! Traître!*' screamed Broussac, her grey face twisted. '*Kill* me! You'll learn nothing from me!'

In agony from the wound in his shoulder he held his forearm across her throat, and pressed her head back into the brick, the weapon in his hand. 'What I want can't be forced from you, Régine,' he said gasping for breath. 'Don't you understand? It has to be given.'

'*Nothing!* Which *terroristes* bought you? Meinhof cowards? Arab pigs? Israeli fanatics? *Brigate Rosse?* Who wants what you can sell? . . . She knew. She found out! And you must kill her! Kill me first, *betrayer!*'

Slowly Havelock released the pressure of his arm and, slower still, he moved his body away from hers. He knew the risk; he did not take it lightly. On the other hand, he knew Régine Broussac. After all, she was one of them; she had survived. He removed his arm and stood in front of her, his eyes steady, looking into hers.

'I've betrayed no one except myself,' he began. 'And through myself a person I love very much. I meant what I said. I can't force you to tell me what I have to know. Among other things, you could lie to me too easily, too successfully, and I'd be back where I was ten days ago. I won't do that. If I can't find her, if I can't have her back, perhaps it doesn't matter. I know what I did and it's killing me. I love her . . . I need her. I think we both need each other more than anything else in the world just now. We're all each other has left. But I've learned something about futility over the years.' He raised the gun in his left hand, taking the barrel with his right. He held it out to her. 'You've fired three times; there are four shells left.'

Broussac stood still, staring at him, studying his face, his eyes. She took the weapon and levelled it at his head, her own eyes questioning, roaming his. Finally her grimacing features softened, astonishment replacing hostility. Slowly she lowered the gun.

'*Déraisonnable,*' she whispered. 'This is the truth, then.'

'The truth.'

Régine looked at her watch. '*Vite!* We must leave. They'll be here in minutes; they'll search everywhere.'

'Where to? There are no taxis – '

'The *Métro*. We'll take it to the Rochereau. There's a small park where we can talk.'

'What about your team? What'll you tell them?'

'That I was testing their alertness,' she said taking his arm as they started up the pavement towards the lighted entrance leading to the underground trains. 'That I wanted to see how they would react in a given situation. It's consistent: it's late, they're off duty and I'm a bitch.'

'You've still got the embassy.'

'I know, I was thorough. I'll have to think about that.'

'Maybe I never showed up,' said Havelock, rubbing his shoulder, grateful that the pain was receding.

'*Merci.*'

The pocket handkerchief park in Denfert Rochereau was a plot of grass dotted with stone benches, sculptured trees and a gravelled path circling a small pool with a fountain in its centre. The only source of light was a street lamp thirty feet away, its spill filtered by the branches of the trees. They sat beside each other on the cold bench. Michael told Broussac what he had seen – and what he had not seen – at the Costa Brava. He then had to ask the question. 'Did she tell you what happened?'

'She was warned, told to follow instructions.'

'By whom?'

'A high government official from Washington.'

'How could she accept him?'

'He was brought to her by a man identified as the senior attaché from Madrid's Consular Operations.'

'Consular . . . *Madrid?* Where was *I?*'

'Madrid.'

'*Jesus*, right down to the hour!'

'What was?'

'The whole goddamned thing. What instructions was she given?'

'To meet a man that night and leave Barcelona with him.'

'Did she?'

'No.'

'Why not?'

'She panicked. In her words, everything had collapsed for her. She didn't feel she could trust *anyone*. She ran.'

'Thank God. I don't know who was killed on that beach, but it was meant to be Jenna. In a way, it makes the whole thing even more obscene. Who was she? Someone who didn't know a damn thing? A woman brought there and told to chase a frisbee in the moonlight, suddenly shot at, knowing she was going to die. *Christ*, what kind of people *are* they?'

'Find out through Madrid. The attaché from Consular Operations.'

'I can't. She was fed another lie. There's no Cons Op unit in Madrid; the climate's too rotten. It operates an hour away out of Lisbon.'

Régine was silent, her eyes on him. 'What's happening, Michael?'

Havelock watched the fountain in the dark pool. Its cascading spray was diminishing, folding, dying; somewhere a hand was turning a dial, shutting it off for the remainder of the night. 'Liars are operating at very high places in my government. They've penetrated areas I used to think were impenetrable. They're controlling, killing – lying. And someone in Moscow is working with them.'

'*Moscow?* Are you sure?'

'I'm sure. On the word of a man who wasn't afraid to die, but was afraid of living the way I promised him he'd be forced to live. Someone in Moscow, someone the controllers of the KGB know nothing about, is in contact with the liars.'

'For what purpose. *You?* To destroy your credibility, then kill you? To avoid some recent accomplishment by maligning the record of a dead man?'

'It's not me; I'm only a part of it. I wasn't important before, but I am now.' Havelock turned his head and looked at old Broussac, her grey face now soft and compassionate, yet still ashen-dark in the dim light. 'Because I saw Jenna; because I found out she was alive. Now they have to kill me. They have to kill her, too.'

'*Why?* You were the best!'

'I don't know. I only know that the Costa Brava is where I have to look for answers. It's where it started for Jenna and me . . . where it was supposed to end. One of us dead, the other dying inside, finished. Out.'

'It is she who is dying inside now. It astonishes me that she can function as she does, move as she does. She's remarkable.' Régine paused. The fountain's spray had collapsed and only trickles of water dripped over its saucer-like basin into the pool. 'She loved you, you know.'

'Past tense?'

'Oh, yes. We all learn to accept new realities, don't we? We're better at it than most people because sudden change is an old acquaintance as well as our enemy. We constantly seek out betrayal in others; we preach it. And all the while we're being tested ourselves, our adversaries intent on seducing our minds and our appetites. Sometimes we succeed, sometimes they do. That's the reality.'

'The futility,' said Havelock.

'You are too much the *philosophe* for this business.'

'It's why I got out.' Michael looked away. 'I saw her face in the window of the plane in Col des Moulinets. Her eyes. Christ, it was awful.'

'I'm certain it was. It happens. Hatred replaces love, doesn't it? It's the only defence in these cases . . . She'll kill you if she can.'

'Oh God . . .' Havelock leaned forward on the bench, his elbows on his knees, hands cupped under his chin, staring at the dead fountain. 'I love her so. I loved her when I killed her that night, knowing a part of me would always be at that beach for the rest of my life, my eyes seeing her running, falling in the sand, my ears hearing her screams . . . wanting to race down and hold her, tell her the whole world was a *lie* and nothing mattered but us! Just *us* . . . Something inside me was trying to tell me that terrible things were being done to us, and I wouldn't listen . . . I was too hurt to listen to myself. I, I, *I! Me!* I couldn't get *me* out of the way and hear the truth she was screaming!'

'You were a professional in a professional crisis,' said Régine softly, touching his arm. 'According to everything you'd learned, everything you'd lived with for years, you were doing what you had to do. A professional.'

Michael turned his head and looked at her. 'Why wasn't I myself?' he asked simply. 'Why didn't I listen to the other screams, the ones I couldn't get out of my throat?'

'We can't always trust what we call instinct, Michael. You know that.'

'I know that I love her . . . loved her when I thought I hated her, when that professional in me expected to see her die because I'd closed the trap on an enemy. I didn't hate her, I loved her. Do you know why I know that?'

'Why, *mon cher?*'

'Because there was no satisfaction in winning, not the slightest. Only revulsion, only sadness . . . only wanting things to be the way they couldn't be.'

'That's when you got out, isn't it? It's what we'd heard, what I found so difficult to believe. I understand now. You loved her very much. I *am* sorry, Michael.'

Havelock shook his head, closing his eyes, the inner darkness comforting for a moment. 'In Barcelona,' he said, opening his eyes again, looking at the quiet pool in front of them, 'what happened to her? Tell me what she told you.'

'She can't understand what happened. Did the Russians actually buy you or did Washington order her execution? It's an enigma to her – a violent enigma. She got out of Spain and went to Italy, going from city to city, seeking out those few people she thought she could trust to help her, hide her. But always there were the questions: Where were *you*? Why was she alone and not with *you*? At first, she was afraid to say, and when she did no one believed her. Whenever she told the story and it was rejected, she felt she had to run again, convinced the few would reach you, and you would come after her. She lives with the nightmare that you're always there, following – hunting her down. And when she had settled briefly into a safe cover, a Russian appeared, someone you both knew in Prague, a KGB butcher. Coincidence? Who was to tell? She ran again, this time stealing a large sum of money from her employer.'

'I wondered about that. How she could buy her way out of Italy, get across the border and up into Paris. Compared with some other routes, she travelled first class.'

Broussac smiled, her blue eyes lively in the shadows, telling him that a brief moment of amusement was to follow. 'She laughed about it – quietly to be sure – but the laughter was good; that she could laugh was good, Michael. Do you see what I mean? For a moment or two she was like a little girl remembering a prank.'

'I hear her laughter in my sleep . . . when I don't hear her screams. Her laugh was always quiet, never loud, but somehow full . . . an echo from deep inside her. She loved to laugh; it was a release for her, something not usually permitted and therefore enjoyed so much more when it happened.' He paused, his eyes again on the still fountain. 'How did she steal the money? Where?'

'Milan.'

'The Russians are crawling all over Milan. Whoever she saw, it was a migratory coincidence . . . Sorry, what happened?'

'She was working in that enormous shop in the Piazza del Duomo, the one that sells books and magazines and newspapers from all over the world. Do you know it?'

'I've seen it.'

'Her languages got her the job, and she tinted her hair, wore glasses, all the usual things. But her figure also got her the undivided attention of the owner, a pig with a large wife he was terrified of and eight children. He was for ever asking her into his office and mauling her and promising her the *Galleria Vittorio* for her favours. One day at noon the Russian came in; she recognized him and knew she had to run; she was afraid that he was connected to you, that you were scouring Europe for her . . . At the lunch hour, she literally assaulted the manager in his office, claiming that she could no longer wait for *his* favours, and that only a small loan stood between them and absolute ecstasy. By this time she had her blouse off and the poor man's wallet under a chair. In a state of utter apoplexy, the idiot opened the safe where several days' receipts were stored – it was a Friday, if you recall.'

'Why should I?' interrupted Havelock.

'We'll get to that,' said Régine, a partial smile on her lips. 'Anyway, when the ageing, perspiring Lothario had the safe open and our Jenna was removing her brassiere, he counted out a few thousand lire in his quivering hands and she struck him on the head with a clock. She then proceeded to empty the safe, positively stunned by the amounts of money filling the bank deposit pouches. That money was her passport and she knew it.'

'It was also an invitation for a police hunt.'

'A hunt that could be delayed, the delay permitting her to get out of Milan.'

'How?'

'Fear, confusion and embarrassment,' replied Broussac. 'Jenna closed the safe, stripped the owner naked and marked him everywhere with streaks of lipstick. She then called his home and speaking to a maid, said an urgent matter required the man's wife to come to the shop in an hour, not before and not later.'

'Fear, confusion and embarrassment,' agreed Michael, nodding. 'She tapped him again, making sure he'd stay where he was, figuring he'd hardly rush to the safe in front of his wife, compounding the mess he was already in . . . And obviously, she took his clothes with her,' added Havelock, smiling, remembering the woman who was Jenna Karras.

'Obviously. She used the next several hours to gather her things together and, realizing that a police warrant would be issued sooner or later, removed the dye from her hair. She then joined the crowds at the Milan railway station.'

'The railway . . . ?' Michael sat back on the bench and looked at Régine. 'The train. She took the train to Rome! That's where I saw her!'

'It's a moment she'll never forget. There you were, standing there, staring at her. The man who had forced her into hiding, into running, who'd caused her to alter her appearance and change the sequence of her languages. The one person on earth she was terrified might find her, kill her . . . and there *she* was, all her disguise gone, recognized by the one she most feared.'

'If the shock hadn't been so paralysing, if only I'd been quicker . . . so much would have been so different.' Michael arched his neck back and brought his hands to his face, covering his eyes. 'Oh, *Christ*, we were so *close*! I yelled to her, I screamed and kept screaming, but she disappeared. I lost her in the crowds; she didn't hear me – she didn't *want* to hear me – and I lost her.' Havelock lowered his hands and gripped the edge of the stone bench. 'Civitavecchia came next. Did she tell you about that?'

'Yes. It was where she saw a crazed animal try to kill her on a pier – '

'It *wasn't* her! How could she think I thought it was? Jesus, a fucking whore from the docks!' Michael checked himself; it served no purpose to lose control.

'She saw what she saw,' said old Broussac quietly. 'She couldn't know what you were thinking.'

'How did she know I'd go to Civitavecchia? A man there told me she thought I'd question the taxi drivers. I didn't. There's a strike, although a few are running, I suppose.'

'There are, and you were the best of hunters. You yourself taught her that the surest way to get out of a country unseen is a busy waterfront in the early hours of the morning. There is always someone willing to broker space, if only in a cargo hold. She asked people on the train, pretending to be a Polish merchant seaman's wife, her husband on a freighter. People are not stupid; they understood; one more couple leaving the arms of the Bear. "Civitavecchia," they said. "Try Civitavecchia!" She assumed you might reach the same conclusion – based on what you'd taught her – and so she made her preparations. She was right; you arrived.'

'By a different route,' said Havelock. 'Because of a guard on the train who remembered a *bella ragazza*.'

'In any case, she assumed the possibility and acted on it, placing herself in a position to observe. As I said, she's remarkable. The strain, the pressures. To do what she did without panic, to mount the strategy alone . . . remarkable. I think you were a splendid teacher, Michael.'

'She had ten years of training before I met her. There was a lot she could teach me . . . and did. You gave her a cover and diplomatic clearance. Where did she go? What arrangements did you make?'

'How did you learn this?'

'Don't make me pay the price, I owe him. Instead, let me send him to you. Don't turn him in; use him for yourself. You won't regret it, but I need the guarantee.'

'Fair enough. Talent should be shared, and I respect the sender. I remember Bonn.'

'Where did she go?'

'Apart from a few remote islands in the Pacific, the safest place in the world for her now. The United States.'

Havelock stared in astonishment at the old woman. 'How did you deduce *that*?'

'I went back over the restricted cables from your State Department looking for any mention of Jenna Karras. Indeed, it was there. A single insertion dated 10 January, detailing briefly the events at the Costa Brava. She was described as an infiltrator caught in a reverse trap in which she had lost her life, her death confirmed by two separate sightings and forensic examination of bloodstained clothing. The file was closed to the satisfaction of Consular Operations.'

'The rotes have it,' said Michael. 'Aye, aye, sir. Next case, please.'

'The implausibility was glaring, of course. Sightings can be erroneous, but a forensic laboratory must work with materials. Yet they couldn't have, not with any legitimacy. Not only was Jenna Karras very much alive and sitting in my office, but she had never gone to that beach on the Costa Brava. The forensic confirmation was a lie, and someone must know it, someone who wanted the lie accepted as the truth.' Broussac paused. 'I assumed it was you. Termination carried out, execution as scheduled. If you had been bought by the Russians, what better proof could they have than the Department of State? If you had been carrying out Washington's instructions, you could not allow them to think you had failed.'

'In the light of what she told you, I can understand.'

'But I wasn't satisfied; the acceptance was too simple, so I looked farther. I went to the data-processing computers and placed her name in the security scanner relating to the past three months ... It was extraordinary. She appeared no less than twelve times, but never on State Department communiqués. It was always on cables from the Central Intelligence Agency, and couched in very odd language. And always the same, cable after cable: the US government had an alert out for a woman matching her description who *might* be using the name of Karras – but it was third or fourth on a list of a half dozen *false* names. It was a highly classified search, but obviously an intense one, the widest co-operation sought. It was strange, almost amateurish. As though one branch of your intelligence community did not want the other to know what it was doing.'

'That didn't exonerate me?'

'On the contrary. You had been found out, the lie had been exposed.'

'Then why wasn't there an alert out for *me*?'

'There was, is. As of five days ago.'

Five days, thought Havelock. The Palatine. 'But you weren't aware of it.'

'Those in the Quai d'Orsay who've listed you as an American liaison knew of it, and in time it would have crossed my desk as a matter of routine. However, neither you nor I have ever listed each other in our reports. That was the understanding between us.'

'It served the purpose. Is the alert specific? Am I given a label?'

'No. Only that it is imperative that you should be located – as a matter of internal security. Again, I presumed: you had been exposed, either as a defector or as someone who had lied to his superiors and disappeared. It really didn't matter which. Because of Jenna Karras, you were the enemy in either case. It was confirmed for me when I called the embassy.'

'I forgot. I'm dangerous.'

'You are. To someone. I checked with London, Brussels, Amsterdam and Bonn. Both alerts have been circulated, both highest priority, but not connected.'

'You still haven't answered the question. Why did you send her to the States?'

'I just did answer you; you weren't listening. The search for her – and now you – is centred in Europe. Rome, the Mediterranean, Paris, London ... Bonn. The curve is arching north, the destination presumed to be the Eastern bloc. This is the line of progress they're concentrating on, where their agents have fanned out, pulling in sources and contacts. They won't think to look in their own barnyard.'

'Back yard,' said Michael absently.

'Que'est-ce que c'est?'

'C'est américain. Peu importe. When did she leave?'

'Three-thirty this afternoon ... yesterday afternoon now. Air France to

New York, diplomatic status, cover name drawn from a dead file – unblemished, of course.'

'And unknown.'

'Yes, it's not relevant. It will be changed.'

'What are the arrangements?'

'She's to see a man; no doubt she's already seen him. *He* will make the arrangements, and it is our policy never to inquire what they are. You have the same sort of men over here – in Paris, London, Amsterdam, wherever. They do not speak with us directly.'

'The landlords of the halfway houses,' said Havelock, 'guiding the people we send them into safe territory, providing identities, papers, families to live with, the towns and cities chosen carefully. We make our payments through blind conduits, and after contact we're not involved. We've never heard of them; ignorance is the order of the day. But there's another side, too, isn't there? We don't really know what happens to those people, do we?'

'With safe transfer, our obligations are fulfilled. They ask no more and we offer no more; that's always been the understanding between us. I, for one, have never been curious.'

'I'm not *curious*, Régine, I'm going out of my mind! She's in sight now, I can find her! I *can find her*! For Christ's sake, help me! Who did you send her to?'

'You ask a great deal, Michael. You're asking me to violate a confidence I've sworn never to break. I could lose a valuable man.'

'I could lose *her*! Look at me! Tell me I wouldn't do the same for you! If it was your husband and I was there and the Gestapo came for him, look at me and tell me I wouldn't *help* you!'

Broussac closed her eyes briefly, as if struck. 'The reference is unkind but not without truth. You and he were much alike . . . Yes, you would have helped.'

'Get me out of Paris. Right away. *Please!*'

Régine was silent for a moment, her eyes again roaming his face. 'It would be better if you did so yourself. I know you can.'

'It could take me days! I'd have to route myself through a back door in Mexico or Montreal. I can't lose the time. With every hour she's farther away. You know what can happen. She could get swallowed up, moving from one circle into the next, no one telling anyone anything. She could disappear and I'd never find her!'

'Very well. Tomorrow, the noon flight on Concorde. You'll be French, a member of the United Nations delegation. Flush the papers down a toilet the minute you're at Kennedy.'

'Thanks. Now for the halfway man. Who is he?'

'I'll get word to him but he may choose to tell you nothing.'

'Get word to him. Who is he?'

'A man named Handelman. Jacob Handelman. Columbia University.'

17

The man with a single strip of surgical tape on each cheek sat at the small table below the curved dais in the underground strategy room of the White House. The flesh on his square face was taut, held in place by the suture beneath the brown adhesive; the effect was robotlike, macabre. His replies in a subdued monotone to the questions put to him heightened the image of a man not totally whole, yet overcontrolled. In truth, he was afraid; the agent-of-record from Col des Moulinets would have been more afraid thirty-five minutes before, when the panel of men facing him was complete. There had been four men then; now there were only three. The President had removed himself. He was observing the proceedings from an unseen cubicle behind the platform, through a pane of coated glass that was part of the inner wall and indistinguishable from it. Words were being said in that room which could not be said in his presence; he could not bear witness to orders of dispatch at an Alpine pass, and prior communications which included the phrase 'beyond-salvage'.

The interrogation was at midpoint, Undersecretary of State Emory Bradford probing the salient points while Ambassador Brooks and General Halyard made notes on their pads under the harsh glares of the Tensor lamps.

'Let me get this clear,' said Bradford. 'You were the field officer-of-record and the only one in contact with Rome. Is that correct?'

'Yes sir.'

'And you're absolutely certain no other member of the unit was in touch with the embassy?'

'Yes, sir. No, sir. I was the only channel. It's standard, not only for the security blackout, but to make sure there's no foul-up in the orders. One man transmits them, one man receives them.'

'Yet you say Havelock referred to two of the unit's personnel as explosives specialists, a fact you were not aware of.'

'I wasn't.'

'But as the field officer-of-record . . .'

'Agent-of-record, sir.'

'Sorry. As the *agent*-of-record shouldn't you have known?'

'Normally, I would have.'

'But you didn't and the only explanation you can give us is that this new recruit, a Corsican named Ricci, hired the two men in question.'

'It's the only reason I can think of. If Havelock was right; if he wasn't lying.'

'The reports from Col des Moulinets stated that there were numerous explosions in the vicinity of the bridge's entrance at the time.' Bradford scanned a typewritten page in front of him. 'Including a massive detonation in the road which occurred approximately twelve minutes after the confrontation, killing three Italian soldiers and four civilians. Obviously Havelock knew what he was talking about; he wasn't lying to you.'

'I wouldn't know, sir. I was unconscious . . . bleeding. The son of – Havelock cut me up.'

'You're getting proper medical attention?' interrupted Ambassador Brooks, looking up from the yellow pad under the Tensor lamp.

'I guess so,' replied the agent, his right hand slipping over his left wrist, his fingers massaging the glistening stainless steel case of his chronometer. 'Except the doctors aren't sure the wounds'll require plastic surgery. I think I should have it.'

'That's their province, of course,' said the statesman.

'I'm . . . valuable, sir. Without that surgery I'm *marked*, sir.'

'I'm sure Undersecretary Bradford will convey your feelings to Walter Reed,' said the general, reading his notes.

'You say you never saw this man Ricci,' continued Bradford, 'prior to the briefing in Rome, just before the unit flew to Col des Moulinets. Is that correct?'

'Yes, sir. No, sir. I never saw him. He was new.'

'And you didn't see him when you regained consciousness after the events at the bridge?'

'No, I didn't.'

'You don't know where he went?'

'No, sir.'

'Neither does Rome,' added the Undersecretary quietly, pointedly.

'I learned that an Italian soldier was hit by a truck and was pretty badly mangled, screaming his head off. Someone said he had blond hair, so I figured it was Ricci.'

'And?'

'A man came out of the woods – someone with a gash in his head – put the soldier in a car and drove him away.'

'How did you learn this?'

'I asked questions, a lot of questions . . . after I got first aid. That was my job, sir. It was a madhouse up there, Italians and French yelling all over the place. But I didn't leave until I found out everything I could – without permitting anyone to ask *me* questions.'

'You're to be commended,' said the ambassador.

'Thank you, sir.'

'Let's assume you're right.' Bradford leaned forward. 'The blond man *was* Ricci, and someone with a head wound got him out of there. Have you any idea who that someone might be?'

'I think so. One of the men he brought with him. The other was killed.'

'So Ricci and this other man got away. But Rome hasn't heard from Ricci. Would you say that's normal?'

'No way, sir. It's not normal at all. Whenever any of those people are damaged, they bleed us for everything they can get, and they don't waste time about it. Our policy in black operations is clear. If we can't evacuate the wounded – '

'I think we understand,' broke in Halyard, an old soldier's antenna picking up a signal couched in a soldier's vocabulary.

'Then it's your opinion that if Ricci and this demolitions expert got away intact, they'd have reached our embassy in Rome as quickly as they could.'

'Yes, sir. With their hands out and shouting all the way. They would have expected attention pronto and threatened us with the kind we don't want if they didn't get it.'

'What do you think happened?'

'I'd say it's pretty obvious. They didn't make it.'

'What was that?' asked Brooks, raising his eyes from the yellow pad.

'There isn't any other explanation. I know those people, sir. They're garbage; they'd kill their mothers if the price was right. They would have been in touch with Rome, believe me.'

'"Didn't make it"?' repeated Halyard, staring at the man from Col des Moulinets. 'What do you mean?'

'The roads, sir. They wind up and down those mountains like corkscrews, sometimes without lights for miles at a time. A wounded man driving, the other one banged up and screaming; that vehicle's a candidate for a long fall up there.'

'Head wounds can be deceptive.' Halyard commented. 'A bloody nose looks a hell of a lot worse than it is.'

'It strikes me,' said Brooks, 'that same man acted with considerable presence of mind amid the chaos. He functioned – '

'Forgive me, Mr Ambassador,' interrupted Bradford, his voice rising slightly but deferentially. The intrusion was not a breach of manners but a signal. 'I think the field officer's point is well taken. A thorough search of those roads will undoubtedly reveal a car somewhere at the bottom of a precipice.'

Brooks exchanged looks with the man from State, the signal acknowledged. 'Yes, of course. Realistically, there is no other explanation.'

'Just one or two more points and we're finished,' said Bradford, rearranging his papers. 'As you know, whatever is said here is confidential. There are no hidden microphones, no recording devices; the words spoken are stored only in our memories. This is for the protection of all of us – not just you – so feel perfectly free to speak candidly. Don't try to soften the truth; we're in the same boat.'

'I understand, sir.'

'Your orders with regard to Havelock were unequivocal. He was officially classified "beyond-salvage" and the word from Rome was to terminate with "extreme prejudice". Is that correct?'

'Yes, sir.'

'In other words, he was to be executed. Killed at Col des Moulinets.'

'That's what it meant.'

'And you received those instructions from the senior attaché, Consular Operations, Rome. A man named Warren. Harry Warren.'

'Yes, sir. I was in constant touch with him, waiting for the determination . . . waiting for Washington to give it to him.'

'How could you be certain the man you spoke to was Harry Warren?'

The agent seemed perplexed as if the question were foolish, but the man who asked it was not foolish at all. 'Among other things, I worked with Harry for over two years. I knew his voice.'

'Just his voice?'

'And the number in Rome. It was a direct line to the embassy's radio room, unlisted and very classified. I knew that, too.'

'Did it occur to you that when he gave you your final instructions he might have been doing so under duress? Against his will?'

'No, sir, not at all.'

'It never crossed your mind?'

'If that had been the case, he would have told me.'

'With a gun at his head?' said Halyard. 'How?'

'The code had been established and he used it. He wouldn't have if there'd been anything wrong.'

'Explain that, please,' said Brooks. 'What code?'

'A word or a couple of words that originate in Washington. They're referred to when decisions are transmitted; that way you know the authorization's there without naming names. If anything had been wrong, Harry wouldn't have used the code, and *I* would have known something wasn't right. I'd have asked for it and he would have given me a different one. He didn't and I didn't. He used the correct one at the beginning.'

'What was the code for Col des Moulinets?' asked Emory Bradford.

'Ambiguity, sir. It came direct from Cons Op, Washington and will be listed in the embassy telephone logs, classified files.'

'Which is proof of authorization,' said Bradford, making a statement.

'Yes, sir. Dates, times and origins of clearance are in those logs.'

Bradford held up an eight-by-ten-inch photograph of a man's face, adjusting the Tensor lamp so it could be seen clearly. 'Is this Harry Warren?'

'Yes, sir. That's Harry.'

'Thank you.' The Undersecretary put down the photograph and made a check mark on the border of his notes. 'Let me go back a bit; there's something I'm not sure is clear. Regarding the woman, she was to be sent across the border unharmed, if possible. Is that correct?'

'The operative words were "if possible". Nobody was going to risk anything for her. She was just a needle.'

'A needle?'

'To stick into the Soviets. Let Moscow know we didn't buy the plant.'

'Meaning she was a Russian device. A woman similar in appearance – perhaps someone who had undergone cosmetic surgery – whom the Russians produced repeatedly at selected locations for Havelock's benefit, letting him get close, but never close enough to take her. Is that what you mean?'

'Yes, sir.'

'The purpose being to shock Havelock into a state of mental instability, to the point of defection?'

'To drive him nuts, yes, sir. I guess it worked; the "beyond-salvage" came from Washington.'

'From Ambiguity.'

'Ambiguity, sir.'

'Whose identity can be traced in the embassy's telephone logs.'

'Yes, sir. The logs.'

'So it was established beyond doubt that the woman at the bridge was *not* Jenna Karras.'

'Beyond doubt. She was killed at the Costa Brava, everyone knew that. Havelock himself was the agent-of-record at that beach. He went crazy.'

Ambassador Brooks slapped down his pencil and leaned forward, studying the man from Col des Moulinets. The sharp, echoing crack of the pencil, and the movement itself, were more than an interruption; they combined to indicate an objection. 'This entire operation, didn't it strike you as . . . well, *bizarre*, to say the least? To be quite candid, was execution the only solution? Knowing what you all knew – presumed you knew – couldn't you have tried to take the man, spare his life, get him back here for treatment?'

'With respect, sir, that's a lot easier said than done. Jack Ogilvie tried in Rome and never left the Palatine. Havelock killed three men on that bridge that we know of; another two may be dead by now and probably are. He dug a knife into my face – he's a psycho.' The agent paused, not finished. 'Yes, sir. All things considered, we kill him. That's "beyond-salvage", and has nothing to do with me. I follow orders.'

'An all too familiar phrase, sir,' said Brooks.

'But justified under the circumstances,' Bradford broke in quickly, writing out the word *Ambiguity* on the page in front of him, continuing before anyone else could speak, or object. 'What happened to Havelock? Did you learn?'

'They said an *uccisore pazzo* . . . crazy man, killer . . . drove the truck hell-bent across the bridge and out of sight. It had to be Havelock. There are alerts out all through the provinces – the towns and cities – and up and down the Mediterranean coast. He worked the coast; he'll get in touch with someone and they'll find him. They said he was wounded; he won't get far. My guess is a couple of days at the outside, and I wish I was there to take him myself.'

'Again quite justified,' said Bradford. 'And we want to thank you for your co-operation this evening. You've been very concise and helpful. You may leave now, and good luck to you.'

The man got out of the chair, nodded awkwardly and walked to the door. He stopped, touching his left cheek and the tape as he turned to face the powerful men on the dais. 'I'm worth the surgery,' he said.

'I'm sure you are,' replied the Undersecretary.

The agent-of-record from Col des Moulinets opened the door and stepped out into the white-walled corridor. The instant the door was shut, Halyard turned to Bradford, and shouted, 'Get hold of Rome! Get those logs and find this *Ambiguity*! It's what you were trying to tell us, isn't it? This is the link to Parsifal!'

'Yes, General,' answered Bradford. 'The Ambiguity code was established by the Director of Consular Operations, Daniel Stern, whose name appears in the embassy logs, entered by the Cons Op senior attaché Harry Warren. Warren was clear in his entry; the transcript was read to me. He wrote the following' – The Undersecretary picked up a note on top of his papers – ' "Code: Ambiguity. Subject: M. Havelock. Decision pending." '

' "Pending"?' asked Brooks. 'When was it *made*?'

'According to the embassy logs, it wasn't. There were no further entries that night making any reference whatsoever to Ambiguity, Havelock or the unit at Col des Moulinets.'

'Impossible,' protested the general. 'You heard that man. The go-ahead was given, the authorization code was delivered. He didn't mince words. That call *must* have come through.'

'It did.'

'Are you saying that the entry was deleted?' asked Brooks.

'It was never made,' said Bradford. 'Warren never made it.'

'Then get him,' said Halyard. 'Nail him. He knows who he talked to. Goddam it, Emory, get on that phone. This is Parsifal!' He turned in his chair, addressing the wall. 'Mr President?'

There was no reply.

The Undersecretary separated the papers in front of him and removed a thin manila envelope from the rest. He opened it, took out a second photograph and handed it to the former ambassador. Brooks studied it, a sharp intake of breath accompanying his first glance. Silently he passed it to Halyard.

'*Jesus* . . .' Halyard placed the photograph under the beam of the Tensor. The surface was grainy, the infinitesimal lines the result of a transmitting machine, but the image was clear. It was a photograph of a corpse stretched out on a white table, the clothes torn and bloody, the face bruised terribly but wiped clean for identification. The face of the dead man was the same as that in the first photograph Bradford had shown the agent from Moulinets only minutes before. It belonged to Harry Warren, Senior Attaché, Cons Op, Rome.

'That was telexed to us at one o'clock this afternoon. It's Warren. He was run down on the via Frascati in the early hours of the morning two days ago. There were witnesses, but they couldn't help much, except to tell our people the car was a large saloon with a powerful engine; it roared down the street, apparently gathering speed just before impact. Whoever drove it wasn't taking any chance of missing; he caught Warren stepping up onto the kerb and hammered him into the pole of a street light, doing considerable damage to the automobile. The police are searching for it, but there's not much hope. It's probably at the bottom of a river in the hills.'

'So the link is gone.' Halyard pushed the photograph towards Addison Brooks.

'I mourn the man,' said the Undersecretary, 'but I'm not sure how much of a link he was.'

'Someone thought so,' said the soldier.

'Or was covering a flank.'

'What do you mean?' asked Brooks.

'Whoever made that final call authorizing "beyond-salvage" couldn't know what Stern told Warren. All *we* know is that the decision hadn't been made.'

'Please be clearer,' the statesman insisted.

'Suppose the strategists of Consular Operations decided they couldn't *reach* a decision. On the surface, it wouldn't appear that difficult – a psychopath, a rogue agent capable of causing extraordinary damage, a potential defector, a killer – the decision wasn't one that stretched their consciences. But suppose they learned something, or suspected something, that called everything into question.'

'The Karras woman,' said Halyard.

'Perhaps. Or maybe a communication, or a signal from Havelock that contradicted the assumption that he was a maniac. Implied that he was as sane as they were; a sane man caught in a terrible dilemma not of his own making.'

'Which is, of course, the truth,' interrupted Brooks quietly.

'The truth,' agreed Bradford. 'What would they do?'

'Get help,' said Halyard. 'Advice.'

'Guidance,' added the statesman.

'Or, practically speaking,' said the Undersecretary, 'especially if the facts weren't clear, to spread the responsibility for the decision. Hours later it was made, and they were dead . . . and we don't know who made it, who placed that final call. We only know it was someone sufficiently cleared, sufficiently trusted to be given the code Ambiguity. That man made the decision; he made the call to Rome.'

'But Warren didn't log it,' said Brooks. 'Why didn't he? How could that happen?'

'The way it's happened before, Mr Ambassador. A routed line traceable only to a single telephone complex somewhere in Arlington is used, the authorization verified by code, and a request made on the basis of *internal* security: there is to be no log, no tape, no reference to the transmission; it's an order actually. The recipient is flattered; he's been chosen, deemed by men who make important decisions to be more reliable than those around him. And what difference does it make? The authorization can always be traced through the code – in this case through the director of Cons Op, Daniel Stern. Only he's dead.'

'It's appalling,' said Brooks, looking down at his notes. 'A man is to be executed because he's right, and when the attempt fails, he's held responsible for the death of those who try to kill him and labelled a killer himself. And we don't know who officially gave the order. We can't *find* him. What kind of people are we?'

'Men who keep secrets.' The voice came from behind the dais. The President of the United States emerged from the white-panelled door set into the white wall. 'Forgive me, I was watching you, listening. It's often helpful.'

'Secrets, Mr President?'

'Yes, Mal,' said Berquist, going to his chair. 'The words are all there, aren't they? Top Secret, Eyes Only, Highly Classified, Maximum Clearance Required, Duplication Forbidden, Authorization to be Accompanied by Access Code . . . so many words. We sweep rooms and telephone lines with instruments that tell us whether bugs and intercepts have been placed, and then develop hardware that misdirects those same scanners when we implant our own devices. We jam radio broadcasts – including satellite transmissions – and override the jamming with laser beams that carry the words we want to send. We put a national security lid on information we don't want made public so we can leak selected sections at will, keeping the rest inviolate. We tell a certain agency or department one thing and another something else entirely, so as to conceal a third set of facts – the damaging truth. In history's most advanced age of communications, we're doing our damnedest to louse it up, to misuse it, really.' The President sat down, looked at the photograph of the dead man in Rome and turned it over. 'Keeping secrets and diverting the flow of accurate information have become prime objectives in our ever-expanding technology . . . of communications. Ironic, isn't it?'

'Unfortunately often vital, sir,' said Bradford.

'Perhaps. If only we could be certain. I often wonder – late at night, watching the lights on the ceiling, trying to sleep – if we hadn't tried to keep a secret three months ago, whether we would be faced with what we're faced with now.'

'Our options were extremely limited, Mr President,' the Undersecretary said firmly. 'We might have faced worse.'

'*Worse*, Emory?'

'Earlier then. Time is the only thing on our side.'

'And we have to use every goddamn minute,' agreed Berquist, glancing first at the general and then at Brooks. 'Now you're both aware of what's happened during the past seventy-two hours and why I had to call you back to Washington.'

'Except the most relevant factor,' said the statesman. 'Parsifal's reaction.'

'None,' replied the President.

'Then he doesn't know,' said Halyard rapidly, emphatically.

'If you'd get that written in stone, I could sleep at night,' said Berquist.

'When did he last communicate with you?' asked Brooks.

'Sixteen days ago. There was no point in reaching you; it was another demand, as outrageous as the others and now as pointless.'

'There's been no movement on the previous demands?' continued the statesman.

'Nothing. Fifteen days ago we funnelled eight hundred million dollars into banks throughout the Bahamas, the Caymans and Central America. We've set up every – ' The President paused as he touched the photograph in front of him, folding a corner until part of a bloodied trouser leg could be seen. ' – every code and counter code he's asked for, so that he could verify the deposits whenever he wished, have the monies sent to blind accounts in Zurich and Bern where they would be accessible to him. He hasn't moved a cent and, except for three verifications, he's made no contact at all with the other banks. He has no interest in the money; it's only a means of confirming our vulnerability. He knows we'll do anything he asks.' Berquist paused again; when he spoke, his voice was barely audible. 'God help us, we can't afford not to.'

There was silence on the dais, an acknowledgement of the unthinkable. It was broken by the general's businesslike comment. 'There are a couple of holes here,' he said reading his notes, then looking at the Undersecretary. 'Can you fill them in?'

'I can speculate,' replied Bradford. 'But to do even that we've got to go back to the very beginning. Before Rome.'

'Costa Brava?' asked Brooks disdainfully.

'Before then, Mr Ambassador. To when we all agreed there had to *be* a Costa Brava.'

'I stand rebuked,' said the statesman icily. 'Please go on.'

'We go back to when we learned that it was Matthias himself who initiated the investigation of Jenna Karras. It was the great man himself, not his aides who relayed information from unnamed informants, sources so deep in Soviet intelligence that even to speculate on their identities was tantamount to exposing our own operations.'

'Don't be modest, Emory,' interrupted the President. '*We* didn't learn that it was Matthias. *You* did. You had the perspicacity to go round the "great man", as you call him.'

'Only with a sense of sadness, sir. It was you, Mr President, who demanded the truth from one of his aides in the Oval Office and he gave it to you. He said they *didn't* know where the information had come from, only that Matthias himself had brought it in. He never would have told me that.'

'The room did it, I didn't,' said Berquist. 'You don't lie to a man sitting in that room . . . unless you're Anthony Matthias.'

'In fairness, Mr President,' said Brooks softly, 'his intention was not to deceive you. He believed he was right.'

'He believed he should have been sitting in my chair, my office! Good Christ, he still *believes* it. Even now! There's no end to his goddamned megalomania! Go on, Emory.'

'Yes, sir.' Bradford looked up. 'We concluded that Matthias's objective was to force Havelock to retire, to get his old student and one of the best men we had out of Consular Operations. We've covered that before; we didn't know why then and we don't know why now.'

'But we went along,' said Berquist, 'because we didn't know what we had. A broken foreign service officer who didn't want to go on, or a fraud – *worse* than a fraud, Matthias's lackey, willing to see a woman killed so that he could work for the *great* man on the outside. Oh, and the work he could have done! The international emissary for Saint Matthias. Or was it Emperor Matthias, ruler of all the states and territories of the republic?'

'Come on, Charley.' Halyard touched the President's arm; no one else in that room would have risked such an intimate gesture. 'It's over. It's not why we're here.'

'If it wasn't for that son of a bitch Matthias we wouldn't *be* here! I find *that* hard to forget. And so could the world one day . . . if there's anyone left with a memory.'

'Then may we return to that infinitely more ominous crisis, Mr President?' said Brooks gently.

Berquist leaned back; he looked at the aristocratic statesman, then at the old general. 'When Bradford came to me and convinced me that there was a pattern of deception at the highest levels of state involving the great Anthony Matthias, I asked for you two – and only you two. At least, for now. I'd better be able to take your criticism, because you'll give it to me.'

'Which I think is why you asked for us,' said Halyard. 'Sir.'

'You're a ball-breaker, Mal.' The President nodded towards the man from State. 'Sorry. All right, we didn't know then, and we don't know now, why Matthias wanted Havelock out. But Emory brought us the scenario.'

'An incredible scenario,' agreed Bradford, his hands on top of the papers, no longer needing his notes. 'The case that Matthias concocted against the

Karras woman was a study in meticulous invention. A reformed terrorist from the Baader Meinhof suddenly appears looking for absolution; he'll trade information for relocation and the cancellation of his death sentence. Bonn agrees – reluctantly – and we buy his story. The woman working with a Cons Op field officer then in Barcelona is actually a member of the KGB. A method of transferring orders is described, which entails the passing of a key, and a small overnight suitcase is located at an airport, *her* suitcase, filled with all the evidence needed to convict her – detailed analyses of the activities she and Havelock had been involved with during the past five weeks, summaries of in-depth, classified information Havelock had sent back to the State Department, and copies of the current codes and radio frequencies we used in the field. Also in that overnight bag were instructions from Moscow, including the KGB code that she was to employ should contact with KGB North-west Sector be required. We tested the code and got a response; it was authentic.'

Brooks raised his left hand no more than a few inches, the gesture of a man used to commanding attention. 'General Halyard and I are familiar with much of this, albeit not the specifics. I assume there's a reason for your restating it in such detail.'

'There is, Mr Ambassador,' agreed Bradford. 'It concerns Daniel Stern. Please bear with me.'

'Then while you're at it,' said the general, 'how did you verify that KGB code?'

'By using the three basic maritime frequencies for that area of the Mediterranean. It's standard procedure for the Soviets.'

'That's pretty damn simple of them, isn't it?'

'I'm no expert, General, but I'd say it's pretty damn smart. I've studied the way we do it – I've had to – and I'm not sure ours is more effective. The frequencies we select are usually the weaker ones, not always clear and easily jammed if discovered. You don't tamper with maritime channels, and no matter how much traffic, the codes get through within a reasonable period of time.'

'You're very impressive,' said Brooks.

'I've had a series of crash courses during the past four months. Thanks to an executive order from the President, I've also had the benefit of the best brains in the intelligence community.'

'The reason for that executive order was not explained,' interrupted Berquist, glancing at the older men. Then he turned back to Bradford: 'All right, you verified the KGB code to be authentic.'

'It was the most incriminating document in that suitcase; it couldn't have been faked. So her name was put through the wheels at Central Intelligence – very deep wheels.' Bradford paused. 'As you may or may not know, General . . . Mr Ambassador, it was at this point that I came on the scene. I didn't seek to be included; I was sought out by men I'd worked with during the Johnson administration . . . and in south-east Asia.'

'Remnants of the benevolent AID in Vientiane who stayed with the Agency?' asked Halyard sardonically.

'Yes,' replied the Undersecretary; there was no apology in his answer. 'Two men whose wide experience in undercover operations – favourable and unfavourable – led them to become what's called source-controls for informants deep within the Soviet apparatus. They phoned me at home one night, said they were at a local bar in Berwyn and why didn't I join them for a drink – old times' sake. When I said it was late, the one I was talking to pointed out that it was also late for them, and Berwyn Heights was a long drive from McLean and Langley. I understood and joined them.'

'I've never heard this,' interrupted the former ambassador. 'Am I to infer that these men did not report back through normal channels but, instead, went directly to you?'

'Yes, sir. They were disturbed.'

'Thank God for the communion of past sinners,' said the President. 'When they returned to those normal channels, they did it our way. It was beyond their scope, they reported. They pulled out and left it in Bradford's lap.'

'The information requested about the Karras woman was a basic intelligence query,' said Halyard. 'Why were they disturbed?'

'Because it was a highly negative inquiry that presupposed the subject was too deep, too concealed for CIA detection. She was going to be found guilty no matter what the Agency came back with.'

'Then it was the arrogance that angered them?' suggested Brooks.

'No, they're used to that from State. What *disturbed* them was that the supposition couldn't possibly be true. They reached five separate sources in Moscow, none aware of the others – moles who had access to every black file in the KGB. Each probe came back negative. She was clean, but someone at State wanted her dirty. When one of the men routinely called an aide of Matthias to get further background from Cons Op, he was told simply to send back a non-productive report – State had everything it needed. In other words, she was hanged no matter what the Agency returned, and the source control had the distinct impression that whatever was sent back to State would be buried. But Jenna Karras was no part of the KGB and never had been.'

'How did your friends explain the KGB code?' asked the soldier.

'Someone in Moscow provided it,' said Bradford. 'Someone working with or for Matthias.'

Again the silence on the dais suggested the unthinkable, and once again it was broken by the general. 'We ruled that *out!*' he cried.

'I'd like to revive it,' said Bradford quietly.

'We've explored the possibility to the point of exhaustion,' said Brooks, staring at Bradford. 'Practically and conceptually, there's no merit in the theory. Matthias is inexorably bound to Parsifal; one does not exist without the other. If the Soviet Union had any knowledge of Parsifal, ten thousand multiple warheads would be in position to destroy half our cities and all our military installations. The Russians would have no choice but to launch, posing their final questions after the first strike. We have intelligence penetration to alert us to any such missile deployment; there's been no such alert. In your words, Mr Bradford, time is the only thing on our side.'

'I'll stay with that judgement, Mr Ambassador. Still the KGB code found its way into the manufactured evidence against the Karras woman even though she was clean. I can't believe it was for sale.'

'Why not?' asked the general. 'What isn't for sale?'

'Not a code like that. You don't *buy* a code that changes periodically, erratically, with no set schedule of change.'

'What's your point?' Halyard interrupted.

'Someone in Moscow *had* to provide that code,' said Bradford, raising his voice. 'We may be closer to Parsifal than we think.'

'What's your thesis, Mr Undersecretary?' Brooks leaned forward.

'There's someone trying to find Parsifal as frantically as we are – for the same reasons we are. Whoever he is, he's here in Washington – he may be someone we see every day, but we don't know who he is. I only know he's working for Moscow, and the difference between him and us right now is that he's been looking longer than we have. He knew about Parsifal *before* we did. And that means someone in Moscow knows.' Bradford paused. 'That's the reason for the most God-awful crisis this country has ever faced . . . the world has ever faced. There's a mole here in Washington who could tip the balance of power – of basic global recognition of our physical and moral superiority – which *is* power – if he reaches Parsifal first. And he may, because he knows who he is and we don't.'

18

The man was wearing a dark overcoat and a low-brimmed hat that partially hid his face. As he climbed out of the two-toned coupé, he only just managed to avoid stepping into a puddle by the driver's door. The sounds of the night rain were everywhere, pinging off the bonnet and splattering against the glass of the windscreen, thumping into the vinyl roof and erupting in the myriad pools all over the deserted parking area on the banks of the Potomac River. The man reached into his pocket, took out a gold-plated butane lighter and ignited it. No sooner had the flame erupted than he extinguished it, replacing the lighter in his pocket, he kept his gloved hand there. He walked to the railing and looked down at the wet foliage and the border of thick mud that disappeared into the black flowing water. Raising his head, he scanned the opposite shoreline; the lights of Washington flickered in the downpour. Hearing the footsteps behind him, leather scraping over the soaked gravel, he turned.

A man approached, coming into view through blocks of darkness. He wore a canvas poncho printed with the erratic shapes of green and black that denoted military issue. On his head was a heavy wide-brimmed leather hat. The face beneath it was thirtyish, hard, with a stubble of a beard and dull eyes set far apart. He had been drinking; the grin that followed recognition was as grotesque as the rest of him.

'Hey, how about it, *huh*!' cried the man in the poncho. '*Wham!* Splat! Boom . . . *Kaboom!* Like a fuckin' gook rickshaw hit by a tank! *Wham!* You never seen nothin' like it!'

'Very fine work,' said the man in the overcoat.

'You betch-er ass! I caught 'em at the pass, and *kaboom*! Hey, I can't hardly see you. It *is* you, ain't it?'

'Yes, but you disappoint me.'

'Why! I did good!'

'You've been drinking. I thought we agreed you wouldn't.'

'A couple of balls, that's all. In my room, not at no gin mill . . . no sir!'

'Did you talk to anyone?'

'Christ, *no*!'

'How did you get out here?'

'Like you said. On a bus . . . three buses . . . and I walked the last couple of miles.'

'In the road?'

'*Off* it. Way off, like it was an S and D in Danang.'

'Good. You've earned your R and R.'

'Hey, Major . . .? Sorry, I mean . . . sir.'

'What is it?'

'How come there was nothin' in the papers? I mean it was one big blow! Musta' burned for hours, seen for a couple of miles. How come?'

'They weren't important, Sergeant. They were only what I told you they were. Bad men who betrayed people like you and me, who stayed over here and let us get killed.'

'Yeah, well, I evened a few scores. I guess I should go back now, huh? To the hospital.'

'You don't have to.' The civilian who had been addressed as 'major' calmly took his gloved hand out of his pocket. In it was a .22 calibre automatic, concealed by the darkness and the rain. He raised it at his side and fired once.

The man fell, his bleeding head sinking into the wet poncho. The civilian stepped forward, wiping the weapon against the cloth of his overcoat. He knelt down and spread the fingers of the dead man's right hand.

The two-tone coupé rounded the curve in the back country road, the headlights sweeping over a rock-strewn Maryland field, the high grass bending under the force of the wind and the night rain. The driver in the dark overcoat and low-brimmed hat saw what he expected to see and slowed down, switching off the lights before coming to a stop. On the shoulder of the road, standing motionless by a barbed wire fence, was a glistening white ambulance, the licence plates those of the federal government, the black lettering on the door proclaiming co-ownership with the taxpayer as well as the identification: *Bethesda Naval Hospital, Emergency Unit 14.*

The driver drew the coupé alongside the long white vehicle. He took out his lighter, flicked the top and held the flame briefly towards the opposite window. The door of the ambulance opened, and a man in his late twenties jumped out into the rain, his government issue raincoat parting to reveal the white uniform of a hospital attendant.

The driver lowered the right window by pressing a button above his armrest. 'Get in!' he yelled through the sound of the downpour. 'You'll get soaked out there!'

The man climbed in, slamming the door shut and wiping his face with his right hand. He was Hispanic, his large eyes two stones of shining hard coal, his hair jet black, matted to the dark skin of his forehead.

'You owe me, mama,' said the Latin. 'Oh, big mama owes me one big *lio grande.*'

'You'll be paid, although I suppose I could say that you simply cancelled an old debt you owed me.'

'No *dados*, mama Major!'

'You would have been executed in the field or still be pushing rocks around Leavenworth if it weren't for me. Don't you forget it, Corporal.'

'I wasted that shrinker for you! You *pay!*'

'You wasted – as you put it – two MPs in Pleiku who caught you stealing narcotics from a Med-Evac truck. Weren't you lucky I was around? Two more MIAs in a river.'

'Sure, mama, *real* lucky! Who was the *puerco* who *told* me about the truck? *You*, Major!'

'I knew you were enterprising. These past years I've kept my eye on you. You never saw me, but I saw you. I always knew where to find you, because debts should be paid.'

'Yeah, well you're wrong, Major. I saw you the other night on the TV news. You were getting out of a big limousine in New York. At the United Nations place, wasn't it? It *was* you, wasn't it?'

'I doubt it.'

'Sure, it was! I know big mama when I see her. You must be something! You pay, mama. You're going to pay a lot.'

'My God, you're irritating.'

'Just pay me.'

'The gun first,' said the man in the overcoat. 'I gave it to you and I want it back. I protected you; no one could trace it ballistically.'

The hospital attendant reached into his raincoat pocket and took out a small gun, identical in size and calibre to the weapon the driver of the coupé had used an hour ago in a parking area overlooking the Potomac.

'You won't find no bullets in it,' said the Hispanic, holding out the automatic in the darkness. 'Here, take it.'

'Give it to me.'

'*Take* it! For Christ's sake, I can't see nothin' in here! *Ouch! Shit!* What the hell . . . ?'

The driver's hand had slipped beyond the short barrel of the weapon, pushing the attendant's wide sleeve partially up his forearm. 'Sorry,' said the man in the overcoat. 'My class ring is twisted. Did I scrape you?'

'Forget it, mama. The money. Give me the fuckin' *dinero!*'

'Certainly.' The man took the gun and slipped it into his pocket. He picked up his lighter from his lap and ignited it; on the seat between them was a stack of money held together with an elastic band. 'There it is. Fifty one-hundred-dollar bills – laundered, of course. Do you want to count it?'

'What for? I know where I can find you now,' said the attendant, opening the door. 'And you're going to see a lot of me, big mama.'

'I look forward to it,' replied the driver.

The wind again whipped the attendant's raincoat away from his white uniform as he slammed the door and started towards the ambulance. The man in the coupé leaned over in the shadows, watching through the opposite window with his fingers on the door latch beside him, prepared to leap out of the car the instant he saw what he expected to see.

The attendant began to stagger, rushing forward off balance, his arms stretched out, his hands clutching the side of the ambulance. He raised his head and screamed, the rain pounding his face; three seconds later he collapsed on the wet grass.

The man in the overcoat jumped out of the coupé and walked around the boot removing a tubular glass object from his left pocket. He reached the attendant, knelt down and pushed the wide sleeve up the immobile arm. He then adjusted the glass vial in his left hand and, with his right, extracted a hypodermic needle. He plunged it into the soft flesh, depressed the shaft until the vial of white liquid was emptied into the arm, and let the long needle remain where it was, firmly embedded in the skin. Reaching across the attendant's body, he pulled the loose, lifeless hand towards the vial, he pressed the fingers around the glass tube, with the thumb firmly down on the plunger and then let the hand fall away.

The man stood up, seeing in the night light the scattered notes, many held in place by the weight of the attendant's body. He turned and opened the door of the ambulance; the inside was neat, the equipment in place, as befitted a trusted employee of the Bethesda Naval Hospital. He took out the small automatic from his pocket and threw it onto the seat. He then reached inside his overcoat for the contents of another pocket. Four additional glass vials, two filled, two empty. He checked the labels; each read the same:

Bethesda Naval Hospital
Security-Control-Supply
Contents: $C_{17}H_{19}NO_3H_2O$
Morphine

He held them out and dropped them on the floor of the ambulance.

Suddenly a gust of wind came swirling off the field forcing the rain to fall in diagonal sheets. The man reached for his hat but it was too late. Caught in an updraught, the hat was lifted off his head and hurled against the side of the coupé. He walked across the grass to retrieve it. Even in the darkness the shock of white could be seen streaking from his forehead through his wavy black hair.

In truth, Nicolai Petrovich Malyekov was annoyed, and his dripping hair was only part of his irritation. Time was running short. In his identity as Undersecretary of State Arthur Pierce, he would have to change his clothes and make himself presentable. A man in his position in the United States government did not run around in the mud and the pouring rain; he would phone for his limousine the minute he reached home. He had agreed to have late night drinks with the British ambassador, as there was another OPEC problem and matters of state to be attended to.

It was not what his people in Moscow wanted, but knowledge of another Anglo-American oil strategy was not to be dismissed. All such information brought the *Voyennaya* closer to the power they had been seeking since Yagoda set them on their path over a half century ago. Yet only the man who could not be found, the man who knew the secret of Anthony Matthias, could lead the *Voennaya* to its destiny – for the good of the world.

Arthur Pierce, raised as an Iowa farmboy but born in the Russian village of Ramenskoye, turned towards his car in the rain. There was no time to be tired for the charade never stopped. Not for him.

Ambassador Addison Brooks stared at Bradford across the dais. 'You say this mole *knows* who Parsifal is, *knew* about him before *we* did!' he exclaimed. 'On what basis do you make that extraordinary statement?'

'Costa Brava,' said the Undersecretary. 'And the past seventy-two hours.'

'Take them in sequence,' ordered the President.

'In the final hours of Costa Brava, Havelock was provided with a radio transmitter whose frequency calibrations had been altered by CIA technicians in Madrid. They were working under blind orders; they had no idea what the transmitter was for or who was going to use it. As you know, the entire Costa Brava assignment was controlled by a man named Steven MacKenzie, the most experienced black-operations officer in Central Intelligence; the security was guaranteed.'

'Completely,' interrupted Berquist. 'MacKenzie died of a coronary three weeks after we pulled him out of Barcelona. There was nothing suspicious. The doctor's a respected, well-known physician and was thoroughly questioned. MacKenzie's death was from natural causes.'

'Only *he* knew all the details,' continued Bradford. 'He'd hired a boat, two men and a blonde woman who spoke Czech and was to scream in the distance – in the dark – during the grisly scene they were performing on that beach. The three of them were the dregs – small-time narcotics dealers and a prostitute – picking up a sizeable fee. They didn't ask questions. Havelock sent out his transmission in KGB code to what he thought was a Baader-Meinhof unit in the boat off-shore. MacKenzie caught it on his scanner and signalled the boat to come in. A few minutes later Havelock saw what we wanted him to see – or he *thought* he saw it. The Costa Brava operation was over.'

'Again,' interrupted the ambassador impatiently, 'General Halyard and I are aware of the essentials – '

'It was over, and except for the President and the three of us, no one else knew about it,' said the Undersecretary, rushing ahead. 'MacKenzie had structured it in fragments, no one group knowing what the other was doing. The only story we issued was the trapped double-agent version, no buried reports, no file within a file that contradicted it. And with MacKenzie's death, the last man on the outside who knew the truth was gone.'

'The last man perhaps,' said Halyard. 'Not the last woman. Jenna Karras knew. She got away from you, but she knew.'

'She knew only what she was told, and I was the one who spoke with her at the hotel in Barcelona. The story she was given had a dual purpose. One, to frighten her into doing exactly what we asked of her so we could ostensibly save her life; and two, to put her into a disturbed frame of mind that would startle Havelock, help convince him she *was* a KGB officer if he had any last doubts or emotional hurdles. If she'd followed my instructions she'd be safe. Or if we'd been able to find her, she wouldn't be running from the men who have to kill her now – and kill Havelock – so the truth about Costa Brava is kept secret. Because they *know* the truth.'

Ambassador Brooks whistled softly; it was a low, swelling whistle, the sound made by a brilliant man genuinely astonished. 'We've reached the last seventy-two hours,' he said, 'beginning with an untraceable call to Rome preceded by an authorization code established by Daniel Stern.'

'Yes, sir. Col des Moulinets. I saw the outlines of the connection when I read the agent-of-record's report, but nothing was clear. Just shapes, shadows. Then it became clearer when he spoke to us here tonight.'

'A man named Ricci he'd never seen before,' said Brooks, 'two demolitions experts he knew nothing about.'

'And a massive explosion which detonated some twelve minutes *after* the gunfire at the bridge,' added Bradford. 'Then his description of the woman as a "needle" for the Soviets, a Russian plant that Moscow could have back and be taught a lesson.'

'Which was a lie,' objected Halyard. 'That bomb was meant for the car she was in. It killed how many? Seven people on the road to the bridge? Christ, it was powerful enough to blow that vehicle out of sight and everyone in it beyond recognition. And our own people weren't to know a goddamned thing about it.'

'By way of a man named Ricci,' said Bradford, 'a Corsican no one knew and two so-called small arms backup personnel who were in reality explosives experts. They were sent by Rome, but the two who escaped never tried to get in touch with the embassy afterwards. In our agent's words, that's not normal. They didn't dare return to Rome.'

'They were sent by our people,' said Berquist. 'But they didn't *come* from our people. They had a separate arrangement with the same person who made the last untraceable call from Washington to Rome. Ambiguity.'

'That same person, Mr President, who was able to reach into Moscow and pull out an authentic KGB code – anything less would never have been accepted by Havelock. Someone who knew the truth about Costa Brava, and was as anxious, perhaps as desperate as we are to keep a blackout on it.'

'Why?' asked the general.

'Because if we went back and examined every aspect of the operation we might find he was there.'

The President and the general reacted as though each had been told of an unexpected death; only Brooks remained passive, watching Bradford carefully, a first-rate mind acknowledging the presence of another.

'That's a hell of a jump, son,' said Halyard.

'I can't think of any other explanation,' said Bradford. 'Havelock's execution had been sanctioned; the sanction was understood even by those who respected his record. He'd turned; he was a "psycho", a killer, dangerous to every man in the field. But why was the woman at Col des Moulinets to be sent across the border? Why was her escape a lesson to the Russians, when all the while a bomb timed to explode minutes later would have blown her away beyond recognition?'

'To maintain the illusion that she had died at the Costa Brava,' said Brooks. 'If she remained alive, she'd ask for asylum and tell her story; she'd have nothing to lose.'

'Forcing a re-examination of the events of that night on the beach,' completed the President. 'She had to be killed away from that bridge while still preserving the lie that she had died at the Costa Brava.'

'And the person who made the call authorizing Havelock's execution,' said Halyard, frowning, the uncertainty in his voice, 'who used the Ambiguity code and put this Ricci and the two nitro men in Col des Moulinets by way of Rome . . . you say he was on the beach that night?'

'Everything points to it, yes, General.'

'For Christ's sake, *why?*'

'Because he knows Jenna Karras is alive,' replied Ambassador Brooks, still watching Bradford. 'At least, he knows she wasn't killed at Costa Brava. No one else did.'

'That's speculation. It may have been kept quiet, but we've been looking for her for nearly four months.'

'Without ever acknowledging it *was* her,' explained the Undersecretary, 'without ever admitting she *was* alive. The alert was for a person, not a name. A woman whose expertise as a deep cover agent could lead her to people she'd worked with previously under multiple identities. The emphasis was on physical appearance and languages.'

'What I can't accept is your jump.' Halyard shook his head, the gesture of a military strategist who sees a practical gap in a plan for field manoeuvre. 'MacKenzie put Costa Brava together in pieces, reporting only to you. The CIA in Langley didn't know about Madrid, and Barcelona was kept away from both. Under those conditions how could someone penetrate what wasn't there? Unless you believe MacKenzie sold you out or loused it up.'

'I don't think either,' the Undersecretary paused. 'I think the man who took the Ambiguity code was already involved with Parsifal three months ago. He knew what to concentrate on and became alarmed when Havelock was ordered to Madrid under a Four-Zero security.'

'Someone with maximum clearance right here in the State Department,' the ambassador broke in. 'Someone with access to confidential memoranda.'

'Yes. He kept tabs on Havelock's activities and saw that something was happening. He flew to Spain, picked him up in Madrid and followed him back to Barcelona. *I* was there; so was MacKenzie. He'd almost certainly recognize me, and as I met MacKenzie twice, it's reasonable to assume we were seen together.'

'And presuming you were, it's also reasonable to assume that Moscow had a file on MacKenzie thick enough to alarm Soviet Intelligence.' Brooks leaned forward, once again locking his eyes with Bradford's. 'A photograph wired to the KGB, and the man we're looking for, who saw you together in Barcelona, knew a black operation was in progress.'

'It could have happened that way, yes.'

'With a lot of conjecture on your part,' said Halyard.

'I don't think the Undersecretary of State is finished, Mal.' The ambassador nodded his head at the papers Bradford had just separated and was scanning. 'I don't believe he'd permit his imagination to wander into such exotic regions unless something triggered it. Am I right?'

'Substantially, yes.'

'How about just plain yes,' said the President.

'Yes,' said the man from State. 'I suppose I could be prosecuted for what

I did this afternoon, but I considered it essential. I had to get away from the phones and the interruptions; I had to re-read some of this material and provoke whatever imagination I have. I went to the classified files of Cons Op, removed Havelock's summary of Costa Brava under chemical therapy and took it home. I've been studying it since three o'clock – and remembering MacKenzie's verbal report after he came back from Barcelona. There are discrepancies.'

'In what way?' asked Brooks.

'In what MacKenzie planned and in what Havelock saw.'

'He saw what we wanted him to see,' said the President. 'You made a point of it a few minutes ago.'

'He may have seen more than we think, more than MacKenzie engineered.'

'MacKenzie was *there*,' protested Halyard. 'What the hell are you talking about?'

'He was approximately seventy yards away from Havelock, with only a peripheral view of the beach. He was more concerned with watching Havelock's reactions than with what was taking place below. He'd rehearsed it a number of times with the two men and the blonde woman. According to those practice sessions everything was to take place near the water, the shots fired into the surf, the woman falling into the wet sand, her body rolling with the waves, the boat close by, within reach. The distance, the darkness – everything was for effect.'

'Visually convincing,' interrupted Brooks.

'Very,' agreed Bradford. 'But it wasn't what Havelock described. What he saw was infinitely *more* convincing. Under chemicals at the clinic in Virginia he literally re-lived the entire experience, including the emotional trauma that was part of it. He described bullets erupting in the sand, the woman running up to the road, not down by the water, and two men carrying the body away. *Two* men.'

'Two men were hired,' said Halyard, perplexed. 'What's the problem?'

'*One* had to be in the boat; it was twenty feet off-shore, the engine running. The *second* man was to have fired the shots and pulled the woman into the water, throwing her "dead body" *into* the boat. The distance, the darkness, a beam of light – these were part of MacKenzie's scene, what he'd rehearsed with the people he'd hired. But the light was the only constant between what MacKenzie planned and what Havelock saw. He didn't witness a performance; he saw a woman actually killed.'

'*Jesus.*' The general sat back in his chair.

'MacKenzie never mentioned any of this?' said Brooks.

'I don't think he saw it. All he said to me was "My employees must have put on a hell of a show". He stayed where he was on that hill above the road for several hours watching Havelock. He left when it began to get light; he couldn't risk Havelock's spotting him.'

Addison Brooks brought his right hand to his chin. 'So the man we're looking for, the man who pulled the trigger at Costa Brava, who was given the Ambiguity code by Stern and put Havelock "beyond-salvage", is a Soviet agent in the State Department.'

'Yes,' said the Undersecretary.

'And he wants to find Parsifal as desperately as we do,' concluded the President.

'Yes, sir.'

'Yet, if I follow you,' said Brooks quickly. 'There's an enormous inconsistency. He hasn't passed on his astonishing information to his normal KGB controls. We'd know it if he had. Good *God*, we'd know it!'

'Not only has he held it back, Mr Ambassador, he's purposely misled a senior director of the KGB.' Bradford picked up the top page of his notes and slid it respectfully towards the silver-haired statesman on his right. 'I've saved this for last. Not, incidentally, to startle you or shock you, but only because it didn't make any sense unless we looked at everything else in relationship to it. Frankly, I'm still not sure I understand. It's a cable from Pyotr Rostov in Moscow. He's Director of External Strategies, KGB.'

'A cable from *Soviet Intelligence*?' said Brooks, astonished, picking up the paper.

'Contrary to what most people believe,' added the Undersecretary, 'strategists from opposing intelligence services often make contact with one another. They're practical men in a deadly practical business. They can't afford wrong signals . . . According to Rostov, the KGB had nothing to do with the Costa Brava and he wanted us to know it. Incidentally, Colonel Baylor in his report said that Rostov trapped Havelock in Athens and, although he could have got him out of Greece and into Russia by way of the Dardanelles, he chose not to.'

'When did you get this?' asked the statesman.

'Twenty-four hours ago,' answered the President. 'We've been studying it, trying to work it out. Obviously no response is called for.'

'Read it, Addison,' said Halyard.

'It was sent to D. S. Stern, Director of Consular Operations, United States Department of – ' Brooks looked up at Bradford. 'Stern was killed *three* days ago. Wouldn't Rostov have *known* that?'

'He wouldn't have sent it if he did. He wouldn't have permitted the slightest speculation that the KGB was involved in Stern's death. He sent that cable because he *didn't* know Stern was dead – or the others.'

'Only Miller's death was released,' said Berquist. 'We couldn't keep it quiet; it was all over Bethesda. We put a blackout on Stern and Dawson, at least for the time being, until we could learn what was happening. We moved their families to the Cheyenne security compound in Colorado Springs.'

'Read it,' said the general.

Brooks held the paper under the glare of the Tensor lamp. He spoke slowly, reading in a monotone:

'The betrayal at Costa Brava was not ours. Nor was the bait taken in Athens. The infamous Consular Operations continues its provocative actions and the Soviet Union continues to protest its disregard for human life as well as the crimes and terrorist acts it inflicts upon the innocent – peoples and nations alike. And should this notorious branch of the American Department of State believe it has collaborators within the walls of Dzerzhinsky, be assured such traitors will be rooted out and face the punishments demanded. I repeat, Costa Brava was not ours.'

The statesman finished; the cable was over. He let his hand drop to the dais, the page was still held between his thumb and forefinger. 'Good *Lord*,' he whispered.

'I understand the words,' said Halyard, 'but not what he's trying to tell us.'

'"Better the denial you know",' replied Brooks. 'There are no walls in Dzerzhinsky Square.'

'That's *it*,' said Bradford, turning to the President. 'That's what we didn't see. The walls are in the *Kremlin*.'

'Outside and inside,' continued the former ambassador. 'He's telling you that he knows Costa Brava could not have taken place without a collaborator or collaborators in Moscow –'

'We understood that,' interrupted Berquist. 'What about the walls? The Kremlin? How do you read that?'

'He's warning us. He's saying he doesn't know who they are and, since he doesn't, they're not controllable.'

'Because they're outside the normal channels of communication?' asked the President.

'Even abnormal channels,' said Brooks.

'A power struggle.' Berquist turned to the Undersecretary of State. 'Has there been anything of a serious nature about this from any of our intelligence departments?'

'Only the usual frictions. The old guard dying, the younger commissars anxious, ambitious.'

'Where do the generals stand?' inquired the general.

'Half wanting to blow up Omaha, half wanting SALT 3.'

'And Parsifal could unite them,' said the statesman. '*All* their hands would be on the nuclear switches.'

'But Rostov doesn't *know* about Parsifal,' protested Bradford. 'He has no *conception* –'

'He senses it,' the ambassador broke in. 'He knows Costa Brava was a Department of State operation somehow in conjunction with elements in Moscow. He's tried to trace them down and can't; that alarms him immensely. There's an imbalance, a shift from the norm at the highest levels.'

'Why do you say that?' The President took the cable from Brooks, scrutinizing it as if trying to see what he had not seen before.

'It's not in there, sir,' said Bradford, nodding at Brooks as he spoke. 'Except for the word "bait", which refers to Havelock. Remember, he didn't take Havelock in Athens. Rostov's aware of the very unusual relationship between Michael Havelock and Anthony Matthias. Czech and Czech, teacher and student, survivors really . . . in many ways father and son; where does one end and the other begin? Is one or both of them dealing with someone in Moscow? And for what purpose? Reasonable objectives can be ruled out; avoiding normal channels would indicate that. Not too many months ago we wondered the same thing: What had Matthias done, and where did Havelock stand? We created Costa Brava because of it.'

'And then Parsifal reached us and it didn't make any difference,' interrupted Berquist. 'We were at the wall. We're still at the wall – only now it's grown larger, broken away from itself until there are two walls, our backs to each no matter which way we turn. The search for Parsifal is joined with another search for another man. Someone right here who's watching every move we make. A Soviet mole capable of pulling a buried code out of Moscow, and deep enough to change the face of Costa Brava . . . My *God*, we've got to blow him out of the ground! If he finds Parsifal before we do, he and the madmen he answers to in the Kremlin can dictate whatever terms they like to this country.'

'You know where he is,' said the general. 'Go after him! He's at State. High up; with access to embassy cables and obviously goddamned close to Matthias. Because if *I* follow you now, he nailed the Karras woman. He supplied that code; he had it placed in her suitcase. He *nailed* her!'

'I think he supplied everything.' Bradford shook his head slowly, arching his brows as if recalling the impossible. 'Including the suitcase, the Baader-Meinhof informer, our own codes and the instructions from Moscow. Everything just appeared in Barcelona . . . out of nowhere. And no one really knows how.'

'I imagine it's pointless to press Matthias further?' said Brooks, asking the question nevertheless.

'Pointless,' replied Bradford. 'He repeats what he's maintained from the beginning. "The evidence was there. It was true. It was channelled to me".'

'The bells are heard by Saint Anthony!' exploded the President.

'The mole at *State*,' Halyard persisted. 'Good *Christ*, he can't be that hard to find. How many people would Stern talk to? What kind of time frame was involved? A few minutes? A few hours? Go back and trace every move he made.'

'The Cons Op strategists operated in total secrecy,' said Bradford. 'There were no appointment calendars, no conference schedules. A call would come to a specific person upstairs, or over at the Agency, or the NSC, and the decks were cleared for whichever strategist it was, but no record of the meeting was ever written down. Internal security again; a great deal could be pieced together by informers with access to such records or memoranda.'

'Misdirect the flow of accurate information at all costs,' said the President softly.

'By our estimates, Stern could have spoken to any of sixty to seventy-five people,' continued Bradford. 'And we could be *underestimating* that figure. There are authorities within teams of specialists, specialists among those considered authorities. The lists are endless, and all those people have maximum clearance.'

'But we're talking about the *State Department*,' said the silver-haired Brooks emphatically. 'Some time between Stern's last conversation with Rome and four hours later when the authorization was given to Col des Moulinets. That narrows down the possibilities considerably.'

'And whoever it is knows that,' said the Undersecretary. 'It further obscures his movements. Even the check-ins and check-outs won't show him to be where he was.'

'Didn't anyone *see* Stern?' persisted Brooks. 'Surely you've asked.'

'As quietly as we could. Not one of those we questioned admitted seeing him within twenty-four hours of the period in question, but then we didn't expect the one who did to say so.'

'*Nobody* saw him?' asked the general, frowning in disbelief.

'Well, yes, someone did,' said Bradford, nodding. 'The outside receptionist on the fifth floor, L Section. Dawson had left a message for Stern; he picked it up on his way to the elevator. He could have been in any of seventy-five offices beyond the reception room door.'

'Who was inside at the time?' The ambassador shook his head the instant he had asked the question, as if to say 'sorry, never mind'.

'Exactly,' said Bradford, accepting the statesman's unspoken afterthought. 'It wasn't any help. Twenty-three people were listed as not having checked out. There were conferences, secretaries taking notes and briefings by division personnel. Everything was substantiated. No one left a meeting long enough to place that call.'

'But, damn it, you've got a floor!' cried the soldier. 'Seventy-five offices, seventy-five people. That's not a hundred and fifty, or a thousand; it's seventy-five and one of them's your mole! Start with those closest to Matthias and pull them in. Put every goddamn one of them into a clinic if you have to!'

'There'd be panic; the entire State Department would be demoralized,' said Brooks. '*Unless* . . . is there a clique, a particular group closest to Matthias?'

'You don't understand him.' Bradford brought his folded hands to his chin, searching for words. 'He's first, last and always *Doctor* Matthias, teacher, enlightener, provoker-of-thought. He's a hustling Socrates on the Potomac, gathering his worshippers wherever he can find them, extolling those who see the light, striking down the disbelievers with the cruellest humour I've ever heard. Cruel but always couched in brilliantly humble phrases. And like most self-appointed arbiters of an élite, his arrogance makes him fickle as hell. A section will catch his eye and they're his fair-haired boys and girls for a while, until another group comes along and flatters him at the right moment and there's suddenly a new court of supplicants he can lecture. Naturally, during the past year it's got worse – but it was always there.' Bradford permitted himself the start of a strained smile. 'Then, of course, I could be biased. I was never allowed into one of those charmed circles.'

'Why do you think you were excluded?' asked the ambassador.

'I'm not sure. I had a certain reputation of my own once; perhaps he was uncomfortable with it. But I think it was because I used to watch him very closely, very hard. I was fascinated, and I know he was uncomfortable with that . . . You see, the "best and the brightest" were led down a lot of strange paths by men like him. Some of us grew up and I don't think Matthias approved of that growth. Scepticism comes with it. The Thomistic leap isn't good enough any more; blind faith can ruin the eyesight – and the perspective.' Bradford leaned forward, his eyes on Halyard. 'I'm sorry,

General. My answer to both you and Ambassador Brooks is that there is no one group I'd zero in on, no guarantee that our mole would be caught before he panicked and ran. And we can't let that happen. I know I'm right. If we can find him, he can lead us to the man we call Parsifal. He may have lost him temporarily, but he knows who Parsifal is.'

The older men were silent; they gazed at each other, then turned back to Bradford. The general frowned, a questioning look in his clear eyes. The President nodded his head slowly, bringing his right hand to his cheek and staring at the man from State.

The ambassador spoke, his slender figure rigid in his chair. 'I commend you, Mr Undersecretary. May I try to reconstruct the new scenario? . . . For reasons unknown, Matthias needed an incontrovertible case against the Karras woman, which would lead to Havelock's retirement. By now, because of what he's done, Matthias is Parsifal's puppet – his prisoner, really – but Parsifal knows it's in his interest to carry out Matthias's obsession. He goes to a well-entrenched Soviet agent in the upper regions of the State Department and the incriminating evidence against the Karras woman is provided, studied and accepted. Except that two source controls from the CIA come to you and tell you it can't be true – any of it – and you, Emory Bradford, enter the picture. In fact, the President, alarmed by what appears to be a conspiracy at State, brings us *all* into the picture – and we in turn recruit a black-operations officer to mount the Costa Brava exercise. That exercise – that scene – is turned into murder and at this juncture, it's your thesis that the mole lost sight of Parsifal.'

'Yes. Parsifal, whoever he is, got what he wanted from the mole, then dropped him. The mole is stunned, possibly frantic. He's undoubtedly made promises to Moscow – based on assurances from Parsifal – that projected a major setback for American foreign policy, conceivably, its collapse.'

'Either,' interjected the President in a quiet monotone, 'would be benevolent alternatives.'

'And whoever has the information contained in Parsifal's documents will assume control of the Kremlin.' Brooks remained rigid, his aristocratic face pale, drawn. 'We're at war,' he added softly.

'I repeat,' said Halyard. 'Go after those seventy-five officers at State. Mount a sweep, call it a medical quarantine; it's simple but effective, even acceptable. Do it in the early evening after they've left work. Round them up in their homes, restaurants; pull them in and get them down to your laboratories. Find your mole!' The general's forceful rendering of the tactic impressed the civilians, who remained silent. Halyard lowered his voice. 'I know it smells, but I don't think you've got a choice.'

'We'd need two hundred men posing as medical technicians and drivers,' said Bradford. 'Between thirty and forty government vehicles. No one knowing anything.'

'We'd also be dealing with families and neighbours with "technicians" knocking on doors at night,' countered Berquist. '*Christ*, that son of a bitch! That *man* for all *seasons!*' The President stopped; he took a deep breath, then continued. 'We'd never get away with it; the rumours would spread like a Mesabi brush fire in a dry July. The press would break it open and call us everything in the book, everything we deserve. Mass arrests without explanation – there's none we could give – interrogations without due process, storm troopers . . . chemicals. We'd be crucified on every editorial page in the country, hanged in effigy on every campus, denounced from every pulpit and soap box, to say nothing of the acid from our legislative brethren. I'd be impeached.'

'More important, Mr President,' said the ambassador, 'and I'm sorry to say I mean that, the action itself would undoubtedly throw Parsifal into panic. He'd see what we were doing, know whom we were trying to unearth in order to find him. He could carry out his threats, carry out the inconceivable.'

'Yes, I know. We're damned if we move, helpless if we don't.'

'It could *work*,' persisted the general.

'Handled correctly, it might, Mr President,' added Bradford.

'For God's sake how?'

'Anyone who objected strenuously, to the point of refusal or evasion, would probably be our man,' replied Bradford.

'Or someone with something else to hide,' said Brooks gently. 'We're in the age of anxiety, Mr Undersecretary, and this is a city with a low threshold for privacy. You might very well corner a person who has nothing more to conceal than an unopened closet. The loathing of a superior, or an unpopular viewpoint, or an office affair. Parsifal will see only what his insanity compels him to see.'

Bradford listened, reluctantly accepting the statesman's judgement. 'There's another approach we haven't had time to implement. An itinerary check. Tracing the whereabouts of every person on that floor during the week of Costa Brava. If we're right . . . if I'm not wrong . . . he wasn't here. He was in Madrid, in Barcelona.'

'He'd cover himself,' objected Halyard.

'Even so, General, he'd have to account for being away from Washington. How many such absences can there be?'

'When can you start?' asked Berquist.

'First thing in the morning – '

'Why not tonight?' the general interrupted.

'If those records were accessible, I could. They're not, and to call someone in to open them at this hour would cause talk. We can't afford that.'

'Even in the morning,' said the ambassador, 'how can you suppress curiosity, keep it quiet?'

Bradford paused before speaking, his eyes cast downward, seeking an answer. 'Time study,' he replied, looking up, the phrase bordering on a question. 'I'll tell whoever controls those records that it's a routine time study. Someone's always doing something like that.'

'Acceptable,' agreed Brooks. 'Banal and acceptable.'

'Nothing's acceptable,' said the President of the United States quietly, staring at the white wall where an hour ago the faces of four dead men had been projected. '"A man for all seasons", they call him. The original was a scholar, a statesman, the creator of Utopia . . . *and* a burner of heretics – they conveniently forget that, don't they? "Condemn the nonbelievers; they don't see what I see, and I'm – inviolate" . . . Goddamn it, if I had my way, I'd do what fat Henry did with Thomas More. I'd cut off Matthias's head, and jam it on top of the Washington Monument as a reminder. Heretics, too, are citizens of the republic, and as such, *holy* man, there is no heresy! *Goddamn* him!'

'You know what would happen, don't you Mr President?'

'Yes, Mr Ambassador, I do. The people would look up at that bleeding neck, at that ever-benign face – no doubt with those tortoiseshell glasses still intact – and in their infinite wisdom they'd say he was right, had been right all along. Citizens – heretics included – would canonize him, and that's the lousy irony.'

'He could still do it, I think,' Brooks mused. 'He could walk out and the cries would start again. They'd offer him the crown and he'd refuse and they'd persist – until it became inevitable. Another irony. Hail not Caesar but Anthony – a coronation. A constitutional amendment would be rammed through the House and the Senate and President Matthias would sit in the Oval Office. As incredible as it might seem, he could probably still do it. Even now.'

'Maybe we should let him,' said Berquist softly, bitterly. 'Maybe the people – in their *infinite* wisdom – are right after all. Maybe *he's* been right all along. Sometimes I don't know any more. Perhaps he really does see things others don't see. Even now.'

The aristocratic statesman and the plainspoken general left the underground room. The four would meet again at noon the next day, each arriving separately at the south portico entrance, away from the inquisitive eyes of the White House press corps. If, in the morning, there were any startling developments in Bradford's research at State, the time would be moved forward, the President's calendar erased. The mole took all precedence. He could lead them to a madman the President and his advisers called Parsifal.

'"I commend you, Mr Undersecretary",' said Berquist, lowering his voice in an amateur's imitation of the ambassador's fluid and graceful speech. It was an imitation with only a trace of rancour; respect was also there. 'He's the last of the originals, isn't he?'

'Yes, sir. There aren't many left, and none that I know of who care that much. Taxes and the great democratization have removed them – or alienated them. They feel uncomfortable and I think it's the country's loss.'

'Don't be sepulchral, Emory, it doesn't suit you. We need him; the power brokers on the Hill are still in awe of him. If there was ever an answer to Matthias, it's Addison Brooks. *The Mayflower* and Plymouth Rock, New York's Four Hundred and fortunes built on the backs of immigrants – leading to the guilt feelings of the inheritors: benevolent liberals who weep at the sight of swollen black bellies in the Mississippi Delta. But for Christ's sake, don't take away the *Château d'Yquem*.'

'Yes, Mr President.'

'You mean "No Mr President". It's in your eyes, Emory; it's always in the eyes. Don't mistake me, I admire old elegant-ass, respect what's in that head of his. Just as I think Tightrope Halyard's one of the few military relics who've actually read the Constitution and understand what civilian authority really means. It's not that war's too important to leave to the generals; that's horseshit. We'd both be rotten pincering up the Rhine. It's the *ending* of wars, the aftermath. The generals are reluctant to accept the first and have no concept of the second. Halyard's different, and the Pentagon knows it. The Joint Chiefs listen to him because he's better than they are. We need him, too.'

'I agree.'

'That's what this office is all about. Need. Not likes or dislikes, only need. If I ever get back to Mountain Iron, Minnesota, alive and in one piece, I can think about whether I like someone or not. But I can't do that now. It's only what I need. And what I need right now is to stop Parsifal, stop what he's done, what he did to Anthony Matthias.' The President paused, then continued, 'I meant what I said – *he* said. I *do* commend you. It was a hell of a job.'

'Thank you, sir.'

'Especially what you didn't say. Havelock. Where is he?'

'Almost certainly in Paris; it's where Jenna Karras was heading. Between pages this afternoon I placed a number of calls to people I know in the Assembly, the Senate, several ministries, the Quai d'Orsay and our own embassy. I applied pressure, hinting that my orders came from the White House, but without mentioning you by name.'

'You could have.'

'Not yet, Mr President. Perhaps never, but certainly not now.'

'Then we understand each other,' said Berquist.

'Yes, sir. Necessity.'

'Halyard might have understood; he's a practical soldier. Brooks wouldn't: underneath that diplomatic exterior he's a thorough moralist.'

'That was my assessment, why I didn't clarify Havelock's status.'

'It remains what it was at Col des Moulinets. If he exposed Costa Brava, it would panic Parsifal more quickly than anything we might do in the State Department. Havelock was at the centre – from the beginning.'

'I understand, sir.'

Berquist's eyes strayed to the blank white screen at the far end of the room. 'In World War Two, Churchill had to make a decision that tore him apart. The German code machine Enigma had been broken by Allied Intelligence, a feat which meant that military strategies issued from Berlin could be intercepted and hundreds of thousands – ultimately perhaps millions – of lives could be saved. Word came that a massive air strike had been called against Coventry. It was a single transmission, coded through Enigma. But to acknowledge it, to evacuate the city or even to mount sudden, abnormal defences, would reveal that the riddle of Enigma had been solved . . . Coventry had to be bombed half out of existence so the secret could be kept. The secret of Costa Brava cannot be exposed for the same reason – millions of lives are in the balance. Find Havelock, Mr Undersecretary. Find him and have him killed. Reinstate the order for his execution.'

19

Havelock knew he had been spotted. A newspaper was abruptly lowered as he walked between the roped stanchions of Air France's disembarkation lounge at Kennedy into the corridor that led to Immigration. He had been pre-cleared on diplomatic status, the papers Broussac had provided guaranteeing a rapid exit through US Customs, and because of this accommodation he understood that he must destroy those papers as quickly as possible. He carried his small suitcase – officially lock-taped and stamped *Diplomatique* in Paris – and once through the corridor he would be admitted through the heavy metal doors that led into the terminal by simply showing his United Nations credentials and declaring that he had no other luggage. A dead-file name would be checked against a dead-file name on the manifest and he would be free to search or be killed in the United States of America. It was all so simple.

However, for Régine Broussac's protection – and ultimately his own – he had to get rid of the false papers that made all this possible. Also, he had to find out who had lowered the newspaper. The grey-faced man had risen slowly from his seat, folded the newspaper under his arm and started for the outer, crowded hall-way that paralleled the inner corridor that led to questionable freedom. Who was that man?

If he could not find out, it was entirely possible that he would be killed before he could search, before he reached a halfway broker named Jacob Handelman. And that was not acceptable.

The uniformed immigration officer was astute, polite. He asked the proper questions while looking Havelock directly in the eyes.

'You have no luggage, sir?'

'*Non monsieur*. Only the one piece here.'

'Then you don't expect to be on First Avenue very long?'

'A day, forty-eight hours,' replied Michael, with a Gallic shrug. '*Une conférence.*'

'I'm sure your government has made arrangements for transportation into the city. Wouldn't you care to wait for the rest of your party?'

The official was *very* good. 'Forgive me, *monsieur*, you force me to be candid.' Michael smiled awkwardly, as though his dignity had been somewhat compromised. 'There is a lady waiting for me; we see each other so seldom. Perhaps it is noted on your information, I was posted at . . . First Avenue for several months last year. Haste, *mon ami*, haste is on my mind.'

Slowly the official returned the smile as he checked off the name and reached for a button. 'Have a good day, sir,' he said.

'Many thanks,' said Havelock walking rapidly through the parting steel checkpoint. *Vive les amours des gentilhommes français*, he thought.

The grey-faced man was standing by a short row of telephones, each occupied; he was second in line behind the third. The newspaper, which had been folded under the arm, was instantly removed and snapped open. He had not been able to make his call, and under the circumstances that was the best sight Michael could hope to see.

He started walking in the man's direction, passing him quickly and looking straight ahead. He took the first turning left, into an intersecting wide corridor crowded with streams of departing passengers heading for their gates. He swung right into a narrower hallway, this one with far fewer people and the majority of these in the uniforms of the various airlines.

Left again, the corridor longer, still narrow, even fewer people, mostly men in white overalls and shirtsleeves; he had entered some kind of freight complex, the office section. There were no passengers, no business suits, no briefcases or carry-on bags.

There were no public telephones. The walls were stark, broken up by widely spaced glass doors. The nearest phones were far behind, around the corner in the first, main hallway. Out of sight.

He found the men's room; it said, *Airport Employees Only*. Michael pushed the door open and walked inside. It was a large tiled room, two air vents whirring on the far wall, no windows. A row of toilet booths was on the left, basins and urinals on the right. A man in overalls with the words *Excelsior Airline Caterers* was positioned in front of the fourth urinal; a flush came from one of the booths. Havelock went to a sink, placing his suitcase under it.

The man at the urinal stepped back and zipped up his overalls; he glanced at Michael, his eyes taking in an expensive dark suit purchased that morning in Paris. Then, as if to say, all right Mr Executive, I'll wash my hands, he ambled to the nearest basin and turned on the water.

A second man emerged from a booth; he pulled his belt taut and started for the door, swearing under his breath, the plastic ID tag pinned to his shirt indicating a harried supervisor.

The man in overalls ripped a paper towel out of a stainless steel machine, cursorily wiped his hands and threw the harsh brown paper into a receptacle. He opened the door, and stepped out. As the door swung back Havelock ran to catch it, holding it open no more than an inch, and peered outside.

The unknown surveillance was fifty-odd feet up the corridor, casually leaning against the wall next to an office door, reading the folded newspaper. He looked at his watch, then glanced at the frosted glass panel; he was the image of a visitor waiting for a friend to come out and join him for a late lunch or drinks, or a drive to a motel near the airport. There was nothing menacing about him, but in that control Michael knew there was menace, professionalism.

Still, two could have control, two could wait, be professional. The advantage belonged to the one behind a door; he knew what was inside. The one outside did not, and could not afford to move away – to a telephone, perhaps – because once out of sight the quarry could escape.

Wait. Keep your control. And get rid of the false papers that could lead the pursuers to Régine Broussac and a halfway man named Jacob Handelman. A dead-file name on an aircraft's manifest was meaningless, inserted by mindless computers that could not say who punched the keys, but the papers could be traced to their origin. Havelock tore the documents into shreds, which he flushed down a toilet. With a penknife he sliced the ribbed

Diplomatique tape which guaranteed the absence of official inspection and opened his suitcase in a booth at the end of the row. He removed the short-barrelled Llama automatic from beneath his folded clothes, and a passport case containing his own very authentic papers. Presented properly, the papers were essentially harmless. The objective, however, was not to have to present them at all, and it was rarely required in the streets of his adopted country, one of the benefits for which he was profoundly thankful.

During the time he destroyed the mocked-up papers and inserted his passport case and weapon in their proper places, the employees' men's room had two more visitors. They came in together – an Air France pilot and his First Officer to judge from their conversation: Michael remained in the stall. They argued, urinated, swore at pre-flight red tape and wondered how much their Havana *Monte Christos* would fetch at the bar of *L'Auberge au Coin*, a restaurant apparently in mid-town Manhattan. They continued talking about their profits on the way out.

Havelock took off the jacket of his suit, rolled it up and waited in the stall. He held the door open no more than a quarter of an inch and looked at his watch. He had been inside the lavatory nearly fifteen minutes. It would happen soon, he thought.

It did. The white metal door swung slowly back, and Havelock saw part of a shoulder first, then the edge of a folded newspaper. The unknown surveillance *was* professional: no folded jacket or coat concealed a gun – no draped cloth that could be grabbed and twisted, to be used against the holder – just a loose newspaper that could be easily discarded and the weapon fired cleanly.

The man whipped around the door, his back against the metal panel, his eyes scanning the walls, the vents, the row of stalls. Satisfied, he bent his knees, lowering himself, but apparently not for the purpose of checking the open spaces under the doors of the first several stalls. His body was turned away from Michael. His eyes darted back and forth. What was he doing?

And then he did it, and the image of another professional on the bridge at Col des Moulinets came to Michael, a blond professional in the uniform of an Italian guard. But the killer 'Ricci' had come prepared, knowing what his landscape was, knowing there was a gatehouse door to be jammed. This grey-faced professional had improvised, the test of on-site ingenuity. He had broken off a piece of wood, a small strip of cheap industrial moulding – found in a dozen places in any airport corridor – and was now wedging it under the door. He stood up, placed his foot against the strip, and pulled on the metal knob. The door was jammed; they were alone. The man turned.

Peering from inside the stall, Havelock studied him. The menace was not at first glance in the man's physical equipment. He was perhaps in his mid-fifties, with thinning hair above a flat grey face with thick eyebrows and high cheekbones. He was no taller than five feet, eight inches, and his shoulders were narrow, compact. But then Michael saw the left hand – the right was concealed beneath the newspaper; it was huge, a peasant's powerful hand, formed by years of working with heavy objects and equipment.

The man started down the row of stalls, the sides of each about two inches above the tiled floor, which made it necessary for him to be within three feet of a front panel to ascertain whether it was occupied. Wearing shoes with thick rubber soles, he moved in total silence. Suddenly he spun his right hand in a circle, flipping off the newspaper. Havelock stared at the gun, as the intruder approached the final three stalls. He was angry but bewildered – the weapon was a Graz-Burya. The Russian bent over . . .

Now. Michael threw his rolled-up suit jacket over the side of the booth on his right. The sound made the Russian leap up, spinning to his left, his gun raised.

Havelock grabbed the handle of his suitcase and simultaneously yanked the door open, then swung the heavy case at the man, body and extended arms following, his eyes on the Graz-Burya, his left hand reaching it, gripping it, tearing it upwards. The Russian spun away, his powerful arms blocking Havelock; Michael used them. He locked the man's left arm under his right, wrenched it forward until the Russian's face was stretched in pain; then he pried the weapon loose, crashing the barrel into the man's head. The Russian started to fall and Havelock crouched and jammed his shoulder into the man's kidney, propelling him back into the row of urinals.

The grey-faced man fell to his knees, supporting himself on his right hand and holding his left arm across his chest in pain. He gasped for breath, shaking his head. '*Nyet, nyet,*' he choked. 'Talk only! Only *talk*.'

'With the door as good as locked and a gun in your hand?'

'Would you have agreed to a conversation if I had come up and introduced myself? In Russian, perhaps?'

'You should have tried me.'

'You did not stay still long enough . . . May I?' The Russian leaned back on his knees, holding his arm and raising one leg as he requested permission to stand.

'Go ahead,' said Havelock, the Graz-Burya steady in his hand. 'You were trying to make a phone call.'

'Certainly. To relay word that you had been found. What would you have done? I don't know, or perhaps I should not ask.'

'What *do* you know? How did you find me?' Michael raised the gun, aiming it at the man's head. 'I'd advise you to tell me the truth. I haven't got a thing to lose with your corpse in here.'

The Russian stared at the barrel and then at Havelock's eyes. 'No, you have nothing to lose; you would not hesitate. A younger man should have been sent out here.'

'How did you know I'd be on that plane?'

'I didn't. No one knows anywhere . . . A VKR officer was shot in Paris; he had nowhere to turn but to us.'

'An importing firm on the Beaumarchais?' interrupted Michael. 'KGB headquarters Paris?'

The Russian overlooked the interruption. 'We knew you had connections throughout the French government. Military intelligence, the Quai d'Orsay, the Deputies. If it was your intention to leave France there was only one way you could do it. Diplomatic cover. All Air France flights listing diplomatic personnel are being watched. Everywhere. London, Rome, Bonn, Athens, the Netherlands, all of South America – everywhere. It's my misfortune that you chose to come back here; it was not expected. You're "beyond-salvage".'

'That seems to be a well-publicized piece of information.'

'It has been circulated in certain quarters.'

'Is that what you wanted to talk about? Because if it is, Moscow's wasting a lot of man hours in all those airports.'

'I bring you a message from Pyotr Rostov. He believes that after Rome, you might listen.'

'*Rome?* What about Rome?'

'The Palatine. It would seem it was conclusive for you. You were meant to die on the Palatine Hill.'

'I was?' Havelock watched the man's eyes, the set of his lips. So Rostov knew about the Palatine; it was to be expected. Bodies had been found there: the corpse of a former American agent known for jugular operations and his two wounded Italian drones who had nothing to lose and something to bargain with by telling the truth. Certainly Moscow knew. But Rostov did not know about Jenna Karras or Col des Moulinets or he would have included them in his opening lure. Under different circumstances, it might have been necessary to shout the words quickly: *Jenna Karras is alive! Col des Moulinets!* Both were far more conclusive. 'What's the message?'

'He says to tell you the bait's been reconsidered. He'll take it now and thinks you should agree. He says he's not your enemy any longer, but others are who may be his as well.'

'What does that mean?'

'I can't answer you,' said the man, his thick eyebrows motionless about his deep-set peasant eyes. 'I'm merely the messenger. The substance is for you to know, not me.'

'You knew about the Palatine.'

'The death of a maniac travels fast, especially if he's your adversary – most especially if he's killed a number of your friends . . . What was the name his own people gave him? The "Gunslinger", I believe. A romantic figure from your Western films, which, incidentally, I enjoy immensely. But in history such a fellow was invariably a filthy, unprincipled pig, devoid of morals or ideology, motivated solely by profit or pathological brutality. In these times he might be the president of an enormous corporation, no?'

'Spare me. Save it for the state schools.'

'Rostov would like a reply, but you don't have to give it at once. I can reach you. A day, two days – a few hours from now. You may name the drop. We can get you out. To safety.'

Again Michael studied the Russian's face. Like Rostov in Athens before him, the man was relaying the truth – as he knew the truth, and as he knew the word of his superior in Moscow. 'What does Rostov offer?'

'I told you. Safety. You know what's ahead of you here. The Palatine Hill.'

'Safety in exchange for what?'

'That's between you and Rostov. Why should I invent conditions? You would not believe them.'

'Tell Rostov he's wrong.'

'About Rome? The Palatine?'

'The Palatine,' said Havelock, wondering briefly whether a KGB director ten thousand miles away would perceive the essential truth within the larger lie. 'I don't need the safety of the Lubyanka.'

'You refuse his offer then?'

'I refuse the bait.'

There was a sudden thud against the men's-room door, followed by a muffled voice swearing, then repeated banging against the metal panel. The strip of wood wedged under the door scraped the tile; it gave less than an inch, which was enough to make the intruder shout, while continuing to pound the door, 'Hey, what the hell *is* this! Open up!'

The Russian glanced at the door; Havelock did not. The man spoke rapidly: 'Should you change your mind, there is a row of trash cans in Bryant Park, behind the Public Library. Place a red mark on the front of one of them – I suggest a felt marker or, better still, a spot of woman's nail polish. Then, starting at ten o'clock that same night, walk north and south on Broadway, between Forty-second and Fifty-third Streets, staying on the east side. Someone will reach you, giving you the address of the contact. It will be outside, naturally. No traps.'

'What's going *on* in there? Fa' *Christ's sake*, open this goddamned *door*!'

'I thought you said I could pick the drop.'

'You may. Simply tell the man who reaches you where you want to meet. Just give us three hours.'

'To sweep it?'

'Son of a bitch! *Open up!*' The metal door was smashed back several inches, the strip of wood scratching against the tiles.

A second, authoritative voice joined that of the angry intruder. 'All right, what's this all about?'

'The door's jammed! I can't get in, but I hear 'em talkin'! They jammed the fuckin' door!' Another crash, another screech, another inch.

'We take precautions, just as you do,' said the Russian. 'What's between you and Rostov . . . is between you and Moscow. We are not in Moscow, *I* am not in Moscow. I do not call for the police when I'm in trouble in New York City.'

'All *right* in there!' shouted the second voice in lower-register officiousness. 'Fair warning, you punks! Obstruction of normal operating procedures at an international airport constitutes a felony, and that includes the toilets! I'm calling Airport Security!' The stern-toned one addressed the angry intruder. 'If I were you, I'd find another men's room. These kids use needles; they can get hopped up and pretty violent.'

'I've gotta' take one pisser of a leak, man! And they don't *sound* like no kids – There's a cop! Hey, *Fuzz!*'

'He can't hear you. He's walking past. I'll get to a phone.'

'*Shit!*'

'Let's go,' said Havelock, reaching down for his jacket. He slipped it on, switching the gun back and forth as he did so.

'My life, then?' asked the Russian. 'No corpse in a men's room?'

'I want my reply delivered. Forget the nail polish on those trash cans.'

'Then, if I may, my weapon, please?'

'I'm not that charitable. You see, you *are* my enemy. You have been for a long time.'

'It's difficult to explain a missing weapon. *You* understand.'

'Tell them you sold it on the open market; it's the first step in capitalism. Buy cheap – or get it for nothing – and sell high. The Burya's a good gun; it'd bring a large profit.'

'*Please!*'

'You don't understand, *Comrade*. You'd be surprised how many hustlers in Moscow would respect you. Come *on!*' Havelock grabbed the grey-faced man by the shoulder, propelling him towards the door. 'Kick out the wood,' he ordered, shoving the weapon into his belt and picking up his suitcase.

The Russian did as he was told. He pressed the side of his shoe on the protruding wedge, moving it back and forth as he pushed the door shut. The wedge came loose; he swept it away with his foot, and pulled the door open.

'Jesus *Christ!*' exclaimed an obese man in sky-blue overalls. 'A couple of fuckin' fairies!'

'They're *coming!*' yelled a shirtsleeved man, running out of an office door across the corridor.

'I think you're too late, Mr Supervisor,' said the wide-eyed freight employee, staring at Havelock and the Russian. 'Here're your fuckin' punks. Two old queens who figured the parking lot was too cold.'

'Let's *go!*' whispered Havelock, grabbing the Russian's elbow.

'Disgusting! Revolting!' shouted the supervisor. 'At your age! Have you no *shame*? Perverts *everywhere!*'

'You won't change your mind about the weapon?' asked the Russian, walking breathlessly up the corridor, wincing as Michael gripped his damaged left arm. 'I'll be severely disciplined. I haven't used it for years; it's really a form of dress, you know.'

'*Perverts!* You should all be in jail, not in public toilets! You're a menace!'

'I'm telling you, you'll get a promotion if the right people think you made a bundle.'

'*Faggots!*'

'Let go of my arm. That idiot's marking us.'

'Why? You're adorable.'

They reached the second hallway, turning left towards the centre of the terminal. There were, as before, men in overalls and shirtsleeves milling about, watching an occasional secretary emerge from an office door. Up ahead was the main corridor, crowds surging in both directions, towards departing gates and luggage areas.

In seconds they were swept into the flow of arrivals. Seconds later a trio of uniformed police could be seen breaking through the stream of departing passengers, pushing aside shoulders and small suitcases and plastic clothes bags. Havelock switched sides with the Russian, yanking him to the left, and as the police came parallel in the opposite aisle Michael crashed his shoulder into his companion, pummelling him into a blue uniform.

'*Nyet! Kishki!*' yelled the Russian.

'*Goddamn* it!' shouted the police officer as he plunged off balance to his right, tripping one of his associates, who in turn fell on top of an elderly blue-haired woman.

Havelock accelerated his pace, threading his way past startled passengers who were rushing towards an escalator on the right that led to the baggage area, where they could retrieve their belongings. On the left was someone's idea of a celestial arch which led into the central terminal; he headed towards it, walking faster still as the path became less congested. In the terminal the bright afternoon sunlight streamed through the huge floor-to-ceiling windows. He looked around as he went towards the exit door marked *Taxis*. There were rows of counters beneath panoplies of white-lettered schedules, isolated slots constantly in motion; circular booths selling knick-knacks and gewgaws were dotted about in the middle of the dome-like building. Along the walls were banks of telephones and indented racks of telephone books. He veered towards the nearest one.

Thirty seconds later he found it: *Handelman, J.* The address was in upper Manhattan, on 116th Street, Morningside Heights.

Jacob Handelman, halfway man, broker of sanctuary for the pursued and the dispossessed. The man who would conceal Jenna Karras.

'Stop over there,' said Havelock, leaning forward in the seat and pointing to a blue canopy emblazoned with a small gold crown and the name *The King's Arms Hotel* across the scalloped valance. He hoped he would not have to spend the night – each hour put greater distance between Jenna and himself – but on the other hand, he could not walk around Columbia University carrying even a small suitcase while tracking down Jacob Handelman. He had told the cab driver to take the Triborough Bridge, head west towards the Hudson and south into Morningside Heights; he wanted to pass the address on 116th, then find a secure place to leave his luggage. It was mid-afternoon and the halfway man could be anywhere within the sprawling urban campus.

Michael had been to Columbia twice while a graduate student at Princeton, once for a lecture on Europe after Napoleon delivered by a visiting bore from Oxford, and the second time for an inter-graduate-school seminar on university placement. Neither occasion was memorable, both were brief, and as a result he really knew nothing about the place. That was probably irrelevant, but the fact that he knew absolutely nothing about Jacob Handelman was not.

The King's Arms was around the corner from Handelman's apartment. It was one of those small hotels that somehow managed to survive tastefully within the environs of a city university, upper Manhattan's answer to the old Taft in New Haven or, stretching a point, the Inn at Princeton. In essence, a campus fixture, temporary quarters for visiting lecturers rather than an undergraduate drinking spot. It had the appearance of dark-leather English comfort and the smell of Academe. It was only an outside possibility, but since the hotel was so close to Handelman's residence, there was a chance someone might know him.

'Certainly, Mr Hereford,' said the clerk, reading the registration card. 'Dr Handelman calls in now and then – a little wine or dinner with friends. A delightful gentleman, a most charming sense of humour. We here, like almost everyone else, call him the Rabbi.'

'I didn't know that. His being a rabbi, I mean.'

'I'm not sure he is formally, although I doubt anyone would question his credentials. He's Jarmaine Professor of Philosophy and I understand he lectures frequently at Jewish Theological. You'll enjoy your interview.'

'I'm sure I will. Thank you.'

'Front,' said the clerk, tapping a bell.

Handelman's apartment was between Broadway and Riverside Drive. The sloping street overlooked Riverside Park and the Hudson. It was a solid structure of heavy white stone – once a monument to New York's exploding upward mobility – which had been permitted to age gently, and to pass through periods of brief renaissance, only to recede into that graveyard of tall, awkwardly ornate edifices too cumbersome for efficient economics. Once there had been a doorman standing in front of the glass-and-ironwork façade; now there were double locks on the inner door and a functioning communications system between visitor and resident.

Havelock pressed the bell, intending merely to make sure Handelman was home; there was no reply from the speaker. He rang again. Nothing.

He went back outside, crossing the street to an opposite door-way, and considered his options. He had telephoned the university's information centre and been given the location and number of Handelman's office. A second call – placed anonymously by an administrations clerk requesting a Thursday *Stat sheet* – revealed the fact that Handelman had doctoral appointments until after 4 p.m. It was now nearly 5 o'clock, and Michael's frustration was growing. Where *was* Handelman? There was, of course, no guarantee that he would come directly home from his office, but a broker of sanctuary who had just placed – or was placing – a woman fugitive from Paris had certain obligations. Havelock had considered going to Handelman's office, or intercepting him on the street; he considered both again. Perhaps an appointment had run late, or dinner been proffered; someone could still be there who might know, who might help him. Coping with the tension of waiting – a practice he was normally superb at – was causing him pain, actual physical pain in his stomach. He breathed deeply; he could not confront the halfway man in an office or on the street or in any public place and he knew it. The meeting must take place where there were names and numbers, maps and codes; these were the tools of a halfway man. They would only be kept where he could store them safely, reach them quickly. Under a floorboard, or deep in a wall, or microscopically reduced and in the toe of a shoe or implanted in shirt buttons.

He had not seen a photograph of Handelman, but he knew what he looked like. The florid-faced bartender at The King's Arms Hotel – himself apparently a fixture, with the flair and verbosity of a fifth-rate poet from Dublin – had described 'the Rabbi'. Jacob Handelman was a medium-tall man with long white hair and a short grey beard, slightly given to overweight and more than slightly to a paunch. His walk was 'slow and stately', the bartender said, 'as if he was the Judaic blood-royal, sir, forever partin' the waters, or mountin' the ark to discourse with the animals. Ah, but he has a gleam in his eye and a lovely heart, sir.'

Havelock had listened to the man and ordered a double scotch.

Three minutes past five. *Breathe deep. Really breathe and think of Jenna, think what you're going to say to her. It could be an hour or two, or longer, perhaps half the night. Half the night for the halfway man. Don't dwell on it.*

Dusk lingered, the orange sun inflaming the New Jersey skyline beyond the Hudson River. The West Side Highway was jammed, and Riverside Drive, parallel to it, was barely less so. The temperature was dropping and grey clouds joined the darkening sky; a March snow was in the air.

And across the street a medium-tall man, wide at the girth, in a full black overcoat, walked slowly down the pavement. His bearing was indeed stately, matching the distinguished image created by his pure white hair, which fell several inches below the brim of his black hat. In the light of a street lamp, Michael could see the grey beard; it was the halfway man.

Jacob Handelman approached the outer glass doors of his apartment building and was now in the stronger light of the large entrance lamps. Havelock stared, at once mesmerized and disturbed; did he know the halfway man? Had 'the Rabbi' been part of an operation eight . . . ten years ago? Perhaps in the Middle East, Tel Aviv, Lebanon? Michael had the distinct feeling that he *did* know him. Was it the walk? The deliberate pace that seemed almost anachronistic, as if the figure should be strolling in mediaeval robes? Or was it the thin steel-rimmed glasses, set so firmly in the centre of the large face?

The moment passed; it was, of course, possible that the halfway man might have crossed his path in any number of situations. They could have been in the same sector at one time or another, a respected professor supposedly on holiday but in reality meeting someone like Régine Broussac. Entirely possible.

Handelman went inside the enclosed entranceway, climbed the inner steps and stopped at the row of mailboxes. It was all Michael could do to restrain himself; the desire to race across the street and confront the halfway man was nearly overpowering.

He may choose to tell you nothing. Broussac.

An old man who did not care to negotiate could scream on a staircase and yell for help. And the one who *needed* help did not know what was behind a door across the street, what devices a group of intelligent city dwellers had mounted to defend themselves from hallway thugs. Security-alarms had flooded the market; he had to wait until Jacob Handelman was safely in his flat. And then a knock on the door and the words 'Quai d'Orsay' would be enough; there was respect for a man who could elude alarms, an inherent threat in someone outside a door who knew that the one inside was a halfway man. Handelman would see him; he could not afford to refuse.

The old man disappeared through the inner door, the heavy panel of ironwork and glass swinging slowly shut behind him. Havelock waited three minutes; the lights went on in several front windows on the fourth floor. It was logical that Handelman's apartment number was 4-A. A halfway man had certain things in common with deep-cover field personnel and the Soviet VKR; he had to be able to watch the streets.

He was not watching now; there was no figure behind the curtains. Michael stepped out of the doorway and crossed the street. Inside the ornate entrance way he struck a match and held it waist-high as he looked down the row of names above the buttons.

R. Charles, Superintendent 1D

He pressed the button and put his lips close to the webbed speaker.

'Yes, what is it?' asked the male voice in clear, well-spoken English.

'Mr Charles?' said Havelock, not knowing why the man's voice struck him as odd.

'Yes, it's Charles. Who's this?'

'United States Government, Department of State – '

'*What?*'

'Nothing to be alarmed about, Mr Charles. If you'll come to the door, you can check my identification through the glass, and either admit me or I can give you a number to call.'

R. Charles paused, then answered slowly. 'Fair enough.'

Thirty seconds later a huge, muscular young man appeared in the hallway beyond the door. He was wearing track shorts and a sweatshirt marked with a large number *20*. It was either a proclamation of age or the gridiron identity of one of Columbia's larger football players. This, then, was the protection the apartment dwellers on Morningside Heights had chosen. Again, logical; take care of your own to take care of you. Free lodgings for an imposing presence. Michael held up his old ID card in its black plastic case; the dates, of course, were blurred.

R. Charles squinted through the glass, shrugged and opened the door. 'What the hell is this?' he asked, more curiosity than hostility in his voice. A man his size did not have to be aggressive; his thick legs and neck and muscular arms were sufficiently intimidating. Also his youth.

'There's a man here I'd like to see on official State Department business, but he's not in. I rang, of course; he's a friend.'

'Who is it?'

'Dr Jacob Handelman. He's a consultant for us but he doesn't advertise it.'

'Nice old guy, Handelman.'

'The best, Mr Charles. However, I think he'd be alarmed if he thought I might be recognized.' Havelock grinned. 'Also, it's damned cold out there.'

'I can't let you in his apartment. I *won't* let you in.'

'And I wouldn't allow you to. I'll just wait here, if it's all right.'

R. Charles hesitated, his eyes dropping to the open ID case still in Michael's hand. 'Yeah, well, okay. I'd ask you into my place but my roommate and I are busting our humps for a mid-term exam tomorrow.'

'Please, I wouldn't think of it . . .'

Havelock was interrupted by the appearance of an even larger young man in a doorway at the end of the hall. He was in a full sweatsuit, a book gripped in one hand, a pair of glasses in the other. 'Hey, man, what is it?'

'Nothing. Someone looking for the Rabbi.'

'Another one? Come on, we're wasting time. You're the brain, I just want to get through tomorrow.'

'Your roommate on the team?' asked Michael, trying to appear contemporary.

'No. He wrestles. That is, he does when they don't throw him out for dirty holds. Okay, Mastiff, coming.' The roommate went inside.

'Thanks again.'

'Sure. You even sound official. The Rabbi ought to show up any minute.'

'Pretty punctual, huh?'

'Like a Swiss clock.' Number *Twenty* turned, then looked back at Havelock. 'You know, I figured something like this. Like you, I mean.'

'How so?'

'I don't know . . . the people who come to see him, I guess. Late at night sometimes; not exactly campus types.'

There was nothing to lose in asking, thought Michael. The young man himself had provided the opening. 'We're most concerned about the woman, I don't mind telling you that. For . . . the Rabbi's sake we hope she got here. Did you by any chance see her? A blonde woman, about five feet five, probably in a raincoat, maybe a hat. Yesterday? Today?'

'Last night,' said the young man. 'I didn't, but Mastiff did. Foxy lady, he told me. But nervous; she rang the wrong bell and got old Weinberg – he's in Four-B and even more nervous.'

'We're relieved she's here. What time last night?'

'About now, I guess. I was on the phone when Weinberg buzzed us on the intercom.'

'Thank you.' *Twenty-four hours. A halfway man upstairs. She was within reach – he could feel it, sense it!* 'Incidentally, by sheer coincidence, you've been given privileged information. Please respect it.'

'Man, you *are* official. I never saw you, Mr Havalatch. But if they institute that draft I may look you up.'

'Do that. Thanks again.'

'Take care.' The huge student walked down the hallway to the open door.

The instant it was closed, Havelock moved quickly to the wide stone staircase in the centre of the foyer, the steps worn smooth, indented from decades of use. He could not use the lift beyond; its sound might well alarm a trusting, muscular student who could suddenly reject the concept of privileged information in favour of less esoteric responsibilities.

In Paris Michael had had the presence of mind to have the expensive black shoes he had purchased to match his suit resoled with hard rubber. They served him well on the staircase; he went up swiftly, silently, taking the steps two and three at a time, rounding the landings without a sound. In less than half a minute he reached the fourth floor; Apartment 4A was at the end of the tiled, dimly lit hallway. He stood for several moments catching his breath, then approached the door and pressed the small button embedded in the moulding. From beyond he heard the bell chime softly and seconds later the sound of footsteps.

'Yes?' said the curiously high-pitched voice, in a rolling European accent.

'Dr Jacob Handelman?'

'Who is this, please?' The speech was Hebrew-rooted German.

'I have news from the Quai d'Orsay. May we talk?'

'Vos?' The silence was brief, the words that followed rushed. 'You are mistaken. I have no idea what you're talking about? I know no one in . . . what you say, the Quai d'Orsay?'

'In that case, I'll have to get in touch with Paris, and tell my contact she's made a dreadful error. Naturally, Jacob Handelman will be removed from the catacomb's computer terminal.'

'Just one minute, please. I must jog this old man's memory.'

Havelock could hear the moving footsteps again, faster now, receding, then returning long before the stated minute was up. The metallic sounds of several locks were heard behind the thick wood; the door opened and the halfway man stared at him, then gestured with his head for Michael to come inside.

What was it? Why was he so certain he knew this man, this old man with the grey beard and the long white hair? The large face was soft but the eyes in the creased flesh behind the heavy-lensed glasses were . . . he was not sure, he could not tell.

'You are in my house, sir,' said Handelman, closing the door and manipulating the locks. 'I've travelled widely, of course, not always by my own wishes, like so many thousands in my situation. Perhaps we have a mutual friend I cannot at the moment recall. At the Quai d'Orsay. Naturally, I know a number of professors at the Sorbonne.'

Was it the high-pitched, sing-song voice? Or the questioning tilt of the head? Or the way the old man stood, feet planted firmly, the posture soft, yet somehow rigid? No, it was not any single thing, it was all of them . . . somehow.

'"A mutual friend" isn't quite accurate. You know a name. Broussac. Ministry of Foreign Affairs, Section Four. She was to have reached you today; she's a person of her word. I think she did.'

'Ah, but my office is filled with scores of messages only my secretary is aware of, Mister . . . Mister . . .?'

'Havelock.'

'Yes, Mr Havellacht. Come in, come in. I knew a Habernicht in Berlin in the old days. Friedrich Habernicht. Quite similar, no?'

'Close, I guess.' *Was it the walk?* The same deliberate stride that he had seen outside. The stately . . . arrogant steps that should be cloaked in mediaeval robes or a high priest's cassock. He had to ask. 'We've met before, haven't we?'

'We?' The halfway man's eyebrows arched; he adjusted his steel-rimmed glasses and peered through them at Michael. 'I cannot imagine where. Unless you were a student in a large class of mine, but that would have to be a number of years ago, I would think. In such a case, you would remember me, I would not necessarily remember you. Age and the sheer mass of numbers, you understand.'

'Never mind.' *A number of years ago. How many years?* 'Are you telling me you haven't heard from Broussac?'

'I'm telling you nothing . . . Sit down, do sit down . . . I am merely saying that I do not know. You say this person Broussac sent me a message today, and *I* am saying I receive dozens of messages *every* day that I frequently do not get to for *many* days. Again, age and the sheer mass of numbers.'

'I heard you before,' interrupted Havelock; he remained standing, his eyes scanning the room. There were bookshelves everywhere, old furniture – overstuffed chairs, fringed lamps, hassocks – nothing Spartan. Once more the smell of Academe. 'Jenna Karras!' said Michael suddenly, raising his voice.

'Another message?' asked Handelman ingenuously, an old man bemused by a younger antagonist. 'So many messages – I must have a talk with my secretary. She overprotects me.'

'Jenna Karras came to see you last night, I know that!'

'Three . . . no, *four* people came to see me last night, each a student of mine. I even have their names over here, and the outlines of two graduate papers.' Handelman walked to a cluttered desk against the wall.

'Cut it out!' shouted Havelock. 'You packaged her and I've got to *find* her! That was Broussac's message.'

'So many messages,' intoned the halfway man, as if chanting a Talmudic response. 'Ahh, here are the names, the graduate outlines,' continued Handelman, bending over the disorganized pile of papers. 'So many visitors . . . so many messages. Who can keep track?'

'*Listen* to me! Broussac wouldn't have given me your name or told me where to find you if I weren't telling you the truth. I have to *reach* her! A terrible thing was done to her – to *us* – and she doesn't understand!'

'"The Filioque Denials in the Councils of Arius",' chanted Handelman, standing erect and holding a sheaf of papers under the light of a floor lamp. 'Those would be the Nicene rejections of the Eastern Church around the fifth century. Very little understood – speaking of understanding.'

He may choose to tell you nothing. 'Goddamn you, where did you *send* her?! Stop *playing* with me! Because – if I have to – I'll – '

'Yes?' Jacob Handelman turned his head in the spill of the floor lamp and peered once again through the steel-rimmed glasses. He took several steps to his left and replaced the papers on the desk.

It was there, at that moment. It was all there. The eyes behind the thin rims of silver, the rigid posture of the soft body . . . the walk. Not the strolling of a high prelate in the church or a mediaeval baron entering a great hall . . . but the strutting of a man in uniform. A black uniform!

Sheets of lightning filled Havelock's eyes. His mind exploded . . . *then and now, now and then!* Not eight or ten years ago, but the early years, the terrible years! He was one of *them*! The images of his memory confirmed it; he saw the man in front of him now as he was then. The large face – without a beard, the hair straight and long, not white but *Aryan yellow*. Walking . . . strutting . . . down to rows of ditches. *Machine-gun fire. Screams.*

Lidice!

As if in a trance, Michael started towards the halfway man, his hands taut and hard, his fingers curving into claws, tensed for combat with another animal – a lower form of animal.

'Vos?' Handelman drew out the sibilant *s* in his high-pitched whine. 'What is the matter with you? Are you crazy, perhaps? Look at you . . . are you sick? Stay away from me!'

'The *Rabbi* . . .? Oh Christ, you son of a bitch. You *incredible son of a bitch!* What were you . . . *Oberstleutnant? Major?* . . . No, it was *Reichsführer*! It was *you*! *Lidice!*'

The old man's eyes widened, magnified by the thick lenses, they looked monstrous. 'You are mad, completely, utterly *mad*! Leave my house! You are not welcome here. With the pain I've suffered, I will not listen to the ravings of a madman!'

The intense sing-song chant of the words covered the halfway man's movement. His right hand slipped down to the desk, to the clutter of papers. Havelock lunged as a gun emerged in Handelman's hand, placed there minutes ago by a *Reichsführer* who could never afford to forget his origins. The halfway man was a killer of Czechs and Poles and Jews, a man who had taken the identity of a ragged inmate he had sent into a shower of gas or a cave of fire.

Havelock grabbed the hand with the gun, jammed his third finger behind the trigger and slammed it repeatedly against the edge of the desk. It would not come loose! The halfway man was arched beneath him, pinning his right arm, the face grotesque, the mouth stretched like a rabid dog's, the soft body suddenly hard, writhing in spasms. Handelman's left hand surged up and clapped on Michael's face, the fingers digging into his eyes.

Havelock twisted violently back and forth and the halfway man slipped out from under him. They were at the edge of the desk, immobilized by each other's arms bent to the breaking point. Suddenly Michael freed his right hand; he clenched it into a fist and brought it crashing down like a hammer into where he could see the blur of Handelman's face.

The steel-rimmed glasses shattered. The German screamed and the gun clattered to the floor as he brought both his hands to his face.

Havelock leaped backward, yanking the German to his feet, and clamped his hand across the ugly mouth. His eyes burned; tears and specks of blood clouded his vision – but he could see and the Nazi could not.

'You raise your voice, old man, I'll kill you the instant you do. Now sit down!'

He pulled the German away from the desk and pushed him into the nearest chair with such force that the halfway man's neck snapped back. The shattered glasses, however, remained secure on Handelman's face; they were a part of that face, part of the ugliness.

'You have blinded me!' whined the soldier from Lidice. 'A madman comes into my house – '

'Forget it!' said Michael. 'I was *there*!'

'Madness!' Gasping through his stretched open mouth, Handelman raised his hands to remove his glasses.

'Leave them alone!' ordered Havelock. 'Let them stay right where they are.'

'Young man, you are – '

'Don't talk! Listen. I can put out a trace on a man named Jacob Handelman going back fifty years. Everything about him – old pictures, Germans still alive who knew him – if he ever existed. Then circulate a photograph of you, minus the beard, of course, in certain sections of Prague. You were there; I saw you later and wanted to kill you. A boy of nine or ten wanted to put a knife in your back in the street. And someone still living in Prague or Rudna or Kladno would want to do the same even now. That's the bottom line, you *bastard*! So don't talk to me about people who weren't here last night, tell me about the one who was. Where *is* she?'

'I am a very valuable man – '

'I'll bet you are. Who'd know more about finding safe territories than someone who did it so well. And who could protect himself better than someone who could expose the whereabouts of so many. You've covered yourself, *Totschläger*. But not with me, do you understand that? Because I don't care. Now, where is *Jenna Karras?*'

'While not addressing myself to the preposterous accusations you make,' whined the German, 'there are considerations of exchange.'

'You have your life,' said Havelock. 'I'm not interested in it. It's enough that you know I'm out there and can end it any time I like. That's your exchange. Where is she?'

'The top drawer of the desk.' The halfway man gestured with his trembling hand, his eyes unseeing behind the shattered glasses. 'Lift up the pencil rack. There's a folded green paper.'

Michael went to the desk, opened the drawer and pulled out the concave receptacle for pens and pencils. There was the light green paper; he picked it up and unfolded it. It was a page of memorandum stationery from the Columbia University Graduate Faculty of Philosophy. In precise, handwritten block letters was the information Havelock would have killed for; it was everything.

Broussac. Applicant for Doctoral Candidate.
Name: Arvidas Corescu. c/o Kohoutek
RFD 3, Mason Falls, Penna.

'Is Corescu the name she's using?' asked Havelock sharply.

'Temporarily. The papers are only temporary; they had to be manufactured in a few hours. Others will follow . . . if they are to follow.'

'Which means?'

'They must be paid for. Nothing is for nothing.'

'Naturally; the hook's sunk in and the line keeps reeling out. You must have some very impressive fish out there.'

'You could say I have powerful – friends. In many places.'

'Who's this Kohoutek?'

'A Slav,' said the halfway man, shrugging derisively. 'He has farm land.'

'When did she leave?'

'She was picked up this morning.'

'What's her cover?'

'Another destitute refugee – a niece, perhaps – got out of the Balkans, or wherever. Away from the Bear, as they say. Kohoutek will get her work; he has friends in the textile unions.'

'From which she pays him *and* you, or the papers don't follow.'

'One needs papers,' whined Handelman, 'to drive a car, or use a bank – '

'Or to be left alone by Immigration,' interrupted Michael. 'That threat's always there, isn't it?'

'We are a nation of laws, sir.'

'You make me *sick*,' said Havelock, approaching the chair. 'I could kill you now, feeling nothing but joy,' he added quietly. 'Can you understand that, philosopher? But I won't because I want you to know what it's like to realize it can happen any moment, any day, any night. With a knock on your door. You live with that, you snake. *Heil Hitler.*'

He turned and started for the door.

The *crack* came from behind him! He spun around to see the long blade of a knife streaking towards him, directly at his chest. The halfway man had torn the shattered glasses off his face and seized the weapon concealed in the overstuffed chair; the musty smell of Academe was suddenly the putrid odour of a no-man's land in a far away battlefield. Havelock jumped back, but not before the blade had ripped through the jacket of his suit, the razor-sharp edge slitting his flesh and marking his white shirt with a line of blood.

His right hand whipped under his coat for the Llama automatic. He kicked wildly in front of him, hoping to make contact with any part of the German's body. As the blade came arching back, he spun away from its trajectory and raised his gun, aiming at the face.

He fired twice; the halfway man fell to the floor, his head soaked in blood, one eye blown away.

A gun had stilled another gun from Lidice. But there was no joy; it had ceased to matter.

There was only Jenna. He had found her! She could not stop him from reaching her now. She might kill him, but first she would have to look into his eyes. That *did* matter.

He shoved the Llama into his belt, the page of green paper into his pocket, and raced out of the apartment.

20

'The name's Broussac, Mr President,' said Emory Bradford into the phone at his desk in the State Department. 'Madame Régine Broussac. The Quai d'Orsay, Foreign Ministry, Section Four. She contacted the embassy the night before last, instructing a radio-car unit to be in the vicinity of Argenteuil for the purpose of picking up a former American intelligence officer who was to meet her there. Under highly unorthodox circumstances, she said.'

'Havelock?'

'She's admitted that much, yes.'

'And?'

'The car drove up and down the streets of Argenteuil all night. It was never contacted.'

'What did this Broussac say? I assume she's been questioned.'

'Angrily. She claims he never showed up.'

'Well?'

'Our people think she's lying.'

'Why?'

'One of our men went round to her flat and asked some questions. He learned that she had returned home by one o'clock in the morning. If that was the case – and apparently it was; two neighbours confirmed it – why didn't she phone the embassy and call off the car?'

'Has she been asked about this?'

'No, sir. Our people are waiting for instructions. It's not customary for embassy personnel to go around asking surreptitious questions about ministers of the Quai d'Orsay.'

Charles Berquist paused, then spoke firmly. 'Ask Ambassador Richardson to call Madame Broussac and respectfully request her to accept an invitation to come to the embassy as soon as it's convenient, preferably within the hour. A car will be sent for her, of course. The President of the United States wishes to speak to her on a confidential basis.'

'Mr *President* – '

'Just do as I say, Mr Undersecretary.'

'Yes, sir.'

'And, Emory?'

'Sir?'

'How's the other task? The seventy-odd diplomats who may have been out of town during the Spanish problem?'

Bradford paused before answering. When he spoke, it was apparent he was trying to control his voice. 'As of this moment, five are missing.'

'*What?*'

'I didn't want to say anything until noon, until I have all the information, but the last report indicates that nineteen personnel were off the premises. Fourteen are accounted for, five aren't.'

'Get it! Get *all* your information!'

'I'm trying.'

'By noon! Get it!'

The cold rain of the night before had lingered with diminishing strength, and the sky outside the Oval Office was dark. A drop of only a degree or two in temperature and there would be thin, erratic patches of snow on the White House lawn. Berquist stood by the window, briefly wondering how deep the drifts were in Mountain Iron, Minnesota. And how he wished to Christ he were back there now! There was a buzzing from his telephone console. He glanced at his watch as he walked to the desk; it was eleven-fifteen.

'Yes?'

'Your call from Paris, sir.'

'Thank you.' Berquist pushed the appropriate red button. 'Madame Broussac?'

'*Oui, Monsieur le Président.* It is an honour, sir. I am flattered to have been summoned to spe~'; with you.' The old woman's voice was strong, but not without astonishment. And a measure of fear.

'And I'm most grateful, Madame. As I instructed, are we alone?'

'Yes, *Monsieur le Président.* Ambassador Richardson most courteously permitted me the use of his office. Quite honestly, I am, as you might say, bewildered.'

'You have the word of the President of the United States that we *are* alone, Madame Broussac. There is no interference on this telephone, no third parties or mechanical devices to record our conversation. Will you accept that word?'

'Assuredly. Why would such an august figure deceive a mere minister of the Quai d'Orsay?'

'For a lot of reasons. But I'm not.'

'*Mais oui.* Then I am convinced.'

'Good. I need your co-operation in a matter of the utmost importance *and* delicacy. It in no way affects the government of France, but any help you might give us could only be in its ultimate interests. Again, you have my word on it, the word of this office.'

'It is sufficient, *Monsieur le Président.*'

'It's imperative we reach a retired foreign service officer recently separated from the Department of State. His name is Michael Havelock.'

'*Mais, Monsieur le . . .*'

'No, please,' interrupted Berquist. 'Let me finish. This office has too many staggering concerns to be involved with the work you do, or with the activities Mr Havelock was engaged in. I only ask you to help us locate him. A destination, a routing, a name he might be using. Whatever you tell me will be held in the strictest confidence; no detail will be compromised, or ever used against you or your operations, I promise you that.'

'*Monsieur –* '

'Lastly,' continued the President, overriding her voice, 'no matter what he may have told you, his government has never meant him harm. We have too much respect for his service record, too much gratitude for his contributions. The tragedy he thinks is his alone is all of ours, and that is all I can tell you, but I hope you consider the source – the office from which it comes. Will you help us, help *me*, Madame Broussac?'

Berquist could hear the breathing over the line from Paris, as well as the pounding tattoo in his own chest. He looked out of the window; fine flecks of white were intermingling with the mottled drizzle. The virgin drifts in the fields of Mountain Iron were at their most beautiful at sundown; one caressed them with the eyes, touched the colours from a distance, never wanting them to change.

'As you are trying to find him,' began Broussac. 'He is looking for someone else.'

'We know that. We've been looking for her, too. To save her life. To save his.' The President closed his eyes; it was a lie he would remember back in the hills of the Mesabi country. But then he would remember, too, Churchill and Coventry. The Enigma . . . Costa Brava.

'There is a man in New York.'

'New *York*?' Berquist sat forward, startled. 'He's *here*? She's . . . ?'

'It surprises you, *Monsieur le Président*?'

'Very much.'

'It was intended to. It was I who sent her. Sent him.'

'This man in New York?'

'He must be approached with a great deal of – as you mentioned – delicacy. He cannot be compromised. You have the same such people in Europe; we all need them, *Monsieur le Président*. Even when we know of those who belong to other – companies, we leave them alone.'

'I understand perfectly.' Berquist did; the warning was clear. 'This man can tell us where he is?'

'He can tell us where *she* is. That's what you need to know. But he must be convinced he is not compromised.'

'I'll send only one man and only he will know. My word.'

'*J'y compte*. I must tell you, I do not know him, except through his dossier.

He is a great man with much compassion, a survivor, *monsieur*. In April of 1945 he was taken out of the Bergen-Belsen camp in Germany.'

'He will be accorded all the respect this office can summon, as well as the confidentiality I promised you. His name, please.'

'Jacob Handelman. Columbia University.'

The three men listened intently as Emory Bradford slowly, methodically delivered his findings in the strategy room of the underground complex of the White House. Speaking in a deliberate monotone, he described the confirmed whereabouts of all nineteen State Department personnel from the fifth floor L Section who were not in Washington during the week of Costa Brava. When he had finished, each man's expression conveyed both pain and frustration, none more so than the President's. He leaned forward on the dais, his heavy Scandinavian face worn and lined, his intelligent eyes angry.

'You were so *sure* this morning.' he said. 'You told me five were missing, five not accounted for. What happened?'

'I was wrong, Mr President.'

'*Goddamn it*, I didn't want to hear that! . . . But go on, who were the five?'

'The woman in hospital. It was an abortion. Her husband's a lawyer and has been in protracted litigation at The Hague for several months. They've been apart. The picture was pretty clear.'

'How could you even consider a woman?' demanded Halyard. 'No double standard implied, but a woman would leave her mark somewhere.'

'Not if she – through Moscow – controlled men. Actually, I was quite excited when her name surfaced. I thought, "Good God, it's perfect." It wasn't.'

'Keep it surgery, and tell that to whomever you spoke to. Who were the others?'

'The two attachés at our embassy in Mexico. They'd been recalled for change-of-policy briefings, then didn't return to Mexico City until the fifth.'

'Explanation?' asked the President.

'Holidays. They went their separate ways and their families joined them. One to ski lodge in Vermont, the other to the Caribbean. Credit-card charges confirmed everything.'

'Who else?' pressed Berquist.

'Arthur Pierce.'

'Pierce?' interrupted the general, startled. 'The fellow at the UN now?'

'Yes, General.'

'I could have straightened you out there. So could have Addison here.'

'So would Matthias,' agreed Bradford. 'If there was anyone at State who maintained clear access to Matthias for a longer period of time, I don't know who it is. He appointed Pierce to the UN with the obvious intention of submitting him for the ambassadorship.'

'If you'll permit me the correction,' said Berquist, '*I* appointed him after Matthias gave him to us and then took him away. He worked over here with the National Security Council for a couple of months last year before the great man said he was needed in New York.'

'And he was one fella *I* told the Pentagon to bribe the hell out of,'

exclaimed the general. 'I wanted to keep him in the army; he was too good
to lose. He didn't like that mess in South-east Asia any more than I did, but
his record was as good as mine . . . Let's face it; it was a damn sight better.'

The ambassador leaned back in his chair. 'I know Pierce. He was brought
to my attention by an old style career foreign officer. I suppose I was as
responsible as anyone for bringing him into the State Department. He was
one of the few in this day and age who really went from rags to riches – well,
influential if not literally rich, but he could have been – Iowa farmboy,
rather humble beginnings, I believe, and then a brilliant academic record,
everything on scholarship. A dozen or so of the country's largest corporations
were after him, not to mention Rand and the Brookings Institute. I was
persuasive and quite practical. Patriotism aside, I pointed out that a tour of
duty with the Department of State could only enhance his value in the
market place. Of course, he's still a relatively young man; with his
accomplishments, if he leaves government, he'll be able to name his own
price anywhere. He's a typical American success story – how could you
possibly conceive of a Moscow connection?'

'I didn't *preconceive* anything, especially not in this case,' said Bradford.
'Arthur Pierce is a friend – and I don't have many. I consider him one of
the best men we have at State. But in spite of our friendship, I went by the
reports given me. Only me, incidentally. Not to my secretary or any
assistant. Only to me.'

'What did you get that made you think Pierce could possibly have
anything to do with Soviet Intelligence? Christ, he's mother, God, apple pie
and the flag.'

'An error in the UN message logs. The initial report showed that during
the last days of December and the first three days of January – the week of
Costa Brava – Pierce hadn't responded to four separate queries from the
Middle East Section. Then, of course, they showed up – four replies that
could be entered in a diplomatic analyst's handbook. They were as penetrating as anything I've read on that area and dovetailed with the specific
proceedings in the Security Council. As a matter of fact, they were used to
block a particularly aggressive Soviet proposal.'

'The error in the logs was the explanation?' said Brooks.

'That's the maddening thing. There's always an explanation, then a
confirmation of an explanation. Message traffic's so heavy, twenty per cent
of it gets misplaced. Pierce's responses had been there all along.'

'Who's the last man?' Berquist was not going to give up. It was clear from
his eyes that he could not readily accept the altered findings, desperation his
electric prod.

'A man I was so convinced might be the mole, I nearly had a White
House secret service detail pick him up. Thank God I didn't; he's volatile, a
screamer.'

'Who?'

'Nikolai Sitmarin. Born and raised in Leningrad, parents dissident
immigrants over a dozen years ago. He's the State Department's most
accomplished analyst of Soviet internal affairs, accurate about seventy per
cent. He's a prize, and in his case I thought, What better way for Moscow
to put a mole into the ground? An eighteen-year-old son of immigrants,

dissidents permitted a family visa when they were damned hard to come by.'

'Is Sitmarin Jewish?' asked the general.

'No, but I expect most people think he is; in my view it added to his cover. Soviet dissidency isn't the exclusive province of Russian Jews, although that seems to be the general impression. Also, he's received a fair amount of media exposure – the thirty-year old *wunderkind* carrying out a personal vendetta. It all seemed so logically convoluted; so right.'

'What were the circumstances?' The President's words were clipped.

'Again, an unexplained absence. He was gone from his office from mid Christmas week until the eighth of January. He just wasn't in Washington and there was no assignment listed for his not being here. I asked a time-stat man to call the section head; the explanation was given.'

'Which was?' pressed Berquist.

'A personal leave was granted. Sitmarin's mother was gravely ill in Chicago.'

'Pretty damned convenient illness, wasn't it?'

'So much so she nearly died. The Cook County General Hospital confirmed it.'

'But she didn't die,' interrupted Brooks.

'I spoke personally to the physician-of-record and he had a very clear idea of the gravity of my inquiry. He quoted from his files.'

'Have them sent to you,' ordered the President. 'There are too damned many explanations; one of them's a lie.'

'I agree, but which one?' added Bradford. 'Not just these five, but the entire nineteen. Someone who thinks he's – or she's – doing a superior a harmless favour is concealing Ambiguity from us, hiding the mole. What's going down as a few extra days' skiing or going to the Caribbean or shacking up . . . excuse me.'

'Oh, for Christ's sake. Go back and dig into every explanation given you. Find one that won't hold up.'

'One that has a discrepancy in it,' added the ambassador. 'Meetings that didn't take place, a conference that was postponed, credit card charges where the signatures are questionable . . . a gravely ill woman who just may have been given an assumed name.'

'It'll take time,' said the Undersecretary.

'You've accomplished a great deal in something over twelve hours,' continued Brooks sympathetically. 'Again, I commend you.'

'And you have the authority of this office to get you what you need, anything you need. Use it! Find the mole!' Berquist shook his head in exasperation. 'He and we are in a race after a madman we call Parsifal. If the Russians reach him first, this country has no viable foreign policy. And if Parsifal panics, it won't make a damn bit of difference.' The President put his hands on the desk. 'Is there anything else? I'm keeping two curious senators waiting and it's no time to do it. They're on the Foreign Relations Committee and I've a gut feeling they've got wind of Matthias.' Berquist stopped; he got up and looked at Bradford. 'Reassure me again – that *every man* at Poole's Island is secure?'

'Yes, sir. Each was screened down to his fingernails, and no one leaves that island for the duration.'

'That, too, will run its course,' said Brooks. 'What *is* the duration? It's an unnatural condition.'

'These are unnatural circumstances,' broke in General Halyard. 'The patrols are armed, the place a fortress.'

'Armed?' the President spoke softly, in his own personal anguish. 'Of course, they're armed. Insane!'

'What about Havelock?' asked the statesman. 'Has there been anything?'

'No,' replied the commander-in-chief, leaving the dais and heading for the door. 'Call me later, Mr Undersecretary,' he said without explanation. 'Call me at three o'clock.'

The snow, though not heavy, was a whipping snow. Tiny white flakes careened off the windscreen, bouncing silently away like thousands of miniature asteroids. Havelock in his rented car had driven past the sign several minutes before, the letters reflected in the headlights: MASON FALLS 3 MILES.

He had checked out of The King's Arms Hotel, relieved to see a different clerk on duty, and had taken a cab to LaGuardia Airport. A hastily purchased map pinpointed Mason Falls, Pennsylvania; his only choice was a domestic flight to Pittsburgh. He was not at the time concerned with further Soviet surveillance. The Russian he had trapped had undoubtedly reported his arrival, but even if he had not, LaGuardia was not an international terminal. No diplomatic personnel came through its gates on overseas flights.

He had been issued a last-moment seat on US Air's 7:56 p.m. plane, reached Pittsburgh by 9:15 and hired a car, the signed credit slip permitting him to drop it off at any Hertz location. By 9:45 he was driving south through the long stretches of dark countryside on Route 51.

MASON FALLS

ESTABLISHED 1858

Through the swirling pockets of snow – thicker now, fuller – Michael could see the glow of a red neon sign ahead on the right. He approached, slowed down and read the letters; a touch of the absurd had intruded: HARRY'S BAR. Either someone along the banks of the Monongahela had a sense of humour, or there was a man named Harry who did not know how far away he was from Venice or Paris. Or perhaps he did.

He obviously did. Inside there were enlarged World War II photographs on the walls depicting Parisian scenes, several showing a soldier standing outside the door of Paris's Harry's Bar on the Left Bank. The place was rustic – thick wood dulled by use and totally untouched by furniture polish – heavy glasses and high-backed bar stools. A juke box in the corner was bleating out country music to the bored half dozen or so patrons at the bar. They were in keeping with their surroundings: everyone male, a profusion of red-checked flannel shirts, wide-ribbed corduroy trousers and ankle-length boots worn in the fields and in barns. These were farmers and farmhands; he might have assumed as much from the pick-up trucks outside, but the biting wind had distracted him – that and the fact that he was in Mason Falls, Pennsylvania.

He looked around for a wall telephone; it was inappropriately placed six feet from the juke box. That did not concern him, but the absence of a telephone book did; he needed an address. There had been no time at LaGuardia to find the correct book for Mason Falls, and as Pittsburgh was an international airport he wanted to get out of the terminal as fast as possible. He walked to the bar, stood between two empty stools and waited for an ageing, morose-looking Harry to serve him.

'Yeah, what'll it be?'

'Scotch-on-the-rocks, and a telephone book, if you've got one, please.'

The owner studied Havelock briefly. 'I don't get much call for Scotch. It ain't the best.'

'I probably wouldn't know the best.'

'It's your throat.' Harry reached under the bar to his right, but instead of coming up with a glass and ice, he put a thin telephone book in front of Michael. He then walked to his left, to a row of bottles on a lighted shelf.

Havelock leafed through the pages rapidly, his index finger descending the row of K's.

Kohoutek, Janos RFD 3 Box 12

Goddamn it!

Rural Free Delivery, routing number *3* could be anywhere in Mason Falls, which although small in population was large in square mileage. Acres and acres of farmland, winding roads that threaded through the countryside. And to call the number was to give an alarm; if there were special words he did not know them and, all things considered, there undoubtedly *were* special words. To mention Jacob Handelman over the phone was asking for a confirmation call to be made to New York. There would be no answer on the dead halfway man's phone until he was found, possibly in the morning, possibly not for several days.

'Here y'are,' said Harry, placing the drink on the bar.

'Would you know a man named Kohoutek?' asked Havelock softly. 'Janos Kohoutek?'

The owner squinted in minor thought. 'Know the name, not him, though. He's one of them foreigners with some land over in the west end.'

'Would you know where in the west end?'

'No. Doesn't it tell you there?' Harry gestured at the telephone book.

'It only gives an RFD and a box number.'

'Call him, for Christ's sake.'

'I'd rather not. As you say, he's a foreigner; he might not understand over the phone.'

'Hey!' yelled Harry over the sounds of the country music. 'Any you assholes know a guy named Kohoutek?'

'Foreigner,' said one red-checked flannel shirt.

'He's got more'n forty acres over west,' added a hunting cap farther down. 'Fuckin' refugees with their government handouts can afford it. We can't.'

'Would you know where?' asked Havelock.

'It's either on Chamberlain or Youngfield, maybe Fourforks, I don't know which. Don't it say in the book?'

'No, just RFD-three, that's all. And a box number.'

'Route three,' said another patron, this one with a growth of beard and bleary eyes. 'That's Davey Hooker's route. He's a carrier, and that son of a bitch soaks 'em. Got the job through his uncle, the fuckin' grafter.'

'Would you know where the route is?'

'Sure. Fourforks Pike. Heads due west from the depot a mile down fifty-one.'

'Thanks very much.' Michael raised the glass to his lips and drank. It was not very good; it was not even Scotch. He reached into his pocket, pulled out his money and left two dollars on the bar. 'Thanks again,' he said to the owner.

'It's sixty cents,' said Harry.

'For old times' sake,' replied Havelock. 'For the other place in Paris.'

'Hey, you *been* there?'

'Once or twice.'

'You shoulda told me! You woulda got decent whisky! Let me tell you, in 'forty-five me and – '

'I'm really sorry, I don't have time.'

Michael pressed himself away from the bar and started for the door. He did not see a man at the far end of the room get off his stool and walk to the telephone.

Fourforks Pike became a slowly curving, interminable back country road less than a mile west of the old railway depot. The first post office box, marked *5*, prominently anchored in the ground on his right, was clearly visible through the snow in the glare of the headlights. The next, however, Havelock would have missed had he not suddenly become aware of a break in the foliage; it was a narrow track on his left, and the box could not be seen from the pike. It was number *7*, negating the theory that odd and even numbers meant different sides of a delivery route. He would have to drive more slowly and keep his eyes more alert.

The next three boxes were all within a half mile, each in sequence, the last number *10*. Two hundred yards beyond, the road split – the first of, presumably, four forks on the pile. He took the straighter line, the fork on the right. Number *11* did not appear until he had driven nearly a mile and a half; when he saw it he briefly closed his eyes in relief. For several agonizing moments he had been convinced he had taken the wrong road. He pressed his foot on the accelerator, his mouth dry, the muscles of his face rigid, his eyes straining.

If the road was interminable – made worse by the spiralling snow against the windscreen – the wait for the final sighting was torturously so. He entered a long, seemingly endless stretch of flat, straight ground, which, as near as he could determine, was bordered by fields or pastures; but there were no houses, no lights anywhere. Had he passed it? Was his vision so distorted by the silent pounding of the snow that the post office box had gone by without his spotting it? Was there an unseen road on his right or his left, a metal receptacle off the shoulder, covered perhaps? It was not logical; the snow was heavier, but not yet heavy, and the wind was too strong for the snow to settle.

It was *there*! On the right. A large black mailbox, shaped like a miniature Quonset hut, the covered opening wide enough to receive small packages. The number *12* was stencilled in white – thick white enamel that threw back the light as though challenging the darkness. Havelock slowed down and peered through the window; again there were no lights beyond, no signs of life whatsoever. There was only what appeared to be a long road that disappeared into a wall of trees and further darkness.

He drove on, eyes straining, looking for something else, something he could not miss if and when he came across it. He only hoped it would be soon, and several hundred yards beyond box number *12*, he found a reasonable facsimile. Not ideal but, with the snow, acceptable. It was a bank of wild foliage that had crept towards the edge of the road, the end of a property line, or a demarcation signifying no responsibility. Whatever it was, it would do.

He drove the hired car off the shoulder and into the cluster of bushes and high grass. He extinguished the headlights and opened his suitcase on the front seat. He removed all identification and shoved it into the elasticized rear pocket, then took out a heavy leaded plastic bag impervious to X-rays, the kind often used for transporting exposed film. He peeled it open and removed the Llama automatic; the magazine was full. Lastly, he reached into the suitcase for the scaling knife he had used at Col des Moulinets; it was sheathed in a thin leather scabbard with a clip. Awkwardly he pulled up the sides of his overcoat and shoved it behind his trousers into the small of his back, clipping it to his belt at the base of his spine. He hoped neither weapon would be called for; words were infinitely preferable, frequently more effective.

He got out of the car, locked it, pushed the snow-swept foliage up around the sides, obliterated the tracks and started down the Fourforks Pike towards PO Box *12*, RFD *3*, Mason Falls, Pennsylvania.

He had walked no more than thirty feet off the highway into the long narrow road that seemed to disappear into a wall of darkness when he stopped. Whether it was the years he had spent instinctively studying alien ground – aware that an unknown path at night might hold lethal surprises – or the wind off the fields that caused him to angle his head downward against it, he could not tell. He was merely grateful that he saw it: a tiny greenish dot of light on his right about two feet above the snow-patched earth. It appeared to be suspended but he knew it wasn't. Instead, it was wired to the end of a thin black metal tube that was sunk at least another two feet into the ground for stability. It was a photo-electric cell, its counterpart across the road, an invisible beam of light crossing the darkness, connecting both terminals. Anything breaking that beam for more than a second or with a weight-density of more than fifty pounds would trigger an alarm somewhere. Small animals could not do it; cars and human beings could not fail to do it.

Michael side-stepped cautiously to his right through the cold, wet overgrowth, to pass beyond the device. He stopped again at the edge of the tangled bushes, aware of a line of flickering white parallel with his shoulders, knowing suddenly that there was another obstacle. It was a barbed wire fence bordering an adjacent field, flakes of snow clinging briefly to the barbs before being whipped away. He had not seen it when he entered the side road marked by post office box number *12*; he looked back and understood. The fence did not begin until the foliage was high enough to conceal it. And that meant he understood something else; again, weight-density. Sufficient pressure against the thinly-spaced wires would set off further alarms. Janos Kohoutek was very security-conscious. Considering his location he had paid for the best he could get.

This, then, was the path, thought Havelock. Between the green trip-light and the shoulder-high barbed wire fence. For if there was one photo-electric alarm, there would be others along the way – the expectation of malfunction was an innate part of protection technology. He wondered how long 'the way' was; he could see virtually nothing but foliage and darkness and swirling snow in front of him. He started literally to push ahead, bending the tangled brushwood and webbed branches with his hands and arms as he kept his eyes riveted on the ground for dots of eerie green light.

He passed three, then four, spaced roughly two hundred and fifty to three hundred feet apart. He reached the wall of tall trees, the fence growing higher as if commanded by nature. He was soaked now, his face cold, his brows iced, but movement was easier through the thick-trunked trees that seemingly had been planted at random but nevertheless formed a visual wall. Suddenly he realized he was heading downwards, descending. He looked over at the road; the decline there was sharper, the mottled surface of earth and snow no longer in sight. There was a break in the trees; the narrow, sloping path he had to take was still overgrown, the high grass and untamed bushes bending in the wind and glazed with white.

And then spread below him was a sight that both hypnotized and disturbed him, in the same way he had reacted to the first sight of Jacob Handelman. He plunged down through the thickets of brush, falling twice into the cold, prickly bushes, his eyes on the bewildering view beyond.

At first glance it was like any farm buried in the deeper countryside, protected in front by sloping fields, endless woods beyond. There was a group of buildings, solid, simple, constructed of heavy wood for severe winters, the lights in various windows flickering in the snowfall: a main house and several barns, a silo, tool sheds and shelters for tractors and ploughs and harvesting equipment. They were indeed what they seemed to be, Havelock was sure, but he knew they were more. Much more.

It began with the gate at the end of the sloping road. It was framed unpretentiously with iron piping; the mesh was ordinary mesh; but it was higher than it had to be, higher than it should be for the entrance to a farm, as if the builder had made a slight error in the height specification and had decided to live with the mistake. Then there was the fence that spanned out from both sides of the unprepossessing gate; it, too, was strange, somehow askew, also higher than it had to be for the purpose of containing animals in the ascending grazing fields before it. Was it just the height? It was no more than seven feet, Michael judged as he drew closer; it had appeared much shorter from above – again nothing strange . . . but somehow wrong. And then he realized what it was, why the word 'askew' had come to mind. The top of the barbed wire fence was angled *inwards*. That fence was not meant to keep animals from breaking in, it was designed to keep people from breaking out!

Suddenly the blinding beam of a searchlight shot out from the upper regions of the silo; it was sweeping round – towards *him*!

This was the 1980s, but he was standing in front of a symbol of human carnage that went back forty years. It was a concentration camp!

'We wondered how long it would take you,' said a voice behind him.

He spun around, reaching for his weapon. It was too late.

Powerful arms gripped him around the neck, arching him backwards as a pair of hands plunged a soft, wet, acrid-smelling cloth into his face.

The beam of the searchlight zeroed in on him. He could see it, feel it, as his nostrils began to burn. Then the darkness came, and he could neither see nor feel.

21

He felt the warmth first; he found it not particularly pleasant but different from the cold. When he opened his eyes, his vision blurred and came into focus slowly; simultaneously he became aware of the nausea in his throat and the stinging sensation on his face. The pungent odour lingered in his nostrils; he had been anaesthetized with pure ethyl ether.

He saw flames, logs burning behind a black-bordered screen, in a large brick fireplace. He was on the floor in front of the slate hearth; his overcoat had been removed, and his wet clothes were heating up uncomfortably. But part of the discomfort was in the small of his back; the scaling knife was still in place, the leather scabbard irritating his skin. He was grateful for the pain.

He rolled over slowly, inch by inch, his eyes half closed, observing what he could by the light of the fire and several table lamps. He heard the sound of muffled voices; two men were standing together in a hallway, talking quietly. They had not noticed his movement. The room itself was in concert with the rustic structures outside – solid, functional furniture, thick plaited rag rugs scattered about over a wide-beamed floor, windows bordered by red-checked curtains that might have come from a Sears-Roebuck catalogue. It was a simple living-room in a country farmhouse, nothing more or less, and nothing suggesting it might be something else – or some place else – to disturb a visitor's eye. If anything, the room was Spartan, lacking a woman's touch, entirely male.

Michael slid his watch slowly into view. It was one o'clock in the morning: he had been unconscious for nearly forty-five minutes.

'Hey, he's awake!' cried one of the men.

'Get Mr Kohoutek,' said the other, walking across the room towards Havelock. He rounded the sofa and reached under his leather jacket to pull out a gun. He smiled; the weapon was the Spanish Llama automatic that had travelled from a mist-laden pier in Civitavecchia, over the Palatine Hill

and Col des Moulinets, to Mason Falls, Pennsylvania. 'This is good
hardware, Mr No-Name. I haven't seen one like it in years. Thanks a lot.'

Michael was about to answer, but was interrupted by the rapid, heavy-
footed entrance of a man who walked out of the hallway carrying a glass of
steaming liquid in his hand.

'You are very free with odds and ends,' thundered Janos Kohoutek. 'Be
careful or you'll walk barefoot in the snow.'

Hocs ne sniegu bez buttow.

Kohoutek's accent was the dialect of the Carpathian Mountains south of
Otrokovice. The words alluding to bare feet in the snow were part of the
Czech-Moravian admonition to wastrels who did not earn their keep or their
clothes. *To understand the cold, walk barefoot in the snow.*

Kohoutek came round the guard and was now fully in view. He was a
bull of a man, his open shirt emphasizing the thickness of his neck and chest,
the stretched cloth marking the breadth of his heavy shoulders; age had not
touched his physique. He was not tall, but he was large, and the only
indication of his years was in his face – more jowl than face – deeply lined,
eyes deeply set, the flesh worn by well over sixty years of driven living. The
hot, dark brown liquid in the glass was tea – black Carpathian tea. The man
holding it was Czech by birth, Moravian by conviction.

'So here is our invader!' he roared, staring down at Havelock. 'A man
with a gun but no identification – not even a driver's licence or credit card,
or a wallet to carry such things in – attacks my farm like a commando! Who
is this stalker in the night? What is his business? His name?'

'Havlicek,' said Michael in a low, sullen voice, pronouncing the name in
an accent close to Moravian. 'Mikhail Havlicek.'

'*Český?*'

'*Ano.*'

'*Obchodní?*' shouted Kohoutek, asking Havelock his business.

'*Mi žena,*' replied Michael, answering 'the woman'.

'*Co žena?*' demanded the ageing bull.

'The one who was brought here this morning,' said Havelock, continuing
in Czech.

'Two were brought in this morning! Which?'

'Blonde hair . . . when we last saw her.'

Kohoutek grinned, but not with amusement. '*Chlipný,*' he said leering.
'*Dobrý těleso!*'

'Her body doesn't interest me, the information she has does.' Michael
raised himself. 'May I get up?'

'*Zadnyne supsobem!*' The mountain bull roared again as he rushed forward,
lashing his right foot out, the boot catching Havelock in the throat, making
him reel back on the slate hearth.

'*Prokili!*' shouted Havelock, grabbing his neck. It was the moment to react
in anger, the beginning of the words that mattered. 'I *paid!*' he yelled in
Czech. 'What do you think you're doing?'

'You paid what? To ask about me on the highway? To sneak up on my
house in the middle of the night? To carry a gun into my farm? I'll pay *you!*'

'I did what I was told!'

'By whom?'

'Jacob Handelman.'

'Handelman?' Kohoutek's full, battered face was stretched into an expression of bewilderment. 'You paid Handelman? *He* sent you?'

'He told me he would phone you, get in touch with you,' said Michael quickly, using a truth from Paris that the halfway man had denied in New York; denied for profit. 'I was not to call you under any circumstances. I was to leave my car on the road past your mailbox and walk down the track to your farm.'

'The highway? You asked questions about me in a café on the highway!'

'I didn't know where the Fourforks Pike was. How could I? Did you have a man there? Did he call you?'

The Czech-Moravian shook his head. 'It doesn't matter. An Italian with a truck. He drives produce for me sometimes.' Kohoutek stopped; the menace returned to his eyes. 'But you did not walk down my road. You came in like a thief, an armed thief!'

'I'm no fool, *pritel*. I know what you have here and I looked for trip-alarms. I was with the *Podzemni*. I found them and so I was cautious; I wanted no dogs on me or men shooting at me. Why do you think it took me so long to get here from that café on the highway?'

'You *paid* Handelman?'

'Very handsomely. May I get up?'

'Get up! Sit, *sit*!' ordered the mountain bull, pointing to a short bench to the left of the fireplace, his expression more bewildered than seconds before. 'You gave him money?'

'A great deal. He said I'd reach a point in the road when I could see the farm below. Someone would be waiting for me by the gate, wave me down with a light. There was nobody I could see, no one at the gate. But then the weather's rotten so I came down.'

Gripping his steaming glass of tea, Kohoutek turned and walked across the room to a table against the wall. There was a telephone on it; he put down the glass, picked up the phone and dialled.

'If you're calling Handelman . . .'

'I do not call Handelman,' the Czech-Moravian broke in. 'I never call Handelman. I call a man who calls another; he phones the German.'

'You mean the Rabbi?'

Kohoutek raised his head and looked at Havelock. 'Yes, the Rabbi,' he said without comment.

'Well, whoever . . . there won't be any answer at his apartment. That's all I wanted to tell you.'

'Why not?'

'He told me he was on his way to Boston. He's lecturing at some place called Brandese or Brandeis.'

'Jew school,' said the bull, then talked into the phone. 'This is Janos. Call New York. The name you will give is Havlicek, have you got that? *Havlicek*. I want an explanation.' He hung up, grabbed his tea and started back towards the fireplace. 'Put that away!' he commanded the guard in the leather jacket who was rubbing the Llama against his sleeve. 'Stand in the hall.' The man walked away as Kohoutek approached the fire, sitting down opposite Michael in a rustic-looking rocking chair. 'Now we wait, Mikhail Havlicek. It won't be long, a few minutes, ten . . . fifteen perhaps.'

'I can't be responsible if he's not at home,' said Havelock, shrugging. 'I wouldn't be here if we didn't have an agreement. I wouldn't know your name or where to find you if he hadn't told me. How could I?'

'We'll see.'

'Where's the woman?'

'Here. We have several buildings,' answered the man from the Carpathians as he sipped his tea and rocked slowly back and forth. 'She's upset, of course. It is not quite what she expected, but she will understand; they all do. We are their only hope.'

'How upset?'

Kohoutek squinted. 'You are interested?'

'Only professionally. I've got to take her out and I don't want trouble.'

'We shall see.'

'Is she all right?' asked Michael, controlling his anxiety.

'Like some others – the educated ones – she lost her reason for a while.' Kohoutek grinned, then coughed an ugly laugh, as he drank his tea. 'We explained the regulations and she told us they were not acceptable. Can you imagine? Not *acceptable*!' The bull roared, then his voice dropped. 'She will be watched carefully, and before she is sent outside she will understand. As they all understand.'

'You don't have to worry. I'm taking her.'

'You say that.'

'I paid.'

Kohoutek leaned forward, stopping the motion of the chair. 'How much?'

It was the question the Czech-Moravian had wanted to ask several minutes ago, but Carpathian progress was serpentine. Michael knew he was on a tightrope; there would be no answer in New York. He was about to negotiate and both men knew it.

'Wouldn't you rather hear it from Handelman? If he's at home.'

'Perhaps I would rather hear it from you, *pritel*.'

'How do you know you can trust me?'

'How do I know I can trust the Rabbi? How do you know *you* can trust him?'

'Why shouldn't I? I found you, found this place. Not in the way I would have preferred, but I'm here.'

'You must represent influential interests,' said Kohoutek, veering quickly, as was the custom of mountain men in negotiations.

'So influential I don't carry identification. But then you know that.'

The ageing lion began rocking again. 'Such influence, however, always carries money.'

'Enough.'

'How much did you pay Handelman?' All movement stopped as the question was asked.

'Twenty thousand dollars American.'

'*Twenty* . . . ?' Kohoutek's weathered face lost some of its colour and his deep-set eyes squinted through the slits of flesh. 'A considerable sum, *pritel*.'

'He said it was reasonable.' Havelock crossed his legs, his damp trousers warmed by the fire. 'We were prepared for it.'

'Are you prepared to learn why he did not reach me?'

'With the complicated arrangements you have for contacting one another, I'm not surprised. He was on his way to Boston, and if someone was not by a phone – '

'Someone is always by a phone; he is a cripple. And you were on your way to a trap that would have cost you your life.'

Michael uncrossed his legs, his eyes riveted on Kohoutek. 'The trip lights?'

'You spoke of dogs; we have dogs. They only attack on command, but an intruder does not know that. They circle him, barking viciously. What would you have done?'

'Used my gun, of course.'

'And for that you would have been shot.'

Both men were silent. Finally, Havelock spoke. 'And the Rabbi has twenty thousand dollars you don't know about and I can't tell you because I'm dead.'

'Now you see.'

'He'd *do* that to you – for twenty thousand dollars?'

The mountain bull again started to rock his chair. 'There could be other considerations. I've had minor troubles here – nothing we cannot control – but this is a depressed area. Certain jealousies arise when you have a successful farm. Handelman might care to replace me, have a reason to replace me.'

'I don't understand.'

'I would have a corpse on my hands, a corpse who might have made a telephone call while he was alive. He could have told someone where he was going.'

'You shot an intruder, a man with a gun, who probably used his gun. You were defending your property, no one would blame you.'

'No one,' agreed Kohoutek, still rocking. 'But it would be enough. The Moravian is a troublemaker, we cannot afford him. Cut him off.'

'From what?'

The mountain man sipped his tea. 'You spent twenty thousand dollars. Are you prepared to pay more?'

'I might be persuaded. We want the woman; she's worked with our enemies.'

'Who is "we"?'

'That I won't tell you. It wouldn't mean anything to you if I did . . . Cut you off from what?'

Kohoutek shrugged his heavy shoulders. 'This is only the first step for these people . . . like the Corescu woman.'

'That's not her name.'

'I'm certain it's not, but that's no concern of mine. Like the others, she'll be pacified, work from here for a month or two, then be sent elsewhere. The south, south-west – the northern midwest, wherever we place her.' The bull grinned. 'The papers are always about to arrive – just another month, one more congressman to pay, a senator to reach. After a while, they're like goats.'

'Even goats can rebel.'

'To what end? Their own? To be sent back to the place where they came from? To a firing squad, or a gulag, or garrotte in an alleyway? You must understand, these are panicked people. It's a *fantastic* business!'

'Do the papers ever arrive?'

'Oh yes, frequently. Especially for the talented, the productive. The payments go on for years.'

'I'd think there'd be risks. Someone who refuses, someone who threatens you with exposure.'

'Then we provide another paper, *pritel*. A death certificate.'

'My turn to ask. Who is "we"?'

'My turn to answer. I will not tell you.'

'But the Rabbi wants to cut you out of this fantastic business.'

'It's possible.' The telephone rang, its bell abrasive. Kohoutek got out of the rocking chair and walked rapidly across the room. 'Perhaps we shall learn now,' he said, placing his tea on the table and picking up the phone in the middle of the second bell. 'Yes?'

Havelock involuntarily held his breath; there were so many probabilities. A curious university athlete whose responsibility was the well-being of his tenants, who might have walked out into the hallway. A graduate student with an appointment. So many accidents . . .

'Keep trying,' said the Carpathian.

Michael breathed again.

Kohoutek came back to the chair, leaving his tea on the table. 'There is no answer on Handelman's phone.'

'He's in Boston.'

'How much could you be persuaded to pay?'

'I don't carry large sums with me,' replied Havelock, estimating the amount of cash in his suitcase. It was close to six thousand dollars – money he had taken out of Paris.

'You had twenty large sums for the Rabbi.'

'It was prearranged. I could give you a down payment. Five thousand.'

'Down payment on what?'

'I'll be frank,' said Michael, leaning forward on the bench. 'The woman's worth thirty-five thousand to us; that was the sum allocated. I've spent twenty.'

'With five, that leaves ten,' said the bull.

'It's in New York. You can have it tomorrow, but I've got to see the woman tonight. I've got to take her tonight.'

'And be on a plane with my ten thousand dollars?'

'Why should I do that? It's a budget item and I don't concern myself with finances. Also, I suspect you can collect a fair amount from Handelman. A thief caught stealing from a thief. You've got him now; you could cut *him* out.'

Kohoutek laughed his bull of a laugh. 'You are from the mountains, *Český*! But what guarantees do I have?'

'Send your best man with us. I have no gun; tell him to keep his at my head.'

'Through an airport? I am not a goat!'

'We'll drive.'

'Why tonight?'

'They expect her in the early morning. I'm to bring her to a man at the corner of Sixty-second Street and York Avenue, at the entrance of the East River Drive. He has the remaining money. He's to take her to Kennedy Airport, where arrangements have been made on an Aeroflot flight. Your man can make sure; she doesn't get into the car until the money is paid. What more do you want?'

Kohoutek rocked, his squint returning. 'The Rabbi is a thief. Is the *Český* as well?'

'Where's the hole? Can't you trust your best man?'

'I am the best. Suppose it was me?'

'Why not?'

'*Done!* We shall travel together, the woman in the back seat with me. One gun at her head, the other at yours. Two guns, *pritel!* Where is the five thousand dollars?'

'In my car up on the road. Send someone with me, but I get it myself; he stays outside. That's the condition or we have no negotiation.'

'You Communists are all so suspicious.'

'We learned it in the mountains.'

'*Český!*'

'Where's the woman?'

'In a back building. She refused to eat, threw the tray at our Cuban. But then, she's educated; it is not always a favourable thing, although it brings a higher price later. First, she must be broken; perhaps the Cuban has already begun. He's a hot-tempered *macho* with balls that clank on the floor. Her type of women are his favourites.'

Michael smiled; it was the most difficult smile he had rendered in his life. 'Are the rooms wired?'

'What for? Where are they going? What plans can they hatch alone? Besides, to install and service such items could raise gossip. The alarms on the road are enough trouble; a man comes from Cleveland to look after them.'

'I want to see her. Then I want to get out of here.'

'Why not? When I see five thousand dollars.' Kohoutek stopped rocking and turned to his left, shouting in English. '*You!* Take our guest up to his car. Make him drive and keep your gun on his head!'

Sixteen minutes later, Havelock counted out the money into the Moravian's hands.

'Go to the woman, *pritel*,' said Kohoutek.

He walked across the fenced-in compound to the left of the silo, the man with the Spanish Llama behind him.

'Over there, to your right,' said the guard.

There was a barn at the edge of the woods, but it was more than a barn. There were lights in several windows above the ground level; there was a second floor. And silhouetted in those lights were straight black lines; they were bars. Whoever was inside those windows could not get out. It was a *Kaserne. Ein Konzentrationslager.*

Michael could feel the welcome pressure of the leather scabbard at the base of his spine; the scaling knife was still in place. He knew he could take the guard *and* the Llama – a slip in the snow, a skid over iced grass and the man in the leather jacket was a dead man – but not yet. It would come later, when Jenna understood, when – and if – he could convince her. One losing his life, the other in a hell that would kill her.

Listen to me! Listen to me, for we are all that's left of sanity! What happened to us? What did they do to us?

'Knock on the door,' said the man behind.

Havelock rapped on the wood. A voice with a Latin accent answered.

'Yes? What is it?'

'Open up, Mr K's orders. This is Ryan. Hurry!'

The door was opened two or three inches by a stocky man in a tee-shirt and dungarees. He stared first at Michael, then saw the guard and opened the door completely.

'Nobody called,' he said.

'We thought you might be busy,' said the man behind Havelock, a snide laugh in his voice.

'With what? Two pigs and a crazy woman?'

'She's the one we want to see. *He* wants to see.'

'He better have a *palo* made like rock, I tell you no lie! I looked in ten minutes ago; she's asleep. I don't think she slept for a couple of days maybe.'

'Then he can jump her,' said the guard, pushing Michael through the door.

They climbed the stairs and entered a narrow corridor with doors on both sides. Steel doors with slits in the centre, sliding panels for peering inside.

We are in our movable prison. Where was it? Prague? Trieste? . . . Barcelona?

'She's in this room,' said the Latin, stopping at the third door. 'You want to look?'

'Just open the door,' said Havelock. 'And wait downstairs.'

'*Esperare* –'

'Mr K's orders,' broke in the leather-jacketed guard. 'Do what the man says.'

The Cuban took a key from his belt, unlocked the cell door and stood aside.

'Get out of here,' said Michael.

The two men walked up the corridor.

Havelock opened the door.

The small room was dark, and the dark light of night grudgingly spilled through the window, the white flakes bouncing off the glass and the bars. He could see her on the bed, more cot than bed. Fully dressed, she was lying face down, her blonde hair cascading over her shoulders, one arm hanging down limply, the hand touching the floor. She lay on top of the covers, her clothes dishevelled, the position of her body and the sound of her deep breathing proof of exhaustion. Watching her, he ached, pain pressing his chest for the pain she had endured, so much of it because of him. Trust had fled, instincts rejected, love repulsed; he had been no less an animal than the animals who had done this to her . . . he was ashamed. And filled with love.

He could see the outline of a floor lamp next to the bed; lighted, it would shine down on her. A cold fear went through him and his throat tightened. He had faced risks before, but never a danger like this, never a moment that meant so much to him. If he lost it – lost her, the bond between them shattered irremediably – nothing mattered except the death of liars. He was profoundly aware that he would willingly give up years of life for the moment to be frozen, not to have to turn on the light – simply to call out her name softly, as he had called it a hundred times a hundred, and have her hand fall into his, her face come against his. But the waiting, too, was self-inflicted torture; what were the words? *Between the acting of a dreadful thing and the first motion, all the interim is like a phantasma, or a hideous dream.* It would end or it would begin when he turned on the lamp. He walked silently to the bed.

An arm shot up in the darkness. Pale skin flashing in the dim light, a hand plunged into his abdomen. He felt the impact of a sharp pointed object – not a knife, something else. He leaped back and grabbed the hand, twisting yet not twisting – to cause her further pain was not in him. He could not hurt her.

She'll kill you if she can. Broussac.

Jenna rolled off the bed, her left leg bent, her knee crashing into his kidney, her sharp fingernails clawing his neck, digging into his skin. He could not strike her, he could not do it. She grabbed his hair, pulling his face down, and her right knee smashed into the bridge of his nose. The darkness was splintered into fragments of white light.

'*Prasátko!*' she cried in a low, muted scream, made guttural by her fury.

He understood; he had taught her well. *Use an enemy. Kill him only if you must. But use him first.* Escape was her intent; it accounted for the dishevelled clothes, the skirt pulled up to expose her thigh. He had attributed it all to exhaustion but he had been wrong; it was a sight for a *prasátko* peering through a slot in the cell door.

'*Stát!*' he whispered harshly, as he held her, twisting nothing, damaging nothing. '*Těší já!*' He freed his left hand and pulled her writhing body across the small room to the lamp. He reached over and found the switch; he snapped it on, her face in front of his.

She stared at him, her wide brown eyes bursting from their sockets with that strange mixture of fear and loathing he had seen in the window of the small plane in Col des Moulinets. The cry that was wrenched from her throat came also from the centre of her life; the scream that grew from it was prolonged and horrible – a child in a cellar of terror, a woman who faced the return of infinite pain. She kicked wildly and spun away, breaking his grip, threw herself across the bed and against the wall. She whipped her hand back and forth, slashing crazily, a wide-eyed animal cornered, with nothing left but to end its life screaming, clawing, thrashing as the trap snapped shut. In her hand she grasped the instrument that had been her only hope for freedom; it was a fork, its tines tinted with his blood.

'*Listen* to me!' he whispered sharply again. 'It was done to both of us! It's what I've come to tell you, what I tried to tell you at Col des Moulinets!'

'It was done to *me*! You tried to *kill* me . . . how many times? If I'm to die, then you – '

He lunged and pinned her hand against the wall, forcing her to stop writhing.

'Broussac *believed* you . . . but then she believed *me*! Try to understand. She knew I told her the truth!'

'You don't know the truth! Liar, *liar*!' She spat in his face, kicking out, twisting, digging the nails of her trapped hand into his back.

'They wanted me out and you were the way! I don't know why, but I know men have been killed . . . a woman, too, who was meant to be you! They want to kill us both now, they *have* to!'

'*Liar!*'

'There are liars, yes, but I'm not one of them!'

'You are, you *are*! You sold yourself to the *zvířata! Kurva!*'

'*No!*' He twisted her hand, the bloodied fork protruding from her clenched fist. She winced in pain as he pulled her wrist down. Then she slowly reduced the counter-pressure, her eyes frightened still, hating still, but wide, too, with confusion. He placed the fork against his throat and whispered. 'You know what to do,' he said carefully, clearly. 'The windpipe. Once punctured there's no way out for me here . . . But there is for you. Pretend to go along with them; be passive, but watch the guard – as you know, he's a goat. The sooner you're co-operative, the sooner they'll find you work on the outside. Remember, all you want are your papers; they're everything to you. But when they let you out, somehow get to a phone and reach Broussac in Paris – you can do it. She'll help you becuse she knows the truth.' He stopped and took his hand away, leaving hers free. 'Now, do it. Either kill me or believe me.'

Her stare was to him a scream, echoing in the dark regions of his mind, and hurling him into the horror of a thousand memories. Her lips trembled, and slowly it happened. Fear and bewilderment remained in her eyes, but the hatred was receding. Then the tears came, welling up slowly; they were the balm that meant the healing could begin.

Jenna dropped her hand and he took it, holding it in his own. The fork fell from her unclenched hand, and her body went limp, as the deep, terrible sobs came.

He held her. It was all he could do, all he wanted to do.

The sobs subsided and the minutes went by in silence. All they could hear was their own breathing, all they felt was each other as they clung together. Finally he whispered, 'We're getting out, but it won't be clean. Did you meet Kohoutek?'

'Yes, a horrible man.'

'He's going with us, supposedly to pick up a final payment for you.'

'But there isn't any,' said Jenna, pulling her face back, studying his, her eyes absorbing him, enveloping him. 'Let me look at you, just look at you.'

'There isn't time – '

'*Shhh.*' She placed her fingers on his lips. 'There must be time, because there's nothing else.'

'I thought the same when I was walking over here, and when I was looking down at you.' He smiled, stroking her hair, his hand gently caressing her lovely face. 'You played well, *překrásný*.'

'I've hurt you.'

'A minor cut and a few major scratches. Don't be insulted.'

'You're bleeding . . . your neck.'

'And my back, and a fork-scrape – I guess you'd call it – on my stomach,' said Michael. 'You can nurse me later and I'll be grateful, but right now it fits the picture they have. I'm taking you back on Aeroflot.'

'Do I continue fighting?'

'No, just be hostile. You're resigned; you know you can't win. It'll go harder for you if you struggle.'

'And Kohoutek?'

'He says you're to stay in the back seat with him. He'll have us both under a gun.'

'Then I shall smoke a great deal. His hand will drop.'

'Something like that. It's a long trip, a lot can happen. A gas station, a breakdown, no lights. He may be a mountain bull but he's close to seventy.' Havelock held her shoulders. 'He may decide to drug you. If he does I'll try to stop him.'

'He won't give me anything dangerous; he wants his money. I'm not concerned, *odvážný*. I'll know you're there and I know what you can do.'

'Come on.'

'*Mikhail*.' She gripped his hands. 'What *happened*? To me . . . to *you*? They said such dreadful things, such *terrible* things! I couldn't believe them, yet I had to believe. It was *there*!'

'It was all there. Down to my watching you die.'

'Oh, *God* . . .'

'I've been running away ever since, until that night in Rome. Then I started running in a different direction. After you, after them – after the liars who did this to us.'

'How did they do it?'

'There's no time now. I'll tell you everything I can later, and then I want to hear *you*. Everything. You have the names, you know the people. Later.'

They stood up and embraced, holding each other briefly, feeling the warmth and the hope each gave the other. Michael pulled a handkerchief from his breast pocket and held it against his neck. Jenna took his hand away and blotted the deep scratches herself; she touched the bridge of his nose where she had struck him with her knee, then smoothed his hair at the temples.

'Remember, my darling,' she whispered. 'Treat me sternly. Push me and shove me and grab my arm firmly as you do it. A man who's been scratched by a woman, whether she's his enemy or not, is an angry man. Especially among other men; his masculinity suffers more than the wounds.'

'Thank you, Sigmund Freud. Let's go.'

The guard in the black leather jacket smiled at the sight of Havelock's bleeding neck while the Cuban nodded his head, his expression confirming a previous judgement. As instructed, Michael held Jenna's arm in a vice-like grip, propelling her forward at his side, his mouth set, his eyes controlled but furious.

'I want to go back to Kohoutek and get out of here!' he said angrily. 'And I don't care for any discussion, is that understood?'

'Did the great big man get hurt by the little bitty girl?' said the guard, grinning.

'Shut up, you goddamned idiot!'

'Come to think of it, she's not that little.'

Janos Kohoutek was dressed in a heavy waterproof jacket, a fur-lined cap on his head. He, too, smiled at the handkerchief held in place on Havelock's neck. 'Perhaps this one's a witch from the Carpathians,' he said, speaking English, his stained teeth showing. 'The old wives' tales say they have the strength of mountain cats and the cunning of demons.'

'Spell it with their *w, pritel*. She's a *bitch*.' Michael pressed towards the door. 'I want to get started; the snow will make for a longer trip.'

'It's not so bad, more wind than anything,' said the bull, taking a roll of thick cord out of his pocket and walking towards Jenna. 'They keep the turnpike clear.'

'What's that?' asked Havelock, gesturing at the cord.

'Hold out her hands,' ordered Kohoutek, addressing the guard. 'You may care to put up with this cat, but I do not.'

'I smoke,' protested Jenna. 'Let me smoke, I'm very nervous. What can I do?'

'Perhaps you would prefer a needle? Then there will be no thought of smoking.'

'My people won't accept drugs,' interrupted Michael firmly. 'The airports are watched, especially our departure gates. No narcotics.'

'Then she'll be tied. Come, take her hand.' The guard in the leather jacket approached Jenna; haltingly she put out her hands, so as not to be touched more than necessary. Kohoutek stopped. 'Has she been to the toilet?' he asked harshly of no one, and no one answered. 'Tell me, woman, have you been to the toilet?'

'I'm all right,' said Jenna.

'For a number of hours? There'll be no stops, you understand? Even to sit on the side of the road with a gun at your head, there'll be no stops. *Rozumět?*'

'I said I'm all right.'

'Tie her, and let's go.' Havelock took several impatient steps towards the door, passing the Moravian and glancing at Jenna. Her eyes were impersonal glass; she was magnificent. 'I assume this refugee from a *žalár* will take us up in the truck.'

The guard looked angry as Kohoutek grinned. 'You are not far wrong, Havlicek. He's been put away for aggravated assault several times. Yes, he'll take us.' The bull pulled the cord tight around Jenna's hands, then turned and shouted, '*Axel!*'

'He has my weapon,' said Michael, gesturing at the man in the leather jacket. 'I'd like it back.'

'You shall have it. At a street corner in New York.'

The second guard entered the room from the hallway, the same man who had first seen Havelock awake on the floor.

'Yes, Mr Kohoutek?'

'You're handling the schedules tomorrow, no?'

'Yes, sir.'

'Stay in radio contact with the northbound trucks and have one pick me up in Monongahela after my plane arrives tomorrow. I will phone from the airport and give you the time of the flight.'

'Right.'

'We go,' said the mountain bull, heading for the door.

Michael took Jenna's arm, the guard in the leather jacket following. Outside, the wind was stronger than before, the snow angrier, whipping in circles and stinging the face. With Kohoutek leading, they ran down the farmhouse path to the vehicle on the drive. A third guard, wearing a white parka, stood by the gate fifty yards away; he saw them and walked to the centre latch.

It was an enclosed van, with facing wooden benches to take five or six people on each side, and with coiled ropes on the walls. At the sight of the covered, windowless quarters Jenna was visibly shaken, and Havelock understood. Her country – his native country – had seen too many such vehicles over the years, heard too many stories told in whispers of convoys carrying away men and women and children who were never seen again. This was Mason Falls, Pennsylvania, USA, but the owners and drivers of these vehicles were no different from their brothers in Prague and Warsaw, late of Moscow – before then Berlin.

'Get in, get *in*!' shouted Kohoutek, now waving a large .45 automatic, as the guard held the handle of the rear door.

'I'm not your prisoner!' yelled Havelock. 'We negotiated! We have an agreement!'

'And part of that agreement, *přítel*, is that you are my guest as well as my hostage until we reach New York. After delivery – both deliveries – I shall be happy to put away the gun and buy you dinner.'

The mountain bull roared with laughter as Jenna and Michael climbed into the van. They sat next to each other, but this was not to Kohoutek's liking.

'The woman sits with me,' he said. 'You move across. *Quickly*.'

'You're paranoid,' said Havelock, moving to the other side, seeking out the shadows.

The door was closed, the latch and lock manipulated by the guard. A dim light came through the windscreen. In seconds, thought Michael, the headlights would be turned on, the reflected spill partially illuminating the van. In the darkness he pulled up his coat and reached behind him with his right hand, inching towards the knife clipped to his belt in the small of his back. If he did not remove it now, it would be infinitely more difficult later when he was behind the wheel of his car.

'What's *that*?' shouted the bull, raising his gun in the shadows, pointing it at Havelock's head. 'What are you doing?'

'The bitch-cat clawed my back; the blood's sticking to my shirt,' said Michael in a normal voice. Then he yelled, 'Do you want to see it, *feel* it!?'

Kohoutek grinned, glancing at Jenna. 'A Carpathian *čarodějka*. The moon's probably full but we can't see it.' He laughed his crude mountain laugh once more. 'I trust the Lubyanka is as tight as it ever was. She'll eat your guards up!'

At the word 'Lubyanka' Jenna gasped, shuddering, drawing out the words. 'Oh, God! Oh, my *God*!'

Kohoutek looked at her again, and again Havelock understood – she was covering for him. He quickly pulled the knife out of the scabbard and palmed it in his right hand. It had all taken less than twelve seconds.

The driver's door opened; the guard climbed in and switched on the lights. He looked behind; the old bull nodded and he turned the ignition key. The vehicle had a powerful engine, and a minute later they had passed through the gate and were climbing the steep hill, the heavy-treaded tyres crunching the snow and the soft earth beneath them, lurching, vibrating, rolling with the uneven pitch of the ground. They reached the wall of trees where the road flattened out; there was perhaps three-eighths of a winding mile to go before the Fourforks Pike. The guard-driver gathered speed, then suddenly stepped on the brake, stopping the truck instantly. A red light was flashing on the dashboard. He reached over for a switch, then a second, and snapped both. There was a prolonged burst of static over the radio as an excited voice shouted through the eruptions: 'Mr Kohoutek! Mr *Kohoutek*!'

'What is it?' asked the guard, grabbing a microphone from the dashboard and depressing a button. 'You're on the emergency channel.'

'The sparrow in New York . . . he's on the phone! Handelman's dead! He heard it on the radio! He was shot in his apartment, and the police are looking for a man . . .'

Havelock lunged, twisting the handle of the knife into his clenched fist, the blade protruding downard, his left hand reaching for the barrel of the .45 automatic. Jenna sprang away; he gripped the long, flat steel as Kohoutek rose, then slamming the gun back down on the wooden bench, he plunged the knife through the mountain bull's hand, embedding the point through flesh and bone into the wood.

Kohoutek screamed; the guard in the front seat spun around as Jenna threw herself at him, crashing her roped hands down on his neck, and pulled the microphone out of his grip, cutting off the transmission. Havelock swung the gun up into the old bull's head; Kohoutek lurched back into the wall and fell forward on the floor of the van, his arm stretched out, his hand still nailed to the wooden bench.

'*Mikhail!*'

The guard had recovered from Jenna's blows and was pulling the Llama out of his leather jacket. Michael sprang forward and jammed the heavy barrel of the .45 into the man's temple; reaching over his shoulder, he pressed down, holding the Llama in place.

'Mr Kohoutek? Have you *got* it?' yelled the voice through the radio static. 'What should the sparrow do? He wants to know!'

'Tell him you've got it,' ordered Havelock, breathing hard, thumbing back the hammer of the gun. 'Say the sparrow should do nothing. You'll be in touch.'

'We've got it.' The guard's voice was a whisper. 'Tell the sparrow not to do anything. We'll be in touch.'

Michael yanked the microphone away and pointed to the Llama. 'Now just hand it to me slowly,' he said. 'Use your fingers, just *two* fingers,' he continued. 'After all, it's mine, isn't it?'

'I was going to give it back,' said the frightened guard, his lips trembling.

'How many years can you give back to the people you drove in this thing?'

'That hasn't anything to do with me, I swear it! I just work for a living. I do what I'm told.'

'You all do.' Havelock took the Llama and moved the automatic around the man's head, pressing it into the base of his skull. 'Now drive us out of here,' he said.

22

The slender, middle-aged man with the straight dark hair opened the door of the telephone booth at the corner of 116th Street and Riverside Drive. The wet city snow was clinging to the glass, blurring the rotating red lights of the police cars up the block. He inserted the coin, dialled *O*, then five additional digits; he heard the second tone and dialled again. In moments a private phone was ringing in the living quarters of the White House.

'Yes?'

'Mr President?'

'Emory? How did it go?'

'It didn't. He's dead. He was shot.'

The silence from Washington was interrupted only by the sound of Berquist's breathing. 'Tell me what happened,' said the President.

'It was Havelock, but the name wasn't reported correctly. We can deny the existence of any such person at State.'

'*Havelock?* At . . .? Oh my God!'

'I don't know all the details, but enough. The shuttle was delayed by the snow and we circled LaGuardia for nearly an hour. By the time I got here there were crowds, police cars, a few press and an ambulance.'

'The *press?*'

'Yes, sir. Handelman's prominent here. Not only because he was a Jew who survived Bergen-Belsen, but because of his standing at the university. He was respected, even revered.'

'Oh, Christ . . . What did you learn? *How* did you learn it? Your name won't surface, will it?'

'No, sir. I used my rank at State and reached the precinct up here; the detective was co-operative. Apparently Handelman had an appointment with a female graduate student who came back to the building twice before ringing the superintendent. They went up to Handelman's apartment, saw the door was unlocked, went inside and found him. The superintendent called the police and, when they got here, he admitted having let in a man who had State Department credentials. He said his name was Havilitch; he didn't recall the first name, but insisted the ID was in order. The police are still in Handelman's apartment getting fingerprints, cloth and blood scrapings.'

'Have the details been made public?'

'In this town they can't wait. It was all released twenty minutes ago. There was no way I could stop it, if I wanted to. But State doesn't have to clarify; we *can* deny.'

The President was silent, then he spoke. 'When the time is right, the Department of State will co-operate fully with the authorities. Until then I want a file built – and circulated on a restricted basis – around Havelock's activities since his separation from the government. It must reflect the government's alarm over his mental state, his apparent homicidal tendencies . . . his loyalty. However, in the interests of national security, that file will remain under restricted classification. It will not be made public.'

'I'm not sure I understand.'

'The facts will be revealed when Havelock is no longer a threat to this country's interests.'

'Sir?'

'One man is insignificant,' said the President softly. 'Coventry, Mr Undersecretary. Enigma . . . Parsifal.'

'I accept the reasoning, sir, not the assumption. How can we be sure we'll find him?'

'He'll find us; he'll find *you*. If everything we've learned about Havelock is as accurate as we believe, he wouldn't have killed Jacob Handelman unless he had an extraordinary reason. And he would never have killed him if he hadn't learned where Handelman sent the Karras woman. When he reaches her, he'll know about you.'

Bradford paused, his breath visible, the vapour briefly interrupted. 'Yes, of course, Mr President.'

'Get back here as fast as you can. We must be ready . . . *you* must be ready. I'll have two men flown up from Poole's Island. They'll meet you at National; stay in airport security until they arrive.'

'Yes, sir.'

'Now, listen to me, Emory. My instructions will be direct, the explanation clear. By presidential order you are to be given round-the-clock protection; your life is in their hands. You are being hunted by a killer who's sold his government's secrets to the enemy. Those will be the words *I* use; *yours* will be different. You will use the language of Consular Operations: Havelock is "beyond-salvage". Every additional hour he lives is a danger to our men in the field.'

'I understand.'

'Emory?'

'Sir?'

'Before this all happened I never really knew you, not personally,' said Berquist softly. 'What's your situation at home?'

'Home?'

'It's where he'll come for you. Are there children at home?'

'Children? No, no there are no children. My older son's in college, my younger boy away at boarding school.'

'I thought I heard somewhere that you had daughters.'

'Two. They're with their mother. In Wisconsin.'
'I see. I didn't know. Is there another wife?'
'There were. Again, two. They didn't last.'
'Then there are no women living in your house?'
'There are frequently, but not at the minute. Very few during the past four months.'
'I see.'
'I live alone. The circumstances are optimum, Mr President.'
'Yes, I guess they are.'

Using the coiled ropes on the wall of the van, they tied the guard to the steering wheel, Kohoutek to the bench.

'Find whatever you can and bind his hand,' said Michael. 'I want him alive. I want someone to ask him questions.'

Jenna found a farmer's kerchief in the glove compartment. She removed the scaling knife from the old mountain bull's huge hand, ripped the cloth in two and expertly bound the wound, stemming the blood at both the gash and the wrist.

'It will hold for three, perhaps four hours,' she said. 'After that, I don't know. If he wakes and tears it, he could bleed to death . . .Knowing what I know, I have no use for prayers.'

'Someone'll find him. Them. This truck. It'll be light in an hour or so, and the Fourforks Pike's a county route. Sit down for a minute.' Havelock started the engine and, reaching his foot over the guard's leg, depressed the clutch and shoved the truck in gear. Wrenching the man back and forth over the steering wheel, he manoeuvred the vehicle so that it was broadside across the road. 'Okay, let's get out.'

'You can't leave me here!' whined the guard. '*Jesus!*'
'Have you been to the toilet?'
'*What?*'
'I hope so, for your sake.'
'Mikhail?'
'Yes?'
'The radio. He'd use it. Someone might come along and free him. We need every minute.'

Havelock picked up the .45 from the seat and smashed the thick, blunt handle repeatedly into the dials and switches until there was nothing but shattered glass and plastic. Finally, he ripped the microphone out of its receptacle, severing the wires; he opened the door and turned to Jenna. 'We'll leave the lights on so no one smashes into it,' he said, stepping out and pulling the seat forward for her. 'One more thing to do. Come on.'

Because of the wind, the Fourforks Pike had less than an inch of snow on the surface except for the intermittent drifts that had been pummelled into the bordering grass. Michael handed the .45 to Jenna and switched the Llama to his right hand. 'That makes too much noise,' he continued. 'The wind might carry it down to the farmhouse. Stay here.'

He ran to the back of the van and fired twice, blowing out both rear tyres. He raced up the other side and fired into the front tyres. The van rocked back and forth as the tyres deflated and settled into the road. To clear the highway, it could be driven into the grass, but it would go no farther than that. He put the Llama into his pocket.

'Let me have the forty-five,' he said to Jenna, pulling his shirt out of his trousers.

She gave it to him. 'What are you going to do?'

'Wipe it clean. Not that it'll do much good, our prints are all over the inside. But they may not brush there; they will this.'

'So?'

'I'm gambling that our driver in his own self interest will yell like hell that it's not his, that it belongs to his employer, your host, Kohoutek.'

'Ballistics,' said Jenna, nodding. 'Killings on file.'

'Maybe something else. That farm will be torn apart and when it is they may start digging around those acres. There could be killings not on file.' He held the automatic with his shirt-tail, opened the door of the truck and arched the weapon over the front seat into the covered van.

'Hey, come *on*, for Christ's sake!' shouted the driver, twisting and turning against the ropes. 'Let me out of here, will ya? I didn't do nothing to you! They'll send me back for ten years!'

'They're a lot easier on people who turn state's evidence. Think about it.' Havelock slammed the door and walked rapidly back to Jenna. 'The car's about a quarter of a mile down on the other side of Kohoutek's road. Are you all right?'

She looked at him; particles of snow stuck to her blonde hair swirling in the wind and her face was drenched, but her eyes were alive. 'Yes, my darling, I'm all right . . . Wherever we are at this moment, I'm home.'

He took her hand and they started down the road. 'Walk in the centre, so our footsteps will be covered.'

She sat close to him, touching him, her arm through his, her head intermittently resting on his shoulder as he drove.

The words between them were few, the silences comforting; they were too tired, too afraid, to talk sensibly, at least for a while. They had been there before; they knew a fraction of peace would come with the quiet – and being with each other.

Remembering Kohoutek's words, Havelock headed north to the Pennsylvania Turnpike, then east towards Harrisburg. The old Moravian had been right; the low-flying winds virtually swept the wide expanse of highway, and the sub-freezing temperature kept the snow dry and buoyant. Although the visibility was poor, the travelling was fast.

'Is this the main autoroute?' asked Jenna.

'It's the state turnpike, yes.'

'Is it wise to be on it? If Kohoutek's found before daybreak, might not men be watching this "turnpike", as they do the *dráhas*?'

'We're the last people on earth he wants the police to find. We know what that farm is. He'll stall, use the intruder story, say *he* was the hostage, the victim. And the guard won't say anything until he hasn't got a choice, or until they find his record, and then he'll bargain. We're all right.'

'That's the police, darling,' said Jenna, her hand gently touching his forearm. 'Suppose it is not the police? You want it to be the police, so you persuade yourself. But suppose it is someone else? A farmer or a driver of a milk truck. I think Kohoutek would pay a great deal of money to get safely back to his home.'

Michael looked at her in the dim light of the dashboard. Her eyes were tired, with dark circles under them; fear was still in the centre of her stare. Yet in spite of the exhaustion and the dread, she was thinking better than he was. But then she had been hunted far more often than he, and more recently. Above all, she would not panic; she knew the value of control even when the pain and the fear were overwhelming. He leaned over and brushed his lips on her face.

'You're magnificent,' he said.

'I'm frightened,' she replied.

'And you're also right. There's a childish song that says "wishing will make it so". It's a lie, and only for children, but I was counting on it, hoping for it. The odds of the police finding Kohoutek, or a citizen reporting what he found to the police, are no better than seventy-thirty. Against. We'll get off at the next exit and head south.'

'To where? Where are we going?'

'First, where we can be alone, and not moving. Not running.'

She sat in a chair by the motel window, the early light spreading up and over the Allegheny Mountains outside in the distance. The yellow rays heightened the gold in the long blonde hair that fell across her shoulders. Alternately she would look at him, then turn her face away and close her eyes, his words too painful to hear in the light.

When he had finished, he was still caught in the anguish that came with the admission: he had been her executioner. He had killed his love and there had been no love left in him.

Jenna rose from the chair and stood silently by the window. 'What did they *do* to us?' she whispered.

Havelock stood across the room watching her; he could not look away. And then, he was drifting back through indeterminate time, through the rolling mists of a haunting, obsessive dream that never left him. The images were there, the moments remembered, but they had been pushed out of his life only to rise up and attack him, inflaming him whenever the memories refused to stay buried. *What's left when your memory's gone, Mr Smith?* Nothing, of course, yet how often had he wished for oblivion, with no images or remembered moments – trading nothingness for the absence of pain. But now he had passed through the nightmare of interrupted sleep and had come to life just as the tears had come to Jenna's eyes, washing away the hatred. But the reality was fragile; its fragments had to be pieced together.

'We must find out why,' said Michael. 'Broussac told me what happened to you, but there were gaps I couldn't understand.'

'I didn't tell her everything,' said Jenna, gazing at the snow outside. 'I didn't lie to her, but I didn't tell her everything. I was afraid she wouldn't help me.'

'What did you leave out?'

'The name of the man who came to see me. He's been with your government for a number of years. He was once quite controversial, but still respected, I think. At least, I'd heard of him.'

'Who was it?'

'A man named Bradford. Emory Bradford.'

'Good *God* . . .' Havelock was stunned. Bradford was a name from the past, a disquieting past. He had been one of the politcal comets born under Kennedy and had won dubious spurs with Johnson. When the comets had faded from the Washington firmament, heading for the international banks and the foundations, the prestigious law offices and the corporate board-rooms, Bradford had remained – less celebrated, to be sure, less influential, certainly – where the political wars had been fought. It was never understood why. A degree of personal wealth aside, he could have done a thousand other things, but he had chosen not to. *Bradford*, thought Havelock, the name echoing in his head. All these years, had Emory Bradford merely been marking time, waiting for another version of Camelot to carry him into another tune of self-professed glory? It had to be. If he had reached Jenna in Barcelona, he was at the core of the deception at Costa Brava, a deception that went far beyond himself and Jenna, two lovers turned against each other. It linked unseen men in Moscow with powerful men in the United States government.

'Do you know him?' asked Jenna, still staring out of the window.

'Not personally. I've never met him. But you're right, he *was* controversial, and almost everyone knows him. The last I heard he was an Undersecretary to State with a low profile but pretty highly regarded – buried but valuable, you could say. He told you he was with Cons Op out of Madrid?'

'He said he was on special assignment with Consular Operations, an emergency involving internal security.'

'Me?'

'Yes. He showed me copies of documents found in a bank vault on the Ramblas.' Jenna turned from the window. 'Do you recall telling me you had to go to the Ramblas on several occasions?'

'It was a drop for Lisbon, I also told you that. Never mind, it was orchestrated.'

'But you can understand. The Ramblas stayed in my mind.'

'They made sure of it. What were the documents?'

'Instructions from Moscow that could only have been meant for you. There were dates, itineraries; everything corresponded to where we'd been, where we were going. And there were codes; if they weren't authentic, then I'd never seen a Russian cipher.'

'The same materials *I* was given,' said Havelock, his anger surfacing.

'Yes, I knew it when you told me what they gave you in Madrid. Not all, of course, but many of the same documents and much of the information they showed you, they showed me. Even down to the radio in the hotel room.'

'The maritime frequency? I thought you'd been careless; we never listened to the radio.'

'When I saw it, a great part of me died,' said Jenna.

'When I found the key in your bag and it matched the one the evidence in Madrid stated that you would have – a key to an airport locker – I couldn't stay in the same room with you.'

'That was it, wasn't it? The final confirmation for both of us. I had changed, I couldn't help it. And when you came back from Madrid, *you* were different. It was as if you were being pulled violently in several directions, but with you only one true commitment, and it was not to me, not to us. You had sold yourself to the Russians for reasons I couldn't understand . . . I even tried to rationalize; perhaps after thirty years there was news of your father – stranger things have happened. Or you were going into deep cover without me; a defector in the process of becoming a double agent. I simply knew that the transition – whatever it was – did not include me.' Jenna turned back to the window. She continued, her voice barely audible, 'Then Bradford reached me again; this time he was panicking, nearly out of control. He said the word had just been intercepted – Moscow had ordered my execution. You were to lead me into a trap, and you were going to do it that night.'

'At the Costa Brava?'

'No, he never mentioned the Costa Brava. He said a man would call around six o'clock while you were out, using a phrase or description I'd recognize as coming only from you. He would say that you could not get to a telephone, but I was to take the car and drive down the coast to Villanueva, that you would meet me by the fountains in the plaza. But you wouldn't, because I'd never get there. I'd be taken on the road.'

'I *told* you I was going to Villanueva,' said Michael. 'It was part of the Cons Op strategy. With me supposedly twenty miles south on business, you had time to get up to the Montebello beach on the Costa Brava. It was the final proof against you. I was to witness it – I demanded that, hoping to Christ you'd never show up.'

'It all fitted, it was *made* to fit!' cried Jenna. 'Bradford said if that call came I was to run. Another American would be in the lobby with him, watching for the KGB. They'd take me to the consulate.'

'But you didn't leave with them. The woman I saw die wasn't you.'

'I couldn't. I suddenly couldn't trust anyone . . . Do you remember the incident that night at the café in the Paseo Isabel just before you went to Madrid?'

'The drunk,' said Havelock, remembering all too well. 'He bumped into you – fell into you, actually – then insisted on shaking your hand and kissing it. He was all over you.'

'We laughed about it. You more than I.'

'I didn't a couple of days later. I was convinced that was when you were given the key to the airport locker.'

'Which I never knew about.'

'And which I found in your bag because Bradford put it there while he was in the hotel room and I was in Madrid. I assume you excused yourself for a moment or two.'

'I was in shock; I was ill. I'm sure I did.'

'It explains the radio, the maritime frequency . . . What about the drunk?'

'He was the other American in the lobby of the hotel. Why was he there? Who *was* he? I went back up as fast as I could.'

'He didn't see you?'

'No, I used the staircase. His face frightened me, I can't tell you why. Perhaps because he had pretended to be someone else before, someone so different, I don't know. I *do* know his eyes disturbed me; they were angry, but they did not look round. He *wasn't* watching the lobby for the KGB; he only kept glancing at his watch. By then I was in a panic myself . . . confused, hurt more than I'd ever been hurt in my life. *You* were going to let me die, and suddenly I couldn't trust *them*.'

'You went back to the room?'

'God, no, I'd have been cornered. I went up to the floor, stayed in the stairwell and tried to think things through. I thought perhaps I was being hysterical, too frightened to act reasonably. Why *didn't* I trust the Americans? I'd just about made up my mind to go back down when I heard noises from the corridor. I opened the door a bit . . . and knew that I was right to do what I did.'

'They came after you?'

'The lift. Bradford knocked on the door several times, and while he was knocking, the other man – the drunk from the café – took out a gun. When there was no answer, they waited until they were sure there was no one in the hallway. Then, with one kick, the man with the gun broke down the door and rushed inside. It was not the action of men who'd come to save someone. I ran.'

Havelock, watching her, tried to think. There were so many ambiguities . . . *ambiguity*. Where were the outlines of the man who had used the code Ambiguity?

'How did they get your suitcase?' he asked.

'As you described it, it was an old one of mine. The last I recall I simply left it in the basement of the flat I leased in Prague. You may have carried it down, in fact.'

'The KGB would find it.'

'The *KGB*?'

'Someone in the KGB.'

'Yes, you said that, didn't you? . . . There has to be someone.'

'What was the phrase or description the man gave you over the phone? The words you were to think came from me.'

'Again Prague. He said there was "a cobblestone courtyard in the centre of the city".'

'*Věrejná mistnostmi*,' said Michael, nodding. 'Prague's Soviet police. They'd know about that. In a report I sent to Washington I described how you got out of that place, how great you were. And how I damn near died watching you from a window three storeys above.'

'Thank you for the commendation.'

'We were putting all our points together, remember? We were going to break out of our movable prison.'

'And you were going to teach.'

'History.'

'And we were going to have children – '

'And send them off to school – '

'And love them and scold them.'

'And go to hockey games.'

'You said there were no such things – '

'I love you . . .'

'*Mikhail?*'

The first steps were tentative, but the pavane was suddenly finished. They ran to each other, and held each other, pushing time away, and hurt, and a thousand moments of anguish. Her tears came, washing away the final barricades mounted by liars and men who served the liars. Their arms grew stronger around each other, the straining of their bodies an exertion each understood; their lips met, swollen, probing, searching for the release they held for each other. They were trapped as never before in their movable prison – they understood that, too – but for the moment they were also free.

The dream had come fully to life, the reality no longer fragile. She was beside him, her face touching his shoulder, her lips parted, the breath of her deep, steady breathing warming his skin. As so often in the past, strands of her hair fell across his chest, somehow a reminder that even in sleep she was a part of him. He turned carefully so as not to awaken her, and looked down at her. The dark shadows beneath her eyes were still there, but they were fading fast as a hint of colour returned to her pale flesh. It would take days, weeks perhaps, for the fear in her wide eyes to disappear, yet in spite of it, her strength was there; it had carried her through unbearable tensions.

She moved, stretching, and her face was bathed in the sunlight that streamed through the windows. As he watched her he thought of what she had been through, what resources she must have had to summon in order to survive. Where had she been? Who were the people who had helped her, hurt her? There were so many questions, so many things he wanted to know. A part of him was a callow adolescent, jealous of the images he did not wish to imagine, while another part of him was a survivor who knew only too well the prices one had to pay to remain alive in their disorderly, so frequently violent world. The answers would come with time, revealed slowly or in eruptions of memory or resentment, but they would not be provoked by him. The healing process could not be forced; it would be too easy for Jenna to sink back and relive the terrors and, by reliving them, prolong them.

She moved again, her face returning to him, her breath warm. And then the absurdity of his thoughts struck him. Where did he think he was . . . *they* were? What did he think would be permitted them? How could he dare to think in terms of any time at all?

Jacob Handelman was dead, his killer as good as identified – certainly known by now to the liars in Washington. The manhunt would be given respectability; he could see the story in the newspapers: a beloved scholar brutally slaughtered by a deranged former foreign service officer wanted by his government for all manner of crimes. Who could possibly believe the truth? That a kindly old Jew who had suffered the horrors of the camps was in reality a strutting man-monster who had ordered up the guns of Lidice? *Insane!*

Broussac would turn; anyone he might have counted on would not touch him now, touch *them* now. There was no time for healing, they needed every hour; the swiftness of their strikes – *his* strikes – was essential. He looked at his watch; it was 2:45, the day three-quarters gone. There were strategies to consider, rapid plans to make . . . liars to reach at night.

Yet there had to be *something*. For them, only themselves; to ease the ache, erase the vestiges of fragility. If there was not, there was nothing.

He did what he had often dreamt of, waking up in sweat whenever the dream recurred, knowing it could never be. It could be now. He whispered her name, calling out to her across the chasms of sleep, and, as if the moments away from each other had vanished, her hand reached for his. She opened her eyes and they roamed his face; then, without speaking, she raised the covers and came to him. She pressed her naked body against his, her arms enveloping him, her lips against his.

They were silent as their excitement grew, except for their throated cries of need and anxiety. The need was each for the other, and the anxiety was not to be feared.

They made love twice more, but the third time was more successful in the attempt than in the completion. The rays of the sun no longer streaked through the window; instead an orange glow reflected a country sundown. They sat up in bed, Michael lighting her cigarette, both laughing softly at their misguided energies, their temporary exhaustion.

'You're going to throw me out for a hot-blooded stag from Ankara.'

'You have nothing at all to apologize for, my darling . . . my Mikhail. Besides, I really don't like their coffee.'

'I'm relieved.'

'You're a love,' she said, touching the bandage on his shoulder.

'I'm *in* love. There's so much to make up for.'

'Both of us, not you alone. You must not think that way. I accepted the lies, just as you did. Incredible lies, incredibly presented. And we don't know why.'

'But we know the purpose, which gives us part of the why. To get me out but keep me under control, under a microscope.'

'With *my* defection, *my* death? There are other ways of terminating a man you no longer want.'

'Killing him?' said Havelock, nodding, then he paused and shook his head. 'It's one way, yes. But then there's no way to control whatever damaging evidence he may have left behind. The possibility that such a man has left that information often keeps him alive.'

'But they want to kill you *now*. You're "beyond-salvage".'

'Someone changed his mind.'

'This person called "Ambiguity",' said Jenna.

'Yes. Whatever I know – or they think I know – has been supplanted by a larger threat much more dangerous to them. Again, me. What I found, what I learned.'

'I don't understand.'

'You,' said Havelock. 'The Costa Brava. It has to be buried.'

'The Soviet connection?'

'I don't know. Who was the woman on the beach? What did she think she was doing there? Why wasn't it you – thank Christ, it wasn't – but *why* wasn't it? Where were they taking you?'

'To my grave, I think.'

'If that was the case, why weren't you sent to that beach? Why weren't you killed then?'

'Perhaps they felt I wouldn't go. I didn't leave the hotel with them.'

'They couldn't have known that then. They thought they had you – frightened, in shock, wanting protection. The point is, they never mentioned the Costa Brava; they didn't even try to *prime* you.'

'I would have driven there that night – all you had to do was call me. I would have come. They could have had their execution; you would have seen what they wanted you to see.'

'It doesn't make sense.' Michael struck a match and lit a cigarette for himself. 'And that's the basic inconsistency, because whoever put Costa Brava together was a hell of a technician, an expert in black operations. It was brilliantly structured, down to split-second timing . . . It doesn't make sense!'

Jenna broke the long silence. 'Mikhail,' she said quietly, sitting forward, her eyes clouded, focused inward. '*Two* operations,' she whispered.

'What?'

'Suppose there were two operations, not one?' She turned to him, her eyes alive now. 'The first set in motion in Madrid – the evidence against *me* – then carried forward to Barcelona – the evidence against *you*.'

'Still one blanket,' said Havelock.

'But then it was *torn*,' insisted Jenna. 'It became *two*.'

'How?'

'The original operation is intercepted,' she said. 'By someone not part of it.'

'Then altered,' he said, beginning to understand. 'The cloth is the same but the stitches are twisted, ending up being something else. A *different* blanket.'

'Still, for what purpose?' she asked.

'Control,' he answered. 'Then you got away and the control was lost. Broussac told me there's been a coded alert out for you ever since Costa Brava.'

'Very coded,' agreed Jenna, crushing out her cigarette. 'Which could mean whoever intercepted the operation and altered it might not have known that I *had* got out of Barcelona alive.'

'Until I saw you and let *everyone* know – everyone who counted. At which point we both had to die; one by the black-operations book – that was me. The other out of strategy – no one in sanction aware – a bomb blowing up a car outside Col des Moulinets. You. Everything buried.'

'Again Ambiguity?'

'No one else could have done it. No one but a man with the clearance code could have infiltrated the strategy at that bridge.'

Jenna looked at him, then across at the windows; the orange glow was fading. 'There are still too many omissions. Too many gaps.'

'We'll fill some of them in, maybe all.'

'Emory Bradford, of course.'

'And someone else,' said Havelock. 'Matthias. Four days ago I tried to reach him from Cagnes-sur-Mer on his private line – very few people have the number. I couldn't understand it, but he wouldn't talk to me. You can't know how crazy it was, in a way unbelievable. But he wouldn't and I thought the worst: the man closest to me had cut me off. Then you tell me about Bradford, and I'm beginning to think I was wrong.'

'How do you mean?'

'Suppose Anton wasn't there? Suppose others had taken over that private place, that very private line?'

'*Bradford?*'

'And whatever's left of his tribe. The return of the political comets, looking for a way to get their fires back. According to *Time* magazine, Matthias is off on an extended holiday, but what if he's not? What if the most celebrated Secretary of State in history is being held incommunicado. In a clinic somewhere, unable to get word out.'

'But that's incredible, Mikhail. A man like that would have to stay in touch with his office. There are daily briefings, decisions – '

'It could be done through second and third parties, aides known to State personnel.'

'It's too preposterous.'

'Maybe it's not. When they told me Anton wouldn't talk to me, I couldn't accept it. I made another call – to an old man, a neighbour of Matthias's whom he saw whenever he went to his lodge in the Shenandoah. His name's Zelienski and he was good for Anton – a retired professor brought over from Warsaw a number of years ago. They used to sit around playing chess, talking about the old days. He was a tonic for Matthias and both of them knew it, especially Anton; but when I spoke to Zelienski he said Anton didn't have time for him these days. Didn't have time.'

'It's entirely possible, Mikhail.'

'But not consistent. Matthias would *make* the time; he wouldn't cut off an old friend without at least some kind of explanation, any more than he would me. It is not like him.'

'How do you mean?'

'I remember Zelienski's words. He said he'd leave messages for Anton and men would call him back expressing Matthias's regrets, saying he rarely drove out to the valley any more. But he did; he was there in the valley when I called. Or he was *supposed* to be. My point is he may not have been.'

'Now *you're* not consistent,' broke in Jenna. 'If what you say is true, why didn't they simply say he wasn't there?'

'They couldn't. I used the private line and it's to be answered only if he's on the premises, and only by him. Someone picked up the phone by mistake and tried to cover it.'

'Someone working for Bradford?'

'Someone who's part of a conspiracy against Matthias, at any rate, and I wouldn't exclude Bradford. Men in Washington are dealing secretly with men in Moscow. Together they built Costa Brava convincing Matthias you're a Soviet agent – his note to me made that clear. We don't know whether everything went off the track or not, but we do know Matthias had nothing to do with it and Bradford did. Anton didn't trust Emory Bradford and his crowd; he considered them the worst sort of opportunists. He kept them away from extremely sensitive negotiations because he believed they'd use them for their own ends. He had a point; they did it before, letting the country know only what they wanted people to hear, using the classification stamp so that it became their signature.' Michael paused, inhaling on his cigarette as Jenna looked at him. 'He may be doing it again, God knows for what purpose. It'll be dark soon and we can drive. We'll head across into Maryland, then down to Washington.'

'To Bradford?'

Havelock nodded. Jenna touched his arm. 'They'll connect you with Handelman,' she said, 'and assume you reached me. They'll know the first name I'd give you is Bradford's. They'll guard him.'

'I know that,' said Michael. 'Let's get dressed. We've got to eat and find a newspaper, one that carries the wire services. We'll talk in the car.' He began walking towards his suitcase, then stopped. 'My God, your clothes. I didn't think; you don't have your clothes.'

'Kohoutek's people took them, took everything. They said foreign labels, European luggage, mementoes – anything like that – had to be confiscated for our own good. There could be no traces of where we came from. They would supply me with something suitable later.'

'Suitable for what?'

'I was too frightened to think.'

'Take all your possessions, and leave you alone in a cell.' *So much to make up for*. 'Let's go,' he said.

'We should stop somewhere and pick up a First Aid kit,' added Jenna. 'That dressing on your shoulder should be changed. I can do it.'

So much to make up for!

23

At a diner on the outskirts of Hagerstown, they saw a dispenser for newspapers reflected in the light of the entrance. There were two papers left, both afternoon editions of the Baltimore *Sun*. They took both, to see whether any photographs had been released that might alert someone inside the roadside restaurant. Shaving the negative odds was instinct.

They sat across from each other in a corner booth. They turned the pages rapidly, and when they had gone through them all they breathed easier. There were no photographs. They would go back and study the article in a moment; it was on page three.

'You must be starved,' said Havelock.

'To tell you the truth, I'd like a drink, if they serve one here.'

'They do. I'll order.' He glanced at the counter and held up his hand.

'I haven't even thought about eating.'

'That's strange. Kohoutek said you wouldn't eat last night, that you threw the tray at his Cuban.'

'A tray full of scraps. I ate; you always told me never to leave food when you're in a bad situation. That you never know when you'll get another meal.'

'Listen to mother.'

'I listened to a child running for his life through the woods.'

'History. Why did you throw the tray? To keep him away from you?'

'To get the fork. There was no knife.'

'You're something, lady.'

'I was desperate. Stop complimenting me.'

A plump, over-made-up waitress approached the table, her eyes appraising Jenna with a mixture of sadness and envy. Michael understood, neither with satisfaction nor in condescension; he merely understood. Jenna Karras was that often-forgotten person, whether she was forced to kill in order to survive or be seduced so she might live. She was a lady. Havelock ordered their drinks.

'Let's get to the bad news,' said Michael, opening the newspaper.

'It's on the third page.'

'I know. Did you read it?'

'Only the bottom line where it said "continued on page eleven". I thought they might have included a photograph there.'

'So did I.' Havelock began reading as Jenna watched him. The waitress placed their drinks on the table. 'We'll order food in a minute,' said Michael, his eyes riveted to the paper. The waitress left as Havelock quickly flipped the pages, snapping the paper in place. As he read on, he experienced relief, then concern, and finally alarm. He finished and leaned back in the booth, staring at Jenna.

'What is it? What does it say?'

'They're covering it up,' he said softly.

'*What?*'

'They're protecting me . . . actually protecting me.'

'You couldn't have read it properly.'

'I'm afraid I did.' He leaned forward, his fingers scanning the lines in the column of the paper. 'Listen to this:

'According to the State Department, no such individual matching the name, the description or the fingerprints is currently or has ever been in the employ of the Department of State. Further, a spokesman for State said that to speculate on the similarity of the reported name of the killer with that of any present or past employee would be grossly unfair and inaccurate. A thorough computer check was made upon receipt of the Manhattan police report and the results were negative. However, the State Department's report revealed that the slain Professor Handelman had acted as a consultant to the Department in the area of European refugee displacement, with emphasis on those persons who had survived the Nazi period. According to a spokesman, the Manhattan police believe that the killer may be a member of a terrorist organization violently hostile to the Jewish community. The State Department pointed out that it is not uncommon for terrorists in all countries to assume the identities of government personnel.'

Havelock stopped and looked up at Jenna. 'That's it,' he said. 'They've thrown everybody off.'

'Could they believe it?'

'Not possible. To begin with, there are a hundred people in and out of State who know I was with Consular Operations. They'd put the names together and come up with mine. Second, my fingerprints must have been all over Handelman's apartment; they're on file. Lastly, Handelman had nothing whatsoever to do with any part of the government; that was his strength. He was a halfway man for the Quai d'Orsay, and they never would have used him if they thought he'd ever be under government scrutiny. It isn't done; we're all off-limits.'

'What do you make of it?'

Michael sank back in the booth, reached for his whisky and drank. 'It's too blatant,' he mused, holding the glass in front of his lips.

'A trap, then,' said Jenna. 'They want you to come in – presumably after Bradford – and take you.'

'To a point "beyond-salvage", to coin a phrase. And once I'm dead, I can't talk, but they can explain they trapped a killer. Reaching Bradford would be easy, coming out with him impossible . . . Unless I could draw *him* out, make him come to *me*.'

'They'd never permit it. He'd be flanked by guards and they'd be watching for you. They'd kill you on sight.'

Havelock drank again, a thought stirring at the bottom of his mind but unclear as yet. 'Watching for me,' he repeated, putting the glass down. '*Looking* for me . . . But no one's *looking* for me except the men who did this to us.'

'The liars, as you call them,' said Jenna.

'Yes. We need help, but I assumed we couldn't get it, that anyone I might want to reach wouldn't touch us. That's not the case now; they called *off* the hunt.'

'Don't be foolish, Mikhail,' interrupted Jenna. 'It's part of the trap. There's an alert out for you as well as for me, and yours isn't coded; there's nothing ambiguous about it. You're you, and every agency that might be of value has you on its list. Who in your government do you think you could trust?'

'No one,' agreed Havelock. 'And no one who could survive a "beyond-salvage" association, if I did trust him.'

'Then what are you saying?'

'Cagnes-sur-Mer,' said Michael, squinting. 'At Salanne's house when I couldn't reach Anton, I called old Zelienski – I told you, remember? He mentioned him. "Alexander the Great", he called him. Raymond Alexander. Not just a mutual friend, but a pretty damned good friend – of mine as well as Matthias. He could do it.'

'How?'

'Because he's *outside* the government. Outside but in a way very much a part of it; Washington needs him and he needs Washington. He's a writer for the *Potomac Review*, and knows as much about the government as anyone I've ever met. But he relies on his contacts; he'd never let me get near him if I'd been identified in the newspapers, but I wasn't.'

'How could he help us?'

'I'm not sure. Maybe draw out Bradford for me. He does in-depth interviews, and to be interviewed by him is a plus for anyone in the government. He's above suspicion. They might drive Bradford out in a tank, but they'd let him go inside the house by himself. I could hint at something unexpected, a substantive change in the State Department with Bradford at the centre. Then suggest an interview – with me in the house to listen, to verify.'

'The house?'

'He works at home; it's part of his mystique. Like James Reston at the *Times*; if a politician or a bureaucrat says he was at Fiery Run, everyone knows what he means; there'll be a story by Scotty Reston. If he says he was out at Fox Hollow, the same people know he was interviewed by Raymond Alexander. Fox Hollow's in Virginia just west of Washington. We could be there in an hour and a half, two hours at the most.'

'Would he do it?'

'He might. I won't tell him why, but he might. We're friends.'

'The university?'

'No, but there's a connection. I met him through Matthias. When I first started at State, Matthias would come down to Washington on one thing or another, building his contacts, charming the asses off influential asses, and I'd frequently get a hurry-up call from Anton, asking me to join them both for dinner. I never refused, not only because of the company, but the restaurants were way beyond my income.'

'That was gracious of your *pritel*.'

'And not very bright for a brilliant man, considering the nature of my training. He was the *učitel* extolling his not-too-gifted student from Praha, when the last thing I needed was any sort of notice. I explained this quietly to Alexander. We both laughed and, as a result, had dinner now and then when Anton was safely back in his tower at Princeton, tending his academic gardens and not trying to grow arbours in Washington. Make no mistake, the great Matthias was not above fertilizing the seeds he'd sown.'

'You'd have dinner at Alexander's home?'

'Always. He understood that he also wasn't someone I wanted to be seen with in public.'

'Then you *are* good friends.'

'Reasonably so.'

'And he's influential?'

'Of course.'

Jenna reached over and touched his arm. 'Mikhail, why not tell him *everything*?'

Havelock frowned and put his hand over hers. 'I don't think he'd want to hear it. It's the sort of thing he runs from.'

'He's a writer. In *Washington*. How can you say that?'

'He's an analyst, a commentator. Not an investigative reporter; not a muck raker. He doesn't like stepping on toes, only on opinions.'

'But what you have to tell him is extraordinary.'

'He'd tell me to go straight to the State Department security bureau in the belief that I'd get a fair hearing. I wouldn't. I'd get a bullet in my head.

Alexander's a sixty-five-year-old curmudgeon who's heard it all – from Dallas to Watergate – and he thinks a hundred and ten per cent of it is a conspiracy of horseshit. And if he found out what I'd done – Handelman excluded – he'd call security himself.'

'He's not much of a friend.'

'By his lights he is; just don't transgress.' Michael paused, turning her hand over. 'But beyond the possibility that he'd bring Bradford out to Fox Hollow, there's something he might clear up. My *pritel*. I'll ask him to find out where Matthias is, say that I don't want to call myself because I may not have time to see him and Anton would be upset. He'd do it; with his connections he *could* do it.'

'Suppose he can't?'

'Then that'll tell us something, won't it? In which case, I'll force him to get Bradford out there, if I have to put a gun to his head. But if he does reach Matthias at a lodge in the Shenandoah . . . we'll know something else, and it frightens the hell out of me. It will mean that the Secretary of State has a Moscow connection in the KGB.'

The village of Fox Hollow was small. The streets were lit by gas lamps and the architecture was colonial by township decree; the stores were called shops, their clientele among the wealthiest in the Washington–New York orbit. The village's charm was not only apparent, it was proclaimed, but it was not for the benefit of outsiders – tourists were discouraged, if not harassed. The minimum police force had maximum arms and a communications system that, proportionately, rivalled that of the Pentagon, where it was probably designed. Fox Hollow was an island in a landlocked area of Virginia as surely as if its square-mileage were surrounded by an impassable sea.

The air had been warmed up by the Potomac River, the snow had receded on the outskirts of Harper's Ferry. It had turned into a cold drizzle at Leesburg, by which time Havelock had prepared his scenario for Raymond Alexander. Its bureaucratic plausibility lent it conviction, plausibility based on genuine anxiety where present or past covert operations were concerned. There had been a killing in New York – if Alexander had not heard of it, he would by morning; he was a voracious reader of newspapers – and the killer had mocked up an impersonation, including an ID and an appearance uncomfortably close to Michael's own. The State Department had flown him back from London on military transport; any assistance the retired foreign service officer could give Consular Operations would be appreciated; also, he *had been* in London, hadn't he?

The Bradford ploy would be refined as their conversation progressed, but the basic thrust would be that the once-controversial Undersecretary of State was about to be rehabilitated and put back in the limelight. In London, Havelock would say, he had been given a detailed report of Bradford's extensive but secret negotiations on the touchy matter of NATO missile deployment; it was a major shift in policy. It was also sufficiently explosive to get Alexander's juices running. It was the sort of advance leak he thrived on, giving him time to put together an exhaustive analysis of the pros and cons. But if the old warhorse wished to interview Emory Bradford

– with on-site but unseen verification, possibly confrontation – he must persuade the Undersecretary to come out to Fox Hollow in the morning. Havelock had a reservation on the afternoon flight back to London – and, of course, time and schedules permitting, he wanted to drop in on his old mentor Anthony Matthias, if only for a few minutes. If Alexander knew where he could find him.

As for Bradford, he had no choice. If summoned by the redoubtable journalist, he would comply. Other things – such as Costa Brava – being paramount, he had to maintain his low profile at all costs, and one way to lose it was to refuse to be interviewed by Raymond Alexander. And when he came into the house in Fox Hollow, with his guards remaining outside in a limousine, Michael would take him. His disappearance would baffle the liars and the guards hired by the liars. The journalist's large, rambling house was surrounded by miles of dense woods, overgrown fields and steep ravines. No one knew the forests the way Mikhail Havlicek knew them; he would take Bradford through them until they came to a back country road somewhere, and a car, and the woman that Bradford had used in Barcelona. After his meeting with Alexander, they would have all night to study the map and travel the roads, watching for the Fox Hollow police, explanations at the ready if they were stopped. They could do it. They *had* to do it.

'It's lovely!' cried Jenna, charmed by the gas-lit streets and the small alabaster columns of the store fronts.

'It's wired,' said Michael, spotting a blue-and-white patrol car at the kerb in the middle of the block.

'Get down!' he ordered. 'Stay out of sight.'

'What?'

'*Please.*'

Jenna did as she was told, curling up on the floor.

He slowed down, pulling alongside the police car; he saw the officer in the window, then eased to his right and parked directly in front.

'What are you doing?' whispered Jenna, bewildered.

'Showing my credentials before anyone asks for them.'

'That's very good, Mikhail.'

Havelock got out of the coupé and walked back to the patrol car. The police officer rolled down the window, first studying the licence plate on Michael's hired car. It was precisely what Michael wanted him to see; it could be of value later that night if a 'suspicious vehicle' were reported.

'Officer, could you tell me where there's a pay phone around here? I thought there was one on the corner, but then I haven't been back here in a couple of years.'

'You've been here before?' asked the policeman, his voice friendly, his eyes not.

'Oh, sure. Used to spend weekends out here a lot.'

'You have business in Fox Hollow, sir?'

'Well . . .' Havelock paused, as if the question bordered on impertinence. Then he shrugged as if to say, After all the police have a job to do. He spoke in a slightly lower tone. 'All right, I understand. My business is with an old friend, Raymond Alexander. I want to call and tell him I'm here . . . Just in case someone's dropping in on him he'd prefer I don't meet. It's standard procedure with Mr Alexander, Officer, but you probably know that. I could drive around for a while. I'll probably have to later on anyway.'

The policeman's posture had visibly improved at the mention of Alexander's name. Limousines and military staff cars were common sights on the road to the venerated political commentator's retreat. There was no such vehicle in front of him now, but the operative phrases were printed in the officer's eyes. 'An old friend. Used to spend weekends . . .'

'Yes, sir. Of course, sir. There's a restaurant five blocks up with a phone in the lobby.'

'The Lamplighter?' said Havelock, remembering.

'That's it.'

'I don't think so, Officer. It could be a busy night. Isn't there a booth on the street?'

'There's one over on Acacia.'

'If you'll tell me how to get there, both RA and I would appreciate it.'

'You can follow me, sir.'

'Thanks very much.' Michael started for his car, then stopped and returned to the window. 'I know this sounds silly, but I was usually driven out here. I think I know the way to his home. I take a left on Webster to Underhill Road, then straight out for two or three miles, isn't that it?'

'It's nearer six miles, sir.'

'Oh? Thanks.'

'After you make your call, I could lead you out, sir. It's quiet in town tonight.'

'That's *very* kind of you. But really, I couldn't ask you.'

'No problem. That's what we're here for.'

'Well, thanks, again. I appreciate it.'

The call to Raymond Alexander brought forth the response Havelock expected. Nothing would do but that he should drop in and see the journalist if only for a drink. Michael said he was glad Raymond was free, not only to renew an old friendship but because he had learned something in London that Alexander might want to know about. It might even make up partially for a great many expensive dinners Havelock had enjoyed at Raymond's expense.

On the way back to his car Michael stopped at the police officer's window. 'Mr Alexander wanted me to get your name. He's very grateful to you.'

'It's nothing, sir. My name's Lewis. Officer Lewis; there's only one.'

Lewis, he thought. *Harry Lewis*, Professor of Political Science, Concord University. He could not think about Harry now, but he would have to think about him soon. Lewis must be convinced he had dropped out of civilization. He had and, to re-enter it, liars would have to be found and exposed.

'Is something the matter, sir?'

'No, nothing at all. I know a man named Lewis. I remembered I was to call him. Thanks once again. I'll follow you.'

Havelock climbed behind the wheel of the rented car and looked at Jenna. 'How are you doing?'

'Uncomfortable and frightened out of my mind! Suppose that man had come over?'

'I would have stopped him, called to him from the booth, but I didn't think it was likely. The police in Fox Hollow stay close to their radios. I just don't want you seen, if we can help it. Not around here, not with me.'

The drive out to Alexander's house took less than twelve minutes. The white post-and-rail fence marking the journalist's property shone in the glare of the headlights of both cars. The home itself was set far back from the road. It was a tasteful combination of stone and wood, with floodlights shining down on the circular drive in front of wide, slate steps that led to the heavy oak entrance door. The grounds were cleared in the front and on the sides of the house; thick, tall trees shot up at random about the close-cropped lawn. But where the lawn ended on either side the dense woods abruptly began. From memory, Michael pictured the rear of the house; the woods were no farther away from the large back patio than they were from the sides of the building. He would use those woods; and Bradford would enter them with him.

'When you hear the police car leave,' he said to Jenna, 'get up and stretch, but don't get out. I don't know what kind of alarms Alexander has around here.'

'It's been a strange introduction to this free country of yours, Mikhail.'

'Also, don't smoke.'

'*Děkuji.*'

'You're welcome.'

Havelock purposely touched the rim of the horn as he got out of the car; the sound was abrupt and short, easily explained. There were no dogs. He walked towards the patrol car in front, hoping the horn would serve its function before he reached the window. It did; the front door opened and a uniformed maid stood in the frame, looking out.

'Hello, Margaret!' yelled Michael over the bonnet of the police car. 'Be right there.' He looked down at the police officer, who had glanced at the door, the scene not lost on him. 'Thanks again, Mr Lewis,' he said, taking a note from his pocket. 'I'd like to – '

'Oh, no, sir, thanks just the same. Have a good evening, sir.' The officer nodded with a smile, pulled the gear in place and drove off.

Havelock waved; no police, no dogs, only unseen alarms. As long as Jenna stayed in the car, she was safe. He walked up the slate steps to the door and the maid.

'Good evening, sir,' said the woman in a distinct Irish brogue. 'My name is Enid, not Margaret.'

'I'm terribly sorry.'

'Mr Alexander is expecting you. I never heard of a Margaret; the girl before me was Gretchen. She lasted four years, may the Lord rest her soul.'

Raymond Alexander got up from the soft easy chair in his book-lined, wood-panelled library and walked towards Michael, his hand outstretched. His gait was more lively than one might have expected from his portly figure; his cherubic face with the clear green eyes was topped by a mass of dishevelled hair that managed to stay darker than the years normally permitted. In keeping with his anachronistic life-style, he wore a deep red velvet smoking jacket, something Havelock had not seen since his adolescent days in Greenwich, Connecticut.

'Michael, how *are* you? My God, it's been four, five years now!' cried the journalist in his clipped, high-pitched voice.

'They've served you well, Raymond. You look great.'

'*You* don't! Forgive me, young man, but you look like something one of my cats would have left outside. I don't think retirement agrees with you.' Alexander released Havelock's hand and quickly raised both of his own. 'Yes, I know all about it. I keep track when friends answer questions. Pour yourself a drink; you know the rules here and you look like you need one.'

'I will, thanks,' said Michael, heading for the familiar copper bar against the wall.

'I suppose you'd look better with some sleep . . .'

It was the opportune opening. Havelock sat down opposite the journalist and told him the story of the killing in New York and State's flying him back from London at 4 a.m., UK time.

'I read about that this morning,' said Alexander, shaking his head. 'Naturally, I thought of you – the name of course – but knew right away it was ridiculous. You, of all people, with *your* background? Did someone steal an old identification of yours?'

'No, it was mocked, that's what we think. At any rate, it's been a long two days. For a while I thought I was a prisoner.'

'Well, they never would have brought you over this way if Anton had been apprised, I can tell you that.'

Only Matthias's closest friends called him by his Czech first name, and because Michael knew it, the statement alarmed him. By necessity, it reversed the sequence that Havelock had intended, but it would have been unnatural not to inquire. The Bradford ploy would come last; Matthias now.

'I wondered about that,' said Havelock, revolving the glass in his hand, his voice casual. 'I simply thought he was too damned busy. As a matter of fact, I was going to ask you if he was in Washington. I'd like to drop in and see him, but my time's limited. I have to get back to London, and if I call him myself . . . well, you know Anton. He'd insist I spend a couple of days.'

Alexander leaned forward in the heavily cushioned chair, his intelligent face expressing concern. 'You don't know, then?'

'Know what?'

'Damn it, that's when government paranoia goes too far! He's the closest thing you have to a father and you're the closest thing he has to a son! You who've kept the secrets of a thousand operations and they haven't told you.'

'Told me what?'

'Anton's ill. I'm sorry you have to hear it from me, Michael.'

'How ill?'

'The rumours range from serious to fatal. Apparently he's aware of whichever it is, and, true to form, thinks of himself last. When State learned that I'd found out, he sent me a personal note swearing me to secrecy.'

'How did you learn of it?'

'One of those odd things you don't really think about . . . until you think about it. I was inveigled into going to a party in Arlington several weeks ago

– you know how I detest those exhausting exercises in verbal endurance, but the hostess was a close friend of my late wife.'

'I'm sorry,' interrupted Havelock, only vaguely remembering the journalist's wife, a willowy thing who had opted for gardens and flower arrangements. 'I didn't know.'

'It's all right. It's been over two years now.'

'The party in Arlington?'

'Yes, well, to my embarrassment a youngish woman who was quite drunk virtually assaulted me. Now, if she'd been a predatory female intent on a sexual liaison, I could have understood her being drawn to the most desirable man on the premises, but I'm afraid it wasn't the case. Apparently she had marital difficulties of a most unusual nature. Her husband was an army officer absent from the household – read "connubial bed" – for nearly three months and no one at the Pentagon would tell her where he was. She feigned illness, which I doubt took a great deal of self-persuasion, and he was brought back on emergency leave. When she got him in her net she demanded to know where he'd been, what he was doing – read "other woman". He refused to tell her, so when soldier-boy was asleep she went through his clothes and found a security pass for a post she'd never heard of; I hadn't either, as a matter of fact. I gather she battered him awake and confronted him, and this time in self-defence he blurted out that it was the highest-priority classification. It was where a very important man was being treated, and he couldn't say any more.'

'Anton?' broke in Michael.

'I didn't piece it together until the next morning. The last thing she said to me – before some charitable or over-sexed guest drove her home – was that the country should be told about such things, that the government was behaving like Mother Russia. That morning she phoned me, quite sober and in serious panic. She apologized for what she described as her "ghastly behaviour" and pleaded with me to forget everything she'd told me. I was entirely sympathetic, but added that perhaps her instincts were right, although I wasn't the person she should appeal to; there were others who would serve her better. She replied something to the effect that her husband could be ruined, a brilliant military career destroyed. So that was that.'

'That was *what*? How did you find out it was Matthias?'

'Because that same morning I read in the *Washington Post* that Anton was prolonging a brief vacation and would not appear before the Senate Foreign Relations Committee. I kept thinking about the woman and what she'd said . . . and the fact that Anton rarely gave up a chance to perform for the Senate newsreels. And then I thought, Why not? Like you, I know where he spends every free moment he has . . .'

'The Shenandoah lodge,' interrupted Havelock, feeling a sense of *déjà vu*.

'Exactly. I reasoned that if the story were true and he was taking an extra few days, we might get together for some valley fishing, or his beloved chess. Like you, again, I have the telephone number so I called him.'

'He wasn't there,' said Michael.

'They didn't say that,' corrected the journalist. 'They said he couldn't come to the phone.'

'*That* phone?'

'Yes . . . *that* phone. It was the private line.'

'The one that goes unanswered unless he's there.'

'Yes.' Alexander raised his brandy glass and drank.

Havelock was close to screaming. He wanted to rush over to the portly writer and shake him. *Go on! Go on, tell me!* Instead, he said quietly, 'That must have been a shock.'

'Wouldn't it have been to you?'

'Certainly.' *It was. Can't you see it in my eyes?* 'What did you do?'

'The first thing was to call Zelienski. You remember old Leon, don't you? Whenever Matthias drove or flew out to the lodge it was standard procedure for Zelienski to be summoned for dinner – has been standard for years now.'

'Did you reach him?'

'Yes, and he told me a very odd thing. He said he hadn't seen Anton in months, that Matthias never answered his calls any more – not personally – and that he didn't think our great man had time for the Valley these days.'

The *déjà vu* was complete for Michael. Then he remembered. 'You're a friend of Zelienski's, aren't you?'

'Through Anton, mainly. Very much the way we met. He comes up now and then for lunch and chess. Never for dinner, though; he won't drive at night. But my point is that the one place where Matthias should have been for a holiday he wasn't. I really can't imagine his not seeing old Leon, can you? After all, Zelienski lets him win.'

'I can't imagine your letting the issue drop, either.'

'You're quite right, I didn't. I called Anton's office and asked to speak with his first assistant. I emphasized that I expected someone who represented the Secretary of State in his absence, as I considered my inquiry to be that substantive. Of *all* people, guess who was put on to me.'

'Who?'

'Emory Bradford. Do you remember him? Bradford the "boomerang", scourge of the warlords where once he'd been their spokesman. I was fascinated because actually I admire him for having had the courage to reverse himself, but I always thought Matthias detested the whole flock. If anything, he was more sympathetic to those who went down in flames because they didn't change their spots.'

'What did Bradford tell you?' Michael gripped the glass in his hand, suddenly terrified that he might break it.

'You mean, what did he tell me after I told him what I thought had happened? Naturally, I never mentioned the woman and, God knows, it wasn't necessary. Bradford was in shock. He begged me not to say anything or write anything, that Matthias himself would be in touch with me. I agreed, and by mid-afternoon, I received Anton's note by messenger. I've abided by his request – until now. I can't for a minute believe he'd want you excluded.'

'I don't know what to say.' Havelock lessened the pressure on the glass, breathing deeply, the moment to be interpreted in any way the journalist wished. But for Michael it was the prelude to perhaps the most important question he had ever asked in his life. 'Do you remember the name of the post where the woman's husband was stationed? The one you'd never heard of before.'

'Yes,' said Alexander, studying Havelock. 'But no one knows I know. Or my source.'

'Will you tell me? No one will ever know *my* source; you have my word on it.'

'For what purpose, Michael?'

Havelock paused, then smiled. 'Send a basket of fruit probably. A letter, of course.'

The journalist nodded his head, smiled and answered, 'It's a place called Poole's Island, somewhere off the coast of Georgia.'

'Thank you.'

Alexander noted his empty glass. 'Come now, we're both out. Freshen yours and do mine while you're at it. That's also part of the rules, remember?'

Michael got out of the chair, shaking his head, smiling still despite the tension he felt. 'Be happy to pour yours, but I really have to get going.' He picked up the journalist's glass. 'I was expected in Maclean an hour ago.'

'You're *leaving*?' exclaimed the old warhorse, his eyebrows arched, turning in the chair. 'What about this piece of information from London you claimed would make up for some of the best meals you ever had, young man?'

Havelock stood at the copper bar, pouring brandy. 'I was thinking about that as I drove out here,' he said pensively. 'I may have been impetuous.'

'Spoilsport,' said Alexander, chuckling.

'Well, it's up to you. It concerns a very complicated, deep cover intelligence operation, which in my judgement will take us nowhere. Do you want to hear it?'

'Stop there, dear boy! You've got the wrong scribbler. I wouldn't touch it. I subscribe to Anton's maxim. Eighty per cent of all intelligence is a chess game played by idiots for the benefit of paranoid morons!'

Michael climbed into the car; there was the faint odour of cigarettes. 'You've been smoking,' he said.

'Feeling like a little boy in a graveyard,' replied Jenna, curled up on the floor. 'What about Bradford? Will your friend bring him out here?'

Havelock started the engine, engaged the gear and swung rapidly around the circular drive towards the entrance. 'You can get up now.'

'What about *Bradford*?'

'We're going to let him sweat for a while, stretch him out.'

Jenna crawled up on the seat, staring at him. 'What are you saying, Mikhail?'

'We're going to drive all night, rest for a while in the morning, then keep going. I want to get there late tomorrow.'

'My God, *where*?'

'A place called Poole's Island, wherever it is.'

24

The island was off the coast, east of Savannah; five years ago it had been a sparsely populated island of less than two square miles, before it was taken over by the government for oceanic research. Several times a week, said the fishermen, helicopters from Hunter Air Force Base could be seen skimming above the water towards an unseen pad somewhere beyond the tall pines that bordered the rocky shoreline.

They had reached Savannah by three-thirty in the afternoon and by four had found a nondescript motel on the ocean highway. At four-twenty they walked onto the piers of a commercial marina across the way in time to watch a dozen or so fishing boats come in with the day's catch. By a quarter past five they had talked to various fishermen, and at five-thirty Havelock had a quiet conversation with the manager of the marina. By ten to six two hundred dollars had exchanged hands, and a fifteen foot skiff with a twelve horsepower outboard had been made available to him, with the hours at his discretion and the night watchman of the marina informed.

They drove back along the highway to a shopping centre in Fort Pulaski where Michael found a sports shop and purchased the items he needed. These included a woollen hat, tight sweater, trousers and thick, rubber-soled ankle boots – all black. In addition to the clothes he bought the following: a waterproof torch and an oilcloth packet, a hunting knife and five packages of seventy-two-inch rawhide shoelaces.

'A sweater, a hat, a torch, a knife,' Jenna said rapidly, angrily. 'You buy one of each. Buy two. I'm going with you.'

'No, you're not.'

'Do you forget Prague and Warsaw? Trieste or the Balkans?'

'No, but you do. In each place – everywhere we went – there was always a secondary we could fall back on, if only to buy time. Someone at an embassy or a consulate who was given the words that constituted a counter-threat.'

'We never used such people.'

'We were never caught.'

She looked at him, her eyes reluctantly accepting his logic. 'What words do *I* have?'

'I'll write them out for you. There's a stationery store across the mall. I want to get a yellow legal pad and carbon paper. Let's go.'

Jenna sat in an armchair next to the motel desk where Havelock wrote. Taking the carbon copies from him as he tore them off the yellow pad, she checked the blue impressions for legibility. He had filled up nine pages, each line in precise block letters, each item numbered, every detail specific, every name accurate. It was a compendium of selected top secret intelligence operations and penetrations perpetuated by the United States government throughout Europe during the past eighteen months. It included sources, informants, deep-cover and double agents, as well as a list of diplomats and attachés in three embassies who in reality were controls for the Central Intelligence Agency. On the tenth page he gave an account of Costa Brava, naming Emory Bradford and the men he had spoken with who had confirmed evidence that could only have been obtained with the co-operation of the KGB and of a VKR officer in Paris who admitted Soviet knowledge of the deception. On the eleventh page he wrote of the fatal meeting on the Palatine Hill, and of an American intelligence officer who had died saving his life and, moments before his death, had exclaimed that there were lies being told by powerful men in Washington. On the twelfth he briefly described the events at Col des Moulinets and the order for execution issued by the codename Ambiguity. On the thirteenth and last page he told the truth about a killer from Lidice who had called himself Jacob Handelman, and the purpose of a farm in Mason Falls, Pennsylvania which sold the services of slaves as efficiently as any camp that provided labour for Albert Speer. The final line was concise: *Secretary of State Anthony Matthias is being held against his will at a government installation called Poole's Island in Georgia.*

'There are your words,' he said, handing Jenna the last page and getting up to stretch. His body ached; he had written furiously for nearly two hours. While Jenna read, he lit a cigarette and walked to the window overlooking the highway and the ocean beyond. It was dark, the moon intermittently shining through a night sky streaked with clouds. The weather was fair, the sea normal; he hoped both would stay that way.

'They're strong words, Mikhail,' said Jenna, placing the last carbon on the desk.

'It's the truth.'

'Forgive me for not approving. You could cost the lives of many people, many friends, with this.'

'Not the last four pages. There're no friends there . . . except the Apache, and he's gone.'

'Then use only the last four pages,' said Jenna.

Havelock turned from the window. 'No, I have to go all the way or not at all. There's no middle ground now; they've got to believe I'll do it. More important, they've got to believe *you'll* do it. If there's the slightest doubt, I'm dead and you might as well be. The threat's got to be real, not hollow.'

'You're assuming you'll be caught.'

'If I find what I think I'm going to find, I intend to be.'

'That's insane!' cried Jenna, quickly getting to her feet.

'No, it isn't. You're not usually wrong, but you are now. That island's the shortcut we've been looking for.' He walked towards the chair where he had dropped the purchases from the sports shop. 'I'll get dressed and we'll work out a telephone relay.'

'You mean this, don't you?'

'I mean it.'

'Booths, then,' she said reluctantly. 'No call over twelve seconds.'

'But only one number.' Michael changed direction and went to the desk. He picked up a pencil, wrote on the pad, tore off the page and gave it to Jenna. 'Here it is; it's the Cons Op emergency reception. Dial direct – I'll show you how – and have a pocket full of change.'

'I have no pocket.'

'And no money, and no clothes,' added Havelock, taking her by the shoulders, pulling her to him. 'Remedy that, will you? It'll take your mind off things for a while. Go shopping.'

'You're mad.'

'No, I mean it. You won't have much time, but most of the shops in that centre stay open until ten-thirty. Then there's a bowling alley, a couple of restaurants and an all-night supermarket.'

'I don't *believe* you,' she exclaimed, pulling her face back and looking at him.

'Believe,' he said. 'It's safer than telephone booths on the highway.' He glanced at his watch. 'It's ten to nine now and Poole's Island is only a mile and a half offshore. It shouldn't take me more than twenty minutes to reach it – say, by ten. At eleven, I want you to start calling that number and say the words "billiards or pool". Got it?'

'Certainly. "Billiards or pool".'

'Good. If you don't get an immediate response, hang up and get to another phone. Call every fifteen minutes.'

'You say a response. What will it be?'

Havelock frowned. ' "We prefer pool".'

' "We prefer pool". Then what?'

'A last call, again fifteen minutes later. Someone else other than the operator will be slotted into the emergency line. He won't use a name but he'll give the response. The second he does, read him the first two lines on the first page. I'll take the carbons with me so that the words match. Do it fast and hang up.'

'And then the waiting begins,' said Jenna, holding him, her cheek against his. 'Now, our immovable prison.'

'Very immovable, stationary, in fact. Pick up food at the supermarket and stay here. Don't go out. I'll reach you.'

'How long will it be, do you think?'

Havelock gently pulled his cheek away from hers and looked at her. 'It could be as long as a day, two days. I hope not but it may be.'

'And if . . .' Jenna could not finish the sentence, and tears came to her eyes. Her pale, striking face looked drawn.

'After three days call Alexander in Fox Hollow and tell him I've been killed or taken, that Anton Matthias is being held prisoner. Say you've got the proof in my own handwriting, plus my voice on the tape I made at Salanne's house in Cagnes-sur-Mer. Under the circumstances, he can't walk away from you. He won't. His beloved republic is being poisoned.' Michael paused. 'Just the last four pages,' he said quietly. 'Burn the first nine. You're right, they don't deserve to die.'

Jenna closed her eyes. 'I cannot promise you that,' she said. 'I love you so. If I lose you, none of them matter. None.'

The water was choppy, as it often was when coastal currents were interrupted by sudden offshore land masses. He was about a quarter of a mile from the island's rocky coastline, approaching from the leeward side, the wind carrying the minimal sound of the engine out to sea. He would cut it

off soon and use the oars, rowing forward towards the darkest section of the
surrounding pines, guided by the soft glow of light beyond the tree tops.

He had made his own separate arrangements with the marina's night
watchman, tenuous arrangements any experienced field man would attempt
to make if he hired a boat knowing he might have to abandon it. One never
gave up means of escape unless it was absolutely necessary, but one obscured
those means as best one could, if only to buy time; five minutes of confusion
was often the difference between capture and escape. So far, however, the
trip had been clean. He could propel the skiff into the blackest inlet and
beach it.

Now was the moment. He pushed in the throttle; the engine coughed
quietly and died. He jumped to the mid-seat, body forward, and lifted the
oars into their locks. The outgoing current was stronger than he expected;
he pressed against the seaward tide, hoping it would alter before his arms
and shoulders weakened. The wound from Col des Moulinets was beginning
to pain him; he had to be careful and use the weight of his body.

Sound. Not his, not the abrasive creaking of oarlocks or the lapping waves
against the bow. A muffled sound . . . an *engine*.

A light, a searchlight, sweeping the water about half a mile to his right. It
was a patrol boat rounding the far point of the island, veering starboard,
directly at him. Did the island's security system include sonar? Sonic beams
shooting over the water, rising and falling with the tides, capable of picking
up small craft approaching the shore? Or was the boat on a routine patrol?
It was not the moment to speculate. Keeping his body low, Havelock swiftly
lifted the oars out of their locks, shoving both under the slatted seats so that
they rested on the floor of the hull. He reached forward for the mooring line,
throwing it over the bow, and then slipped over the side into the ocean,
breathing deeply and tensing his muscles to ward off the cold. He slid back
and held onto the propeller shaft, splashing water over the outboard motor,
cooling the top surface. He had travelled at very low throttle; in minutes
only a sensitive hand would be able to determine whether the engine had
been running – if anyone thought to check.

The searchlight suddenly blinded him; the skiff had been spotted. The
far-away engine roared through the wind, joined by the wobbling wail of a
siren. The patrol boat accelerated, bearing down on him. He dived under
the water, swimming out, away from the island, the current propelling him.
The skiff was still nearly a quarter-mile from the shoreline, too far for a
swimmer to attempt comfortably in these waters; it was a fact that might
weigh in his favour when the boat was found.

By the time the large patrol boat had side-slipped in to the skiff and cut
its motors, Michael was twenty yards behind its stern, breaking the surface,
pulling the wet woollen hat down over his head. The searchlight was
crisscrossing the water everywhere; he went under twice, his eyes open, re-
emerging when the beam had passed. It continued scanning the area, but
no longer behind, only in the front and to the sides. Two men with grappling
hooks had the skiff in tow; the one at the bow shouted.

'Leo's Marina, Lieutenant! Out of Savannah! Marker number GA-zero-
eight-two!'

'Tell base to raise Leo's Marina in Savannah and cut us in!' yelled the officer to an unseen radio operator in the open cabin. 'The number's GA-zero-eight-two! Get a reading!'

'Yes, sir!' came the reply.

'And inform base of our location. Have a security check run on sector four.'

'This thing couldn't have got in there, Lieutenant,' said the man with the stern hook. 'It'd be tripped by the flat nets. Everywhere there ain't no rocks we got flat nets.'

'Then what the hell's it doing here? Are there any clothes, any equipment? Anything?'

'Nothin', sir!' yelled the first man, climbing down into the skiff. 'Stinks of fish, that's all.'

Havelock watched while treading and bobbing in the water. He was struck by an odd thing: the men on the patrol boat were in khaki fatigues, the officer in a field jacket. They were army, not navy. Yet the boat had a naval registration.

'Lieutenant!' The voice came from within the cabin as a face with a headset framing it appeared in the open archway. 'The watchman at Leo's said a couple of drunks had that skiff out and brought it in late. He figured they didn't tie it up proper and it went out with the tide. He'd appreciate it if we towed it in; it'd be his ass. The boat's shit, but the outboard's worth money.'

'I don't like it,' said the officer.

'Hey, come on, sir. Who's gonna swim a half mile in these waters? The fishermen've seen sharks around here.'

'Suppose it's *been* in?'

'With the flat nets?' asked the man with the stern hook. 'No place else to park, Lieutenant.'

'Fuck it! Throw up the line and let's circle around nearer the nets and rocks. This Leo owes us.'

And Havelock knew he owed a night watchman far more than the hundred dollars he had given him. The patrol boat's engines roared as the first man climbed aboard and another tied the skiff's mooring line to a stern cleat. In seconds the surface prowler was heading towards the shoreline, crisscrossing the waters as its powerful searchlight roamed the darkness.

Flat nets. Fields of lightweight fabric, stretched and held afloat just below the surface by buoyant cork or styrofoam, woven together with strands of piano wire. Fish could not break the wire but propellers could, and would activate alarms accordingly. *Rocks.* Stretches of the island's coastline that were prohibitive to vessels of any size. He had to keep the patrol boat in sight; it was approaching the rocks.

Sharks. He did not care to think about them; there simply was no point.

What he must concentrate on was reaching land. The current was almost intolerable, but by breast-stroking between the waves and the undertow beneath he made slow progress, and when he could see the beams of a dozen torches shining through the pines he knew he was getting closer. Time was irrelevant, its passage reflected only in the straining pain in his arms and legs, but his concentration was complete. He had to reach a net or a rock, or some other obstruction beneath him that told him he could stand.

A net came first. He worked himself to the right, hand over hand, slipping on the thick nylon cord, until he felt a huge floating styrofoam barrel shaped like an ocean buoy. He rounded it and pulled himself in on the border of cord until his knees struck two sharp objects that told him he had reached the rocks. He held onto the net, his body battered by the incoming surf, and waited, gasping for air. The torch beams were receding into the pines; the security check in sector four had proved fruitless. When the last beam disappeared between the trunks, he inched his way towards the shore, holding on to the wire net with all his strength as the waves crashed over him. He must stay away from the rocks! They loomed above him – sharp white, jagged points of stone made razor sharp by millennia of rushing waters. One enormous wave and he would be impaled.

He lurched to his left, spreading himself over the net, when suddenly it was gone. It was gone! He could feel the sand under him. He had crossed the manmade barrier reef and was on land.

He crawled out of the water, barely able to lift his arms, while his legs kept collapsing into the wet softness beneath him. The moon made one of its sporadic appearances, illuminating a dune of wild grass twenty yards ahead; he crept forward, each foot bringing him nearer a resting place. He reached the dune and climbed up onto its dry sand; he rolled over on his back and stared at the dark sky.

He remained motionless for the better part of half an hour, until he could feel the blood filling his arms again, the weight returning to his legs. Ten years ago, even five, he reflected, the gauntlet he had struggled through would have taken him fifteen minutes, at most, from which to recover. Now, he would appreciate several hours', if not a night's, sleep and a hot bath.

He lifted his hand and looked at the dial of his watch. It was 10:43. In seventeen minutes Jenna would place her first call to Cons Op emergency reception. He had wanted an hour on the island – to explore, to make decisions – before that first call, but it was not to be. He was forty-three minutes behind schedule. On the other hand, there would have been no schedule at all to adhere to if he had failed to cross the island's barrier reef.

He got to his feet, tested his legs, shook his arms and twisted his torso back and forth, barely noticing the discomfort of his soaked clothing and the abrasive scraping of sand over his entire body. It was enough that he could function, that signals from brain to muscle still filtered through the proper motor controls. He could move – swiftly if he had to – and his mind was clear; he needed nothing else.

He checked his gear. The waterproof torch was hooked into a strap around his waist next to the oilcloth packet on his left; the hunting knife in its scabbard was on the right. He removed the packet, unzipped the waterproof flap and felt the contents. The thirteen folded pages were dry. So was the small Spanish automatic. He took out the weapon, shoved it under his belt, and replaced the packet on the strap. He then checked his trouser pockets; the rawhide shoelaces were soaked but intact – each lace separate, rolled into a ball – five in his right hand pocket, five in the left. If more than ten were needed, then none would be needed. They would all be worthless. He was ready.

Footsteps . . . Were there *footsteps*? If so, the sound was incongruous with the sand and the soft earth that must lie beneath the ocean pines. It was a slow tattoo of sharp cracks – leather heels beating a hard surface. Havelock crouched, then raced towards the cover of the tall trees and peered diagonally to his right in the direction of the sound.

A second tattoo, now on his left, farther away, but coming closer. It was similar to the first – slow, deliberate. He crawled deeper into the pines until he came within several feet of the edge, where he dived to the ground and immediately raised his head to take advantage of the sudden new light. What he saw explained the sound of the footsteps, but nothing else. Directly ahead was a wide, smoothly surfaced concrete road, with just beyond it a stockade fence at least twelve feet high extending as far as the eye could see in both directions. The light came from behind it; a roof of light hung everywhere. It was the glow he had seen from the water, now much brighter, but still oddly soft, lacking intensity.

The first soldier appeared on the right, walking slowly. Like the crew on the patrol boat, he wore army fatigues, but strapped to his waist was a government-issue Colt .45 automatic. He was a young foot soldier on guard duty, his bored face reflecting the waste of time and motion. His counterpart emerged from the shadows on the left, perhaps fifty yards away; his walk, if anything, was slower than that of his comrade. They approached each other like two robots on a treadmill, meeting no more than thirty feet from Havelock.

'Did anyone fill you in?' asked the soldier on the right.

'Yeah, some rowboat with a motor drifted out from Savannah with the tide, that's all. No one in it.'

'Anybody check the engine?'

'What do you mean?'

'The oil. The oil stays warm if it's been running. Like any motor.'

'Hey, come on. Who the hell could get in here anyway?'

'I didn't say they could. I just said it was one way to tell.'

'Forget it. They're still doing a three-sixty search – in case somebody's got wings, I guess. The whips around here are all swacked in the head.'

'Wouldn't you be?'

The guard on the left looked at his watch. 'You've got a point. See you inside.'

'If Jackson shows up you will. Last night he was half an hour late. Can you believe it? He said he had to see the end of a lousy TV movie.'

'He pulls that a lot. Willis told him the other night that someday someone's going to just walk off and say he took over. Let him hang.'

'He'd talk his way out of it.'

Each man turned and began trudging back on his familiar, useless course. Michael pieced together the essentials of their conversation. A search party was combing the island and the guards' watch was almost over – a watch that was apparently loose, if a midnight relief could be half an hour late. It was an inconsistency; the island was a security fortress, yet guard duty was treated as though it were a futile if necessary performance. Why?

The answer, he surmised, might be found in an old observation. The ordinary soldier is the first to perceive an unnecessary duty. Which could only mean the shoreline alarms were matched by interior sensors. Michael studied the high stockade fence. It was new, the wood a pale tan, and it took little imagination to picture the trips wired behind it – dual beams set off by mass, weight and body heat, impossible to tunnel under or vault over or cut through. And then he saw what he had not concentrated on: the fence curved – as the concrete road curved – on both sides. Gates must be beyond the sightlines, entrances manned by personnel at the only points of penetration. Not casual at all.

A three-sixty search.

Soldiers with torches treading through the pines and over the beaches, looking for the shadow of a possibility. They had begun directly behind him, on a stretch of the coastline called sector four, moving quickly – a dozen men, or maybe thirteen, in a squad. Wherever they had come from, they would undoubtedly return to the same place once they had completed the circle . . . and the night was dark, the moonlight increasingly infrequent. Using the search party as part of his strategy was an outside possibility – the only one he could think of – but for the tactic to work, he had to move. *Now.*

The soldier on the right not only was closest but was the most logical to deal with first. He was nearly out of sight, rounding the bend in the road, disappearing beyond the angle of the fence. Havelock got up and ran across the road, then started racing down the sandy shoulder, furious at the sound of his waterlogged boots. He reached the bend; there were gate lights up ahead, perhaps six hundred feet away. He ran faster, closing the gap between himself and the slow-moving guard, hoping the wind rustling through the trees muffled the sponge-like crunching beneath him.

He was within twelve feet when the man stopped, alarmed, his head whipping to the side. Havelock sprang, covering the final six feet in mid-air; his right hand clamped onto the soldier's mouth and his left grabbed the base of the man's skull, controlling both their falls to the ground. He held the soldier firmly, his knee under the young man's back, arching the body over it.

'Don't try to shout!' he whispered. 'This is only a security exercise – like war games, you understand? Half the garrison here knows about it, half doesn't. Now, I'm going to take you across the road and tie you up and gag you, but nothing'll be too tight. You're simply out of manoeuvres. Okay?'

The young guard was too shocked to respond except with his large, frightened eyes, which blinked repeatedly. Michael could not trust him – more accurately, he could not trust him not to panic. He reached for the fallen barracks cap and rose with the soldier, pulling the young man up, his hand still clamped on his mouth; they both dashed across the road, turning right, heading for the pines. Once in the darkness under the branches, Havelock stopped and tripped the soldier to the ground; they were far enough into sector four.

'Now, I'm going to take my hand away,' said Michael, kneeling, 'but if you make a sound, I'll have to chop you out, you got that? If I didn't I'd lose points. Okay?'

The young man nodded and Havelock slowly removed his hand, prepared to clamp it back at the first loud utterance. The guard rubbed his cheeks and said quietly, 'You scared the shit out of me. What the hell's going on?'

'Just what I told you,' said Michael, unstrapping the soldier's weapons belt and yanking off his field jacket. 'It's a security-exercise,' he added, reaching into his own pocket for a rawhide lace and pulling the guard's arms behind him. 'We're going to get inside.' He tied the guard's wrists and forearms together, lacing the rawhide up to the elbows.

'Into the compound?'

'That's right.'

'No way, man. You lose!'

'The alarm system?'

'It's seven ways to Memphis and back. A pelican got burned on the fence the other night; it sizzled for a goddamn half an hour. Son of a bitch if we didn't have chicken the next day.'

'What about inside?'

'What about it?'

'Are there alarms inside?'

'Only in Georgetown.'

'What? What's Georgetown?'

'Hey, I know the rules. All I've got to give you is my name, rank and serial number!'

'The gate,' said Havelock menacingly. 'Who's on the gate?'

'The gate detail, who else? What goes out comes in.'

'Now, you *tell* me – '

A faint glow of light caught Michael's eye; it was far away, through the trees, the distant beam of a torch. The search party was rounding the island. There was no more time for conversation. He tore off part of the soldier's shirt, rolled it up and stuffed it into the protesting mouth, then strung another rawhide lace around the young man's face and tied it at the back of his neck, holding the gag in place. A third lace bound his ankles.

Havelock put on the field jacket, strapped the weapons belt around his waist, removed his knitted hat and shoved it into a pocket. He put the barracks cap on his head, pulling it down as far as he could, then reached under his soaked sweater and unhooked the waterproof torch. He judged the angles of passage through the trees, the distance of the emerging beams of light, and started running diagonally to his right through the pines – towards an edge of rock or beach, he had no idea which.

He clung to the rock, the crashing sea beneath him, the wind strong, and waited until the last soldier passed above. The instant he did, Michael pulled himself up and raced towards the receding figure; with the experience born of a hundred such encounters, he grabbed the man around the neck, choking off all sound as he yanked him to the ground. Thirty seconds later the unconscious soldier was bound – arms, legs and mouth. Havelock ran to catch up with the others.

'All right, you guys!' shouted an authoritative voice. 'Screw-off time is over! Back to your kennels!'

'Shit, Captain,' yelled a soldier. 'We thought you were bringing in a boatload of broads and this was a treasure hunt!'

'Call it a trial run, *gumbar*. Next time you may score.'

'He can't even score at pinball!' shouted another. 'What's he gonna do with a broad?'

Havelock followed the beams of light through the pines. The road appeared – the light-coloured smooth concrete reflecting the harsh glare of the gate lights. The squad crossed the road in a formless group, Michael jostling himself ahead so there would be soldiers behind him. They passed through the steel structure, a guard shouting off the numbers as each man went past.

'*One, two, three, four . . .*'

He was number eight; he put his head down, rubbing his eyes.

'*Seven, eight, nine . . .*'

He was inside. He took his hands away from his eyes as he moved with the squad across an oddly smooth surface, and looked up.

His breathing stopped, his legs froze. He was barely able to move forward, for he was in another time, another place. What he saw in front of him and around him was surreal. Abstract images, isolated fragments of an unearthly scene.

He was not inside a compound on a small land mass off the Georgia coast called Poole's Island. He was in Washington, DC.

25

It was something out of a macabre dream, reality twisted, abstracted, deformed to fulfil a demonic fantasy. Scaled-down models of familiar sights were alongside six-foot-high photographic blow-ups of places he knew only too well. There were small, narrow tree-lined streets, abruptly starting, suddenly ending, falling off into dirt, and street signs and street lamps – all in miniature. The soft glow of light that came from the lamps washed over massive, life-sized doorways and on buildings – which were not buildings but only the façades of buildings.

There were the glass doors of the Department of State. And over there, the stone entrance of the new FBI building, and across the way, beyond a tiny park dotted with small white benches, the brown steps leading to the main doors of the Pentagon. Far to his left he could see a tall black wrought-iron fence, with an opening in the centre to accommodate a drive flanked by two tiny glass-enclosed guardhouses. It was the South Portico entrance to the White House.

Incredible!

And cars of normal size, glistening. A taxi, two army staff cars, two outsized limousines, all parked separately, stationary symbols of another place. And there were the unmistakable symbols, seen in the distance to his right beyond the miniature park: small alabaster models – no more than four feet in size – of the Jefferson Memorial, the Washington Monument and small compact duplicates of the Reflecting Pools on the mall.

It was all there, all *insane*! It was a spread-out film set, filled with outlandish grainy photographs, miniaturized models, partial structures. The whole scene could have been the product of a mad imagination, a film maker intent on exploring a white-light nightmare that was his warped, personal statement about Washington, DC.

Uncanny.

A bizarre, false world had been created to duplicate a distorted version of the real one hundreds of miles away!

It was more than Havelock could absorb. He had to break away and find a few moments of sanity, to try to piece together the meaning of the macabre spectacle. To find Anton Matthias.

The squad began to separate, several to the left, others to the right. Beyond the false façade of State was a receding lawn and low-hanging willows, then darkness. Suddenly a prolonged burst of cursing came from behind, from the entrance gate, and Michael tensed.

'Goddamned son-of-a-bitch-fuck-off, where *is* he!'

'Who, Sergeant?'

'Jackson, Lieutenant! He's late again!'

'He goes on report, Sergeant. This duty's become far too lax. I want it tightened up.'

There were amused rumblings from the search party squad, a number looking behind, laughing quietly. Havelock took advantage of the moment to slip down the street and around the corner into the shadows of the lawn.

He leaned against a wall; it was solid. It enclosed something within and was not part of the false façade in front. He crouched in the darkness, trying to think, trying to understand. And that was the problem: it was beyond his understanding. He knew, of course, about the Soviet training centre in Novgorod called the American Compound, a vast complex where everything was 'Americanized', where there were stores and supermarkets and motels and gas stations, where everyone used US currency and spoke American-English, slang and different dialects. And he had heard about further Soviet experiments in the Urals, where entire US Army camps had been built, American military customs and regulations followed with extraordinary accuracy, and where, again, only American-English was spoken, barracks language encouraged, everything authentic down to the most minute detail. Then, of course, there were the *paminyatchiks* – the so-called Travellers – a deep-cover operation scorned as a paranoid fantasy by Rostov in Athens, but still alive, still functioning. These were men and women who had been brought over as infants and placed in homes as sons and daughters, growing up entirely within the total American experience, but whose mission as adults was to serve the Soviet Union. It was said – and confirmed by Rostov – that the *paminyatchik* apparatus had been absorbed by the *Voennaya*, that maniacally secretive cult of fanatics which even the KGB found difficult to control. It was further rumoured that some of these fanatics had reached positions of power and influence. Where did rumour stop and reality begin? What was the reality here?

Was it possible? Was it even conceivable that Poole's Island was peopled by graduates of Novgorod and the Urals, whose lower ranks were filled by *paminyatchiks* coming of age, and whose highest ranks were run by still other *paminyatchiks* who had risen to positions of power at State, who were capable of abducting Anton Matthias? Emory Bradford . . . was *he* . . .?

Perhaps it was all rumour. Men in Washington were working with men in Moscow; there was madness enough in that acknowledged connection.

He was not going to learn anything crouched in the shadows of a wall; he must move, explore – above all, not be caught. He edged his way to the corner of the building and peered around it at the softly lit tree-lined streets and the tiny structures that surrounded it. Beyond the guard detail at the gate a trio of officers strolled through the miniature park in the direction of the alabaster monuments in the distance, and four enlisted men hurried towards a large Quonset hut set back on a lawn between two unfamiliar brick structures that looked like the ground floor of some tasteful apartment complex. Then, to Havelock's surprise, a civilian emerged from the doorway of the brick building on the left, followed by another in a white laboratory coat, who seemed to be speaking quietly but emphatically. Michael wondered briefly whether the language were Russian. The two men walked down the path and turned right to a set-piece 'intersection', whose simulated traffic lights, however, were not operating. They turned right again, continuing their conversation, the first civilian now upbraiding his white-coated companion, but not obstreperously. Nothing was loud; the scene was still, with only the penetrating cacophony of the crickets breaking the stillness. Whatever secrets Poole's Island held, they were buried beneath a peaceful exterior . . . itself a lie created by liars.

As the two civilians walked down the allée and out of sight, Havelock noticed the metal sign affixed to a post on the other side of the street. Had he seen it before? Of course he had! Every time he had driven or taken a cab out of Matthias's house in Georgetown. There was a blue arrow preceded by the words: CHESAPEAKE AND OHIO CANAL. It was the picturesque waterway that separated the stridency of Washington from the tranquillity of the residential enclaves in Georgetown, whose quiet streets housed the wealthiest and most powerful men in the nation's capital.

Georgetown.

Are there alarms inside?

Only in Georgetown.

Anton Matthias was somewhere down that street, somewhere over a bridge, with or without water, in a house that was a lie. My *God*! Had they simulated his house so as to rehearse his abduction? It was entirely possible; Anton's residence was protected by presidential order, guards were on duty around the clock, as befitted the nation's most valuable living asset. It was not only possible, it was the only way it could have been done. Matthias *must* have been taken at home, the alarms circumvented, the guards pulled away and replaced by State Department orders – orders issued by liars. A mission had been rehearsed and executed.

He moved out into the street, walking casually – an enlisted man getting some air or getting away from his fellow soldiers. He reached the brick building on the left and crossed over the lawn to the sidewalk; the receding street was dark, no lamps shone above the line of short trees. He walked faster, feeling more comfortable in the shadows, and noted the paths that turned to the right, leading to a row of three Quonset huts – there were lights in several windows and the glow of a few television sets. He assumed these were the living quarters of whatever officers there were and their civilian counterparts. Graduates of Novgorod and the Urals?

Suddenly, civilization stopped. The street and the sidewalk ended, and there was nothing ahead but a dirt road bordered by high foliage and darkness. But it was a road; it led somewhere. Havelock began a slow lope; jogging would be his excuse if stopped – before he took out his interrogator. He thought of Jenna, going from telephone to telephone on the mainland, reaching a bewildered Cons Op emergency operator and saying words that brought no response: there might never be a response. Michael understood that, and, strangely, it only served to infuriate him. One accepted the risks in his profession and treated them with respect, for they induced fear and caution – a valuable protection – but one could not accept betrayal by one's own. It was the final circle of futility, proof of the ultimate sham – of a wasted life.

A glow of light. Far down the road, to the left. He broke into a run, and as he came nearer, he knew what it was: the outlines of a house, part of a house that stopped at the first floor. It was, unmistakably, the façade of Anton's home in Georgetown, the area of the street accurate in every detail. He approached the end of the dirt road and halted where the tarred surface began on the left. He stared in disbelief.

The brick steps were the same brick steps that led up to the porticoed entrance with the white door and the carriage lamps and the brass hardware. Everything was identical to its original hundreds of miles away, even to the lace curtains in the windows; he could picture the rooms inside and knew that they, too, were the same. The lessons of Novgorod had been learned well, their fruits transplanted to a small island minutes away from the coast of the United States, *seconds* by air. *My God, what's happened?*

'Stay right where you are, soldier!' the command came from behind. 'What the *hell* do you think you're doing out here!'

Havelock turned, covering the .45 as best he could. A guard stepped out of the foliage, with a gun in his hand, but he was not military; he was dressed in civilian clothes. Havelock said, 'What's wrong with you? A guy can't take a walk?'

'You weren't walking, you were running.'

'Jogging, pal. Ever heard of it?'

'Every morning, *pal*, when I don't pull this late night crap. But on the island road with everybody else, not down here. You know the rules. No one goes past sector six; you don't go off the macadam.'

'Hey, come on, man,' said Havelock. 'Don't be a hard nose – '

A sudden swelling of music burst from the house, filling the night and drowning out the crickets. Michael knew it well; it was one of Matthias's favourites. Handel's Water Music. His *pritel* was there!

'Every night, a goddamn concert,' said the civilian.

'How come?'

'How the hell do I know? He goes into the garden and plays that stuff for an hour or more.'

Music is for thought, Mikhail. The better the music the better the thinking. There's a causal relationship, you know.

'Nice of you people to let him have it.'

'Why not? What else has he got, and where's he going to go? But *you're* going to get your GI ass in a sling if you don't get out of here.' The guard holstered his gun inside his jacket. 'You're lucky I don't – Hey, wait a minute! You've got a weapon!'

Havelock lunged, gripped the man's throat and hurled him to the ground over his left leg. He fell on the guard and rammed his knee into the man's chest as he ripped the field jacket open and pulled out the hunting knife. 'You're not lucky at all!' he whispered. 'Where are you from, *zapanka*? Novgorod? The Urals? A *paminyatchik*?' Michael held the point of the knife's blade between the guard's nostrils and lips. 'I'm going to cut your face off unless you tell me what I want to know. First, how many men are up there? *Easy!*' He released the pressure on the man's throat; the guard coughed.

'You'll . . . never get off here,' he choked.

Havelock drew blood, the trickle covering the man's lips. 'Don't push me, butcher! I have a lot of memories, *ponimayu*. How many *men*?'

'One.'

'*Liar!*'

'No, *one*! The two of us are on till four. One outside, one inside!'

'Alarms. Where are they? *What* are they?'

'Crossbeams, shoulder to knee. In the door.'

'That's *all*?'

'It's all that's on. To keep him in.'

'The garden?'

'Wall. Too high. For Christ's sake, where's he going to *go*? Where are *you* going to go?'

'We'll see.' Michael pulled the guard's head up by his hair, then dropped the knife and struck him, a sharp, hard blow behind the right ear; the man collapsed. Havelock took out a rawhide lace, cut it in two with the knife and bound his hands and feet. Finally, he gagged the man with his own handkerchief, tying the cloth in place with one of the three remaining laces. He dragged the unconscious body into the foliage and started for the 'house'.

The Water Music soared into its thematic march, horns and strings intermingling, reverberating above and behind the half-house. Havelock climbed the short hill that bordered the brick steps until he was within ten feet of the first lace-curtained window. He crouched and crept to it, his head below the sill, then stepped to the side and stood up. He inched his face to the glass. The room was exactly as he remembered it from another time and place. The worn, fine oriental rugs, the heavy, comfortable arm chairs, the brass lamps – it was Matthias's sitting-room – his parlour, as he called it – a place to greet visitors. Michael had spent many pleasant hours in that room, yet this was not that room.

He crouched and made his way to the edge of the strange structure, rounded the corner and started towards the rear – towards a wall he could picture in his mind, a wall that enclosed a garden – hundreds of miles away. There were three windows to pass, to duck under, to check, and the second window told him what he had to know. Inside, a heavy-set man sat on a couch, smoking a cigarette, his feet on a coffee table, watching television. The volume was high, apparently to counteract the stereophonic sound of the music.

Havelock ran to the wall and jumped; he clung to the top with both hands and then, his chest aching and the wound close to tearing apart, he pulled himself up. He lay prone, catching his breath, letting the pain subside.

Below, the eerily lit garden was as he remembered it. Soft light coming from the house, a single lamp on the all-important chess table between two brown wicker chairs, other white wicker furniture, and a slate path roaming in circles around the beds of flowers.

There he was, his beloved *pritel*, sitting in a chair at the end of the garden, his eyes closed, seeing images the music evoked in his mind. The tortoiseshell glasses were still in place, the silver hair waved back over his strong head.

Silently Havelock swung his legs over the side, rolled on his stomach and dropped to the ground. He stayed in the shadows for several moments; the music had dropped to pianissimo and the sound of the television could be heard distinctly. The guard would remain inside; that was to say, he would remain inside until Michael wanted him. And when he had taken the hired gun of liars, he would use him or kill him. Somehow.

Havelock came away slowly from the wall and walked down the circular path towards Matthias.

For no apparent reason the statesman suddenly opened his eyes. Michael rushed forward, holding up both hands, the gesture a command for silence – but it was ignored. Matthias spoke, his deep voice rising with the music. '*Dobré Srovnani*, Mikhail. So good of you to come round. I was thinking about you the other day, about that paper you wrote several weeks ago. What was it? The "Effects of Hegelian Revisionism" or some such immodest and inappropriate title. After all, my *darebak akademik*, Hegel is his own best revisionist, no? The *revisionist maximus*! How do you like that?'

'Anton . . .?'

Again suddenly, without warning or indication, Matthias rose from his chair, eyes wide, face contorted. He began backing away unsteadily, his arms crossed in front of his chest, his voice now a horrible whisper: '*No!* You *cannot* . . . you *must not* . . . come near me! You don't understand, you can never understand! *Get away from me!*'

Havelock stared; the shock was as unbearable as the truth.

Anthony Matthias was insane.

BOOK III

'Raise your hands! Walk to the wall and spread your legs! *Move!* . . . *Now!* Lean into the brick, palms straight out!'

As if in a trance, his eyes still on Matthias, who was crouching like a child on one knee by a rosebush, Havelock did as the guard ordered. He was in shock, his impressions a blur, his thoughts suspended. His *pritel*, his mentor . . . his father . . . was mad. The shell of the man who had astonished the world with his brilliance, with his perceptions, was cowering by the flowers, his head trembling, the frightened eyes behind the glasses filled with a terror no one knew but himself.

Havelock had heard the guard's footsteps on the slate and had known the blow was coming. Somehow it had not mattered. Nothing mattered.

A spreading web of pain shuddered through his head, and the darkness came.

He was on a parlour rug, circles of bright white light spinning in front of his eyes, his temples throbbing, his drenched, sand-filled trousers pressing against his skin. He could hear men rushing up the steps outside, barking orders in panic. As they came through the door he felt his jacket, his waist; his gun had been taken, but he had not been searched. That process and the interrogation would presumably be left to the guard's superiors.

Two men approached: one in uniform, a major; the other, a civilian. He knew the latter; he was from State, an agent from Cons Op with whom he had worked in London or Beirut, or Paris or . . . he could not recall.

'That's him,' said the civilian. 'Bradford told me it might be – he didn't know how – but it is. He gave me the details; you're not involved.'

'Just get him out of here,' replied the soldier. 'What you do is your business.'

'Hello, Havelock.' The man from State looked down with contempt. 'You've been busy. It must have been fun killing that old guy in New York. What were you doing? Setting him up for contingency funds, with a little more of the same down here? Get on your feet, you bastard!'

Body and head racked, Michael slowly rolled onto his knees and pushed himself up. 'What happened to him? What *happened*?'

'I don't answer questions.'

'Somebody has to . . . for Christ's sake, *somebody* has to!'

'And give you a free ticket? No way, you son of a bitch.' The civilian addressed the guard who was standing across the room. 'Did you search him?'

'No, sir. I just removed his weapon and punched the alarm. There's a flashlight on his belt and some kind of pouch.'

'Let me help you, Charley,' said Havelock, spreading the field jacket and reaching for the oilcloth packet. 'It is Charley, isn't it? Charley Loring . . . was it Beirut?'

'It was, and keep your goddamned hands still!'

'What you want's in there. Go on, take it. It won't detonate.'

The man from State nodded at the major; the soldier stepped forward and grabbed Michael's hands as Charles Loring ripped the packet off the webbed belt.

'Open it,' continued Havelock. 'It's from me to you. All of you.'

The Cons Op agent unzipped the packet and took out the folded yellow pages. The major released his grip as the civilian walked to a floor lamp and began reading. He stopped, looked over at Michael, then spoke to the soldier. 'Wait outside, Major. And you,' he added, glancing at the guard. 'In the other room, please.'

'Are you sure?' asked the officer.

'Very,' said Charley. 'He's not going anywhere, and I'll shout if I need you.' The two men left, the soldier by the front door, the guard into the next room. 'You're the lowest piece of garbage I've ever known,' said the man from State.

'It's a carbon, Charley.'

'I can see that.'

'Call Cons Op emergency. Every fifteen minutes since eleven o'clock they've got a message. It's in the form of a question. "Billiards or pool?" The response is "We prefer pool". Tell them to give it.'

'Then what?'

'Patch yourself into the next call, give the response and listen.'

'So some other piece of garbage can read this to me.'

'Oh, no, just twelve seconds' worth. No way to trace. And don't bother to think about giving me a needle. I've been in therapy before, so I took precautions. I have no idea where the calls are coming from, take my word.'

'I wouldn't take your word for a goddamn thing, *garbage*!'

'You'd better right now, because if you don't, copies of those pages will be sent to appropriate addresses all over Europe. From Moscow to Athens, from London to Prague – from Paris to Berlin. Get on the phone.'

Twenty-one minutes later the man from State stared at the wall as he gave the response to Jenna Karras. Eleven seconds after that he hung up and looked over at Havelock. 'You're everything they said you were. You're below filth.'

'And "beyond-salvage"?'

'That's right.'

'Then so are you, because you're programmed, Charley. You're useless. You forgot how to ask questions.'

'*What?*'

'You just accepted the verdict on me. You knew me – knew my record – but it didn't make any difference. The word came down and the good little sheep said "Why not?"'

'I could *kill* you.'

'And live with the consequences? Don't do that. Call the White House.'

* * *

He could hear the deafening roar of the giant helicopter's rotating blades and knew that the President of the United States had arrived at Poole's Island. It was mid-morning, and the Georgia sun was burning the pavements outside the open window. He was in a room and there was no question that it was a cell even though there were no bars in the single window. He was two storeys off the ground; there were four soldiers beneath, and the eerie façades and photographs of familiar buildings could be seen beyond. A world of lies, of artifice, of transplanted, warped reality.

Havelock walked back to the bed – more cot than bed – and sat down. He thought of Jenna, what she must be going through – again what resources she must summon to survive the unbearable tension. And of Matthias – good *God*, what had *happened*? Michael relived the horrible scene in the garden, trying to find a thread of sense.

You must not come near me. You don't understand. You can never understand!

Understand *what*?

He had no idea how long he sat there thinking; he only knew that his thoughts were interrupted by the crack of the glass panel in the centre of the door. A face appeared; it was under the gold braid of a visor cap, another military liar. The door opened and a broad-shouldered, middle-aged colonel walked in, gripping a pair of handcuffs.

'Turn around,' he ordered. 'Extend your arms.'

Havelock did as he was told, and the cuffs were clamped on his wrists. 'What about my feet?' asked Michael curtly. 'Aren't they considered weapons?'

'I'll have a much more effective one in my hand,' said the officer, 'and I'll be watching you every second. You pull one thing I could even misinterpret, I'm inside, and you're dead.'

'A one-to-one conference. I'm flattered.'

The colonel spun Havelock around. 'I don't know who you are, or what you're doing, or what you've done, but you remember this, cowboy. That man is my responsibility and there's no way I wouldn't blow you out of this room and ask questions later.'

'Who's the cowboy?'

As if to punctuate his threat, the officer shoved Michael back into the wall. 'Stay there,' he commanded, and left the room.

Thirty seconds later the door opened again, the President Charles Berquist walked in. In his hand were the thirteen carbons of Havelock's indictment. The President stopped and looked at Michael. He raised the yellow pages.

'This is an extraordinary document, Mr Havelock.'

'It's the truth.'

'I believe you. I find a great part of it beneath contempt, of course, but then I tell myself that a man with your record would not cavalierly cause the exposure and death of so many. That, basically, this is a threat – an irresistible threat – to get yourself heard.'

'Then you'd be telling yourself another lie,' said Michael, motionless against the wall. 'I was placed "beyond-salvage". Why should I concern myself with anyone?'

'Because you're an intelligent man who knows there must be explanations.'

'Lies, you mean?'

'Some are lies and they will remain lies for the good of this country.'

Havelock paused, studying the hard Scandinavian face of the President, the steady eyes that were somehow a hunter's eyes. 'Matthias?'

'Yes.'

'How long do you think you can bury him here?'

'For as long as we possibly can.'

'He needs help.'

'So do we. He had to be stopped.'

'What have you done to him?'

'I was only part of it, Mr Havelock. So were you. We all were. We made him an emperor when there were no personal empires to be allocated by divine right, much less ours. We made him a god when we didn't own the heavens. There's only so much the mind can absorb and act upon when elevated to such heights in these very complicated times. He was forced to exist in the perpetual illusion of being unique, above all other men. We asked too much. He went mad. His mind – that extraordinary instrument – snapped, and when it could no longer control itself, it sought control elsewhere. To compensate, perhaps, to convince himself that he was what we said he was, although a part of him told him he wasn't. Not any longer.'

'What do you mean "sought control elsewhere"? How could he do that?'

'By committing this nation to a series of obligations that were, to say the least, unacceptable. Try to understand, he had feet of quicksilver, not of clay like you and me. Yes, even I, the President of the United States, some say the most powerful man in the world. It's not true. I'm bound by the body politic, subject to the goddamn polls, guided by the so-called principles of a political ideology, with my head on a congressional chopping block. Checks and balances, Mr Havelock. But not him. We made him a superstar; he was bound to nothing, accountable to no one. His word was law, all other judgements subordinate to his brilliance. And then there was his charm, I might add.'

'Generalities,' said Michael. 'Abstractions.'

'Lies?' asked Berquist.

'I don't know. What are the specifics?'

'I'm going to show you. And if after what you've seen you still feel compelled to carry out your threat, let it be on your head, not mine.'

'I don't have a head. I'm "beyond-salvage".'

'I told you, I've read these pages. All of them. The order's been rescinded. You have the word of the President of the United States.'

'Why should I accept it?'

'If I were you I probably wouldn't. I'm simply telling you. There are many lies and there will continue to be lies, but that's not one of them . . . I'll have the handcuffs removed.'

The scene in the large, dark windowless room was an unearthly depiction of a science-fiction nightmare. There were a dozen television screens mounted in a row on the wall, monitors that recorded and taped the activities seen by the various cameras. Below the screens was an enormous console manned by four technicians, several white-jacketed doctors entered, watching a scene or scanning tapes, writing notes, leaving quickly or conferring with colleagues. And the object of the whole sophisticated operation was to record and analyse every movement made and every word spoken by Anthony Matthias.

His face and body were projected on seven screens at once, and under each monitor was a green digital read-out showing the exact hour and minute of the filming; the screen on the far left was marked 'Current'. The day was an illusion for Matthias, starting with morning coffee in the garden identical to his own in Georgetown.

'Before he wakes he's given two injections,' said the President, sitting next to Havelock at a second, smaller console at the rear wall. 'One's a muscle-relaxant that reduces physical and mental tensions, the other a stimulant that accelerates the heart, pumping blood without interfering with the first narcotic. Don't ask me the medical terms, I don't know them, I just know it works. He's free to associate with a degree of simulated confidence . . . in a way, a replica of his former self.'

'Then his day begins? His . . . simulated day?'

'Exactly. Read the monitors from right to left. His day starts with breakfast in the garden. He's brought intelligence reports and newspapers corresponding to the dates of whatever issue is being probed. Then in the next screen you see him walking out of *his* home and down *his* steps with an aide who's talking to him, refining the options of the problem, building up the case, whatever it is. Everything, by the way, is taken from his logs; that remains constant throughout "the day".' Berquist paused, and gestured at the third monitor from the right. 'There you see him in his limousine, the aide still talking, bringing his focus back. He's driven around for a while, then gradually brought in sight of places that are familiar to him, the Jefferson Memorial, the monument, certain streets, past the South Portico . . . the sequence is irrelevant.'

'But they're not *whole*,' insisted Michael. 'They're fragments!'

'He doesn't see that; he sees only the impression. But even if he did see that they were fragments, as you call them, or miniatures of the existing places, the doctors tell me his mind would reject them and accept the reality of the impressions. Just as he refused to accept his own deterioration, and kept pressing for wider and wider responsibilites, until he simply reached out and took them . . . Watch the fourth screen. He's getting out at the State Department, going inside and telling his aide something; it will be studied. In the fifth, you can see him walking into his office – the same in every respect as his own on the eighth floor – and immediately scanning the cables and reading the day's appointments, again identical to those that were there at the time. The sixth shows him taking a series of phone calls, the same calls he has taken before. Often his responses are meaningless, a part of him rejecting a voice or a lack of authentic repartee, but at other times what we learn is mind-blowing . . . He's been here nearly six weeks and there are times when we think we've only scratched the surface. We're only beginning to learn the extent of his massive excesses.'

'You mean the things he's done?' asked Havelock, recoiling from the frightening turn of events.

Berquist looked at Michael in the glow of the console and the flickering light emanating from the screens across the room. 'Yes, Mr Havelock, the – "things" – he's done. If ever a man in the history of representative government exceeded the authority of his office, Anthony Matthias is that man. There were no limits to what he promised – what he *guaranteed* – in the name of the United States government. Take today. A policy was set and in the process of being implemented, but it did not suit the Secretary of State at this particular moment of irrationality, so he altered it . . . Watch the seventh screen, the one marked "Current". Listen. He's at his desk and in his mind he's back about five months, when a bipartisan decision was made to close an embassy in a new African country slaughtering its citizens with mass hangings and death squads, revolting the civilized world. The aide is explaining.'

Mr Secretary. The President and the Joint Chiefs as well as the Senate have gone on record as opposing any further contact at this time . . .

Then we won't tell them, will we? Antediluvian reactions cannot be a keystone of a coherent foreign policy. I shall make contact myself and present a cohesive and judicious plan. Arms and well-sweetened butter are international lubricants, and we shall provide them.

Michael was stunned. 'He said that? He *did* that?'

'He's reliving it now,' replied Berquist. 'In a few minutes he'll place a call to the mission in Geneva, and another unbelievable commitment will be made . . . This, however, is only a minor example, one they're working on this morning. Actually, as outrageous as it is, it's insignificant compared to so many others. So many . . . so dangerous . . . so incredible.'

'Dangerous?'

'One voice overriding all others, entering unthinkable negotiations, processing agreements contrary to everything this nation supposedly stands for, agreements which an outraged Congress would impeach me for even considering. But even that fact – and it *is* a fact – is insignificant. We can't let the world know what he's done. We'd be humiliated, a giant on its knees, begging forgiveness and, if it was not forthcoming, answered with guns and bombs. You see, he's put it all in writing.'

'Could he *do* that?'

'Not constitutionally, no. But he was the superstar. The uncrowned king of the republic had spoken, a god had given his word. Who questions kings or gods? The mere existence of such documents is the most fertile grounds on earth for international extortion. If we can't quietly invalidate those negotiations – diplomatically void them by anticipated congressional rejection – they *will* be exposed. If they are, every treaty, every agreement we've concluded during the past decade – all the sensitive alliances we're currently negotiating everywhere in the world – will be called into question. This country's foreign policy will collapse; we'd never be trusted again. And when a nation such as ours has no foreign policy, Mr Havelock, it has war.'

Michael leaned over the console, staring at the 'Current' screen, and brought his hand to his forehead; he felt the beads of perspiration. 'He's gone this far?'

'Beyond. Remember, he's been Secretary of State for nearly six years, and before he took office his influence was significant, perhaps too much so, in the two previous administrations. He was nothing short of an ambassador-plenipotentiary for both, roaming the globe, cementing his power bases.'

'But they were for *good*, not this!'

'They were, and no one knew it better than I did. I'm the one who persuaded him to chuck the consulting business and take over. I said the world needed his imprimatur, the time was right. You see, I appealed to his ego; all great men have outrageous egos. De Gaulle was right: the man of destiny knows it before anybody else. What he doesn't know is the limit of his capabilities. God knows Matthias didn't.'

'You said it a few minutes ago, Mr President. We made him a god. We asked too much of him.' Havelock shook his head slowly, overwhelmed.

'Just hold it there,' answered Berquist, his voice cold, his eyes penetrating in the incandescent reflections of light. 'I said it by way of an oversimplified explanation. No one makes a man a god unless that man wants to *be* one. And, Christ-on-a-raft, Matthias has been looking for that divine appointment all his life! He's been tasting the holy water for years – in his mind *bathing* in it . . . You know what someone called him the other day? A hustling Socrates on the Potomac, and that's exactly what he was. A hustler, Mr Havelock. A grade A, high I-Q'd, brilliant opportunist. A man with extraordinarily persuasive words, capable of first-rate global diplomacy – the best we could field – so long as *he* was the eye of the world-wide hurricane. He could be magnificent and, as I also said, no one knew it better than I did, and I used him. But for all that, he was a hustler. He never stopped pushing, the omniscient Anthony Matthias.'

'And knowing this,' said Michael, refusing to permit Berquist's stare to cower him, 'you still used him. *You* pushed him as much as he pushed himself. You appealed to a "man of destiny", wasn't that it?'

The President lowered his eyes to the dials on the console. 'Yes,' he said softly. 'Until he blew apart. Because I was watching a performance, not the man, and I was blinded. I didn't see what was really happening.'

'*Jesus!*' exclaimed Havelock, his whisper a cry. 'It's all so hard to believe!'

'On that assumption,' interrupted Berquist, regaining his composure, 'I've had several tapes prepared for you. They're re-enactments of actual conversations that took place during his final months in office. The psychiatrists tell me they're valid, and the papers we've unearthed bear them out. Put on the earphones and I'll press the appropriate buttons . . . The images will appear on the last monitor on the right.'

What took place on that screen during the next twelve minutes was a portrait of a man Havelock did not know. The tapes showed Matthias at emotional extremes, as he was psychologically stimulated by the combined effects of the chemicals and the visual trappings, and prodded by aides using his own words. He was screaming one moment, weeping the next, cajoling a diplomat over the phone with charm and flattery – and brilliant humility – then condemning the man as a fool and a moron once the conversation was finished. Above all were the lies where once there had been essential truth. The telephone was his instrument, his resonant voice with its European cadence the organ.

'This first,' said Berquist, angrily stabbing a button, 'is his response to me when I had just told him I wanted a reassessment of foreign aid in San Miguel.'

Your policy is firm, Mr President, a clear call for decency and human rights. I applaud you, sir. Goodbye . . . Idiot! Imbecile! One does not have to endorse a brother, one must merely accept geopolitical realities! Get me General Sandoza on the line. Set up a very private appointment with his ambassador. The colonels will understand we back them!

'This little number followed a joint House and Senate resolution, which I thoroughly endorsed, to withhold diplomatic recognition . . .'

You understand, Mr Prime Minister, that our existing accords in your part of the world prohibit what you suggest, but you should know that I am in agreement with you. I'm meeting with the President . . . no, no, I assure you he will have an open mind . . . and I have already convinced the chairman of the Senate Foreign Relations Committee. A treaty between our two countries is desirable progress, and should it be in contradistinction to prior agreements . . . well, enlightened self-interest was the essence of Bismarck's reign.

'I can't believe this,' said Havelock, mesmerized.

'Neither did I, but it's true.' The President pushed a third button. 'We're now in the Persian Gulf . . .'

You are, of course, speaking unofficially, not as your country's Minister of Finance but as a friend, and what you are seeking are additional guarantees of eight hundred and fifty million for your current fiscal year, and one billion two hundred million for the next . . . Contrary to what you may believe, my good friend, they are entirely plausible figures. I say this confidentially, but our territorial strategies are not what they appear. I shall prepare, again on a confidential basis, a memorandum-of-intent.

'Now we're in the Balkans, a Soviet satellite, loyal to Moscow, and at our throats . . . Insanity!'

Mr Premier, the restrictions on arms sales to your nation, if they cannot be lifted outright, will be overlooked. I find specific and considerable advantages in our co-operating with you. 'Equipment' can and will be funnelled through certain North African regimes considered to be in our adversary's camp but with whom I've met – shall we say ex-et non officio – recently and frequently. Confidentially, a new geopolitical axis is being formed . . .

'Being formed!' exploded Berquist. 'Suicide! Here's a *coup* in the Yemen. Headlong instability, wholesale bloodshed guaranteed!'

The emerging of a great new independent nation, Sirach Bal Shazar, though slow to gain the recognition you deserve, will have the quiet support of this administration. We recognize the necessity of dealing firmly and realistically with internal subversion. You may be assured that the funds you ask for will be allocated. Three hundred million, once transferred, will indicate to the legislative branch of our government the faith we place in you.

'Finally,' said the President, touching a last button, his whisper strained, his lined face looking exhausted. 'The new madman of Africa.'

To speak frankly and in the utmost confidence, Major-General Halafi, we approve of your proposed incursion north into the Straits. Our so-called allies there have been weak and ineffectual, but, naturally, our disassociation must, because of the current treaties, be gradual. The educating process is always difficult, the re-educating of the entrenched unfortunately a maddening chess game, fortunately played by those of us who understand. You shall have your weapons. Salaam, my warrior friend.

The scenes were paralysing. Alliances not in the interests of the United States had been tacitly formed or half-formed, treaties proposed or negotiated that were in violation of existing agreements; guarantees of billions had been made that Congress would never authorize, nor the American taxpayer tolerate; military obligations had been assumed that were immoral in concept, crossed the bounds of national honour, and were irrationally provocative to boot. It was a portrait of a brilliant mind that had fragmented itself into a profusion of global commitments, each a lethal missile.

Michael slowly recovered from his state of shock. Suddenly, the gap came into focus; it must be filled, explained. Havelock took off the earphones and turned to the President. 'Costa Brava,' he whispered harshly. '*Why?* Why "beyond-salvage"?'

'I was part of the first, but I did not call for the second. As near as we can determine, it was not officially sanctioned.'

'Ambiguity?'

'Yes. We don't know who he is. However, I should tell you, I personally confirmed the salvage order later.'

'*Why?*'

'Because I accepted one aspect of the oath you signed when you entered the service of your government.'

'Which was?'

'To lay down your life for your country, should your country need it desperately enough to ask for it. Any of us would, you know that as well as I do. Nor do I have to remind you that untold thousands have done so even when the needs were questionable.'

'Meaning the need for my life – my death – was not questionable?'

'When I gave the order, no it was not.'

Michael held his breath. 'And the Czechoslovakian woman? Jenna Karras?'

'Her death was never sought.'

'It *was*!'

'Not by us.'

'Ambiguity?'

'Apparently.'

'And you don't know . . . Oh, my *God*. But my execution was sanctioned. By *you*.'

The President nodded, his Nordic face less hard then before, his eyes still level, still steady, but no longer a hunter's eyes.

'May the condemned man ask why?'

'Come with me,' said Berquist, rising from the console in the dim, flickering light. 'It's time for the last phase of your education, Mr Havelock. I hope to God you're ready for it.'

They left the monitor room and entered what appeared to be a short, white corridor, guarded by a huge master sergeant whose face and display of ribbons indicated many tours and many battles. He cracked to attention the instant he saw the President; his commander-in-chief nodded and proceeded towards a wide black door at the end of the enclosure. However, it was not a door, Michael realized as he drew nearer behind Berquist. It was a vault, its wheel-of-entry in the centre, a small hand-sensor plate to the right of the frame. The President pressed his right palm against it; a tiny row of coloured lights raced back and forth above the plate, settling on green and white. He then reached over with his left hand and gripped the wheel; the lights were tripped again, a combination of three greens this time.

'I'm sure you know more about these devices than I do,' said Berquist, 'so I'll only add that it can be released solely by myself . . . and one other person in the event of my death.'

The significance was obvious and required no comment. The President swung the heavy door back, reached up and pressed an unseen plate on the inner frame; somewhere cross-beam trips were deactivated. Once again he nodded at the soldier, gesturing for Havelock to enter. They stepped inside as the master sergeant approached the steel panel and closed it, then spun the wheel into its locked position.

It was a room, but not an ordinary room, for there were no windows, no prints on the walls, no extraneous furniture, no amenities, only the quiet whir of ventilating machines. There was an oblong conference table in the centre with five chairs around it, note pads, pencils and ashtrays in place, a paper shredder in the far left corner; it was a table in a room pre-set for immediate consultation and instant destruction of whatever came from a given meeting. Whereas the room they had just left had twelve television monitors across the wall, this had a single large reflector screen, an odd-shaped projector bracketed into the far wall next to a panel of circular switches.

Without speaking, Charles Berquist went directly to the panel, dimmed the overhead lights and snapped on the projector. The screen across the dark room was instantly filled with a double image, a straight black line dividing the two photographs. Each was a single page of two separate documents, both obviously related, the forms nearly identical. Havelock stared at them in growing terror.

'This is the essence of what we call "Parsifal",' said the President quietly. 'Do you recall Wagner's last opera?'

'Not well,' replied Havelock, barely able to speak.

'No matter. Just bear in mind that whenever Parsifal took up the spear used at Christ's crucifixion and held it against wounds, he had the power to heal. Conversely, whoever holds these has the power to rip them open. All over the world.'

'I . . . don't . . . *believe* this,' whispered Havelock.

'I wish to God I didn't have to,' said Berquist, raising his hand and pointing to the projected document on the left. 'This first agreement calls for a nuclear strike against the People's Republic of China, executed by the combined forces of the United States of America and the Soviet Union. Objective: the destruction of all military installations, government centres, hydro-electric plants, communications systems and seven major cities ranging from the Manchurian border to the China Sea.' The President paused and gestured at the document on the right. 'This second agreement calls for a nearly identical strike against the Union of Soviet Socialist Republics carried out by the combined forces of the United States and the People's Republic of China. The differences are minor, vital only to a few million people who will be burnt to death in the nuclear fires. There are an additional five cities, including Moscow, Leningrad and Kiev. Total destruction: twelve cities obliterated from the face of the earth . . . This nation has entered into two separate agreements, one with the Soviet Union, the other with the People's Republic of China. In each instance, we have committed the full range of our nuclear weapons to a combined strike with a partner to destroy the mutual enemy. Two diametrically opposed commitments, and the United States is the whore serving two studs gone berserk. Mass annihilation. The world has its nuclear war, Mr Havelock, engineered with brilliant precision by Anthony Matthias, superstar.'

27

'These are . . . *insane!*' whispered Havelock, his eyes riveted on the screen. 'And we're a partner to *each*? Each commits us to a nuclear strike – a *first* strike?'

'A second also, and a third, if necessary, from submarines ringing the coasts first of China then of Russia. Two insane agreements, Mr Havelock, and we are, indeed a party to each. There it is in writing.'

'My *God* . . .' Michael scanned the lines of both documents as if studying the deformed appendages of an obscene, horrible thing. 'If these are ever exposed, there's nothing left.'

'Now you understand,' said Berquist, his gaze, too, fixed on the agreements that filled both sides of the screen, his face drawn, his eyes hollow. 'That's the unendurable threat we're living with. Unless we follow to the letter the instructions delivered to my office, we face global catastrophe in the truest sense. The threat is simple: the nuclear pact with Russia will be shown to the leaders of the People's Republic of China, and our agreement with the PRC will be given to Moscow. Each will know they've been betrayed – by the richest whore in history. That's what they'll believe, and the world will go up in a thousand nuclear explosions. The last words heard will be: "This is not an exercise, this is *it!*" And that is the truth, Mr Havelock.'

Michael felt the trembling in his hands, the throbbing at his temples. Something Berquist had just said triggered a sudden uneasiness but he could not concentrate to identify its source. He could only stare at the two documents projected on the screen. 'There's nothing here about dates,' he said, almost pointlessly.

'It's on a separate page – these are memoranda-of-intent. Conferences are to be held during the months of April and May, at which the precise dates of the strikes will be determined. The Russians are scheduled for April, May is for China. Next month and the month after. The strikes are to occur within forty-five days of each conference.'

'It's . . . beyond belief.' Overwhelmed, Havelock suddenly felt the paralysis again. He stared at Berquist. 'You connected *me* with *this*? These?'

'You *were* connected. God knows not through your own doing, but dangerously connected. We know how; we don't know why. But the how was enough to place you "beyond-salvage".'

'For Christ's sake, *how?*'

'To begin with, Matthias built the case against your friend Jenna Karras.'

'*Matthias?*'

'It was he who wanted you out. But we couldn't be sure. Were you out, or were you simply changing jobs? From the government of the United States to the holy empire of Matthias the Great.'

'Which is why I was watched. London, Amsterdam, Paris . . . God knows where else.'

'Everywhere you went. But you gave us nothing.'

'And that was grounds for "beyond-salvage"?'

'I told you, I had nothing to do with the original order.'

'All right, it was this Ambiguity. But later it was *you*. You reconfirmed it.'

'Later, much later; when we learned what *he* had learned. Both orders were given, one in sanction, one not, for the same reason. You were penetrating the manipulation – the structure – behind these documents, the link between men in Washington and their unknown counterparts in the KGB. We're in a race. One miscalculation on your part, one exposure of the flaw in that structure, and we have every reason to believe that these agreements, these invitations to Armageddon, would be shown to the leaders in Moscow and Peking.'

'*Wait* a minute!' cried Havelock, bewildered, angry. 'That's what you said before! Goddamn it, these were *negotiated* with Moscow and Peking!'

The President of the United States did not reply. Instead, he walked to the nearest chair at the table and sat down, the back of his large head and his thinning blond hair reflected in the shaft of light. And then he spoke. 'No, they were not, Mr Havelock,' he said, looking at the screen. 'These are the detailed fantasies of a brilliant but mad mind, the words of a superb negotiator.'

'Good *God*, then *deny* them! They aren't real!'

Berquist shook his head. 'Read the language!' he said sharply. 'It's literally *beyond* deniability. There are detailed references to the most secret weapons in our arsenals. Locations, activating codes, specifications, logistics – information that men would be labelled traitors for revealing, their lives ended in prison, none sentenced to less than thirty years for their acts. In Moscow or Peking those even remotely associated with the armaments data in these documents would be shot without a hearing on the mere possibility they had divulged, knowingly or unknowingly, even a part of it.' The President paused, turning his head slightly to the left, his eyes still on the screen. 'What you must understand is that should the leaders in either Moscow or Peking be shown the adversary document, they would be convinced beyond doubt of its authenticity. Every strategic position, each missile capability, every area of destructive responsibility has been hammered out down to the last detail, nothing left to debate . . . even to the hours of vehicular robot-controlled occupation of territories.'

'Hammered out?' asked Michael, the phrase a glaring intrusion.

Berquist turned around, his eyes once again the hunter's, but wary, afraid. 'Yes, Mr Havelock, hammered out. Now you've reached the core of Parsifal.

These agreements were negotiated by two extraordinary – and extraordinarily informed – minds. *Two* men *hammering out* every detail, each step, each point as though his stature in history depended on the task. A nuclear chess game, the universe to the winner . . . what's left of it.'

'How do you know that?'

'Language again. It's the product of two minds. It doesn't take a psychiatrist, or a pathologist, to spot the different inputs. More to the point, Matthias couldn't have created these by himself, he didn't have the in-depth information so readily available. But with another – a Russian, as knowledgeable about Chinese capabilities as we are – together they could do it. *Did* it. Two men.'

His gaze fixed on the President, Havelock spoke in a monotone. 'Parsifal is that other man, isn't he?' he asked quietly. 'The one who could rip open wounds . . . all over the world.'

'Yes. He has the original set of these agreements, the only other set that exists, he claims. We must believe him. He's got a nuclear gun to our heads – my head.'

'Then he's been in touch with you,' said Michael, his eyes shifting to the screen. 'You got these from *him*, not Anton.'

'Yes. His demands at first were financial, growing with each contact, until they were beyond being outrageous; they were astronomical. Millions upon millions . . . and millions after that. We assumed his motive was political. He had the resources to buy lesser governments, to finance revolutions throughout the Third World, to promote terrorism. We kept dozens of unstable countries under the closest intelligence scrutiny, penetrating their most entrenched elements with our best people, telling them only to look for the slightest substantive change. We thought we might trace him, trap him. And then we learned that Parsifal had not gone near the money; it was merely the means that told him we would do as he ordered. He's not interested in money; he never was. He wants control, power. He wants to dictate to the strongest nation on earth.'

'He *has* dictated. That's where you made your first mistake.'

'We were buying time. We're still buying it.'

'At the risk of annihilation?'

'In the all-consuming hope of preventing it. You still don't understand, Mr Havelock. We can and probably will parade Anthony Matthias before the world as a madman, destroying the credibility of ten years of treaties and negotiations, but it will not answer the fundamental question. How in the name of *God* did the information in these agreements get there? Was it given to a man certifiably insane? If it was, whom else has he divulged it to? And do we willingly deliver to potential enemies the innermost secrets of our offence and defence capabilities? Or let them know how deeply we've penetrated their own weapons systems?. . . We have no monopoly on nuclear maniacs. There are men in Moscow and Peking who at the first perusal of these would reach for the buttons and launch. Do you know why?'

'I'm not sure . . . I'm not sure of anything.'

'Welcome to a very élite club . . . Let me tell you why. Because it's taken all of us forty years and uncountable billions to get where we are today. Atomic knives at each other's throats. There's no time and not enough money left to begin again. In short, Mr Havelock, in the desperate attempt to avert a global nuclear holocaust, we might start one.'

Michael swallowed, conscious of doing so, the blood draining from his throat. 'Simplistic assumptions are out,' he said.

'They're not even fashionable,' replied Berquist.

'Who is Parsifal?'

'We don't know. Any more than we know who Ambiguity is.'

'You don't *know*?'

'Except that they're connected. We can assume that.'

'*Wait* a minute!'

'You keep saying that.'

'You've got *Matthias*! You're running him through a computerized charade here. Tear into his head! You've got a hundred therapies! Use them. Find out!'

'You think we haven't tried? There's nothing in the annals of therapy that hasn't been used . . . isn't *being* used. He's erased reality from his mind; he's convinced himself he negotiated with the militarists in Peking and Moscow. He can't allow it to be otherwise; his fantasies have to be real to him. They protect him.'

'But Parsifal's *alive*, he's *not* a fantasy! He has a face, eyes, features! Anton's got to be able to give you *something*!'

'Nothing. Instead, he describes – accurately to be sure – known extremists in the Soviet Presidium and China's Central Commission. Those are the people he sees when these agreements are mentioned . . . with or without chemicals. That mind of his – that incredible instrument – is as creative in protecting him now as it was when he was instructing the world of lesser mortals before.'

'*Abstractions!*' cried Havelock.

'You've said that, too.'

'This Parsifal's *real*! He exists! He's got you under a *gun*!'

'My words, I believe.'

Michael ran to the table and pounded it with his clenched fist. 'I can't *believe* this!'

'Believe or not,' said the President, 'but don't do that again. There's some kind of sonic thing that registers solid decibels, not conversations. If I don't speak immediately, the vault is opened and you could lose your life.'

'Oh, my *God*!'

'I don't need your vote. There's no third term any longer – if there is any longer – and I wouldn't seek it anyway.'

'Are you trying to be funny, Mr President?'

'Possibly. In times like these, and if circumstances permit you to grow older, you may find a certain comfort in the rare attempt. But I'm not sure . . . of anything any longer. Millions to build this place, secrecy unparalleled, the finest psychiatrists in the country. Am I being sold an illusion? I don't know. I just know I have nowhere else to go.'

Havelock sank into the chair at the end of the table, vaguely uncomfortable at sitting down in Berquist's presence without having been instructed to do so. 'Oh,' he said meaninglessly, his voice trailing off, looking abjectly at Berquist.

'Forget it,' said the President. 'I ordered up your own personal firing squad, remember?'

'I still don't understand why. You say I penetrated something, a flaw in some structure or other. That if I kept going, these – ' Michael looked up at the screen, wincing – 'would be given to Moscow or Peking.'

'Not would, *might*. We couldn't take the slightest chance that Parsifal might panic. If he did, he'd undoubtedly head for Moscow. I think you know why.'

'He has a Soviet connection. The evidence against Jenna, everything that happened in Barcelona; none of it could have taken place without Russian intelligence.'

'The KGB denies it; that is, a man denies it on an official basis. According to the Cons Op records and a Lieutenant-Colonel Lawrence Baylor, that man met you in Athens.'

'Rostov?'

'Yes. He didn't know what he was denying, of course, but he as much as told us that if there was a connection it wasn't sanctioned. We think he's a worried man; he has no idea how justified he is.'

'He may,' said Havelock. 'He's telling you it could be the VKR.'

'What the hell is that? I'm no expert in your field.'

'*Voennaya Kontr Razvedka*. A branch of the KGB, an élite corps that frightens anyone possessing a scrap of sanity. Is that what I penetrated?' Michael stopped and shook his head. 'No, it couldn't be. I broke it in Paris, after Col des Moulinets. A VKR officer from Barcelona who came after me. I was placed "beyond-salvage" in Rome, not Paris.'

'That was Ambiguity's decision,' said Berquist. 'Not mine.'

'But for the same reason. Your words . . . sir.'

'Yes.' The President leaned forward. 'It was the Costa Brava. That night on the Costa Brava.'

The frustration and the anger returned; it was all Michael could do to control himself. 'The Costa Brava was a sham! A fraud! I was *used*, and for that you pinned the label on me! You knew about it. You said you were a *part* of it!'

'You saw a woman killed on that beach.'

Havelock got up swiftly and gripped the back of the chair. 'Is this another attempt to be funny . . . Mr *President*!'

'I don't remotely feel like being amusing. No one was to be killed that night on the Costa Brava.'

'No one . . . *Christ!* You *did* it! You and Bradford and those bastards in Langley I spoke with from Madrid! Don't tell me about Costa Brava, I was *there*! And you were responsible, all of you!'

'We initiated it, we set it in motion, but we didn't finish it. And that, Mr Havelock, is the truth.'

Michael wanted to rush to the screen and smash his hands against the terrible images. Instead, the words, Jenna's words, came back to him. *Not one operation, but two.* Then his own. *Intercepted. Altered.*

'Wait a minute,' he said.

'Find another expression.'

'No, please. You started it, and without your knowing it the scenario was read, then taken over, the threads altered, going into another weave.'

'Those phrases aren't in my lexicon.'

'They're very clear. You're making a rug and the birds in the pattern are swans; suddenly they turn into vultures.'

'I stand corrected. That's what happened.'

'*Shit!* Excuse me.'

'I'm from Minnesota. I've shovelled more than you've ever seen, most of it in Washington.' Berquist leaned back in his chair. 'Do you understand now?'

'I think so. It's the flaw that could trap him. Parsifal was at Costa Brava.'

'*Or* his Soviet connection,' amended the President. 'When you saw the Karras woman three months later you began probing that night. If you exposed it, you might have alarmed Parsifal. We don't *know* that you would have, but as long as the possibility existed, we couldn't risk the consequences.'

'Why didn't anyone tell me? Why didn't anyone reach me and spell it out?'

'You wouldn't come in. The strategists at Consular Operations went to extreme lengths to bring you in. You eluded them.'

'Not because of – ' Havelock gestured helplessly, angrily at the screen – '*these*. You could have *told* me, not tried to kill me!'

'There was no time, nor could we send couriers with any part of this information or with the slightest intimations as to Matthias's mental condition. We didn't know what you'd do at any given moment, what you might say about that night, or whom you might say it to. In our judgement – in my judgement – if the man we call Parsifal *was* at Costa Brava, or was part of the altered strategy, and he thought he was being identified with that night, he could well have been provoked into doing the unthinkable. We could not permit even the possibility of that.'

'So many questions . . .' Michael blinked in the harsh glare of light. 'So much I can't fit together.'

'You may when and if the decision is made on both our parts to bring you all the way in.'

'The Apache,' said Havelock, avoiding Berquist's comment. 'The Palatine Hill . . . Jack Ogilvie. Was it an accident? Was that shot meant for me, or was it really meant for him because he knew about something back here. He mentioned a man who died of a heart attack on the Chesapeake.'

'Ogilvie's death was exactly what it appeared to be. A mistake. The bullet was meant for you . . . The others, however, were not accidents.'

'What others?'

'The remaining three strategists at Consular Operations were murdered in Washington.'

Havelock stood motionless, absorbing the information in silence.

'Because of me?' he asked finally.

'Indirectly. But then you're at the core of everything because of the single, imponderable question. Why did Matthias do what he did to you?'

'Tell me about the strategists, please.'

'They knew who Parsifal's Soviet connection was,' said the President. 'Or they would have known the next night if you had been killed at Col des Moulinets.'

'Code name. Ambiguity. He's here?'

'Yes. Stern gave him the clearance code. We know where he is, not who he is.'

'Where?'

'You may or may not be given that information.'

'For *God's sake*! In all due respect, Mr President, hasn't it occurred to you even now to *use* me? Not kill me, but *use* me!'

'Why should I? Could you help me? Help us?'

'I've spent sixteen years in the field, hunting and being hunted. I speak five languages fluently, three marginally and more dialects than I can count. I know one side of Anthony Matthias better than anyone else alive; I know his *feelings*. More to the immediate point, I've uncovered as many double entries – agents – as any other man in Europe. Yes, I think I can help.'

'Then you must give me your answer. Do you intend to carry out your threat? These thirteen pages that could . . .'

'Burn them,' interrupted Havelock; he was watching the President's eyes, believing him.

'They're carbons,' said Berquist.

'I'll reach her. She's a couple of miles away in Savannah.'

'Very well. Code name Ambiguity is on the fifth floor of the State Department. One of sixty-five, maybe seventy, men and women. The word, I believe, is "mole".'

'You've narrowed it down that *far*?' asked Michael, sitting down.

'Emory Bradford did. He's a better man than you think. He never wanted to harm the Karras woman.'

'Then he was incompetent.'

'He'd be the first to agree with that. Still, if she'd followed his instructions, she'd eventually have been told the truth; the two of you would have been brought in.'

'Instead, I was put "beyond-salvage".'

'Tell me something, Mr Havelock,' said the President, once again leaning forward in the chair. 'If you were I, knowing what you know now, what would you have done?'

Michael looked at the screen, the astonishing words burning into his mind. 'The same thing you did. I was expendable.'

'Thank you.' The President rose. 'Incidentally, no one here on Poole's Island knows anything about these. Not the doctors, the technicians or the military. Only five other men are aware of them. Or of Parsifal. One of them is a psychiatrist from Bethesda, a specialist in hallucinatory disorder who flies down once a week to work with Matthias only in this room.'

'I understand.'

'Now, let's get out of here while we're still sane,' said Berquist as he walked to the projector; he snapped it off, then turned on the overhead lights. 'Arrangements will be made to fly the two of you to Andrews Air Force Base this afternoon. We'll find you a place somewhere in the country, not in Washington. We can't risk your being seen.'

'If I'm going to be effective, I must have access to records, logs, files. They can't be moved to the country, Mr President.'

'If they can't be, we'll bring you in under very controlled circumstances . . . There'll be two more chairs placed at the table. You'll be given clearance for everything under another name. And Bradford will brief you as soon as possible.'

'Before I leave here, I want to talk to the doctors. I'd also like to see Anton, but I understand; it'll be brief, only a few minutes.'

'I'm not sure they'll permit it.'

'Then overrule them. I want to talk to him in Czech, his own language. I've got to dig around something he said to me. He said, "You don't understand. You can never understand." It's deep inside him, something between himself and me. Maybe I'm the only one who can get it out. It could be everything, why he did what he did, not only to me but to himself. Somewhere in my head there's a bomb, I've known it from the beginning.'

'The doctors are overrruled. But I remind you, you spent twelve days at a clinic, a total of eighty-five hours in chemical therapy, and you couldn't help us.'

'You didn't know where to look. God help me, neither do I.'

The three doctors were not able to tell him anything he could not have guessed from Berquist's descriptions, and in fact the psychiatric terminology tended to obscure the picture for him. The President's characterization of a delicate, remarkable instrument exploding under the inhuman pressures of responsibilities was far more graphic than the dry explanation of the limits of stress-tolerance. Then one of the analysts interrupted – the youngest, as it happened.

'There is no reality for him in the accepted sense of the word. He filters his impressions, permitting only those that support what he wants to see and hear. These are his reality – more real to him, perhaps, than anything was before – because they're his fantasies and they've got to protect him now. He has nothing else, only fragmented memories.'

President Charles Berquist was not only adept at description, thought Michael. He also listened.

'The deterioration can't be reversed?' asked Havelock.

'No,' said another psychiatrist. 'The cellular structure has degenerated. It's irreversible.'

'He's too old,' said the younger man.

'I want to see him. I'll be brief.'

'We've registered our objections,' said the third doctor, 'but the President feels differently. Please understand, we're working here under virtually impossible conditions, with a patient who's failing – how rapidly is difficult to tell. He has to be both artificially repressed and stimulated for us to achieve any results at all. It's extremely delicate, and a prolonged trauma could set us back days. We haven't the time, Mr Havelock.'

'I'll be quick. Ten minutes.'

'Make it five. *Please*.'

'All right. Five minutes.'

'I'll take you over,' said the younger psychiatrist. 'It's where you saw him last night. The garden.'

Outside on the street, the white-jacketed doctor directed Michael to an army jeep behind the red brick building. 'You were getting pissed off in there,' he said. 'You shouldn't have. They're two of the best men in the country and nobody was exaggerating. Sometimes this place seems like Futilityville.'

'Futility – what?'

'The results don't come fast enough. We'll never catch up.'

'With what?'

'With what he's done.'

'I see. You can't be too much of a slouch yourself,' said Havelock as they drove down the tree-lined street towards the track that approached Matthias's mocked-up house.

'I've written a couple of papers, and I'm good with stats, but I'm happy to fetch and carry for these guys.'

'Where'd they find you?'

'I worked with Dr Schramm at Menninger's – he's the one who insisted on the five minutes, and the finest neuropsychiatrist in the business. I operated machines for him – brain scanners, electro-spectrographs, that sort of thing. I still do.'

'There's a lot of machinery around here, isn't there?'

'No expense spared.'

'I can't get over it,' exclaimed Michael, glancing around at the receding scenery, the macabre façades and alabaster models, and the miniature streets and street lamps and odd-shaped blow-ups placed on manicured lawns. 'It's incredible. It's something out of a movie – a *weird movie*! Who the hell built it and how were they persuaded not to say anything? The rumours must be flying all over south Georgia.'

'Not because of them – the people who built it, I mean.'

'How could you stop them?'

'They're nowhere near here. They're hundreds of miles away working on a half-dozen other projects.'

'*What?*'

'You just said it,' explained the young doctor, grinning. 'A movie. This whole complex was built by a Canadian film company that thinks it was hired by a cost-conscious producer on the West Coast. They started the scenic construction twenty-four hours after the Corps of Engineers threw up the stockade and converted the existing buildings for our use.'

'What about the helicopters that fly in from Savannah?'

'They're routed on a path and into a threshold beyond the stockade; they can't see anything. And anyway, except for the President and one or two others, they're all from Quartermaster, bringing in supplies. They've been told it's an oceanic research centre and have no reason to think otherwise.'

'What about the personnel?'

'We doctors, the technicians who can handle just about everything, a few aides, the guards and a platoon of enlisted men and five officers. These last are all army, even the ones who man the patrol boat.'

'What have they been told?'

'As little as possible. Apart from us, the technicians and the aides know more than anyone else, but they were screened as if they were being sent to Moscow. Also the guards, but I guess you know that. I gather you're acquainted.'

'With one anyway.' The jeep entered the rutted dirt road, the island dust billowing behind them. 'I can't understand the army. How do they keep it quiet?'

'To begin with, they don't go anywhere. None of us do, that's the official word. And even if they did they wouldn't worry about the officers. They're all from the Pentagon Rolladex and each one sees himself as a future Chairman of the Joint Chiefs. They wouldn't say anything; silence is their guarantee of quick promotion.'

'And the enlisted men? They must be a boiling pot.'

'That's stereotypical thinking, isn't it? Young guys like that took a lot of beaches once, fought in a lot of jungles.'

'I only meant there's got to be gossip, wild tales all over the place. How are they contained?'

'For a start, they don't see that much, not of anything that counts. They're told Poole's Island is a simulated exercise in survival, everything top secret, ten years in a stockade if the secrecy's broken. They're also screened, and they're all regular army; they've got a home here. Why louse it up?'

'It still sounds loose.'

'Well, there's always the bottom line. I mean, before too long it's not going to make a hell of a lot of difference, is it?'

Havelock whipped his head around and stared at the psychiatrist. *Incidentally, no one here on Poole's Island knows anything about these. Neither the doctors, the technicians . . .* Berquist's words. Had that vault, that very odd room, been entered? 'What do you mean?'

'One of these days Matthias will quietly slip away. When he's gone the rumours won't make any difference. All great men and women have post-mortem stories told about them; it's part of the ball game.'

If there is a ball game, Doctor.

'*Dobrý odpoledne, přítel,*' said Michael softly as he walked out of the house into the sun-drenched garden. Matthias was sitting in the same chair at the end of the winding slate path where he had been seated the night before, protected from the sun by the shade of a palm tree that fanned out in front of the wall. Havelock continued speaking, quickly, ever so gently, in Czech. 'I know you're upset with me, my dear friend, and I wish only to put to rest the difficulty between us. After all, you are my beloved teacher, the only father I have left, and it isn't right for fathers and sons to be estranged.'

At first Matthias recoiled in the chair, pulling himself farther into the shadows of the palm, the intermittent streaks of light crossing his frightened contorted face. But a mist began to cover the wide eyes behind the tortoiseshell glasses, a film of uncertainty; perhaps he was remembering words from long ago – perhaps a father's words in Prague, or a child's plea. It did not matter. The language, the soft, deliberate cadence – they were having their effect. It was crucial now to touch. The touch was vital, a symbol of so much that was of another language, of another country – of remembered trust. Michael approached, the words flowing softly, the cadence rhythmic, evoking another time, another land.

'There are the hills above Moldau, our great Vltava with its beautiful bridges and the Wenceslas when the snow falls . . . the Striba Lake in summer. And the valleys of the Váh and the Nitra, sailing with the currents towards the mountains.'

They touched, the student's hand on the teacher's arm. Matthias trembled, breathing deeply, his own hand rising haltingly from his lap and covering Havelock's.

'You told me I didn't understand, that I could never understand. It's not so, my teacher . . . my father . . . I *can* understand. Above all, I *must* understand. There should be nothing between us . . . ever. I owe everything to you.'

The mist in Matthias's eyes began to clear, the focus returning, and in that focus there was something suddenly wild – something mad.

'No, *please*, Anton,' said Michael quickly. 'Tell me what it is. Help me, help me to understand.'

The hollow whisper began as it had in the darkness of the garden before. Only now there was blinding sunlight and the language was different, the words different.

'The most dreadful agreements on earth are the ultimate *solutions*. That is what you could never understand . . . But you saw them all . . . all coming and going, the negotiators of the world! Coming to me! Pleading with me! The world knew I could do it and it came to *me*!' Matthias stopped and then, as suddenly as it had the night before, the deep whisper was replaced by a scream that seemed to block out the sunlight, a nightmare in the middle of the afternoon. '*Get away from me!* You will betray me! You will betray us *all*.'

'How can I?'

'Because you *know*!'

'I *don't* know!'

'Betrayer! Betrayer of your countrymen! Your father! Betrayer of the world!'

'Then why not *kill me*!' roared Michael, knowing there was nothing left, nowhere else to go with Anton Matthias. 'Why didn't you have me *killed*?'

'Havelock, cut it out!' shouted the young doctor from the doorway.

'Not now!' yelled Michael in English.

'*Yes*, goddamn it!'

'*Slyšet ja!*' screamed Havelock into Matthias's face, returning to Czech. 'You could have killed me but you didn't! Why not? I'm nothing compared to the world, to *your solutions* for the world! What *stopped* you?'

'That's it, mister!'

'Let me alone! He's got to tell me!'

'Tell you *what*?'

'*Ted'*, *starý pán*.' Michael gripped the arms of Matthias's chair, locking him into it. 'What *stopped* you?'

The hollow whisper returned, the wild eyes now clear of uncertainty. 'You left the conference and we did not see you, we could not find you. We had to know what you had done, whom you had told.'

Madness.

'You're finished here, Havelock!' said the psychiatrist, gripping Michael's arm and pulling him away from the chair. 'What were you two talking about? I know it's Czech, but that's *all* I know. What did he tell you? I want it verbatim!'

Havelock tried to shake the numbness from his mind, the utter sense of futility. He looked at the doctor, remembering his use of the word; he would not corrupt it as the young man had. 'It wouldn't do you any good. He was back in his childhood; it was meaningless rambling . . . an angry, frightened child. I thought he was going to tell me something. He didn't.'

The doctor nodded, his eyes those of a learned, older man. 'He does that a lot,' said the psychiatrist, voice and face relaxing. 'It's a degenerative syndrome in old people born in another country, with a different language. It doesn't make much difference whether they're sane or insane; they go back. And why not? They're entitled to the comfort . . . Sorry. Nice try. Come on, I have to get you out of here. There's a chopper waiting for you at the pad.'

'Thanks.' Michael backed away on the slate path and looked, he knew, for the last time at Anton Matthias . . . *pritel*, mentor, father. The once great man was cowering again, seeking sanctuary in the shadows of the palm tree.

Madness. Or was it?

Was it *possible*? Did he – Mikhail Havlicek – know the answer? *Did he know Parsifal?*

28

It was called Sterile House Five – Sterile Five for short – and was ten miles south of Alexandria in the Fairfax countryside. Once the estate of a horse breeder, it had been purchased by an elderly, apparently wealthy, retired couple who were in fact buyers-of-record for the United States government. They were appropriate 'owners' because they had spent their adult lives in the Foreign Service; they had been attached to various embassies and given various titles, but in reality they were two of the most proficient cryptoanalysts in US Intelligence. Their cover was simple; he had been an investment banker living in Europe for several decades. It was eminently acceptable to the distant, affluent neighbours and accounted for the frequent sight of limousines turning off the country road into the half-mile drive that led to the house. Once a visitor arrived, the 'owners' were rarely visible – unless visibility was pre-arranged – for their quarters were in the north wing, a separate section of the house, with a separate entrance and independent facilities.

Sterile Five was another form of halfway house, serving clients who had far more to offer the United States government than the castaway inmates of Mason Falls, Pennsylvania. Over the years it had seen a procession of high-level defectors pass through its doors for a period of interrogation and debriefing. Scientists, diplomats, espionage agents, military men – all had been residents at one time or another. Sterile Five was reserved for those people Washington felt were vital to the immediate interests of the country at given moments of crisis. Havelock and Jenna Karras arrived in an unmarked government vehicle at twenty minutes past four. Undersecretary of State Emory Bradford was waiting for them.

The recriminations were brief; there was no point in going over past errors. Bradford had spoken with the President and understood that there would be 'two new chairs'. At Sterile Five, however, they sat in the 'owner's study', a small room outfitted for a country squire: a couch and thick armchairs; leather, brass, and expensive wood in harmony; mementoes signifying little of substance on the walls. There was a heavy pine table behind the single couch, with a silver tray bearing bottles, glasses and ice. Havelock made himself and Jenna drinks; Bradford declined.

'What have you told Miss Karras?' asked the Undersecretary.

'Everything I learned at Poole's Island.'

'It's difficult to know what to say . . . what to think,' said Jenna. 'I suppose I'm awe-struck and terrified at the same time.'

'It's a good combination,' agreed Bradford.

'What I want from you,' Havelock said to Bradford as he went around the couch with the drinks and sat down beside Jenna, 'is everything you have, the names of everyone involved – no matter how remotely – from the beginning. I don't care how long it takes; we can be here all night. As you go along I'll ask questions, make notes, and when you're finished I'll give you a list of what I need.'

It took less than four minutes for Michael's first question: 'MacKenzie? CIA? Black operations. One of the best out of Langley.'

'I was told *the* best,' Bradford said.

'He set up Costa Brava, then?'

'Yes.'

'He was the second sighting, the one who brought back the bloodstained clothing for forensic?'

'I was about to – '

'Tell me,' interrupted Havelock. 'Did he die of a stroke – a coronary – on the Chesapeake?'

'In his boat, yes.'

'Was there an inquest? An autopsy?'

'Not formally, but again, the answer is yes.'

'What does that mean?'

'With a man like that you don't promote speculation. The doctor was co-operative and thoroughly questioned; he's a highly respected physician. X-rays were examined by him and our own people, the conclusion was unanimous. A massive aortal haemorrhage.' Bradford lowered his voice. 'It was the first thought we had when we heard the news. We didn't overlook a thing.'

'Thanks,' said Havelock, writing a note to himself. 'Go on.'

Jenna placed her drink on the coffee table. 'Was he the man with you in the lobby of the hotel in Barcelona?'

'Yes, it was his operation.'

'He was an angry man. His eyes were angry, not concerned, just angry.'

'He was in an angry occupation.'

'He crashed my door in; he had a gun in his hand.'

'He was worried, we both were. Miss Karras, if you'd come downstairs or even stayed in your room – '

'Please, go on,' Michael broke in.

The Undersecretary continued as Havelock and Jenna listened intently, interrupting whenever either had a question or felt details should be clarified. Within the hour it was apparent to Bradford that Jenna Karras had a mind to contend with and the experience to match. She asked nearly as many questions as Michael, frequently pursuing specifics until possibilities not previously considered were suddenly brought to light.

Bradford reached the night when the three strategists were killed, when the unknown Ambiguity routed the call to Rome placing Havelock 'beyond-salvage'. The Undersecretary of State was thorough, detailing the checks he had made on the personnel in the L Section of the fifth floor during the hours in question. None, he was certain, could be Ambiguity.

'Because the conferences and briefings they held were . . . how do you say it?' Jenna looked at Michael. '*Potvrdit?*'

'Confirmed,' said Havelock, watching her. 'Logged in the official records.'

'Yes, official.' She turned back to Bradford. 'Is this the reason you rule out these people?'

'None left their meetings long enough to have reached Rome on a code circuit.'

'Forgive me,' continued Jenna, 'but do you exclude the possibility that this Ambiguity might have associates? Persons who would lie for them?'

'I don't even want to think about it,' said the Undersecretary. 'But considering the diversity of those who were there, I *do* think it's mathematically impossible. I know too many of those people, have known them for years, some for nearly two decades.'

'Still . . .'

'*Paminyatchiks?*' asked Havelock, his eyes on Jenna.

'*Proč ne? Jestli mužete.*'

'*Čí slos.*'

'*Jest malý.*'

'What are you talking about?' asked Bradford.

'We're being rude,' said Jenna. 'Sorry. I thought – '

'She thought it was something to think about,' interrupted Michael. 'I explained that the numbers didn't add up. Go on, please.'

Jenna looked at Havelock and reached for her drink.

The Undersecretary of State spoke for nearly four hours, half the time answering questions and refining countless details, until the elegant den came to seem like a quietly-charged courtroom. Bradford was the reluctant hostile witness facing two agile and relentless prosecuting lawyers.

'How are you handling Jacob Handelman?'

'Unsolved. The President read me what you wrote over the phone. It's incredible . . . about Handelman, I mean. Are you sure you weren't mistaken?'

'It was his gun, his knife. There was no mistake.'

'Berquist said you must have had extraordinary reason to kill him.'

'Oddly enough, I didn't. I wanted him to sweat – for years, if I could. He came after me. Are you going to tell the truth about him?'

'The President says no. What purpose would it serve? He says the Jews have been through enough; let it be.'

'Another necessary lie?'

'Not necessary, but compassionate, I think.'

'Kohoutek? That farm in Mason Falls?'

'He's being taken now.'

'His clients?'

'Each case will be studied individually and decisions made, again compassionately.'

Havelock leafed through the pages of his notebook, then put it down on the coffee table and reached for his empty glass. He glanced at Jenna; she shook her head. He got up and walked round the couch to pour himself a drink. 'Let me try to put this together,' he began quietly. 'Ambiguity's somewhere on the fifth floor of the State Department, and he's probably been there for years, feeding Moscow everything he gets his hands on.' Michael paused and walked aimlessly to the thick-paned window; outside the floodlights illuminated the landscaped grounds. 'Matthias meets this Parsifal and together they create these incredible – no, not incredible – *unthinkable* agreements.' Havelock stopped, turning suddenly from the window and looking hard at Bradford. 'How could it have happened? For Christ's sake, where *were* all of you? You saw him every day, talked to him, watched him! Couldn't you see what was happening to him?'

'We never knew what role he was playing,' said the Undersecretary of State, returning the stare, slow anger finally surfacing. 'Charisma has many facets, like a diamond seen in different lights, different turns. Was he Dean Matthias sitting in academic judgement, or Dr Matthias at a lectern, holding forth for an enraptured convocation? Or was he simply Mr Chips, over sherry, with Handel in the background, enlightening his favourite idolators of the moment? He did that very well. Then there was the *bon vivant*, the darling of Georgetown, Chevy Chase and the Eastern Shore. My God, what a coup for a hostess! And how magnificently he performed . . . what charm! What wit! The sheer force of his personality, a paunchy little man who suddenly emanated power! If he'd been capable, he could have had any woman he wanted. Then, of course, there was the office tyrant. Demanding, petulant, self-seeking, jealous . . . so conscious of his image he scoured the papers for the most minor mention, swelling up with the headlines, furious at the slightest criticism. And speaking of criticism, what did he do last year when a lowly senator questioned his motives at the Geneva conference? He went on television, voice choking, close to tears, and said he would remove himself from public life. *Jesus*, what an uproar! That senator's a pariah today!' Bradford paused, shaking his head, embarrassed at his outburst. He continued, lowering his voice. 'Then there was Anthony Matthias, the most brilliant Secretary of State in this nation's history . . . No, Mr Havelock, we saw him but we didn't see him. We didn't know him because he was too many people.'

'You're nit-picking at a man's vanity,' said Michael, walking towards the couch. 'Those're called shortcomings; you may not have any, the rest of us do. He *was* many people; he had to be. Your problem is that you hated him.'

'No, you're wrong.' Again Bradford shook his head. 'You don't hate a man like Matthias,' he continued, glancing at Jenna. 'You may be awe-struck, or frightened, or mesmerized – but you don't hate.'

'Let's get back to Parsifal,' said Havelock, sitting on the arm of the couch. 'Where do you think he came from?'

'He came from nowhere and he disappeared into nowhere.'

'The second he may have done, the first he couldn't have. He came from somewhere. He met Matthias time after time, certainly for weeks, possibly months.'

'We've checked Matthias's diaries over and over again. Also his logs, his telephone records, his classified appointments, his every travel itinerary – where he went, whom he met, from diplomats to doormen. There were no consistent repeats. Nothing.'

'I'll want them all. Can you arrange it?'

'It's arranged.'

'Anything on a time span?'

'Yes, spectroanalysis of the copy page type indicates recent impressions. Within six months.'

'Very good.'

'We could have assumed it.'

'Do me a favour,' said Michael, sitting down and reaching for his notebook.

'What's that?' asked the Undersecretary.

'Never assume.' Havelock wrote on the pad and added, 'Which is exactly what I'm going to do right now. Parsifal's a Russian. Most likely an untouched, unlisted defector.'

'We've . . . assumed that. Somebody with extraordinary knowledge of the Soviet Union's strategic arms capabilities.'

'Why do you say that?' asked Jenna Karras.

'The agreements. They contain offensive and defensive nuclear-strike data that matches our deepest and most accurate penetrations of their systems.'

Michael wrote another note for himself. 'Just as important,' he said. 'Parsifal knew where to find "Ambiguity". The connection is made, the mole reaches Moscow, and the evidence against you is provided – for my benefit. Then "Ambiguity" moves into Costa Brava, rewriting the scenario on the beach.' Michael turned back to the Undersecretary of State. 'It's here you think the break came, isn't it?'

'I do, and I agree with you. I think it was "Ambiguity" on that beach, not Parsifal. I believe further that "Ambiguity" returned to Washington and found he'd lost Parsifal. He'd been used, then discarded, a situation that must have panicked him.'

'Because in order to get the KGB to co-operate he obviously had to promise something extraordinary?' asked Havelock.

'Yes, but then there's Rostov's cable and it's a snag. He as much as told us that if there was a connection it wasn't sanctioned, or even controllable.'

'He was right. I explained it to Berquist, and it fits . . . from the beginning.

It's the answer to Athens. Rostov was referring to a *branch* of the KGB, a descendant of the old OGPU slaughter-house maniacs, a pack of wolves.'

'*Voennaya Kontr Razvedka*,' said Jenna, adding quietly, 'VKR.'

'"Ambiguity" isn't just a major or a colonel in the KGB, he's a member of the wolf pack. Those are the men he's dealing with, and that, Mr Bradford, is about the worst news you could hear. The KGB with all its paranoia is a stable intelligence-gathering organization compared to the fanatics of the *Voennaya*.'

'Fanatics and anything nuclear are a combination this world can't afford.'

'If the *Voennaya* reach Parsifal first, that's precisely the combination the world is stuck with.' Michael drank, swallowing more than he intended to, fear enveloping him. He picked up the notebook. 'So we have a mole called Ambiguity who co-operated with a fellow Russian we've labelled Parsifal, Matthias's partner in creating these insane agreements that could blow up the globe. Matthias virtually collapses, is taken into custody – and therapy – at Poole's Island, and Parsifal goes on alone. But now really alone because he's dropped the mole.'

'You agree with me then,' said Bradford.

Havelock looked up from the pad. 'If you were wrong, we'd know it. Or maybe we wouldn't; maybe we'd be a pile of ashes . . . Or, from a less melodramatic though hardly less tragic point of view in my judgement, the Soviet Union would be running this country with the blessings of the rest of the world. "The giant ran amok; for God's sake, chain him." Moscow might even get a vote of confidence from our own citizens. "Better dead than Red" is not a euphemism I care to test. When push comes to shove, people opt for living.'

'But you and I know what that living is, Mikhail,' broke in Jenna. 'Would you opt for it?'

'Of course,' said the Undersecretary of State, mildly surprising the other two. 'You can't change anything by dying – unless you're a martyr – or by taking yourself out. Especially when you've seen the worst.'

Havelock looked again at Bradford, now studying him. 'I think the jury just came back in for you, Mr Undersecretary. That's why you stayed in this city isn't it? You saw the worst.'

'I'm not the issue.'

'You were for us for a while. It's nice to know the terrain's firmer. Call me Havelock, or Michael, or whatever you like, but why not drop the mister?'

'Thanks. I'm Emory – or whatever you like.'

'I'm Jenna, and I'm starved.'

'There's a fully stocked kitchen with a cook in residence. He's also one of the guards. When we're finished, I'll introduce you.'

'Just a few more minutes.' Havelock tore off a page from his notebook. 'You said you were checking the whereabouts of everyone on the fifth floor at the time of Costa Brava.'

'Re-checking,' interrupted Bradford. 'The first check was negative all the way. Everyone was accounted for.'

'But we know someone wasn't,' said Michael. 'He was at Costa Brava.

One of those checks of yours ran into a smokescreen, the man inside leaving and returning while supposedly in place.'

'Oh?' It was the Undersecretary's turn to write a note, which he did on the back of one of his countless pages. 'I hadn't thought of it that way. I was looking for an absence where the explanation might not hold up. You're saying something quite different.'

'Yes, I am. Our man's better than that; there won't be any explanation. Don't look for someone missing; look for someone who wasn't there, who wasn't where he was supposed to be.'

'Someone on assignment, then.'

'It's a place to start,' agreed Havelock, tearing off a second page. 'The higher the profile the better, incidentally. Remember we're looking for a man who's got maximum clearance, and the more prominent the man the better the smokescreens work. Don't forget Kissinger's diarrhoea in Tokyo; he was really in Peking.'

'I'm beginning to understand your accomplishments.'

'Considering the mistakes I've made,' replied Michael, writing on the page he had just torn out of the notebook, 'I wouldn't qualify for a code ring on the back of a cereal box.' He got up, stepped around the coffee table to Bradford, and held out the two pages. 'This is the list. Do you want to look it over and see if there are any problems?'

'Sure.' The Undersecretary of State took the papers and settled back into the chair. 'By the way, I'll have that drink now, if you don't mind. Bourbon on the rocks, please.'

'I thought you'd never ask.' Havelock looked at Jenna; she nodded. He took her glass from the coffee table and walked round the couch as Bradford spoke.

'There are a couple of surprises here,' he said, glancing up and frowning. 'There's no problem with the Matthias material – the appointments, logs, itineraries – but why do you need all this stuff on the doctor in Maryland? Background, financial statements, employees, laboratories. We *were* thorough, believe me.'

'I do believe you. Call it a throwback. I know a doctor in the south of France and he's one hell of a surgeon. But he gets brain fever when he's near the gaming tables; he's crashed a couple of times and had to be bailed out.'

'There's no parallel here. Randolph hasn't had to work since his mother first saw him in the hospital. His family owns half the Eastern Shore, the richer half.'

'But not the people who work for him,' said Michael, pouring drinks. 'They may not even own a boat.'

Bradford's gaze again dropped to the page. 'I see,' he said, more bewilderment in his voice than conviction. 'I'm not sure I understand this. You want the names of people in the Pentagon who form the Nuclear Contingency Committees.'

'I read somewhere that there were three,' added Havelock, carrying the drinks back. 'They play war games, changing sides and cross-checking their strategies.' He handed Bradford his bourbon, then sat down next to Jenna; she took her drink, her eyes on Michael.

'You think Matthias used them?' asked the Undersecretary.

'I don't know. He must have used somebody.'

'For what purpose? There's nothing in our arsenals he didn't know about, had on file somewhere. He *had* to know; he negotiated.'

'I just want to be thorough.'

Bradford nodded with an embarrassed smile. 'I've heard that before. Okay.' He went back to the page, reading aloud. '"List of negative-possibles going back ten years. Follow-ups on each. Sources: CIA, Cons Op, Army Intelligence." I don't know what this means.'

'They will. There'll be dozens of them.'

'What are "they"?'

'Men and women who were priority targets for defection but never came over.'

'Well, if they didn't come over – '

'Moscow doesn't announce those who got out themselves,' interrupted Havelock. 'The computer follow-ups will clarify current statuses.'

Bradford paused, then nodded again, reading silently.

Jenna touched Michael's arm; he looked at her. She spoke softly, her eyes questioning. '*Proč ne paminyatchik?*'

'*Ne Ted'.*'

'I beg your pardon?' The Undersecretary glanced up as he shifted the pages in his hands.

'Nothing,' said Havelock. 'She's hungry.'

'I'll be finished in a minute, get back to Washington and leave you alone; the rest of this is routine. The DC psychiatrists' reports on Matthias will have to be signed over by the President and additional security put on here, but it can be done. I'm seeing him when I get back tonight.'

'Why don't you just take me over to Bethesda?'

'Those records aren't there. They're down at Poole's Island locked away with the other psychiatric probings and very special. They're in a steel container and can't be removed without presidential clearance. I'll have to get them. I'll fly down tomorrow.' Bradford stopped reading and looked up, startled. 'This last item . . . are you sure? What can they tell you? They couldn't tell *us* anything.'

'Put it down as my own personal Freedom of Information Act.'

'It could be very painful for you.'

'What is it?' asked Jenna.

'He wants the results of his own twelve days in therapy,' Bradford said.

They ate by candlelight in the country-elegant dining room, the scene somehow shifting from the deadly sublime to the faintly ridiculous. Adding to the contrast was a large, reticent man who was a surprisingly accomplished cook; but the bulge of a weapon beneath his white jacket did little to emphasize his talents in the kitchen. There was, however, nothing humorous about his eyes; he was a military guard and as accomplished with a gun as he was at preparing Beef Wellington. Yet whenever he left the room after serving and clearing, Jenna and Michael looked across the table at each other, trying unsuccessfully not to laugh. Although even these brief minutes of laughter did not last; the unthinkable never left them.

'You trust Bradford,' said Jenna, over coffee. 'I know you do. I can tell when you trust a person.'

'You're right, I do. He has a conscience and I think he's paid for it. You can trust a man like that.'

'Then why did you stop me from bringing up the *paminyatchiks* – the travellers?'

'Because he couldn't handle it and it can't help him. You heard him; he's the methodical man, one step at a time, each step exhaustingly analysed. That's his value. With the *paminyatchiks* he's suddenly asked to question everything geometrically.'

'I don't understand. Geometrically?'

'In a dozen different directions at once. Everyone's immediately suspect; he wouldn't be looking for one man, he'd be studying whole groups. I want him to concentrate on smokescreens, bore into every assignment on the fifth floor, whether eight blocks or eight hundred miles away from the State Department, until he finds someone who might not have been where he was supposed to be.'

'You explained it very well.'

'Thanks.'

'You might have added the use of a puppet, however.'

Havelock looked at her through the glow of the candles, a half smile coming to his lips. She levelled her eyes with his, smiling also. 'Damn it, you know you're absolutely right,' he said, laughing softly.

'I wasn't making a list, you were. You can't be expected to think of everything.'

'Thanks for the kindness, I'll bring it up in the morning. Incidentally, why didn't you? You weren't shy in there.'

'That was asking questions, not giving orders or advice. There's a difference. I wouldn't care to give orders or advice to Bradford until he accepted me. And if I were forced to, it would be in the form of questions, leading to a suggestion.'

'That's an odd thing to say. You're accepted; Bradford heard it from Berquist. There's no higher authority.'

'I don't mean in that sense. I mean him. He's uncomfortable with women, impatient, perhaps. I don't envy his wife or his women; he's a deeply troubled man.'

'He couldn't have more to be troubled about.'

'Long before this, Mikhail. He reminds me of a brilliant, talented man whose brilliance and talent don't mix very well. I think he feels impotent, and that touches his women . . . all women, really.'

'Am I with Sigmund again?'

'*Limburský syr!*' Jenna laughed. 'I watch people, you know I do. Do you remember the jeweller in Trieste, the bald-headed man whose shop was MI Six drop? You said he was – what's the peculiar word you have? Like *houkacka*?'

'Horny. I said he was horny, that he walked round the women in his store with a spike in the middle of his trousers.'

'And I said he was gay.'

'And you were right, because you unbuttoned your blouse a few inches and the son of a bitch kept following me.'

They both laughed, the laughter echoing off the veloured walls. Jenna reached over and touched his hand.

'It's good to laugh again, Mikhail.'

'It's good to laugh with you. I don't know how often we'll be able to.'

'We must make time for it. I think it's terribly important.'

'I love you, Jenna.'

'Then why don't we ask our gun-bearing Escoffier where we sleep? I don't want to appear *doslat*, my darling, but I love you, too. I want to be close to you, not with a table between us.'

'You figured I wasn't gay.'

'Latent, perhaps. I'll take what I can get.'

'Direct. I always said you were direct.'

The gun-bearing Escoffier walked in. 'More coffee?' he asked.

'No thank you,' said Havelock.

'Some brandy?'

'I think not,' said Jenna.

'How about television?'

'How about the sleeping quarters?'

'The reception's lousy up there.'

'We'll manage,' said Michael.

He sat on the antique bench in front of the dying fire in the bedroom, stretching his neck and moving his shoulder in circles. He was sitting there under orders, Jenna's favours to be withheld for seven years or some such nonsense if he disobeyed. She had gone downstairs to find bandages, antiseptic, and no doubt whatever else she could lay her hands on in pursuit of her immediate medical aims.

Ten minutes ago they had walked into the room together, hands clasped, bodies touching, both laughing softly. When she leaned into him, Michael suddenly winced from the pain in his shoulder, and she had looked into his eyes. She had then unbuttoned his shirt and studied the dressing underneath on his shoulder in the light of a table lamp. An accommodating guard had started the fire over an hour before; it was nearly out, but the coals were glowing, the stone hearth throwing off heat.

'Sit down here and stay warm,' Jenna had said, leading him to the bench. 'We never did pick up a Red Cross kit. They must have something downstairs.'

'You'd better call it first aid or they'll think you're taking up a collection.'

'Just be still, my darling. That shoulder's raw.'

'I haven't thought about it, I haven't felt it,' said Havelock, watching her go to the door and let herself out.

It was true, he had neither thought about the wound from Col des Moulinets nor, except for mild spasms, been aware of the pain. There had been no time. It hadn't been important enough to think about. Too much had been too overwhelming too quickly. He looked over at the large bedroom window, a window with the same thick, bevelled glass as the one below in the study. He could see the wash of floodlights beyond – distorted by the glass – and wondered briefly how many men prowled the grounds protecting the sanctity of Sterile Five. Then his eyes wandered back to the burning coals that were the end of the fire. So much . . . so overwhelming . . . so quickly. The mind had to catch up before it was drowned in the on-rushing revelations released by floodgates no longer holding back unthinkable – *unbearable* – truths. If he was going to keep his sanity, he had to find time to think.

It's good to laugh with you. I don't know how often we'll be able to.

We must make the time for it. I think it's terribly important.

Jenna was right. Laughter was not inconsequential. *Her* laugh was not; he suddenly wanted so desperately to hear it. Where was she? How long did it take to find a roll of elastoplast and a couple of bandages? Every sterile house was fully equipped with all manner of medical supplies, they went with the territory. Where *was* she?

He got up from the antique bench, suddenly alarmed. Perhaps other men – men not assigned to Sterile Five – were prowling the grounds outside. He had a certain expertise in such matters. Infiltration was made easier by a profusion of woods and underbrush, and Sterile Five was a country house, surrounded by trees and foliage – natural cover for unnatural experts bent on penetration. *He* could intrude, invade, undoubtedly take out opposition silently, and if he could, others could. Where *was she*?

Havelock walked rapidly to the window, realizing as he approached it that the thick glass which was impervious to bullets would also distort any movement outside. It did; he turned swiftly for the door. Then he realized something else: he had no weapon!

The door opened before he reached it. He stopped, his breath cut short, relief sweeping through him as Jenna stood there with one hand on the knob and the other holding a plastic tray filled with bandages, scissors, tape and antiseptic.

'Mikhail, what is it? What's the matter?'

'Nothing. I . . . I felt like getting up.'

'Darling, you're perspiring,' said Jenna, closing the door and coming to him, touching his forehead, then his right temple. 'What *is* it?'

'I'm sorry. My imagination went a little off the track. I . . . I thought you were gone longer than . . . I expected. I'm sorry.'

'I was gone longer than *I* expected.' Jenna took his arm and led him to the bench. 'Let's get the shirt off,' she said, placing the tray down and helping him.

'Just that?' asked Havelock, sitting down and looking at her, removing his arms from his sleeves. 'Just longer than you expected? That's it?'

'Well, apart from two brief affairs under the staircase and a mild flirtation with the cook, I'd say it was sufficient . . . Now, stay still while I take this off.' Jenna carefully, expertly, sliced through the borders of the dressing on his shoulder, peeled it back and removed the bandage. 'Actually, it's healing quite well, considering what you've put it through,' she said, as she stripped off the tape and reached for the spirit and cotton wool. 'More irritation than anything else. The salt water probably prevented infection . . . This will sting a bit.'

'It *does*,' said Michael, wincing as Jenna swabbed the flesh around the wound, then stroked the remains of the elastoplast away. 'Apart from that activity under the staircase, what the hell were you doing?' he asked while she placed squares of gauze over his skin.

'Concentrating on the mild flirtation,' she replied, reeling out the surgical tape and strapping the clean dressing in place. 'There. You won't feel any better, but you look better.'

'And you're avoiding me.'

'Don't you like surprises?'

'Never did.'

'*Koláče!*' she said, drawing out the word, while laughing, and pouring alcohol over his exposed skin. 'In the morning we'll have *koláče*,' she added, massaging his back.

'Sweet rolls?. . . You're crazy. You're positively out of your mind! We've spent twenty-four hours in a goddamned hell and you're talking about hot cross buns!'

'We must live, Mikhail,' said Jenna, her voice suddenly soft beside him, the movement of her hands slowing to a halt. 'I did speak with our armed-to-the-teeth cook, and I'm sure I flirted. In the morning he'll make sure we have apricots and dry yeast; nutmeg he has . . . and ground mace. He'll order it all tonight. In the morning, *koláče.*'

'I don't believe you – '

'Try and you'll see.' She laughed again, and held his face in her hands. 'In Prague you found a bakery that made *koláče*. You loved it and asked me to bake some for you.'

'In Prague, there was another set of problems, not what's facing us now.'

'But it *is us*, Mikhail. *Us* once more, and we must have our moments. I lost you once, and now you're here, with me again. Let me have these moments, let *us* have them . . . even knowing what we know.'

He reached for her, pulling her to him. 'You have them. We have them.'

'Thank you, my darling.'

'I love to hear you laugh, have I told you that?'

'A number of times. You said I laughed like a small child watching a marionette show. Do you remember saying that?'

'I do, and I was right.' Michael tilted her head back. 'It fits, a child and sudden laughter . . . a nervous child sometimes. Broussac saw it too. She told me what happened in Milan, how you stripped that poor bastard, coloured him red, and stole his clothes.'

'As well as an enormous sum of money!' interrupted Jenna. 'He was a dreadful man.'

'Régine said you laughed about it like a small child remembering a joke or a prank or something like that.'

'I suppose I did.' Jenna glanced at the fire. 'I was so frightened, hoping so much that she would help me, thinking she might not. I think I was holding on to a memory that amused me, that might calm me down. I don't know, but it's happened before.'

'What do you mean?' asked Michael.

Jenna turned back to him, her wide eyes inches from his but not looking at him – instead, looking beyond, seeing images from the past. 'When I ran away from Ostrava, when my brothers were killed, and I was marked by the anti-Dubčeks – when my life there was finished – I came into the world of Prague. It was a world filled with hatred, a world so violent that I thought at times I couldn't stand it any more. But I knew what I had to do, I couldn't turn back to a life that wasn't mine any longer . . . So I used to remember things, relive the memories as if I were actually *there*, not in Prague, not in that world of fear. I was back in Ostrava, my adoring brothers taking me for rides, telling their sister outrageous stories to make me laugh. During those moments I was free, I wasn't afraid.' She looked at him. 'Those memories were hardly like Milan, were they? But I could laugh, I *did* laugh . . . Enough! I'm not making sense.'

'You're making sense,' said Michael, pulling her to him again, his face against hers. 'Thank you for that. Not much sense is being made these days. Anywhere.'

'You're tired, my darling. More than tired, you're exhausted. Come on, let's go to bed.'

'I always obey my doctors.'

'You need rest, Mikhail.'

'I always obey my doctors up to a point.'

'*Zlomený*,' said Jenna, laughing softly against his ear.

Strands of her blonde hair were layered over his face, her arm across his chest, but neither was asleep. The spendid, warm comfort of their love-making did not bring sleep; the unthinkable was too much with them. A soft shaft of light came from the partially closed bathroom door.

'You didn't tell me everything that happened to you on Poole's Island, did you?' said Jenna, her head next to his on the pillow. 'You told Bradford that you did, but you didn't.'

'Almost everything,' replied Havelock, staring at the ceiling. 'I'm still trying to figure it out.'

Jenna took her arm away and, supporting herself on her elbow, faced him. 'Can I help you?' she asked.

'I don't think anybody can. It's the bomb in my head.'

'What is, my darling?'

'I know Parsifal.'

'You *what* . . . ?'

'That's what Matthias said. He said I saw them all coming and going, the "negotiators of the world", he called them. But there was only one and I must have seen him. I must know him.'

'That was the reason he did what he did to you? To us? Why he wanted you out?'

'He said I could never understand . . . the deadliest treaties were the only solution.'

'And I was the sacrifice.'

'Yes. What can I say? He's not sane; he wasn't when he ordered the case against you. You were to die and I was to live, live and be watched.' Michael shook his head in frustration. '*That's* what I can't understand.'

'My death?'

'No, my *living*.'

'Even in his insanity, he loved you.'

'Not *him*. Parsifal. If I was a threat why didn't Parsifal kill me? Why was it left to the mole to put out the order three months later?'

'Bradford explained that,' said Jenna. 'You'd seen me; you were reopening Costa Brava, and it could have led you back to the mole.'

'It still doesn't explain Parsifal. He could have had me taken out twenty times over. He didn't. That's the gap. What kind of a man are we dealing with?'

'Certainly not rational. It's what's so terrifying.'

Havelock turned his head and looked at her. 'I wonder,' he said.

The ringing was harsh, unexpected, reverberating throughout the room. He bolted up from a deep sleep, his hand reaching for a non-existent weapon. It was the telephone, and Michael stared at it before picking it up from the bedside table. He glanced at his watch as he spoke. It was 4:45 in the morning.

'Yes?'

'Havelock, it's Bradford.'

'What's the matter? Where are you?'

'In my office. I've been here since eleven. Incidentally, I've had people working through the night. Everything you wanted will be at Sterile Five by eight o'clock, except the records at Poole's Island. There'll be a few hours' delay with those.'

'You called at this hour to tell me that?'

'Of course not.' Bradford paused, an intake of breath filling the moment. 'I may have found him,' he said rapidly. 'I did as you suggested. I looked for someone who might not have been where he was supposed to be. I won't know for certain until late this morning; that's the delay with Poole's Island. If it's true, it's incredible; his record is as clean as they come, his military service – '

'Don't say any more,' ordered Michael.

'Your phone is as sterile as that house.'

'Mine may be. Yours may not be. Or your office. Just listen to me.'

'What is it?'

'Look for a puppet. He could be alive or dead.'

'A what?'

'Someone filling in, the strings leading back to your man. Do you understand that?'

'Yes, I think so. As a matter of fact, I do. It's part of what I've found already.'

'Call me when you know. From the street, from a booth. But don't close in, don't do anything.' Havelock hung up and looked at Jenna. 'Bradford may have found "Ambiguity". If he has, you were right.'

'*Paminyatchik?*'

'A traveller.'

29

It was a morning such as Sterile Five had never experienced and would probably never see again. A persuasive inmate had taken over the sombre asylum. In spite of the tension, despite the anticipated call from Bradford, by 8:30 Jenna had commandeered the kitchen, the gun-bearing Escoffier relegated to the position of assistant. Ingredients were measured and mixed to the accompaniment of glances of approval and the gradual breaking down of culinary barriers; the armed cook began to smile. Pans were selected and the outsized oven turned on; then two additional guards emerged on the scene as if their nostrils belonged to hounds and the kitchen had become a meat market.

'Please call me Jenna,' said Jenna to the others, as Havelock was demoted to a corner table and dismissed with a newspaper.

First names were exchanged, wide grins appeared, and before long there was conversation interspersed with laughter. Home towns were compared – bakeries the basis of comparison – and a kind of frivolity took over the kitchen at Sterile Five. It was as though no one had ever before dared lighten the oppressive atmosphere of the security-conscious compound. It was lightened now and Jenna was the bearer of that light. To say that the men – these professionals familiar with the deadly arts – were taken with her was too modest an observation. They were actually having fun, and fun was not normal at Sterile Five. The world was going to hell in a galactic basket and Jenna Karras was baking *koláče*.

At 9:55, however, after quantities of sweet rolls had been eaten in the kitchen and dispensed throughout the grounds, the serious air of the sterile house returned. Static on a dozen radios erupted as inside bells and television monitors became operational. An armoured van from the Department of State had entered the long, guarded drive from the highway. It was expected.

By 10:30 Havelock and Jenna were back in the ornate study to examine the papers and photographs, which were separated by classification. There were six stacks, some thicker than others: four on the desk in front of Michael; two on the coffee table, where Jenna sat reading on the couch. Bradford had been thorough, and if more-was-more his only error was in duplication. An hour and twenty minutes passed, the near-noon sun filling the windows, refracted in the bullet-proof glass, the rays scattered across the walls. There was silence, except for the turning of pages.

The approach they used was standard when dealing with such a mass of diverse information. They read everything rapidly, concentrating on the totality, not on specifics, trying first to get a feel of the landscape; they would get to the details later and relentlessly scrutinize them. Despite the concentration on reading, a comment was inevitable now and then.

'Ambassador Addison Brooks and General Malcolm Halyard,' said Michael, reading a page that contained the names of all those involved –

however remotely, with or without knowledge – with the Parsifal mosaic. 'They're the President's back-ups if he's forced to expose Matthias.'

'In what sense?' asked Jenna.

'After Anton, they're among the most respected men in the country. Berquist will need them.'

Several minutes later Jenna spoke. 'You're listed here.'

'Where?'

'An entry in an early Matthias calendar.'

'How early?'

'Eight – no, nine months ago. You were a house guest of his. It was when you were flown over for the Cons Op personnel-evaluation, I think. We hadn't known each other very long.'

'Long enough for me to want to get back to Prague as fast as I could. Those sessions were usually a monumental waste of time.'

'You told me once they served a purpose, that the field often had strange effects on certain men and they should be periodically checked.'

'I wasn't one of them. Anyway, I said usually, not always. On occasions they'd pick out a . . . a gunslinger.'

Jenna put the page down on her lap. 'Mikhail, could it have been then? That visit to Matthias? Could you have seen Parsifal then?'

'Anton was himself nine months ago. There was no Parsifal.'

'You said he was tired – "terribly tired" were the words you used. You were worried about him.'

'His health, not his sanity. He was sane.'

'Still –'

'You think I haven't gone over every minute in my mind?' interrupted Havelock. 'It was in Georgetown, and I was there two days, two nights, the length of the evaluation. We had dinner twice, both times alone. I didn't see anybody.'

'Certainly people came to the house.'

'They certainly did; they never gave him a moment's peace, day or night.'

'Then you saw them.'

'I'm afraid I didn't. You'd have to know that old place; it's a maze of small rooms in the front. There's a parlour to the right in the hallway, a library on the left that one goes through to get to his office. I think Anton liked it; he could keep people waiting who probably wouldn't see each other. Petitioners in stages, moved from one area to the next. He'd greet them in the parlour, then they'd be taken to the library and, finally, to the *sanctum-sanctorum*, his office.'

'And you were never in those rooms.'

'Not with anybody else. When he was interrupted at dinner, I remained in the dining-room in the back. I even used a separate side entrance when coming or going from the house, never the front door. We had an understanding.'

'Yes, I remember. You didn't care to be seen with him.'

'I'd put it differently. I'd have been honoured – I mean that, honoured – to have been seen with him. It just wasn't a very good idea, for either of us.'

'But if it wasn't during those two days, when was it? When *could* you have seen Parsifal?'

Michael looked at her, feeling helpless. 'I'd have to go back over half a lifetime, that's part of the madness. In his fantasy he sees me leaving a conference; that could be anything from a classroom to a seminar to a lecture hall. How many were there? Fifty, a hundred, a thousand? Post-graduate degrees take time. How many have I forgotten? Was it there, in one of those? Was Parsifal somewhere in the past?'

'If he was, you could hardly be considered a threat to him now.' Jenna sat forward, recognition suddenly in her eyes. '"He could have taken me out twenty times over but he didn't,"' she repeated. 'Parsifal *didn't* try to kill you.'

'Exactly.'

'Then he could be someone you knew years ago.'

'Or there's another possibility. I said he could have taken me out, and he would have, but regardless of how careful or how removed a person is, there's always a risk in killing someone, or contracting for a gun, no matter how slight. Maybe he can't tolerate even the hint of a risk. Maybe he's in a crowd of faces right in front of me and I can't pick him out. But if I knew who he was, or what he looked like, I'd know where to find him. *I'd* know, but not necessarily many others, probably no one in our line of work.'

'The mole could supply you with both, an identity and a description.'

'Good hunting, Mr Undersecretary,' said Havelock. 'And I wish to hell he'd *call*! . . . Anything else in there?' he added, going back to the material on a Maryland physician.

'I haven't got that far with the diaries. But there's something in the itineraries and it's repeated frequently. I'm not sure I understand. Why is the Shenandoah mentioned so often, Mikhail?'

Havelock looked up from the page as a dissonant chord echoed in the recesses of his brain.

Emory Bradford struggled to keep his eyes open. Except for brief catnaps, taken when he could no longer function, he had not slept in nearly thirty-six hours. Yet he *had* to stay awake; it was past noon. The newsreel tapes and photographs from New York would be arriving any minute, rushed down by an accommodating television station that accepted an innocuous explanation in exchange for a new and confidential source at the Department of State. The Undersecretary had ordered up the proper equipment; he could run the tapes within minutes of receiving them. And then he would know.

Incredible. Arthur Pierce! *Was* it Pierce, after all? The senior State Department official at the United Nations delegation, chief aide to the ambassador, a career officer with a service record to be envied by just about anyone working in the upper regions of the government, a record that fairly screamed 'advancement'! And prior to his arrival in Washington there was a superb military record. Had he stayed in the army he would have been on his way to the Joint Chiefs of Staff. Pierce had arrived in South-east Asia as a second-lieutenant from the University of Michigan, his Master's degree *summa cum laude* and an experienced officer cadet. Thereafter during five voluntarily uninterrupted tours of duty he had risen to the rank of major, replete with decorations for bravery, citations for leadership and recommen-dations for further strategic studies. And before *that*, before Vietnam, there was a dossier that exemplified the young American achievement of a farm boy: church acolyte, Eagle Scout, high school valedictorian, college scholarship with academic honours – even membership of the most envied student clubs. As General Halyard had put it, Arthur Pierce was flag, mother, apple pie and God. *Where* was the connection with Moscow?

Yet there was one if there was validity in Havelock's use of the term 'smokescreen' and especially in his next phrase 'the puppet who might be dead or alive'. It was the initial suggestion, however, that had first caught Bradford's attention: *Look for a man who wasn't there, who wasn't where he was supposed to be.*

He had been studying routinely – too routinely for the thought seemed too farfetched – the recommendations and positions taken by the American delegation at the Security Council's meetings during the week of Costa Brava. These included the confidential discussions within the delegation, as summarized by an attaché named Carpenter. His superior Pierce, the man second only to the Ambassador, was mentioned frequently, his suggestions concise, astute, very much in character. Then Bradford came upon a parenthetical abbreviated phrase deep in the text of that Thursday's meeting: '(*Del./F.C.*).'

It followed a strong and lengthy recommendation presented to the ambassador by Pierce. Bradford had not picked it up before, probably because of the unnecessarily complicated diplomatic verbiage, but seven hours ago he had looked hard at it. '(Del./F.C.) *Delivered by Franklyn Carpenter.*'

Translation: not offered by the ambassador's senior aide, Arthur Pierce, whose words they were, but, instead, relayed by a subordinate. Meaning: Pierce was not there, not where he was supposed to be.

Bradford had then studied every subsequent line in the delegation report. He'd found two additional bracketed *F.C.*s for Thursday and three more for Friday. *Friday*. Then he had remembered the obvious and gone back to the beginning of the week. It had been the end of the year; the operation at Costa Brava had taken place on the night of 4 January. Sunday. *A weekend*.

There had been no Security Council meeting that Wednesday because the majority of the delegations who were still on speaking terms were holding diplomatic receptions for New Year's Eve. On Thursday, the first day of the New Year, as if to show the world the UN meant to greet it seriously, the Council had resumed, then again on Friday . . . but not Saturday or Sunday.

Therefore, if Arthur Pierce was not where he was supposed to be, and had instructed a subordinate to deliver his words, he could have left the country on Tuesday evening, allowing five days for the Costa Brava. If, if . . . if. *Ambiguity?*

He had called Havelock, who told him what to look for next. The puppet.

The lateness of the hour was irrelevant. Bradford had raised an operator on the all-night tracing switchboard and told him to reach one Franklyn Carpenter, wherever he might be. Eight minutes later the operator had called back; Franklyn Carpenter had resigned from the Department of State a little over three months ago. The number on file was useless; the telephone had been disconnected. Bradford had then given the name of the only other person listed as at the American desk during that Thursday meeting of the Security Council, a lower level attaché no doubt still in New York.

The tracing operator had called back at 5:15 a.m., the UN attaché on the line.

'This is Undersecretary of State Bradford . . .'

The man's initial response had been one of astonishment mixed with the fuzziness of sleep, and more than a touch of fear. Bradford had to spend several minutes reassuring him, trying to bring him back to those few days nearly four months ago.

'Can you remember them?'

'Reasonably, I suppose.'

'Did anything strike you as unusual during the end of that week?'

'Nothing that comes to mind, no, sir.'

'The American team for those sessions – and I'm mainly concerned with Thursday and Friday – consisted of the ambassador, the senior State Department official, Arthur Pierce, yourself and a man named Carpenter, is that right?'

'I'd reverse the last two. I was low man on the totem pole then.'

'Were all four of you there every day?'

'Well . . . I think so. It's hard to recall every day four months ago. The attendance rolls would tell you.'

'Thursday was New Year's Day, does that help you?'

There was a pause before the attaché answered. When he did so, Bradford closed his eyes. 'Yes,' the aide said. 'I *do* remember. I may have been listed at the desk, but I wasn't there. The White Flash had – Excuse me, I'm sorry, sir.'

'I know who you mean. What did Undersecretary Pierce do?'

'He asked me to fly down to Washington to compile an analysis of the entire Middle East position. I spent damn near the whole weekend on it. Then, wouldn't you know, he didn't use it. Never has to this day.'

'I have a last question,' Bradford said quietly, trying to control his voice. 'When a team member's recommendations are given to the ambassador by someone else at the desk, what exactly does it signify?'

'That's easy. The senior members try to anticipate adversary proposals and write up strategies or counterproposals to block them. In the event he's out of the council room when a controversial proposal is brought up, his advice is there for the ambassador.'

'Isn't that dangerous? Couldn't someone simply write up something under an official title and hand it to a member?'

'Oh, no, it doesn't work that way. You don't just drop those deliveries and disappear. You've got to be on the premises, that's a must. Suppose the ambassador likes an argument, uses it, and gets hit with a reply that he can't handle. He wants the man responsible back in session to get him away from the fan.'

'Undersecretary Pierce gave a number of deliveries, as you call them, during the Thursday and Friday meetings.'

'That's standard. He's out of that room as much as he's in it. He's terrific in the Diplomats' Lounge, I've got to say it. He's there a lot, button-holing

God knows who, but it works. I think he's as effective as anyone up here; I mean he's really impressive. Even the Soviets like him.'

Yes, they do, Mr Attaché. So much so that controversial proposals could be avoided by pre-arrangement, Bradford said to himself.

'I know I said a last question; may I have one more?'

'I'm not going to argue, sir.'

'What happened to Carpenter?'

'I wish to hell I knew. I wish I could find him. I guess he just fell apart.'

'What do you mean?'

'I guess you didn't know. His wife and kids were killed in an automobile accident a couple of days before Christmas. How'd you like to have three coffins in front of a Christmas tree with the presents unopened?'

'I'm sorry.'

'He showed a lot of guts coming back as soon as he did. Of course, we all agreed it'd be the best thing for him. To be with people who cared; not alone.'

'I imagine that Undersecretary Pierce concurred.'

'Yes, sir. He was the one who persuaded him to come back.'

'I see.'

'Then one morning he just didn't show up. The next day a telegram arrived; it was his resignation, effective immediately.'

'That was unusual, wasn't it? Actually improper, I believe.'

'After what he'd been through, I don't think anyone wanted to pursue formalities.'

'And again the Undersecretary concurred.'

'Yes, sir. It was Pierce's idea, Carpenter just disappeared. I hope he's all right.'

He's dead, Mr Attaché. The puppet is dead.

Bradford had continued until the sun was up, until his eyes ached from the strain. The next items he examined were the time sheets for the night the Ambiguity code had been stolen, the 'beyond-salvage' sent to Rome. He saw what he expected to see: Arthur Pierce had been not in New York but in Washington, at his office on the fifth floor – and, naturally, he had checked out shortly after five o'clock in the evening, the time corresponding to half a dozen others. How simple it must have been to walk out in a crowd, sign the security sheet and go right back inside. He could have stayed there all night, signed in in the morning and no one would have known the difference. Just as he, Undersecretary Emory Bradford, could do the same thing *this* morning.

He had gone back to the military transcripts – a *nonpareil* army record – to the State Department dossier – an inventory of achievement – to an early life that read like an officially documented tribute to Jack Armstrong, All-American Boy. Where in God's name was the connection with Moscow?

By eight o'clock it had become impossible to concentrate so he leaned back in his chair and slept. At eight thirty-five he was stirred awake by the hum of life beyond his office door. The day had begun for the Department of State. Coffee was made and poured, appointments checked, schedules set up as secretaries awaited the arrival of their crisp, starched superiors. There was an unwritten but understood dress code at State these days; frizzled hair, loud ties and unkempt beards were out. He had got up, walked outside and greeted his own middle-aged secretary, startling her by his appearance. At that moment he realized what an impression he must have made – tieless, in shirtsleeves, dark circles under his eyes, his hair rumpled and the black stubble of a beard on his face.

He had asked for coffee and headed for the men's room to relieve himself, wash and straighten up as best he could. And as he walked through the large office, past desks and secretaries and arriving executives, he felt the stares levelled at him. If they only knew, he thought to himself.

By ten o'clock, remembering Havelock's admonition, he went out to a public phone and made arrangements for the tapes and the photographs to be flown down from New York. He was tempted to call the President. He did not; he spoke to no one.

Now he glanced at his watch. It was twenty-two minutes past twelve, three minutes later than it was when he last checked. The shuttle flights were every hour from New York; which one was the shipment on?

His thoughts were interrupted by a quiet rapping on his door and a corresponding acceleration in his heartbeat. 'Come in!'

It was his secretary, and she looked at him the way she had looked at him early in the morning, concern in her deep-set eyes. 'I'm off to lunch, okay?'

'Sure, Liz.'

'Can I get you anything?'

'No, thanks.'

The woman stood awkwardly in the door frame, pausing before she continued. 'Are you feeling all right, Mr Bradford?' she asked.

'Yes, I'm fine.'

'Is there anything I can do?'

'Stop worrying about me and go to lunch,' he said, attempting a smile; it was not successful.

'See you later then.'

If she only knew, he thought.

His telephone rang. It was lobby security; the unmarked delivery from New York had arrived. 'Sign for it and send it up with a guard, please.'

Seven minutes later the tape was inserted into the video recorder and an interior view of the Security Council of the United Nations appeared on the screen. On the bottom of the picture a date was flashed: *Tues. December 30. 2:56 P.* The occasion was an address by the Saudi Arabian ambassador. A few minutes into the speech there was a pan shot for reaction, first the Israeli delegation, then the Egyptian, followed by the American team. Bradford stopped the tape with the remote control and studied the picture. The four men were in place; the ambassador and his senior aide, Arthur Pierce, in front, two men seated behind. There was no point in listening or watching further for Tuesday the 30th; Bradford resumed the movement, pulling the remote mechanism up in front of him to locate the forward button. He pressed it and a rushing blur appeared on the screen. He released the button; the Saudi was still speaking. He was about to resume the forward motion when a quick-cut shot revealed the American delegation again. Arthur Pierce was not there.

Bradford pressed the reverse several times until he found the action that he was looking for, that he knew would be there. An official from State did not walk out on a friendly speech without at least some explanation. There it was. Pierce was looking at his watch as he rose, leaning first towards the ambassador and whispering, then to the man behind him, presumably the lower-level attaché, who nodded. A female announcer's voice came from the speaker. 'We understand that a telephone call has been received by the United States delegation, quite possibly from the Secretary of State, who may care to register his comments on Ibn Kashani's most laudatory speech.'

Bradford pressed the forward button again, and again, and once again. The address was over; many delegations rose in an ovation. Arthur Pierce had not returned to his chair.

Thurs. Jan. 1 10:43 A. The welcoming of the New Year by the President of the Security Council. Pierce was not at the American desk. In his place was the man – presumably Franklyn Carpenter – who had been seated behind the amabassador; he was beside him now, a sheaf of papers in his hands.

Fri. Jan. 2 4:10 P. A provocative speech by the PCR delegate, necessitating the use of the translation earphones. Pierce was not at the American desk.

Mon. Jan. 5 11:43 A. Arthur Pierce was absent.

Mon. Jan. 5 2:16 P. Arthur Pierce was absent.

Mon. Jan. 5 4:45 P. Arthur Pierce was in his chair, shaking his head in response to comments by the ambassador from Yemen.

Bradford turned off the video tape and looked at the manila envelope containing photographs of the New Year's Eve receptions. He did not really need them; he knew the Undersecretary of the American delegation would appear in none.

He had been at the Costa Brava.

There was a final check, and with computer scanners it would take less than a minute. Bradford reached for his phone; he asked for transport backlog information, made his request and waited, rubbing his eyes, aware that a tremble had developed in his breathing. Forty-seven seconds later the reply came: 'On Tuesday, 30 December there were five flights out of New York to Madrid. Ten o'clock, twelve, one-fifteen, two-thirty and five-ten . . . On Monday, 4 January, Spanish time, there were four flights from Barcelona routed through Madrid, starting at seven-thirty, a.m., arrival Kennedy Airport, EST, twelve-twenty-one; nine-fifteen, a.m., arrival Kennedy, EST, three o'clock . . .'

'Thank you,' said Bradford, interrupting. 'I have what I need.'

He did. Pierce had taken the 5:10 Tuesday flight to Madrid and had returned on the 9:15 Monday flight from Barcelona, permitting him to appear at the United Nations by 4:45, Eastern Standard Time. Somewhere in the passenger manifests there would be a single traveller whose name on a passport would in no way correspond to that of the Undersecretary of the delegation.

Bradford pivoted in his chair, breathing deeply, staring out of the large window at the tree-lined streets of Washington below. It was time to go out into one of those streets and find another telephone. Havelock had to know. He got up and walked around his desk towards his jacket and overcoat, both draped carelessly over a straight-backed chair against the wall.

The door opened without a knock, and the Undersecretary of State froze, his every muscle paralysed. Standing there, closing the door and leaning against the frame, was another Undersecretary of State, a shock of white streaking through his dark hair. It was Pierce. He stood erect, his eyes level, cold, somehow weary, his voice flat as he said, 'You look exhausted, Emory,' he said. 'You're also inexperienced. Exhaustion and inexperience are a bad combination; together they cause lapses. When you ask questions of sub-ordinates, you should remember to demand confidentiality. That young man, the one who took Carpenter's place, was really quite excited this morning.'

'You killed Carpenter,' whispered Bradford, finding a part of his voice. 'He didn't resign, you killed him.'

'He was in great emotional pain.'

'Oh, *Christ* . . . His wife and children, you did that, too!'

'You have to plan, create circumstances, foster need . . . dependence. You can accept that, can't you? Good Lord, in the old days you never gave it a thought. And how many did *you* kill? Before your celebrated conversion, that is. I was out there, Emory. I saw what you did.'

'But you *were* there . . .'

'Hating every minute of it. Sickened by the waste, the body counts – on both sides – and the lies. Always the lies, from Saigon and Washington. It was the slaughter of children, yours and theirs.'

'Why *you*? There's nothing anywhere to *explain*! Why *you*?'

'Because it's what I was meant to do. We're on different sides, Emory, and I believe in mine far more than you believe in yours. That's understand-able; you've seen what it's like here, and you can't do anything about it. I can and I will. There's a better way for this world than yours. We'll bring it about.'

'*How?* By blowing it *up*? By plunging us all into a nuclear war that was never meant to *be*?!'

Pierce stood motionless, his eyes boring into Bradford's. 'It's true then,' he said quietly. 'They did it.'

'You didn't *know* . . . Oh, my *God*!'

'Don't blame yourself, we were close. We were told – *I* was told – that he was going mad, that he was creating a strategy so intolerable the world would be revolted, the United States would never be trusted again. When it was completed, and the documents were in our hands, we would have the ammunition to dictate or destroy, the option would be ours, in either case your system would be finished, wiped from the face of the earth you've raped.'

'You're so *wrong* . . . so misguided.' Bradford's voice was a whisper. 'Great mistakes, yes! Massive errors of judgements, *yes*! . . . But we *face* them. In the end we always face them!'

'Only when you're caught. Because you haven't the courage to fail, and without that you can't win.'

'You think suppression's the answer? You think because you silence people they won't be heard?'

'Not where it matters; that's the practical answer. You've never under-stood us, anyway. You read our books but you don't grasp their meaning; you even choose to overlook specific points. Marx said it, Lenin reconfirmed it, but you didn't listen. Our system is in constant transition, phases to be passed through until change isn't needed any longer. One day our freedom will be complete, not like yours. Not hollow.'

'You're spoonfed! No change? People *have* to change. Every day! According to the weather, to birth, to death . . . to needs! You can't turn them into automatons; they won't stand for it! That's what you can't understand. You're the ones who are afraid of failure. You won't let anybody argue with you!'

'Not those who would undo more than sixty years of hope, of progress. Our great scientists, the doctors, the engineers . . . the vast majority of their parents weren't able to read.'

'So you taught the children and banned the books.'

'I thought you were better than that.' Pierce took several steps forward away from the door. 'You can't find him, can you? He delivered his nuclear blueprints, then went underground. You don't know who he's shown them to, or sold them to. You're in panic.'

'You can't find him either. You lost him.'

'But we know who he is. We've studied his habits, his needs, his talents. Like all men with outstanding minds, he's complicated but predictable. We'll find him. We know what to look for; you don't.'

'He defected from you, didn't he?'

'A temporary condition. His quarrel was with the bureaucracy, with unimaginative superiors, not the objectives of the state. When he came to me, I could have taken him, but I chose not to; he offered me too high a price. You see, he believes in us not you – certainly not you, *never* you. His father was a tenant serf on the lands of Prince Voroshin. He was hanged by that grand nobleman for stealing a wild pig in winter to feed his family. He won't turn on us.'

'Who's "us"? Moscow doesn't acknowledge you, we've learned that much through Costa Brava. The KGB had nothing to *do* with Costa Brava; it was never sanctioned.'

'Not by anyone you deal with. They're old and tired; they accommodate. They've lost sight of our promise, our destiny, if you like. We haven't.' Pierce looked at the television set and the video recorder beneath it; then at the box on Bradford's desk. 'A network film library – or is it archives? Images recorded so they can be studied to settle disputes or investigate death. Very good, Emory.' The mole glanced up. 'Or we could add a third *d*. Disappearance. Yes, those would tell you; that feeble excuse for a diplomat we call an ambassador certainly couldn't. He'd check his records, find that I'd given him the best arguments for those sessions and swear I was there. It might amuse you to know that I frequently talk with my true associates in the lounge and tell them to go easy on him, let him win a few. He was heaven-sent for me.'

'It doesn't amuse me.'

Pierce approached Bradford, standing directly in front of him. 'Havlicek's come back, hasn't he?'

'Who?'

'We prefer his real name. Mikhail Havlicek, son of Václav, an enemy of the state and named for a grandfather from Rovno, across the Carpathians.

Mikhail is a Russian name, you know. Not Czech. On the other hand, you probably *don't* know that; you put such little emphasis on heritage. Under different circumstances, he might be standing where I am at this moment. He's a talented man; I'm sorry he was so misguided. He's here, isn't he?'

'I don't know what you're talking about.'

'Oh, come on, Emory. That outrageous newspaper story, that very opaque whitewash done so very badly by State in response to the killing on Morningside Heights. That old Jew knew something, didn't he? And the pathological Havlicek shot his head off finding out what it was. Then you covered for him because he'd found *you* out, and no doubt found the girl as well. You need him now; he could blow you apart. You made your accommodation with him. You told him the truth, you had to. It all goes back to the Costa Brava doesn't it?'

'*You* go back to the Costa Brava!'

'Certainly. We were on our way to the total compromise of one of the most powerful men in the Western world. We wanted to make sure it was done right. You didn't have the stomachs for it. We did.'

'But you didn't know why. You still *don't*!'

'It never mattered, can't you see that? He was going insane. You, with your extraordinary expectations, were driving him insane; he was a gifted man doing the work of twenty. The Georgian syndrome, Emory. Stalin was a babbling idiot when he was killed. All we had to do with Matthias was fuel his fantasies, gratify his every whim, grievance and suspicion . . . encourage his madness. Because that madness compromised this country into its own madness.'

'There's no compromise now. Only annihilation. Extinction.'

Pierce nodded his head slowly. 'There's the risk, of course, but one can't be afraid to fail.'

'Now *you're* the one who's insane!'

'Not at all. The extinction would be yours, the annihilation yours. That court of world opinion you whiningly appeal to so frequently would see to it. And right now all that matters is that we find the man who singlehandedly ushered Anton Matthias into his disintegration, those documents given to us. Don't worry about Havlicek; you were going to put him "beyond-salvage", we weren't.'

'You did. *You* did!'

'At the time it was right. It isn't now. Now he'll help us. I wasn't joking before; he's one of the most talented men you've ever fielded, a very accomplished hunter. With *his* expertise and what *we* know, we'll find the man who'll bring this government to its knees.'

'I've told people who you are!' whispered Bradford. '*What* you are!'

'I'd have been followed at the airport – especially the airport – and I wasn't. You didn't tell anyone because you didn't know until a few minutes ago. I'm far too important a figure for such speculations from a man like you. You've made too many mistakes; you can't afford any more. This city doesn't like you, Mr Undersecretary.'

'Havelock will kill you on sight.'

'I'm sure he would if he could see us, but that's his problem, isn't it. We *know* Havlicek; he doesn't know us; he doesn't know me. That puts him at quite a disadvantage. We'll just watch him; it's all we have to do.'

'You'll never find him!' Bradford lurched to his left, instantly blocked by Pierce, who shoved him against the wall.

'Don't, Emory. You're tired and very weak. Before you could raise your voice you'd be dead. As for finding him, how many safe houses are there? Steriles one to seventeen? And who wouldn't tell a man like me – a man involved with numerous diplomatic "defections" – which ones are available? I've brought in several enviable catches – or presumed catches.' Pierce took several steps, once again standing in front of Bradford. 'Now, don't die. Tell me. Where is this catastrophic document? I assume it's a photostat. The original is held over your head, a nuclear sword on a very thin thread.'

'Where you could never find it.'

'I believe you,' said the traveller. 'But you could.'

'There's no way . . . could or would.'

'Unfortunately, I believe that, too.'

There was a brief snapping sound as Pierce suddenly thrust out his right hand, gripping Bradford's bare arm, pressing his palm into the flesh. With his left, the mole simultaneously reached up and clamped his fingers over Bradford's mouth, twisting the Undersecretary's body, arching him to the side. In seconds, Bradford's eyes widened, then closed as the choking sounds from his throat were muted. He collapsed to the floor, as Pierce withdrew the palmed needle. The mole raced behind the desk and picked up the tape container; beneath it was a note on headed stationery. He reached for the telephone, pressed the outside-line button and dialled.

'Federal Bureau of Investigation, New York Office,' a voice answered.

'Internal Security, please. Field Agent Abrams.'

'Abrams,' said a male voice seconds later.

'Your travels went well, I hope.'

'A smooth flight,' was the reply. 'Go ahead.'

'There's a network executive,' continued Pierce, reading the note, 'an R. B. Denning at the Trans American News Division. He supplied library footage to the wrong man at State, an unbalanced man named Bradford whose motives were offensive to the interests of the United States government. The tapes were destroyed by Bradford in a rage, but for the good of Trans Am's news department – the entire company as well, of course – Denning's officially advised to say nothing. The Department of State feels it mandatory to contain the embarrassment, et cetera, et cetera. This is a very green light.'

'I'll reach him right away even if he's into his second martini.'

'You could add that State might be reluctant to deal with Trans Am in the future, insofar as they delivered company materials without checking the source of the request through proper channels. However, if everyone co-operates for the good of the country . . .'

'The picture will be clear,' interrupted the *paminyatchik* from New York. 'I'll get on to it.'

Pierce hung up, walked to the television set and carefully moved it back against the wall. He would have the video-recorder taken away, sent to another office. There would be no hint of the newsreel tapes or any way to trace them.

There was no prolonged, agonized scream, no cry of protest against offending gods or mortals – only the sound of shattering of glass in the huge window as a body plummeted downward from the seventh floor of the State Department.

It was said by those who had seen him that morning that it was the way he had to go – in a moment of frenzy, of total despair, wanting it over with, not wanting to think any longer. The pressures had become overpowering; he had never really recovered from those soul-searching days of the late 'sixties, everyone knew that. He was a man whose time had come and gone, and he had never reasoned out the role he had played in its arrival and departure. Substance had eluded him; at the end he was a voice in the shadows, a voice disturbing to many, but dismissed by many others because he couldn't *do* anything.

The press printed it all in the evening editions, the obituaries ranging from kind to cool, depending on their editorial stripe. But it should be noted that none were very long; no one really cared. Inconsistency was not compatible with that most desirable of political sins: type-casting. To change was to be weak. We want Jesus or the strong-jawed cowboy. Who the hell can be both?

Undersecretary of State Emory Bradford, committed hawk turned passionate dove, was dead. By his own hand, of course.

And there was no odd piece of equipment such as a video recorder in the stand beneath the television set. It had been delivered to the wrong office, a G-12 on the third floor confirming his original request. The set was pushed back against the wall. Apparently unused.

30

'You couldn't have prevented it,' said Jenna firmly, standing in front of Havelock at the desk. 'You're not permitted to go to the State Department and it's a condition you accept. If the mole saw you he'd either kill you quietly and remain where he was, or bolt and run to Moscow. You want him, and your being seen isn't the way to find him.'

'Maybe I couldn't have prevented it but I might have let his death – his life – mean more than it did. He wanted to tell me and I told him not to say any more. He said this phone was as sterile as the house and I wouldn't accept that.'

'That's not what you said. You told him *his* phone, *his* office, might not be sterile. From everything you've learned over the years, everything you've seen, you made the logical decision. And I still believe there are *paminyatchiks* in your State Department who would lie for this man, tap an office for him.'

'You know, a paranoid named McCarthy said things like that and tore this country apart thirty years ago. Tore it apart with fear and frenzy.'

'Perhaps he was one himself. Who could have done it better?'

'It's possible. The *paminyatchik* is the total patriot. He'll call for a loyalty oath every time because he had no compunction about signing one.'

'That's what you must look for now, Mikhail. A total patriot, a man with an unblemished record. He will be the mole.'

'If I could find out what it was Bradford was waiting for yesterday, I think I'd have both. He said he wouldn't know until "late morning". That means he expected something that would tell him where a man wasn't, proof someone on the fifth floor wasn't where he was supposed to be. The security desk said Bradford received a package at 12:25, but no one knows what it was, and naturally it wasn't there later.'

'There was no return address or company name?'

'If there was, nobody noticed. It was delivered by messenger.'

'Check the firms who provide those services. Certainly someone can recall the colour of the uniform; that would narrow it down.'

'She wasn't that kind of messenger. She wore a fur-collared tweed coat and the only thing security remembers is that she was pretty high-toned for delivering packages.'

'High-toned?'

'Attractive, well-spoken, direct. I think that covers it.'

'Someone's secretary.'

'Yes, but whose? What sort of person would Bradford go to, what kind of proof?'

'What was the size of the package?'

'The guard who took it up said it was a large, padded envelope with a bulge in the bottom, and thick throughout. Papers and something else.'

'Papers?' said Jenna. 'Newspapers? Could he have gone to a newspaper?'

'He might have. Four-month-old clippings that would describe an event or events during that time. Or he could have pulled in data from the CIA; he had friends there: something from the files that pertained to the evidence against you, or perhaps Costa Brava . . . something we've overlooked. Or he could have been checking hospitals, or ski lodges, or home towns, small town neighbourhoods or divorce court dockets – representation *in absentia*, or Caribbean resort reservations – signatures on meal and bar checks, a *maître d'hôtel* or a beach boy who makes his money by remembering. It's all possible because everything I've said pertains to someone in these records.' Michael touched the sheaf of pages on the desk, running his thumb along the edge. 'And a dozen other possibilities I haven't even thought about.' Havelock leaned back in the chair, folding his hands under his chin. 'Our man's good, Jenna. He'll cover himself with a layer of invisible paint.'

'Then go on to something else.'

'I am. A doctor in Maryland. Talbot County's most revered physician.'

'Mikhail?'

'Yes?'

'Before . . . you were reading the reports of your own therapy at the clinic. After the Costa Brava.'

'How did you know?'

'Every now and then you'd close your eyes. Those pages weren't easy for you.'

'They weren't easy.'

'Did they tell you anything?'

'No. Other than describing your execution and my reactions to it, nothing.'

'May I seem them.'

'I wish to Christ I could think of a reason to stop you. I can't.'

'Your not wanting me to is reason enough.'

'No, it's not. You were the one being killed; you have to know.' He opened the drawer on his right, reached in and pulled out a thick, black-bordered manila envelope. He gave it to her, their eyes briefly locking. 'I'm not proud of it,' he said. 'And I'll have to live with it for the rest of my life. I know what that means now.'

'We'll help each other . . . for the rest of both our lives. I believed them too.'

She carried the envelope to the couch, sat down and opened it, removing the file folders inside. They were in sequence; she picked up the first and leaned slowly back, looking at the object in her hands as though it were some horrible yet holy thing. She opened the cover and began reading.

Havelock could not move, could not concentrate. He sat rigid in the chair, the papers in front of him blurred, dark lines without meaning. While Jenna read, he relived that terrible night; images flashed across his inner vision and exploded inside his head. Just as he had watched her die, she was now witnessing the naked thoughts of a mind in chemical therapy – *his* mind, his deepest emotions – and was watching him die also.

The phrases – the screams – came back to him; she was hearing them too. She had to be, for it was she who now closed her eyes and held her breath, a tremor developing in her hands as she went on . . . and on. She finished the third folder and he could feel her staring at him. It was a look he could not return. The screams were pounding in his ears, thunderbolts of intolerable violence, unforgiveable errors. Betrayal.

Go quickly! Die quickly! Leave me quickly! You were never mine. You were a lie and I loved a lie but you were never part of me! . . . How can you be what you are, yet so much that you are not? Why did you do this to us? To me? You were the only thing I had and now you're my personal hell . . . Die now, go now! . . . No! For God's sake, let me die with you! I want to die . . . but I won't die for you! . . . Only for myself, against myself! Never for you. You gave yourself to me but you gave me a whore and I took a whore . . . and I believed in the whore. A rotten slut of a whore! . . . Oh, Christ, she's hit! She's hit again. Go to her! For God's sake, go to her! Hold her! . . . No, never to her! It's over! It's all over and it's history and I won't listen to the lies any longer. Oh, Jesus, she's crawling, crawling in the sand like a cut up, bleeding animal. She's alive! Go to her! Hold her! Lessen the final pain – with a bullet if you have to! No! . . . She's gone. There's no movement now, only blood on her hands and streaked through her hair. She's dead and a part of me is dead, too. Still, it's got to be history, as the early days are history . . . Oh, my God, they're dragging her away, dragging the lanced, dead animal away. Who? Who are they? Have I seen . . . photographs, files . . . it doesn't matter. Do they know what they've done? Did she? Killer, slut, whore! . . . My one, my only love. It's history now, it has to be history. A killer is gone . . . love gone. A fool survives.

She had finished. She placed the last file on the coffee table in front of her and turned to him; she was crying, silently. 'So much love and so much hatred. Hatred and self-hatred. I wasn't forced to go through what you did; perhaps it was easier, if more bewildering, to be the victim. But when the bewilderment was replaced by anger, I *felt* the way you did. Hating you so very much, yet loathing myself for the hatred, never forgetting the love that I knew – I *knew* – had been there. It couldn't have been false, not so much, not all of it. The anger took over at the border and later at the airfield in Col des Moulinets when I thought you had come to finally kill me. Kill me with the violence you had shown that woman on the pier at Civitavecchia. I saw your face through the window of the plane and – if there's a God may He forgive me – you were my enemy. My love was my enemy.'

'I remember,' said Michael. 'I saw your eyes and I remember the cold, immaculate hatred. I tried to shout, tried to tell you, but you couldn't hear me; I couldn't hear myself through the sound of the engines. But your eyes were weapons that night, more frightening than any I'd ever faced. I wouldn't have the courage to see them again, but I suppose in a way I always will.'

'Only in your memory, Mikhail.'

The telephone rang. Havelock let it ring again. He could not take his gaze off Jenna. Then he picked it up.

'Yes?'

'Havelock?'

'Mr President.'

'Did you get the information on Emory?' asked Berquist, the Minnesotan's voice laced with sadness and exhaustion, yet forcing an illusion of strength.

'Nowhere near what I need.'

'What you need is a liaison. I'll pick someone here at the White House, someone with authority and a man I can trust. I'll have to bring him on board, but that can't be helped. Bradford's gone and you *do* need a funnel.'

'Not yet, sir. And not anyone at the White House.'

There was a pause from Washington. 'Because of what Rostov told you in Athens?'

'Possibly. The percentages are minor but I'd rather not test them. Not now.'

'You *believed* him?'

'With all due respect, Mr President, he was the only one who told me the truth. From the beginning.'

'Why would he tell you a truth like that?'

'I'm not sure. On the other hand, why did he send Cons Op that cable? In both instances the information was sufficiently startling to force us all to pay attention. That's the first step in sending a signal.'

'Addison Brooks said very much the same thing.'

'He was talking diplomatically, and he was right. The *Voennaya* doesn't speak for Moscow.'

'I understand. Bradford –' Berquist paused, as if he suddenly remembered he was referring to a dead man. 'Bradford explained it to me last night. So you really believe there's a Soviet agent operating inside the White House?'

'As I said, I'm not sure. But there may be – or more than likely, may have been. I don't think Rostov would have brought it up unless he could have substantiated the reality, present or past. He was probing, looking for responses. The truth provokes the most genuine answers in this business; he learned that when he brought up Costa Brava. In this case, I don't want to take the risk.'

'All right, but then, how can you function? You can't be seen walking around questioning people.'

'No, but I can't question them without being seen. I can use the phone if it's set up properly. I know what I want to ask and I'll know what to listen for. From these conversations I'll refine whom I want to see and set up contacts . . . I'm experienced in this, Mr President.'

'I don't have to take your word for that. How is it set up . . . properly?'

'Give me a name, and call me an assistant counsel to the President, or something like that. It's not unusual for the Oval Office to make its own discreet inquiries into certain matters, is it?'

'Hell, no, I've got a staff for that, and it's not necessarily discreet. Hundreds of reports are sent to the White House every week. They have to be checked out, experts questioned, figures substantiated. Without it all, responsible decisions can't be made. In Lincoln's time he had two young men and they took care of everything including the drafting of letters. Now we have scores of aides and assistants to aides and secretaries to assistants and they can't handle half the volume. The answer is yes.'

'What happens if someone is called by an aide or an assistant aide and that someone doubts the authority of the person questioning him?'

'It happens a lot, especially at the Pentagon; there's a simple solution. He's told to call the White House switchboard and ask to be connected to the aide's or the assistant's office. It works.'

'It *will* work,' said Michael. 'Along with the lines already on this phone can you add another one, listing me in the White House index, the extension routed here?'

'Havelock, one of the more exotic pleasures in being President, or close to a President, is the trunk full of electronic gimmickry available on short notice. You'll be indexed and patched into the switchboard within the hour. What name do you want to use?'

'You'll have to choose one, sir. I might duplicate someone already there.'

'I'll call you back.'

'Mr President, before you hang up.'

'What is it?'

'I'll need another one of those things that may not be in your lexicon. A context back-up.'

'It sure as hell isn't. What is it?'

'In the event someone calls the White House index and wants to know exactly what I do, there should be someone else there who can tell him.'

Again there was the pause from Washington. 'You were right down on Poole's Island,' said Berquist pensively. 'The words say exactly what they mean, don't they? You need someone to back you up in the context of what you're presuming to do, or be.'

'That's right, sir.'

'Call you back.'

'May I suggest something?' said Michael quickly.

'What?'

'Within the next few days – if we have a few days – someone is going to come up to that someone else in the White House and ask where my office is. When he or she does, hold him – or her – because whoever it is will bring us a step closer.'

'If that happens,' said Berquist angrily, 'whoever-it-is may be strangled by a Minnesota farm boy before you get a chance to talk to him. Or her.'

'I'm sure you don't mean that, Mr President.'

'I'm not going to throw a nuclear warhead on Leningrad either. Call you back.'

Havelock replaced the phone and looked over at Jenna. 'We can begin narrowing down the names. We'll start calling in an hour.'

'Your name is Cross. Robert Cross. Your title is special assistant to the President, and all inquiries as to your status and functions are to be directed to Mrs Howell, she's counsel to White House internal affairs. She's been told what to do.'

'What about my office?'

'You've got one.'

'What?'

'You've even got an assistant. In the security area of the east office block. You need a key to get in the main corridor over there, and your man is instructed to take into custody anyone who comes around looking for Mr Cross. He's a member of the secret service detail and if anyone does show up asking for you he'll alert you and bring that person down to Fairfax under guard. I assumed that's what you wanted.'

'It is. What about the other offices in that area? Will the people in them be curious?'

'Unlikely. By and large those assignments are temporary, everyone working on his own quiet project. Curiosity's discouraged. And if it surfaces, you've got your man in place.'

'It sounds tight.'

'I think so. Where are you going to start? . . . Emory showed me the list of the items you wanted and assured me you'd have it all in the morning. Did you get everything?'

'Everything. Bradford's secretary is first, then the doctor in Maryland. MacKenzie's death.'

'We were extremely thorough with him,' said Berquist. 'Under the circumstances we were able to bring in the Central Intelligence Agency and those people were aggressive. What are you looking for?'

'I'm not sure. Someone who's not around any more, perhaps. A puppet.'

'I won't try to follow that.'

'I may need your direct intervention in one area, however. You said before that the Pentagon frequently balks at being questioned by White House personnel.'

'It goes with the uniforms; they're not worn over here. I expect you're referring to the Nuclear Contingency Committees. I saw them on your list.'

'I am.'

'They're touchy. Rightly so, I'd say.'

'I have to talk to every member of those three teams; that's fifteen senior officers. Can you get word to the chairman that you expect them all to co-operate with Mr Cross? Not in the area of maximum restricted information, but in terms of . . . progress evaluation.'

'One of those phrases again.'

'It says it Mr President. It would help if you could work Matthias in.'

'All right,' said Berquist slowly. 'I'll lay it on the great man. It's not in character, but he can hardly deny it. I'll have my military aide convey the word: the Secretary of State wants those committees to provide an in-depth progress report for the Oval Office. A simple memorandum ordering co-operation within the limits of maximum classification should do it . . . They'll say there's a cross-over, of course. You can't have one without violating the other.'

'Then tell them to err on the side of classification. The final report's for your eyes only anyway.'

'Anything else?'

'The psychiatric file on Matthias. Bradford was to have got it for me.'

'I'm going to Camp David tomorrow. I'll take a detour by Poole's Island and bring it back with me.'

'One thing more. This Mrs Howell; apart from calling in the secret service if anyone approaches her about me, what has she been told to say? About me, my functions?'

'Only that you're on a special assignment for the President.'

'Can you change it?'

'To what?'

'Routine assignment. Researching old agendas so that White House files can be completed on various matters.'

'We have people doing that. It's basically political – how is this position defended, or why did that senator buck us and how do we stop him from doing it again?'

'Put me in with the crowd.'

'You're in it. Good luck . . . but then you'll need a great deal more than luck. This world needs more than luck. Sometimes I think we need a miracle to last another week . . . Keep me informed; my orders are that whenever Mr Cross calls, I'm to be interrupted.'

Bradford's secretary, one Elizabeth Andrews, was at home, the sensational death of her superior having had its emotional impact. A number of newspaper people had telephoned her and she had relayed the events of the morning calmly, sadly, but clearly, until a gossip-oriented reporter, noting Bradford's marital track record, hinted at a sexual entanglement.

'You sick bitch,' Elizabeth had said, slamming down the phone.

Havelock's call came twenty minutes later and Elizabeth Andrews was not eager to recount the tale again. He suggested she call him back at the White House when she felt better; the ploy worked. The phone in the study in Fairfax rang six minutes after Michael had hung up.

'I'm sorry, Mr Cross. It's been a very trying time and some very trying reporters.'

'I'll be as brief as possible.'

She described the morning, beginning with Bradford's sudden and unexpected emergence from his office shortly after she had arrived.

'He looked dreadful. He'd obviously been up all night and was exhausted, but there was something else. A kind of manic energy; he was excited about something. I've seen him like that lots of times, of course, but somehow yesterday it was different. He spoke louder than he usually did.'

'That could have been the exhaustion,' said Havelock. 'It often works that way. A person compensates because he feels weak.'

'Perhaps, but I don't think so, not with him, not yesterday morning. I know it sounds ghastly, but I think he'd made up his mind . . . that's a horrible thing to say, but I believe it. It was as though he were exhilarated, actually looking forward to the moment when it was going to happen. It's ghoulish, but he left the office shortly before ten, said he was going out for a few minutes, and I have this terrible picture of him out on the street, looking up at the window . . . and thinking to himself, Yes, this is it.'

'Could there be another explanation? Could he have been going to see someone?'

'No, I don't think so. I asked him if he'd be in another office in case a call came for him and he said no, he was going out for some air.'

'He never mentioned why he'd been there all night?'

'Only that he'd been working on a project that he'd fallen behind on. He'd been doing a fair amount of travelling recently – '

'Did you set up the transportation arrangements for him?' interrupted Havelock.

'No, he usually did that himself. As you probably know, he often . . . took someone with him. He was divorced, several times actually. He was a very private person, Mr Cross. And so very unhappy.'

'Why do you say that?'

Ms Andrews paused, then spoke firmly. 'Emory Bradford was a brilliant man, and they didn't pay attention to him. He was once very influential in this city until he told the truth – as he saw the truth – and as soon as the applause died down, they all ran away from him.'

'You've been with him a long time.'

'A long time. I saw it all happen.'

'Could you give me examples of this running away from him?'

'Sure. To begin with he was consistently overlooked when his experience, his expertise could have been of value. Then he'd frequently write position papers, correcting powerful men and women – senators, congressmen, secretaries of this and that – who had made stupid mistakes in interviews and press conferences; but if one out of ten ever responded or thanked him, I never knew about it, and I would have. He'd monitor the early morning television programmes, where the worst gaffes are made – just as he was doing yesterday, right up to the end – and dictate what he called clarifications. They were always gentle, even kind, never offensive, and sure enough "clarifications" were usually issued, but never any thanks.'

'He was watching television yesterday morning?'

'For a while . . . before it happened. At least the set was rolled out to the front of his desk. He moved it back . . . before it happened. Right up until the end he couldn't break the habit. He wanted people to be better than they were; he wanted the government to be better.'

'Were there any notes on his desk that could have told you whom he was watching?'

'No, nothing. It was like his final gesture, leaving this world tidier than he'd found it. I've never seen his desk so neat, so clean.'

'I'm sure you didn't.'

'I beg your pardon.'

'Nothing. I was agreeing with you . . . I know you were at lunch, but were there any people in the vicinity of his office door who might have seen someone go in or out?'

'The police covered that, Mr Cross. There are always people milling around; we all have different lunch breaks depending on what's happening in what time zone, but no one saw anything unusual. Actually, our section was pretty much cleared out. We had a secretarial pool meeting at one-thirty, so most of us – '

'Who called that meeting, Miss Andrews?'

'This month's chairman; then, of course, he said he didn't, so we sat around drinking coffee.'

'Didn't you get a memo about the meeting?'

'No, the word was just passed around this morning. It frequently is; that's standard.'

'Thank you very much. You've been most helpful.'

'It's all such a waste, Mr Cross. Such a goddamned terrible waste.'

'I know. Goodbye.' Havelock hung up and spoke, his eyes still on the phone. 'Our man *is* good,' he said. 'Invisible paint.'

'She couldn't tell you anything?'

'Yes, she did. Bradford listened to me. He went outside to a phone and called for whatever it was he wanted. The number we need won't be found charged to his office; it's among a couple of million lost in the underground trunk lines.'

'Nothing else?'

'Maybe something.' Michael looked over at Jenna, a frown on his face, his eyes clouded. 'See if you can find a copy of yesterday's paper around here, will you? I want to know the name of every senior official at State who was interviewed on the morning television programmes. It's crazy. The last thing on Bradford's mind was television.'

Jenna found the newspaper. No one from the Department of State had been on television that morning.

31

If Talbot County, Maryland, had an esteemed physician in Dr Matthew Randolph, it also had an extremely unpleasant man. Born to Eastern Shore money, raised in the tradition of privilege which included the finest schools and clubs, and possessing what amounted to unlimited funds, he nevertheless abused everyone and everything within these rarefied circles in the pursuit of medicine.

When he was thirty, having graduated *magna cum laude* from Johns Hopkins and completed pathological and surgical residencies at Massachusetts General and New York, he decided he could not function at his talented best within the stultifying, politicized confines of a normal hospital. The answer for him was simple; he bullied and extorted monies from the legions of the Chesapeake privileged, threw in an initial two million dollars himself and opened his own fifty-bed medical centre.

It was run his way, which amounted to a none too benevolent dictatorship. There was no exclusivity with regard to admission but there was a rule-of-thumb policy: the rich was soaked outrageously for services rendered, and the poor given financial consideration only after having endured the ignominy of disclosing overwhelming proof of poverty and listening to a lecture on the sins of indolence. Rich and poor alike, however, continued in growing numbers to put up with these insults for, over the years, the Randolph Medical Center had established a reputation that was second to none. Its laboratory equipment was the finest money could buy; its generously paid staff physicians were the brightest graduates from the best schools and toughest residencies; the visiting surgical and pathological specialists were flown in from all over the globe, and the talents of the overpaid technicians and nursing corps far in excess of normal hospital standards. In essence, treatment at Randolph was both medically superb and personally gratifying. The only way it might be improved upon, some said, was to remove the abrasive personality of the now sixty-eight-year-old Matthew Randolph. However, others pointed out that one way to cripple a smoothly running craft in rough waters was to tear out the throttle because the engine pitch was grating to the ears. And in Randolph's case, short of his own death – which seemed unlikely for several centuries – physically tearing him out was the only way to remove him.

Besides, who else could look down at a nephew of Emile du Pont just before an operation and ask: 'how much is your life worth to you?'

In the du Pont case, it was a million-dollar-plus tie-in computer with four of the nation's leading research centres.

Havelock learned these details from CIA files as he researched the death of a black operations officer named Steven MacKenzie, the 'engineer' of Costa Brava. In Cagnes-sur-Mer, Henri Salanne had by implication questioned the veracity of the doctor who signed MacKenzie's death certificate. In his own mind Michael had gone further; he had considered altered laboratory reports, autopsy findings not consistent with the state of the corpse and, after the President had mentioned X-rays, the obvious switching of photographic plates. However, in the light of the information on Randolph and his Medical Center, it was difficult to credit these possibilities. Everything connected to and with the official cause of death was processed under Randolph's personal on-site attendance and his own laboratories. The abrasive doctor might well be dictatorial, certainly petulant, most definitely opinionated and unpleasant, but if ever there was a person who deserved to be called a man of integrity it was Matthew Randolph. The same was true of his Medical Center. All things considered – *all* things – there was no reason on earth for either to be otherwise.

And for Havelock, that was the flaw. It was simply too symmetrical. Pieces rarely, if ever, fell in place – even negatively – so precisely. There were always caves to explore that might lead to hidden pools – whether they did or not was irrelevant, the caves were *there*. Here, there were none.

The first indication Michael had that there might be substance to his doubts was the fact that Matthew Randolph did not return his first call. In every other instance, including calls to eight senior officers of the Pentagon's Nuclear Contingency Committees, Bradford's secretary, CIA and NSC personnel, the phone in Fairfax had rung minutes after he had placed the contact call. One did not dismiss lightly a request to reach a presidential aide at the White House.

Dr Matthew Randolph apparently felt no such compulsion. And so Havelock had phoned a second time only to be told: 'The doctor is extremely busy today. He said to say he'll get back to you, Mr Cross, when he has the free time.'

'Did you explain that I'm to be reached at the White House?'

'Yes, sir.' The secretary had paused, embarrassment in her brief silence. 'He said to tell you the Center's painted white, too,' she added in a very soft voice. '*He* said that, Mr Cross, *I* didn't.'

'Then tell Genghis Khan from me that I'll either hear from him within the hour or he may find the sheriff of Talbot County escorting him to the DC–Maryland border, where a White House detail will pick him up and bring him down here.'

Matthew Randolph returned the call, in fifty-eight minutes.

'Who the *hell* do you think you are, Cross?'

'An extremely overworked nonentity, Dr Randolph.'

'You threatened me! I don't like threats, whether they come from the White House or a blue house or an outhouse! I trust you get my meaning.'

'I'll convey your feelings to the President.'

'Do that. He's not the worst, but I could think of better.'

'You might even get along.'

'I doubt it. Sincere politicians bore me. Sincerity and politics are diametrically opposed. What do you want? If it's any kind of endorsement, you can start with a healthy government research grant.'

'I have an idea President Berquist might entertain that idea only if you openly opposed him.'

Randolph paused. 'Not bad,' he said. 'What do you want? We're busy here.'

'I want to ask you several questions about a man – a dead man – named Steven MacKenzie.'

Again the doctor paused, but it was a different silence. And when he resumed speaking, it was in a different tone. Previously his hostility was genuine; now it was forced.

'Damn it, how many times do we have to go over that? MacKenzie died of stroke – a massive aortal haemorrhage to be precise. I turned over the pathology report and conferred with your spook doctors till hell froze over. They've got it all.'

'*Spook* doctors?'

'They sure as hell weren't from Mary-General or Baltimore's Mother of Mercy, I can tell you. Nor did they claim to be.' Randolph paused again; Michael did not fill the moment. He was listening with a trained ear, silences and audible breathing being a part of the abstract tonal picture he was trying to define. The doctor continued, his phrases too rushed, the edge of his voice too sharp; his previous confidence was waning, replaced by volume alone. 'You want any information on MacKenzie, you get it from them. We all concurred; there was never any doubt. Aortal haemorrhage, plain and simple, and I don't have the time to rehash this sort of thing. Do I make myself clear?'

'More than you know, Dr Randolph.' It was Havelock's turn to pause. He did so until he could see in his mind's eye a mouth that had dropped open, and hear the aggressive breathing of a man with something to hide. 'I'd find the time, if I were you. The file isn't closed here, Doctor, and for reasons of specific external pressures we can't shut it – much as we'd like to. You see, we *want* to conclude it precisely the way you determined, but we have to co-operate with each other. Do *I* make myself clear?'

'The pathology was unequivocal, you all agree with that?'

'We *want* to. Please understand that. Be convinced of it.'

'What do you mean "external pressures"?' The doctor's confidence was returning, the question asked sincerely.

'Let's say in-house intelligence trouble makers. We'd like to shut them up.'

Costa Brava was never far away. Even in deceit.

Randolph's final pause was brief. 'Come up tomorrow,' he said. 'Be here at noon.'

Havelock sat in the back seat of the nondescript, armour-plated car; three secret service men were his companions. Conversation was at a minimum. The two men in front and the pleasant but quiet agent beside Michael had obviously been ordered to make no direct inquiries.

The Randolph Medical Center was indeed painted white. It was a glistening complex of three buildings connected by enclosed walkways set down in the middle of a generous acreage of lawns, paths and a central winding driveway. They parked in the nearest available space to the entrance labelled Admissions and Administration. Michael got out of the car, walked up the smooth concrete path that led to the glass double doors and went inside; he was expected.

'Dr Randolph's in his office, Mr Cross,' said a uniformed nurse behind the marble counter. 'Take the first corridor to your right; his is the last door at the end of the hall. I'll tell his secretary you're on your way.'

'Thank you.'

As he walked down the spotless white corridor towards Randolph's office, Havelock considered the options available to him. How much he told the doctor depended upon how much Randolph already knew about Steven MacKenzie. If what he knew was little, Michael's words would be laced with security-conscious innuendo. If a great deal, there was no harm in corroborating parts of the truth. However, what primarily concerned

Havelock was the reason behind the doctor's extraordinary behaviour. The man as much as admitted having twisted or concealed *some* aspect of MacKenzie's death and, regardless of whether he considered it minor or not, it was a dangerous act. Tampering with cause-of-death or withholding pertinent information was a criminal act. What had the physician done and why had he done it? Even to consider Matthew Randolph as part of an intelligence conspiracy was absurd, irrational. What had he done?

A stern-visaged secretary with disciplined angry hair pulled back and lashed into a bun rose from her chair, but her voice contradicted her appearance; it was the same voice that had relayed the doctor's comment about his medical centre being the same colour as the White House. It was obvious that she had thrown up a wall to protect herself from the Randolph hurricane.

'He's very upset today, Mr Cross,' she said in that frail, intense tone. 'You'll do better getting straight to your business. He hates to waste time.'

'So do I,' replied Michael, as the woman escorted him to an ornate, panelled door. She rapped twice – not once or three times, but precisely twice, standing motionless with splendid posture as though she were about to refuse a blindfold.

The cause of her stoicism was soon apparent. The door opened, revealing a tall, slender, angular man with a fringe of light grey hair circling a bald head, the eyes behind the steel-rimmed glasses alive and impatient. Dr Matthew Randolph was rich American Gothic, with not a little of Savonarola thrown in, his long graceful hands somehow appropriate for holding a pitchfork, a torch or a scalpel. He looked past his secretary and barked; he did not speak.

'You Cross?'

'Yes.'

'You're eight minutes late.'

'Your watch is fast.'

'Maybe. Come on in.' He now looked at his secretary, who had stepped aside. 'No interruptions,' he instructed.

'Yes, Dr Randolph.'

The physician closed the door and nodded at the chair in front of his large, cluttered desk. 'Sit down,' he said, 'but before you do, I want to make sure you don't have one of those recording machines on you.'

'You have my word.'

'Is it any good?'

'Is yours?'

'You called me. I didn't call you.'

Havelock shook his head. 'I have no taping device on me for the simple reason that our conversations could be far more harmful to us than to you.'

'Maybe,' muttered Randolph, going behind the desk as Michael sat down. 'Maybe not. We'll see.'

'That's a promising beginning.'

'Don't get smart ass, young fella.'

'I apologize if I sounded that way. I meant it. We have a problem and you could put it to rest.'

'Meaning I didn't before.'

'Let's say there are new questions and, frankly, they may be valid. Certainly they could be embarrassing, not only politically, but in terms of morale in certain areas of the intelligence community. Someone might even care to go into print. That's our problem.'

'That's what I want to hear.' The physician nodded, adjusting his glasses so as to look over the steel rims. 'Your problem. Spell it out.'

Havelock understood. Randolph wanted an admission of guilt from the White House before he would implicate himself in any conceivable wrong-doing. Therefore, it was reasonable to assume that the more serious Havelock's first admission, the more latitude Randolph would permit himself regarding his own possible duplicity. Thieves in concert and conversation; who could go screaming to a judge?

'Do you know the kind of work MacKenzie was involved in?'

'I've known Mac and his family for over forty years. His parents were close friends of mine and his three children were born right here at the Center. I delivered them myself – probably delivered his wife, Midge, too.'

'That doesn't answer my question.'

'It should. I've been caring for the MacKenzies most of their lives and that included young Steve, as well as the adult Steve – as far as you permitted him to live as an adult. Actually, to be more accurate, these past years I more or less double-checked whatever the doctors did at Walter Reed; by and large they were damned good. You could hardly tell from the scars that four of them were bullet wounds.'

'Then you did know,' said Michael, nodding.

'I told him to get out. My God, I told him that over and over again for the last five, six years now. The strain on him was something fierce – worse, I think, for Midge. Him flying all over the world, she never knowing whether he'd come back; not that he ever told her a hell of a lot, he wouldn't do that . . . Yes, Mr Cross, I knew what Steve did – not the specifics or his title or anything like that, but I knew it wasn't your everyday desk job.'

'It's strange,' mused Havelock, indeed sensing the strangeness. 'I never thought of MacKenzie as having a wife and children, coming from a relatively normal background.' *He was not a survivor. Why did he do it?*

'Maybe that's why he was so good. You looked at him and saw a pretty average successful executive . . . something like you, in fact. But underneath he had a fever because you bastards poisoned him.'

The suddenness of the charge, its harshness, and the fact that it was delivered in a conversational tone was unnerving. 'That's quite a statement,' said Michael, his eyes roaming over the doctor's face. 'Would you care to explain it? To the best of my knowledge, no one held a gun to MacKenzie's head and told him to do whatever it was he was doing.'

'You didn't have to, and you're damn right I care to explain it. I figure it's your blueprint for *narcotizing* a man so that he turns away from a normal, productive, reasonably happy life to one where he wakes up in a cold sweat in the middle of the night because he probably hasn't had the luxury of sleeping for the past several weeks. Or, if he does sleep, the first sharp sound sends him lunging for protection. Or a gun.'

'You're very dramatic.'

'It's what you did.'

'How?'

'You fed him a diet of tension, excitement – even frenzy – with fair doses of blood to go with it.'

'Now you're melodramatic.'

'You know where it started for him?' Randolph went on, as if Havelock had not spoken. 'Thirteen, fourteen years ago Mac was one of the best sailors on the Eastern Shore, probably the Atlantic coast and the Caribbean, too. He could sense a new wind and smell the currents. He could look at the stars in a dark sky and helm a craft – engine or sail – all through the night and take you within sight of where he said you'd be by dawn. It was a gift . . . Then came the war in Vietnam and he was a naval officer. Well, it didn't take those brass boys long to spot a good thing. Before you could pronounce one of those unpronounceable places, he was ferrying men and supplies up the coast and the inland waterways. That's where it started. He was the best there was; he could read gook maps and get anybody anywhere.'

'I'm not sure I understand.'

'Then you're thick. He was taking assassination and sabotage teams behind enemy lines. Fleets of small craft were under his command; he was a secret navy all by himself. Then it happened.'

'What?'

'One day he didn't just ferry those people, he became one of them.'

'I see.'

'I wonder if you do. It's where the fever first touched him. Men who were nothing more than cargo became friends he made plans with, fought beside, who died in front of his eyes. He did that for twenty-eight months until he was wounded and sent home. Midge was waiting for him; they got married and he went back to finish law school. Only, he couldn't stand it. Before a year was up, he left, and began talking with people in Washington. A part of him missed that crazy – Christ, I don't know what you call it.'

'It doesn't make any difference,' said Havelock quietly. 'I know what you mean.'

The doctor looked hard at Michael. 'Maybe you do. Maybe that's why you're here . . . Like a lot of men, Mac came back from that war a different person; not on the surface, but underneath. There was an anger in him I'd never seen before, a need to compete – angrily – for the highest stakes he could find. He couldn't sit still for twenty minutes at a time much less absorb the finer points of law. He had to keep moving.'

'Yes, I know,' interrupted Michael involuntarily.

'And you bastards in Washington knew just what to feed him. Get him back into the excitement, the tension. Promise him the best – or worst – competition *you* could find, and make the stakes so high no normal man would consider them. And all the while keep telling him he was the best, the best, the *best!* He thrived on it . . . and at the same time it was tearing him apart.'

Havelock brought his hands together, gripping them, moved both to anger and understanding. It was no time, however, to betray either; he wanted information. 'What should we . . . bastards in Washington . . . have done then?' he asked calmly.

'That's such a stupid question only one of you sons of bitches would ask.'

'Would you mind answering?'

'Get him medical attention! Psychiatric care!'

'Why didn't you? You were his doctor.'

'Damn it, I *tried*! I even tried to *stop* you!'

'I beg your pardon?'

'Somewhere in a number of old files there are letters from me to the Central Intelligence Agency describing – goddamn it, *diagnosing* – a troubled man, a disturbed man. Mac would have come home and for a few weeks he'd cover it, driving back and forth to Langley like a regular commuter. Then you could see it happening; he'd go into a kind of depression, wouldn't talk very much and, when he did, he sure as hell wasn't listening. Then he became restless, impatient . . . his mind always somewhere else. You see, he was *waiting*, waiting for his next *fix!*'

'And we gave it to him,' said Michael.

'Right on, as the youngsters say! You knew exactly how long he could take it. You were priming him, honing his machine until he'd either blow apart or get back into – whatever the hell you call it.'

'The field,' said Havelock.

'That's it, the goddamned *field*! Midge would come to me and tell me Mac was going to pieces, couldn't sleep, wouldn't communicate, and I'd write another letter. You know what I'd get back? A "thank-you-for-your-interest", as though I'd suggested you bastards change your laundry service! Midge and those kids were going through hell, and you people thought your shirts had just the right amount of starch in 'em!'

Michael's eyes strayed to bare white walls behind Randolph. *How many buried letters were there in how many unopened files? How many MacKenzies . . . and Ogilvies . . . and Havelocks? What was the Gunslinger count these days? Men primed, machines honed in the cause of futility. Deadly talents kept in the field because somewhere it was written they could do the job regardless of the mind and body count . . . their own and others. Who profited?*

'I'm sorry,' said Havelock. 'With your permission, I'll report this conversation where it won't be overlooked.'

'So far you've got my permission. Up to now.'

'Up to now,' agreed Michael.

The physician leaned back in his chair. 'I've drawn a picture for you. It's not pretty, but I've got my reasons. Now, you draw one for me and we'll see where we stand.'

'All right.' Havelock crossed his legs, then spoke, choosing his words cautiously. 'As I'm sure you're aware, most intelligence work is dull, pedestrian. It's routine digging for facts, reading newspapers, reports, scientific journals, and gathering information from a wide variety of other sources, the majority of which are reasonable people, perfectly amenable to imparting what they know because they see no reason to conceal it. Then, of course, there are others who are in the business of making a profit by selling the facts they've bought; buy low, sell higher, a time-honoured principle. These people generally deal with a different kind of intelligence officer, one trained to distinguish between fact and fiction; the buy-low, sell-highers can be pretty imaginative.' Michael paused, knowing that the timing of his delivery was vital. 'Normally,' he continued, 'the combination of these sources and the sheer volume of the information they provide is sufficient for specialists to put together an accurate pattern of facts and events, like fitting the pieces of a puzzle together. That's an abused expression, but it says it.' Again Havelock paused. What Randolph wanted – needed – to hear called for a silent introduction. Three seconds were enough. 'Finally, there's a last category of potential information. It's the most difficult to obtain because it has to be extorted from sources that know they possess secrets that could cost them their lives if their superiors knew they had revealed them. These require an entirely different sort of intelligence officer, a specialist himself. He's trained to manipulate, to engineer situations in which individuals are convinced they have no choice but to take a specific course of action, in the end revealing secrets – or doing something – they would not previously have considered. Steven MacKenzie was that kind of specialist, and he *was* one of the best; no one had to convince him. But on his last, his final assignment, someone intercepted and altered the situation MacKenzie had created. And in order for that original situation to remain the accepted one, he was marked for take-out.'

'What the hell is that, a plate of spaghetti?'

'He was killed.'

Randolph shot forward in his chair. 'He was *what?*'

'Murdered. We might have prevented it if we'd taken the proper precautions. That's our problem, Doctor, and a growing number of people know it. "Mac", as you call him, didn't die of a stroke on his boat, he was killed. We're aware of it, but we don't want to acknowledge it . . . Now, you can understand why I don't have any taping device concealed anywhere. The picture I just painted is uglier than yours.'

'It sure as hell is – if it were true. But I'm afraid it isn't. We'll stick to the aortal haemorrhage because it works. You bastards couldn't be farther off base. You blew it.'

'What does that mean?'

'Steven MacKenzie committed suicide.'

32

'That's impossible!' cried Havelock, rising to his feet. 'You're *wrong!*'

'Am I? Are you a doctor, too, Mr Cross?'

'I don't have to be. I know men like MacKenzie. *I* am one!'

'I figured as much, and that statement is about on a par with my assessment of the lot of you.'

'No, don't mistake me,' said Michael quickly, shaking his head emphatically. 'It's no adolescent generalization. I'm the first to admit that the thought of packing it in can become a recurrent fixation, obsessive, but not *this* way. Not alone on a boat. That doesn't work!'

'Sorry. The pathology – the evidence – is against you. I wish to almighty God it wasn't, but it is.'

Havelock could not help himself; he leaned over Randolph's desk and shouted, 'There was evidence against a woman very close to me and that evidence was a lie!'

'I don't know what that's got to do with the price of perfume in Alaska, but it doesn't change anything.'

'In this case, it does. There's a connection!'

'You're downright incoherent, young fella.'

'*Please*. Listen to me. I'm not a "young fella"' and I'm not a raving idiot. Whatever you found you were *meant* to find.'

'You don't even know what it was.'

'I don't *have* to! Try to understand me, Doctor. A black operations officer like MacKenzie . . .'

'A *what*? Mac was white!'

'Oh, Jesus! An engineer, a manipulator . . . a man in sanction, with the authority to bring about events in which people might be killed, usually *are* killed – because it has to be done. More often than I can tell you, men like this have very painful doubts, enormous feelings of guilt, feelings of . . . goddamn it, *futility*! Certainly, depression sets in, sure they've considered blowing their brains out, but not *this* way. There are other ways that make sense because if there's one thing ingrained in such men it's function, function, *function*! For Christ's sake, *take* yourself out, but *accomplish* something when you do it! And do it *right*.'

'That's sub-kindergarten psychobabble,' protested Randolph.

'Call it whatever you like but it's true. It's the first thing, the most *important* thing recruiters look for in a candidate. It's the single overriding factor . . . You said it yourself. You said MacKenzie had to compete – angrily compete – for the highest stakes he could find.'

'Ultimately, he did. Himself.'

'No, that's waste! That's not even making a statement . . . Look, I'm *not* a doctor, not a psychiatrist, and I probably can't convince you, but I know I'm right, so let it pass. Just tell me what you found, what you did.'

'Mac gave himself a needle and let it all drift away.'

'*Never*.'

'Sorry. He was damned smart about it too. He used a steroid compound of digoxin combined with enough alcohol to float an elephant. The alcohol bloodcount overshadowed everything else, but the digoxin blew the heart. It's one hell of a combination.'

'Then the X-ray was valid?'

Randolph did not reply at first. Instead, he pursed his thin lips and fingered his glasses. Then he spoke. 'No.'

'You *did* switch the plates?'

'Yes.'

'Why?'

'To carry out what Mac intended. To make sure.'

'Go back.'

The doctor leaned forward. 'He knew what he'd put Midge and the kids through all these years and it was his way of trying to make up for it, make peace with himself. Midge had had about all she could take; she was finished with pleading. She told him he had to get out of the Agency or get out of the house.' Randolph stopped briefly, shaking his head. 'Mac knew he couldn't do either so he decided to get out, period.'

'You've skipped something.'

'He had a whale of an insurance policy and, considering the work he did – work the insurance company didn't know a damned thing about – it was understandable. Those kinds of policies don't pay on suicide. I was going to be damned before Midge and those kids were cheated out of what they deserved . . . That's the story, Mr Cross. You made him what he was and, together, he and I made him better.'

Havelock stared at the physician, then turned and sat down in the chair, his eyes still on Randolph. 'Even if you were right,' he began wearily, 'and believe me you weren't then – you're not now – you could have spelled it out for the Agency and they'd have gone along with you; the last thing they want is for this sort of killing to get into print. Instead, you put everyone off, wasted valuable time and the damage you've done is incalculable.'

'What in *hell*! Twenty minutes ago you said you *wanted* it my way! Yesterday on the phone you said you wanted to shut up some troublemakers!'

'I lied. Just as you lied. But at least I knew what I was doing; you didn't. If you'd told the truth – if only to one person – every minute of MacKenzie's day would have been examined; something might have turned up, somewhere a connection . . . No one even bothered to go over the boat. Oh, *Christ*!'

'Maybe you didn't *hear* me!' shouted the physician, his eyes wild, his face apoplectic. 'Midge MacKenzie had given her last ultimatum! He was between a rock and a hard place. He couldn't, as you put it, *function* any more! He fell apart!'

'That accounted for the alcohol, I don't doubt it.'

'And when he was plastered he made his final decision. It's all there!'

'It's not there,' said Michael, feeling far older than the elderly doctor in front of him. 'I don't expect you to accept this, but the last thing a man like MacKenzie would do is make a decision when he's drunk.'

'Hogwash!'

'Let me ask you something. I assume you take a drink now and then, and when you do, you know when you've had a few.'

'Certainly.'

'Would you ever operate when you knew you were high?'

'Certainly not, but there's no parallel!'

'Yes, there is, Dr Randolph. Because when men like MacKenzie or myself – twenty or thirty more I could mention – are in the field, *we're* surgeons. They even call most of the jobs we do "operations". It's hammered into us from our first day of training that every reflex, every observation, every reaction has to be as accurate and as fast and as clear as we can make them. We're primed – our machines are honed.'

'You're playing with words – yours *and* mine! Mac wasn't in the field.'

'If what you believe is true, he was. The highest stakes. Himself.'

'*Goddamn* it, you're twisting everything I said!'

'No, I'm not. Because a lot of what you said was as perceptive as I've ever heard it expressed. I respect it . . . Don't you *understand*? MacKenzie wouldn't have killed himself this way because – everything else aside – the digoxin might not have *worked*! And that he *couldn't* accept. It was too much a part of him, had been for far too many years. If it was going to be his final decision, the one thing he couldn't afford was a mistake! Can't you *see* that?'

It was as though Matthew Randolph had been struck. His eyes were wide and fixed, the muscles of his face taut, his mouth rigid. When he spoke, it was a whisper. 'God *almighty* . . .' he said, his voice drifting off into silence. Then softly, unexpectedly, he rose from his chair and stood motionless, a helpless old man struggling with a massive error he did not want to confront. 'Oh, my God,' he added, taking off his glasses, breathing deeply.

Havelock watched him, moved to make things easier. 'You did the right thing by your lights. Mine, too, if I'd been you. But at the wrong time, the wrong way. Still, we can go back over everything. We might find something.'

'Shut up!'

It was the last thing Michael expected to hear. 'What?'

'I said *shut up!*'

'You're full of surprises.'

'I may have a real one for you.'

'MacKenzie?'

Randolph did not answer. Instead, he walked rapidly to a filing cabinet against the wall, taking out a small chain of keys; he selected one and literally jammed it into the upper lock. 'These are my private files, *very* private. A lot of broken marriages and altered wills could result if they were read. Mac's in here.'

'What about him?'

'Not *him*. The staff pathologist who put it all together, who worked with me to convince those fellas from Langley it was a haemorrhage, pure and simple.'

'A question,' interrupted Havelock. 'The CIA report says everything was processed here. Your laboratories, your equipment . . . your staff. Why didn't they remove the body to Bethesda or Walter Reed?'

The physician turned, his hands in an open file drawer, his long fingers inserted between the folders. 'Some pretty strong language on my part with the promise of a lot stronger from Midge MacKenzie if they tried. I told them she'd kick up a mess of feathers such as they haven't seen since the Bay of Pigs, that she hated their guts, figured the strain killed Mac and the least they could do was leave him in peace.'

'Did they talk to her?'

'They tried to. She gave them five minutes, answered their questions, and told them to go to hell. They got the picture; they didn't want any loud trouble from her.'

'I'll bet they didn't.'

'Also,' said Randolph, turning back to the files, 'we've got a hell of a reputation here, treat some of the most important people in the country. Who's going to call us liars?'

'You counted on that, didn't you?'

'You're damn right . . . Here it is.'

'What did your pathologist find that you think might help?'

'It's not what he found. Like I said, it's *him*. He was a temporary.'

'A what?' Michael could feel a sudden, hollow suspension of breath in his chest.

'You heard me,' went on Randolph, carrying the file back to his desk and sitting down. 'He was a temporary replacement, took over for our regular man who was out with a case of mono.'

'Mononucleosis?'

'Infectious glandular fever. Easy thing to transmit, if you've a mind to.'

'You're losing me.'

'Catch up,' said the surgeon, turning the pages in the folder. 'Several days before Mac's death our pathologist comes down with mono. Then, thank-you-very-much, a highly qualified man shows up; he's in the middle of a transfer, has a month or so free, and is staying with a sister in Easton. Jesus, I grabbed him.'

'And?'

'Mac's body's brought in; he does the initial work, and asks to see me in my office. I'll never forget it; the first thing he says to me is, "How well did you know this MacKenzie?"'

Havelock nodded. 'One thing led to another and the bottom line was that MacKenzie's body couldn't stand an independent autopsy.'

'He'd found minute traces of digoxin,' said Randolph.

'And a puncture wound, the position and angle indicating that it was probably self-inflicted,' Havelock added.

'You've got it.'

'I'm sure he also inquired about MacKenzie's work, his mental state, his family . . . and somewhere along the line brought up the subject of insurance.'

'He did. Oh, *Christ!*'

'Don't cut your throat, Doctor. These people do their homework like no one else on earth.'

'What people?'

'If I'm right, they're called *paminyatchiks*.'

'Who?'

'Never mind. And don't bother looking for holes in there. He covered himself; he didn't tell a single lie, that's his blanket. He simply knew it all in advance. You couldn't touch him without incriminating yourself and ruining your centre.'

'I'm not looking for holes,' replied the doctor, rapidly scanning pages.

'A sister in Easton? Forget it. She never was, and he's gone, and you won't find him.'

'That's just it. I know where he is.'

Michael bolted forward. 'You *what?*'

'His name came up several weeks ago. I was talking to a salesman from a surgical supply house and he mentioned that he had to check our purchase orders because a pathologist wanted to duplicate a piece of equipment we had. I recognized the name, of course, but not the place. It wasn't where I thought he'd transferred to.' Randolph stopped and looked up from the file. 'I did an odd thing,' he continued. 'Childish, I suppose. It was as though I didn't want to acknowledge him, or think about what he and I had done . . . just wanted to keep tabs on him. I didn't tell my secretary – as I usually do

– to list his current position in our personnel records. Instead, I came in here and wrote it in Mac's file. Somewhere.' The doctor went back to the pages.

Stunned, Havelock sat rigidly on the edge of the chair. Over the years in his shadow world, he had learned that the most incredible turns of circumstance generally had the most credible reasons for happening. He barely found his voice as he explained. 'Your pathologist kept the name because he knew that you of all people could never come after him. Conversely, he had his hooks into you *with* the name, not without it. Believe me, Doctor, sooner or later he would have pulled you in, viciously and effectively.'

'I've got it,' said Randolph, raising his eyes and staring at Michael. 'He still could, you know. Pull me in, I mean.'

'So could I, but I won't unless you destroy the information on that page. It's not likely because I wouldn't give you the chance. On the other hand, he'll never come near you because I won't give *him* the chance. He's made the one fatal mistake he can't afford to make in his very strange life. It's fatal. The name, please.'

'Colin Shippers. Chief Pathologist, The Regency Foundation. It's a private research centre.'

It's far more than that, Doctor. It's where a paminyatchik *can be found. The first concrete step towards Ambiguity. Towards Parsifal.*

'This is what I want you to do,' said Havelock. 'And I'm afraid you'll have to do it.'

It was vital to operate not only once removed but almost blindly, and that was the most difficult thing in the world for Michael to do. The highly concentrated surveillance had to be left to others, something Havelock hated because his team was operating totally in the dark, told only to follow instructions, given no clear reason for the job they were doing. There were always built-in risks in such methods; responsibility without knowledge or authority led to resentments, and resentment was the first cousin to carelessness. That could *not* be permitted. Nor, unfortunately, could inquiries be made regarding routine habits, friends, medical associates, places frequented . . . all the *minutiae* that might help them was denied.

For if MacKenzie's death linked Dr Colin Shippers back to the initial cover-up of Costa Brava – a cover-up that was no part of the White House strategy – he was at the medical centre under orders from the mole at State, a *paminyatchik* who had assumed the Ambiguity code. And a *paminyatchik* in that position would never entrust an assignment as sensitive as the killing of a CIA black-operations officer to any but one of his own. Therefore, they had to operate on the assumption that Shippers himself was a traveller, and that even the hint of an alarm would send him underground, severing the connection to Ambiguity and, with it, any possibility of tracing the mole through the link. Sources of information were continuously covered by the travellers; personnel offices, bank and credit references, professional records . . . even FBI checks . . . all were assiduously scrutinized by informants – willing and unwilling, Russian plants and blackmailed clerks – who alerted the thoroughly Americanized Soviet agents that someone was interested in them. This practice, in concert with Amendments IV, V and VI of the Bill of Rights, made it virtually impossible to trap the *paminyatchik*; he was a citizen and entitled to the protection of the Constitution of the United States. By the time probable cause eliminated unreasonable search, or a grand jury returned a presentment or an indictment and the accused was informed of the nature and cause of his possible crime the traveller had long since departed, only to surface in weeks or months with another identity, a wholly original *curriculum vitae* and, not infrequently, a new face, courtesy of surgeons in Moscow.

However, as Rostov had pointed out in Athens, the irony of this long-range Soviet penetration was found in the practical results. Far too often the American 'experience' served to undermine the Soviet commitment. During his rare but necessary trips to Moscow's Dzerzhinsky Square, the *paminyatchik* was made aware of the inevitable comparisons between the two countries. In the final analysis, the travellers were far less productive than the KGB felt it had a right to expect in the light of the money and effort it had expended. Yet to threaten one was to court exposure of the whole programme.

Futility was not always the province of those with a god on their side, thought Havelock.

Yet again, there were the exceptions, and exposure would never come from them. A mole called Ambiguity who roamed the sacrosanct corridors of the State Department, and a bright, persuasive pathologist named Colin Shippers who could grasshop from laboratory to laboratory – how often were these laboratories branches of United States intelligence – ? These justified the expense and whatever manpower Moscow allotted to the *paminyatchik* operation. Ambiguity was obviously Shippers's superior, the on-site control, and without doubt a respected satellite in the KGB firmament – but he was not keeping his normal KGB channels informed of the present crisis. Costa Brava, and all the madness it represented was not only disavowed by Dzerzhinsky Square, but what little they did know about it alarmed men like Pyotr Rostov.

It must do; events had taken place which could *not* have taken place without complicity in Moscow. A VKR officer had been trapped and wounded in Paris by the central figure at Costa Brava, and it took little imagination to know that the orders the officer followed were obfuscated so as to be untraceable within the complex machinery of Russian intelligence. Of course Rostov was alarmed; the spectre of the fanatical VKR was enough to frighten the most dedicated Marxist, just as it frightened Havelock. For the unknown Ambiguity obviously sent routine dispatches to his controls in the KGB, but he reserved his most explosive information for his masters in the *Voennaya*.

Rostov sensed it, but he could not pin it down, much less expose it. It was the reason for his offer to a former counterpart in Consular Operations. *He says he's not your enemy any longer, but others are who may be his as well.*

If Rostov had any idea how valid his instincts were, he would risk a firing squad to make contact, thought Michael. But Rostov was wrong; the Russian *was* his enemy. Essentially neither could trust the other because neither Washington nor Moscow would permit such trust, and not even the horror of Parsifal could change that.

Futility in a world gone mad . . . as mad as its former saviour, Anthony Matthias. Superstar.

'How long do you think it will take?' asked Jenna, sitting across from Havelock in the small, sunlit alcove off the kitchen where they had their morning coffee.

'It's difficult to tell. It'll depend on how convincing Randolph is and how quickly Shippers suspects that an insurance company may be something else, something that alarms him. It could be today, tonight, tomorrow . . . the day after.'

'I'd think you'd want Randolph to force him to react immediately. Can you afford the time?'

'I can't afford to lose him; he's the only link we've got. His name didn't appear in the laboratory report – which was easy for him to insist on in the light of Randolph's decision to cover up what he thought was a suicide. Shippers knows the only way he could surface would be for Randolph to incriminate himself, which he'd never do. Apart from practical considerations his ego wouldn't permit it.'

'But swiftness is everything, Mikhail,' objected Jenna. 'I'm not sure I understand your strategy.'

Havelock looked into her eyes, his own eyes questioning. 'I'm not sure I do, either. I've always known that to make things work in this business – this so-called profession of ours – was to think as your enemy thinks, to *be* him, then do what you're convinced he doesn't expect. Now, I'm asked to think like someone I can't possibly relate to, a man who literally has to be *two people*.' Michael sipped his coffee, staring now at the rim of the cup. 'Think about it. An American childhood, adolescence . . . baseball, hockey, books and music . . . friends at school and college; going out with girls, talking about yourself, confiding in people you really like. These are the years when secrets are for telling; it's against human nature to keep them to yourself . . . part of growing up to reveal yourself. So explain it to me. How does a man like this, a *paminyatchik*, keep the one secret he can never reveal so deep inside him.'

'I don't know, but you've just described someone I do know very well.'

'Who?'

'You, my darling.'

'That's crazy.' Havelock put his cup down. He was anxious to leave the table; that, too, was in his eyes.

'Is it?' Jenna reached over, putting her hand briefly over his. 'How many friends at school and in college, how many girls and people you really liked did you tell about Mikhail Havlicek, and Lidice? How many know about the agonies of Prague and a child who hid in the forests and carried secret messages and explosives strapped to his person? Tell me, how many?'

'It was pointless. It was history.'

'I would never have known – *we* would never have known – except that our leaders insisted on a thorough background check. Your intelligence services have not always sent the best people into our part of Europe and we paid for the mistakes. But when the dossier of Havlicek and the Havlicek family was brought to us – all easily verified – it came sealed with a man from the highest office of your State Department who took it away with him. It was apparent that your immediate superiors – our normal contacts – were not aware of your early days. For some reason they were concealed; for some reason . . . you were two people. Why, Mikhail?'

'I just told you. Matthias and I agreed; it was history.'

'You didn't want to live with it, then. You wanted that part of your life to remain hidden, out of sight.'

'That'll do.'

'I was with you so many times when older people spoke of those days and you never said anything, never let on that you were there. Because if you had, it could have led to your secret, the years you didn't care to talk about.'

'That's consistent.'

'Like this Shippers, you'd been there and you were staying out of sight. You *were there* but your signature didn't appear anywhere.'

'It's a far-fetched parallel.'

'Different, perhaps; not far-fetched,' insisted Jenna. 'You can't make even the usual inquiries about Shippers because informants might alert him and he'd disappear, protecting his secret. You're waiting for him to consider Randolph's call, finally perhaps – you hope – he'll decide that he should find out whether or not this insurance company is really . . . how do you say it?'

'Balking,' offered Michael. 'Asking last questions before agreeing to the final settlement on MacKenzie's policy. It's standard; they hate like hell paying money.'

'Yes, you believe he'll do this. And when he discovers there *are* no questions, he'll be alarmed, then make his move to contact his control: again you hope, Ambiguity.'

'I think that's the way he *will* behave. It's the best and safest way I can come up with. Anything else would send him underground.'

'And each hour he . . .' Jenna shook her head, searching for words.

'Thinks about it,' said Havelock. 'Concentrates.'

'Yes, concentrates. Every moment is a lost moment, giving him time to spot his surveillance, the men who worry you because you don't know them and you can't give them the true background material on their subject.'

'I don't like it, but it's been done before.'

'Hardly under these conditions, never with such terrible consequences for error. Swiftness *is* everything, Mikhail.'

'You're trying to tell me something and I don't know what it is.'

'You're afraid of alarming Shippers, afraid he might disappear.'

'"Terrified" is a better word.'

'Then don't go after *him*. Go after the man who was silent, who was at the medical centre when MacKenzie died but whose signature did not appear. Just as you were two men in Prague, he is two men here. Go after the one you *see* because you have no reason to believe he *is* two men, or has a secret to conceal.'

Havelock touched his cup, his eyes fixed on Jenna's eyes. 'Go after a laboratory pathologist,' he said quietly. 'On the assumption that someone had to be there with Randolph . . . Corroboration. The insurance company insists on a corroborating physician.'

'In my country five signatures are barely adequate for any one document.'

'He'll refuse, of course.'

'Can he? He *was there.*'

'He'll tell Randolph he can't support him, can't agree openly to the diagnosis of aortal haemorrhage.'

'Then I think the doctor should be quite firm. If that's Shippers's medical position, why didn't he take it before?'

Michael smiled, the realization clear. 'That's very good. Blackmail an extortionist with his own material.'

'Why not? Randolph has . . . how do you say it? . . . the leverage. Age, reputation, wealth; who is this Shippers to oppose him?'

'And none of it makes a damn bit of difference anyway. We're simply forcing him to move quickly. For his own protection – not even as a traveller, but as a doctor – he'll have to determine how serious the insurance people are. Whether it's a routine measure or whether they meant it. Then he finds out there's nothing: he's got to move again.'

'What's today's schedule?' asked Jenna.

'Initial surveillance will pick up Shippers when he leaves his apartment this morning. Secondary will take over inside the Regency buildings.'

'How? . . . I'm sorry, I wasn't listening last night when you were on the phone.'

'I know you weren't, I was watching you. Are you going to have something for me?'

'Later, perhaps. How did you get them inside the buildings?'

'The Regency Foundation's a private firm with its share of classified government contracts. That's obviously the reason Shippers went there; a lot of those contracts are defence orientated. Regency was the company that first projected the radius burn-level of napalm . . . It's common for government technocrats and General Accounting Office personnel to be around there, shuffling papers and looking official. From this morning there are two more.'

'I hope no one asks them questions.'

'They wouldn't answer if anyone did; that's standard. Also they've got briefcases and plastic IDs on their lapels to identify them. They're covered if anyone checks.' Havelock looked at his watch as he got up from the table. 'Randolph's making his call between ten and ten-thirty. Let's go. I'll reach him and give him the new words.'

'If Shippers reacts,' said Jenna, following Michael down the hall towards the panelled study, 'he won't use his office phone.'

'There are three mobile units in the streets, separated by blocks, everyone in radio contact, wrist cameras activated by arm movements. They can move out on foot or by car – cars alternating in traffic. If they're any good, they won't lose him.'

'They *do* worry you, don't they?'

'They worry me.' Havelock opened the door of the study, holding it for Jenna. 'They'd worry me more if it wasn't for a fellow named Charley who wanted to put a bullet in my head down on Poole's Island.'

'The one from Consular Operations?'

Michael nodded, going to the desk. 'He flew up last night; my personal request, which didn't exactly thrill him. But he's good, he's thorough, and he knows that Shippers is involved with the Matthias crisis. That's enough to make him better than he ever was. He's in charge, and if he doesn't choke on the mobile phone he'll keep me posted, let me know if anything breaks.'

Jenna had gone to her own desk – the couch; on the coffee table in front of it there were neat, narrow stacks of papers and several pages of handwritten notes. She sat down and picked up a bound typewritten report from the pile on the left. She spoke while reading, her voice indefinite her concentration split. 'Have you got in touch with the insurance company?'

'No, that's a risk I don't want to take,' replied Havelock, sitting down at the desk and watching Jenna, but his interest diverted. 'MacKenzie's policy might be flagged.'

'You're probably right.'

'What have you got there? It's the same thing you were looking at last night.'

'It's the report from your Central Intelligence Agency. The list of potential Soviet defectors over the past ten years, none of whom materialized.'

'Look for a nuclear scientist or an armaments strategist who disappeared.'

'Others disappeared too, Mikhail,' said Jenna, reading and reaching for a pencil.

Havelock kept his eyes on her for several moments, then looked down at a sheet of paper on which were scribbled various telphone numbers. He checked one, picked up the phone, and dialled.

'He's a cold son of a bitch, I can tell you,' snapped Dr Matthew Randolph. 'When I put it to him he clammed up, asked a couple of questions like a mortician settling with a family lawyer and said he'd get back to me.'

'How did you put out, and what were his questions?' asked Michael, putting down the page of Pentagon stationery on which were written the identities of the senior officers on the Nuclear Contingency Committees. He had circled a name. 'Try to be as accurate as possible.'

'I'll be *completely* accurate,' objected the surgeon testily.

'I only meant in terms of the words, the phrases he used.'

'It won't be hard; they were damned few and damned short. As you suggested, he said I had no right to involve him, that was our understanding. He simply brought me his findings and how I altered them was my responsibility, not his. So I said I wasn't a goddamned lawyer but if my memory for trivia served me, he was an accessory and there was no way round it and I was going to be fried in hell before Midge MacKenzie and those kids got screwed out of what was coming to them.'

'So far very good. What was his response?'

'He didn't have any, so I blasted along. I told him he was a damned fool if he thought he was invisible around here four months ago and a bigger fool if he thought anyone on the staff would believe I'd spend hours in a pathology laboratory over the body of a friend all by myself.'

'*Very* good.'

'He had an answer to that. Like a talking piece of dry ice, he asked who specifically knew.'

Havelock felt a sudden spasm in his chest, the spectre of unnecessary execution rising. 'What did you say? Did you mention anybody?'

'Hell, I said probably *everybody*!'

Michael relaxed. 'You can come on the payroll, Doctor.'

'You couldn't afford me, son.'

'Please, go on.'

'I backed down a bit, told him he was getting all worked up over nothing. I said the fellow who came to see me from the insurance company said it was just a formality, that they required a second signature on the path-report before sending the cheque. I even suggested he call Ben Jackson over at Talbot Insurance if he was worried, that Ben was an old friend.'

'You gave him a *name*?'

'Sure. Ben *is* an old friend; he set up Mac's policy. I figured if anyone phoned Ben he'd call me and ask what the hell was going on.'

'And what were *you* going to say?'

'That whoever it was got it backwards. *I* was the one who wanted the second signature for our own records.'

'What did *Shippers* say?'

'Just a few words, spoken like a frozen computer. He asked whether I had told either Ben or the man from the insurance company who he was.'

'And?'

'I said no I didn't. Fair was fair, and I guessed the best way was to handle it quietly. For him to get over here and sign the damned report without any fanfare.'

'His response here?'

'Again, damned short and bloodless.' Randolph paused and, spacing his words apart in a monotone, continued, ' "Have you told me everything?" he wanted to know. I tell you he was a zombie.'

'What did you say?'

'I said of course I had, what else was there? That's when he told me he'd call me back. Just like that, "I'll call you back", in that God-awful voice.'

Havelock breathed deeply, his eyes dropping to the names on the Pentagon stationery, to one name in particular. 'Doctor, either you've done a remarkable job or I'm going to have your inflated head.'

'What the hell are you *talking* about?'

'If you'd done it my way, just using the insurance company alone, without any other name, Shippers would have assumed MacKenzie's death was being re-examined by a third party without telling you. Now, if he calls this Jackson he'll know you're lying.'

'So what? Same result, isn't it?'

'Not for you, Doctor, and we can't bring in your friend; we can't take the risk. For your sake I hope he's gone fishing. And I mean it – if you've given me another complication, I'll see your head rolling down the street.'

'Well, now, young fellow, I've been doing some thinking about that. There could be a *couple* of heads rolling down a *two*-way street, couldn't there? Here you are, a mucka-muck from the White House telling me the executive branch of our government is trying to cover up the brutal killing of a heroic veteran, an employee of the CIA, and I'm just a country doctor trying to protect the interests of his bereaved widow and fatherless orphans because they've suffered more than anyone had a right to ask them to suffer. You want to tangle with me, you bastard?'

'Please call me if you hear anything further, Dr Randolph.'

Special Detachment Officer Charles Loring, Consular Operations, late of Poole's Island, rubbed his eyes and raised the thermos of black coffee to his lips as he sat in the front seat of the grey car. The driver was for all intents and purposes a stranger; that was to say, Loring had not seen him before 10 o'clock last night, when he had met the entire unit selected by Havelock from thirty-odd service records submitted by the Federal Bureau of Investigation at the Justice Department's request. The unit was now his responsibility, the assignment of continuity-surveillance understood, the reasons behind it withheld – which was not the smartest thing to do when dealing with superior talent.

And despite Havelock's minor – very minor – attempt to flatter him, Charley Loring knew that the former Cons Op field man was getting some of his own back by claiming privilege. The only clue Havelock gave him was that this Shippers was tied in with Poole's Island, and it was – with reluctance – enough for Charley. Havelock was a low-blow-dealing prick, and he had made fools of Savannah, but if he was running some part of the Matthias show in Washington he had more problems than they did. Loring would do what he could to help. There were times when likes and dislikes just did not mean very much, the catastrophe – the tragedy – of Poole's Island was such a time.

The unit had met at 10 o'clock at Sterile Eleven down in Quantico, and had stayed up until 4 o'clock in the morning covering the variables of total surveillance . . . without knowing a damn thing about the subject. They had a photograph but, apart from an inadequate description furnished by Randolph, that was about all they had, and it too was inadequate. It was a blow-up made at Sterile Eleven from a 1971 Jefferson Medical School Yearbook that had been located by the FBI office in Philadelphia. No reason was given to the agents who found it, only that they should observe complete secrecy. Actually, it had been stolen out of the university's library by an agent who had concealed it under his coat. Examining the grainy blow-up the unit had to imagine a face considerably older than that in the photograph and, since no one they could speak to had seen Shippers in four months, the possibility of a beard or a moustache could not be discounted. And they could speak to no one about Dr Colin Shippers, no one at all. Havelock's orders.

Initial surveillance had disposed of the conjecture about any hirsute additions to the subject's face; tinted glasses and a heavier frame were the essential differences between his appearance now and the yearbook photograph. The men inside the Regency Foundation had radioed out twice; they had picked up Shippers. One man was down the hall from the laboratory where the pathologist worked; the other covered his office on the floor below. The waiting had begun, thought Loring. But waiting for what?

The hours or days would tell. All Charles Loring knew was that he had done everything he could to position the unit effectively: spaced apart and in contact to ensure maximum concealment. The cars were at one-way intersections, his own down the street and across from the research centre with a full view of the entrance and the adjacent garage used for personnel parking.

A sharp, high-pitched hum came from the dashboard console; it was a signal from one of the men inside. Loring reached for the microphone, depressed the switch, and spoke. 'S-Five. What is it?'

'S-Three. He just left the lab, seems in a hurry.'

'Any clues?'

'I heard a telephone ring in there a few minutes ago. He's alone so he could have talked, but that's spec. I wasn't able to overhear any conversation.'

'It's good enough. Stay where you are and stay out of sight.'

Loring replaced the microphone, only to hear a second jarring signal before he could lean back in the seat.

'S-Five.'

'S-Two. Subject went into his office. From the way he walked – his general demeanour – he's agitated.'

'Good description; it fits upstairs. We may be moving faster than any of us – '

'Hold it! Stay on the line,' instructed Surveillance-Two as static filled the speaker. The man had concealed his radio under his clothing without breaking the open circuit. In seconds his voice was back. 'Sorry. Subject came right back out and I had to spin. He chucked the white coat and is in his street clothes. Same tan raincoat, same soft, floppy hat. I guess he's yours.'

'I guess he is. Out.' Loring held the microphone in his hand and turned to the driver. 'Get ready, the package is coming our way. If I have to go on foot take over. I'll stay in touch.' He reached under his jacket and took out the small compact hand-held radio, checking by habit the battery charge. He then pulled back his left sleeve, revealing the flat miniaturized high-speed camera attached to the underside of his wrist. He twisted his hand and heard the muted click; he was ready. 'I wonder who this Shippers is,' he said, watching the entrance of the Regency Foundation.

The telephone rang, breaking Havelock's concentration on his Pentagon notes. He picked it up.

'Yes?'

'Cross?'

Michael blinked, recognizing Randolph's strident voice. 'Yes, Doctor?'

'Maybe we can both keep our heads. Ben Jackson just called, angrier than a Point Judith squall.'

'What about?'

'Seems this lawyer phoned him asking why the final payment on Mac-Kenzie's policy was being held up.'

'Shippers,' said Havelock.

'You got it, and Ben was madder'n hell. There *was* no final payment. The entire settlement was mailed to Midge's lawyer about eight weeks ago.'

'Why did Jackson call you and not Mrs MacKenzie's attorney?'

'Because Shippers – I figure it was Shippers or someone calling for him – got shook up and said there was some confusion over signatures on a medical report and did Ben know anything about it. Naturally, Ben said he didn't; the money was paid – processed through his agency – and that was that. He also added that he didn't appreciate his reputation –'

'Listen to me,' interrupted Havelock. 'I won't lose *my* head, but you may have blown yours away. I want you to stay in your office, and don't see anybody until I can get a couple of men up there. If anyone tries to reach you, ask the desk to say you're operating.'

'Forget it!' shot back Randolph. 'A mealy-mouth snot like Shippers doesn't worry me. He comes near here I'll have one of the guards throw him into a padded cell.'

'If he did and you could, I'd kiss your feet at this point, but it won't *be* Shippers. He may call you; that's as near as he'll come and it'd be the best thing that could happen to you. If he does, say you're sorry for the white lie, but after long consideration you wanted to cover yourself on that report.'

'He wouldn't believe it.'

'Neither would I, but it's a stall. I'll have men up there within the hour.'

'I don't want them!'

'You have no choice, Dr Randolph,' said Michael, hanging up and immediately drawing his page of telephone numbers in front of him.

'Do you really think Shippers will go after him?' asked Jenna, standing by the window with the CIA report in her hand.

'*He* won't, but others'll be sent up there, not at first to kill him, but to take him. Take him and get him alone where they can press his head until they find out who he's dealing with, who he's lying for. Killing could be nicer.' Havelock reached for the phone, his eyes on the page below.

'On the other hand,' observed Jenna, 'knowing Randolph lied, knowing he was involved, made Shippers move faster than we thought possible. How long ago was Loring's last call?'

'Over an hour. Shippers took a taxi downtown; they're with him on foot by now. We should be hearing soon.' Michael dialled; the line answered quickly. 'This is Sterile Five, Fairfax. Under that code name I was taken under escort up to the Randolph Medical Center yesterday. Talbot County, Maryland, Eastern Shore. Will you confirm, please?' While waiting, Havelock covered the phone and said to Jenna, 'I just thought of something. With any luck we might turn a liability into an asset,' then returned to the phone: '. . . Yes, that's right. Three man team; departure was eleven hundred hours. Are you ready for instructions? . . . Return two men up there immediately on a priority basis. Subject is Dr Matthew Randolph; he's to be given protection, maximum visual contact, but there's a hook. I want the men to be part of the local scenery, orderlies or staff or whatever I can work out with Randolph. Tell them to get en route and call me on the mobile phone in twenty minutes; patch it through.' Michael paused again, looking again at Jenna as the Secret Service dispatcher checked schedules. 'Randolph may have done us another favour at a risk to himself he'll never understand.'

'*If* he co-operates.'

'He hasn't got a choice, I meant that.' The dispatcher returned; Havelock listened, then spoke. 'No, that's fine. Actually, I prefer men who weren't up there yesterday. By the way, the code will be – ' Michael stopped, his thoughts going back to the Palatine Hill, to a dead man whose words had sent him to Maryland's Eastern Shore. 'Apache,' he said. 'They were hunters. Tell Apache to call me in twenty minutes.'

Dr Matthew Randolph roared his objections to no avail. He would either co-operate, Havelock told him, or they could all take their chances *and* the fallout 'tangling' with each other. 'Mr Cross' was prepared to press his suit to the limit even if it meant admitting the murder of a CIA operations officer named Steven MacKenzie. And Randolph, understanding that he was now between a rock and a hard place, entered into the dangerous charade with a fair degree of inventiveness. The Apache team would be two visiting cardiologists from California, complete with white jackets and stethoscopes.

Havelock's orders were explicit, no room for error. Whoever came for Matthew Randolph – and someone was bound to come – he or they were to be taken alive. Wounds were permitted, but only in the legs, the feet, nothing above the waist.

It was a four-zero order, none more sacrosanct in the clandestine services.

'Havelock, it's Loring.'

'How goes it?'

'My driver said he wasn't able to raise you.'

'I was talking with an irascible doctor, but if there was an emergency, your man could have broken in. He knows that.'

'It wasn't and it isn't. It's just weird.' Loring stopped. The pause was uncomfortable.

'What's going on, Charley?'

'That's just it. Nothing. Shippers' taxi let him off in front of Garfinckle's Department Store. He went inside, made a call from one of the phones on the ground floor, and for the past hour or so he's been wandering around the men's shop on the fifth. I'm calling from there; I've got him in sight.'

'He's waiting for someone.'

'If he is, it's an odd way of doing it quietly.'

'What do you mean?'

'He's buying clothes like he was going on a cruise, trying on things and laughing with the clerks. He's a one-man gross for the day.'

'It's not usual, but be patient. The main point is he made the call, made his first outside move. You're doing fine.'

'Who the hell is he, Havelock?'

Michael reflected. Loring deserved to be told more than he had; it was the moment to bring him nearer to the truth. So much depended on the sharp, plainspoken Cons Op officer.

'A deep cover entry who's going to meet a man who could blow Poole's Island out of Savannah harbour. I'm glad you're there, Charley. We *have* to know who that man is.'

'Good enough, and thanks. All the floors and exits here are covered, we're in contact and our cameras are ready . . . If it's a question of choice, do we drop Shippers and stay with his contact?'

'You may not have to. You may recognize him. The others probably wouldn't, but you might.'

'Jesus, from *State*?'

'That's right. My guess is fairly high-level, forty-five to middle fifties, and some kind of specialist. If you *do* recognize him, stay far back until they separate, then pick up Shippers and bring him down here. But when you close in, be very fast and very careful and check for capsules.'

'Shippers is that deep? Christ, how do they do it?'

'Past tense, Charley. Did. A long time ago.'

The waiting would have been intolerable had it not been for Havelock's growing fascination with a Lieutenant-Commander Thomas Decker, Annapolis '61, former skipper of the submarine *Starfire* and a member of the Pentagon's Nuclear Contingency Committees. Decker was a liar with no apparent reason for lying.

Michael had spoken to all fifteen NCC senior officers, calling several twice, a few three times, ostensibly to put together a clear picture of the committees' working methods for updated presidential comprehension. In most of the conversations, the initial remarks were guarded – each, of course, demanding White House switchboard verification – but as the words flowed and the officers realized Havelock knew what he was talking about, they grew less wary and more specific within the bounds of maximum security. Hypothetical events were matched with theoretical responses, and beyond his fundamental reason for speaking to each man, Havelock was impressed. If the laws of physics determined that for every action there was an equal and opposite reaction, the NCC Teams had come up with a better equation. For any nuclear action on the part of an enemy the reaction was anything but equal; it was devastatingly superior. Even Lieutenant-Commander Decker's contributions were electric in this sense. He made it clear that a ring-perimeter of undersea nuclear marauders could demolish all major enemy installations from the north Atlantic to the Black Sea and most points in between in a matter of minutes. In this area he did not lie; he did in another. He said he had never met Secretary of State Anthony Matthias.

His name had appeared on three separate telephone logs from Matthias's office, all within the past six months.

It was, of course, possible that Decker's statement *was* true, that he had not actually *met* Matthias, merely spoken with him on the phone. But if that was the case, why had he not volunteered the information? A man who was asked whether or not he knew a statesman of Matthias's stature did not deny it readily without quickly offering the qualification that he *did* know him by way of the telephone. It was not natural, actually contradictory for an obviously ambitious naval officer rising fast in the Pentagon, who could be expected to clutch ferociously at the coat-tails of Anthony Matthias.

Thomas Decker, USN, had lied. He did know Matthias and, for obscure reasons, did not care to admit it.

It was time for the fourth call to Lieutenant-Commander Decker.

'You know, Mr Cross, I've given you about all I can or should in these matters. I'm sure you're aware that there are restrictions placed on me that can only be countered by the President himself – in his presence, I might add.'

'I'm aware of that, Commander, but I'm confused by one of my notes. It probably has nothing to do with anything we've talked about, but the Secretary of State didn't understand it, either. You said you didn't know him, never met him.'

Decker's pause was as electric as his data on undersea nuclear warfare. 'That's the way he wanted it,' he said quietly. 'That's the way he said it had to be.'

'Thank you, Commander. Incidentally, Secretary of State Matthias was trying to pin-point it this morning. He couldn't recall where you and he last talked with each other.'

'The lodge, of course. Sometime in August or September, I think.'

'Of course. The lodge. The Shenandoah.'

'That's where it was, where it always was. No one knew anything. It was just ourselves. How is it possible he can't remember?'

'Thank you, Commander. Goodbye.'

The *Shenandoah*.

The bell was piercing, the ring unbroken; it was the switchboard's way of signalling emergency! Havelock had been pacing, thinking; he rushed across the room and grabbed the phone. It was Loring.

'You've got my tail on a plate and I'll start carving it for you! *Jesus*, I'm *sorry!*'

'You lost him,' said Michael, drained, his throat dry.

'*Christ.* I'll turn in my cards! Every fucking one of them!'

'Calm down, Charley. What happened?'

'A switch. A *goddamned switch!* I . . . I just wasn't *looking* for it! I *should* have, but I *wasn't!*'

'Tell me what happened,' repeated Michael, sitting down as Jenna got up from the couch and started towards the desk.

'Shippers paid for the stuff he bought, arranging for most of it to be delivered except for a couple of boxes he took with him. He went into the fitting room and came out dressed for the street, same raincoat, same soft hat, carrying the boxes.'

'Held high,' Havelock broke in, wearily, again the sense of futility spreading through him.

'Naturally,' agreed Loring. 'I followed him to the elevator, staying several aisles away – frankly looking at every son of a bitch in the men's department, figuring one of them might be your man. One lousy son of a bitch who might have brushed up against Shippers and got something from him . . . The lift door closed, and I raised the men on each floor, every stop covered, each man to head below and join the others at the outside exits the second that lift passed his floor . . . My S-Nine picked him up at the 14th Street entrance and followed him, radioing the rest of us his position; we spread out in cars and on foot. *Jesus!*'

'When did it happen?' asked Michael.

'On the corner of 11th Street, four minutes after I left the store, and I was the last one out. The man hailed a cab, threw the boxes inside and, just before he got in, took off his hat. It wasn't Shippers at all. It was some guy ten, fifteen years older and mostly bald.'

'What did your Nine do?'

'The best he could. He tried to stop the cab but he couldn't; it shot right in a break in traffic. He called us, spelling everything out, giving the cab's number and description. Five of us ran back to the store, covering what exits we could, but we all knew we'd lost him. S-Eleven and Twelve went after the cab; I told them to stay with it if they had to break every traffic law on the books – since we'd lost the subject, we could still grab the plant. They picked it up six blocks west and there was no one inside. Only the raincoat, the hat and the two boxes lying on the floor.'

'The driver?'

'He said some nut got in, took off his coat, gave him five dollars, and jumped out at the next light. The men are taking the boxes in for possible prints.'

'They won't find any matching anything in the Bureau's computers.'

'I'm *sorry*. Havelock, I'm really sorry. Shippers' whole act was a diversion, and I bought it. Of all the goddamned times to lose an instinct, I had to pick this one.'

Michael shook his head, as he spoke. 'You didn't lose it, Charley, I pushed it out of your head. At least you sensed a break in the pattern and I told you to forget it. I told you to be patient and concentrate on a man who never intended to be there.'

'You don't have to do this,' said Loring. 'I wouldn't if I were you.'

'You don't know that. Besides, I need you. You're not off the hook, Charley, I want those instincts of yours. There's a naval officer at the Pentagon, a Lieutenant-Commander Thomas Decker. Under a very thick screen find out everything you can about him. Everything.'

'An entry?'

'No. A liar.'

Jenna Karras supported herself on the desk at Michael's side, looking over his shoulder as he studied the names and brief summaries of the men she had selected from the CIA, Cons Op and Army Intelligence reports. Out of a hundred and thirty-five potential Soviet defectors who neither came over to the West nor whose current whereabouts were known she had chosen eight for priority consideration.

Michael looked at the list, put it down and slowly turned to her. 'This has been a rotten day. It's no time for jokes.'

'I'm not joking, Mikhail,' said Jenna.

'There's not an armaments expert, or a high-ranking military man, or even an atomic scientist here. These are doctors, specialists – old men now, none of whom was remotely connected with any sort of strategic planning or nuclear strike capabilities.'

'Parsifal needs no such connections.'

'Then perhaps I wasn't clear about what those documents *say*. They spell out a series of nuclear moves – first and second strikes, interceptor counterstrikes, territorial neutralization and automated reclamation – detailed strategies that could only be conceived and negotiated by experts.'

'Matthias didn't carry around such details in his head, you've said as much.'

'Of course not, which is why I'm going after the men on the contingency committees – one in particular. But Parsifal *did*. He must have had those projections available to him. They were chips, his bargaining points in their insane game.'

'Then someone is missing,' insisted Jenna, walking round the desk, then suddenly turning to face Havelock. 'Who spoke for the People's Republic? Who bargained China's position? Who gave *its* projections, *its* strategic details? According to your theory, there has to be a *third* negotiator.'

'No, there doesn't. Their combined sources would be enough to build a totally convincing case for a China strategy. It's common knowledge in intelligence circles that if US and Soviet penetration of the PRC arsenals were linked up, we'd know more about China's nuclear capabilities than anyone in Peking.'

'A convincing *case*?'

'Totally.'

'*Combined* sources, Mikhail? Why?'

Havelock studied Jenna's face, gradually understanding what she was trying to say. '*One* source,' he said quietly. 'Why not?'

The telephone rang, its strident signal producing an abrupt tightness in Michael's throat. He reached for it; the President of the United States was on the line, his first words as ominous as Havelock had ever heard.

'The Russians know about Matthias. There's no way to tell their next move.'

'Parsifal?' asked Michael, with no breath in him.

'They can smell him and what they smell is flaring their nostrils. They're close to panic.'

'How did you find out?'

'They reached one of our high diplomatic personnel. They told him that they were prepared to expose Matthias. Our only hope now is that the man they contacted is one of the best we've got. They respect him; he could be our single hope for containment. I'm bringing him on board; he's taking Bradford's place. He's got to be told everything, understand everything.'

'Who is he?'

'A man named Pierce. Arthur Pierce.'

33

The *paminyatchik* sat in the underground strategy room of the White House as the President of the United States and two of the nation's most influential men briefed him. The conference had taken precedence over all Charles Berquist's prior appointments and obligations. It had so far lasted nearly three hours, the incredulous Undersecretary of State for the UN delegation rapidly taking brief notes, his intelligent grey eyes conveying a deep awareness of impending catastrophe, while at the same time his mind remained in complete control, seeking answers, avoiding panic.

The tension was electric, intermittently broken by expressions of courtesy and respect. Arthur Pierce could not be called a friend of either the President or of Addison Brooks, but nor was he a stranger. He was a professional with whom both men had worked, and in whom both had confidence. They remembered with gratitude his penetrating analyses in previous crises. As for General Malcolm Halyard, 'Tightrope' had met Major Pierce in Saigon years ago and was so impressed with his performance that he had cabled the Pentagon recommending that the War College make a serious appraisal of the major's potential for permanent, as opposed to reserve, status.

Yet despite these extremely favourable appraisals, the outstanding citizen-soldier had chosen civilian status, albeit government orientated. And since, to its dismay, the military establishment was frequently part of the government, the word had gone out: an exceptional man was available and looking for challenging work; someone should come up with something before the commerical headhunters descended on him. Washington needed all the genuine talent it could find.

It had happened so easily, so logically in its arithmetic: one plus one plus one. People became steps and the steps led to a high place. An elderly career officer at State said he just happened to be at a dinner party in Alexandria where his military host mentioned Pierce to him. Naturally the career officer felt compelled to mention Pierce's name at a conference attended by Addison Brooks. State was perpetually scouting for that rare man with proven abilities who also had a potential for further intellectual growth. Arthur Pierce was summoned for an interview, which evolved into a lengthy lunch with the aristocratic statesman. This, in turn, led to an offer of employment, an entirely feasible decision in the light of the record.

The mole was in place. There had in fact been no dinner party in Alexandria, no host who had discussed in uniquely flattering terms an outstanding soldier from Saigon. It did not matter; others were discussing him; Brooks had verified that. A dozen corporations were about to make offers to the brilliant young man, so Addison Brooks spoke first.

As the years went by, the decision to recruit Arthur Pierce could only be applauded. He *was* outstanding, with an increasingly apparent ability to comprehend and counter Soviet manoeuvres, especially in face-to-face confrontations. There were, of course, specialists who studied *Tass* and the various Russian journals and communiqués to interpret often obscure Soviet positions, but where Pierce was most effective was at the conference table, whether in Helsinki, Vienna or Geneva. At times his perceptions were uncanny; he frequently seemed to be ten steps ahead of the spokesmen sent by Moscow, preparing counter-proposals before the Soviet position had even been made clear, thus giving the US team the advantage of an immediate response. His presence was increasingly sought by upper-level diplomats until the inevitable took place: he was brought into Matthias's orbit, and the Secretary of State lost little time making Arthur Pierce an upper-level diplomat himself.

The *paminyatchik* had arrived. An infant, genetically selected in Moscow and sent covertly into the heartland of America, was in place after a lifetime of preparation, and at this moment was being addressed by the President of the United States.

'You now have the whole ungodly picture, Mr Undersecretary.' Berquist stopped as a painful memory flooded his mind. 'It's strange using that title,' he continued softly. 'Only days ago another Undersecretary sat on this same dais.'

'I hope I can contribute even a fraction of what he did,' said Pierce, studying his notes. 'The fact that he was killed is appalling. Emory was a friend of mine . . . he didn't have many friends.'

'He said the same thing about himself,' observed Addison Brooks. 'And about you.'

'Me?'

'That you were his friend.'

'I'm flattered.'

'You might not have been at the time,' said General Halyard. 'You were one of nineteen people he was looking into.'

'In what way?'

'He was trying to find someone on the fifth floor of State who might have been out of the country, who might have been at the Costa Brava,' explained the President.

'The man who later used the Ambiguity code?' asked Pierce, frowning.

'That's right.'

'How did my name come up? Emory never told me, never called me.'

'Under the circumstances,' said the ambassador, 'he couldn't. Several query-responses between you and Washington during that week had been misplaced. I don't have to tell you what a shock it was to him at first. They were found, of course.'

'Those misfilings are a constant irritant,' said Pierce, going back to his notes, checking off items with his gold-plated ballpoint pen. 'I don't even know that there's a solution. The volume of traffic is simply too great and there are too few people cleared for the material at that level.' The Undersecretary circled a note, adding as an afterthought, 'On the other hand, I'd rather put up with the irritation than take the chance that some of those confidential memoranda ever got out.'

'How much of what you've learned here in this room do you think the Russians know?' Berquist's Nordic face was set, his eyes hard and level, the muscles in his jaws pulsating.

'Less than I've learned here in this room but probably more than we suspect. The Russians are so damned elliptical. What's more, they're also working themselves up into a frenzy. I can't form a judgement until I've had a chance to study those – incredible documents.'

'*False* documents,' said Halyard emphatically. 'Agreements between two madmen, that's what they are.'

'I'm not sure either Moscow or Peking would believe that, General,' said Pierce, shaking his head. 'One of those madmen is Anthony Matthias, and the world isn't ready to accept him as insane.'

'Because it doesn't want to,' interrupted Brooks. 'It's afraid to.'

'That's right, sir,' agreed the Undersecretary of State. 'But apart from Matthias, these so-called nuclear aggression pacts, as the President has described them, contain extraordinary classified information: locations, megatonnage, detailed delivery capabilities, launching codes . . . even abort systems. From what I can gather, the gates of the arsenals of the two superpowers and their runner-up in China have been opened, the most secret hardware in each camp there for anyone who reads the agreements to see.' Pierce turned to the soldier. 'What would be the Pentagon's recommendation if a similar Sino-Soviet pact against *us* were brought in by clandestine services, General?'

'Launch,' answered Halyard flatly. 'There'd be no alternative.'

'Only if you were convinced it was authentic,' interjected Brooks.

'I'd be convinced,' said the general. 'So would you be. Who else but men with access to that information could include it? Also, there are the projected dates. I'd be *damned* convinced.'

'When you say the Russians are elliptical,' said the statesman, 'I concur wholeheartedly, but how do you mean it in the current sense?'

'They threw phrases at me – disjointed *non-sequiturs* – watching me to see if I'd follow up on any of them. We've been confronting each other for a number of years now, whether in Vienna or Bern or New York; you get to spot even concealed reactions.'

'But first they told you they knew Matthias was insane,' said Berquist. 'That was their opening, wasn't it?'

'Yes, sir. I don't think I used the exact words before. I will now. I was in the Russian ambassador's office at his request – summons, really – along with his senior aide. Frankly, I thought he'd asked to see me so we might work out a compromise on the Pan-Arab resolution, but instead he greeted me with a statement that could only refer to Matthias: "We understand from a most reliable source that a holiday has been extended because the mental condition of the vacationer has deteriorated to a point beyond recovery."'

'What was your reply?' asked Brooks. 'The exact words, please.'

'"The Russian compulsion for brooding, self-serving fantasy is no different now from what it was when Dostoevski described it." Those were my exact words.'

'Provocative yet insouciant,' said the statesman. 'Very good.'

'That's when the fireworks started. "He's mad!" shouted the ambassador. "Matthias is mad! He's done insane things, undermined what's left of *détente*." Then his aide joined in, demanding to know where the next meetings were being held, which unstable governments Matthias had been in contact with and whether they knew he was insane, or was a madman sending out secret communications, concealing his insanity from the people he was reaching? What frightens me, Mr President, Mr Ambassador, General Halyard, is that *they* described what you've described to *me*. If I understood correctly, Matthias had been doing just that for the past six months. Reaching unstable regimes, instant prime ministers, revolutionary juntas we shouldn't be touching.'

'That's where the Russians got their information, of course,' said Berquist. 'They think a demented Matthias is implementing a number of his well-known "geopolitical realities". Moving in on them.'

'They think far more than that, sir,' corrected Pierce. 'They believe he may have funnelled nuclear materials to extremist regimes and fanatic camps – Islamic, for example, or Afghan, or anti-Soviet Arab factions – that we've all agreed shouldn't have them. They're paranoid about it. We can protect ourselves from each other by the sheer magnitude of our arsenals; but neither of us can protect ourselves from an irrational partisan junta or sect that possesses launch and nuclear capability. Actually, we're far safer; we're separated by oceans. Strategic Russia is part of the Euro-Asian land mass; its borders are vulnerable if only by proximity to potential enemies. If I read them correctly, it's these concerns that are pushing them towards the panic button.'

'But not Parsifal,' said Brooks. 'In your judgement, the man we call Parsifal has *not* made contact with Moscow.'

'I can't rule *anything* out,' said Pierce. 'There are so many phrases, threats, implications – as I said, elliptical references. For instance, they mentioned "next meetings", "unstable governments", "nuclear materials". All of these – again if I understood correctly – are actually a part of these agreements. If I could study them I'd be able to spot parallels with the original texts.' The Undersecretary paused, then spoke quietly, firmly. 'I think it's possible this Parsifal *has* made contact, delivering provocative hints, perhaps nothing more. And I think it's urgent that we know even this.'

'He wants to blow us all up,' said the President. 'My God, that's all he wants to do.'

'The sooner I can get to Poole's Island, Mr – ' Pierce was interrupted by the humming of the white telephone on the white dais, a red light flashing on its miniaturized console. Berquist picked it up. 'Yes?'

The President listened in silence for nearly thirty seconds, then answered, nodding. 'I understand. Let me know what happens as soon as it happens.' He replaced the phone and turned to the others. 'That was Havelock. He won't get here this afternoon.'

'What *is* happening?' asked the soldier.

'Too many things for him to leave the phone.'

'I'm sorry,' said Arthur Pierce. 'I wanted to meet him. I think it's vital we stay in touch. I can tell him what's going on with the Soviets and he can keep me up to date. I have to know when to press forward, when to back off.'

'You'll be kept informed; he has his orders from me . . . They lost the pathologist.'

'*Damn!*' exploded the general.

'He either picked up the surveillance or, knowing things were out of control, decided to disappear.'

'Or was ordered to disappear,' added the statesman.

'That's what I can't understand,' said Berquist, turning to the silent Undersecretary of State. 'The Russians gave you no indication that they were *aware* of any Soviet involvement in this whole damn thing? They didn't mention the Costa Brava or Rostov's cable to us?'

'No, sir. That may be the one advantage we have. We know, but they don't.'

'*Rostov* knows,' insisted the President.

'Then he's too frightened to act,' replied Pierce. 'It's often the case with entrenched KGB personnel; they're never sure whose toes they may be stepping on. Or if he is searching, he's not getting anywhere.'

'You're talking as though we were speaking about two different Moscows,' objected Halyard.

'I agree with Havelock,' said the mole. 'We are. And until the Moscow that wants to get its hands on Matthias's documents succeeds, the one I'm dealing with speaks for the Kremlin. Otherwise, that won't be the case. It's all the more reason why I've *got* to be kept current. If Havelock caught even one man we could trace to that other Moscow, it would be leverage. I could use it.'

'He's already told us,' interrupted Brooks. 'A branch of Soviet intelligence known as the VKR. Rostov as much as admitted it.'

Pierce looked bewildered. 'I didn't hear that mentioned.'

'Perhaps I overlooked it,' said Berquist.

'In any event, it's too general. The VKR is a consolidation of many units. I'd need specifics. Which unit? Which directors?'

'You may get them.'

'I beg your pardon, sir?' Pierce's gold-plated pen was suspended above his notes.

'It's one of the things that's keeping Havelock at Sterile Five.'

'Sterile Five . . .'

'They may have lost this Shippers but Havelock expects that whoever gave him orders will send men up to Maryland to find out who Matthew Randolph's been working with. He's got his own people in place with orders to wound and take. As I told you, the doctor lied about MacKenzie's death but for the wrong reasons.'

'Yes, I know.' Pierce looked down at his notes as he replaced the pen inside the coat of his dark, pin-stripe suit. 'It helps me to write things out; I didn't expect to take these with me.'

'I'm glad,' said the President. 'I wouldn't let you . . . You've got a lot to think about, Mr Undersecretary, and not much time. How do you plan to handle the Russians?'

'Cautiously,' replied the mole. 'With your permission, I'd like to substantiate a part of what they told me.'

'You're out of your *mind*,' said the general.

'Please, General, only a very minor part. They obviously have a fairly accurate source, so to deny the whole would only make them more suspicious, more hostile. We can't afford that now. In the President's words, we must contain them as much as possible for as long as possible.'

'How do you think you can do it?' asked Berquist, his eyes squinting, wary.

'By admitting that Matthias collapsed from exhaustion. Everything else has been exaggerated way out of proportion to the medical diagnosis, which is of minor consequence. He's been ordered to rest for several weeks; that's all. The rest is rumour and wild gossip, the sort of thing that goes with a man like Matthias. Don't forget, they have their memories of Stalin; they can't dismiss them. By the time Stalin was dead most of Moscow believed he was certifiably insane.'

'Excellent,' interjected Ambassador Brooks.

'They can't dismiss the other sources,' said Halyard, obviously wanting to agree but the strategist in him prohibiting it. 'The leaks from unstable regimes – instant prime ministers or whatever you called them. Matthias *reached* them.'

'Then they must be more specific with *me*. I think I can handle them case by case. At the least, they'd have to confer with Moscow, double check the origins. Every case could buy us time.' Pierce stopped, turning to Berquist. 'And time, Mr President, is what's on my mind now. I think the sooner I get back to New York and ask – no, demand – a meeting with the Soviet ambassador, the better chance I have of pushing their hands away from the buttons. I *do* believe they'll listen to me. I can't guarantee how long, but for a while – a few days, a week – they will.'

'Which prompts the obvious question,' said the statesman, his well-tailored elbows on the table, his slender hands folded beneath his chin. 'Why do you think they contacted you and not the more direct, crisis-oriented channels in Washington?'

'I'd like to know that too,' added Berquist. 'There's a phone never more than fifty feet away from me for such contingencies.'

Arthur Pierce did not at first reply, his eyes shifting back and forth between the President and the ambassador. 'It's difficult for me to answer that without appearing arrogant or overly ambitious, and I don't believe I'm either.'

'We'll accept that,' said Berquist. 'Just give us your opinion.'

'With all due respect to our ambassador in New York – and I'm sincere; he has an extremely likeable presence, which is terribly important, and he's had an outstanding career in government – '

'*Had*,' the President broke in. 'He's a soft bush in a high wind, but the roots are deep. He's there because of his *lovable* presence, and the fact that he doesn't make a goddamn decision. We'll accept that, too. Go on.'

'The Soviets know you appointed me – at Matthias's request – to be the State Department's spokesman. To be *your* spokesman, sir.'

'And the spokesman for Anthony Matthias,' said Brooks, nodding his head. 'Which assumes a close relationship with our Secretary of State.'

'I enjoyed such a relationship until a number of months ago – when apparently all relationships were terminated by his illness.'

'But they think you still have it,' observed Halyard. 'And why the hell not? You're the closest thing we could have there *except* Matthias.'

'Thank you, General. Basically, I think they came to me because they thought I'd know if there was any substance to the Matthias rumours. The madness.'

'And if they thought you knew but were lying, what would be their response?'

'They'd disregard the hot-line, Mr President. They'd put the world on nuclear alert.'

'Get back to New York and do what you can. I'll make the security arrangements for you to get down to Poole's Island. Study those arrangements until you know them word by word.'

The *paminyatchik* rose from the dais, leaving his unnecessary notes behind.

* * *

The limousine passed through the White House gates as Arthur Pierce shot forward in his seat, his hand gripping the strap and, in a harsh voice, spoke to the driver assigned to him by the Department of State. 'Get me to a phone booth as fast as you can.'

'The mobile phone's in working order, sir. It's in the case in the centre of the floor.' The driver removed his right hand from the wheel and gestured at the black leather receptacle behind him. 'Just pull up the latch.'

'I don't care to use this phone! A booth, please.'

'Sorry, sir, just trying to be helpful.'

The Undersecretary checked himself. 'I apologize. It's those mobile operators; they can take for ever and I'm in a great hurry.'

'Yeah, I've heard that complaint before.' The driver accelerated briefly, only to apply the brakes seconds later. 'There's one, sir. On the corner.'

Pierce got out of the car and walked rapidly to the glass box, coins in his hand. Inside, he pulled the door shut, inserted a quarter and dialled. 'Your trip?' he asked curtly.

'Smooth flight. Go ahead.'

'Has the detail left for Maryland?'

'About fifteen minutes ago.'

'*Stop* them!'

'How?'

The *paminyatchik* bit his lip. There could be no mobile phones for them, no system where numbers could be recorded. He had only one question left before issuing the order. 'Is there any way you can reach them once they're on the premises? Any way at all?'

The initial silence was his answer. 'Not the way it's orchestrated,' was the quiet reply.

'Send a second detail immediately. Police vehicle, automatic weapons, silencers. Kill them; kill them all. No one must be left alive.'

'You *sent* them!'

'It's a trap.'

'Oh, *Christ* . . . Are you sure?'

'I've just left the White House.'

A low whistle was the astonished response. 'It really paid off, didn't it?'

'They had no choice. As we say over here, I had all the marbles and I was shooting from the top of the circle. I'm inside. There's also something else.'

'What?'

'Reach Mother. Rostov's centred in on Victor. Find out how deep; elimination must be considered.'

Loring walked down the steps of the Pentagon thinking about Lieutenant-Commander Thomas Decker. He was not sure what Havelock was looking for, but he was fairly certain he had not got it. After having read Decker's complete service record, including endless evaluation and fitness reports over at the Department of the Navy, Charley had decided to pull in a few debts owed him at the Pentagon. On the pretext that the officer was being considered for a sensitive embassy position that required tact and a fair degree of personality, he called on several friends in Army Intelligence and said he needed a few confidential interviews. Could they help and did they remember when he had helped them? They did and they could.

Five people, each held accountable for confidentiality, were brought separately to him for informal, very off-the-record conversations. There were three fellow naval officers who had served with Decker aboard the submarine *Starfire*, a secretary who had worked in his office for six months and a marine who was on his Nuclear Committee team.

Havelock had said Decker was a liar. If he was, Loring had found no evidence to support it. He was, if anything, something of a moralizer, who had run a taut ship on the basis of strict Judeo-Christian principles to the point where he read the Lessons at each weekly interdenominational religious service he insisted should be part of the *Starfire*'s schedule. His reputation was that of a firm but fair skipper; like Solomon, he weighed all sides of an issue before rendering his decision, which he then proceeded to justify on the basis of what he had heard. As a fellow officer put it, one might disagree with a given course of action on Decker's part, but one understood how he had arrived at it. His 'engineer's mind', said another, grasped the 'blocks and tackles' of a complicated argument quicker than most and he was adept at spotting fallacies. Yet he never, according to the third officer, used another man's honest error to assert his own superiority; he accepted others' mistakes compassionately, so long as a man had given his best. This, thought Loring, was not a liar's approach. Liars jumped on the failings of others when they were gratuitously provided.

It was the secretary, however, who shed light on another side of Thomas Decker not readily perceived from his service record and the statements of his fellow naval officers. The Lieutenant-Commander apparently went to great lengths to please and support his own superiors.

He was always so tactful, so generous in his appraisals of other people's work even when you knew he thought it wasn't very good. There was this admiral . . . Then the White House put out a directive that choked him, but still he . . . And he gave his full endorsement to a Joint Chiefs of Staff position which he told me was really counterproductive . . . You talk about tact – well, the commander is about the most diplomatic man I've ever known.

The last person to talk with Charley Loring was the marine, a major and a member of Decker's Nuclear Contingency Committee. He put his own assessment of his colleague somewhat more succinctly.

He kisses ass something fierce, but what the hell, he's damned good. Also, that's not exactly an unknown exercise around here. Tact? . . . Christ, yes, he's got tact, but he's not going to hang himself over something really important. I mean, he'll find ways of greasing an issue so the oil's all over the table.

Translation: spread the responsibility for disagreement, preferably as high as it will flow, but if this attitude made for a dangerous liar, there were few truthful men at the Pentagon – or anywhere else, for that matter.

Loring reached his car in the side parking area, settled back in the seat and pulled out the microphone from its cradle beneath the dashboard. He flipped the power switch and pressed the transmission button, making contact with the White House mobile operator.

'Patch me through to Sterile Five, please,' he instructed. While everything was fresh in his mind he would relay it all to Havelock. For all the good it might do.

The Apache unit roamed the corridors of the medical centre, one or other of the two men keeping Dr Matthew Randolph in sight wherever he went. Neither man approved of the arrangements and let Sterile Five know it; they were inadequate for this particular subject. Randolph was an ageing jack rabbit who darted in and out of doors and hallways and outside exits with determined alacrity. Whatever had prompted the doctor to co-operate initially had evaporated as his contrariness reasserted itself. It was as though he were consciously trying to draw attention to himself, to *make* something happen, to challenge any one who might be waiting for him in an empty room or darkened corner to show himself. Beyond the intrinsic difficulty of protecting such a person, the two men found it senselessly unsafe to be forced to show *themselves*. Professionals were, by training and nature, cautious, and Randolph was making them behave otherwise. Neither man relished the thought of being picked off by a sharpshooter a hundred-odd yards away as he followed the cantankerous doctor down a driveway or across a lawn. There was nothing amusing about the situation. Two men were not enough. Even one other man covering the outside would relieve the pressure; more than one, they understood, might defeat the purpose of the strategy by making the whole operation too obvious. One more, however, was mandatory.

Sterile Five accommodated. The emergency call from Apache had interrupted Loring's report to Havelock on Decker. Since Loring was free, he would be flown up by a Pentagon helicopter to within a few miles of the medical centre, where a car would be waiting for him. He would be there in thirty-five to forty minutes.

'How will we know when he gets here?'

'Check the desk by an intercom phone. He'll come inside and ask directions to – Easton. Then he'll drive out and return on foot.'

'Thank you, Sterile Five.'

The sun was at the tree-top mark in the western sky, bathing the Virginia countryside in soft bursts of yellow and gold. Havelock wearily got up from the desk, his hand still warm from clutching the ever-present telephone.

'The Agency will dig all night, cross-checking with Cons Op and G-Two. They've located two photographs; six are still missing.'

'I'd think photographs would be the first consideration in these files' said Jenna, standing by the silver tray, pouring Michael a drink. 'You can't bring over such people if you don't know what they look like.'

He watched over her as she repeated the words he had heard over the phone.

'The men you chose were never considered that important,' Havelock said. 'They were marginal, to begin with, their value limited.'

'They were specialists.'

'Psychiatrists, psychologists and a couple of professors of philosophy. Old men who were permitted the privilege of expressing their views – some vaguely offensive, none earthshaking to the Kremlin.'

'But they all questioned theories promoted by Soviet strategists. Their questions were relevant to everything you've learned about Anthony Matthias.'

'Yes, I know. We'll keep looking.'

Jenna carried the short glass of straight whisky to the desk. 'Here, you need this.'

'Thanks.' Havelock took the glass and walked slowly towards the window. 'I want to pull in Decker,' he said. 'I've got to bring him down here. He'll never tell me over the phone. Not everything.'

'You're convinced he's your man, then?'

'No question about it. I just had to understand why.'

'Loring told you. He fawns on superiors, says he agrees with them even when he doesn't. Such a man would do Matthias's bidding.'

'Strangely enough, that's only part of it,' said Michael, shaking his head, then sipping his drink. 'That description fits most ambitious men everywhere; the exceptions are rare. Too rare.'

'Then what?'

Havelock stared out of the window. 'He makes a point of justifying everything he does,' began Michael slowly. 'He reads the Lessons at services instituted at his command; he plays at being Solomon. Underneath that tactful, unctuous exterior there has to be a zealot. And only a zealot in his position would commit a crime for which – as Berquist says – he'd be summarily executed in most countries, and even here he would spend thirty years in prison ... It wouldn't surprise me if Lieutenant-Commander Thomas Decker did it all. If I had my way, he'd be taken out and shot. For all the good it would do.'

The sun had dropped below the trees, mottled orange rays filtered by branches, spreading across the lawns and bouncing off the alabaster walls of the Randolph Medical Center. Charles Loring crouched by the trunk of a tall oak at the far end of the parking area, the front entrance and rear emergency ramp in clear view, his radio in his hand. An ambulance had just brought in the victim of a traffic accident and his wife from *US50*; the injured man was being examined by Dr Randolph and the Apache unit was in place in the corridor outside the examining room.

The Cons Op agent looked at his watch. He'd been at his post for nearly three-quarters of an hour – after a hastily arranged flight from the Pentagon helicopter pad to a car waiting for him at a private field on the outskirts of Denton, eight minutes away. He understood the Apache team's concerns. The man they were assigned to protect was making things difficult, but Charley would have handled it differently. He would have sat on this Randolph and told the doctor he didn't give a good goddamn whether he was chopped down or not, that the primary objective of the stake-out was to take even one of those coming after him, that *that* man's life was far more important than his. Such an explanation might have made Randolph more co-operative. And Loring might have been having a decent dinner somewhere, instead of waiting for God knew what on a cold, wet lawn in Maryland.

Charley looked up towards the intruding sound. A black and white patrol car swerved into the rear parking area, turned abruptly and came to a sudden stop at the side of the emergency ramp. Two police officers got out quickly and raced up towards the doors, one leaping onto the platform, both awkwardly holding their sides. Loring lifted the radio to his lips.

'Apache, this is Outside. A police car just drove up to the emergency dock in a hurry. Two cops are entering.'

'We see them,' came the reply, accompanied by static. 'We'll let you know.'

Charley looked again at the patrol car, and what he saw struck him as odd. Both doors were left open, something the police rarely did unless they intended to stay close to their vehicle. There was always the possibility that a radio might be tampered with, or a signal book stolen, or even concealed weapons.

The static erupted, words following. 'Interesting, but no sweat,' said an Apache as yet unseen by the Cons Op agent. 'Seems the wreck on Highway Fifty was traced to a prominent member of a Baltimore family. Mafia all the way, wanted on a dozen counts. They've just been admitted for identification and any possible last statements.'

'Okay. Out.' Loring lowered the radio and considered a cigarette, deciding against it for fear the light would give him away. His eyes strayed again to the stationary patrol car, his mind wandering. Suddenly, there was something to think about, something immediate.

He had passed a police station on the road to the medical centre, not five minutes away. He had recognized it not at first from the sign but by the cluster of three or four patrol cars in the side lot – not black-and-whites, but *red*-and-whites, the kind of bright colour scheme often adopted by shore resort areas. And if a sought-after, major league Mafioso had been taken minutes ago to a local hospital after a collision, there certainly would be more than one patrol car covering the action.

Open doors, men racing, arms at their sides – concealed weapons. Oh, my *God*!

'Apache! Apache, come in!'

'What is it, Outside?'

'Are those police still in there?'

'They just *went* in.'

'Go in after them! *Now!*'

'What?'

'Don't argue, just *do* it! With weapons!'

By the time the radio was in his pocket and the .38 in his hand, Charley was halfway across the parking area, racing as fast as he could towards the emergency dock. He reached the platform and sprang up with one hand, legs scrambling, body lunging for the wide metal doors. He crashed them open and dashed past a startled nurse behind a glass-partitioned reception counter, his head turning in all directions, his eyes choosing the corridor straight ahead; it conformed to the Apaches' position, their immediate sighting of the policemen. He ran down to an intersecting hallway, staring first to his left, then his right. There it was, ten feet away! EXAMINING ROOM. The door was shut; it did not make sense.

Loring approached swiftly, silently, taking long cautious steps, his back pressed against the wall. Suddenly he heard two muted spits and the start of a terrible, throated scream from behind the heavy steel door, and he knew his instincts had been as right as he now wished they had been wrong. He spun around the frame, so as to give his left hand free access to the metal handle, then jammed the handle down and threw his shoulder against the panel, crashing the door open, then turned back for the protection of the frame.

The shots came, exploding into the wall in front of him; they were high, the spits from deep inside the room, not close by. Charley crouched and dived, rolling as he hit the floor, and fired into a blue uniform. He fired low, bullets ricocheting off obstructing steel. *Legs, ankles, feet! Arms, if you have to, but not the chest, not the head! Keep him alive!*

The second blue uniform lunged over an examining table – a rushing blur of dark colour – and Loring had no choice. He fired directly at the attacking man who held a pipe-stock repeating weapon in his arms. The killer spun off the padded table, plummeting to the floor, his throat ripped open. Dead.

Keep the other alive, keep the other alive! The order kept screaming in his head as Charley kicked the door shut and lurched, rolling, firing at the ceiling and blowing out the bright overhead fluorescent tubes, leaving only the harsh glow of a small high-intensity lamp on a far-away table.

Three spits erupted from the shadows, the bullets embedding themselves into the plaster and wood above him. He rolled furiously to his left and collided with two lifeless bodies – were they Apaches? He could not tell; he only knew he could not let the man who was alive escape. And there were only two alive in that room, blood, shattered flesh and corpses everywhere.

It had been a massacre.

A spitting burst of gunfire staccatoed across the floor and he could feel the searing heat of the bullet that had punctured his stomach. But the pain did an odd thing to him, which he had no time to think about. He could only experience the reaction. His mind exploded in anger, but the anger was controlled, the fury directed. He had lost before. He could not lose again. He simply *could not!*

He sprang diagonally to his right, crashing into a stretcher table and sending it rolling towards the shadows from which the staccato burst had come; he heard the impact and rose swiftly, held his gun in both hands and aimed at another hand in the shadows. He fired as the screams swelled in the corridors beyond the closed door.

He had one last thing to do. And then he would not have lost.

34

Lieutenant-Commander Thomas Decker walked into the study of Sterile Five, escorted by two men from the White House Secret Service. His angular face was set, and he looked both purposeful and a trifle anxious. The broad-shouldered frame under the well-tailored blue uniform was that of a man who kept in shape not from enjoyment but from compulsion; the body was too rigid, with too little fluidity in its movement. But it was the face that fascinated Havelock. It was a hard-shelled mask about to crack, and once that process started, it would shatter. Strength, purpose and anxiety aside, Decker was petrified, and try as he might he could not conceal his inner terror.

Michael spoke, addressing the Secret Service detail. 'Thanks very much, gentlemen. The kitchen is outside to the right, at the end of the hallway. The cook will find you something to eat – beer, coffee, whatever you want. I'm sure I've interrupted your dinner break and I don't know when we'll be finished here. Make any phone calls you like, of course.'

'Thank you, sir,' said the man on Decker's left, nodding to his companion as they both turned and started for the door.

'You've also interrupted *my* dinner, and I expect – '

'Shut up, Commander,' broke in Havelock quietly.

The door closed, and Decker took several angry steps towards the desk but the anger was too contrived, too forced. It had been summoned to replace the fear. 'I have an engagement this evening with Admiral James at the Fifth Naval District!'

'He's been informed that pressing naval business precludes your being there.'

'This is outrageous! I *demand* an explanation!'

'You're entitled to a firing squad.' Havelock rose as Decker gasped. 'I think you know why.'

'*You!*' The officer's eyes grew wide; he swallowed as the colour left his mask of a face. 'You're the one who's been calling me, asking me those questions! Telling me . . . a very *great man* . . . doesn't remember! It's a *lie!*'

'It's the truth,' said Michael simply. 'But you can't understand and it's been driving you up the wall. It's all you've been thinking about since I told you – because you know what you've done.'

Decker became rigid again, brows arched, eyes clouded, a military man having given his serial number but refusing any subsequent interrogation despite impending torture. 'I have nothing to say to you. Mr Cross. It *is* Cross, isn't it?'

'It'll do,' said Havelock, nodding once. 'But you've got a great deal to say, and you *are* going to say it. Because if you don't, a presidential order will send you to the deepest cell in Leavenworth and the key will be thrown away. To put you on trial would be far too dangerous to the security of this country.'

'No! . . . You *can't*! I did nothing wrong! I was right, *we* were right!'

'The Joint Chiefs and key members of the House and Senate will agree,' continued Michael. 'It'll be one of the few times when the umbrella of national security will be completely valid.'

The mask cracked; the face shattered. Fear turned to desperation as Decker whispered, 'What do they say I've done?'

'In violation of your oath as an officer and the codes of secrecy you've sworn to uphold, you reproduced dozens of the most sensitive documents in this country's military history and removed them from the Pentagon.'

'And to *whom* did I deliver them? Answer me that.'

'It doesn't matter.'

'It *does*! It's everything!'

'You had no authorization.'

'*That* man has all the authority he needs!' Decker's voice trembled as he tried to regain control. 'I demand that you get Secretary of State Matthias on the phone.'

Havelock walked away from the desk, away from the telephone. The movement was not lost on the naval officer. It was the moment to retreat slightly.

'I've been given *my* orders, Commander,' said Michael, permitting a degree of uncertainty in his own voice. 'By the President and several of his closest advisers. The Secretary of State is not to be consulted in this matter under any circumstances whatsoever. He's not to be informed. I don't know why, but those are my orders.'

Decker took a halting step, then another, zeal joining the desperation in his stretched, frantic eyes. He began barely above a whisper, the words growing louder with a zealot's conviction. 'The *President*? His *advisers* . . . ? For God's sake, can't you *see*? Of course they don't want him informed because he's right and they're *wrong*. They're afraid and he isn't! Do you think for a moment if I disappeared he wouldn't know what had happened? Do you think he wouldn't confront the President and his advisers and force a showdown? You talk about the Joint Chiefs, members of the House and the Senate. My God, do you think he couldn't call them together and show what a weak, ineffective, *immoral* administration this really *is*? There'd *be* no administration! It would be repudiated, crippled, thrown out!'

'By whom, Commander?'

Decker straightened his broad-shouldered body, a condemned man knowing that ultimate justice would bring a pardon. 'The people, Mr Cross. The people of this nation recognize a giant. They won't turn their backs on him because a hack politician and his weak-kneed advisers say so. They won't stand for it! The world has lamented the loss of great leadership these past few decades. Well, we produced a great leader and the world knows it. And my advice to you is to get Anthony Matthias on the telephone. You don't have to say anything, I'll speak to him.'

Havelock stood motionless, something more than uncertainty now in his voice. 'You believe there could be a showdown? The President – impeached?'

'Look at Matthias. Can you doubt it? Where in the last thirty years has there been a man like him?'

Michael slowly walked back to the desk and lowered himself into the chair, glancing up at Decker. 'Sit down, Commander,' he said.

Decker quickly sat in the chair that Havelock had purposely placed in front of the desk. 'We've used some harsh words with each other, and for my part I apologize. But you *must* understand. We *are* right.'

'I need more than that,' said Havelock. 'We know you removed copies of detailed strategies developed by the Nuclear Contingency Committees, documents that spelled out everything in our own arsenals as well as the results of our deepest penetrations of both the Soviet and the Chinese systems. You delivered these to Matthias over a period of months, but we've never understood why. If you could tell me, give me a reason. *Why*?'

'For the most obvious reason in the world! It goes back to the key word in the title of those committees. Contingency. *Contingency*, Mr Cross, always contingency! *Reaction* – reaction to *this*, reaction to *that*! Always replying, never *initiating*! We only *respond*. We need a master plan, to let them know we have a master plan that will ensure their total destruction should they transgress. Our strength, our survival, can no longer be based on defence, Mr Cross, it must be based on *offence*! Anthony Matthias understands this. The others are afraid to face it.'

'And you helped him develop this – master plan?'

'I'm proud to say I contributed,' said the officer, his words rushed – the pardon was in sight. 'I sat with him hour after hour going over every conceivable nuclear option, every possible Soviet and Chinese response, not a single capability overlooked.'

'When did you meet?'

'Every Sunday, for weeks on end.' Decker lowered his voice, confidentiality joined now with zeal and desperation. 'He impressed on me the highly classified nature of our relationship, so I used to drive out in a rented car to his lodge in West Virginia, to a cabin on the secondary road where we'd meet alone.'

'The "Woodshed",' said Michael, the word escaping from him.

'You know it, then?'

'I've been there.' Havelock briefly closed his eyes; he knew the 'Woodshed' only too well: a small cabin retreat where Anton went to work on his projected memoirs – to talk out his thoughts, every phrase picked up by a voice-activated tape recorder. 'Is there anything else? I want you to know I'm listening, Commander. You're very impressive – and I'm listening.'

'He's such a truly *brilliant* man,' continued Decker, his tone close to an awestruck whisper, his eyes gazing on some unseen holy light. 'That probing mind, the depth of his every observation, his grasp of global realities – all *truly* remarkable. A statesman like Anthony Matthias can take this nation to its zenith, bring us to where we were meant to be in the eyes of man and God. Yes, I did what I did and I'd do it again, because I'm a patriot. I love this country as I love the scriptures, and I would lay down my life for it, knowing that I would retain my honour . . . There really is no choice, Mr Cross. We *are* right. Pick up the phone and call Matthias, tell him I'm here. And *I'll* tell him the truth. Small men who worship graven images have crawled out of the ground and are trying to destroy him. He'll stamp them out – with our help.'

Michael leaned back in the chair, the weariness, the futility, as complete as they had ever been. ' "With our help",' he repeated in a voice so low he was barely aware he had spoken.

'Yes, of course!'

Havelock shook his head slowly back and forth. 'You sanctimonious son of a bitch,' he said.

'What?'

'You heard me. *You sanctimonious son of a bitch!*' Michael roared. Then he breathed deeply and continued quietly, rapidly, 'You want me to call Matthias? I wish to hell I could, just to watch your goddamn face, to see your steely, self-righteous eyes grow wild when you learned the truth.'

'What are you talking about?' whispered Decker.

'Matthias wouldn't know who you *are*! Any more than he knows who the President is, or his aides, or the undersecretaries, or the diplomats he works with every day – or *me*, who's known him for over twenty years, closer to him than any other person alive.'

'No . . . no, you're wrong. No!'

'*Yes*, Commander! He broke. More precisely, *we broke him*. That mind is gone! It's shattered. He's insane. He couldn't take it any longer. And, by Christ, you did your part. You gave him his ultimate authority, his final responsibility. You stole the world's – yes, the *world's* secrets – and told him his genius could handle them. You took a thousand facts and a hundred theoretical strategies, mixed them up and turned them into the most terrifying weapon this earth has ever known. A blueprint for global annihilation.'

'That's *not* what I did!'

'Granted, not all by yourself, but you provided the – what the hell's that God-awful Pentagonese? – support-structure, that's it. You provided the support structure for a fiction that's so real there's not a nuclear expert alive who wouldn't accept it as truth. *Gospel* truth, if you like, Commander.'

'We only discussed, analysed, tore apart options! The final plan was to be his; you can't *understand*. His grasp was brilliant! There was nothing he couldn't comprehend; it was incredible!'

'It was the act of a mind dying, on the edge of becoming its own convoluted vegetable. He wanted you to believe, and he was still good enough to make you believe. He had to, and you wanted to.'

'I did! So would *you*!'

'That's what I've been told by a better man than you'll ever be.'

'I don't deserve that. He appealed to a truth I *do* believe in. We *must* be strong!'

'I don't know any sane person who would argue with that, but there are different kinds and degrees of strength. Some work – usually quietly; others don't, because they're swollen with bellicosity. The savage explodes from his own tension; he can't contain himself, he's got to flex. And somewhere along the line he blows up, setting in motion a dozen responses that are explosions in themselves.'

'Who *are* you? *What* are you?'

'A student of history who went astray. But I'm not the issue. You are. Everything you gave Matthias is within arm's reach of the Russians, Commander. That master plan, which you're so convinced we must let the world know we have, may in all its details be on its way to Moscow. Because the man you gave it to is insane, was on his way to becoming insane when you delivered the materials to him.'

Decker rose slowly from the chair. 'I don't believe you,' he said, his voice hollow, the words spoken in dread.

'Then why am I here? Why should I say it? Personal considerations aside, do you think anyone with the brains to get out of the rain wants to make that statement? Have you any idea what it means to this country to know that the mind of its Secretary of State has been destroyed? I'd like to remind you, Commander, that you don't have an exclusive claim to patriotism. None of you do.'

Decker stared down at Havelock until he could no longer bear the contact. He turned away, the broad-shouldered body somehow shrinking beneath the tunic. 'You tricked me. You made me say things I never would have said.'

'It's my job.'

'Everything's over for me. I'm finished.'

'Maybe not. As of this moment, I'd guess you were the least likely candidate for a security risk in the Pentagon. You've been burned by a legend and it's a pain you'll never forget. Nobody knows better than I do how persuasive Matthias could be . . . We need help, not prison sentences. Packing you off to Leavenworth would only raise questions no one wants raised. We're in a blind race; maybe you can help.'

Decker turned, swallowing, his face ashen. 'In any way I can. How?'

Michael got out of the chair and came round the desk to face the officer. 'For starters, nothing I've told you can be repeated.'

'My God, of *course* not.'

'No, of course not. You'd be hanging yourself.'

'I'd be hanging the country. I have no exclusivity on patriotism, but I am a patriot, Mr Cross.'

Havelock walked past the coffee table and the couch, and was reminded of Jenna's absence. Since they had agreed her presence would be inhibiting, she was upstairs; more accurately, she had insisted on not being there. He reached the wall, aimlessly studied a brass plaque, and spoke. 'I'm going to guess again, Commander. There came a time when Matthias wouldn't see you any more. Am I right?'

'Yes. I phoned repeatedly – not at State, of course – but he never returned my calls.'

'Not at State?' asked Michael, turning. 'But you *did* call there. It's how I found you.'

'Only three times. Twice to say there were Sunday conferences at the Pentagon, and once to tell him I was going into hospital for minor surgery on a Friday and expected to be there until Tuesday or Wednesday. He was very solicitous, but that was when he told me never again to contact him at the State Department.'

'You called the lodge, then?'

'And his house in Georgetown.'

'This is later?'

'Yes. I called night after night, but he wouldn't come to the phone. Try to understand, Mr Cross. I was aware of what I'd done, of the enormity of the violation I'd committed. Mind you, until a few minutes ago I've never regretted it. I can't change my beliefs; they're ingrained in me. But back then – five or six months ago – I was bewildered, frightened perhaps, I'm not sure. I'd been left stranded – '

'You were in withdrawal,' interrupted Havelock. 'You'd been on a high, on one of the most potent narcotics in the world: Anthony Matthias. Suddenly he wasn't there any longer.'

'Yes, that's it. Those were heady days, magnificent memories. Then without knowing why my connection to greatness was severed. I thought perhaps it was something I'd done that displeased him, or information I'd brought him that was deficient, incomplete. I didn't know, I just knew that I'd been cut off, with no explanation.'

'I understand,' said Michael, remembering so clearly the night in Cagnes-sur-Mer when his *pritel* did not come to the telephone five thousand miles away. 'I'm surprised you didn't force the issue, confront him somehow, somewhere. You were entitled to that explanation.'

'I didn't have to. It was finally given to me.'

'*What?*'

'One evening, after I'd tried to reach him again, to no avail again, a man called me back. A very strange man – '

The prolonged outburst of the phone shattered the moment, blowing apart the taut line of concentration. Havelock ran to it, to the sustained ring that signalled *Emergency*.

'It's Loring,' said the strained voice in a half-whisper. 'I'm hit. I'm okay, but I'm hit.'

'Where are you?'

'A motel on Highway Three-seventeen, near Harrington. The Pheasant Run Motel. Cabin Twelve.'

'I'll send a doctor.'

'A very *special* doctor, Havelock. Use the field in Denton.'

'What do you mean?'

'I had to get out of there. I grabbed a police car – '

'A police . . . ? *Why?*'

'I'll tell you later. Everything . . . Special doctor with a bag full of needles.'

'For Christ's sake, spell it *out*, Charley!'

'I've got one of those sons of bitches. He's strapped naked on the bed – no capsules, no razors. I've *got* one!'

Havelock stabbed the buttons on the Sterile Five telephone one after another, issuing orders one after another as Lieutenant Commander Decker stood rigidly across the room, watching, listening, a helpless shell of a crusader whose cause had collapsed. The President was informed, and a very special doctor was being tracked down, to be sent to Maryland by helicopter, a Secret Service detail accompanying him. A second helicopter was prepared for take off, waiting for Michael at the field in Quantico six miles away; he would be driven there by the Secret Service escorts who had brought Decker to Sterile Five. The final call placed by Havelock was within the house itself. Upstairs. To Jenna Karras.

'I have to leave. It's Loring in Maryland. He's wounded, but he may have picked up a traveller – don't ask me how. And you were right. One source. He's here and has more to say; please come down and take it. I have to go . . . Thanks.'

Michael got up from the desk and addressed the frightened naval officer. 'A lady's on her way here, and I'm ordering you – ordering you, Commander – to tell her everything you were going to tell me and answer fully any questions she may ask. Your escort will be back in twenty minutes or so. When you're finished, and only if she agrees, you may go. But once you reach your house you're not to leave it for any reason whatsoever. You'll be watched.'

'Yes, Mr Cross.'

Havelock grabbed his jacket off the back of the chair and started towards the door. He stopped and turned to Decker, his hand on the knob. 'Incidentally, her name is Mrs Cross.'

All low-flying traffic was diverted as the two helicopters roared into the small private field in Denton, Maryland, the aircraft from the Bethesda Naval Hospital arriving eleven minutes before the chopper from Quantico. Havelock raced across the tarmac to the staff car sent over from Annapolis, the driver an ensign reputed to know the roads on the Eastern Shore of Chesapeake Bay. The ensign knew nothing else; no one did; not even the doctor whose orders were to take care of Charles Loring first and not to administer anything to Loring's prisoner until Sterile Five was on the scene. Two state police patrol cars had been sent to the Pheasant Run Motel; they would be given their instructions by the Secret Service.

If the name Pheasant Run gave rise to images of squiredom and hunt country, it was misapplied to the sleazy motel's row of run-down cabins just off the main road. Apparently, the motel's primary function was to serve as a meeting place for assignations lasting an hour or so; cars were parked in small unpaved areas at the rear, out of sight of the main road. The management catered to its clientele's idiosyncrasies if not their comforts, and Loring had used his head. A man in pain, concealing wounds, without luggage but with a prisoner he wanted to rush surreptitiously into hiding, could hardly hope to register at a brightly lit Howard Johnson's Motor Lodge.

Havelock thanked the ensign and told him to return to Annapolis, reminding him that the present emergency called for the utmost secrecy. Washington had his name, and his co-operation would not be overlooked. The young man, obviously impressed by the sight of searchlights and military helicopters at night, as well as by his own participation, replied in a monotone, 'You may be assured of my silence, sir.'

'Just say you went out for a beer, that's good enough. Better, maybe.'

A government man, holding up an encased silver badge in his palm, intercepted Michael as he ran along the row of cabins looking for number *12.*

'Sterile Five,' said Havelock, noticing for the first time the two state police cars parked in the shadows twenty feet apart to his left. Number *12* was nearby.

'This way,' said the man, pocketing his badge as he led Michael between two cabins towards the rear of the motel's grounds. Beyond was a shorter row of cabins, which were not visible from the front. Loring had spent precious moments of pain and anxiety studying the motel's layout – again an indication that he was in control.

In the distance, behind the cabin on the left, the bonnet of a stationary car could be seen, but it was not an ordinary car. A streak of white ending in an arrowhead was stencilled over the black chassis at midpoint. It was the patrol car Loring had stolen, the only indication that perhaps he had lost a part of the control that had served them all so well. Someone in

Washington would have to reach a panicked police headquarters and call off the hunt.

'This is it,' said the federal agent, pointing to the door of a cabin which opened on to a verandah three steps above ground level. 'I'll be out here,' added the man. 'Watch those steps; they're loose.'

'Thanks,' said Havelock, going cautiously up to the door. He tried the knob; it was locked. In answer to his knock, someone inside asked, 'Who is it?'

'Sterile Five,' replied Michael.

The door was opened by a stocky, red-haired man in his middle thirties, his Celtic face freckled, his eyes wary, his sleeves rolled up. 'Havelock?'

'That's right.'

'Name's Taylor. Come on in, we've got to talk fast.'

Michael walked inside the room with the soiled wallpaper; the doctor closed the door. On the bed was a naked man, spread-eagled, bloody hands and feet tied to the frame, belts around the wrists, a torn sheet lashed to his ankles. His mouth was pulled taut by a striped blue tie to inhibit any loud sound and his eyes were wide with anger and fear.

'Where's . . . ?'

Taylor gestured towards the far corner of the room. There on the floor, his head on a pillow and a blanket over him, was Charles Loring, his eyes only partially open; he was dazed or in shock. Havelock started across the filthy grey carpet but was stopped by the doctor's grip on his arm.

'That's what we have to talk about. I don't know what's going on here, but I do know I can't be responsible for that man's life unless we got him to a hospital an hour ago. Do I make myself clear?'

'As soon as we can, not right now,' said Michael, shaking his head. 'I've got to question him. He's the only person who can give me the information I need. Everyone else is dead.'

'Maybe you didn't hear me. I said an hour ago.'

'I heard you, but I know what I have to do. I'm sorry.'

'I don't *like* you,' said Taylor, staring at Havelock, removing his hand as if he had touched something loathsome.

'I wish that could concern me, Doctor, because I like *him*. I'll be as brief and as quiet as I can. He'd want it this way, take my word for it.'

'I have to. I couldn't persuade him to get out of here ten minutes ago.'

Michael walked over to Loring and knelt down, putting his face close to the wounded man's. 'Charley, it's Havelock. Can you hear me?'

Loring opened his eyes wider, his lips trembling, struggling to form the words. Finally the whisper came. 'Yes. Hear . . . you . . . fine.'

'I'll tell you what I've learned, which is damned little. Nod your head if I'm on the track, shake it if I'm not. Don't waste words or breath. Okay?' The Cons Op agent nodded and Michael continued, 'I spoke with the police who are trying to put it together. As they tell it, an ambulance brought in a traffic accident with his wife, and Randolph, a staff doctor and a nurse were cleaning him up, checking the extent of injuries.' Loring shook his head, but Havelock went on, 'Let me finish, then we'll go back. They weren't in there five minutes when two state troopers came running in and spoke with our cardiologists. No one knows what was said, but they were admitted into the examining room.' Again the Cons Op agent shook his head. 'A couple of minutes later a third man – I assume that was you – crashed through emergency doors, and that's when everything went down.' Loring nodded; Havelock took a breath and continued softly, rapidly.

'The staff heard gunshots, perhaps five or six, no one's sure. Most of them ran out of the building. The rest hid in the corridors and patients' rooms behind locked doors, everyone trying to reach a phone. When the gunfire stopped, someone outside saw you and one of the state police come running down the ramp – you were bent over with a gun in your hand, the officer was bleeding, limping and holding his arm. You forced him into the patrol car and got out of here. The police are trying to find out who the other trooper was, but identifications were taken off some of the bodies, not all.' Loring shook his head violently. Michael touched his shoulder. 'Take it easy; we'll go back. I don't have to tell you the body count was full. Randolph, the staff doctor, the nurse, the accident victim and his wife and our Apache unit. Two automatic weapons equipped with silencers were found; they're still counting the shells. Yours was the gunfire that was heard; they're tracing the weapons, matching prints. Beyond what I've told you, no one knows what happened ... Now, let's go back.' Havelock squinted, remembering. 'The traffic accident.'

Loring shook his head, whispering. 'No accident.'

'Why not?'

'They *weren't* troopers.'

Michael looked up at the naked man strapped to the bed, and at the uniform rumpled on the floor. 'Of course they weren't. And the patrol car was a mock-up; they've got the money for that kind of thing. I should have known; you wouldn't have taken it otherwise.'

The wounded agent nodded, his hand emerging from under the blanket, gesturing for Havelock to lean closer. 'The man and the woman ... from the ambulance ... the accident. Any IDs?'

'No.'

'Same with the troopers ... right?'

'Right.'

'The accident,' whispered Loring, stopping for breath. 'Too easy. Man hurt ... a woman who won't leave his side. They get in ... to a room .... doctor, nurse ... Randolph. They got him.'

'How could they know Randolph would be there?'

'Doesn't matter. They'd tell the doctor ... or the nurse to call for him ... under a gun. Probably did. They *got* him. Too easy.'

'And the troopers?'

'In a hurry ... running like hell. They were sent to break it up, break it *all* up ... in a hurry.'

'How did you figure that?'

'They left the doors open, ran funny ... heavy weapons under their coats. The pattern wasn't normal, wasn't right ... Apache said the accident was a big-balled Mafioso the cops came to question. If he was, there'd be ten vehicles there, not one.' Loring expelled his breath, coughing; blood trickled out of the corners of his mouth. He gasped, and resumed breathing. The doctor was now behind Havelock.

'For Christ's sake,' said Taylor quietly but with angry intensity. 'Why don't you just put a bullet in his head?'

'Why don't I put one in yours?' Michael leaned back towards Loring. '*Why*, Charley? Why do you think they were sent in to break it up?'

'I'm not sure. Maybe I was spotted . . . maybe I blew it again.'

'I don't believe that.'

'Don't be so goddamn nice, I can't stand it . . . I probably did blow it . . . I'm getting old.'

'Then just pass on your instincts, Methuselah, we need them. You didn't blow anything. You brought us one, you *brought* us one, Charley.'

Loring tried to raise his shoulders, Michael gently holding him down. 'Tell me something, Havelock. You said this morning . . . about Shippers. "A long time ago". You said he was programmed a long time ago. Tell me. Is that son of a bitch over there a . . . a traveller?'

'I think he is.'

'Goddamn . . . maybe I'm not so old.'

Michael got to his feet and turned to the doctor behind him. 'All right, Taylor, he's yours. Get him over to the field and have him taken to the best facilities at Bethesda. And get on the phone and tell those mothers the White House wants the finest team of surgeons you've got ready and waiting for this man.'

'Yes, *sir*,' said the doctor sardonically. 'Anything else, *sir*?'

'Oh, yes, physician. Prepare your bag of magic. You're about to go to work.'

Loring was carried out on a stretcher by two male nurses who had been standing by; they were given firm instructions by the doctor as they took away the wounded Cons Op agent. Taylor turned to Havelock.

'Do we start now?'

'What about the wounds?' asked Michael, looking down at the naked man's bandaged but blood-streaked right arm and left foot.

'Your friend put tourniquets where they were needed, and I added dressings; the bleeding's arrested. Also, he was damned accurate. Bone was shattered, but apart from the pain, nothing'll drain him. Naturally, I gave him a couple of locals to ease him, keep his head clearer.'

'Will they interfere with the chemicals?'

'I wouldn't have administered them if they did.'

'Then shoot him up, Doctor. I can't waste time.'

Taylor went to his large black leather case which was open and on a table near the window under the glow of a lamp. He studied the contents for several moments, took out three vials and three cased syringes and placed them on the edge of the bed next to the naked man's thigh. The prisoner raised his head, his features contorted, his eyes glazed, frenzied; he was close to hysterics. Suddenly he began to writhe furiously, and muffled animal-like howls came from his throat. He stopped, overwhelmed, by the pain in his right arm, and, gasping for breath, he stared at the ceiling. Then abruptly he held the air in his lungs, his face becoming redder by the second, eyes now bulging.

'What the hell is he – '

'Get out of my *way!*' shouted Havelock, pushing the doctor aside and crashing his clenched fist down on the killer's bare stomach. The breath exploded out of the traveller's bound mouth, and the eyes and flesh tone began returning to normal.

'*Jesus,*' said Taylor, rushing forward to steady the vials which were about to roll off the edge of the bed. 'What was *that?*'

'You're dealing with something you may never have dealt with before, Doctor. They're programmed like robots, killing whomever they're told to kill – without any feeling at all, without the slightest concern. Not even for themselves.'

'Then he won't negotiate. I thought maybe if he saw these things, he might.'

'No way. He'd stall us, throw us off with every plausible lie in the books, and they know them all. They're masters of the craft. Let's go, Doctor.'

'How do you want to progress? In stages, which will bring him back one step at a time, or do you want to chance a maximum? It's the fastest, but there's a risk.'

'What's the worst with it?'

'Incoherence. Disjointed rambling, no logical pattern.'

'No logical . . . ? That's it. I'll chance the incoherence, just get him away from any patterns that might trigger programmed responses.'

'It doesn't work quite that way. The flow becomes formless; dissociation is the first reaction. The key is to hit certain words – '

'You're saying everything I want to hear, Doctor, and you're also wasting time.'

'You think so?' With the swiftness of a surgeon stemming a sudden internal eruption, Taylor broke off a vial's tiny glass casing, inserted the syringe, withdrew it and plunged it into the traveller's thigh before the bound man knew it was happening. The killer writhed violently, yanking at the belts and the torn sheets in an effort to break them, rolling from side to side as muffled cries filled the room. 'The more he does that, the quicker it'll take effect,' added Taylor, pressing his hand on the side of the stretched, whipping neck. 'Only a minute or so.'

Michael watched, fascinated and revolted, as he always was when observing the effect of these chemicals on a human being. He had to remind himself that this killer had brutally taken the lives of men and women less than three hours ago – his own people and others, the guilty and the totally innocent. How many would mourn for them and never understand? And how many were laid at the feet of one Michael Havelock, courtesy of Anton Matthias? Two career officers, a young doctor, a younger nurse, a man named Randolph, whose only crime was to try to right a terrible wrong.

Futility.

'He's about ready now,' said Taylor, studying the filmy, partially closed eyes of the prisoner, whose movements had contracted into slow, weaving motions accompanied by moans.

'You must be happy in your work, Doctor.'

'I was always a nosy kid,' answered the red-haired man, gently removing the striped tie from the traveller's mouth. 'Besides, someone's got to do it and big uncle paid for my medical degree. My old man couldn't pay for a bucket of suds in Paddy O'Rourke's saloon. I'll pay my debt and get out.'

Havelock leaned over the bed as Taylor backed away. 'May I begin?' he asked.

'Talk, he's your crossword puzzle.'

'*Orders*,' began Michael, his hand on the headboard, his lips near the traveller's ear, his voice firm, steady, low. 'Orders, orders, *orders*. None of us can move without our *orders*! But we have to be certain, we can't make a mistake. Who can clear our *orders*, clear our orders *now*?'

The prisoner's head moved back and forth, his mouth alternately opening and closing, stretching the bruised flesh. But no sound came.

'It's an emergency,' continued Havelock. 'Everybody *knows* it's an emergency . . . an *emergency*. We've got to hurry, hurry . . . hurry up.'

'Hurry . . . hurry *up*.' The whisper emerged, tentative, uncertain.

'But how can we be *sure*?' Michael raced on. 'We have to be *certain*.'

'The flight . . . the flight was *smooth*. We heard it twice. That's all we have to know. The flight . . . *smooth*.'

'Of course. A *smooth flight*. We're all right now. We can hurry . . . Now, let's float back . . . before the emergency. Relax. Sleep.'

'Very good,' said the doctor from across the dimly lit, squalid room. 'You centred him as quickly as I've ever seen it done. That was a response.'

'It wasn't difficult,' replied Havelock, rising from the bed and studying the traveller. 'Since he's been given his orders he's had three things on his mind. Emergency, speed and clearance. His instructions were to kill – an extreme order, also a dangerous one – so clearance was vital. You heard him, he had to hear it twice.'

'The code was a "smooth flight". He gave it to you, and now you'll give it back to him. You're closer.'

'And you're no amateur, Doctor. Get me a chair, will you? I've also got speed and emergency on my mind. Things may get rough.' Taylor brought a straight-backed chair over to the bed; Michael sat down; the chair was unsteady but serviceable. He leaned forward, arms on the edge of the bed, and spoke again to the bound man. 'We have a smooth flight . . . a smooth flight . . . a *very smooth flight! Now* kill your partner!'

The traveller whipped his head to the right, his clouded eyes blinking, his lips moving – protest without sound.

'You heard me!' shouted Havelock. 'We have a smooth flight, so *kill him*!'

'What . . . ? *Why*?' The whispered words were guttural.

'Are you married? Tell me, since we're on a smooth flight, are you *married*?'

'Yes . . . yes, married.'

'Kill your *wife*!'

'Why?'

'We're on a *smooth flight*! How can you *refuse*?'

'Why . . . *why*?'

'Kill your partner! Kill your wife! Do you have children?'

'*No*!' The traveller's eyes widened, the glaze within on fire. 'You could never ask . . . *never*!'

'I do! A smooth flight! What more do you need?'

'*Clearance*. I demand clearance! I . . . must have it!'

'From where? From whom? I've already told you. We're on a smooth flight! That's *it*!'

'*Please* . . . ! Me, kill *me*. I'm . . . confused!'

'Why are you confused? You heard my orders, just as you heard the orders for today. Did I give you those orders?'

'No.'

'*No*? You don't remember? If not me, *who*?'

'The trip . . . the smooth flight. The . . . control.'

'The *control*?'

'The source.'

'The source-control! *Your* source-control. I *am* your source-control! Kill your partner! Kill your wife! *Kill the children! All* the children!'

'I . . . *I*. You can't ask me . . . please don't ask me.'

'I don't ask. I demand, I give orders! Do you want to sleep?'

'Yes.'

'You *can't* sleep!' Michael turned his head and spoke to Taylor, his voice soft, barely audible. 'How long will the dose last?'

'The way you're eating it up, half the normal time. Another ten minutes, tops.'

'Prepare another. I'm taking him up.'

'It'll blow him into space.'

'He'll come down.'

'You're the doctor,' said the doctor.

'*I* am your source-control!' shouted Havelock, getting out of the chair, leaning over the traveller's face. 'You have no one else, *paminyatchik*! You will do as I tell you and *only* what I tell you! Now, your *partner*, your *wife*, the *children* . . .'

'*Ahhhh* . . . !' The scream was prolonged, a cry beyond helplessness.

'I've only *begun* . . .'

The bound, drugged killer, strained against the leather and the cloth, body and features twisted, his mind in a labyrinth of terror, with sacrifice demanded upon sacrifice, pain upon pain, no way out of the impossible maze.

'*Now*,' said Havelock to the doctor beside him.

Taylor plunged the hypodermic needle into the traveller's arm; the reaction was there in moments, drug accelerating drug. The screams turned into animal screeches, saliva flowing from the killer's mouth – violence the only answer to violence.

'*Give* it to me!' yelled Michael. '*Prove* it to me! Or be killed with everyone else! Partner, wife, children . . . you all die unless you can prove yourself to me. Right now, this moment! . . . *What is the code for your source-control*?'

'*Hammer-zero-two*! You *know* it!'

'Yes, I know it. Now tell me, where can I be reached – don't *lie*!'

'Don't know . . . don't *know*! I'm called . . . we're all called.'

'When you want clearance! When you have information to deliver. How do you reach me when you want clearance, when you have information that has to be relayed.'

'Tell them . . . need it. We all do. Everyone.'

'Who?'

'Orphan. Reach . . . Orphan.'

'*Orphan?*'

'Ninety-six.'

'Orphan-ninety-six? Where is he? *Where?*'

'*O . . . r . . . p . . . h . . .*' The final scream was shattering. The traveller thrashed his full strength and weight against the belts and broke one, releasing his left arm. He lunged upwards, then arched his back in a spasm and fell unconscious over the far side of the bed.

'He's had it,' said Taylor, reaching across Havelock and holding the prisoner's wrist in his fingers. 'His pulse is a jackhammer; it'll be eight hours before he can sustain another jolt. Sorry – Doctor.'

'It's all right, Doctor,' said Michael, walking away from the bed and reaching into his pocket for cigarettes. 'We could have done worse. You're a hell of a good chemist.'

'I don't consider it my life's work.'

'If it weren't right now, you might not have – ' Havelock stopped to light a cigarette.

'What?'

'Nothing. I meant *you* might not have time for a drink, but I do.'

'Sure, I do. I'll get Boris here down to a clinic.'

'Boris? . . . You know?'

'Enough to know he's not a Boy Scout.'

'That's the funny thing. He probably was.'

'Tell me,' asked the red-haired doctor, 'would a source-control order him to do that? Kill his wife and kids, people that close to him?'

'Never. Moscow wouldn't risk it. These people are like robots, but it's blood inside, not oil. They're monitored continuously, and if the KGB wants them taken out, an execution squad is sent in to do it. A normal family is part of the cover; it's also a powerful secondary hook. If a man's ever tempted, he knows what will happen.'

'You used it the same way, didn't you? Only in reverse.'

'I'm not wildly proud of the accomplishment, but yes.'

'Jesus, Mary and Paddy O'Rourke,' muttered the doctor.

Michael watched as Taylor reached for the bedside phone to issue his instructions through Bethesda Central. The *telephone. Orphan-96.* 'Wait a minute!' Michael cried suddenly.

'What's the matter?'

'Let me use that phone!' Havelock rushed to the table, picked up the telephone and dialled, talking out loud as he did so. 'O, r, p, h, a, n . . . *nine six.*'

'Operator,' said the female voice on the line.

'What?'

'Is this a collect call, billed to a credit card, or to another number?'

'Credit card.' Michael stared at the wall to remember his untraceable, State-assigned number. He gave it to the operator and heard the subsequent ringing.

'Good evening and thank you for calling the Voyagers Emporium, luggage for the sophisticated globe-trotter. If you'll state the numbered item or items

from our catalogue you wish to purchase, you will be connected to the
proper representative in our twenty-four-hour service department.'

Havelock replaced the phone. He needed another code; it would be found
in a clinic. It *had* to be found . . . *We all do. Everyone* . . . Ambiguity was at
the end of that code.

'Anything?' asked the bewildered Taylor.

'That'll be up to you, Doctor. Ever heard of the Voyagers Emporium? I
don't know it, but then for years I've bought my stuff in Europe.'

'The Voyagers? Sure. They've got branches all over the place. They're
the Tiffany of the luggage business. My wife bought one of those carry-on
bags and I swear to God when I got the bill I thought she'd picked up a car.
They're first class.'

'They're also trade marked KGB. That's what you're going to work on.
Whatever your schedule is, scratch it. I want you down at the clinic with
our globe-trotter here. We need another series of numbers. Just one more
set.'

There was a sound of heavy footsteps outside the cabin, followed by a
harsh rapping on the door.

'What is it?' asked Havelock, loud enough to be heard outside.

'Sterile Five, you're wanted. Urgent call over the state police vehicles.
You're to be taken to the airfield pronto.'

'On my way.' Havelock turned to Taylor. 'Make your arrangements. Stay
with it – with *him*. I'll be in touch. Sorry about the drink.'

'So's Paddy O'Rourke.'

'Who the hell is Paddy O'Rourke?'

'A little man who sits on my shoulder and tells me not to think too much.'

Michael climbed into the marine helicopter, the giant overhead blades
thundering, the pilot beckoning him forward to the flight deck.

'There's a patch-phone back there!' shouted the pilot. 'It'll be quieter
when the hatch is closed. We'll put your call through.'

'Who is it?'

'We'll never know!' yelled the radio-man, turning from his console against
the bulkhead. 'Our link is filtered. We're by-passed.'

The heavy metal door was electronically swung into place, shutting out
the spill of the airfield's searchlights and reducing the thunder of the rotors
to a muffled roar. Havelock crouched in the flashing darkness and gripped
the phone, holding it to his right ear, his free hand covering the other. The
voice that came last on the line was that of the President of the United
States.

'You're being flown directly to Andrews Air Force Base to meet with
Arthur Pierce.'

'What's happened, sir?'

'He's on his way to Poole's Island with the vault specialist, but wants to
talk with you first. He's a frightened man, and I don't think he frightens
easily.'

'The Russians?'

'Yes. He can't tell whether they accepted his story or not. They listened
to him in silence, nodded and showed him the door. He has an idea that

during the past eighteen hours they've learned something major, something they won't talk about – something that could blow everything apart. He warned them not to make any precipitous moves without communication at the highest levels.'

'What was their response?'

'Deadly. "Look to yourselves", they said.'

'They've got something. Pierce knows his enemy.'

'In the last extremity, we'll be forced to parade Matthias . . . hoping to deter a launch, no guarantee that it will. I don't have to tell you what it will mean – we'll be a government of lepers, never trusted again. If we're on the map.'

'What can I do? What does Pierce want?'

'All you've got, everything you've learned. He's trying to find something, *anything*, he can use as a lever. Every hour he can present a counter charge and prevent escalation, every day he can buy us, is a day for you. You *are* making progress?'

'Yes. We know the Ambiguity connection now, where he sends and receives. By mid-morning we should learn just how he does it, through whom. When we do we'll find him.'

'Then you *could* be a step away from Parsifal.'

'I think so.'

'I don't want to hear that! I want to hear *yes*.'

'Yes, Mr President.' Havelock paused, thinking about the few, brief words they needed to break the Voyagers code. They would be heard and recorded in a clinic. 'I believe it.'

'You wouldn't say it otherwise, thank *God*. Get down to Pierce. Give him everything you've got. *Help* him!'

35

The intersecting runways were lined with amber airstrip lamps. Searchlight beams crisscrossed and penetrated the dense cloud cover as routine patrols and check-out flights soared off into the night sky and swooped down from the darkness on to the floodlit open field. Andrews was a vast, guarded military city unto itself. The activity was intense, both on the field and off. As headquarters of the US Air Force Systems Command, its responsibilities were as far-ranging as they were endless. For thousands there was no such thing as day or night – merely duty hours and assignments. Banks of computers in a dozen buildings coexisted with the constant flow of expertise from the human interpreters, all forming judgements that affected NORAD, CONAD, the DEW line stations and SAC. The base occupied some 4,400 acres east of the Potomac and west of Chesapeake Bay, but its interests circled the globe, its purpose being the defence of the North American continent.

The marine helicopter was given clearance to enter a low-altitude pattern and set down on a pad north of the main field. Searchlights caught them a quarter of a mile away from ground-zero as radar, radio and a pilot's sharp eyes eased them into the threshold from which they could make the vertical descent. Among the instructions radioed from the control tower was a message for Sterile Five. A jeep would be standing by to take Havelock to a runway on the south perimeter. It would wait there until his business was concluded and return him to the helicopter.

Havelock climbed out of the hatch and jumped to the ground. The damp chill of the air was accentuated by the rushing wash of the decelerating rotors, and as he walked rapidly away from it he pulled the lapels of his overcoat around his throat, wishing he had worn a hat – but then he remembered that the only hat he owned at the moment was a ragged knit cap that he'd left somewhere down on Poole's Island.

'Sir! *Sir!*' The shout came from Michael's left, beyond the tail assembly of the helicopter. It was the driver of the jeep, the vehicle itself barely visible in the shadows between the blinding arc lights of the pad.

Havelock ran over as the sergeant behind the wheel started to get out as a gesture of courtesy. 'Forget it,' said Michael, approaching the side panel, his hand on the windscreen frame. 'I didn't see you,' he added, stepping over and lowering himself into the seat.

'Those were my instructions,' explained the air force non-com. 'Stay out of sight as much as possible.'

'Why?'

'You'll have to ask the man who gives the orders, sir. I'd say he's careful, and since nobody's got a name I don't ask questions.'

The jeep shot forward, expertly manoeuvred by the driver onto a narrow asphalt road fifty yards east of the helicopter pad. He turned left and accelerated, the road virtually circled the massive field, passing lighted buildings and enormous parking lots – flickering black structures and dark, spacious blurs – interspersed with the glare of onrushing headlights; everything at Andrews was apparently always at triple time. The wind whipped through the open vehicle, the slapping damp air penetrating Michael's coat, making him tense his muscles against the cold.

'I don't care if he calls himself Little Bo Peep,' said Havelock, as much for conversation as for anything else. 'So long as there's heat wherever we're going.'

The sergeant glanced briefly at Michael. 'Sorry again,' he replied, 'but the man doesn't have it that way. My instructions are to take you to a runway on the south perimeter. I'm afraid that's it. A runway.'

Havelock folded his arms and kept his eyes on the road ahead, wondering why the Undersecretary of State was being so cautious within a military compound. Then his thoughts dwelt briefly on the man himself and he found part of the answer – the blind part, but nevertheless intrinsic; there had to *be* a reason. From what he had read about Arthur Pierce in the State Department dossier, coupled with what he had known from a distance, the Undersecretary was a bright, persuasive spokesman for American interests at the United Nations, as well as around the international conference tables, with an avowed and profound mistrust of the Russians. This mistrust, however, was couched in a swift, aggressive wit and woven in deceptively pleasant frontal assaults that drove the stolid Russians wild for they had no matching counter-attacks, except for bluster and defiance. Perhaps Pierce's outstanding credential was that he had been hand-picked by Matthias himself when Anton was at the height of his intellectual powers. But the characteristic that stood out in Havelock's mind while racing down the dark airfield road was the highly regarded self-discipline attributed to Arthur Pierce by just about everybody who had contributed to his service dossier. He was never known to say anything unless he had something to say. By extension, thought Michael, he would not do something unless there was a reason for doing it.

And he had chosen to meet on a runway.

The driver swung left into an intersecting road that ran the distance of a huge maintenance hangar, then turned right onto the border of a deserted airstrip. In the distance, silhouetted in the glare of the headlights, was the figure of a man standing alone. Behind him, perhaps five hundred feet beyond and off the strip, was a small prop-jet with interior and exterior lights on and a fuel truck alongside it.

'There's the man,' said the sergeant, slowing down. 'I'll drop you off and wait back by the junk shop.'

'The what?'

'The maintenance hangar. Just shout when you want me.'

The jeep came to a stop thirty feet from Arthur Pierce. Havelock got out and saw the Undersecretary of State starting towards him, a tall, slender man in a dark overcoat and hat, his stride long and energetic. Protocol was obviously unimportant to Pierce; there were too many with his title in the State Department who, regardless of the crisis, would expect a mere foreign service officer to approach *them*. Michael began walking, noticing that Pierce was removing the glove from his right hand.

'Mr Havelock?' said the diplomat, hand extended, as the jeep sped away.

'Mr Undersecretary?'

'But of course it's you,' continued Pierce, his grip firm and genuine. 'I've seen your photograph. Frankly, I've read everything I could get my hands on about you. Now, I suppose I should get this over with.'

'What?'

'Well, I guess I'm a little awe-struck, which is a pretty silly thing for a grown man to say. But your accomplishments in a world I don't claim to understand are *very* impressive.' The Undersecretary paused, looking embarrassed. 'I imagine the exotic nature of your work evokes this kind of reaction quite a lot.'

'I wish it would; you make me feel terrific. Especially considering the mistakes I've made – particularly during the last few months.'

'The mistakes weren't yours.'

'I should also tell you,' Michael went on, overlooking the comment, 'I've read a great deal about you, too. There aren't many people in your league at State. Anthony Matthias knew what he was doing – when he knew what he was doing – when he pulled you out of the pack and put you where you are.'

'That's one thing we have in common, isn't it? Anthony Matthias. You far more than me in depth, and I'd never pretend otherwise. But the privilege, the goddamn *privilege* – there's no other way I can put it – of having known him the way I knew him makes the years, the tensions, the sweat worthwhile. It was a time of my life when everything jelled for me; he made it come together.'

'I think we both feel the same way.'

'When I read the material on you, you have no idea how I envied you. I was close to him but I could never be what you were to him. What an extraordinary experience those years must have been.'

'It was – they were. But nothing's there for either of us any longer.'

'I know. It's unbelievable.'

'Believe. I saw him.'

'I wonder if they'll let me see him. I'm on my way to Poole's Island, you know.'

'Do yourself a favour. Don't. It sounds trite, but remember him – especially him – the way he was, not the way he is.'

'Which brings us to now.' Pierce shook his head while staring at Havelock in the chiaroscuro light of the runway. 'It's not good. I don't think I really described to the President how close we are to the edge.'

'He understood. He told me what they said to you when you warned them. "Look to yourselves", wasn't that it?'

'Yes. When they get that simple, that direct, I shake. They'll strike out at shadows; one violent shove and we're over. I'm a fair debater and not bad at negotiations, but you know the Russians better than I do. How do you read it?'

'The same as you. Understatement isn't their way, bombast is. When they don't bother to threaten, they're threatening. Moves will take the place of words.'

'That's what frightens me. The only thing I cling to is that I really don't believe they've brought in the men who push the buttons. Not yet. They know they have to be absolutely accurate. If they have concrete proof, not just hints, that Matthias entered into nuclear aggression pacts against the USSR and if they even smell China, they won't hesitate to push the decision up where it won't be theirs any longer. That's when we can all start digging into the ground.'

'Nuclear aggression . . . ?' Havelock paused, alarmed more than he thought possible. 'You think they've assumed *that* much?'

'They're close to it. It's what's been working them into a frenzy. Pacts negotiated by a maniac . . . with other maniacs.'

'And now the frenzy's gone. They keep quiet and show you the door. You warn them and they tell you we should look to ourselves. I'm frightened, too, Mr Undersecretary.'

'You know what I'm thinking, then?'

'Parsifal.'

'Yes.'

'Berquist said you thought the Soviets had learned something during the past eighteen hours. Is this it?'

'I'm not sure,' said Pierce. 'I'm not even sure I'm working the right side of the street, but *something's* happened. It's why I wanted to see you. You're the only one who knows what's going on hour by hour. If I could pick something out, piece it together with something they said or reacted to, I might find a connection. What I'm looking for is a person or an event, anything that I can use to interdict them, to bring up before they do and deflect them. *Anything* to keep them from alarming the warlords in the Presidium.'

'They're not fools; they know those men. They'd know what they were delivering.'

'I don't think that would stop them.' Pierce hesitated, as if debating with himself whether or not to cite an example, then decided to speak. 'You know General Halyard?'

'I've never met him. Or Ambassador Brooks. I was supposed to meet them both this afternoon. What about him?'

'I consider him one of the most thoughtful, *sceptical* military men in this country.'

'Agreed. Not only from his reputation but I was given his dossier. And?'

'I asked him this afternoon what he thought the reaction would be – his included – if our clandestine services unearthed a Sino-Soviet pact against us, one that projected attack dates within forty-five days and contained the kind of information found in those documents on Poole's Island. His reply was one word: "Launch". If he can say that, what about the lesser, far more insecure men?'

Arthur Pierce did not dramatize the question but asked it calmly, and the chill Michael felt was now only partially due to the damp, cold air. Forces were closing in; time was running out. 'The President said to help you,' he began. 'I don't know if I can, but I'll try. You say you're looking for something to deflect them; I may have it. There's a long-standing KGB operation that goes back to the days of the NKVD – to the nineteen-thirties. It's called *Aspiratsiya Paminyatchik* – '

'Sorry,' interrupted the man from State. 'My Russian's not very good without an interpreter.'

'It doesn't matter, it's just a name. It stands for a strategy that calls for young children, even infants, to be selected by doctors and brought over here. They're placed with specific families – deep-cover Marxists – and grow up as Americans, in every superficial way normal, the more successful the better. But all through the years they're being trained – programmed, if you like – for their adult assignments, which are dependent on their given skills and developments. It comes down to infiltration – again, the higher the better.'

'Good *Lord*,' said Pierce quietly. 'I'd think there'd be enormous risks in such a strategy. Such people have to be instilled with extraordinary belief.'

'Oh, they believe, it's the essential part of their programming. They're also monitored; the slightest deviation and they're either eliminated or brought back to Mother Russia where they're re-educated while training others at the American compounds in the Urals and in Novgorod. The main point is that we've never really been able to crack the operation, the few we've taken have been the least competent and so low on the ladder they haven't been able to shed any light. But we may have cracked it now. We've got ourselves an honest-to-God *paminyatchik* who's sanctioned for killing, as part of an execution unit. His kind has access – *must* have access – to clearance centres and source-controls. There's too much risk in killing, too many possibilities for over-reaction, to say nothing of being caught. Orders have to be rechecked, authorization confirmed.'

'You've *got* such a man? My God, where?'

'He's being flown now to Bethesda – he's wounded – and later tonight will be transferred to a clinic in Virginia.'

'Don't *lose* him! Is there a doctor with him? A good one.'

'I think so. He's a clinic specialist named Taylor; he'll stay with him.'

'Then by morning you think you'll be able to give me something I can use with the Russians? This could be the deflection I need. I counter their attack with an attack of my own. I accuse –'

'I can give it to you now,' interrupted Havelock, 'but you can't use it until I tell you. Tomorrow night at the earliest. Can you stall that long?'

'I think so. What is it?'

'We put him under chemicals an hour ago. I don't know how the right people are reached, but I know the cover identity of their clearance centre. Also the code name for the *paminyatchik* source-control for this area – which I have to assume includes the Washington operation, the most vital in the US.'

Arthur Pierce shook his head in astonishment and admiration. 'You floor me,' he said, with respect in his quiet voice. 'I told you I was a little awe-struck. Well, I take it back, I'm *a lot* awe-struck. What can I use?'

'Whatever you have to. After tomorrow I'll trade the whole *Aspiratsiya Paminyatchik* for another few days.'

'The President told me a few minutes ago . . . he called after speaking to you. You think you're that close to Parsifal?'

'We'll be closer still when we get Taylor's patient down to the clinic. With a few words he can put us within arm's reach of the man we call Ambiguity. And unless everything that we've projected – that Bradford projected – is wrong – and I don't think it is, it *can't* be – once we have Ambiguity we'll know who Parsifal is. *I'll* know.'

'Christ, *how?*'

'Matthias as good as told me I knew him. Are you familiar with a company, a chain of stores, called the Voyagers Emporium?'

'Most of my luggage is, I regret to say. At least, my bank account regrets it.'

'Somewhere inside, in a department or a section, is the KGB clearing centre. Ambiguity has to stay in touch; it's where he gets his orders, transmits information. We'll break it quietly – *very* quietly – tear it apart and find him. We don't need much; we know where he's located.'

'Right where you see him every day,' said Pierce, nodding. 'What about the code name for the source-control?'

'Hammer-zero-two. It doesn't mean anything to us, and it can be changed by the network overnight; but the fact that we broke it, broke the *paminyatchik* circle so decisively, has got to make someone sweat inside the Kremlin.' Michael paused, then added, 'When I give you the go-ahead, use what you need, all of it or any part. It's basically a diversion, what you call deflection, but I think it's a strong one. Create a diplomatic rhubarb, cause a storm of cables between Moscow and New York. Just buy us time.'

'You're sure?'

'I'm sure we don't have a choice. We *need* time.'

'You could lose the source-control.'

'Then we'll lose him. We can live with a source-control – we've all got them in more than sixty countries. We can't live with Parsifal. Any of us.'

'I'll wait for your call.' The Undersecretary of State glanced at his watch, squinting in the dim light to read the radium dial. 'I still have a few minutes before we leave. The vault specialist had to be flown in from Los Alamos; he's meeting with one of the men from his company who brought him the internal diagrams . . . There're so many things I want to ask, so much I need to know.'

'I'm here as long as you are; when you leave, I leave. I heard it from the President.'

'I like him. I haven't always liked presidents.'

'Because you know he doesn't give a damn whether you do or not – not while he's in the Oval Office. That's the way I read him. I like him too, and I have every reason in the book not to.'

'Costa Brava? They told me everything.'

'It's history. Let's deal with the present. What else can I tell you that may help?'

'The obvious,' said Pierce, his voice descending to a reluctant hollow sound. 'If Parsifal *has* reached the Russians what can I say – if I'm given the chance to say it? If he's hinted at the China factor, or at the vulnerabilities in their own counter-strike capabilities, how can I explain it? Where did he *get* it all? Exposing Matthias is only part of the answer. Frankly, it's not enough, and I think you know that.'

'I know it.' Havelock tried to collect his thoughts, to be as clear and concise as possible. 'What's in those so-called agreements is a mix of a thousand moves in a triple-sided chess game, the anchor player being us. Our penetration of the Russian and Chinese systems is far deeper than we've ever hinted at, and there are strategy committees set up to study and evaluate every conceivable option in the event some goddamn fool – on *any* side – gives the order to launch.'

'Such committees, I'm sure, exist in Moscow and Peking.'

'But neither Moscow nor Peking could produce an Anthony Matthias, the man with geopolitical panaceas, respected, even worshipped – there is no one on either side of the world like him.'

Pierce nodded. 'The Soviets treat him as a valued go-between, not as an adversary. The Chinese throw banquets for him and call him a visionary.'

'And when he began to fall apart, he still had the imagination to conceive of the ultimate nuclear chess game.'

'But *how*?'

'He found a zealot. A naval officer on one of the Pentagon committees who's up to his eyeballs in overkill theories. He gave Matthias everything. He made copies of all the strategies and counter-strategies the three committees exchanged with one another. They contained authentic data – they *had* to contain it; those war games are very real on paper. Everything can be checked by computers – the extent of megaton damage inflicted, damage sustained, the limits of punishment before the ground is useless. It was all there, and Matthias put it together. Matthias and the man who's got us by the throat. Parsifal.'

'I'd say the naval officer is scheduled to begin a long period of confinement.'

'I'm not sure what that would accomplish. At any rate, I'm not finished with him; he's still got more to give – may have given it by now.'

'Just a minute,' said the Undersecretary of State, his face suddenly alive. 'Could *he* be Parsifal?'

'No, not possible.'

'Why not?'

'Because in his own misguided way he believed in what he was doing. He has a permanent love affair with his uniform and his country; he'd neither allow the possibility of compromise nor give the Russians an ounce of ammunition. Decker's not an original, but he's genuine. I doubt the Lubyanka could break him.'

'Decker . . . You've got him put away, haven't you?'

'He's not going anywhere. He's at home with an escort unit outside.'

Pierce shook his head while reaching into his pocket. 'It's all so insane!' he said as he pulled out a packet of cigarettes and matches. 'Care for one?' he asked, proffering the pack.

'No, thanks. I've had my quota of five hundred for the day.'

The man from State struck a match, holding the flame under the cigarette. Without the protection of a second hand, the wind extinguished it. He struck another; left palm up, and inhaled, the smoke from his mouth mingling with the vapour of his breath. 'At the meeting this afternoon, Ambassador Brooks brought up something I didn't understand. He said an intelligence officer from the KGB had made contact with you and speculated on the identity of the faction in Moscow who'd worked with Matthias at the Costa Brava.'

'He meant with Parsifal; Matthias was being led by then. And Rostov – his name's Rostov – didn't speculate. He knew. They're a collection of fanatics in a branch called the VKR, the *Voennaya*. They make even our Deckers look like flower children. He's trying to break it open and I wish him luck. It's crazy, but a dedicated enemy may be one of our hopes.'

'What do you mean, "break it open"?'

'Get names, find out who did what and let the saner people deal with them. Rostov's good; he may do it and, if he does, he'll somehow get word to me.'

'He *will*?'

'He's already offered me a white contact. It happened at Kennedy Airport when I flew in from Paris.'

There was the sound of a gunning engine in the distance. Pierce threw down his cigarette and crushed it under his foot as he spoke. 'What more do you think this Decker can give you?'

'He may have spoken to Parsifal but doesn't know it, or someone speaking for Parsifal. In either case, he was reached at home, which means that somewhere in a couple of hundred thousand long distance records is a specific call made to a specific number at a specific time.'

'Why not a couple of million records?'

'Not if we've got a general location.'

'*Do* you?'

'I'll know more by tomorrow. When you get back – '

'Mr Undersecretary! *Mr Undersecretary!*' The shouting was accompanied by the roar of the jeep's motor and the screeching of its tyres as it came to a stop only a few feet from them. 'Undersecretary Pierce?' said the driver.

'Who gave you my name?' asked Pierce, icily.

'There's an urgent telephone call for you, sir. They said it was your office at the United Nations and they must speak to you.'

'The Russians,' said Pierce under his breath to Havelock; his alarm was apparent. 'Please, wait for me.'

The Undersecretary of State swung himself rapidly into the Air Force jeep and nodded to the driver; his eyes were on the lights of the maintenance hangar. Michael pulled his coat around him, his attention drawn to the small prop-jet aircraft several hundred feet away in the opposite direction. The left engine had been started and the pilot was revving it. The right coughed into operation seconds later. Then Havelock saw another jeep; it had taken the place of the fuel truck next to the plane. The vault specialist had arrived; the departure for Poole's Island was imminent.

Arthur Pierce returned six minutes later, climbed out of the open vehicle and dismissed the driver. 'It *was* the Russians,' he said, approaching Michael. 'They wanted an unrecorded, unlogged meeting tomorrow morning; that means an emergency. I reached the senior aide of the delegation and told him I had called my own emergency conference tomorrow on the strength of their reactions late this afternoon. I also suggested I might have information for them that would necessitate a storm of cables – I used your phrase – between New York, their embassy in Washington and Moscow. I hinted that perhaps the pounding shoe was in another hand.' The Undersecretary stopped, hearing the preliminary warm-up of the jets from the plane in the distance; the second jeep was leaving the area. 'That's my signal; the vault specialist's here. You know, it's going to take at least three hours to break into that room. Walk over with me, will you?'

'Sure. What was the Russians' reaction?'

'Very negative, of course. They know me; they sense a deflection, a diversion – to use your word. We agreed to meet tomorrow evening.' Pierce paused and turned to Havelock. 'For God's sake, give me the green light, then. I'll need every argument, every weapon I can have. Among them a medical report diagnosing exhaustion for Matthias . . . God knows, not the psychiatric file I'm bringing back to you.'

'I forgot. The President was to have got it to me yesterday – today.'

'I'm bringing it up.' Pierce started walking again as Michael kept pace. 'I can see how it happens.'

'What happens?'

'The days blending into one another. Yesterday, today . . . tomorrow, if there is a tomorrow. One long, unending sleepless night.'

'Yes,' said Havelock, feeling no need to amplify.

'How many weeks have you been living it?'

'More than a few.'

'*Jesus.*' The roar of the combined engines grew louder as they drew nearer to the plane. 'I suppose this is actually the safest place to talk,' said Pierce, raising his voice to be heard. 'No device could filter that noise.'

'Is that why you wanted to meet on the runway?' asked Michael.

'You probably think I'm paranoid, but yes it is. I wouldn't care if we were in the control room of a NORAD base, I'd want the walls swept before having a conversation like the one we just had. You probably *do* think I'm paranoid. After all, this is Andrews – '

'I don't think you're paranoid at all,' interrupted Havelock. 'I think I should have thought of it.'

The door of the small aircraft was open, the metal steps in place. The pilot signalled from his lighted window; Pierce waved back, nodding agreement. Michael walked with the Undersecretary to within ten feet of the door where the wash of the propellers was strong and growing stronger.

'You said something about having a general location in mind regarding that call to Decker,' shouted Pierce. 'Where is it?'

'Somewhere in the Shenandoah,' yelled Havelock. 'It's only speculation, but Decker delivered the materials there.'

'I see.'

The engines roared a sudden crescendo and the wind from the propeller blades reached gale force, whipping the hat from Arthur Pierce's head. Michael crouched, scrambling after it through the powerful wash. He stopped it with his foot and carried it back to the Undersecretary of State.

'Thanks very much!' shouted Pierce.

Havelock stared at the face in front of him, at the streak of white that sprang up from the forehead and shot through the mass of wavy dark hair.

36

It was an hour and forty-five minutes before he saw the floodlights that marked the entrance to the drive at Sterile Five. The flight from Andrews to Quantico and the trip by car to Fairfax had been oddly disturbing, and he did not know why. It was as though a part of his mind were refusing to function; he was conscious of a gap in his own thought process but was blocked by a compulsion not to probe. It was like a drunk's refusal to face the gross embarrassments of the night before: something not remembered did not exist. And he was incapable of doing anything about it; he did not know what it was, only that it was not, and therefore, it was.

One long, unending, sleepless night. Perhaps that was it. He needed sleep . . . he needed Jenna. But there was no time for sleep, no time for them to be together in the way they wanted to be together. No time for anything or anyone but Parsifal.

What was it? Why had a part of him suddenly died?

The marine car pulled up in front of the ornate entrance of the estate. He got out, thanked the driver and the armed guard, and walked up to the door. He thought as he stood there, with a finger on the bell, that like so many other doors in so many other houses he had entered he had no key with which to open it. Would he ever have a key to a house that was his – theirs – and be able to open it as so many millions opened theirs every day? It was a silly thought, foolishly pondered. Where was the significance of a house and a key? Still, the thought – the need, perhaps – persisted.

The door opened abruptly, and Jenna Karras, her striking lovely face so taut, brought him back to the urgent present, her eyes burning into his.

'Thank *God*!' she cried, reaching for him, clutching him and pulling him inside. 'You're *back*! I was going out of my mind!'

'What is it?'

'Mikhail, come with me. Quickly!' She gripped his hand as they walked rapidly down the foyer past the staircase to the study, which she had left open. Going to the desk, she picked up a note and said, 'You must call the Bethesda Hospital. Extension Six-seven-one. But first you have to know what happened!'

'What – '

'The *paminyatchik* is dead.'

'Oh, *Christ*!' Michael grabbed the phone that Jenna held out for him. He dialled, his hand trembling. 'When?' he shouted. '*How*?'

'An execution,' she replied as he waited for Bethesda to answer. 'Less than an hour ago. Two men. They took out the guard with a knife, got into the room and killed the traveller while he was sedated. Four shots in the head. The doctor's beside himself.'

'Six-seven-one! *Hurry*, please!'

'I couldn't stand it,' whispered Jenna, staring at him, touching his face. 'I thought you were there . . . outside somewhere . . . seen, perhaps. They said you weren't, but I didn't know whether to believe them or not.'

'*Taylor*? How did it *happen*?'

As Havelock listened to the doctor, a numbing pain spread through him, stealing his breath. Taylor was still in shock and spoke disjointedly. Jenna's brief description had been clearer. There was nothing further to learn. Two killers in the uniforms of naval officers had come to the sixth floor, found Taylor's patient and proceeded professionally with the execution, killing a marine guard in the process.

'We've lost Ambiguity,' said Michael, hanging up, his hand so heavy the phone fell into the cradle, clapping into place. '*How*? That's what I can't understand! . . . We had maximum security, military transport, every precaution!' He looked helplessly at Jenna.

'Was it all highly visible?' she asked. 'Could the precautions and the transport have drawn attention?'

Havelock nodded wearily. 'Yes. Yes, of course. We commandeered an airfield, flew in and out of there like a commando raid, diverting the other traffic.'

'And not that far from the medical centre,' completed Jenna. 'Someone alerted to the disturbance would be drawn to the scene. He would see what you didn't want him to see. In this case, a stretcher would be enough.'

Michael slipped off his overcoat and listlessly dropped it on a chair. 'But that doesn't explain what happened at the medical centre itself. An execution team was sent in to abort a trap, to kill their own people, no chance that anyone would be taken alive.'

'*Paminyatchiks*,' said Jenna. 'It's happened before.'

'But how did their controls *know* it was a trap? I spoke only to the Apache unit and to Loring. *No one* else! How *could* they? How could they have been so sure that they sent in sanctioned killers? The risk is enormous!' Havelock walked round the desk, looking at the scattered papers, hating them, hating the terror they evoked. 'Loring told me that he was probably spotted, that it was his fault; but I don't believe it. That mocked-up patrol car didn't just emerge from round the block, it was sent from somewhere by someone in authority who had made the most dangerous decision he could make. He wouldn't have made it on the strength of one man seen in a parking lot – that man, incidentally, was too damned experienced to show himself so obviously.'

'It doesn't seem logical,' agreed Jenna. 'Unless the others were spotted earlier.'

'Even if the cardiologist cover was blown, at best they'd be considered protection. No, the control *knew* it was a trap, knew that the primary objective – let's face it, the sole objective – was to take even one of them alive ... Goddamn it, *how*?' Michael leaned over the desk, his hands gripping the edge, his head pounding. He pushed himself away and walked towards the wide, dark windows with the thick, bevelled glass. And then he heard the words, spoken softly by Jenna Karras.

'Mikhail, you did speak to someone else. You spoke to the President.'

'Of *course*, but ...' He stopped, staring at the distorted image of his face in the window, but slowly *not* seeing his face ... seeing, instead, the formless outline of another. Then the night mist that had rolled in through the trees and over the lawns outside became another mist, from another time. The crashing of waves suddenly filled his ears, thundering, deafening, unbearable. Lightning shattered across the luminous, unseen screen in his mind, and then the sharp cracks came, one after another until they grew into earsplitting explosions, blowing him into a frenzied galaxy of flashing lights ... and *dread*.

Costa Brava. He was *back* at the *Costa Brava*!

And the face in the mirror took on form ... distant form ... unmistakable form. And the shock of white hair sprang up from that face, surrounded by waves of black, framed, isolated ... an image unto itself.

'No ... *no*!' He heard himself screaming; he could feel Jenna's hands on his arms, then his face ... but *not* his face! The face in the window! The face with the sharp path of white in the hair ... his hair, but *not* his hair, his face but *not* his face! Yet both were the faces of *killers*, his and the one he had seen that night on the Costa Brava!

A fisherman's cap had suddenly been blown away in the ocean wind; a hat had been whipped off the head of a man by the sudden wash of propellers. On a runway ... in a shadowed light ... two hours ago!

The same man? Was it *possible*? Even *conceivable*?'

'Mikhail!' Jenna held his face in her hands. 'Mikhail, what *is* it? What's wrong?'

'It's *not* possible!' he screamed. 'It can't be!'

'What, my darling? *What* can't be?'

'*Jesus*. I'm losing my mind!'

'Darling, *stop it!*' shouted Jenna, shaking him, holding him.

'No . . . no, I'll be all right. Let me alone. Let me *alone!*' he spun away from her and raced to the desk. 'Where is it? Where the *hell is it?*'

'Where is what?' asked Jenna calmly, now beside him.

'The file.'

'What file?'

'*My* file!' He yanked the top right-hand drawer open, rummaging furiously among the papers until he found the black-bordered folder. He pulled it out, slammed it on the desk and opened it; breathing with difficulty, he leafed through the pages, eyes and fingers working maniacally.

'What's troubling you, Mikhail? Tell me. Let me help you. What started this? What's making you go back? . . . We agreed not to punish each other.'

'Not me! *Him!*'

'Who?'

'I can't make a mistake! I *can't!*' Havelock found the page he was looking for. He scanned the lines using his index finger, his eyes riveted on the page. He read in a flat voice: '"They're killing her. Oh, my God, he's killed her and I can't bear the screams. Go to her, stop them . . . stop them. No, not me, never me. Oh, Christ, they're pulling her away . . . she's bleeding so, but not in pain now. She's gone. Oh, my God, she's gone, my love is gone . . . The wind is strong, it's blown his cap away . . . The face? Do I know the face? A photograph somewhere? A dossier? The dossier of a killer . . . No, it's the hair. The streak of white in the hair."' Michael stood up and looked at Jenna; he was perspiring. 'A streak . . . of . . . white,' he said slowly, desperately trying to enunciate the words clearly. 'It *could be him!*'

Jenna leaned into him and held his shoulders. 'You must take hold of yourself, my darling. You're not being rational; you're in some kind of shock. Can you understand me?'

'No time,' he said, removing her hands and reaching for the phone. 'I'm okay, and you're right. I am in shock, but only because it's so incredible. *Incredible!*' He dialled, breathed deeply, and spoke. 'I want to be connected to the main switchboard of Andrews Air Force Base, and I want you to give instructions to the duty officer to comply with any requests I make with regard to information.'

Jenna watched him, then backed away to the table with the decanters. She poured him some brandy and handed it to him. 'You're pale,' she said. 'I've never seen you so pale.'

Havelock waited, listening as the head of the White House Secret Service gave his instructions to Andrews and, conversely, the electronic verification check was made by the colonel in charge of field communications. The incredible was always rooted in the credible, he thought. For the most credible reasons on earth he had been on that beach at the Costa Brava that night, observing the extraordinary; and the simple phenomenon of a gust of wind had blown a man's cap away. Now he must know whether there was substance in the observation. *Both* observations.

'There are calls from New York constantly,' said the colonel in answer to his question.

'I'm talking about those five to ten minutes,' countered Michael. 'Transferred to a maintenance hangar on the south perimeter. It was less than two
hours ago; someone must remember. Check every operator on the boards.
Now!'

'Christ, take it easy.'

'You take it fast!'

No operator at Andrews Air Force base had transferred a call to a
maintenance hangar on the south perimeter.

'There was a sergeant driving a jeep, ordered to pick up cargo labelled
Sterile Five, Marine equipment. Are you with me?'

'I'm aware of the Sterile classification and of the flight. Helicopter, north
pad.'

'What's his name?'

'The driver?'

'Yes.'

The colonel paused, obviously concerned as he answered. 'We understand
the original driver was replaced. Another relieved him on verbal orders.'

'Whose?'

'We haven't traced it.'

'What was the second driver's name?'

'We don't know.'

'Thank you, Colonel.'

Paminyatchik.

'Find me the dossier on Pierce,' said Havelock, looking up at Jenna, his
hand on the telephone button.

'*Arthur Pierce?*' asked Jenna, astonished.

'As quickly as you can.' Michael dialled again. 'I can't make a mistake, I
can't make a mistake. Not here, not *now.*' Then 'Mr President? It's Havelock.
I've been with Pierce and tried to help him . . . Yes, sir, he's bright, very
bright and very good. We'd like a point clarified; it's minor but it would
clear something up for both of us. He had a lot on his mind, a lot to absorb.
At the meeting this afternoon, after I called, did you bring up the Apache
operation at the Randolph Medical Center? . . . Then everyone's current.
Thank you, Mr President.' Michael replaced the phone as Jenna handed
him a dark brown file folder.

'Here's Pierce's dossier.'

Havelock opened it and immediately turned to the synopsis of personal
characteristics.

*The subject drinks moderately at social occasions, and has never been known to abuse
alcohol. He does not use any form of tobacco.*

The match, the open flame unprotected, extinguished by the wind . . . A
second flame, the flare of light prolonged, unmistakable. The sequence as
odd and unmistakable as the cigarette smoke emerging solely from the
mouth and mingling with the curling vapour of breath, a non-smoker's
exhalation. A *signal.* Followed moments later by an unknown driver delivering an urgent message, using a name he was not supposed to know, angering
the man he was addressing. Every sequence had been detailed, timed,
reactions considered. Arthur Pierce had not been called to the phone, he
had been *making* a call.

Or had he? There could be *no* mistake, not now. Had an operator transferring rapidly incoming calls throughout the vast expanse of an Air Force base forgotten one among so many? And how often did soldiers take over innocuous assignments for friends without informing their superiors? How frequently did highly visible men appear to be on the side of the avenging medical angels by never smoking in public but in a crisis pulling out a concealed pack of cigarettes, a habit they were sincerely trying to break, the act of smoking actually awkward? . . . How many men had streaks of premature white in their hair?

No mistakes. Once the accusation was made it could not be taken back and if it could not be sustained, trust at the highest level would be eroded, possibly destroyed, the very people who *had* to communicate would become guarded, wary, commanders in silent conflict. Where was the ultimate proof?

Moscow?

There is first the KGB; all else follows. A man may gravitate to the VKR, but first he must have sprung from the KGB. Rostov, Athens.

He says he is not your enemy . . . but others are who may be his as well. A Soviet agent. Kennedy Airport.

'I can see it in your eyes, Mikhail.' Jenna touched his shoulder, forcing him to look at her. 'Call the President.'

'I must be absolutely certain. Pierce said it would take at least three hours for the vault to be opened, another two to sort out the documents. I've got some time. If he's Ambiguity, he's trapped.'

'How can you be absolutely certain about a *paminyatchik*?'

'At the source. Moscow.'

'Rostov?'

'I can try. He may be as desperate as I am, but if he isn't, I'll tell him he should be. We've got our maniacs, and he's got his.' Havelock picked up the phone and dialled the three digits for the White House switchboard. 'Please get me the Russian consulate in New York. I'm afraid I don't know the number . . . No, I'll hold on.' Michael covered the mouthpiece, speaking to Jenna. 'Go over Pierce's file. Look for something we can trace. Parents, if they're alive.'

'A wife,' said Jenna.

'He's not married.'

'Convenient. Lovers, then.'

'He's discreet.'

'Naturally.' Jenna picked up the file from the desk.

'*Dobriy vyecher*,' said Havelock into the phone, his hand removed. 'I need to speak to the director of street security.' Every operator at every Soviet embassy and consulate understood when a caller asked to be connected to the street security director. A deep male voice got on the line, acknowledging merely that he had picked up the phone. Michael continued in Russian: 'My name is Havelock and I have to assume I'm speaking to the right person, the one who can put me in touch with the man I'm trying to reach.'

'Who might that be, sir?'

'I'm afraid I didn't get his name, but he knows mine. As I'm quite sure you do.'

'That's not much help, Mr Havelock.'

'I think it's enough. The man met me at Kennedy Airport and we had a lengthy conversation, including the means I might employ to reach him again; a forty-eight-hour time span and the New York Public Library figured prominently among them. There was also some discussion about a missing Graz-Burya automatic, a splendid weapon, I think you'll agree. It's urgent I speak with that man – as urgent as his message was for me.'

'Perhaps if you could recall the message, it might be more helpful, sir.'

'An offer of sanctuary from the Director of External Strategies, Pyotr Rostov, KGB, Moscow. And I wouldn't say those words if I were taping this. *You* can, but I can't afford it.'

'There is always the possibility of a reverse order of events.'

'Take the chance, comrade. You can't afford not to.'

'Then why not talk with me . . . comrade?'

'Because I don't know you.' Michael looked down at the list of the direct, unlisted numbers he had been assigned; he repeated one to the Russian. 'I'll be here for the next five minutes.' He hung up and reached for the brandy.

'Will he call back, do you think?' asked Jenna, sitting in the chair in front of the desk, the Pierce file in her hand.

'Why not? He need not say anything, just listen . . . Anything there we can use?'

'The mother died in nineteen-sixty-eight. The father disappeared eight months later and has never been seen since. He wrote to his son in Vietnam saying that he "didn't care to go on without his wife, that he'd join her with God".'

'Naturally. But no suicide, no body. Just a Christian fade out.'

'Naturally. *Paminyatchik*. He had too much to offer in Novgorod.'

The telephone rang, the lighted button corresponding to the number he had given the Soviet consulate in New York.

'You understand, Mr Havelock,' began the sing-song voice, the English unmistakably that of the Soviet agent from Kennedy Airport, 'that the message delivered to you was offered in the spirit of compassion for the great injustice done by those in your government who called for the execution of a man of peace – '

'If you're doing this,' interrupted Havelock, 'for the benefit of any recording on this end, forget it. And if you're auditioning for the consulate, do it later. I haven't got time. I'm accepting a part of Rostov's offer.'

'I was not aware that it was divided into parts.'

'I'm assuming prior communication.'

'I assume that's reasonable,' said the Russian. 'Under extremely limited circumstances.'

'Any circumstances you like, just use this telephone number and get him back to me within the hour.' Michael looked at his watch. 'It's not quite seven o'clock in the morning in Moscow. Reach him.'

'I don't believe those circumstances are acceptable.'

'They've got to be. Tell him I may have found the enemy. *Our* enemy, the word's temporary, of course – assuming again there's a future for either of us.'

'I really don't think – '

'*Don't* think. Reach him. Because if you don't, I'll try myself and that could be acutely embarrassing – to you, comrade, not to me. I don't care any more. I'm the *prize.*' Havelock replaced the phone, aware of the beads of perspiration that had broken out on his forehead.

'What can Rostov actually tell you?' Jenna got up from the chair and placed Pierce's dossier on the desk. 'There's nothing here, incidentally. Just a brilliant, modest hero of the republic.'

'Naturally.' Michael wiped his forehead with the back of his hand and leaned forward, supporting himself on his elbows. 'Rostov told me in Athens that one of his sources for Costa Brava was a mole operating from the White House. I didn't believe him; it's the kind of shock treatment that makes you listen harder. But suppose he was telling me the truth – a past truth – because he knew the mole was out and untraceable. The perfect traveller.'

Jenna raised her hand, pointing to the dossier on the desk. 'Pierce was assigned to the National Security Council. He had an office in the White House for several months.'

'Yes. And Rostov meant what he said; he couldn't understand, and what you can't understand in this business is cause for alarm. Everything he had learned about Costa Brava – which I confirmed – told him it couldn't have taken place without the co-operation of someone in Moscow. But *who*? These operations are under his direct control, but he didn't have anything to do with it, knew nothing about it. So he tested me, thinking I could tell him something, bringing in the mole for credibility, knowing that we both accepted a mole's information as being reliable. The truth – as he was told the truth – except it was a lie.'

'Told by a KGB officer, a *paminyatchik* mole, who had transferred his allegiance from the KGB to the *Voennaya*,' said Jenna. 'He throws off his former superiors for his new ones.'

'Then proceeds to intercept and take over Costa Brava. *If* he was at Costa Brava. If . . . *if.*'

'How will you handle Rostov? He'll be taped; he'll be monitored.'

'It'll be light. He is, after all, Director of External Strategies. I'll play on the power struggle. KGB versus VKR. He'll understand.'

'He won't talk about the *paminyatchik* operation over the telephone. You know that. He can't.'

'I won't ask him to. I'll name the name and listen. He'll tell me somehow. We've both been around a long time – too long – and the words we use have never been written to mean what we say they mean, the silences we use never understood except by people like us. He wants what I have – if I have it – as much as I want what he can confirm. It'll work. Somehow. He'll tell me whether Arthur Pierce is the mole . . . if he's convinced the mole has gone behind his back and joined the maniacs.'

Jenna walked to the coffee table, picked up a note pad, then sat down in the leather armchair. 'While you're waiting, do you want to talk about Commander Decker?'

'*Christ!*' Havelock's right hand shot out for the phone, his left stabbing the list of numbers in front of him. He dialled as he spoke, his voice strained. 'I mentioned him to Pierce. Oh, *God*, did I mention him! . . . Raise the Decker escort, please. *Hurry*.'

'Naval escort. In position.'

The words over the radio phone were clear, and the sudden throbbing in Michael's temples began to subside. 'This is Sterile Five. We have reason to believe there could be hostile activity in your area.'

'No signs of it,' was the reply. 'Everything's quiet and the street's well lighted.'

'Nevertheless, I'd like additional personnel.'

'We're stretched pretty thin at Sixteen Hundred, Sterile Five. Why not call in the locals? They don't have to know any more than we do, and we don't know a damn thing.'

'Can you do it?'

'Sure. We'll label it diplomatic and they'll get overtime. By the way, how do you read the activity?'

'Abduction. Neutering you first, then taking Decker.'

'Thanks for the warning. We'll get right on it. Out.'

Havelock leaned back in the chair, his neck stretched over the rim, and stared at the ceiling. 'Now that we know there still *is* a Commander Decker, what did he tell you?'

'Where did you leave off? I went back over everything.'

Michael closed his eyes, remembering. 'A phone call,' he said slowly. 'It was later, after their Sunday meetings at the lodge. He tried for days, weeks, to get in touch with Matthias, but Anton wouldn't talk to him. Then someone called him . . . with an explanation. That was it, he said it was an explanation.'

Jenna flipped through her notes, stopping at a page, then going back two. 'A man with a strange voice, an odd accent – "clipped and rushed" was the way Decker described it. I asked him to recall as thoroughly as possible every word the man said. Fortunately, that call was very important to him; he remembered nearly everything, I think. I wrote it down.'

'Read it, will you?'

Jenna rolled the page over. 'The man identified himself as a colleague of the Secretary of State, and asked Decker several questions about his naval career, obviously to make sure it *was* Decker . . . Then here it begins – I tried to write it down as though I'd heard it myself . . . "Secretary Matthias appreciates everything you've done, and wants you to know that you will be mentioned prominently and frequently in his memoirs. But you must understand the rules, the rules can't be broken. For the Secretary's global strategy to be effective, it must be developed in total secrecy, the element of surprise paramount, no one *in* or *out* of government – "' Jenna paused. 'The emphases were Decker's,' she added. '" . . . *in* or *out* of government aware that a master plan has been created."' Again Jenna stopped and looked up. 'Here Decker wasn't precise, the man's reasons for excluding people in government were apparently based on the assumption that there were too many who couldn't be trusted, who might divulge secrets regardless of their clearance.'

'Of course he wasn't precise. He was talking about himself and it was a painful reference.'

'I agree . . . This last part I'm sure was accurate, probably word-for-word. "The Secretary of State wants you to know that when the time comes you will be summoned and made his chief executive officer, all controls in your hands. But because of your superb reputation in the field of nuclear tactics, there can't be even a hint of any association between you. If anyone ever asks you if you know the Secretary of State, you must say you do not. That's also part of the rules."' Jenna put the note pad down on her lap. 'That's it. Decker's ego was thoroughly flattered, and by his lights his place in history was assured.'

'Nothing else was needed,' said Havelock, straightening himself up in the chair. 'Did you write that out, so I can read it?'

'I write more clearly in English than I do in Czech. Why?'

'Because I want to study it – over and over and over again. The man who spoke those words is Parsifal, and somewhere in the past I've heard that man speak before.'

'Go back over the years, Mikhail,' said Jenna, sitting forward, raising the note pad and flipping the pages. 'I'll go back with you. *Now*! It's not impossible. A Russian who speaks English rapidly, clipping his words. It's *there*. That's what Decker said. "Clipped and rushed." Those were his words. How many such men can you have known?'

'Let's do it.' Havelock got up from the desk as Jenna tore off the two pages that contained her notes on the call to Thomas Decker. Michael came round and took them from her. 'Men I *know* who've met Matthias. We'll start with this year and work backwards. Write down every name I come up with.'

'Why not do it geographically? City by city. You can eliminate some quickly, concentrate on the others.'

'Association,' he added. 'We scratch Barcelona and Madrid; we never touched the Soviets . . . Belgrade – a river warehouse on the Sava, the attaché from the Russian consulate. Vasili Yankovitch. He was with Anton in Paris.'

'Yankovitch,' said Jenna, writing.

'And Ilitch Borin, visiting professor at the University of Belgrade; we had drinks, dinner. He knew Matthias from the cultural exchange conferences.'

'Borin.'

'No one else in Belgrade . . . Prague. There must be at least a dozen men in Prague. The Russians are crawling all over Prague.'

'Their names? Start alphabetically.'

The names came, some rapidly, others slowly, some striking chords of possibility, others completely improbable. Nevertheless, Jenna wrote them all down, prodding Michael, forcing him to jolt his memories, one name leading to another.

Krakow. Vienna. Paris. London. New York. Washington.

The months became a year, then two, and finally three. The list grew as Havelock probed, pushing his conscious, permitting the free association of his subconscious, digging, straining, forcing his mind to function as if it were a finely-tuned instrument. And again the sweat broke out on his forehead, his pulse oddly quickening as he reached the end of his energies.

'God, I'm tired,' said Michael quietly, staring at the bevelled windowpane where over an hour ago two faces had appeared, one replacing the other, both killers, both from the Costa Brava. Or were they?

'You have thirty-nine names,' said Jenna, coming to him, touching the back of his neck, massaging it gently. 'Sit down and study them, study the telephone conversation. Find Parsifal, Mikhail.'

'Do any match the names on your list? I thought of that when I mentioned Ilitch Borin; he's a doctor of philosophy. Is there anyone?'

'No.'

'I'm sorry.'

'So am I.'

'He hasn't called. Rostov hasn't called.'

'I know.'

'I said an hour; the deadline was an hour.' Havelock looked at his watch. 'It's thirty-four minutes past the deadline.'

'There could be mechanical troubles in Moscow. It would be nothing new.'

'Not for him. He's pulled in the white contract; he doesn't want to acknowledge.'

'How often have you stretched a deadline? Waiting until the one who expected your call was filled with anxiety, his defences eroded.'

'He knows my dossier too well for that.' Michael turned to her. 'I must make a decision. If I'm right Pierce can't be allowed off that island. If I'm wrong they'll think I've crashed, gone over the edge. Berquist won't have any choice, he'll have to remove me.'

'Not necessarily.'

'Of course necessarily. I'm seeing monsters in dark closets, wasting valuable hours on delusions. That's not a man you want giving orders. My God, Arthur Pierce! The most valuable asset we have – if we have him.'

'Only you know what you *did* see.'

'It was night, a night that was racking me. Look through that clinic file. Is that a rational man talking or thinking? What *was* he seeing? . . . I need one word, one silence from Rostov.'

'Wait, Mikhail,' said Jenna, touching his arm and urging him back to the armchair. 'You still have time. Study the list of names, the words spoken to Decker. It may happen to you. A name, a voice, a phrase. It could happen.'

Scholars. Soldiers. Lawyers. Doctors. Attachés. Diplomats . . . Defectors. All Russians who at one time or another had direct contact with Anthony Matthias. Havelock pictured each man, each face, his inner ear hearing dozens of voices speaking in English, matching the voices with the faces, listening for phrases that were spoken rapidly, words that were clipped, consonants harsh. It was maddening, faces and voices intermingling, lips moving, suddenly no sound followed by shouts. *You will be mentioned prominently and frequently.* Did *he* say that, *would* he say that? *You will be summoned* . . . how many times had that phrase been used. So many. But who used it? *Who?*

An hour passed, then most of another and a second packet of cigarettes with it. The expired deadline for Moscow was approaching the final deadline for Poole's Island. A decision – *the* decision – would have to be made. Nothing was forgotten, only submerged, eyes straying to watches as the inner search for Parsifal reached a frightening level of intensity.

'I can't find him!' cried Michael, pounding his hand on the coffee table. 'He's here, the *words* are here, but I can't find him!'

The telephone rang. *Rostov?* Havelock shot up from the chair, staring at it, motionless. He was drained, and the thought of finding the resources to fence verbally with the Soviet intelligence officer eight thousand miles away drained him further. The abrasive bell sounded again. He went to the phone and picked it up, Jenna watching him.

'Yes?' he said quietly, marshalling his thoughts for the opening moves on both sides.

'It is your friend from Kennedy Airport, who no longer has his weapon –'

'Where's Rostov? I gave you a deadline.'

'It was met. Listen to me carefully. I'm calling from a phone booth on Eighth Avenue and must keep my eyes on the street. The call came through half an hour ago. Fortunately, I took it, as my superior had an engagement for the evening. He will expect to find me when he returns.'

'What are you driving at?'

'Rostov is dead. He was found at nine-thirty in the morning, Moscow time, after repeated calls failed to rouse him.'

'How did he *die?*'

'Four bullets in the head.'

'Oh, *Christ!* Have they any idea who killed him?'

'The rumour is *Voennaya Kontr Razvedka,* and I, for one, believe it. There have been many such rumours lately, and if a man like Rostov can be taken out, then I am too old, and must call from a phone booth. You are fools here, but it's very much better to live with fools than lie among jackals who will rip your throat open if they don't care for the way you laugh or drink.'

At the meeting this afternoon . . . something I didn't understand . . . An intelligence officer from the KGB made contact . . . speculated on the identity . . . Arthur Pierce, while awkwardly smoking a cigarette on a deserted runway.

'Rostov didn't speculate. He knew. A collection of fanatics in a branch called the VKR, the Voennaya *. . . He'll break it open . . .'* A fellow killer from the Costa Brava.

Had Pierce's call encompassed more than the death of a *paminyatchik?* Had he demanded the execution of a man in Moscow? Four bullets in the head. It had cost Rostov's life, but it could be the proof he needed. Was it conclusive? Could anything be conclusive?

'Code name Hammer-zero-two,' said Michael, thinking, reaching. 'Does it mean anything to you?'

'A part of it possibly, not all of it.'

'What *part?*'

'The "hammer". It was used years ago, and very restricted. Then it was abandoned, I believe. Hammarskjöld, Dag Hammarskjöld. The United Nations.'

'*Jesus*! . . . Zero, zero . . . two. A zero is a circle . . . a circle. A council!
Two . . . double, twice, *second*. The second voice in the delegation! That's it!'

'As you gather,' interrupted the Soviet, 'I must cross over.'

'Call the New York office of the FBI. Go there. I'll get word to them.'

'That is one place I will *not* go. It is one of the things I can tell you.'

'Then keep moving and call me back in thirty minutes. I have to move
quickly.'

'Fool or jackals. Where is the choice?'

Havelock pressed the adjacent button on the phone, disconnecting the
line. He looked up at Jenna. 'It's Pierce. Hammer-zero-two. I told him – we
all told him – about Rostov closing in on the *Voennaya*. He had Rostov killed.
It's *him*.'

'He's trapped,' said Jenna. 'You've got him.'

'I've got him. I've got Ambiguity, the man who called us dead at Col des
Moulinets . . . And when I get him to a clinic I'll shoot him into space.
Whatever he knows I'll know.' Michael dialled quickly. 'The President,
please. Mr Cross calling.'

'You must be very quiet, Mikhail,' said Jenna, approaching the desk.
'Very quiet and precise. Remember, it will be an extraordinary shock to him
and, above all, he must believe you.'

Havelock nodded. 'That's the hardest part. Thanks. I was about to plunge
in with conclusions first. You're right. Take him up slowly . . . Mr
President?'

'What is it?' asked Berquist anxiously. 'What's happened?'

'I have something to tell you, sir. It will take a few minutes, and I want
you to listen very closely to what I've got to say.'

'All right. Let me get on another phone; there are people in the next room
. . . By the way, did Pierce reach you?'

'What?'

'Arthur Pierce. Did he call you?'

'What *about* Pierce?'

'He telephoned about an hour ago; he needed a second clearance. I told
him about your call to me, that you both wanted to know whether I'd
brought up the Randolph Medical Center business – lousy goddamned mess
– and I said I had, that we all knew about it.'

'*Please*, Mr President! Go back. What *exactly* did you say?'

'What's the matter with you?'

'What did he say to you?'

'About what?'

'Just *tell* me! First, what you said to him!'

'Now, just a minute, Havelock – '

'*Tell* me! You don't have time, *none* of us has time! What did you *say*?'

The urgency was telegraphed. Berquist paused, then answered calmly, a
leader aware of a subordinate's alarm, not understanding it but willing to
respect its source. 'I said that you'd phoned me and specifically asked if I
had brought up the Randolph Medical Center at the meeting this afternoon.
I said that I had, and that you seemed relieved that everyone knew about
it.'

'What did *he* say?'

'He seemed confused, frankly. I think he said "I see", then asked me if you'd given any reason for wanting to know.'

'Know *what?*'

'About the Medical – What *is* wrong with you?'

'What did you *say?*'

'That I understood you were both concerned, although I wasn't sure why.'

'What was his reply?'

'I don't think he had one . . . Oh, yes. He asked if you'd made any progress with the man you've got at Bethesda.'

'Which wasn't until tomorrow and he knew it!'

'What?'

'Mr President, I don't have time to explain and you can't lose a moment. Has Pierce got into that vault, that room?'

'I don't know.'

'Stop him! He's the mole!'

'You're *insane!*'

'Goddamn it, Berquist, you can have me shot, but right now I'm *telling* you! He's got cameras you don't know about! In rings, watches, cuff-links! Stop him! Take him! Strip him and check for capsules, *cyanide!* I can't give that order but you can! You *have* to! *Now!*'

'Stay by the phone,' said the President of the United States. 'I *may* have you shot.'

Havelock got out of the chair, if for no other reason than the need to move, to keep in motion. The dark mists were closing in again; he had to get out from under them. He looked at Jenna, and her eyes told him she understood.

'Pierce found me. I found him, and he found me.'

'He's trapped.'

'I could have killed him at Costa Brava. I wanted to kill him, but I wouldn't listen. I wouldn't listen to myself.'

'Don't go back. You've got him. You're within the time span.'

Michael walked away from the desk, away from the dark mists that pursued him. 'I don't pray,' he whispered. 'I don't believe. I'm praying now, to what I don't know.'

The telephone rang and he lunged for it. 'Yes?'

'He's gone. He ordered the patrol boat to take him back to Savannah.'

'Did he get into that *room?*'

'No.'

'Thank Christ!'

'He's got something else,' said the President in a voice that was barely audible.

'What?'

'The complete psychiatric file on Matthias. It says everything.'

37

The police swept through the streets of Savannah, patrol cars roaring out to the airport and screeching into bus and train stations. Car-rental agencies were checked throughout the city and road blocks set up on the major highways and back country routes – north to Augusta, south to Saint Marys, west to Macon and Valdosta. The man's description was radioed to all units – municipal, county, state – and the word spread down through the ranks from the highest levels of authority: *Find him. Find the man with the streak of white in his hair. If seen approach with extreme caution, weapons drawn. If movements are unexpected, shoot. Shoot to kill.*

The manhunt was unparalleled in numbers and intensity, the federal government assuring the state, the cities and townships that all costs would be borne by Washington. Men off duty were called in by precincts and station houses; vehicles in for minor repairs were put back on the streets, and private cars belonging to police personnel were issued magnetic, circling roof lamps and sent out to prowl the dark country roads. Everywhere cars and pedestrians were stopped; anyone even vaguely approaching the man's description was politely requested to remove hats where they were worn, and torches roamed over faces and hairlines, searching for a hastily, imperfectly dyed streak of white hair rising above a forehead. Hotels, motels and rural inns were descended upon; registers were checked for late arrivals, desk clerks questioned, the interrogators alerted to the possibility of evasion or deception. Farmhouses where lights remained on were entered – courteously to be sure – but the intruders were aware that the inhabitants could be hostages, that an unseen child or wife might be held somewhere on the premises by the man with the streak of white in his hair. Rooms and barns and silos were searched, nothing left to speculation.

Morning came and weary thousands reported back to points of dispatch, angry, frustrated, bewildered by the government's ineffectual methods. For no photographs or sketches were issued; the only name given was that of an elusive 'Mr Smith'. The alarm was still out, but the *blitzkrieg* search was essentially over, and the professionals knew it. The man with the streak in his hair had slipped through the net. He could be blond or bald or grey by now, limping with a cane or a crutch and dressed in tattered clothes, or in the uniform of the police or the army, without a vestige of his former appearance.

The newspapers carrying early-morning stories of the strange, massive hunt abruptly called off their reporters. Owners and editors had been reached by respected men in government who claimed no special knowledge of the situation but had profound trust in those higher up who had appealed to them. *Play it down, let the story die.* In second editions the search was relegated to a few lines near the back pages, and those papers with third editions carried no mention of it at all.

And an odd thing happened at a telephone exchange beginning with the digits *0-7 7 4 2* . . . Since midnight, it had not functioned and by 8 a.m., when service was suddenly, inexplicably, resumed, telephone 'repairmen' were in the building of the Voyagers Emporium annex, where orders were received, and every incoming call monitored and taped, all tapes *under* fifteen seconds in length played instantly over the phone to Sterile Five. The brevity reduced the number to a very few.

International airports were infiltrated by federal agents using sophisticated X-ray equipment that scanned briefcases and hand luggage to look for a two-inch thick metal case with a combination lock on the side. There were two assumptions: one, the devastating file would not be entrusted to a cargo hold and, two, it would remain in its original government container for authenticity. Even so, in case container and file were separated, either shape was sufficient cause for examination. By eleven thirty a.m. over 2,700 attaché cases had been opened and searched, from Kennedy to Atlanta to Miami International.

'Thanks very much,' said Havelock into the phone, forcing energy into his voice, feeling the effects of the sleepless night. He hung up and looked over at Jenna, who was pouring coffee. 'They can't understand and I can't tell them. Pierce wouldn't call Orphan-ninety-six unless he thought he could get his message across with a very few words, spoken quickly. He knows I've got the place wired and manned by now.'

'You've done everything you can,' said Jenna, carrying the coffee to the desk. 'All the airports are covered – '

'Not for him,' Michael broke in. 'He wouldn't risk it, and besides, he doesn't want to leave. He wants what I want. Parsifal . . . It's that *file*! One small single-engined plane crossing the Mexican border or a fishing boat meeting another between here and Cuba, or out of Galveston towards Matamoros, and that file's on its way to Moscow, into the hands of the overkill specialists in the *Voennaya*. And there's not a damn thing I can do about it.'

'The Mexican border is being patrolled, the agents doubled. The piers and marinas are watched both here and in the Gulf, all boats tracked, stopped if directions are in question. You insisted on these things and the President issued the orders.'

'It's a long border and those are large bodies of water.'

'Get some rest, Mikhail. You can't function if you're exhausted; it's one of your rules, remember.'

'One of the rules . . . ?' Havelock brought both hands to the sides of his head, massaging his temples with his fingers. 'Yes, that's one of the rules, part of the rules.'

'Lie down on the couch and close your eyes. I can take the calls, let you know what they are. I slept for a while, you didn't.'

'When did you sleep?' asked Michael, looking up, doubting.

'I rested before the sun was up. You were talking to your Coast Guards.'

'They don't belong to me,' said Havelock wearily, pushing himself up. 'Maybe I will lie down . . . just for a few minutes. It's part of the rules.' He walked round the desk, then stopped; his eyes roamed the elegant study strewn with papers, notebooks and file folders. 'God, I hate this room!' he said, heading for the couch. 'Thanks for the coffee, but no thanks.'

The telephone rang, and Michael steeled himself, wondering whether the bell would stop before a second ring, or whether it would remain unbroken, the signal of an *emergency*. It stopped, then resumed ringing. Havelock lowered himself down on the couch as Jenna answered, speaking calmly.

'This is Sterile Five . . . Who's calling?' She listened, then covered the phone and looked over at Michael. 'It's the State Department, New York City, Division of Security. Your man's come in from the Soviet consulate.'

Havelock rose unsteadily, briefly finding it necessary to centre his balance. 'I must talk to him,' he said, walking towards the desk. 'I thought he'd be there hours ago.' He took the phone from Jenna and, after peremptory identifications, made his request. 'Let me have the candidate, please.' The Russian came on the line. 'Where the hell have you been?'

'Apparently it is considered in poor taste over here to defect except during business hours,' began the Russian in a weary, sing-song voice. 'I arrived down here at the Federal Plaza at four o'clock this morning, after having survived an attempted mugging on the subway, only to be told by one of the night guards that there was nothing he could do until the *office* opened! I explained my somewhat precarious position and the kind, vacuous idiot offered to buy me a cup of coffee – in a public restaurant. Finally getting into the building by myself – your security is ludicrous – I waited in a dark, draughty hallway until nine o'clock when your militia arrived. I then presented myself and the imbeciles, they wanted to call the *police*! They wanted to have me *arrested* for breaking and entering and the possible destruction of government property!'

'All right, you're there now – '

'I haven't *fin-nished*!' yelled the Russian. 'Since that auspicious beginning I have been filling out uncountable forms – with Russian nursery rhymes, incidentally – and have repeatedly given your number, asking to be put in touch with you. What *is* the matter with you people? Do you limit *toll calls*?'

'We're in touch now – '

'Not *fin-nished*! This past hour I have been sitting alone in a room so poorly wired I was tempted to lower my trousers and fart into the microphones. And I have *just* been given additional forms to fill out, including one inquiring about my hobbies and favourite recreational pastimes! Are you sending me to *camp*, perhaps?'

Michael smiled, grateful beyond words for a momentary break in the tension. 'Only where you'll be safe,' he said. 'Consider the source. We're fools, remember, not jackals. You made the right choice.'

The Russian sighed audibly. 'Why do I work myself up? The *frukti galavas* are no better in the Dzerzhinsky . . . why not admit it? They're worse. Your Albert Einstein would be on his way to Siberia, assigned to lead mules in a gulag. Where is the sense in it all?'

'There's very little,' said Havelock softly. 'Except to survive. All of us.'

'A premise I subscribe to.'

'So did Rostov.'

'I remember the words he sent you. "He's not my enemy any longer but others are who may be mine as well." They are ominous words, Havelock.'

'The *Voennaya.*'

'Maniacs!' was the guttural reply. 'In their heads they march with the Third Reich.'

'How operational are they here?'

'Who knows? They have their own councils, their own methods of recruitment. They touch too many you can't see.'

'The *paminyatchiks*? You can't see them.'

'Believe me when I tell you I was trusted but never that trusted. However, one can speculate . . . on rumours. There are always rumours, aren't there? You might say the speculation has persuaded me to take the action I have.' The Russian paused. 'I *will* be treated as a valuable asset, will I not?'

'Guarded and housed as a treasure. What's the speculation?'

'In recent months certain men have left our ranks – unexpected retirements to well-earned dachas, untimely illnesses . . . disappearances. None so crudely as Rostov, but perhaps there was no time to be clever. Nevertheless, it seems there is a disturbing sameness about the departed. They were generally categorized as quiet realists, men who sought solutions and knew when to pull back from confrontation. Pyotr Rostov exemplified this group; he was in fact their spokesman in a way. Make no mistake, you were his enemy, he despised your system – too much for the few, too little for the many – but he understood there was a point where enemies could no longer push forward. Or there was nothing. He knew time was on our side, not bombs.'

'Are you saying those who replaced the Rostovs think otherwise?'

'That is the rumour.'

'The *Voennaya*?'

'That is the speculation. And should they take over the power centres of the KGB, can leadership of the Kremlin be far behind? This cannot happen. If it does . . .' The Russian did not finish the statement.

'There'll be nothing?' offered Havelock.

'That is the judgement. You see, they think *you'll* do nothing. They believe they can chew you up, first in one area, then in another.'

'That's nothing new.'

'With tactical nuclear weapons?'

'That's very new.'

'It's insane,' said the man from the KGB. 'You'll *have* to react; the world will demand it.'

'How can we stop the VKR?'

'By giving them little or no ammunition.'

'What do you mean, "ammunition"?'

'Knowledge of provocative or inflammatory actions that they can use to threaten the tired old men in the Presidium. It is the same as over here; you have your jackals, beribboned generals and wild-eyed colonels closeting themselves with overweight, over-aged senators and congressmen, making pronouncements of disaster if you don't strike first. The wisest men do not always prevail; actually, you're better at that than we are. Your controls are better.'

'I hope so,' said Michael, thinking fleetingly of men like Lieutenant-

Commander Thomas Decker. 'But you say the *Voennaya* has filtered into your ranks, into the KGB.'

'Speculation.'

'If it's true it means that at least several of them could be walking around the embassy here or the consulate in New York.'

'I'm not even sure of my own superior.'

'And a *paminyatchik* outside would know them, could reach them, make a delivery.'

'You assume I know something. I don't. What delivery?'

Havelock paused, trying to still the throbbing in his temples. 'Suppose I were to tell you that just such ammunition as you describe was stolen last night by a mole so deep and entrenched he had access to information released only by executive order. He disappeared.'

'Willing to give up his entrenched position?'

'He was found out. You were instrumental; you told me about Rostov's death and the VKR. He *is* a *Voennaya*. He's the enemy.'

'Then look for the sudden diplomatic departure of a low-level attaché, a street security man or a communications officer. If there is a VKR recruit, he would be among these. Intercept, if you can, hold up the plane, if you have to. Claim stolen property, espionage, go to the limit. Don't let them have that ammunition.'

'If we're too late.'

'What can I tell you without knowing the nature of the delivery?'

'The worst.'

'Can you deny?'

'It's beyond deniability. Part of it's false – the worst part – but it will be accepted as the truth . . . by the beribboned generals and the wild-eyed colonels.'

The Russian was silent, then replied quietly. 'You must speak with others much higher, much wiser. We have, as you say here, a rule-of-thumb when dealing with such matters. Go to substantial men in the Party between the ages of fifty and seventy who went through Operation Barbarossa and Stalingrad. Their memories are acute; they may help you. I'm afraid I can't.'

'You have. We know what to watch for at the embassy and the consulate . . . You'll be brought down here for debriefing, you understand that.'

'I understand. Will I be permitted to see American films on the television, perhaps. After the interrogation sessions, of course.'

'I'm sure something can be arranged.'

'I do so like the Westerns . . . Havelock, stop the delivery to Moscow. You don't know the *Voennaya*.'

'I'm afraid I do know it,' said Michael, rounding the desk and sinking once again into the chair. 'And I'm afraid,' he added, hanging up.

There was no rest for the next three hours, coffee, aspirin and cold water compresses serving to keep him awake and numb the piercing ache that pounded through his head. Every department in every intelligence and investigatory agency that had information on or access to the Soviet embassy or the consulate in New York was contacted and ordered to divulge whatever Sterile Five requested. The schedules for Aeroflot, LOT Airlines, Czechoslovak CSA and all the carriers to the Eastern bloc were studied, their manifests checked for diplomatic passengers. The cameras were doubled on both Soviet buildings in Washington and New York, personnel leaving the premises placed under surveillance, the units told to keep their subjects in sight even at the risk of being seen themselves. Everything was designed to inhibit contact, to cut off the delivery on its way to Moscow, and nothing could achieve this more effectively than a VKR agent knowing he might expose the fugitive if he kept a rendezvous, or Pierce realizing he might be caught if he made one.

Helicopters criss-crossed along the Mexican border by the score, following small aircraft; radio checks were constant, and those planes making unsatisfactory replies were ordered to return to be searched. Off the coasts of Florida, Georgia and the Carolinas navy jets soared low over the water, tracking boats that veered too far south-east; radios were used here, too; either explanations were satisfactory or directions were altered. Out of Corpus Christi, other jets and Coast Guard patrols spotted and intercepted fishing and pleasure craft on their way towards Mexican waters; fortunately, inclement weather in the western Gulf had reduced their numbers. None made contact with other boats; none went beyond Port Isabel or Brazos Island.

It was a quarter to four when an exhausted Havelock returned to the couch. 'We're holding,' he said. 'Unless we've missed something, we're holding. But we may have . . .' He fell onto the pillows. 'I've got to go back to the names. He's there. Parsifal's *there* and I must find him! Berquist says we can't go beyond tonight, he can't take the chance. The *world* can't take the chance.'

'But Pierce never got into that room,' protested Jenna. 'He never saw the agreements.'

'The psychiatric file on Matthias spells them out – in all their insanity. In some ways, it's worse. A diagnosed madman running the foreign policy of the most powerful, most feared country on earth. We're lepers . . . Berquist said we'll be lepers. If we're alive.'

The telephone rang; Michael expelled his breath and buried his head. The mists were closing in again, now enveloping him, suffocating him.

'Yes, thank you very much,' said Jenna into the phone across the room.

'What is it?' asked Havelock, opening his eyes, staring at the floor.

'The Central Intelligence Agency unearthed five more photographs. That leaves only one, and that man they're quite sure is dead. Others may be also, of course.'

'Photographs? Of what, whom?'

'The old men on *my* list.'

'Oh?' Michael turned over; his eyes, fixed on the ceiling, were closing. 'Old men,' he whispered. 'Why?'

'Sleep, Mikhail. You *must* sleep. You're no good to yourself or anyone else this way.' Jenna walked to the couch and knelt beside him. She pressed her lips lightly against his cheek. 'Sleep, my darling.'

Jenna sat at the desk, and each time the phone began to ring she pounced on it like a breathless blonde cat protecting its lair from predators. The calls

came from everywhere – progress reports issued by men who were following
orders blindly.

They were holding.

The handsome couple in riding breeches, boots and emblazoned red jackets
galloped across the field on their hunters, the horses straining, nostrils
flared, long legs pounding the hard earth and plunging through the tall
grass. In the distance to their right was a split-rail fence signifying the
property line of an adjacent estate, beyond it another field that disappeared
into a wall of giant maples and oaks. The man gestured at the fence,
laughing and nodding his head. The woman at first feigned surprise and
maidenly reluctance, then suddenly whipped her mount to the right and
raced ahead of her companion, high in the saddle as she approached the
fence. She soared over it, followed by the man only yards behind and to her
left; they rode swiftly towards the edge of the woods, where both reined in
their horses. The woman grimaced as she came to a stop.

'*Damn!*' she shouted. 'I pulled a muscle in my calf! It's screaming!'

'Get off and walk around. Don't sit on it.'

The woman dismounted as the man reached over for the reins of her
horse. His companion walked in circles, her limp pronounced, swearing
under her breath.

'Good God, where are we?' she asked, half-shouting.

'I think it's the Heffernans' place. How's the leg?'

'Murder, absolute murder! *Christ!*'

'You can't ride on it.'

'I can hardly walk on it, you damn fool.'

'Temper, temper. Come on, let's find a phone.' The man and woman
started through the edge of trees, the man leading both horses, threading
them past several thick trunks. 'Here,' he said, reaching for a low branch on
a thick bush. 'I can tie them up here and come back for them; they won't go
anywhere.'

'Then you can help me. This really is excruciating.'

The horses tied and grazing, the couple began to walk. Through the trees
they could see the outlines of the wide semicircular drive at the front
entrance of the large house. They also saw the figure of a man who seemed
to emerge from nowhere. He was in a gabardine overcoat, with both hands
in his pockets. They met and the man in the overcoat spoke.

'May I help you? This is private property.'

'I trust we *all* have private property, old man,' replied the sportsman
supporting the woman. 'My wife pulled a muscle over our last jump. She
can't ride.'

'What?'

'Horses, sport. Our horses are tied up back there. We were doing a little
pre-hunt work over the course before Saturday's meet and I'm afraid we
came a cropper, as they say. Take us to a phone, please.'

'Well, I . . . I . . .'

'This *is* the Heffernans' house, isn't it?' demanded the husband.

'Yes, but neither Mr or Mrs Heffernan is here, sir. Our orders are not to
allow anyone inside.'

'Oh, shit!' exploded the wife. 'How tacky can you be? My leg hurts, you ass! I need a ride back to the club.'

'One of the men will be happy to drive you, ma'am.'

'And my chauffeur can bloody well come and pick me up! Really, just who *are* these Heffernans? Are they members, darling?'

'I don't think so, Buff. Look, the man has his orders, and tacky as they are, it's not his fault. You go along and I'll take the horses back.'

'They'd better not try to *become* members,' said the wife as the two men helped her across the drive to a car.

The man walked back through the woods to the horses, untied them and led them across the field, where he removed the rails and prodded them through into the tall grass. He replaced the rails, mounted his hunter and, with the woman's horse in tow, trotted south over the course of Saturday's hunt – as he understood the course to be from his first and only study of the charts as a guest of the club.

He reached under his saddle and pulled out a powerful hand-held radio; he pressed a switch and raised the instrument to his lips.

'There are two cars,' he said into the radio. 'A black Lincoln, licence plate seven-four-zero, MRL; and a dark green Buick, licence one-three-seven, GMJ. The place is ringed with guards, and there are no rear exit roads. The windows are thick; you'd need a cannon to blow through them, and we were picked up by density infrareds.'

'Got it,' was the reply, amplified over the tiny speaker. 'We're mainly interested in the vehicles . . . By the way, I can see the Buick now.'

The man with various saws clipped to and dangling from his wide leather belt was high up in the tall pine tree bordering the road, his safety strap around it and clamped to his harness. He shoved the hand-held radio into its holster and adjusted the binoculars to his eyes, looking diagonally down through the branches, focusing on the car coming out of the tree-lined drive.

The view was clean, all angles covered. No cars could enter or leave the premises of Sterile Five without being seen – even at night; the capabilities of infrared applied to lenses as well as trip lights.

The man whistled; the door of the truck far below opened, and on its panel were the words HIGH TOP TREE SURGEONS. A second man stepped out and looked up.

'Take off,' said the man above, loud enough to be heard. 'Relieve me in two hours.'

The driver of the truck headed north for a mile and a half to the first intersection. There was a garage on the right; the doors of its repair shop were open, and a car was inside on a hydraulic lift, facing the front. The driver reached for the switch and snapped his headlights on and off. Instantly, within the garage's shop the headlights of the car on the lift flashed on and off – the signal had been acknowledged, the vehicle was in position. The station's owner believed he was co-operating – confidentially – with the Narcotics Division of the State Police. It was the least a citizen could do.

The driver swung to his right, then immediately to the left, making a U-turn between the converging roads; he headed south. Three minutes later he passed the pine tree that concealed his companion beyond the branches near the top. Under different circumstances he might have touched his horn; he couldn't now. There could be no sound, no sight that marked in any way that area of the road. Instead, he accelerated, and in fifty seconds came to another intersection, the first south of Sterile Five.

Diagonally across on the left was a small old country inn, Southern style, like a large doll house built to bring back memories of an old plantation. Behind was a black asphalt parking area, where perhaps a dozen cars were lined up like large brightly-coloured toys. Except for one, the fourth from the end, which had a clear view of the intersection and swift access to the exit. Facing the front, it was layered with dirt, and dark, a poor relation in the company of its shiny, expensive cousins.

Again the driver leaned forward and flicked his headlights on and off. The dirty, worn-looking car – with an engine more powerful than any other in the lot – did the same. Another signal was acknowledged. Whatever emerged from Sterile Five could be picked up in either direction.

Arthur Pierce studied his face in the mirror of the run-down motel on the outskirts of Falls Church, Virginia; he was satisfied with what he saw. The fringe of grey circling his shaved head was in concert with the rimless glasses and the shabby brown cardigan worn over the soiled white shirt with the frayed collar. He was the image of the loser, whose minor talents and lack of illusion kept him securely, if barely, above the poverty level. Nothing was ventured because it was useless. Why bother? No one stopped such men on the street; they walked too slowly; they were inconsequential.

Pierce turned from the mirror and walked across the room to the road map spread out under the light of a plastic lamp on the cheap, stained desk against the wall. On the right, holding the map in place, was a grey metal container with the emblem of the United States Navy stamped on the top, the medical insignia below it and a brass, built-in combination lock on the side. In it was a document as lethal as any in history. The psychiatric diagnosis of a statesman the world revered, a diagnosis proving that man insane – to have *been* insane while functioning as the international voice of one of the two most powerful nations on earth. And the nation that permitted this intolerable condition to exist could no longer serve as the leader of the cause it espoused. A madman had betrayed not only his government but the world; lying, deceiving, misleading, forging alliances with enemies, scheming against supposed allies. No matter that he was insane, it had happened. It was all there.

The contents of the grey metal container was an incredible weapon, but for it to be used with devastating effect it had to reach the proper hands in Moscow. Not the tired old compromisers, but the visionaries with the strength and the will to move swiftly to bring the corrupt, incompetent giant to its knees. The possibility that the Matthias file might fall into soft, wrinkled hands in Moscow was insufferable; it would be bartered, *negotiated*, finally thown away by weak men frightened of the very people they controlled. No, thought Arthur Pierce, this metal container belonged to the VKR. Only the *Voennaya*.

He could not risk otherwise, and several phone calls had convinced him that there *was* risk in channelling it out with the few he could trust. As expected, embassy and consulate personnel were under heavy surveillance; all international flights were being monitored, and hand and cargo luggage X-rayed. Too much risk.

He would take it out himself, along with the ultimate weapon, the terminal weapon, documents that called for successive nuclear strikes against Soviet Russia and the People's Republic of China, agreements signed by the great American Secretary of State. They were nuclear fantasies conceived by an insane genius, working with one of the most brilliant minds ever produced by the Soviet Union. Fantasies so real that the tired old men in the Kremlin would run for their dachas and their vodka, leaving decisions to those who could cope, to the men of the *Voennaya*.

Where *was* the brilliant mind that had made it all possible? The man who had turned on his homeland only to learn the truth – that he had been wrong. *So wrong!* Where was Parsifal? Where was Alexi Kalyazin?

With these thoughts Pierce turned to the map again. The inept – and not so inept – Havelock had mentioned the Shenandoah – that the man they called Parsifal was somewhere in the Shedandoah area, by implication within a reasonable distance of Matthias's country home. The implied reasonable distance, however, was the variable quotient. The Shenandoah Valley was more than a hundred miles long, over twenty wide, from the Allegheny to the Blue Ridge Mountains. What might be considered reasonable? There was no reasonable answer, so the solution must be found in the opposite direction: in the plodding mind of Michael Havelock – Mikhail Havlicek, son of Václav, named for a Russian grandfather from Rovno – a man whose talents lay in persistence and a degree of imagination, not brilliance. Havelock would reduce the arc, put in use a hundred computers to trace a single telephone call made at a specific time to a specific place to a man he called a zealot. Havelock would do the work and a *paminyatchik* would reap the benefits. Lieutenant-Commander Decker would be left alone; he was a key that might well unlock a door.

Pierce bent over the map, his index finger shifting from one line to another. The arc, the semi-circle that blanketed the Shenandoah from Sterile Five, was covered, with men and vehicles in position. From Harper's Ferry to the Valley Pike, Highways 11 and 66, Routes 7, 50, 15, 17, 29 and 33, all were manned, waiting for a word that a specific car was approaching at a specific time heading for a specific place. That place was to be determined and reported; nothing else was required of the men in those vehicles. They were hirelings, not participants, their time paid for in money, not purpose or destiny.

Arthur Pierce, born Nicolai Petrovitch Malyekov in the village of Ramenskoye, Union of Soviet Socialist Republics, suddenly thought about that destiny, and the years that had led to his own electrifying part in it. He had never wavered, never forgotten who he was or why he had been given the supreme opportunity to serve the ultimate cause, a cause so meaningful and so necessary for a world where the relative few tyrannized the many, where millions upon millions lived on the edge of despair or in hopeless poverty so that the capitalist manipulators could laugh over global balance sheets while

their armies burned pyjama-clad children in far away lands. These were not
the blatant, provocative conclusions of banal propagandists, they were
truths. He had seen it all for himself – from the burning villages in South-
east Asia to the corporate dining-rooms where offers of employment were
accompanied by grins and winks and promises of stock options that were
the first steps towards wealth to the inner corridors of government power
where hypocrites and incompetents encouraged yet more hypocrisy and
incompetence. How he hated it all! Hated the corruption and the greed and
the sanctimonious liars who deceived the masses to whom they were
responsible, abusing the powers given them, lining their pockets and the
pockets of their own . . . There *was* a better way. There was *commitment*.
There was the *Voennaya*.

He had been thirteen years old when he was told by the loving couple he
called 'Mother' and 'Father'. They explained while holding him and gazing
into his eyes to let him see their love. He was theirs, they said, but he was
also not theirs. He had been born to a chosen couple thousands of miles
away who loved him so much they gave him to the State, to a cause that
would make a better world for generations to come. And as his 'mother' and
'father' spoke, so many things in Arthur Pierce's young memory began to
fall into place. All the discussions – not only with his 'mother' and 'father',
but with the scores of visitors who came so frequently to the farm house –
discussions that told of suffering and oppression and of a despotic form of
government that would be replaced by a government dedicated to the people
– *all* the people.

He was to be part of that change. Over the early years certain other
visitors had come and had given him games to play, puzzles to work,
exercises to read – tests that graded his capabilities. And one day when he
was thirteen he was pronounced extraordinary; on that same day he was
told his real name. He was ready to join the cause.

It would not be easy, his 'mother' and 'father' had said, but he was to
remember when pressures seemed overwhelming that *they* were there, *always*
there. And should anything happen to them, others would take their place
to help him, encourage him . . . guide him, knowing that others still were
watching. He was to be the best in all things; he was to be *American* – kind,
generous and above all, seemingly fair; he was to use his gifts to rise as far
as he was capable of rising. But he was never to forget who and what he
was, or the cause that gave him the gift of life and the opportunity to help
make the world better than it was.

Things after that auspicious day were not as difficult as his 'mother' and
'father' had predicted. Through his high school years and college, his secret
served to prod him – because it was *his* secret and he *was* extraordinary.
They were years of exhilaration: each new prize and award was proof of his
superiority. He found it easy to be liked, as though in a never-ending
popularity contest, the crown was always his. Yet there were self-denials,
too, and they served to remind him of his commitment. He had many friends
but no deep friendships, no relationships. Men liked him but accepted his
basic distance, ascribing it usually to his having to find jobs to pay his way
through school. Women he used only for sexual release; he formed no
attachments whatsoever.

During his post-graduate studies at Michigan he was contacted by Moscow and told his new life was about to begin. The meeting was not without amusement, the contact a recruitment executive from a large conservative corporation who had supposedly read the graduate student files and wanted to meet one Arthur Pierce. But there was nothing amusing in his news; it was deadly serious – and exhilarating.

He was to join the army, where certain opportunities would lead to advancement, further advancement and contact with civilian and military authorities. He would serve an appropriate amount of time and return not to the mid-west but to Washington, where word of his record and talents would be spread. Companies would be lined up, anxious to employ him, but the government would step in. He was to accept.

But first the army – and he was to give it everything he had, he was to continue to be the *best*. His 'father' and 'mother' had thrown him a farewell party on the farm inviting all his friends, including most of the old Boy Scout Troop 37. And it *was* a farewell party in more than one sense. His 'father' and 'mother' told him at the end of the night that they would not see him again. They were getting old and they had done their job: him. And he would make them proud. Besides, their talents were needed elsewhere. He understood; the cause was everything.

For the first time since he was thirteen, he had cried that night. But it was permitted – and, besides, they were tears of joy.

All those years, thought Arthur Pierce, glancing in the cheap motel mirror at the fringe of grey and the frayed collar around his neck. They had been worth it; the proof would be found in the next few hours.

The waiting had begun. The reward would be a place in history.

Michael opened his eyes, a sea of dark brown leather confronting him, moisture everywhere, the heat oppressive. He turned over and raised his head, suddenly aware that it was not sunlight but the glow of a distant lamp that washed the room. He was drenched with sweat. It was night, and he was not ready for night. What had *happened*?

'*Dobriy den.*' The greeting floated over to him.

'What time is it?' he asked, sitting up on the couch.

'Ten past seven,' said Jenna, at the desk. 'You slept a little over three hours. How do you feel?'

'I don't know. Left out, I think. What's going on?'

'Not a great deal. As you said, we're holding. Did you know that the lights on these buttons actually go on before the telephone rings? Only a split-second, but they do.'

'It's not comforting. Who called?'

'Very serious, bewildered men reporting nothing, reporting that they had nothing to report. Several asked how long they were to keep up what they referred to as their "reconnaissance". I said until they were told otherwise.'

'That says it.'

'The photographs arrived.'

'What . . . ? Oh, your list.'

'They're on the coffee table. Look at them.'

Havelock focused on the row of five grainy faces staring at him. He rubbed his eyes and wiped the perspiration from his hairline, blinking repeatedly as he tried to concentrate. He began with the face on the far left; it meant nothing to him. Then the next, and the next, and the . . . next.

'Him,' he said, not knowing why he said it.

'Who?'

'The fourth one. Who is he?'

Jenna glanced down at a paper in front of her. 'It's a very old picture, taken in nineteen-forty-eight. The only one they could find. It's over thirty years old.'

'Who is he? Who was he?'

'A man named Kalyazin. Alexi Kalyazin. Do you recognize him?' Jenna got up from the desk.

'Yes . . . no. I don't know.'

'It's an *old* photograph, Mikhail. *Look* at it. *Study* it. The eyes, the chin, the shape of the mouth. Where? *Who?*'

'I don't know. It's there . . . and it's not there. What did he do?'

'He was a clinical psychotherapist,' said Jenna, reading. 'He wrote definitive studies evaluating the effects on men of the stress of combat or prolonged periods of enduring unnatural conditions. His expertise was used by the KGB; he became what you call here a strategist, but with a difference. He screened information sent in to the KGB by people in the field, looking for deviations that might reveal either double agents or men no longer capable of functioning in their jobs.'

'An evaluator. A fake with a penchant for overlooking the obvious.'

'I don't understand you.'

'Gunslingers. They never spot the gunslingers.'

'I still don't know what you're talking about.'

'I don't know him. It's a face like so many other faces, so many dossiers. God, the *faces!*'

'But there's *something!*'

'Maybe, I'm not sure.'

'Keep looking at it. *Concentrate.*'

'Coffee. Is there any coffee?'

'I forgot,' said Jenna. 'The first rule upon waking is coffee. Black and strong. You *are* Czech, Mikhail.' She went to the table behind the couch, where an accommodating guard had plugged in the silver pot.

'The first rule,' repeated Havelock, suddenly disturbed. 'The first *rule?*'

'What?'

'Where are your notes on Decker's telephone call?'

'You had them.'

'Where *are* they?'

'Down there. On the table.'

'*Where?*'

'Under the last photograph. On the right.'

Get yourself a drink. You know the rules.

Michael threw the photograph of an unknown face off the table and gripped the two notebook pages in his hand. He stared at them, shifting them back and forth.

'Oh, my *God!* The rules, the goddamned *rules!*'

Havelock got up and lurched towards the desk, his legs unsteady, his balance fragile.

'What is it?' asked Jenna, alarmed, the cup in her hand.

'*Decker!*' shouted Michael. 'Where are the notes on *Decker?*'

'Right there. On the left. The pad.'

Havelock riffled through the pages, his hand trembling again, his eyes seeing and not seeing, looking for the words. He found them.

'"An odd accent",' he whispered. '"An *odd* accent", but *what* accent?'

He grabbed the phone, barely able to control his finger as he dialled. 'Get me Lieutenant-Commander Decker, you've got his number on your index.'

'Mikhail, get hold of yourself.'

'Shut *up!*' The elongated buzz signified the ring, the wait intolerable.

'Hello?' said the tentative voice of a woman.

'Commander Decker, please.'

'I'm . . . terribly sorry, he's not here.'

'He's there to *me!* This is Mr Cross calling. Get him on the phone.'

Twenty seconds elapsed, and Michael thought his head would explode.

'What is it, Mr Cross?' Decker asked.

'You said an "odd accent". What did you mean?'

'I beg your pardon?'

'The call! The call you got from Matthias, from the one who said he was speaking for Matthias! When you said he had an odd accent, did you mean foreign, Russian?'

'No, not at all. It was high pitched and very Anglicized. Almost British, but not British.'

'Good night, Commander,' said Michael, hanging up.

Pour yourself a drink . . . you know the rules here . . . Come now, we're both out. Freshen yours and do mine while you're at it. That's also part of the rules, remember?

Havelock picked up the phone again, pulling the list of numbers in front of him. He dialled. The waiting was almost a pleasure, but it was too short; he needed time to adjust. Poole's Island!

'This is Mr Cross. Let me have Security please.'

Two short hums were heard, and a voice answered. 'Checkpoint,' said the officer on duty.

'This is Cross. Executive order, priority-zero. Please confirm.'

'Start counting,' said the voice.

'One, two, three, four, five, six – '

'Okay. Scanners match. What is it, Mr Cross?'

'Who was the officer who took emergency leave approximately six weeks ago?'

The silence was interminable; when the reply came, it was a matter-of-fact response by a knowledgeable man. 'Your information's incorrect, Mr Cross. There's been no request for emergency leave from the officer corps or anyone else. No one's left the island.'

'Thank you, Security.'

Alexander the Great . . . *Raymond Alexander!*

Fox Hollow!

38

'It's him,' said Michael, leaning over the desk, his hand still gripping the phone. 'He's Parsifal. Raymond Alexander.'

'*Alexander?*' Jenna took several steps away from the table and stared at Havelock, shaking her head slowly.

'It *must* be! It's in the words – "the *rules*". "One of the rules, part of the rules." Always rules; his life is a series of unbreakable rules! The odd accent wasn't foreign, *wasn't* Russian. It was 'thirties-Harvard with Alexander's pretentious emphasis. He's used it in a thousand lecture halls, hundreds of debates. Points made quickly, retorts thrown in unexpectedly, thrust and parry. That's Alexander!'

'As you've described him,' said Jenna calmly but firmly, 'there's an enormous contradiction I don't think you can explain. Are you prepared to accuse him of knowing the identity of a Soviet mole and doing nothing about it? Especially one so dangerous as an Undersecretary of State?'

'No, I *can't* explain it, but he can. He will. He sent me to Poole's Island, telling me a bullshit story about an army officer on emergency leave who let it slip to his wife. There wasn't any such person; no emergency leaves were taken.'

'Perhaps he was protecting another source.'

'Then why the elaborate lie? Why not a simple refusal to disclose? No, he wanted me to believe it, put me on my word to protect him – knowing I *would* protect him!'

'For what *purpose?*' said Jenna, coming to the desk. 'Why did he tell you in the first place? To have you *killed?*'

'Let him answer that.' Havelock picked up the phone, pressing the house intercom button. 'I want a car and an escort to follow me. It's about an hour's drive from here. Right away.' He replaced the phone and, for a moment, looked at it, then shook his head. 'No,' he said.

'The President?' asked Jenna.

'I'm not going to call him. Not yet. The state he's in he'd send in a battalion of commandos. We won't learn the truth that way. Cornered like that, Alexander might blow his brains out.'

'If you're right, what more is there to learn?'

'*Why!*' said Michael furiously, opening the top drawer and taking out the Llama automatic. 'And how,' he added, checking the magazine and cracking it back in place. 'That large contradiction you mentioned. His beloved republic.'

'I'm going with you.'

'No.'

'*Yes!* This time you have no right to refuse me. My life is in this room – my death as well. I have a right to *be* there.'

'You may have a right but you're not going. That son of a bitch set you up, he marked you for extinction.'

'I have to know *why*.'

'I'll tell you.' Michael started to leave.

'Suppose you can't!' cried Jenna, blocking him. 'Yes, Mikhail, look at me! Suppose you do not come back – it's possible, you know. Would you finally rob me of my sanity?'

'We've been out there. There are no alarms, no dogs or guards. Besides, he doesn't expect me. I'll come back – with *him*! . . . What the hell do you mean, your "sanity"?'

'I lost you once – I loved you and lost you! Do you think I can take even the risk of losing you again and never knowing *why*? How much do you *want* from me?'

'I want you to live.'

'I can't live, I *won't* live unless you're with me! I've tried it – it simply doesn't appeal to me. Whatever's out there is for both of us, not you alone. It's not fair, Mikhail, and you know it.'

'I don't give a damn about being fair!' He reached for her and pulled her into his arms; aware of the gun in his hand, wishing they were somewhere else where there were no guns – *ever*. 'I only care about you. I know what you've been through, what I *did* to you. I want you here, where I'll know you're all right. I can't risk *you*, don't you understand?'

'Because you love me?'

'So much . . . so very much.'

'Then respect me!' cried Jenna, whipping her head back, her blonde hair swirling over her shoulders. 'Damn you, Mikhail, *respect* me!'

Havelock looked at her, at the anger and the pleading in her eyes. *So much to make up for.* 'Come on,' he said. 'Let's get our coats. Let's go.'

Jenna turned and went to the coffee table, where she picked up the photograph, including the one on the floor. 'All right,' she said.

'Why?' asked Michael, gesturing at the pictures.

'Why not?' she replied.

The man concealed high up in the darkness of the tall pine drove his spikes deeper into the trunk, adjusting his harness to relax the pressure of the straps. Suddenly, in the distance far below, he saw the beams of headlights streaking out of the tree-lined drive at Sterile Five. He raised the infrared binoculars to his eyes with his right hand as his left pulled out the radio from its holder. He brought it to his lips and pressed the switch.

'Activity,' he said. 'Stay alert. Respond.'

'North in touch,' came the first reply.

'South also,' was the second.

Pushing the open-channel radio into the leather collar around his throat, the man focused the binoculars on the car emerging from the drive. It was the Buick; he refined the focus, and the images beyond the windshield sharpened.

'It's our man and the woman,' he said. 'Turning north. It's yours, North.'

'We're ready.'

'South, take off and assume your alternate position.'

'Leaving now. North keep us posted. Let us know when you want relief.'

'Will do.'

'*Hold* it! There's a second car . . . It's the Lincoln, two federals in the front. I can't see in the back . . . Now I can. No one else.'

'It's an escort,' said one of the two men in the car a mile and a half north. 'We'll wait till he passes.'

'Give him plenty of room,' ordered the man in the tree. 'They're curious people.'

'Don't worry.'

The Buick reached the intersection and turned left, the Lincoln Continental several hundred feet behind and following, a prowling behemoth protecting its young. Both vehicles headed west.

Inside the dark repair shop of the gas station, a hissing sound accompanied the lowering of the hydraulic lift; the engine of the descending car was turned on and gunned. The driver raised his radio and spoke.

'South, they've taken the B route. Head west on the parallel road and pick us up six miles down.'

'Heading across into west parallel,' was the reply.

'Hurry,' said North. 'They are.'

The white fence that marked the start of Alexander's property shone in the glare of the headlights. Seconds later the floodlights beaming on the trees scattered throughout the immense front acreage could be seen on the left, the wood and stone house beyond. Havelock then saw what he hoped he would see. There were no cars in the circular drive, very few lights in the windows. He slowed down and pulled the microphone from its dashboard recess.

'Escort, this is it,' he said, depressing the transmission switch. 'Stay up here on the road. There are no visitors and I want the man we're seeing to think we're alone.'

'Suppose you need us?' asked Escort.

'I won't.'

'That's not good enough. Sorry, sir.'

'All right, you'll hear me. I'm not shy; I'll fire a couple of shots.'

'That's good enough, as long as we're down there at the house.'

'I want you up here on the road.'

'Sorry, again. We'll leave the Abraham up here, but we'll be down there, right outside. On foot.'

Michael shrugged, replacing the microphone; it was pointless to argue. He snapped off the headlights and turned into the drive, idled the engine and let the Buick glide to within thirty feet of the entrance. The car came to a stop and he looked at Jenna. 'Ready?'

'I think more than my life. Or death. He wanted both.' She slipped the photographs under her coat. 'Ready,' she said.

They got out, closed the doors quietly, and walked up the broad steps to the huge panelled oak door. Havelock rang the bell; again the waiting was unbearable. The door opened and the uniformed maid stood there, startled.

'Good evening. It's Enid, isn't it?'

'Yes, sir. Good evening, sir. I didn't know Mr Alexander was expecting guests.'

'We're old friends,' said Michael, his hand on Jenna's arm, as both stepped inside. 'Invitations aren't required. It's part of the rules.'

'I've never heard that one.'

'It's fairly new. Is Mr Alexander where he usually is at this hour? In his library?'

'Yes, sir. I'll tell him you're here. The name, please?'

There was a sudden hollow echo preceding the voice that filled the large hall. 'It won't be necessary, Enid.' It was the clipped, high-pitched voice of Raymond Alexander pouring out of an unseen speaker. 'And I *have* been expecting Mr Havelock.'

Michael's eyes darted about the walls, his hand now gripping Jenna's arm. 'Is this another rule, Raymond? Make sure the guest is who he says he is?'

'It's fairly new,' replied the voice.

Havelock walked with Jenna through the elegant living-room filled with antiques from the far corners of the earth to the hand-carved door of the library. He guided her to his left, beyond the frame; she understood. He reached under his jacket for the Llama automatic and held it at his side before turning the heavy brass knob. He shoved the door open, his back pressed against the wall, his weapon ready.

'Is that really necessary, Michael?'

Havelock moved slowly into the frame, quickly adjusting his eyes to the shadowy, indirect lighting of the library. The source was two lamps: one fringed and on the large desk at the far end of the room; the other a floor lamp above the soft, leather armchair, shining down on the wild, unkempt head of Raymond Alexander. The old warhorse sat motionless, and in his bloated, pale white hands was a brandy glass held in front of his deep red velvet smoking jacket.

'Come in,' he said, turning to a small box-like device on the side table. He pressed a button, and somewhere overhead, on the wall above the door, the dim glow of a television monitor faded away. 'Miss Karras is a handsome woman. Very lovely . . . Come in, my dear.'

Jenna appeared, standing next to Michael. 'You're a monster,' she said simply.

'Far worse.'

'You wanted to kill us both,' she continued. 'Why?'

'Not him, never him. Not . . . *Mikhail.*' Alexander raised his glass and drank. 'Your life – or death – was never really considered one way or the other. It was out of our hands.'

'I could kill you for that,' said Havelock.

'I repeat. Out of our hands. Frankly, we thought she'd be retired, returned to Prague and eventually cleared. Don't you see, Michael, she wasn't important. Only you; you were the only one that mattered. You had to go and we knew they'd never let you, you were too valuable. You had to do it yourself, insist on it yourself. Your revulsion had to be so deep, so painful that there was no other way for you. It worked. You left. It was necessary.'

'Because I knew you,' said Havelock. 'I knew the man who led a sick, disintegrating friend down the road of insanity, turning him into some kind of grotesque thing – Belial with his finger on the nuclear switch. I knew the man who did this to Anton Matthias. I knew Parsifal.'

'Is that the name they've given me? Parsifal? Exquisite irony. No healing wounds with this fellow, only tearing them apart. Everywhere.'

'It's why you did what you did, isn't it? *I* knew who you were.'

Alexander shook his head, the unkempt hair a thousand coiled springs in motion, his green eyes under the full, arched brows, briefly closing. 'I wasn't important, either. Anton insisted; you became an obsession with him. You were what was left of his failing integrity, his decaying conscience.'

'But you knew how to *do* it. You knew a Soviet double agent so high in the government he could have been made Secretary of State. *Would* have been if he hadn't been there on that beach at the Costa Brava. You knew where he was, you knew his name, you *reached* him!'

'We had no part of the Costa Brava! I learned of it only after inquiring about you. We couldn't understand, we were shocked.'

'Not Matthias. He was beyond being shocked.'

'It was when we knew everything was out of control.'

'Not we! *You!*'

The old journalist again stopped all movement, his hands gripping the glass. He locked his eyes with Michael's and answered. 'Yes. Me. I knew.'

'So you sent me to Poole's Island, expecting me to be killed, and once dead I was guilty by reason of silence.'

'*No!*' Alexander shook his head, now violently. 'I never thought you'd *go* there, never thought you'd be *permitted* to go there.'

'That very convincing story about a soldier's wife you met and how she told you. It was all a lie. There've been no emergency leaves, no one's left that island. But I believed you, gave you my word I'd protect the source. Protect *you*. I never said anything, not even to Bradford.'

'Yes, yes, I wanted to convince you, but not *that* way. I wanted you to go up the ladder, using your regular channels, confront them, make them tell you the truth . . . And once you learned the truth, the *entire* truth, you might see, you might understand. You might be able to stop it . . . Without me.'

'How? For Christ's sake, *how?*'

'I think I know, Mikhail,' said Jenna, touching Havelock's arm as she stared down at Alexander. 'He did mean "we". Not "I". This man is not Parsifal. His servant, perhaps, but not Parsifal.'

'Is that true?' asked Havelock.

'Pour yourself and Miss Karras a drink, Michael. You know the rules. I have a story to tell you.'

'No drinks. Your rules don't apply any longer.'

'At least sit down, and put that gun away. You have nothing to fear here. Not from me. Not any longer.'

Havelock looked at Jenna; he nodded, leading them both to adjacent chairs across from Alexander. They sat down, Jenna removing the photographs from her coat and placing them beside her. Michael shoved the weapon into his pocket. 'Go on,' he said curtly.

'A number of years ago,' began the journalist, staring at the glass in his hands, 'Anton and I committed a crime. In our minds it was far more serious than any punishment might indicate, and the punishment would have been severe in the extreme. We were fooled ... "gulled" is the innocuous word, "deceived" more appropriate, "betrayed" more appropriate still. But the fact that it could have happened to us – two pragmatic intellectuals, as we believed we were – was intolerable to us. Still, it had happened.' Alexander drained his glass and placed it on the table next to his chair. He folded his puffed, delicate hands and continued. 'Whether it was because of my friendship with Matthias, or for whatever standing I might have had in this city, a man called me from Toronto saying he had obtained a false passport and was flying to Washington. He was a Soviet citizen, an educated man in his early sixties, and an employee in a reasonably high position in the Soviet government. His intention was to defect and could I put him in touch with Anthony Matthias.' The journalist paused and leaned forward, gripping the arms of the chair. 'You see, in those days everyone knew Anton was about to be tapped for extraordinary things; his influence was growing with every article he wrote, every trip to Washington. I arranged a meeting; it took place in this room.' Alexander leaned back and kept his eyes on the floor. 'That man had remarkable insights to offer, a wide knowledge of internal Soviet affairs. A month later he was working for the State Department. Three years after that Matthias was special assistant to the President, two years later Secretary of State. The man from Russia, by way of Toronto, was still in the Department, his talents so appreciated that by then he was processing highly classified information as the director of Eastern Bloc debriefings and reports.'

'When did you find out?' asked Havelock.

The journalist looked up. 'Four years ago,' he said quietly. 'Again, in this room. The defector asked to meet us both; he said that what he had to say was urgent and our schedules for that very night must be cleared – there could be no delays. He sat where Miss Karras is sitting now and told us the truth. He was a Soviet agent and had been continuously funnelling the most sensitive information to Moscow for the past six years. But something had happened and he could no longer function in his role. He felt old and worn out, the pressures were too great. He wanted to disappear.'

'And since you and Anton – the pragmatic intellectuals – had been responsible for six years of infiltration, he had you exactly where he wanted you.' Michael spoke sharply, revolted by the ineptitude and essential corruption that Alexander was describing. 'God forbid that great men should be tarnished.'

'That was part of it, surely, but then there was a certain justification. Anthony Matthias was at his zenith, reshaping global policies, reaching secure accommodation and *détente*, making the world somewhat safer than it was before him. Such a revelation would have been politically disastrous; it would have destroyed him ... and the good he was doing. I myself presented this argument strongly.'

'I'm sure it didn't take long to convince him,' said Havelock.

'Longer than perhaps you think,' replied Alexander, a trace of weary anger in his voice. 'You seem to have forgotten what he was.'

'Perhaps I never really knew.'

'You say this was part of it,' interrupted Jenna. 'What was the other part?'

The journalist shifted his gaze to rest on Jenna before he spoke. 'That man was given an order with which he could not – would not – comply. He was told to be prepared for a series of shocking Eastern Bloc reports and to shape them in such a way that would force Anton to request a naval blockade of Cuba along with a presidential Red Alert.'

'Nuclear?'

'Yes, Miss Karras. A replay of the 'sixty-two missile crisis, but far more provocative. These startling reports would corroborate photographic "evidence" purporting to show the jungles and southern coastal regions of Cuba ringed with offensive nuclear weapons, the first bridge of an imminent attack.'

'For what *purpose?*' asked Jenna.

'A geopolitical trap,' said Michael. 'He walks into it, he's finished.'

'Precisely,' agreed Alexander. 'Anton brings the full military might of the United States to the brink of war, and suddenly the gates of Cuba are opened and inspection teams from the world over invited to see for themselves. There is nothing, and Anthony Matthias is humiliated, portrayed as an hysterical alarmist – the one thing he never was – all his brilliant negotiations thrown away. The healing with them, I might add.'

'But this Soviet agent,' said Jenna, bewildered, 'this man who had for six years fed Moscow secrets, was a professional, if nothing else; he refused. Did he say why?'

'Quite movingly, I thought. He said Anton Matthias was too valuable to be sacrificed to a cabal of hotheads in Moscow.'

'The *Voennaya*,' said Havelock.

'Those shocking reports came in and they were ignored. No crisis ever took place.'

'Would Matthias have accepted them as authentic even if he hadn't known,' asked Michael.

'Somebody would have forced him to. Perfectly conscientious men and women in the section would have become alarmed, would possibly have come to someone like me – if they hadn't been told in advance what to expect, what the intemperate strategy was. Anton called in the Soviet ambassador for a long confidential talk. Men were replaced in Moscow.'

'They've come back,' said Havelock.

The journalist blinked; he did not understand, nor did he pretend to. He continued. 'The man who had deceived us, but who ultimately would not betray some voice inside himself, disappeared. Anton made it possible. He was given a new identity, a new life, beyond those who would have had him killed.'

'He came back, too,' said Michael.

'He never really went away. But yes, he came back. A little over a year ago, without calling, without warning, he came to see me and said we had to talk. But not in this room; he wouldn't talk in here and I think I appreciated that. I remembered too well that night when he told us what we'd done. It was late afternoon and we walked along the ridge above the ravine – two old men making their way slowly, cautiously over the ground, one profoundly frightened, the other curiously intense . . . in a quiet way, possessed.' Alexander paused. 'I'd like some more brandy; this isn't easy for me.'

'I'm not interested,' said Michael.

'Where is it?' asked Jenna, getting up and going to the table, reaching for the glass.

'The copper bar,' said the old man, looking up at her. 'Against the wall, my dear.'

'Go on,' said Havelock impatiently. 'She can hear you; we can both hear you.'

'I meant what I said. I *need* the brandy . . . You don't look well, Michael. You look tired; you're unshaven and there are dark circles under your eyes. You should take better care of yourself.'

'I'll make a note of it.'

Jenna returned. 'Here you are,' she said, handing Alexander his drink and going to her chair.

It was the first time Havelock noticed that Raymond's hand shook. It was why he held the glass in both hands, gripping it to reduce the tremble. '"In a quiet way, possessed." That's where you were.'

'Yes, I remember,' Alexander drank, then looked again at Jenna. 'Thank you,' he said.

She nodded. 'Please, go on.'

'Yes, of course . . . We walked along the ridge, we two old men that late afternoon, when suddenly he stopped and said to me, "You must do as I ask, for we have an opportunity that will never be presented to the world again." I replied that I was not in the habit of acceding to such requests without knowing what was being asked of me. He said it was not a request but a demand, that if I refused he would reveal the roles Matthias and I had played in his espionage activities. He would expose us both, destroy us both. It was what I feared most – for both of us, Anton more than myself, of course. But still myself, I can't say otherwise.'

'What did he want you to do?' asked Havelock.

'I was to be the Boswell; my journals would record the deterioration and collapse of a man with such power that he could plunge the world into the insanity that was down the road for him. My Samuel Johnson was, of course, Anthony Matthias, and the message to mankind was to be a sobering one: "This must not be allowed to happen again; no one man should ever again be elevated to such heights."'

'"We made him a god",' said Michael, recalling Berquist's words, '"when we didn't own the heavens."'

'Well put.' The journalist nodded his head. 'I wish I'd written it. But then, to borrow from Wilde, I probably will, if I ever get the chance.'

'This man, this Russian,' said Jenna, 'told you that afternoon what was happening to Matthias?'

'Yes. He'd seen him, been with him, knew the signs. Sudden tirades followed by weeping, constant self-justification, false humility that only served to point up his accomplishments . . . . growing suspicions about everyone around him, yet in public there was always the façade of normality. Then there were the lapses of memory – mainly concerning failures and, when prodded, the need to blame others for those failures . . . I came to see it all, write it all. I'd drive to the Shenandoah every week or so – '

'On Sundays?' broke in Havelock.

'Sundays, yes.'

'Decker?'

'Oh, yes, Commander Decker. By then, you see, the man you call Parsifal had persuaded a deteriorating Anton that all his policies, all his visions, would find their ultimate justification in total strength. The Master Plan they called it . . . and they found the man who could provide them with what they needed.'

'For the ultimate chess game,' said Michael.

'Yes. Decker would use the back road and meet Matthias in the cabin he used when he wanted to be alone.'

'The Woodshed,' said Havelock. 'A voice-activated tape system.'

'It never failed,' agreed Alexander in a voice barely above a whisper. 'Never. Even afterwards, when Matthias and . . . Parsifal played their dreadful game, all the more terrifying because Matthias was one of the players. It was frightening in another aspect, too, for Anton would become the warlord statesman, the brilliant negotiator, not seeing the man you call Parsifal but seeing others, addressing others. Russian generals and scientists who weren't there, Chinese army commanders and commissars half way across the globe. During those moments he *saw* them, they were *there*. It was a running pattern of self-induced seances, therapy of the most destructive kind. And each time he came out of it he was a little bit worse, his eyes guarded by those tortoiseshell glasses a little less focused. He was a man who'd been on some sort of drug trip, his mind a touch less clear for it. Yet he could still function in both worlds . . . I saw it all, wrote it all.'

'When did I come up?' asked Havelock. 'Why me?'

'You were there all the time, photographs of you were on his desk, his bureau . . . in the Woodshed. An album of the two of you on a camping trip through the Canadian far west.'

'I'd forgotten,' said Michael. 'It was so long ago. I was in graduate school, Anton was my adviser.'

'Far more than that. You were the son he never had, speaking to him in his native language, recalling another place, another time.' Alexander raised his head from the cradle of his chest, riveting his eyes on Havelock. 'Above all you were the son who refused to believe that his visions, his solutions for the world, were the right ones. He couldn't convince you. Your voice kept telling him he was wrong, and he couldn't stand that. He couldn't stand being told he was wrong, especially by you.'

'He was. He knew I'd tell him.'

'His eyes would stray to your pictures, and suddenly he would see you and be talking to you, tormented by your arguments, your anger. He was afraid of you really . . . and the work would stop.'

'So I had to be put out of reach.'

'Where you could no longer judge him, I think. You were part of his everyday reality, the Department of State. You had to be separated from that reality. It began to consume him; he couldn't tolerate your interference. You had to go; he wouldn't have it any other way.'

'And Parsifal knew how to do it,' said Michael bitterly. 'He knew the mole at State. He reached him and told him what to do.'

'I had no part of that. I knew it was being done but I didn't know how . . . You had spoken to Anton about Miss Karras. About your devotion to her and how, after the long years of your own inner turmoil – going back to your childhood – you were ready to come out. With her. Getting out was very important to you. Your decision had been made.'

'You thought I'd come out *without* her? Why?'

'Because Parsifal was experienced in such matters,' said Jenna. She selected one of the photographs and handed it to Michael. 'A clinical psychologist attached to the KGB. A man named Alexi Kalyazin – the face that struck a chord with you.'

'I don't *know* him!' shouted Havelock, getting out of the chair and turning on Raymond Alexander. 'Who *is* he?'

'Don't ask me to say the name,' whispered the journalist, shaking his head, shrinking back into the chair. 'Don't ask me. I can't be involved.'

'Goddamn you, you *are* involved!' yelled Michael, throwing the photograph on Alexander's lap. 'You're the *Boswell*! . . . Wait a minute!' Michael looked at Jenna. 'He was a defector. Forget the fact that he was a plant, he was a *defector*. He must have been listed!'

'All references to the defection of Alexi Kalyazin were expurgated,' said Alexander quietly. 'All files were removed; a man with another name simply disappeared.'

'Naturally. So the great man couldn't possibly be tarnished!' Havelock approached Alexander's chair; he reached down and gripped the lapels of the journalist's jacket, yanked him up. 'Who *is* he? *Tell* me!'

'Look at the photograph.' Alexander's body was trembling. 'Look at it. Remove much of the hair, the eyebrows as well. Give him many lines around his face, his eyes . . . a small white beard, speckled with grey.'

Michael grabbed the photograph and stared at it. 'Zelienski . . . Leon *Zelienski*!'

'I thought you'd see, I thought you'd understand. Without me. The ultimate chess game . . . the finest chess player Anton knew.'

'He isn't Russian, he's a Pole! A retired professor of history from Berkeley . . . brought over here years ago from the University of Warsaw!'

'A new identity, a new life, papers in place in locations obscured. Living on a back country road less than two miles from Matthias. Anton always knew where he was.'

Havelock brought his hands to his temples, trying to contain the racking pain in his head. 'You . . . you and Zelienski. Two *demented old men*! Do you know what you've *done*?'

'It's out of control. Everything's out of control.'

'You never had it *in* control! The instant Zelienski reached the mole you lost! We all lost! Couldn't you see what was happening? Did you think it would end with a goddamn *message*? Couldn't you *stop* him? You knew Matthias was at Poole's Island . . . *how* did you know?'

'A source. One of the doctors – he's frightened.'

'Then you knew he'd been diagnosed insane! How could you let it go on?'

'You just said it. I couldn't stop him. He wouldn't listen to me – he *won't* listen to me. I *can't stop him*! He's as crazed as Anton now. He has a Christ complex – his is the only light, the only way.'

'And you traded your holy name in print so he could have it! What the *hell* are you made of?'

'Leave me something, Michael. He had me caged. Zelienski told me that if I went to anyone, if anyone came for him, a telephone call which he made daily from varioius phones would *not* be made, and those so-called nuclear agreements – *signed* by Anthony Matthias – would be on their way to Moscow and Peking.'

Havelock watched the uneasy green eyes of the old journalist and looked at the bloated hands gripping the arms of the chair. 'No, Raymond, that's only part of it. You couldn't stand being exposed, being wrong. You're like Anton, frightened by the truth of your own mistakes. The blind but omniscient Tiresias, seeing things others can't see, the myth to be sustained whatever the cost.'

'*Look* at me!' shouted Alexander suddenly, his whole body shaking. 'I've lived with this – *through* this – for nearly a year! What would *you* have done?'

'God help me, I don't know. I can only hope better than you . . . but I don't know. Pour yourself a lot of brandy, Raymond. Maintain the myth; keep saying to yourself over and over again that you're infallible. It may help. It also may not make any difference any more. Go out with a grin on that pompous face of yours. Just go.' Michael turned to Jenna. 'Let's get out of here,' he said. 'We've got a long drive.'

'South to North, come in.'

'North in touch. What is it?'

'Get to a phone and call Victor. There's movement. Our people came out fast and spoke with the escort; they were on the grounds. Both cars raced out of here a few moments ago, heading west, pedals to the floor.'

'Don't lose them.'

'No chance. The escort left the Lincoln up on the road and we placed a directional homer under the chassis. An earthquake couldn't move it. We've got them tracked up to twenty miles and down to a hundred yards. We've got them.'

39

The night sky was oddly divided – clear moonlight behind, a ceiling of darkness ahead. The two cars raced along the country roads, the men in the Lincoln committed to protection without understanding, and Michael and Jenna understanding too well and afraid.

'There are no rules now,' said Michael. 'The book hasn't been written.'

'He's capable of change, that's all you really know. He was sent here for one purpose and walked over to the other side.'

'Or did he stumble? Alexander said Zelienski – Kalyazin – told them he felt old and worn out, the pressures too great. Maybe he just gave up and walked into sanctuary.'

'Until he found another commitment and accepted an entirely different set of pressures,' said Jenna. 'Exhilarating pressures for a man of his age, I imagine. He's over seventy, isn't he?'

'About that, I'd guess.'

'Think of it. The end may not come for a long time but, still, it's in sight. And as you approach it you suddenly find you've discovered an extraordinary solution you believe the world needs desperately, a lesson it must be taught. What do you do?'

Havelock glanced at her. 'That's what frightens me. Why should you move off centre? How can I make him move?'

'I wish I could answer that.' Jenna looked up at the windscreen, at the myriad tiny globules of water forming over the glass. 'We're heading into the rain,' she said.

'Unless there's another solution,' said Michael quietly, switching on the wipers. 'Exchange one lesson for another.'

'What?'

'I'm not sure, I don't know. There aren't any rules.' Havelock reached for the microphone and pulled it to his lips. 'Escort, are you with me?'

'About four hundred feet behind, Sterile Five.'

'Slow down and make it at least a mile and a half. We're getting into the area and to a lot of people you're an obvious government vehicle. I don't want any connection between us or any startled eyes. If the man I'm making contact with gets even a hint of you, I don't want to think about the consequences.'

'We don't like the distance,' said the escort.

'Sorry to offend, but it's an order. Stay out of sight. You know the destination; just take the mountain road as I described it. Seneca something-or-other. Go up about half a mile. We'll be there.'

'Would you mind repeating the order, sir?'

Michael did so. 'Is that clear?'

'Yes, Sterile Five. It's also on tape.'

The dirt-layered car met the blanket of rain, dust and mud dissolving under the downpour. The driver swung into a long curve as the red signal light on the powerful radio amplifier suddenly glowed.

'We're on a different frequency,' said the man in the passenger seat as he reached for the microphone. He pressed the scanner for contact. 'Yes?' he said.

'South?'

'We're here.'

'It's Victor. I'm approaching Warrenton on Sixty-six. Where are you?'

The man with the microphone studied the map on his lap with a pencil light. 'North on Seventeen, heading into Marshall. You can pick it up in Warrenton.'

'Status?'

'Normal. We reckon once they reach Marshall, they'll either continue north on Seventeen or head west on the Front Royal Road. The turns are getting hairy; we're going into the mountains.'

'We've got men covering both routes up there. I want to know which road they take and the distance between Sterile Five and his escort. Use this channel. I should catch up with you in ten to fifteen minutes.'

'What flight plan?'

'My own.'

The blond man sitting in the brown saloon in front of the Blue Ridge Diner slumped back in the seat, the microphone in his hand, his eyes on the road. He depressed the button and spoke.

'It's the Front Royal Road,' he said as the Buick coupé rushed by in the rain. 'Right on time and in a hurry.'

'How far behind is the Lincoln?' asked the voice from the speaker.

'No sign of it yet.'

'You're sure?'

'No headlights, and anyone damn fool enough to drive up here in this mess isn't going to roll in the dark.'

'It's not normal. I'll be right back.'

'It's your equipment.'

The blond man lowered the microphone and reached for the cigarettes on the seat beside him. He jerked one out of the pack, put it to his lips and snapped his butane lighter. Thirty seconds went by and still the Lincoln Continental had not come into view; nothing was in view but sheets of rain. Forty-five seconds. Nothing. A minute, and the voice, accompanied by static, burst out of the speaker. 'Front Royal, where are you?'

'Here and waiting. You said you'd be right back, remember?'

'The escort. Has it gone by?'

'Nope. If it had I would have rung you up, pal . . . Wait. Stay there. We may have it.' A stream of light came out of the curve and seconds later the long, dark car roared by in the downpour. 'He just went by, old buddy. I'll roll now.' The blond man sat up and eased the car out into the road.

'I'll be right back,' said the voice.

'You keep repeating yourself, pal,' said the blond man, stepping on the accelerator. Gathering speed while watching the rain-soaked road closely, he saw the red tail-lights of the Lincoln flickering in the distance through the downpour. He breathed easier.

'Front Royal,' erupted the voice from the speaker.

'Right here, li'l darlin'.'

'Scan to seventeen-twenty megahertz for separate instructions.'

'Scanning now.' The blond man reached down and pressed the metal button; the digital read-outs appeared on the narrow horizontal strip above the radio's dial. 'Front Royal in position,' he said.

'This is the man you don't know, Front Royal.'

'Nice not to know you, old buddy.'

'How much are you being paid for tonight?' asked the new voice.

'Since you're the man I don't know, I figure you ought to know how much.'

'How good are you?'

'Very. How good's your money?'

'You've been paid.'

'Not for what you want now.'

'You're perceptive.'

'You're kind of obvious.'

'That big fellow up ahead. He knows where the little fellow's going, wouldn't you agree?'

'Sure would. There's a lot of space between them, 'specially for a night like this.'

'Do you think you could get between them?'

'Can do. Then what?'

'A bonus.'

'For what?'

'The little fellow's going to stop somewhere. After he does, I don't want the big fellow around him any longer.'

'You're talking about a pretty big bonus, Mr No-name. That car's an Abraham.'

'Six figures,' said the voice. 'A reckless driver. Very reckless and very accurate.'

'You're on, li'l darlin'.'

Arthur Pierce nodded through the window and the rain as he passed the old car four miles down the Front Royal Road. He lifted the microphone and spoke on the 1720 frequency.

'All right, South, here's the manual. You stay with me, everyone else is dismissed. Thank them all for their time and say we'll be in touch.'

'What about North? They travel.'

'I want them back with the naval contingent. It's theirs now; they can alternate. Sooner or later – tonight, tomorrow, the next day – they'll let him out. When they do, terminate. We don't want to hear his voice.'

Havelock stopped the car and lowered the window; he peered through the rain at the sign nailed to the tree, feeling certain it was the one. It was:

SENECA'S NOTCH
Dead End

He had driven Leon Zelienski home twice, once in the afternoon when the old man's car would not start, and then several years later on a night like tonight, when Matthias was worried that Leon might get stuck in the mud. Zelienski had not got stuck, but Michael had; it had been a long, wet walk back to Anton's house. He remembered the roads.

He had taken Leon Zelienski home; he was coming after Alexi Kalyazin. Parsifal.

'Here we go,' said Havelock, turning up into the rocky road with only remnants of long-eroded tar on its surface. 'If we stay in the centre we should make it.'

'Stay in the centre,' said Jenna.

They lurched and skidded up the narrow road, drenched darkness all around them, tyres spinning, hurling loose stones behind and up into the metal fenders. The jarring ride did nothing to steady their nerves or set the tone for awesome negotiations. Michael had been brutal with Raymond Alexander, knowing he was right, but only partly right. He began to understand the other aspect of the journalist's profound fear, fear that was driving him to the edge of hysteria. Zelienski's threat was clear and terrifying. Should Alexander betray the Russian or interfere in any way, the daily telephone call that Zelienski placed from various phones would not be made. The silence would be the signal for the nuclear agreements to be sent to Moscow and Peking.

And chemicals could not be used to force Zelienski to reveal the number that he was calling. There was too great a risk with a man of his age. One cubic-centimetre of excess dosage and his heart could blow apart, the number lost with the internal explosion. There were only words. What *were* the words one found for a man who would save the world with a blueprint for its annihilation? There was no reason in such a mind, nothing but its own distorted vision.

The small house came into view above them on the right; it was hardly larger than a cabin, square in design and made of heavy stone. A sloping stony driveway ended in a carport, where a nondescript vehicle stood motionless, protected from the downpour. A single light shone through a bay window, which was oddly out of place in the small dwelling.

Havelock switched off the headlights and turned to Jenna. 'It all began here,' he said. 'In the mind of the man up there. All of it. From the Costa Brava to Poole's Island, from Col des Moulinets to Sterile Five; it started here.'

'Can we end it here, Mikhail?'

'Let's try. Let's go.'

They got out of the car and walked through the rain up the wet, soft mud of the driveway, rivulets of water racing down around their feet. They reached the carport; there was a door centred under the attached roof with a concrete step below. Havelock walked to the door; he looked briefly at Jenna and then knocked.

Moments later the door opened, and a slight, stooped old man with only a few strands of hair and a small white beard peppered with grey stood in the open space. As he stared at Havelock his eyes grew wide and his mouth parted, lips trembling.

'*Mikhail,*' he whispered.

'Hello, Leon. I bring you Anton's affection.'

The blond man had seen the sign, the only part with any meaning to him were the words 'Dead End.' It was all he needed to know. With his headlights still extinguished, he manoeuvred the brown saloon several hundred feet down the smooth wet road, and stopped on the far right, the engine idling. He turned the headlights back on and reached under his coat to remove a large automatic with a silencer attached. He understood Mr No-name's instructions; they were in sequence. The Lincoln would be along any moment now.

There it was! Two hundred yards away at the mouth of the road that branched off the highway. The blond man released the brake and began coasting, spinning the wheel back and forth, weaving, the unmistakable sign of a drunken, reckless driver. Cautiously, the limousine slowed down, pulling as far to the right as possible. The blond man accelerated, and the weaving became more violent as the Lincoln's horn roared through the torrents of rain. When he was within thirty feet, the blond man suddenly pressed the accelerator to the floor and swung to the right before making a sharp turn to the left.

The impact came, the saloon's radiator grill ramming the left rear door of the Lincoln. The car skidded and crashed into the other car, pinning the driver's door.

'Goddamn you sons of *bitches*!' screamed the blond man through the open window, slurring his words, his head swaying back and forth. 'Holy *Christ*, I'm bleeding! My whole stomach's *bleeding*!'

The two men lurched out of the limousine from the other side. As they came running around the bonnet in the blinding glare of the headlights, the blond man leaned out the window and fired twice. Accurately.

'Do I call you Leon or Alexi?'

'I can't *believe* you!' cried the old Russian, sitting in front of the fire, his eyes rheumy and blinking, riveted on Havelock. 'It was degenerative, irreversible. There was no *hope*.'

'There are very few minds, very few wills, like Anton's. Whether he'll ever regain his full capacities no one can tell, but he's come back a long way. Drugs helped, electro-therapy as well; he's cognizant now . . . And appalled at what he did.' Havelock sat down in the straight-backed chair opposite Zelienski-Kalyazin. Jenna remained standing by the door that led to the small kitchen.

'It's never *happened*!'

'There's never been a man like Matthias, either. He asked for me; they sent me to Poole's Island and he told me everything. Only me.'

'Poole's Island?'

'It's where he's being treated. Is it Leon or Alexi, old friend?'

Kalyazin shook his head. 'Not Leon, it's never been Leon. Always Alexi.'

'You had good years as Leon Zelienski.'

'Enforced sanctuary, Mikhail. I am a Russian, nothing else. Sanctuary.'

Havelock and Jenna exchanged glances, her eyes telling him that she approved – approved with enormous admiration – the course he had suddenly chosen.

'You came over to us . . . Alexi.'

'I did not come over to you. I fled others. Men who would corrupt the soul of my homeland, who went beyond the bounds of our convictions, who killed needlessly, wantonly, seeking only power for its own sake. I believe in our system, Mikhail, not yours. But these men did not; they would have changed words into weapons and then no one would have been proved right. We'd all be gone.'

'Jackals,' said Havelock, repeating the word he had heard only hours ago, 'fanatics who in their heads marched with the Third Reich, who didn't believe time was on your side, only bombs.'

'That will suffice.'

'The *Voennaya*.'

Kalyazin's head snapped up. 'I never told Matthias that!'

'I never told him, either. I've been in the field for sixteen years. Do you think I don't know the VKR?'

'They do not speak for Russia, not *our* Russia . . . Anton and I would argue until the early hours of the morning. He couldn't understand; he came from a background of brilliance and respectability, money and a full table. Over here none of you will ever understand, except the black people, perhaps. We had nothing and were told to expect nothing, not in this world. Books, schools, simple reading – these were not for us, the millions of us. We were placed on this earth as the earth's cattle, worked and disposed of by our "betters" – decreed by God . . . My father was hanged by a Voroshin prince for stealing game. Stealing *game*! All that was changed – by the millions of us, led by prophets who had no use for a God who decreed human cattle.' An odd smile appeared on Kalyazin's thin, white lips. 'They call us atheistic communists. What would they wish us to be? We *knew* what it was like under the *Holy Church*! A God who threatens eternal fires if one rises up against a living hell is no God for nine-tenths of mankind. He can and should be replaced, dismissed for incompetence and unwarranted partiality.'

'That argument is hardly restricted to pre-revolutionary Russia,' said Michael.

'Certainly not, but it's symptomatic . . . and we were *there*! It's why you'll lose one day. Not in this decade or the next – perhaps not for many, many years, but you'll lose. Too many tables are bare, too many stomachs swollen and you care too little.'

'If that proves to be true then we deserve to lose. I don't think it is.' Havelock leaned forward, elbows on knees and looked into the old Russian's eyes. 'Are you telling me you were given sanctuary but you gave nothing in return?'

'Not of my country's secrets, nor did Anton ever ask me a second time. I think he considered the work I did – the work you did before you resigned – to be in the main quite pointless. Our decisions counted for very little, our accomplishments were not important at the summits. I did, however, give you a gift that served us both, served the world as well. I gave you Anthony Matthias. I saved him from the Cuban trap; it would have driven him from office. I did so because I believed in him, and not in the madmen who temporarily had far too much control of my government.'

'Yes, he told me. He would have been destroyed, his influence finished . . . . It's on that basis . . . your belief in him – that he asked me to come and see you. It's got to stop, Leon – excuse me – Alexi. He knows why you did what you did, but it's got to *stop*.'

Kalyazin's gaze strayed to Jenna. 'Where is the hatred in your eyes, young lady? Surely, it must be there.'

'I won't lie to you, it's close to my thoughts. I'm trying to understand.'

'It had to be done; there was no other way. Anton had to be rid of the spectre of Mikhail. He had to know he was far away from the government, with other interests, other pursuits. He was so afraid his . . . his son . . .

would learn of his work and come to stop him.' Kalyazin turned to Havelock. 'He couldn't get you out of his mind.'

'He approved of what you did?' asked Michael.

'He looked away, I think, a part of him revolted by himself, another part crying to survive. He was failing rapidly by then, his sanity pleading to be left intact whatever the cost. Miss Karras became the price.'

'He never asked you how you did it? How you reached the men in Moscow to provide what you needed?'

'Never. That, too, was part of the price. Remember, the world you and I lived in was very unimportant to him. Then, of course, everything became chaos . . .'

'Out of control?' suggested Jenna.

'Yes, young lady. The things we heard were so unbelievable, so horrible. A woman killed on a beach . . .'

'What did you expect?' asked Havelock, controlling himself and not finding it easy. *Two . . . three demented old men.*

'Not that. We weren't killers. Anton had given orders that she was to be sent back to Prague and watched, her contacts observed and eventually, her innocence to be established.'

'Those orders were intercepted, changed.'

'By then he could do nothing. You had disappeared and he finally went completely, totally mad.'

'Disappeared? *I* disappeared?'

'That's what he was told. And when they told him he collapsed, his mind went. He thought he'd killed you, too. It was the final pressure he could not withstand.'

'How do you know this?' pressed Michael.

Kalyazin balked, his rheumy eyes blinking. 'There was someone else. He has sources, a doctor. He found out.'

'Raymond Alexander,' said Havelock.

'Anton told you, then?'

'Boswell.'

'Yes, our Boswell.'

'You mentioned him when I called you from Europe.'

'I was frightened. I thought you might speak to someone who had seen him at Anton's house; he was there so often. I wanted to give you a perfectly acceptable reason for his visits, to keep you away from him.'

'Why?'

'Because Alexander the Great has become Alexander the Diseased. You've been away, you don't know. He rarely writes any more. He drinks all day and most of the night; he can't stand the strain. Fortunately, for his public, there's the death of his wife to blame it on.'

'Matthias told me you had a wife,' said Michael, his ear picking up something in Kalyazin's voice. 'In California. She died and he persuaded you to come here to the Shenandoah.'

'I had a wife, Mikhail. In Moscow. And she was killed by the soldiers of Stalin. A man I helped destroy, a man who came from the *Voennaya*.'

'I'm sorry.'

A brief rattling somewhere in the small house was louder than the pounding rain outside. Jenna looked at Havelock.

'It's nothing,' said Kalyazin. 'There's a piece of wood, a wedge, I place in that old door on windy nights. The sight of you made me forget.' The old man leaned back in his chair and brought his thin, veined hands to his chin. 'You must be very clear with me, Mikhail, and you must give me time to think. It's why I did not answer you a few moments ago.'

'About Anton?'

'Yes. Does he really know why I did what I did? Why I took him through those terrible nights? Auto and external suggestion, swelling him up until he performed like the genius he was, debating with men who weren't there. Does he *really* understand?'

'Yes, he does,' replied Havelock, feeling a thousand pounds on the back of his neck. He was so close, but a wrong response would send this Parsifal back into self-imposed, unbreakable silence. Alexander was right after all; Kalyazin had a Christ complex. Beneath the old Russian's mild speech was a commitment forged in steel. He knew he was right. 'No single man,' said Michael, 'should be given such power, and the strains of that power, ever again. He begs you, pleads with you on the strength of all the talks you and he had before his illness, to give me those incredible agreements you both created and whatever copies exist. Let me burn them.'

'He understands then, but is it enough? Do the others? Have *they* learned?'

'Who?'

'The men who allocate such power, who permit the canonization of would-be saints only to find that their heroes are simple mortals, broken by swollen egos and by the demands made on them.'

'They're terrified. What more do you want?'

'I want them to know what they've done, how this world can be set on fire by a single brilliant mind caught in the vortex of unbearable pressures. The madness is contagious; it does not stop with a broken saint.'

'They understand. Above all, the one man most people consider the most powerful on earth, he understands. He told me they had created an emperor, a god, and they had no right to do either. They took him up too high; he was blinded.'

'And Icarus fell to the sea,' said Kalyazin. 'Berquist is a decent man, hard but decent. He's also in an impossible job, but he handles it better than most.'

'There's no one I'd rather see there now.'

'I'm inclined to agree.'

'You're killing him,' said Havelock. 'Let him go. Free him. The lesson's been taught, and it won't be forgotten. Let him get back to that impossible job and do the best he can.'

Kalyazin looked at the glowing embers of the fire. 'Twenty-seven pages, each document, each agreement. I typed them myself, using the form employed by Bismarck in the treaties of Schleswig-Holstein. It so appealed to Anton . . . I was never interested in the money, they know that, don't they?'

'They know that. He knows that.'

'Only the lesson.'

'Yes.'

The old man turned back to Michael. 'There are no copies except the one I sent to President Berquist in an envelope from the State Department, from Matthias's office, with the word *Restricted* stamped across the front. It was marked, of course, for his eyes only.'

Havelock tensed, recalling so clearly Raymond Alexander's statement that Kalyazin had 'caged' him, that if a telephone call was not made the documents would be sent to Moscow and Peking. The numbers added up to four, not two. 'No other copies at all, Alexi?'

'None.'

'I would think,' remarked Jenna unexpectedly, taking two hesitant steps towards the frail, old Russian, 'that Raymond Alexander, your Boswell, would have insisted on one. It's the core of his writing.'

'It's the core of his fear, young lady. I control him by telling him that if he divulges anything to anyone copies will be sent to your enemies. That was never my intention, on the contrary, the thought farthest from my mind. It would bring about the very cataclysm I pray will be avoided.'

'Pray, Alexi?'

'Not to any god you know, Mikhail. Only to a collective conscience. Not to a Holy Church with a biased Almighty.'

'May I have the documents?'

Kalyazin nodded. 'Yes,' he said, drawing out the word. 'But not in the sense of possession. We will burn them together.'

'Why?'

'You know the reason; we were both in the same profession. The men who allowed the Matthiases of this world to soar so high they're blinded by the sun, those men will never know. Did an old man lie? I deceived them before. Am I deceiving them again? *Are* there copies?'

'Are there?'

'No, but they won't know that.' Kalyazin struggled out of the chair; he stood up and breathed deeply, planting his feet firmly on the floor. 'Come with me, Mikhail. They're buried in the woods along the path to the Notch. I pass them every afternoon, seventy-three steps to a dogwood tree, the only one in Seneca's burial ground. I often wonder how it got there . . . Come, let's get it over with. We will dig in the rain and get terribly wet and return with the weapons of Armageddon. Perhaps Miss Karras might make us some tea. Also, glasses of vodka . . . with buffalo grass, always buffalo grass. Then we shall burn the evidence and rekindle the fire.'

The door to the kitchen crashed open like a sudden explosion of thunder, and a tall man with a fringe of grey around his bald head stood there, a gun in his hand.

'They lie to you, Alexi. They *always* lie and you never know it. *Don't move*, Havelock!' Arthur Pierce reached out, gripped Jenna's elbow and yanked her to him, lashing his left arm around her neck, the automatic pressed against her head. 'I'm going to count to five,' he said to Michael. 'By which time you will have removed your weapon with two fingers and thrown it on the floor or you will see this woman's skull blown into the wall. *One, two, three – '*

Havelock unbuttoned his coat, spreading it open, and using two fingers like pincers, took the Llama from its holster. He dropped it on the floor.

'Kick it over!' yelled the traveller.

Michael did so. 'I don't know how you got here, but you can't get out,' he said quietly.

'Really?' Pierce released Jenna, shoving her towards the astonished old Russian. 'Then I should tell you that your Abraham was cut down by an ungrateful Ishmael. *You* can't get out.'

'Others know where we are.'

'I doubt that. There'd be a hidden army out there on that road if they did. Oh, no, you went in solo – '

'*You?*' cried Kalyazin, shaking, then nodding his trembling head. 'It *is* you!'

'Glad you're with us, Alexi. You're slowing down in your old age. You don't hear lies when you're told them.'

'What lies? How did you *find* me?'

'By following a persistent man. Let's talk about the lies.'

'What *lies?*'

'Matthias recovering. That's the biggest lie of all. There's a metal case in my car the contents of which will make remarkable reading all over the world. It shows Anthony Matthias for what he is. A screaming, hollow shell, a maniac, violent and paranoid, who has no working concept of reality. He builds delusions out of images, fantasies out of abstractions – he can be programmed like a deranged robot, re-enacting his crimes and offences. He's insane and getting worse.'

'That can't be true!' Kalyazin looked at Michael. 'The things he told me . . . only Anton would know them, recall them.'

'Another lie. Your convincing friend failed to mention that he's just driven down from the village of Fox Hollow, the residence and dateline of a well-known commentator. One Raymond Alexander . . . what did Miss Karras just call him? Your Boswell, I think. I'll visit him. He can add to our collection.'

'*Mikhail?* Why? Why did you say these things? Why did you lie to me?'

'I had to. I was afraid you wouldn't listen to me. And because I believe that the Anton we both knew once would have wanted me to.'

'Still another lie,' said Pierce, lowering himself cautiously, his gun extended as he picked up the Llama from the floor and shoved it into his belt. 'All they want are those papers so business can go on as usual. So their nuclear committees can go on designing new ways to blow the godless out of existence. That's what they call us, Alexi. Godless. Perhaps they'll make Commander Decker the next Secretary of State. His type is very much in vogue, ambitious zealots are the order of the day.'

'That couldn't happen and you know it, Traveller.'

Pierce looked at Havelock, studying him. 'Yes, a traveller. How did you do it? How did you find me?'

'You'll never know that. Or how deeply we've penetrated the *paminyatchik* operation. That's right. Penetrated.'

The traveller stared at Michael. 'I don't believe you.'

'That doesn't matter.'

'It won't make any difference. We'll have the documents. All the options will be ours, nothing left to you. *Nothing*. Except burning cities if you make a wrong turn, a wrong judgement. The world won't tolerate you any longer.' Pierce stabbed the air with his gun. 'Let's go, all of you. You're going to dig them up for me, Havelock. "Seventy-three steps to a dogwood tree".'

'There are a dozen paths up to the Notch,' said Michael quickly. 'You won't know which one.'

'Alexi will show me. When it comes down to it he chooses us, not you. Never you. Not business as usual, conducted by liars. He'll tell me.'

'Don't do it, Kalyazin.'

'You lied to me, Mikhail. If there must be ultimate weapons – even on paper – they can't be yours.'

'I told you why I lied, but there's a final reason. Him. You came over to us not because you believed in us but because you couldn't believe in *them*. They've come back. He was the man at the Costa Brava – he killed at the Costa Brava.'

'I carried out what you only pretended! You had the stomach only for pretence. It had to be *done*, not faked!'

'No, it didn't. But where there's a choice, you kill. You killed the man who set up the operation, an operation where *no one's* death was called for.'

'I did exactly what you would have done but with far more finesse and inventiveness. His death had to be credible, accepted for what it appeared to be. MacKenzie was the only one who could retrace the events of that night, who knew his personnel.'

'Also killed!'

'Inevitable.'

'And Bradford? Inevitable, too?'

'Of course. He'd found me.'

'You see the pattern, Kalyazin?' shouted Havelock, his eyes on Pierce. 'Kill, kill, *kill*! . . . Do you remember Rostov, Alexi?'

'Yes, I remember him.'

'He was my enemy, but he was a decent man. They killed him, too. Only hours ago. They've come back and they're marching.'

'Who?' asked the old Russian haltingly, memories stirred.

'The *Voennaya*. The maniacs of the VKR!'

'*Not* maniacs,' said Pierce firmly, quietly. 'Dedicated men who understand the nature of your hatred, your mendacity. Men who will not compromise the principles of the Soviet Union only to watch you spread your sanctimonious lies, turning the world against us . . . Our time has come, Alexi. You'll be with us.'

Kalyazin blinked, his watery eyes staring at Arthur Pierce. Slowly he shook his head, his words whispered. 'No . . . no I will never be part of you.'

'What?'

'You do not speak for Russia,' said the old man, his voice growing until it filled the room. 'You kill too easily . . . you killed someone very dear to me. Your words are measured and there's truth in what you say . . . but not in what you *do* or the *way* you *do it*! You are *animals*!' Without the slightest warning, Kalyazin lunged at Pierce, hurling his frail body at the traveller, his gaunt hands gripping the weapon. '*Mikhail*, run! *Run*, Mikhail!' There was a muffled roar as the gun exploded into the old man's stomach. Still he would not let go. '*Run* . . . !' The whisper was a shout, a final command.

Havelock spun around and propelled Jenna towards the open kitchen door. He turned, prepared to throw himself on Pierce, but stopped, holding himself in check, for what he saw caused him to make an instantaneous decision. The dying Kalyazin held on fiercely, but the bloody gun was coming free; in an instant it would be aimed at him, fired into his head.

He lurched for the kitchen door and slammed it shut as he raced inside, colliding with Jenna. She held two kitchen knives in her hand; Michael grabbed the shorter blade, and they ran for the outside door.

'The woods!' he shouted in the carport. 'Kalyazin can't hold him. Hurry *up*! You go to the right, I'll head left!' They ran across the drenched grass in the downpour. 'We'll converge a couple of hundred yards inside!'

'Where is the path? Which *is* it?'

'I don't know!'

'He'll be looking for it!'

'I know.'

Five gunshots exploded, but not from a single gun, there were two. They separated, Michael zig-zagging towards the darkness of the trees on his left, spinning quickly to look behind him. Three men. Pierce was shouting orders to two others who had raced up the muddy drive. They ran from the carport, fanning out, torches on, weapons ready.

He reached the edge of the tall grass and plunged into the protective cover of the woods; he removed his coat and scrambled to his right, diving for the thickest underbrush. He crawled forward, his eyes on the field, on the beam of the middle light, and worked his way back towards the edge. His body was soaked, mud and wet foliage were everywhere. The border of the grass was his battle line; the downpour was loud enough to drown out the sound of quick movements. The man would come swiftly, then be stopped by the undergrowth and by his own caution.

As the beam approached, Havelock inched towards the last bank of tangled bush; he waited, crouching. The man slowed down, sweeping the area with light. Then he entered the woods quickly, the beam moving up and down as he used his arm to open a path through the thick brush.

Now. Michael rolled out on the grass and rushed ahead; he was directly behind the traveller. He sprang, the knife gripped in his hand. As he plunged the blade into the killer's back, his left hand yanked back the man's neck and clamped over his mouth. Both fell into mud and brush, Michael working the knife brutally until there was no movement beneath him. He yanked the head up as he ripped the gun from the lifeless hand; it was not Arthur Pierce. He lunged for the torch and snapped it off.

Jenna raced into the dark, narrow alleyway cut through the trees and foliage. Was this *it*? she wondered. Was it the path to Seneca's Notch . . . 'seventy-three steps to a dogwood tree'. If it was, it was her responsibility. No one could be allowed to pass through, and the surest way of preventing it was as distasteful as it was frightening.

Yet she had done it before, always terrified by the prospect, sickened with the results, but there was no time to think of such things. She looked behind her; the torch beam was veering to its left, towards the path! She let out a short cry loud enough to be heard through the pounding rain. The light halted and was briefly immobile before shifting, now focusing directly on the entrance of the path. The man rushed into it.

Jenna lurched into the tangled branches on the border and crouched, holding the long blade of the kitchen knife rigid, diagonally up from her knees. The oscillating beam of light drew nearer, the figure behind it running hard, slipping on the mud, his concentration up ahead on the path, a killer racing after the remembered cry of an unarmed woman.

Ten feet, five . . . now!

Jenna lunged up through the brush with her eyes and blade centred on the body directly behind the light. The contact was sickening. A rush of blood erupted as the long blade sank into the flesh, impaling the body that had raced into it.

The man screamed, a terrible scream that filled the woods, drowning the downpour for a long moment.

Jenna lay gasping for air beside the dead man, rubbing her blood-soaked hand in the soft mud. She grabbed the torch and switched it off. Then she rolled to the border of the path and vomited.

Havelock heard the sudden scream and closed his eyes – then opened them, grateful beyond life itself to realize it was a man's scream. Jenna had done it; she had taken out the man whose orders were to kill her. And that man was not Pierce. He knew it. He had seen the positions in the carport. Pierce had been on the left, closest to the door, the angles consistent when the chase had begun.

Arthur Pierce was somewhere between the middle ground and the road beyond Kalyazin's house, an acre of drenched forest, rain surging downward, dripping everywhere from the imperfect roof of the trees.

Where was the last beam of light? It was not there – of course it wasn't there! Light was a target and Pierce was no fool. They were two animals now, two predators stalking each other in the waterlogged darkness. But one had the advantage, and Michael knew it instinctively, felt it strongly: The forests had been good to Mikhail Havlicek; they were his friend and sanctuary. He did not fear the webbed darkness, for it had saved him too often, protected him from uniformed hunters who would shoot a child because of his father.

He crawled swiftly through undergrowth, eyes straining, ears alert, trying to pick up sounds that were not part of the rain and the creaking weight of drenched limbs above. He semicircled the area, noting among a thousand other intuitively-gathered bits of information that there were no paths, no breaks in the forest leading to Seneca's Notch. Inside the house he had said there were a dozen such paths to confuse Pierce, not knowing whether there were any, never having been beyond Zelienski-Kalyazin's front door.

He swept the arc again, closing it, snaking through the overgrowth; the trunks of the trees were his intermittent fortress walls – he used them like parapets, as he peered around them.

Movement! The sound of suction, not weight. A foot or a knee pressing into and rising from the mud.

Light was a target . . . light *was* a target.

He crawled out of the arc, fifteen, twenty, thirty, forty feet beyond the perimeter, knowing what he was looking for, feeling for – a branch. He found it.

A sapling – strong, supple, no more than four feet high, its roots deep, clawing the earth beneath.

Havelock reached into his belt and pulled out the torch he had taken from the dead traveller. He placed it on the ground and removed his shirt, spreading it in front of him, moving the torch to the centre of the cloth.

Thirty seconds later the torch was securely tied, wrapped in the shirt, the sleeves wound around it, sufficient cloth remaining for the final attachment. He knelt next to the small tree and lashed the package laterally against the thin shaft of the trunk; he crisscrossed what remained of the sleeves so it was held firmly in place. He pulled the trunk back and let it go, testing it.

He snapped on the light and pulled the trunk back for the last time, then raced into the woods to his right. He spun around a thick tree and waited, watching the beam of light as it eerily swept back and forth over the ground. He levelled the traveller's gun, steadying it against the bark.

His ears picked up the sound of suction again, footsteps coming through the rain. Then the figure emerged, looming grotesquely through the webbed branches.

Pierce crouched, trying to avoid the light, and fired his automatic; the ear-shattering explosions echoed throughout the dripping forest.

'You lose,' said Michael as he pulled the trigger and watched the killer of Costa Brava reel backwards, screaming. He fired again, and the man from the *Voennaya* fell to the ground motionless, silent. Dead. 'You didn't know the woods,' said Michael. 'I learned them from people like you.'

'Jenna! *Jenna!*' he yelled, lurching through the trees towards the open grass. 'It's *over!* The field, the *field!*'

'Mikhail? *Mikhail!*'

He saw her walking slowly, unsteadily, in the distance through the sheets of the downpour. Seeing him, she quickened her pace and broke into a run. He, too, raced over the wet grass, wanting – needing – the distance between them to vanish.

They held each other; the world for a few brief moments was no part of them. The cold rain on his bare skin was only cool water, warmed by her embrace, her face against his face.

'Were there other paths?' she asked, breathless.

'None.'

'Then I found it. Come, Mikhail. *Hurry!*'

They stood in Kalyazin's house. The old Russian's body was covered with a blanket, his tortured face mercifully hidden. Havelock walked to the telephone. 'It's time,' he said, dialling.

'What's *happened?*' asked the President of the United States, his voice tense. 'I've been trying to reach you all night!'

'It's over,' said Michael, 'Parsifal's dead. We've got the documents. I'll write a report telling you what I think you'll have to know.'

There was a stunned silence on the line, then Berquist whispered simply, 'I know you wouldn't lie.'

'I would, but not about this.'

'What *you* think *I* have to know?' said Berquist, finding a part of his voice.

'Yes. I'll leave out nothing that's essential to you, for that impossible job you're in.'

'Where are you? I'll send an army for you – just get those documents here.'

'No, Mr President. We have a last stop to make, to a man they called Boswell. But before we leave I'm going to burn them. There's only one set and I'm burning it. The psychiatric file as well.'

'*You've* . . . ?'

'It'll be in the report . . . There's a practical reason for my doing what I'm doing. I don't know what's out there – I think I know, but I can't be certain. It started here and it's going to end here.'

'I see.' Berquist paused. 'I can't change your mind and I can't stop you.'

'That's true.'

'Very well, I won't try. I like to think I'm a judge of men. You have to be to sit in this office. At least, you should be . . . What can a grateful nation, a very grateful President do for you?'

'Leave me alone, sir. Leave us alone.'

'Havelock?'

'Yes?'

'How can I be certain? The burning?'

'Parsifal didn't want you to be. You see, he never wanted it to happen again. No more Matthiases. Superstars are out. He never wanted you to be absolutely sure.'

'I'll have to think about that, won't I?'

'It'd be a good idea.'

'Matthias died this evening. It's why I tried to call you.'

'He died a long time ago, Mr President.'

Epilogue

Autumn. New Hampshire alternately chilled into grey submission by the gathering arctic winds and then warmed by the vibrant colours of fall, the persistent sun giving life to the fields and refusing to submit to the slow approach of winter.

Havelock hung up the phone in the enclosed porch that Jenna had insisted be his study . . . She had seen him, had watched his eyes, as he had walked through the living-room door of the old house and stood there, mesmerized by the expanse of glass and the framed countryside beyond. A desk, bookshelves against the inner brick wall, and an odd assortment of comfortable furniture had transformed the bare porch into an airy room, protected by transparent walls that allowed a wide view of the fields and the woods that meant so much to him. She had understood, and he loved her for understanding. What he could see from that very unusual place was not what others would see, not simply the tall grass and vastly taller trees in the distance, but an ever-changing landscape of sanctuary.

And memories of tension and survival, they were there, too, suddenly welling up until he had to move – physically move – to overcome them . . . to suppress them. It would take time; normality was not to be found in a matter of weeks, even months.

Underneath he had a fever because you bastards poisoned him. You fed him a diet of . . . frenzy. He needed his fix! Dr Matthew Randolph, dead man, talking about another dead man . . . and so many others.

They had discussed it, Jenna and he, had defined the fever that gripped him every now and then, and she was the only doctor he needed. They would take long walks; sudden bursts of running frequently became necessary for him, until the sweat came and his chest pounded. But the fever would pass, the explosions in his head dissolve – the guns would be stilled.

Sleep came easier these days, and his fits of restlessness caused him to reach only for her and not for a weapon. There were no weapons in the house. There never would be in any house they would ever live in.

'*Mikhail?*' The cheerful shout was accompanied by the opening and closing of the door beyond the living-room.

'In here!' He turned in the leather swivel chair that was her last addition to his study.

Jenna walked into the sun-drenched room, the light catching her long blonde hair that fell from beneath a dark wool cap, her tweed coat buttoned to ward off the autumn chill outside. She lowered a canvas bag to the floor and kissed him lightly on the lips. 'There are the books you wanted. Anybody call?' she asked, taking off her coat. 'They put me on the student foreign exchange committee and I think I'm supposed to be at a meeting tonight.'

'You are. Eight o'clock. Dean Crane's place.'

'Good.'

'You enjoy it, don't you?'

'I can help, I *do* help. Not only because of the languages, but mainly with the government papers. All those years falsifying documents does give one an advantage. At times I find it terribly difficult to be so honest. As if I'm doing something wrong.'

They both laughed. Havelock reached for her hand. 'Someone else called.'

'Who?'

'Berquist.'

Jenna stiffened. 'He hasn't tried to reach you since you sent in your report.'

'He honoured my request. I told him to leave us alone.'

'Then why call you now? What does he want?'

'He doesn't want anything. He thought I should be brought up to date.'

'About what?'

'Loring's all right, but he'll never get back in the field again.'

'I'm glad. On both counts.'

'I hope he can handle it.'

'He will. They'll make him a strategist.'

'That's what I suggested.'

'I thought you would.'

Michael released her hand. 'Decker didn't make it.'

'What?'

'It happened months ago, but they covered it up. It was the most generous thing they could do. He walked out of his house the morning after Seneca's Notch and was caught in the crosshairs. The guards moved in on the killer's car – the one sent by Pierce – and so did Decker. He just kept walking into the fire, so help me God, singing "The Battle Hymn of the Republic". He wanted to die.'

'The death of a zealot.'

'Futility. He'd learned a lot; in his twisted way he had a lot to offer.'

'It's history, Mikhail.'

'History,' agreed Havelock.

Jenna walked back to the canvas bag and took out the books. 'I had coffee with Harry Lewis. I think he's working up the courage to tell you.'

'"Birchtree"?' Michael smiled. 'It'll be something he can tell his grand-children. Professor Harry Lewis, undercover man, complete with a code name.'

'I don't think he's terribly proud of it.'

'Why not? He didn't do anything wrong and he did it better than most. Besides, he got me a job I happen to like very much . . . Let's have Harry and his wife to dinner, and when the phone rings – believe me, it'll ring – I'll say it's for "Birchtree".'

'You're outrageous,' said Jenna, laughing.

Havelock stopped smiling. 'I'm restless,' he said.

'It was the call.'

'I get so goddamned . . . *restless*.' He looked at her.

'Let's take a walk.'

They climbed the steep hill several miles west of the house, the high grass bending with the breezes, the hard earth sunbaked, the sky an eloquent blue, speckled with the tassels of wind-swept clouds. Below to the north was a winding stream, the waters curling gently around the bends, flirting with the low-hanging branches and heading south with a purpose on the other side of the hill.

'We had a picnic in Prague,' said Michael, looking down. 'Remember? The Moldau was below then.'

'We'll have a picnic here,' said Jenna, watching him closely. 'Chilled wine, salad – those dreadful sandwiches you like so much.'

'Ham and cheese, with celery, onions and mustard.'

'Yes,' she said, smiling. 'Unfortunately I remember.'

'If I were famous, they'd name it after me. It'd sweep the country, be on every menu.'

'Then keep a low profile, my darling.'

His smile waned. 'You're stronger than I am, Jenna.'

'If you want to believe that, fine, but it isn't true.'

'It keeps coming back . . . the restlessness.'

'Depression, Mikhail. And less and less, we both know that.'

'Still, it comes back and I turn to you. You don't have to turn to me.'

'But I do.'

'Not this way.'

'I never went through what you did for the length of time you did. And there's something else. It was always your responsibility, not mine. Every decision you made had to cost you a part of yourself. It was yours, you were there. I could hide – behind you. I couldn't have done what you did. Quite simply, I don't have the strength.'

'That's not true.'

'Stamina, then, and that *is* true. All those weeks I was running, every now and then I had to stop, stay where I was and do nothing, think of nothing. I couldn't go on, not during those times, and I didn't question myself. I just knew I couldn't. You did; you could. As a child and as a man, and a price has to be paid for what you did . . . what was done to you. It will pass; it *is* passing.'

'A child,' said Havelock, glancing down at the stream below. 'I see him, I feel him, but I don't really know him. But I remember him. When he was frightened or awfully hungry or tired and afraid to sleep, he'd climb a tree at daybreak and check for patrols. If there were none, he'd climb down and run through the fields as fast as he could, faster and faster and *faster*. After a while he felt good again, somehow – confident. Then he'd find a trench in a ravine or a deserted, bombed-out barn and sleep. A six-year-old getting a shot of whisky, all that oxygen in his lungs. It worked, and that was the only thing that mattered. The fever went down.'

Jenna touched his arm, studying his face and began to smile. 'Run *now*, Mikhail. Run down the hill and wait for me, but run by yourself. Go on, you lazy thing! *Run!*'

He ran, his legs scissoring the air, his feet pounding the earth, the wind whipping his face and cooling his body, taking the breath from him, replacing it with new breath. He reached the bottom of the hill far below, his chest expanding with each gasp, quiet laughter coming from his throat. The fever was passing, soon it would be gone. Again.

He looked up at Jenna, the sun behind her, the blue sky above. He shouted between swallows of air. 'Come *on*, you lazy *thing*! I'll race you back to the house. *Our* house!'

'I'll trip you at the last moment!' yelled Jenna, coming down the hill rapidly, but not running. 'You know I can do it!'

'It won't do you any good!' Michael took out a bright metal object from his pocket. 'I've got the key to the door. *Our* door!'

'Silly!' Jenna shouted, breaking into a run. 'You didn't lock it! We've *never* locked it!'

She came to him and they held each other.

'We don't have to,' he said. 'Not any longer.'

THE AQUITAINE
PROGRESSION

For Jeffrey Michael Ludlum
Welcome, friend. Have a great life.

PART I

1

Geneva. City of sunlight and bright reflections. Of billowing white sails on the lake – sturdy, irregular buildings above, their rippling images on the water below. Of myriad flowers surrounding blue-green pools of fountains – duets of exploding colours. Of small quaint bridges arching over and beneath the glassy surfaces of man-made ponds to man-made sanctuaries that are tiny islands for lovers and friends and quiet negotiators. Reflections.

Geneva, the old and the new. City of high medieval walls and glistening tinted glass, of sacred cathedrals and less holy institutions. Of sidewalk cafés and lakeside concerts, of miniature piers and gaily-painted boats that chug around the vast shoreline, the guides extolling the virtues – and the estimated value – of the lakefront estates which surely belonged to another time – ogled by tourists very much of the present.

Geneva. City of purpose, dedicated to the necessity of dedication, frivolity tolerated only as it is intrinsic to the agenda or the deal. Laughter is measured, controlled – glances conveying approval of sufficiency or silently admonishing excess. The canton by the lake knows its soul. Its beauty coexists with industry, the balance not only accepted but jealously guarded.

Geneva. City also of the unexpected, predictability in conflict with sudden unwanted revelation, the violence of the mind accompanied by striking bolts of personal lightning.

Cracks of thunder follow; the skies grow dark and the rains come. A deluge, pounding the angry waters taken by surprise, distorting vision, crashing down on the giant spray, Geneva's trademark on the lake, the *Jet d'Eau*, that geyser designed by man to dazzle man. When sudden revelations come, the gigantic fountain dies. All the fountains die and the flowers wither without the sunlight. The bright reflections are gone and the mind is frozen.

Geneva. City of inconstancy.

Joel Converse, attorney at law, walked out of the Hotel Richemond into the blinding morning on the Jardin Brunswick. Squinting, he turned left, shifting his attaché case to his right hand, conscious of the value of its contents, but thinking primarily about the man he was to meet for coffee and croissants at *Le Chat Botté*, a sidewalk café across from the waterfront. Re-meet was more accurate, thought Converse, if the man had not confused him with someone else.

A. Preston Halliday was Joel's American adversary in the current negotiations, the finalizing of last minute details for a Swiss-American merger that had brought both men to Geneva. Although the remaining work was minimal – formalities, really, discoveries having established that the agreements were in accord with the laws of both countries and acceptable to the International Court in the Hague – Halliday was an odd choice. He had not been part of the American legal team fielded by the Swiss to keep tabs on Joel's firm. That, in itself, would not have excluded him, fresh observation was frequently an asset, but to elevate him to the position of point, or chief spokesman, was to say the least unorthodox. It was also unsettling.

Halliday's reputation – what little Converse knew of it – was as a trouble-shooter, a legal mechanic from San Francisco who could spot a loose wire, rip it out and short an engine. Negotiations covering months and costing hundreds of thousands had been aborted by his presence, that much Converse recalled about A. Preston Halliday. But that was all he recalled. Yet Halliday said they knew each other.

'It's Press Halliday,' the voice had announced over the hotel phone. 'I'm pointing for Rosen in the Comm Tech-Bern merger.'

'What happened?' Joel had asked, a muted electric razor in his left hand, his mind trying to place the name; it had come to him by the time Halliday replied.

'The poor bastard had a stroke, so his partners called me in.' The lawyer had paused. 'You must have been mean, counsellor.'

'We rarely argued, counsellor. Christ, I'm sorry, I like Aaron. How is he?'

'He'll make it. They've got him in bed and on a dozen versions of chicken soup. He told me to tell you he's going to check your finals for invisible ink.'

'Which means *you're* going to check because I don't have any and neither did Aaron. This marriage is based on pure greed, and if you've studied the papers you know that as well as I do.'

'The larceny of investment write-offs,' agreed Halliday, 'combined with a large chunk of technological market. No invisible ink. But since I'm the new boy on the block, I've got a couple of questions. Let's have breakfast.'

'I was about to order room service.'

'It's a nice morning, why not get some air? I'm at the Président so let's split the distance? Do you know the *Chat Botté*?'

'American coffee and croissants. Quai du Mont Blanc.'

'You know it. How about twenty minutes?'

'Make it a half hour, okay?'

'Sure.' Halliday had paused again. 'It'll be good to see you again, Joel.'

'Oh? Again?'

'You may not remember. A lot's happened since those days . . . more to you than to me, I'm afraid.'

'I'm not following you.'

'Well, there was Vietnam and you were a prisoner for a pretty long time.'

'That's not what I meant, and it was years ago. Where do we know each other from? What case?'

'No case, no business. We were classmates.'

'Duke? It's a large law school.'

'Farther back. Maybe you'll remember when we see each other. If you don't, I'll remind you.'

'You must like games . . . Half an hour. *Chat Botté*.'

As Converse walked towards the Quai du Mont Blanc, the vibrant boulevard fronting the lake, he tried to fit Halliday's name into a time frame, the years to a school, a forgotten face to match an unremembered classmate. None came, and *Halliday* was not a common name, the short form *Press* even less so . . . unique, actually. If he had known someone named

'Press Halliday', he could not imagine forgetting it. Yet the tone of voice had implied familiarity, even closeness.

It'll be good to see you again, Joel. He had spoken the words warmly, as he had the gratuitous reference to Joel's POW status. But then those words were always spoken softly, sympathy implied if not overtly expressed. Also, Converse understood why under the circumstances Halliday felt he had to bring up the subject of Vietnam, even fleetingly. The uninitiated assumed that all men imprisoned in the North Vietnamese camps for any length of time had been mentally damaged, *per se*, that a part of their minds had been altered by the experience, their recollections muddled. To a degree, some aspects were undeniable, but not with respect to memory, that was a false assumption. Memories were sharpened because they were searched, compulsively, often mercilessly. The accumulated years, the layers of experience . . . faces with eyes and voices, bodies with sizes and shapes; scenes flashing across the inner screen, the sights and sounds, images and smells – touching and the desire to touch . . . nothing of the past was too inconsequential to peel away and explore. Frequently it was all they had, especially at night – *always* at night, with the cold, penetrating dampness stiffening the body and the infinitely colder fear paralysing the immediate – memories were everything. They helped block out the distant screams in the dark, mute the sharp reports of small-arms fire, gratuitously explained in the mornings as necessary executions of the uncooperative and unrepentant. Or of even more unfortunate prisoners forced to play games too obscene to describe, demanded by captors in search of amusement.

Like most men kept isolated for the greater part of their imprisonment, Converse had examined and re-examined every stage of his life, trying to piece them together, to understand . . . to *like* . . . the cohesive whole. There was much that he did not understand – or like – but he could live with the product of those intensive investigations. Die with it, if he had to; that was the peace he had to reach for himself. Without it the fear was intolerable.

And because these self-examinations went on night after night and required the discipline of accuracy, Converse found it easier than most men to remember whole segments of his life. Like a spinning disc attached to a computer that suddenly stops, his mind could isolate a place or a person or a name, given only basic information. Repetition had simplified and accelerated the process, and that was what bewildered him now. Unless Halliday was referring to a time so far back as to have been only a brief, forgotten childhood acquaintance, no one of that name belonged to his past.

It'll be good to see you again, Joel. Were the words a ruse, a lawyer's trick?

Converse rounded the corner, the brass railing of *Le Chat Botté* glistening, hurling back tiny explosions of sunlight. The boulevard was alive with gleaming small cars and spotless buses; the pavements were washed clean, the strollers in various stages of hurried but orderly progress. Morning was a time for benign energy in Geneva. Even the newspapers above the tables in the sidewalk cafés were snapped with precision, not crushed or mutilated into legible positions. And vehicles and pedestrians were not at war; combat was supplanted by looks and nods, stops and gestures of acknowledgment. As Joel walked through the open brass gate of *Le Chat Botté*, he wondered briefly if Geneva could export its mornings to New York. But then the City

Council would vote the import down, he concluded, the citizens of New York could not stand the civility.

A newspaper snapped directly below him on the left, the precision apparently contagious, as the paper was lowered revealing a face Converse knew. It was a . . . coordinated face, unlike his own, the features compatible and in place. The hair straight and dark, neatly parted and brushed, the nose sharp, above sharply defined lips. The face belonged to his past, thought Joel, but the name he remembered did not belong to the face.

The familiar-looking man raised his head; their eyes met and 'A. Preston Halliday' rose, his short compact body obviously muscular under the expensive suit.

'Joel, how are you?' said the now-familiar voice, a hand outstretched above the table.

'Hello . . . Avery,' replied Converse staring, awkwardly taking the necessary steps and shifting his attaché case once again to grip the hand. 'It *is* Avery, isn't it? Avery Fowler. Taft, early 'sixties. You never came back for the senior year, and no one knew why; we all talked about it. You were a wrestler.'

'Twice All New England,' said the attorney, laughing, gesturing at the chair across from his own. 'Sit down and we'll catch up. I guess it's sort of a surprise for you. That's why I wanted us to meet before the conference this morning. I mean, it'd be a hell of a note for you to get up and scream "impostor!" when I walked in, wouldn't it?'

'I'm still not sure I won't, but I won't scream.' Converse sat down, attaché case at his feet, studying his legal opponent. 'What's this Halliday routine? Why didn't you say something on the phone?'

'Oh, come on, what was I going to say? By the way, old sport, you used to know me as Tinkerbell Jones. You never would have showed up.'

'Is Fowler in jail somewhere?'

'He would have been if he hadn't blown his head off,' answered Halliday, not laughing.

'You're full of surprises. Are you a clone?'

'No, the son.'

Converse paused. 'Maybe I should apologize.'

'No need to, you couldn't have known. It's why I never came back for the senior year . . . and, goddamn it, I wanted that trophy. I would have been the only mat-jock to win it three years in a row.'

'I'm sorry. What happened . . . or is it privileged information counsellor? I'll accept that.'

'Not for you, counsellor. Remember when you and I broke out to New Haven and picked up those pigs at the bus station?'

'We said we were Yalies . . .'

'And only got taken, never got laid.'

'Our eyebrows were working overtime.'

'Preppies,' said Halliday. 'They wrote a book about us. Are we really that emasculated?'

'Reduced in stature, but we'll come back. We're the last minority, so we'll end up getting sympathy . . . What happened, Avery?'

A waiter approached, the moment broken. Both men ordered American coffee and croissants, no deviation from the stated norm. The waiter folded two red napkins into cones, placing them in front of each.

'What happened?' said Halliday quietly, rhetorically after the waiter left. 'The beautiful son of a bitch who was my father embezzled four hundred thousand from the Chase Manhattan while he was a trust officer, and when he was caught, went bang. Who was to know a respected, if transplanted, commuter from Greenwich, Connecticut, had two women in the city, one on the upper East Side, the other on Bank Street. He was beautiful.'

'He was busy. I still don't understand the Halliday.'

'After it happened – the suicide covered up – mother raced back to San Francisco with a vengeance. We were from California, you know ... but then why would you? With even more vengeance she married my step-father, John Halliday, all traces of Fowler assiduously removed during the next few months.'

'Even to your first name?'

'No, I was always "Press" back in San Francisco. We Californians come up with catchy names. Tab, Troy, Crotch ... The 1950s Beverly Hills syndrome ... At Taft, my student ID read Avery Preston Fowler so you all just started calling me Avery or that awful "Ave". Being a transfer student I never bothered to say anything. When in Connecticut follow the gospel according to Holden Caulfield.'

'That's all well and good,' said Converse, 'but what happens when you run into someone like me? It's bound to happen.'

'You'd be surprised how rarely. After all, it was a long time ago, and the people I grew up with in California understood. Kids out there have their names changed according to matrimonial whim, and I was in the East for only a couple of years, just long enough for the fourth and fifth forms at school. I didn't know anyone in Greenwich to speak of, and I was hardly part of the old Taft crowd.'

'You had friends there. We were friends.'

'I didn't have many. Let's face it, I was an outsider and you weren't particular. I kept a pretty low profile.'

'Not on the mats, you didn't.'

Halliday laughed. 'Not very many wrestlers become lawyers, something about mat-burns on the brain ... Anyway, to answer your question, maybe five or six times over the past ten years has anyone said to me, "Hey, aren't you so-and-so and not whatever you said your name was?" When they do, I tell them the truth. My mother remarried when I was sixteen and the questions stop.'

The coffee and croissants arrived. Joel broke his pastry in half. 'And you thought I'd ask the question at the wrong time, specifically when I saw you at the conference. Is that it?'

'Professional courtesy. I didn't want you dwelling on it – or me – when you should be thinking about your client. After all, we tried to lose our virginities together that night in New Haven.'

'Speak for yourself,' Joel smiled.

Halliday grinned. 'We got pissed and both admitted it, don't you remember? Incidentally, we swore each other to secrecy while throwing up in the can.'

'Just testing you, counsellor, I remember. So you left the grey-flannel crowd for orange shirts and gold medallions?'

'All the way. Berkeley, then across the street to Stanford.'

'Good school . . . How come the international field?'

'I liked travelling and figured it was the best way of paying for it. That's how it started, really . . . How about you? I'd think you would have had all the travelling you ever wanted.'

'I had early delusions of the foreign service, diplomatic corps, legal section. That's how it started . . . really.'

'After all that travelling you did?'

Converse levelled his pale blue eyes at Halliday, conscious of the coldness of his look. It was unavoidable, if misplaced – as it usually was. 'Yes, after all that travelling. There were too many lies and no one told us about them until it was too late. We were conned and it shouldn't have happened.'

Halliday leaned forward, his elbows on the table, hands clasped, his gaze returning Joel's. 'I couldn't figure it,' he began softly. 'When I read your name in the papers, then saw you paraded on television, I felt awful. I didn't really know you that well, but I liked you.'

'It was a natural reaction. I'd have felt the same way if it had been you.'

'I'm not sure you would. You see, I was one of the honchos of the protest movement.'

'You burned your draft card while extolling the Yippie label,' said Converse gently, the ice gone from his eyes. 'I wasn't that brave.'

'Neither was I. It was an out-of-date library card.'

'I'm disappointed.'

'So was I . . . in myself. But I was visible.' Halliday leaned back in his chair and reached for his coffee. 'How did *you* get so visible, Joel? I didn't think you were the type.'

'I wasn't. I was squeezed.'

'I thought you said conned.'

'That came later.' Converse raised his cup and sipped his black coffee, uncomfortable with the direction the conversation had taken. He did not like discussing those years and all too frequently he was called upon to do so. They had made him out to be someone he was not. 'I was a sophomore at Amherst and not much of a student . . . Not much, hell, I was borderline-negative, and whatever deferment I had was about to go down the tube. But I'd been flying since I was fourteen.'

'I didn't know that,' interrupted Halliday.

'My father wasn't beautiful and he didn't have the benefit of concubines, but he *was* an airline pilot, later an executive for Pan Am. It was standard in the Converse household to fly a plane before you got your driver's licence.'

'Brothers and sisters?'

'A younger sister. She soloed before I did and she's never let me forget it.'

'I remember. She was interviewed on television.'

'Only twice,' broke in Joel, smiling. 'She was on your turf and didn't give a damn who knew it. The White House bunker put the word out to stay away from her. Don't tarnish the cause, and check her mail while you're at it.'

'That's why I remember her,' said Halliday. 'So a lousy student left college and the Navy gained a hot pilot.'

'Not very hot, none of us were. There wasn't that much to be hot against. Mostly we burned.'

'Still you must have hated people like me back in the States. Not your sister of course.'

'Her, too,' corrected Converse. 'Hated, loathed, despised . . . furious. But only when someone was killed, or went crazy in the camps. Not for what you were saying – we all knew Saigon – but because you said it without any real fear. You were safe, and you made us feel like assholes. Dumb, frightened assholes.'

'I can understand that.'

'So nice of you.'

'I'm sorry, I didn't mean it the way it sounded.'

'How did it sound, counsellor?'

Halliday frowned. 'Condescending, I guess.'

'No guess,' said Joel. 'Right on.'

'You're still angry.'

'Not at you, only the dredging. I hate the subject and it keeps coming back up.'

'Blame the Pentagon PR. For a while you were a *bona fide* hero on the nightly news. What was it, three escapes? On the first two you got caught and put on the racks, but on the last one you made it all by yourself, didn't you? You crawled through a couple of hundred of miles of enemy jungle before you reached the lines.'

'It was barely a hundred and I was goddamned lucky. With the first two tries I was responsible for killing eight men. I'm not very proud of that. Can we get to the Comm Tech-Bern business?'

'Give me a few minutes,' said Halliday, shoving his croissant aside. 'Please. I'm not trying to dredge. There's a point in the back of my mind, if you'll grant I've got a mind.'

'Preston Halliday had one, his rep confirms it. You're a shark, if my colleagues are accurate. But I knew someone named Avery, not Press.'

'Then it's Fowler talking, you're more comfortable with him.'

'What's the point?'

'A couple of questions first. You see, *I* want to be accurate because you've got a reputation, too. They say you're one of the best on the international scene, but the people I've talked to can't understand why Joel Converse stays with a relatively small if entrenched firm when he's good enough to get flashier. Or even go out on his own.'

'Are you hiring?'

'Not me, I don't take partners. Courtesy of John Halliday, attorney at law, San Francisco.'

Converse looked at the second half of his croissant and decided against it. 'What was the question, counsellor?'

'Why are you where you're at?'

'I'm paid well and literally run the department; no one sits on my shoulder. Also I don't care to take chances. There's a little matter of alimony, amiable but demanding.'

'Child support, too?'

'None, thank heavens.'

'What happened when you got out of the Navy? How did you feel?' Halliday again leaned forward, his elbow on the table, chin cupped in his hand – the inquisitive student. Or something else.

'Who are the people you've talked to?' asked Converse.

'Privileged information, for the moment, counsellor. Will you accept that?'

Joel smiled. 'You *are* a shark . . . Okay, the gospel according to Converse. I came back from that disruption of my life wanting it all. Angry to be sure, but wanting everything. The non-student became a scholar of sorts, and I'd be a liar if I didn't admit to a fair amount of preferential treatment. I went back to Amherst and raced through two and a half years in three semesters and a summer. Then Duke offered me an accelerated programme and I went there, followed by some specializations at Georgetown while I clerked.'

'You clerked in Washington?'

Converse nodded. 'Yes.'

'For whom?'

'Clifford's firm.'

Halliday whistled softly, sitting back. 'That's golden territory, a passport to Blackstone's heaven as well as the multinationals.'

'I told you I had preferential treatment.'

'Was that when you thought about the foreign service? While you were at Georgetown? In Washington?'

Again Joel nodded, squinting as a passing flash of sunlight bounced off a grille somewhere on the lakefront boulevard. 'Yes,' he replied quietly.

'You could have had it,' said Halliday.

'They wanted me for the wrong reasons, *all* the wrong reasons. When they realized I had a different set of rules in mind, I couldn't get a twenty cent tour of the State Department.'

'What about the Clifford firm? You were a hell of an image, even for them.' The Californian raised his hands above the table, palms forward. 'I know, I know. The wrong reasons.'

'Wrong numbers,' insisted Converse. 'There were forty-plus lawyers on the masthead and another two hundred on the payroll. I'd have spent ten years trying to find the men's room and another ten getting the key. That wasn't what I was looking for.'

'What were you looking for?'

'Pretty much what I've got. I told you, the money's good and I run the international division. The latter's just as important to me.'

'You couldn't have known that when you joined,' objected Halliday.

'But I did. At least I had a fair indication. When Talbot, Brooks and Simon – as you put it, that small but entrenched firm I'm with – came to me we reached understanding. If after four or five years I proved out, I'd take over for Brooks. He was the overseas man and was getting tired of adjusting to all those time zones.' Again Converse paused. 'Apparently I proved out.'

'And just as apparently somewhere along the line you got married.'

Joel leaned back in the chair. 'Is this necessary?'

'It's not even pertinent, but I'm intensely interested.'

'Why?'

'It's a natural reaction,' said Halliday, his eyes amused. 'I think you'd feel the same way if you were me and I were you, and I'd gone through what you went through.'

'Shark dead ahead,' mumbled Converse.

'You don't have to respond, of course, counsellor.'

'I know, but oddly enough I don't mind. She's taken her share of abuse because of that what-I've-been-through business.' Joel broke the croissant but made no effort to remove it from the plate. 'Comfort, convenience, and a vague image of stability,' he said.

'I beg your pardon?'

'Her words,' continued Joel. 'She said that I got married so I'd have a place to go and someone to fix the meals and do the laundry, and eliminate the irritating, time-consuming foolishness that goes with finding someone to sleep with. Also by legitimizing her, I projected the proper image . . . "and, Christ, did I have to play the part" . . . also her words.'

'Were they true?'

'I told you, when I came back I wanted it all and she was part of it. Yes, they were true. Cook, maid, laundress, bedmate, and an acceptable, attractive appendage. She told me she could never figure out the pecking order.'

'She sounds like quite a girl.'

'She was. She is.'

'Do I discern a note of possible reconciliation?'

'No way.' Converse shook his head, a partial smile on his lips but only a trace of humour in his eyes. 'She was also conned and it shouldn't have happened. Anyway, I like my current status, I really do. Some of us just weren't meant for a hearth and roast turkey, even if we sometimes wish we were.'

'It's not a bad life.'

'Are you into it?' asked Joel quickly so as to shift the emphasis.

'Right up with orthodontists and scholastic aptitude tests. Five kids and one wife. I wouldn't have it any other way.'

'But you travel a lot, don't you?'

'We have great homecomings.' Halliday again leaned forward, as if studying a witness. 'So you have no real attachments now, no one to run back to.'

'Talbot, Brooks and Simon might find that offensive. Also my father. Since mother died we have dinner once a week when he's not flying all over the place, courtesy of a couple of lifetime passes.'

'He still gets around a lot?'

'One week he's in Copenhagen, the next in Hong Kong. He enjoys himself; he keeps moving. He's sixty-eight and spoiled rotten.'

'I think I'd like him.'

Converse shrugged, again smiling. 'You might not. He thinks all lawyers are piss ants, me included. He's the last of the white-scarved flyboys.'

'I'm sure I'd like him . . . But outside of your employers and your father, there are no – shall we say – priority entanglements in your life.'

'If you mean women, there are several and we're good friends, and I think this conversation has gone about as far as it should go.'

'I told you, I had a point,' said Halliday.

'Then why not get to it, counsellor? Interrogations are over.'

The Californian nodded. 'All right, I will. The people I spoke with wanted to know how free you were to travel.'

'The answer is that I'm not. I've got a job and a responsibility to the company I work for. Today's Wednesday; we'll have the merger tied up by Friday, I'll take the weekend off and be back on Monday . . . when I'm expected.'

'Suppose arrangements could be made that Talbot, Brooks and Simon found acceptable?'

'That's presumptuous.'

'And you found very difficult to reject.'

'That's preposterous.'

'Try me,' said Halliday. 'Five hundred thousand for accepting on a best-efforts basis, one million if you pull it off.'

'Now you're insane.' A second flash of light blinded Converse, this one remaining stationary longer than the first. He raised his left hand to block it from his eyes as he stared at the man he had once known as Avery Fowler. 'Also, ethics notwithstanding because you haven't a damn thing to win this morning, your timing smells. I don't like getting offers – even crazy offers – from attorneys I'm about to meet across a table.'

'Two separate entities, and you're right, I don't have a damn thing to win or lose. You and Aaron did it all, and I'm so ethical I'm billing the Swiss only for my time – minimum basis – because no expertise was called for. My recommendation this morning will be to accept the package as it stands, not even a comma changed. Where's the conflict?'

'Where's the sanity?' asked Joel. 'To say nothing of those arrangements Talbot, Brooks and Simon will find acceptable. You're talking roughly about two and a half top years of salary *and* bonuses for nodding my head.'

'Nod it,' said Halliday. 'We need you.'

'*We*? That's a new wrinkle, isn't it? I thought it was *they*. *They* being the people you spoke with. Spell it out, *Press*.'

A. Preston Halliday locked his eyes with Joel's. 'I'm part of them and something is happening that shouldn't be happening. We want you to put a company out of business. It's bad news and it's dangerous. We'll give you all the tools we can.'

'What company?'

'The name wouldn't mean anything, it's not registered. Let's call it a government in exile.'

'A *what*?'

'A group of like-minded men who are in the process of building a portfolio of resources so extensive it'll guarantee them influence where they shouldn't have it . . . authority where they shouldn't have it.'

'Where is that?'

'In places this poor inept world can't afford. They can do it because no one expects them.'

'You're pretty cryptic.'

'I'm frightened. I know them.'

'But you have the tools to go after them,' said Converse. 'I presume that means they're vulnerable.'

Halliday nodded. 'We think they are. We have some leads, but it'll take digging, piecing things together. There's every reason to believe they've broken laws, engaged in activities and transactions prohibited by their respective governments.'

Joel was silent for a moment, studying the Californian. 'Governments?' he asked. 'Plural?'

'Yes.' Halliday's voice dropped. 'They're different nationalities.'

'But one company?' said Converse. 'One corporation?'

'In a manner of speaking, yes.'

'How about a simple yes?'

'It's not that simple.'

'I'll tell you what is,' interrupted Joel. 'You've got leads, so you go after the big bad wolves. I'm currently and satisfactorily employed.'

Halliday paused, then spoke. 'No, you're not,' he said softly.

Again there was silence, each man appraising the other. 'What did you say?' asked Converse, his eyes blue ice.

'Your firm understands. You can have a leave of absence.'

'You presumptuous son of a bitch! Who gave you the right even to *approach* . . .'

'General George Marcus Delavane,' broke in Halliday. He delivered the name in a monotone.

It was as if a bolt of lightning had streaked down through the blinding sunlight burning Joel's eyes, turning the ice into fire. Cracks of thunder followed, exploding in his head.

The pilots sat around the long rectangular table in the wardroom, sipping coffee and staring down into the brown liquid or up at the grey walls, no one caring to break the silence. An hour ago they had been sweeping over Pak Song, firing the earth, interdicting the advancing North Vietnamese battalions, giving vital time to the regrouping ARVN and American troops who soon would be under brutal siege. They had completed the strike and returned to the carrier – all but one. They had lost their commanding officer. Lieutenant Senior Grade Gordon Ramsey had been hit by a fluke rocket that had winged out of its trajectory over the coastline and zeroed in on Ramsey's fuselage; the explosion had filled the jet streams, death at 600 miles an hour in the air, life erased with the blinking of an eye. A severe weather front had followed hard upon the squadron; there would be no more strikes, perhaps for several days. There would be time to think and that was not a pleasant thought.

'Lieutenant Converse,' said a sailor by the open wardroom door.

'Yes?'

'The captain requests your presence in his quarters, sir.'

The invitation was so nicely phrased, mused Joel, as he got out of his chair, acknowledging the sombre looks of those around the table. The request was expected, but unwelcome. The promotion was an honour he would willingly have forgone. It was not that he held longevity or seniority or even age over his fellow pilots; it was simply that he had been in the air longer than anyone else and with that time came the experience necessary for the leader of a squadron.

As he climbed the narrow steps up toward the bridge he saw the outlines of an immense army Cobra helicopter in the distant sky stuttering its way toward the carrier. In five minutes or so it would be hovering over the threshold and lower itself to the pad; someone from land was paying the navy a visit.

'It's a terrible loss, Converse,' said the captain standing over his chart table, shaking his head sadly. 'And a letter I hate like hell to write. God knows they're never easy, but this one's more painful than most.'

'We all feel the same way, sir.'

'I'm sure you do.' The captain nodded. 'I'm also sure you know why you're here.'

'Not specifically, sir.'

'Ramsay said you were the best and that means you're taking over one of the crack squadrons in the South China Sea.' The telephone rang, interrupting the carrier's senior officer. He picked it up. 'Yes?'

What followed was nothing Joel expected. The captain at first frowned, then tensed the muscles of his face, his eyes both alarmed and angry. 'What?' he exclaimed, raising his voice. 'Was there any advance notice – anything in the radio room?' There was a pause, after which the captain slammed down the phone, shouting, 'Jesus Christ!' He looked at Converse. 'It seems we have the dubious honour of an unannounced visitation by Command-Saigon, and I do mean visitation!'

'I'll return below, sir,' said Joel, starting to salute.

'Not just yet, Lieutenant,' shot back the captain quietly but firmly. 'You are receiving your orders and as they affect the air operations of this ship, you'll hear them through. At the least, we'll let Mad Marcus know he's interfering with navy business.'

The next thirty seconds were taken up with the ritual of command-assignment, a senior officer investing a subordinate with new responsibilities. Suddenly, there was a sharp two-rap knock, as the captain's door opened and the tall, broad-shouldered General of the Army, George Marcus Delavane, intruded, breaking the space in front of him with the sheer force of his presence.

'Captain?' said Delavane courteously, saluting the ship's commander first despite the navy man's lesser rank. The somewhat high-pitched voice was courteous, but not the eyes; they were intense, instantly hostile.

'General,' replied the captain, saluting back along with Converse. 'Is this an unannounced inspection by Command-Saigon?'

'No, it's an urgently-demanded conference between you and me – between Command-Saigon and one of its lesser forces.'

'I see,' said the four-striper, anger showing through his calm. 'At the moment I'm delivering urgent orders to this man . . .'

'You saw fit to countermand mine!' broke in Delavane vehemently.

'General, this has been a sad and trying day,' said the captain. 'We lost one of our finest pilots barely an hour ago . . .'

'Running away?' Again Delavane interrupted, the tastelessness of his remark compounded by the nasal pitch of his voice. 'Was his goddamned tail shot off?'

'For the record, I resent that!' said Converse, unable to control himself. 'I'm replacing that man and I resent what you just said – General!'

'You? Who the hell are you?'

'Easy, Lieutenant. You're dismissed.'

'I respectfully request to answer the general, sir!' shouted Joel, in his anger refusing to move.

'You what, prissy flyboy?'

'My name is . . .'

'Forget it, I'm not interested!' Delavane whipped his head back toward the captain. 'What I want to know is why you think you can disobey my orders – the orders from Command-Saigon! I called a strike for fifteen hundred hours! You "respectfully declined" to implement that order!'

'A weather front's moved in and you should know it as well as I do.'

'My meteorologists say it's completely flyable!'

'I suspect if you asked for that finding during a Burma monsoon they'd deliver it.'

'That's gross insubordination!'

'This is my ship and military regulations are quite clear as to who's in command here.'

'Do you want to connect me to your radio room? I'll reach the Oval Office and we'll see just how long you've got this ship!'

'I'm sure you'll want to speak privately – probably over a scrambler. I'll have you escorted there.'

'Goddamn you, I've got four thousand troops – maybe twenty per cent seasoned – moving up into Sector Five! We need a low-altitude combined strike from land and sea and we'll have it if I have to get your ass out of here within the hour! And I can do it, Captain! . . . We're over here to win, win, and win it all! We don't need sugar-coated Nellies hedging their goddamned bets! Maybe you never heard it before, but all war is a risk! You don't win if you don't risk, Captain!'

'I've been there, General. Common sense cuts losses and if you cut enough losses you can win the next battle.'

'I'm going to win this one, with or without you, Blue Boy!'

'I respectfully advise you to temper your language, General.'

'You what?!' Delavane's face was contorted in fury, his eyes the eyes of a savage wild animal. 'You advise me? You advise Command-Saigon! Well, you do whatever you like – Blue Boy in your satin pants – but the incursion up into the Tho Valley is on.'

'The Tho,' interrupted Converse. 'That's the first leg of the Pak Song route. We've hit it four times. I know the terrain.'

'You know it?' shouted Delavane.

'I do, but I take my orders from the commander of this ship – General.'

'You prissy shit-kicker, you take orders from the President of the United States! He's your commander-in-chief! And I'll get those orders!'

Delavane's face was inches from Joel's, the maniacal expression challenging every nerve ending in his body; hatred was matched with loathing. Barely realizing the words were his, Converse spoke. 'I, too, would advise the General to be careful of his language.'

'Why, shit-kicker? Has Blue Boy got this place wired?'

'Easy, Lieutenant! I said you were dismissed!'

'You want me to watch my language, big fella with your little gold bar? No, sonny boy, you watch it, and you read it! If that squadron of yours isn't in the air at fifteen hundred hours, I'll label this carrier as the biggest yellow streak in Southeast Asia! You got that, satin-pantsed Blue Boy, third class?'

Once more Joel replied, wondering as he spoke where he found the audacity. 'I don't know where you come from, sir, but I sincerely hope we meet under different circumstances sometime. I think you're a pig.'

'Insubordination! Also, I'd break your back.'

'Dismissed, Lieutenant!'

'No, Captain, you're wrong!' shouted the general. 'He may be the man to lead this *strike after all. Well, what'll it be, Blue Boys? Airborne, or the President of the United States – or the label?'*

At 1520 hours Converse led the squadron off the carrier deck. At 1538, as they headed at low altitude into the weather, the first two casualties occurred over the coastline; the wing planes were shot down – fiery deaths at 600 miles an hour in the air. At 1546, Joel's right engine exploded; his altitude made the direct hit easy. At 1546.30, unable to stabilize, Converse ejected into the downpour of the storm clouds, his parachute instantly swept into the vortex of the conflicting winds. As he swung violently down toward the earth, the straps digging into his flesh with each whipping buffet, one image kept repeating its presence within the darkness. The maniacal face of General George Marcus Delavane. He was about to begin an indeterminate stay in hell courtesy of a madman. And as he learned, the losses were infinitely greater on the ground.

Delavane! The Butcher of DaNang and Pleiku. Waster of thousands, throwing battalion after battalion into the jungles and the hills with neither adequate training nor sufficient fire power. Wounded, frightened children had been marched into the camps, bewildered, trying not to weep and, finally understanding, weeping out of control. The stories they told were a thousand variations on the same sickening theme. Inexperienced, untried troops had been sent into battle within days after disembarkation, the weight of sheer numbers expected to vanquish the often unseen enemy. And when the numbers did not work, more numbers were sent. For three years command headquarters listened to a maniac. *Delavane!* The warlord of Saigon, fabricator of body-counts, denyer of blown-apart faces and severed limbs, liar and extoller of death without a cause! A man who had proved to be too lethal even for the Pentagon zealots – a zealot who had outdistanced his own, in the end revolting his own, recalled and retired only to write diatribes read by fanatics in search of their own personal furies.

Men like that can't be allowed any more, don't you understand? He was the enemy, OUR enemy! Those had been Converse's own words, shouted in a fever of outrage in front of a panel of uniformed questioners who had looked at one another, avoiding him, not wanting to respond to those words. They had thanked him perfunctorily, told him that the nation owed him and thousands like him a great debt, and with regard to his final comments, he should try to understand that there were often many sides to an issue, and that the complex execution of command frequently was not what it appeared. In any event, the President had called upon the nation to bind its wounds; what good was served by fuelling old controversies? And then the final kicker, the threat.

'You yourself briefly assumed the terrible responsibility of leadership, Lieutenant,' said a pale-faced Army lawyer, barely glancing at Joel, his eyes scanning the pages of a file folder. 'Before you made your final and successful escape – by yourself, from a pit in the ground away from the main camp – you led two previous attempts involving a total of seventeen prisoners of war. Fortunately you survived, but eight men did not. I'm sure that you, as their leader, their tactician, never anticipated a casualty risk of nearly fifty per cent. It's been said often, but perhaps not often enough: command is awesome, Lieutenant.'

Translation: *Don't join the freaks, soldier. You survived but eight were killed. Were there circumstances the military is not aware of, tactics that protected some more than others, one more than others? One man who managed to break out – by himself – eluding guards that shot loose prisoners on sight at night. Merely to raise the question by reopening a specific file will produce a stigma that will follow you for the rest of your life. Back off, soldier. We've got you by simply raising a question we all know should not be raised, but we'll do it because we've taken enough flak. We'll cut it off wherever we can. Be happy you survived and got out. Now, get out.*

At that moment, Converse had been as close to consciously throwing away his life as he would ever think possible. Physically, hysterically, assaulting that panel of sanctimonious hypocrites had not been out of the question . . . until he studied the face of each man, his peripheral gaze taking in rows of tunic ribbons, battle stars on most. Then a strange thing had happened: an odd admixture of disgust, revulsion . . . and compassion swept over him. These were panicked men, a number having committed their lives to the call of their country's practice of war . . . only to have been conned, as he had been conned. If to protect what was decent meant protecting the worst, who was to say they were wrong? Where were the saints? Or the sinners? Could there be any of either when all were victims?

Disgust, however, won out. Lieutenant Joel Converse, USNR could not bring himself to give a final salute to that aggregate council of his superiors. In silence, he had turned, with no military bearing whatsoever, and walked out of the room as if he had pointedly spat on the floor.

A flash of light again from the boulevard, a blinding echo of the sun from the Quai du Mont Blanc. He was in Geneva, not in a North Vietnamese camp holding children who vomited while telling their stories, or in San Diego being separated from the United States Navy. He was in Geneva . . . and the man sitting across the table knew everything he was thinking and feeling.

'Why *me?*' asked Joel.

'Because, as they say,' said Halliday, 'you could be motivated. That's the simple answer. A story was told. The Captain of an aircraft carrier refused to put his planes in the air for a strike demanded by Delavane. Several storms had moved in; he called it suicidal. But Delavane forced him to, threatened to call the macho White House and have the Captain removed of command. You led that strike. It's where you got it.'

'I'm alive,' said Converse, flatly. 'Twelve hundred kids never saw the next day and maybe a thousand more wished they never had.'

'And you were in the Captain's quarters when Mad Marcus Delavane made his threats and called the shots.'

'I was there,' agreed Converse, no comment in his voice. Then he shook his head in bewilderment. 'Everything I told you – about myself – you've heard it before.'

'Read it before,' corrected the lawyer from California. 'Like you – and I think we're the best in the business under fifty – I don't put a hell of a lot of stock in the written word. I have to hear a voice, or see a face.'

'I didn't answer you.'

'You didn't have to.'

'But *you* have to answer *me. Now* . . . You're not here for Comm Tech-Bern, are you?'

'Yes, that part's true,' said Halliday. 'Only the Swiss didn't come to me, I went to them. I've been watching you, waiting for the moment. It had to be the right one, perfectly natural, geographically logical.'

'Why? What do you mean?'

'Because I'm being watched . . . Rosen did have a stroke. I heard about it, contacted Bern, and made a plausible case for myself.'

'Your reputation was enough.'

'It helped, but I needed more. I said we knew each other, that we went way back – which God knows was true – and much as I respected you, I implied that you were extremely astute with finals . . . and that I was familiar with your methods. I also put my price high enough.'

'An irresistible combination for the Swiss,' said Converse.

'I'm glad you approve.'

'But I don't,' contradicted Joel. 'I don't approve of you at all, least of all *your* methods. You haven't told me anything, just made cryptic remarks about an unidentified group of people you say are dangerous, and brought up the name of a man you knew would provoke a response. Maybe you're just a freak after all, still pushing that safe, Yippee label.'

'Calling someone a "freak" is subjectively prejudicial in the extreme, counsellor, and would be stricken from the record.'

'Still the point's been made with the jury, lawyer-man,' said Converse in quiet anger. 'And I'm making it now.'

'Don't prejudge the safety,' continued Halliday, with equally quiet sincerity. 'I'm not safe, and outside of a proclivity for cowardice, there's a wife and five children back in San Francisco I care deeply about.'

'So you come to me because I have no such . . . what was it? Priority entanglements?'

'I came to you because you're invisible, you're not involved, and because you're the best and I can't do it! I *legally* can't do it, and it's got to be done *legally*.'

'Why don't you say what you mean?' demanded Converse. 'Because if you don't, I'm getting up and we'll see each other later across a table.'

'I represented Delavane,' said Halliday quickly. 'God help me I didn't know what I was doing, and very few people approved, but I made a point we used to make all the time. Unpopular causes and people also deserve representation.'

'I can't argue with that.'

'You don't know the cause. I do. I found out.'

'What cause?'

Halliday leaned forward. 'The generals,' he said, his voice barely audible. 'They're coming back.'

Joel looked closely at the Californian. 'From where? I didn't know they'd been away.'

'From the past,' said Halliday. 'From years ago.'

Converse sat back in the chair, his own eyes now amused. 'Good Lord, I thought your kind were extinct. Are you talking about the Pentagon menace, *Press* . . . it is "Press", isn't it? The San Francisco short-term, or was it from Haight Ashbury, or the Beverly Hills something or other? You're a little behind the times; you already stormed the Presidio.'

'Please, don't make jokes. I'm not joking.'

'Of course not. It's *Seven Days in May*, or is it *Five Days in August*? It's August now, so let's call it *The Old Time Guns of August*. Nice ring, I think.'

'Stop it!' whispered Halliday. 'There's nothing remotely funny, and if there were, I'd find it before you did.'

'That's a comment, I suppose,' said Joel.

'You're goddamned right it is, because I *didn't* go through what you went through. I stayed out of it, I wasn't conned, and that means I can laugh at fanatics because they never hurt me and I still think it's the best ammunition against them. But not now. There's nothing to laugh at now!'

'Permit me a small chuckle,' said Converse without smiling. 'Even in my most paranoid moments I never subscribed to the conspiracy theory that had the military running Washington. It couldn't happen.'

'It might be less apparent than in other countries, but that's all I'll grant you.'

'What does that mean?'

'It would undoubtedly be much more obvious in Israel, certainly in Johannesburg, quite possibly in France and Bonn, even the UK – none of them takes its pretences that seriously. But I suppose you've got a point. Washington will drape the constitutional robes around itself until they become threadbare and fall away . . . revealing a uniform, incidentally.'

Joel stared at the face in front of him and heard the voice that shot quietly, intensely across the table. 'You're *not* joking, are you? And you're too bright to try to snow me.'

'Or con you,' added Halliday. 'Not after that label I wore while watching you in pyjamas halfway across the world. I couldn't do it.'

'I think I believe you . . . You mentioned several countries, specific countries. Some aren't speaking, others barely; a few have bad blood and worse memories. On purpose?'

'Yes,' nodded the Californian. 'It doesn't make any difference because the group I'm talking about thinks it has a cause that will ultimately unite them all. And run them all . . . their way.'

'The generals?'

'And admirals, and brigadiers, and field marshals . . . old soldiers who pitched their tents in the right camp. So far right there's been no label since the Reichstag.'

'Come *on*, Avery!' Converse shook his head in quiet consternation. 'A bunch of tired old warhorses . . .'

'Recruiting and indoctrinating young, hard, capable new commanders,' interrupted Halliday.

'. . . coughing their last bellows . . .' Joel stopped. 'Have you proof of that?' he asked, each word spoken slowly.

'Not enough . . . but with some digging . . . maybe enough.'

'Goddamn it, stop being elliptical.'

'Among the possible recruits, twenty or so names at the State Department and the Pentagon,' said Halliday. 'Men who clear export licences and who spend millions upon millions because they're allowed to spend it, all of which, naturally, widens any circle of friends.'

'And influence,' stated Converse. 'What about London, Paris, and Bonn . . . Johannesburg and Tel Aviv?'

'Again names.'

'How firm?'

'They were there, I saw them myself. It was an accident. How many have taken an oath I don't know, but they were there and their stripes fit the philosophical pattern.'

'The Reichstag?'

'All they need is a Hitler.'

'Where does Delavane fit in?'

'He may appoint one. He may designate the Führer.'

'That's ridiculous. Who'd take him seriously?'

'He was taken seriously before. You saw the results.'

'That was then, not now. You're not answering the question.'

'Men who thought he was right before, and don't fool yourself, they're out there by the thousands. What's mind-blowing is that there are a few dozen with enough seed money to finance his and their delusions – which, of course, they don't see as delusions at all, only as the proper evolution of current history, all other ideologies having failed miserably.'

Joel started to speak, then stopped, his thoughts suddenly altered. 'Why haven't you gone to someone who can stop them? Stop him.'

'Who?'

'I shouldn't have to tell you that. Any number of people in the government – elected and appointed – and more than a dozen departments. For starters, there's Justice.'

'I'd be laughed out of Washington,' said Halliday. 'Beyond the fact that we have no proof – as I told you, just names, suppositions – don't forget that Yippy label I once wore. They'd pin it on me again and tell me to get lost.'

'But you *represented* Delavane.'

'Which only compounds the legal aspects, I shouldn't have to tell you that.'

'The lawyer-client relationship,' completed Converse. 'You're in a morass before you can make a charge. Unless you've got hard evidence against your client, proof that he's going to commit further crimes and that you're aiding the commission of those crimes by keeping silent.'

'Which proof I don't have,' interrupted the Californian.

'Then no one will touch you,' added Joel. 'Especially ambitious lawyers at Justice; they don't want their post-government avenues cut off. As you say, the Delavanes of this world have their constituencies.'

'Exactly,' agreed Halliday. 'And when I began asking questions and tried to reach Delavane, he wouldn't see me or talk to me. Instead, I got a letter telling me I was fired . . . that if he had known what I was he never would have retained me. "Smoking dope and screaming curses while brave young men answered their country's call".'

Converse whistled softly. 'And you think you weren't conned? You provide legal services for him, a structure he can use for all intents and purposes within the law, and if anything smells, you're the last person who can blow the whistle. He drapes the old soldier's flag around himself and calls you a vindictive freak.'

Halliday nodded. 'There was a lot more in that letter – nothing that could damage me except where *he* was concerned – but it was brutal.'

'I'm certain of it,' Converse took out a pack of cigarettes; he held it forward as Halliday shook his head. 'How did you represent him?' asked Joel.

'I set up a corporation, a small consulting firm in Palo Alto specializing in imports and exports. What's allowed, what isn't, what are the quotas, and how to legitimately reach the people in DC who will listen to your case. Essentially it was a lobbying effort, trading in on a name, if anyone remembered. At the time, it struck me as kind of pathetic.'

'I thought you said it wasn't registered,' remarked Converse, lighting a cigarette.

'It's not the one we're after. It'd be a waste of time.'

'But it's where you first got your information, isn't it? Your leads?'

'That was the accident and it won't happen again. It's so legitimate it's legal Clorox, clean as a whistle.'

'Still it's a front,' insisted Joel. 'It has to be if everything – or anything – you've said is true.'

'It's true, and it is. But nothing's written down. It's an instrument for travel, an excuse for Delavane and the men around him to go from one place to another, carrying on legitimate business. But while they're in a given area, they do their real thing.'

'The gathering of the generals and the field marshals?' said Converse.

'We think it's a spreading missionary operation. Very quiet and very intense.'

'What's the name of Delavane's firm?'

'Palo Alto International.'

Joel suddenly crushed out his cigarette. 'Who's *we*, Avery? Who's putting up this kind of money when amounts like that mean they're people who can reach anyone they want to in Washington?'

'Are you interested?'

'Not in working for someone I don't know . . . or approve of. No, I'm not.'

'Do you approve of the objectives as I've outlined them to you?'

'If what you've told me is true, and I can't think of any reason why you'd lie about it, of course I do. You knew I would. That still doesn't answer my question.'

'Suppose,' went on Halliday rapidly. 'I were to give you a letter stating that the sum of five hundred thousand dollars to be allocated to you from a blind account on the island of Mykonos was provided by a client of mine whose character and reputation are of the highest order. That his . . .'

'Wait a minute, *Press*,' broke in Converse harshly.

'Please don't interrupt me, *please*!' Halliday's eyes were riveted on Joel, a manic intensity in his stare. 'There's no other way, not *now*. I'll put my name – my professional life on the line. You've been hired to do confidential work within your specialization by a man known to me to be an outstanding citizen who insists on anonymity. I endorse both the man and the work he's asked you to do, and swear not only to the legality of the objectives but to the extraordinary benefits which would be derived by any success you might have. You're covered, you've got five hundred thousand dollars and – I expect just as important to you, perhaps more so – you have the chance to stop a maniac – *maniacs* – from carrying out an unthinkable plan. At the least, they'd create widespread unrest, political crises everywhere, enormous suffering – both individual and group. At the worst, they might change the course of history to the point where there wouldn't *be* any history.'

Converse sat rigid in his chair, his gaze unbroken. 'That's quite a speech. Practise it long?'

'No, you son of a bitch! It wasn't necessary to practise. Any more than you rehearsed that little explosion of yours twelve years ago in San Diego. "Men like that can't be allowed any more, don't you understand? He was the enemy, *our* enemy." . . . Those were the words, weren't they?'

'You did your homework, counsellor,' said Joel, his anger controlled. 'Why does your client insist on being anonymous? Why doesn't he take his money, make a political contribution, and talk to the Director of the CIA, or the National Security Council, or to the White House, any of which he could do easily. A half a million dollars isn't chopped chicken liver even today.'

'Because he can't be involved officially in any way whatsoever.' Halliday frowned as he expelled his breath. 'I *know* it sounds crazy, but that's the way it is. He *is* an outstanding man and I went to him because I was concerned. Frankly, I thought he'd pick up the phone and do what you just said. Call the White House, if it came to it, but he wanted to go this route.'

'With *me*?'

'Sorry, he didn't know you. He said a strange thing to me. He told me to find someone to shoot down the bastards without giving them the dignity of the government's concern, even its recognition. At first I couldn't understand, but then I did. It fitted in with my own theory that laughing at the Delavanes of this world renders them impotent more thoroughly than any other way.'

'It also eliminates the spectre of martyrdom,' added Converse. 'Why would this . . . outstanding citizen . . . do what he's doing? Why is it worth the money to him?'

'If I told you, I'd be breaking the confidence.'

'I didn't ask you his name. I want to know why.'

'By telling you,' said the Californian, 'you'd know who he is. I can't do that. Take my word for it, you'd approve of him.'

'Next question,' said Joel, a sharp edge to his voice. 'Just what the *hell* did you say to Talbot-Brooks that they found so acceptable?'

'Resigned to finding acceptable,' explained Halliday. 'I had help. Do you know Judge Lucas Anstett?'

'Second Court of Appeals,' said Converse, nodding. 'He should have been tapped for the Supreme Court years ago.'

'That seems to be the general consensus. He's also a friend of my client, and as I understand it, he met with John Talbot and Nathan Simon – Brooks was out of town – and without revealing my client's name, told them there was a problem that might well erupt into a national crisis if immediate legal action wasn't taken. Several US firms were involved, he explained, but the problem basically lay in Europe and required the talents of an experienced international lawyer. If their junior partner, Joel Converse, was selected and he accepted, would they consent to a leave of absence so he could pursue the matter on a confidential basis. Naturally, the judge strongly endorsed the project.'

'And naturally Talbot and Simon went along,' said Joel. 'You don't refuse Anstett. He's too damned reasonable, to say nothing of the power of his court.'

'I don't think he'd use that lever.'

'It's there.'

Halliday reached into his jacket pocket and took out a long white business envelope. 'Here's the letter. It spells out everything I said. There's also a separate page defining the schedule in Mykonos. Once you make arrangements at the bank – how you want the money paid or where you want it transferred – you'll be given the name of a man who lives on the island; he's retired. Phone him; he'll tell you when and where to meet. He has all the tools we can give you. The names, the connections as we think they are, and the activities they're most likely engaged in that violate the laws of their respective governments, sending arms, equipment, and technological information where they shouldn't be sent. Build just two or three cases that are tied to Delavane – even circumstantially – and it'll be enough. We'll turn it all into ridicule. It *will* be enough.'

'Where the *hell* do you get your nerve?' said Converse angrily. 'I haven't agreed to anything! You don't make decisions for me, and neither do Talbot or Simon, or the holy Judge Anstett, *or* your goddamned client! What did you think you were doing? Appraising me like a piece of horseflesh, making arrangements about me behind my back! Who do you people think you are?'

'Concerned people who think we've found the right man for the right job at the right time,' said Halliday, dropping the envelope in front of Joel. 'Only there's not that much time left. You've been where they want to take us and you know what it's like.' Suddenly the Californian got up. 'Think about it. We'll talk later. By the way, the Swiss know we were meeting this morning. If anyone asks what we talked about, tell them I agreed to the final disposition of the Class A stock. It's in our favour even though you may think otherwise. Thanks for the coffee. I'll be across the table in an hour . . . It's good to see you again, Joel.'

The Californian walked swiftly into the aisle and out through the brass gate of the *Chat Botté* into the sunlight of the Quai du Mont Blanc.

The telephone console was built into the far end of a long, dark conference table. Its muted hum was in keeping with the dignified surroundings. The Swiss *arbitre*, the canton of Geneva's legal representative, picked it up and spoke softly, nodding his head twice, then replaced the phone in its cradle. He looked around the table; seven of the eight attorneys were in their chairs talking quietly with one another. The eighth, Joel Converse, stood in front of an enormous window flanked by drapes and overlooking the Quai Gustave Ador. The giant *Jet d'Eau* erupted beyond, its pulsating spray filling the corridor above, cascading to the left under the force of a north wind. The sky was growing dark; a summer storm was on its way from the Alps.

'Messieurs,' said the *arbitre*, as conversations trailed off and faces were turned to the Swiss. 'That was Monsieur Halliday. He had been detained, but urges you to proceed. His associate, Monsieur Rogeteau has his recommendations and it is understood that he met with Monsieur Converse earlier this morning to resolve one of the last details. Is that not so, Monsieur Converse?'

Heads turned again, now in the opposite direction toward the figure by the window. There was no response. Converse continued to stare down at the lake.

'Monsieur *Converse?*'

'I beg your pardon?' Joel turned, a frown creasing the upper regions of his face, his thoughts far away, nowhere near Geneva.

'It is so, Monsieur?'

'What was the question?'

'You met earlier with Monsieur Halliday?'

Converse paused. 'It is so,' he replied.

'*And?*'

'And . . . he agreed to the final disposition of the Class A stock.'

There was a quiet but audible expression of relief on the part of the Americans, and a silent acceptance from the Bern contingent, their eyes non-committal. Neither reaction was lost on Joel, and under different circumstances he might have tabled the item for additional consideration. Halliday's judgment of Bern's advantage notwithstanding, the acceptance was too easily achieved; he would have postponed it anyway, at least for an hour's worth of analysis. Somehow it did not matter. *Goddamn him*! thought Converse.

'Then let us proceed as Monsieur Halliday suggested,' said the *arbitre*, glancing at his watch.

An hour stretched into two, then three, the hum of voices mingling in counterpoint as pages were passed back and forth, points clarified, paragraphs initialled. And still Halliday did not appear. Lamps were turned on as the darkness filled the midday sky outside the huge windows; there was talk of the approaching storm.

Then suddenly like an unexpected bolt of lightning, screams came from beyond the thick oak door of the conference room, swelling in volume until images of horror filled the minds of all who heard the prolonged, terrible sounds. Some around the enormous table lunged beneath it, others got out of their chairs and stood in shock, in stunned bewilderment, and a few rushed to the door, among them Converse. The *arbitre* twisted the knob and yanked it back with such force that the door crashed into the wall. What they saw was a sight none of them would ever forget. Joel lashed out his hands, gripping, pulling, parting the bodies in front of him as he raced into the anteroom.

Avery Fowler's striped jacket fell away from his chalk white fingers, his white shirt covered with blood, his chest a mass of tiny, bleeding holes. He fell, grabbing a secretary's desk, his upturned collar separating, revealing more blood on his throat. The expulsions of breath were too well known to Joel; he had held the heads of children in the camps as they had wept in anger and the ultimate fear. He held Avery Fowler's head now, lowering him to the floor.

'My God, what *happened*?' cried Converse, cradling the dying man in his arms.

'They're . . . back,' coughed the classmate from long ago. 'The elevator. They trapped me in the elevator! . . . They said it was for Aquitaine, that was the name they used . . . *Aquitaine*. Oh, Christ! Meg . . . the *kids* . . .!' Avery Fowler's head twisted spastically into his right shoulder, then the final eruption of air came from his bloodied throat.

A. Preston Halliday was dead.

Converse stood in the rain, his clothes drenched, staring at the unseen place on the water where only an hour ago the fountain had shot up to the sky proclaiming *this* was Geneva. The lake was angry, an infinity of whitecaps had replaced the graceful white sails. There were no reflections anywhere. But there was distant thunder from the north. From the Alps.

And Joel's mind was frozen.

2

He walked past the long, marble counter of the Hotel Richemond's front desk and headed for the winding staircase on the left. It was habit; his suite was on the second floor and the brass-grilled elevators with their wine-coloured velvet interiors were things of beauty, but not swiftness. Also, he enjoyed passing the casement displays of outrageously priced, brilliantly-lighted jewels that lined the walls of the elegant staircase – shimmering diamonds, blood-red rubies, webbed necklaces of spun gold. Somehow they reminded him of change, of extraordinary change. For him. For a life he had thought would end violently, thousands of miles away in a dozen different yet always the same rat-infested cells, with muted gunfire and the screams of children in the dark distance. Diamonds, rubies, and spun gold were symbols of the unattainable and unrealistic, but they were there, and he passed them, observed them, smiling at their existence . . . and they seemed to acknowledge him, large shining eyes of infinite depth staring back, telling him they were there, he was there. Change.

But he did not see them now, nor did they acknowledge him. He saw nothing, felt nothing; every tentacle of his mind and body was numbed, suspended in airless space. A man he had known as a boy under one name had died in his arms years later under another, and the words he had whispered at the brutal moment of death were as incomprehensible as they were paralysing. *Aquitaine. They said it was for Aquitaine* . . . Where was sanity, where was reason? What did the words mean and why had he been drawn into that elusive meaning? He *had* been drawn in, he knew it, and there was reason in that terrible manipulation. The magnet was a name, a man. George Marcus Delavane, warlord of Saigon.

'*Monsieur!*' The suppressed shout came from below; he turned on the stairs and saw the formally-attired *directeur* rushing across the lobby and up the steps. The man's name was Henri, and they had known each other for nearly five years. Their friendship went beyond that of hotel executive and hotel guest; they had gambled together frequently at Divonne, across the French border.

'Hello, Henri.'

'*Mon Dieu*, are you all right, Joel? Your office in New York has been calling you repeatedly. I heard it on the radio, it is all over Geneva! *Narcotiques*! Drugs, crime, guns . . . *murder*! It touches even us now!'

'Is that what they say?'

'They say small packages of cocaine were found under his shirt, a respected *avocat international* a suspected connection . . .'

'It's a lie,' Converse broke in.

'It's what they say, what can I tell you? Your name was mentioned; it was reported that he died as you reached him . . . You were not implicated, of course; you were merely there with the others. I heard your name and I've been worried sick! Where have you *been*?'

'Answering a lot of unanswerable questions down at police headquarters.' *Questions that were answerable, but not by him, not to the authorities in Geneva. Avery Fowler – Preston Halliday – deserved better than that. A trust had been given, accepted in death.*

'Christ, you're drenched!' cried Henri, intense concern in his eyes. 'You've been walking in the rain, haven't you? There were no taxis?'

'I didn't look, I wanted to walk.'

'Of course, the shock, I understand. I'll send up some brandy, some decent Armagnac. And dinner, perhaps; I'll release your table at the *Gentilhommes*.'

'Thanks. Give me thirty minutes and have your switchboard get New York for me, will you? I never seem to dial it right.'

'Joel?'

'What?'

'Can I help? Is there something you should tell me? We have won and lost together over too many bottles of *grand cru classé* for you to go alone when you don't have to. I know Geneva, my friend.'

Converse looked into the wide brown eyes beneath him, at the lined, concerned face, rigid in its concern. 'Why do you say that?'

'Because you so quickly denied the police reports of cocaine, what else? I watched you. There was more in what you said than what you said.'

Joel blinked, and for a moment shut his eyelids tight, the strain in the middle of his forehead acute. He took a deep breath and replied. 'Do me a favour, Henri, and don't speculate. Just get me an overseas line in a half hour, okay?'

'*Mais oui, Monsieur*,' said the Frenchman, nodding his head on the staircase. '*Le directeur du Richemond* is only to serve her guests, special guests accorded special service, of course . . . I'm here if you need me, my friend.'

'I know that. If I turn a wrong card, I'll let you know.'

'If you have to turn *any* card in Switzerland, call me. The suits vary with the players.'

'I'll remember that. Thirty minutes? A line?'

'*Certainement, Monsieur*.'

* * *

The shower was as hot as his skin could tolerate, the steam filling his lungs, cutting short the breath in his throat. He then forced himself to endure an ice-cold spray until his head shivered, the cold pain real. He reasoned that the shock of extremes might clear his mind, at least reduce the numbness. He had to think; he had to decide; he had to listen.

He came out of the bathroom, his white terrycloth robe blotting the residue of the shower, and shoved his feet into a pair of slippers on the floor beside the bed. He removed his cigarettes and lighter from the bureau top, and walked out into the sitting room. The concerned Henri had been true to his word; on the coffee table a floor-steward had placed a bottle of expensive Armagnac, the two glasses for appearance, not function. He sat down on the soft, pillowed couch, poured himself a drink, and lighted a cigarette. Outside, the heavy August rain pounded the casement windows, the tattoo harsh and unrelenting. He looked at his watch; it was a few minutes past six – shortly past noon in New York. Joel wondered if Henri had been able to get a clear trans-Atlantic line. The lawyer in Converse wanted to hear the words spoken from New York, words that would either confirm or deny a dead man's revelation. It had been twenty-five minutes since Henri had stopped him on the staircase; he would wait another five and call the switchboard.

The telephone rang, the blaring, vibrating European bell unnerving him. He reached for the phone on the table next to the couch; his breath was short and his hand trembled. 'Yes? Hello?'

'New York calling, Monsieur,' said the hotel operator. 'It's your office. Should I cancel the call listed for six-fifteen?'

'Yes, please. And thank you.'

'Mr *Converse*?' The intense, high pitched voice belonged to Lawrence Talbot's secretary.

'Hello, Jane.'

'Good God, we've been trying to reach you since ten o'clock! Are you all *right*? We got the news then, around ten. It's all so horrible!'

'I'm fine, Jane. Thanks for your concern.'

'Mr Talbot's beside himself. He can't believe it!'

'Don't believe what they're saying about Halliday. It's not true. May I speak with Larry, please?'

'If he knew you were on the phone talking to me, I'd be fired.'

'No, you wouldn't. Who'd write his letters?'

The secretary paused briefly, her voice calmer when she spoke. 'Oh, God, Joel, you're the end. After what you've been through, you still find something funny to say.'

'It's easier, Jane. Let me have Bubba, will you?'

'You *are* the limit!'

Lawrence Talbot, senior partner of Talbot, Brooks and Simon, was a perfectly competent attorney but his rise in law was as much due to his having been one of the few All American football players from Yale as from any prowess in the courtroom. He was also a very decent human being, more of a coordinating coach than the driving force of a conservative yet highly competitive law firm. He was also eminently fair and fairminded; he kept his word. He was one of the reasons Joel had joined the firm; another was Nathan Simon, a giant of a man and an attorney. Converse had learned more about the law from Nate Simon than from any other lawyer or professor he had ever met. He felt closest to Nathan yet Simon was the most difficult to get close to; one approached this uniquely private man with equal parts of fondness and reserve. Lawrence Talbot burst over the phone.

'Good *Lord*, I'm appalled! What can I *say*? What can I *do*?'

'To begin with, strike that horseshit about Halliday. He was no more a drug connection than Nate Simon.'

'You haven't heard, then? They've backed off on that. The story now is violent robbery; he resisted and the packets were stuffed under his shirt after they shot him. I think Jack Halliday must have burned the wires from San Francisco, threatened to beat the crap out of the whole Swiss government . . . He played for Stanford, you know.'

'You're too much, Bubba.'

'I never thought I'd enjoy hearing that from you, young man. I do now.'

'Young man and not so young, Larry . . . Clear something up for me, will you?'

'Whatever I can.'

'Anstett. Lucas Anstett.'

'We talked. Nathan and I listened, and he was most persuasive. We understand.'

'*Do* you?'

'Not the particulars certainly; he wouldn't elaborate. But we think you're the best in the field, and granting his request wasn't difficult. T, B and S *has* the best and when a judge like Anstett confirms it through such a conversation we have to congratulate ourselves, don't we?'

'Are you doing it because of his bench?'

'Christ, *no*. He even told us he'd be harder on us in appeals if we agreed. He's one rough cookie when he wants something. He tells you you'd be worse off if you give it to him.'

'Did you believe him?'

'Well, Nathan said something about billy-goats having certain identifiable markings that were not removed without a great deal of squealing, so we should go along. Nathan frequently obfuscates issues, but goddamnit, Joel, he's usually right.'

'If you can take three hours to hear a five-minute summation,' said Converse.

'He's always thinking, young man.'

'Young and not so young. Everything's relative.'

'Your wife called . . . Sorry, your ex-wife.'

'Oh?'

'Your name came up on the radio or television or something, and she wanted to know what happened.'

'What did you tell her?'

'That we were trying to reach you. We didn't know any more than she did. She sounded very upset.'

'Call her and tell her I'm fine, will you, please? Do you have the number?'

'Jane does.'

'I'll be leaving then.'

'On full pay,' said Talbot from New York.

'That's not necessary, Larry. I'm being given a great deal of money, so save the bookkeeping. I'll be back in three or four weeks.'

'I could do that, but I won't,' said the senior partner. 'I know when I've got the best and I intend to hold him. We'll bank it for you.' Talbot paused, then spoke quietly, urgently. 'Joel, I have to ask you. Did this thing a few hours ago have anything to do with the Anstett business?'

Converse gripped the telephone with such force his wrist and fingers ached. 'Nothing whatsoever, Larry,' he said. 'There's no connection.'

Mykonos, the sun-drenched, white-washed island of the Cyclades, neighbouring worshipper of Delos. Since Barbarossa's conquest it had been host to successive brigands of the sea who sailed on the Meltemi winds – Turks, Russians, Cypriots, finally Greeks – placed and displaced over the centuries, a small land mass alternately honoured and forgotten until the arrival of sleek yachts and shining aircraft, symbols of a different age. Low-slung automobiles – Porsches, Maseratis, Jaguars – now sped over the narrow roads past starched-white windmills and alabaster churches; a new type of inhabitant had joined the laconic, tradition-bound residents who made their livings from the sea and the shops. Free-spirited youths of all ages, with their open shirts and tight pantsuits, their sunburned skins serving as backdrops for adornments of heavy gold, had found a new playground. And ancient Mykonos, once a major port to the proud Phoenicians, became the St Tropez of the Aegean.

Converse had taken the first Swiss Air flight out of Geneva to Athens, and from there a smaller Olympic plane to the island. Despite the fact that he had lost an hour in the time zones, it was barely four o'clock in the afternoon when the airport taxi crawled through the streets of the hot, blinding white harbour and pulled up in front of the smooth white entrance of the bank. It was on the waterfront, and the crowds of flowered shirts and wild print dresses, and the sight of launches chopping over the gentle waves towards the slips on the main pier, were proof that the giant cruise ships far out in the harbour were managed by knowledgeable men. Mykonos was a dazzling snare for tourists; money would be left on the white-washed island; the *tavernas* and the shops would be full from the early sun to burning twilight. The ouzo would flow and Greek fishermen's caps would disappear from the shelves, placed on the swaying or embarrassed heads of suburbanites from Grosse Pointe and Short Hills. And when night came and the last *efharisto* and *parakalo* had been awkwardly uttered by the visitors, other games would begin, the courtiers and courtesans, the beautiful, ageless, self-indulgent children of the blue Aegean would start to play. Peals of laughter would be heard as *drachmas* were counted and spent – especially spent – in amounts that would stagger those who had opulent suites on the highest decks of the most luxurious ships. Where Geneva was contrary, Mykonos was accommodating . . . in ways the long-ago Turks might have envied.

Joel had called the bank from the airport, not knowing its business hours, but knowing the name of the banker he was to contact. Kostas Laskaris greeted him cautiously over the phone, making it clear that he expected not only a passport that would clear a spectrograph, but the original letter from A. Preston Halliday with his signature, said signature to be subjected to scanner, matching the signature the bank had been provided by the deceased Mr A. Preston Halliday.

'*We hear he was killed in Geneva. It is most unfortunate.*'

'*I'll tell his wife and children how your grief overwhelms me.*'

Converse paid the taxi and climbed the short, white steps of the entrance, carrying his suitcase and attaché case, grateful that the door was opened by a uniformed guard whose appearance brought to mind a long-forgotten photograph of a mad sultan who whipped his harem's women in a courtyard when they failed to arouse him.

Kostas Laskaris was not at all what Joel had expected from the short, disconcerting conversation over the phone. He was a balding, pleasant-faced man in his late fifties, with warm dark eyes and relatively fluent in English but certainly not comfortable with the language. His first words upon rising from his desk and indicating a chair in front of it for Converse contradicted Joel's previous impression.

'I apologize for what might have appeared as a cal*loos* statement on my part regarding Mr Halliday. However, it *was* most unfortunate, and I don't know how else to phrase it. And it is difficult, sir, to grieve for a man one never knew.'

'I was out of line. Forget it, please.'

'You are most kind, but I'm afraid I cannot forget the arrangements . . . mandated by Mr Halliday and his associate here on Mykonos. I must have your passport and the letter, if you please?'

'Who is he?' asked Joel, reaching into his jacket pocket for his passport billfold; it contained the letter. 'The associate, I mean.'

'You are an attorney, sir, and surely you are aware that the information you desire cannot be given to you until the barriers . . . have been leaped, as it were. At least I think that's right.'

'It'll do. I just thought I'd try.' He took out his passport and the letter, handing them to the banker.

Laskaris picked up his telephone and pressed a button. He spoke in Greek and apparently asked for someone. Within seconds the door opened and a bronzed, stunning dark-haired woman entered and walked gracefully over to the desk. She raised her downcast eyes and glanced at Joel, who knew the banker was watching him closely. A sign from Converse, another glance – from him directed at Laskaris – and introduction would be forthcoming, accommodation silently promised, and a conceivably significant piece of information would be entered in a banker's file. Joel offered no such sign; he wanted no such entry. A man did not pick up a half a million dollars for nodding his head, and then look for a bonus. It did not signify stability; it signified something else.

Inconsequential banter about flights, customs and the general deterioration of travel covered the next ten minutes, at which time his passport and the letter were returned. However, not by the striking, dark-haired woman but by a young, blond Adonis who was slightly balletic as he moved toward the desk. The pleasant-faced Laskaris was not missing a trick; he was perfectly willing to supply one, whichever route his wealthy visitor required.

Converse looked into the Greek's warm eyes, then smiled, the smile developing into quiet laughter. Laskaris smiled back and shrugged, dismissing the beach boy.

'I am chief manager of this branch, sir,' he said, as the door closed, 'but I do not set the policies for the entire bank. This is, after all, Mykonos.'

'And a great deal of money passes through here,' added Joel. 'Which one did you bet on?'

'Neither,' replied Laskaris, shaking his head. 'Only on exactly what you did. You'd be a fool otherwise, and I do not think you are a fool. In addition to being chief manager on the waterfront, I am also an excellent judge of character.'

'Is that why you were chosen as the intermediary?'

'No, that is not the reason. I am a friend of Mr Halliday's associate here on the island. His name is Beale, incidentally. Dr Edward Beale . . . You see, everything is in order.'

'A doctor?' asked Converse leaning forward and accepting his passport and the letter. 'He's a doctor?'

'Not a medical man, however,' clarified Laskaris. 'He's a scholar, a retired professor of history from the United States. He has an adequate pension and he moved here from Rhodes several months ago. A most interesting man, most knowledgeable. I handle his financial affairs – in which he is not very knowledgeable, but still interesting.' The banker smiled again, shrugging again.

'I hope so,' said Joel. 'We have a great deal to discuss.'

'That is not my concern, sir. Shall we get to the disposition of the funds? How and where would you care to have them paid?'

'A great deal in cash. I bought one of those sensorized money belts in Geneva – the batteries are guaranteed for a year. If it's ripped off me, a tiny siren goes off that splits your eardrums. I'd like American currency – except for a few thousand, of course.'

'Those belts are effective, sir, but not if you are unconscious, or if there is no one around to hear them. Might I suggest traveller's cheques?'

'You could and you'd probably be right, but I don't think so. I may not care to write out a signature.'

'As you wish. The denominations for yourself, please?' said Laskaris, pencil in hand, pad below. 'And where would you like the remainder to be sent?'

'Is it possible,' asked Converse slowly, 'to have accounts set up, not in my name, but accessible to me?'

'Of course, sir. Frankly, it is often standard in Mykonos . . . as well as in Crete, Rhodes, Athens, Istanbul, and also much of Europe. A description is wired, accompanied by words written out in your handwriting – another name, or numbers . . . one man I knew used a nursery rhyme – and they are matched. One must use a sophisticated bank, of course.'

'Of course. Name a few.'

'Where?'

'In London . . . Paris . . . Bonn . . . maybe Tel Aviv,' said Joel, trying to remember Halliday's words.

'Bonn is not easy; they are so inflexible. A wrong apostrophe and they summon whomever they consider their authorities . . . Tel Aviv is simple;

money is as free-wheeling and as serpentine as the Knesset. London and Paris are standard and, of course, their greed is overwhelming. You will be heavily taxed for the transfers because they know you will not make an issue over covert funds. Very proper, very mercenary, and very much thievery.'

'You know your banks, don't you?'

'I've had experience, sir. Now, as to the disbursements?'

'I want a hundred thousand for myself – nothing larger than five hundred dollar bills. The rest you can split up and tell me how I can get it if I need it.'

'It is not a difficult assignment, sir. Shall we start writing names, or numbers . . . or nursery rhymes?'

'Numbers,' said Converse. 'I'm a lawyer. Names and nursery rhymes are in dimensions I don't want to think about right now.'

'As you wish,' said the Greek, reaching for a pad. 'And here is Dr Beale's telephone number. When we have concluded our business, you may call him . . . Or not, as you wish. It is not my concern.'

Dr Edward Beale, resident of Mykonos, spoke over the telephone in measured words and the slow, thoughtful cadence of a scholar. Nothing was rushed, nothing accelerated for the moment; everything was deliberated and deliberate.

'There is a beach – more rocks than beach, and not frequented at night – about seven kilometres from the waterfront. Walk to it. Take the west road along the coast until you see the lights of several buoys riding the waves. Come down to the water's edge. I'll find you.'

The night clouds sped by, propelled by high altitude winds, letting the moonlight penetrate rapidly, sporadically, illuminating the desolate stretch of beach that was the meeting ground. Far out on the water, the red lamps of four buoys bobbed up and down. Joel climbed over the rocks and into the soft sand, making his way to the water's edge; he could both see and hear the small waves lapping forward and receding. He lit a cigarette, assuming the flame would announce his presence. It did; in moments a voice came out of the darkness behind him, but the greeting was hardly what he expected from an elderly, retired scholar.

'Stay where you are and don't move,' was the first command, spoken with quiet authority. 'Put the cigarette in your mouth and inhale, then raise your arms and hold them straight out in front of you . . . Good. Now smoke; I want to see the *smoke*.'

'Christ, I'm choking!' shouted Joel, coughing, the smoke, blown back by the ocean breeze, stinging his eyes. Then suddenly he could feel the sharp, quick movements of a single hand stabbing about his clothes, reaching across his chest up and down his legs. 'What are you *doing*?' he cried, spitting the cigarette out of his mouth involuntarily.

'You don't have a weapon,' said the voice.

'Of *course* not!'

'I do. You may lower your arms and turn around now.'

Converse spun, still coughing, and rubbed his watery eyes. 'You crazy son of a bitch!'

'It's a dreadful habit, those cigarettes. I'd give them up if I were you. Apart from the terrible things they do to your body, now you see how they can be used against you in other ways.'

Joel blinked and stared in front of him. The pontificator was a slender, white-haired old man of medium height, but standing very erect in what looked like a white canvas jacket and trousers. His face – what could be seen of it in the intermittent moonlight – was deeply lined and there was a partial smile on his lips. There was also a gun in his hand, held in a firm grip, levelled at Converse's head. 'You're *Beale*?' asked Joel. 'Dr *Edward* Beale?'

'Yes. Are you calmed down now?'

'Considering the shock of your warm welcome, I guess so.'

'Good. I'll put this away then.' The scholar lowered the gun and knelt down on the sand next to a canvas satchel. He shoved the weapon inside and stood up again. 'I'm sorry, but I had to be certain.'

'Of what? Whether or not I was a commando?'

'Halliday's dead. Could a substitute have been sent in your place? Someone to deal with an old man in Mykonos? If so, that person would most certainly have a gun.'

'Why?'

'Because he would have had no idea that I *was* an old man. *I* might have been a commando.'

'You know, it's possible – just *possible* – that I could have had a gun. Would you have blown my goddamned head off?'

'A respected attorney coming to the island for the first time, passing through Geneva's airport security? Where would you get it? Whom would you know on Mykonos?'

'Arrangements could have been made,' protested Converse with little conviction, realizing it was useless.

'I've had you followed since you arrived. You went directly to the bank, then to the Kouneni hotel where you sat in the garden and had a drink before going to your room. Outside of the taxi driver, my friend Kostas, the desk clerk, and the waiters in the garden, you spoke to no one. As long as you *were* Joel Converse I was safe.'

'For a product of an ivory tower, you sound more like a hit man from Detroit.'

'I wasn't always in the academic world, but yes, I've been cautious. I think we must all be very cautious. With a George Marcus Delavane it's the only sound strategy.'

'Sound strategy?'

'Approach, if you like.' Beale reached between the widely-separated buttons of his jacket and withdrew a folded page of paper. 'Here are the names,' he said, handing it to Joel. 'There are five key figures in Delavane's operation over here. One each from France, West Germany, Israel, South Africa and England. We've identified four – the first four – but we can't find the Englishman.'

'How did you get these?'

'Originally from notes found among Delavane's papers by Halliday when the General was his client.'

'That was the accident he mentioned, then? He said it was an accident that wouldn't happen again.'

'I don't know what he told you, of course, but it certainly was an accident. A faulty memory on Delavane's part, an affliction I can personally assure you touches the ageing. The General simply forgot he had a meeting with Halliday and when Preston arrived, his secretary let him into the office so he could prepare papers for Delavane, who was expected in a half hour or so. Preston saw a file folder on the General's desk; he knew that folder, knew it contained material he could cross check. Without thinking twice, he sat down and began working. He found the names and knowing Delavane's recent itinerary in Europe and Africa, everything suddenly began to fall into place – very ominously. For anyone politically aware those four names are frightening – they dredge up frightening memories.'

'Did Delavane ever learn that he'd found them?'

'In my judgement, he could never be certain. Halliday wrote them down and left before the General returned. But then Geneva tells us something else, doesn't it?'

'That Delavane did find out,' said Converse grimly.

'Or he wasn't going to take any further chances, especially if there was a schedule, and we're convinced there is one. We're in the countdown now.'

'To what?'

'From the pattern of their operations – what we've pieced together – a prolonged series of massive, orchestrated conflagrations designed to spin out of control destabilizing governments.'

'That's a tall order. In what way?'

'Guesswork,' said the scholar, frowning. 'Probably widespread, coordinated eruptions of violence led by terrorists everywhere – terrorists fuelled by Delavane and his people. When the chaos becomes intolerable, it's their excuse to march in with military units and assume the controls, initially with martial law.'

'It's been done before,' said Joel. 'Feed and arm a presumed enemy, then send out provocateurs . . .'

'With massive sums of money and material,' interrupted Beale.

'And when they rise up,' completed Converse, 'pull out the rug, crush them, and take over. The citizens give thanks and call the heroes saviours, as they start marching to their drums. But how could they *do* it?'

'That's the all-consuming question. What are the targets? Where are they, *who* are they? We have no idea. If we had an inkling, we might approach from that end, but we don't and we can't waste time hunting for unknowns. We must go after what we do know.'

'Again, time,' Joel broke in. 'Why are you so sure we're in a countdown?'

'Increased activity everywhere – in many cases frantic. Shipments originating in the States are funnelled out of warehouses in England, Ireland, France, and Germany to groups of insurgents in all the troubled areas. There are rumours out of Munich, the Mediterranean and the Arab states. The talk is in terms of final preparations but no one seems to know what exactly for – except that they must be ready. It's as though such groups as Baader Meinhoff, the Brigate Rosse, the PLO, and the red legions of Paris and Madrid are all in a race with none knowing the course, only the moment when it begins.'

'When is that?'

'Our reports vary but they're all within the same time span. Between three to five weeks.'

'Oh, my *God*!' Joel felt the rush of anger and fear. Suddenly, he remembered. 'Avery – *Halliday* whispered something to me just before he died. Words that were spoken by the men who shot him. "Aquitaine . . . They said it was for Aquitaine". Those were the words he whispered. What do they mean, Beale?'

The old scholar was silent, his eyes alive in the intermittent moonlight. He slowly turned his head and stared out at the water in thought. 'It's *madness*,' he whispered.

'That doesn't tell me anything.'

'No, of course not,' said Beale quickly, apologetically, turning back to Converse. 'It's simply the magnitude of it all. It's so incredible.'

'I'm not reading you.'

'Aquitaine . . . Aquitania as Julius Caesar called it . . . was the name given to a region in southern France that at one time in the first centuries after Christ was said to have extended from the Atlantic, across the Pyrenees to the Mediterranean, and as far north as the mouth of the Seine west of Paris on the coast . . .'

'I'm vaguely aware of that,' Joel broke in, too impatient for an academic dissertation.

'If you are, you're to be commended. Most people are only aware of the later centuries, say from the eighth on, when Charlemagne conquered the region, formed the kingdom of Aquitaine and bestowed it on his son Louis, and *his* sons Pepins One and Two. Actually, these and the following three hundred years are the most pertinent.'

'To what?'

'The *legend* of Aquitaine, Mr Converse. Like many ambitious generals, Delavane sees himself as a student of history – in the tradition of Caesar, Napoleon, Von Clausewitz . . . even Patton. I was rightly or wrongly considered a scholar, but he remains a student, and that's as it should be. Scholars can't take liberties without substantive evidence – or they shouldn't – but students can and usually do.'

'What's your point?'

'The legend of Aquitaine becomes convoluted, the What-If syndrome riding over the facts until theoretical assumptions are made that distort the evidence. You see, the story of Aquitaine is filled with sudden, massive expansions and abrupt contractions. To simplify, an imaginative student of history might say that had there not been political, marital and military miscalculations on the part of Charlemagne and his son, the two Pepins, and later Louis the Seventh of France and Henry the Second of England, *both* of whom were married to the extraordinary Eleanor, the kingdom of Aquitaine might have encompassed most if not all of Europe.' Beale paused. 'Do you begin to understand?' he asked.

'Yes,' said Joel. 'Christ, *yes*.'

'That's not all,' continued the scholar. 'Since Aquitaine was once considered a legitimate possession of England, it might have in time enveloped all of her foreign colonies, including the original thirteen across the Atlantic. Later the United States of America . . . Of course, miscalculations or not, it could never have happened due to a fundamental law of western civilization, valid since the deposition of Romulus Augustulus and the collapse of the Roman Empire. You cannot crush, then unite by force and rule disparate peoples and their cultures – not for any length of time.'

'Someone's trying to now,' said Converse. 'George Marcus Delavane.'

'Yes. In his mind he's constructed the Aquitaine that never was, never could be. And it's profoundly terrifying.'

'Why? You just said it couldn't happen.'

'Not according to the old rules, not in any period since the fall of Rome. But you must remember, there's never *been* a time in recorded history like this one. Never such weapons, such anxiety. Delavane and his people know that, and they will play upon those weapons, those anxieties. They *are* playing upon them.' The old man pointed to the sheet of paper in Joel's hand. 'You have matches. Strike one and look at the names.'

Converse unfolded the page, reached into his pocket and took out his lighter. He snapped it, the flame illuminating the paper, as he studied the names. 'My *God*,' he said, frowning in the sharp spill of light. 'They fit in with Delavane. It's a gathering of warlords, if they're the men I think they are.' Joel extinguished the flame.

'They are,' replied Beale, 'starting with General Jacques Louis Bertholdier in Paris, a remarkable man, quite extraordinary. A Resistance fighter in the War, given the rank of major before he was twenty, but later an unreconstructed member of Salan's OAS. He was behind an assassination attempt on de Gaulle in August of '62, seeing himself as the true leader of the Republic. He nearly made it. He believed then as he believes now that the Algerian generals were the salvation of an enfeebled France. He has survived not only because he's a legend, but because his voice isn't alone – only he's more persuasive than most. Especially with the élite crowd of promising commanders produced by St Cyr. Quite simply, he's a fascist, a fanatic hiding behind a screen of eminent respectability.'

'And the one named Abrahms,' said Converse. 'He's the Israeli strong man who struts around in a safari jacket and boots, isn't he? The screecher who holds rallies in front of the Knesset and in the stadiums, telling everyone there'll be a blood bath in Judea and Samaria if the children of Abraham are denied. Even the Israelis can't shut him up.'

'Many are afraid to; he's become electrifying, like lightning, a symbol. Chaim Abrahms and his followers make the Begin regime seem like reticent, self-effacing pacifists. He's a Sabra tolerated by the European Jews because he's a brilliant soldier, proven in two wars, and has enjoyed the respect – if not the affection – of every Minister of Defence since the early years of Golda Meir. They never know when they might need him in the field.'

'And this one,' said Joel, again using his lighter. 'Van Headmer, South African, isn't it? The "hangman in uniform" or something like that.'

'Jan van Headmer, also the "slayer of Soweto", as the Blacks call him. He executes *offenders* with alarming frequency and government tolerance. His family is old-line Afrikaner, all generals going back to the Boer War, and he sees no reason on earth to bring Pretoria into the twentieth century. Incidentally, he's a close friend of Abrahms and makes frequent trips to Tel Aviv. He's also one of the most erudite and charming general officers ever to attend a diplomatic conference. His presence denies his image and reputation.'

'And Leifhelm,' completed Converse, again shutting down the flame. 'A mixed bag, if I'm accurate. Supposedly a great soldier who followed too many orders, but still respected. I'm weakest on him.'

'Entirely understandable,' said Beale, nodding in the moonlight. 'In some ways his is the oddest story – the most monstrous, really, because the truth has been consistently covered up so as to use him and avoid embarrassment. Field Marshal Erich Leifhelm was the youngest general ever commissioned by Adolf Hitler. He foresaw Germany's collapse and made a sudden about face. From brutal killer and a fanatic super Aryan to a contrite professional who abhorred the Nazis' crimes as they were "revealed" to him. He fooled everyone and was absolved of all guilt; he never saw a Nuremberg courtroom. During the cold war the Allies used his services extensively, granting him full security clearances, and later, in the 'fifties, when the new German divisions were mounted for the NATO forces, they made sure he was put in command.'

'Weren't there a couple of newspaper stories about him a few years ago? He had several run-ins with Helmut Schmidt, didn't he?'

'Exactly,' agreed the retired soldier. 'But those stories were soft and carried only *half* the story. Leifhelm was quoted as saying merely that the German people could not be expected to carry the burden of past guilt into future generations. It had to stop. Pride should once more be established in the nation's heritage. There was some sabre-rattling aimed at the Soviets, but nothing substantively beyond that.'

'What was the other half?' asked Converse.

'He wanted the *Bundestag*'s restrictions on the armed forces lifted completely, and fought for the expansion of the intelligence services, patterned after the *Abwehr*, including rehabilitation sentences for political troublemakers. He also sought widespread deletions in German text books throughout the school systems. "Pride has to be restored," he kept saying, claiming everything in the name of virulent anti-communism.'

'The Third Reich's first strategy in everything when Hitler took over.'

'You're quite right. Schmidt saw through him and knew there'd be chaos if he had his way – and he *was* influential. Bonn could not afford the spectre of painful memories. Schmidt forced Leifhelm to resign and literally removed his voice from all government affairs.'

'But he keeps speaking.'

'Not openly. However, he's rich and retains his friends and contacts.'

'Among them Delavane and his people.'

'Foremost among them now.'

Joel once more snapped his lighter, as if remembering something he had seen, and scanned the lower part of the page. There were two lists of names, the row on the left under the title of *State Department*, the right beneath the word *Pentagon*. There were perhaps twenty-five people in all. 'Who are the

Americans?' He released the lever; the flame died and he put the lighter back in his pocket. 'The names don't mean anything to me.'

'Some should, but it doesn't matter,' said Beale elliptically. 'The point is that among those men are disciples of George Delavane. They carry out his orders. How many of them is difficult to say, but at least several from each grouping. You see, these are the men who make the decisions – or conversely, do not oppose decisions – without which Delavane and his followers would be stopped in their tracks.'

'Spell that out.'

'Those on the left are key figures in the State Department's Office of Munitions Control. They determine what gets cleared for export, who under the blanket of "national interest" can receive weapons and technology withheld from others. On the right are the senior officers at the Pentagon on whose word millions upon millions are spent for armament procurements. All are decision makers . . . and a number of those decisions have been questioned, a few openly, others quietly by diplomatic and military colleagues. We've learned that much.'

'Questioned why?' interrupted Converse.

'There were rumours – there always *are* rumours – of large shipments improperly licensed for export. Then there's surplus military equipment – excess supplies – lost in transfers, using temporary warehouses and out-of-the-way storage depots. Surplus equipment is easily unaccounted for; it's an embarrassment in these days of enormous budgets and cost overruns. Get rid of it and don't be too particular. How fortunate in these instances – and coincidental – if a member of the Aquitaine shows up, willing to buy and with all his papers in order. Whole depots and warehouses are sent where they shouldn't be sent.'

'A *Libya* connection!'

'There's no doubt of it. A great many connections.'

'Halliday mentioned it and you said it a few moments ago. Laws broken – arms, equipment, technological information – sent to people who shouldn't have them. They break loose on cue and there's disruptions, terrorism . . .'

'Justifying military responses,' broke in old Beale. 'That's part of Delavane's concept. Justifiable escalation of armed might, the commanders in charge, the civilians helpless, forced to listen to them, obey them.'

'But you just said questions were raised.'

'And answered with such worn out phrases as "national security" and "adversarial disinformation" to stop or throw off the curious.'

'That's obstruction. Can't they be caught at it?'

'By whom? With what?'

'Damn it, the questions themselves!' replied Converse. 'Those improper export licences, the military transfers that got lost, merchandise that can't be traced.'

'By people without the clearances to go around security classifications, or lacking the expertise to understand the complexities of export licensing.'

'That's nonsense,' insisted Joel. 'You said some of those questions were asked by diplomatic personnel, military colleagues, men who certainly had the clearances *and* the expertise.'

'And who suddenly, magically, didn't ask them any longer. Of course, many may have been persuaded that the questions were, indeed, beyond their legitimate purviews; others may have been too frightened to penetrate for fear of involvement, others still, forced to back off – frankly threatened. Regardless, behind it all there are those who do the convincing, and they're growing in numbers everywhere.'

'Christ, it's a . . . a *network*,' said Converse softly.

The scholar looked hard at Joel, the night light off the water reflecting across the old man's pale, lined face. 'Yes, Mr Converse, a "network". The word was whispered to me by a man who thought I was one of them. "The network," he said. "The network will take care of you." He meant Delavane and his people.'

'Why did they think you were part of them?'

The old man paused. He looked briefly away at the shimmering Aegean, then back at Converse. 'Because *that* man thought it was logical . . . Thirty years ago I took off a uniform, trading it for the Harris tweeds and unkempt hair of a university professor. Few of my colleagues could understand, for you see I was one of the élite, perhaps a later, American version of Erich Leifhelm – a brigadier-general at thirty-eight, the Joint Chiefs were conceivably my next assignment. But where the collapse of Berlin and the disembodiment of the bunker had one effect on Leifhelm, the evacuation of Korea and the disembowelment of Panmunjong had another effect on me. I saw only the waste, not the cause I once saw, only the futility where once there'd been sound reasons. I saw death, Mr Converse, not heroic death against animalistic hordes, or even on a Spanish afternoon with the crowds shouting "*Olé*", but just plain death. Ugly death, shattering death, and I knew I could no longer be a part of those strategies that called for it . . . Had I been qualified in belief, I might have become a priest.'

'But your colleagues who couldn't understand,' said Joel, mesmerized by Beale's words, words that meant so very much to him. 'They thought it was something else?'

'Of course they did. I'd been praised in evaluation reports by the holy MacArthur himself. I even had a label: The Red Fox of Inchon – my hair was red then. My commands were marked by quick, decisive moves and countermoves, all reasonably well thought out and swift in execution. And then one day, south of Chunchon, I was given an order to take three adjacent hills that comprised dead high-ground – vantage points that served no strategic purpose – and I radioed back that it was useless real estate, that whatever casualties we sustained were not worth it. I asked for clarification, a field officer's way of saying "You're crazy, why should I?" . . . The reply came in something less than fifteen minutes. "Because it's there, General." That was all. "Because it's there." A symbolic point was to be made for someone's benefit or someone else's macho news briefing in Seoul . . . I took the hills, and I also wasted the lives of over three hundred men – and for my efforts I was awarded another cluster of the Distinguished Service Cross.'

'Is that when you quit?'

'Oh, Lord no, I was too confused, but inside, my head was boiling. The end came, and I watched Panmunjong, and was finally sent home, all manner of extraordinary expectations to be considered my ordinary rewards . . . However, a minor advancement was denied me for a very good reason:

I didn't speak the language in a sensitive European post, but another did. By then my head had exploded; I used the rebuke and I took my cue. I resigned quietly and went my way.'

It was Joel's turn to pause and study the old man in the night light. 'I've never heard of you,' he said finally. 'Why haven't I ever heard of you?'

'You didn't recognize the names on the two lower lists, either, did you? "Who are the Americans?" you said. "The names don't mean anything to me." Those were your words, Mr Converse.'

'They weren't young decorated generals – heroes – in a war.'

'Oh, but several *were*,' interrupted Beale swiftly, 'in several wars. They had their moments in a fleeting sun, and then they were forgotten, the moments only remembered by them, relived by them. Constantly.'

'That sounds like an apology for them.'

'Of course it is! You think I have no feelings for them? For men like Chaim Abrahms, Bertholdier, even Leifhelm? We call upon these men when the barricades are down, we extol them for acts beyond our abilities . . .'

'*You* were capable. You performed those acts.'

'You're right and that's why I *understand* them. When the barricades are rebuilt, we consign them to a very dull oblivion. Worse, we force them to watch inept civilians strip the gears of reason, and through oblique vocabularies plant the explosives that will blow those barricades apart again. Then when they're down once more, we summon our commanders.'

'Jesus, whose side are you on?'

Beale closed his eyes tightly, reminding Joel of the way he used to shut his own when certain memories came back to him. 'Yours, you idiot,' said the scholar quietly. 'Because I know what they can do when we ask them to do it. I meant what I said before. There's never been a time in history like this one. Far better that inept, frightened civilians are still talking, still searching, than one of us . . . Forgive me, one of them.'

A gust of wind blew off the sea; the sand spiralled about their feet. 'That man,' said Converse, 'the one who told you the network would take care of you. Why did he say it?'

'He thought they could use me. He was one of the field commanders I knew in Korea, a kindred spirit then. He came to my island – for what reason I don't know, perhaps a vacation, perhaps to find me, *who* knows – and found me on the waterfront. I was taking my boat out of the Plati Harbour when suddenly he appeared, tall, erect and very military in the morning sun. "We have to talk," he said, with that same insistence we always used in the field . . . I asked him aboard and we slowly made our way out of the bay. Several miles out of the Plati he presented his case, *their* case. *Delavane's* case.'

'What happened then?'

The scholar paused for precisely two seconds, then answered simply. 'I killed him. With a scaling knife, dropping his body over a cluster of sharks beyond the shoals of the Stephanos.'

Stunned, Joel stared at the old man, the iridescent light of the moon contributing to the macabre revelation. 'Just like that?' he said in a monotone.

'It's what I was trained to do, Mr Converse. I was the Red Fox of Inchon.

I never hesitated when the ground could be gained, or an adversarial advantage eliminated.'

'You *killed* him?'

'It was a necessary decision, not a wanton taking of life. He was a recruiter and my response was in my eyes, in my silent outrage. He saw it, and I understood. He could not permit me to live with what he'd told me. One of us had to die, and I simply reacted more swiftly than he did.'

'That's pretty cold reasoning.'

'You're a lawyer, you deal every day with options. Where was the alternative?'

Joel shook his head, not in reply but in astonishment. 'How did Halliday find you?'

'We found each other. We've never met, never talked, but we have a mutual friend.'

'In San Francisco?'

'He's frequently there.'

'Who is he?'

'It's a subject we won't discuss. I'm sorry.'

'Why not? Why the secrecy?'

'It's the way he prefers it. Under the circumstances, I believe it's a logical request.'

'Logic? Find me logic in any of this! Halliday reaches a man in San Francisco who just happens to know you, a former general thousands of miles away on a Greek island who just *happens* to have been approached by one of Delavane's people. Now that's coincidence, but damned little logic!'

'Don't dwell on it. Accept it.'

'Would you?'

'Under the circumstances, yes, I would. You see, there's no alternative.'

'Sure there is. I could walk away five hundred thousand dollars richer, paid by an anonymous stranger who could only come after me by revealing himself.'

'You could but you won't. You were chosen very carefully.'

'Because I could be motivated? That's what Halliday said.'

'Frankly, yes.'

'You're off the wall, all of you!'

'One of us is dead. You were the last person he spoke with.'

Joel felt the rush of anger again, the sight of a dying man's eyes burned into his memory. 'Aquitaine,' he said softly. '*Delavane* .... All right, I was chosen carefully. Where do I begin?'

'Where do you think you should begin? You're the attorney, everything must be done legally.'

'That's just it. I'm an attorney, not the police, not a detective.'

'No police in any of the countries where those four men live could do what you can do, even if they agreed to try, which frankly I doubt. More to the point, they would alert the Delavane network.'

'All right, I'll try,' said Converse, folding the page with the list of names and putting it in his inside jacket pocket. 'I'll start at the top. In Paris. With this Bertholdier.'

'Jacques Louis Bertholdier,' added the old man, reaching down into his

canvas bag and taking out a thick manila envelope. 'This is the last thing
we can give you. It's everything we could learn about those four men,
perhaps it can help you. Their addresses, the cars they drive, business
associates, cafés and restaurants they frequent, sexual preferences where
they constitute vulnerability . . . anything that could give you an edge. Use
it, use everything you can. Just bring us back briefs against men who have
compromised themselves, broken laws – above all, evidence that shows they
are not the solid, respectable citizens their lifestyles would indicate. Embarrassment, Mr Converse, *embarrassment*. It leads to ridicule, and Preston
Halliday was profoundly right about that. Ridicule is the first step.'

Joel started to reply, to agree, then stopped, his eyes riveted on Beale. 'I
never told you Halliday said anything about ridicule.'

'Oh?' The scholar blinked several times in the dim light, he was
momentarily unsure of himself, caught by surprise. 'But, naturally, we
discussed . . .'

'You never met, you never *talked*!' broke in Converse.

'. . . through our mutual friend the strategies we might employ,' completed
the old man, his eyes now steady, unblinking. 'The aspect of ridicule is a
keystone. Of course, we discussed it.'

'You just hesitated.'

'You startled me with a meaningless statement. My reactions are not
what they once were.'

'They were in a boat beyond the Stephanos,' corrected Joel.

'An entirely different situation, Mr Converse. Only one of us could leave
that boat. Both of us will leave this beach tonight.'

'All right, I may be reaching. You would, too, if you were me.' Converse
withdrew a pack of cigarettes from his shirt pocket, shook one up nervously
to his lips and took out his lighter. 'A man I knew as a kid under one name
approaches me years later calling himself something else.' Joel snapped his
lighter and held the flame under the cigarette, inhaling. 'He tells a wild
story that's just credible enough so I can't dismiss it. The believable aspect
is a maniac named Delavane. He says I can help stop him – stop *them* – and
there's a great deal of money for nodding my head – provided by a man in
San Francisco who won't say who he is, expedited by a former general on a
fashionably remote island in the Aegean. And for his efforts, this man I
knew under two names is murdered in daylight, shot a dozen times in an
elevator, dying in my arms, whispering the name "Aquitaine". And then
this other man, this ex-soldier, this doctor, this *scholar* tells me another story
that ends with a "recruiter" from Delavane killed with a scaling knife, his
body thrown overboard into a school of sharks beyond the Stephanos –
whatever that is.'

'The Aghios Stephanos,' said the old man. 'A lovely beach, far more
popular than this one.'

'Goddamn it, I *am* reaching, Mr Beale, or Professor Beale, or *General*
Beale! It's too much to absorb in two lousy days! Suddenly I don't have
much confidence. I feel way beyond my depth – let's face it, overwhelmed
and underqualified . . . and damned frightened.'

'Then don't overcomplicate things,' said Beale. 'I used to say that to
students of mine more often than I can remember. I would suggest they not

look at the totality that faced them, but rather each thread of progression, following each until it met and entwined with another thread, and then another, and if a pattern did not become clear, it was not their failure but mine. One step at a time, Mr Converse.'

'You're one hell of a Mr Chips. I would have dropped the course.'

'I'm not saying it well, I used to say it better. When you teach history, threads are terribly important.'

'When you practise law, they're everything.'

'Go after the threads then, one at a time. I'm certainly no lawyer, but can't you approach this as an attorney whose client is under attack by forces that would violate his rights, cripple his manner of living, deny his pursuit of peaceful existence – in essence, destroy him?'

'Not likely,' replied Joel. 'I've got a client who won't talk to me, won't see me, won't even tell me who he is.'

'That's not the client I had in mind.'

'Who else? It's his money.'

'He's only a link to your real client.'

'Who's that?'

'What's left of the civilized world, perhaps.'

Joel studied the old scholar in the shimmering light. 'Did you just say something about not looking at totalities, but at threads? You scare the hell out of me.'

Beale smiled. 'I could accuse you of misplaced concretion, but I won't.'

'That's an antiquated phrase. If you mean out-of-context, say it, and I'll deny it. You're securely in *well-placed* contradiction, Professor.'

'Good heavens, you were chosen carefully. You won't even let an old man get away with an academic bromide.'

Converse smiled back. 'You're a likeable fellow, General . . . or Doctor. I'd hate to have met you across a table if you'd taken up law.'

'That could truly be misplaced confidence,' said Edward Beale, his smile gone. 'You're only about to begin.'

'But now I know what to look for. One thread at a time . . . until the threads meet and entwine, and the pattern's there for everyone to see. I'll concentrate on export licences, and whoever's shuffling the controls, then connect three or four names with one another and trace them back to Delavane in Palo Alto. At which point we blow it apart *legally*. No martyrs, no causes, no military men-of-destiny crucified by traitors, just plain bloated, ugly profiteers who've professed to be super patriots when all the while they were lining their unpatriotic pockets. Why *else* would they have done it? Is there another *reason*? . . . That's ridicule, Dr Beale. Because they *can't answer*.'

The old man shook his head, his lined brows indicating bewilderment. 'The professor becomes a student,' he said, hesitantly. 'How can you do this?'

'The way I've done it dozens of times in corporate negotiations . . . only I'll take it a step farther. In those sessions, I'm like any other lawyer, I try to figure out what the fellow across the table is going to ask for and then why he wants it. Not just what *my* side wants, but what *he* wants. What's going through his mind? . . . . You see, Doctor, I'm trying to think like him; I'm putting myself in his place, never for a second letting him forget that

I'm doing just that. It's very unnerving, like making notes on margins whenever your opponent says anything, whether he's saying anything or not . . . But this time it's going to be different. I'm not looking for opponents. I'm looking for allies. In a cause, *their* cause. I'll start in Paris, then on to Bonn, or Tel Aviv, then probably Johannesburg. Only when I reach these men I won't try to think like them, I'm going to *be* one of them.'

'That's a very bold strategy, I compliment you.'

'Talking of options, it's the only one open. Also, I've got a lot of money I can spend around, not lavishly but effectively, as befits my unnamed client. Very unnamed, very much in the background, but always there.' Joel stopped, a thought striking him. 'You know, Dr Beale, I take it back. I don't want to know who my client is – the one in San Francisco, I mean. I'm going to create my own, and knowing him might distort the portrait I've got in mind. Incidentally, tell him he'll get a full accounting of my expenses: the rest will be returned to him the same way I got it. Through your friend Laskaris at the bank here on Mykonos.'

'But you've accepted the money,' objected Beale. 'There's no reason . . .'

'I wanted to know if it was real. If *he* was real. He is, and he knows exactly what he's doing. I'll need a great deal of money because I'm going to have to become someone I'm not, and money is the most convincing way to do it . . . No, Doctor, I don't want your friend's money. I want Delavane. I want the warlord of Saigon . . . But I'll use his money, just as I'm using him – the way I want him to be. To get inside that network.'

'If Paris is your first stop and Bertholdier is going to be your intitial contact, there's a specific munitions transfer we think is directly related to him. It might be worth a try. If we're right, it's a microcosm of what they intend doing everywhere.'

'Is it in here?' asked Converse, tapping the thick manila envelope containing the dossiers.

'No, it came to light only this morning – early this morning. I don't imagine you listened to the news broadcasts.'

'I don't speak any language but English. If I heard a news programme I wouldn't know it. What happened?'

'All Northern Ireland is on fire, the worst riots, the most savage killing in fifteen years. In Belfast and Ballyclare, Dromora and in the Mourne Mountains, outraged vigilantes – on *both* sides – are roaming the streets and the hills, firing indiscriminately, slaughtering in their anger everything that moves. It's utter chaos. The Ulster government is in panic, parliament tied down, emotionally disrupted, everyone trying to find a solution. That solution will be a massive infusion of troops and their commanders.'

'What's it got to do with Bertholdier?'

'Listen to me carefully,' said the scholar, taking a step forward. 'Eight days ago a munitions shipment containing three hundred cases of cluster bombs and two thousand cartons of explosives was air freighted out of Beloit, Wisconsin. Its destination was Tel Aviv by way of Montreal, Paris and Marseilles. It never arrived and an Israeli trace – employing the Mossad – showed that only the cargo's paperwork reached Marseilles, nothing else. The shipment disappeared in either Montreal or Paris, and we're convinced it was diverted to provisional extremists – again on both sides – in Northern Ireland.'

'Why do you think so?'

'The first casualties – over three hundred men, women and children – were killed or severely wounded, ripped to shreds by cluster bombs. It's not a pleasant way to die, perhaps worse to be hurt; the bombs tear away whole sections of the body. The reactions have been fierce and the hysteria's spreading. Ulster's out of control, the government paralysed. All in the space of one day, *one single day*, Mr Converse!'

'They're proving to themselves they can do it,' said Joel quietly, the fear in his throat.

'Precisely,' agreed Beale. 'It's a test case, a microcosm of the full scale horror they can bring about.'

Converse frowned. 'Outside of the fact that Bertholdier lives in Paris, what ties him to the shipment?'

'Once the plane crossed into France, the French insurers were a firm in which Bertholdier is a director. Who would be less suspect than a company that had to pay for the loss, a company, incidentally, which has access to the merchandise it covers? The loss was upward of four million francs, not so immense to create headlines, but entirely sufficient to throw off suspicion. And one more lethal delivery is made – death, mutilation, and chaos to follow.'

'What's the name of the insurance company?'

'*Compagnie Solidaire*. It would be one of the operative words, I'd think. *Solidaire*, and perhaps Beloit and Belfast.'

'Let's hope I get to confront Bertholdier with them. But if I do, I've got to say them at the right time. I'll catch the plane from Athens in the morning.'

'Take the urgent good wishes of an old man with you, Mr Converse. And urgent is the appropriate word. Three to five weeks, that's all you've got before everything blows apart. Whatever it is, wherever it is, it will be Northern Ireland ten thousand times more violent. It's real and it's coming.'

Valerie Charpentier woke up suddenly, her eyes wide, her face rigid, listening intently for sounds that broke the dark silence around her and the slap of the waves in the distance. Any second she expected to hear the shattering bell of the alarm system which was wired into every window and door of the house.

It did not come, yet there had been other sounds, intrusions on her sleep, penetrating enough to wake her. She pulled the covers back and got out of bed, walking slowly, apprehensively to the glass doors that opened onto her balcony – the rocky beach, the jetty, and the Atlantic Ocean beyond.

There it was *again*. The bobbing, dim lights were unmistakably the same, washing over the boat which was moored exactly where it had been moored before. It was the sloop that for two days had cruised up and down the coastline, always in sight, with no apparent destination other than this particular stretch of the Massachusetts' shore. At twilight on the second evening it had dropped anchor no more than a quarter of a mile out in the water in front of her house. It was back. After three days it had returned.

Three nights ago she had called the police, who in turn reached the Cape Ann Coast Guard patrols, who came back with an explanation that was no more lucid than it was satisfactory. The sloop was a Maryland registry, the owner an officer in the United States Army, and there were no provocative or suspicious movements that warranted any official action.

'I'd call it damned provocative *and* suspicious,' Val had said firmly. 'When a strange boat sails up and down the same stretch of beach for two days in a row, then parks in front of my house within shouting distance – shouting distance being swimming distance.'

'The water rights of the property you leased don't extend beyond two hundred feet, mam,' had been the official reply. 'There's nothing we can do.'

At the first light of the next morning, however, Valerie knew that *something* had to be done. She had focused her binoculars on the boat, only to have gasped and moved back away from the glass doors. Two men had been standing on the deck of the sloop, their own binoculars – far more powerful than hers – directed at the house, at the bedroom upstairs. At her.

A neighbour down the beachside *cul-de-sac* had recently installed an alarm system. She was a divorced woman, too, but with a hostile ex-husband and three children; she deemed the alarm necessary. Two phone calls and Val was speaking to the owner of Watchguard Security. A temporary system had been hooked up that day while a permanent installation was designed.

A bell – not shattering but instead soft and gentle. It was the quiet clanging of a ship's bell out on the dark water, its clapper swinging with the waves. It was the sound that had awakened her and it was both a relief, yet strangely disturbing. Men out on the water at night who intended harm did not announce their presence. On the other hand, those same men had come back to her house, the boat only several hundred yards off shore. They had returned in the darkness, the moon blocked by a sky thick with clouds, no moonlight to guide them. It was as if they wanted her to know they were there and they were watching. They were waiting.

For what? What was happening to her? A week ago her phone had gone dead for seven hours and when she had called the telephone company from her friend's house, a supervisor in the service department told her he could find no malfunctions. The line was operative.

'Maybe for you, but not for me, and you're not paying the bills.'

She had returned home; the line was still dead. A second, far angrier call brought the same response. No malfunctions. Then two hours later the dial tone was inexplicably there, the phone working. She had put the episode down to less than best equipment over at the rural telephone complex. She did not know what to ascribe to the sloop now eerily bobbing in the water in front of her house.

Suddenly, in the boat's dim light, she could see a figure crawl up out of the cabin. For a moment or two it was hidden in the shadows, then there was a brief flare of intense light. A match. A cigarette. A man was standing motionless on the deck smoking a cigarette. He was facing her house, as if studying it. Waiting.

Val shivered as she dragged a heavy chair in front of the balcony door – but not too close, away from the glass. She pulled the light blanket off the bed and sat down, wrapping it around her, staring out at the water, at the boat, at the man. She knew that if the man or that boat made the slightest move toward the shore she would press the buttons she had been instructed to press in the event of an emergency. When activated, the huge circular alarm bells – both inside and outside – were ear-piercing, erupting in concert, drowning out the surf and the waves crashing on the jetty, heard thousands of feet away – the only sound on the beach, frightening, overwhelming. She wondered if she would cause them to be heard tonight – this morning.

She would not panic. Joel had taught her not to panic, even when she thought a well-placed scream was called for on the dark streets of Manhattan. Every now and then the inevitable had happened. They had been confronted by drug addicts or punks and Joel would remain calm – icily calm – moving them both back against a wall and offering a cheap, spare wallet he kept in his hip pocket with a few bills in it. *God*, he was ice! Maybe that was why no one had ever actually assaulted them, not knowing what was behind that cold, brooding look.

'I should have screamed!' she once had cried.

'No,' he had said. 'Then you would have frightened him, panicked him. That's when those bastards can be lethal.'

Was the man on the boat lethal – were the *men* on the boat deadly? Or were they simply novice sailors hugging the coastline, practising tacks, anchoring near the shore for their own protection – curious, perhaps concerned, that the property owners might object? An Army officer was not likely to be able to afford a captain for his sloop, and there were marinas only miles away north and south – marinas without available berths but with men who could handle repairs.

Was the man out on the boat smoking the cigarette merely a land-locked young officer getting his sailing legs, comfortable at a familiar anchor away from deep water? It was possible, of course – anything was possible, and summer nights held a special kind of loneliness that gave rise to strange imaginings. One walked the beach alone and thought too much.

Joel would laugh at her and say it was all those demons racing around her artist's head in search of regimen and logic. And he would undoubtedly be right. The men out on the boat were probably more up-tight than she was. In a way they were trespassers who had found a haven in sight of hostile natives; one inquiry of the Coast Guard proved it. And that clearance, as it were, was another reason why they had returned to the place where, if not welcome, at least they were not harassed. If Joel were with her she knew exactly what he would do. He would go down to the beach and shout across the water to their temporary neighbours and ask them to come in for a drink.

Dear Joel, foolish Joel, ice-cold Joel. There were times you were comforting – when you were comfortable. And amusing, so terribly amusing – even when you weren't comfortable. In some ways I miss you, darling. But not enough, thank you.

And yet why did the feeling – the instinct, perhaps – persist? The small boat out on the water was like a magnet, pulling her toward it, drawing her into its field, taking her where she knew she did not want to go.

Nonsense! Demons in search of logic! She was being foolish – *Foolish Joel, ice-cold Joel* – stop it, for God's sake! Be *reasonable!*

Then the shiver passed through her again. Novice sailors did not navigate around strange coastlines at night.

The magnet held her until her eyes grew heavy and troubled sleep came.

She woke up again, startled by the intense sunlight streaming through the glass doors, its warmth enveloping her. She looked out at the water. The boat was gone – and she wondered for a moment whether it had really been there.

Yes, it had. But it was gone.

3

The 747 lifted off the runway at Athens Helikon Airport, soaring to the left in its rapid ascent. Below in clear view, adjacent to the huge field, was the US Naval Air Station, permitted by treaty although reduced in size and in the number of aircraft during the past several years. Nevertheless, far-reaching, jet-streamed American eyes still roamed the Mediterranean, Ionian and Aegean seas, courtesy of a resentful yet nervous government all too aware of other eyes to the north. Staring out of the window, Converse recognized the shapes of familiar equipment on the ground. There were two rows of Phantom F-4T's and A-6E's on opposite sides of the dual strip, updated versions of the F-4G's and A-6A's he had flown years ago.

It was so easy to slip back, thought Joel, as he watched three Phantoms break away from the ground formation; they would head for the top of the runway, and another patrol would be in the skies. Converse could feel his hands tense, in his mind he was manipulating the thick, perforated shaft, reaching for switches, his eyes roaming the dials, looking for right and wrong signals. Then the power would come, the surging force of pressurized tons beside him, behind him, himself encased in the centre of a sleek, shining beast straining to break away and soar up into its natural habitat. *Final check, all in order; cleared for take-off. Release the power of the beast, let it free. Roll! Faster, faster; the ground is a blur, the carrier deck a mass of passing grey, blue sea beyond, blue sky above. Let it free! Let me free!*

He wondered if he could still do it, if the lessons and the training of boy and man still held. After the Navy, during the academic years in Massachusetts and North Carolina, he had frequently gone to small airfields and taken up small insignificant single-engined aircraft just to get away from the pressures, to find a few minutes of blue freedom, but there were no challenges, no taming of all-powerful beasts. Later still, it had all stopped . . . for a long, long time. There were no airfields to visit on weekends, no playing around with sleek company planes; he had given his promise. His wife had been terrified of his flying. Valerie could not reconcile the hours he had flown – civilian and in combat – with her own evaluation of the averages. And in one of the few gestures of understanding in his marriage, he had given his word not to climb onto a wing and into a cockpit. It had not bothered him until he knew – they knew – the marriage had gone sour, at which point he began driving out to a field called Peterboro in New Jersey every chance he could find and had flown whatever was available, any time, any hour, in search of the blue freedom. Still, even then – especially then – there had been no challenges, no beasts . . . other than himself.

The ground below disappeared as the 747 stabilized and began to climb to its assigned altitude. Converse turned away from the window and settled back in his seat. The lights were abruptly extinguished on the *No Smoking* sign, and Joel took out a pack of cigarettes from his shirt pocket, extracting one to his lips. He snapped his lighter, the smoke diffusing instantly in the rush of air from the vents above. He looked at his watch; it was 12.20. They were due in Orly Airport at 3.35, French time. Allowing for the zones, it was a three hour flight, and during those three hours he would commit to memory everything he could about General Jacques Louis Bertholdier – if Beale and the dead Halliday were right, the arm of Aquitaine in Paris.

At Helikon he had done something he had never done before, something that had never occurred to him, an indulgence that was generally attributed to romantic fiction or movie stars or idols of the rock mania. Fear and caution had joined with an excess of money and he had paid for two adjoining seats in First Class. He wanted no one's eyes straying to the pages he would be reading. Old Beale had made it frighteningly clear on the beach last night. If there was the remotest possibility that the materials he carried might fall into other hands – *any* other hands – he was to destroy them at all costs. For they were in-depth dossiers on men who could order multiple executions by placing a single phone call.

He reached down for his attaché case, the leather handle still dark from the sweat of his grip since Mykonos early that morning. For the first time he understood the value of a device he had seen and read about in films and novels. Airport security aside, had he been able to chain the handle of his attaché case to his wrist, he would have breathed far more comfortably.

Jacques Louis Bertholdier, age 59, only child of Alphonse and Marie Therese Bertholdier, was born at the military hospital in Dakar. Father a career officer in the French army, reputedly autocratic and a harsh disciplinarian. Little is known about the mother, significance perhaps to be found in that Bertholdier never speaks of her, as if dismissing her existence. He retired from the army four years ago at the age of 55, and is now a director of *Juneau et Cie*, a conservative firm on the *Bourse des Valeurs*, Paris's Stock Exchange.

Early years appear to be typical of a commanding officer's son, moving from post to post, accorded the privileges of the father's rank and influence. He was used to servants and fawning military personnel. If there was a difference, it was in the boy himself. It is said that he could execute the full dress manual-of-arms by the time he was five and at ten could recite by rote the entire book of regulations.

In 1938, the Bertholdiers were back in Paris, the father a member of the General Staff. They were chaotic times, as the war with Germany was imminent and the elder Bertholdier one of the few commanders aware that the Maginot could not hold. His outspokenness so infuriated his fellow officers that he was transferred to the field, commanding the 4th Army, stationed along the north-eastern border.

The war came and the father was killed in the fifth week of combat. Young Bertholdier was then 16 years old and going to school in Paris.

The fall of France in June of 1940 could be called the beginning of our subject's adulthood. Joining the Resistance first as a courier, he fought for four years, rising in the underground's ranks until he commanded the Calais-Paris sector. He made frequent undercover trips to England coordinating espionage and sabotage operations with the Free French and British Intelligence. In February of 1944, de Gaulle conferred on him the temporary rank of Major. He was 20 years of age.

Several days prior to the Allied occupation of Paris, Bertholdier was severely wounded in a street skirmish between the Resistance fighters and the retreating German troops. Hospitalization relieved him from further activity for the remainder of the European war. Following the surrender he was appointed to the national military academy at St Cyr, a compensation deemed proper by de Gaulle for the young hero of the underground. Upon graduation he was elevated to the permanent rank of captain. He was 24 and given successive commands in the Dra Hamada, French Morocco; Algiers; then across the world to the garrisons at Haiphong, and, finally, the Allied Sectors in Vienna and West Berlin. (Note this last post with respect to the following information on Field Marshal Erich Leifhelm. It's where they first met and became friends, at first openly, subsequently denying the relationship after both had resigned from military service.)

Setting Erich Leifhelm aside for the moment, Converse thought about the young legend that was Jacques Louis Bertholdier. Though Joel was as unmilitary as a man could be, in an odd way he could identify with the military phenomenon described in these pages. Although no hero, he had been accorded a hero's return from a war in which very few were so acclaimed, these generally from the ranks of those who had endured capture more than they had fought. Nevertheless, the attention – the sheer *attention* – that led to privileges was a dangerous indulgence. Although initially embarrassed, one came to accept it all . . . then expect it all. The recognition could be heady, the privileges soon taken for granted. And when the attention began to dwindle away a certain anger came into play; one wanted it all back.

These were the feelings of someone with no hunger for authority – success, yes; power, no. But what of a man whose whole being was shaped by the fabric of authority *and* power, whose earliest memories were of privilege and rank, and whose meteoric rise came at an incredibly young age? How does such a man react to recognition and the ever increasing spectrum of his own ascendancy? One did not lightly take away much from such a man; anger could turn into fury. Yet Bertholdier had walked away from it all at fifty-five, a reasonably young age for one so prominent. It was not consistent. Something was missing from the portrait of this latter-day Alexander. At least so far.

Timing played a major part in Bertholdier's expanding reputation. After posts in the Dra Hamada and pre-crisis Algiers, he was transferred to French Indochina where the situation was deteriorating rapidly for the colonial forces, then in violent guerilla warfare. His exploits in the field were instantly the talk of Saigon and Paris. The troops under his command provided several rare but much needed victories, which although incapable of altering the course of the war convinced the hard-line militarists that the inferior Asian forces could be defeated by superior Gallic courage and strategy; they needed only the materials withheld by Paris. The surrender at Dienbienphu was bitter medicine for those men who claimed that traitors in the Quai d'Orsay had brought about France's humiliation. Yet out of the defeat Colonel Bertholdier emerged as one of the few heroic figures, but he was wise enough or cautious enough to keep his own counsel, and did not, at least in appearance, join the 'hawks'. Many say that he was waiting for a signal that never came. Again he was transferred, serving tours in Vienna and West Berlin.

Four years later, however, he broke the mould he had so carefully constructed. In his own words, he was 'infuriated and disillusioned' by de Gaulle's accords with the independence-seeking Algerians; he joined General Raoul Salan's rebellious OAS, which violently opposed policies it termed betrayals. During this revolutionary interim of his life, he was implicated in an assassination attempt on de Gaulle. With Salan's capture in April of 1962, and the insurrectionists' collapse, once again Bertholdier emerged stunningly intact out of defeat. In what can only be described as an extraordinary move – and one which has never really been understood – de Gaulle had Bertholdier released from prison and brought to the Quai d'Orsay. What was said between the two men has never been revealed, but Bertholdier was returned to rank. De Gaulle's only comment of record was given during a press conference on 4 May, 1962. In reply to a question regarding the reinstated rebel officer, he said (verbatim translation): 'A great soldier-patriot must be permitted and forgiven a single misguided interlude. We have conferred. We are satisfied.' He said no more on the subject.

For seven years Bertholdier was stationed at various influential posts, rising to the rank of general, more often than not the chief military *chargé d'affaires* at major embassies during France's participation in the NATO Alliance. He was frequently recalled to the Quai d'Orsay, accompanying de Gaulle to international conferences, always visible in newspaper photographs, usually within several feet of the great man himself. Oddly enough, although his contributions appear to have been considerable, after these conferences – or summits, if you will – he was invariably sent back to his previous station while internal debates continued and decisions were reached without him. It was as though he was constantly being groomed but never permanently summoned. Was that ultimate summons the signal he had been waiting for seven years before at Dienbienphu? It is a question for which we have no answer here, but we believe it's vital to pursue it.

With de Gaulle's dramatic resignation over his demands for constitutional reform in 1969, Bertholdier's career went into an eclipse. His assignments were far from the centres of power and remained so until his resignation. Research into bank and credit card references as well as passenger manifests shows that during the past eighteen months our subject made trips to the following: London, 3; New York, 2; San Francisco, 2; Bonn, 3; Johannesburg, 1; Tel Aviv, 1 (combined with Johannesburg). The pattern is clear. It is compatible with the rising geographical pressure points of General Delavane's operation.

Converse rubbed his eyes and rang for a drink. While waiting for the Scotch he scanned the next few paragraphs, his memory of the man now jogged; they were familiar history and not terribly relevant. Bertholdier's name had been put forward by several ultra-conservative factions, hoping to pull him out of the military into the political wars, but nothing came of the attempts. The ultimate summons had passed him by; it never came. At fifty-five, he resigned from the army to become a director of a large firm on the Paris stock exchange, basically a figurehead capable of overwhelming the wealthy, and keeping the socialistically-inclined at bay by the sheer weight of his own legend.

He travels everywhere in a company limousine (read: staff car) and wherever he goes his arrival is expected, the proper welcome arranged. The vehicle is a dark blue American Lincoln Continental, Licence Plate 100-1. The restaurants he frequents are: Taillevent, The Ritz, Julien and Lucas Carton. For lunches, however, he consistently goes to a private club called *Les Étalons Blancs* three to four times a week. It is a very off-the-track establishment whose membership is restricted to the highest-ranking military, what's left of the rich nobility, and wealthy fawners who, if they can't be either, put their money on both so as to be in with the crowd.

Joel smiled; the author of the report was not without humour. Still, something was missing. His lawyer's mind looked for the lapse that was not explained. What was the signal Bertholdier had not been given at Dienbienphu? What had the imperious de Gaulle said to the rebellious officer, and what had the rebel said to the great man? Why was he consistently accommodated – but only accommodated – never summoned to power? An Alexander had been primed, forgiven, elevated, then dropped? There was a message buried in these pages, but Joel could not find it.

Converse reached what the writer of the report considered relevant only in that it completed the portrait, adding little, however, to previous information.

Bertholdier's private life appears barely pertinent to the activities that concern us. His marriage was one of convenience in the purest La Rochefoucauld sense: It was socially, professionally and financially beneficial for both parties. The marriage itself, however, appears to be solely a business arrangement. There have been no children, and although Madame Bertholdier appears frequently at her husband's side for state and social occasions, they have rarely been observed in close conversation.

Also, as with his mother, Bertholdier has never been known to discuss his wife. There might be a psychological connection here, but we find no evidence to support it. Especially since Bertholdier is a notorious womanizer, supporting at times as many as three separate mistresses as well as numerous peripheral assignations. Among his peers there is a soubriquet which has never found its way into print: Le Grand Timon, and if the reader here needs a translation, we recommend drinks on the Montparnasse.

On that compelling note the report was finished. It was a dossier that raised more questions than it answered. In broad strokes it described the *whats* and the *hows* but few of the *whys*; these were buried and only imaginative speculation could unearth even the probabilities. But there were enough concrete facts to operate on. Joel glanced at his watch; an hour had passed. He had two more to reread, think, and absorb as much as possible. He had already made up his mind who he would contact in Paris.

René Mattilon was not only an astute lawyer frequently called upon by Talbot, Brooks and Simon when they needed representation in the French courts, he was also a friend. Although he was older than Joel by a decade, the roots of their friendship were traced back to a common experience, common in the sense of global geography, futility and waste. Thirty years ago Mattilon was a young attorney in his twenties conscripted by his government and sent to French Indochina as a legal officer. He witnessed the inevitable and could never understand why it cost so much for his proud, intractable nation to perceive it. Also, he could be scathing in his comments about the subsequent American involvement.

'*Mon Dieu*! You thought you could do with arms what we could not do with arms *and* brains? *Déraisonnable*!'

It had become standard that whenever Mattilon flew to New York or Joel to Paris, they found time for dinner and drinks. Also, the Frenchman was amazingly tolerant of Converse's linguistic limitations; Joel simply could not learn another language. Even Val's patient tutoring had fallen on deaf and dead ears and an unreceptive brain. For four years his ex-wife, whose father was French and mother German, tried to instil in him the simplest phrases but found him hopeless.

'How the hell can you call yourself an international lawyer when you can't be understood beyond Sandy Hook?' she had asked.

'Hire interpreters trained by Swiss banks and put them on a point system,' he had replied. 'They won't miss a trick.'

Whenever he came to Paris, he stayed in a suite of two rooms at the opulent George V Hotel, an indulgence permitted by Talbot, Brooks and Simon he had assumed more to impress clients than to satisfy a balance sheet. The assumption was only half right, as Nathan Simon had made clear.

'You have a fancy sitting room,' Nate had told him sepulchrally. 'Use it for conferences and you can avoid those ridiculously expensive French lunches and – God forbid – the dinners.'

'Suppose they want to eat?'

'You have another appointment. Wink and say it's personal: no one in Paris will argue.'

The impressive address could serve him now, mused Converse, as the taxi maniacally weaved through the mid-afternoon traffic on the Champs-Elysées toward the Avenue George V. If he made any progress – and he intended to make progress – with men around Bertholdier or Bertholdier himself, the expensive hotel would fit the image of an unknown client who had sent his personal attorney on a very confidential search. Of course, he had no reservation, an oversight to be blamed on a substituting secretary.

He was greeted warmly by the assistant manager, albeit with surprise and, finally, apologies. No telexed request for reservations had come from Talbot, Brooks and Simon in New York, but, naturally, accommodation would be found for an old friend. They were; the standard two-room suite on the second floor, and before Joel could unpack, a steward brought a bottle of the Scotch whisky he preferred, substituting it for the existing brand on the small bar. He had forgotten the accuracy of the copious notes such hotels kept on recurrent guests. Second floor, the right whisky, and no doubt during the evening he would be reminded that he usually requested a wake up call for seven o'clock in the morning. It would be the same.

But it was close to five o'clock in the afternoon now. If he was going to reach Mattilon before the lawyer left his office for the day, he had to do so quickly. If René could have drinks with him, it would be a start. Mattilon either was his man or he was not, and the thought of losing even an hour of any kind of progress was disturbing. He reached for the Paris directory on a shelf beneath the phone on the bedside table; he looked up the firm's number and dialled.

'Good *Christ*, Joel!' exclaimed the Frenchman. 'I read about that terrible business in Geneva! It was in the morning papers and I tried to call you – Le Richemond, of course – but they said you'd checked out. Are you all right?'

'I'm fine. I was just there, that's all.'

'He was American. Did you know him?'

'Only across the table. By the way, that crap about his having something to do with narcotics was just that. Crap. He was cornered, robbed, shot and set up for post-mortem confusion.'

'And an overzealous *préfet* leapt at the obvious, trying to protect his city's image. I know; it was made clear . . . It's all so horrible. Crime, killing, terrorism; it spreads everywhere. Less so here in Paris, thank God.'

'You don't need muggers, the taxi drivers more than fill the bill. Except nastier, maybe.'

'You are, as always, *impossible*, my friend! When can we get together?'

Converse paused. 'I was hoping tonight. After you left the office.'

'It's very short notice, *mon ami*. I wish you had called before.'

'I just got in ten minutes ago.'

'But you left Geneva . . .'

'I had business in Athens,' interrupted Joel.

'Ah, yes, the money flees from the Greeks these days. Precipitously, I think. Just as it was here.'

'How about drinks, René? It's important.'

It was Mattilon's turn to pause; it was obvious he had caught the trace of urgency in Converse's brevity, in his voice. 'Of course,' said the Frenchman. 'You're at the George V, I assume?'

'Yes.'

'I'll be there as soon as I can. Say forty-five minutes.'

'Thanks very much. I'll get a couple of chairs in the gallery.'

'I'll find you.'

That area of the immense marble-arched lobby outside the tinted glass doors of the George V Bar was known informally as the 'gallery' by habitués, its name derived from the fact that there *was* an art gallery narrowly enclosed within a corridor of clear glass on the left. However, just as reasonably, the name fitted the opulent room itself. The deeply-cushioned, cut velvet chairs, settees and polished, low dark tables that lined the marble walls were beneath works of art – mammoth tapestries from long-forgotten châteaux and huge, heroic canvases by artists, both old and new. And the smooth, quarried stone of the floor was covered by giant Oriental rugs, while affixed to the high ceiling was a series of intricate chandeliers, throwing soft light through filigrees of lacelike gold.

Quiet conversations took place between men and women of wealth and power at these upholstered enclaves, in calculated shadows under spotlit paintings and woven cloth from centuries ago. Frequently they were opening dialogues, testing questions that as often as not were finalized in boardrooms, peopled by chairmen and presidents, treasurers, and prides of lawyers. The movers and the shakers felt comfortable with the initial informality – the uncommitted explorations – of first meetings in this very formal room. The ceremonial environs somehow lent an air of ritualized disbelief; denials were not hard to come by later. The 'gallery' also lived up to its caveat: within the fraternity of those who had achieved success on the international scene, it was said that if such a person spent any length of time in these elegant surroundings sooner or later he would invariably run into almost everyone he knew. Therefore, if one did not care to be seen, one should go somewhere else.

The room was filling up, waiters from the discreetly raucous bar roving outside and taking orders, knowing where the real money was. Converse found two chairs at the far end, the dim light more pronounced. He looked at his watch, barely able to read it – seen and not seen; he had settled for the middle ground. Forty minutes had passed since his call to René, a shower taking up the time and the sweat-stained dirt of his all-day journey from Mykonos. Placing his cigarettes and lighter on the table, he ordered a drink from an alert waiter, his eyes on the marble entrance to the room.

Twelve minutes later he saw him. Mattilon walked energetically out of the harsh glare of the street lobby into the soft light of the gallery. He stopped for a moment, squinting, then nodded. He started down the centre of the carpeted floor, his eyes levelled at Joel from a distance, a broad, genuine smile on his face. René Mattilon was in his mid to late fifties, but his stride, like his outlook, was that of a younger man. There was about him that aura peculiar to successful trial lawyers; his confidence was apparent because it was the essence of his success, yet it was born of diligence, not merely ego and performance. He was the secure actor comfortable in his role, his greying hair and blunt, masculine features all part of his considered appearance. Beyond that appearance, however, there was also something else, thought Joel, as he rose from his chair. René was a thoroughly decent man; it was a disarming conclusion. God knew they both had their flaws, but they were both decent men; perhaps that was why they enjoyed each other's company.

A firm handshake preceded a brief embrace. The Frenchman sat down across from Converse, as Joel signalled an attentive waiter. 'Order in French,' he said. 'I'd end up getting you a hot fudge sundae.'

'This man speaks better English than either of us. Campari and ice, please.'

'*Merci, Monsieur.*' The waiter left.

'Thanks again for coming over,' said Converse. 'I mean it.'

'I'm sure you do . . . You look well, Joel, tired but well. That shocking business in Geneva must give you nightmares.'

'Not really, I told you, I was simply there.'

'Still, it might have been *you*. The newspapers said he died while you held his head.'

'I was the first one to reach him.'

'How horrible.'

'I've seen it happen before, René,' said Converse quietly, no comment in his voice.

'Yes, of course. You were better prepared than most, I imagine.'

'I don't think anyone's ever prepared . . . But it's over. How about you? How are things?'

Mattilon shook his head, pinching his rugged, weather-beaten features into a sudden look of exasperation. 'France is madness of course, but we survive. For months and months now, there are more plans than are stored in an architect's library, but the planners keep colliding with each other in government hallways. The courts are full, business thrives.'

'I'm glad to hear it.' The waiter returned with the Campari; both men nodded silently. Mattilon's eyes on Joel. 'No, I really am,' Converse continued, as the waiter walked away. 'You hear so many stories.'

'Is that why you're in Paris?' The Frenchman studied Joel. 'Because of the stories of our so-called upheavals? They're not so earth-shaking, you know, not so different from before. Not *yet*. Most private industry here was publicly financed through the government. But naturally not managed by government incompetents, and for that we may pay. Is that what's bothering you or, more to the point, your clients?'

Converse drank. 'No, that's not why I'm here. It's something else.'

'You're troubled, I can see that. Your customary glibness doesn't fool me. I know you too well. So tell me, what's so important? That was the word you used on the telephone.'

'Yes, I guess it was. It may have been too strong.' Joel drained his glass and reached for his cigarettes.

'Not from your eyes, my friend. I see them and I don't see them. They're filled with clouds.'

'You've got it wrong. As you said, I'm tired. I've been on planes all day, with some ungodly layovers.' He picked up his lighter, snapping it twice until the flame appeared.

'We haggle over foolishness. What is it?'

Converse lit a cigarette, consciously trying to sound casual as he spoke. 'Do you know a private club called *Les Étalons Blancs*?'

'I know it, but I couldn't get in the door,' replied the Frenchman laughing. 'I was a young, inconsequential lieutenant – worse, attached to the *juge-avocat* – essentially with our forces to lend an appearance of legality, but mind you only an appearance. Murder was a misdemeanour, and rape to be congratulated. *Les Étalons Blancs* is a refuge for *les grands militaires* . . . and those rich enough or foolish enough to listen to their trumpets.'

'I want to meet someone who lunches there three or four times a week.'

'You can't call him?'

'He doesn't know me, doesn't know I want to meet him. It's got to be spontaneous.'

'Really? For Talbot, Brooks and Simon? That sounds most unusual.'

'It is. We may be dealing with someone we don't want to deal with.'

'Ahh, missionary work. Who is he?'

'Will you keep it confidential? I mean that, not a word to anyone?'

'Do I breathe? If the name is in conflict with something on our schedule, I will tell you and, frankly, be of no help to you.'

'Fair enough. Jacques Louis Bertholdier.'

Mattilon arched his brows in mock astonishment, less in mockery than astonishment. 'The emperor has all his clothes,' said the Frenchman, laughing quietly. 'Regardless of who claims otherwise. You start at the top of the line, as they say in New York. No conflict, *mon ami*; he's not in our league – as you also say.'

'Why not?'

'He moves with saints and warriors. Warriors who would be saints, and saints who would be warriors. Who has time for such façades?'

'You mean he's not taken seriously?'

'Oh no, he *is*. Very seriously, by those who have the time and the inclination to move abstract mountains. He is a pillar, Joel, grounded in heroic marble and himself immovable. He was the de Gaulle who never followed and some say it is a pity.'

'What do you say?'

Mattilon frowned, then cocked his head in a Gallic shrug. 'I'm not sure. God knows the country needed someone, and perhaps Bertholdier could have stepped in and steered a far better course than the one we embarked upon, but the times were not right. The Elysée had become an imperial court, and the people were tired of royal edicts, imperial sermons. Well, we don't have *those* any longer; they've been supplanted by the dull, grey banalities of the workers' credo. Perhaps it *is* a pity, although he could still do it, I imagine. He began his climb up Olympus when he was very young.'

'Wasn't he part of the OAS? Salan's rebels in Algeria? They were discredited, called a national disgrace.'

'*That* is a judgment even the intellectuals must reluctantly admit could be subject to revision. The way all of North Africa and the Middle East has gone, a French Algeria could be a trump card today.' Mattilon paused and brought his hand to his chin, his frown returning. 'Why on earth would Talbot, Brooks and Simon walk away from Bertholdier? He may be a monarchist at heart, but God knows he's honour personified. He's regal, perhaps even pompous, but a very acceptable client for all of that.'

'We've heard things,' said Converse quietly, shrugging now himself, as if to lessen the credibility of hearsay evidence.

'*Mon Dieu*, not his *women*?' exclaimed Mattilon laughing. 'Come now, when will you grow up?'

'Not women.'

'What then?'

'Let's say some of his associates, his acquaintances.'

'I hope you make the distinction, Joel. A man like Bertholdier can choose his associates certainly, but not his acquaintances. He walks into a room and everyone wants to be his friend, most claim he *is* a friend.'

'That's what we want to find out. I want to bring up some names, see whether they *are* associates . . . or unremembered acquaintances.'

'*Bien*. Now you're making sense. I can help; I *will* help. We shall have lunch at *Les Étalons Blancs* tomorrow and the next day. It is the middle of the week and Bertholdier will no doubt choose one or the other to dine there. If not, there's always the day after.'

'I thought you couldn't get in the door?'

'Not by myself, no. But I know someone who can, and he will be most obliging, I can assure you.'

'Why?'

'He wishes to talk with me whenever and wherever he can. He's a dreadful bore and unfortunately speaks very little English – numbers mainly, and words like "In and Out", or "Over and Out", and "Dodger-Roger" or "Rodger-Dodger" and 'Runway Six" or "Lift-off-Five" and all manner of incomprehensible phrases.'

'A *pilot*?'

'He flew the first *Mirages*, brilliantly I might add, and never lets anyone forget it. I shall have to be the interpreter between you, which at least eliminates my having to initiate conversation. Do you know anything about the *Mirage*?'

'A jet's a jet,' said Joel. 'Pull and sweep out, what else is there?'

'Yes, he's used that one, too. Pull and sweep something. I thought he was cleaning a kitchen.'

'Why does he always want to talk with you? I gather he's a member of the club.'

'Very much so. We're representing him in a futile case against an aircraft manufacturer. He had his own private jet, and lost his left foot in one of your crash landings . . .'

'Not mine, pal.'

'The door was jammed. He couldn't ground-eject where he wished to, when the plane's speed was sufficiently reduced for him to avoid a final collision.'

'He didn't slap the right buttons.'

'He says he did.'

'There are at least two back-ups, including an instant manual, even on your equipment.'

'We've been made aware of that. It's not the money, you understand; he's enormously wealthy. It's his pride. To lose brings into question his current – or if you will, latter day – skills.'

'They'll be a lot more in question under cross examination. I assume you've told him that.'

'Very gently. It's what we're leading up to.'

'But in the meantime every conference is a hefty fee.'

'We're also saving him from himself. If we did it swiftly or too crudely, he'd simply dismiss us and be driven to someone far less principled. Who else would take such a case? The government owns the plant now, and God knows it won't pay.'

'Good point. What'll you tell him about me? About the club?'

Mattilon smiled. 'That as a former pilot *and* an attorney you can bring an expertise to his suit that might be helpful. As to *Les Étalons Blancs*, I shall suggest it, tell him you'd be impressed. I shall describe you as something of an Attila the Hun of the skies. How does that appeal to you?'

'With very little impact.'

'Can you carry it off?' asked the Frenchman. The question was sincere. 'It would be one way to meet Bertholdier. My client and he are not simply acquaintances, they *are* friends.'

'I'll carry it off.'

'Your having been a prisoner of war will be most helpful. If you see Bertholdier enter, and express a desire to meet him, such requests are not lightly refused former POWs.'

'I wouldn't press that too hard,' said Converse.

'Why not?'

'A little digging could turn up a rock that doesn't belong in the soil.'

'Oh?' Mattilon's brows arched again, neither in mockery nor astonishment, simply surprise. '"Digging", as you use it, implies something more than a spontaneous meeting with odd names spontaneously thrown about.'

'Does it?' Joel revolved his glass, annoyed with himself, knowing that any argument would only enlarge the lapse. 'Sorry, it was an instinctive reaction. You know how I feel about that topic.'

'Yes, I do, and I forgot. How careless of me. I apologize.'

'Actually, I'd just as soon not use my own name. Do you mind?'

'You're the missionary, not I. What shall we call you?' The Frenchman was now looking hard at Converse.

'It doesn't matter.'

Mattilon squinted. 'How about the name of your employer, Simon? If you meet Bertholdier, it might appeal to him. *Le duc de St Simon* was the purest chronicler of the monarchy . . . Henry Simon. There must be ten thousand lawyers named Henry Simon in the States.'

'Simon it is.'

'You've told me everything, my friend?' asked René, his eyes non-committal. 'Everything you care to.'

'Yes, I have,' said Joel, his own eyes a blue-white wall. 'Let's have another drink.'

'I think not. It's late and my current wife has *malaise* if her dinner is cold. She's an excellent cook, incidentally.'

'You're a lucky man.'

'Yes, I am.' Mattilon finished his drink, placed the glass on the table and spoke casually. 'So was Valerie. I shall never forget that fantastic duck *à l'orange* she fixed for us three or four years ago in New York. Do you ever hear from her?'

'Hear and see,' answered Converse. 'I had lunch with her in Boston last month. I gave her the alimony cheque and she picked up the tab. By the way, her paintings are beginning to sell.'

'I never doubted that they would.'

'She did.'

'Unnecessarily . . . I always liked Val. If you see her again, please give her my affectionate best.'

'I will.'

Mattilon rose from the upholstered chair, his eyes no longer non-committal. 'Forgive me, I thought so often you were such a . . . matched pair, I believe is the expression. The passions dwindle, of course, but not the *de suite*, if you know what I mean.'

'I think I do, and speaking for both of us, I thank you . . . for the misplaced concretion.'

'*Je ne comprends pas.*'

'Forget it, it's antiquated – doesn't mean anything. I'll give her your affectionate best.'

'*Merci.* I'll phone you in the morning.'

Les Étalons Blancs was a pacifist's nightmare. The club's heavy dark wood walls were covered with photographs and prints, interspersed with framed citations and glistening medals – red ribbons and gold and silver discs cushioned on black velvet, throwing back the light, drawing all eyes, which then strayed to the pictures. They were a visual record of heroic carnage going back two centuries. The linear drawings evolved into products of film, as the horses and caissons and sabres became motorcycles, tanks, planes and guns, but the scenes were not all that different, the themes constant. Victorious men in uniform were depicted in moments of glory; whatever suffering there might have been was strangely absent, only stern purpose and awareness shining in their eyes and apparent in their postures. These men did not lose, no missing limbs or shattered faces here; these were the privileged warriors, somehow unscathed yet scathing, genuine arrogance found in their life-long missions. And Joel felt a profound fear as he studied the martial array. These were not ordinary men, nor did they care to be; they scorned the ordinary as unthinkable for them, perhaps only to be commanded by them. They were hard and strong and the word 'capability' was written across their countless faces. What had Beale said on Mykonos? What had been the judgment of the Red Fox of Inchon, a man who knew whereof he spoke?

. . . *I know what they can do when we ask them to do it.* Yet how much more could they do if they asked it of themselves, wondered Joel. Without the searching, vacillating impediments of civilian authorities?

'Luboque has just arrived,' said Mattilon quietly, coming up behind Converse. 'I heard his voice in the lobby. Remember, you don't have to overdo it – I'll translate what I think is appropriate anyway – but nod profoundly when he makes one of his angry remarks. Also laugh when he tells jokes; they're dreadful, but he likes it.'

'I'll do my best.'

'I'll give you an incentive. Bertholdier has a reservation for lunch. At his usual place, table eleven, by the window.'

'Where are *we*?' asked Joel, seeing the pressed lips of minor triumph on the Frenchman's face.

'Table twelve. Now.'

'If I ever need a lawyer, I'll call you.'

'We're terribly expensive. Come now, as they say in all those wonderful films of yours. "You're on, Monsieur Simon." Play the role of Attila but don't overplay it.'

'You know, René, for someone who speaks English as well as you do, you gravitate to the tritest phrases.'

'The English language and American phrases have very little in common, Joel, trite or otherwise.'

'Smart ass.'

'Need I say more? . . . *Ahh*, Monsieur Luboque, Serge, *mon ami*!'

Mattilon's third eye had spotted the entrance of Serge Luboque; he pivoted in place as the thumping became louder on the floor – lending also a certain credibility to the lawyer's hearing. Luboque was a short, slender man, his physique giving rise to the images of those early jet pilots when compactness was a requirement. He was also very close to being a caricature of himself. His short, waxed moustache was affixed to a miniaturized face that was pinched in vaguely hostile dismissal. It was directed both at no one and everyone. The effect was important, not the content. Whatever he had been before, Luboque was now a *poseur* who knew his postures; it was all he had to know. A brilliant and exciting past had disappeared for him; he had only the memories, the rest was anger.

'*Et voici l'expert légal des compagnies aériennes*,' he said, looking at Converse, extending his hand for Joel's grasp.

'Serge is delighted to meet you and is sure you can help us,' explained Mattilon.

'I'll do what I can,' said Converse. 'And apologize for my not speaking French.'

The lawyer obviously did so, as Luboque shrugged, speaking rapidly, incomprehensibly; the word *anglais* repeated several times.

'He, too, apologizes for not speaking English,' said Mattilon glancing at Joel, mischievousness in his look, as he added, 'If he's lying, Monsieur Simon, we may both be placed against these decorated walls and shot?'

'No way,' said Converse, smiling. 'Our executioners might dent the medals and blow up the pictures. Everybody knows you're lousy shots.'

'*Qu'est-ce que vous dites?*'

'*Monsieur Simon tient à vous remercier de ce déjeuner*,' said Mattilon, turning to his client. '*Il en est très fier car il estime que l'officier français est le meilleur du monde*.'

'What did you say?'

'I explained,' said the lawyer, turning again, 'that you were honoured to be here as you believe the French military – especially the officer corps – to be the finest on earth.'

'Not only lousy shots but rotten pilots,' said Joel, smiling and nodding profoundly.

'*Est-il vrai que vous avez pris part à de nombreuses missions dans l'Asie du Sud?*' asked Luboque, his eyes fixed on Converse.

'I beg your pardon?'

'He wants it confirmed that you are really an Attila of the skies, that you flew many missions.'

'Quite a few,' answered Joel.

'*Beaucoup,*' said Mattilon.

Luboque again spoke rapidly, even more incomprehensibly, as he snapped his fingers for a steward.

'What now?'

'He'd rather tell you about *his* exploits – in the interests of the case, of course.'

'Of course,' said Converse, his smile now fixed. 'Lousy shots, rotten pilots and insufferable egos.'

'Ah, but our food, our women, our incomparable understanding of life.'

'There's a very explicit word in French – one of the few I learned from my ex-wife – but I don't think I should use it.' Joel's smile was now cemented to his lips.

'That's right, I forgot,' said Mattilon. 'She and I would converse in *la belle langue*; it used to irritate you so . . . Don't use it. Remember your incentive.'

'*Qu'est-ce que vous dites encore? La belle langue?*' Luboque spoke as a steward stood by his side.

'*Notre ami, Monsieur Simon, suivra un cours à l'école Berlitz et pourra ainsi s'entretenir directement avec vous.*'

'*Bien!*'

'What?'

'I told him you would learn the Berlitz French so you could dine with him whenever you flew into Paris. You're to ring him up. Nod . . . smart ass.'

Converse nodded.

And so it went. Point, non-counter point, *non sequitur*. Serge Luboque held forth during drinks in the warrior's playroom, Mattilon translating, in each case advising Joel as to the expression that should appear on his face as well as suggesting an appropriate reply, which he would deliver at any event.

Finally Luboque stridently described the crash which had cost him his left foot and the obvious equipment failures for which he should be compensated. Converse looked properly pained and indignant, and offered to write a legal opinion for the court, based on his expertise as a pilot of jet aircraft. Mattilon translated; Luboque beamed and rattled off a barrage of consonated vowels that Joel took for thanks.

'He's forever in your debt,' said René.

'Not if I write that opinion,' replied Converse. 'He locked himself in the cockpit and threw away the key.'

'Write it,' countered Mattilon, smiling. 'You've just paid for my time. We'll use it as a wedge to open the door of retreat. Also, he'll never ask you to dinner when you're in Paris.'

'When's lunch? I'm running out of expressions.'

It came, or more precisely, they marched in hesitant lock-step into it, matching Luboque's thumping foot against the hard, ornate parquet floor. The ridiculous, three-sided conversation continued as wine was proffered – a bottle sent back by the sneering *poseur* – and Converse's eyes kept straying to the dining room's entrance.

The moment came. Bertholdier arrived. He stood in the open archway, his head turned slightly to his left as another man in a light brown gabardine topcoat spoke without expression. The general nodded his head and the subordinate retreated. Then the soldier walked in with a quiet vitality, with a grandiosity born of his own self-understood impact, no flourishes required. Heads turned and they were acknowledged, the man's eyes piercing into each, accepting each as a great dauphin, who will soon be king, accepts the attention of the ministers of a failing monarch. The effect was extraordinary, for there were no kingdoms, no monarchies, no lands to be divided through conquest to the knights of Crécy or anybody else, but this *man* was quietly being accorded the arrival of . . . *goddamn it*, thought Joel . . . an *emperor* of his own.

Jacques Louis Bertholdier was of medium height, between 5' 9" and 5' 11", certainly no more, but his bearing – the sheer straight shaft of his posture, the breadth of his shoulders and the length of his strong neck made him appear much taller, much more imposing than another might to a less anticipatory group. He was among his own, and here, indeed, he was above the others, elevated by their own consensus.

'Say something reverential,' said Mattilon, as Bertholdier approached, heading for the table next to theirs. 'Glance up at him and look suitably awed. I'll do the rest.'

Converse did as he was told, uttering Bertholdier's full name under his breath, but loud enough to be heard. He followed this quiet exclamation by leaning toward Mattilon and saying, 'He's a man I've always wanted to meet.'

There followed a brief exchange in French between René and his client, whereupon Luboque nodded, his expression that of an arrogant man pleased to dispense a favour to a new friend.

Bertholdier reached his chair, the *maître* and his head waiter hovering on either side. The pavane took place less than four feet away.

'*Mon Général*,' said Luboque, rising.

'*Serge*,' replied Bertholdier, stepping forward, hand extended, a superior officer aware of a worthy subordinate's disability. '*Comment ça va?*'

'*Bien, Jacques. Et vous?*'

The greetings were brief, the direction of the conversation changed quickly by Luboque, who gestured at Converse, as he continued speaking. Instinctively, Joel got to his feet, posture straight, his eyes level, unblinking, staring at Bertholdier, his look as piercing as the general's, professional but without awe . . . He had been right – in an unexpected way. The South-east Asian connection had validity for Jacques Louis Bertholdier. And why not? He, too, had his memories. Mattilon was introduced almost as an afterthought, the soldier nodding, as he crossed behind René to shake hands with Joel.

'A pleasure, Monsieur Simon,' said Bertholdier, his English precise, his grip firm, a comrade acknowledging another comrade, the man's imperious charm instantly apparent.

'I'm sure you've heard it thousands of times, sir,' said Joel, maintaining the steady, professional burn in his eyes, 'but this is an occasion I never expected. If I may, General, it's an honour to meet you.'

'It is an honour to meet *you*,' rejoined Bertholdier. 'You gentlemen-of-the-air did all you could, and I know something about the circumstances. So many missions! I think it was easier on the ground!' The general laughed quietly, the celebrated now acknowledging a worthy *un*celebrated comrade-in-arms.

Gentlemen-of-the-air; the man's unreal, thought Converse. But the connection was firm; *it* was real, he felt it, he *knew* it. The combination of words and looks had brought it about. So simple; a lawyer's ruse, taming an adversary – in this case an enemy. The enemy.

'I couldn't agree with that, General; it was a lot cleaner in the air. But if there'd been more like you on the ground in Indochina, there never would have been a Dienbienphu.'

'A flattering statement, but I'm not sure it could stand the test of reality.'

'I'm sure,' said Joel, quietly, clearly. 'I'm convinced of it.'

Luboque, who had been engaged in conversation by a knowing Mattilon, interrupted. '*Mon Général, voulez vous vous joindre à nous?*'

'*Je m'excuse. Je suis occupé . . . mes invités,*' answered Bertholdier, turning back to Converse. 'I must decline Serge's invitation, I'm expecting guests. He tells me you are an attorney, a specialist in aircraft litigation.'

'It's part of the broader field, yes. Air, ground, ocean-going craft . . . we try to represent the spectrum. Actually, I'm fairly new at it – not the expertise, I hope – but the representation.'

'I see,' said the general, obviously bewildered. 'Are you in Paris on business?'

This was it, thought Joel. The words, the eyes, and the voice had to join in subtle evocation. Especially the eyes; they had to convey the unspoken. 'No, I'm just here to catch my breath. I flew from San Francisco to New York and on to Paris. Tomorrow I'll be in Bonn for a day or so, then off to Tel Aviv.'

'How tiring for you.' Bertholdier was now returning his stare.

'Not the worst, I'm afraid,' said Converse, a half-smile on his lips. 'After Tel Aviv, there's a night flight to Johannesburg.'

'Bonn, Tel Aviv, Johannesburg . . .' The soldier spoke softly, his eyes much louder. 'A most unusual itinerary.'

'Productive, we think. At least, we hope so.'

'We?'

'My client, General. My new client.'

'*Déraisonnable!*' cried Mattilon, laughing at something Luboque had said, and, just as obviously, telling Joel he could no longer keep his impatient litigant in conversation.

Bertholdier, however, did not take his eyes off Converse. 'Where are you staying, my young fighter-pilot friend?'

'Young and not so young, General.'

'Where?'

'The George V. Suite two-three-five.'

'A fine establishment.'

'It's habit. My previous firm always posted me there.'

'Posted? As in garrisoned?' asked Bertholdier, a half smile now on his lips.

'An unconscious slip,' said Joel. 'But then again, it says it, doesn't it, sir?'

'It does, indeed . . . Ah ha, my guests arrive!' The soldier extended his hand. 'It's been a pleasure, Monsieur Simon.'

Swift *au revoirs* accompanied nods and rapid handshakes, as Bertholdier returned to his table to greet his luncheon companions. Through Mattilon, Joel thanked Luboque for the introduction; the disabled pilot gestured with both hands, palms in the giving position, and Converse had the distinct feeling that he had been baptized. The insane, three-sided dialogue then resumed at high speed, and it was all Joel could do to maintain even minimum concentration.

Progress had been made; it was in Bertholdier's eyes, and he could feel those eyes straying over to him through the animated conversation taking place at both tables. The General was diagonally to Converse's left; the slightest turning of either face and the line of sight between them was direct. Twice it happened. The first time, Joel felt the forceful gaze resting on him as if two shafts of magnified sunlight were burning the flesh at his temple. He shifted his head barely inches; their eyes locked, the soldier's penetrating, questioning, severe. The second occasion took place a half hour later, this exchange prompted by Converse himself. Luboque and Mattilon were discussing legal strategy and, as if drawn by a magnet, Joel slowly turned to his left and watched Bertholdier, who was quietly, emphatically making a point with one of his guests. Suddenly, as a voice replied across the adjacent table, the General snapped his head in Converse's direction, his eyes no longer questioning, only cold and ice-like. Then just as abruptly, there was warmth in them; the celebrated soldier nodded, a half-smile on his face.

Joel sat in the soft leather chair by the window in the dimly-lit sitting room; what light there was came from a fringed lamp on the desk. Alternately, he stared at the telephone in front of the lamp, and then turned and looked out of the window at the weaving night traffic of Paris, and the lights on the wide boulevard below – but not for very long. He kept returning to the phone, his focus isolating it, framing it, giving it a substance he so frequently gave telephones when waiting for a call from a legal adversary he expected to capitulate, knowing that man or woman *would* capitulate. It was simply a question of time.

He expected no capitulation now, only communication, a connection, *the* connection. What form it would take, he had no idea, but it would come. It had to come.

It was nearly 7.30, four hours since he had left *Les Étalons Blancs*, and a final, firm handshake exchanged with Jacques Louis Bertholdier. The look in the soldier's eyes was unmistakable: If nothing else, Converse reasoned, Bertholdier would have to satisfy his sheer curiosity.

Joel had covered himself with the hotel's front desk, distributing several well-placed 100-franc notes. The device was not at all unusual in these days of national and financial unrest – had not been for years, actually, unrest notwithstanding. Visiting businessmen frequently chose to use *noms de commerce* for any number of reasons, ranging from negotiations best kept quiet to amorous engagements best left untraceable. In Converse's case, the use of the name, Simon, made it appear logical, if not eminently respectable. If Talbot, Brooks and Simon preferred that all communications be made in the surname of one of the senior partners, who could question the decision? Joel, however, carried the ploy one step farther. After telephoning New York, he explained, he was told that his own name was not to be used at all: no one knew he was in Paris and that was the way his firm wanted it. Obviously, the delayed instructions accounted for the mix up in the reservation, which was void at any rate. There was to be no billing; he would pay in cash, and since this was Paris, no one raised the slightest objection. Cash was infinitely preferable, delayed payment a national anathema.

Whether anyone believed this nonsense or not was irrelevant. The logic was sufficiently adequate and the franc notes persuasive; the original registration card was torn up and another placed in the hotel file. H. Simon replaced J. Converse. The permanent address of the former was a figment of Joel's imagination, a numbered house on a numbered street in Chicago, Illinois, said house and said street most likely non-existent. Anyone asking or calling for Mr Converse – which was highly unlikely – would be told no guest of that name was currently at the George V. Even René Mattilon was not a problem for Joel had been specific. Since he had no further business in Paris, he was taking the 6 o'clock shuttle to London and staying with friends for several days before flying back to New York. He thanked René profusely, telling the Frenchman that his firm's fears about Bertholdier had been groundless. During their quiet conversation he had brought up three key names with the general, each greeted with a blank look from Bertholdier, who proceeded to apologize if his memory was faulty.

'He wasn't lying,' Joel had said.

'I can't imagine why he would,' Mattilon had replied.

I can, Converse had thought to himself. They call it *Aquitaine*.

A crack! There was a sudden intrusion of sound, a harsh metallic snap then another, and another . . . the tumblers of a lock falling out of place, a knob being turned. It came from beyond the open door to the bedroom. Joel bolted forward in his chair; then, looking at his watch, just as rapidly he expelled his breath and relaxed. It was the hour when the floor maid turned down the bed; the tension of the expected call and what it represented had frayed his nerves. Again he leaned back, his gaze resting on the telephone. When would it ring? *Would* it ring? The minutes were passing so slowly, the hours too quickly.

'*Pardon, Monsieur*,' said a feminine voice, accompanied by a light tapping on the open door frame. Joel could not see the speaker.

'Yes?' Converse forced his eyes away from the silent phone.

What greeted him, however, was not the appearance of a uniformed maid, but instead a sight that caused him to silently gasp. It was the figure of Jacques Louis Bertholdier, his posture erect, his angled head rigid, his eyes a strange mixture of cold appraisal, condescension, and – if Joel was not mistaken – a trace of fear. He walked through the door and stood motionless; when he spoke his voice was a rippling sheet of ice.

'I was on my way to a dinner engagement on the fourth floor, Monsieur Simon. By chance, I remembered you were in this very hotel. You did give me the number of your suite. Do I intrude?'

'Of course not, General,' said Converse, on his feet.

'Did you expect me?'

'Not this way.'

'But you did expect me?'

Joel paused. 'Yes.'

'A signal sent and received?'

Again Joel paused. 'Yes.'

'You are either a provocatively subtle attorney or a strangely obsessed man. Which is it, Monsieur Simon?'

'If I provoked you into coming to see me and I was subtle about it, I'll accept that gladly. As to being obsessed, the word implies an exaggerated or unwarranted concern. Whatever concerns I have, I know damned well they're neither exaggerated nor unwarranted. No obsession, General. I'm too good a lawyer for that.'

'A pilot cannot lie to himself. If he does so blindly, he crashes to his death.'

'I've been shot down. I've never crashed through pilot error.'

Bertholdier walked slowly to the brocaded couch against the wall. 'Bonn, Tel Aviv and Johannesburg,' he said quietly as he lowered himself, sitting down and crossing his legs. 'The signal?'

'The signal.'

'My company has interests in those areas.'

'So does my client,' said Converse.

'And what do *you* have, Monsieur Simon?'

Joel stared at the soldier. 'A commitment, General.'

Bertholdier was silent, his body immobile, his eyes searching. 'May I have a brandy?' he said finally. 'My escort will remain in the corridor outside this door.'

4

Converse walked to the small bar against the wall, conscious of the soldier's gaze, wondering which tack the conversation would take. He was oddly calm, the way he frequently was before a merger conference, or a pre-trial examination, knowing he knew things his adversaries were not aware of – buried information that had surfaced through long hours of hard work. In the present circumstances, there had been no work at all on his part, but the results were the same. He knew a great deal about the legend across the room named Jacques Louis Bertholdier. In a word, Joel was prepared, and over the years he had learned to trust his on-the-feet instincts . . . as he had once trusted those that had guided him through the skies years ago.

Also, as it was part of his job, he was familiar with the legal intricacies of import-export manipulations. They were a maze of often disconnected authorizations, easily made baffling for the untrained ear, and during the next few minutes he intended to baffle this disciple of George Marcus Delavane – warlord of Saigon – until the soldier's trace of fear became something far more pronounced.

Clearances for foreign shipments came in a wide variety of shapes and colours, from the basic export licence with specific bills of lading, to those with the less specific generic limitations. Then up – or out – to the more coveted licences entailing a wide variety of products subject to governmental reviews and usually shunted back and forth between vacillating departments until deadlines forced bureaucratic decisions – often based on whose influence was the strongest, or whom among the bureaucrats were the weakest.

Finally, there was the most lethal authorization of all, a document too frequently received in corruption and delivered in blood. It was called the *End-User's Certificate*, an innocuously-named permit that was a licence to ship the most abusive merchandise in the nation's arsenals into air and sea lanes beyond the controls of those who should have them.

In theory, this deadly equipment was intended solely for allied governments with shared objectives, thus the 'use' at the discretion of the parties at the receiving 'end' – calculated death legitimized by a 'certificate' that obfuscated everyone's intentions. But once *en route*, diversion was the practice. Shipments destined for the Bay of Haifa or Alexandria would find their way to the Gulf of Sidra and a precocious madman in Libya, or to an assassin named Carlos training killer teams anywhere from Beirut to the Sahara. Fictional corporations with non-existent – yet strangely influential – officers operated through obscure brokers in shadows and out of hastily-constructed or out-of-the-way warehouses in the US and abroad. Millions upon millions were to be made; death was merely a consequence and there was a phrase for it all. Boardroom terrorism. It fitted, and it would be the way of Aquitaine. There was no other.

These were the thoughts, the methods of operation that rapidly, like flashes of cards, leaped through Converse's mind as he poured the drinks. He was ready; he turned and walked across the room.

'What are you seeking, Monsieur Simon?' asked Bertholdier, taking the brandy from Converse.

'Information, General.'

'About what?'

'World markets – expanding markets that my client might service.' Joel crossed back to the chair by the window and sat down.

'And what sort of service does he render?'

'He's a broker.'

'Of what?'

'A wide range of products.' Converse brought his glass to his lips; he drank, then added, 'I think I mentioned them in general terms at your club this afternoon. Planes, vehicles, ocean-going craft, munitions material. The spectrum.'

'Yes, you did. I'm afraid I did not understand.'

'My client has access to production and warehouse sources beyond anyone I've ever known or ever heard of.'

'Very impressive. Who is he?'

'I'm not at liberty to say.'

'Perhaps I know him.'

'You might, but not in the way I've described him. His profile is so low in this area, it's non-existent.'

'And you won't tell me who he is,' said Bertholdier.

'It's privileged information.'

'Yet in your own words, you sought me out, sent a signal to which I responded, and now say you want information concerning expanding markets for all manner of merchandise, including Bonn, Tel Aviv, and Johannesburg. But you won't divulge the name of your client who will benefit if I have this information – which I probably do not. Surely you can't be serious.'

'You *have* the information, and yes, I'm very serious. But I'm afraid you've jumped to the wrong conclusion.'

'I have no fear of it at all. My English is fluent and I heard what you said. You came out of nowhere, I know nothing about you; you speak elusively of this unnamed influential man . . .'

'You *asked* me, General,' interrupted Joel firmly, without raising his voice, 'what I was seeking.'

'And you said information.'

'Yes, I did, but I didn't say I was seeking it from you.'

'I beg your pardon?'

'Under the circumstances – for the reasons you just mentioned – you wouldn't give it to me anyway, and I'm well aware of that.'

'Then what is the point of this . . . shall I say induced conversation? I do not like my time trifled with, Monsieur.'

'That's the last thing on earth we'd do – *I'd* do.'

'Please be specific.'

'My client wants your trust. *I* want it. But we know it can't be given until you feel it's justified. In a few days – a week at the outside – I hope to prove that it is.'

'By trips to Bonn, Tel Aviv . . . Johannesburg?'

'Frankly, yes.'

'Why?'

'You said a few minutes ago. The signal.'

Bertholdier was suddenly wary. He shrugged too casually; he was pulling back. 'I said it because my company has considerable investments in those areas. I thought it was entirely plausible you had a proposition, or propositions, to make relative to those interests.'

'I intend to have.'

'Please be specific,' said the soldier, controlling his irritation.

'You know I can't,' replied Joel. 'Not yet.'

'When?'

'When it's clear to you – all of you – that my client, and by extension myself, have strong motives for being a part of you as the most dedicated among you.'

'A part of my company? *Juneau et Cie*?'

'Forgive me, General, I won't bother to answer that.'

Bertholdier glanced at the brandy in his hand, then back at Converse. 'You say you flew from San Francisco.'

'I'm not based there,' broke in Joel.

'But you came from San Francisco. To Paris. Why *were* you there?'

'I'll answer that if for no other reason than to show you how thorough we are . . . and how much more thorough others are. We traced – *I* traced – overseas shipments back to export licences originating in the northern California area. The licencees were companies with no histories and warehouses with no records – chains of four walls erected for brief, temporary periods of convenience. It was a mass of confusion leading nowhere and everywhere. Names on documents where no such people existed, documents themselves that came out of bureaucratic labyrinths virtually *un*traceable – rubber stamps, official seals, and signatures of authorization where no authority was granted. Unknowing medium-level personnel told to expedite departmental clearances . . . That's what I found in San Francisco. A morass of complex, highly questionable transactions that could not bear intense scrutiny.'

Bertholdier's eyes were fixed, too controlled. 'I would know nothing about such things, of course,' he said.

'Of course,' agreed Converse. 'But the fact that my client does – through me – and the additional fact that neither he nor I have any desire whatsoever to call attention to them must tell you something.'

'Frankly, not a thing.'

'Please, General. One of the first principles of free enterprise is to cripple your competition, step in, and fill the void.'

The soldier drank, gripping the glass firmly. He lowered it and spoke. 'Why did you come to me?'

'Because you were there.'

'*What?*'

'Your name was there – among the morass, way down deep, but there.'

Bertholdier shot forward. 'Impossible! *Preposterous!*'

'Then why am I here? Why are *you* here?' Joel placed his glass on the table by the chair, the movement that of a man not finished speaking. 'Try to understand me. Depending upon which government department a person's dealing with, certain recommendations are bound to be helpful. You wouldn't do a damn thing for someone appealing to Housing and Urban Development, but over at the State Department's Munitions Controls or at Pentagon procurements, you're golden.'

'I have never lent my name to any such appeals.'

'Others did. Men whose recommendations carried a lot of weight, but who perhaps needed extra clout.'

'*Qu'est ce que vous dites?* This clout.'

'A final push for an affirmative decision . . . without any apparent personal involvement. It's called support for an action through viable second and third parties. For instance, a memo might read: "We – the department, not a person – don't know much about this, but if a man like General Bertholdier is favourably disposed, and we are informed that he is, why should we argue?"'

'*Never*. It could not happen.'

'It did,' said Converse softly, knowing it was the moment to bring in reality to support his abstractions. He would be able to tell instantly if Beale was right, if this legend of France was responsible for the slaughter and chaos in the cities and towns of a violently upended Northern Ireland. 'You were there, not often but enough for me to find you . . . Just as you were there in a different way when a shipment was air freighted out of Beloit, Wisconsin, on its way to Tel Aviv. Of course it never got there, somehow diverted to maniacs on both sides in Belfast. I wonder where it happened? Montreal? Paris? Marseilles? The Separatists in Quebec would certainly follow your orders, as would men in Paris and Marseilles. It's a shame a company named Solidaire had to pay off the insurance claim. Oh, yes, you're a director of the firm, aren't you? And it's so convenient that insurance carriers have access to the merchandise they cover.'

Bertholdier was frozen to the chair, the muscles of his face pulsating, his eyes wide and staring at Joel. His guilt was suppressed, but no less for that control. 'I cannot believe what you are implying. It's shocking and incredible!'

'I repeat, why am I here?'

'Only you can answer that, Monsieur,' said Bertholdier, abruptly getting to his feet, the brandy in his hand. Then slowly, with military grace, he leaned over and lowered the glass to the coffee table; it was a gesture of finality; the conference was over. 'Quite obviously I made a foolish error,' he continued, straightening up, shoulders square again, head rigid again, but now with a strained yet oddly convincing smile on his lips. 'I am a soldier, not a businessman; it is a late direction in my life. A soldier tries to seize an initiative and I attempted to do just that, only there was – there *is* – no initiative. Forgive me, I misread your signal this afternoon.'

'You didn't misread anything, General.'

'Am I contradicted by a stranger – I might even say a devious stranger – who arranges a meeting under false pretences and proceeds to make outrageous statements regarding my honour and my conduct? I think not.' Bertholdier strode across the room toward the hallway door; Joel rose from his chair. 'Don't bother, Monsieur, I'll let myself out. You've gone to enough trouble, for what purpose I haven't the faintest idea.'

'I'm on my way to Bonn,' interrupted Converse. 'Tell your friends I'm coming. Tell them to expect me. And please, General, tell them not to prejudge me. I mean that.'

'Your elliptical references are most annoying . . . Lieutenant. It was "lieutenant" wasn't it? Unless you also deceived poor Luboque as well.'

'Whatever deception I employed to meet you can only be for his benefit. I've offered to write a legal opinion for his case. He may not like it, but it'll save him a lot of pain and money. And I have not deceived you.'

'A matter of judgment, I think.' Bertholdier turned and reached for the outsized brass knob.

'*Bonn*, Germany,' pressed Joel.

'I heard you. I haven't the vaguest notion what you . . .'

'Leifhelm,' said Converse quietly. 'Erich Leifhelm.'

The soldier's head turned slowly; his eyes were banked fires, the coals glowing, about to erupt with a gust of wind. 'A name known to me, but not the man.'

'Tell him I'm coming.'

'Good night, Monsieur,' said Bertholdier, opening the door, his face ashen, his eyes inflamed by that sudden uncontrollable wind.

Joel raced into the bedroom, grabbed his suitcase which was against the wall and threw it on the luggage rack. He had to get out of Paris immediately, tonight. Within hours, perhaps minutes, Bertholdier would have him watched, and if he was followed to an airport, his passport would expose the name Simon as a lie. He could let not that happen, not yet.

It was so strange, so unsettling. He had never had any reason to leave a hotel surreptitiously, on short notice, *without* notice. He was not sure he knew how to do it, only that it had to be done. The altering of the registration card came instinctively; there were occasions when legal negotiations had to be kept quiet for everyone's benefit – not the least, in reverse, the stock manipulators – but this was different. It was so . . . abnormal. He had said to Beale on Mykonos that he was going to become someone he was not. It was an easy thing to say, not at all easy to do.

His suitcase packed, he checked the battery charge on his electric razor and absently turned it on, moving it around his chin, as he walked to the bedside telephone. He shut the switch off as he dialled, unsure of what he would say to the assistant *directeur* nevertheless instinctively orienting his mind to a business approach. After initial remarks, mutually flattering, the words came.

'There's an extremely sensitive situation, and my firm is anxious that I leave for London just as soon as possible . . . and as discreetly as possible. Frankly, I would prefer not to be seen checking out.'

'Discretion, Monsieur, is honoured here, and haste is a normal request. I shall come up and present your bill myself. Say, ten minutes?'

'I've only one piece of luggage, I'll carry it, but I'll need a cab. Not in front.'

'Not in front, of course. The freight elevator, Monsieur. It connects below with our corridor for deliveries. Arrangements will be made.'

'I've made arrangements!' said Jacques Louis Bertholdier harshly into the limousine's mobile phone, the glass partition between him and the chauffeur tightly shut. 'One man remains in the gallery in sight of the elevators, another in the cellars where the hotel supplies are brought in. If he attempts to leave during the night, it is the only other exit available to him. I've used it myself on several occasions.'

'This . . . is all *most* difficult to absorb.' The voice on the line spoke with a clipped British accent, the speaker obviously astonished, his breathing audible, a man suddenly afraid. 'Are you *sure*? Could there be some other linkage?'

'Imbecile! I repeat. He knew about the munitions shipment from Beloit! He knew the routing, even the method of theft, going so far as to identify *Solidaire* and my position as a board member! He made a *direct* reference to our business associate in *Bonn*! Then to Tel Aviv . . . *Johannesburg*! What other linkage *could* there be?'

'Corporate entanglements, perhaps. One can't rule them out. Multinational subsidiaries, munitions investments, our associate in West Germany also sits on several boards . . . and the locations – money *pours* into them.'

'What in the name of God do you think I'm talking about? I can say no more now, but what I've told you, my English *flower*, take it to be the worst!'

There was a brief silence from London. 'I understand,' said the voice of a subordinate rebuked.

'I hope you do. Get in touch with New York. His name is Seemón, Henri Seemón.'

'What?'

'*Henree Seemón*. He's an attorney from Chicago. I have the address; it's from the hotel's registration file.' Bertholdier squinted under the glare of the reading lamp, haltingly deciphering the numbers and the numbered street written down by a senior page, well paid by one of the general's men to go into the office and obtain information on the occupant of Suite two-three-five. 'Do you have that?'

'Yes,' was the reply, the voice now speaking sharply, a subordinate about to redress a grievance. 'Was it wise to get it that way? A friend or a greedy employee might tell him someone was inquiring about him.'

'*Really*, my British *daffodil*? An innocuous page checking the registry so as to post a lost garment to a recent guest?'

Again the brief silence. 'Yes, I see. You know, Jacques, we work for a great cause – a *business* cause, of course – more important than either of us, as we did once years ago. I must constantly remind myself of that, or I don't think I could tolerate your insults.'

'And what would be your recourse, *Anglais*?'

'To cut your arrogant Frog balls off in Trafalgar Square and stuff them in a lion's mouth. The repository wouldn't have to be large; an ancient crack would do . . . I'll ring you up in an hour or so.' There was a click and the line went dead.

The soldier held the mobile phone in his hand. He lowered it in front of his eyes, a smile slowly emerging on his lips. They were the *best, all* of them! They were the hope, the only hope of a very sick world.

Then the smile faded, the blood again draining from his face, arrogance turning into fear. What did this Henry Simon want, *really* want? Who was the unknown man with access to extraordinary sources . . . planes, vehicles, *munitions*? What in God's name did they know? What were they *doing*?

The padded elevator descended slowly, its interior designed for moving furniture and luggage, its speed adjusted for room service deliveries. The assistant *directeur* stood beside Joel, his face pleasantly impassive; in his right hand was the leather *bourse* containing a copy of Converse's bill and the franc notes covering it – as well as a substantial gratuity for the Frenchman's courtesy.

A slight whirring sound preceded the stop; the panel light shone behind the letters *Sous-sol* and the heavy doors parted. Beyond in the wide hallway was a platoon of white-jacketed waiters, maids, porters, and few maintenance personnel, commandeering tables, racks of linens, luggage and assorted cleaning materials. Loud, rapid chatter, heightened by bursts of laughter and guttural expletives, accompanied the bustling activity. At the sight of the assistant *directeur*, there was a perceptible lessening of volume and an increase of concentrated movement, nods and fawning smiles directed at the man who, with the flick of a pen, could eliminate their jobs.

'If you'll just point me in the right direction, I'll be on my way,' said Joel, not wishing to call further attention to himself in the company of the *directeur*. 'I've taken up too much of your time.'

'*Merci*. If you will follow that corridor, it will lead to the service exit,' replied the Frenchman, pointing to a hallway on the left, beyond the bank of elevators. 'The guard is at his desk and is aware of your departure. Outside in the alley, turn right and walk to the street; your taxi is waiting for you.'

'I appreciate – my *firm* appreciates – your cooperation. As I mentioned upstairs, there's nothing really that secretive, or unusual . . . just sensitive.'

The hotel man's impassive countenance did not change, except for a slightly sharper focus in his eyes. 'It is of no matter, Monsieur, an explanation is not required. I did not request it and, if you'll forgive me, you should not feel an obligation to offer one. *Au'voir*, Monsieur Simon.'

'Yes, of course,' said Converse, maintaining his composure despite the fact he felt like a schoolboy admonished for speaking out of turn, for offering an answer when he had not been called upon. 'See you next time I'm in Paris.'

'We await the day, Monsieur. *Bon soir.*'

Joel turned quickly, making his way through the uniformed crowd toward the hallway, apologizing whenever his suitcase made contact with a body. He had just been taught a lesson, one he should not have had to learn. He knew it in a courtroom and in conference: Never explain what you don't have to. Shut up. But this was not a court, or a conference. It was, it suddenly dawned on him, something quite different. It was an escape, and the realization was a little frightening, certainly very strange. Or was it? Escape was in his vocabulary, in his experience. He had tried it three times before in his life – years ago. And death had been everywhere. He put it out of his mind and walked down the corridor toward the large metal door in the distance.

He slowed down; something was wrong. Ahead, standing in front of the security desk talking to the guard, was a man in a light coloured topcoat. Joel had seen him before but he did not know where; then the man moved and Converse began to remember; an image came back to him. Another man had moved the same way – taking several steps backward before turning – in the previous instance to disappear from an archway, now to cross the corridor to lean against the wall. Was it the same man? Yes, it *was*! It was the one who had accompanied Bertholdier to the dining-room entrance of *Les Étalons Blancs*. Joel had thought at the time that a subordinate was taking leave of a superior. He was here now under orders from that same superior.

The man looked up, the flash of recognition instantly in his eyes. Stretching, he raised himself to his full height and turned away, his hand slowly moving toward the fold in his coat. Converse was stunned. Was the man actually reaching for a *gun*? With an armed guard barely ten feet away? It was insane! Joel stopped; he considered racing back into the crowd by the elevators but knew it was pointless. If Bertholdier had posted a watchdog in the basement, others would be upstairs, in the corridors, in the lobby. He could not turn and run; there was no place to go, nowhere to hide. So he kept walking, now faster, directly toward the man in the light brown topcoat, his mind confused, his throat tight.

'*There* you are!' he cried out loud, not sure the words were his. 'The general told me where to find you!'

If Converse was stunned, the man was in shock, numbed speechless but still in shock. '*Le général?*' he said barely above a whisper. 'He . . . tell you . . .?'

The man's English was not good and that was very good. He could understand, but not well. Rapidly spoken words, persuasively delivered, might get them both out the door. Joel turned to the guard, while angling his attaché case into the small man's back. 'My name's Simon. I believe the *directeur* spoke to you about me.'

The juxtaposition of the name and the title was sufficient for the bewildered guard. He glanced at his papers, nodding. '*Oui, Monsieur. Le directeur* . . .'

'Come *on!*' Converse shoved the attaché case into the man in the light brown topcoat, propelling him toward the door. 'The general's waiting for us outside. Let's go! Hurry *up!*'

'*Le général* . . .?' The man's hands instinctively shot out at the crash bar of the exit door; in less than five seconds he and Joel were alone in the alley. '*Qu'est-ce que c'est? Où est le général?* . . . Where?'

'Here! He said to wait here. *You*. You're to wait here! *Ici!*'

'*Arrêtez!*' The man was recovering. He stood his ground, thrusting his left hand out, pushing Converse back against the wall, his right hand surging into his overcoat.

'Don't!' Joel dropped his attaché case, gripping his suitcase and pulling it up in front of him, about to rush forward. He stopped. The man did not pull out a gun; instead, it was a thin, rectangular object bound in black leather. An unseen switch was pressed and a long metallic needle rose from the narrow flat top. An antenna . . . A *radio!*

All thought was blurred for Converse, only motion counted. He could not permit the man to use the radio, no second switch or button could be pressed, emitting a signal, alerting those with other radios elsewhere in the hotel. With a sudden, uncontrollable surge of strength, he rammed his suitcase into the man's knees, tearing the radio away with his left hand, whipping his right arm out and over the man's shoulder. He cracked his elbow, vicing the Frenchman's neck, as he spun on the pavement. Then without thinking, he yanked Bertholdier's soldier forward, both bodies rushing toward the wall, and crashed the man's head into the stone. Blood spread throughout the Frenchman's skull, matting his hair and streaking down his face in deep red rivulets. Joel could not think, he could not *allow* himself to think. If he did, he would be sick and he knew it. Motion, *motion!*

The man went limp. Converse angled the unconscious body by the shoulders, propelling it against the wall, shoving it away from the metal door and letting it drop in the farther shadows. He leaned down and picked up the radio, snapping off the antenna, and shoving the case into his pocket. He stood up, confused, frightened, trying to orient himself; then he saw what he had to see and rushed forward. Grabbing his attaché case and suitcase off the ground, he raced breathlessly out of the alley, conscious of the blood that had somehow erupted over part of his face. The taxi was at the kerb, the driver smoking a cigarette in the darkness, oblivious to the violence that had taken place only thirty yards away.

'De Gaulle Airport!' shouted Joel, opening the door, and throwing his luggage inside. 'Please, I'm in a hurry! *Pressé!*' He lurched into the seat, gasping, his neck stretched above the cushioned rim, swallowing the air that would not fill his lungs.

The rushing lights and shadows that bombarded the interior of the cab served only to coil out his suspended thought, allowing his racing pulse to decelerate and the air to reach him, slowly drying the perspiration that had broken out at his temples and his neck. He leaned forward, wanting a cigarette but afraid he would vomit from the smoke trapped in his throat. He shut his eyes, his lids pressing against one another so tightly a thousand specks of white light assaulted the dark screen of his mind. He felt ill, nauseatingly ill, and he knew it was not simply fear alone. It was something quite apart, something that was in and of itself as paralysing as fear. He had committed an act of utter brutality and it both shocked and appalled him. He had actually, *physically* attacked a man, wanting to punish him, cripple him, perhaps kill him – which he might very well have done. No matter why, he might have *killed* another human being! Did the presence of a hand-held radio justify a shattered skull? Did it constitute self-defence? *Goddamn it*, he was a man of words, of logic, not blood! *Never* blood, that was in the past, so long ago and so painful.

Those memories belonged to another time, to an uncivilized time, when men became what they were not – in order to survive. Converse never wanted to go back. Above all things, he had promised himself he never would, a promise he made when the terror and the violence were all around him, at their shattering worst. He remembered so vividly, with such pain the final hours before his last escape – and the quiet, generous man without whom he would have died twenty feet down in the earth, a shaft in the ground designed for troublemakers.

Colonel Sam Abbott, US Air Force, would always be a part of his life no matter how many years might separate them. At the risk of death preceded by torture, Sam had crawled out at night and had thrown a crudely-fashioned metal wedge down the 'punishment hole'; it was that primitive tool that allowed Joel to build a crude ladder out of earth and rock and finally to freedom. Abbott and he had spent the last twenty-seven months in the same camp, both officers trying to hold what sanity there was together. But Sam understood the burning inside him; the Colonel had stayed behind, and during those final hours before break-out, Joel was racked by the thoughts of what might happen to his friend.

Don't worry about me, sailor. Just keep your minimum wits about you and get rid of that wedge.

Take care, Sam.

You take care. This is the last shot you've got.

I know.

Joel moved over toward the door and rolled down the window several inches, letting the rush of wind from the highway cool him. Christ, he needed Sam Abbott's quiet objectivity now! His lawyer's mind told him to get hold of himself; the brain had to give rise to thought, thought to whatever imagination he was capable of. First things first. Think! The radio; he had to get rid of the *radio*. But not at the airport . . . it might be found in the airport; it was evidence, worse a means of tracing him. He rolled the window down several more inches and threw it out, his eyes on the rear-view mirror above the windscreen. The driver glanced up at him, briefly concerned; Joel took repeated deep breaths – a man wanting air to suspend the discomfort of acid or anxiety – and then rolled the window back up. Think. He had to *think*! Bertholdier expected him to go from Paris to Bonn and when the general's soldier was found – and he had undoubtedly been found by now – all flights to Bonn would be watched . . . whether or not the man was alive or dead.

He would buy a ticket for somewhere else, some place where connections to Köln-Bonn were accessible on a regular basis. As the stream of air brushed his face he thought, composing himself sufficiently to remove the handkerchief from his breast pocket and wipe away the moist blood that covered his right cheek and lower chin.

'Scandinavian Air Lines,' he said raising his voice to the driver. '*SAS*. Do you . . . *comprenez?*'

'Very clearly, Monsieur,' said the bereted man behind the wheel in well-spoken English. 'Do you have a reservation for Stockholm, Oslo, or Copenhagen? They are different gates.'

'I'm . . . I'm not sure.'

'We have time, Monsieur. At least fifteen minutes.'

The voice over the telephone from London was frigid, the words and the delivery an impersonal rebuke, made extremely personal because of familiarity. 'There is no attorney by that name in Chicago, and certainly not at the address you gave me. In fact, the address does not exist. Do you have something else to offer, or do we put this down as one of your most paranoid fantasies, *mon général?*'

'You are a fool, *Anglais*, with no more comprehension than a frightened rabbit. I *heard* what I *heard*!'

'From whom? A non-existent man?'

'A non-existent man who has put my guard in a hospital! A fractured skull with a great loss of blood and severe brain damage. He may not live, and if he does, it will no doubt be as a vegetable. Speak to me not of fantasies, *daffodil*. The man is real.'

'Are you serious?'

'Call the hospital! *L'hôpital de St Jérôme.* Let the doctors tell you.'

'All right, all right, compose yourself. We must think.'

'I am perfectly composed,' said Bertholdier, getting up from the desk of his study, and carrying the phone to the window, the extension cord snaking across the floor. He looked out; it had begun to rain, the street lights diffused in the spattered glass. 'He's on his way to Bonn,' continued the general. 'It was his next stop, he was very clear about it.'

'Intercept him. Call Bonn, reach Köln, give them his description. How many flights can there be from Paris with a lone American on board? Take him at the airport.'

Bertholdier sighed audibly into the phone, his tone one of discouragement bordering on disgust. 'It was never my intention to *take* him. It would serve no purpose and probably cut us off from what we have to learn. I want him followed, I want to know where he goes, whom he calls, whom he meets with; these are the things we must learn.'

'You said he made a direct reference to our associate. That he was going to reach him.'

'Not *our* people. *His* people.'

'I'll say it again,' insisted the voice from London. 'Call Köln, reach Bonn. Listen to me, Jacques, he can be found, and once he is, surveillance can be put in place.'

'Yes, yes, I'll do as you say, but it may not be as easy as you think. Three hours ago I would have thought otherwise, but that was before I knew what he was capable of. Someone who can take another man and rush that man's head into a stone wall at full force is either an animal, a maniac, or a zealot who will stop at nothing. In my judgment, he is the last. He said he had a commitment . . . and it was in his eyes. And he'll be clever; he's already proved he can be clever.'

'You say *three* hours?'

'Yes.'

'Then he may already *be* in Bonn.'

'I know.'

'Have you called our associate?'

'Yes, he's not at home and the maid could not give me another number. She doesn't know where he is, or when he's expected.'

'Probably in the morning.'

'No doubt . . . *Attendez!* There was another man at the club this afternoon. With Luboque and this Simon whose name is not Simon. He *brought* him to Luboque! Good bye, *Anglais.* I'll keep you informed.'

René Mattilon opened his eyes. The streaks of light on the ceiling seemed to shimmer, myriad tiny clots bursting, breaking up the linear patterns. Then he heard the sound of the rain on the windows and understood. The shafts of light from the streetlamps had been intercepted on their journeys through the glass, distorting the images he knew so well. It was the rain, he concluded; that was what had awakened him. That and perhaps the weight of his wife's hand between his legs. She stirred and he smiled, trying to make up his mind – or find the energy – to reach for her. She had filled a void for him he never thought could be filled after his first wife had died. He was grateful, and along with his feeling of gratitude came excitement, two emotions satisfyingly compatible. He was becoming aroused; he rolled over on his side and pulled down the covers, revealing the swell of her breasts encased in laced silk, the diffused light and the pounding on the windows heightened his sensuality. He reached for her.

Suddenly, there was another sound, not the rain, yet intruding on the rain, and from within the mists of sleep he recognized it. Quickly, he withdrew his hand and turned away from his wife. He had heard that noise only moments before; *it* was the sound that had awakened him, an insistent tone that had broken the steady rhythm of the downpour. It was the chimes of his apartment doorbell.

Mattilon climbed out of bed as carefully and as silently as he could, reaching for his bathrobe on a nearby chair and sliding his feet into the slippers beneath. He walked out of the bedroom, closing the door quietly behind him, and found the wall switch that turned on the lamps in the living room. He glanced at the ornate clock on the fireplace mantel; it was nearly 2.30 in the morning. Who could possibly be calling on them at this hour? He tied the sash around his robe and walked to the door.

'Yes, who is it?'

'*Sûreté*, Monsieur. Inspector Prudhomme. My state identification is zero-five-seven-two-zero.' The man's accent was Gascon, not Parisian. It was often said they made the best police officials. 'I shall wait while you call my station, Monsieur. The telephone number is . . .'

'No need,' said Mattilon, alarmed, unlatching the door. He knew the man was genuine not only from the information offered, but anyone from the *Sûreté* calling on him at this hour would know he was an attorney. The *Sûreté* was legally circumspect.

There were two men, both in raincoats spotted by the downpour, their hats drenched; one was older than the other and shorter. Each held out an open identification card for René's inspection. He waved the cards aside and gestured the two men to come in, adding, 'It's an odd time for visitors, gentlemen. You must have pressing business.'

'Very pressing, Monsieur,' said the older man entering first. He was the one who had spoken through the door, giving his name as Prudhomme, and was obviously the senior. 'We apologize for the inconvenience, of course.' Both men removed their hats.

'Of course. May I take your coats?'

'It won't be necessary, Monsieur. With your cooperation we'll only be a few minutes.'

'And I shall be most interested to know how I can cooperate with the *Sûreté* at this time of night.'

'A matter of identification, sir. Monsieur Serge Antoine Luboque is a client of yours, we are informed. Is this so?'

'My God, has something happened to Serge? I was with him only this afternoon!'

'Monsieur Luboque appears in excellent health. We left his country house barely an hour ago. And to the point, it is your meeting with him this afternoon – *yesterday* afternoon – that concerns the *Sûreté*.'

'In what way?'

'There was a third party at your table. As yourself, an attorney, introduced to Monsieur Luboque as a man named Simon. Henry Simon, an American.'

'And a pilot,' said Mattilon warily. 'With considerable expertise in aircraft litigation. I trust Luboque explained that; it was the reason he was there at my request. Monsieur Luboque is the plaintiff in just such a lawsuit. That of course, is all I can say on the subject.'

'It is not the subject that interests the *Sûreté*.'

'What is then?'

'There is no attorney by the name of Henry Simon in the city of Chicago, Illinois, in the United States.'

'I find that hard to believe.'

'The name is false. At least, it is not his. The address he gave the hotel does not exist.'

'The address he *gave* the hotel?' asked René, astonished. Joel did not have to give an address to the George V; it knew him well, knew the firm of Talbot, Brooks and Simon very well indeed.

'In his own handwriting, Monsieur,' added the younger man stiffly.

'Has the hotel management confirmed this?'

'Yes,' said Prudhomme. 'The assistant *directeur* was very cooperative. He told us he escorted Monsieur Simon down the freight elevator to the hotel cellars.'

'The cellars?'

'Monsieur Simon wished to leave the hotel without being seen. He paid his bill in his room.'

'A minute, please,' said Mattilon, perplexed, his hands protesting, as he turned and walked aimlessly around an armchair, stopping, his hands on the rim. 'What *precisely* do you want from me?'

'We want you to help us,' answered Prudhomme. 'We think you know who he is. You brought him to Monsieur Luboque.'

'On a confidential matter entailing a legal opinion. He agreed to listen and to evaluate on the condition that his identity should be protected. It's not unusual when seeking expertise if one is involved with, shall we say, an individual as wealthy and as temperamental as Monsieur Luboque. You've spoken with him; need I say more?'

'Not on that subject,' said the older man from the *Sûreté*, permitting himself a smile. 'He thinks all government personnel work for Moscow. We were surrounded by dogs in his foyer, all salivating, I might add.'

'Then you can understand why my American colleague prefers to remain unnamed. I know him well, he's a splendid man.'

'Who is he? And do you know where we can find him?'

'Why do you want him?'

'We wish to question him about an incident that took place at the hotel.'

'I'm sorry. As Luboque is a client, so by extension is Simon.'

'That is not acceptable to us under the circumstances, Monsieur.'

'I'm afraid it will have to be, at least for a few hours. Tomorrow I shall try to reach him through his office in . . . in the United States . . . and I'm sure he'll get in touch with you immediately.'

'We don't think he will.'

'Why not?'

Prudhomme glanced at his starchly-postured associate and shrugged. 'He may have killed a man,' he said matter-of-factly.

Mattilon stared at the *Sûreté* officer in disbelief. 'He . . . *what?*'

'It was a particularly vicious assault, Monsieur. A man's head was rammed into a wall; there are extensive cranial injuries and the prognosis is not good. His condition as of midnight was critical, the chances of recovery less than half. He may be dead by now, which one doctor said could be a blessing.'

'No . . . *no*! You are mistaken! You're wrong!' The lawyer's hands gripped the rim of the chair. 'A terrible error has been made!'

'No error. The identification was positive – that is Monsieur *Simon* was identified as the last person seen with the man who was beaten. He forced the man out into an alley; there were sounds of scuffling and minutes later that man was found, his skull fractured, bleeding, near death.'

'Impossible! You don't *know* him! What you suggest is inconceivable. He *couldn't*.'

'Are you telling us he is disabled, physically incapable of assault?'

'No,' said Mattilon, shaking his head. Then suddenly he stopped all movement. '*Yes*,' he continued thoughtfully, his eyes pensive, now nodding, rushing ahead. 'He's incapable, yes, but not physically. *Mentally*. In that sense he is disabled. He could not do what you say he did.'

'He's mentally deranged?'

'My *God*, no! He's one of the most lucid men I've ever met. You have to understand. He went through a prolonged period of extreme physical stress and mental anguish. He endured punishment, both to his body and his mind. There was no permanent damage but there are indelible memories. As so many men like him – men who've been subjected to such treatment – he avoids all forms of physical confrontation or abuse. It is repugnant to him. He can't inflict punishment because too much was inflicted on him.'

'You mean he would not defend himself, his own? He would turn the other cheek if he, or his wife, or his children were attacked?'

'Of course not, but that's not what you described. You said "a particularly vicious assault" implying something quite different. And if it were otherwise – if he were threatened or attacked and defended himself – he most certainly would not have left the scene. He's too fine a lawyer.' Mattilon paused. '*Was* that the case? Is that what you're saying? Is the injured man known to you from the police files? Is he . . .'

'A limousine chauffeur,' interrupted Prudhomme. 'An unarmed man who was waiting for his assigned passenger of the evening.'

'In the *cellars?*'

'Apparently it is a customary service and not an unfamiliar one. These firms are discreet. This one sent another driver to cover before inquiring as to their employee's condition. The client would not know.'

'Very chic, I'm sure. What do they say happened?'

'According to a witness, a guard who's been with the hotel for eighteen years, this Simon approached in a loud voice, speaking English – the guard thinks angrily, although he does not understand the language – and forced the man outside.'

'The guard is wrong! It must have been someone else.'

'Simon identified himself. The assistant *directeur* had cleared his departure. The description fits; it was the one who called himself Simon.'

'But *why*? There has to be a reason!'

'We should like to hear it, Monsieur.'

René shook his head in bewilderment; nothing made sense. A man could register at any hotel under any name he wished, of course, but there were charges, credit cards, people calling; a false name served no purpose. Especially at a hotel where one was presumably known, and if one *was* known and chose to travel incognito, that status would not be protected if a front desk was questioned by the *Sûreté*. 'I must ask you again, Inspector, have you checked thoroughly with the hotel?'

'Not personally, Monsieur,' replied Prudhomme, looking at his associate. 'My time was taken up interrogating those in the vicinity of the assault.'

'I checked with the *concierge* myself, Monsieur,' said the younger, taller man, speaking like a programmed robot. 'Naturally, the hotel is not anxious for the incident to receive atttention, but the management was cooperative. The night *directeur* is newly employed from the Hotel Meurice and wished to minimize the incident, but he himself showed me the registration form.'

'I see.' And Mattilon did, at least insofar as Joel's identity was concerned. Hundreds of guests at a large hotel and a nervous night *directeur* protecting his new employer's image. The obvious source was accepted as truth, another truth no doubt forthcoming in the morning from more knowledgable men. But that was all René understood – nothing else. He needed a few moments to think, to try and understand. 'I'm curious,' he said, reaching for words. 'At worst, this is an assault with severe results, but nevertheless an assault. Why isn't it a simple police matter? Why the *Sûreté*?'

'My first question, Monsieur,' said the plain-spoken Prudhomme. 'The reason given us was that the incident involved a foreigner, obviously a wealthy foreigner. One does not know these days where such things lead. We have certain controls not available to the *arrondissement* police.'

'I see.'

'Do you?' asked the man from the *Sûreté*. 'May I remind you that as an attorney you have an obligation to uphold the courts and the law? You have been offered our credentials and I have suggested you call my station for any further verification you might wish. Please, Monsieur, who is Henry Simon?'

'I have other obligations, as well, Inspector. To my word, to a client, to an old friendship . . .'

'You put these above the law?'

'Only because I know you're *wrong*.'

'Then where is the harm? If we are, we shall find this Simon undoubtedly at an airport and he will tell us himself. But if we are not wrong, we may find a very sick man who needs help. Before he harms others. I am no psychiatrist, Monsieur, but you have described a troubled man – a once-troubled man, in any event.'

Mattilon was uncomfortable with the blunt official's logic . . . and also something else he could not define. Was it Joel? Was it the clouds in his old friend's eyes, the unconscious verbal slip about a blemished rock in the dirt?

René looked again at the clock on the mantel; a thought occurred to him. It was only 8.42 in New York.

'Inspector, I'm going to ask you to wait here while I go into my study and make a phone call on my private line. The line, incidentally, is not connected to the telephone on the table.'

'That was unnecessary, Monsieur.'

'Then I apologize.'

Mattilon walked rapidly to a door on the opposite side of the room, opened it, and went inside. He crossed to his desk, sat down and opened a red leather telephone index. He flipped the pages to the letter *T*, scanning the names until he reached *Talbot, Lawrence.* He had both the office and the house number; it was necessary as the courts in Paris were in operation before the East Coast of America was out of bed. If Talbot was not there, he would try Nathan Simon, then Brooks, if he had to. Neither was necessary. Lawrence Talbot answered the phone.

'I'll be damned, how are you, René? You in New York?'

'No, Paris.'

'Sounds like you're down the block.'

'So do you. It's always startling.'

'It's also late where you are, if I'm not mistaken.'

'It's very late, Larry. We may have a problem, that's why I'm calling.'

'A problem? I didn't even know we had any business going. What is it?'

'Your missionary work.'

'Our what?'

'Bertholdier. His friends.'

'*Who?*'

'Jacques Louis Bertholdier.'

'Who is he? I've heard the name but I can't place him.'

'You can't . . . place him?'

'Sorry.'

'I've been with Joel. I arranged the meeting.'

'Joel? How is he? Is he in Paris now?'

'You weren't aware of it?'

'Last time I spoke with him was two days ago in Geneva – after that awful business with Halliday. He told me he was all right, but he wasn't. He was shaken up.'

'Let me understand you, Larry. Joel is not in Paris on business for Talbot, Brooks and Simon, is that what you're saying?'

Lawrence Talbot paused before answering. 'No, he's not,' said the senior partner softly. 'Did he say he was?'

'Perhaps I just assumed it.'

Again Talbot paused. 'I don't think you'd do that. But I do think you should tell Joel to call me.'

'That's part of the problem, Larry. I don't know where he is. He said he was taking the 6 o'clock plane for London, but he didn't. He checked out of the George V quite a bit later under very odd circumstances.'

'What do you mean?'

'His hotel registration was altered, changed to another name – a name I suggested, incidentally, as he didn't wish to use his own at lunch. Then he insisted on leaving by way of some basement delivery entrance.'

'That's strange.'

'I'm afraid it's the least of the oddities. They say he assaulted a man. He may have killed him.'

'*Jesus!*'

'I don't believe it, of course,' said Mattilon quickly. 'He wouldn't, he couldn't . . .'

'I *hope* not.'

'Certainly you don't think . . .'

'I don't know *what* to think,' interrupted Talbot. 'When he was in Geneva and we talked, I asked him if there was any connection between Halliday's death and what he was doing. He said there wasn't, but he was so remote, so distant; his voice sounded hollow.'

'What he's *doing* . . . ? What *is* he doing?'

'I don't know. I'm not even sure I can find out, but I'll do my damndest. I tell you, I'm worried. Something's happened to him. His voice was like an echo chamber, do you know what I mean?'

'Yes, I do,' said Mattilon quietly. 'I heard him, I saw him. I'm worried, too.'

'Find him, René. Do whatever you can. Give me the word and I'll drop everything and fly over. He's hurting somewhere, somehow.'

'I'll do what I can.'

Mattilon walked out of his study and faced the two men from the *Sûreté*.

'His name is Converse, Joel Converse,' he began.

'His name is Converse, first name Joel,' said the younger, taller man from the *Sûreté*, speaking into the mouthpiece of a pay phone on the Boulevard Raspail, as the rain pounded the booth. 'He's employed by a law firm in New York: Talbot, Brooks and Simon; the address is on Fifth Avenue. The assumed name Simon, however, was apparently a convenience, and not related to the firm.'

'I don't understand.'

'Whatever this Converse is involved with has nothing to do with his employers. Mattilon spoke to one of the partners in New York and it was made clear to him. Also both men are concerned, worried; they wish to be kept informed. If Converse is found, Mattilon insists on immediate access to him as the attorney of record. He may be holding back, but in my judgment he's genuinely bewildered. In shock, might be more accurate. He knows nothing of consequence, I could tell if he did.'

'Nevertheless, he *is* holding back. The name Simon was used for my benefit, so that I would not learn the identity of this Converse. Mattilon knows that; he was there and they are friends and he brought him to Luboque.'

'Then he was manipulated, General. He did not mention you.'

'He might if he's questioned further. I cannot be involved in any way.'

'Of course not,' agreed the man from the *Sûreté* with quiet emphasis.

'Your superior, what's his name? The one assigned to the incident.'

'Prudhomme. Inspector First Grade Prudhomme.'

'Is he frank with you?'

'Yes. He thinks I'm something of a mechanical ex-soldier whose instincts may outdistance his intellect, but he sees that I'm willing. He talks to me.'

'You'll be kept with him for a while. Should he decide to go back and see Mattilon, let me know immediately. Paris may lose a respected attorney. My name must not surface.'

'He would only go back to Mattilon if Converse was found. And if word came to the *Sûreté* as to his whereabouts, I'd reach you instantly.'

'There could be another reason, Colonel. One that might provoke a persistent man into re-examining his progress – or lack of it – in spite of orders to the contrary.'

'Orders to the contrary, sir?'

'They will be issued. This Converse is solely our concern now. All we needed was a name. We know where he's heading. We'll find him.'

'I don't understand, General.'

'News has come from the hospital. Our chauffeur has taken a turn for the better.'

'Good news indeed.'

'I wish it were. The sacrifice of a single soldier is abhorrent to any field commander, but the broader tactics must be kept in view, they must be served. Do you agree?'

'Yes, of course.'

'Our chauffeur must not recover. The larger strategy, Colonel.'

'If he dies, the efforts to find Converse will be intensified. And you're right, Prudhomme will re-examine everything, including the lawyer, Mattilon.'

'Orders to the contrary will be issued. But watch him.'

'Yes, sir.'

'And now we need your expertise, Colonel. The talents you developed so proficiently while in the service of the Legion before we brought you back to a more civilized life.'

'My gratitude isn't shallow. Whatever I can do.'

'Can you get inside the hospital of St Jérôme with as little notice as possible?'

'With no notice. There are fire escapes on all sides of the building and it's a dark night, heavy with rain. Even the police stay in doorways. It's child's play.'

'But man's work. It has to be done.'

'I don't question such decisions.'

'A blockage in the windpipe, a convulsion in the throat.'

'Pressure applied through cloth, sir. Gradually and with no marks, a patient's self-induced trauma . . . But I would be derelict if I didn't repeat what I said, General. There'll be a search of Paris, then a large scale manhunt. The killer will be presumed to be a rich American, an inviting target for the *Sûreté*.'

'There'll be no search, no manhunt. Not yet. If it is to be, it will come later, and if it does, a convicted corpse will be trapped in the net . . . Go into

the field, my young friend. The chauffeur, Colonel; the broader strategy
must be served.'

'He's dead,' said the man in the telephone booth, hanging up.

5

Erich Leifhelm ... born 15 March 1912, in Munich to Dr Heinrich
Leifhelm and his mistress, Marta Stoessel. Although the stigma of his
illegitimacy precluded a normal childhood in upper-middle-class, moral-
ity-conscious Germany of those years, it was the single most important
factor in his later pre-eminence in the National Socialist movement. At
birth, he was denied the name of Leifhelm; until 1931 he was known as
Erich Stoessel.

Joel sat at a table in the open café in Copenhagen's Kastrup Airport, trying
to concentrate. It was his second attempt within the past twenty minutes,
the first he abandoned when he realized he was absorbing nothing, seeing
only black letters forming an unending string of vaguely recognizable words
relating to a figure in the outer reaches of his mind. He could not focus on
that man; there were too many interferences, real and imagined. Nor had he
been able to read on the two-hour flight from Paris, having opted for
economy class, hoping to melt in with the greater number of people in the
larger section of the aircraft. The concept at least was valid; the seats were
so narrow and the plane so fully occupied that elbows and forearms were
virtually immobile. The conditions prohibited his taking out the report, both
for reasons of space and for fear of the proximity to straying eyes.

Heinrich Leifhelm moved his mistress and their son to the town of
Eichstatt, 50-odd miles north of Munich, visiting them now and then, and
providing an adequate but not over comfortable standard of living. The
doctor was apparently torn between maintaining a successful practice –
with no social blemishes – in Munich, and a disinclination to abandon the
stigmatized mother and child. According to close acquaintances of Erich
Stoessel-Leifhelm, these early years had a profound effect on him.
Although too young to grasp the full impact of World War I – a memory
that was later to haunt him – the small household's subsistence level fell
as the elder Leifhelm's ability to contribute lessened with the burden of
wartime taxes. Also, his father's visits served to heighten the fact that he
could not be acknowledged as a son and was not entitled to the privileges
accorded two stepbrothers and a stepsister, strangers he was never to
know and whose home he could not enter. Through the absence of proper
lineage, certified by hypocritical documents and more hypocritical church
blessings, he felt he was denied what was rightfully his, and so there were
instilled in him a furious sense of resentment, competitiveness, and a
deep-seated anger at existing social conditions. By his own admission, his

first conscious longings were to get as much as he could for himself – both materially and in the form of recognition – through the strengths of his own abilities, and by doing so strike out at the status quo which had tried to emasculate him. By his mid-teens, Stoessel-Leifhelm's anger consumed him.

Converse stopped reading, suddenly aware of the woman across the half-deserted café; she was seated alone at a table, looking at him. Their eyes met and she turned away, placing her arm on the low white railing that enclosed the restaurant, studying the thinning, late night crowds in the terminal, as if waiting for someone. Startled, Joel tried to analyse the look she had given him. Was it recognition? Did she know him? Know his face? Or was it appraisal? A well-dressed whore cruising the airport in search of a mark, seeking out a lonely businessman far away from home. Airports at night frequently served as sexual meeting grounds, appetites born of distance and loneliness, monies exchanged as often as not for conversation as for copulation, foreplay extended, vacuums filled. She turned her head slowly and looked at him again, now obviously upset that his eyes were still on her. Then abruptly, in two swiftly defined motions, she glanced at her watch, tugged at her wide-brimmed hat, and opened her purse. She took out a Krone note, placed it on the table, got up, and walked rapidly toward the entrance of the café. Beyond the open gate she walked faster, her strides longer, heading for the arch that led to the baggage claim area. Converse watched her, shaking his head, annoyed at his alarm; he was seeing shadows in the dull white neon light of the terminal. With his attaché case and leather-bound report, the woman had probably thought he was some kind of airport official. Who was the mark then?

He was seeing too many shadows, he thought, as he followed the graceful figure nearing the arch. Too many shadows that held no surprises, or alarms. There had been a man on the plane from Paris sitting several rows in front of him. Twice the man had got up and gone to the toilet, and each time he came back to his seat he had looked hard at Joel, studied him, actually. Those looks had been enough to prime his adrenalin. Had he been spotted at the de Gaulle airport? Was the man an employee of Jacques Louis Bertholdier? . . . As a man in an alley had been – *don't think about that*! He had flicked off an oval of dried blood on his shirt as he had given himself the command.

'I can always tell a good ole Yank! Never miss!'

That had been the antiquated salutation in Copenhagen, as both Americans waited for their luggage.

'Well, I missed once. Some son of a bitch on a plane in Geneva. Sat right next to me. A real guinea in a three-piece suit, that's what he was! He spoke English to the stewardess, so I figured he was one of those rich Cuban spicks from Florida, you know what I mean?'

An emissary in salesman's clothes. One of the diplomats.

Geneva. It had started in Geneva.

Too many shadows. No surprises, no alarms. The woman went through the arch and Joel pulled his eyes away, forcing his attention back to the report on Erich Leifhelm. Then a slight, sudden movement stopped him; he looked back at the woman. A man had stepped out of an unseen recess; his hand had touched her elbow. They exchanged words briefly, swiftly, and parted as abruptly as they had met, the man continuing into the terminal as the woman disappeared. Did the man glance over in his direction? Converse watched closely; *had* that man looked at him? It was impossible to tell; his head was turning in all directions, looking *at* or *for* something. Then, as if he had found it, the man hurried toward a bank of airline counters. He approached the Japan Air Lines desk, taking out his wallet as he began speaking to an oriental clerk.

No surprises, no alarms. A harried traveller had asked directions; the interferences were more imagined than real. Yet even here his lawyer's mentality intervened. Interferences were real whether based in reality or not. *Oh, Christ!* Leave it alone! Concentrate!

At the age of 17, Erich Stoessel-Leifhelm had completed his studies at the Eichstaff II Gymnasium, excelling both academically and on the playing field where he was known as an aggressive competitor. It was a time of universal financial chaos, the American stock market crash of '29 further aggravating the desperate economy of the Weimar Republic, and few but the most well-connected students went on to universities. In a move he later described to friends as one of youthful fury, Stoessel-Leifhelm travelled to Munich to confront his father and demand assistance. What he found was not only a shock, but turned out to be a profound opportunity, strangely arrived at. The doctor's staid, placid life was in a shambles. His marriage, from the beginning unpleasant and humiliating, had caused him to drink heavily with increasing frequency until the inevitable errors of judgment occurred. He was censured by the medical community (with a high proportion of Jews therein), charged with incompetence and barred from the Karlstor Hospital. His practice was in ruins; his wife had ordered him out of the house; an order expedited by an old but still powerful father-in-law, also a doctor and member of the hospital's board of directors. When Stoessel-Leifhelm found his father, he was living in a cheap apartment house in the poorer section of the city picking up pfennigs by dispensing prescriptions (drugs) and Deutsch-marks by performing abortions.

In what apparently (again according to friends from the time) was a watershed of pent-up emotions, the elder Leifhelm embraced his illegiti-mate son and told him the story of his tortured life with a disagreeable wife and tyrannical in-laws. It was the classic syndrome of an ambitious man of minimal talents and maximum connections. But withal, the doctor claimed he had never abandoned his beloved mistress and their son. And during this prolonged and undoubtedly drunken confession, he revealed a fact Stoessel-Leifhelm had never known. His father's wife was Jewish. It was all the teenager needed to hear.

The disenfranchised boy became father to the ruined man.

There was an announcement in Danish over the airport's loudspeakers and Joel looked at his watch. It came again, now in German., He listened intensely for the words, he could barely distinguish them, but they were there. Hamburg-Köln-Bonn. It was the first boarding call for the last flight of the night to the capital of West Germany by way of Hamburg. The flying time was less than two hours, the layover in Hamburg justified for those executives who wanted to be at their desks by the start of the business day. Converse had checked his suitcase through to Bonn, making a mental note as he did so to replace the heavy black leather bag with a carry-on. He was no expert in such matters but common sense told him that the delays required by waiting for one's luggage – in the open for anyone to see – was no way to travel swiftly or to avoid eyes that might be searching for him. He put Erich Leifhelm's dossier in his attaché case, closed it and spun the brass combination discs. He then got up from the table, walked out of the café, and across the terminal toward the Lufthansa gate.

Sweat matted his hairline; the tattoo inside his chest accelerated until it became a hammering fugue for kettledrums. He *knew* the man sitting next to him, but from where or from what period in his life he had no idea. The crag-lined face, deep ridges that creased the sun-tanned flesh, the intense blue-grey eyes beneath the thick, wild brows and brown hair streaked with white; he *knew* him, but no name came, no clue to the man's identity.

Joel kept waiting for some sign of recognition directed at himself. None came, and involuntarily he found himself looking at the sun-tanned man out of the corner of his eye – 'stealing glances' was the embarrassing phrase that came to him. The man did not respond; instead his attention was on a bound sheaf of typewritten pages, the type larger than the print normally associated with legal briefs of even summonses. Perhaps, thought Converse, the man was half blind, wearing contact lenses to conceal his infirmity. But was there something else? Not an infirmity, but a connection being concealed. Had he seen this man in Paris – as he had seen another wearing a light brown topcoat in a hotel basement corridor? Had this man beside him also been at *Les Étalons Blancs*? Had he been part of a stationary group of ex-soldiers in the warriors' playroom . . . in a corner, innocuous because of the numbers? Or at Bertholdier's table, his back to Joel, presumably unseen by the American he was now following? *Was* he following him at this moment? wondered Converse, gripping his attaché case. He turned his head barely inches and studied his seatmate.

Suddenly the man looked up from the bound, typewritten pages and over at Joel. His eyes were non-committal, expressing neither concern nor curiosity.

'Sorry,' said Converse, awkwardly.

'Sure, it's okay . . . why not?' was the strange, laconic reply, the accent American, the dialect distinctly Texas-Western. The man returned to his pages.

'Do we know each other?' asked Joel, unable to back off from the question.

Again the man looked up. 'Don't think so,' he said tersely, once more going back to his report, or whatever it was.

Converse looked out the window, at the black sky beyond, flashes of red light illuminating the silver metal of the wing. Absently he tried to calculate the digital degree heading of the aircraft but his pilot's mind would not function. He *did* know the man, and the oddly-phrased 'why not?' served only to disturb him further. Was it a signal, a warning? As his words to Jacques Louis Bertholdier had been a signal, a warning that the general had better contact him, recognize him.

The voice of a Lufthansa stewardess interrupted his thoughts. 'Herr Dowling, it is a pleasure, indeed, to have you on board.'

'Thank you, darlin',' said the man, his lined face creasing into a gentle grin. 'You find me a little bourbon over ice and I'll return the compliment.'

'Certainly, sir. I'm sure you've been told so often you must be tired of hearing it, but your television show is enormously popular in Germany.'

'Thanks again, honey, but it's not *my* show. There are a lot of pretty little fillies runnin' around that screen.'

An actor. *A goddamned actor*! thought Joel. No alarms, no surprises. Just intrusions, far more imagined than real.

'You're too modest, Herr Dowling. They're all so alike, so disagreeable. But you are so kind, so manly . . . so understanding.'

'Understandin'? Tell you somethin', I saw an episode in Cologne last week while on this picture and I didn't understand a word I was sayin'.'

The stewardess laughed. 'Bourbon over ice, is that correct, sir?'

'That's correct, darlin'.'

The woman started down the First Class aisle toward the galley as Converse continued to look at the actor. Haltingly, he spoke. 'I *am* sorry. I should have recognized you, of course.'

Dowling turned his sun-tanned head, his eyes roaming Joel's face, then dropping to the hand-tooled leather attaché case. He looked up with an amused smile. 'I could probably embarrass you if I asked where you knew me from. You don't look like a *Sante Fe* groupie.'

'A *Sante Fe* . . .? Oh, sure, that's the name of the show.' And it was, reflected Converse. One of those phenomena on television that by sheer force of incredible ratings and extraordinary network profits had been featured on the covers of *Time* and *Newsweek*. He had never seen it.

'And, naturally,' continued the actor. 'You follow the tribal rites . . . and wrongs . . . the dramatic vicissitudes of the imperious Ratchet family, owners of the biggest spread north of Santa Fe as well as the historic Chimaya Flats, which they stole from the impoverished Indians.'

'The who? What?'

Dowling's leathery face again laminated itself into a grin. 'Only Pa Ratchet, the Indians' friend, doesn't know about the last part, although he's being blamed by his red brothers. You see, Pa's no-good sons heard there was oil shale beneath the Chimayas and did their thing . . . Incidentally, I trust you catch the verbal associations inherent in the name Ratchet; you can take your choice. There's just plain "rats", or Ratchet as in "wretched", or Ratchet as in the tool – screwing everything in front of it by merely pressing forward.'

There was something different about the actor now, thought Joel, bewildered. Was it his words – ? No, not the words, his voice. The Western inflections were greatly diminished. 'I don't know what you're talking about, but you sound different.'

'Wal, Ah'll jes' be *hornswoggled*!' said Dowling, laughing. Then he returned to the unaccented tones he had begun to display. 'You're looking at a renegade teacher of English and college dramatics who said a dozen years ago to hell with old age tenure, let's go after a very impractical dream. It led to a lot of funny and not very dignified jobs, but the god Thespis moves in mysterious ways. An old student of mine, on one of those undefinable jobs like "production-coordinator" spotted me in a crowd scene; it embarrassed the hell out of him. Nevertheless, he put my name in for several small parts. A few panned out and a couple of years later an accident called *Sante Fe* came along. That's when my perfectly respectable name of Calvin was changed to Caleb. "Fits the image better," said a pair of Gucci loafers who never got closer to a horse than a box at Santa Anita . . . It's crazy, isn't it?'

'Crazy,' agreed Converse, as the stewardess walked back up the aisle toward them.

'Crazy or not,' added Dowling, under his breath. 'This good old rancher isn't going to offend *anyone*. They want Pa Ratchet, they've got him.'

'Your bourbon, sir,' said the woman, handing the actor a glass.

'Why, *thank* you, li'l darlin'.! My oh my, you're purtier than any filly on the show!'

'*Mein Herr*, you're too kind.'

'May I have a Scotch, please,' said Joel.

'That's better, son,' said Dowling, grinning again as the stewardess left. 'And now that you know my crime, what do you do for a living?'

'I'm an attorney.'

'At least you've got something legitimate to read. This screenplay sure as hell isn't.'

Although considered by most of Munich's respectable citizens to be a collection of misfits and thugs, the National Socialist Workers Party, with its headquarters in Munich, was making itself felt throughout Germany. The radical-populist movement was taking hold by basing its inflammatory message on the evil, un-German 'them'. It blamed the ills of the nation on a spectrum of targets ranging from the Bolsheviks to the ingrate Jewish bankers; from the foreign plunderers who had raped an Aryan land to, finally, all things not 'Aryan', namely-in-focus, the Jews and their illgotten-wealth.

Cosmopolitan Munich and its Jewish community laughed at the absurdities; they were not listening. The rest of Germany was; it was hearing what it wanted to hear. And Erich Stoessel-Leifhelm heard it, too. It was his passport to recognition and opportunity.

In a matter of weeks, the young man literally whipped his father into shape. In later years he would tell the story with heavy doses of cruel humour. Over the dissolute physician's hysterical objections, the son removed all alcohol and smoking materials from the premises, never letting his father out of his sight. A harsh regimen of exercise and diet was enforced. With the zeal of a puritanical athletic trainer, Stoessel-Leifhelm started taking his father out to the countryside for 'Gewaltmärsche' – forced marches – gradually working up to all-day hikes through the exhausting trails of the Bavarian mountains, continuously shouting at the older man to keep moving, to rest only at his son's commands, to drink water only with permission.

So successful was the rehabilitation that the doctor's clothes began to hang on him like seedy-old-fashioned garments purchased for a much fatter man. A new wardrobe was called for, but good clothing in Munich in those days was beyond the means of all but the wealthy, and Stoessel-Leifhelm had only the best in mind for his father – not out of filial devotion but, as we shall see, for a quite different purpose.

Money had to be found, which meant it had to be stolen. He interrogated his father at length about the house the doctor had been forced to leave, learning everything there was to learn. Several weeks later Stoessel-Leifhelm broke into the house on the Luisenstrasse at three o'clock one morning, stripping it of everything of value, including silver, crystal, oil paintings, gold place-settings, and the entire contents of a wall safe. Sales to 'fences' were not difficult in Munich of 1930, and when everything was disposed of, father and son had the equivalent of nearly eight thousand American dollars, virtually a fortune in those times.

The restoration continued; clothes were tailored in the Maximilien-strasse, the best footwear purchased at bootsmiths on the Odeonsplatz and, finally cosmetic changes were effected. The doctor's unkempt hair was trimmed and heightened by colouring into masculine Nordic blond, and his shabby inch-long beard shaved off, leaving only a small, unbroken, well-manicured moustache above his upper lip. The transformation was complete; what remained was the introduction.

Every night during the long weeks of rehabilitation, Stoessel-Leifhelm had read aloud to his father whatever he could get his hands on from the National Socialists' headquarters, and there was no lack of material. There were the standard inflammatory pamphlets, pages of ersatz biological theory purportedly proving the genetic superiority of Aryan purity and, conversely, the racial disintegration resulting from indiscriminate breeding – all the usual Nazi diatribes – plus generous excerpts from Hitler's *Mein Kampf*. The son read incessantly until the doctor could recite by rote the salient outrages of the National Socialists' message. Throughout it all, the seventeen-year-old kept telling his father that this was the way to get back everything that had been stolen from him, to avenge the years of humiliation and ridicule. As Germany itself had been humiliated by the rest of the world, the Nazi party was the avenger, the restorer of all things truly German. It was, indeed, the New Order for the Fatherland, and it was waiting for men of stature to recognize the fact.

The day came, a day when Stoessel-Leifhelm had learned that two high-ranking party officials would be in Munich. They were the crippled Josef Goebbels, and the would-be aristocrat, Rudolph Hess. The son accompanied the father to the National Socialist headquarters where the well-tailored, imposing, obviously rich and Aryan *Doktor* requested an audience with the two Nazi leaders on an urgent and confidential matter. It was granted, and according to early party historical archives, his first words to Hess and Goebbels were the following.

'Gentlemen, I am a physician of impeccable credentials, formerly head surgeon at the Karlstor Hospital and for years I enjoyed one of the most successful practices in Munich. That was in the past. I was destroyed by

Jews who stole everything from me. I am back, I am well, and I am at your service.'

The Lufthansa plane began its descent into Hamburg and Joel, feeling the drag, dog-eared the page of Leifhelm's dossier and reached down for his attaché case. Beside him, the actor Caleb Dowling stretched, script in hand, then jammed his screenplay into an open flight bag at his feet.

'The only thing sillier than this movie,' he said, 'is the amount of money they're paying me to be in it.'

'Are you filming tomorrow?' asked Converse.

'Today,' corrected Dowling, looking at his watch. 'It's an early shoot, too. Have to be on location by five-thirty – dawn over the Rhine, or something equally inspiring. Now if they'd just turn the damn thing into a travelogue, we'd all be better off. Nice scenery.'

'But you were in Copenhagen.'

'Yep.'

'You're not going to get much sleep.'

'Nope.'

'Oh.'

The actor looked at Joel, the crow's feet around his generous eyes creasing deeper with his smile. 'My wife's in Copenhagen and I had two days off. This was the last plane I could get.'

'Oh? You're married?' Converse immediately regretted the remark; he was not sure why, but it sounded foolish.

'Twenty-six years, young fella. How do you think I was able to go after that impractical dream? She's a whizz of a secretary; when I was teaching, she'd always be this or that dean's Gal Friday.'

'Any children?'

'Can't have everything. Nope.'

'Why is she in Copenhagen? I mean why isn't she staying with you . . . on location?'

The grin faded from Dowling's sun-tanned face; the lines were less apparent, yet somehow deeper. 'That's an obvious question, isn't it? That is, you being a lawyer would pick it up quickly.'

'It's none of my business, of course. Forget I asked it.'

'No, that's okay. I don't like to talk about it – rarely do – but friendly seat-mates on airplanes are for telling things. You'll never see them again, so why not slice off a bit and feel better.' The actor tried haltingly to smile; he failed. 'My wife's name was Mühlstein – it means a millstone. She's Jewish. Her story's not much different from a few million others, but for her it's . . . well, it's hers. She was separated from her parents and her three younger brothers in Auschwitz. She watched them being taken away – away from her – while she screamed, not understanding. She was lucky; they put her in a barracks, a fourteen-year-old sewing uniforms until she showed other endowments that could lead to other work. A couple of days later, hearing the rumours, she got hysterical and broke out, racing all over the place, trying to find her family. She ran into a section of the camp they called the *Abfall*, the garbage, corpses hauled out of the gas chambers. And there they were, the bodies of her mother and her father and her three brothers, the sight and stench so sickening it's never left her. It never will. She won't set foot in Germany and I wouldn't ask her to.'

No alarms, just surprises . . . and another Iron Cross for the Erich Leifhelms of the past, retroactively presented.

'Christ, I'm sorry,' murmured Converse. 'I didn't mean to . . .'

'You didn't. I did . . . You see, she knows it doesn't make sense.'

'Doesn't make *sense*? Maybe you didn't hear what you just described.'

'I heard, I know, but I didn't finish. When she was sixteen, she was loaded into a truck with five other girls, all on their way to that different type of work, when they did it. Those kids took their last chance and beat the hell out of a *Wehrmacht* corporal who was guarding them in the van. Then with his gun they got control of the truck from the driver and escaped.' Dowling stopped, his eyes on Joel.

Converse, silent, returned the look, unsure of its meaning, but moved by what he had heard. 'That's a marvellous story,' he said quietly. 'It really is.'

'And,' continued the actor, 'for the next two years they were hidden by a succession of German families, who surely knew what they were doing and what would happen to them if they got caught. There was a pretty frantic search for those girls – a lot of threats made, more because of what they could tell than anything else. Still, those Germans kept moving them around, hiding them, until one by one they were taken across the border into occupied France where things were easier. They were smuggled across by the underground, the *German* underground.' Dowling paused, then added, 'As Pa Ratchet would say, "Do you get my drift, son?"'

'I'd have to say it's obvious.'

'There's a lot of pain and a lot of hate in her and God knows I understand it. But there should be some gratitude, too. Couple of times clothing was found, and some of those people – those German people – were tortured, a few shot for what they did. I don't push it, but she could level off with a little gratitude. It might give her a bit more perspective.' The actor snapped on his seat belt.

Joel pressed the locks on his attaché case, wondering if he should reply. Valerie's mother had been part of the German underground. His ex-wife would tell him amusing stories her mother had told her about a stern, inhibited French Intelligence officer forced to work with a high-spirited, opinionated German girl, a member of the *Untergrundbewegung*. How the more they disagreed, and the more they railed against each other's nationality, the more they noticed one another. The Frenchman was Val's father; she was proud of him, but in some ways she was prouder of her mother. There had been pain in that woman too. And hate. But there had been a reason, and it was unequivocal. As there had been for one Joel Converse years later.

'I said it before and I mean it,' began Joel slowly, not sure he should say anything at all. 'It's none of my business, but I wouldn't ever push it, if I were you.'

'Is this a lawyer talkin' to ole Pa?' asked Dowling in his television dialect, his smile false, his eyes far away. 'Do I pay a fee?'

'Sorry, I'll shut up.' Converse adjusted his seat belt and pushed the buckles in place.

'No, *I'm* sorry. I laid it on you. Say it. Please.'

'All right. The horror came first, then the hate. In sidewinder language that's called *prima facie* – the obvious, the first sighting . . . the real, if you like. Without these, there'd be no reason for the gratitude, no call for it. So, in a way, the gratitude is just as painful because it never should have been necessary.'

The actor once again studied Joel's face, as he had done before their first exchange of words. 'You're a smart son of a bitch, aren't you?'

'Professionally adequate. But I've been there . . . that is, I *know* people who've been where your wife has been. It starts with the horror.'

Dowling looked up at the ceiling light, and when he spoke his words floated in the air, his harsh voice quietly strained. 'If we go to the movies, I have to check them out; if we're watching television together, I read the TV section . . . sometimes on the news – with some of those fucking nuts – I tense up, wondering what she's going to do. She can't see a swastika, or hear someone screaming in German, or watch soldiers marching in a goosestep; she can't stand it. She runs and throws up and shakes all over . . . and I try to hold her . . . and sometimes she thinks I'm one of them and she screams. After all these years . . . *Christ!*'

'Have you tried professional help – not my kind – but the sort she might need?'

'Oh, hell, she recovers pretty quick,' said the actor defensively, as if slipping into a role, his teacher's grammar displaced for effect. 'Also, until a few years ago we didn't have the money for that kind of thing,' he added sombrely, without effect.

'What about now? That can't be a problem now.'

Dowling dropped his eyes to his flight bag at his feet. 'If I'd found her sooner . . . maybe. But we were both late bloomers; we got married in our forties – two oddballs looking for something. It's too late now.'

'I'm sorry.'

'I never should have made this goddamn picture. *Never.*'

'Why did you?'

'She said I should. To show people I could play something more than a drivelling, south-forty dispenser of fifth-rate bromides. I told her it didn't matter . . . I was in the war, in the Marine Corps. I saw some crap in the South Pacific but nothing to compare with what she went through, not a spit in the proverbial bucket. *Jesus!* Can you imagine what it must have been like?'

'Yes, I can.'

The actor looked up from the flight bag, a half-drawn smile on his lined, sun-tanned face. 'You, good buddy? Not unless you were caught in Korea . . .'

'I wasn't in Korea.'

'Then you'd be hard put to imagine it any more than I. You were too young and I was too lucky.'

'Well, there was . . .' Converse fell silent; it was pointless. It had happened so often he did not bother to think about it anymore. 'Nam had been erased from the national conversational psyche. He knew that if he reminded a man like Dowling, a decent man, the air would be filled with apologies, but nothing was served by a jarring remembrance. Not as it pertained to Mrs Dowling, born Mühlstein. 'There's the no smoking sign,' said Joel, covering. 'We'll be in Hamburg in a couple of minutes.'

'I've taken this flight a half-dozen times over the past two months,' said Caleb Dowling, 'and let me tell you, Hamburg's a bitch. Not German customs, that's a snap, especially this late. Those rubber stamps fly and they push you through in ten minutes tops. But then you wait. Twice, maybe three times, it was over an hour before the plane to Bonn even got here. By the way, care to join me for a drink in the lounge?' The actor suddenly switched to his southern dialect. 'Between you and me, they make it mighty pleasant for ol' Pa Ratchet. They Telex ahead and Ah got me my own gaggle of cowpokes, all ridin' hard to git me to the waterin' hole.'

'Well . . .' Joel felt flattered. Not only did he like Dowling, but being the guest of a celebrity was a pleasant high. He had not had many pleasant things happen to him recently.

'I should also warn you,' added the celebrity, 'that even at this hour the groupies crawl out of the walls, and the airline PR people manage to roust out the usual newspaper photographers, but none of it takes too long.'

Converse was grateful for the warning. 'I've got some phone calls to make,' he said casually, 'but if I finish them on time, I'd like very much to join you.'

'Phone calls? At this hour?'

'Back to the States. It's not this hour back in . . . Chicago.'

'Make them from the lounge; they keep it open for me.'

'It may sound crazy,' said Joel, reaching for words, 'but I think better alone. There are some complicated things I have to explain. After customs I'll find a phone booth.'

'Nothing sounds crazy to me, son. I work in *Holl*-eee-wood.' Suddenly, the actor's amused exuberance faded. 'In the States,' he said softly, his words floating again, eyes distant again. 'You remember that crap in Skokie, Illinois. They did a television show on it . . . I was in the study learning lines when I heard the screams and the sound of a door crashing open. I ran out and saw my wife racing down to the beach. I had to drag her out of the water. Sixty-seven years old, and she was a little girl again, back in that goddamn camp, seeing the lines of hollow-eyed prisoners, knowing which lines were which . . . seeing her mother and father, her three kid brothers. When you think about it, you can understand why those people say over and over . . . "never again". It can't ever happen again. I wanted to sell that fucking house; I won't leave her alone in it.'

'Is she alone now?'

'Nope,' said Dowling, his smile returning. 'That's the good part. After that night we faced it; we both knew she couldn't be. Got her a sister, that's what we did. Bubbly little thing with more funny stories about Cuckooburg than ever got into print. But she's tough as they come; she's been bouncing around the studios for forty years.'

'An actress?'

'Not so's anyone could tell, but she's a great face in the crowd. She's a good lady, too, good for my wife.'

'I'm glad to hear it,' said Joel, as the aircraft's wheels made bouncing contact with the runway, and the jet engines screeched into reverse thrust. The plane rolled forward, then started a left turn toward its dock.

Dowling turned to Converse. 'If you finish your calls, ask someone for the VIP lounge. Tell them you're a friend of mine.'

'I'll try to get there.'

'If you don't,' added the actor in his Santa Fe dialect, 'see y'awl back in the steel corral. We got us another leg on this here cattle drive, pard'ner. Glad you're riding' shotgun.'

'On a cattle drive?'

'What the hell do I know? I hate horses.'

The plane came to a stop and the forward door opened in less than thirty seconds as a number of excited passengers rapidly jammed the aisle. It was obvious from the whispers and the stares and the few who stood up on their toes to get clearer views, that the reason for the swift exodus of this initial crowd was the presence of Caleb Dowling. And the actor was playing his part, dispensing Pa Ratchet benedictions with warm smiles, broad infectious winks and deep-throated laughter, all with good old wrangler humility. As Joel watched, he felt a rush of compassion for this strange man, this actor, this risk-taker with a private hell he shared with the woman he loved.

Never again. It can't ever happen again. Words.

Converse looked down at the attaché case he held with both hands on his lap. Inside was another story, one that held the sound of distant thunder, far off bolts of lightning filling the air with deadly electricity.

I am back, I am well, and I am at your service. Also words – from another time – but also swollen with thunder for the present, for they were part of the story of a living man's silent return. A spoke in the wheel of Aquitaine.

The first rush of curious passengers filed through the exit door after the television star, and Joel slipped rapidly into the less harried line. He would go through customs as rapidly and as unobtrusively as possible, then find a dark corner of the airport and wait in the deepest shadows until the loudspeakers announced the plane for Köln-Bonn.

Goebbels and Hess accepted Dr Heinrich Leifhelm's offer with enthusiasm. One can easily imagine Goebbels visualizing the image of this blond, Aryan physician of 'impeccable credentials' spread across thousands of pamphlets confirming the specious theories of Nazi genetics, as well as his all-too-willing condemnation of the inferior, avaricious Jew; he was heaven-sent. Whereas for Rudolph Hess, who wanted more than his little boys to be accepted by the Junkers and the monied class, the *Herr Doktor* was his answer; the physician was obviously a true aristocrat, and in time, quite possibly a lover.

The confluence of preparation, timing and appearance turned out to be more than young Stoessel-Leifhelm could have imagined. Adolf Hitler returned from Berlin for one of his Marienplatz rallies, and the imposing *Doktor*, along with his intense, well-mannered son, was invited to dinner with the Führer. The national proclivity was consistent; Hitler heard everything he wanted to hear, and from that day until his death in 1934, Heinrich Leifhelm was Hitler's personal physician.

There was nothing that the son could not have, and in short order he had everything he wanted. In June of 1931, a ceremony was held in the *Heiligtum Hof* at the National Socialists' headquarters where Heinrich Leifhelm's marriage to 'a Jewess' was held to be invalid due to a 'concealment of Jewish blood' on the part of an 'opportunistic Hebrew family', and all rights, claims and inheritances of the children of the 'insidious union' were deemed void. A civil marriage was performed between Leifhelm and Marta Stoessel, and the true inheritor, the only child who could claim the name of Leifhelm, was an eighteen-year-old called Erich.

Munich and the Jewish community still laughed, but not as loudly, at the absurd announcement the Nazis inserted in the legal columns of the newspaper. It was considered nonsense; the Leifhelm name was a discredited name, and certainly no paternal inheritance was involved; finally it was all outside the law. What they were only beginning to understand was that the laws were changing in changing Germany; they were not to remain constant. In two short years there would be only one law: Nazi determination.

Erich Leifhelm had arrived and his ascendancy in the party was swift and assured. At eighteen he was *Jugendführer* of the Hitler Youth movement, photographs of his strong, athletic face and body challenging the children of the New Order to join the national crusade. During his tenancy as a symbol, he was sent to the University of Munich where he completed his courses of study in three years with high academic honours. By this time, Adolf Hitler had been swept into power; he controlled the Reichstag which gave him dictatorial powers. The Thousand Year Reich had begun and Erich Leifhelm was sent to the Officers' Training Centre in Magdeburg.

In 1935, a year after his father's death, Erich Leifhelm, now a youthful favourite of Hitler's inner circle, was promoted to the rank of Oberstleutnant in the Vergeltungswaffen Korps, the youngest field commander in the *Wehrmacht*. He was deeply involved in the vast military expansion that was taking place in Germany, and as the war drew nearer he entered what we can term the third phase of his complicated life, one that ultimately brought him to the centre of Nazi power and at the same time provided him with an extraordinary means of separating himself from the leadership of which he was an intrinsic and influential part. This is briefly covered in the following final pages, a prelude to the fourth phase which we know is his fanatic allegiance to the theories of George Marcus Delavane.

But before we leave the young Erich Leifhelm of Eichstatt, Munich and Magdeburg, two events should be recorded here that provide insights into the man's psychotic mentality. Mentioned above was the robbery at the Luisenstrasse house and the resulting profits of the theft. Leifhelm to this day does not deny the incident, taking pleasure in the tale because of the despicable images he paints of his father's first wife and her overbearing parents. What he does not speak of – nor does anyone in his presence – is the original police report in Munich, which as near as can be determined was destroyed some time in August, 1934, a date corresponding to Hindenburg's death and Hitler's rise to absolute power as both President and Chancellor of Germany with the title of *Der Führer* raised to offical mandatory status.

All copies of the police report were removed from the files, but two elderly pensioners from the Munich department remember it clearly. They are both in their late seventies, have not seen each other in years, and were questioned separately.

Robbery was the lesser crime that early morning on the Luisenstrasse; the more serious one was never spoken of at the insistence of the family. The fifteen-year-old Leifhelm daughter was raped and severely beaten, her face and body battered so violently that upon admission to the Karlstor Hospital the doctors gave her little chance of recovery. She did recover physically, but remained emotionally disturbed for the rest of her short life. The man who committed the assault must have been familiar with the interior of the house, had to know there was a back staircase that led to the girl's room, which was separated from her two brothers and her mother in the front. Erich Leifhelm had questioned his father in depth regarding the inside design of that house; he was there by his own admission, and was aware of the fierce pride and strict moral code held by the 'tyrannical in-laws'. There is no question; his compulsion was such that he had to inflict the most degrading insult he could imagine, and he did so, knowing the influential family would and could insist on official silence.

The second event took place during the months of January or February, 1939. The specifics are sketchy insofar as there are few survivors of the time who knew the family well, and no offical records, but from those who were found and interviewed, certain facts surfaced. Heinrich Leifhelm's legal wife, his children and her family tried without success for several years to leave Germany. The official party line was that the old patriarch's medical skills – having been acquired in German universities – were owed to the State. Also, there were unresolved legal questions arising from the disbanded union between the late Doktor Heinrich Leifhelm and a member of the family, questions specifically relating to commonly-shared assets and the rights of inheritance as they affected an outstanding officer of the *Wehrmacht*.

Erich Leifhelm was taking no chances. His father's 'former' wife and children were virtually held prisoners, their movements restricted, the house on the Luisenstrasse watched, and for weeks following any renewed applications for visas, they were all kept under full 'political surveillance' on the chance that they had plans of vanishing. This information was revealed by a retired banker who recalled that orders came from the Finanzministerium in Berlin instructing the banks of Munich to immediately report any significant withdrawals by the former Frau Leifhelm and/or her family.

During what week or on what day it happened, we did not learn, but some time in January or February of 1936, Frau Leifhelm, her children and her father disappeared.

However, the Munich court records, impounded by the Allies on 23 April 1945, give a clear, if incomplete, picture of what took place. Obviously driven by his compulsion to validate his seizure of the estate in the eyes of the law, a brief was filed on behalf of Oberstleutnant Erich Leifhelm listing the articles-of-grievance suffered by his father, Dr Heinrich Leifhelm, at the hands of the family cabal, said family of criminals having fled the Reich under indictment. The charges, as expected, were outrageous lies: from outright theft of huge non-existent bank accounts to character assassination in order to usurp a great doctor's practice. There was the legal certificate of the 'official' divorce, and a copy of the elder Leifhelm's last will and testament. There was only one true union and one true son, all rights, privileges and inheritances passed on to him: Oberstleutnant Erich Stoessel Leifhelm.

Possessing reasonably accurate dates, survivors were found. It was confirmed that Frau Leifhelm, her three children and her father perished at Dachau, ten miles outside Munich.

The Jewish Leifhelms were gone; the Aryan Leifhelm was now the sole inheritor of considerable wealth and property that under existing conditions would have been confiscated. Before the age of thirty, he had wiped his personal slate clean and avenged the wrongs he was convinced had been visited on his superior birth and talents. A killer had matured.

'You must have one hell of a case there,' said Caleb Dowling, grinning and poking Joel with his elbow. 'Your butt burned up in the ashtray a while ago. I reached over to close the goddamned lid and all you did was raise your hand like I was out of order.'

'I'm *sorry*. It's . . . it's a complicated brief. Christ, I wouldn't raise my hand to you, you're a celebrity.' Converse laughed because he knew it was expected.

'Well, my second bit of news for you, good buddy, is that celebrity or no, the smoking lamp's been on for a couple of minutes now and you still got a reefer in your fingers. Now, I grant you, you didn't light it, but we're getting a lot of Nazi looks over here.'

'Nazi . . . ?' Joel spoke the word involuntarily, as he pressed the unlighted cigarette into the receptacle; he was not aware that he had been holding it.

'A figure of speech and a bad line,' said the actor. 'We'll be in Köln before you put all that legal stuff away. Come on, good buddy, he's going in for the approach.'

'No,' countered Joel without thinking. 'He's making a pitch-out until he gets the tower's instructions. It's standard; we've got at least three minutes.'

'You sound like you know what the hell you're talking about.'

'Vaguely,' said Converse, putting the Leifhelm dossier into his attaché case. 'I used to be a pilot.'

'No kidding? A *real* pilot?'

'Well, I got paid.'

'For an airline? I mean, one of these *real* airlines?'

'Larger than this one, I think.'

'Goddamn, I'm impressed. I wouldn't have thought so. Lawyers and pilots don't seem compatible.'

'It was a long time ago.' Joel closed his case and snapped the locks.

The plane rolled down the runway, the landing having been so unobtrusive that a smattering of applause erupted from the rear of the aircraft.

Dowling spoke as he unfastened his seat belt. 'I used to hear some of that after a particularly good class.'

'Now you hear a lot more,' said Converse.

'For a hell of a lot less. By the way, where are you staying, counsellor?'

Joel was not prepared for the question. 'Actually, I'm not sure,' he replied, again reaching for words, for an answer. 'This trip was a last-minute decision.'

'You may need help. Bonn's crowded. Tell you what, I'm at the Königshof and I suspect I've got a little influence. Let's see what we can do.'

'Thanks very much but that won't be necessary.' Converse thought rapidly. The last thing he wanted was the attention focused on anyone in the actor's company. 'My firm's sending someone to meet me and he'll have seen to the accommodation. As a matter of fact, I'm supposed to be one of the last people off the plane, so he doesn't have to try and find me in the crowd.'

'Well, if you've got any time and you want a couple of laughs with some actor types, call me at the hotel and leave a number.'

'I probably will. I enjoyed riding shotgun.'

'On the cattle drive, pard'ner?'

Joel waited. The last stragglers were leaving the plane nodding at the flanking stewardesses, some yawning, others in awkward combat with shoulder bags, camera equipment, and suitcarriers. The final passenger exited through the aircraft's concave door and Converse got up, gripping the handle of his attaché case and sliding into the aisle. Instinctively, without having a conscious reason to do so, he glanced to his right, into the rear section of the plane.

What he saw – and what saw him – caused him to freeze, his breath exploding silently within his chest. Seated in the last row of the long fuselage was a woman. The pale skin under the wide brim of the hat, and the frightened, astonished eyes that abruptly looked away – all formed an image he vividly remembered. She was the woman in the café at the Kastrup Airport in Copenhagen! When he last saw her she was walking rapidly into the baggage claim area, *away* from the row of airline counters. She had been stopped by a man in a hurry; words had been exchanged – and now Joel knew they had concerned him.

The woman had doubled back, unnoticed in the last-minute rush for boarding. He felt it, he *knew* it! She had followed him from Denmark!

6

Converse rushed up the aisle and through the metal door into the carpeted tunnel. Fifty feet down the passageway the narrow walls opened into a waiting area, the plastic seats and the roped-off stanchions designating the gate. There was no one; the place was empty, the other gates shut down, the lights off. Beyond, suspended from the ceiling, were signs in German,

French, and English directing passengers to the main terminal and the downstairs baggage claim. There was no time for his luggage; he had to run; he had to get away from the airport as fast as possible, get away without being seen. Then the obvious struck him, and he felt sick. He *had* been seen; they knew he was on the flight from Hamburg – whoever *they* were. The instant he walked into the terminal, he would be spotted, and there was nothing he could do about it. They had found him in Copenhagen; the woman had found him and she had been ordered on board to make certain he did not stay in Hamburg, or switch planes to another destination.

How? How did they *do* it?

There was no time to think about it; he would think about it later – if there was a later. He passed the arches of the closed-down metal detectors and the black conveyor belts where hand luggage was X-rayed. Ahead, no more than 75 feet were the doors to the terminal. What was he going to do, what *should* he do?

Nur für hier Beschäftigte
Männer

Joel stopped. The sign on the door was emphatic, the German print forbidding. Yet he had seen those words before. Where? What was it? Zurich! He had been in a department store in Zurich when a stomach attack had descended to his bowels. He had pleaded with a sympathetic clerk who had taken him to a nearby employees' men's room. In one of those odd moments of gratitude and relief, he had focused on the strange words as they had drawn nearer. Nur für hier Beschäftigte Männer.

No further memory was required. He pushed the door open and went inside, not sure what he would do other than collect his thoughts. A man in green overalls was at the far end of the line of sinks against the wall; he was combing his hair while inspecting a blemish on his face in the mirror. Converse walked to the row of urinals beyond the basins, his demeanour that of an airline executive. The affectation was accepted; the man mumbled something courteously and left. The door swung shut and he was alone.

Joel stepped back from the urinal and studied the tiled enclosure, hearing for the first time the sound of several voices . . . outside, somewhere outside, beyond . . . the *windows*. Three-quarters up from the floor and recessed in the far wall were three frosted glass windows, the painted white frame melting into the whiteness of the room. He was confused. In these security-conscious days of airline travel with the constant emphasis on guarding against smuggled arms and narcotics, a room inside a gate area that had a means of getting outside before entering customs did not make sense. Then the obvious fact occurred to him. It could be his way out! The flight from Hamburg was a *domestic* flight, this part of the Köln-Bonn airport a *domestic* terminal – there were no customs. Of *course* there were exterior windows in an enclosure like this. What difference did it make? Passengers still had to pass through the electronic arches, and conversely, authorities wanting to pick up a passenger flying domestically would simply wait by a specific gate.

But no one waited for him. He had been the last – the *second* to last – passenger off the late night flight. The roped-off gate had been deserted;

anyone sitting in one of the plastic chairs or standing beyond the counter would be obvious. Therefore, those who were keeping him in their sights did not want to be seen themselves. Whoever they were, they were waiting, watching for him from some remote spot inside the terminal. They could wait.

He approached the far right window and lowered his attaché case to the floor. Standing erect, the sill was only inches above his head. He reached for the two white handles and pushed; the window slid easily up several inches. He poked his fingers through the space; there was no screen. Once the window was raised to its full height, there would be enough room for him to crawl outside.

There was a clattering behind him, rapid slaps of metal against wood. He spun around as the door opened revealing a hunched-over old man in a white maintenance uniform carrying a mop and pail. Slowly, with deliberation, the old man took out a pocket watch, squinted at it, said something in German, and waited for an answer. Joel was not only aware that he was expected to speak, he assumed that he had been told the employees' men's room was being closed until morning. He had to think; he could not leave; the only way out of the airport was through the terminal. If there was another, he did not know where and it was no time to be running around a section of an airport shut down for the remainder of the night. Patrolling guards might compound his problems.

His eyes dropped, centring on the metal pail, and in desperation he knew what he had to do, but not whether he could do it. With a sudden grimace of pain, he moaned and grabbed his chest, falling to his knees. He cried louder, his face contorted, and sank further to the floor.

'Doctor, doctor . . . *Doctor!*' he shouted over and over again in muted tones of pain.

The old man dropped the mop and the pail; a guttural stream of panicked phrases accompanied several cautious steps forward. Converse rolled to his right against the wall; he gasped for breath as he watched the German with wide, blank eyes.

'Doctor . . . !' he whispered.

The old man trembled and backed away toward the door; he turned, opened it, and ran out, his frail voice raised for help.

There would only be seconds! The gate was no more than two hundred feet to the left, the entrance to the terminal perhaps a hundred to the right. Joel got up quickly, raced to the pail, turned it upside down, and brought it back to the window. He placed it on the floor and stepped up with one foot, his palms making contact with the base of the window; he shoved. The glass rose about four inches and stopped, the frame lodged against the sash. He pushed again with all the strength he could manage in his awkward position. The window would not budge; breathing hard he studied it, his intense gaze zeroing in on two small steel objects he wished to God were not in place, but they were. Two protective braces were screwed into the opposing sashes, preventing the window from being opened more than six inches. Köln-Bonn might not be an international airport with a panoply of sophisticated security devices, but it was not without its own.

There were distant shouts from beyond the door; the old man had reached someone. The sweat rolled down Converse's face as he stepped off the pail and reached for his attaché case on the floor. Movement and decision were intertwined, neither preceding the other, only instinct unconsciously governing both. Joel picked up the leather case, stepped forward, and crashed it repeatedly into the window, shattering the glass, finally breaking away the lower wooden frame. He stepped back up on the pail and looked out. Beyond – below – was a cement path bordered by a guardrail, floodlights in the distance, no one in sight. He threw the attaché case out of the window, and pulled himself up, his left knee kicking fragments of glass and what was left of the frame to the concrete below. Awkwardly, he hunched his whole body, pressing his head into his shoulder blades, and plunged through the opening. As he fell to the ground, he heard shouts from inside; they grew in volume, all in counterpoint, mixtures of anger and bewilderment. He ran.

Minutes later, at a sudden curve in the cement path, he saw the floodlit entrance of the terminal and the line of taxis waiting for the passengers of Flight 817 from Hamburg to collect their luggage before the drivers collected their inflated night prices to Bonn and Köln. There were entrance and exit roads leading to the platform, broken by pedestrian crosswalks, and beyond these an immense parking lot with several lighted booths still operating for those driving their own cars. Converse slipped over the guardrail and ran across the intersecting lawn until he reached the first road, racing into the shadows at the first blinding glare of a floodlight. He had to reach a taxi, a taxi with a driver who spoke English; he could not remain on foot . . . he had been captured on foot once, years ago. On a jungle trail, where if he had only been able to commandeer a jeep – an enemy jeep – he might have . . . *Stop it*! This is not 'Nam, it's a goddamn airport with a million tons of concrete poured between flowers, grass, and asphalt! He kept moving in and out of the shadows, until he had made a complete semi-circle – one-eight zero. He was in darkness, the last of the taxis in the line ahead of him. He approached the first, which was the last.

'English? Do you speak English?'

'*Englisch? Nein.*'

The second cab driver was equally negative, but the third was not.

'As you Americans say, only the asshole would drive a taxi here wizzout the English reasonable. Is so?'

'It's reasonable,' said Joel, opening the door.

'*Nein*! You cannot do that!'

'Do what?'

'Come in the taxi.'

'Why not?'

'The line. Allviss is the line.'

Converse reached into his jacket pocket and withdrew a folded layer of Deutschmarks. 'I'm generous. Can you understand that?'

'Is also urgent sickness. Get in, *Mein Herr.*'

The cab pulled out of the line and sped toward the exit road. 'Bonn or Köln?' asked the driver.

'Bonn,' replied Converse, 'but not yet. I want you to drive into the other lane and stop across the way in front of that parking lot.'

'*Vas* . . . ?'

'The other *lane*. I want to watch the entrance back there. I think there was someone on the Hamburg plane I know.'

'Many have come out. Only those with luggage . . .'

'She's still inside,' insisted Joel. '*Please*, just do as I say.'

'She . . . *Ach, ein Fräulein*. Is yoor Deutschmarks, *Mein Herr*.'

The driver swung the cab into the cut off that led to the incoming road and the parking lot. He stopped in the shadows beyond the second booth; the terminal doors were on the left, no more than a hundred yards away. Converse watched as weary passengers, carrying assorted suitcases, golfbags, and the ever-present camera equipment, began to file out of the terminal's entrance, most raising their hands for taxis, a few walking across the pedestrian lanes toward the parking lot.

Twelve minutes passed and still there was no sign of the woman from Copenhagen. She could not have been carrying luggage, so the delay was voluntary, or instructed. The driver of the cab had assumed the role of non-observer; he had turned off the lights, and with a bowed head he appeared to be dozing. Silence . . . Across the parallel roads, the travellers from Hamburg had dwindled down. Several young men, undoubtedly students, two in scissored jeans, their companions drinking from cans of beer, were laughing as they counted the bills of Deutschmarks between them. A yawning businessman in a three-piece suit struggled with a bulging suitcase and an enormous cardboard box wrapped in a floral print, while an elderly couple argued, their dispute emphasized by two shaking heads of grey hair. Five others, men and women, were by the kerb at the far end of the platform apparently waiting for prearranged transportation. But where . . . ?

Suddenly, she was there, but she was not alone. Instead, she was flanked by two men, a third directly behind her. All four walked slowly, casually out of the automatic glass doors, moving to the left, their pace quickening until they reached the dimmest area of the canopied entrance. Then the three men angled themselves in front of the woman, as if mounting a wall of protection, their heads turning, talking to her over their shoulders while studying the crowd. Their conversation became animated but controlled, anger joining confusion, tempers held in check. The man on the right broke away and crossed to the corner of the building, then walked beyond into the shadows. He pulled an object out of an inside pocket and Joel instantly knew what it was; the man raised it to his lips. Someone in or around the airport was being contacted by radio.

Barely seconds passed when the beams of powerful headlights burst through the glass over Converse's right shoulder, filling the back of the taxi. He pressed himself into the seat, his head turned, neck arched, his face at the edge of the rear window. Beyond, by the exit booth of the parking lot, a dark red limousine had stopped, the driver's arm extended, a bill clutched in his hand. The attendant took the money, turned to give change, when the large car lurched forward leaving the man in the booth bewildered. It careened around the taxi and headed for the curve in the road that led to the airport terminal's entrance. The timing was too precise; radio contact had been made and Joel spoke to the driver.

'I told you I was generous,' he said, startled by the words he was forming in his head. 'I can be *very* generous if you'll do as I ask you.'

'I am an honest man, *Mein Herr*,' replied the German, uncertainty in his voice, his eyes looking at Joel in the rear-view mirror.

'So am I,' said Converse. 'But I'm also honestly curious, and there's nothing wrong with that. You see that dark red car over there, the one that's stopping at the corner of the building?'

'*Ja.*'

'Do you think you could follow it without being seen? You'd have to stay pretty far behind, but keep it in sight. Could you do it?'

'Is not a reasonable request. How generous is the *Amerikaner*?'

'Two hundred Deutschmarks over the fare.'

'You are generous, *Mein Herr*, and I am a superior driver.'

The German did not underestimate his talents behind the wheel. Skilfully, he weaved the cab unobtrusively through a cut off, swinging abruptly left into the parallel exit road and bypassing the entrance to the terminal.

'What are you doing?' asked Joel, confused. 'I want you to follow . . .'

'Is only way out,' interrupted the driver, glancing back at the airport platform while maintaining moderate speed. 'I shall let him pass me. I am just one more insignficant taxi on the *Landstrasse*.'

Converse sank back into the corner of the seat, his head away from the windows. 'That's reasonably good thinking,' he said.

'Superior, *Mein Herr*.' Again the driver looked briefly back out of the window, then concentrated on the road and the rear view mirror. Moments later he gradually accelerated his speed; it was not noticeable; there was no breaking away, instead merely a faster pace. He eased to the left, passing a Mercedes coupé, staying in the lane to overtake a Volkswagen, then returning to the right.

'I hope you know what you're doing,' muttered Joel.

No reply was necessary as the dark red vehicle streaked by on the left.

'Directly ahead the road separates,' said the driver. 'One way to Köln, the other to Bonn. You say you are going to Bonn, *Mein Herr*, but what if your friend goes to Köln?'

'Stay with him.'

The limousine entered the road for Bonn and Converse lighted a cigarette, his thoughts on the reality of having been found, which meant his name was known from the passenger manifest. So be it; he would have preferred otherwise but once the initial contact had been made with Bertholdier, it was not a vital point. He could operate as himself; his past might even be an asset. Also, there was a positive side to the immediate situation; he had learned something, several things. Those following him – who now had lost him – were no part of the authorities; they were not connected with either the German or the French police, or the coordinating Interpol. If they were, they would have taken him at the gate or on the plane itself, and that told him something else. Joel Converse was not wanted for assault or – God forbid – murder back in Paris. And this assumption could only lead to a third probability: the violent, bloody struggle in the alley was being covered up. Jacques Louis Bertholdier was taking no chances that because of his severely wounded aide his own name might surface in any connection whatsoever with a wealthy guest of the hotel who had made such alarming insinuations to the revered general. The protection of Aquitaine was paramount.

There was a fourth possibility, so realistically arrived at it could be considered fact. The men in the dark red limousine who had met the Hamburg plane were also part of Aquitaine, underlings of Erich Leifhelm, the spoke of Aquitaine in West Germany. Some time during the last five hours, Bertholdier had learned the identity of the ersatz Henry Simon – probably through the management of the George V – and contacted Leifhelm. Then, both alarmed that no passenger manifest listed an American named Converse flying from Paris to Bonn, they checked the other airlines and found he had gone to Copenhagen. The alarms must have been strident. Why Copenhagen? He said he was going to Bonn. Why did this strange man with his extraordinary information go to Copenhagen? Who are his contacts, who will he meet? Find him. Find *them*! Another phone call had been made, a description given, and a woman had stared at him in a café in the Kastrup Airport. It was all so through-the-looking-glass.

He had flown to Denmark for one reason, but another purpose had been revealed. They had found him, but in the finding they revealed their own panic. An agitated reception committee, the use of a radio at night to reach an unseen vehicle only a few hundred feet away, a racing limousine; these were the ingredients of anxiety. The enemy was off-balance and the lawyer in Converse was satisfied. At this moment, that enemy was a quarter of a mile down the road, speeding into Bonn, unaware that a taxi behind them, skilfully manoeuvred by a driver slipping around the intermittent traffic was keeping them in sight.

Joel crushed out his cigarette as the driver slowed down to let a pick-up truck pass, the large dark red car seen clearly ahead on the long curve. The German was no amateur; he knew the beneficial moves to make, and Converse understood. Whoever was in that limousine might well be an influential owner, and even two hundred Deustschmarks were not worth the probable enmity of a powerful man.

Probabilities . . . everything was probabilities. He had built his legal reputation on the study of probabilities and it was a simpler process than most of his colleagues believed. The approach, that is, was simple, not the work; that was never easy. It demanded the dual discipline of both concentrating on the minute, and prodding the imagination to expand until the minutiae were arranged and rearranged into dozens of different equations. The exhaustive what-if syndrome was the keystone of legal thinking; it was as simple as that. It was also a verbal trap, Joel reflected, as he thought back several years, an uncomfortable smile forming. In one of her moments of pique, Val had told him that if he would spend one iota of the time on the two of them that he spent on his 'goddamned probabilities', he would 'probably' come to realize that the 'probability' of their surviving together was 'very probably nil'.

She had never lacked for being succinct, nor sacrificed her humour in the pursuit of candour. Her striking looks aside, Valerie Carpentier Converse was a very funny lady. Unable not to, he had smiled at her explosion that night years ago, then they had both laughed quietly until she turned away and left the room, too much sadness in the truth she had spoken.

Large picturesque buildings gradually replaced the quiet countryside, so many somehow reminding Converse of huge Victorian houses with filigreed borders and overlapping eaves and grilled balconies beneath large rectangular windows – geometric shapes starkly defined. These in turn gave way to a contradictory stretch of attractive but perfectly ordinary residential homes, the sort that could be found in any traditional wealthy suburb on the outskirts of a major American city. Scarsdale, Chevy Chase, Grosse Pointe, or Evanston. Then came the centre of Bonn where narrow, gas-lit streets ran into wider avenues with modern lighting, quaint squares only blocks away from banks of contemporary stores and boutiques. It was an architectural anachronism – old world ambience coexisting with up-to-the minute structure – but with no sense of a city, no sense of electricity or grandeur. Instead it appeared to be a large town, growing rapidly larger, the town fathers uncertain of its direction. The birthplace of Beethoven and the gateway to the Rhine Valley was the most unlikely capital of a major government imaginable. It was anything but the seat of a hard-nosed Bundestag, and a series of astute, sophisticated prime ministers who faced the Russian bear across the borders.

'*Mein Herr!*' cried the driver. 'They take the road to Bad Godesberg. *Das Diplomatenviertel.*'

'What does that mean?'

'Embassies. They have *Polizeistreifen*! We could be, how do you say, *known*?'

'Spotted,' explained Joel. 'Never mind. Do what you've been doing, you're great. Stop, if you have to; park, if you have to. Then keep going. You now have three hundred Deutschmarks over the fare. I want to know where they stop.'

It came six minutes later, and Converse was stunned. Whatever he had thought, wherever his imagination had led him, he was not prepared for the driver's words.,

'That is the American Embassy, *Mein Herr.*'

Joel tried to focus his thoughts. 'Take me to the Hotel Königshof,' he said, remembering, not knowing what else to say.

'Yes, I believe Herr Dowling left a note to that effect,' said the desk clerk, reaching below the counter.

'He *did*?' Converse was astonished. He had used the actor's name in the outside hope of some possible preferential treatment. He expected nothing else, if, indeed, that.

'Here it is.' The clerk extracted two small telephone memos from the thin stack in his hand. 'You are John Converse, an American attorney.'

'Close enough. That's me.'

'Herr Dowling said you might have difficulty in finding appropriate accommodation here in Bonn. Should you come to the Königshof tonight, he requested that we be as helpful as possible. It is possible, Herr Converse. Herr Dowling is a very popular man.'

'He deserves to be,' said Joel.

'I see he also left a message for you.'

The clerk turned and retrieved a sealed envelope from one of the mailboxes behind him. He handed it to Converse, who opened it.

Hi, pard'ner.

If you don't pick this up, I'll get it back in the morning. Forgive me, but you sounded like too many of my less fortunate colleagues who say no when they want to say yes. Now collectively in their case, it's some kind of warped pride because they think I'm suggesting a handout – it's either that or they don't want to meet someone who may be where they're going. By the looks of you, I'd have to rule out the former and stick with the latter. There's someone you don't want to meet here in Bonn, and you don't have to. The room's taken care of and in my name – change that if you like – but don't argue about the bill. I owe you a fee, counsellor, and I always pay my debts. At least during the last four years I have.

Incidentally, you'd make a lousy actor. Your pauses aren't at all convincing.

Pa Ratchet

Joel put the note back in the envelope, resisting the temptation to go to a house phone and call Dowling. The man would have little enough sleep before going to work; thanks could wait until morning. Or evening.

'Mr Dowling's arrangements are generous and completely satisfactory,' he said to the clerk behind the counter. 'He's right. If my clients knew I'd come to Bonn a day early, I'd have no chance to enjoy your beautiful city.'

'Your privacy will be respected, sir. Herr Dowling is a most thoughtful man, as well as generous, of course. Your luggage is outside with a taxi, perhaps?'

'No, that's why I am so late. It was put on the wrong plane out of Hamburg and will be here in the morning. At least that's what I was told at the airport.'

'*Ach*, so inconvenient, but all too familiar. Is there anything you might require?'

'No thanks' replied Converse raising his attaché case slightly. 'The bare necessities travel with me . . . Well, there is one thing. Would it be possible to order a drink?'

'Of course.'

Joel sat up in bed, the dossier at his side, the drink in his hand. He needed a few minutes to think before going back into the world of Field Marshal Erich Leifhelm. With the help of the switchboard, he had called the all-night number for Lufthansa and had been assured that his suitcase would be held for him at the airport. He gave no explanation other than the fact that he had been travelling for two days and nights and simply did not care to wait for his luggage. The attendant could read into his words whatever she liked; he did not care. His mind was on other things.

The American Embassy! What appalled him was the stark reality of old Beale's words . . . *Behind it all are those who do the convincing, and they're growing in numbers everywhere . . . We're in the countdown – three to five weeks, that's all you've got . . . It's real and it's coming.* Joel was not prepared for the reality. He could accept Delavane and Bertholdier, certainly Leifhelm, but the shock of knowing the ordinary embassy personnel – *American* personnel – were on the receiving end of orders from Delavane's network was paralysing. How far *had* Aquitaine progressed? How widespread were its followers, its influence? Was tonight the frightening answer to both questions? He would think about it all in the morning. First, he had to be prepared for the man he had come to find in Bonn. As he reached for the dossier, he remembered the sudden deep panic in Avery Fowler's eyes – Preston Halliday's eyes. How long had he known? How much had he known?

It is pointless to recount Erich Leifhelm's exploits in the early to middle years of the war other than to say his reputation grew, and – what is most important – that he was one of the very few superior officers to come up through Nazi party ranks to be accepted by the old line professional generals. Not only did they accept him but they sought him out for their commands. Men like Rundstedt and von Falkenhausen, Rommel and von Treskow; at one time or another each asked Berlin for Leifhelm's services. He was unquestionably a brilliant strategist and a daring officer, but there was something else. These generals were aristocrats, part of the ruling class of pre-war Germany and by and large loathed the National Socialists, considering them thugs, exhibitionists and amateurs. It is not difficult to imagine Leifhelm, sitting among these men, modestly expounding on what was clearly noted in his military record. He was the son of the late prominent Munich surgeon Dr Heinrich Leifhelm, who had left him considerable wealth and property. We need no conjecture, however, to understand how much further he went to ingratiate himself, for the following is extracted from an interview with General Rolf Winter, Standortkommandant of the Wehrbereichskommando in the Saar sectors.

'We would sit around having coffee after dinner, the talk quite depressing. We knew the war was lost. The insane orders from Berlin – most we agreed we would never carry out – guaranteed wholesale slaughter of troops and civilians. It was madness, a *Götterdämmerung*. And always, this young Leifhelm would say things like, "Perhaps the fools will listen to me. They think I'm one of them, they've thought so from the early days in Munich" . . . And we would wonder. Could he bring some sanity to the collapsing front? He was a fine officer, highly regarded, and the son of a well-known doctor, as he constantly reminded us. After all, young men's heads were turned in those early days – the cavernous roars of *Sieg Heil*, the fanatic crowds; the banners and drums and marching beside ten thousand torches at night; it was all so melodramatic, so Wagnerian. But Leifhelm was different; he wasn't one of the gangsters; patriotic, of course, but not a hoodlum . . . So we sent dispatches with him to our closest comrades in Berlin, dispatches that would have resulted in our execution if they fell into the wrong hands. We were told he tried very hard, but he could not pull sanity out of the minds of men who lived in daily fear of death from rumour and gossip. But he maintained his own sanity – and loyalty – which were constant. We were informed by one of his adjutants, not him, mind you, that he was confronted by an SS colonel who had followed him in the street and demanded the contents of his briefcase. He refused, and when threatened with immediate arrest, he shot the man so as not to betray us. He was one of us. It was a noble risk and only a night bombing raid saved his own life.'

It is clear what Leifhelm was doing and equally clear that the dispatches were never shown to anyone, nor was there an SS colonel shot in the streets during a bombing raid. According to Winter, those dispatches from Saar were so explosive in content someone would have remembered them; no one does. Once again, Leifhelm saw an opportunity. The war was lost, and the Nazis were about to become the ultimate twentieth century villains. But not the élite, German general corps – there was a distinction. He wiped another slate clean and joined the 'Prussians'. He was so successful that he was rumoured to have been part of the plot to assassinate Adolph Hitler at Wolfsschanze, and called upon to be a member of Doenitz's surrender team.

During the cold war, Allied Central Command asked him to join other key elements of the *Wehrmacht* officer corps in the *Bundes Polizei*. He became a privileged military consultant with full security clearance. A mature killer had survived and history, with the Kremlin's help, took care of the rest.

In May 1949 the Federal Republic was established, and the following September the Allied occupation formally came to an end. As the cold war escalated and West Germany began its remarkable recovery, the NATO forces demanded material and personnel support from their former enemies. The new German divisions were formed under the command of ex-Field Marshal Erich Leifhelm.

No one had dredged up the questionable decisions of the Munich courts from nearly two decades past; there were no other survivors and his services were desired by the victors. During the post-war reconstruction when countless settlements and labyrinthine legal resolutions were being sought throughout Germany, he was quietly awarded all assets and property previously decreed, including some of the most valuable real estate in Munich. So ends the third phase of Erich Leifhelm's story. The fourth phase – which concerns us most – is the one we know least about. The only certainty is that he has become as deeply entrenched in General Delavane's operation as any name on the primary list.

There was a rapping on the door. Joel lunged off the bed, the Leifhelm dossier cascading to the floor. He looked at his watch, fear paramount, confusion not far behind. It was nearly four o'clock. Who wanted him at *this* hour? Had they *found* him. Oh, *Christ!* The *dossier!* The *briefcase!*

'Joe . . .? *Joe*, you *up?*' The voice was both a whisper and a shout . . . an actor's *sotto voce*. 'It's me, Cal Dowling.'

Converse ran to the door and opened it, his breath coming in gasps Dowling was fully dressed, holding up both his hands for silence, as he glanced up and down the corridor. Satisfied, he walked rapidly inside pushing Joel back and closing the door.

'I'm *sorry*, Cal,' said Converse. 'I was asleep. I guess the sound startle me.'

'You always sleep in your trousers with the lights on?' asked the actor quietly. 'Keep your voice down. I checked the hallways, but you can never be clear about what you didn't see.'

'Clear about what?'

'One of the first things we learned on Kwajalein in 'forty-four. A patrol doesn't mean shit unless you've got something to report. All it means is that they were better than you were.'

'I was going to call you, to thank you . . .'

'*Cut* it, good buddy,' broke in the lined, sun-tanned Dowling, his expression serious. 'I'm timing this down to the last couple of minutes, which is about all we've got. There's a limo downstairs waiting to take me out to the cameras over an hour away. I didn't want to come out of my room before in case anyone was hanging around, and I didn't want to call you because a switchboard can be watched or bribed – ask anyone in Cuckooburg. I don't worry about the desk; they're not too fond of our crowd over here.' The actor sighed and shook his head. 'When I got to my room, all I wanted was sleep, and all I got was a visitor. I'm down the hall and I was hoping to Christ – *if* you came here – he wouldn't see you.'

'A visitor?'

'From the embassy. The *US* embassy. Tell me, Joe . . .'

'Joel,' interruped Converse. 'Not that it matters.'

'Sorry, I've an obstruction in my left ear and that doesn't matter, either . . . He spent damn near twenty-five minute with me asking questions about you. He said we were seen talking together on the plane. Now, you *tell* me, counsellor, are you okay, or are my instincts all fucked up?'

Joel returned Dowling's steady gaze. 'Your instincts are perfectly fine,' he said without emphasis. 'Did the man from the embassy say otherwise?'

'Not exactly. As a matter of fact, he didn't *say* a hell of a *lot*. Just that they wanted to talk to you, wanted to know why you'd come to Bonn, where you were.'

'But they knew I was on the plane?'

'Yep, said you'd flown out of Paris.'

'Then they *knew* I was on that plane.'

'That's what I just said – what he said.'

'Then why didn't they meet me at the gate and ask me themselves?'

Dowling's face creased farther, his eyes narrowing within the wrinkles of bronzed flesh. 'Yeah, why didn't they?' he asked himself.

'Did he say?'

'No, but then Paris didn't come up until he was about to leave.'

'What do you mean?'

'It was like he figured I was holding back something – which I certainly was – but he couldn't be sure. I'm pretty good at what I do, Joe . . . Joel.'

'You also took a risk,' said Converse, remembering that he was talking to a risk-taker.

'No, I covered myself. I specifically asked if there were charges against you or anything like that. He said there weren't.'

'Still, he was . . .'

'Besides, I didn't like him. He was one of those pushy official types. He kept repeating things, and when he couldn't come up with anything, he said, "We know he flew out of Paris," as if challenging me. I said *I* didn't.'

'There's not much time, but can you tell me what else he asked you?'

'I told you, he wanted to know everything we talked about. I said I didn't have a tape recorder in my head, but it was mainly small talk, the kind of chatter I get all the time from people I meet on planes. About the show, the business. But he didn't want to settle for that; he kept pushing, which gave me the opportunity to get a little pissed off myself.'

'How so?'

'I said, yes, we did talk about something else but it was very personal, and none of his damn business. He got pretty upset at that, and that let me get even angrier. We exchanged a few barbs but his weren't very sharp; he was too uptight. Then he asked me for about the tenth time if you'd said anything about Bonn, especially where you were staying. So I told him for the tenth time the truth – at least what you said. That you were a lawyer and here to see clients and I didn't know where the hell you were. I mean I didn't actually know you were here.'

'That's fine.'

'Is it? Instincts are okay for first reactions, counsellor, but then you have to wonder. An aggravating Ivy League government man, waving an embassy ID and acting obnoxious, may be very annoying in the middle of the night, but he *is* from the Department of State. What the hell's this all about?'

Joel turned and walked to the foot of the bed; he looked down at the Leifhelm dossier on the floor. He turned again and spoke clearly, hearing the exhaustion in his voice. 'Something I wouldn't for the life of me involve you in. But for the record, those instincts of yours were right on, pard'ner.'

'I'll be honest,' said the actor, his clear eyes amused, peering out from behind the craglines. 'I thought as much. I said to that bastard if I remembered anything else, I'd phone Walter what's-his-name – except I called him Walt – and let him know.'

'I don't understand.'

'He's the ambassador here in Bonn. Can you imagine, with all the troubles they've got over here, that diplomtic yo-yo had a luncheon for *me*, a lousy television actor? . . . Well, that bit of volunteerism on my part made our Preppie more upset than anything else; he didn't expect it. He said – three times, as I recall – that the ambassador wasn't to be bothered with this problem. It wasn't that important, and he had enough on his mind, and actually he wasn't even aware of it. And catch this, Mr Lawyer. He said you were an in-house, State Department "queery", as if a simple-minded actor couldn't possibly understand bureaucratic jingoism. I think that's when I said "bullshit".'

'Thank you,' said Converse, not knowing what else to say, but knowing what he wanted to find out.

'That's when I figured my instincts weren't so bad.' Dowling looked at his watch, then hard at Converse, his eyes now penetrating. 'I was a Marine, but I'm no flag-waver, good buddy. However, I *like* the flag. I wouldn't live under any other.'

'Neither would I.'

'Then you make it plain. Are you working for it?'

'Yes, the only way I know how and that's all I can tell you.'

'Are you looking into something here in Bonn? Is that why you didn't want to be seen with me? Why you stayed away from me in Hamburg . . . and even getting off the plane here?'

'Yes.'

'And that son of a bitch didn't want me to call the ambassador.'

'No, he didn't. He doesn't. He can't afford it. And, please, I ask you not to.'

'Are you – oh, *Christ*! Are you one of those undercover people I read about? I walk into a guy on a plane who can't be seen when he gets to an airport.'

'It's not that melodramatic. I'm a lawyer and simply following up on some alleged irregularities. Please accept that. And I appreciate what you did for me. I'm kind of new at this myself.'

'You're cool, good buddy. *Man*, are you cool.' Dowling turned and walked to the door. He stopped and looked back at Converse. 'Maybe I'm crazy,' he said. 'At my age it's allowed, but there's a streak in you, young fella. Part go-ahead, part stay-where-you-are. I saw it when I talked about my wife. Are you married?'

'I was.'

'Who isn't? *Was* married, that is. Sorry.'

'I'm not. We're not.'

'Who is? Sorry, again. My instincts were right. You're okay.' Dowling reached for the knob.

'Cal?'

'Yes?'

'I have to know. It's terribly important. Who was the man from the embassy. He must have identified himself.'

'He did,' said the actor. 'He pushed an ID in front of my face when I opened the door, but I didn't have my glasses on. But when he was leaving I made it clear I wanted to know who the hell he was.'

'Who was he?'

'He said his name was Fowler. Avery Fowler.'

7

'*Wait!*'

'What?'

'*What* did you say?' Converse reeled under the impact of the name. He physically had to steady himself, grabbing the nearest solid object, a bedpost, to keep from buckling.

'What's the matter, Joe? What's wrong with you?'

'That name! Is this some kind of joke – a bad joke – a bad *line*! Were you *put* on the plane? Did I walk into *you*! Are you part of it, Mr *Actor*? You're damned good at what you do!'

'You're either juiced or sick. What are you talking about?'

'This *room*, your note! *Everything!* That *name!* Is this whole goddamned night a set up?'

'It's morning, young man, and if you don't like this room you can stay wherever you like as far as I'm concerned.'

'Wherever . . . ?' Joel tried to push the blinding flashes of light from the Quai du Mont Blanc from his eyes and clear the searing blockage in his throat. 'No . . . I *came* here,' he said hoarsely. 'There's no way you could have known I'd do that. In Copenhagen, on the plane . . . I got the last ticket in First Class; the seat next to me had been sold, an aisle seat.'

'That's where I always sit. On the aisle.'

'Oh, *Jesus!*'

'Now you're rambling.' Dowling glanced at the empty glass on the bedside table, then over at the bureau top where there was a silvery tray and a bottle of Scotch whisky provided by an accommodating desk clerk. 'How much sauce have you had?'

Converse shook his head. 'I'm not drunk . . . I'm sorry. *Christ*, I'm *sorry!* You had nothing to do with it. They're using you – trying to use you to find me! You *saved my* . . . my job . . . and I went after you. Forgive me. You've been so helpful.'

'And you don't look like someone who's that worried about a job,' said the actor, his scowl more one of concern than anger.

'It's not the employment, it's . . . pulling it off.' Joel silently took a deep breath, imposing control, postponing the moment when he would have to confront the awesome implications found in what he had just heard. *Avery Fowler!* 'I want to succeed in what I'm doing; I want to win,' he added limply, hoping to conceal the slip he saw Dowling had spotted. 'All lawyers want to win.'

'Sure.'

'I *am* sorry, Cal.'

'Forget it,' said the actor, his voice casual, his look not casual at all. 'Where I'm at these days screeching's an hourly occurrence, only they don't say anything. I think you just did.'

'No, I over-reacted, that's all. I told you I was new at this. Not the law, just this . . . not talking directly, I guess says it.'

'Does it?'

'Yes. Please believe that.'

'All right, if you want me to.' Dowling again looked at his watch. 'I've got to go, but there's something else that might be helpful in saving that . . .' The actor paused convincingly. 'That job of yours.'

'What is it?' asked Converse tightly, trying not to leap at the question.

'As this Fowler was leaving I had a couple of thoughts. One was that I'd been pretty hard on a fellow who was simply doing *his* job, and the other was just plain selfish. I hadn't cooperated and that could come back and snap me in the ass. Of course if you never showed up here, I'd get my note back and it wouldn't matter. But if you did, and you wore a black hat, my tail could be in a bucket of boiling lead.'

'That should have been your first concern,' said Joel truthfully.

'Maybe it was, I don't know. At any rate, I told him that in the course of our conversation I asked you for drinks, to come out on location if you wanted to. He seemed puzzled at the last part, but he understood the first. I asked whether I should call him at the embassy if you took me up on either invitation, and he said no, I shouldn't do that.'

'*What?*'

'In short words, he made it very plain that my calling him would only louse up this "in-house queery". He told me to wait for *his* call. He'd phone me around noon.'

'But you're filming. You're on location.'

'That's the beauty part, but the hell with it. There are mobile telephone hook-ups; the studio insist on them these days. It's another kind of screeching called budgetary controls. We get our calls.'

'You're losing me.'

'Then find me. When he calls me, I'll call *you*. Should I tell him you reached me?'

Surprised, Converse stared at the ageing actor, the risk-taker, 'You're way ahead of me, aren't you?'

'You're pretty obvious. So was he, when I put it together – which I just did. This Fowler wants to reach you, but he wants to do it solo, away from those people you don't want to meet. You see, when he was at the door and we had our last words, I was bothered by something. He couldn't sustain the role – anymore than you did on the plane – but I couldn't be certain. He kind of fell apart on his exit, and that you never do even if you've got to hold in a sudden attack of diarrhoea . . . What do I tell him, Joe?'

'Get a telephone number, I guess.'

'Done. You get some sleep. You look like a coked-up starlet who's just been told she's going to play Medea.'

'I'll try.'

Dowling reached into his pocket, taking out a scrap of paper. 'Here,' he said approaching Converse and handing it to him. 'I wasn't sure I was going to give this to you but I damn well want you to have it now. It's the mobile number where you can reach me. Call me after you've talked to this Fowler. I'm going to be a nervous wreck until I hear from you.'

'I give you my word . . . Cal, what did you mean when you mentioned "the beauty part" and forgetting about it?'

The actor's head shifted back in perfect precision, at just the right angle for any in the audience. 'The son of a bitch asked me what I did for a living . . . As they say in the Polo Lounge, "Ciao, baby".'

Converse sat on the edge of the bed, his head pounding, his body tense. Avery Fowler! *Jesus*! Avery Preston Fowler *Halliday*! *Press* Fowler . . . *Press Halliday*! The names bombarded him, piercing his temples and bouncing off the walls of his mind, screaming echoes everywhere. He could not control the assault; he began to sway back and forth, his arms supporting him, a strange rhythm emerging, the beat accompanying the name – names – of the man who had died in his arms in Geneva. A man he had known as a boy, the adult a stranger who had manipulated him into the world of George Marcus Delavane and a spreading disease called Aquitaine.

This Fowler wants to reach you, but he wants to do it solo, away from those people you don't want to meet . . . The judgment of a risk-taker.

Converse stopped, his eyes on the Leifhelm dossier on the floor. He had assumed the worst because it was beyond his comprehension, but there was an alternative, an outside possibility, perhaps under the circumstances even a probability. The geometrics were there; he could not trace them but they *were there*! The name Avery Fowler meant nothing to anyone but him – at least not in Bonn, not as it pertained to a murder in Geneva. Was Dowling right? Joel's request to the actor to get the man's telephone number had been made without conviction, the stigma of the American Embassy on his mind, the sight of a dark red limousine driving through the embassy's gates refusing to leave him. *That* was the connection that had enveloped the shock of Avery Fowler's name. The man using it was from the *embassy* and at least part of the embassy was part of *Aquitaine*, therefore the impostor was part of the *trap*. That was the logic; it was simple arithmetic . . . but it was not geometry. Suppose there was a break in the line, an insertion from another plane that voided the arithmetic progression? If there was, it was in the form of an explanation he could not possibly perceive unless it was given to him.

The shock was receding; he was finding his equilibrium again. As he had done so many times in courtrooms and boardrooms, he began to accept the totally unexpected, knowing he could do nothing about it until something happened, something over which he had no control. The most difficult part of the process was forcing himself to function until it *did* happen, whatever it was. Conjecture was futile; all the probabilities were beyond his understanding.

He reached down for the Leifhelm dossier.

Erich Leifhelm's years with the *Bundes Polizei* were unique and require a word about the organization itself. In the aftermath of all wars, a subjugated national police force is required in an occupied country for reasons ranging from simple language to the understanding of local customs and traditions. There must be a buffer between the occupation troops and a vanquished people to maintain order. There is also a side issue rarely elaborated upon or analysed in the history books, but no less important for that lack. Defeated armies possess talent and unless that talent is utilized, the humiliation of defeat can ferment, at the minimum distilling itself into hostilities that are counterproductive to a stabilized political climate, or at the maximum, into internal subversion that can lead to violence and bloodshed at the expense of victors and whatever new government that is being formed. To put it bluntly, the Allied General Staff recognized that it had on its hands another brilliant and popular military man who would not suffer the anonymity of early retirement or a corporate boardroom. The *Bundes Polizei* – literally translated: Federal Police – like all police organizations was, and is, a paramilitary force, and as such the logical repository for men like Erich Leifhelm. They were the leaders; better to use them than be abused by them. And as always among leaders, there are those few who surge forward, leading the pack. During these years foremost among those few was Erich Leifhelm.

His early work with the *Polizei* was that of a military consultant during the massive German demobilization, then afterwards as the chief liaison between the police garrisons and the Allied occupation forces. Following demobilization, his duties were mainly concentrated in the trouble-spots of Vienna and Berlin where he was in constant touch with the commanders of the American, British and French sectors. His zealous anti-Soviet feelings were spread rapidly by Leifhelm throughout the command centres and duly noted by the senior officers. More and more he was taken into their confidence until – as had happened before with the Prussians – he was literally considered one of them.

It was in Berlin that Leifhelm first came in contact with General Jacques Louis Bertholdier. A strong friendship developed but it was not an association either one cared to parade due to the age-old animosities between the German and French militaries. We were able to trace only three former officers from Bertholdier's command post who remembered – or would speak of – seeing the two men frequently at dinner together in out-of-the-way restaurants and cafés, deep in conversation, obviously comfortable with one another. Yet during those occasions when Leifhelm was summoned to French headquarters in Berlin, the formalities were icily proper, names rarely used and certainly never first names, only ranks and titles. In recent years, as noted above, both men have denied knowing each other personally, albeit admitting their paths may have crossed.

Whereas previously acknowledgement of their friendship was discouraged because of traditional prejudices, the current reasons are far more understandable. Both are spearheads in the Delavane organization. Their names are on the primary list with good reason. They are influential men who sit on the boards of multilingual corporations which deal in products and technology ranging from the building of dams to the construction of nuclear plants; in between are a hundred likely subsidiaries throughout Europe and Africa which could easily expedite sales of armaments. As detailed in the following pages, it can be assumed that Leifhelm and Bertholdier communicate through a woman named Ilse Fishbein in Bonn. Fishbein is her married name, the marriage itself questionable in terms of motive insofar as it was dissolved years ago when Yakov Fishbein, a survivor of the camps, emigrated to Israel. Frau Fishbein, born in 1942, is the youngest illegitimate daughter of Hermann Goering.

Converse lowered the dossier and reached for a memo pad next to the telephone on the bedside table. He then unclipped the gold Cartier ballpoint pen Val had given him years ago from his shirt pocket and wrote down the name 'Ilse Fishbein'. He looked at both the pen and the name, having singular thoughts about each. The Cartier status symbol was a remembrance of better days – no, not really better, he considered, but at least more complete. Valerie, at his insistence, had finally quit the New York advertising agency with its insane hours, and gone freelance. On her last day of formal work, she had walked across town to Cartier and spent a considerable portion of her last pay cheque on his gift. When he asked her what he had done outside of his meteoric rise in Talbot, Brooks and Simon to deserve such impractical opulence she had replied: 'For making me do what I should have done a long time ago. On the other hand, if free-lancing doesn't pay off, I'll steal it back and pawn it . . . What the hell, you'll probably lose it.'

Free-lancing had paid off very well, indeed, and he had never lost the pen.

Ilse Fishbein gave rise to another kind of thought. Much as he would like to confront her, it was out of the question. Whatever Erich Leifhelm knew had been provided by Bertholdier in Paris and relayed by Frau Fishbein here in Bonn. And it obviously contained a detailed description as well as a warning; the American was dangerous. Ilse Fishbein, as a trusted confidante in Aquitaine, could undoubtedly lead him to others in Germany who were part of Delavane's network, but to approach her was to ask for his own . . . whatever it was they intended for him at the moment, and he was not ready for that. Still, it was a name, a piece of information, a fact he was not expected to have, and experience had taught him to keep such details up front and reveal them, spring them quietly when the moment was right. Or use them himself when no one was looking. He was a lawyer and the ways of adversary law were labyrinthian; whatever was withheld was no man's land. On either side; to the more patient, the spoils.

Yet the temptation was so damned *inviting*. The bloodline of Hermann Goering involved with the contemplated resurrection of the generals! In *Germany*. Ilse Fishbein could be an immediate threat to unlock a floodgate of unwanted memories. He held in his hand a spiked club; the moment would come when he would swing it.

Leifhelm's commanding duties in the field with the West German NATO divisions lasted seventeen years, whereupon he was elevated to SHAPE headquarters, near Brussels, as military spokesman for Bonn's interests.

Again his tenure was marked by extreme anti-Soviet postures, frequently at odds with his own government's pragmatic approach to coexistence with the Kremlin, and throughout his final months at SHAPE, he was more often appreciated by the Anglo-American right-wing factions than by the political leadership in Bonn.

It was only when the Chancellor concluded that American Foreign Policy had been taken out of the hands of professionals and usurped by bellicose ideologies that he ordered Leifhelm home, creating an innocuous post for the soldier to keep him at bay.

Leifhelm, however, had never been a gullible fool, nor was he one now in his new, improvised status. He understood why the politicians had created it and, thereby, his own subtle strengths. People everywhere were looking to the past, to men who spoke clearly, with candour, and did not obfuscate the problems facing their countries and the world, especially the western world.

So he began to speak. At first to veterans' groups, and splinter organizations where military pasts and preformed partisan politics guaranteed him a favourable reception. Spurred by the enthusiastic reponse he evoked, Leifhelm began to expand, seeking larger audiences, his position more strident, his statements more provocative.

One man listened and was furious. The Chancellor learned that Leifhelm had carried his quasi-politicking into the Bundestag itself, implying a constituency far beyond what he really had, but by the sheer force of his personality swaying members who should not have been swayed. Leifhelm's words came back to the Chancellor of the Federal

Republic: an enlarged army in far greater numbers than the NATO commitments; an intelligence service patterned after the once-extraordinary *Abwehr*; a general revamping of text-books, deleting injurious and slanderous materials; rehabilitation camps for political trouble-makers and subversives pretending to be 'liberal thinkers'. It was all there.

The Chancellor had had enough. He summoned Leifhelm to his office where he demanded his resignation in the presence of three witnesses. Further, he ordered Leifhelm to remove himself from all aspects of German politics, accepting no further speaking engagements, neither lending his name nor his presence to any cause whatsoever. He was to retire totally from public life. We have reached one of those witnesses whose name is not pertinent to this report. The following is his recollection.

'The Chancellor was furious. He said to Leifhelm: "Herr General, you have two choices, and, if you'll forgive me, a final solution. Number one, you may do as I say. Or you can be stripped of your rank and all pensions and financial accruals afforded therein, as well as the income from some rather valuable real estate in Munich, which in the opinion of any enlightened court would be taken from you instantly. That is your second choice."

I tell you, the field marshal was apoplectic! He demanded his rights, as he called them, and the Chancellor shouted. "You've had your rights, and they were wrong! They're still wrong!" Then Leifhelm asked what was the final solution, and I swear to you, as crazy as it sounds, the Chancellor opened a drawer of his desk, took out a pistol, and aimed it at Leifhelm. "I myself, will kill you right now," he said. "You will not, I repeat, *not* take us back."

I thought for a moment that the old soldier was going to rush forward and accept the bullet, but he didn't. He stood there staring at him, such hatred in his eyes, matched by the other man's cold appraisal. Then Leifhelm did a stupid thing. He shot his arm forward – not at the Chancellor, but away from him – and cried "Heil Hitler". Then he turned in military fashion and walked out the door.

We were all silent for a moment or two. Then the Chancellor broke our silence. "I should have killed him," he said. "I may regret it. We may all regret it."'

Five days after this confrontation, Jacques Louis Bertholdier made the first of his two trips to Bonn following his retirement. On his initial visit he stayed at the Schlosspark Hotel. As hotel records are kept for a period of three years, we were able to obtain copies of his billing charges. There were numerous calls to various firms doing business with *Juneau et Cie*, too numerous to examine individually, but one number kept being repeated, the name having no apparent business connections with Bertholdier or his company. It was Ilse Fishbein. However, upon checking Erich Leifhelm's telephone bills for the dates in question, it was found that he too had placed calls to Ilse Fishbein, identical in number to those placed by Bertholdier. Inquiries and brief surveillance further established that Frau

Fishbein and Leifhelm have known each other for a number of years. The conclusion is apparent: She is the conduit between Paris and Bonn in Delavane's apparatus.

Converse lit a cigarette. There was the name again, the temptation again. Ilse Fishbein could be the shortcut. Threatened with exposure, this daughter of Hermann Goering could reveal a great deal. Not only could she confirm that she was the liaison between Leifhelm and Bertholdier, but conceivably much more, for the two ex-generals had to transmit information to each other. The names of companies, of buried subsidiaries, firms doing business related to Delavane in Palo Alto might surface, names he could pursue legally, looking for the illegalities that had to be there. If there only was a way, his presence felt, not seen.

An intermediary. He had used intermediaries in the past, often enough to know the value of the procedure. It was relatively simple. A third party was employed to make contact with an adversary carrying information that could be of value to the latter insofar as it might be deemed damaging to his interests – and was in the hands of his opponent. If the facts were strong enough, an equitable solution was usually forthcoming. The ethics were questionable, but contrary to accepted beliefs, ethics were in three dimensions, if not four. The ends did not justify the means, but justifiable means that brought about a fair and necessary conclusion were not to be dismissed.

And nothing could be fairer or more necessary than the dismantling of Aquitaine. Old Beale was right that night on the moonlit beach of Mykonos. His client was not an unknown man in San Francisco, but instead a large part of this so-called civilized world. Aquitaine had to be stopped, aborted.

An intermediary? It was another question he would put off until the morning. He picked up the dossier, his eyes heavy.

Leifhelm has few intimate friends that appear to be constant, probably due to his awareness that he is under watch by the government. He sits on the boards of several prominent corporations which have stated frankly that his name justifies his stipend . . .

Joel's head fell forward. He snapped it back, widened his eyes, and scanned the final pages rapidly, impressions made, not really absorbed; his concentration was waning. There were several restaurants, the names meaningless; a marriage during the war that ended when Leifhelm's wife disappeared in November 1943, presumed killed in a Berlin bombing raid, no subsequent wife or wives, his private life extraordinarily private, if not austere. The exception here was his proclivity for small dinner parties, the guest lists always varied, again names, again meaningless. The address of his residence on the outskirts of Bad Godesberg . . . Suddenly, Converse's neck stiffened, his eyes briefly alive and steady.

The house is in the remote countryside, on the Rhine River and far from any shopping areas or suburban concentration. The grounds are fenced and guarded by attack dogs who bark viciously at all approaching vehicles except Leifhelm's dark red Mercedes limousine.

A dark red Mercedes! It was Leifhelm himself who had been at the airport! Leifhelm who had driven directly to the embassy! How could it happen? *How?*

It was too much to absorb, too far beyond his understanding. The darkness was closing in, Joel's brain telling him it could no longer accept further input; it simply could not function. The dossier fell to his side; he closed his eyes and sleep came.

He was plunging headlong down through a cavernous hole in the earth, jagged black rocks on all sides, infinite darkness below. The walls of irregular stone kept screaming in frenzy, screeching at him like descending layers of misshapen gargoyles, sharp beaks and raised claws lunging at his flesh. The hysterical clamour was unbearable. Where had the silence gone? Why was he falling into black nothingness?

He flashed his eyes open; sweat lined his sockets, his forehead drenched, his breath coming in gasps. The telephone by his head was ringing, the erratic bell jarring, panic in its dissonance. He tried to shake the sleep and the fear from his semi-consciousness; he reached for the blaring instrument, glancing at his watch as his hand shot out above the bedside table. It was 12.15, a quarter past noon, the sun streaking through the hotel window.

'Yes? Hello . . .?'

'Joe? *Joel?*'

'Yes.'

'It's Cal Dowling. Our boy called.'

'What? Who?'

'This Fowler. Avery Fowler.'

'Oh, *Jesus!*' It was coming back, it was *all* coming back. He was seated at a table in *Chat Botté* on the Quai du Mont Blanc, flashes of sunlight bouncing off the grills from the lakeside boulevard. No . . . he was not in Geneva. He was in a hotel room in Bonn and only hours ago he had been plunged into madness by that name. 'Yes,' he choked, catching his breath. 'Did you get a telephone number?'

'He said there wasn't time for games, and besides, he doesn't have one. You're to meet him at the east wall of the Alter Zoll as fast as you can get there. Just walk around; he'll find you.'

'That's not good enough!' cried Converse. 'Not after Paris! Not after the airport last night! I'm not stupid!'

'I didn't get the impression he thought you were,' replied the actor. 'He told me to tell you something; he thought it might convince you.'

'What is it?'

'I hope I get this right; I don't even like saying it . . . He said to tell you a judge named Anstett was killed last night in New York. He thinks you're being cut loose.'

8

The Alter Zoll, that ancient bulwark once Bonn's southern fortress on the Rhine only to be razed to the ground three centuries ago, a toll house now standing where the last of the great fortification's towers stood. Antique cannons were dotted about the green lawns, remembrances of a might that had slipped away under the squabblings of emperors and kings, priests and princes. A winding mosaic wall of red and grey stone overlooked the massive river below where boats of varied descriptions ploughed furrows in the open water, caressing the shorelines on both sides, diligent and sombre in their appointed rounds; no Lake Geneva here, far less the blue-green waters of the mischievous Como.

Joel stood by the low wall, trying to focus on the view, trying to accept it really, hoping it would calm him, but the exercise was futile. The beauty before him was lost, it would not penetrate his thoughts; nothing could. Lucas Anstett, Second Circuit Court of Appeals, judge extraordinary and intervening negotiator between one Joel Converse and his employers and an unknown man in San Francisco. Apart from that unknown man and a retired scholar on the island of Mykonos, the only other person who knew what he was doing and why. How in the space of eighteen hours or less could he have been *found*? Found and killed!

'Converse?'

Joel turned, whipping his head over his shoulder, his body rigid. Standing twenty feet away on the far edge of a gravel path was a sandy-haired man several years younger than Converse, in his early to mid-thirties, his face a boyish face that would grow old slowly, giving the illusion of youth long after its time. He was also shorter than Joel, but not much, perhaps 5' 10" or 11", and dressed in light grey trousers and a cord jacket, his white shirt open at the neck.

'Who are you?' asked Converse hoarsely.

A couple strolled between them on the path as the younger man moved his head to his left, gesturing for Joel to follow him onto the lawn beyond. Converse did so, joining him by the huge iron wheel of a bronze cannon.

'All right, who are you?' repeated Joel.

'My sister's name is Meagen,' said the sandy-haired man. 'And so neither one of us makes a mistake, you tell me who I am.'

'How the *hell* . . . ?' Converse stopped, the words coming back to him, words whispered by a dying man in Geneva. *Oh, Christ! Meg, the kids . . .* 'Meg, the kids,' he said out loud. 'Fowler called his wife Meg.'

'Short for Meagen, and she was Halliday's wife, only you knew him as Fowler.'

'You're Avery's brother-in-law.'

'Press's brother-in-law,' corrected the man, his hand extended – in seriousness not conviviality. 'Connal Fitzpatrick,' he added.

'Then we're on the same side.'

'I hope so.'

'I've got a lot of questions to ask you, Connal.'

'No more than I've got for you, Converse.'

'Are we going to start off belligerently?' asked Joel, noting the harsh use of his own last name and releasing Fitzpatrick's hand.

The younger man blinked, then reddened, embarrassed. 'Sorry,' he said. 'I'm one angry brother – on both sides – and I haven't had much sleep. I'm still on San Diego time.'

'San Diego? Not San Francisco?'

'Navy. I'm a lawyer stationed at the naval base there.'

'Whew,' whistled Converse softly. 'It's a small world.'

'I know all about the geography,' agreed Fitzpatrick. 'And also you, Lieutenant. How do you think Press got his information? Of course, I wasn't in San Diego then, but I had friends.'

'Nothing's sacred then.'

'You're wrong; everything is. I had to pull some very thick strings to get that stuff. It was about five months ago when Press came to me and we made our . . . I guess you'd call it the contract between us.'

'Clarification, please.'

The naval officer placed his right hand on the barrel of the cannon. 'Press Halliday wasn't just my brother-in-law, he came to be my best friend, closer than any blood brother, I think.'

'And you with the militaristic hordes?' asked Joel, only half joking, a point of information on the line.

Fitzpatrick smiled awkwardly, boyishly. 'That's part of it, actually. He stood by me when I wanted to go for it. The services need lawyers too, but the law schools don't tell you much about that. It's not where they're going to get any endowments from. Me, I happen to like the Navy, and I like the life; and the challenges, I guess you'd call them.'

'Who objected?'

'Who didn't? In both our families the pirates – who go back to skimming the earthquake victims – have always been attorneys. The two current old men knew Press and I got along and saw the writing they wrote on their own wall. Here's this sharp Wasp, and this Catholic boy; now if they ring in a Jew and a light-skinned black and maybe even a not-too-offensive gay, they've got half the legal market in San Francisco in their back pockets.'

'What about the Chinese and the Italians?'

'Certain country clubs still have remnants of the old school ties in their lockers. Why soil the fabric? Deals are made on the fairways, the accent on "ways", not "fair".'

'And you didn't want anything to do with that, counsellor?'

'Neither did Press, that's why he went international. Old Jack Halliday pissed bright red when Press began corralling all those foreign clients; then purple when he added a lot of US sharks who wanted to operate overseas. But old Jack couldn't complain; his wild-eyed stepson was adding considerably to the bottom line.'

'And you went happily into uniform,' said Converse, watching Fitzpatrick's eyes, impressed by the candour he saw in them.

'*Back* into uniform, and very happy – with Press's blessings, legal and otherwise.'

'You were fond of him, weren't you?'

Connal lifted his hand off the cannon. 'I loved him, Converse. Just as I love my sister. That's why I'm here. That's the contract.'

'Incidentally,' said Joel kindly, 'speaking of your sister, even if I were somebody else I could easily have found out her name was Meagen.'

'I'm sure you could; it was in the papers.'

'Then it wasn't much of a test.'

'Press never called her Meagen in his life, except for that one phrase in the wedding ceremony. He wasn't averse to talking about her, but it was always "Meg". I would have asked you about that somehow, and if you were lying I'd have known it. I'm very good on direct.'

'I believe you. What's the contract beween you and . . . Press?'

'Let's walk,' said Fitzpatrick, and as they strolled toward the wall with the winding river below and the seven hills of Westerwald in the distance, Connal began. 'Press came to me and said he was into something pretty heavy and he couldn't let it go. He'd come across information that tied a number of well-known men – or once well-known men – together in an organization that could do a lot of harm to a lot of people in a lot of countries. He was going to stop it, stop them, but he had to go outside the usual courtroom ballparks to do it – do it legally.

'I asked him the normal questions: Was he involved, culpable, that sort of thing, and he said no, not in any indictable sense, but he couldn't be sure whether or not he was entirely safe. Naturally, I said he was crazy; he should take his information to the authorities and let them handle it.'

'Which is exactly what I told him,' interrupted Converse.

Fitzpatrick stopped walking and turned to Joel. 'He said it was more complicated than that.'

'He was right.'

'I find that hard to believe.'

'He's dead. Believe it.'

'That's no answer!'

'You didn't ask a question,' said Converse. 'Let's walk. Go on. Your contract.'

Bewilderment on his face, the naval officer began. 'It was very simple,' he continued. 'He told me he would keep me up to date whenever he travelled, letting me know if he was seeing anyone related to his major concern – that's what we called it, his "major concern". Also anything else that could be helpful if . . . if . . . goddamn it, *if*!'

'If what?'

Fitzpatrick stopped again, his voice harsh. 'If anything *happened* to him!'

Converse let the emotion of the moment pass. 'And he told you he was going to Geneva to see me. The man who knew Avery Preston Fowler Halliday as Avery Fowler roughly twenty-odd years ago in school.'

'Yes. We'd been over that before when I got him the security material on you. He said the time was right, the circumstances right. By the way, he thought you were the best.' Connal permitted himself a brief uncomfortable smile. 'Almost as good as he was.'

'I wasn't,' said Joel, a half smile returned. 'I'm still trying to figure out his position on some Class A stock in the merger.'

'What?'

'Nothing. What about Lucas Anstett? I want to hear about that.'

'It's in two parts. Press said they'd worked through the judge to spring you if you'd agree to take on the . . .'

'*They?* Who's they?'

'I don't know. He never told me.'

'Goddamn it! Sorry, go ahead.'

'That Anstett had talked to your firm's senior partners and they said okay if you said okay. That's part one. Part two is a personal idiosyncrasy; I'm a news freak and like most of my ilk I'm tuned into the hourly AFR.'

'Clarification.'

'Armed Forces Radio. Oddly enough it's probably got the best news coverage on the air; it pools all the networks. I have one of those small transistorized jobs with a couple of shortwave bands I pack when I'm travelling.'

'I used to do that,' offered Converse. 'For the BBC, mainly because I didn't speak French – or anything else for that matter.'

'They've got good coverage but they shift bands too much. Anyway I had AFR on early this morning and heard the story, such as it was.'

'What was it?'

'Short on details. His apartment on Central Park South was broken into around two in the morning, New York time. There were signs of a struggle and he was shot in the head.'

'That's it?'

'Not quite. According to a housekeeper nothing was taken so robbery was ruled out. *That's* it.'

'*Jesus.* I'll call Larry Talbot. He may have more information. There wasn't anything else?'

'Only a quick sketch of a brilliant jurist. The point is nothing was *taken.*'

'I understand that,' broke in Joel. 'I'll talk to Talbot.' They started walking again south along the wall. 'Last night,' continued Converse, 'why did you tell Dowling you were an embassy man? You must have been at the airport.'

'I'd been at the airport for seven hours going from counter to counter asking for passenger information, trying to find out what plane you were on.'

'You knew I was on my way to Bonn?'

'Beale thought you were.'

'*Beale?*' asked Joel, startled. 'Mykonos?'

'Press gave me his name and the number but said I wasn't to use either unless the worst happened.' Fitzpatrick paused. 'The worst happened,' he added.

'What did Beale tell you?'

'That you went to Paris, and, as he understood it, you were going to Bonn next.'

'What else?'

'Nothing. He said he accepted my credentials, as he called them, because I had his name and knew how to reach him; only Press could have given me that information. But anything else I'd have to learn from you, if you felt there was something to tell me. He was pretty damned cold.'

'He had no choice.'

'Although he did say that in case I couldn't find you, he wanted to see me on Mykonos before I began raising my voice . . . "for everything Mr Halliday stood for". That's the way he put it. I was going to give you two more days to get here, if I could hold up.'

'Then what? Mykonos?'

'I'm not sure. I figured I'd call Beale again but he'd have to tell me a lot more than he did to convince me.'

'And if he didn't? Or couldn't?'

'Then I'd have flown straight to Washington and gone to whoever the top floor of the Navy Department suggested. If you think for one goddamned minute I'm going to let this thing pass for what it isn't, you're wrong and so is Beale.'

'If you'd have made that clear to him, he would have come up with something. You'd have gone to Mykonos.' Converse reached into his shirt pocket for his cigarettes; he offered one to Fitzpatrick, who shook his head. 'Avery didn't smoke either,' said Joel aimlessly as he snapped his lighter. 'Sorry . . . Press.' He inhaled.

'It's okay; that name's how I got you to see me.'

'Let's go back to that a minute. There's a slight inconsistency in your testimony, counsellor. Let's clear it up – just so neither one of us makes a mistake.'

'I don't know what you think you're crowding in on, but go ahead.'

'You said you were going to give me two more days to get here, is that right?'

'Yes, if I could make arrangements, get some sleep and hold up.'

'How did you know I didn't get here two days *before* you did?'

Fitzpatrick glanced at Joel. 'I've been a legal officer in the Navy for the past eight years, both as defence counsel and judge advocate in any number of situations – not always court martials. They've taken me to most of the countries where Washington has reciprocal agreements.'

'That's a mouthful, but I'm not in the Navy.'

'You were, but I wasn't going to use it if I didn't have to, and I didn't. I flew into Düsseldorf, showed my naval papers to the *Inspektor* of immigration, and asked for his cooperation. There are seven international airports in West Germany. It took roughly five minutes with the computers to find out that you hadn't entered any of them during the past *three* days, which was all I was concerned about.'

'But then you had to get to Köln-Bonn.'

'I was there in forty minutes and called him back. No Converse had been admitted and unless you were crossing the border incognito – which I suspect I know more about than you do – you had to fly in sooner or later.'

'You're tenacious.'

'I've given you my reasons.'

'What about Dowling and that embassy routine at the hotel?'

'Lufthansa had you listed on the passenger manifest from Hamburg – you'll never know how relieved I was. I hung around the counter in case there was a delay or anything like that when these three embassy guys showed up flashing their IDs, the head man speaking rotten German.'

'You could tell?'

'I speak German . . . and French, Italian and Spanish. I have to deal with different nationalities.'

'I'll let that pass.'

'I suppose that's why I'm a lieutenant-commander at thirty-four. They move me around a lot.'

'Pass again. What caught you about the embassy people?'

'Your name, naturally. They wanted confirmation that you were on Flight Eight-eleven. The clerk sort of glanced at me and I shook my head; he cooperated without a break in his conversation. You see, I'd given him a few Deutschmarks but that wasn't it. These people don't really dig the official US over here.'

'I heard that last night. From Dowling. How did he come up?'

'Dowling himself, but later. When the plane arrived I stood at the rear of the baggage claim; the embassy boys were by the entrance to the gates about fifty feet away. We all waited until there was only one piece of luggage on the conveyor belt. It was yours but you never showed up. Finally a woman came out and the embassy contingent surrounded her, everyone excited, upset. I heard your name mentioned, but that's all I heard because by that time I'd decided to go back and speak to the clerk.'

'To see if I'd really been on the plane?' asked Converse. 'Or whether I turned out to be a no-show.'

'Yes,' agreed Fitzpatrick. 'He was cute; he made me feel like I was suborning a juror. I paid him and he told me this Caleb Dowling – who I think I was expected to know – had stopped at the desk before going out to the platform.'

'Where he left instructions,' said Joel, interrupting quietly.

'How did you know?'

'I picked up a set at the hotel.'

'That was it, the *hotel*. Dowling told him he'd met this lawyer on the plane, a fellow American named Converse who'd sat with him since Copenhagen. He was worried that his new friend might not have accommodation in Bonn and, if he asked Lufthansa for suggestions, the clerk should send him to the Königshof Hotel.'

'So you totalled up the figures and decided to become one of the embassy people who'd lost me,' said Converse, smiling. 'To confront Dowling. Who among us hasn't taken advantage of a hostile witness?'

'Exactly. I showed him my naval ID and told him I was an attaché. Frankly, he wasn't very cooperative.'

'And you weren't very convincing, according to his theatrical critique. Neither was I. Strangely enough, that's why he got us together.' Joel stopped, crushed out his cigarette against the wall and threw it over the stone. 'All right, Commander, you've passed muster or roster or whatever the hell you call it. Where do we stand? You speak the language and you've got government connections I don't have. You could help.'

The naval officer stood motionless; he looked hard at Joel, his eyes blinking in the glare of the sunlight, but not from any lack of concentration. 'I'll do whatever I can,' he began slowly, 'as long as it makes sense to me. But you and I have to understand each other, Converse. I'm not backing away from the two days. That's all you've got – *we've* got if I come on board.'

'Who made the deadline?'

'I did. I do now.'

'It can't work that way.'

'Who says?'

'I did. I do now.' Converse started walking along the wall.

'You're in Bonn,' said Fitzpatrick, catching up, neither impatience nor supplication in either his gait or his voice, only control. 'You've been to Paris and you came to *Bonn*. That means you have names, areas of evidence, both concrete or hearsay. I want it all.'

'You'll have to do better than that, Commander.'

'I made a *promise*.'

'To whom?'

'My sister. You think she doesn't know? It was tearing Press apart! For a whole goddamned year he'd get up in the middle of the night and wander around the house, talking to himself but shutting her out. He was obsessed and she couldn't crack the shell. You'd have to know them to appreciate this, but they were good, I mean *good* together. I know it's not very fashionable these days to have two people with a passel of kids who really like each other, who can't wait to be with each other when they're apart, but that's the way they were.'

'Are you married?' asked Joel, without breaking his stride.

'No,' answered the navy man, obviously confused by the question. 'I expect to be. Perhaps. I told you, I move around a lot.'

'So did Press . . . Avery.'

'What's your point, *counsellor*?'

'Respect what he was doing. He knew the dangers and he understood what he could lose. His life.'

'That's why I want the facts! His body was flown back yesterday. The funeral's tomorrow and I'm not there because I gave Meagen a promise! I'm coming back, too, but with everything I need to blow this whole fucking thing apart!'

'You'll only *implode* it, sending it way down deep if you're not stopped before that.'

'That's *your* judgment.'

'It's all I've got.'

'I don't buy it!'

'Don't. Go back and talk about rumours, about a killing in Geneva that nobody will admit was anything but a robbery, or a murder in New York that remains, and probably will remain something it wasn't. If you mention a man on Mykonos, believe me, he'll disappear. Where are you, commander? Are you just a freak, after all, a philosophical blood brother of Press Halliday who stormed the Presidio and burned his draft card in the good old days of muscatel and grass?'

'That's a crock of shit!'

'It's on the record, Commander. By the way, as a judge-advocate how many officers did you prosecute?'

'What . . . ?'

'As a defence counsel how many cases did you lose?'

'I've had my share of wins and losses, mostly wins, frankly.'

'Mostly? Frankly? You know there are certain people who can take fifteen numbers, insert what they call variables, and make the statistics say anything they want them to say.'

'What's that got to do with anything? How is it connected to Press's death, his *murder*?'

'Oh, you'd be surprised, Commander Fitzpatrick. Beneath that brass could be a very successful infiltrator, perhaps even an *agent-provocateur* in a uniform you shouldn't be wearing.'

'What the *hell* are you talking about . . . Forget it, I don't want to know. I don't have to listen to you but you have to listen to me! You've got two days, Converse. Am I on board or not?'

Joel stopped and studied the intense young face beside him – young and not so young. There were hints of creases around the angry eyes. 'You're not even in the same fleet,' said Converse wearily. 'Old Beale was right. It's my decision and I choose to tell you nothing. I don't want you on board, sailor. You're a hot-headed piss ant and you bore me.'

Joel turned and walked away.

'All right, *cut*! That's a print! Nice work, Cal, I almost believed that drivel.' The director, Roger Blynn, checked the clipboard thrust in front of him by a script girl and issued instructions to the camera crew's interpreter before heading over to the production table.

Caleb Dowling remained seated on the large rock on the slope of the hill above the Rhine; he patted the head of an odoriferous goat which had just defecated on the toe of his boot. 'I'd like to kick the rest of the shit out of you, li'l partner,' he said quietly, 'but it wouldn't be congruous with my well-developed image.'

The actor got up and stretched, aware that the on-lookers beyond the roped-off set were staring at him, chattering away like tourists in a zoo. In a few minutes he would walk over – no, not walk, amble over – and pull the rope off the carriage of an arc light so that he could mingle with the fans. He never tired of it, probably because it came so late in his life and was, after all, symbolic of what he and his wife could currently afford. Also every now and then there was a bonus: one of his former students, who usually approached him cautiously, obviously wondering if the good-natured rapport he had established in the classroom had survived the onslaught of national recognition or been drowned in the tidal wave of so-called stardom. Cal was good at remembering faces, and not too bad with at least one of a person's two names, so when these occasions arose, he invariably would eye his former charge and ask him if he had completed yesterday's assignment. Or walk up to him – or her – and pedagogically inquire something like: 'Of the chronicles Shakespeare drew from for his histories, which had the greatest impact on his language, Daniel, Holinshed, or Froissart?' If the answer came back naming the last, he would slap his thighs and exclaim words akin to: 'Hot damn, li'l wrangler, you busted a tough bronc there!' Laughter followed, and frequently drinks and reminiscences later.

It was a good life these days, almost perfect. If only some sunlight would reach into the painfully dark corners of his wife's mind. If it could, she'd be here on a hillside in Bonn chatting in her quietly vivacious way with the people beyond the rope – mostly women, mostly those around her age – telling them that her husband was really quite like their own. He never picked up his socks and was a disaster in the kitchen; people liked to hear that even if they didn't believe it. But the sunlight did not reach those far, dark corners. Instead, his Frieda remained in Copenhagen, walking along the beaches of Sjaelland Island, having tea in the botanical gardens, and waiting for a call from her husband saying that he had a few days off and would come out of hated Germany. Dowling looked around at the efficiently enthusiastic crew and the curious spectators; laughter punctuated their conversations, a certain respect as well. These were not hateful people.

'Cal?' The voice belonged to Blynn, the film's director, who was walking rapidly across the slope of the hill. 'There's someone here to see you.'

'I hope more than one, Roger, otherwise the men who go under the dubious title of our employers are grossly overpaying me.'

'Not for this pile of kitsch.' The director's smile disappeared, as he approached the actor. 'Are you in any trouble, Cal?'

'Constantly, but not so it's noticeable.'

'I'm serious. There's a man here from the German police – the Bonn police. He says he has to talk to you, claims it's urgent.'

'What about?' Dowling felt a rush of pain in his stomach; it was the fear he lived with.

'He wouldn't tell me. Just that it was an emergency and he had to see you alone.'

'Oh, *Christ*!' whispered the actor. 'Freddie! . . . where is he?'

'Over in your trailer.'

'*In* my . . .'

'Rest easy,' said Blynn. 'That stunt-jock Moose Rosenberg's with him. If he moved an ashtray, I think that gorilla would throw him through the wall.'

'Thanks, Roger.'

'He meant it when he said "alone"!'

Dowling did not hear this; he had started running across the hill toward the small camper he used for brief periods of relaxation. He prayed to no one in particular for the best, preparing himself for the worst.

It was neither, simply another complication in an enigma. Frieda Dowling was not the subject; instead it was Joel Converse, an American attorney at law. The stunt man climbed out of the trailer, leaving Caleb and the police officer alone. The man was in civilian clothes, his English fluent, his manner vaguely officious yet courteous.

'I'm sorry to have upset you, Herr Dowling,' said the German in response to Caleb's initial, intense inquiry about his wife. 'We know nothing of Frau Dowling. Is she ill, perhaps?'

'She's had a few spells lately, that's all. She's in Copenhagen.'

'Yes, so we understand. You fly there frequently, don't you?'

'Whenever I can.'

'She does not care to join you here in Bonn?'

'Her name was Mühlstein and the last time she was in Germany she wasn't considered much of a human being. Her memories are, let's say memorable in the extreme. They come back with a lot of acid.'

'Yes,' said the police officer, his eyes as steady as Caleb's. 'We will live with that for generations.'

'I hope so,' said the actor.

'I wasn't alive, Herr Dowling. I'm very happy she survived, I mean that.'

Dowling was not sure why but he lowered his voice, the words nearly inaudible, if not involuntary. 'Germans helped her.'

'I would hope so,' said the German quietly. '*My* business, however, concerns a man who sat next to you last night on the planes from Copenhagen to Hamburg and from Hamburg to Bonn. His name is Joel Converse, an American attorney.'

'What about him? By the way, may I see your identification?'

'Certainly.' The police officer reached into his pocket, removed his plastic ID case and handed it to the actor who had his glasses firmly in place. 'I trust everything is in order,' added the man.

'What's this "*Sonder Dezernat*"?' asked Dowling, squinting at the small print on the card.

'It is best translated as "special branch" or "department". We are a unit of the *Bundes Polizei*, the Federal Police. It is our job to look into matters the government feels are more sensitive than the normal jurisdictional complaints.'

'That doesn't say a damn thing, and you know it,' said the actor. 'We can use lines like that in movies and get away with it because we write in all those reactions, but you're not Helmut Dantine or Martin Kosleck and I'm not Elisa Landi. Spell it out.'

'Very well, I shall spell it out. Interpol. A man died in a Paris hospital as a result of head injuries inflicted by the American, Joel Converse. His condition was diagnosed as improving, but unfortunately it was only temporary; he was found dead this morning, his death attributed to an unprovoked attack by Herr Converse. We know he flew into Köln-Bonn, and according to the airline stewardesses you sat with him for three and a half hours. We want to know where he is. Perhaps you can help us.'

Dowling removed his glasses, lowering his chin and swallowing as he did so. 'And you think I know?'

'We have no idea, but you talked with him. And we hope you *do* know that there are severe penalties for withholding information about a fugitive, especially one sought for a killing.'

The actor fingered the stems of his glasses, his instincts in conflict, erupting. He walked over to the bed against the wall and sat down, looking up at the police officer. 'Why don't I trust you?' he asked.

'Because you think of your wife and will trust no German,' replied the

German. 'I am a man of law and *peace*, Herr Dowling. Order is something the people decide for themselves, myself among them. The report we have received states clearly that this Converse may be a very disturbed man.'

'He didn't sound disturbed to me. In fact, I thought he had a damned good head on his shoulders. He said a lot of very perceptive things.'

'That you wanted to hear?'

'Not all of them.'

'But a good percentage, leading *up* to all of them.'

'What does that mean?'

'A madman is convincing; he plays on all sides, eventually weighing everything in his favour. It's the essence of his madness, his psychosis, his *own* convictions.'

Dowling dropped the glasses on the bed, exhaling audibly, feeling the pain of fear again in his stomach. 'A madman?' he said – without conviction. 'I don't believe that.'

'Then let us have a chance to disprove it. Do you know where he is?'

The actor squinted at the German. 'Give me a card or a number where I can reach you. He may get in touch with me.'

'Who was responsible?' The man in the red velvet jacket behind the large desk sat in semi-darkness, a brass lamp serving only to throw a harsh circle of light on the surface in front of him. Beyond, the light was dim. Yet the glow was sufficient to reveal the outlines of a huge map centred on the wall behind the man and the desk. It was a strange map, not of the global world, but instead fragmented. The shapes of nations were clearly defined yet oddly shadowed, eerily coloured, as if an attempt had been made to create a single land mass out of disparate geographical areas. They included all of Europe, most of the Mediterranean and selected portions of Africa. And, as if the wide expanse of the Atlantic Ocean was merely a pale blue connector, Canada and the United States of America were part of this arcane entity.

The man stared straight ahead, his lined, square-jawed face with its aquiline nose and thin, stretched lips seemed moulded from parchment, his close-cropped salt-and-pepper hair a proper garland for a head set atop such a rigidly framed torso. He spoke again; his voice was rather higher in the vocal register than lower, with no resonance, but with a secure sense of command. One could easily imagine this voice raised in volume – even to fever pitch, like a tom cat screeching across a frozen lake. It was not raised now, however; it was the essence of quiet urgency. 'Who was reponsible?' he repeated. 'Are you still on the line, London?'

'Yes,' replied the caller from Great Britain. 'Yes, of course. I'm trying to think, trying to be fair.'

'I admire that, but decisions have to be made. In all likelihood the responsibility will be shared, we simply have to know the sequence.' The man paused; when he continued his voice suddenly took on an intensity that was a complete departure from his previous tone. It was the shrill call of the cat across the ice-bound lake. 'How was Interpol involved?'

Startled, the Englishman answered quickly, his phrases clipped, the words rushing headlong over one another. 'Bertholdier's aide was found dead at four in the morning, Paris time. Apparently he was to receive hospital medication at that hour. The nurse called the *Sûreté* . . .'

'The *Sûreté*?' shouted the man behind the desk in front of the fragmented map. 'Why the *Sûreté*? Why not Bertholdier? It was *his* employee, not the *Sûreté*'s!'

'That was the lapse,' said the Britisher. 'No one realized instructions to that effect had been left at the hospital desk . . . apparently by an inspector named Prudhomme, who was awakened and told of the man's death.'

'And *he* was the one who called Interpol?'

'Yes, but too late to intercept Converse at German immigration.'

'For which we can be profoundly grateful,' said the man lowering his voice.

'Normally, of course, the hospital would have waited and reached Bertholdier in the morning, telling him what had happened. As you say, the patient was an employee, not a member of the family. After that undoubtedly the *arrondissement* police would have been informed and finally the *Sûreté*. By then our people would have been in place and fully capable of preventing Interpol's involvement. We can still stop them but it will take several days. Personnel transfers, new evidence, amendments to the case file; we need time.'

'Then don't waste any.'

'It was those *damned* instructions.'

'Which no one had the brains to look for,' said the man in front of the shadowed map. 'This Prudhomme's instincts were aroused. Too many rich people, too much influence, the circumstances too bizarre. He smells something.'

'We'll get him off the case, just a few days,' said the Englishman. 'Converse is in Bonn, we know that. We're closing in.'

'So may Interpol and the German police. I don't have to tell you how tragic that would be.'

'We have certain controls through the American Embassy. The fugitive is American.'

'The *fugitive* has information!' insisted the man behind the desk, his fist clenched in the circle of light. 'How much and supplied by whom we don't know and we *must* know.'

'Nothing was learned in New York? The judge?'

'Only what Bertholdier suspected and what I knew the moment I heard his name. After forty years Anstett came back, still hounding me, still wanting my neck. The man was a bull, but only a go-between; he hated me as much as I hated him, and up to the end he shielded those behind him. Well, he's gone and his holy righteousness with him. The point is, Converse is *not* what he pretends to be. Now, *find* him!'

'As I say, we're closing in. We have more sources, more informers than Interpol. He's an American fugitive in Bonn who, we understand, doesn't speak the language. There are only so many places he can hide. We'll find him; we'll break him and learn where he comes from. After which, we'll terminate immediately, of course.'

'*No!*' The sleek male cat again shrieked across the frozen lake. 'We play *his* game! We welcome him, embrace him. In Paris he talked about Bonn,

Tel Aviv, Johannesburg; therefore you'll accommodate him. Bring him to Leifhelm – even better have Leifhelm go to him. Fly in Abrahms from Israel, van Headmer from Africa, and, yes, Bertholdier from Paris. He obviously knows who they are anyway. He'll claim ultimately to want a council meeting, to be a part of us. So we'll hold a conference and listen to his lies. He'll tell us more with his lies than he can with the truth.'

'I really don't understand.'

'Converse is a *point*, but *only* a point. He's exploring, studying the forward terrain, trying to understand the tactical forces ahead of him. If he were anything else, he'd deal directly through legitimate authorities and legitimate methods. There'd be no reason for him to use a false name, or give false informtion . . . or to run away, forcibly overcoming a man he thinks is trying to stop him. He's an infantry point who has certain information but doesn't know where he's going. Well, a point can be sucked into a trap, the advancing company ambushed. Oh, yes, we must give him his conference.'

'I submit that's extraordinarily dangerous. He *must* know who recruited him, who gave him the names, his sources. We can break him physically or chemically and get that information.'

'He probably doesn't have it,' explained the man patiently. 'Infantry points are not privileged to command decisions; frankly, they might turn back. We have to know more about this Converse, and by six o'clock tonight I'll have every report, every résumé, every word ever written about him. There's something here we can't see.'

'We already know he's resourceful,' said the Britisher. 'From what we can piece together in Paris, he's considered an outstanding attorney. If he sees through us, or gets away from us, it could be catastrophic. He will have met with our people, *spoken* with them.'

'Then once you find him don't let him out of your sight. By tomorrow I'll have other instructions for you.'

'Oh?'

'Those records that are being gathered from all over the country. For a man to do what Converse is doing he had to be manipulated very carefully, very thoroughly, a driving intensity instilled in him. It's the manipulators we have to find. They're not even who we think they are. I'll be in touch tomorrow.'

George Marcus Delavane replaced the telphone in its cradle and slowly, awkwardly twisted his upper body around in the chair. He gazed at the strange, fragmented map as the first light of dawn fired the eastern sky, its orange glow filling the windows. Then, with effort, his hands gripping the arms of the steel chair, he pivoted himself around again, his eyes on the stark pool of light on the desk. He moved his hands to his waist and carefully, trembling, unbuttoned his dark red velvet jacket, forcing his gaze downward, ordering himself to observe the terrible truth once more. He stared past the 5-inch-wide leather strap that diagonally held him in place, now *commanding* his eyes to focus, to accept with loathing what had been done to him.

There was nothing but the edge of the thick, steel seat, the polished wood of the floor the next plane of vision. The long, sturdy legs that had carried his trained, muscular body through battles in the snow and the mud, and triumphant parades in the sunlight, through ceremonies of honour and defiance had been stolen from him, said by the doctors to have been diseased instruments of death that would kill the rest of him. He clenched his fists and pressed them slowly down on the desk, his throat filled with a silent scream.

9

'*Goddamn you*, Converse, who do you think you are?' cried Connal Fitzpatrick, his voice low, furious, as he caught up with Joel who was walking rapidly between the tall trees of the Alter Zoll.

'Someone who knew Avery Fowler as a boy and watched a man named Press Halliday die a couple hundred years later in Geneva,' replied Converse, quickening his pace, heading toward the gates of the national landmark where there were taxis.

'Don't pull that crap on me! I knew Press far better and far longer than you *ever* did. For Christ's sake, he was married to my sister! We were close friends for fifteen years!'

'You sound like a little kid playing one-upmanship. Get lost.'

Fitzpatrick rushed forward, pivoting in front of Joel, blocking him. 'It's true! Please, I can help, I *want* to help! I know the language; you don't! I have connections here; you don't.'

'You also have your own idea about a deadline which *I* don't. Get out of my way, sailor.'

'*Come* on,' pleaded the naval officer. 'So I didn't get everything I wanted. Don't crowd me out.'

'I beg your pardon?'

Fitzpatrick shifted his weight awkwardly. 'You've come on strong before yourself, haven't you, counsellor?'

'Not if I didn't know the circumstances.'

'Sometimes it's a way of finding them out.'

'Not with me it isn't.'

'Then my error was in not knowing you; the circumstances were beyond that scope. With someone else it might have worked.'

'Now you're talking tactics, but you meant it when you said two days.'

'You're damned right I did,' agreed Connal, nodding. 'Because I want whatever it is exposed. I want *whoever* it is to *pay*! I'm mad, Converse, I'm mad as hell. I don't want this thing to linger and die away. The longer nothing is done the less people care; you know that as well as I do and probably better. Have you ever tried to reopen an old case? I have with a few courts-martial where I thought things had been screwed up. Well, I learned something: the system doesn't like it! You know why?'

'Yes, I do,' said Joel. 'There are too many new cases in the dockets, too many rewards in going after the current ones.'

'Bingo, counsellor. Press deserves better than that. Meagen deserves better.'

'Yes, he does – they do. But there's a complication that Press Halliday understood better than either of us. Put simply – and cruelly – his life wasn't terribly important compared to what he was going after.'

'That's pretty damned cruel,' said the officer.

'It's very damned accurate,' said Converse. 'Your brother-in-law would have wrestled you to the mat for walking into this and trying to call the shots. Back off, Commander. Go back to the funeral.'

'*No*. I want to come on board. I withdraw the deadline.'

'How considerate of you.'

'Oh, Christ, you know what I mean.'

'No, I don't know what you mean.'

'You call the shots,' said Fitzpatrick, nodding again, exhaling in defeat. 'I'll do what you tell me to do.'

'Why?' asked Joel, their eyes locked.

The Navy lawyer did not flinch; he spoke simply. 'Because Press trusted you. He said you were the best.'

'Except for him,' completed Converse, permitting his expression to relax slightly, a hint of a smile apparent. 'All right, I believe you, but there are ground rules. You either accept them or, as you put it, on board you're not.'

'Let's hear them. I'll wince inside so you can't see it.'

'Yes,' agreed Joel, 'you'll wince. To begin with I'll tell you only what I think you have to know in a given situation. Whatever you develop will be on your own; that way it's free-wheeling, no way can you tip the evidence we've compiled.'

'That's rough.'

'That's the way it is. I'll give you a name now and then when I think it will open a door, but it will *always* be a name you heard second or third hand. You're inventive; figure out your own unidentifiable sources so as to protect yourself.'

'I've done that on quite a few waterfronts.'

'You have? How good are you at play acting?'

'What?'

'Never mind, I think you just answered that. You didn't go down to those waterfronts in your dress whites as a lieutenant-commander.'

'Hell, no.'

'You'll do.'

'You've got to tell me *something*.'

'I'll give you an overview, a lot of abstractions and a few facts. As we progress – *if* we progress – you'll learn more. If you think you've put it together, tell me. That's essential. We can't risk blowing everything while you operate under wrong assumptions.'

'Who's we?'

'I wish to hell I knew.'

'That's comforting.'

'Yes, isn't it.'

'Why don't you tell me everything now?' asked Fitzpatrick.

'Because Meagen Halliday lost a husband. I don't want to see her lose a brother.'

'I'll accept that.'

'By the way, how long have you got? I mean you're on active duty.'

'My initial leave is thirty days, with extensions as warranted. Christ, an only sister with five kids and her husband is killed. I could probably write my own ticket.'

'We'll stick to the thirty days, Commander. It's more than we're allowed.'

'Start talking, Converse.'

'Let's walk,' said Joel, heading back to the Alter Zoll wall and the view of the Rhine below.

The 'overview' delivered by Converse described a current situation in which like-minded individuals in various countries were coming together and using their considerable influence to get around the laws and ship armaments and technology to hostile governments and organizations.

'For what purpose?' asked Fitzpatrick.

'I could say profits but you'd see through it.'

'As the only motive, yes,' said the Navy lawyer pensively. 'Influential people – as I understand the word "influential" as related to existing laws – would operate singly or at best in small groups within their own countries. That is if profits were the primary objective. They wouldn't coordinate outside; it isn't necessary. It's a sellers' market; they'd only water down the profits.'

'Bingo, counsellor.'

'So?' Fitzpatrick looked at Joel as they strolled toward a break in the stone wall where a bronzed cannon was in place.

'Destabilization,' said Converse. 'Mass destabilization. A series of flash-points in highly volatile areas that will call into question the status quo's ability to cope with the violence.'

'I've got to ask you again, for what purpose?'

'You're quick,' said Joel, 'so I'll let you answer that. What happens when an existing political structure is crippled by disorder, when it can no longer function because things have got out of control?'

The two men stopped by the cannon, the naval officer's eyes following the line of the huge, threatening barrel. 'It's restructured or replaced,' he said, pulling his gaze back to look at Converse.

'Bingo again,' said Converse softly. 'That's the overview.'

'It doesn't make sense.' Fitzpatrick creased his eyes in the sunlight, as well as in thought. 'Let me recap. Am I allowed?'

'You're allowed.'

'"Influential individuals" connotes people in pretty good standing in very high places. Assuming we're not talking about an out-and-out criminal element – which the lack of a pure profit motive would seem to eliminate – we're talking about reasonably respectable citizens. Is there another definition I'm not aware of?'

'If there is I'm not aware of it, either.'

'Then why would they want to destabilize the political structures that guarantee them their influence? It *doesn't* make sense.'

'Ever hear of the phrase "everything's relative"?'

'To a fare-thee-well. So what?'

'So think.'

'About what?'

'Influence.' Joel took out his cigarettes, shook one to his lips, and lit it. The younger man stared at the seven hills of Westerwald in the distance.

'They want *more*,' said Fitzpatrick slowly, turning back to Converse.

'They want it all,' said Joel. 'And the only way they can get it is to prove that their solutions are the only solutions, all others having proved worthless against the eruptions of chaos suddenly everywhere.'

Connal's expression was fixed, immobile, as he absorbed Converse's words. 'Holy *Mary* . . .' he began, his voice a whisper, yet still a cry. 'An international plebiscite – the peoples' will – for the almighty state. Fascism. It's multinational *fascism*.'

'I'm sick of saying "bingo", so I'll say "right-on", counsellor. You've just said it better than any of us.'

'*Us*? Which is "*we*", but you don't know who you are!' added Fitzpatrick, bewilderment and anger coming together with his creased, linked eyebrows.

'Live with it,' said Joel. 'I have. I do.'

'*Why*?'

'Avery Fowler. Remember him?'

'Oh, *Jesus!*'

'And an old man on the island of Mykonos. That's all we have. But what they said is true. It's real. I've seen it, and that's all I need to know. In Geneva, Avery said there was very little time left. Beale refined it; he called it a countdown. Whatever's going to happen will happen before your leave is up – two weeks and four days is the earliest report. That's what I meant before.'

'Oh my God,' whispered Fitzpatrick. 'What else can you tell me – *will* you tell me?'

'Very little.'

'The embassy,' Connal interrupted. 'It's been a couple of years, but I *was there*. I worked with the military attaché. I don't need any introductions. We can get help there.'

'We can also get killed there.'

'*What*?'

'It's not clean. Those three men you saw at the airport, the ones from the embassy . . .'

'What about them?'

'They're on the other side.'

'I don't believe you!'

'Why do you think they were at the airport?'

'To meet you, talk to you. There could be a dozen different reasons. Whether you know it or not you're considered a hot shot lawyer on the international scene. Foreign service personnel frequently want to touch base with guys like you.'

'I've had this conversation before,' said Converse, irritated.

'What does *that* mean?'

'If they wanted to see me why didn't they go to the gate?'

'Because they thought you'd come into the terminal like everybody else.'

'And when I didn't – according to you – they were upset, angry. That's what you said.'

'They were.'

'All the more reason to meet me at the gate.'

Fitzpatrick frowned. 'Still, that's kind of flimsy . . .'

'The woman. Do you remember the woman?'

'Of course.'

'She spotted me in Copenhagen. She followed me . . . Also, there's something else. Later, on the platform, all four were picked up by a car belonging to a man we know – we *know* – is part of everything I've described to you. They drove to the embassy and you'll have to take my word for that. I saw them.'

Connal fixed his gaze on Joel, accepting what he had heard. 'Oh, *Jesus*,' he said, astonished. 'Okay, no embassy. What about Brussels, SHAPE? There's a Navy Intelligence unit; I've dealt with those people before.'

'Not yet. Maybe not at all.'

'I thought you wanted to use the uniform, my connections.'

'Maybe I will. It's nice to know they're there.'

'Well, what do you want me to do? I've got to do *something*.'

'Are you really fluent in German?'

'*Hochdeutsch, Schwäbisch, Bayerisch*, and several dialects in between. I told you, I can handle five languages . . .'

'You've made it obnoxiously clear,' interrupted Converse. 'There's a woman named Fishbein here in Bonn. That's the first name I'm going to give you. She's involved; we're not sure how, but she's suspected of being what they call a conduit – a relayer of information. I want you to meet her, talk with her, establish a relationship. We'll have to think of something that'll be convincing in order for you to do it. She's in her forties, and she's the youngest daughter of Hermann Goering. She married a survivor of the holocaust for obvious reasons; he's long gone. Any ideas?'

'Sure,' said Fitzpatrick without hesitating. 'Inheritance. There are a couple of thousand last wills and testaments every year that the deceased want processed through the military. They're from crazies who leave everything they've got to the *other* survivors. The true Aryan Germanic stock and all that horseshit. We bounce them back to the civil courts who don't know what to do with them, so they end up in limbo and eventually in the Treasury Department's coffers.'

'No kidding?'

'*Ein, zwei, drei*. Believe me, those people mean it.'

'Can you use the device?'

'How about a million-plus legacy from a small Midwest brewer of lager beer?'

'You'll do,' said Joel. 'You're on board.'

There was no mention of Aquitaine or of George Marcus Delavane or Jacques Louis Bertholdier or Erich Leifhelm, or of twenty-odd names at the State Department and the Pentagon. Nor was there any detailed analysis of the 'network' progress as it appeared in the dossiers in Converse's possession, or as described by Dr Edward Beale on Mykonos. Connal Fitzpatrick was given the barest bones of the body of information. Joel's reasoning was far less benign than he had stated. If the navy lawyer was taken and interrogated – no matter how brutally – there was little of substance he could reveal.

'You're not really telling me a hell of a lot,' said Fitzpatrick.

'I've told you enough to get your head blown off, and that's not a phrase normally in my lexicon.'

'Nor mine.'

'Then consider me a nice fellow,' said Converse, as the two men headed for the entrance gate of the Alter Zoll.

'On the other hand,' continued Halliday's brother-in-law, 'you've been through a lot more than I ever have. I read that stuff about you in the security files – files, not file – they were cross-correlated with the files of a lot of other prisoners. You were something else. According to most of the men in those camps, you held them together . . . until they put you into solitary.'

'They were wrong, sailor. I was shaking and scared to death and would have fucked a Peking duck to save my skin.'

'That's not what the files say. They say . . .'

'I'm not really interested, Commander,' said Joel, as they passed through the ornate gate. 'But I've got an immediate problem you can help solve.'

'What is it?'

'I gave my word I'd call Dowling on some mobile phone line. I wouldn't know how to ask for it.'

'There's a booth over there,' said Connal, pointing to a white plastic bubble that protruded from a concrete pylon on the pavement abutting the drive. 'Do you have the number?'

'It's here somewhere,' replied Converse, crawling through various pockets. 'Here it is,' he said as he separated the scrap of paper from several credit card charges.

'*Vermittlung, bitte.*' The naval officer sounded authentic as he spoke crisply into the telephone. '*Fräulein, geben Sie mir bitte sieben, drei, vier, zwei, zwei.*' Fitzpatrick then inserted a series of coins into the metal box and turned to Joel. 'Here you are. They're ringing.'

'Stay there. Ask for him . . . say it's his lawyer calling, the one at the hotel.'

'*Guten Tag, Fräulein. Ist Herr* . . . Oh, no, I speak English. Do you speak English? No, I'm not calling from California, but it's an emergency . . . Dowling, I have to reach . . .'

'*Caleb,*' said Joel quickly.

'Caleb Dowling.' The Navy man covered the mouthpiece. 'What kind of name is that?'

'Something to do with Gucci shoes.'

'What? . . . *Oui, ja* – yes, thanks. They're getting him. Here take it.' Fitzpatrick handed the phone to Converse.

'*Joe?*'

'Yes, Cal. I said I'd call you after I met with Fowler. Everything's okay.'

'No, it's not, Mister Lawyer,' said the actor quietly. 'You and I had better have a very serious talk, and I don't mind telling you a hunk of beef named Rosenberg will be just a few feet away.'

'I don't understand.'

'A man died in Paris. Does that clear things up for you?'

'Oh, *God*.' Converse felt the blood draining from his head and a hollowness in his throat. For a moment he thought he was going to be sick. 'They came to you?' he whispered.

'A man from the German police a little over an hour ago and this time I didn't have any doubts about my visitor. He was the real item.'

'I don't know what to say,' stammered Joel.

'Did you do it?'

'I . . . I guess I did.' Converse stared at the telephone dial, seeing the bloodied face of the man in the alleyway, feeling the blood on his own fingers.

'You *guess*? That's not something you guess about.'

'Then yes . . . The answer is yes. I did it.'

'Did you have a reason?'

'I thought I did.'

'I want to hear it, but not now. I'll tell you where to meet me.'

'No!' exclaimed Joel, confused but emphatic. 'I can't involve you. You can't be involved!'

'This fellow gave me a card and wants me to call him if you get in touch with me. He was very specific about withholding information; how it's considered aiding a fugitive.'

'He was right, *absolutely* right! For God's sake, tell him everything, Cal! The truth. You got me a room for the night because you thought I might not have a reservation and we had a pleasant few hours on the plane. You put it in your name because you didn't want me to pay. Don't hide *anything*! Not even this call.'

'Why didn't I tell him before?'

'That's all right, you're telling him now. It was a shock and I'm a fellow American and you're in a foreign country. You wanted time to think, to reflect. My phone call shook you into behaving rationally. Tell him you confronted me with the accusation and I didn't deny it. Be honest with him, Cal.'

'How honest? Should I include my session with Fowler?'

'That's all right, too, but it's not necessary. Let me back up and clarify. Fowler's a false name and he's not relevant to Paris, I give you my word. Bringing him in is only volunteering an unnecessary complication.'

'Should I tell him you're at the Alter Zoll?'

'It's where I'm calling you from. I just admitted it.'

'You won't be able to go back to the Königshof.'

'It doesn't matter,' said Joel, speaking rapidly, wanting to get off the phone and start thinking. 'My luggage is at the airport and I can't go back there either.'

'You had a briefcase.'

'I've taken care of that. It's where I can get it.'

The actor paused, then spoke slowly. 'So your advice to me is to level with the police, to tell them the truth.'

'Without volunteering extraneous and unrelated material. Yes, that's my advice, Cal. It's the way you can stay clean and you *are* clean.'

'It sounds like fine advice, Joe – Joel, and I certainly wish I could take it, but I'm afraid I can't.'

'What? *Why?*'

'Because bad men like thieves and killers don't give advice like that. It's not in any script I ever read.'

'That's nonsense! For Christ's sake, do as I tell you!'

'Sorry, partner, it's not good dramaturgy. So you do as I tell *you*. There's a big stone building at the university – beautiful place, a restored palace actually – with a layout of gardens you don't see very often. They're on the south side with benches here and there on the main path. It's a nice place on a summer's night, kind of out of the way and not too crowded. Be there at ten o'clock.'

'Cal, I won't involve you in this!'

'I'm already involved. I've withheld information and I've aided a fugitive.' Dowling paused again. 'There's someone I want you to meet,' he said.

'*No.*'

There was a click and the line went dead.

10

Converse hung up the phone and braced himself on the sides of the plastic booth, trying to clear his head. He had killed a man, not in a war anyone knew about, and not in the heat of survival in a Southeast Asian jungle, but in a Paris alleyway because he had to make an instant decision based on probabilities. Rightly or wrongly the act had been done and he could not dwell on it. The German police were looking for him, which meant that Interpol had entered the picture, transmitting from Paris information somehow supplied by Jacques Louis Bertholdier, who remained out of sight, beyond the scope of the hunt. Joel recalled his own words spoken only minutes ago. If Press Halliday's life was not terribly important compared to what he was going after, neither was the life of a minion who worked for Bertholdier, Delavane's disciple, Aquitaine's arm in France. There were no options, thought Converse. He had to go on; he had to stay free.

'What's the matter?' asked Fitzpatrick, standing anxiously several feet to Joel's left. 'You look like you got kicked by a mule.'

'I got kicked,' agreed Converse.

'What happened to Dowling? Is he in trouble?'

'He *will* be!' exploded Joel. 'Because he's a misguided idiot who thinks he's in some kind of goddamned movie!'

'That wasn't your opinion a little while ago.'

'We met; it came out all right. This can't, not for him.' Converse pushed himself away from the booth and looked at the Navy lawyer, his mind now trying desperately to concentrate on the immediate. 'I may tell you and I may not,' he said glancing around for an available taxi. 'Come on, we're going to put your awesome linguistic abilities to work. We need shelter, expensive but not showy, especially *not* a place where the well-heeled tourists go who don't speak German. If there's one thing they'll spread about me it's that I can't talk my way through the five boroughs of New York. I want a rich hotel that doesn't need foreigners, doesn't cater to them. Do you know the kind of place I mean?'

Fitzpatrick nodded. 'Exclusive, clubby, German business oriented. Every large city has them and they're always twenty times my *per diem* for breakfast.'

'That's okay, I've got money here in Bonn. I might as well try to get it out.'

'You're full of surprises,' said Connal. 'I mean *real* surprises.'

'Do you think you can handle it? Find a hotel like that?'

'I can explain what I want to a cab driver; he'll probably know. Bonn's small, nothing like New York or London or Paris . . . There's a taxi letting people out.' The two men hurried to the kerb and the cab with a quartet of discharging passengers, balancing camera equipment and outsized Louis Vuitton handbags.

'How will you do it?' asked Converse, as they nodded to the tourists, two couples in the midst of an argument, male versus female, Nikon versus Vuitton.

'A combination of what we both said,' answered Fitzpatrick. 'A quiet, nice hotel away from the *Ausländerlärm*.'

'What?'

'The clamour of tourists – and worse. I'll tell him we're calling on some very important German businessmen – bankers, say – and we'd like a place they'd be most comfortable in for confidential meetings. He'll get the drift.'

'He'll see we don't have any luggage,' objected Joel.

'He'll see the money in my hand first,' said the naval officer, holding the door for Converse.

Lieutenant-Commander Connal Fitzpatrick, USN, member of the military bar and limited thereby, impressed Joel Converse, vaunted international attorney, to the point where the latter felt foolish. Effortlessly, the Navy lawyer got them situated in a two-bedroom suite at an inn on the banks of the Rhine called *Das Rektorat*. It was one of those converted pre-war estates where most of the guests seemed to have at least a nodding acquaintance with several others and the clerks rarely looked anyone in the eye, as if silently announcing their subservience – or confirming the fact that they would certainly not acknowledge having seen Herr So-and-So should someone ask them.

Fitzpatrick had begun his campaign with the taxi driver, leaning forward in the seat and speaking in rapid, quiet phrases. Their exchanges seemed to grow more confidential as the cab sped toward the heart of the city; then it abruptly veered away, crossing the railroad tracks that intersected the capital and entered a smooth road paralleling the river north. Joel had started to speak, to ask what was happening, but the Navy lawyer had held up his hand, telling Converse to be quiet.

Once they had stopped at the entrance of the inn, reached by an interminably long, manicured drive, Fitzpatrick got out.

'Stay here,' he said to Joel. 'I'll see if I can get us a couple of rooms . . . And don't say anything.'

Twelve minutes later Connal returned, his demeanour stern, his eyes, however, lively. His mission had been accomplished. 'Come on, Chairman of the Board, we're going straight up.' He paid the driver handsomely and once again held the door for Converse – now a touch more deferentially, thought Joel.

The lobby of *Das Rektorat* was unmistakably German with odd overtones of the more delicate Victorian; thick heavy wood and sturdy leather chairs were beside and below filigrees of brass ornamentation forming arches over doorways, elegant borders for large mirrors, and valances above thick bay windows where none were required. One's first impression was of a quiet, expensive spa from decades ago, its initial solemnity lightened by the flashes of reflecting metal and glass. It was a strange mixture of the old and the very old, money its underpinnings.

Fitzpatrick led Converse to a panelled elevator recessed in the panelled corridor, no bellboy – or manservant – in attendance. It was a small enclosure, room for no more than four people, the walls of tinted, marbled glass; they vibrated as the elevator ascended two storeys.

'I think you'll approve of the accommodation,' said Connal. 'I checked it out; that's why it took me so long.'

'We're back in the nineteenth century, you know,' countered Joel. 'I trust they have telephones and not just the Hessian express.'

'All the most modern communications, I made sure of that, too.' The elevator door opened. 'This way,' said Fitzpatrick, gesturing to the right. 'The suite's at the end of the hall.'

'The suite?'

'You said you had money in Bonn.'

Two bedrooms flanked a tastefully furnished sitting room, with French doors that opened onto a small balcony overlooking the Rhine. The rooms were sunlit and airy, the decor of the walls again an odd mixture; Impressionist reproductions of floral arrangements were beside dramatic prints of past champion horses from leading German tracks and breeding farms.

'All right, wonder boy,' said Converse, looking out of the open French doors, then turning back to Connal Fitzpatrick who stood in the middle of the room, the key still in his hand. 'How did you do it?'

'It wasn't hard,' replied the Navy lawyer, smiling. 'You'd be surprised what a set of military papers will do for a person in this country. The older guys sort of stiffen up and look like boxer puppies smelling a pot roast, and there aren't that many people here much under sixty.'

'That doesn't tell me anything unless you're enlisting us.'

'It does when I combine it with the fact that I'm an aide assigned by the US Navy to accompany an important American financier over here to hold confidential meetings with his German counterparts. While in Bonn, naturally, incognito is the best means for my eccentric financier to travel. Everything's in *my* name.'

'What about reservations?'

'I told the manager that you'd rejected the hotel reserved for us as having too many people you might know. I also hinted that those countrymen of his you're going to meet might be most appreciative of his cooperation. He agreed that I might have a point there.'

'How did we hear about this place?' asked Joel, still suspicious.

'Simple. I rememberd it from several conversations I had at the International Economic Conference in Düsseldorf last year.'

'You were *there*?'

'I didn't know there was one,' said Fitzpatrick, heading for the door on the left. 'I'll take this bedroom, okay? It's not as large as the other one and that's the way it should be since I'm an aide – which Jesus, Mary, and Joseph all know is the truth.'

'*Wait* a minute,' broke in Converse, stepping forward. 'What about our luggage? Since we don't have any, didn't that strike your friend downstairs as a little odd for such important characters?'

'Not at all,' said Connal, turning. 'It's still in the city at that unnamed hotel you rejected so emphatically after twenty minutes. But only I can pick it up.'

'Why?'

Fitzpatrick brought his index finger to his lips. 'You also have a compulsion for secrecy. Remember, you're eccentric.'

'The manager *bought* all that swill?'

'He calls me *Kommandant*.'

'You're quite a bullshitter, sailor.'

'I remind you, sir, that in the land of *Erin go Bragh* it's called good healthy blarney. And although you lack certain qualifications, Press said you were a master of it in negotiations.' Connal's expression became serious. 'He meant it in the best way, counsellor, and that's not bullshit.'

As the Navy lawyer turned again and walked through the door to the bedroom, Joel felt an odd sense of recognition but could not define it. What was it about the younger man that struck a chord in him? Fitzpatrick had that boldness that came with the untried, that lack of fear in small things that caution would later teach him often led to larger things. He tested waters bravely; he had never come close to drowning.

Suddenly, Converse understood the recognition. What he saw in Connal Fitzpatrick was himself . . . before things happened. Before he knew the meaning of fear, raw terrible fear. And finally the loneliness.

It was agreed that Connal would return to the Köln-Bonn airport, not for Joel's luggage but for his own, which was stored in a locker in the baggage claim area. He would then go into Bonn proper, buy an expensive suitcase and fill it with half a dozen shirts, underwear, socks, and the best off-the-rack clothing he could find in Joel's sizes, namely three pairs of trousers, a jacket or two and a raincoat. It was further agreed that casual clothes were most appropriate; an eccentric financier was permitted such lapses of sartorial taste, and also such attire more successfully concealed its non-custom-made origins. Finally the last stop he would make before returning to *Das Rektorat* was at a second locker in the railroad station where Converse had left his attaché case. Once the case was in the Navy lawyer's possession and the taxi waiting outside, there were to be no further stops. He was to drive directly to the countryside inn.

'I wanted to ask you something,' said Fitzpatrick, just before leaving. 'Back at the Alter Zoll you said something about how "they" would spread the word that you couldn't talk your way through the five boroughs of New York. I gathered that referred to the fact that you don't speak German.'

'That's right. Or any other language, adequate English excepted. I tried but it never took. I was married to a girl who spoke fluent French and German and even she gave up. I don't have the ear, I guess.'

'Who did "*they*" refer to?' asked Connal, barely listening to Converse's explanation. 'The embassy men?'

Joel hesitated. 'A little wider, I'm afraid,' he said, choosing his words carefully. 'You'll have to know but not now, not yet. Later.'

'Why later? Why not now?'

'Because it wouldn't do you a damned bit of good, and it might raise questions you wouldn't want raised under shall we say, adverse circumstances.'

'That's elliptical.'

'It certainly is.'

'Is that it? Is that all you'll say?'

'No. There's one other thing. I want my briefcase.'

Fitzpatrick had assured him that the switchboard of *Das Rektorat* was eminently capable of handling telephone calls in English – as well as at least six other languages including Arabic – and he should have no qualms about placing a call to Lawrence Talbot in New York.

'Christ, where *are* you, Joel?' Talbot shouted into the phone.

'Amsterdam,' replied Converse, not wanting to say Bonn and having had the presence of mind to make the call station-to-station. 'I want to know what happened to Judge Anstett, Larry. Can you tell me anything?'

'I want to know what's happened to *you*! René called last night . . .'

'Mattilon?'

'You told him you were flying to London.'

'I changed my mind.'

'What the hell *happened*? The police were with him; he had no choice. He had to tell them who you were.' Talbot suddenly paused, then spoke in a calmer voice, a false voice. 'Are you all right, Joel? Is there something you want to tell me, something bothering you?'

'Something bothering me?'

'Listen to me, Joel. We all know what you went through, and we admire you, *respect* you. You're the finest we've got in the international division . . .'

'I'm the *only* one you've got,' Converse broke in, trying to think, trying to buy time as well as information. 'What did René say? Why did he call you?'

'You sound like your old self, fella.'

'I *am* my old self, Larry. What did René call you about? Why were the police with him?' Joel could feel the slippage; he was entering another sphere and he knew it, accepted it. The lies would follow, guile joining deceit, time and freedom of movement paramount. He had to *stay* free; there was so much to do, so little time.

'He called me back after the police left to fill me in – incidentally, they were from the *Sûreté*. As he understood it, the driver of a limousine was assaulted outside the George V's service entrance . . .'

'The driver of a limousine . . . ?' interrupted Converse involuntarily. 'They said he was a *chauffeur*?'

'From one of those high-priced services that ferry around people who make odd stops at odd hours. Very posh and very confidential. Apparently the fellow was pretty well smashed up and they say you did it. No one knows why but you were identified and they say the man may not live.'

'Larry, this is preposterous!' objected Joel, his protestation accompanied by feigned personal outrage. 'Yes, I *was* there – in the area – but it had nothing to do with *me*! Two hot heads got into a fight and since I couldn't stop them I wasn't going to get my head handed to me. I got out of there and before I found a taxi I yelled at the doorman to call for help. The last thing I saw he was blowing his whistle and running toward the alley.'

'You weren't even involved then,' said Talbot. The statement was a lawyer's positive fact.

'Of course not! Why would I be?'

'That's what we couldn't understand. It didn't make sense.'

'It *doesn't* make sense. I'll call René and fly back to Paris, if I have to.'

'Yes, do that,' agreed Talbot haltingly. 'I should tell you I may have aggravated the situation.'

'You? How?'

'I told Mattilon that perhaps you were . . . well, not yourself. When I spoke with you in Geneva you sounded awful, Joel. Just plain *awful*.'

'Good God, how did you think I'd feel? A man I was negotiating with dies in front of me bleeding from a dozen bullet wounds. How would *you* feel?'

'I understand,' said the lawyer in New York, 'but then René thought he saw something in you – heard something – that disturbed him, too.'

'Oh, come on, will you people get off it!' Converse's thoughts raced; every word he spoke had to be credible, his now diminished outrage rooted in believability. 'Mattilon saw me after I'd been flying in and out of airports for damn near fourteen hours. Christ, I was exhausted!'

'Joel?' Talbot began, obviously not quite ready to get-off-it. 'Why did you tell René you were in Paris for the firm?'

Converse paused, not for lack of a response, but for effect. He was ready for the question; he had been ready when he first approached Mattilon. 'A white lie, Larry, and no harm to anyone. I wanted some information and it seemed the best way to get it.'

'About this Bertholdier? He's the general, isn't he?'

'He turned out to be the wrong source. I told René as much and he couldn't have agreed with me more.' Joel lightened his tone of voice. 'Also it would have appeared strange if I said I was in Paris for somebody else, wouldn't it? I don't think it would have done the firm any good. Rumours and speculation run rampant down our corridors; you told me that once.'

'Yes, and it's true. You did the right thing . . . Damn it, Joel, why the *hell* did you leave the hotel the way you did? From the basement, or wherever it was.'

It was the moment for total conviction, a small inconsequential untruth that if not carried off would lead to the larger, far more dangerous lie. Connal Fitzpatrick could do it well, reflected Converse. The Navy lawyer had not learned to fear the small things; he did not know they were spoors that could lead one back to a rat cage in the Mekong River.

'Bubba, my friend and sole support,' said Joel, as cavalierly as he could muster. 'I owe you many things, but not the intimacies of my private life.'

'The what of your what?'

'I am approaching middle age – at least it's not far off – and I have no matrimonial incumbrances or guilt by reasons of fidelity.'

'You were avoiding a *woman*?'

'Fortunately for the firm not a man.'

'Jee-*sus*! I'm so well into middle age I don't think about those things. Sorry, young fella.'

'Young and not so young, Larry.'

'We were all off-base then. You'd better call René right away and get this thing cleared up. I can't tell you how relieved I am.'

'You can tell me about Anstett. That's why I called you.'

'Of course.' Talbot lowered his voice. 'A terrible thing, a tragedy. What did the papers over there say?'

Converse was caught; he had not anticipated the question. 'Very little,' he replied, trying to remember what Fitzpatrick had told him. 'Just that he was shot and apparently nothing was taken from his apartment.'

'That's right. Naturally, the first thing Nathan and I thought of was you, and whatever the hell you're involved with, but that wasn't the case. It was a Mafia vendetta, pure and simple. You know how rough Anstett was on appeals from those people; he'd throw them out as fast as he'd call their attorneys a disgrace to the profession.'

'It was a confirmed Mafia killing?'

'It will be, and that's straight from O'Neil down at the commissioner's office. They know their man; he's an executioner for the Delvecchio's family and last month Anstett threw the key away on Delvecchio's oldest son. He's in for twelve years with no appeals left, the Supreme Court won't touch him.'

'They *know* the man?'

'It's only a matter of picking him up.'

'How come it's so clear-cut?' asked Joel, confused.

'The usual way,' said Talbot. 'An informer who needs a favour. And since everything's happened so fast and so quietly it's assumed that the ballistics will prove out.'

'So fast? So quietly?'

'The informer reached the police first thing this morning. A special hunt was dispatched and only they know the man's identity. They figure the gun will still be in his possession. He'll be picked up any time now; he lives in Syosset.'

Something was wrong, thought Converse. There was an inconsistency but he could not spot the flaw. Then it came to him. 'Larry, if everything's so quiet, how do you know about it?'

'I was afraid you'd ask that,' said Talbot uneasily. 'I might as well tell you: it'll probably by in the newspaper follow-ups anyway. O'Neil's keeping me posted; call it courtesy, and also because I'm nervous.'

'Why?'

'Except for the man who killed him, I was the last person to see Anstett alive.'

'*You?*'

'Yes. After René's second call I decided to phone the judge, after conferring with Nathan, of course. When I finally reached Anstett, I said I had to see him. He wasn't happy about it but I was adamant. I explained that it concerned you. All I knew was that you were in terrible trouble and something had to be done. I went over to his apartment on Central Park South and we talked. I told him what had happened and how frightened I was for you, frankly letting him know that I held him responsible. He didn't say much but I think he was frightened, too. He said he'd get in touch with me in the morning. I left, and according to the coroner's report, he was killed approximately three hours later.'

Joel's breath was short, his head splitting, his concentration absolute. 'Let me get this straight, Larry. You went over to Anstett's apartment after René's call – his second call. *After* he told the *Sûreté* who I was.'

'That's right.'

'How long was it?'

'How long was what?'

'Before you left for Anstett's. After you spoke with Mattilon.'

'Well, let me see. Naturally, I wanted to talk to Nathan first but he was out to dinner, so I waited. Incidentally, he concurred and offered to join me . . .'

'How *long*, Larry?'

'An hour and a half, two hours at the outside.'

Two hours plus three hours totalled five hours. More than enough time for the puppets to be put in place. Converse did not know how it had been done, only that it *had* been done. Things had suddenly erupted in Paris, and in New York an agitated Lawrence Talbot had been followed to an apartment on Central Park South, where someone, somewhere, recognized a name and a man and the part he had played against Aquitaine. Were it otherwise, Talbot would be the corpse, not Lucas Anstett. All the rest was a smoke screen behind which the disciples of George Marcus Delavane manipulated the puppets.

'. . . and the courts owed so much to him, the country owed so much.' Talbot was speaking but Joel could no longer listen.

'I have to go, Larry,' he said, hanging up.

The killing was obscene, and the fact that it was carried out so quickly, so efficiently and with such precise deception was as frightening as anything Converse could imagine.

Joseph (Joey the Nice) Albanese drove his Pontiac down the quiet, tree-lined street on Syosset, Long Island, waving to a couple in a front yard. The husband was trimming the hedge under his wife's guidance. They stopped what they were doing, smiled and waved back. Very nice. His neighbours liked him, thought Joey. They considered him a sweet guy and very generous, what with letting the kids use his pool, and serving their parents only the best booze when they dropped over, and the biggest steaks money could buy when he had weekend barbecues – which he did often, rotating the neighbours so that no one should feel left out.

He *was* a sweet guy, mused Joey. He was always pleasant and never raised his voice in anger to anyone, offering only a glad hand, a nice word and a happy smile to everybody, no matter how lousy he really felt. That was it, *goddamn it*! thought Joey. Irre – fuckin – gardless of how upset he was he never let it show! Joey-the-Nice was what they called him and they were right. Sometimes he figured he had to be some kind of saint – may Jesus Christ forgive him for having such thoughts. He had just waved to neighbours but in truth he felt like smashing his fist through the windscreen and shoving the glass down their throats.

It wasn't them, it was last *night* that did it! A crazy night, a crazy *hit*, everything *crazy*! And that *gumbar* they brought in from the West Coast, the one they called 'Major', he was the nuttiest fruitcake of them all! And a sadist to boot, the way he beat the shit out of that old man and the crazy questions he asked, and shouting all the time. *Tutto pazzo!*

One minute he's playing cards in the Bronx, the next the phone is ringing. Get down to Manhattan *in frette e furia*! A bad heat is needed *subito*! So he goes and what does he find? It's that iron-balled judge, the one who closed steel doors on Delvecchio's boy! What craziness! They'll trace it back to the old man for sure. He'll know such *afflizione* from the cops and the courts he'll be lucky to own a small whorehouse in Palermo – if he ever gets back.

Then maybe . . . just maybe . . . thought Joey at the time, there was a turning muscle in the organization. Old Delvecchio was losing his grip; just maybe it was being called for, this *afflizione* that surely would follow. And possibly – just possibly – Joey himself was being tested. Maybe he was *too* nice, too *soave*, to put the bad heat on someone like the old judge who gave them all such a hard time. Well, he wasn't. No siree, the nice stopped with the handle of a gun. It was his job, his profession. The Lord Jesus decided who should live and who should die, only He spoke through mortal men on earth who told people like Joey whom to hit. There was no moral dilemma for Joey the Nice. It was important, however, that the orders always came from a man with respect; that was necessary.

They did last night; the order came from a man with great respect. Although Joey did not know him personally, he had heard for years about the powerful *padrone* in Washington, DC. The name was whispered, never spoken out loud.

Joey touched the brakes of his car, slowing down so as to swing into his driveway. His wife, Angie, would be pissed off at him, maybe shout a little because he didn't come home last night. One more irritation on top of all the craziness, but what the hell was he going to say? Sorry, Angie, but I was gainfully employed throwing six bullets into an old guy who definitely discriminated against Italians. So you see, Angie, I had to stay across the bridge in Jersey where one of the *paesani* I played cards with and who'll swear I was there all night happens to be the chief of police.

But, of course, he would never go into such details with his wife. That was his own law. No matter how aggravated he was he never brought his job home. More husbands should be like him and there would be happier households in Syosset.

Shit! One of the fucking kids had left a bicycle in front of the attached garage; he wouldn't be able to open the automatic door and drive inside. He'd have to get out. Shit! One more aggravation. He couldn't even park by the Millers' kerb next door; some creep's car was there but it wasn't the Millers' Buick. Double shit!

Joey brought the Pontiac to a stop halfway into the sloping driveway and got out. He went up to the bike and leaned down. The rotten kid didn't even use the kickstand and Joey hated bending over what with his heavy gut and all.

'*Joseph Albanese!*'

Joey the Nice spun around, crouching, reaching under his jacket. That tone of voice was used by only one type of slime! He pulled out his .38 and dived toward the grille of his car.

The explosions reverberated throughout the neighbourhood. Birds fluttered out of trees and there were screams along the block in the bright afternoon sunlight. Joseph Albanese was sprawled against the grille of the Pontiac, rivulets of blood slowly rolling down the shiny chrome. Joey the Nice had been caught in the vectored fire, and gripped in his hand was the gun he had used so effectively the night before. Ballistics would prove out. The killer of Lucas Anstett was dead. The judge had been the victim of a gangland assassination, and so far as the world was concerned, it had nothing to do with events taking place eight thousand miles away in Bonn, Germany.

Converse stood on the small balcony, his hands on the railing, looking down at the majestic river beyond the forest of trees that formed the banks of the Rhine. It was past seven o'clock; the sun was going below the mountains in the west, its orange rays shooting up, creating blocks of shadows over the earth – moving shadows that floated across the waters in the descending distance. The vibrant colours were hypnotic, the breezes cooling, but nothing could stop the pounding echo in his chest. *Where was Fitzpatrick? Where was his attaché case? The dossiers?* He tried to stop thinking, to stop his imagination from catapulting into frightening possibilities . . .

There was a sudden harsh echo, not from his chest, but from inside the room. He turned quickly as the door opened and Connal Fitzpatrick stood there, removing his key from the lock. He stepped aside letting a uniformed porter enter with two suitcases, instructing the man to leave them on the floor while he reached into his pocket for a tip. The porter left and the Navy lawyer stared at Joel. There was no attaché case in his hand.

'Where is it?' said Converse, afraid to breathe, afraid to move.

'I didn't pick it up.'

'Why *not?*' cried Joel, rushing forward.

'I couldn't be sure . . . maybe it was just a feeling, I don't know.'

'What are you talking about?'

'I was at the airport for seven hours yesterday, going from counter to counter asking about you,' said Connal softly. 'This afternoon I passed the Lufthansa desk and the same clerk was there. When I said hello he didn't seem to want to acknowledge me; he looked nervous, and I couldn't understand. I came back out of the baggage claim with my suitcase and watched him. I remembered how he had glanced at me last night, and as I passed him I swore his eyes kept shooting to the centre of the terminal, but there were so many people, so much confusion, I couldn't be certain.'

'You think you were picked up? *Followed*?'

'That's just it, I don't *know*. When I was shopping in Bonn I went from store to store and every now and then I'd turn around, or shift my head, to see if I could spot anyone. A couple of times I thought I saw the same people twice, but then again it was always crowded, and – again – I couldn't be sure. But I kept thinking about that Lufthansa clerk; something *was* wrong.'

'What about when you were in the taxi? Did you . . .'

'Naturally. I kept looking out of the rear window. Even during the drive out here. Several cars made the same turns we did, but I'd tell the driver to slow down and they passed us.'

'Did you watch where they went after they passed you?'

'What was the point?'

'There is one,' said Joel, recalling a clever driver who followed a deep red Mercedes limousine.

'All I knew was that you're pretty uptight about that attaché case. I don't know what's in it and I figure you don't want anyone else to know, either.'

'Bingo, counsellor.'

There was a knocking at the door, and although it was soft, it had the intrusion of a staccato burst of thunder. Both men stood motionless, their eyes riveted on the door.

'Ask who it is,' whispered Converse.

'*Wer ist da, bitte?*' said Fitzpatrick, loud enough to be heard. There was a brief reply in German and Connal breathed again. 'It's okay. It's a message for me from the manager. He probably wants to sell us a conference room.' The Navy lawyer went to the door and opened it.

However, it was not the manager, or a bellboy, or a porter bringing a message from the manager. Instead, standing there, was a slender, elderly man in a dark suit with erect posture and very broad shoulders. He glanced first at Fitzpatrick, then looked beyond at Converse.

'Excuse me, please, Commander,' he said courteously, walking through the door and approaching Joel, his hand outstretched. 'Herr Converse, may I introduce myself? The name is Leifhelm. Erich Leifhelm.'

11

Stunned, Joel took the German's hand, too paralysed to do anything else. 'Field Marshal ... ?' he uttered, instantly regretting it – he could have had the presence of mind at least to say 'General.' It was Leifhelm's dossier, that incredible story of an incredibly polished monster. The pages flashed across Converse's mind as he looked at the man – his straight hair, still more blond than white, his pale blue eyes glacial, his pinkish skin lined, waxed, set it seemed for decades.

'An old title and one thankfully I have not heard in many years. But you flatter me. You were sufficiently interested to learn something of my past.'

'Not very much.'

'I suspect enough.' Leifhelm turned to Fitzpatrick. 'I apologise for my little ruse, Commander. I felt it was best.'

Fitzpatrick shrugged, bewildered. 'You know each other, apparently.'

'Of one another,' corrected the German. 'Mr Converse came to Bonn to meet with me, but I imagine he's told you that.'

'No, I haven't told him that,' said Joel.

Leifhelm turned back, studying Converse's eyes. 'I see. Perhaps we should talk privately.'

'I think so,' Joel looked over at Fitzpatrick. 'Commander, I've taken up too much of your time. Why not go downstairs to dinner and I'll join you in a while?'

'Whatever you say, sir,' said Connal, an officer assuming the status of an aide. He nodded and left, closing the door firmly behind him.

'A lovely room,' said Leifhelm, taking several steps toward the open French doors. 'And with such a lovely view.'

'How did you find me?' asked Converse.

'Him,' replied the former field marshal, looking at Joel. '*Ein Offizier*, according to the front desk. Who is he?'

'How?' repeated Connal.

'He spent hours last night at the airport inquiring about you; many remembered him. He was obviously a friend.'

'And you knew he'd checked his luggage? That he'd be back for it?'

'Frankly no. We thought he might come for yours. We knew you wouldn't. Now, please, who is he?'

Joel understood that it was vital he maintain a level of arrogance, as he had done with Bertholdier in Paris. It was the only route he could take with such men; to be accepted by them they had to see something of themselves in him. 'He's not important and he knows nothing. He's a legal officer in the Navy who's worked in Bonn before and is over here now I gather on personal business. A prospective fiancée, I think he mentioned. I saw him the other week; we chatted and I told him I was flying in today or tomorrow and he said he'd make a point to meet me. He's obsequious, and persistent.

I'm sure he has delusions of a civilian practice. Naturally – under the circumstances – I used him. As you did.'

'Naturally.' Leifhelm smiled; he *was* polished. 'You gave him no arrival time?'

'Paris changed any possibility of that, didn't it?'

'Oh, yes, Paris. We must discuss Paris.'

'I spoke to a friend who deals with the *Sûreté*. The man died.'

'Such men do. Frequently.'

'They said he was a driver, a chauffeur. He wasn't.'

'Would it have been wiser to say he was a trusted associate of General Jacques Louis Bertholdier?'

'Obviously not. They say I killed him.'

'You did. We gather it was an uncontrollable miscalculation, no doubt brought on by the man himself.'

'Interpol's after me.'

'We, too, have friends; the situation will change. You have nothing to fear – as long as *we* have nothing to fear.' The German paused, glancing around the room. 'May I sit down?'

'Please. Shall I ring for a drink?'

'I drink only light wine and very sparingly. Unless you wish . . . it's not necessary.'

'It's not necessary,' said Converse, as Leifhelm sat in a chair nearest the balcony doors. Joel would sit when he felt the moment was right, not before.

'You took extraordinary measures at the airport to avoid us,' continued the youngest field marshal ever to be so designated by Adolf Hitler.

'I was followed from Copenhagen.'

'Very observant of you. You understand no harm was intended.'

'I didn't understand anything. I just didn't like it. I didn't know what effect Paris would have on my arrival in Bonn, what it meant to you.'

'What Paris meant?' asked Leifhelm rhetorically. 'Paris meant that a man, an attorney using a false name, said some very alarming things to a most distinguished figure many consider a brilliant statesman. This attorney, who called himself Simon, said he was flying to Bonn to see me. On his way – and I'm sure with provocation – he kills a man, which tells us something; he's quite ruthless and very capable. But that is all we know; we would like to know more. Where he goes, who he meets? In our position, would you have done otherwise?'

It was the moment to sit down. 'I would have done it better.'

'Perhaps if we'd known how resourceful you were we might have been less obvious. Incidentally, what happened in Paris? What did that man do to provoke you?'

'He tried to stop me from leaving.'

'Those were not his orders.'

'Then he grossly misunderstood them. I've a few bruises on my chest and neck to prove it. I'm not in the habit of physically defending myself, and I certainly had no intention of killing him. In fact, I didn't know I had. It was an accident purely in self-defence.'

'Obviously. Who would want such complications?'

'Exactly,' agreed Converse bluntly. 'As soon as I can rearrange my last hours in Paris so as to eliminate any mention of my seeing General Bertholdier, I'll return and explain what happened to the police.'

'As the adage goes, that may be easier said than done. You were seen talking together at *Les Étalons Blancs*. Undoubtedly, the general was recognized later when he came to the hotel; he's a celebrated man. No, I think you'd be wiser to let us handle it. We *can*, you know.'

Joel looked hard at the German, his eyes cold yet questioning. 'I admit there are risks doing it my way. I don't like them and neither would my client. On the other hand I can't go around being hunted by the police.'

'The hunt will be called off. It will be necessary for you to remain out of sight for a few days, but by then new instructions will be issued from Paris. Your name will disappear from the Interpol lists; you'll no longer be sought.'

'I'll want assurances, guarantees.'

'What better could you have than my word? I tell you nothing when I tell you that we could have far more to lose than you.'

Converse controlled his astonishment. Leifhelm had just told him a great deal whether he knew it or not. The German had as good as admitted he was part of a covert organization that could not take any chance of exposure. It was the first concrete evidence Joel had heard. Somehow it was too easy. Or were these elders of Aquitaine simply frightened old men?

'I'll concede that,' said Converse, crossing his legs. 'Well, General, you found me before I found you, but then, as we agreed, my movements are restricted. Where do we go from here?'

'Precisely where you wanted to go, Mr Converse. When you were in Paris you spoke of Bonn, Tel Aviv, Johannesburg. You knew whom to reach in Paris and whom to look for in Bonn. That impresses us greatly; we must assume you know more.'

'I've spent months in detailed research – on behalf of my client, of course.'

'But who are you? Where do you come from?'

Joel felt a sharp, sickening ache in his chest. He had felt it many times before; it was his own response to imminent danger and very real fear. 'I am who I want people to think I am, General Leifhelm. I'm sure you can understand that.'

'I see,' said the German, watching him closely. ' Sworn companion of the prevailing winds, but with the power beneath to carry you to your own destination.'

'That's a little heavy, but I guess it says it. As to where I come from I'm sure you know that by now.'

Five hours. More than enough time to put the puppets in place. A killing in New York; it had to be dealt with.

'Only bits and pieces, Mr Converse. And even if we knew more, how could we be certain it's true? What people think you are you may not be.'

'Are you, General?'

'*Ausgezeichnet!*' said Leifhelm, slapping his knee and laughing. It was a genuine laugh, the man's waxen face creasing with humour. 'You are a fine lawyer, *Mein Herr*. You answer – as they say in English – a pointed question with another question that is both an answer and an indictment.'

'Under the circumstances, it's merely the truth. Nothing more.'

'Also modest. Very commendable, very attractive.'

Joel uncrossed his legs, then crossed them again impatiently. 'I don't like compliments. General, I don't trust them – under the circumstances. You were saying before about where I wanted to go, about Bonn, Tel Aviv, and Johannesburg. What did you mean?'

'Only that we have complied with your wishes,' said Leifhelm, spreading his hands in front of him. 'Rather than your making such tedious trips we have asked our representatives in Tel Aviv and Johannesburg, as well as Bertholdier, of course, to fly to Bonn for a conference. With you, Mr Converse.'

He had *done* it! thought Joel. They *were* frightened, *panicked* perhaps the better description. Despite the pounding and the pain in his chest, he spoke slowly, quietly. 'I appreciate your consideration, but in all frankness, my client isn't ready for a summit. He wanted to understand the parts before he looked further at the whole. The spokes support the wheel, sir. I was to report how strong they were – how strong they appeared to me.'

'Oh, yes, your client. Who is he, Mr Converse?'

'I'm sure General Bertholdier told you I'm not at liberty to say.'

'You were in San Francisco, California . . .'

'Where a great deal of my research was done,' interrupted Joel. 'It's not where my client lives. Although I readily admit there's a man in San Francisco – Palo Alto, to be exact – whom I'd like very much to *be* a client.'

'Yes, yes, I see.' Leifhelm put the ends of his fingers together, as he continued. 'Am I to understand that you reject the conference here in Bonn?'

Converse had taken a thousand such questions in opening gambits with attorneys seeking accommodation between corporate adversaries. Both parties wanted the same thing; it was simply a question of flattening out the responsibility so that no one party would be the petitioner.

'Well, you've gone to a lot of trouble,' Joel began. 'And as long as it's understood that I have the option of speaking to each individually should I wish, I can't see any harm.' Converse permitted himself a strained smile – as he had done a thousand times. 'In the interests of my client, of course.'

'Of course,' said the German. 'Tomorrow, say four o'clock in the afternoon. I'll send a car for you. I assure you, I set an excellent table.'

'A table?'

'Dinner, naturally. After we have our talk.' Leifhelm rose from the chair. 'I wouldn't think of your coming to Bonn and forgoing the experience. I'm known for my dinner parties, Mr Converse. And if it concerns you, make whatever . . . security arrangements . . . you like. A platoon of personal guards, if you wish. You'll be perfectly safe. *Mein Haus ist dein Haus.*'

'I don't speak German.'

'Actually, it's an old Spanish saying. *Mi casa, su casa.* "My house is your house". Your comfort and well-being are my most urgent concerns.'

'Mine, too,' said Joel, rising. 'I wouldn't think of having anyone accompany me, *or* follow me. It'd be counterproductive. Of course, I'll inform my client as to my whereabouts, telling him approximately when he can expect my subsequent call. He'll be anxious to hear from me.'

'I should think so.' Leifhelm and Converse walked to the door; the German turned and once more offered his hand. 'Until tomorrow then. And may I again suggest while you're here you be careful, at least for several days.'

'I understand.'

The puppets in New York. The killing that had to be dealt with – the first of two obstacles, two sharp, sickening aches in his chest.

'By the way,' said Joel, releasing the field marshal's hand. 'There was a news item on the BBC this morning that interested me – so much that I phoned an associate. A man was killed in New York, a judge. They say it was a revenge killing, a contract put out by organized crime. Do you know anything about it?'

'*I?*' asked Leifhelm, his blond-white eyebrows raised, his wax-like lips parted. 'It seems people are killed by dozens every day in New York, judges included, I presume. Why should I know anything about it? The answer, obviously, is no.'

'I just wondered. Thank you . . .'

'But . . . but you. You must have a . . .'

'Yes, General?'

'Why does this judge interest you? Why did you think I would know him?'

Converse smiled, but without a trace of humour. 'I won't be telling you anything when I tell you he was our mutual adversary – enemy, if you like.'

'Our . . .? You really must explain yourself!'

'As you, and as I said, I am what I want people to think I am. This man knew the truth. I'm on leave of absence from my firm, working confidentially for a personal client. He tried to stop me, tried to get the senior partner to cancel my leave and call me back.'

'By giving him *reasons?*'

'No, just veiled threats of corruption and impropriety. He wouldn't go any farther; he's on the bench and couldn't back it up; his own conduct would be suspect. My employer is completely ignorant – angry as hell and confused – but I've calmed him down. It's a closed issue, the less explored the better for us all.' Joel opened the door for Leifhelm. 'Till tomorrow . . .' He paused for a brief moment, loathing the man standing in front of him, but with only respect in his eyes. 'Field Marshal,' he added.

'*Gute Nacht,*' said Erich Leifhelm, nodding his head sharply once in military acknowledgement.

Converse persuaded the switchboard operator to send someone into the dining room for the American, Commander Fitzpatrick. The task was not easy for the naval officer was neither in the dining room nor the bar, but outside on the *Spanische Terrasse* having a drink with friends, watching the Rhine in twilight.

'What goddamned friends?' demanded Joel over the phone.

'Just a couple I met out there. He's a nice guy – an executive type, pretty much into his seventies, I think.'

'And she?' asked Converse, his lawyer's antennae struck by a vocal signal.

'Maybe . . . thirty, forty years younger,' replied Connal with less elaboration.

'Get up here, sailor!'

* * *

Fitzpatrick leaned forward on the couch, his elbows on his knees, his expression a mixture of concern and astonishment as he looked over at Joel, who was smoking a cigarette in front of the open balcony doors. 'Let me run this again,' he said warily. 'You want me to stop someone from getting your service record?'

'Not all of it, just part of it.'

'Who the hell do you think I am?'

'You did it for Avery – for *Press*. You can do it for me. You *have* to!'

'That's backwards. I *opened* those files for him, I didn't keep them closed.'

'Either way it's control. You've got access; you've got a key.'

'I'm *here*, not there. I can't scissor out something you don't like eight thousand miles away. Be reasonable!'

'Somebody can, somebody *has* to! It's only a short segment, and it's got to be at the end. The final interview.'

'An *interview*?' said Connal, startled, getting to his feet. 'In a service record? You mean some kind of operational report? Because if you do, I wouldn't be . . .'

'Not a report,' interrupted Converse, shaking his head. 'The discharge . . . my *discharge* interview. That stuff Press Halliday quoted to me.'

'Wait a minute, *wait* a minute!' Fitzpatrick held up his hands. 'Are you referring to the remarks made at your discharge *hearing*?'

'Yes, that's it. The hearing!'

'Well, relax. They're not part of your service record, or anyone else's.'

'Halliday had them – *Avery* had them! I just told you, he quoted my words verbatim!' Joel walked to a table where there was an ashtray; he crushed out his cigarette. 'If they're not part of the record, how did he get them? How did *you* get them for him?'

'That's different,' said Connal, obviously remembering as he spoke. 'You were a POW and a lot of those hearings were put under a debriefing classification, and I *do* mean classified. Even after all these years, many of those sessions are still touchy. A lot of things were talked about that no one to this day wants made public – for everyone's good, not just the military's.'

'But *you* got them! I heard my own words, goddamn it!'

'Yes, I got them,' admitted the Navy lawyer without enthusiasm. 'I got the transcript, and I'd be busted to a Seaman 3rd Class if anyone knew about it. You see, I believed Press. He swore to me he needed it, needed everything. He couldn't make any mistakes.'

'How did you do it? You weren't even in San Diego at the time, that's what you said!'

'By calling the vaults and using my legal release number to have a photostat made. I said it was a Four-Zero emergency and I'd take responsibility. The next morning when the authorization came in by pouch for counter signature, I had the Chief Legal Officer at the base sign it with a lot of other things. It simply got buried in the paper work.'

'But how did you know about it in the first place?'

'Selected POW records have flags on their discharge sheets.'

'Clarification, please?'

'Just what I said, flags. Small blue seals that denote additional information still held under tight security. No flags, everything's clean; but if there is one, that means there's something else. I told Press and he said he had to have whatever it was, so I went after it.'

'Then anyone else could, too.'

'No, not anyone. You need an officer with a legal release number and there aren't many of us. Also there's a minimum forty-eight hour delay so the material can be vetted. That's almost always in the area of weapons and technology data that still might be classified.'

'*Forty-eight* . . . ?' Converse swallowed as he tried to count the hours since Paris, since the first moment his name had surfaced. 'There's still time!' he said, his voice taut, his words clipped. 'If you can do it there's still *time*. And if you can I'll tell you everything I know because you'll deserve it. No one will deserve it more.'

'Spell it out.'

Joel turned aimlessly, shaking his head. 'That's funny. I said the same thing to Avery. I said "spell it out, Avery" . . . Sorry, his name was Press.' Converse turned back to the Navy lawyer, a military lawyer with a mystifying military privilege called a legal-release-number. 'Listen to me and hear me clearly. A few minutes ago something happened that I wasn't sure would or *could* happen – something your brother-in-law was killed to prevent. Tomorrow at four o'clock in the afternoon I'm going to walk into the middle of those men who are coming together to promote some kind of violence that'll stun this world, toppling governments, allowing *these* people to step in and fill the voids, running things their way, shaping the *laws* their way. One big Supreme Court, each chair owned by a fanatic with specific convictions as to who and what has value and who and what doesn't, and those who don't can go to hell, no appeals on the agenda . . . I'm going to meet them face to face! I'm going to *talk* to them, *hear* their *words*! I admit I'm the most amateurish fox you've ever heard of in a chicken coop – only in this case it's a vultures' nest, and I mean the type that swoop down and tear the flesh off backs with one pass . . . But I've got something going for me: I'm one hell of a good lawyer and I'll learn things they won't know I've learned. Maybe enough to piece together a couple of cases that will blow it all apart – blow *them* apart. Before I told you I rejected your deadline. I still reject it, but *now* it doesn't seem so far out of the ballpark. Certainly not two days, but perhaps not ten! But, you see I thought I was going to have to fly to Tel Aviv, then Johannesburg. Prime everyone, frighten them. Now I don't! We've already done it! They're coming to me because they're frightened *now*! They don't know what to think and that means they're panicked.' Converse paused, sweat forming on his hairline; then he added. 'I don't have to tell you what a good lawyer can do with panicked hostile witnesses. The materials he can collect for evidence.'

'Your plea's accepted, counsellor,' said Fitzpatrick, not without awe. 'You're convincing. Now tell me why my intercession can help? What does it accomplish?'

'I want those men to think I'm *one* of them! I can live with everything they can put together about me – I'm not proud of it all; I've made my compromises – but I *can't* live with that transcript of my discharge! . . . Don't you *see*? It's what Avery – Press – understood! I understand now. He knew me nearly twenty five years ago, and when I think back we were actually pretty damned good friends. And no matter what happened to us individually, he was banking on the fact that I hadn't really changed that much, not in the deeper things. By the time we reach the voting age we're pretty well set, all of us. The real changes come later, much later, dictated by such things as acceptance and rejection and the state of our wallets – the prices we pay for our convictions, or to support our talents – defending success or explaining failure. That transcript confirmed what Halliday believed, at least enough so for him to want to meet me, talk with me, and finally to recruit me. Only he did it – finally – by dying with me holding his head. I couldn't walk away after that.'

Connal Fitzpatrick was silent as he walked out on the balcony. He leaned over and gripped the railing, Converse watching him. Then he tood up, raised both his hands, and pulled back the sleeve of his left wrist; he turned. 'It's 12.15 in San Diego. No one in legal goes to lunch before one o'clock; the Coronado's bar doesn't begin to jump until then.'

'Can you *do* it?'

'I can try,' said the naval officer, crossing through the French doors toward the telephone. 'No, damn it, if you've got your times straight, I can do better than try, I can issue an order. That's what rank's all about.'

The first five minutes were excruciating for Joel. There were delays on all overseas calls, but somehow the bi-, tri- or quadrilingual Fitzpatrick, speaking urgently, unctuously in German, managed to get through, the phrase *dringende Not* repeated frequently.

'Lieutenant Senior Grade Remington, David. Legal Division, SAND PAC. This is an emergency, sailor, Commander Fitzpatrick calling. Break in if the lines are occupied.' Connal covered the mouthpiece and turned to Converse. 'If you'll open my suitcase, there's a bottle of bourbon in the middle.'

'I'll open your suitcase, Commander.'

'*Remington*? . . . Hello, David, it's Connal . . . Yes, thanks very much, I'll tell Meagen . . . No, I'm not in San Francisco, don't call me there. But something's come up I want you to handle, something on my calendar that I didn't get to. For openers, it's a Four-Zero emergency. I'll fill you in when I get back, but until I do you have to take care of it. Got a pencil? . . . There's a POW service record under the name of Converse, Joel . . . Lieutenant, one and a half stripes, Air Arm, pilot – carrier-based, Vietnam duty. He was discharged in the sixties . . .' Fitzpatrick looked down at Converse, who held up his right hand and three fingers of his left. '. . . Nineteen sixty-eight, to be exact . . .' Joel stepped forward, his spread right hand still raised, his left now showing only the index finger. '. . . June of 'sixty-eight,' added the Navy lawyer, nodding. 'Point of separation our old home town, San Diego. Have you got all that? Read it back to me, please, David.'

Connal nodded sporadically, as he listened. 'C-O-N-V-E-R-S-E, that's right . . . June 'sixty-eight, Air Arm, pilot, Vietnam, POW section, San Diego separation; that's it, you've got it. Now here's the wicket, David. This Converse's SR is flag status; the flag pertains to his discharge hearing, no weapons of high tech involved . . . Listen carefully, David. It's my understanding that there may be a request pending accompanied by a legal release code for the discharge transcript. Under *no* circumstances is that transcript to be released. The flag stays fixed and can't be removed by anyone without my authorization. And if the release *has* been processed it'll still be within the forty-eight hour vet-delay. *Kill* it. Understood?'

Again Fitzpatrick listened, but instead of nodding, he shook his head. 'No, not under any circumstances. I don't care if the secetaries of State, Defense and the Navy all sign a joint petition on White House stationery, the answer is no. If anyone questions the decision tell him I'm exercising my authority as Chief Legal Officer of SAND PAC. There's some goddamned article in the "shoals" that says a station CLO can impound materials on the basis of conceivably-privileged information relative to the security of the sector, *et cetera, et cetera*. I don't recall the time element – seventy-two hours or five days or something like that – but find that statute. You may need it.'

Connal listened further, his brows creasing, his eyes straying to Joel. He spoke slowly, as Converse felt the sickening ache again in his chest. 'Where can you reach me . . . ?' said the naval officer, perplexed. Then suddenly he was no longer bewildered. 'I take back what I said before; call Meagen in San Francisco. If I'm not with her and the kids, she'll know where to reach me . . . thanks again, David. Sweep your decks and get right on this, okay. Thanks . . . I'll tell Meg.' Fitzpatrick hung up the phone and exhaled audibly. 'There,' he said, slouched in relief, pushing his hand through his loose, light brown hair. 'I'll phone Meagen and give her this number, tell her to say I've gone up to the Sonoma hills, if Remington calls – Press had some property there.'

'Give her the telephone number,' said Joel, 'but don't tell her anything else.'

'Don't worry, she's got enough on her mind.' The naval officer looked at Converse, frowning. 'If your hourly count is right, you've got your time now.'

'My count's all right. Is Lieutenant Remington? I mean that only in the sense that he wouldn't let anyone override your order, would he?'

'Don't mistake my officiousness where he's concerned,' replied Connal. 'David isn't easily pushed around. The reason I chose him and not one of four other senior lawyers in the department is that he's got a reputation for being a stickler-prick. He'll find that statute and nail it to the forehead of any four-striper who tries to countermand that order . . . I like Remington; he's very useful. He scares the hell out of people.'

'We all have case-partners like that. It's called the good guy-bad guy routine.'

'David fits. He's got an eye that keeps straying to the right.' Fitzpatrick suddenly stood erect, his bearing military. 'I thought you were going to get the bourbon, *Lieutenant?*'

'Yes, *sir*, Commander!' shot back Joel, heading for Fitzpatrick's suitcase.

'And if I remember correctly, after you pour us a drink, you're going to tell me a story I want very much to hear.'

'*Aye, aye,* sir!' said Converse, lifting the suitcase off the floor and putting it on the couch. 'And if I may suggest, sir,' continued Joel. 'A room-service dinner might be in order. I'm sure the Commander needs nourishment after his trying day at the wheel.'

'Good thinking, Lieutenant. I'll phone down to the *Empfang*.'

'Before calling your bookie, may I also suggest that you first call your sister?'

'Oh, Christ, I forgot!'

Chaim Abrahms walked down the dark street in Tel Aviv, his stocky frame draped in his usual safari jacket, boots beneath his khaki trousers, and a beret covering his nearly bald head. The beret was the only concession he made to the night's purpose; normally he enjoyed being recognized, accepting the adulation shouted at him with well-rehearsed humility. In daylight, his head uncovered and held erect, his familiar safari stared at and the heavy sound of his boots heard, he would listen to the words and respond with a nod, his eyes boring in on the speakers, acknowledgment in his looks.

'*First a Jew!*' was the phrase with which he was always greeted, whether in Tel Aviv or Jerusalem, sections of Paris and most of New York.

The phrase had been born years ago when as a young terrorist for the Irgun, he had been condemned to death *in absentia* by the British for the slaughter of a Palestinian village, the Arab corpses put on display for *Nakama!* He had then issued a cry heard around the world.

'I am first a Jew, a son of Abraham! All else follows, and rivers of blood will follow if the children of Abraham are denied!'

The British, in 1948, not caring to create another martyr, commuted his sentence and he joined a kibbutz. Yet the acreage of the settlement could not confine the militant Sabra. Three wars had unleashed his agricultural shackles as well as his ferocity – and his brilliance in the field. It was a brilliance developed and refined through the early years of racing with a fugitive, fragmented army. Where the tactics of surprise, shock, hit and melt away were constant, when out-manned and out-gunned were the accepted odds, but only victory the acceptable outcome. He later applied the strategies and the philosophy of those years to the ever-expanding war machine that became the Army, Navy and Air Force of a mighty Israel. Mars was in the heavens of Chaim Abrahms's vision and, for the prophets aside, the god of war was his strength, his reason for being. From Ramat Aviv to Har Hazeytim, from Metullah to Masada of the Negev, *Nakama!* was the cry. *Retribution* to the enemies of Abraham's children!

If only the Poles and the Czechs, the Hungarians and the Romanies, as well as the haughty Germans and the impossible Russians had not immigrated by such tens of thousands. They arrived and the complications came with them. Faction against faction, culture against culture, each screaming louder than the last, all trying to prove they were more entitled to the name *Jew* than the others. It was all nonsense! They were there because they had to be; they had succumbed to Abraham's enemies, permitted – yes *permitted* – the slaughter of millions rather than rising as millions and slaughtering in return. Well, they found out what their *civilized* ways brought them, and how much their Talmudic convolutions earned them. So they came to the Holy Land – *their* Holy Land, so they proclaimed. Well, it wasn't theirs. Where were they when it was being clawed out of rock and arid desert by strong hands with primitive tools – biblical tools? Where were they when the hated Arab and the despised English first felt the wrath of the tribal Jew? They were in the capitals of Europe, in their banks and their fancy drawing rooms, making money and drinking expensive brandy out of crystal goblets. No, they came here because they had to; they came to the Holy Land of the Sabra.

They brought with them money and dandy ways and elegant words and confusing arguments and influence and the guilt of the world. But it was the Sabra who taught them how to fight. And it was a Sabra who would bring all Israel into the orbit of a mighty new alliance.

Abrahms reached the intersection of Ibn Gvirol and Arlosoroff streets. There was a mist in the air; the street lamps were haloed, their lights constricted. It was just as well; he should not be seen. He had another block to go, to an address on Jabotinsky, an unprepossessing apartment house where there was an undistinguished flat leased by a man who appeared to be no more than an unimportant bureaucrat. What few realized, however, was that this man, this specialist who operated sophisticated computer equipment with communications throughout most of the world, was intrinsic to the global operations of the Mossad, Israel's intelligence service which many considered the finest on earth. He, too, was a Sabra. He was one of them.

Abrahms spoke his name quietly into the mouthpiece above the mail slot in the outer lobby; he heard the click of the lock of the heavy door, and walked inside. He began the climb up the three flights of steps that would take him to the flat.

'Some wine, Chaim?'

'Whisky,' was the curt reply.

'Always the same question and always the same answer,' said the specialist. 'I say "Some wine, Chaim?" and you say one word. "Whisky" you say. You would drink whisky at the Seder, if you could get away with it.'

'I can and I do.' Abrahms sat in a cracked leather chair, looking around the plain, dishevelled room with books everywhere, wondering, as he always did, why a man with such influence lived this way. It was rumoured that the Mossad officer did not like company, and larger, more attractive quarters might invite it. 'I gathered from your grunts and coughs over the telephone that you have what I need.'

'Yes, I have it,' said the specialist, bringing in a glass of very good Scotch to his guest. 'I have it, but I don't think you're going to like it.'

'Why not?' asked Abrahms, drinking, his eyes alert over the rim of the glass, holding them on his host as the latter sat down opposite him.

'Basically because it's confusing, and what's confusing in this business is to be approached delicately. You are not a delicate man, Chaim Abrahms, forgive the indelicacy of my saying it. You tell me this Converse is your enemy, a would-be infiltrator, and I tell you I find nothing to support the conclusion. Before anything else there must be a deep personal motive for a non-professional to engage in this kind of deception, this kind of behaviour, if you will. There has to be a driving compulsion to strike out at an image of a cause he loathes ... Well, there is a motive, and there is an enemy for which he must have great hatred, but neither is compatible with what you suggest. The information, incidentally, is completely reliable. It comes from the *Quanq Dinh* . . .'

'What in hell is that?' interrupted the general.

'A specialized branch of North Vietnamese – now, of course, Vietnamese – intelligence.'

'You have sources *there*?'

'We fed them for years – nothing terribly vital, but sufficient to gain a few ears . . . and voices. There were things we had to know, weapons we had to understand; they could be turned against us.'

'This Converse was in North Vietnam?'

'For several years as a prisoner of war; there's an extensive file on him. At first, his captors thought he could be used for propaganda, radio broadcasts, television . . . imploring his brutal government to withdraw and stop the bombing – all the usual garbage. He spoke well, presented a good picture, and was obviously very American. Initially they televised him as a murderer from the skies, saved from the angry mobs by humane troops, then later while eating and exercising; you see, they were programming him for a violently sudden reversal. They thought he was a soft, privileged young man who could be broken rather easily to do their bidding in exchange for a more comfortable treatment – after having experienced a period of harsh depriva- tion. What they learned, however, was quite different. Under that soft shell the inner lining was made of hard metal, and the odd thing was that as the months went by it grew harder, until they realized they had created – created was their word – a hellhound of sorts, somehow forged in steel.'

'Hellhound? Was that their word, too?'

'No, they called him an ugly troublemaker, which considering the source is not without irony. The point is they recognized the fact that they *had* created him. The harsher the treatment the more volatile he became, the more resilient.'

'Why not?' said Abrahms sharply. 'He was angry. Prod a desert snake and watch him strike.'

'I can assure you, Chaim, it is not the normal human response under such conditions. A man can go mad and strike in crazed fury, or he can become reclusive to the point of catatonia, or fall apart weeping, willing to compromise anything and everything for the smallest kindness. He did none of these things. His was a calculated and inventive series of responses drawing on his own inner resources to survive. He led two escapes – the first lasting three days and the second five – before the groups were recaptured. As the leader, he was placed in a cage in the Mekong River and devised a way to kill the water rats by grabbing them from beneath the surface like a shark. He was then thrown into solitary confinement, a pit in the ground twenty feet deep with barbed wire anchored across the top. It was from there, during a heavy rainstorm at night, that he clawed his way up, bent the wire back and escaped alone. He made his way south through the jungles and in the river streams for over a hundred miles until he reached the American lines. It was no easy feat. They created a savagely obsessed man who won his own personal war.'

'Why didn't they simply kill him before that?'

'I wondered myself,' said the specialist, 'so I phoned my source in Hanoi, the one who provided the information. He said a strange thing, something quite profound in its way. He said he wasn't there, of course, but he thought it was probably respect.'

'For an ugly troublemaker?'

'Captivity in war does odd things, Chaim, to both the captured and the captors. There are so many factors at work in a vicious game. Aggression, resistance, bravery, fear, and not the least, curiosity – especially when the players come from such diverse cultures as the Occident and the Orient. An abnormal bond is often formed, as much from the weariness of the testing-game as anything else, perhaps. It doesn't lessen the national animosities, but a subtle recognition sets in that tells these men, these players, that they are not really in the game by their own choosing. In depth analyses further show us that it is the captors not the captured that first perceive this commonality. The latter is obsessed with freedom and survival, while the former begin to question their absolute authority over the lives and conditions of other men. They start to wonder what it would be like to be in the other player's shoes. It's all part of what the psychiatrists call the Stockholm syndrome.'

'What in the name of *God* are you trying to say? You sound like one of those bores in the Knesset reading a position paper. A little of this, a little of that and a lot of wind!'

'You are definitely not delicate, Chaim. I'm trying to explain to you that while this Converse nurtured his hatreds and his obsessions, his captors wearied of the game, and as our source in Hanoi suggests, they grudgingly spared his life out of respect, before he made his final and successful escape.'

To Abrahms' bewilderment the specialist had apparently finished. 'And?' said the Sabra.

'Well, there it is. There is the motive and the enemy, but they are also *your* motive and *your* enemy – arrived at from different routes, of course. Ultimately, you wish to smash insurgentism wherever it erupts, curb the spread of Third World revolutions, especially Islamic because you know they're being fostered by the Marxists – read Soviets – and are a direct threat to Israel. One way or another it's the global threat that's brought you all together and in my judgment rightfully so. There is a time and a place for a military-industrial complex, and it is now. It must run the governments of the free world before that world is buried by its enemies.'

Again the specialist stopped. Chaim Abrahms squinted and tried not to shout. '*And?*'

'Can't you see? This Converse is one of you. Everything supports it. He has the motive and an enemy he's seen in the harshest light. He is a highly regarded attorney who makes a great deal of money with a very conservative firm, and his clients are among the wealthiest corporations and conglomerates. Everything he's been and everything he stands for can only benefit from your efforts. The confusion lies in his unorthodox methods and I can't explain them except to say that perhaps they are *not* unorthodox in the specialized work he does. Markets can plummet on rumours; concealment and diversion are surely respected. Regardless, he doesn't want to destroy you, he wants to join you.'

The Sabra put his glass down on the floor and struggled out of the chair. With his chin tucked into his breastbone and his hands clasped behind his back, Abrahms paced back and forth in silence. He stopped and looked down at the specialist.

'Suppose, just *suppose*,' he said, 'the almighty Mossad has made a mistake, that there's something you didn't find?'

'I would find that hard to accept.'

'But it's a possibility?'

'In the light of the information we've gathered, I doubt it. Why?'

'Because I have a sense of smell, *that's* why!'

The man from the Mossad kept his eyes on Abrahms, as if studying the soldier's face – or thinking – from a different viewpoint. 'There is only one other possibility, Chaim. If this Converse is not who and what I've described, which would be contrary to all the data we've compiled, then he is an agent of his government.'

'That's . . . what I smell,' said the Sabra softly.

It was the specialist's turn to be silent. He breathed deeply, then responded. 'I respect your nostrils, old friend. Not always your conduct but certainly your sense of smell. What do the others think?'

'Only that he's lying, that he's covering for others he may or may not know, who are using him as a scout, an "infantry point" was the term used by Palo Alto.'

The Mossad officer continued to stare at the Sabra, but his eyes were no longer focused; he was seeing abstract, twisted patterns, convolutions few men would comprehend. They came from a lifetime of analysing seen and unseen, legitimate and racial enemies, parrying dagger thrusts and counterthrusts in the blackest darkness. 'It's possible,' he whispered, as if replying to an unspoken question heard only by himself. 'Almost inconceivable, but possible.'

'What is? That Washington is behind him?'

'Yes.'

'Why? You just said it.'

'As an outrageous alternative I did not subscribe to, but the only one left that has the slightest plausibility. Simply put, he has too much information.'

'And?'

'Not Washington in the usual sense, not the government in the broader sense, but within a *branch* of the government a *section* that has heard whispers but cannot be sure. If there is such an organization, they must invade it to expose it. So they choose a man with the right history, the right memories, even the right profession to do the job. He might even believe everything he says.'

The Sabra was transfixed but impatient. 'That has too many complications for me,' he said bluntly.

'Try it my way first. Try to accept him; he may be genuine. He'll have to give you *something* concrete; you can force that. Then again he may not because he cannot.'

'*And?*'

'And if he can't you'll know you're right. Then put as much distance between him and his sponsors as is humanly and brutally possible. He must become a pariah, a man hunted for crimes so insane his madness is unquestioned.'

'Why not just kill him?'

'By all means, but not before he's been labelled so mad that no one will step forward to claim him. It will buy you the time you need. The final phase of Aquitaine is when? Three, four weeks away?'

'That's when it begins, yes.'

The specialist got up from the chair and stood pensively in front of the soldier. 'I repeat, first try to accept him, see if what I said before is true. But if that sense of smell of yours is provoked further, if there's the slightest possibility he has been willingly or unwillingly, wittingly or unwittingly, made a *provocateur* by men in Washington, then build your case against him and throw him to the wolves. Create that pariah as the North Vietnamese created a hellhound. Then kill him quickly, before anyone else reaches him.'

'A Sabra of the Mossad speaks?'

'As clearly as I can.'

The young Army captain and the somewhat older civilian came out of the Pentagon from adjacent glass doors and glanced briefly at each other, no recognition in their looks. They walked separately down the short bank of steps and turned left on the cement path that led to the enormous parking lot; the army officer was perhaps ten feet ahead of the civilian. Upon reaching the huge asphalt area, each veered in a different direction toward his car. If these two men had been the subject of photographic surveillance during the past fifty seconds, there was no indication whatsoever that they knew each other.

The green Buick coupé turned right in the middle of the block, going through the open chasm that was the entrance to the hotel's underground parking lot. At the bottom of the ramp the driver showed his room key to the attendant, who raised the yellow barrier and waved him along. There was an empty space in the third column of stationary automobiles. The Buick eased into it and the Army captain got out.

He circled through the revolving door and walked to a bank of elevators in the hotel's lower lobby. The panels of the second elevator opened, revealing two couples who had not intended to reach the underground level; they laughed as one of the men repeatedly pressed the Main Lobby button. The officer, in turn, touched the button for the fourteenth floor. Sixty seconds later he walked out into the corridor toward the Exit staircase. He was heading for the eleventh floor.

The blue Toyota station wagon came down the ramp, the driver's hand extended, a room key held out, the number visible. Inside the parking area the driver found an empty space in the sixth column and carefully steered the small station wagon into it.

The civilian stepped out and looked at his watch. Satisfied, he started toward the revolving door and the elevators. The second elevator was empty and the civilian was tempted to press the button for the eleventh floor; he was tired and did not relish the additional walk. However, there would be other occupants on the way up; he held to the rules and placed his index finger over the button opposite the number *nine*.

* * *

Standing in front of the hotel room door, the civilian raised his hand, rapped once, waited several beats, then rapped twice more. Seconds later the door was opened by the Army captain. Beyond him was a third man, also in uniform, the colour and the insignia denoting a Lieutenant, junior grade, in the Navy. He stood by the desk, above a telephone.

'Glad you got here in time,' said the Army officer. 'The traffic was rotten. Our call should be coming through in a few minutes.'

The civilian entered, nodding to the Navy man as he spoke. 'What did you find out about Fitzpatrick?' he asked.

'He's where he shouldn't be,' replied the Lieutenant.

'Can you bring him back?'

'I'm working on it, but I don't know where to begin. I'm a very low man on a very big totem pole.'

'Aren't we all?' said the captain.

'Who'd have thought Halliday would have *gone* to him?' asked the naval officer, frustration in his voice. 'Or if he was going to bring him in why didn't he go to him *first*? Or tell him about *us*?'

'I can answer the last two questions,' said the Army man. 'He was protecting him from a Pentagon backlash. If we go down his brother-in-law stays clean.'

'And I can answer the first question,' said the civilian. 'Halliday went to Fitzpatrick because, in the final analysis, he didn't trust us. Geneva proved he was right.'

'*How?*' asked the captain defensively, but without apology. 'We couldn't have prevented it.'

'No, we couldn't,' agreed the civilian. 'But we couldn't do anything about it afterwards, either. That was part of the trust and there was no way we could live up to it. We couldn't afford to.'

The telephone rang. The lieutenant picked it up and listened. 'It's Mykonos,' he said.

PART II

12

Connal Fitzpatrick sat opposite Joel at the room service table drinking the last of his coffee. The dinner was finished, the story completed, and all the questions the Navy lawyer could raise answered by Converse because he had given his word; he needed a complete ally.

'Except for a few identities and some dossier material,' said Connal, 'I don't know an awful lot more than I did before. Maybe I will when I see those Pentagon names. You say you don't know who supplied them?'

'No. Like Topsy, they're just there. Beale said a number of them are probably mistakes, but others aren't; they have to be linked to Delavane.'

'They had to be supplied by someone, too. There had to be reasons why they were listed.'

'Beale called them "decision makers" in military procurements.'

'Then I *have* to see them. I've dealt with those people.'

'*You?*'

'Yes. Not very often, but enough to know my way around.'

'Why *you?*'

'Basically, translating legal nuances from language to language where navy tech was involved. I think I mentioned that I speak . . .'

'You did,' broke in Joel.

'*Goddamn* it!' cried Fitzpatrick, crushing his napkin in a fist.

'What's the matter?'

'Press *knew* I had dealings with those committees, with the technology and armaments boys! He even asked me about them. Who I saw, who I liked . . . who I trusted. *Jesus!* Why didn't he come to *me?* Of all the people he knew, I was the logical one! I'm down the pike and his closest friend.'

'That's why he didn't come to you,' said Converse.

'Stupid *bastard!*' Connal raised his eyes. 'And I hope you hear that, Press. You might still be around to see Connal Two win the Bay Regatta.'

'I think you really believe he might hear you.'

Fitzpatrick looked across the table at Joel. 'Yes, I do. You see, I believe, counsellor. I know all the reasons why I shouldn't – Press enumerated them to a fare-thee-well when we were in our cups – but I believe. I answered him once with a quote from one of his laid-back Protestant forebears.'

'What was that?' asked Joel, smiling kindly.

'"There's more faith in honest doubt than is held by all the archangels in the mind of God".'

'It's very nice. I've never heard it before.'

'Maybe I didn't get it right . . . I've got to see those names!'

'And I have to get my attaché case, but I can't go myself.'

'Then I'm elected,' said the Navy man. 'Do you think Leifhelm's right? You think he can really call off Interpol?'

'I'm of two thoughts about it. For my immediate manoeuvrability I hope he can. But if he does, it'll scare the hell out of me.'

'I'm on your side about that,' agreed Connal, getting out of the chair. 'I'll call the desk and get a taxi. Give me the key to the locker.'

Converse reached into his pocket and pulled out the small, rounded key with the German numerals. 'Leifhelm's seen you. He could have you followed; he did before.'

'I'll be ten times more careful. If I see the same pair of headlights twice, I'll go to a *Bierkeller*. I know a few here.'

Joel looked at his watch. 'It's twenty minutes to ten. Do you think you could swing around to the university first?'

'Dowling?'

'He said he had someone he wanted me to meet. Just walk by him – or them – and say everything's under control, nothing else. I owe him that much.'

'Suppose he tries to stop me?'

'Then pull out your ID and say it's high priority, or ultrasecret, or whatever bullshit security phrases that come to that very inventive mind of yours.'

'Do I sense a touch of legal envy?'

'No, just recognition. I know where you're coming from. I've been there.'

Fitzpatrick walked slowly along the wide path on the south façade of the immense University Building, once the great palace of the all powerful Archbishops of Köln. The unimpeded moonlight swelled over the area, reflecting off the myriad rows of cathedral windows and lending a luminous dimension to the light stone walls of the majestic structure. Beyond the path the winding gardens of August seemed to possess an eerie night elegance – sleeping circles of floral wonder totally unaware of their beauty. Connal was so struck by the tranquil loveliness of the nocturnal setting that he nearly forgot why he was there.

The reason was brought sharply back into focus when he saw the figure of a long, slender man slouched alone on a bench. The man's legs were extended and crossed at the ankles, his head covered by a soft cloth hat, but not sufficiently to hide the flowering grey-blond hair that protruded slightly over his temples and the back of his neck. So this Caleb Dowling was an actor, thought the Navy lawyer, amused by the fact that Dowling had feigned protestations of shock when he realized Connal did not know him. But then neither did Converse; they were obviously a minority in a world of television addicts. A College professor who had fulfilled the fantasies of youth, a risk-taker, according to Joel, who had won a battle against astronomical odds was a nice thing to think about, saddened by the knowledge of a haunted wife he loved dearly. Also a marine who had fought in the bloody mess that was Kwajalein was a man to be reckoned with; he was not to be underestimated.

Fitzpatrick walked over to the bench and sat down several feet away from Dowling. The actor glanced at him, then did a perfectly natural double-take, his head snapping, no rehearsal required.

'*You?*'

'I'm sorry about last night,' said Connal. 'I gather I wasn't very convincing.'

'You lacked a certain finish, young fella. Where the hell is Converse?'

'Sorry again. He couldn't make it, but not to worry. Everything's A-okay and under control.'

'Whose okay and whose control?' countered the actor, annoyed. 'I told Joel to come here, not a cub scout interlocutor.'

'I resent that. I'm a lieutenant-commander in the United States Navy and the Chief Legal Officer at a major naval base. Mr Converse accepted an assignment from us which has an element of personal risk for him and the highest priority of classification for us. Back off, Mr Dowling. We appreciate – and I speak for Converse as well as myself – your interest and your generosity, but it's time for you to recede. For your own benefit, incidentally.'

'What about Interpol? He killed a man.'

'Who tried to kill *him*,' added Fitzpatrick quickly, a lawyer rejoining a negative statement by a witness on the stand. 'That will be clarified internally and the charges dropped.'

'You're pretty smooth, Commander,' said Dowling, sitting up. 'Better than you were last night – this morning, actually.'

'I was upset. I'd lost him and I had to find him. I had to deliver vital information.'

The actor now crossed his legs at the knees and leaned back, his arm slung casually over the slatted rim of the bench. 'So this thing Converse and you are involved with is a real hush-hush operation?'

'It's highly classified, yes.'

'And you and he being lawyers it's got something to do with legal irregularities over here that somehow reach into the military, is that right?'

'In the broadest sense, again yes. I'm afraid I can't be any more specific. Converse mentioned that there was someone you wanted him to meet.'

'Yes, there is. I said a couple of harsh things about him, but I take them back; he was doing his thing. He didn't know who the hell I was anymore than you did; his wife told him. He's one smart man, tough but fair.'

'I hope you understand that under the circumstances Converse can't comply with your request.'

'You'll do,' said Dowling calmly, removing his arm from the back of the bench.

Connal was suddenly alarmed. There was movement behind him in the shadowed moonlight; he whipped his head around, peering over his shoulder. Out of the protective darkness of the building from within the pitch black cover of a doorway, the figure of a man began walking across the dark green lawn . . . An *arm* thrown casually over the rim of the bench! Then just as casually removed. Both movements had been signals! Identity confirmed; move in.

'What the hell have you *done*?' asked the navy lawyer harshly.

'Bringing you two bucks to your senses,' replied Dowling. 'If my celebrated instincts are valid, I did the right thing. If they're wrong, I still did the right thing.'

'*What*?'

The man crossing the lawn entered the spill of clear moonlight. He was heavy-set and in dark suit and tie, his scowling, late-middle-aged face and straight grey hair giving him the air of a prosperous businessman, who at the moment was intensely angry. Dowling spoke, as he got up from the bench.

'Commander, may I introduce the Honourable Walter Peregrine, United States Ambassador to the Federal Republic of Germany?'

Lieutenant David Remington wiped his steel-rimmed glasses with a silicone-treated tissue, then threw the tissue into the waste basket and got up from his desk. Returning the glasses to his face, he walked to a mirror secured to the back of his office door and checked his appearance. He smoothed his hair, shoved the knot of his tie in place, and looked down at the failing crease of his trousers. All things considered, considering it was 1730 hours and he had been harassed at his desk since 0800 in the morning, including that crazy Four-Zero emergency from Fitzpatrick, he looked as presentable as possible. And anyway, Rear-Admiral Hickman was not a stickler for spit-'n'-polish where the desk corps were concerned. He knew damn well most of the legal execs would bolt in a minute for much higher paying jobs in the civilian sector if the dress and other disposable codes were taken too seriously. Well, David Remington wouldn't. Where the hell else could a man travel all over the world, housing a wife and three kids in some of the nicest quarters imaginable, with all the medical and dental bills paid for, and not have the terrible pressures of rising in private or corporate practice? His father had been an attorney for one of the biggest insurance companies in Hartford, Connecticut, and his father had had ulcers at forty-three, a nervous breakdown at forty-eight, his first stroke at fifty-one, and a final, massive coronary at fifty-six – when everyone said he was so terrific at his job he might even be in line for the presidency. But then people always said things like that when a man died in the line of corporate duty – which men did too goddamned frequently.

None of that for David Remington, no sir! He was simply going to be one of the best lawyers in the US Navy, serve his thirty years, get out at fifty-five with a generous pension, and become a well-paid legal-military consultant at fifty-six. At the precise age when his father died, he would start living very nicely, indeed. It was simply a matter of building a reputation as a man who knew more about naval and maritime law – and stuck to it – than any other lawyer in the Navy. If he stepped on toes in his performance, so be it; it could only enhance that reputation. He didn't give a damn about being popular, only right. And he never made a decision until he was certain of its correct legal position. Consultants like that were prized commodities in civilian practice.

Remington wondered why Admiral Hickman wanted to see him, especially at this hour when most of the desk corps had gone for the day. There was a court martial pending that could become a sensitive issue. A black officer, an Annapolis graduate, had been caught selling cocaine off a destroyer berthed in the Philippines; that was probably it. Remington had pre-prepared the case for the judge-advocate, who frankly did not care to prosecute; the amount was not that large, and certainly others were selling far more, and they were probably white. That was not the point, Remington had insisted. If there were others, they had not been caught; if there was evidence, it had not been found. The law was colour-blind.

He would say the same thing to Hickman. The 'stickler-prick', a derisive nickname Remington knew was used behind his back, would stand firm. Well, at fifty-six – the age at which his father had been killed by company policy – a stickler-prick would have all the comforts of an exclusive country club without paying the corporate price. Lieutenant Remington opened the door, walked out into the grey hallway, and started for the elevator that would take him to the floor of the office of the highest ranking man at the San Diego naval base.

'Sit down, Remington,' said Rear-Admiral Brian Hickman, shaking the rigidly-postured lieutenant's hand and indicating a chair in front of the large desk. 'I don't know about you but this has been what I used to call at your age one fucked-up day. Sometimes I wish Congress wouldn't appropriate so damn much money down here. Everyone gets on such a high you'd think they'd smoked everything in Tijuana. They forget they're supposed to have architects before they start bribing the contractors.'

'Yes, sir, I know what you mean, sir,' said Remington, sitting down with proper deference as Hickman stood several feet to his left. The mere reference to Tijuana and drugs confirmed his suspicions; the admiral was about to launch into the everybody-does-it routine, so why should the navy stir up a racial controversy with something that took place in the Philippines. Well, he was prepared. The law – naval law – was colour blind.

'I'm going to have a well-deserved drink, Lieutenant,' said Hickman, heading for a copper bar against the wall. 'Can I get you something?'

'No, thank you, sir.'

'Hey, look, Remington, I appreciate your staying late for this . . . conference, I guess you'd call it, but I don't expect any version of corporate military behaviour. Frankly, I'd feel foolish drinking by myself, and what we've got to talk about isn't so almighty important. I just want to ask you a couple of questions.'

'Corporate behaviour, sir? I'll have some white wine, if you have it, sir.'

'I always have it,' said the admiral with resignation. 'It's usually for personnel who are about to get divorced.'

'I'm happily married, sir.'

'Glad to hear it. I'm on my third wife – should have stuck with the first.'

The drinks poured, the seating arrangements in order, Hickman spoke from behind the desk, his tie loosened, his voice casual. But what he said evoked anything but casualness in David Remington.

'Who the hell is Joel Converse?' asked the admiral.

'I beg your pardon, sir?'

The admiral sighed, the sound indicating that he would begin again. 'At twelve hundred hours, twenty-one minutes today, you placed a CLO negative on all inquiries regarding a flag on one Lieutenant Joel Converse's service record. He was a pilot in the Vietnam action.'

'I know what he was, sir,' said Remington.

'And at fifteen hundred hours, two minutes,' continued Hickman looking at a note on his desk. 'I get a teletype from the Fifth Naval District requesting that the flag be removed in their favour and the material released immediately. The basis for their request was – and it always is – national security.' The admiral paused to sip his drink; he appeared to be in no hurry, simply weary. 'I ordered my adjutant to call you and ask why you did it.'

'And I answered him completely, sir,' broke in Remington. 'It was at the instructions of the Chief Legal Officer of SAND PAC and I cited the specific regulation that states clearly that the CLO of a naval base can withhold files on the basis that his own inquiries can be compromised by the entrance of a third party. It's standard in civil law, sir. The Federal Bureau of Investigation rarely gives a local or metroplitan police force the information it's collected in an investigation for the simple reason that the investigation could be compromised by leaks or corrupt practices.'

'And our Chief Legal Officer, Lieutenant Commander Fitzpatrick, is currently carrying out an investigation of an officer who left the service *eighteen years* ago?'

'I don't know, sir,' said Remington, his eyes non-committal. 'I only know those were his orders. They're in force for seventy-two hours. After that, you, of course, can sign the order of release. And the President, naturally, can do so anytime in a national emergency.'

'I thought it was forty-eight hours,' said Hickman.

'No, sir. The forty-eight hours is standard with the release of every flag regardless of who asks for it – except, of course, the President. It's called the vet delay. Naval Intelligence cross checks with the CIA, the NSA and G-Two to make sure there's no material being released that's still considered classified. That procedure has nothing to do with the prerogatives of a Chief Legal Officer.'

'You know your law, don't you?'

'I believe as well as any attorney in the United States Navy, sir.'

'I see.' The admiral leaned back in his upholstered swivel chair and placed his legs on the corner of the desk. 'Commander Fitzpatrick's off the base, isn't he? Emergency leave, if I recall.'

'Yes, sir. He's in San Francisco with his sister and her children. Her husband was killed in a robbery in Geneva; the funeral's tomorrow morning, I believe.'

'Yes, I read about it. Goddamned lousy . . . But you know where to reach him.'

'I have a telephone number, yes, sir. Do you want me to call him, Admiral? Apprise him of the Fifth Naval request.'

'No, no,' said Hickman, shaking his head. 'Not at a time like this. They can dry their mops at least until tomorrow afternoon. I've got to assume they also know the regulations; if security's so damned jeopardized they know where the Pentagon is – and the latest rumour out of Arlington is that they found out where the White House is.' The Admiral stopped, and looked over at the lieutenant. 'Suppose you didn't know where to reach Fitzpatrick?'

'But I do, sir.'

'Yes, but suppose you didn't? And a legitimate request was received – below presidential involvement, but still pretty damned urgent – *you* could release that flag, couldn't you?'

'Theoretically, as next in authority yes I could. As long as I accepted the legal responsibility for my judgment.'

'The what?'

'That I believed the request was sufficiently urgent to override the Chief Legal Officer's prior order which granted him seventy-two hours for whatever action he deemed necessary. He was adamant, sir. Frankly, short of presidential intervention, I'm legally bound to uphold the CLO's privilege.'

'I'd say morally, too,' agreed Hickman.

'Morality has nothing to do with it, sir. It's a clear legal position. Now, shall I make that call, Admiral?'

'No, the hell with it.' Hickman removed his feet from the desk. 'I was just curious and, frankly, you've convinced me. Fitz wouldn't have given you the order unless he had a reason. The Fifth D can wait three days, unless those boys want to run up telephone bills to Washington.'

'May I ask, sir, who specifically made the request?'

The admiral looked pointedly at Remington. 'I'll tell you in three days. You see, I've got a man's privilege to uphold, too. You'll know then anyway because in Fitz's absence you'll have to countersign the transfer.' Hickman finished his drink and the lieutenant understood. The conference was over. Remington got up and returned the half-filled wine glass to the copper bar; he stood at attention and spoke.

'Will that be all, sir?'

'Yes, that's it.' said the admiral, his gaze straying to the window and the ocean beyond.

The lieutenant saluted sharply as Hickman brought a casual hand to his forehead. The lawyer then did an about-face and started for the door.

'Remington?'

'Yes, sir?' replied the lieutenant, turning.

'Who the hell *is* this Converse?'

'I don't know, sir. But Commander Fitzpatrick said the status of the flag was a Four-Zero emergency.'

'*Jesus* . . .'

Hickman picked up his phone and touched a combination of buttons on the console. Moments later he was speaking to a fellow ranking officer in the Fifth Naval District.

'I'm afraid you'll have to wait three days, Scanlon.'

'Why is that?' asked the admiral named Scanlon.

'The CLO negative holds the Converse flag as far as SAND PAC is concerned. If you want to go the DC route, be my guest. We'll cooperate.'

'I told you, Brian, my people don't want to go through Washington. You've had these things happen before. DC makes waves and we don't want waves.'

'Well then, why don't you tell me why you want the Converse flag? Who is he?'

'I'd tell you if I could, you know that. Frankly, I'm not all that clear on it myself, and what I do know I've sworn to keep secure.'

'Then go to Washington. I'm standing behind my Chief Legal, who, incidentally, isn't even here.'

'He isn't . . . ? But you talked to him.'

'No, to his next in line, a lieutenant named Remington. He took the direct order from the CLO. Believe me, Remington won't budge. I gave him the chance and he covered himself with legalities. Around here he's known as a stickler-prick.'

'Did he say why the negative was put out?'

'He didn't have any idea. Why don't you call him yourself? He's probably still downstairs and maybe you can . . .'

'You didn't use my *name*, did you?' interrupted Scanlon, apparently agitated.

'No, you asked me not to, but he'll know it in three days. He'll have to sign the release and I'll have to tell him who requested it.' Hickman paused, then without warning exploded. 'What the *hell* is this all about, Admiral? Some pilot who was discharged over eighteen years ago is suddenly on everybody's most-wanted list. I get a departmental priority teletype from the big Fifth D and you follow it up with a personal call, playing the old Annapolis memory game, but you won't tell me anything. Then I find out my own CLO without my knowing about it has put a negative on this Converse flag and labelled it a Four-Zero emergency status! Now I know he's got personal problems and I won't bother him until tomorrow, and I realize you've given your word to stay secure, but goddamn it, somebody had better start telling me *something!*'

There was no response from the other end of the line. But there was the sound of breathing; and it was tremulous.

'Scanlon!'

'What did you just say?' said the voice of the admiral 3,600 miles away.

'I'm going to find out anyway . . .'

'No, the status. The status of the flag.' Scanlon could barely be heard.

'Four-Zero emergency, that's what I said!'

The interruption was abrupt; there was only an echoing click. Admiral Scanlon had hung up the phone.

Walter Peregrine, United States Ambassador to the Federal Republic of Germany, was an angry man. 'What's your name, Commander?'

'Fowler, sir,' answered Fitzpatrick, glancing briefly but hard at Dowling. 'Lieutenant-Commander Avery Fowler, United States Navy.' Again Connal looked at the actor, who stared at him through the moonlight.

'I understand there's some question about that,' said Peregrine, his glare as hostile as Dowling's. 'May I see your identification, please?'

'I'm not carrying identification, sir. It's the nature of my assignment not to do so, sir.' Fitzpatrick's words were rapid, precise, his posture squared and erect.

'I want verification of your name, your rank, and your branch of service! *Now!*'

'The name I've given you is the name I was instructed to give should any beyond the scope of the assignment inquire.'

'*Whose* instructions?' barked the diplomat.

'My superior officers, sir.'

'Am I to infer that Fowler is not your correct name?'

'With respect, Mr Ambassador. My name is Fowler, my rank is lieutenant-commander, my branch of service is the United States Navy.'

'Where the *hell* do you think you are? Behind the lines, captured by the enemy? "Name, rank, and serial number – that's all I'm required to say under the Rules of the Geneva Convention!"'

'It's all I'm *permitted* to say, sir.'

'We'll damn well find out about that, Commander – if you are a commander. Also about this Converse, who appears to be a very odd liar – one minute the soul of propriety, the next a very strange man on the run.'

'Please try to understand, Mr Ambassador, our assignment is classified. In no way does it involve diplomacy or will it impair your efforts as the chief American representative of our government, but it *is* classified. I will report this conversation to my superiors and you will undoubtedly hear from them. Now, if you gentlemen will forgive me, I'll be on my way.'

'I don't think so, Commander – or whoever you are. But if you are who you say, nothing's compromised. I'm not a damn fool. Nothing will be said to anyone on the embassy staff. Mr Dowling insisted on that and I accepted the condition. You and I will be locked in a communications room with a phone on a scrambler and you're going to place a call to Washington. I didn't take this job at a loss of three-quarters of a million a year to find shoe clerks running an investigation of my own company without my knowing about it. If I want an outside audit, I'll damn well order it myself!'

'I wish I could comply, sir; it sounds like a reasonable request. But I'm afraid I can't.'

'I'm afraid you will!'

'Sorry.'

'Do as he says, Commander,' interjected Dowling. 'As he told you, nothing's been said to anyone, and nothing will be. But Converse needs protection; he's a wanted man in a foreign country and he doesn't even speak the language. Take Ambassador Peregrine's offer. He'll keep his word.'

'With respect, sirs, the answer is negative.' Connal turned away and started up the wide path.

'*Major!*' shouted the ambassador, his voice furious. '*Stop* him! *Stop* that man!'

Fitzpatrick looked behind him; for reasons he could not explain to himself he saw what he never expected to see, and the instant he did, he knew he should have expected it. From out of the distant shadows of the immense, majestic building, a man rushed forward, a man who was obviously a military aide to the ambassador – a member of the *embassy staff!* Connal froze, Joel's words coming back to him.

Those men you saw at the airport, the ones from the embassy . . . they're on the other side.

Under almost any other circumstances, Fitzpatrick would have remained where he was and weathered it out. He hadn't actually done anything wrong; there was nothing illegal, no laws broken of which he was cognizant, and no one could force him to discuss personal matters where no law had

1. Then he realized how wrong he was! The generals of George
vane would force him, *could* force him! He spun around and

gunfire erupted. Two shots – splitting cracks of broken air
him! He dived to the ground and rolled into the shadows of the
bushes, as a man's voice roared over the already disturbed stillness of the
peaceful night and the sleeping gardens.

'You goddamned son of a *bitch!* What do you think you're *doing!'*

There were further shouts, a further barrage of obscenities, and the sounds
of struggle filled the quiet enclave of the university.

'You don't *kill* a man . . . ! Besides, you *bastard*, there could be other
people! Don't say a *word*, Mr Ambassador!'

Connal scrambled across the gravel path, raising his hands to spread the
bordering foliage. In the clear, unimpeded moonlight of the distant bench,
the actor, Caleb Dowling – the former marine from Kwajalein – stood over
the figure of the major who had run out of the shadow, his boot on the
supine man's throat, his hand grasping the man's extended arm, the weapon
wrenched free of the major's offending grip.

'You are one dumb son of a bitch, Major! Or, goddamn you, maybe
you're something else!'

Fitzpatrick got to his knees, then his feet, and, crouching, raced into the
receding darkness of the wide path toward the exit.

13

'I didn't have any choice!' said Connal, the attaché case on the couch, the
Navy lawyer in an adjacent chair, leaning forward, still shaking, still intense.

'Calm down, try to relax.' Converse walked to the elegant antique hunt
table against the wall where there was a large silver tray with whisky, ice
and glasses. Joel had learned to make use of room service in England. 'You
need a drink,' he said, pouring Fitzpatrick's bourbon.

'Do I *ever!* I've never been shot at. You have. Christ, is that what it's *like?'*

'That's what it's like. You can't believe it. It's unreal, just mind-blowing
sounds that can't really have anything to do with you, until – until you see
the evidence for yourself. It's real, it's meant for you, and you're sick.
There's no swelling music, no brass horns, just vomit.' Converse brought
the naval officer his drink.

'You're omitting something,' said Connal, taking the glass and looking up
at Joel.

'No, I'm not. Let's think about tonight. If you heard Dowling right, the
ambassador won't say anything around the embassy . . .'

'I remember,' interrupted Fitzpatrick, taking several swallows of the
bourbon, his eyes still on Converse. 'It was in one of the other flags. During
your second escape a man got killed; it was sundown. You reached him
when it happened and the flag said you went crazy for a couple of minutes.

Somehow, according to this guy – a sergeant, I think – you circled around in the jungle, caught the North Vietnamese, killed him with his own knife and got his repeating rifle. Then you blew away three other Viets in the area.'

Joel held his place in front of the Navy lawyer. He answered the younger man, his voice quiet, his look angry. 'I hate descriptions like that,' he said flatly. 'It raises all the images I loathe . . . Let me tell you the way it was – like it was, counsellor. A kid, no more than nineteen, had to relieve himself, and although we stuck together he had the dignity to go ten or fifteen feet away to take care of his private functions, using leaves because squeezable toilet paper wasn't available. The maniac – I won't use the word soldier – who killed him waited for the precise moment, then fired off a burst that cut the kid's face apart. When I reached him, half of that face in my hands, I heard the cackle, the obscene laughter of an obscene man who personified for me everything I found despicable – whether North Vietnamese or American. If you want to know the truth, whatever I did I did against both – because both were guilty, all of us turned into animals, myself included. Those other three men, those enemies, those uniformed robots probably with wives and children back in villages somewhere up north, had no idea I got behind them, I shot them in the back, counsellor. What would Johnny Ringo say about that? Or John Wayne?'

Connal was silent as Joel walked over to the hunt table to pour himself a whisky. The Navy lawyer drank, then spoke. 'A few hours ago you said you knew where I was coming from because you'd been there. Well, I haven't been where you were, but I'm beginning to see where *you're* coming from. You really despise everything that Aquitaine stands for, don't you? Especially those running it.'

Converse turned. 'With everything that's in me,' he said. 'That's why we've got to talk about tonight.'

'I told you, I had no choice. You said the embassy people I saw at the airport were with Delavane. I couldn't take the chance.'

'I know. Now we're both running, hunted by our own people and protected by the men we want to trap. We've got to *think* Commander.'

The telephone rang; two abrasive, static-like bells. Fitzpatrick leaped from the chair, his initial reaction one of shock. Joel watched him, calming him with his look. 'Sorry,' said Connal. 'I'm still edgy. I'll get it; I'll be all right.' He crossed to the phone and picked it up. '*Ja?*' He listened for several seconds, covered the mouthpiece and looked at Converse. 'It's the overseas operator. San Francisco. It's Meagen.'

'Which means Remington,' said Joel, his throat suddenly dry, his pulse accelerating.

'Meagan? Yes, I'm here. What is it?' Fitzpatrick stared straight ahead as his sister talked; he nodded frequently, the muscles of his jaw working as he concentrated. 'Oh, *Christ!* . . . No, it's all right. I *mean* it, everything's okay. Do you have the number?' Connal looked down at the small telephone table, there was a message pad but no pencil. He glanced over at Joel, who had already started for the desk and a hotel pen. Fitzpatrick held out his hand, took the pen, and wrote out a series of numbers. Converse stood aside, conscious that he was barely breathing, his fingers gripping the glass which remained immobile. 'Thanks, Meagen. I know it's a hell of a time for you; you don't need this, but if you have to call again, make it station-to-station, okay? . . . I will, Meg. I give you my word. Goodbye.' The Navy lawyer hung up, his hand for a moment remaining on the telephone.

'Remington called, didn't he?' said Joel.

'Yes.'

'What *happened?*'

'Someone tried to get the flag on your service record released,' said Fitzpatrick, turning, looking at Converse. 'It's okay. Remington stopped it.'

'Who was it?'

'I don't know, I'll have to reach David. Meagen doesn't have any idea what a flag is, much less who you are. The message was only that "a release was sought for the flag" but he stopped it.'

'Then everything's all right.'

'That's what I said, but it's not.'

'Clarification, goddamn it!'

'There's a time limit on how long my order stands. It's only a day or two after the vetting process . . .'

'Which is forty-eight hours,' interrupted Joel.

'Yes, I'm sure of that; it's *after* that. You see, you thought this would happen, but frankly I didn't. Whoever's asking for that flag isn't small potatoes. You could walk out of that meeting and a few hours later your new associates could have that stuff in their hands. Converse the Delavane-hater. Is he now the Delavane-*hunter?*'

'Call Remington.' Joel went to the French doors, opened them, and walked out on the small balcony. Drifting wisps of cloud filtered the moonlight, and far to the east there were flashes of heat lightning reminding Converse of the silent artillery fire he and the other escaping prisoners would see in the hills, knowing it was both sanctuary and unreachable. He could hear Fitzpatrick inside; from the sound of his voice he was getting a line through to San Diego. Joel reached into a pocket for his cigarettes; he lighted one. Whether it was the bright glow of the flame that illuminated the movement, he did not know, but he looked in the direction of that movement. Two balconies away, about thirty feet to his right, a man stood watching him. The figure was a silhouette in dark light; he nodded in that dim light and went back inside. Was the man simply another guest who had coincidentally gone outside for a breath of air? Or had Aquitaine posted a guard? Converse could hear the Navy lawyer talking conversationally; he turned and walked back into the room.

Connal was seated in the chair on the other side of the table. He held the phone to his ear with his left hand, his right held the pen above the message pad. He made a note, interrupting.

'Wait a minute. You say Hickman told you to let it ride but he wouldn't tell you who specifically made the request? . . . I see. All right, David, thanks very much. Are you going out tonight? . . . So if I need you I can reach you at this number . . . Yes, I know, it's these damn phones up in Sonoma. One heavy rain in the hills and you're lucky to get a line, forget a clear one. Thanks again, David. Goodbye.' Fitzpatrick hung up the phone and looked strangely, almost guiltily at Joel. Instead of speaking, he shook his head, breathing out and frowning.

'What is it? What's the matter?'

'You'd better get everything you can at that meeting tomorrow. Or is it today?'

'It's past midnight. It's today. Why?'

'Because twenty-four hours later that flag will be released to a section in the Fifth Naval District – that's Norfolk, and it's powerful. They'll know everything you don't want them to know about you. The time limit is seventy-two hours.'

'Get an extension!'

Connal stood up, helplessness in his expression. 'On what basis?'

'What else? National security.'

'I'd have to spell out the reasons, you know that.'

'I *don't* know that. Extensions are granted for all sorts of contingencies. You need more time to prepare. A source or a witness has been postponed – illness or an injury. Or personal matters – goddamn it, your brother-in-law's funeral, your sister's grief – they've delayed your progress!'

'Forget it, Joel. If I tried that, they'd tie you in with Press and goodbye, Charlie. They killed him, remember?'

'No,' said Converse firmly. 'It's the other way around. It separates us farther.'

'What are you talking about?'

'I've thought about this, tried to put myself in Avery's shoes. He knew his every move was being watched, his telephone probably tapped. He said the geography, the Comm Tech-Bern merger, the breakfast, Geneva itself, everything had to be logical; it couldn't be any other way. At the end of that breakfast he said if I agreed we'd talk later.'

'So?'

'He knew we'd be seen together – it was unavoidable – and I think he was going to give me the words to say if someone in Aquitaine asked me about him. He was going to turn everything around and give me the push I needed to reach these men.'

'What the hell are you talking about?'

'Avery was going to stamp me with the label I had to wear to get inside Delavane's network. We'll never know, but I have an idea he was going to tell me to say that he, A. Preston Halliday, suspected me of being one of *them*, that he had inserted himself in the Comm Tech-Bern merger to threaten me with exposure, to *stop* me.'

'Wait a minute.' Connal shook his head. 'Press didn't know what you were going to do or how you were going to do it.'

'There was only one way *to* do it, he knew that! He also knew I'd reach the same conclusion once I understood the particulars. The only way to stop Delavane and his field marshals is to infiltrate Aquitaine. Why do you think that money was put up front? I don't need it and he knew he couldn't buy me. But he knew it could be used – would *have* to be used to get inside and start talking, start gathering evidence . . . Call Remington again. Tell him to prepare an extension.'

'It's not Remington, it's the commander of SAND PAC, an admiral named

Hickman. David said I could expect a call from him tomorrow, I'll have to figure that one out and phone Meagan back. Hickman's uptight; he wants to know who you are and why all the interest.'

'How well do you know this Hickman?'

'Fairly well. I was with him in New London and Galveston. He requested me as his CLO in San Diego, that's what gave me the stripe.'

Converse studied Fitzpatrick's face, then without any apparent reason kept silent as he turned and walked to the open balcony doors. Connal did not interrupt; undoubtedly he understood. He had seen too many attorneys, himself included, struck by a thought they had to define for themselves, an idea upon which a case might hinge. Joel turned around slowly, haltingly, the dim, abstract shadows of a possibility coming into focus.

'Do it,' he began. 'Do what I think your brother-in-law might have done. Finish what he might have said but never got a chance to say. Assume he and I had that meeting after the merger conference. Give me the springboard I need.'

'In your words, clarification, please, counsellor.'

'Present Hickman with a scenario as it might have been written by A. Preston Halliday. Tell him that flag's got to remain in place because you have reason to believe I was connected with your brother-in-law's murder. Explain that before Halliday flew to Geneva he came to see you – as he did – and told you he was meeting me, an opposing attorney he suspected of being involved with corrupt export licensing, a legal front for some board-room profiteers. Say he said he was going to confront me. Preston Halliday had a history of causes.'

'Not for the past ten or twelve years, he didn't,' corrected Fitzpatrick. 'He joined the establishment with a vengeance and with a healthy respect for the dollar.'

'It's the history that counts. He knew that; it was one of the reasons he came to me. Say you're convinced he did contact me, and since millions are made out of that business, you think I methodically had him removed, covering myself by being there when he died . . . I have a certain reputation for being methodical.'

Connal lowered his head and ran his hand through his hair, then walked in thought toward the antique hunt table. He stopped, raising his gaze to one of the racehorse prints and turned back to Converse.

'Do you know what you're asking me to do?'

'Yes. Give me the springboard that'll catapult me right in the middle of those would-be Genghis Khans. To do it you'll have to go farther with Hickman. Because you're so personally involved so goddamn angry – which again is the truth – tell him to explain your position to whoever wants the flag released. It's a non-military matter, so you're taking what you know to the civilian authorities.'

'I understand all that,' said Fitzpatrick. 'Everything I say *is* the truth, as I saw it when I flew over here to find you. Except that I reverse the targets. Instead of being the one who can help me, you're now the one I want nailed.'

'Right on, counsellor. And I'm met by a welcoming committee at Leifhelm's estate.'

'Then I guess you don't see.'

'What?'

'You're asking me to go on record implicating you in first degree murder. I'll be branding you a killer. Once I say it, I can't take the words back.'

'I know that. Do it.'

George Marcus Delavane twisted his torso in his chair behind the desk in front of the strangely coloured fragmented map on the wall. It was not a controlled movement; it was an action in search of control. Delavane did not care for obstructions and one was being explained to him now by an admiral in the Fifth Naval District.

'The status of the flag is Four-Zero,' said Scanlon. 'To get it released we'd have to go through Pentagon procedures and I don't have to tell you what that means. Two senior officers, one from Naval Intelligence, plus a supporting signature from the National Security Agency; all would have to appear on the request sheet, the level of the inquiry stated, thus escalating the request to a sector demand. Now, General, we can do all this, but we run the risk . . .'

'I know the risk,' interrupted Delavane. 'The signatures are the risk, the identities a risk. Why the Four-Zero? Who placed it and *why?*'

'The Chief Legal Officer of SAND PAC. I checked him out. He's a lieutenant-commander named Fitzpatrick, and there's nothing in his record to give us any indication as to why he did it.'

'I'll tell you why,' said the warlord of Saigon. 'He's hiding something. He's protecting this Converse.'

'Why should a Chief Legal Officer in the navy protect a civilian under these circumstances? There's no connection. Furthermore, why would he exercise a Four-Zero condition? It only calls attention to his action.'

'It also clamps a lid down on that flag.' Delavane paused, then continued before the admiral could interrupt. 'This Fitzpatrick,' he said. 'You've checked the master list?'

'He's not one of us.'

'Has he ever been considered? Or approached?'

'I haven't had time to find out.' There was the sound of a buzzer, not part of the line over which the two men spoke. Scanlon could be heard punching a button, his voice clear, officious. 'Yes?' Silence followed and seconds later the admiral returned to Palo Alto. 'It's Hickman again.'

'Maybe he has something for us. Call me back.'

'Hickman wouldn't give us anything if he had the slightest idea we existed,' said Scanlon. 'In a few weeks, he'll be one of the first to go. If it were up to me he'd be shot.'

'Call me back,' said George Marcus Delavane, looking at the map of the new Aquitaine on the wall.

Chaim Abrahms sat at the kitchen table in his small stone Mediterranean villa in Tzahala, a suburb of Tel Aviv favoured by the retired military and those with adequate incomes or influence to live there. The windows were open and the breeze from the garden stirred the oppressive summer's night air. There was air conditioning in two other rooms, and ceiling fans in three more, but Chaim liked the kitchen. In the old days they would sit in primitive kitchens and plan raids; ammunition was often passed about while desert chicken boiled on a wood stove in the Negev. The kitchen was the soul of the house. It gave warmth and sustenance to the body, clearing the mind for tactics – so long as the women left after performing their chores and did not interrupt the men with their incessant trivialities. His wife was asleep upstairs; so be it. He had little to say to her any more, or she to him; she could not help him now. And if she could, she would not. They had lost a son in Lebanon, *her* son she said, a teacher, a scholar, not a soldier, not a killer by choice. Too many sons were lost on both sides, she said. For old men, she said, old men who infected the young with their hatreds and who used biblical legends to justify death by questionable real estate. Death, she cried. Death before *talk!* She had forgotten the early days; too many forgot too quickly. Chaim Abrahms did not forget, nor would he ever.

And his sense of smell was as acute as ever. This lawyer, this Converse, this talk! It was all too clever; it had the stench of cold, analytical minds, not the heat of believers. The Mossad specialist was the best, but even the Mossad made mistakes. The specialist looked for a motive, as if one could dissect the human brain and say this action caused that reaction; this punishment that commitment to vengeance. Too damned *clever!* A believer was fuelled by the heat of his convictions. They were his only motive, and they did not call for clever manipulations.

Chaim knew he was a plain-spoken man, a direct man, but it was not because he was unintelligent or lacked subtle perceptions; his prowess on the battlefield proved otherwise. He was direct because he knew what he wanted, and it was a waste of time to pretend to be clever. In all the years he had lived with his convictions he had never met a fellow believer who allowed himself to waste time.

This Converse knew enough to reach Bertholdier in Paris. He showed how much more he knew when he mentioned Leifhelm in Bonn, and specifically named the cities of Tel Aviv and Johannesburg. What more did he have to prove? *Why* should he prove it if his belief was there? Why did he not plead his case with his first connection and not waste time? . . . No, this lawyer, this Converse, was from somewhere else. The Mossad specialist said the motive was there for affiliation. He was wrong. The redhot heat of the believer was *not* there. Only cleverness, only talk.

And the specialist had not dismissed Chaim's sense of smell. As well he should not, for the two Sabras had fought together for years, as often as not against the Europeans and their conniving ways – those immigrants who held up the Old Testament as if they had written it – calling the true inhabitants of Israel uneducated, ruffian clowns. The Mossad specialist *respected* his Sabra brother; it was in his look, that respect. No one could dismiss the instincts of Chaim Abrahms, son of Abraham, archangel of darkness to the enemies of Abraham's children. Thank God his wife was asleep.

It was time to call Palo Alto.

'My General, my friend.'

'Shalom, Chaim,' said the warlord of Saigon. 'Are you on your way to Bonn?'

'I'm leaving in the morning – we're leaving. Van Headmer is in the air now. He'll arrive at Ben Gurion at eight-thirty and together we'll take the ten o'clock flight to Frankfurt where Leifhelm's pilot will meet us with the Cessna.'

'Good. You can talk.'

'*We* must talk now,' said the Israeli. 'What more have you learned about this Converse?'

'He becomes more of an enigma, Chaim.'

'I smell a fraud.'

'So do I, but perhaps not the fraud I thought. You know what my assessment was. I thought he was no more than an infantry point, someone being used by more knowledgeable men – Lucas Anstett among them – to learn far more than they knew or heard rumours about. I don't discount a degree of minor leaks; they're to be anticipated and managed, scoffed at as paranoia.'

'Get to the point, Marcus,' said the impatient Abrahms, who always called Delavane by his middle name. He considered it a Hebrew name, in spite of the fact that Delavane's father had insisted on it for his first son in honour of the Roman Caesar – philosopher, Marcus Aurelius, a proselytizer of moderation.

'Three things happened today,' continued the former general in Palo Alto. 'The first infuriated me because I could understand it, and frankly disturbed me because it portended a far greater penetration than I thought possible from a sector I thought *impossible*.'

'What was it?' broke in the Israeli.

'A firm prohibtion was placed on getting part of Converse's service record.'

'Yes!' cried Abrahms, in his voice the sound of triumph.

'What?'

'Go on, Marcus! I'll tell you when you're finished. What was the second calamity?'

'Not a calamity, Chaim. An explanation so blatantly offered it can't be turned aside. Leifhelm called me and said Converse himself brought up Anstett's death, claiming to be relieved, but saying little else except that Anstett was his enemy – that was the word he used.'

'So instructed!' Abrahms' voice reverberated around the kitchen. 'What was the third gift, my General?'

'The most bewildering as well as enlightening – and, Chaim, do not shout into the phone. You are not in one of your stadium rallies or provoking the Knesset.'

'I am in the field, Marcus. Right *now!* Please continue my friend.'

'The man who clamped the lid down on Converse's military record is a naval officer who was the brother-in-law of Preston Halliday.'

'Geneva! Yes!'

'*Stop* that!'

'My apologies, my dear friend. It's just all so perfect!'

'Whatever you have in mind,' said Delavane, 'may be negated by the man's reason. This naval officer, this brother-in-law, believes Converse engineered Halliday's murder.'

'Of course! *Perfect!*'

'You *will* keep your *voice* down!' The cry of the cat on a frozen lake was heard.

'Again my deepest and most sincere apologies, my General . . . Was that all this naval officer said?'

'No, he made it clear to the commander of his base in San Diego that Halliday had come to him and told him he was meeting a man in Geneva he believed was involved with illegal exports to illegal destinations. An attorney for profiteers in armaments. He intended to confront this man, this international lawyer named Converse, and threaten to expose him. What do we have?'

'A *fraud!*'

'But on whose *side*, Sabra? The volume of your voice doesn't convince me.'

'Be convinced. I'm right. This Converse is the desert scorpion!'

'What does that mean?'

'Don't you *see?* The Mossad sees!'

'The Mossad?'

'Yes! I talked with our specialist and he senses what I smell – he admits the possibility! I grant you, my General, my honoured warrior, that he has information that led him to think this Converse might be genuine, that he wanted truly to be with us, but when I said I smelled bad meat, he granted one other, exceptional possibility. Converse may or may not be programmed, but he could be an agent for his government!'

'A *provocateur?*'

'Who knows, Marcus? But the pattern is so perfect. First, a prohibition is placed on his military record – it will tell us something, we know that. Then he responds in the negative about the death of an enemy – not his, but *ours* – and he claims it is his enemy too – so simple, so instructable. Finally, this Converse is insinuated to be the killer in Geneva – so orderly, so precisely to his advantage . . . We are dealing with very analytical minds who watch every move in the chess game, and match every pawn with a king.'

'Yet everything you say can be reversed. He could be . . .'

'He *can't* be!' cried Abrahms.

'Why, Chaim? Tell me why?'

'There is no *heat*, no *fire* in him! It is not the way of a believer! We are not clever, we are adamant!'

George Marcus Delavane said nothing for several moments, and the Israeli knew better than to speak. He waited until the quiet cold voice came back on the line.

'Have your meeting tomorrow, General. Listen to him and be courteous; play the game he plays. But he must not leave that house until I give the order. He may never leave it.'

'Shalom, my friend.'

'Shalom, Chaim.'

14

Valerie approached the glass doors of her studio – identical to the doors of her balcony upstairs – and looked out at the calm, sunwashed waters of Cape Ann. She thought briefly of the boat that had dropped anchor so frighteningly in front of her house several nights ago. It had not come back; whatever had happened was past, leaving questions but no answers. If she closed her eyes she could still see the figure of a man crawling up out of the cabin light, and the glow of the cigarette, and she still wondered what that man was doing, what he was thinking. Then she remembered the sight of the two men in the early light, framed in the dark rims of her binoculars – staring back at her with far more powerful lenses. Questions. No answers. Were they novices finding a safe harbour? Amateurs navigating the dark waters of a coastline at night? Questions, no answers.

Whatever, it was past. A brief, disturbing interlude that gave rise to black imaginings – demons in search of logic, as Joel would say.

She tossed her long, dark hair aside and returned to her easel, picking up a brush and putting the final dabs of burnt umber beneath the shadowed sand dunes of wild grass. She stepped back, studied her work, and swore to herself for the fifth time that the oil painting was finished. It was another seascape; she never tired of them and fortunately she was beginning to get a fair share of the market. Of course there were those painters in the Boston-Boothbay axis who claimed she had virtually cornered the market but that was rubbish. It was true that her prices had risen satisfactorily as a result of the critical approval accorded her two showings at the Copley Galleries, but if the truth were known she could hardly afford to live where she lived and how she lived without at least a part of Joel's cheque every month.

Then again not too many artists had a house on the beach with an attached twenty by twenty foot studio enclosed by full-length glass doors and with a ceiling that was literally one entire skylight. The rest of the house, the original house, on the northern border of Cape Ann was more rambling-quaint than functional. The initial architecture was early-coast-confusion, with lots of heavy bleached wood and curlicues, the balustraded balcony and outsized bay windows in the front room that were charming to look at and look out of, but leaked something fierce when the winter winds came off the ocean. No amount of putty or sashing compound seemed to work; nature was extracting a price for observing her beauty.

Still it was Val's dream house, the one she had promised herself years ago she would some day afford. She had come back from the École des Beaux Arts in Paris prepared to assault New York's art world via the Greenwich Village-Woodstock route only to have stark reality alter her plans. The family circumstances had always been sufficiently healthy for her to live comfortably, albeit not lavishly, throughout three years in college and two more in Paris. Her father was a passably good, if excessively enthusiastic amateur painter who always complained that he had not taken the risk and gone totally into the fine arts rather than architecture. As a result, he supported his only child both morally and financially, in a very real sense living through her progress and devoted to her determination. And her mother – slightly mad, always loving, *always* supportive in anything and everything – would take terrible photographs of Val's crudest work and send the pictures back to her sister and cousins in Germany, writing outrageous lies that spoke of museums and galleries and insane commissions.

'The crazy *Berlinerin*,' her father would say fondly, in his heavy Gallic accent. 'You should have seen her during the war. She frightened us all to death! We half expected she would return to headquarters some night with a drunken Goebbels or a doped-up Goering in tow, then tell us if we wanted Hitler to give her the word!'

Her father had been the Free French liaison between the Allies and the German-Berlin underground. A rather stiff Parisian autocrat who happened to speak German, he had been assigned to the cell in the Charlottenburg which coordinated all of Berlin's underground's activities. He frequently said that he had more trouble with the wild *Fräulein* with the impetuous ideas than he had avoiding the Nazis. Nevertheless they married each other two months after the end of the war. In Berlin. Where neither his family would talk to hers, nor hers to his. 'We had two small orchestras,' her mother would say. 'One played pure, beautiful Viennese *Schnitzel*, the other some white cream sauce with deer droppings.'

Whether family animosities had anything to do with it, neither ever said, but the Parisian and the Berliner emigrated to St Louis, Missouri, in the United States of America, where the Berliner had distant relations.

The stark reality. A frightened, tearful father had flown to New York and told Val a terrible truth. His beloved crazy Berliner had been ill for years; it was the cancer and it was about to kill her. In desperation, he had spent nearly all the money he had, including unpaid second and third mortgages on the rambling house in Bellefontaine, to stem the disease. Among the profiteers were clinics in Mexico; there was nothing else he could say. He could only weep and his losses had nothing to do with his tears. And she could only hold her father and ask him why he had not told her before.

'It was not your battle, *ma chérie*. It was ours. Since Berlin, it was always we two. We fought then together; we fight now as always – as one.'

Her mother died six days later, and six months after that her father lighted a Gauloise on the screened-in-porch and mercifully fell asleep, not to wake up. Valerie could not cry. It was a shock but not a tragedy. Wherever he was he wanted to be there, not alone.

So Valerie Charpentier looked for a job, a paying job that did not rely on the sales of an unknown artist. What astonished her was not the fact that employment was so easy to find, but that it had very little to do with the thick portfolio of sketches and line drawings she presented. The second advertising agency she applied to seemed more interested in the fact that she spoke both German and French fluently. It was the time of corporate take-overs, of multi-national alliances where profits could be made on both sides of the Atlantic by single entities. Valerie Charpentier, artist-in-residence inside, became a company hack on the outside. Someone who could draw and sketch rapidly and make presentations and speak the languages and she hated it. Still, it was a remarkable living for a woman who had anticipated a period of years before her name meant something on a canvas.

Then a man came into her life who made whatever affairs she had had totally forgettable. A nice man, a *decent* man – even an exciting man – who had his own problems but did not talk about them, *would* not talk about them, and that should have given her a clue. Joel, her Joel, effusive one moment, withdrawn the next, but always with that shield, that façade of quick humour which was as often biting as it was amusing. For a while they had been good for each other. Both were ambitious for entirely different reasons – she for the independence that came with recognition, he for the wasted years he could never reclaim – and each acted as a buffer when the other faced disappointment or delay. But it all began to fall apart. The reasons were painfully clear to her but not to him. He became mesmerized by his own progress, by his own determination to the exclusion of everything else, starting with her. He never raised his voice or made demands, but the words were ice and the demands were increasingly there. If there was a specific point when she recognized the downhill slide it was a Friday night in November. The agency had wanted her to fly to West Berlin; a *Telefunken* account required some fast personal service and she was elected to calm the churning waters. She had been packing when Joel came home from work. He had walked into the bedroom of their apartment and asked her what she was doing, where she was going. She told him and he had replied.

'You can't. We're expected at Brook's house in Larchmont tomorrow night. Talbot and Simon'll be there, too. I'm sure they'll talk international. You've got to be there.'

She had looked at him, at the quiet desperation in his eyes. She did not go to Germany. It was the turning point, the downhill race had begun and, within a brief few months, she knew it was irreversible. She quit the agency, giving up authority for the dog days of free-lancing, hoping the extra time she had to devote to him might help. It did not; he seemed to resent any overt act of sacrifice, no matter how she tried to conceal it. His periods of withdrawal and disinterest multiplied and in a way she felt sorry for him. His furies were driving him and it was so obvious that he disliked what was happening; he disliked himself but could not help himself. He was on his way to a burn-out and she could not help him, either.

If there had been another woman she could have fought, staking out her claim and insisting on the right to compete fiercely, but there was no one else, only himself and his silent compulsions. Finally she could not penetrate his shield; he had nothing left for anyone else emotionally. That was what she had hurled at him. 'Emotional burn-out!' she had cried. He had agreed in that quiet, kind voice and the next day he was gone.

So she took him. Four years, she demanded, the exact amount of time he had taken from her. Those four years of heady generosity were about to come to an end, Val reflected, as she cleaned her brushes and scraped the palette. In January they were over, the last cheque as always posted by the fifteenth. Five weeks ago during lunch at the Ritz in Boston Joel had offered to continue the payments. He claimed he was used to them and was making more in salary and bonuses than he could spend soberly. The money was no hardship and besides it gave him a certain stature among his peers and was a marvellous ploy to avoid prolonged entanglements. She had declined, borrowing words from her father or more likely her mother, saying that things were far better than they were. He had smiled that half-sad, yet still infectious smile and said, 'If they turn out otherwise, I'm here.'

Goddamn him!

Poor Joel. Sad Joel. He was a good man caught in the vortex of his conflicts. And Val had gone as far as she could go – to go farther was to deny her own identity. She would not do that; she had not done it.

She placed her brushes in the tray and walked to the glass doors that looked over the dunes and the ocean. He was out there, far away, still somewhere in Europe. Valerie wondered if he had given a thought to the day. It was the anniversary of their marriage.

To summarize, Chaim Abrahms was moulded in the stress and chaos of fighting for daily survival. They were years of never ending violent skirmishes, of out-thinking and out-living enemies bent on killing not only whole Sabra settlements but on the destruction of the desert Jew's aspirations for a homeland as well as political freedom and religious expression. It is not difficult to understand where Abrahms came from and why he is what he is, but it is frightening to think about where he is going. He is a fanatic with no sense of balance or compromise where other peoples with identical aspirations are concerned. If a man has a different stripe, whether of the same species or not, he is the enemy. Armed force takes precedence over negotiations in all matters, and even those in Israel who plead for more moderate stands based on totally secure borders are branded traitors. Abrahms is an imperialist who sees an ever-expanding Israel as the ruling kingdom of the entire Middle East. An appropriate ending to this report is a comment he made after the well-known statement issued by the Prime Minister during the Lebanon invasion: 'We covet not one inch of Lebanon.' Abrahms' reply in the field to his troops – by no means the majority sympathetic – was the following.

'Certainly not an inch! The whole damned country! Then Gaza, the Golan, and the West Bank! And why not Jordan, then Syria, and Iraq! We have the means and we have the will! We are the mighty children of Abraham!'

He is Delavane's key in the volatile Middle East.

It was nearly noon, the overhead sun beating down on the small balcony beyond the french doors. The late-breakfast remnants had been cleared away by room service; only a silver pot remained on the hunt table. They had been reading for hours, since the first coffee was brought to the suite at 6.30. Converse put down the dossier, and reached for his cigarettes on the table by the armchair. *It is not difficult to understand where Abrahms came from . . . but frightening to think about where he is going*. Joel looked over at Connal Fitzpatrick who was seated on the couch, leaning forward over the coffee table and reading a single page while making notes on the telephone message pad; the Bertholdier and Leifhelm dossiers were in two neat piles on his left.

The Navy lawyer had said practically the same words to him, thought Converse, lighting a cigarette. *I'm beginning to see where you're coming from* . . . The inherent question put to Joel's legal mind was simple: Where was he himself going? He hoped to hell he knew. Was he an inept gladiator marching into a Roman arena facing far stronger, better armed and superior talent? Or were the demons from his own past turning him into his own sacrifice, leading him into the arena's hot sand where huge angry, half-starved cats waited for him, ready to pounce and tear him apart. So many questions, so many variables he was incapable of addressing. He just knew he could not turn back.

Fitzpatrick looked up. 'What's the matter?' he asked, obviously aware that Converse was staring in his direction. 'You worried about the Admiral?'

'Who?'

'Hickman, San Diego.'

'Among other things. In the clear light of day you're sure he bought the extension?'

'No guarantees, but I told you he said he'll call me if any emergency heat came down. I'm damn sure he won't do anything before consulting me. If he tries to reach me, Meagen knows what to do and I'll lean harder. If need be, I'll claim point of personal privilege and demand a meeting with those unnamed people in the Fifth District, maybe go so far as to imply they could be part of Geneva. *That'd* be a full circle. We could end up with a stand-off – the release of that flag only with a full-scale investigation of the circumstances. Irony and stand-off.'

'You won't have a stand-off if he's with them. He'll override you.'

'If he was *with* them he wouldn't have told Remington he was going to call me. He wouldn't have said anything; he'd have waited the extra day and let it go. I know him. He wasn't just non-plussed, he was mad. He stands by his people and he doesn't like outside pressures, especially Navy pressures. We're on hold, and as long as it's hold, the flag's in place. I told you, he's a lot angrier with Norfolk than with me. They won't even *give* him a reason; they claim they can't.'

Converse nodded. 'All right,' he said. 'Call it a case of nerves on my part. I just finished the Abrahms' dossier. That maniac could blow up the whole Middle East all by himself and drag the rest of us in with him . . . What did you think of Leifhelm and Bertholdier?'

'As far as the information goes they're everything you said and then some. They're more than just influential ex-generals with fistfuls of money, they're powerful rallying symbols for what a lot of people think are justifiable extremes. That's as far as the information goes – but the operative word for *me* is the information itself.'

'That's a step back. It's there.'

'It sure is, but how come? You say Beale gave it to you, that Press used the phrase "we" – "the ones *we're* after", "the tools *we* can give you", "the connections *we* think they are".'

'And we went over this,' insisted Joel. 'The man in San Francisco, the one he went to who provided the five hundred thousand and told him to build cases against these people legally, and together they'd turn them into plain-

and-simple profiteers. It's the ultimate ridicule for super-patriots. It's sound reasoning, counsellor, and that's the *we*.'

'Press and this unknown man in San Francisco?'

'Yes.'

'And they could pick up a phone and hire someone to put together *these?*' Fitzpatrick gestured at the two dossiers on his left.

'Why not? This is the age of the computer. Nobody today lives on an unmapped island or in an undiscovered cave.'

'*These*,' repeated Connal, 'are not computer print-outs. They're well-researched, detailed, in-depth dossiers that take in the importance of political nuances and personal idiosyncrasies.'

'You have a way with words, sailor. Yes, they are. A man who can forward half a million dollars to the right bank on an Aegean island can hire just about anyone he likes.'

'He can't hire these.'

'What does that mean?'

'Let me take a real step back,' said the Navy lawyer, getting to his feet and reaching down for the single page he had been reading. 'I won't reiterate my relationship with Press because right now it hurts a little to think about it.' Fitzpatrick paused, seeing the look in Converse's eyes that rejected this kind of sentimentality in their discussion. 'Don't mistake me,' he continued. 'It's not his death, not the funeral; it's the other way around. It's not the Press Halliday I knew. You see, I don't think he told us the truth, either you or me.'

'Then you know something I don't know,' said Converse quietly.

'I know there's no man in San Francisco that even vaguely fits the description or the image he gave you. I lived all my life there, including Berkeley and Stanford, just like Press. I knew everyone he knew, especially the wealthiest and the more exotic ones; we never held back on those with each other. I was legal worlds away and he always filled me in if new ones came along. It was part of the fun for him.'

'That's tenuous, counsellor. I'm sure he kept certain associations to himself.'

'Not those kinds,' said Connal. 'It wouldn't be like him. Not with me.'

'Well, I . . .'

'Now let me step forward,' interrupted Fitzpatrick. 'These dossiers – I haven't seen them before, but I've seen hundreds like them, maybe a couple of thousand on their way to becoming full-fledged versions of them.'

Joel sat up. 'Please explain that, Commander.'

'You just hit it, Lieutenant. The rank says it.'

'Says *what?*'

'Those dossiers are the reworked, finished products of intelligence probes. They've been bounced around the community, each branch contributing its in-put – from straight biographical data to past surveillances to psychiatric evaluation – and put together by teams of specialists. They were taken from way down in the government vaults and rewritten with current additions and conclusions, then shaped to appear as the work of an outside, non-government authority. But they're not. They've got *Classified*, *Top Secret* and *Eyes Only* written all over them.'

From simply sitting up, Converse sat forward. 'That could be a subjective judgement based on limited familiarity. I've seen some very detailed, very in-depth reports put together by high-priced firms specializing in that sort of thing.'

'Describing precise military incidents during time of war? Pinpointing bombing raids and specifying regiments and battalions and the current strategies employed? Detailing through *interviews* the internal conflicts of ranking enemy officers, and the tactical reasons for shifting military person- nel into civilian positions after the cessation of hostilities? No firm would have access to that material.'

'They could be researched,' said Joel, suddenly not convinced himself.

'Well, *these* couldn't,' Connal broke in, holding up the page of typewritten names, his thumb on the lower two columns listing the 'decision-makers' from the Pentagon and the State Department. 'Maybe five or six – three from each side at maximum – but not the rest. These are people *above* the ones I've dealt with, men who do their jobs under a variety of titles so they can't be reached – bribed, blackmailed, or threatened. When you said you had names I assumed I'd know most of them, or at least half of them. I don't. I only know the departmental execs, upper-echelon personnel who have to go even higher, who obviously report to these people. Press couldn't have gotten these names himself or through others on the outside. He wouldn't know where to look and they wouldn't know where to look – *I* wouldn't know.'

Converse rose. 'Are you sure you know what you're talking about?'

'Yes. Someone – probably more than one – deep in the Washington cellars provided these names just as he or they provided the material for those dossiers.'

'Do you know what you're saying?'

Connal stood still and nodded his head. 'It's not easy for me to say,' he began grimly. 'Press lied to us. He lied to you by what he said, and to me by what he didn't say. You're tied to a string and it goes right back to Washington. And I wasn't to know anything about it.'

'The puppet's in place . . .' Joel spoke so softly he could barely be heard as he walked aimlessly across the room toward the bright sunlight streaming through the balcony doors.

'What?' asked Fitzpatrick.

'Nothing, just a phrase that kept running through my head when I heard about Anstett.' Converse turned. 'But if there's a string why have they hidden it? Why did *Avery* hide it? For what purpose?'

The Navy lawyer remained motionless, his face without expression. 'I don't think I have to answer that. You answered it yourself yesterday afternoon when we were talking about me – and don't kid yourself, Lieutenant, I knew exactly what you were saying. "I'll give you a name now and then that may open a door . . . . but that's all." Those were your words. Freely translated, you were telling yourself that the sailor you took on board might stumble on to something, but in case he was taken by the wrong people, they couldn't beat out of him what he didn't know.'

Joel accepted the rebuke, not merely because the essence was accurate, but because it made clear a larger truth, one he had not understood on

Mykonos. Beale told him that among those raising questions in Washington had been military men who for one reason or another had not pursued their inquiries; they had kept silent. They had kept silent where they might be overheard, perhaps, but they had not kept their silence. They had talked in quiet voices until another quiet voice from San Francisco – a man who knew whom to reach courtesy of his close friend and brother-in-law in San Diego – made contact. They had talked together and out of their secret conversations had come a plan. They needed an infiltrator, a man with the expertise who had a loathing they could fuel, and once fired send out into the labyrinth.

The realization was a shock, but oddly enough Joel could not fault the strategy. He did not even fault the silence that remained even after Preston Halliday's murder; loud accusing voices would have rendered that death meaningless. Instead, they had stayed quiet, knowing their puppet had the tools to make his way through the maze of illegalities and do the job they could not do themselves. He understood that, too. But there was one thing Converse could not accept and that was his own expendability as the puppet. He had tolerated being left unprotected under the conditions outlined by Avery Fowler-Preston Halliday. Not under these. If he was on a string he wanted the puppeteers to know he knew it. He also wanted the name of someone in Bonn he could call, someone who was a part of them. The old rules did not apply any longer, a new dimension had been added.

In four hours he would be driven through the iron gates of Erich Leifhelm's estate; he wanted someone on the outside, a man Fitzpatrick could reach if he did not come out by midnight. The demons were pressing hard – even furiously, thought Joel. Still he could not turn back. He was so close to trapping the warlord of Saigon, so close to making up for so much that had warped his life in ways no one would ever understand . . . No, not 'no one', he reflected. One person did, and she said she could not help him any longer. Nor had it been fair any longer to seek her help.

'What's your decision?' said Connal.

'Decision?' asked Joel, startled.

'You don't have to go this afternoon. Throw it all *back!* This belongs stateside with the FBI in conjunction with the Central Intelligence Agency overseas. I'm appalled they didn't take that route.'

Converse breathed the start of a reply, then stopped. It had to be clear, not only to Fitzpatrick but to himself. He thought he understood. He had seen the look of profound panic in Avery Fowler's eyes – Preston Halliday's eyes – and he had heard the cry in his voice. The lies were his strategy, but the look and the cry were his innermost feelings.

'Has it occurred to you, Commander, that they can't take that route? That, perhaps, we're not talking about men who can pick up a phone – as you said before – and put those wheels in motion? Or if they tried, they'd have their heads cut off, perhaps literally, with an official rebuke and a bullet in the back of their skulls? Let me add that I don't think they're afraid for themselves any more than I believe they chose the best man for the job, but I *do* think they came to a persuasive conclusion. They couldn't work from the inside because they didn't know whom they could trust.'

'Christ, you're a cold son of a bitch.'

'Ice, Commander. We're dealing with a paranoid fantasy called Aquitaine, and it's controlled by proven, committed, highly intelligent and resourceful men who if they achieve what they've set out to do will appear as the voices of strength and reason in a world gone mad. They'll control that world – our world – because all other options will pale beside their stability. *Stability*, counsellor, as opposed to destabilization and chaos. What would you choose if you were an everyday nine-to-fiver with a wife and kids, and you could never be sure when you went home at night whether or not your house had been broken into, your wife raped, your kids strangled? You'd opt for tanks in the street.'

'With justification,' said the Navy lawyer, the two words spiralling quietly off into the air of the sunlit room.

'Believe that, sailor. They're banking on it and that's just what they're planning to do on an international scale. It's only a few days or a few weeks away – whatever it is, wherever it is. If I can just get an inkling . . .' Converse turned and started for the door of his bedroom.

'Where are you going?' asked Connal.

'Beale's telephone number on Mykonos; it's in my briefcase. He's my only contact and I want to talk to him. I want him to know the puppet was just granted some unexpected free will.'

Three minutes later Joel stood over the table, the phone to his ear as the Greek operator in Athens routed his call to the island of Mykonos. Fitzpatrick sat on the couch, Chaim Abrahms' dossier in front of him on the coffee table, his eyes on Converse.

'Are you getting through all right?' asked the Navy lawyer.

'It's ringing now.' The erratic, stabbing signals kept repeating – four, five, six times. On the seventh the telephone in the Aegean was picked up.

'*Kherete?*'

'Dr Beale, please. Dr Edward Beale.'

'*Tee thelate?*'

'Beale. The owner of the house. Get him for me, *please!*' Joel turned to Fitzpatrick. 'Do you speak Greek?'

'No, but I've been thinking about taking it up.'

'You do that.' Converse listened again to the male voice in Mykonos. Greek phrases were spoken rapidly, none comprehensible. 'Thank you! Goodbye.' Joel tapped the telephone bar several times hoping the overseas line was still open and that the English-speaking Greek operator was still there. 'Operator? Is this the operator in Athens? . . . Good! I want to call another number on Mykonos, the same billing in Bonn.' Converse reached down on the table for the instructions Preston Halliday had given him in Geneva. 'It's the Bank of Rhodes. The number is . . .'

Moments later the waterfront banker, Kostas Laskaris, was on the line. '*Kherete.*'

'Mr Laskaris, this is Joel Converse. Do you remember me?'

'Of course . . . Mr Converse?'

The banker sounded distant, somehow strange, as if wary or bewildered. 'I've been trying to call Dr Beale at the number you gave me, but all I get is a man who can't speak English. I wondered if you could tell me where Beale is.'

A quiet expulsion of breath could be heard over the phone. 'I wondered,' said Laskaris quietly. 'The man you reached was a police officer, Mr Converse. I had him placed there myself. A scholar has many valuable things.'

'*Why?* What do you mean?'

'Shortly after sunrise this morning, Dr Beale took his boat out of the harbour accompanied by another man. Several fishermen saw them. Two hours ago Dr Beale's boat was found crashed on the rocks beyond the Stephanos. There was no one on board.'

I killed him. With a scaling knife, dropping his body over a cluster of sharks beyond the shoals of the Stephanos.

Joel hung up the phone. Halliday, Anstett, Beale, all of them gone – all his contacts dead. He was a puppet on the loose, his strings gone haywire, leading only to shadows.

15

Erich Leifhelm's wax-like skin paled further as his eyes narrowed and his starched, white lips parted. There followed a rush of blood to his head as he sat forward in his chair at the desk in his library and spoke into the telephone.

'What was that name again, London?'

'Admiral Hickman. He's the . . .'

'*No,*' interrupted the German sharply. 'The other one! The officer who has refused to release the information.'

'Fitzpatrick, an Irish name. He's the ranking legal officer at the naval base in San Diego.'

'A Lieutenant-Commander Fitzpatrick?'

'Yes, how did you know?'

'*Unglaublich! Diese Stümper!*'

'*Wieso?*' asked the Englishman. 'In what sense?'

'He may be what you say he is in San Diego, *Engländer*, but he is not *in* San Diego! He's here in Bonn!'

'Are you mad? No, of course, you're not. Are you *certain?*'

'He's *with* Converse! I spoke to him myself. The two are registered in *his* name at *Das Rektorat!* He is how we found Converse!'

'There was no attempt to conceal the name?'

'On the contrary, he used his papers to gain entrance!'

'How bloody third-rate,' said London, bewildered. 'Or how downright sure of himself,' added the Britisher, his tone changing. 'A signal? No one dares touch him?'

'*Unsinn!* It's not so.'

'Why not?'

'He spoke to Peregrine, the ambassador. Our man was there. Peregrine wanted to take him, wanted him brought forcibly to the embassy. There were complications; he got away.'

'Our man wasn't very good, then.'

'An obstruction. Some *Schauspieler* – an actor. Peregrine will not discuss the incident. He says nothing.'

'Which means no one will touch this naval officer from California,' concluded London. 'There's a very good reason.'

'What is it?'

'He's the brother-in-law of Preston Halliday.'

'Geneva! *Mein Gott*, they are onto us!'

'Someone is, but not anyone with a great deal of information. I agreed with Palo Alto, who also agrees with our specialist in the Mossad – with Abrahms, as well.'

'The Jew? What does the Jew say? What does he *say?*'

'He claims this Converse is an agent flying blind out of Washington.'

'What more do you *need?*'

'He is not to leave your house. Instructions will follow.'

Stunned, Undersecretary of State Brewster Tolland hung up the phone, sank briefly back in his chair then shot forward, his hand rushing toward his console, his fingers pressing the appropriate buttons.

'Chesapeake,' said the female voice. 'Code, please?'

'Six Thousand,' said Tolland. 'May I speak with Consular Operations, Station Eight, please?'

'Station Eight requires . . .'

'Plantagenet,' interrupted the Undersecretary.

'Right away, sir.'

'What is it, Six Thousand?'

'Cut the horseshit, Harry, this is Brew. What have you got running in Bonn we don't know about?'

'Off the top of my head, nothing.'

'How far off the top is that?'

'No, it's straight. You're current on everything we're doing. There was an FRG review yesterday morning and I'd remember if there was anything that excluded you.'

'You might remember but if I'm excluded, I'm out.'

'That's right and I'd tell you as much if only to keep you out, you know that. What's your problem?'

'I just got off the scrambler with a very angry ambassador, who may just call a very old friend at Sixteen Hundred.'

'Peregrine? What's *his* problem?'

'If it's not you, then someone's playing Cons-Op. It's supposedly a covert investigation of the embassy – his embassy – somehow connected with the Navy Department.'

'The *Navy* . . . ? That's crazy – I mean *dumb* crazy! Bonn's a port?'

'Actually, I suppose it is.'

'I never heard of the *Bismark* or the *Graf Spee* steaming around the Rhine. No way, Brew. We don't have anything like that and we wouldn't have. Do you have any names?'

'Yes, one,' replied Tolland, looking down at a pad with hastily scribbled notes on it. 'An attorney named Joel Converse. Who is he, Harry?'

'For Christ's sake, I never *heard* of him. What's the naval angle?'

'Someone who claims to be the Chief Legal Officer of a major Navy base with the rank of Lieutenant-Commander.'

'*Claims* to be?'

'Well, before that he passed himself off as a military attaché working at the embassy.'

'Somewhere the inmates broke out of a home.'

'This isn't funny, Harry. Peregrine's no fool. He may be a vanity appointment but he's damned good and he's damned smart. He says these people aren't only real but may know something he doesn't.'

'What does he base that on?'

'First, the opinion of a man who's met this Converse . . .'

'Who?' interrupted Harry of Station Eight.

'He won't say, just that he trusts him, trusts his judgement. This person with no name says Converse is a highly qualified, very troubled man, not a black hat.'

'A what?'

'That was the term Peregrine used. Obviously someone who's okay.'

'What else?'

'What Peregrine calls isolated odd behaviour in his personnel ranks. He wouldn't elaborate; he says he'll discuss it with the Secretary or Sixteen Hundred if I can't satisfy him. He wants answers fast and we don't want to rock the boat over there.'

'I'll try to help,' said Harry. 'Maybe it's something from Langley or Arlington – the *bastards!* I can run a check on the navy's chief legals in an hour, and I'm sure the American Bar Association can tell us who Converse is – *if* he is. At least narrow him down if there's more than one.'

'Get back to me. I haven't got much time and we don't want the White House raising its voice.'

'The last thing ever,' agreed the Director of Consular Operations, the State Department's branch of foreign clandestine activities.

'Try *that* on for legal size!' shouted Rear-Admiral Hickman, standing by the window, angrily addressing a rigid, pale-faced David Remington. 'And tell me with as few goddamned details as possible how it fits!'

'I find it impossible to believe, sir. I spoke with him yesterday – at noon – and then again last evening. He was in Sonoma!'

'So did *I*, Lieutenant. And whenever there was a scratching or an echo, what were the words? All that rain in the hills screwed up the telephone lines!'

'Those were the words, sir.'

'He passed through Düsseldorf immigration two *days* ago! He's now in Bonn, Germany, with a man he swore to me had something to do with his brother-in-law's death. The *same* man he's protecting by putting a clamp on that flag. This *Converse!*'

'I don't know what to say, sir.'

'Well, the State Department does and so do I. They're pushing through that vet-delay or whatever the hell you called it in your legalese.'

'It's vetted material, sir. It simply means . . .'

'I don't want to *hear*, Lieutenant,' said Hickman, heading back to his desk, adding under his breath. 'Do you know how much you bastards cost me for the two divorces?'

'I beg your pardon, sir?'

'Never mind. I want that flag released. I brought Fitz on board here. I gave him his striper and the son of a bitch lied to me. He not only *lied*, he did it ten thousand miles away – lying about where he was when he knew he shouldn't be there without my authorization! He *knew* it! . . . Do you have any objections, Lieutenant? Something you can put into a sentence or two that won't require my bringing in three other legals to translate?'

Lieutenant Remington, one of the finest lawyers in the United States Navy, knew when to put the engines in reverse. Legal ethics had been violated by misinformation; the course was clear. Aggressive retreat with full boilers – or nuclear power, he supposed, although he did not really know. 'I'll personally accelerate the vet-delay, Admiral. As the officer responsible for the secondary CLO statute, I'll make it clear that the direct order is now subject to immediate cancellation. No such order can or should originate under questionable circumstances. Legally . . .'

'*That* will be all, Lieutenant,' said the Admiral, cutting off his subordinate and sitting down.

'Yes, sir.'

'No, that *isn't* all!' continued Hickman, abruptly leaning forward. 'How's that transcript released and how soon can you expect it?'

'With State's input it'll only be a matter of hours, sir, noon or shortly afterwards, I'd guess. A classified teletype will be sent to those requesting the flag. However, since SAND PAC has only placed a restriction and not a request . . .'

'*Request* it, Lieutenant. Bring it up to me the minute it gets here and don't leave the base until it does.'

'Aye, aye, sir!'

The deep red Mercedes limousine weaved down the curving road inside the massive gates of Erich Leifhelm's estate. The late afternoon orange sun filtered diagonally through the tall trees, which not only bordered the road but were everywhere beyond on both sides. The drive might have been restful, even awesomely so – shafts of sunlight bursting down through immense, verdant foliage – except for a sight that made the whole scene grotesque. For racing alongside the car were at least half a dozen giant Dobermanns, not one of them making a sound. There was something unearthly about their running furiously in silence, black eyes flashing up at the windows, their jaws wide with rapid, erratic breathing, teeth bared, but no sound emerging from their throats. Somehow Converse knew that if he stepped out of the car without the proper commands being issued, the huge dogs would tear him to pieces.

It was true. The limousine pulled into a long circular drive that fronted wide brown marble steps leading to an arched doorway, the heavy panels in dark *bas relief* – a remnant of some ancient pillaged cathedral. Standing in the centre on the lower step was a man with a silver whistle raised to his lips. Again there was no sound, but suddenly the animals abandoned the car and ran to him, flanking him, facing forward on their haunches, jaws slack, bodies pulsating.

'Please wait, sir,' said the chauffeur, in Germanic English, climbing out and running round to Joel's door. He opened it. 'If you will step out, please, and take two paces away from the car. Only two paces, sir.' The chauffeur now held in his hand a black object with a rounded metal tube extending from the front of the instrument, not unlike a miniaturized electric starter.

'What's that?' asked Converse, not kindly.

'Protection, sir. For you, sir. The dogs, sir. They are trained to sense heavy metal.'

Joel stood there as the German moved the electronic detector over his clothes, including his shoes, his inner thighs and the back of his waist. 'Do you people really think I'd come out here with a gun?'

'I do not think, sir. I do as I am told.'

'How original,' mumbled Converse, as he watched the man on the marble step raise the silver whistle again to his lips. As one, the phalanx of Dobermanns suddenly lurched forward. In panic, Joel grabbed the chauffeur, spinning the German in front of him. There was no resistance; the man simply turned his head and grinned as the dogs veered to the right and raced around the circular drive into the approach road cut out of the forest.

'Don't apologize, *Mein Herr*,' said the chauffeur. 'It happens often.'

'I wasn't going to apologize,' said Converse flatly, as he released the man. 'I was going to break your neck.' The German moved away as Joel remained motionless, stunned by his own words. He had not spoken words like that in over fifteen years. Before then, yes, but he tried never to remember.

'This way, sir,' said the man on the steps, his accent oddly yet distinctly British.

Inside, the great hall was lined with medieval banners hanging down from an interior balcony. The hall led into an immense sitting room, the motif again medieval, made comfortable by soft leather, gaily fringed lamps and silver salvers everywhere on thin polished tables. It was also made ugly by the profusion of protruding animals' heads on the upper walls; large cats, elephants and boar looked down in defiant anger. It was a field marshal's lair.

But it was not the trimmings that absorbed him, it was the sight of the four men who stood beside four separate chairs facing him.

The next few seconds were like extended minutes, his mind racing as he defined them – two really. He knew Bertholdier and Leifhelm; they stood beside each other on the right. It was the two on the left he stared at. The medium-sized, stocky man with the fringe of close-cropped hair beneath a balding head and wearing a rumpled safari jacket, the ever-present boots beneath his khaki trousers, could be no one but Chaim Abrahms. His pouched, angry face with its slits of glaring eyes was the face of an avenger. The very tall man with the gaunt, aquiline features and the straight grey hair was General Jan van Headmer, the *Slayer of Soweto*. Joel had read the van Headmer dossier quickly: fortunately it was the briefest, the final summary saying it all.

In essence, van Headmer is a Capetown aristocrat, an Afrikaner who has never really accepted the British, to say nothing of the tribal blacks. His convictions are rooted in a reality that for him is unshakable. His forebears carved out a savage land under savage conditions and at a great loss of life brutally taken by savages. His thinking is unalterably late nineteenth and early twentieth century. He will not accept the sociological and political inroads made by the more educated Bantu because he will never consider them anything more than bush primitives. When he orders austere deprivations and mass executions, he thinks he is dealing only with semi-verbalizing animals. It is this thinking that led him to be jailed along with Prime Ministers Verwoerd and Vorster during World War II. He concurred wholeheartedly with the Nazi concept of superior races. His close association with Chaim Abrahms is his single difference with the Nazis, and not a contradiction for him. The Sabras carved a land out of primitive Palestine; they are one in that parallel history, and both take pride in their strength and respective accomplishments. Van Headmer, incidentally, is one of the most charming men one could meet. On the surface, he is cultured, extremely courteous and always willing to listen. Underneath he is an unfeeling killer and he is Delavane's key figure in South Africa with its vast resources.

'*Mein Haus ist dein Haus*,' said Leifhelm, walking towards Joel, his hand outstretched.

Converse stepped forward to accept the German's hand. Their hands clasped. 'That was an odd greeting outside for such a warm sentiment,' said Joel, releasing Leifhelm's hand and immediately, abruptly, walking past the former field marshal to Bertholdier. 'Good to see you again, General. My apologies for the unfortunate incident in Paris the other night. I don't mean to speak lightly of a man's life but in those few split seconds I didn't think he had much regard for mine.'

Joel's boldness had the desired effect. Bertholdier stared at him, momentarily unsure of what to say. And Converse was aware that the other three men were watching him intently, without question struck by his audacity, both in manners and words.

'To be sure, Monsieur,' said the Frenchman, pointlessly but with composure. 'As you know, the man disregarded his orders.'

'Really? I was told he misunderstood them.'

'It is the same!'

The sharp, deep, heavily accented voice came from behind. Joel turned. 'Is it?' he asked coldly.

'In the field, yes,' said Chaim Abrahms. 'Either one is an error, and errors are paid for with lives. The man paid with his.'

'May I introduce General Abrahms?' broke in Leifhelm, touching Converse's elbow and leading him across the room. Hands were extended.

'General Abrahms, it's a privilege,' said Joel sincerely. 'Like everyone here, I've admired you tremendously, although perhaps your rhetoric has been excessive at times.'

The Israeli's face reddened as soft, throated laughter crept quietly around the large room. Suddenly, van Headmer stepped forward, Converse's eyes drawn to his strong face, the brows frowning, his muscles taut.

'You are addressing one of my closest associates, sir,' he said: the rebuke was unmistakable. Then he stopped, a thin smile creasing his gaunt, chiselled face. 'And I could not have said it better myself. A pleasure to know you, young man.' The Afrikaner's hand was stretched out towards Joel, who accepted it as the laughter swelled.

'I am insulted!' cried Abrahms, his thick eyebrows raised, his head bobbing in mock despair. 'By *talkers*, I'm insulted! Frankly, Mr Converse, they agree with you because none of them has had a woman in a quarter of a century. They may tell you otherwise – others may tell you otherwise – but believe me they hire whores to play cards with them or read stories into their old grey ears just to fool their friends!' The laughter grew louder and the Israeli, with an audience, went on, leaning forward and pretending to speak *sotto voce* to Joel. 'But, you see, *I* hire the whores to tell me the truth while I *Shtup* them! They tell me these fancy talkers nod off by nine o'clock, whining for warm milk. With the *Ovaltine*, if it's possible!'

'My dear Sabra,' said Leifhelm, talking through his laughter. 'You read your own romantic fiction too assiduously.'

'You see what I mean, Converse?' asked Abrahms, palms extended, his thick neck and head shrugging. 'You hear that? "Assiduously". Now you know why the Germans lost the war. They forever spoke so dramatically of the *Blitzkrieg* and the *Angriffe*, but actually they were talking – *assiduously* – about what to do next!'

'They should have given you a commission, Chaim,' said Bertholdier, enjoying himself. 'You could have changed your name, called Rommel and von Rundstedt Jews and taken over both fronts.'

'The High Command could have done worse,' agreed the Israeli.

'I wonder, though,' continued the Frenchman, 'if you would have stopped there? Hitler was a fine orator, as you are a fine orator. Perhaps you would have claimed he, too, was a Jew and moved into the Chancellery.'

'Oh, I have it on good authority that he *was* a Jew. But from a *very* bad family. Even we have them: of course they're all from Europe.'

The laughter grew again and then rapidly began to subside. Joel took the cue.

'Sometimes I speak too frankly, General,' he said, addressing the Israeli. 'I should learn better, but believe me no insult was intended. I have nothing but admiration for your stated positions, your policies.'

'And that's precisely what we shall discuss,' said Erich Leifhelm, drawing everyone's attention. 'Positions, policies, overall philosophy, if you will. We will stay as far away from specifics as we can, although a few will undoubtedly intrude. However, it is our approach to the larger abstractions that count. Come, Mr Converse, have a chair. Let us begin our conference, the first of many I trust.'

* * *

Rear-Admiral Hickman put the transcript slowly down on his desk and looked aimlessly past his propped-up feet at the window and the ocean under a grey sky beyond. He crossed his arms, lowered his head and frowned, the combined gestures matching his thoughts. He was as bewildered now as he had been when he first read the transcript, as convinced now as he was then that Remington's conclusion was off the mark. But then the legal officer was too young to have any real knowledge of the events as they had actually happened: no one who had not been there could really understand. Too many others did: it was the reason for the flag, but it made no sense to apply that reasoning to this Converse eighteen years later. It was exhuming a corpse that had died from a fever, whether the shell of a man lived on or not. It had to be something else.

Hickman looked at his watch, unfolded his arms and removed his feet from the edge of the table. It was 3.10 in Norfolk; he reached for the telephone.

'Hello, Brian,' said Rear-Admiral Scanlon of the Fifth Naval District. 'I want you to know how much we appreciate SAND PAC's help in this thing.'

'SAND PAC's?' asked Hickman, bemused that no credit was given to the State Department.

'All right, Admiral, *your* help. I owe you one, old Hicky.'

'Start paying by dropping that name.'

'Hey, come on, don't you remember the hockey games? You'd come racing up the ice and the whole cadet corps would shout: "Here comes *Hicky!* Here comes *Hicky!*"'

'May I unblock my ears now?'

'I'm just trying to thank you, pal.'

'That's just it, I'm not sure for what? Have you read the transcript?'

'Naturally.'

'What the hell's *there?*'

'Well,' answered Scanlon tentatively. 'I read it pretty quickly. It's been an awful day and frankly I just passed it on. What do *you* think is there? Between you and me, I'd like to know, because I barely had time to skim through it.'

'What do I think is there? Absolutely *nothing*. Oh, sure we kept flags on stuff like that back then because the White House passed the order to put the lid on officially-recorded criticism and we all went along. Also we were pretty sick and tired of it ourselves. But there's nothing in that transcript that hasn't been heard before, or that has any value for anyone but military historians a hundred years from now as a very small footnote.'

'Well . . .' repeated Scanlon, even more tentatively, 'this Converse had some pretty harsh things to say about Command-Saigon.'

'About *Mad Marcus?* Christ, I said worse during the Force-Tonkin conferences and *my* CO did me ten times better. We ferried in those kids up and down the coast when all they were ready for was a day at the beach with hot dogs and Ferris wheels . . . I don't get it. You and my legal zero in on the same thing, and I think it's old hat and discredited. Mad Marcus is a relic.'

'Your who?'

'My legal exec. I told you about him, Remington.'

'Oh, yes. The stickler-prick.'

'He picked up on the Saigon thing, too. "That's it," he said. "It's in those remarks. It's Delavane." He wasn't around to know Delavane was fair game for every anti-war group in the country. Hell, *we* gave him the name "Mad Marcus". No, it's not Delavane, it's something else. Perhaps it's in those escapes, specifically Converse's last escape. Maybe there's some MIA input we don't know about.'

'Well,' repeated the Admiral in Norfolk for the third time, but now far less tentatively. 'You may have something there but it doesn't concern us. Look, I'll be honest with you. I didn't want to say anything because I didn't want you to think you went to a lot of trouble for nothing, but the word I get is that the whole thing is a bust-negative.'

'Oh?' said Hickman, suddenly listening very carefully. 'How so?'

'It's the wrong man. Apparently an over-enthusiastic junior grade officer was doing some digging in the same time period, the same general circumstances. He saw the flag and drew six wrong conclusions. I hope he enjoys taking five a.m. muster.'

'And that's it?' asked SAND PAC's admiral, controlling his astonishment.

'That's the feedback we get here. Whatever your CLO had in mind hasn't anything to do with our people.'

Hickman could not believe what he was hearing. Of course Scanlon had not mentioned the State Department's efforts. He knew nothing about them! He was quickly putting as much distance between himself and the Converse flag as he could, lying because he had not been told. State was working quietly – probably through Cons Op – and Scanlon had no reason to think 'old Hicky' knew a damn thing about Bonn or Converse or Connal Fitzpatrick's whereabouts. Or about a man named Preston Halliday who had been murdered in Geneva. What was *happening?* He would not find out from Scanlon. Nor did he care to.

'To hell with it then. My CLO will be back in three or four days and maybe I'll learn something.'

'Whatever it is, it's back in your sandbox, Admiral. My people had the wrong man.'

'Your people couldn't navigate a row boat in the DC Reflecting Pool.'

'Can't blame you for that, Hicky.'

Hickman hung up the phone and resumed his standard position when in thought, gazing beyond his propped-up shoes to the window and the ocean beyond. The sun was trying to break through the overcast without much success.

He had never liked Scanlon for reasons too petty to examine. Except one: he knew Scanlon was a liar. What he had not known was that he was such a stupid liar.

Lieutenant David Remington was flattered by the call. The well-known four-striper had invited him to lunch, not only invited him but had apologized for the lateness of the invitation and told him that it was perfectly understandable if it was not convenient. Further the captain wanted him to know that the call was of a personal nature, having nothing to do with naval business. The high-ranking officer, although a resident of La Jolla, was in port for only a few days and needed legal advice. He had been told that Lieutenant Remington was just about the best lawyer in the United States Navy. Would the lieutenant accept?

Of course Remington had made it perfectly clear that whatever advice he might offer would be offered on the basis of *amicus curiae*; no remuneration could possibly be considered as that would be a violation of Statute . . .

'May I buy you lunch, Lieutenant, or do we have to split the cheque?' the four-striper had asked, somewhat impatiently, thought Remington.

The restaurant was high in the hills above La Jolla, an out-of-the-way roadside inn that apparently catered to diners of the area and those from San Diego and University City who did not care to be seen together in the usual places. Remington had not been too pleased: he would have preferred being seen at the Coronado with the captain than travelling ten miles north so as *not* to be seen in the hills of La Jolla. Nevertheless, the four-striper had been politely adamant: it was where he wanted to meet. David had checked him out. The much-decorated captain was not only in line for promotion, but was considered a potential candidate for the Joint Chiefs of Staff. Remington would have ridden a bicycle on the exposed Alaskan pipeline to keep the appointment.

Which was exactly what he thought he was doing, as he spun the steering wheel right, then left, then right and right again as he made his way up the steep narrow roads. It was important to keep in mind, he thought, as he whipped the car to the left, that *personal* advice was nevertheless *professional* advice, and *without* payment of any sort whatsoever constituted a *debt* that would one day be acknowledged. And if a man was elevated to the Joint Chiefs . . . Remington could not help it. In a glow of self-importance he had let it drop to a fellow legal officer – the one who had coined the name 'stickler-prick' – that he was lunching with a highly-regarded four-striper in La Jolla and might be late returning to the office. Then to drive his point home, he asked his associate for directions.

Oh, my *God!* What *was* it!? Oh, my *God!*

In the apex of the hairpin curve was an enormous black rig, thirty feet in length, and out of control. It weaved right and left on the narrow incline, its speed gathering with every foot, measured in racing yards, a black behemoth swerving, crashing down on everything in front of it, a wild beast gone mad!

Remington whipped his head to his right as he spun the wheel to avoid impact. There were only thin trunks of young trees and saplings in late summer bloom; beneath was a floral abyss. These were the last images he saw as the car careened on its side and began to plunge.

Far above on another hill, a man kneeled, binoculars in his hands, raised to his face as the explosion below confirmed the kill. His expression was neither one of joy nor sadness, merely acceptance. A mission had been accomplished. After all, it was war.

And Lieutenant David Remington, whose life was so ordered and orderly, who knew exactly where and how he was going in this world, who knew above all that he would never be trapped by the forces that had killed his father in the name of corporate policy, was put to death by the policy of a company he had never heard of. An enterprise called Aquitaine. He had seen the name, Delavane.

* * *

Their view is that it's the proper evolution of current history, all other ideologies having failed ... The words spoken by Preston Halliday in Geneva kept repeating themselves in Converse's inner ear as he listened to the four voices of Aquitaine. The frightening thing was that they believed those words without equivocation, morally and intellectually, their convictions rooted in observations going back decades, their arguments persuasive, illuminating past global mistakes of judgment that resulted in horrible suffering and unnecessary loss of life.

The simple objective of their coming together – allies and former enemies alike – was to bring benevolent order to a world in chaos, to permit the industrial states to flourish, their economies strong for the benefit of all people, spreading the strengths and benefits of multinational trade to the impoverished, uncommitted Third World and by so doing secure its commitment. Only in this way, in this coming together, could the tide of Communism be stopped – stopped and reversed until its systems collapsed under the sheer force of superior armed might and financial resources.

To bring all this about required a shift of values and priorities. Industrial decisions everywhere must be coordinated to bring about the total strength of the free states. Government treasuries, multinational corporations and giant conglomerates must look to a stratum of interlocking committees, agree to be directed by these committees, to accept their decisions – which would in effect be their respective governments' decisions, each keeping the others apprised of its current agenda. What was this stratum of ultimate negotiators? Who comprised these committees which would in effect speak for the free nations and set their policies?

Throughout history only one class of people remained constant in its excellence, who when called upon in times of crisis performed far beyond human expectations – even in defeat. The reasons for their segment's unique contributions in war and, unfortunately, less so in peace, were historically clear: they were selfless. They belonged to a class that was trained to serve without thought of reward except *by* excellence. Wealth was irrelevant because their needs were furnished and prerequisites granted only through the outstanding performance of duty. This class of people was not subject to the corruption of the market place. In reality it was unusually equipped to deal with such corruption for it could not be touched by them. The mere presence of any excessive benefactions within its ranks would instantly be recognized and condemned, resulting in courts-martial. This class of society, this novel branch of the human race was not only incorruptible at the highest levels, it was the ultimate saviour of mankind as we know it today.

It was the military. The world over, even encompassing one's enemies. Together – even as enemies – they best understood the catastrophic results of weakness.

To be sure, certain minor liberties would perforce have to be withheld from the body politic but these were small sacrifices for survival. Who could argue?

None of the four spokesmen for Aquitaine raised his voice. They were the quiet prophets of reason, each with his own history, his own identity ... allies and enemies together in a world gone mad.

Converse replied in the affirmative to everything that was said – it was not difficult to do so – and asked abstract questions of philosophy – as he was expected to ask. Even the court jester, Chaim Abrahms, became deeply serious and answered quietly.

'You think we Jews are the only ones in the Diaspora, my friend? You are wrong. The whole human race is dispersed everywhere, all of us locking rams' horns and not knowing where to go. Certain rabbis claim we Jews shall not see salvation until the Messianic era, the time of divine redemption when a god will appear to show us the way to our own promised land. He was far too late arriving: we could not wait for Him any longer. We created Israel. Do you see the lesson? We – we *here* – are now the divine intervention on earth. And I – even *I*, a man of accomplishment and ego – will give up my life in silence so we may succeed.'

Jacques Louis Bertholdier. 'You must understand, Mr Converse, that Locke said it best in his *Essay concerning Human Understanding*. Essentially he wrote that man attained his highest freedom only when he understood the parameters of his behaviour. We will establish those parameters. Is anything more logical?'

Erich Leifhelm. 'Goethe said it perhaps better when he insisted that the *Romantik* of politics was best used to numb and quell the fears of the uninformed. In his definitive *Aus Meinem Leben* he states clearly that all governing classes must be imbued above all with discipline. Where is it more prevalent?'

Jan van Headmer. 'My own country, sir, is the living embodiment of the lesson. We took the beast out of the savage and formed a vast, productive nation. The beast returns and my nation is in turmoil.'

And so it went for several hours. Quiet dissertations delivered thoughtfully, reflectively, passions apparent only in the deep sincerity of their convictions. Twice Joel was pressed to reveal the name of his client and twice he demurred, stating the legal position of confidentiality – which could change in a matter of days, perhaps less.

'I'd have to offer my client something concrete. An approach, a strategy that would warrant his immediate involvement, his commitment, if you will.'

'Why is that necessary at this juncture?' asked Bertholdier. 'You've heard our reasoning. Certainly an approach can be discerned.'

'All right, scratch approach. A strategy then. Not the "why" but the "how".'

'You ask for a plan?' asked Abrahms. 'On what basis?'

'Because you'll be asking for an investment surpassing anything in our experience.'

'That's an extraordinary statement,' interjected van Headmer.

'He has extraordinary resources,' replied Converse.

'Very well,' said Leifhelm, glancing at each of his associates before he continued. Joel understood; permission was being sought based on prior discussions. It was granted. 'What would you say to the compromising of certain powerful individuals in specific governments?'

'Blackmail?' asked Joel. 'Extortion? It wouldn't work. There are too many checks and balances. A man's threatened, the threat's discovered and he's out anyway. Then the purification rites set in and where there was once weakness, suddenly there's a great deal of strength.'

'That's an extremely narrow interpretation,' said Bertholdier.

'You do not take into consideration the time element!' cried Abrahms defiantly, for the first time raising his voice. '*Accumulation*, Converse! Rapid *acceleration!*'

Suddenly Joel was aware that the three other men were looking at the Israeli, but not simply watching him. Within each composed pair of eyes was a glare, a warning. Abrahms shrugged. 'It's merely a point.'

'Well taken,' said Converse, without emphasis.

'I'm not even sure it applies,' added the Israeli, compounding his error.

'Well, *I'm* sure it's time for dinner,' said Leifhelm, unobtrusively removing his hand from the side of his chair. 'I've boasted so about my table to our guest that I admit to a shortness of breath – concern, of course. I trust the chef has upheld my honour.' As if answering a signal – which Joel knew was the case – the British manservant appeared beneath an archway at the far end of the room. 'I am clairvoyant!' Leifhelm rose. 'Come, come, my friends. Saddle-of-lamb *cicatrisé*, a dish created by the gods for themselves and stolen by the irrepressible thief who rules my kitchen.'

The dinner was, indeed, superb, each dish an isolated effort into which had gone great concentration, both in taste and setting. Converse was more gourmand than gourmet, his culinary education having been force-fed in expensive restaurants where his mind was only mildly distracted by the food, but he knew when a dish was the best in its class. There was nothing second-rate about Leifhelm's table, including the table itself, an enormous solid mass of mahogany perched on two huge, delicately carved tripods that swept out, legs surging for their grips on the intricate parquet floor in the high-ceilinged room with oils of hunting scenes on the deep red velour walls. Low candelabra were placed in front of the silver-mirrored placemats, but the flames of the candles did not obstruct one's view of another person, a feat Joel wished could be mastered by most of the hostesses in New York, London and Geneva.

The talk veered away from the serious topics explored in the sitting room. It was as if a recess had been called, a diversion to ease the burdens of statesmanship and replenish the reservoirs of thought. If that was the aim, it was eminently successful, and it was the Afrikaner, van Headmer, who led the way. In his soft-spoken, charming way (the dossier had been accurate; the 'unfeeling killer' *was* charming) he described a safari he had taken Chaim Abrahms on in the Veldt.

'Do you realize, gentlemen, that I bought this poor Hebrew his first jacket at Safarics' in Johannesburg and there's never been a day I haven't regretted it. It's become our great general's trademark! Of course, you know why he wears it. It absorbs perspiration and requires very little washing, simply large applications of bay rum. This *is* a different jacket, isn't it, great general?'

'Bleach, *bleach*, I tell my wife!' replied the Sabra court jester, grimacing. 'It takes out the smell of the godless slave traders!'

'Talking of slaves, let me tell you,' said the Afrikaner, warming to his story with a glass of wine, changed with each new course.

The story of Chaim Abrahms' first and only safari was worthy of good vaudeville. Apparently the Israeli had been stalking a male lion for hours with his gun bearer, a Bantu he constantly abused, not realizing the black understood and spoke English as well as he. Abrahms had zeroed-in each of his four rifles prior to the hunt, but whenever he had the lion in his sights, he missed. This supposedly superb marksman, this celebrated general with the rifle-eye of the hawk, could not hit eight feet of flesh a hundred yards away. At the end of the day, an exhausted Chaim Abrahms bribed the gun bearer, using broken English and a multiplicity of hand gestures, not to tell the rest of the safari of his misses. The hunter and the Bantu returned to camp, the hunter crying the woes of non-existent cats and stupid gun bearers. The native had gone to van Headmer's tent and as the Afrikaner told it in perfectly mimicked Bantu English, said the following.

'I liked the lion more than the Jew, sir. I altered his sights, sir, but apparently I will be forgiven my indiscretion, sir. Among other enticements, he has offered to have me *bar mitzvahed*.'

The diners collapsed in laughter, Abrahms to his credit loudest of all. Obviously he had heard the story before and relished the telling. It occurred to Joel that only the most secure could hear such telling tales of themselves and respond with genuine laughter. The Israeli was a rock in the firmament of his convictions and could easily tolerate a laugh at himself. That, too, was frightening.

The British servant intruded, walking silently on the hard wood floor and spoke into Erich Leifhelm's ear.

'Forgive me, please,' said the German, rising to take a call. 'A nervous broker in Munich who consistently picks up rumours from Riyadh. A sheik goes to the toilet and he hears thunder from the east.'

The ebullient conversation went on without a break in the flow, the three men of Aquitaine behaving like old comrades sincerely trying to make a stranger feel welcome. The appearance, too, was frightening. Where were the fanatics who wanted to destroy governments, ruthlessly grabbing controls and shackling whole societies, channelling 'body-politics' into their vision of the military state? These were men of intellect. They spoke of Rousseau and Goethe, and had compassion for suffering and pain and unnecessary loss of life. They had humour and could laugh at themselves, and talk quietly of sacrificing their own lives for the betterment of a world gone mad. Joel understood. These were persuaders assuming the mantles of statesmen. What had Leifhelm said, quoting Goethe? 'The romance of politics was best used to numb and quell the fears of the uninformed.'

Frightening.

Leifhelm returned, followed by the British servant carrying two open bottles of wine. If the call from Munich brought unfavourable news, the German gave no indication of it. His spirits were as before, his waxen smile at the ready and his enthusiasm for the next course unbridled. 'And now, my friends, the lamb *cicatrisé* – medallions of ambrosia and, hyperbole aside, actually rather good. Also, in honour of our guest we have a bonus this evening. My astute English friend and companion was in Siegburg the other day and ran across several bottles of Östreicher Lenchen Beerenauslese, 'Seventy-one. What could be a more fitting tribute?'

The men of Aquitaine glanced at one another, then Bertholdier spoke. 'Certainly a find, Erich. It's one of the more acceptable German varieties.'

'The 'Eighty-two Klausberg Riesling in Johannesburg promises to be among the finest in years,' said van Headmer.

'I doubt it will rival the Richon Zion Carmel,' added the Israeli.

'You are all impossible!'

A be-hatted chef rolled in a silver service trolley, uncovered the saddle of lamb and, under appreciative looks, proceeded to carve and serve. The Englishman presented the various side dishes to each diner, then poured the wine.

Erich Leifhelm raised his glass, the flickering light of the candles reflecting off the carved crystal and the edges of the silver-mirrored placemats. 'To our guest and his unknown client both of whom we trust will soon be in our fold.'

Converse nodded his head and drank.

He took the glass from his lips and suddenly was aware of the four men of Aquitaine. They were staring at him, their own glasses firmly on the table. None had drunk the wine.

Leifhelm spoke again, his voice nasal, cold, a fury held in check by an intellect in control.

'"General Delavane was the enemy, *our* enemy! Men like that can't be allowed any more, can't you understand!" Those were the words, were they not, Mr Converse?'

'*What?*' Joel heard his voice but was not sure it was his. The flames of the candles suddenly erupted; fire filled his eyes and the burning in his throat became an unbearable pain. He grabbed his neck as he struggled out of the chair, hurling it back, hearing the crash, yet not hearing it, hearing only a succession of echoes. He was falling, layers of black earth passed his eyes broken by flashes of lightning. The pain surged into his stomach; it was intolerable; he clutched his groin trying to force the pain back up and out of his body. Then he felt his own movement on a hard surface and somehow knew he was writhing wildly on the floor, held in check by overpowering arms.

'The gun. Step back. Hold him.' The voice, too, was a series of echoes, sharply enunciated in a searing British accent. 'Now. *Fire!*'

An explosion blew up the universe. The rest was silence.

16

The telephone rang, jolting Connal Fitzpatrick out of a deep sleep. He had fallen back on the couch, the van Headmer dossier in his hand, both feet still angled on the floor. Shaking his head and rapidly blinking and widening his eyes, he tried to orient himself. Where *was* he? What *time* was it? The phone rang again, now a prolonged, shattering bell. He lurched off the couch, his legs unsteady, his breathing erratic – his exhaustion too complete to shake off in a few seconds. He had not really slept since California; his body and mind could barely function. He grabbed the phone, nearly dropping it as he momentarily lost his balance.

'Yes . . . *hello!*'

'Commander Fitzpatrick, if you please,' said a male voice in a clipped British accent.

'This is he.'

'Philip Dunstone here, Commander. I'm calling for Mr Converse. He wanted me to tell you that the conference is going extremely well, far better than he thought possible.'

'You're *who?*'

'Dunstone. Major Philip Dunstone. I'm senior aide to General Berkeley-Greene.'

'Berkeley-Greene . . . ?'

'Yes, Commander. Mr Converse said to tell you that along with the others he's decided to accept General Leifhelm's hospitality for the night. He'll be in touch with you first thing in the morning.'

'Let me talk to him. Now.'

'I'm afraid that's not possible. They've all gone out on the motor launch for a spin down river. Frankly, they're a secretive lot, aren't they? Actually, I'm not permitted to attend their discussions any more than you are.'

'I'm not settling for this, Major!'

'Really, Commander, I'm simply relaying a message . . . Oh yes, Mr Converse did mention that if you were concerned I should also tell you that, if the admiral called, you were to thank him and give him his regards.'

Fitzpatrick stared at the wall. Converse would not bring up the Hickman business unless he was sending a message. The request made no sense to anyone but the two of them. Everything *was* all right. Also there could be several reasons why Joel didn't care to talk directly on the phone. Among them, thought Connal resentfully, was probably the fact that he didn't trust his 'aide' to say the proper words in the event their conversation was being overheard.

'All right, Major . . . what was the name again? Dunstone?'

'That's right, Philip Dunstone. Senior aide to General Berkeley-Greene.'

'Leave word for Mr Converse that I'll expect to hear from him by eight o'clock.'

'Isn't that a little harsh, old boy? It's nearly two a.m. now. The breakfast buffet usually starts about nine-thirty out here.'

'Nine o'clock then,' said Fitzpatrick firmly.

'I'll tell him myself, Commander. Oh, one final thing, Mr Converse asked me to apologize for his not having reached you by midnight. They've really been at it hammer and tongs in there.'

That was it, thought Connal. Everything was under control. Joel certainly would not have made that remark otherwise. 'Thanks, Major, and by the way I'm sorry I was rude. I was asleep and tried to get it together too fast.'

'Lucky chap. You can head back to the pillows while I stand watch. Next time you can take my place.'

'If the food's good, you're on.'

'It's not, really. A lot of pansy cooking, to tell you the truth. Good night, Commander.'

'Good night, Major.'

Relieved, Fitzpatrick hung up the phone. He looked over at the couch, thinking briefly of going back to the dossiers but decided against it. He felt hollow all over, hollow legs, hollow chest, a hollow ache in his head. He needed sleep badly.

He gathered up the papers and took them into Converse's room, placing them in the attaché case, locking it and turning the combination tumblers. Gripping the handle he went back into the sitting room, checked the door, turned off the lights and headed for his own bedroom. He threw the case on the bed and removed his shoes, then his trousers, but that was as far as he got. He collapsed on the pillow, somehow managing to wrap part of the bedspread around him. The darkness was welcome.

'*That* was hardly necessary,' said Leifhelm to the Englishman, as the latter replaced the phone. '"Pansy cooking" is not the way I would describe my table.'

'He undoubtedly would,' said the man who had called himself Philip Dunstone. 'Let's check the patient.'

The two walked out of the library and down the hall to a bedroom. Inside were the three other men of Aquitaine along with a fourth, his black bag and the exposed hypodermic needles denoting a physician. Below on the bed was Joel Converse, his eyes wide and glass-like, saliva oozing from the sides of his mouth, his head moving back and forth as if in a trance, unintelligible sounds emerging from his lips. The doctor glanced up and spoke.

'There's nothing more he can give us because there *is* nothing more,' said the physician. 'The chemicals don't lie. Quite simply, he's a blind sent out by men in Washington but he has no idea who they are. He didn't even know they existed until this naval officer convinced him they had to exist. His only referrals were Anstett and Beale.'

'Both dead,' interrupted van Headmer. 'Anstett is public and I can vouch for Beale. My employee on Santorini flew into Mykonos and confirmed the kill. There can be no trace, incidentally. The Greek is back on the chalk cliffs selling laces and inflated whisky in his *taverna*.'

'Prepare him for his odyssey,' said Chaim Abrahms, looking down at Converse. 'As our specialist in the Mossad put it so clearly, distance is now the necessary requirement. A vast separation between this American and those who would send him out.'

Fitzpatrick stirred, the bright morning sunlight from the windows piercing the darkness – expanding shades of white forcing his eyelids open. He stretched, his shoulder digging into a hard corner of the attaché case, the rest of him constricted by the bedspread which was tangled about his legs. He kicked it off and flung his arms on both sides of the bed, breathing deeply, feeling the relaxed swelling of his chest. He swung his left hand above his head, twisted his wrist and looked at his watch. It was 9.20; he had slept for seven and a half hours, but the uninterrupted sleep seemed much longer. He got out of bed and took several steps; his balance was steady, his mind clearing. He looked at his watch again, remembering. The major named Dunstone had said breakfast at Leifhelm's estate was served from 9.30 on, and if the conference had moved to a boat on the river at 2.00 a.m. Converse probably would not call before ten o'clock.

Connal walked into the bathroom; there was a phone on the wall by the toilet if he was wrong about the call. A shave followed by a hot and cold shower and he would be fully himself again.

Eighteen minutes later Fitzpatrick walked back into the bedroom, a towel around his waist, his skin still smarting from the harsh sprays of water. He crossed to his open suitcase on a luggage rack next to the closet where he had hung his clothes. He took out his miniaturized radio, placed it on the bureau and deciding against the Armed Forces band, dialled into what was left of a German newscast. There were the usual threats of strikes in the industrial south, as well as charges and counter charges hurled around the Bundestag, but nothing earthshaking. He selected comfortable clothes – lightweight slacks, an Oxford blue shirt and his cord jacket. He got dressed and walked out into the sitting room, heading for the phone; he would call room service for a small breakfast and a great deal of coffee.

He stopped. Something was wrong. What was it? The pillows on the couch were still rumpled, a glass half filled with stale whisky still on the coffee table, as were pencils and a blank telephone message pad. The balcony doors were closed, the curtains drawn, and across the room the silver ice bucket remained in the centre of the silver tray on the antique hunt table. Everything was as he had last seen it, yet there was something . . . The *door!* The door to Converse's bedroom was shut. Had he closed it? No, he had *not!*

He walked rapidly over, twisted the knob and pushed the door open. He studied the room, conscious of the fact that he had stopped breathing. It was immaculate, cleaned and smoothed to a fare-thee-well, no indication whatsoever that it was occupied. The suitcase was gone, the few articles Converse had left on the bureau no longer there. Connal rushed to the closet, yanking it open. It was empty. He went into the bathroom; it was spotless, new soap in the receptacles, the glassses wrapped in clinging paper ready for incoming guests. He walked out of the bathroom stunned. There was not the slightest sign that anyone except a maid had been in that bedroom for days.

Fitzpatrick ran out to the sitting room and the telephone. Seconds later the manager was on the line; it was the same man Connal had spoken with yesterday.

'Yes, indeed, your businessman was even more eccentric than you described, Commander. He checked out at three-thirty this morning, paying all the bills, incidentally.'

'He was *here?*'

'Of course.'

'You *saw* him?'

'Not personally. I don't come on duty until eight o'clock. He spoke with the night manager and settled your account before going up to pack.'

'How could your man know it was *him?* He never saw him before!'

'Really, Commander, he identified himself as your associate and paid the bill. He also had his key; he left it at the desk.'

Fitzpatrick paused, astonished, then spoke harshly. 'The room was cleaned! Was that also done at three-thirty this morning?'

'No, *Mein Herr*, at seven o'clock. By the first housekeeping shift.'

'But not the outer room?'

'The connection might have disturbed you. Frankly, Commander, that suite must be prepared for an early afternoon arrival. I'm sure the staff felt it would not bother you if they got a head start on the task. Obviously it did not.'

'Early afternoon . . . ? *I'm* here!'

'And welcome to stay until twelve noon; the bill has been paid. Your friend has departed and the suite has been reserved.'

'And I don't suppose you have another room.'

'I'm afraid there's nothing available, Commander.'

Connal slammed down the phone. *Really, Commander* . . . Those same words had been spoken by another over the same telephone at two o'clock in the morning. There were three directories in a wicker rack by the table; he pulled out the one for Bonn and found the number.

'*Guten Morgen. Hier bei General Leifhelm.*'

'*Herrn Major Dunstone, bitte.*'

'*Wem?*'

'Dunstone,' said Fitzpatrick, then continuing in German. 'He's a guest. Philip Dunstone. He's the senior aide to . . . to a General Berkeley-Greene. They're English.'

'English? There are no Englishmen here, sir. There's no one here – that is to say there are no guests.'

'He was there last night! They both were. I *spoke* with Major Dunstone.'

'The General had a small dinner party for a few friends, but no English people, sir.'

'Look, I'm trying to reach a man named Converse.'

'Oh, yes, Mr Converse. *He* was here, sir.'

'Was?'

'I believe he left . . .'

'Where's *Leifhelm?*' shouted Connal.

There was a pause before the German replied coldly. 'Who should I say is calling *General* Leifhelm?'

'Fitzpatrick. Lieutenant-Commander Fitzpatrick!'

'I believe he's in the dining room. If you'll stay on the telephone.' The line was put on hold, the dead, suspended silence unnerving. Finally there was a click and Leifhelm's voice reverberated over the phone.

'Good morning, Commander. Bonn has provided a lovely day, no? The seven hills are as clear as in a picture postcard. I believe you can see them . . .'

'Where's Converse?' interrupted the Navy lawyer.

'I would assume at *Das Rektorat.*'

'He was supposed to be staying at your place.'

'No such arrangements were made. They were neither requested nor offered. He left rather late, but he did leave, Commander. My car drove him back.'

'That's not what I was told! A Major Dunstone called me around two this morning . . .'

'I believe Mr Converse left shortly before then . . . *Who* did you say called?'

'Dunstone. A Major Philip Dunstone. He's English. He said he was the senior aide to General Berkeley-Greene.'

'I don't know this Major Dunstone; there was no such person here. However, I'm familiar with just about every general in the British Army and I've never heard of anyone named Berkeley-Greene.'

'Stow it, Leifhelm!'

'I beg your pardon.'

'I *spoke* to Dunstone! He . . . he said the right words. He said Converse was staying at your place – with the *others!*'

'I think you should have spoken directly with Herr Converse, because there was no Major Dunstone or General Berkeley-Greene at my home last night. Perhaps you should check with the British Embassy, certainly they'd know if these people were in Bonn. Perhaps you heard the words incorrectly: perhaps they met later at a café.'

'I *couldn't* speak to him! Dunstone said you were out on the river in a boat.' Fitzpatrick's breath was now coming in short gasps.

'Now that's ridiculous, Commander. It's true I keep a small launch for guests, but it's a well-known fact that I am not partial to the water.' The General paused, adding with a short laugh. 'The great field marshal gets seasick in a flat boat six feet from shore.'

'You're *lying!*'

'I resent that, sir. Especially about the water. I never feared the Russian Front, only the Black Sea. And if we had invaded England, I assure you I would have crossed the Channel in a plane.' The German was toying: he was enjoying himself.

'You know exactly what I mean!' Again Connal shouted. 'They said Converse checked out of here at three-thirty this morning! I say he never came *back!*'

'And I say this conversation is pointless. If you are truly alarmed, call me back when you can be civil. I have friends in the *Staats Polizei*.' Again a click; the German had hung up.

As Fitzpatrick replaced the phone, another thought suddenly struck him, frightening him. He walked quickly into the bedroom, his eyes instantly zeroing in on the attaché case. It was half under the pillow; oh *God*, he had been in such a sound sleep! He went to the bed, yanked the case out and examined it. Breathing again, he saw that it was the same case, the combination locks secure, no amount of pressure on the small brass buttons would release the plates. He lifted the case up and shook it; the weight and the sounds were proof that the papers were inside and intact, proof also that Converse had not returned to the inn and checked out. All other considerations aside and regardless of whatever emergencies that might have arisen, he never would have left without the dossiers and the list of names.

Connal carried the case back into the sitting room, trying to collect his thoughts, putting them in numerical sequence so as to impose some kind of order. *A*. He had to assume the flag on Joel's service record had been lifted or the damaging information unearthed in some other way and that Converse was now being held by Leifhelm and the contingent from Aquitaine that had flown in from Paris, Tel Aviv and Johannesberg. *B*. They would not kill him until they had used every means possible to find out what he knew – which was far less than they imagined and could take several days. *C*. The Leifhelm estate, according to his dossier, was a fortress, thus the chances of going in and bringing Converse out were nil. *D*. Fitzpatrick knew he could not appeal to the American Embassy. To begin with Walter Peregrine would place him under territory-arrest and those doing the arresting might put a bullet in his head. One had tried. *E*. He could not risk seeking help from Hickman in San Diego, which under different circumstances might be a logical course of action. Everything in the admiral's make-up ruled out any connection with Aquitaine; he was a fiercely independent officer whose conversations were laced with scepticism about the Pentagon's policies and mentality. But if that flag had been officially released – whether with his consent or over his objections – Hickman would have no choice but to call him back to the base for a full inquiry. Any contact at all could result in the immediate cancellation of his leave, but if there was no contact and no way to reach him the order could not be given.

Connal sat down on the couch, the attaché case at his feet, and picked up a pencil; he wrote out two words on the telephone message pad: *Call Meagen*. He would tell his sister to say that after Press's funeral he had left for parts unknown without explanation. It was consistent with what he had said to the admiral, that he was taking his information to 'the authorities' investigating Preston Halliday's death.

F. He could go to the Bonn police and tell them the truth. He had every reason to believe that an American colleague was being held against his will inside the gates of General Erich Leifhelm's estate. Then, of course, the inevitable question would arise: Why didn't the Lieutenant-Commander contact the American Embassy? The unspoken was just below the surface: Regardless of one's opinion General Leifhelm was a prominent figure and such a serious charge should have diplomatic support. The embassy again. Strike out. Then again if Leifhelm said he had 'friends' in the *Staats Polizei*, he probably owned the key men in the Bonn Police. If he was alarmed Converse could be moved. Or killed. *G*. . . . was insane, thought the Navy lawyer as a legal phrase crept slowly into his consciousness, suddenly taking on a blurred viability. *Trade off*. It was a daily occurrence in pre-trial examinations, both civilian and military. *We'll drop this if you accept that. We'll stay out of this area if you stay out of that one*. Standard practice. Trade off. Was it possible? Could it even be considered? It was crazy and it was desperate, but then nothing was sane, nothing sanguine. Since force was out of the question . . . could an exchange be made? Leifhelm for Converse. A general for a lieutenant.

Connal did not dare analyse; there were too many negatives. He had to act on instinct because there was nothing else left, nowhere he could turn that did not lead to a blank wall or a bullet. He got up from the couch and went to the table with the telephone, sitting down in the chair, and reached for the directory on the floor. What he had in mind was insane but he could not think about that. He found the name. *Fishbein, Ilse.* The illegitimate daughter of Hermann Goering.

The rendezvous was set: a back table at the Hansa-Keller café on the Kaiserplatz, the reservation in the name of Parnell. Fitzpatrick had had the presence of mind in California to pack a conservative civilian suit; he wore it now as the American attorney, Mr Parnell, who was fluent in German and sent by his firm in Milwaukee, Wisconsin, to make contact with one Ilse Fishbein in Bonn, West Germany. He also had the presence of mind in Bonn, West Germany, to have managed a single room at the Schlosspark on the Venusbergweg and he had placed Converse's attaché case where it was safe for a considerable length of time, a trail left for Converse should everything blow apart. A trail he would recognize.

Connal arrived ten minutes early, not merely to secure the table but to familiarize himself with the surroundings and silently practise his approach within them. He had done the same thing many times before, walking into military courtrooms before a trial, testing the chairs, the height of the tables, the scan of vision of the tribunal on the dais. It all helped.

He knew it was she when the woman arrived and spoke to the *maître* at his lectern. She was tall and full-formed, not obese but fleshed out, statuesque in a way, conscious of her mature sensuality, but smart enough not to parade it. She was dressed in a light grey summer suit, the jacket buttoned above her generous breasts, a wide white collar demurely angled over the fabric. Her face too was full but not soft, the cheekbones high, lending an appearance of character that might not otherwise have been there; her hair was dark and shoulder length, with slight streaks of early grey. She was escorted to the table by the head waiter. Fitzpatrick rose as she approached.

'*Guten Tag, Frau Fishbein,*' he said, extending his hand. '*Bitte, setzen Sie sich.*'

'It's not necessary for you to speak German, Herr Parnell,' said the woman, releasing his hand and sliding into the chair under the guidance of the waiter who bowed and left. 'I make my living as a translator.'

'Whatever you feel most comfortable with,' said Connal.

'I think under the circumstances I should prefer English, and spoken softly, if you please. Now what is this incredible thing you alluded to over the telephone, Mr Parnell?'

'Quite simply an inheritance, Mrs Fishbein,' replied Fitzpatrick, his expression sincere, his eyes steady. 'If a few technical questions can be settled, and I'm sure they can be, as a rightful legatee you will receive a substantial sum of money.'

'From someone in America I never knew?'

'He . . . knew your father.'

'I did not,' said Ilse Fishbein quickly, her eyes darting about at the adjacent tables. 'Who is this man?'

'He was a member of your father's staff during the war,' answered Connal, lowering his voice still further. 'With your father's help – certain contacts in Holland – he got out of Germany before the Nuremberg trials with a great deal of money. He came to the United States by way of London, his funds intact, and started a business in the Midwest. It became enormously successful. He died recently, leaving sealed instructions with my firm, his attorneys.'

'But why me?'

'A debt. Without your father's influence and assistance our client would probably have withered for years in jail instead of flourishing as he did in America. As far as anyone was concerned he was a Dutch immigrant from the Netherlands whose family business was destroyed in the war and who sought his future in America. That future included considerable real estate holdings and a very successful meat packing plant – all in the process of being sold. Your inheritance is in excess of two million American dollars. Would you care for an aperitif, Mrs Fishbein?'

The woman could not at first reply. Her eyes had grown wide, her full jaw slackened, her stare trance-like. 'I believe I will, Herr Parnell,' she said in a monotone, finding her voice. 'A large whisky, if you please.'

Fitzpatrick signalled the waiter, ordered drinks and tried several times to make idle conversation, commenting on the beautiful weather and asking what sites he should see while in Bonn. It was no use. Ilse Fishbein was as close to being in a catatonic state as Connal could imagine. She had gripped his wrist, clutching it in silence with extremely strong fingers, her lips parted, her eyes two blank glass agates. The drinks came, the waiter left, and still she would not let go of him. Instead, she drank somewhat awkwardly, lifting the glass with her left hand.

'What are these questions to be settled, *Mein Herr?* Ask anything, *demand* anything. Do you have a place to stay? Things are so crowded in Bonn.'

'You're very kind; yes, I do. Try to understand, Mrs Fishbein, this is an extremely sensitive matter for my firm. As you can well imagine it's not the sort of legal work American attorneys are too happy with, and frankly had our client not made certain provisos connecting the successful completion of this aspect of his last will and testament to the full execution of other aspects we might have . . .'

'The questions! What are the *questions?*'

Fitzpatrick paused before answering, the thoughtful lawyer permitting the interruption but still intent on making his point. 'Everything will be handled confidentially, the probate court operating *in camera* . . .'

'With *photographs?*'

'In private, Mrs Fishbein. For the good of the community, in exchange for specific state and local taxes which might not be paid in the event of confiscation. You see, the higher courts might decide the entire estate is open to question.'

'Yes, the questions! What *are* they?'

'Really quite simple. I've prepared certain statements which you will sign and to which I can swear to your signature. They establish your bloodline. Then there is a short deposition required substantiating the claim. We need only one but it must be given by a former high-ranking member of the German forces, preferably a man whose name is recognizable, whom the recent history books or war accounts establish as a working colleague of your natural father. Of course, it would be advantageous to have someone known to the American military in the event the judge decides to call the Pentagon and ask "who is this fellow?"'

'I know the man!' whispered Ilse Fishbein. 'He was a Field Marshal, a brilliant *General!*'

'Who is he?' asked the Navy lawyer, then instantly shrugging, dispensing with the question of identity as irrelevant. 'Never mind. Just tell me why you think he's the right man, this field marshal.'

'He is greatly respected, although not everyone agrees with him. He was one of the *grossmächtigen* young commanders, once decorated by my father himself for his brilliance!'

'But would anyone in the American military establishment know him?'

'*Mein Gott!* He worked for the Allies in Berlin and Vienna after the war!'

'Yes?'

'And at SHAPE Headquarters in Brussels!'

Yes, thought Connal, we're talking about the same man. 'Fine,' he said, casually but seriously. 'Don't bother giving me his name. It doesn't matter and I probably wouldn't know it anyway. Can you reach him quickly?'

'In minutes! He's here in Bonn.'

'Splendid. I should catch the plane back to Milwaukee by tomorrow noon.'

'You will come to his house and he will dictate what you need to his secretary.'

'I'm sorry I can't do that. The deposition must be countersigned by a notary. I understand you have the same rules over here – and why not, you invented them – and the Schlosspark Hotel has both typing and notary services. Say this evening, or perhaps early in the morning? I should be more than happy to send a taxi for your friend. I don't want this to cost him a *Pfennig.* Any expenses he incurs my firm will be happy to repay.'

Ilse Fishbein giggled – a silent, hysterical giggle, but a giggle never the less. 'You do not know my friend, *Mein Herr.*'

'I'm sure we'll get along. Now how about lunch?'

'I have to go to the toilet,' said the German woman, her eyes glass agates again. As she rose, Connal rising with her, her whisper could be heard. '*Mein Gott! Zwei Millionen Dollar!*'

'He does not even care to know your *name!*' cried Ilse Fishbein into the phone. 'He's from a place called Milwaukee, Wisconsin, and is offering me *two million dollars American!*'

'He did not even ask who I was?'

'He said it didn't matter! He probably wouldn't know you, in any event. Can you imagine? He offered to send a taxi for you! He said you should not spend a penny!'

'It's true Goering was excessively generous during the last weeks,' mused Leifhelm. 'Of course he was more often drugged than not, and those who supplied him with narcotics which were difficult to obtain were rewarded with the whereabouts of priceless art treasures. The one who later smuggled him the poisoned suppositories still lives like a Roman emperor in Luxembourg.'

'So you see, it's true! Goering *did* these things!'

'Rarely knowing what he was doing, however,' agreed the general reluctantly. 'This is really most unusual and very inconvenient, Ilse. Did this man show you any documents, any proof of his assignment?'

'*Naturally!*' lied Fishbein close to panic, picking remembered words out of the air. 'There was a formal page of legal statements and a . . . *deposition* – all to be handled by the courts confidentially! In *private!* You see there is a question of taxes which would not be paid if the estate was confiscated . . .'

'I've heard it all before, Ilse,' Leifhelm broke in wearily. 'There are no statutes for so-called war criminals and expatriated funds. So the hypocrites choke on their hypocritical rules the instant they cost money.'

'You are always so perceptive, my general, and I have always been so loyal. I've never refused you a single request whether it was professional in nature or far more intimate. *Please*. Two million American! It will take but ten or fifteen minutes!'

'You've been like a good niece, I can't deny it, Ilse. And there is no way anyone could know about you in other matters . . . Very well, this evening then. I'm dining at the Steinberger at nine o'clock. I'll stop at the Schlosspark at eight-fifteen or thereabouts. You can buy me a gift with your – shall we say, ill-conceived new riches.'

'I'll meet you in the lobby.'

'My driver will accompany me.'

'*Ach*, bring twenty men!'

'He's worth twenty-five,' Leifhelm said.

Fitzpatrick sat in the chair in the small conference room on the first floor of the hotel and examined the gun, the manual of instructions on his lap. He tried to match what the clerk had told him to the diagrams and words below his eyes, satisfied that he knew enough. There were basic similarities to the standard Navy issue Colt .45, the only handgun he was familiar with, and the technical information was extraneous to his needs. The weapon he had purchased was a *Heckler und Koch PGS auto pistol*, about six inches long, its calibre nine millimetres, and with a nine-shell magazine clip. The instructions emphasized such points as 'polygonal rifling' and 'sliding roller lock functions'; he let the manual slip to the floor, and practised removing the clip and slapping it back into place. He could load the weapon, aim it and fire it; those movements were all that was necessary and he trusted the last would *not* be necessary.

He glanced at his watch; it was almost eight o'clock. He shoved the automatic into his belt, reached down for the instructions and stood up, looking around the room, mentally checking off the movements and the locations he had designed for himself. As he expected, the Fishbein woman had told him Leifhelm would be accompanied by someone, a 'driver' in this case, and it could be assumed the man had other functions. If so, he would have no chance to practise them.

The room – one of twenty-odd conference rooms in the hotel and which he had reserved under the name of a fictitious company – was not large but there were structural arrangements that could be put to advantage. The usual rectangular table was in the centre, three chairs on each side and two at the ends, one with a telephone. There were additional chairs against the walls for stenographers and observers – all this was normal. However, in the centre of the left wall was a doorway that led to a very small room apparently used for private conversations. Inside was another telephone which when off the hook caused a button on the first telephone on the conference table to light up; confidentiality had its limits in Bonn. Further, the hallway door opened into a short foyer, thus prohibiting those entering from scanning the room while standing in the corridor.

Connal folded the Heckler and Koch instructions, put them in his jacket pocket, and walked over to the table surveying his set pieces. He had gone to an office supply store and purchased the appropriate items. On the far end of the table by the telephone – which was placed parallel to the edge, the buttons in clear view – were several file folders next to an open brief case (from a distance its dark plastic looked like expensive leather). Scattered about were papers, pencils and a yellow legal pad, the top pages looped over. The setting was familiar to anyone who had ever kept an appointment with an attorney, said learned counsel having put his astute observations down on paper prior to the conference.

Fitzpatrick retraced his steps to the chair, moved it forward several feet, and crossed to the door of the small side room. He had turned on the lights – two table lamps flanking a short couch; now he went to the nearest with the telephone and turned it off. He then walked back to the open door and stood between it and the wall, peering through the narrow vertical space broken up by upper and lower hinges. He had a clear view of the foyer's entrance; three people would pass into the conference room and he would come out.

There was a knock on the hallway door, the rapid, impatient tapping of an heiress unable to control herself. He had told the Fishbein woman the location of the room, but nothing else. No name or number and, in her anxiety, she had not asked about either. Fitzpatrick took the necessary steps to the telephone table in the small room; he lifted the phone out of its cradle and placed it on its side. He returned to his position behind the door, angling himself so as to look through the crack, his body in the shadows. He took the pistol from his belt, held it in front of his mouth and shouted loud enough to be heard outside in the hotel corridor, but pleasantly, not angrily.

'*Bitte, kommen Sie herein! Die Tür ist offen. Ich telefoniere gerade.*'

The sound of the door as it opened preceded Ilse Fishbein as she walked rapidly into the room, her eyes directed at the conference table. She was followed by Erich Leifhelm, who glanced about then turned slightly, nodding his head. A third man in the uniform of a chauffeur came into view, his hand in the pocket of his black jacket. Connal then heard the second sound he needed to hear. The hallway door was slammed shut.

The Navy lawyer yanked back the small door and quickly stepped around it, the gun extended, aimed directly at the chauffeur.

'*You!*' he cried in German. 'Take your hand out of your pocket! *Slowly!*' The woman gasped, then began the start of a scream. Fitzpatrick interrupted harshly. 'Be *quiet!* As your friend will tell you, I haven't anything to lose. I can kill the three of you and be out of the country in an hour, leaving the police to look for a Mr Parnell who doesn't exist.'

The chauffeur, the muscles of his jaws rippling, removed his hand from his pocket, his fingers rigid. Leifhelm stared in anger and fear at Connal's gun, his face no longer ashen but flushed.

'You *dare* . . . ?'

'I dare, Field Marshal,' said Fitzpatrick. 'Just as you dared forty years ago to rape a young kid and make damned sure that she and her whole family never walked out of the camps. You bet your ass I dare and, if I were you, I wouldn't give me the slightest cause to be any angrier than I am.' Connal spoke to the woman. '*You.* Inside that briefcase on the table are eight strands of rope. Start with the driver. Bind his hands and feet, I'll tell you how. Now! *Quickly!*'

Four minutes later the chauffeur and Leifhelm sat in two conference chairs, their ankles and wrists bound, the driver's weapon removed from his pocket. The Navy lawyer checked the ropes, the knots having been tied under his instructions. Everything was secure; the more one writhed the tighter the knots would become. Fitzpatrick ordered the panicked Fishbein woman into a third chair; he lashed her hands to the arms and her feet to the legs.

Rising, Connal picked up the automatic from the table and approached Leifhelm who was sitting in the chair next to the lighted telephone. 'Now,' he said, the gun pointed at the German's head. 'As soon as I hang up the phone in the other room we're going to make a call from here.' The Navy lawyer walked quickly into the small side room, hung up the telephone, and returned. He sat down next to the bound Leifhelm and took a scrap of paper out of the open briefcase. On it was written the phone number of the general's estate on the Rhine beyond Bad Godesberg.

'What do you think you'll accomplish?' asked Leifhelm.

'Trade off,' replied Fitzpatrick, the barrel of the gun pressed against the German's temple. 'You for Converse.'

'*Mein Gott!*' whispered Ilse Fishbein, petrified, as the chauffeur winced, his hands straining against the ropes which were now biting into the flesh of his wrists.

'You believe anyone will listen to you, much less carry out your orders?'

'They will if they want to see you alive again. You know I'm right, General. This gun isn't so loud, I made sure of that. I can turn on the radio and kill you and be on a plane out of Germany before you're found. This room is reserved for the night with instructions that we're not to be disturbed for any reason whatsoever.' Connal shifted the weapon to his left hand, picked up the telephone, and dialled the number written on the scrap of paper.

'*Guten Tag. Hier bei General Leifhelm.*'

'Put someone in authority on this phone,' said the Navy lawyer in perfect high-German. 'I have a gun less than a foot away from General Leifhelm's head and I'll kill him right now unless you do as I say.'

There were muffled shouts over the line while a hand was held against the mouthpiece. In seconds a crisp British accent was speaking slowly, deliberately in English.

'Who is this and what do you want?'

'Well, what do you know? This sounds like Major Philip Dunstone – that *was* the name, wasn't it? You don't sound half so friendly as you did last night.'

'Don't do anything rash, Commander. You'll regret it.'

'And don't you do anything stupid or Leifhelm will regret it sooner – that is until he can't regret anything any longer. You've got one hour to get Converse to the airport and inside the Lufthansa security gate. He has a reservation on the ten o'clock flight to Washington, DC, by way of Frankfurt. I've made arrangements. I'll be calling a number in a room where he'll be taken and I'll expect to talk with him. After I do, I'll leave here and call you on another phone, telling you where your employer is. Just get Converse to that security gate. One hour, Major!' Fitzpatrick shoved the phone in front of Leifhelm's face, and once again pressed the barrel of the gun into the German's temple.

'Do as he says,' said the General, choking on his words.

The minutes went by slowly, stretching into a quarter of an hour, then thirty minutes, the silence finally broken by Leifhelm.

'So you found her,' he said, gesturing his head at Ilse Fishbein, who trembled as tears of fear and gargantuan loss streaked down her full-blown cheeks.

'Just as we found out about Munich forty years ago, and a hell of a lot of other things. You're all on your way to that great big war room in the sky, Field Marshal, so don't worry about whether I'll go back on my word to your English butler, I wouldn't miss seeing you bastards paraded for everyone to see what you really are. People like you give the military everywhere a goddamned rotten name.'

There was a slight commotion from the hallway beyond the door. Connal looked up, raising the gun and holding it directly at Leifhelm's head.

'*Was ist?*' said the German, shrugging.

'*Keine Bewegung!*'

From beyond the door the strains of a melody filled the hotel corridor sung by several male voices more off key than on. Another conference in one of the other rooms had broken up, obviously as much due to the intake of alcohol as from the completion of a business agenda. Raucous laughter pierced a refrain as unsuccessful harmony was attempted. Fitzpatrick relaxed, lowering the automatic; no one on the outside knew the name or number of the room.

'You say men like me give your profession – which is my profession as well – a seriously bad name,' said Leifhelm. 'Has it occurred to you, Commander, that we might elevate that profession to one of indispensable greatness in a world that needs us badly?'

'Needs us?' asked Connal. 'We need the world first and not your kind of world. You tried it once and blew it, don't you remember?'

'That was one nation led by a madman trying to impose his imprimatur over the globe. This is many nations with one class of self-abnegating professionals coming together for the good of all.'

'Whose definition? Yours? You're a funny fellow, General Municher. Somehow I question your benevolent tendencies.'

'Indiscretions of a deprived youth whose name and rightful opportunities were stolen from him should not be held against the man a half century later.'

'Deprived or depraved? I think you made up for lost time pretty quickly and as brutally as you could. I don't like your remedies.'

'You have no vision.'

'Thanks be to Jesus, Mary and Joseph it's not yours.' The singing out in the corridor faded briefly, then swelled again, the harmony and the volume more discordant and louder than before. 'Maybe that's some of your old Dachau playboys having a beer bust.'

Leifhelm shrugged.

Suddenly, shatteringly, the door burst open, crashing into the wall as three men raced in, spits filling the air as silenced guns fired, hands jerking back and forth, the surface of the table chewed up, splinters of wood flying everywhere. Fitzpatrick felt the searing repetitions of pain in his arm as the automatic was blown out of his grip. He looked down and saw the blood rising to the surface, drenching the fabric of his right sleeve. In his shock he winced, glancing to his left. Ilse Fishbein was dead, her bleeding skull shattered by a fusillade of bullets; the chauffeur was smiling obscenely.

The door was closed as if nothing had happened, the last moments a faded, unremembered incident. Leifhelm spoke.

'*Stümper*,' he said, as one of the invaders cut the ropes around his wrists. 'I used that term only yesterday, Commander, but I did not know how right I was. Did you think a single telephone call could not be traced to a single room? . . . It was all too coincidentally symmetrical. Converse is ours and suddenly this poor whore comes into immense riches – *American* riches. I grant you it was entirely possible – such bequests are made frequently by sausage-soaked idiots who don't realize the harm they do – but the timing was too perfect, too . . . amateurish.'

'You're one son of a bitch.' Connal briefly closed his eyes, trying to force the pain out of his mind, unable to move his fingers.

'Why, Commander,' said the general getting out of the chair, 'do I sense the bravado of fear? Do you think I'm going to have you killed?'

'You sense it. I won't give you any more than that.'

'You're quite wrong. Considering the nature of your military leave, you can be of minor but unique service to us. One more statistic to disrupt a pattern. You'll be our guest, Commander, but not in Germany proper. You are going on a trip.'

17

Converse opened his eyes, dead, flat iron weighed on his lids, nausea in his throat, blurred darkness everywhere. And there was a terrible stinging at his side – on his arm – flesh separated from flesh, stretched and inflamed. Blindly he tried to touch the offending spot, but gasped, pulling back in pain. Then somewhere light was creeping around the dark space above him, picking its way through moving obstructions, peering into the shadows. Objects slowly came into focus – the metal rim of the cot-like bed next to his face, two wooden chairs opposite each other at a small table in the distance, a door also in the distance, but farther away and shut . . . then another door, this one open, a white basin with a pair of dull taps on the left in a far away cubicle. The light? It was still moving. Now dancing, flickering. Where was it?

He found it; he found them. High in the wall on either side of the closed door were two rectangular windows, the short curtains billowing in the breezes. The windows were open, but oddly not open, not clear, the spaces interrupted. Joel raised his head, supporting himself on his forearm and squinted, trying to see more clearly. He focused on the interruptions behind the swelling curtains – thin black metal shafts vertically connecting the window frames. They were bars. He was in a cell.

He fell back on the bed, swallowing repeatedly to lessen the burning in his throat, and moving his arm in circles trying to lessen the pain of the . . . wound? Yes, a wound, a gunshot! The realization jarred his memory: a dinner party had turned into a battleground filled with hysteria. Blinding lights and sudden jolts of pain were accompanied by low, strident voices bombarding him, incessant echoes pounding in his ears as he tried desperately to repel the piercing assaults. Then there were moments of peaceful calm, the drone of a single voice in the mists. Converse closed his eyes, pressing his lids tightly together with all his strength as another realization struck him and disturbed him deeply. That voice in the swirling mists was *his* voice; he had been drugged and he knew he had given up secrets.

He had been drugged before, a number of times in the North Vietnamese camps, and as always there was the sickening feeling of numbed outrage. His mind had been stripped and violated, his voice made to perform obscenities against the last vestiges of his will.

And, again as always, there was the empty hole in his stomach, a vacuum that ran deep and produced only weakness. He felt starved and probably was. The chemicals usually induced vomiting, the linings of the intestines screaming for a coating of destiny that could not be found. It was strange, he reflected, opening his eyes and following the moving shafts of light, but those memories from years ago evoked the same protective instincts that had helped him then – so many years ago. He could not waste energy; he had to conserve what strength he had. Regain new strength. Otherwise there was nothing but the numbed outrage and neither his mind nor his body could do anything about it.

There was a sound across the room! Then another and another after that. The sliding, grating metal told him that a bolt was being released; the sharp sound of a key followed by the twisting of a knob meant that the door in the far distant wall was about to be opened. It was, and a wide, blinding burst of sunlight filled the room that was his cell. Converse shielded his eyes, peering between his fingers. The blurred, frazzled silhouette of a man stood in the doorframe carrying a flat object in his left hand, bracing it from beneath. The figure walked in and Joel, blinking, saw it was the chauffeur who had electronically searched him in the driveway.

The uniformed driver crossed to the table and deftly lowered the flat object; it was a tray, its contents covered by cloth. It was only then that Converse's attention was drawn back to the sunlit doorway. Outside, milling about in anxious contempt, was the pack of Dobermanns, their shining black eyes continuously shifting towards the door, their lips curled, teeth bared in unending quiet snarls.

'*Guten Morgen, Mein Herr,*' said Leifhelm's chauffeur, shifting instantly to English. 'Another beautiful day on the northern Rhine, no?'

'It's bright out there, if that's what you mean,' replied Joel, his hand still cupping his eyes. 'I suppose I should be grateful to notice after last night.'

'Last night?' The German paused, then added quietly, 'It was two nights ago, Amerikaner. You've been here for the past thirty-three hours.'

'*Thirty* . . . ?' Converse pushed himself up and swung his legs over the side of the bed. He had to stop all motion; the dizziness was too much, too much strength had been drained. *Oh Christ! He remembered so clearly! Don't waste movement. They'll be back. The bastards!* 'You bastards,' he said out loud but without any real meaning. Then for the first time he realized he was shirtless, and noticed the bandage on his left arm between his elbow and his shoulder. It covered the gunshot wound. 'Did somebody miss my head?' he asked.

'I'm told you inflicted the injury yourself. You tried to kill General Leifhelm, when the others took your gun away.'

'I tried to kill . . . ? With my non-existent gun? The one you made sure I didn't *have?*'

'You were too clever for me, *Mein Herr.*'

'What happens now?'

'Now? Now you eat. I have instructions from the doctor. You begin with the *Hafergrütze* . . . how do you say? The porridge.'

'Hot mush or cereal,' completed Joel. 'With skim or powdered milk. Then some kind of soft-boiled eggs taken with pills. And if it all goes down a little ground meat, and if *that* stays down a few spoonfuls of crushed turnips or potatoes or squash. Whatever's available.'

'How do you know this?' asked the uniformed man, genuinely surprised.

'It's a basic diet,' said Converse cynically. 'Variations with the territory and the supplies. I once had some comparatively good meals . . . You're planning to put me under again.'

The German shrugged. 'I do what I'm told. I bring you food. Here, let me help you.'

Joel looked up as the chauffeur approached the bed. 'Under other circumstances I'd spit in your goddamned face. But if I did I wouldn't have that slight, *slight* possibility of spitting in it some other time. You may help me. Be careful of my arm.'

'You are a very strange man, *Mein Herr.*'

'And you're all perfectly normal citizens catching the early train to Larchmont so you can put down ten martinis before going to the PTA meeting.'

'*Was?* I know of no such meeting.'

'They're keeping it a secret; they don't want you to know. If I were you, I'd get out of town before they make you president.'

'*Mich? Präsident?*'

'Just help me to the chair, like a good ole' Aryan boy, will you?'

'Hah, you are being amusing, *ja?*'

'Probably not,' said Converse easing into the wooden chair. 'It's a terrible habit I wish I could break.' He looked up at the bewildered German. 'You see, I keep trying,' he said in utter seriousness.

Three more days passed, his only visitor the chauffeur accompanied by the sullen, high-strung pack of Dobermanns. His well-searched suitcase was given to him, scissors and a nail file removed from the travelling kit – his electric razor intact. It was their way of telling him that his presence had been removed from Bonn, leaving to painful speculation the whereabouts and the life or death of Connal Fitzpatrick. Yet there was an inconsistency and as such the basis for hope. No allusions were made to his attaché case, either with visual evidence – the page of a dossier, perhaps – or through his brief exchanges with Leifhelm's driver. The generals of Aquitaine were men of immense egos; if they had those materials in their possession, they would let him know.

As to his conversations with the chauffeur, they were limited to questions on his part and disciplined pleasantries on the German's part, no answers at all – at least none that made any sense.

How long is this going to go on? When am I going to see someone other than you?

There is no one here, sir, except the staff. General Leifhelm is away – in Essen, I believe. Our instructions are to feed you well and restore your health.

Incommunicado. He was in solitary.

But the food was not like that given to prisoners anywhere else. Roasts of beef and lamb, chops, poultry and fresh fish; vegetables that must have come directly from a nearby garden . . . and wine – which at first Joel was reluctant to drink – but when he did even he knew it was superior.

On the second day, as much to keep from thinking as anything else, he had begun to perform mild exercises – as he had done so many years ago. By the third day he had actually worked up a sweat during a running-in-place session, a healthy sweat, telling him the drugs had left his body. The wound on his arm was still there but he thought about it less and less. Curiously, it was not serious.

On the fourth day questions and reflections were no longer good enough. Confinement and the maddening frustration of having no answers forced him to turn elsewhere, to the practical, to the most necessary consideration facing him. Escape. Regardless of the outcome the attempt had to be made. Whatever plans Delavane and his disciples in Aquitaine had for him, they obviously included parading a drugless man – more than likely a dead man with no narcotics in his system. Otherwise they would have killed him at once, disposing of his body in any number of untraceable ways. He had done it before. Could he do it again?

He was not rotting in a rat-infested cell and there was no terrible gunfire in the distant darkness, but it was far more important that he succeed now than it ever was eighteen years ago. And there was an extraordinary irony: eighteen years ago he had wanted to break out and tell whomever would listen to him about a madman in Saigon who sent countless children to their deaths – and worse, to broken minds and hollow feelings that would follow them for the rest of their lives. Now he had to tell the world about that same madman.

He had to get out. He had to tell the world what he knew. He had to escape!

Converse stood on the wooden chair, the short curtain pulled back, and peered through the black metal bars outside. His cabin, or cottage, or jailhouse, whatever it was, seemed to have been lowered from above into a cleared-out patch of the forest. There was a wall of tall trees and thick foliage as far as he could see in either direction, a dirt path angling to the right beneath the window. The clearing itself extended no more than twenty feet in front of the structure before the dense greenery began; he presumed it was the same on all sides – as it was from the other window to the left of the door, except that there was no path below, only a short, coarse stubble of brown grass. The two front windows were the only views he had. The rest of this isolated jailhouse consisted of unbroken walls, a small ceiling vent in the bathroom, but no other openings.

All he could be certain of, since the chauffeur and the dogs and the warm meals indicated he was still within the grounds of Leifhelm's estate, was that the river could not be far away. He could not see it but it was there and it gave him hope – more than hope, a sense of morbid exhilaration rooted in his memory. Once before the waters of a river had been his friend, his guide, ultimately the lifeline that had taken him through the worst of his journey. A tributary of the Huong Khe south of Duc Tho had rushed him silently at night under the bridges and by patrols and past the encampments of three battalions. The waters of the Rhine, like the currents of the Huong Khe years ago, were his way out.

The multiple sounds of animal feet clawing the earth preceded the streaking dark coats of the Dobermanns as they raced below the window, instantly stopping and crowding angrily in front of the door. The chauffeur was on his way with a breakfast no prisoner in isolation should expect. Joel climbed off the chair and quickly carried it back to the table, setting it in place and going to his bed. He sat down, kicked off his shoes, and lay back on the pillow, his legs stretched out over the rumpled blanket.

The bolt was slid back, the key inserted and the heavy knob turned; the door opened. As he did every time he entered, the German pushed the centre of the door with his right hand as he supported the tray with his left. However, this morning he was gripping a bulging object in his right hand, the blinding sunlight obscuring it for Converse. The man walked in and, more awkwardly than usual, placed the tray on the table.

'I have a pleasant surprise for you, *Mein Herr*. I spoke with General Leifhelm on the telephone last night and he asked about you. I told him you were recovering splendidly and that I had changed the bandage on your unfortunate injury. Then it occurred to him that you had nothing to read and he was very upset. So an hour ago I drove into Bonn and purchased three days of the *International Herald Tribune*.' The driver placed the rolled-up newspapers next to the tray on the table.

But it was not the issues of the *Herald Tribune* that Joel stared at. It was the German's neck and the upper outside pocket of his uniform jacket. For looped around that neck and angled over to that pocket was a thin silver chain, the top of a tubular silver whistle protruding, clearly visible against the dark fabric. Converse shifted his eyes to the door; the huge Dobermanns were sitting on their haunches, each breathing breathlessly, salivating, but reasonably quiet, for all intents and purposes immobile. Converse remembered his arrival at the general's monumental lair, and the strange Englishman who had controlled the dogs with a silver whistle.

'Tell Leifhelm I appreciate the reading material but I'd be even more grateful if I could get out of this place for a few minutes.'

'*Ja*, with a plane ticket to the beaches in the south of France, *nein?*'

'For Christ's sake, just to take a walk and stretch my legs! What's the matter? Can't you and that drooling band of mastiffs handle one unarmed man getting a little air? . . . No, you're probably too frightened to try.' Joel paused, then added in an insulting mock-German accent. '"I do vot I am tolt".'

The driver's smile faded. 'The other evening you said you would not apologize but instead break my neck. That was a joke, *Mein Herr*. Do you understand? A joke I find so amusing I can laugh at it.'

'Hey, come on,' said Converse, changing his tone as he swung his legs off the bed and sat up. 'You're ten years younger than I am and twenty times stronger. I felt insulted and reacted stupidly, but if you think I'd raise a hand against you you're out of your mind. I'm sorry. You've been decent to me and I was stupid again.'

'*Ja*, you were stupid,' said the German without rancour. 'But also you were right. I do as I am told. And why not? It is a privilege to take orders from General Leifhelm. He has been *gut* to me.'

'Have you been with him long?'

'Since Brussels. I was a sergeant in the Federal Republic's border patrols. He heard about my problem and took an interest in my case. I was transferred to the Brabant garrison and made his chauffeur.'

'What was your problem? I'm a lawyer, you know.'

'The charge was that I strangled a man. With my arm.'

'Did you?'

'*Ja*. He was trying to put a knife in my stomach – and lower. He said I took advantage of his daughter. I took no advantage; it was not necessary. She was a whore – it was in the clothes she wore, the way she walked – *es ist klar!* The father was a pig.'

Joel looked at the man, at the clouded malevolence in his eyes. 'I can understand General Leifhelm's sympathies,' he said.

'Now you know why I do as I am told.'

'Clearly.'

'He is calling for his messages at noon. I shall ask him about your walking. You understand that one word from me and the Dobermanns will rip your body from its bones.'

'Nice puppies,' said Converse, addressing the pack of dogs outside.

Noon came and the privilege was granted. The walk was to take place after lunch, when the driver returned to remove the tray. He returned and after several warnings Joel ventured outside, the Dobermanns crowding around him, black nostrils flared, white teeth glistening, bluish-red tongues flattened out in anticipation. Converse looked around; for the first time he saw that the small house was made of thick, solid stone. The unique squad began its constitutional up the path, Joel growing bolder as the dogs lost a degree of interest in him under the harsh admonitions of the German's commands. They began racing ahead and regrouping in circles, snapping at one another, but always whipping their huge heads back or across at their master and his prisoner. Converse walked faster.

'I used to jog a lot back home,' he lied.

'*Was ist?* Jog?"

'Run. It's good for the circulation.'

'You run now, *Mein Herr*, you will have no *Zirkulation*. The Dobermanns will see to it.'

'I've heard of people getting coronaries from jogging, too,' said Joel, slowing down, but not reducing the speed with which his eyes darted in all directions. The sun was directly overhead; it was no help in determining direction.

The dirt path was like a marked single line in an intricate network of hidden trails. It was bordered by thick foliage, more often than not roofed by low-hanging branches, then breaking open into short stretches of wild grass that might or might not lead to other paths. They reached a fork, the leg to the right curving sharply into a tunnel of greenery. The dogs instinctively raced into it, stopped by the chauffeur who shouted commands in German. The Dobermanns spun around, bouncing off each other, and returned to the fork, then raced into the wider path on the left. It was an incline and they started up a steep hill, the trees shorter and less full, the bramble bushes wilder, coarser, lower to the ground. Wind, thought Converse. A valley wind; a wind whipping up from a trough, a long narrow slice in the earth, the kind of wind a pilot of a small plane avoided at the first sign of weather. A river.

It was there. To his left; they were travelling east. The Rhine was below, perhaps a mile beyond the lower line of tall trees. He had seen enough. He began breathing audibly. The exhilaration inside him was intense; he could have walked for miles. He was back on the banks of the Huong Khe, the dark watery lifeline that would take him away from the Mekong cages and the cells and the chemicals. He had done it before; he *was* going to do it again!

'Okay, Field Marshal,' he said to Leifhelm's driver, looking at the silver whistle in the German's pocket. 'I'm not in as good shape as I thought I was. This is a mountain! Don't you have any flat pastures or grazing fields?'

'I do as I am told, *Mein Herr*,' replied the man grinning. 'Those are nearer the main *Haus*. This is where you must walk.'

'This is where I say thank you and no thank you. Take me back to my little grass shack and I'll play you a simple tune.'

'*Wie bitte?*'

'I'm bushed and I haven't finished the newspapers. Seriously, I want to thank you. I really needed the air.'

'*Serh gut*. You are a pleasant fellow.'

'You have no idea, good ole Aryan boy.'

'*Ach*, so amusing. *Der Jude ist in Israel, nicht wahr?* Better than in Germany, Mein Herr.'

'Nate Simon would love you. He'd take your case for nothing just to blow it . . . No, he wouldn't. He'd probably give you the best defence you ever had.'

Converse stood on the wooden chair under the window to the left of the door. All he had to hear and see was the sound and the sight of the dogs; after that he had twenty or thirty seconds. The taps in the bathroom were turned on, the door open; there was sufficient time to run across the room, flush the toilet, close the door and return to the chair. But he would not be standing on it. Instead, it would be gripped in his hands, literally. The sun was descending rapidly; in an hour it would be dark. Darkness had been his friend before – years ago – as the waters of a river had been his friend – years ago. They had to be his friends again. They *had* to be!

The sounds came first – racing paws and nasal explosions – then the sight of gleaming dark coats of animal fur rushing in circles in front of the jailhouse. Joel ran to the bathroom, concentrating on the instants as he waited for the sliding of the bolt. It came and he flushed the toilet, pivoting in the small space, closing the bathroom door, and racing back to the chair. He raised it and stood in place, his legs and feet locked to the floor. The door was opened several inches – only seconds now – then the German's right hand pushed it back.

'Herr Converse? *Wo ist . . . ? Ach, die Toilette.*'

The chauffeur walked in with the tray, and Joel swung the chair with all his strength into the German's head. The driver arched back off his feet, tray and dishes crashing to the floor. He was stunned, nothing more. Converse kicked the door shut and brought the heavy chair repeatedly down on the chauffeur's skull until the man went limp, blood and saliva pouring down his eyes and face.

The phalanx of dogs had lurched as one at the suddenly closed door, the roars of fury and protest and clawing, scratching feet-on-wood, the sounds of maniacal behemoths.

Joel grabbed the silver chain, slipped it over the unconscious German's head, and pulled the silver whistle out of the pocket. There were four tiny holes on the tube: each meant something. He pulled the remaining chair to the window at the right of the door, climbed up and put the whistle to his lips. He covered the first hole and blew into the mouthpiece. There was no sound but it made no difference.

The Dobermanns went mad! They began to attack the door in suicidal assaults. He removed his finger, placed it over the second hole and blew.

The dogs were confused; they circled around each other, snapping, yelping, snarling, but still they would not take their concentration off the door. He tried the third tiny hole and blew into the whistle with all the breath he had.

Suddenly, the dogs stopped all movement, their tapered, close-cropped ears upright, shifting – they were waiting for a second signal. He blew it again, again with all the breath that was in him. It was the second they were waiting for, and again, as one, the pack raced to the right beneath the window, pounding to some other place where they were meant to be by command.

Converse leaped down from the chair and knelt by the unconscious German. He went rapidly through the driver's pockets, taking his billfold and all the money he had, as well as his wristwatch . . . and his gun. For an instant Joel looked at the weapon, loathing the memories it evoked. He shoved it under his belt and went to the door.

Outside, he pulled the heavy door shut, heard the click of the lock and slid the bolt in place. He ran up the dirt path estimating the distance to the fork where the right leg was *verboten* and the left led to the steep hill and the sight of the Rhine below. It was actually no more than two hundred yards away, but the winding curves and the thick bordering foliage made it seem longer. If he remembered accurately – and on the walk back he had been like a pilot without instruments relying on sightings – there was a flat stretch of about eighty feet below the fork.

He reached it, the same flat area, the same diverging paths up ahead. He ran faster.

Voices! Angry, questioning? Not far away and coming nearer! He dived into the brush to his right, rolling over the needle-like bushes until he could barely see through the foliage. Two men walked rapidly into his limited view, talking loudly, as if arguing but somehow not with each other.

'*Was haben die Hunde?*'

'*Die sollten bei Heinrich sein!*'

Joel had no idea what they were saying; he only knew that as they passed him they were heading for the isolated cabin. He also knew that they would not spend much time trying to raise anyone inside before they took more direct methods. And once they did all the alarms in Leifhelm's fortress would be activated. Time was measured for him in minutes and he had a great deal of ground to cover. He crept cautiously out of the brush on his hands and feet. The Germans were out of sight, beyond a rounding curve. He got up and raced for the fork and the steep hill to the left.

The three guards at the immense iron gate that was the entrance to Leifhelm's estate were bewildered. The pack of Dobermanns were circling around impatiently in the rough grass, obviously confused.

'*Was haben die Hunde denn?*' asked one man.

'*Ich verstehe das nicht,*' replied a second.

'*Heinrich hat sie losgelassen, aber warum?*' said the third.

'*Das werden wir schon noch hören,*' muttered the first guard, shrugging. '*Sonst, rufen wir in ein paar Minuten an.*'

'*Mir gefällt das nicht!*' shouted the second guard. '*Ich rufe jetzt an!*'

The first guard walked into the gate house and picked up the telephone.

Converse ran up the steep hill, his breath short, his lips dry, his heartbeat thundering in his chest. There it was! He had a clear line of sight, pilotage confirmed! He could take the equipment that was his body into the huge watery airstrip below, no contact with a tower necessary. He started running down, gathering speed, the wind sweeping his face, stinging in exhilaration. He *was* back! He was racing through the sudden, open clearings of another jungle, no fellow prisoners to worry about, only the numbed outrage within himself to prod him, to make him break through the barriers and somehow, somewhere strike back at those who had stripped him naked and raped an innocence and . . . *goddamn it* . . . turned him into an animal! A reasonably pleasant human being without hatred had been turned into a half-man with more hatreds than a person should live with. He would get back at them all, all enemies, all *animals!*

He reached the bottom of the open slope of gnarled grass and bush, the trees and intertwining underbrush once more a wall to be penetrated. But he had his bearings; no matter how dense the woods he simply had to keep the last rays of the sun on his left, heading due north, and he would reach the river.

Rapid explosions made him spin around. Five gunshots followed one upon the other in the distance. It was easy to imagine the target: a circle of wood around the cylinder of a lock in the door of an isolated cabin in the forest. His jailhouse was being assaulted, entrance gained. The minutes were growing shorter.

And then two distinctly different sounds pierced the twilight, interwoven in dissonance. The first was a series of short, staccato bursts of a high-pitched siren. The second, between and under the repeated blasts, was the hysterical yelping of running dogs. The alarms had been set off; scraps of discarded clothing and slept-on sheets would be pressed into inflamed nostrils and the Dobermanns would come after him, no quarter considered – no cornered prey – only animal teeth ripping human flesh a satisfactory reward.

Converse plunged into the wall of green and ran as fast as he could, dodging, crouching, lurching from one side to the other, his arms outstretched, his hands working furiously against the strong, supple impediment of the woods. His face and body were repeatedly whipped by slashing branches and obstinate limbs, his feet continuously tripped by fallen debris and exposed roots. He stumbled more than he could count, each time – each brief instant of surrounding silence – serving only to emphasize the sound of the dogs somewhere between the fork and the hill and the lower forest. They were no farther away, perhaps nearer. They *were* nearer! They had entered the woods, the echoes of their hysteria all around him, punctuated by howling yelps of animal frustration as one or another or several were caught in the tangled ground cover, straining and roaring maniacally to be free to pursue the hated object implanted in their nostrils.

The *water!* He could see the water through the trees! Sweat was now rolling down his face, the salt blinding his eyes, stinging the scrapes on his neck and chin, his shirt drenched, his hands bleeding from the sharp briars and the coarse bark everywhere.

He fell, his foot plunging into a hole burrowed by some river bank animal, his ankle twisted and in pain.

He got up, pulling at his leg, freeing his foot, and, limping badly, tried to resume running. The Dobermanns were gaining, the yelping and the harsh barking louder and more furious; they had picked up his direct scent, the trail of undried sweat maddening them, preparing them for the kill.

The river bank! It was filled with soft mud and floating debris, a webbing of nature's garbage caught in a cavity, whirling slowly, waiting for a strong current to pull it all away. Joel grabbed the handle of the chauffeur's gun, not to pull it out but to secure it as he limped down the bank, selecting the quickest way into the water.

He heard nothing until the last instant when the massive roar came out of the shadows and the huge body of an animal flew through the air over the river bank directly at him. The monstrous face of the dog was a contorted study in fury, the eyes on fire, the enormous jaws wide, all teeth and a gaping, shining black mouth. Converse fell to his knees as the Dobermann whipped past his right shoulder, ripping his shirt with its upper eye teeth and flipping over on its back in the mud. The momentary defeat was more than the animal could stand. It writhed furiously, rolling over, snarling, then literally raising itself on its hind legs, simultaneously lunging up from the mud for Joel's groin.

The gun was in his hand. Converse fired, blowing the top of the attack dog's head off, blood and tissue spraying the shadows. The slack, huge jaws fell into his crotch.

The rest of the pack was now racing towards the bank – ear-shattering crescendos of animal violence announcing its arrival. Joel threw himself into the water and swam as rapidly as he could away from the shoreline; the weapon was an impediment but he knew he could not let it go.

Years ago – centuries ago – he had desperately needed a weapon, knowing it could be the difference between survival and death, and for five days none could be had. But on that fifth day, he had found one on the banks of the Huong Khe. He had floated half under water past a squad on patrol, and found the point ten minutes later down river – too far from the scout's unit to be logical – a man perhaps thinking angry thoughts that made him walk faster, or bored with his job and wanting to find a few moments to be by himself and out of it all. Whichever, it made no difference to that soldier. Converse had killed him with a rock from the river and had taken his gun. He had fired that gun twice, twice saved his life before he reached an advance unit south of Phu Loc.

As he pushed against the shoreline currents of the Rhine, Joel suddenly remembered. This was the fifth day of his imprisonment in Leifhelm's compound, no jungle cell to be sure, but no less imprisonment. He had done it! And on the fifth day a weapon was his! There were omens wherever one wished to find them; he did not believe in omens but for the moment he accepted the possibility.

He was in the shadows of the river now, the surrounding mountains blocking the dying sun. He paddled in place and turned. Back on shore, at the cavity in the bank that had been his plank to the water, the dogs were circling in confused anger, snarling, yelping, as several ventured down to sniff their slain leader, each urinating as it did so – territory and status were being established. The beams of powerful flashlights suddenly broke through the trees. Converse swam farther out; he had survived searchlights in the Mekong. He had no fear of them now; he had been there – here – and he knew when he had won.

He let the outer currents carry him east along the river. Somewhere there would be other lights, lights that would lead him to shelter and a telephone. He had to get everything in place and build his brief quickly but he could do it. Yet the attorney in him told him that a man with a bandaged gunshot wound in soaked clothing and screaming a foreign language in the streets was no match for the disciples of George Marcus Delavane; they would find him. So it would have to be done another way – with whatever artifices he could muster. He had to get to a telephone. He had to place an overseas call. He could do it; he would do it! The Huong Khe faded; the Rhine was now his lifeline.

Swimming breaststroke, the gun still gripped in his hand, his arm smarting in the water, he saw the lights of a village in the distance.

18

Valerie frowned as she listened on the phone in her studio, the spiralling cord outstretched as she reached over and placed a brush in the track of her easel. Her eyes scanned the sunlit dunes outside the glass doors, her thoughts, however, were on the words she was hearing, words that implied things without saying them. 'Larry, what's *wrong* with you?' she interrupted, unable to hold herself in check any longer. 'Joel's not just an employee or a junior partner, he's your friend! You sound like you're trying to build a case against him. What's that term you all use? . . . . Circumstantial, that's it. He was here, he was there; someone said this and somebody else said that.'

'I'm trying to *understand*, Val,' protested Talbot from his office in New York. 'You've got to try to understand, too. There's a great deal I can't tell you because I've been instructed by people whose offices I have to respect to say very little or preferably nothing at all. I'm bending those instructions because Joel *is* my friend and I want to help.'

'All right, let's go back,' said Valerie. 'What exactly were you leading up to?'

'I know it's none of my damned business and I wouldn't ask it if I didn't think I had to . . .'

'I'll accept that,' agreed Val. 'Now what is it?'

'Well, I know you and Joel had your problems,' continued the senior partner of Talbot, Brooks and Simon, as though he were referring to an inconsequential spat between children. 'But there are problems and there are problems.'

'Larry,' interrupted Val again. 'There were problems. We're divorced. That means the problems were serious.'

'Was physical abuse one of them?' asked Talbot quickly in a low voice, the words obviously repugnant to him.

Valerie was stunned; it was a question she would never have considered. '*What?*'

'You know what I mean. In fits of anger did he strike you? Cause you bodily harm?'

'You're not in a courtroom, and the answer is no, of course not. I might have welcomed it – at least the anger.'

'I beg your pardon?'

'Nothing,' said Valerie, recovering from her astonishment. 'I don't know what prompted you to ask, but it couldn't be farther from the truth. Joel had far more effective ways to deflate my ego than hitting me. Among them, dear Larry, was his dedication to the career of one Joel Converse in Talbot, Brooks and Simon.'

'I'm aware of that, my dear, and I'm sorry. Those complaints are perennial in the divorce courts and I'm not sure there's anything we can do about them – not in this day and age, perhaps not ever. But that's different. I'm talking about his black moods – we knew he had them.'

'Do you know any rational person who doesn't?' asked the former Mrs Converse. 'This isn't really the best of all possible worlds, is it?'

'No, it isn't. But then Joel lived through a period of time in a far worse world than most of us will ever know or could imagine. I can't believe he emerged from it without a scar or two.'

Valerie paused, touched by the older man's unadorned directness; it did have its basis in concern. 'You're sweet, Larry, and I suspect you're right – in fact I know it. So I think you should tell me more than you have. The term "physical abuse" is what you lawyers call a leading something-or-other. It's not fair because it could also be misleading. Come on, Larry, be fair. He's not my husband any more, but we didn't break apart because he chased girls or bashed my head in. I may not want to be married to him but I respect him. He's got his problems and I've got mine, and now you're implying his are a lot bigger. What's happened?'

Talbot was silent for a moment, then blurted out the words again quickly, quietly; once more they were obviously repugnant to him. 'They say he assaulted a man in Paris without provocation. The man died.'

'*No*, that's impossible! He didn't, he *couldn't*!'

'That's what he told me, but he lied. He told me he was in Amsterdam, but he wasn't. He said he was going back to Paris to clear things up but he didn't. He was in Germany – he's *still* somewhere in Germany. He hasn't left the country and Interpol has a warrant for him; they're searching everywhere. Word reached him to turn himself into the Amsterdam Embassy but he refused. He's disappeared.'

'Oh, my *God*, you're all so *wrong!*' exploded Valerie. 'You don't *know* him! If what you say happened, he was attacked first – *physically* attacked – and had no choice but to hit back!'

'Not according to an impartial witness who didn't know either man.'

'Than he's not impartial, he's lying! . . . Listen to me. I lived with that man for four years and, except for a few trips, all of them here in New York City. I've seen him accosted by drunks and street garbage – punks he could have pushed through the pavements, and perhaps some of them he should have – but I never saw him so much as take a step forward. He'd simply raise the palms of his hands and walk away . . . A few times some damn fools would call him names and he'd just stand there and look at them. And let me tell you, Larry, that look was enough to make you feel cold all over. But that's all he'd do, never anything more.'

'Val, I want to believe you. I want to believe it was self-defence, but he ran away, he's disappeared. The embassy can help him, protect him, but he won't come in.'

'Then he's frightened. That *can* happen, but it was always for only a few minutes, usually at night when he'd wake up. He'd bolt up, his eyes shut so tight his whole face was a mass of wrinkles. It never lasted long and he said it was perfectly natural and not to worry about it – he didn't, he said. And I don't think he really did; he wanted all that in the past, none of it was ever mentioned.'

'Perhaps it should have been,' said Talbot softly.

Valerie replied with equal softness. '*Touché*, Larry. Don't think I haven't thought about that these last couple of years. But whatever's happened he's acting this way only because he's afraid – or you know its quite possible he's been hurt. Or, oh my *God* . . .'

'All the hospitals and registered doctors have been checked,' broke in Talbot.

'Well, damn it, there's got to be a *reason!* This isn't like him and you know it!'

'That's just it, Val. Nothing he's done is like the man I know.'

The ex-Mrs Converse stiffened. 'To use one of Joel's favourite expressions,' she said apprehensively. 'Clarification, please?'

'Why not?' answered Talbot, the question was directed as much at himself as her. 'Perhaps you can shed some light, nobody else can.'

'What about this man in Paris, the one who died?'

'There's not much to tell; apparently he was a chauffeur for one of those limousine services. According to the witness, a basement guard in the hotel, Joel approached him, yelled something at him and pushed him out the door. There were sounds of a scuffle and a few minutes later the man was found severely beaten in an alley.'

'It's *ridiculous!* What did Joel say?'

'That he walked out the door, saw two men fighting and ran to tell the doorman on the way to his taxi.'

'That's what he'd have done,' said Val firmly.

'The doorman at the George V says it didn't happen. The police say follicles of hair found on the beaten man matched those in Joel's shower.'

'Utterly unbelievable!'

'Let's say there was provocation we don't know about,' went on Talbot rapidly. 'It doesn't explain what happened later, but before I tell you I want to ask you another question. You'll understand.'

'I don't understand a single thing! What is it?'

'During those periods of depression, his dark moods, did Joel ever fantasize? I mean did he indulge in what psychiatrists call role-playing?'

'You mean did he assume other personalities, other kinds of behaviour?'

'Exactly.'

'Absolutely not.'

'Oh.'

'Oh what? Let's have it, Larry.'

'Talking about what's believable and what isn't, you're in for a jolt, my dear. According to those people who don't want me to say very much – and you'll have to take my word they know – Joel flew into Germany claiming he was involved in an undercover investigation of the embassy in Bonn.'

'Perhaps he was! He was on a leave of absence from T, B and S, wasn't he?'

'On an unrelated matter in the private sector, that much we know. There *is* no investigation – undercover or otherwise – of the embassy in Bonn. Frankly, the people who reached me were from the State Department.'

'Oh, my *God* . . .' Valerie fell silent, but before the lawyer could speak, she whispered. '*Geneva*. That horrible business in Geneva!'

'If there's a connection – and both Nathan and I considered it first – it's so buried it can't be followed.'

'It's there. It's where it all started.'

'Assuming your husband's rational.'

'He's not my husband and he *is* rational!'

'The scars, Val. There had to be scars. You agreed with me.'

'Not the kind you're talking about. Not killing, and lying and running away! That's *not* Joel! That isn't – *wasn't* – my husband!'

'The mind is a highly complex and delicate instrument. The stresses of the past can leap forward from years ago . . .'

'Get off it, Larry!' shouted Valerie. 'Save it for a jury, but don't pin that nonsense on Converse!'

'You're upset.'

'You're damned right I am. Because you're looking for explanations that don't fit the man! They fit what you've been *told*. By those people you say you have to respect.'

'Only in the sense that they're knowledgeable – they have access to information we don't have. Then there's the overriding fact that they hadn't the faintest idea who Joel Converse was until the American Bar Association gave them the address and telephone number of Talbot, Brooks and Simon.'

'And you *believed* them? With everything you know about Washington you simply accepted their word? How many times did Joel come back from a trip to Washington and say the same thing to me? "Larry says they're lying. They don't know what to do so they're lying."'

'Valerie,' said the attorney sternly. 'This wasn't a case of bureaucratic clearance, and after all these years I think I can tell the difference between someone playing games and a man who's genuinely angry – angry and frightened, I should add. The man who reached me was an Undersecretary of State, Brewster Tolland – I had a call-back confirmation – and he wasn't putting on an act. He was appalled, furious, and, as I say, a very worried man.'

'What did you tell him?'

'The truth, of course. Not only because it was the right thing to do, but it wouldn't help Joel to do anything else. If he's ill he needs help, not complicity.'

'And you deal with Washington every week.'

'Several times a week, and of course it was a consideration.'

'I'm sorry, Larry, that was unfair.'

'But realistic, and I meant what I said. It wouldn't help Joel to lie for him. You see, I really believe something's happened. He's not himself.'

'Wait a minute,' cried Valerie, the obvious striking her. 'Maybe it's *not* Joel!'

'It's him,' said Talbot simply.

'Why? Just because people you don't know in Washington say it is?'

'No, Val,' replied the lawyer. 'Because I spoke with René in Paris before Washington entered the picture.'

'*Mattilon?*'

'Joel went to Paris to ask for René's help. He lied to him just as he lied to me, but it was more than the lies – Mattilon and I agreed on that. It was something he saw in Joel's eyes, something I heard in his voice. An unhinging, a form of desperation; René saw it and I heard it. He tried to conceal it from both of us but he couldn't . . . When I last spoke to him, he hung up before we'd finished talking, in the middle of the sentence, his voice echoing like a zombie's.'

Valerie stared at the harsh, dancing reflections of sunlight off the waters of Cape Ann. 'René agreed with you?' she asked, barely above a whisper.

'Everything I've just told you we said to each other.'

'Larry, I'm frightened.'

Chaim Abrahms walked into the room, his heavy boots pounding the floor. 'So he did it!' shouted the Israeli. 'The Mossad was right, he's a hellhound!'

Erich Leifhelm sat behind his desk, the only other person in the book-lined study. 'Patrols, alarms, *dogs!*' cried the German slamming his frail hand on the red blotter. 'How did he *do* it?'

'I repeat – a hellhound – that's what our specialist called him. The longer he's restricted, the angrier he gets. It goes back a long time. So our *provocateur* starts his odyssey before we planned. Have you been in touch with the others?'

'I've called London,' said Leifhelm, breathing deeply. 'He'll reach Paris and Bertholdier will have the units flown up from Marseilles, one to Brussels, the other here to Bonn. We can't waste an hour.'

'You're looking for him now, of course.'

'*Natürlich!* Every inch of the shoreline for miles in both directions. Every back road and path that leads up from the river and into the city.'

'He can elude you, he's proved it.'

'Where can he go, Sabra? To his own embassy? There he's a dead man. To the Bonn police or the *Staats Polizei?* He'll be put in an armoured van and brought back here. He goes nowhere.'

'I heard that when he left Paris and I heard it again when he flew into Bonn. Errors were made in both places, both costing a great *many* hours. I tell you I'm more concerned now than at any moment in three wars and a lifetime of skirmishes.'

'Be reasonable, Chaim, and try to be calm. He has no clothes but what he wears in the river and the mud; he possesses no identification, no passport, no money. He doesn't speak the language . . .'

'He *has* money!' yelled Abrahms, suddenly remembering. 'When he was under the needle he spoke of a large sum of money promised in Geneva and delivered on Mykonos.'

'And where is it?' asked Leifhelm. 'In this desk, *that's* where it is. Nearly seventy thousand American dollars. He hasn't got a Deutschmark in his pocket, or a watch or a piece of jewellery. A man in filthy, soaked clothing, with no identification, no money, no coherent use of the language, and telling an outlandish tale of imprisonment involving The General Leifhelm, would undoubtedly be put in jail as a vagrant or a psychopath or both. In which case, we shall be informed instantly and our people will bring him to us. And bear in mind, Sabra, by ten o'clock tomorrow morning it won't make any difference. That was *your* contribution, the Mossad's ingenuity. We simply had the resources to make it come to pass . . . as is said in the Old Testament.'

Abrahms stood in front of the enormous desk, arms akimbo above the pockets of his safari jacket. 'So the Jew and the Field Marshal set it all in motion. Ironical, isn't, Nazi?'

'Not as much as you think, *überlegener Jude*. Impurity (as with beauty) is in the eye of the frightened beholder. You are not my enemy, you never were. If more of us in the old days had your commitment, your audacity, we never would have lost the war.'

'I know that,' said the Sabra. 'I watched and listened when you reached the English Channel. You lost it then. You were weak.'

'It was not *us!* It was the frightened *Debutant* in Berlin!'

'Then keep them away when we create a *truly* new order, German. We can't afford weakness.'

'You do try me, Chaim.'

'I mean to.'

The chauffeur felt the bandages on his face, the swelling around his eyes and his lips painful to the touch. He was in his own room, the doctor having put on the television – probably as an insult as he could barely see it.

He was disgraced. The prisoner had escaped in spite of his own formidable talents and the supposedly impassable pack of Dobermanns. The American had used the silver whistle, that much the other guards had told him, and the fact that it had been removed from his neck was a further embarrassment.

He would not add to his disgrace. With blurred vision he had gone through his pockets – which no one in the panic of the chase had thought to do – and found that his billfold, his expensive Swiss watch and all his money had been taken. He would say nothing about them. He was embarrassed enough and any such revelations might be cause for dismissal, conceivably his death.

Joel headed for the shoreline as fast as he could, submerging his head underwater whenever the beam of the searchlight swept towards him. The boat was a large motor launch, its bass-toned engines signifying power, its sudden turns and circles evidence of rapid manoeuvrability. It hugged the overgrown banks then would sweep out towards the open water at the slightest object in the river.

Converse felt the soft mud below; he half swam, half trudged towards the darkest spot on the shore, the chauffeur's gun securely in his belt. The boat approached, its penetrating beam studying every foot, every moving branch or limb or cluster of river weeds. Joel took a deep breath and slowly lowered himself beneath the water, his face angled up towards the surface, his eyes open, his vision a muddy dark blur. The searchlight grew brighter and seemed to hover above him for an eternity; he inched his way to the left and the beam moved away. He rose to the surface, his lungs bursting, but suddenly realized he could make no sound; he could not fill his chest with gasps of air. For directly above him, less than five feet away loomed the broad stern of the motor launch, bobbing in the water as if idling. The dark figure of a man was peering through very large binoculars at the river bank.

Converse was bewildered; it was too dark now to see anything even with magnification. Then he remembered and the memory accounted for the size of the binoculars. The man was focusing through infra-red lenses; they had been used by patrols in Southeast Asia and often made the difference, he had been told, between search-and-destroy, and search-and-be-destroyed. They revealed objects in the darkness, soldiers in the darkness.

The boat moved forward, but the idle increased only slightly, entering the slowest of trawling speeds. Again Joel was confused. What had brought Leifhelm's searching party to this particular spot on the river front? There were several other boats behind and out in the distance, their searchlights sweeping the water, but they kept moving, circling. Why did the huge motor launch concentrate on this stretch of the shore? Could they have spotted him through infra-red binoculars? If they had, they were proceeding very strangely; the North Vietnamese had been far swifter – more aggressive, more effective.

Silently, Converse lowered himself beneath the surface and breast-stroked out beyond the boat. Seconds later he raised his head above the water, his vision clear, and he began to understand the odd manoeuvrings of Leifhelm's patrol. Beyond the darkest part of the river bank into which he had lurched for concealment were the lights he had seen eight or nine minutes ago, before the launch and its searchlight monopolized his attention. He had thought they were the lights of a small village but he was in the wrong part of the world. Instead they were the inside lights of four or five small houses, a river colony with a common dock, summer homes perhaps of those fortunate enough to own waterfront property.

If there were houses and a dock, there had to be a drive – an open passage up to the road or roads leading into Bonn and the surrounding towns. Leifhelm's men were combing every inch of the riverbank, cautiously, quietly, the searchlights angled down so as not to alarm the inhabitants or forewarn the fugitive in case he had reached the cluster of cottages and was on his way up to the unseen road or roads. A ship's radio would be activated, its frequency aligned to those in cars roaming above, ready to spring the trap. In ways it was the Huong Khe again for Joel, the obstacles far less primitive, but no less lethal. And then as now there was a time to wait, wait in the black silence and let the hunters make their moves.

They made them quickly. The launch slid into the dock, the powerful twin screws quietly churning in reverse, as a man jumped off the bow with a heavy line and looped it around a pile. Three others followed, instantly racing off the short pier up onto the sloping lawn, one heading diagonally to the right, the other two towards the first house. What they were doing was obvious: one man would position himself in the bordering woods of the downhill entrance drive while his colleagues checked the houses, looking for signs of entry – nervousness, eyes filled with fear, mud on the floors.

Converse's arms and legs began to feel like weights, each an anvil he could barely support much less keep moving, but there was no choice. The beam of the searchlight kept moving up and down the base of the riverbank, its spill illuminating everything in its vicinity. A head surfacing at the wrong moment would be blown out of the water. *Huong Khe. Tread water in the reeds. Do it! Don't die!*

He knew the waiting was no longer than thirty minutes, but it seemed more like thirty hours or thirty days suspended in a floating torture rack. His arms and legs were now in agony; sharp pains shot through his body everywhere; muscles formed cramps that he dispersed by holding his breath and floating in a foetal position, his thumbs pressing relentlessly into the core of the knotted muscles. Twice, gasping for air, he swallowed water, coughing it out below the surface, his nostrils drowning, and twice finding the air silently again. There were moments when it crossed his inner consciousness that it would be so simple to drift away. *Huong Khe. Don't do it! Don't die!*

Finally through water-logged eyes he saw the men returning. One, two . . . three? . . . they ran down to the dock, to the man with the rope. *No!* The man with the rope had rushed forward! His eyes were playing blurred tricks! Only two men had run onto the dock, the first man joining them, asking questions. The line man returned to the pile and released the rope; the other two jumped on board. The first man once again joined his companions, now on the bow of the launch – leaving another on shore, a lone observer somewhere unseen between the riverbank and the road above. *Huong Khe. An infantry scout separated from his patrol.*

The motor launch swung away from the dock and sped within feet past Joel, who was buffeted under water by its wake. Once more the boat veered towards the shoreline and slowed down, its searchlight peering into the dense foliage of the bank, heading west, back towards Leifhelm's estate. Converse held his head above the surface, his mouth wide open swallowing all the air he could as he made his way slowly – very slowly – into the mud. He pulled himself up through the wet reeds and branches until he felt dry ground. *Huong Khe.* He pulled the undergrowth over him as best he could, finally covering his upturned face. He would rest until he felt the blood flowing steadily if painfully through his limbs; until the muscles of his neck lost their tension – it was always the neck; the neck was the warning signal – and then he would consider the man on the dark hill above him.

He dozed, a slapping wave below stirring him. He pushed the branches and the leaves away from his face and looked at the chauffeur's watch on his wrist, squinting at the weak radium dial. He had slept for nearly an hour – fitfully to be sure, the slightest sounds forcing his eyelids briefly open, but he had rested. He rolled his neck back and forth, then moved his arms and his legs. Everything still hurt but the excruciating pain was gone. And now he faced a man on a hill above him. He tried to examine his thoughts. He was frightened, of course, but his anger – his outrage – would control that terrible fear; it had done so before, it would do so now. The objective was all that mattered – some kind of sanctuary, a place where he could think and put things together and somehow make the most important telephone call in his life. To Larry Talbot and Nathan Simon in New York. Unless he could do these things he was dead . . . as Connal Fitzpatrick was undoubtedly dead. *Jesus!* What had they *done* to him? A man with the purity of vengeance purely sought caught in a diseased web called Aquitaine! It was a very unfair world . . . He could not think about it; he had a man on the hill to think about.

He crept on his hands and knees. Stretch by stretch he crawled through the woods bordering the dirt road that wound up the hill from the lawn and the riverbank. Whenever a twig crunched or a rock was displaced he stopped, waiting for the moment to dissolve back into the sounds of the forest. He kept telling himself he had the advantage; he was the unexpected. It helped counteract the fear of the darkness and the knowledge that a physical confrontation was before him. Like the patrol scout years ago in the Huong Khe, that man above him now had things he needed. The combat could not be avoided, so it was best not to think about it, simply force his mind into a time-set without feelings, and do it. But do it completely, his mind had to understand that, too. There could be no hesitation, no intrusions of conscience – and no sound of a gun, only the use of the steel.

He saw him, oddly enough silhouetted in the distant glare of a single street lamp far above on a road. The man was standing – leaning actually – against the trunk of a tree facing down, his sweep of vision taking in everything below. The stretches between Joel's hands and knees became inches, the stops more frequent, silence more vital. Slowly he made his way in an arc above the tree and the man and started down, a large cat descending on its prey, his mind in a time-set, no feeling, only the instinct for survival. He was the predator he had once been long ago, everything blocked out but the requirement of the lifeline.

He was within six feet; he could hear the man's breathing. There was a snap beneath him! A branch! The scout turned, his eyes alive in the dim glare of light. Converse lunged, the barrel of the gun gripped in his hand. He crashed the steel handle into the German's temple, withdrew his arms and smashed it up into the scout's throat. The man fell backward, dazed but not unconscious; he started to scream. Joel sprang, the fingers of his left hand spread, surging for his enemy's neck, the weapon aimed accurately, the handle impacting directly into the German's forehead, blood and red tissue erupting.

Silence. No movement. Another scout separated from his patrol had been taken out. And, as he had years ago, Converse permitted himself no feeling. It was done and he had to go on.

The man's dry clothes fitted reasonably well including the dark leather jacket. Like most small or medium-sized commanders, Leifhelm surrounded himself with tall men, as much for protection as to proclaim his superiority over his large compatriots. There was also another gun; Joel struggled with the clip, removed it, and threw it along with the weapon into the woods. The bonus came with the German's billfold; it contained a sizeable sum of money as well as a frayed, much-stamped passport. Apparently, this trusted employee of Leifhelm travelled widely for Aquitaine – probably knowing nothing and very expendable – but always available at the moment of decision. The man's shoes did not fit; they were too small. So Converse used his drenched clothing to wipe his own, the German's dry socks absorbing some of the soft, wet moisture of the leather. He covered the man with branches and walked up the hill to the road.

He stayed out of sight between the trees as five cars passed by, all sedans, all possibly belonging to Erich Leifhelm. Then he saw a bright yellow Volkswagen come into view, weaving slightly. He stepped out and held up his hands, the gesture of a man in trouble.

The small car stopped, a blonde girl in the passenger seat, the driver no more than eighteen or twenty, another young man in the back, also blond; he looked as though he might be the girl's brother.

'*Was ist los, Opa?*' asked the driver.

'I'm afraid I don't speak German. Can you speak any English?'

'I speak some English,' said the boy in the back, slurring his words. 'Better than these two! All they want to do is get to our place and make love. See! I do speak English?'

'You certainly do, and very well, indeed. Would you explain to them, please? Frankly, I've had a fight with my wife at a party down there – you know, at those cottages – and I want to get back to Bonn. I'll pay you, of course.'

'*Ein Streit mit seiner Frau! Er will nach Bonn gehen. Er wird uns bezahlen.*'

'*Warum nicht? Sie hat mich heute sowieso schon zuviel gekostet,*' said the driver.

'*Nicht für was du kriegst, du Drecksack!*' cried the girl, laughing.

'Get in, *Mein Herr!* We are your chauffeurs. Just pray he stays on the road, *ja!* What hotel are you staying at?'

'Actually, I'd rather not go back there. I'm really very angry. I'd like to teach her a lesson by staying away tonight. Do you think you could find me a room? I'll pay you even more, of course. Frankly, I've been drinking a bit myself.'

'*Ein betrunkener Tourist. Er will ein Hotel. Fahren wir ihn ins Rosencafé?*'

'*Dort sind mehr Nutten als der alte Knacker schafft.*'

'We are your guides, *Amerikaner,*' said the young man beside Converse. 'We are students from the university who will not only find you a room, but with excellent prospects of getting back at your wife with some pleasure! There's also a café. You'll buy us a lager or six, *ja?*'

'All you want. But I'd also like to make a telephone call. To the United States – it's business. Will I be able to?'

'Most everyone in Bonn speaks English, *Mein Herr*. If they don't at this *Rosencafé*, I, myself, will take care of it. Six lagers, though, remember that!'

'Twelve, if you like.'

'*Da wird es im Pissoir eine Überschwemmung geben!*'

He knew the rate of exchange and once inside the raucous café – actually a run-down bar favoured by the university crowd – he counted the money he had taken from the two Germans. It was roughly five hundred dollars, over three from the man on the hill. The seedy clerk at the registration desk explained in convoluted English that, indeed, the switchboard could place a call to America, but it might take several minutes. Joel left fifty dollars in Deutschmarks for his youthful Good Samaritans and excused himself, heading up to his room – such as it was. An hour later the call came through.

'Larry?'

'Joel?'

'Thank *God* you're there!' cried Converse in relief. 'You'll never know how I kept hoping you weren't out of town. Getting a call through from here is a bitch.'

'I'm here,' said Talbot, his voice suddenly calm and in control. 'Where are *you* Joel?' he asked quietly.

'Some poor excuse for a hotel in Bonn. I just got here. I didn't get the name.'

'You're in a hotel in Bonn but you don't know which one?'

'It doesn't matter, Larry! Get Simon on the line. I want to talk to you both. Quickly.'

'Nathan's in court. He should be back here by four o'clock – our time. That's about an hour from now.'

'*Goddamn* it!'

'Take it easy, Joel. Don't upset yourself.'

'Don't *upset* . . .? For Christ's sake. I've been locked up in a stone cabin with bars in the windows for five days! I broke out a couple of hours ago, and ran like hell through the woods with a pack of dogs and lunatics carrying guns chasing me. I spent an hour in the water damn near drowning before I could reach land without getting my head shot off, and then I had to – I had to . . .'

'You had to what, Joel?' asked Talbot, a strange passivity in his voice. 'What did you have to do?'

'Goddamn it, Larry. I may have *killed* a man to get out of there!'

'You had to kill someone, Joel? Why did you think you had to do that?'

'He was waiting for me! They were searching for me! On the land, in the woods along the river banks – he was a scout separated from his patrol. *Scouts, patrols!* I had to get out, get *away!* And you tell me not to be upset!'

'Calm down, Joel, try to get hold of yourself . . . You escaped before, didn't you? A long time ago . . .'

'What's that got to do with anything?' broke in Converse.

'You had to kill people then, didn't you? Those memories must always be with you.'

'Larry, that's bullshit! Listen to me and take down everything I say – the names I give you, the facts – get it all down.'

'Perhaps I should bring Janet on the line. Her shorthand . . .'

'No! Only you, no one else! They can trace people, anyone who knows anything. It's not that complicated. Are you ready?'

'Of course.'

Joel sat down on the narrow bed and took a deep breath. 'The best way to put it – as it was put to me, but you don't have to write this down, just understand – is that they've come back.'

'Who?'

'The generals . . . field marshals, admirals, colonels . . . allies and enemies, all field commanders and above. They've come together from everywhere to change things, change governments and laws and foreign policies, everything to be based on military priorities and decisions . . . It's crazy, but they could do it. We'd live out their fantasies because they'd be in control, believing they're right and selfless and dedicated – as they've always believed.'

'Who are these people, Joel?'

'Yes, write this down. The organization is called Aquitaine. It's based on an historical theory that the region in France once known as Aquitaine might have become all of Europe and by extension – as colonies – the North American continent as well.'

'Whose theory?'

'It doesn't *matter*, it's just a theory. The organization was conceived by General George Delavane – he was known as "Mad Marcus" in Vietnam – and I saw only a fraction of the damage that son of a bitch did! He's pulled in military personnel from all over the place, all commanders, and they're fanning out recruiting their own kind, fanatics who believe as they do, that theirs is the only way. For the past year or so, they've been shipping illegal weapons and armaments to terrorist groups, encouraging destabilization wherever they can, the ultimate purpose being that they'll be called in to restore order, and when they do, they'll take over . . . Five days ago I met with Delavane's key men from France and Germany, Israel and South Africa – and I think possibly England.'

'You met with these people, Joel? Did they invite you to a meeting?'

'They thought I was one of them, that I believed in everything they stood for. You see, Larry, they didn't know how much I hated them. They hadn't been where I'd been, hadn't seen what I saw . . . as you said, years ago.'

'When you *had* to escape,' added Talbot sympathetically. 'When you had to kill people – times you'll never forget. They must have been terrible for you.'

'Yes, they were. Goddamn it, *yes!* Sorry, let's stay on course. I'm so tired – still frightened, too, I think.'

'Relax, Joel.'

'Sure. Where was I?' Converse rubbed his eyes. 'Oh, yes, I remember. They got information on me, information from my service record, my status as a POW, which wasn't actually part of the record but they got it and they found out what and who I was. They heard the words that told them how much I hated them, hated what Delavane had done, what they all had done. They drugged me, got whatever they could and threw me into a godforsaken stone house set in the middle of the woods above the Rhine. While under the chemicals I must have told them everything I knew . . .'

'Chemicals?' asked Talbot, obviously never having heard the term.

'Amatols, Pentothals, scopolamine. I've been the route, Larry. I've been there and back.'

'You *have?* Where?'

'In the camps. It's immaterial.'

'I'm not sure it is.'

'It is. The point is they found out what I know. That means they'll move up their schedule.'

'Schedule?'

'We're in the countdown. *Now!* Two weeks, three weeks, four at the outside! No one knows how or where or what the targets are but there'll be eruptions of violence and terrorism all over the place, giving them the excuse to move in and take over. "Accumulation" . . . "rapid acceleration", those were the words they used! Right now in Northern Ireland – everything's blown apart, nothing but chaos – whole armoured divisions are moving in. *They* did it, Larry! It's a test, a trial run for them! . . . I'm going to give you the names.' Converse did so, both surprised and annoyed that Talbot produced no reaction to any of the men of Aquitaine. 'Have you got them?'

'Yes, I have.'

'Those are the salient facts and the names I can vouch for. There's a lot more – people in the State Department and the Pentagon, but the lists are in my briefcase and it's been stolen, or hidden somewhere. I'll get some rest and start writing out everything I know then call you in the morning. I have to get out of here. I'm going to need help.'

'I agree, so may I talk now,' said the lawyer in New York in that odd flat voice. 'First, where are you, Joel? Look on the phone or read the print on an ashtray – or check the desk; there must be stationery.'

'There's no desk and the ashtrays are chipped glass . . . Wait a minute, I picked up some matches from the bar when I bought cigarettes.' Converse reached into the pocket of the leather jacket and pulled out the book of matches. 'Here it is. "*Riesendrinks*".'

'Look below that. My German is limited but I think it means "big drinks" or something.'

'Oh? Then its must be this. *Rosencafé*.'

'That sounds more like it. Spell it for me, Joel.'

Converse did, an undefined feeling disturbing him. 'Have you got it?' he asked. 'Here's a telephone number.' Joel read off the numbers printed on the cover.

'Good, that's splendid,' said Talbot. 'But before you get off the line – and I know you need rest badly – I have a couple of questions.'

'I would hope to hell you do!'

'When we spoke after that man was hurt in Paris, after that fight you saw in the alley, you told me you were in Amsterdam. You said you were going to fly back to Paris and see René, straighten everything out. Why didn't you, Joel?'

'For God's sake, Larry, I just told you what I've been through! It took every minute I had to set things up. I was going after these people – this goddamned Aquitaine – and it could only be done one way. I had to work myself in, I couldn't waste time!'

'That man died. Did you have anything to do with his death?'

'Christ, yes, I killed him! He tried to stop me, they all tried to stop me! They found me in Copenhagen and had me followed. They were waiting for me at the airport here. It was a trap!'

'To stop you from reaching these men, these generals and field marshals?'

'Yes!'

'Yet you just told me these same men invited you to meet with them.'

'I'll spell it all out for you in the morning,' said Converse wearily, the tension of the last hours – days really – culminating in exhaustion and a racking headache. 'By then I'll have everything down on paper, but you may have to come over here to get it – and me. The main thing is we're in

touch. You've got the names, the overview, and you know where I am. Talk
with Nathan, think about everything I've said and the three of us will figure
out what to do. We have contacts in Washington, but we'll have to be
careful. We don't know who's with whom. But there's a plus here. Some of
the material I have – I *had* – could only have come from people down there.
One view is that I was set in motion by them, that men I don't know are
watching every move I make because I'm doing what they can't do.'

'By yourself,' said Talbot, agreeing. 'Without Washington's help. Without
their help.'

'That's right. They can't show themselves; they have to stay in the
background until I bring out something concrete . . . That was the plan.
When you and Nathan talk, if you have questions call me. I'm just going to
lie down for an hour or so anyway.'

'I've got another question now, if you don't mind. You know Interpol has
an international warrant for you.'

'I do.'

'And the American Embassy is looking for you.'

'I know that, too.'

'I was told that word reached you to come into the embassy.'

'*You* were told . . .?'

'Why haven't you done it, Joel?'

'Jesus, I *can't!* Don't you think I would if I could? The place is crawling
with Delavane's people. Well, that's an exaggeration, but I know of three. I
saw them.'

'It's my understanding that Ambassador Peregrine himself got word to
you, guaranteeing you protection, confidentiality. Wasn't that enough?'

'Your *understanding* . . . The answer is *no!* Peregrine hasn't any idea what
he's got inside that place . . . Or maybe he does. I saw Leifhelm's car go
through those gates like he had a lifetime pass. At three o'clock in the
morning. Leifhelm's a Nazi, Larry, he's never been anything else! So what
does that make Peregrine?'

'Come on, Joel. You're maligning a man by implication who doesn't
deserve it. Walter Peregrine was one of the heroes of Bastogne. His command
at the Battle of the Bulge is a legend of the war. And he was a reserve officer,
not part of the regular army. I doubt that Nazis are his favourite guests.'

'His command? Another *commander?* Then maybe he knows *exactly* what
he's got in that embassy!'

'That's not fair. His outspoken criticisms of the Pentagon are a documented part of his post-war career. He's called them megalomaniacs with
too damn much money feeding their egos at the taxpayers' expense. No,
you're not being fair, Joel. I think you should listen to him. Call him on the
phone, talk to him.'

'Not being fair?' said Converse softly, the undefined feeling coming into
focus, now a warning. 'Wait a minute! You're the one who's not being fair.
"*I* was told" . . . "It's *my* understanding?" What oracle have you been in
touch with? Who's imparting these pearls of wisdom about me? On what
basis and where from?'

'All right, Joel, all right . . . calm down. Yes, I have talked to people –
people who want to help you. A man is dead in Paris, and now you say

there's another in Bonn. You talk of scouts and patrols and those horrible chemicals, and how you ran through the woods and had to hide in the river. Don't you understand, son? Nobody's blaming you or even holding you responsible. Something happened; you're living it all over again.'

'My God!' broke in Converse, stunned. 'You don't believe a word I've *said!*'

'You believe it and that's all that matters. I saw my share in North Africa and Italy, but nothing to compare with what you went through later. You have a deep, understandable hatred for war and all things military. You wouldn't be human if you didn't, not with the suffering you experienced and the terrible things you endured.'

'Larry, everything I've told you is *true!*'

'Fine, splendid. Then reach Peregrine, go to the embassy and tell them. They'll listen to you. *He'll* listen.'

'Are you denser than I think?' shouted Joel. 'I just told you, I can't! I'd never get to *see* Peregrine! I'd get my head blown away!'

'I spoke to your wife – sorry, your ex-wife. She said you'd have these moments at night . . .'

'You spoke to *Val?* You brought *her* into this! Christ, are you out of your mind! Don't you know they trace everyone *down?* It was right under your nose, counsellor! *Lucas Anstett!* Stay away from her! Stay away or I'll . . . I'll . . .'

'You'll what, son?' asked Talbot quietly. 'Kill me, too?'

'Oh, *Jesus!*'

'Do as I say, Joel. Call Peregrine. Everything will be all right.'

Suddenly Converse heard an odd sound over the line, odd in context but one he had heard hundreds of times before. It was a short buzz, barely significant but there was significance to it. It was Lawrence Talbot's courteous signal to his secretary to come into his office and pick up a revised letter or a corrected brief or a dictation tape. Joel knew what it was now. The address of a seedy hotel in Bonn.

'All right, Larry,' he said, feigning an exhaustion that was all too real. 'I'm so *damned* tired. Let me lie down for a while and maybe I will call the embassy. Maybe I should get in touch with Peregrine. Everything's so confused.'

'That's the way, son. Everything's going to be fine now. Just splendid.'

'Goodbye, Larry.'

'Goodbye for now, Joel. See you in a couple of days.'

Converse slammed down the phone and looked around the dimly-lit room. What was he checking for? He had come with nothing and he would leave with nothing but what was on his back – what he had stolen. And he had to leave quickly. He had to run. In minutes men would be speeding in cars from the embassy, and at least one of those men would have a gun and a bullet meant for him!

What in hell was *happening* to him? The truth was a fantasy bolstered by lies and the lies were his only means of survival. *Insanity!*

19

He ran past the elevator to the staircase, descending the steps two and three at a time, his hand on the iron railing as he lurched around the landings, and reached the lobby door four storeys below. He swung it open, suddenly gripping the edge and slowing his pace so as not to call attention to himself; he need not have been concerned. The small band of people milling about in front of the benches against the wall and wandering around the warm tile floor were the neighbourhood elderly looking for nightly companionship and a few drunks walking in and out of the neon-lighted door to the noisy café. Oh, *Christ!* His mind was in a frenzy! He could walk around in the night, hiding in alleys, but a lone man in unfamiliar streets was too easily spotted by unofficial hunters or by the official police. He had to get inside somewhere, somehow. Out of sight.

The café! His Samaritans! He pulled up the collar of the leather jacket, and forced the belt of the trousers lower, inching down the gap around his ankles. He then approached the door casually, permitting himself a slight stagger as he pushed it open. He was greeted by floating levels of smoke – not all of it tobacco by any means – and adjusted his stinging eyes to the erratically flashing lights, as he tried to block out the offending noise – a combination of guttural roars and disco music blaring from hi-tech speakers. His Good Samaritans were gone; he looked for the young blonde girl as his focal point but she was not there. The table they had occupied was taken by another foursome – no, not four *different* people, only three – they had joined the English-speaking student who had sat beside him in the car, three other young men in various stages of collegiate release. Joel approached them, passing an empty chair in his path; he gripped the rim and unobtrusively pulled it behind him to the table. He sat down and smiled at the blond-haired student.

'I didn't know if I'd left enough money for those twelve beers I promised,' he said pleasantly.

'*Ach!* I was just talking about you, *Mein Herr Amerikaner!* These are my friends – like me, all dreadful students!' The three newcomers were introduced rapidly, the names lost in the music and the smoke. Everyone nodded; the American was welcome.

'Our other two friends left?'

'I told you,' shouted the blond youngster through the noise. 'They wished to drive to our house and make love. That's all they *do!* Our parents went to Bayreuth for the music festival, so they shall make their own music on her bed and I shall come home late!'

'Nice arrangement,' said Converse, trying to think of how to broach the subject that had to be broached quickly. He had very little time.

'Very *good*, sir!' said a dark-haired young man on his right. 'Hans would have missed that; his English is understandably inferior. I was an exchange student in the state of Massachusetts for two years. "Arrangement" is also a musical term. You combined the two! *Very* good, sir!'

'I keep trying,' said Joel aimlessly, looking at the student. 'You really speak English?' he asked sincerely.

'Very well, *Mein Herr*. My scholarship depends upon it. My friends here are good people, make no mistake, but they are rich and come here for amusement. As a boy, I lived two streets away from this place. But they protect the lads here, and why not? Let them have fun; nobody is hurt and money is spread.'

'You're sober,' said Converse, the statement bordering on a question.

The young man laughed, as he nodded. 'Tonight, yes. Tomorrow afternoon I have a difficult exam and need a clear head. The summer session examinations are the worst. The professors would rather be on holiday.'

'I was going to talk to *him*,' said Joel, nodding at the blond student, who was arguing with his two companions, his hands waving in the smoke, his voice strident. 'But that doesn't make sense. You do.'

'In *what* sense, sir, if you will forgive the redundancy of the expression?'

'"Redundancy"? What's your major?'

'Preliminary law, sir.'

'I don't need that.'

'It is a difficulty, sir?'

'Not for me . . . Listen, I haven't much time and I have a problem. I have to get out of here. I need to find another place to stay – just until tomorrow morning. I assure you I've done nothing wrong, nothing illegal – in case my clothes or my appearance give another impression. It's strictly a personal matter. Can you help me?'

The dark-haired young German seemed to hesitate, as if reluctant to answer, nevertheless doing so, leaning forward to be heard. 'Since you bring up the subject, *Mein Herr*, I'm sure you can understand that it would not be seemly for a student of the law to help a man under questionable circumstances.'

'That's exactly why I brought it up,' said Converse rapidly, speaking into the student's ear. 'I'm an attorney and under these clothes a reasonably respectable one. I simply took on the wrong American client over here and can't wait to get a plane out tomorrow morning.'

The young man listened, studied Joel's face and nodded. 'Then these are not lodgings you would normally seek?'

'To be avoided wherever possible. I just thought it would be a good idea to be inconspicuous for the night.'

'There are very few places such as this in Bonn, sir.'

'To Bonn's credit, counsellor.' Glancing about the café and its predominant clientele, Converse had another thought. 'It's summer!' he said urgently to the student through the bedlam. 'Are there any youth hostels around here?'

'Those in the vicinity of Bonn or Köln are filled, sir, mostly with Americans and the Dutch. The others which might have spaces are quite far north towards Hanover. However, there is another solution, I think.'

'What?'

'Summer, sir. The rooming houses usually filled by those attending the university have many spaces during the summer months. In the house where I stay there are two empty rooms on the second floor.'

'I thought you lived around here.'

'That was long ago. My parents are retired and live with my sister in Mannheim.'

'I'm in a great hurry. May we go? I'll pay you what I can tonight and more tomorrow morning.'

'I thought you said you were taking the plane in the morning.'

'I have two stops to make first. You can come with me: you can show me where they are.'

The young man and Joel excused themselves, knowing they would not be missed. The student started towards the lobby door, but Converse grabbed his elbow, gesturing at the street entrance.

'Your luggage, sir!' shouted the German through the din and the flashing lights.

'You can lend me a razor in the morning!' yelled back Converse, pulling the young man through the mingling bodies towards the door. Several tables before the entrance was an empty chair, on the seat a soft, rumpled cloth cap. He reached down and picked it up, holding it in front of him as he reached the door and walked outside to the pavement, the student behind him. 'Which way?' he asked, pulling the cap over his head.

'This way, sir,' replied the young German, pointing beneath the shabby canopy of the adjacent hotel entrance.

'Let's go,' said Joel, stepping forward.

They stopped – that is Converse stopped first, gripping the student's shoulder and turning him into the building. A black sedan had come speeding down the street, swerving into the open space in front of the canopy. Two men got out of the back doors and rushed towards the entrance, the second man running around the car to catch up with the first. Joel angled his head as the young German stared at him. He recognized both men; both were Americans. They had been at the Köln-Bonn airport eight nights ago hoping to trap him then as they were coming to trap him now. The black car moved forward out of the glare of the lights, into the shadows. It pulled into the kerb and waited, a hearse prepared to receive its cargo.

'*Was ist los?*' asked the German youth, unable to conceal his fear.

'Nothing really.' Converse removed his hand and gave the student two friendly claps on the shoulder. 'Just let this be a lesson to you, counsellor. Know who your client is before you get greedy and accept too large a retainer.'

'*Ja,*' said the young German, attempting a smile but not suceeding, his eyes on the black sedan.

They walked rapidly past the parked automobile with the driver inside, the glow of a cigarette seen in the darkness of the front seat. Joel pulled down the cloth cap and again angled his head, now away from one of his countrymen.

The truth was a fantasy bolstered by lies . . . Survival was in running and concealment. Insanity!

* * *

The early morning was mercifully uneventful except for his thoughts, which were raging. The student, whose name was Johann, had secured him a room at the boarding house, the proprietress delighted with a hundred Deutschmarks for the rental. It more than made up for the gauze, tape and antiseptic she gave him to rebandage his wound. Converse had slept soundly if intermittently, awakened by fears transposed into macabre dreams. By seven o'clock sleep was impossible.

There was an urgent piece of business that had to be taken care of; he understood the risk but the money was necessary, now more than ever. On Mykonos, the knowledgeable if serpentine Laskaris had forwarded $100,000 to banks in Paris, London, Bonn and New York, using the accepted practice of written-out numbers as a signature to withdraw the funds. Laskaris had suggested further that Joel should not attempt to carry with him or try to memorize four sets of lengthy and entirely different digits. Instead the banker would wire the American Express travel offices in the four cities to hold for a period of three months a message for – *who, Mr Converse? It should be a name meaningful to you but not to others. It will be your code, no other identification necessary – as with certain telephone banking facilities in your own country . . . Make it Carpentier. J. Carpentier.*

Joel understood that he might have revealed the device while under narcotics. Also he might not; his mind was not on money. He had a great deal in his possession and the chemicals tended to elicit only feverish priorities. He had learned that in the camps a lifetime ago, twice astonished that he had not mentioned far-off tactics down the roads of escape. There was also a back-up, ethics notwithstanding. The young German, Johann, would be his intermediary. The risks could not be avoided, only minimized; he had also learned that a lifetime ago. If the boy was taken, his conscience would be stricken, but then what could be the worst that would happen to him? There was no point in thinking about it.

'Go inside and ask if there's a message for J. Carpentier,' said Joel to the student. They were in the back seat of a taxi across the street from the American Express office. 'If the answer is yes, say the following words. "It must be a wire from Mykonos",' he added, recalling Laskaris' precise instructions.

'That is necessary, sir?' asked the dark-haired Johann, frowning.

'Yes, it is. Without mentioning Mykonos and the fact that the message is a cable, they won't give it to you. Also it identifies you. You won't have to sign anything.'

'This is all very strange, *Mein Herr*.'

'If you're going to be a lawyer, get used to odd forms of communication. There's nothing illegal, simply a means of protecting your client's and your firm's confidentiality.'

'I have much to learn, it seems.'

'You're not doing anything wrong,' continued Joel quietly, his eyes level with Johann's. 'On the contrary, you're doing something very right and I'll pay you very well for doing it.'

'*Sehr gut*,' said the young man.

Converse waited in the taxi, his eyes scanning the street, concentrating on stationary automobiles and those pedestrians walking too slowly or not at all, or anyone whose glances even seemingly strayed to American Express' storefront, Johann went inside and Joel swallowed repeatedly, a tightness in his throat: the waiting was awful, made worse by the knowledge that he was using the student in a high-risk situation. Then he thought briefly of Avery Fowler-Halliday and Connal Fitzpatrick; they had lost. The young German had an infinitely greater chance of living for many years.

The minutes went by as the sweat crawled through Converse's hair and down his neck; time was suspended in fear. Finally, Johann came outside, blinking in the sunlight, innocence personified. He crossed the street and climbed into the taxi.

'What did they say to you?' asked Joel, trying to sound casual, his eyes still roaming the street.

'Only if I had been waiting long for the message. I replied that I expected it was a cablegram from Mykonos. I didn't know what else to say.'

'You did fine.' Joel tore open the envelope and unfolded the wire. There was an unbroken series of written out numbers, well over twenty he judged at a glance. Again he remembered Laskaris' instructions: *Pick every third number beginning with the third and ending with the third from the last. Think merely in terms of three. It's quite simple – these things usually are – and in any event no one else can sign for you. It's merely a precaution.*

'Is everything all right?' asked Johann.

'So far we're ahead one step and you're one step nearer a bonus, counsellor.'

'I'm also nearer my examination.'

'What time do you take it?'

'Three-thirty this afternoon.'

'Good omen. Think in terms of three.'

'I beg your pardon?'

'Nothing. Let's find a pay telephone. You've only got one more thing to do and tonight you can buy your friends the biggest dinner in Bonn.'

The taxi waited at the corner while Converse and the young German stood outside the booth, Johann having written down the bank's number from the telephone book. The student was reluctant to go any farther; the exotic chores asked of him now were more than he cared to accept.

'All you have to do is tell the truth!' insisted Joel. '*Only* the truth. You met an American attorney who doesn't speak German and he's asked you to make a call for him. This attorney has to withdraw funds for a client from a confidential accounts-transfer and wants to know whom he should see. That's all. No one will ask your name, or mine, either, for that matter.'

'And when I do this there will be something else, *Mein Herr? Nein*, I think not. You call yourself . . .'

'I can't make a mistake! I can't misunderstand a word. And there is nothing else. Just wait wherever you like around the bank or near the bank. When I come out I'll give you two thousand Deutschmarks, and, as far as I'm concerned – as far as *anyone*'s concerned – we never met.'

'So much for so little, sir. You can understand my fears.'

'They're nothing compared to mine,' said Converse, quietly yet urgently. 'Please, do this. I need your help.'

As he had done the night before through the noise and the smoke and the flashing lights of the raucous bar, the young German looked hard at Joel, as if trying to see something he could not be sure was there. Finally, he nodded once without enthusiasm. '*Sehr gut*,' he said, stepping into the booth with several coins in his hand.

Converse watched through the glass as the student dialled and obviously had brief conversations with two or three different people before reaching the correct party. The one-sided dialogue as observed by Joel seemed interminable – far too long and too complicated for the simple request of a name in the transferred accounts department. At one point, as he wrote something down on the scrap of paper with the bank's number on it, Johann appeared to object and Converse had to restrain himself from opening the door and terminating the call. The German youth hung up and came out, his expression confused and angry.

'What happened? Was there a problem?'

'Only with the hour and institutional policy, sir.'

'What does that mean?'

'Such accounts are serviced only after twelve noon. I made it clear that you had to be at the airport by then but *Herr Direktor* said the bank's policy would stand.' Johann handed Converse the slip of paper. 'You're to see a man named Lachmann on the first floor.'

'I'll catch a later plane.' Joel looked at the chauffeur's watch on his wrist. It was 10.35; an hour and a half to go.

'I was hoping to be at the university library long before noon.'

'You can still be there,' said Converse sincerely. 'We can stop, get a stamped envelope, and you can write out your name and address. I'll mail the money to you.'

Johann glanced at the pavement, his hesitation all too obvious. 'I think, perhaps . . . the examination is not so difficult for me. It's one of my better subjects.'

'Of course,' agreed Joel. 'There's no reason on earth why you should trust me.'

'You mistake me, sir. I believe you would mail the money to me. It's just that I'm not sure it's such a good idea for me to receive the envelope.'

Converse smiled; he understood. 'Fingerprints?' he asked kindly. 'Accepted rules of evidence?'

'It's also one of my better subjects.'

'Okay, you're stuck with me for another couple of hours. I've got about seven hundred Deutschmarks left until I reach the bank. Do you know some clothing store away from the main shopping district where I can buy a pair of trousers and a jacket?'

'Yes, sir. And if I may suggest, if you are going to withdraw enough funds to give me two thousand Deutschmarks, perhaps a clean shirt and a tie might be in order.'

'Always check your client's appearance. You may go far, counsellor.'

The ritual at the *Bonner Sparkasse* was a study in awkward but adamant efficiency. Joel was ushered into Herr Lachmann's office on the first floor, where neither a handshake nor small talk was offered. Only the business at hand was addressed.

'Origin of transfer, please?' asked the blunt, corpulent executive.

'Bank of Rhodes, Mykonos branch, waterfront office. The name of the . . . "dispatcher", I guess you'd call him . . . is Laskaris. I don't recall his first name.'

'Even his last is unnecessary,' said the German, as though he did not care to hear it. The transaction itself seemed somehow to offend him.

'Sorry, I just wanted to be helpful. As you know, I'm in a great hurry. I have a plane to catch.'

'Everything will be done according to the regulations, *Mein Herr.*'

'Naturally.'

The banker shoved a sheet of paper across the desk. 'You will write out your numerical signature five times, one below the other, as I read you the regulations which constitute the policy of the *Bonner Sparkasse* as they pertain to the laws of the Federal Republic of Germany. You will then be required to sign – again in your numerical signature – an affidavit that you thoroughly understood and accept these prohibitions.'

'I thought you said "regulations".'

'One and the same, *Mein Herr.*'

Converse took the cablegram out of the inside pocket of his newly-purchased sports jacket and placed it beside the blank page of stationery. He had underlined the correct numbers and began writing.

'"You, the numerically undersigned, traceable from the origin of transfer,"' droned the obese Lachmann, leaning back in his chair and reading from a single page, '"swear to the fact that whatever funds withdrawn from the *Bonner Sparkasse* from this confidential account have been subject to all taxes, individual and corporate, from whatever sources of revenue. That they are not being processed through differing currencies to avoid said taxes, or for the purpose of making unlawful payments to individuals, companies, or corporations trafficking in illegal and . . ."'

'Forget it,' broke in Joel. 'I know it; I'll sign it.'

'". . . egregious activities outside the laws of the Federal Republic of Germany or the laws of the nation of which the undersigned is a legal resident with full citizenship."'

'Ever tried half-full or resident alien status?' said Converse, starting the last line of numbers. 'I know a law student who would punch holes in that affidavit.'

'There is more, but you say you'll sign?'

'I'm sure there's more and of course I'll sign.' Joel pushed the page with the handwritten numbers back to the banker. 'There. Just get me the money. One hundred thousand American, minus your fee. Split it two-thirds and a third. US and German, no bills over a thousand Deutschmarks or five hundred American.'

'That is quite a bit of paper, *Mein Herr.*'

'I'll handle it. Please, as quickly as possible.'

'Is that amount the entire account? I would not know, of course, until the scanners verify your "signature".'

'It's the entire account.'

'It could take several hours, *natürlich.*'

'What?'

'The regulations, the *policy, Mein Herr.*' The fat man extended his arms in supplication.

'I don't *have* several hours!'

'What can I do?'

'What *can* you do? A thousand American . . . for *you.*'

'One hour, *Mein Herr.*'

'Five thousand?'

'Five minutes, my good friend.'

Converse walked out of the elevator, the abrasive newly-acquired money belt far less comfortable than the one he had purchased in Geneva. However, it was pointless to refuse it. It was a courtesy of the bank, according to Lachmann, as the German pocketed nearly twelve thousand Deutschmarks for himself. The 'five minutes' had been a persuasive exaggeration, thought Joel as he glanced at the clock on the wall; it was nearly 12.45. The ritual had taken over half an hour, from his 'indoctrination' to the verification of his 'signature' by electronic scanners capable of picking the slightest 'fundamental' variation in the writing characteristics. Apparently no one dared make any mistakes in the German banks where questionable practices were concerned. The regulations were followed right to the borders of illegality, everyone covered by following orders that placed the burden of innocence solely on the recipients.

Converse started for the bronze-bordered doors of the entrance when he saw the student, Johann, sitting on a marble bench, looking out of place but not uncomfortable. The young man was reading some sort of pamphlet put out by the bank. Or more precisely he was pretending to read it, his eyes, however, darting above the paper, watching the crowds criss-crossing the marble floor. Converse nodded as Johann saw him; the student got up from the bench and waited until Joel reached the entrance before he began to follow.

Something had happened. Outside on the pavement people were rushing in both directions, but mainly to the right; voices were raised, questions shouted, replies blurred with anger and angry ignorance.

'What the hell is it?' asked Converse.

'I don't know,' replied Johann, next to him. 'Something ugly, I think. People are running to the kiosk on the corner. The newspapers.'

'Let's get one,' said Joel, touching the young man's arm, as they started towards the growing crowd on the block.

'*Attentat! Mord! Amerikanischer Botschafter ermordet!*'

The news-stand vendors were shouting, handing out papers as they grabbed coins and bills with little or no attempt to give change. There was a sense of the swelling panic that comes with sudden unexplained events that presage greater disasters. All around them people were snapping papers, their eyes riveted on the headlines and the stories beneath.

'*Mein Gott!*' cried Johann, glancing at a folded newspaper on his left. 'The American ambassador has been assassinated!'

'*Christ!* Get one of those!' Converse threw a number of coins into the kiosk as the young German grabbed a paper from the extended hand of a news vendor. 'Let's get out of here!' yelled Joel, gripping the student's arm.

But Johann did not move. He stood there in the middle of the shouting crowd, staring at the newspaper, his eyes wide, his lips trembling. Converse shoved two men away with his shoulders as he pulled the young man forward, now both of them surrounded by anxious, protesting Germans obsessed with getting papers.

'*You!*' Johann's scream was muted by some intolerable fear.

Joel ripped the newspaper from the student's hands. In the upper centre of the front page were photographs of two men. On the left was the murdered Walter Peregrine, American ambassador to the Federal Republic. On the right was the face of an American *Rechtsanwalt* – one of the few words in German Converse knew; it meant attorney. The photograph was of himself.

20

'*No!*' roared Joel, crushing the paper in his left fist, his right hand gripping Johann's shoulder. 'Whatever it says, it's a *lie!* I'm not any part of this! Don't you see what they're trying to *do?* Come on with me!'

'*Nein!*' screamed the young German, looking frantically around, realizing his voice was lost in the enveloping bedlam.

'I said *yes!*' Converse shoved the newspaper inside his jacket and threw his right arm around Johann's neck, vicing the student into him. 'You can think and do what you like but first you come with *me!* You're going to read me every goddamned word!'

'*Da ist er! Der Attentäter!*' shrieked the young German, reaching out, clutching the trousers of a man in the crowd who cursed and swung his arm down on the offending hand.

Joel wrenched the student's neck to his left, pulling him away while shouting into the student's ear, his words stunning himself as much as they did the young man. 'You want it this way you can *have* it! I've got a gun in my pocket and if I have to use it I will! Two decent men have been killed already – now three – why should you be the exception? Because you're *young?* That's no reason! When you come right down to it, who the hell are we *dying* for?'

Converse yanked the youth back and forth, dragging him out of the crowd. Once on the clear pavement he released his armlock, replacing it with a strong grip on the back of Johann's neck. He propelled the student forward, his eyes roving the street, trying to find a secluded area where they could talk – where Johann could talk, reading a string of lies put out by the men of Aquitaine. The newspaper slipped down beneath his jacket; he reached in and grabbed it by the edge, pulling the paper out intact. He could not just keep walking, pushing his reluctant captive down the pavement; several people had glanced at them, fuel for the curious. Oh,

Christ! The photograph – his *face!* Anyone might recognize him, and he was calling attention to himself by keeping the boy in tow.

Up ahead, on the right, there was a bakery or a coffee shop or a combination of both with tables under umbrellas on the sidewalk; several were empty at the far end. He would have preferred a deserted alley or a cobblestoned side street too narrow for vehicles, but he could not keep doing what he was doing, walking so rapidly with a prisoner in his grip.

'Over there! That table in the rear. You sit facing out. And remember, I wasn't joking about the gun; my hand will be in my pocket.'

'*Please,* let me *go!* You've done enough to me! My friends know we left together last night; my landlady knows I got you a room! The police will *question* me!'

'Get in there,' said Converse, shoving Johann between the chairs to the table at the rear of the pavement. Both sat down, the young German no longer trembling; instead his eyes were pivoting in all directions. 'Don't even think about it,' continued Joel. 'And when a waiter comes over speak in English. *Only* English.'

'There are no waiters. Customers go inside and bring out their own sweet rolls and coffee.'

'We'll do without – you can get something later. I owe you money and I pay my debts.'

. . . I always pay my debts. At least during the last four years I have. Words from a note left by a risk-taker. An actor named Caleb Dowling.

'I want no money from you,' said Johann, his English guttural with fear.

'You think it's tainted, makes you a true accessory, is that right?'

'You are the lawyer, I am merely a student.'

'Let me set you straight. It's not tainted because I didn't do whatever they said I did and there's no such thing as an accessory to innocence.'

'You are the lawyer, sir.'

Converse pushed the newspaper in front of the young German and with his right hand reached into his pocket where he had put the ten thousand Deutschmarks in ascending denominations for his immediate use. He counted out seven thousand and reached over, placing it in front of Johann. 'Put that away before I shove it down your throat.'

'I will not take your money!'

'You'll take it and tell them I gave it to you, if you want to. They'll have to give it back.'

'*Was ist?*'

'The truth, counsellor. You'll find out one day that it's the best shield you've got. Now, read what the paper *says!*'

'The ambassador was killed some time last night,' began the student haltingly, as he awkwardly put the Deutschmarks in his pocket. '. . . the approximate time of death is difficult to establish until further examinations,' he continued, translating the words in the article in fits and starts, trying to find the appropriate meanings. '. . . The fatal wound was . . . *Schädel* – cranial, a head wound – the body in the water for many hours, washed up on the riverbank in the Plittersdorf and found early this morning . . . The military *chargé d'affaires* was quoted as saying that the last person known to have been with the ambassador was an American by the name of Joel

Converse. When that name appeared there were . . .' The young German squinted, shaking his head nervously. 'How do you *say* it?'

'I don't know,' said Joel coldly, his voice flat. 'What am I trying to say?'

'. . . very excited – frantic – communications between the governments of Switzerland, France and the Federal Republic, all in coordination with the International Criminal Police, otherwise known as Interpol, and the . . . pieces of the tragic . . . *Rätsel* . . . puzzle fell into place – became clear, it means. Unknown to Ambassador Peregrine, the American Converse had been the object of an Interpol . . . *Suche* . . . search as a result of killings in Geneva and Paris as well as several attempted murders not yet clarified.' Johann looked up at Converse. There was a throbbing in his throat.

'Go on,' ordered Joel. 'You don't know how enlightening this is. Go *on!*'

'According to the ambassador's office a confidential meeting was arranged at the request of this man Converse, who claimed to have information injurious to American interests and which has subsequently proven to be false. The two men were to meet at the entrance of the Adenauer Bridge, between 7.30 and 8 o'clock last evening. The *chargé d'affaires* who accompanied Ambassador Peregrine confirmed that the two men met at 7.51 P.M. and started across the bridge on the pedestrian walkway. It was the last time anyone from the embassy saw the ambassador alive.' Johann swallowed, his hands trembling. He took several deep breaths and went on, his eyes rushing forward across the print, beads of perspiration breaking out on his hairline. 'Below are more complete . . . *eingehendere* . . . details as they are known, but a statement issued by Interpol described the suspect, Joel Converse, as an apparently normal man who is in reality a . . . *wandernde* . . .' The young German lowered his voice to a whisper. '. . . a walking explosive with severe mental disturbances. He is judged by several behavioural experts in the United States to be psychopathically ill as a result of nearly four years as a prisoner of war during the Vietnam conflict . . .'

As Johann stammered on, frightened by his own voice, the telling words and damning phrases came with staccato regularity, backed up by hastily-contacted departmental 'sources' and unnamed, faceless 'authorities'. The portrait was that of a mentally deranged man who had been thrown back in time, his derangement triggered by some violent event that left him with his intelligence intact but without moral or physical control. In addition, Interpol's search for him was spoken of in clouded terms, implying a secret manhunt that had been in progress for a number of days, if not weeks.

'. . . His homicidal tendencies are channelled,' continued the now near-panicked student, the article quoting another 'authoritative' source. '. . . He has a pathological hatred for present or former high-ranking military personnel, especially those who had gained prominent public stature . . . Ambassador Peregrine was a celebrated battalion commander in World War II's Bastogne campaign during which many American lives were lost . . . Authorities in Washington have speculated that the disturbed man, who after several harrowing attempts finally escaped from a maximum security camp in North Vietnam years ago, travelling over a hundred miles through enemy . . . *Dschungel* . . . jungle to reach his lines, is reliving his own experiences . . . His justification for survival – according to a military psychiatrist – is the killing of superior officers, past or present, who gave orders in combat, or in the extreme even civilians who in his imaginings bore some responsibility for the suffering he and others endured. Yet he is outwardly a normal man, as so many like him . . . Guards have been placed in Washington, London, Brussels, and here in Bonn . . . As an international lawyer, he is presumed to have access to numerous criminal elements who deal in illegal passports . . .'

It was a brilliantly executed trap, the crucial lies supported by truths, half truths, distortions and complete falsehoods. Even the precise timing of the evening was considered. The *chargé d'affaires* at the embassy stated unequivocally that he had seen Joel at the Adenauer Bridge 'at 7.51 P.M.', approximately twenty-five minutes after he had broken out of the stone jailhouse on Leifhelm's estate, and less than ten minutes after he had plunged into the Rhine. Every fragment of the hour was accounted for. That he was 'officially' placed at the bridge by '7.51' denied his story of capture and escape any credibility.

The incident in Geneva – the death of A. Preston Halliday – was introduced as a possible explanation for the violent act that had hurled him back in time, triggering Joel's maniacal behaviour. '. . . It has been learned that the attorney who was shot to death had been a well-known leader in the American protest movement in the 'sixties . . .' The veiled conclusion was that Converse might have hired the killers. Even the death of the man in Paris was given a much different and far more important dimension – oddly enough based in reality. '. . . Initially the victim's true identity was withheld in hopes of aiding the manhunt, as suspicions were aroused as a result of an interview the *Sûreté* had with a French lawyer who has known the suspect for a number of years. The attorney, who had lunched with the suspect that day, indicated that his American friend was in "serious trouble" and needed "medical attention" . . .' The dead man in Paris, of course, was an outstanding colonel in the French army, and an aide successively to several 'prominent generals'.

Finally, as if to convince any remaining unbelievers in this public trial by 'authoritative' journalism, references were made not only to his conduct but to the remarks he made upon his separation from service over a decade and a half ago. These were released by the United States Department of the Navy, Fifth Naval District, which included its own recommendation at the time that one Lieutenant Converse be placed under voluntary psychiatric observation; it was refused. His conduct had been insulting in the extreme to the panel of officers who wished only to help him, and his remarks were nothing short of violent threats against numerous high-ranking military personnel whom, as a carrier pilot, he could have known nothing about.

It all completed the portrait as painted by the artists of Aquitaine. Johann finished the article, the newspaper now clutched in his hands, his eyes wide and frightened. 'That's all there is . . . sir.'

'I'd hate to think there's any more,' said Joel. 'Do you believe it?'

'I have no thoughts. I'm too frightened to think.'

'That's an honest answer. Uppermost in your mind is the fact that I might kill you, so you can't face what you think. That's what you're really saying. You're afraid that by a look or a wrong word I could take offence and pull a trigger.'

'*Please*, sir, I am not adequate!'

'Neither was I.'

'Let me *go*.'

'*Johann*. My hands are on the table. They've been on the table since we sat down.'

'*Was . . . ?*' The young German blinked and looked at Converse's forearms, both of which were in front of him, his hands clasped on the white metal surface. 'You have no gun?'

'Oh, yes, I have a gun. I took it from a man who would have killed me if he'd had the chance.' Joel reached into his pocket as Johann stiffened. 'Cigarettes,' said Converse, taking out a pack and a book of matches. 'It's a terrible habit. Don't start if you haven't.'

'It's very expensive.'

'Among other things . . . We've talked off and on since last night.' Joel struck a match, lighting a cigarette, his eyes remaining on the student. 'Except for a few moments back there in the crowd when you could have had me lynched, do I look or sound like the man described in that newspaper story?'

'I am no more a doctor than a lawyer.'

'Two points for the opposition. The burden of sanity's on me. Besides, it said I appeared perfectly normal.'

'It said you suffered a great deal.'

'Several hundred years ago, but no more than thousands of others and far, far less than some fifty-eight thousand who never came back. I don't think an insane man is capable of making a rational remark like that under these circumstances, do you?'

'I don't know what you're talking about.'

'I'm trying to tell you that everything you just read to me is an example of a man being tried by negative journalism. Truths mixed with half-truths, distortions and implausible judgements were slanted to support the lies that are meant to convict me. There's not a court in any civilized country that would admit that kind of testimony or permit a jury to hear it.'

'Men have been killed,' said Johann, again his words whispered. 'The ambassador was killed.'

'Not by me. I wasn't anywhere near the Adenauer Bridge at eight o'clock last night. I don't even know where it is.'

'Where were you?'

'Not where anyone saw me, if that's what you mean. And those who know I couldn't have been at the bridge would be the last people on earth to say so.'

'There has to be some evidence of where you were.' The young German nodded at the cigarette in Converse's hand. 'Perhaps one of those. Perhaps you finished a cigarette.'

'Or finger or footprints? Pieces of clothing? There's all of that but they don't tell the time.'

'There are methods,' corrected Johann. 'The advances in the technology of . . . *Forschung* . . . the investigation techniques have been rapid.'

'Let me finish that for you. I'm not a criminal lawyer but I know what you're saying. Theoretically, for example, the ground depression of a footprint matched with the scrapings off my shoes could put me where I was within the hour.'

'*Ja!*'

'No. I'd be dead before a scrap of evidence reached a laboratory.'

'*Why?*'

'I can't tell you. I wish to God I could but I can't.'

'Again, I must ask why?' The fear in the young man's eyes was joined by disappointment, the last glimpse of believability, perhaps, gone with Joel's refusal to explain.

'Because I can't, I won't. You said a few minutes ago that I'd done enough to you and without meaning to, I have. But I won't do this. You're not in a position to do anything but get yourself killed. That's as frankly as I can put it, Johann.'

'I see.'

'No you don't, but I wish there was a way to convince you that I have to reach others. People who *can* do something. They're not here; they're not in Bonn, but I'll reach them if I can get away.'

'There's something else? You would have me do something *else?*' The young German stiffened again and again his hands trembled.

'No. I don't want you to do anything. I'm asking you *not* to do anything – at least for a while. Nothing. Give me a chance to get out of here and somehow get in touch with people who can help me – help all of us.'

'All of us?'

'I mean that and it's all I'll say.'

'These people are not to be found in your own embassy, *Amerikaner?*'

Converse looked hard at Johann, his eyes as steady as he could manage in light of the snapping newspapers at most of the nearby tables. 'Ambassador Walter Peregrine was killed by one or more men at that embassy. They came to kill me last night at the hotel.'

Johann breathed deeply, taking his eyes off Joel and staring down at the table. 'Back at the kiosk, in the crowd, when you threatened me . . . you said three men had been killed already – three decent men.'

'I'm sorry. I was desperate.'

'It wasn't simply that, it was what you said right afterwards. You said why should I be the exception? Because I was young? That was no reason, you claimed, and then you shouted very strange words – I remember them precisely. You said: "When you come right down to it, who the hell are we dying for?" It was more than a question, I think.'

'I won't discuss the implications of that remark, counsellor. And I can't tell you what to do. I can only tell you what I've told dozens of clients over the years. When a decision is reduced to several strong opposing arguments – mine included – and you've listened to them all, put them behind you and follow your own gut instinct. Depending upon who and what you are, it'll be the right one for you.' Converse paused, pushing back his chair. 'Now I'm going to get up and walk out of here. If you start screaming, I'll run and try to hide somewhere where I'll be safe before anyone recognizes me. Then I'll do whatever I can do. If you don't set off an alarm, I'll have a better chance, and in my view that would be best . . . for all of us. You could go to the university library and come out in an hour or so, buy a paper, and go to the police. I'd expect you to do that, if you felt you had to. That's my view. I don't know what yours is. Goodbye, Johann.'

Joel rose from the table, bringing his hand instantly to his face, his fingers spread, touching his eyebrows. He turned and walked through the tables to the pavement, veering right, heading for the first intersection. He barely took a breath, his lungs bursting for air but he dared not let even a breath impair his hearing. He waited as he walked, his pulse accelerating, his ears so alive that the slightest dissonance would have burned them.

There were only the sounds of the excited street conversation in counterpoint with the blaring horns of taxis – but these were not the dissonance he was prepared for; that would come with the screams of a young male voice raising an alarm. It did not come; he walked faster, entering the flow of pedestrians crossing the square – faster, *faster* – passing strollers who saw no need to rush. He reached the kerb of the opposite pavement and slowed down – a rapidly walking man called attention to himself; he dared not do that either. Yet the impulse to break into a run was almost uncontrollable the farther he distanced himself from the tables of the sidewalk bakery café. His ear had picked up no alarm and every split second of that absence told him to race into whatever secluded side streets he could find.

Nothing. Nothing broke the excitable discordant sounds of the square – no hysterical voice raised above the din – but there *was* a change, a discernible change, and it had nothing to do with strident alarms provoked by a single screaming voice. The discordant sounds *themselves* had been lowered, replaced by a growing symphony of shrugs and gestures of incomprehensibility and obvious relaxation. The words *Amerikaner – Amerikaner* were repeated everywhere. The panic of the first news had passed. An American had killed an American; it was not a German assassin, or a communist, or even a terrorist who had eluded the Federal Republic's security arrangements. Life could go on; Deutschland could not be held responsible for the death – and a sigh of relief could be felt among the citizens of Bonn.

Converse spun around the corner of a brick building and stared across the square at the tables of the bakery-café. The student, Johann, remained in his chair, his head bowed, supported by both hands, reading the newspaper. Then he got up and walked into the bakery itself. *Was there a telephone inside? Would he talk to someone?*

How long can I wait? thought Converse, prepared to run, as instinct held him back.

Johann came out of the bakery carrying a tray of coffee and rolls. He sat down and meticulously separated the plates from the tray and once again stared at the newspaper in front of him. Then he looked up at nothing in particular – as if he knew he was being watched by unseen eyes – and nodded once.

Another risk-taker, thought Joel, as he turned and looked and listened to the unfamiliar sights and sounds of the side street he had entered. He had been given a few hours; he wished he knew how to use them – he wished he knew what to *do*.

*   *   *

Valerie ran to the phone. If it was another reporter, she would say the same thing she had said to the last five. *I don't believe a word of it and I've nothing more to say!* And if it was one more person from Washington – from the FBI or the CIA or the VA or any other combinations of the alphabet, she would scream! She had spent three hours being interviewed that morning until she had literally ordered the crucifiers out of the house. They were liars trying to force her to support their lies. It would be far easier to take the phone off the hook but she could not do that. She had called Lawrence Talbot in New York twice, telling his office to trace him wherever he was and have him call her back. It was all madness. *Insanity!* as Joel used to say with such quiet intensity she thought his voice was a wild roar of protest.

'Hello?'

'*Valley?* It's Roger.'

'*Dad!*' Only one person had ever called her by that name and that man was her former father-in-law. The fact that she was no longer married to his son had made no difference in their relationship. She adored the old pilot and knew he felt the same about her. 'Where *are* you? Ginny didn't know and she's frantic. You forgot to turn on your answering machine.'

'I didn't forget, Valley. Too damned many people to call back. I just flew in from Hong Kong when I got off the plane I was upwinded by fifty or sixty screaming newspaper people and so many lights and cameras I won't be able to see or hear for a week.'

'Some enterprising airline clerk let out the word you were on board. Whoever it was will eat for a week off a generous expense account. Where are you?'

'Still at the airport – in the traffic manager's office. I'll say this for 'em they got me out of there . . . Valley, I just read the papers. They got me the latest editions. What the *hell* is this all about?'

'I don't know, Dad, but I do know it's a lie.'

'That boy's the sanest thing I ever had anything to do with! They're twisting everything, making the good things he did into something . . . I don't know, sinister or something. He's too damned *up-front* to be crazy!'

'He's not crazy, Roger. He's being taken, he's being put through a wringer.'

'What *for?*'

'I don't know. But I think Larry Talbot does – at least more than he's told me.'

'What *has* he told you?'

'Not now, Dad. Later.'

'Why?'

'I'm not sure . . . Something I feel, perhaps.'

'You're not making sense, Valley.'

'I'm sorry.'

'What did Ginny say? I'll call her, of course.'

'She's hysterical.'

'She always was – a little bit.'

'No, not that way. She's blaming herself. She thinks people are striking out at her brother for the things *she* did in the 'sixties. I tried to tell her that was nonsense but I'm afraid I made it worse. She asked me perfectly calmly if I believed what was being said about Joel. I told her of course I didn't.'

'The old paranoia. Three kids and an accountant for a husband and it still comes back. I never could handle that girl. Damned good pilot, though. Soloed before Joel, and she was two years younger. I'll phone her.'

'You may not be able to reach her.'

'Oh?'

'She's having her number changed and I think you should do the same thing. I know I'm going to the minute I hear from Larry.'

'Valley . . .' Roger Converse paused. '. . . don't do that.'

'Why not? Have you any idea what it's been *like* here?'

'Look, you know I've never asked what happened between you and Joel, but I usually have dinner with that piss ant lawyer once a week when I'm in town. He thinks it's some kind of filial necessity but I'd knock it off in a minute if I didn't like him. I mean he's a likeable guy, kind of funny sometimes.'

'I know all that, Roger. What are you trying to say?'

'*They* say he disappeared, that no one can find him.'

'And?'

'He may call you. I can't think of anyone else he would call.'

Valerie closed her eyes; the afternoon sun through the skylight was blinding. 'Is that based on your weekly dinner conversations?'

'It's not intuition. I never had any except in the air . . . Of course it is. It was never said outright, but it was always just below the cloud cover.'

'You're impossible, Dad.'

'Pilot error's like any other. There are times when you can't afford it . . . Don't change your number, Valley.'

'I won't.'

'Now what about me?'

'Ginny's husband had a good idea. They're referring all questions to their attorney. Maybe you should do the same. Do you have one?'

'Sure,' said Roger Converse. 'I got three. Talbot, Brooks and Simon. Nate's the best, if you want to know the truth. Did you know at the age of sixty-seven that son of a bitch took up flying? He's qualified in multi-engines now – can you imagine?'

'*Dad!*' broke in Valerie, suddenly. 'You're at the airport?'

'That's what I said. Kennedy.'

'Don't go home. Don't go to your apartment. Take the first plane you can to Boston, Use another name. Call me back and let me know what flight you're on. I'll pick you up.'

'*Why?*'

'Just do as I say, Roger. *Please!*'

'What for?'

'You're staying here. I'm leaving.'

21

Converse hurried out of the clothing store on the crowded Bornheimer Strasse and studied his reflection in the window. He surveyed the overall effect of his purchases, not as he had done inside in front of the full length mirror for fit and appearance, but as one of the strolling pedestrians on the sidewalk. He was satisfied; there was nothing about the clothes that called attention to him. The photograph in the papers – the only one in the past fifteen years that would be in a wire service or newspaper file – was taken about a year ago when he was one of several merger attorneys interviewed by Reuters. It was a head-and-shoulders shot, showing him in his lawyer's wardrobe – a dark suit and waistcoat, white shirt and a striped tie, the image of a rising international specialist. It was also the image everyone who read the papers had of him, and since it would not change, only spread, then he was the one who had to change.

Also, he could not continue to wear the clothes he had worn to the bank. A panicked Lachmann would undoubtedly give a complete description to the police, but even if his panic rendered him silent, those clothes were dark, the shirt white, the tie striped. Unconsciously or not, thought Joel, he had sought a patina of respectability. Perhaps all men running for their lives did so, their essential dignity stolen from them. Regardless, dressed in those clothes he was the man in the newspaper photograph.

The appearance he had in mind belonged to a history professor at college, a man whose various articles of clothing were all related. His jackets were always subdued tweeds with elbow patches, the trousers grey – heavy and light flannel, never anything else – and his shirts were button-down Oxford blue, again without exception. Above his thick horn-rimmed glasses was perched a soft Irish walking hat, the brim sloped downward front and back. Wherever that man went, whether down a street in Boston or on New York's Fifth Avenue or Beverly Hills' Rodeo Drive – which Joel was sure he never saw – one would know he belonged to academic New England.

Converse had managed to duplicate the outward appearance of the man in his memory, tinted glasses replacing the horn-rims, but only for a while. He had passed a large variety store, Bonn's equivalent of an American Five-and-Dime, and he knew that there would be a counter with different sizes and shapes of glasses, a few slightly magnified for reading, others clear.

For reasons that were only beginning to come into focus, those glasses were now vital to him. Then he understood. He was preoccupied with what he knew he *could* do – change his appearance. He was procrastinating, uncertain what to do next, not sure he was capable of doing anything.

He looked at his face in the oval mirror of the variety store, again satisfied with what he saw. The ersatz tortoiseshell rims were thick, the glass clear; the effect was owlish, scholarly. He was no longer the man in the newspaper photograph and, equally important, the concentration he had devoted to his appearance had begun to clear his mind. He could think again, sit down somewhere and sort things out. He also needed food and a drink.

The café was crowded, the stained glass windows muting the summer sunlight into shafts of blue and red piercing the smoke. He was shown to a table against the black-leathered upholstered banquette, assured by the *maître*, or whoever he was, that all he had to do was request a menu in English; the items were numbered. Whisky on the Continent, however, was universally accepted as Scotch; he ordered a double, and took out the pad and ballpoint pen he had picked up at the variety store. His drink came and he proceeded to write.

> Connal Fitzpatrick?
> Briefcase?
> $93,000.00 plus
> Embassy out
> No Larry Talbot et al
> No Beale
> No Anstett
> No man in San Francisco
> Men in Washington. Who?
> Caleb Dowling? No.
> Hickman, Navy, San Diego? Possible.
> . . . Mattilon?

René! Why hadn't he thought of Mattilon *before?* He understood why the Frenchman made the remarks attributed to him anonymously in the newspaper story. René was trying to be protective. If there was no defence, or if it was so weak as not to be viable, the most logical back-up was temporary insanity. Joel circled Mattilon's name and wrote the number 1 on the left, circling it also. He would find a telephone exchange in the street, the kind where operators assigned booths to bewildered tourists, and call René in Paris. He drank two swallows of whisky, relaxing as the warmth spread through him then went back to his list, starting at the top.

Connal . . . ? The presumption that he had been killed was inevitable but it was not conclusive. If he was alive, he was being held for whatever information could be pried out of him. As the Chief Legal Officer of the West Coast's largest and most powerful naval base, and a man who had a history of meetings with the State Department's Office of Munitions Control as well as its counterparts at the Pentagon, Fitzpatrick could be an asset to the men of Aquitaine. Yet to call attention to him was to guarantee his execution if he had not been killed already. If he *was* alive, the only way to save him was to find him, but not in any orthodox or official manner; it had to be done secretly. Connal had to be rescued secretly. Suddenly, Joel saw the figure of a man in the uniform of the United States Army across the café talking with two civilians at the bar. He did not know the man. It was the uniform that struck him. It brought to mind the military *chargé d'affaires* at the embassy, that extraordinarily observant and precise officer who was capable of seeing a man who was not at a bridge at the exact moment he was not there. A liar for Aquitaine, someone whose lies identified him. If that liar did not know where Fitzpatrick was, he could be made to find out. Perhaps there was a way, after all. Converse drew a line on the right side of his list, connecting Connal Fitzpatrick with Admiral Hickman in San Diego. He did not give it a number; there was too much to consider.

Briefcase? He was still convinced that Leifhelm's men had not found it. If the generals of Aquitaine had that attaché case, they would have let him know. It was not like those men to conceal such a prize, not from the prisoner who had thought he was a match for them. No, they would have told him one way or the other, if only to make clear to him how totally he had failed. If he was right, Connal had hidden it. At the inn called *Das Rektorat?* It was worth a try. Joel circled the word *Briefcase* and numbered it *2*.

'*Speisekarte, Mein Herr?*' said a waiter who had come up to the table before Converse knew it.

'English, please?'

'Certainly, sir.' The waiter separated his menus as though they were an outsize deck of cards. He selected one and handed it to Joel as he spoke. 'The *Spezialität* for today is *Wienerschnitzel* – it is the same in English.'

'That's fine. Keep the menu, I'll take it.'

'*Danke.*' The man swept away before Joel could order another drink. It was just as well, he thought.

$93,000.00 plus. There was nothing more to be said; the irritating bulge around his waist said it all. He had the money; it was to be used.

Embassy out . . . No Larry Talbot, et al . . . No Beale . . . No Anstett . . . No man in San Francisco. Throughout the meal he thought about each item, each statement, wondering how it all could have happened. Every step had been considered carefully, facts absorbed, dossiers memorized, caution uppermost. But everything had been blown away by complications far beyond the simple facts provided by Preston Halliday in Geneva.

Build just two or three cases that are tied to Delavane – even circumstantially – and it'll be enough.

In the light of the revelations on Mykonos, then in Paris, Copenhagen and Bonn, the simplicity of that remark was almost criminal. Halliday would have been appalled at the depth and breadth of influence Delavane's legions had attained, at the penetrations they had made at the highest levels of the military, the police, Interpol and, obviously now, those who controlled the flow of news from so-called 'authoritative sources' in western governments. It *was* appalling.

Converse abruptly checked his racing thoughts. He suddenly realized that he was thinking about Halliday in the context of a man who saw only a pair of eyes at night in the jungle, unaware of the size or the ferocity of the unseen animal in the darkness. That was wrong. Halliday knew the materials Beale was handing over to him on an island in the Aegean; he knew about the connections between Paris, Bonn, Tel Aviv and Johannesburg; he knew about the decision-makers in the State Department and the Pentagon – he knew it *all!* He had *arranged* it all with unknown men in Washington! Halliday had lied in Geneva. A Californian wrestler he had befriended years ago in school named Avery Fowler was the manipulator, and in the name of A. Preston Halliday, he had lied.

Where were those subterranean men in Washington who had the audacity
to raise half a million dollars for an incredible gamble but were too frightened
to come out in the open? What kind of men *were* they? Their scout had been
killed, their puppet accused of being a psychopathic assassin. How long
could they *wait*. *What* were they?

The questions enraged Converse, so much so that he tried not to pursue
them as they led only to fury. They blinded his reason. He needed reason
and, above all, the protection that came with awareness. He could not risk
blindness. It was time to find a telephone exchange and reach Mattilon in
Paris. René would believe him, René would help him. It was unthinkable
that his old friend would do anything else.

The civilian walked in silence to the hotel window, knowing he was expected
to deliver a pronouncement that would form the basis of a miracle – not a
solution but a miracle, and there were no such things in the business he
knew so well. Peter Stone was by all the rules a relic, a castaway who had
seen it all, and in the final years of seeing had finally fallen apart. Alcohol
had taken the place of true audacity, at the end rendering him a professional
mutant, a part of him still proud of past accomplishments, another part
sickened by the waste, by the knowledge of wasted lives, wasted strategies –
morality thrown into a gargantuan wastebasket of a collective non-
conscience.

Still, he had once been one of the best – he could not forget that. And
when it was all over he had faced the fact that he was killing himself with a
plethora of bourbon and self-pity; he had pulled out. But not before he had
gained the enmity of his past employers in the Central Intelligence Agency,
not for speaking out publicly, but for telling them privately who and what
they were. Fortunately, as sobriety returned, he learned that his past
employers had other enemies in Washington, enemies having nothing to do
with foreign entanglements or competition. Simply men and women serving
the Republic who wanted to know what the hell was going on when Langley
wouldn't tell them. He had survived – was surviving. He thought about
these things knowing that the two other men in the room believed he was
concentrating on the issue at hand.

There was no issue. The file was closed, the border rimmed in black.
They were so young – God, so *damned* young! – they would find it too terrible
to accept. He remembered – vaguely – when such a conclusion appalled
him. But that was nearly forty years ago; he was almost sixty now and he
had heard such conclusions repeated too often to sweat the bullets of regret.
The regret, the sadness were there – but time and repetition had dulled his
senses; clear evaluation was everything. Stone turned and spoke.

'We can't do *anything*,' he said with quiet authority. The Army captain
and the Navy lieutenant were visibly upset. Peter Stone continued. 'I spent
twenty-three years in the tunnels, including a decade with Angleton, and
I'm telling you there's absolutely nothing we can do. We have to let him
hang out, we can't touch him.'

'Because we can't *afford* to?' asked the naval officer scathingly. 'That's
what you said when Halliday was killed in Geneva. We can't *afford* to!'

'We can't. We were outmanoeuvred.'

'That's a *man* out there,' insisted the lieutenant. '*We sent* him out . . .'

'And they set him up,' broke in the civilian, his voice calm, his eyes sadly knowledgeable. 'He's as good as dead. We'll have to start looking elsewhere.'

'Why is that?' asked the Army captain. 'Why is he as good as dead?'

'They have too many controls, we can see that now. If they don't have him locked up in a cellar, they know pretty much where he is. Whoever finds him will kill him. A riddled body of a crazed killer is delivered up and there's a collective sigh of relief. That's the scenario.'

'And that's the most cold-blooded analysis of a murder I've ever heard! *Murder*, an unwarranted execution!'

'Look, Lieutenant,' said Stone, stepping away from the window. 'You asked me to come with you – convinced me I should – because you wanted some experience in this room. With that experience comes the moment when you recognize and accept the fact that you've been beaten. It doesn't mean you're finished, but you've been punched out of the round. We've been punched out, and it's my guess the punches haven't stopped yet.'

'Maybe . . .' began the captain haltingly. 'Maybe we should go to the Agency, tell them everything we know – everything we *think* we know – and what we've done. It might get Converse out alive.'

'Sorry,' countered the former CIA man. 'They want his head and they'll get it. They wouldn't have gone to all this trouble if "dead" wasn't written all over him. That's the way it works.'

'What kind of world do you live in?' asked the naval officer quietly, shaking his head.

'I don't live in it any more, Lieutenant, you know that. I think it's one of the reasons you came to me. I did what you two – and whoever else is with you – are doing now. I blew a whistle, only I did it with two months of bourbon in my veins and ten years of disgust in my head. You say you might go to the Company? Good, go ahead, but you'll do it without me. No one worth a quarter in Langley will touch me.'

'We can't go to G-2 or Naval Intelligence,' said the Army officer. 'We know that, we've all agreed. Delavane's people are there; they'd shoot us down.'

'Aptly put, Captain. Would you believe with real bullets?'

'I do now,' said the naval man, nodding at Stone. 'The report out of San Diego is that the legal, Remington, was killed in an automobile accident in La Jolla. He's the one who last spoke to Fitzpatrick, and before he left the base, he asked another legal the directions to a restaurant in the hills. He'd never been there – and I don't think it was an accident.'

'Neither do I,' agreed the civilian. 'But it takes us to the somewhere-else we can look.'

'What do you mean?' said the Army captain.

'Fitzpatrick. SAND PAC can't find him, right?'

'He's on leave,' interjected the naval officer. 'He's got another twenty days or so. He wasn't ordered to list his itinerary.'

'Still they've tried to find him but they can't.'

'And I still don't understand,' objected the captain.

'We go after Fitzpatrick,' said Stone. 'Out of San Diego, not Washington.

We find a reason to *really* want him back. A SAND PAC emergency, routed strictly through Eyes-Only, a base problem – nobody else's.'

'I hate to repeat myself,' said the Army man, 'but you've lost me. Where do we start? Whom do we start with?'

'With one of your own, Captain. Right now he's a very important person. The *chargé d'affaires* at the Mehlemer House.'

'The what?'

'The American Embassy in Bonn. He's one of them. He lied when it counted most,' said Stone. 'His name is Washburn. Major Norman Anthony Washburn, the Fourth.'

The telephone complex was off the lobby of an office building. It was a large square room with five enclosed booths built into three walls and a high, squared counter in the centre where four operators sat in front of consoles, each woman obviously capable of speaking two or more languages. Telephone directories of the major European cities and their suburbs were on racks to the left and right of the entrance, small pads with attached ballpoint pens on ledges above for the convenience of those seeking numbers. The routine was familiar: A caller delivered a written-out number to an operator, specified the manner of payment – cash, credit card, or collect – and was assigned a booth. There were no lines; a half dozen booths were empty.

Joel found the number of Mattilon's law firm in the Paris directory. He wrote it out, brought it to an operator and said he would pay cash. He was told to go to booth number seven and wait for the ring. He entered it quickly, the soft cloth brim of his hat falling over his forehead above the tortoiseshell glasses. Any enclosure, whether a toilet stall or a glass booth, was preferable to being out in the open. He felt his pulse accelerating; it seemed to explode when the bell rang.

'*Saint Pierre, Nelli et Mattilon*,' said the female voice in Paris.

'Monsieur Mattilon, please – *s'il vous plaît*.'

'*Votre . . . ?*' The woman stopped, undoubtedly recognizing an American's abysmal attempt at French. 'Who may I say is calling, please?'

'His friend from New York. He'll know. I'm a client.'

René did know. After several clicks his strained voice came on the line. 'Joel?' he whispered. 'I don't *believe* it!'

'Don't,' said Converse. 'It's not true – not what they say about Geneva or Bonn, not even what *you* said. I had nothing to do with those killings, and Paris was an accident. I had every reason to think – I *did* think – that man was reaching for a gun.'

'Why didn't you stay where you were then, my friend?'

'Because they wanted to stop me from going on. It's what I honestly believed, and I couldn't let them do that. Let me talk. . . At the George V you asked me questions and I gave you evasive answers and I think you saw through me. But you were kind and went along. You have nothing to be sorry about, take my word for it – my very *sane* word. Bertholdier came to me that evening in my room; we talked and he panicked. Six days ago I saw him again here in Bonn – only this time it was different. He was ordered to be there, along with three other very powerful men, two generals and a former field marshal. It's a cabal, René, an international cabal, and they can pull it off. Everything's secret and moving fast. They've recruited key military personnel all over Europe, the Mediterranean, Canada, and the US. There's no way to tell who's with them and who isn't – and there isn't time to make a mistake. They've got millions at their disposal, warehouses all over filled with munitions ready to ship to their people when the moment comes.'

'The moment?' broke in Mattilon. 'What moment?'

'Please,' insisted Joel, rushing ahead. 'They've been funnelling weapons and explosives to maniacs everywhere – terrorists, provos, certified lunatics – with one purpose only: Destabilization through violence. It's their excuse to move in. Right now they're blowing up Northern Ireland.'

'The madness in *Ulster?*' interrupted the Frenchman again. 'The horrors going on . . .'

'It's *their* horror! It's a trial run. They did it with one massive shipment from the States – to prove they *can* do it! But Ireland's only a test, a minor exercise. The big explosion's coming in a matter of days, a few weeks at most. I've got to reach the people who can stop them and I can't do that if I'm dead!' Converse paused, only to catch his breath, giving Mattilon no chance to speak. 'These are the men I was after, René – after *legally*, to build a few cases against them, expose them in the courts before they got anywhere. But then I found out. They're already there. I was too late.'

'But why *you?*'

'It started in Geneva – with Halliday, the man who was shot to death. He was killed by their gunmen, but not before he recruited me. You asked me about Geneva and I lied to you, but that's the truth . . . Now you'll either help me, or try to help me, or you won't. Not for me – I'm insignificant – but what I got roped into isn't. And I *was* roped into it, I know that now. But I've seen them, *talked* to them, and they're so goddamned logical, so fucking persuasive, they'll turn all Europe fascist; they'll set up a military federation with my country the progenitor. Because it started in my country; it started in San Francisco with a man named Delavane.'

'Saigon? The Mad Marcus of *Saigon?*'

'Alive and well and living in Palo Alto, pushing his military buttons all over the place. He's still a magnet and they're drawn to him like flies to a pig.'

'Joel, are you . . . are you . . . all *right?*'

'Let's put it this way, René. I took a lousy watch off a man who guarded me – a paranoid who nevertheless was nice to me – and it's got a sweep hand. You've got thirty seconds to think about what I've told you, then I'll hang up. *Now*, old friend, twenty-nine seconds.'

Ten passed and Mattilon spoke. 'An insane man does not deliver such a precise explanation so precisely. Nor does he use such words as "progenitor"; it is not in his vocabulary . . . Very well, perhaps I am mad, too, but what you speak of – God knows the times are right, what else can I say? *Everything* is crazy!'

'I've got to get back to the States alive, to Washington. I know people there. If I can reach them and show myself for what I am, they'll listen to me. Can you help?'

'I have contacts in the Quai d'Orsay. Let me go to them.'

'No,' objected Converse strenuously. 'They know we're friends. One word to the wrong person and you'd be killed. Forgive me, but more important, your talking would set off alarms. We can't afford that.'

'Very well,' said Mattilon. 'There is a man in Amsterdam – don't ask me how I know him – who can arrange such things. I assume you have no passport.'

'I have one but it's not mine. It's German. I took it off a guard who was ready to put a bullet in my head.'

'Then I'm sure he's not in a position to complain to the authorities.'

'He's not.'

'In your mind you really did go back, didn't you, my friend?'

'Let's not talk about it, okay?'

'*Bien*. You are you. Keep that passport; it will be useful.'

'Amsterdam. How do I get there?'

'You are in Bonn, no?'

'Yes.'

'There is a train to Emmerich on the Dutch border. In Emmerich switch to local transport – streetcars, autobuses, whatever. The customs are lax, especially during the peak hours when workers go back and forth. No one looks, so just show the passport you have quickly, partially covering the photograph, perhaps. It's good that it's German. You should have no trouble.'

'Suppose I do?'

'Then I can't help you, my friend. I'm being honest. And then I *must* go to the Quai d'Orsay.'

'All right. I get across, then what?'

'You'll reach Arnhem. From there you take the train to Amsterdam.'

'And then?'

'The man. His name is on a card in my bottom drawer. Do you have something to write on – write with?'

'Go ahead,' said Converse, reaching for the notepad and the ballpoint pen on the ledge beneath the telephone.

'Here it is. Thorbecke. Cort Thorbecke. The apartment house is on the south-west corner of Utrechtse and Kerk Straats. The telephone number is zero-two-zero, four-one-one-three-zero. When you call for an appointment, tell him you are a member of the Tatiana family. Do you have that? *Tatiana*.'

'René . . . ?' said Joel, writing. 'I never would have guessed. How come you know someone like this?'

'I told you not to ask but on the other hand he may probe and you should have at least vague answers – everything was always vague. Tatiana is a Russian name, one of the Czar's daughters reputedly executed at Ekaterinburg in 1918. I say reputedly because many believe she was spared along with her sister Anastasia and smuggled out with a nurse who had a fortune of jewels on her. The nurse favoured Tatiana and once free gave everything to the child and nothing to her sister. It's said she lived anonymously in great wealth – may even be living today – but no one knows where.'

'That's what I have to know?' asked Converse.

'No, it's merely the origin of its present meaning. Today it is a symbol of trust given to very few people in recent years, people who themselves are trusted by the most suspicious men on earth, men who cannot afford to make mistakes.'

'Good Lord, who?'

'Russians, powerful Soviet commissars who have a fondness for Western banking, who broker money out of Moscow for investments. You can understand why the circle is small. Few are called and fewer chosen. Thorbecke is one of them and he does an extensive business in passports. I'll reach him and tell him to expect your call. Remember, no name, just Tatiana. He'll have you on a KLM to Washington in short order. You'll need money, however, so we must think how I can . . .'

'Money's one thing I don't need,' interrupted Converse. 'Just a passport and a plane ticket to Dulles Airport without being picked up.'

'Get to Amsterdam. Thorbecke will help.'

'Thank you, René. I wanted to count on you and you came through. It means a lot to me. It means my life.'

'You're not in Washington yet, my friend. But call me when you get there, no matter the hour.'

'I will. Thanks, again.'

Joel hung up, put the notepad and the pen into his pocket, and went out of the booth to the counter. He asked for his charges and while the English-speaking operator was getting them, he remembered the item he had marked 2 on his list. His attaché case with the dossiers and the names of the decision-makers at the Pentagon and the State Department. *Das Rektorat.* Through some extraordinary oversight on Leifhelm's part, had Connal managed to hide it somewhere? Could it have been found perhaps by an employee at the country inn? Converse spoke to the operator who was handing him his bill.

'There's a place called *Das Rektorat*. It's a hotel in the countryside – where I'm not sure, but I'd like to call it and reach the manager. I'm told he speaks English.'

'Yes, sir. *Das Rektorat* has splendid accommodation, if any is available.'

'I'm not looking for a reservation. A friend of mine stayed there last week and thinks he may have left a valuable item in his room. He called me and asked me to check for him, to speak with the manager. If I find the number, would you place the call for me and get him on the line? I'm sorry to say I don't speak German; I'd probably reach the chef.'

'Certainly, sir,' replied the woman, smiling. 'It would be easier for me to get the number. Return to booth seven and I'll ring you. You can pay for both calls when you are finished.'

Inside the glass enclosure Joel lighted a cigarette, thinking about what he was going to say. He barely had time to formulate his words when the ring came.

'This is the *Vorsteher* – the manager – of *Das Rektorat*, sir,' said the operator. 'And he does speak English.'

'Thank you.' The operator broke off her connection. 'Hello?'

'Yes, may I help you, sir?'

'I hope so. I'm an American friend of Commander Connal Fitzpatrick, Chief Legal Officer of the San Diego Naval Base in California. I understand he stayed there last week.'

'Indeed he did, sir. We were so sorry we could not have extended his visit with us but there was a prior reservation.'

'Oh? He left unexpectedly?'

'I shouldn't put it that way. We spoke in the morning and I believe he understood our situation. I myself made arrangements for a taxi.'

'He was alone when he left?'

'Yes, sir.'

'Oh. Then if you'll tell me which hotel he went to, I can check there as well.'

'Check, sir?'

'The Commander misplaced one of his briefcases, a flat leather type with two combination locks. The contents are of no value except to him, but he very much wants to find it. It was a present from his wife, I think. Have you come across it?'

'No, *Mein Herr.*'

'Are you *sure?* The Commander has a habit of concealing his legal papers, sometimes under a bed or in the back of a closet.'

'He left nothing here, sir. The room was thoroughly examined and cleaned by our staff.'

'Perhaps someone came to see him and took the wrong case.' Converse knew he was pressing but there was no reason not to.

'He had no visitors . . .' The German paused. 'Just one moment, I do recall now.'

'Yes?'

'You say a flat briefcase, what is generally referred to as an attaché case?'

'*Yes!*'

'He carried it with him. It was in his hand when he left.'

'Oh . . .' Joel tried to recover quickly. 'Then if you'll just tell me what forwarding address he left, what hotel he went to.'

'I'm sorry sir. There were no such instructions.'

'Somebody had to make a reservation for him! Rooms are tight in Bonn!'

'Please, *Mein Herr.* I myself offered to try but he refused my aid, somewhat discourteously I might add.'

'I'm sorry.' Joel was annoyed that he had lost control. 'Those legal papers were important. Then you have no idea where he went?'

'But I do, sir, if one wishes to be humoured. I made a point of asking. He said he was going to the *Bahnhof*, the train station. If anyone asked for him, we were to say he was sleeping in a baggage locker. I'm afraid it was also meant discourteously.'

The *train* station? A locker! It was a *message!* Fitzpatrick was telling him where to look! Without speaking further, Converse hung up the phone, left the booth, and went to the counter. He paid for both calls and thanked the operator, wanting to leave her a tip but knowing it would only call attention to him. 'You've been very kind and, if I may, one last favour.'

'Sir?'

'Where is the train station?'

'You can't miss it. Turn left out of the building and walk four streets, then left again for two more. It is one of the more uncertain prides of Bonn.'

'You've been very kind.'

Joel hurried down the pavement constantly reminding himself to check his speed. Everything depended on control now, *everything*. Every move he made had to be normal, even casual, nothing to cause anyone to take a second glance at him. It was another omen! He was beginning to think they *did* exist. Mattilon had told him to take a train; Fitzpatrick had told him to go to the train station. A locker!

He walked through the large open doors of the entrance and turned to his right towards the row of lockers where he had left the attaché case before heading out to the Alter Zoll to meet 'Avery Fowler'. He reached the locker itself; there was a key in it, nothing inside. He began scrutinizing the lockers around it, on both sides, below, not at all sure what he was looking for but knowing he was looking for *something*. He found it! Two rows above on the left! The initials were small but clear, scratched into the metal by a strong, precise hand. *C. F.* Connal Fitzpatrick!

The Navy lawyer had done it! He had put the explosive papers back where only the two of them knew where they would be. Suddenly Converse felt sick. How could he get them out? How could he get *inside?* He looked around the station, peering between the summer crowds. The huge clock read 2.30; in two and a half hours the offices would be closed, the business day over, the crowds fuller. Mattilon had told him to reach Emmerich during the busiest time, when workers travelled back and forth across the border at the end of the day, and it took nearly two hours to reach Emmerich, *if* there was a train. He had less than a half hour to get inside the locker.

There was an information booth at the far end of the cavernous station. He walked towards it, his mind again racing, choosing words that might produce a key. The abrasive weight of the money belt around his waist gave him a glimpse of hope.

'Thank you very much,' he said to the clerk, his tortoiseshell glasses perched on his nose, the cloth hat falling over his forehead. He had been assigned an English-speaking, middle-aged information-dispenser with a pinched face and bored, irritated expression. 'Quite simply I've lost the key to the locker in which I stored my luggage and I have to get a train to Emmerich. By the way, when is the next one?'

'*Ach*, it is always ze case,' replied the cat-faced clerk, thumbing a schedule. 'Nozzing but trouble wiz zer sommer people. You lose ziss, you lose zat; and you expect everyone to help you! Zer train for Emmerich left twenty-seven minutes ago. Zer iss another in nineteen *minuten*, but nozzing after that for an hour.'

'Thank you. I have to be on it. Now, about the locker?' Joel removed a hundred Deutschmark note below the counter, and raised it slowly above the ledge. 'It's very important that I get my luggage and take that train. May I shake your hand for helping me?'

'It will be done!' exclaimed the clerk quietly, looking to his right and left as he grasped Converse's hand and the money. He picked up the phone at his side and dialled abusively. '*Schnell! Wir müssen ein Schliessfach öffnen. Standort zehn Auskunft!*' He slammed down the phone and looked up at Joel, a smile sculpted onto his rigid lips. 'A man will be here instantly to be of service, *Mein Herr*. We are always eager to be of service. The *Amerikaner*, so thoughtful.'

The man came, bulging out of his railroad uniform, his eyes dull, his authority questionable. '*Was ist los?*'

The clerk explained in German, then looked again at Converse. 'He speaks some English, not well, of course, but adequately, and he will assist you.'

'Zer are regulations,' said the official keeper of the locker keys. 'Come, show me.'

'Happy Birthday,' said Joel to the clerk behind the information booth.

'It is not my birthday, *Mein Herr*.'

'How would you know?' asked Converse, smiling, taking the fat man's arm.

'Zer are procedures,' said the railroad bureaucrat, opening the locker with a master key. 'You will sign for zer contents at zer office.'

It was *there!* His attaché case was on its side, nothing broken or slashed. He reached into his pocket and took out his money. 'I'm in a great hurry,' he said as he slipped out first a hundred Deutschmarks, then, with hesitation, another. 'My train leaves in a few minutes.' He shook the German's hand, passing the money, and asked calmly but with enthusiasm in his eyes. 'Couldn't you say it was a mistake?'

'It *was* a mistake!' answered the uniformed man enthusiastically. 'You must catch a train!'

'Thank you. You're a nice person. Happy Birthday.'

'*Was?*'

'I know, don't bother. Thank you again.'

Glancing around rapidly, subtly, hoping against hope that no one was watching him, Joel walked to an unoccupied wooden bench against the wall, sat down, and opened the attaché case, everything was there. But he could not keep it. Again he looked around the station, knowing what he had to find; he saw it. A drug store, or its equivalent; there would be envelopes somewhere inside. He closed the briefcase and got up, starting towards the store, trusting someone would speak English.

'Nearly all of us speak English, *Mein Herr*,' said the matronly woman behind the counter near the stationery section. 'It is practically a requirement, especially during the summer months. What are your needs?'

'I have to send a business report back to the United States,' answered Converse, a large, thick envelope and a roll of tape in his right hand, the attaché case in his left, 'but my train leaves in a few minutes and I don't have time to get to a post office.'

'There are several post-collection boxes in the *Bahnhof*, sir.'

'I need stamps, postage. I don't know how much,' said Joel helplessly.

'If you will put your materials in the envelope, seal it and address it, I shall weigh the package and suggest the appropriate amount of stamping. We keep sheets here for convenience, but they are more expensive than in the *Postamt*.'

'It doesn't matter. I'd like it to go air mail, and more postage rather than less.' Five minutes later Converse handed the accommodating clerk the heavily sealed package for weighing. He had written a note on the top of the first dossier, and printed the address clearly on the front of the envelope. The woman returned with the appropriate postage. He paid her and placed the envelope on the counter in front of him.

'Thank you,' he said, looking at his watch, as he began frantically licking the stamps and securing them. 'Would you by any chance know where I can buy a ticket to . . . Emmerich, or Arnhem, I guess?'

'Emmerich is *deutsch*, Arnhem is *holländisch*. Any stall, sir.'

'I may not have time,' said Joel, in the last three stamps. 'I suppose I could buy one on the train.'

'They will not stop it if you have money.'

'There.' He had finished, 'Where's the nearest mail box – collection box?'

'At the other end of the *Bahnhof, Mein Herr.*'

Again Joel looked at his watch, again the pounding in his chest as he ran out into the station, instantly checking himself again, watching the crowds for any who might be watching him. He had less than eight minutes to mail the envelope, buy a ticket and find the train. Depending on the complications, perhaps he could eliminate the second step. But to pay his fare on board would mean engaging in conversation, conceivably finding someone to translate – the possibilities and the possible consequences were frightening.

As he feverishly looked for the mail box, he kept repeating to himself the exact words he had scribbled on the top of the first dossier's cover: *Do not – repeat do not – let anyone know you have this. If you don't hear from me within five days, send it to Nathan S. I'll call him if I can. Your once and obedient HUSBAND. Love, J.* He then looked down at the name and the address he had written on the envelope in his hand and wondered, a dull, sickening pain of concern spreading through him.

> Ms Valerie Charpentier
> R. F. D. 16
> Dunes Ridge
> Cape Ann, Massachusetts
> USA

Three minutes later he found a mail box and deposited the envelope, opening and closing the slot several times to make sure it had fallen inside. He looked around at the signs everywhere, the Germanic lettering confusing him, the lines in front of the windows discouraging him. He felt so goddamned *helpless*, wanting to ask questions but afraid of stopping anyone, afraid that someone would study his face.

There was a window across the station, far away on the other side; two couples had left the line – four people with a sudden change of plans. Only one person was left. Converse hurried through the crowds, once again trying to hold himself in check, minimizing his movements, gliding, as it were.

'Emmerich, please,' he said to the clerk, as the lone customer finally left the window.

The attendant briefly turned and looked at the clock on the wall behind him. Then he spoke in German, the phrases fast and guttural. '*Verstehen Sie?*' he asked, the word a question.

'*Nein* . . . Here!' Converse put three one-hundred Deutschmark notes on the ledge of the counter, shaking his head, shrugging. 'Please, a ticket! I know, I've only got a few minutes.'

The man took two of the bills, shoving the third back. He made change and pressed several buttons beneath him; a ticket spewed out and he handed it to Joel. '*Danke. Zwei Minuten!*'

'The track. What *track?* Can you understand? Where?'

'*Wo?*'

'Yes, yes that's it! Where?'

'*Acht.*'

'What?' Then Converse held up his right hand, raising and lowering the fingers, as if indicating numbers.

The attendant responded by holding up both hands, a five-finger spread and three middle fingers. '*Acht,*' he repeated, pointing across the station to Joel's left.

'Eight! Thank you.' Gripping his attaché case Converse walked as fast as possible without breaking into a run. He saw the gate through the throngs of people; a conductor was making an announcement while looking at his watch and backing into the archway.

A woman carrying packages collided with him, careening into his left shoulder, the bundles plummeting out of her arms, scattering on the floor. He tried to apologize through the abuse she hurled at him, loud words that caused the surrounding travellers to stop and gape. He picked up several shopping bags as the woman's barking voice reached a crescendo.

'Up yours, lady,' he mumbled, dropping the packages and turning, now running to the closing gate. The conductor saw him and pushed it open.

He got to his seat, gasping, trying not to, his soft hat pulled down over his forehead, the wound in his left arm aching sharply. He thought he might have ripped it open in the collision. He felt under his jacket, past the handle of the gun he had taken from Leifhelm's chauffeur, to his shirt. There was no blood and he closed his eyes briefly in relief.

He was oblivious of the man across the aisle who stared at him.

In Paris, the secretary sat at her desk, the telephone held against her head, her voice low, muted further by her cupped hand over the mouthpiece.

'That is everything,' she said quietly. 'Do you have it?'

'Yes,' said the man on the other end of the line. 'It's extraordinary.'

'Why? It's the reason I'm here.'

'Of course. I should say *you're* extraordinary.'

'Of course. What are your instructions?'

'The gravest, I'm afraid.'

'I thought so. You have no choice.'

'Can you?'

'It's done. I'll see you at Taillevent. Eight o'clock?'

'Wear your black Galanos. I adore it so.'

'The Great Spike anticipates.'

'It is ever so, my dearest. Eight o'clock.'

The secretary hung up the phone, rose from the chair, and smoothed her dress. She opened a drawer and took out a bag with long straps, unlatching the snaps as she slipped it over her shoulder and walked to her employer's closed door. She knocked.

'Yes?' asked Mattilon inside.

'It is Suzanne, Monsieur.'

'Come in, come *in*,' said René, leaning back in his chair as the woman entered. 'The last letter is filled with incomprehensible language, no?'

'Not at all, Monsieur. It's just that I . . . well I'm not sure it's proper to say.'

'What could be improper? And if it is, at my age I'd be so flattered I'd probably tell my wife.'

'Oh, Monsieur . . .'

'No, really, Suzanne, you've been here what now, a week, ten days? One would think you had been here for months. Your work is excellent and I appreciate your filling in.'

'Your secretary is a dear friend, Monsieur. I could do no less.'

'Well, thank you. I hope the good Lord sees His way to pull her through. Young people today, they drive so fast – so terribly fast and so dangerously. I'm sorry, what is it, Suzanne?'

'I've had no lunch, sir. I was wondering . . .'

'My *God*, I'm inconsiderate! I'm afraid it goes with two partners who take August seriously and go on holiday! Please, as long as you like, and I insist you bring the bill to me and let me reimburse you.'

'That's not necessary, but thank you for the offer.'

'Not an offer, Suzanne, an order. Have lots of wine and let's both of us make messes of my partners' clients. Now, off you go.'

'Thank you, Monsieur.' Suzanne turned towards the door, opened it slightly, and then stopped. She turned her head and saw that Mattilon was absorbed in reading. She closed the door silently, reached into her bag, and withdrew a large pistol with the perforated cylinder of a silencer attached to the barrel. She pivoted slowly and walked towards the desk.

The lawyer looked up as she approached. '*What?*'

Suzanne fired four times in rapid succession. René Mattilon sprang back in his chair, his skull pierced from his right eye to his left forehead. Blood streaked down his face and over his white shirt.

22

'Where in God's name have you been?' cried Valerie into the phone. 'I've been trying to reach you since early this morning!'

'Early this morning,' said Lawrence Talbot, 'when the news broke, I knew I had to get the first plane to Washington.'

'You don't *believe* what they're saying? You *can't!*'

'I do, and worse, I feel responsible. I feel as if I'd unwittingly pulled the trigger myself, and in a way that's exactly what happened.'

'Goddamn you, Larry, explain that.'

'Joel called me from a hotel in Bonn, only he didn't know which one. He wasn't rational, Val. He was calm one moment, shouting the next, finally admitting to me that he was confused and frightened. He rambled on – most of the time incoherently – telling some incredible story of having been captured and thrown into a stone house in the woods, and how he escaped, hiding in the river, eluding guards and patrols and killing a man he called a "scout". He kept screaming that he had to get away, that men were searching for him, in the woods, along the river bank . . . Something's happened to him. He's gone back to those terrible days when he was a prisoner of war. Everything he says, everything he describes is a variation of those experiences – the pain, the stress, the tensions of running for his life through the jungle and down rivers. He's sick, my dear, and this morning was the horrible proof.'

Valerie felt the hollowness in her throat, the sudden, awful vacuum below. She was beyond thinking; she could only react to words. 'Why did you say you were responsible, that in some ways you pulled the trigger?'

'I told him to go to Peregrine. I convinced him that Peregrine would listen to him, that he wasn't the man Joel thought he was.'

'. . . "Thought he was?" What did Joel say?'

'Very little that made sense. He ranted about generals and field marshals and some obscure historical theory that brought all the commanders from various wars and armies together in a combined effort to take control of governments. He wasn't lucid. He'd pretend to be but the minute I questioned a statement he made or a point in his story, he'd blow up and tell me it didn't matter, or I wasn't listening, or I was too dense to understand. But at the end he admitted he was terribly tired and confused and how badly he needed sleep. That was when I made my last pitch about Peregrine, but Joel didn't trust him. He was actually hostile towards him because he said he saw a former German general's car go through the embassy gates and, as you may or may not know, Peregrine was an outstanding officer during the Second World War. I explained as patiently and as firmly as I could that Peregrine was not one of "them", that he was no friend of the military . . . Obviously I failed. Joel reached him, set up a rendezvous and killed him. I had no *idea* how sick he was.'

'Larry,' began Valerie slowly, her voice weak. 'I hear everything you say but it doesn't ring true. It isn't that I don't believe you – Joel once said you were an embarrassingly honest man – but something's missing. The Converse I know and lived with for four years never bent the facts to support abstractions he wanted to believe. Even when he was angry as hell he couldn't do that. I told him he'd make a lousy painter because he couldn't bend a shape to fit a concept. It wasn't in him and I think he explained it. At five hundred miles an hour, he said, you can't mistake a shadow on the ocean for a carrier if your instruments are out.'

'You're telling me he doesn't lie.'

'I'm sure he does – I'm sure he did – but never about important things. It simply isn't in him.'

'That was before he became ill, violently ill . . . He killed that man in Paris, he admitted it to me.'

Valerie gasped. '*No!*'

'Yes, I'm afraid. Just as he killed Walter Peregrine.'

'Because of some obscure historical *theory?* It's all wrong Larry!'

'Two psychiatrists at the State Department explained it, but in phrases I'm sure I'd mangle if I tried to repeat them. "Progressive latent retrogression", I think was one of them.'

'Bullshit!'

'But you may be right about one thing. Geneva. Remember you said it all had something to do with Geneva?'

'I remember. What about Geneva?'

'It's where it started, everyone in Washington agrees with that. I don't know if you've read the papers . . .'

'Only *The Globe*; it's delivered. I haven't left the phone.'

'It was Jack Halliday's son – stepson, actually. He was the lawyer who was killed in Geneva. It seems he was a prominent leader of the anti-war movement in the 'sixties and he was Converse's opponent in the merger. It was established that they met for breakfast before the conference. The theory is that he baited Joel, and we can assume it was brutal as he had a reputation of going for the jugular.'

'Why would he do that?' asked Val, her frayed nerves now suddenly alert.

'To throw Joel off. To distract him. Remember, they were dealing in millions and the attorney who came off best could do very well for himself – clients lining up all over Wall Street to retain him. There's even evidence that Halliday succeeded.'

'What evidence?'

'The first part's technical so I won't try to explain it except to say that there was a subtle transfer of voting stock which under certain isolated market conditions might give Halliday's clients more say in management than the merger intended. Joel accepted it; I don't think he would have normally.'

'Normally? What's the other part?'

'Joel's behaviour at the conference itself. According to the reports – interviews with everyone in that room – he wasn't himself, he *was* distracted, some said agitated. Several lawyers on both sides commented on the fact that he kept to himself, standing by a window most of the time, looking out as if he expected something. His concentration was so lax that questions addressed to him had to be repeated and, when they were, he appeared as though he didn't understand them. His mind was somewhere else, on something that consumed him.'

'Larry!' shouted Valerie. 'What are you *saying?* That Joel had something to do with this Halliday being *killed?*'

'It can't be ruled out,' said Talbot sadly. 'Either psychologically or in light of what people saw in the anteroom when Halliday died.'

'What they *saw?*' whispered Valerie. 'The paper said he died with Joel holding his head.'

'I'm afraid there's more, my dear. I've read the reports. According to a receptionist and two other attorneys, there was a violent exchange between them just before Halliday died. No one's sure what was said, but they all agree it seemed vicious, with Halliday clutching Joel's lapels, as though accusing him. Later, when questioned by the Geneva police, Joel claimed there was no coherent conversation, only the hysterical words of a dying man. The police report added that he was not a cooperative witness.'

'My God, he was probably in *shock!* You know what he went through – the sight of that man dying literally in his arms must have been traumatic for him!'

'Admittedly this is hindsight, Valerie, but everything must be examined, above all his behaviour.'

'What do they think he did? What's the theory *now?* That Joel went out into the street, saw someone who fitted the bill and hired him to *kill* a man? Really, Larry, this is ludicrous.'

'There are more questions than there are answers, certainly, but what's happened – what we know has happened – isn't ludicrous at all. It's tragic.'

'All right, all right,' said Valerie, her words rushed. 'But why would he do it? Why would he want Halliday killed. *Why?*'

'I think that's obvious. How he must have despised someone like Halliday. A man who stayed safely at home, who condemned and ridiculed everything men like Joel went through, calling them goons and murderers and lackeys . . . and unnecessary sacrifices. Along with his hated "commanders", the Hallidays of this world must have stood for everything else he loathed. One group ordering them into battle – to be maimed, killed, captured . . . tortured, the other making a mockery of everything they endured. Whatever Halliday said at that breakfast table must have made something snap in Joel's head.'

'And you think,' said Valerie, quietly, the words echoing in her throat, 'that's why he wanted Halliday dead?'

'Latent vengeance. It's the prevalent theory, the consensus, if you will.'

'I don't "will". Because it's not true, it couldn't be true.'

'These are highly qualified experts, Val, doctors in the behavioural sciences. They've analysed everything in the records and they feel the pattern is there. Shock-induced, instant pathological schizophrenia.'

'That's very impressive. They should embroider it on their Snoopy baseball caps because that's where it belongs.'

'I don't think you're in a position to dispute . . .'

'I'm in a hell of a position,' interrupted the ex-Mrs Converse. 'But nobody bothered to ask me, or Joel's father, or his sister – who just happened to have been one of those wild-eyed protesters you all speak of. There's no way Halliday could have provoked Joel the way they say he did – at breakfast, lunch *or* dinner.'

'You can't make such a statement, my dear. You simply don't know that.'

'I *do* know, Larry. Because Joel thought the Hallidays of this world, as you put it, were *right*. He wasn't always crazy about the way they did things but he thought they were *right!*'

'I don't believe that. Not after what he went through.'

'Then go to another source – if that's what you call it. To some of those records your high priests of the behavioural sciences conveniently overlooked . . . When Joel came back, there was a parade for him at Travis Air Force Base in California, where he was given everything but the keys to every starlet's apartment in Los Angeles. Am I right?'

'I recall there was a military welcome for a man who had escaped under extraordinary circumstances. The Secretary of State greeted him at the plane, in fact.'

'In absolute fact, Larry. Then what? Where else was he paraded?'

'I don't know what you mean?'

'Look at the records. Nowhere. He wouldn't do it. How many invitations did he get? From how many towns and cities and companies and organizations – all pushed like *hell* by the White House? A hundred, five hundred, five *thousand?* At least that many, Larry. And do you know how many he accepted? Tell me, Larry, do you know? Did those high priests talk about this?'

'It wasn't the issue.'

'Of course it wasn't. It warped the pattern; it bent the shapes Joel Converse wouldn't bend! The answer is *zero*, Larry. He wouldn't do it, any of it! He thought one day more of that war was one more day in hell too long. He refused to lend his name.'

'What are you trying to say?' said Talbot sternly.

'Halliday wasn't his enemy, not the way you're trying to paint him. The brush strokes aren't there. They're not on the canvas.'

'Your metaphors are more than I can handle, Val. What are you trying to tell me?'

'That something smells, Larry. It's so rotten I can hardly breathe, but the stench isn't coming from my former husband. It's coming from all of you.'

'I have to take exception to that. All I want to do is help, I thought you knew that.'

'I do, really I do. It's not your fault. Goodbye, Larry.'

'I'll call you the minute I learn anything.'

'Do that. Goodbye.' Valerie hung up the phone and looked at her watch. It was time to get down to Logan Airport in Boston to pick up Roger Converse.

'In Köln um zehn nach drei!' shouted the voice over the loudspeaker.

Converse sat by the window, his face next to the glass, as the towns sped by on the way to Köln: Bornheim, Wesel, Brühl. The train was perhaps three-quarters full, which was to say that each double seat had at least one occupant, many two, but certainly not all. When they pulled out of the station a woman had been sitting where he sat now, a fashionably dressed suburbanite. Several seats behind them another woman – a friend – spotted her. His seatmate spoke to Joel. The brief attention she had called to both of them when he could not reply unnerved him. He shrugged and shook his head; she exhaled impatiently, got up in irritation and joined her friend.

She had left a newspaper behind, the same newspaper with his photograph on the front page, which remained flat out on the seat. He stared at it until he realized what he was doing and instantly shifted seats, picking up the paper and folding it so that the picture would be out of sight. He glanced around cautiously, holding his hand casually above his lips, frowning, pensive, trying to seem a man in thought whose eyes saw nothing. But he had seen another pair of eyes and they were studying him – staring at him while the owner was engaged in what appeared to be a lively conversation with an elderly woman next to him. The man had looked away, and

Converse had a brief half second to observe the face before he turned to the window. He knew that face; he had talked to that man but he could not remember where it was or when it was, only that they had spoken. The realization was as maddening at it was frightening. *Where* was it? *When* was it? Did the man know him, know his *name?*

If the face did, he had done nothing about it. He had returned his concentration to the woman, the conversation still lively. Joel tried to picture the whole man; perhaps it would help. He was large, not so much in height as in girth, and on the surface jovial, but Converse sensed a meanness to him. Was that now or before? When was before? *Where?* Ten minutes or so had passed since the exchange of looks, and Joel was no further ahead in peeling away the layers of memory. He was stymied and afraid.

'*Wir kommen in zwei Minuten in Köln an. Bitte achten Sie auf Ihr Gepäck!*'

A number of passengers got up from their seats, tugging at their jackets and skirts, reaching for luggage. As the train began to slow down Converse literally pressed himself into the window, the glass cooling the right side of his forehead. He let his mind go slack, unfocused, expecting the next few minutes to tell him what to do.

The minutes passed, the suspension on hold, his mind blank as passengers got off and others got in, many carrying briefcases – attaché cases – several very much like his own which he had left in a trash can in Bonn. He had wanted to keep it but he could not. It had been a gift from Valerie, as his gold pen was a gift, both initialled in those better days . . . No, not better, he told himself, simply different. Nothing was better or worse; there were no comparisons where commitments were concerned. They either stuck or they did not. Theirs came unstuck.

Then why, he asked himself, as the train ground its wheels to a stop at Köln, had he sent the contents of his briefcase to Val? His answer was the essence of logic, he thought. She would know what to do: the others would not. Talbot, Brooks and Simon were out. His sister, Virginia, was even farther out. His father? The fly-boy with a sense of responsibility that went as far as his last wing dip? It could not be the pilot. He loved old Roger, more than he suspected Roger loved him, but the pilot could never come to grips with the ground. Hard earth meant relationships and old Roger never knew how to handle them, even with a wife he claimed to have loved dearly. The doctors said she had died of a coronary occlusion; her son thought it was from neglect. Roger was not on the scene, had not been for several weeks. So that left Valerie . . . his once and former Valerie.

'*Entschuldigen Sie. Ist der Platz frei?*' The intruding voice came from a man about his own age, carrying an attaché case.

Joel nodded, assuming the words referred to the empty seat beside him.

'*Danke,*' said the man, sitting down, the attaché case at his feet. He withdrew a newspaper from under his left arm and snapped it open. Converse tensed as he saw his photograph, his own serious face staring at him. He turned again to the window, pulling the soft brim of the hat lower, his face down, hoping he looked like an exhausted traveller wishing only to catch a few minutes' sleep. Moments later, as the train started forward, he had an inkling that he had succeeded.

'*Verrückt, nicht wahr?*' said the man with the attaché case reading the newspaper.

Joel stirred and blinked open his eyes beneath the brim of the hat. 'Umm?'

'*Traurig,*' added the man, his right hand separated from the paper in a gesture of apology.

Converse settled back into the window, the coolness of the glass an anchor, his eyes closed, the darkness more welcome than he could ever remember . . . No, that was not true; he remembered to the contrary. In the camps there were moments when he was not sure he could keep up the façade of strength and revolt. When everything in him wanted to capitulate, to hear even a few kind words, to see a smile that had meaning. Then the darkness would come and he would cry, the tears drenching his face. And when they stopped the anger was inexplicably restored. Somehow the tears had cleansed him, purged the doubts and the fears and made him whole again. And angry again. The darkness was so inviting.

'*Wir kommen in fünf Minuten in Düsseldorf an!*'

Joel bolted forward, his neck painfully stiff, his head cold. He had dozed for a considerable distance judging from the stiffness above his shoulder blades. The man beside him was reading and marking a report of some kind, the attaché case on his lap, the newspaper folded neatly between himself and Converse, folded maddeningly so that his photograph stared up at the ceiling of the train in clear view. The man opened his case, put the report inside, and snapped it shut. He turned to Converse.

'*Der Zug ist pünktlich,*' he said, nodding his head.

Joel nodded back, suddenly aware that the passenger across the aisle had got up with the elderly woman, shaking her hand and replying to something she said. But he was not looking at her; his eyes had strayed over to Converse. Joel slumped back into the seat and the window, resuming the appearance of a weary traveller, the soft brim of his hat pulled down to the rims of his glasses. Who *was* that man? If they knew each other how could he be silent under the circumstances? How could he simply look over now and then and casually return to his conversation with the woman? At the very least, he would have to betray some sense of alarm or fear, or at the minimum, excited recognition.

The train began to slow down, the metallic grinding of the steel plates against the huge wheels swelling; soon the whistles would commence for their arrival at Düsseldorf. Converse wondered whether the German next to him would get off. He had closed his attaché case but he made no preliminary moves to rise and join the line forming at the forward door. Instead, he picked up the newspaper, mercifully opening it to an inside page.

The train stopped, passengers disembarked and others got on board – mostly women with shopping boxes and plastic bags emblazoned with the logos of expensive boutiques and recognizable names in the fashion industry. The train to Emmerich was a suburban 'mink run', as Val used to call the afternoon trains from New York to Westchester and Connecticut. Joel saw that the man from across the aisle had walked the elderly woman up to the rear of the line, again shaking her hand solicitously before sidestepping his way back toward his seat. Converse turned his face to the glass, his head bowed, and closed his eyes.

'*Bitte, können wir die Plätze tauschen? Dieser Herr ist ein Bekannter. Ich sitze in der nächsten Reihe.*'

'*Sicher, aber er schläft ja doch nur.*'

'*Ich wecke ihn,*' said the German next to Converse, while laughing and getting up. The man from across the aisle had changed seats. He sat down next to Joel.

Converse stretched, covering a yawn with his left hand, his right slipping under his jacket to the handle of the gun he had taken from Leifhelm's chauffeur. If it became necessary he would show that gun to his new yet familiar companion. The train started, the noise below growing in volume; it was the moment. Joel turned to the man, his eyes knowing but conveying nothing.

'I *figured* it was you,' said the man, obviously an American, grinning broadly but not attractively.

Converse had been right, there was a meanness about the obese man; he heard it in the voice as he had heard it before – but where he did not remember. 'Are you sure?' asked Joel.

'Sure I'm sure. But I'll bet you're not, are you?'

'Frankly, no.'

'I'll give you a hint. I can always spot a good ole Yank! Only made a couple of mistakes in all the years of hopping around selling my li'l ole line of look-alike, almost originals.'

'Copenhagen,' said Converse, remembering with distaste, waiting for his luggage with the man. 'And one of your mistakes was in Rome when you thought an Italian was an Hispanic from Florida.'

'You *got* it! That guinea bastard had me buffaloed, figured him for a spic with a lot of bread – probably from running dope, you know what I mean? You know how they are, how they cornered the market from the Keys up . . . Say, what's your name again?'

'Rogers,' replied Joel for no other reason than the fact he had been thinking about his father a while ago. 'You speak German,' he added, making a statement.

'Shit, I'd better. West Germany's just about our biggest market. My old man was a Kraut; it's all he spoke.'

'What do you sell?'

'The best imitations on Seventh Avenue, but don't get me wrong, I'm not one of the Jew boys. You take a Balenciaga, right? You change a few buttons and a few pleats, put a ruffle maybe where the Latino doesn't have one. Then farm the patterns out to the Bronx and Jersey, lower Miami and Pennsylvania, where they sew in a label like "Valenciana". Then you wholesale the batch at a third of the price and everybody's happy – except the Latino. But there's not a fucking thing he can do that'd be worth his time in court because for the most part it's legal.'

'I wouldn't be so sure about that.'

'Well, a guy would have to plough through a road of *hazzerai* to prove it *wasn't* legal.'

'Sadly, that's true.'

'Hey, don't get me wrong! We provide the merchandise and a service for thousands of nice l'il ole housewives who can't afford that Paris crap. And I earn my bread, ole Yankee Doodle. Take that wrinkled old broad I was with; she owns a half dozen speciality shops in Köln and Düsseldorf, and now she's looking into Bonn. Let me tell you, I waltz her . . .'

The towns and small cities went by. Leverkusen . . . Lagenfeld . . . Hilden, and still the salesman went on, one tasteless anecdote leading to the next, his voice grating, repetitive.

'*Wir kommen in fünf Minuten in Essen an!*'

It happened in Essen.

The commotion came first but it was not sudden. Instead, it grew in volume as an immense rolling wave gathers force approaching a ragged coastline, a sustained crescendo arriving with its crash over the rocks, the sound sustained because of the unseen wave behind it. The embarking passengers all seemed to be talking with one another, heads turned, voices excited, necks craned to hear a stranger's words. Several carried small transistor radios, some held against ears, other held out, the volumes turned up at the request of those nearby. The more crowded the train became, the louder and more electric the conversations, heightened by the shrill, metallic tones from the radios. A thin young girl in the uniform of a private school, her books in a canvas beach bag, and a blaring radio in her left hand sat down in the seat in front of Joel and the salesman. Passengers gathered around, shouting, apparently asking the girl if she could make the radio louder.

'What's it all about?' asked Converse, turning to the obese man.

'Wait a minute!' replied the salesman, leaning forward with difficulty, and in greater discomfort rising partially up from the seat. 'Let me listen.'

There was a perceptible lull, but only among the crowd around the seat where the girl now held the radio in the air. Suddenly there was a burst of static and Converse could hear two voices, in addition to that of the newscaster, a remote report from somewhere away from the radio. And then Joel heard the words spoken in English; they were nearly impossible to pick out as an interpreter kept rushing in to give the German translation.

'A full inquiry . . . *Eine gründliche Untersuchung* . . . entailing all security forces . . . *die alle Sicherheitsbelagschaften* . . . *erfordert* . . . has been ordered . . . *wurde veranlasst.*'

Converse grabbed the salesman's coat. 'What is it – tell me what happened?' he asked rapidly.

'That *nut* hit again! . . . Wait, they're going back. Lemme hear this.' Again there was a short burst of static and the excited newscaster came back on the air. A terrible sense of dread spread through Joel as the onslaught of German crackled out of the small radio, each phrase more breathless than the last. Finally the guttural diatribe ended. The passengers straightened their backs. Some stood up, turning to one another, their voices raised in counterpoint, excited conversations resumed. The salesman lowered himself into the seat, breathing hard, not apparently because of the alarming news he had heard but out of sheer physical discomfort.

'Would you *please* tell me what this is all about?' asked Converse, controlling his anxiety.

'Yeah, sure,' said the heavy set man, taking a handkerchief from his breast pocket and mopping his forehead. 'This mother-loving world is filled with crazies, you know what I mean? For Christ's sake, you can't tell who the fuck you're talking to! If it was up to me, every kid who was born cross-eyed or couldn't find a tit would be buried in dirt. I'm just sick of the weirdos, you know what I mean?'

'That's very enlightening, now what *happened?*'

'Yeah, okay.' The salesman put the handkerchief back in his pocket, then loosened his belt and undid the buttons above his zippered fly. 'The soldier boy, the one who runs the headquarters in Brussels . . .'

'The Supreme Commander of NATO,' said Joel, his dread complete.

'Yeah, that one. He was shot, his head blown off right in the goddamned street when he was leaving some little restaurant in the old section. He was in civilian clothes, too.'

'When?'

'A couple of hours ago.'

'Who do they say did it?'

'The same creep who knocked off that ambassador in Bonn. The *nut!*'

'How do they know that?'

'They got the gun.'

'The what?'

'The gun. It's why they didn't release the news right away: they wanted to check the fingerprints with Washington. It's his, and they figure the ballistics will show it's the same gun that was used to kill what's-his-name.'

'Peregrine,' said Converse quietly, aware that his dread was not complete. The worst part was only coming into focus. 'How did they get the gun?'

'Yeah, well that's where they've marked the bastard. The soldier boy had a guard with him who shot at the nut and hit him – they think on the left arm, When the weirdo grabbed his arm the gun dropped out of his hand. The hospitals and the doctors have been alerted and all the borders all over the place are being checked, every fucking American male passport made to roll up his sleeves, and anyone looking anywhere's near like him hauled off to a customs tank.'

'They're being thorough,' said Joel, not knowing what else to say, feeling only the pain of his wound.

'I'll say this for the creep,' continued the salesman, eyes wide and nodding his head in some obscene gesture of respect. 'He's got 'em chasing their asses from the North Sea to the Mediterranean. They got reports he was seen on planes in Antwerp, Rotterdam and back there in Düsseldorf. It only takes forty-five minutes to get from Düsseldorf to Brussels, you know. I got a friend in Munich who flies a couple times a week to have lunch in Venice. Every place over here's a short hop. Sometimes we forget that, you know what I mean?'

'Yes, I do. Short flights . . . Did you hear anything else?'

'They said he could be heading for Paris or London or maybe even Moscow – he could be a Commie, you know. They're checking the private airfields, too, figuring he's got friends who are helping him – some friends, huh? A regular happy group of drooling psychos. They're even comparing him to that Carlos, the one they call "the jackal", what do you think of that?

They say if he does go to Paris, the two of them might link up and there could be a few more executions. This Converse, though, he's got his own regular trademark. He puts bullets in their heads. Some kind of Boy Scout, huh?'

Joel stiffened, feeling the tension throughout his slumped body, a sharp hollow pain in the centre of his chest. It was the first time he had heard his name spoken casually by a stranger, identifying him as the psychopathic killer, an assassin hunted by governments whose border patrols were scrutinizing everyone at every checkpoint, private airfields watched, a dragnet in progess. The generals of Aquitaine had done their job with precision, right down to his fingerprints on a gun and a flesh wound in his arm. But the timing – how could they *dare?* How did they know he was not in an embassy somewhere asking for temporary asylum until he could make a case for himself? How could they take the *chance?*

Then the realization came to him and he had to dig his fingers into his wrist to control himself, to contain his panic. The call to *Mattilon!* How easily René's phone could have been tapped, by either the *Sûreté* or Interpol and how quickly would Aquitaine's informers spread the word! Oh, *Christ!* Neither one of them had thought of it! They *did* know where he was, and no matter where he went he was trapped! As the offensive salesman accurately phrased it 'every place over here's a short hop'. A man could fly from Munich to Venice to lunch and be back in his office for a 3.30 appointment. Another man could kill in Brussels and be on a train in Düsseldorf forty-five minutes later. Distances were measured in half hours. From ground-zero in Brussels, 'a couple of hours ago' covered a wide circle of cities and a great many borders. Were his hunters on the train? They might be but there was no way they could know which train he had taken. It would be easier and far less time-consuming to wait for him in Emmerich. He had to think, he had to *move.*

'Excuse me,' said Converse, getting up. 'I have to use the men's room.'

'You're lucky.' The salesman moved his heavy legs, holding his trousers as he let Joel pass. 'I can hardly squeeze into those boxes. I always take a leak before . . .'

Joel made his way up the aisle, abruptly stopping, swallowing, trying to decide whether to continue or turn around. He had left the newspaper on his seat, photograph easily revealed by unfolding the top page. He had to continue; any change of movement, however minor, might attract attention. His objective was not the men's room, it was the passageway between the cars; he had to see it. A number of people had opened the door and gone through, several apparently looking for someone they expected to find on the train. He would look down at the lock on the toilet door and proceed.

He stood in the swerving, vibrating passageway studying the metal door. It was a standard two-tiered exit; the top opened first before the lower part could be unlocked and pulled back, revealing the steps. It was all he had to know.

He returned to his seat and to his relief the salesman was splayed back, his thick lips parted, his eyes closed, a high-pitched wheeze emanating from his throat. Converse cautiously lifted one foot after the other over the fat man's legs and manoeuvred himself into his seat. The newspaper had not been touched. Another relief.

Diagonally above and in front of him, he saw a small receptacle in the curved wall with what appeared to be a sheaf of railroad schedules fanned out by disuse. Limp, bent pieces of paper ignored because these commuters knew where they were going. Joel raised himself off the seat, reached out, and took one, apologizing with several nods of his head to the young girl below. She giggled.

Oberhausen . . . Dinslaken . . . Voerde . . . Wesel . . . Emmerich.

Wesel. The last stop before Emmerich. He had no idea how many miles Wesel was from Emmerich but he had no choice. He would get off the train at Wesel, not with whatever departing passengers there were, but by himself. He would disappear in Wesel.

He felt a slight deceleration beneath him, his pilot's instincts telling him it was the outer perimeter of an approach, the final path to touchdown in the scope. He stood up and carefully manoeuvred both feet between the fat man's legs, pivoting at the last second as the salesman snorted, shifting his position. Squinting under the brim of his hat, Joel casually glanced around, as if he were momentarily unsure of which way to go. He moved his head slowly, his eyes recording rapidly; as far as he could see no one was paying the slightest attention to him.

He walked wearily up the aisle, a tired passenger in search of relief. He reached the toilet door and was greeted by an ironic sign of that relief. The white slot below the handle spelled out *Besetzt*. His first manoeuvre had its basis in reality. The toilet was in use. He turned towards the heavy passageway door, pulled it open and stepped outside, crossing the vibrating, narrow coupling area to the opposite door. He pushed it open, but instead of going inside he took a single stride forward, then lowered his body, turning as he did so, and stepped back into the passageway, into the shadows. He stood up, his back against the external bulkhead and inched his way to the edge of the thick glass window. Ahead was the inside of the rear car and by turning he had a clear view of the car in front. He waited, watching, turning, at any moment expecting to see someone lowering a newspaper, or breaking off a conversation and looking over at his empty seat.

None did. The excitement at the news of the assassination in Brussels had tapered, as had the rush of near panic in Bonn when the streets learned that an ambassador had been killed. A number of people were obviously still talking about both incidents, shaking their heads and grappling with the implications and the future possibilities, but their voices were lowered: the crisis of the first reports had passed. After all, it was not fundamentally the concern of these citizens. It was American against American. There was even a certain gloating in the air; the gunfight at OK Corral had new significance. The colonists were, indeed, a violent breed.

'*Wir kommen in* . . .' The rapid clacking of the wheels below, echoing in the metal chamber, obscured the distant announcement over the loudspeakers. Only moments now, thought Converse as he turned and looked at the exit door. When the train slowed sufficiently and the lines began to form at both inner doors, he would make his moves.

'Wir kommen in drei Minuten in Wesel an!'

Several passengers in both cars got out of their seats, adjusted their briefcases and shopping bags and started up the aisle. The grinding of the huge wheels underneath signified the approach to touchdown. *Now.*

Joel turned to the exit door and finding the upper latch snapped it open, pulling the upper section back: the rush of air was deafening. He spotted the handle of the lower release and gripped it, prepared to yank it up as soon as the ground beyond slowed down. It would be in only seconds. The sounds below grew louder and the sunlight outside created a racing silhouette of the horizontal train. Then the sharp, abusive words broke through the dissonance and he froze.

'*Very* well thought out, Herr Converse! Some win, some lose. You *lost.*'

Joel spun around. The man yelling at him in the metal chamber was the passenger who had got on the train at Düsseldorf, the apologetic commuter who sat next to him until the obese salesman had asked him to exchange seats. In his left hand was a gun held far below his waist, in his right the ever-respectable attaché case.

'You're a surprise,' said Converse.

'I would hope so. I barely made the train in Düsseldorf. *Ach,* three cars I walked through like a madman – but not the madman you are, *ja?*'

'What happens now? You fire that gun and save the world from a madman?'

'Nothing so simplistic, pilot.'

'Pilot?'

'Names are immaterial, but I am a colonel in the West German Luftwaffe. Pilots only kill one another in the air. It is embarrassing on the ground.'

'You're comforting.'

'I also exaggerate. One disconcerting move on your part and I shall be a hero of the Fatherland, having cornered a crazed assassin and killed him before he killed me.'

'"Fatherland"? You still call it that?'

'*Natürlich.* Most of us do. From the father comes the strength, the female is the vessel.'

'They'd love you in a Vassar biology class.'

'Is that meant to be amusing?'

'No, just disconcerting – in a very minor way, nothing serious.' Joel had moved in inches until his back was against the bulkhead, his whole mind, his entire thinking process, on pre-set. He had no choice except to die, now or a matter of hours from now. 'I suppose you have an itinerary for me,' he asked, as he swung his left arm forward with the question.

'Quite definitely, pilot. We will get off the train at Wesel and you and I will share a telephone, my gun firmly against your chest. Within a short time a car will meet us and you will be taken . . .'

Converse slammed his concealed right elbow into the bulkhead, his left arm in plain sight. The German glanced at the door of the forward car. *Now!*

Joel lunged for the gun, both hands surging for the black barrel as he crashed his right knee with all the force he could command into the man's testicles. As the German fell back, he grabbed his hair and smashed the man's head down onto a protruding hinge of the opposite door.

It was over. The German's eyes were wide, alarmed, glassy. Another scout was dead, but this man was no ignorant conscript from an impersonal government, this was a soldier of Aquitaine.

A stout woman screamed in the window, her lips separated by her screams, her face hysterical.

'*Dies ist Wesel* . . . !'

The train had slowed down and other excited faces appeared at the window, the frenzied crowd now blocking those who tried to open the door.

Converse lunged across the vibrating metal enclosure to the exit panel. He grasped the latch and pulled it open, crashing the door into the bulkhead. The steps were below, gravel and tar beyond. He took a deep breath and plunged outside, curling his body to absorb the hard ground, and when he made contact he rolled over, and over, and over.

23

He careened off a rock and into a cluster of bushes. Nettles and coarse tendrils enveloped him, scraping his face and his hands. His body was a mass of bruises, the wound in his left arm stinging and moist – unbearable, untouchable – but there was no time even to acknowledge pain. He had to get away: in minutes the whole area would be swarming with men searching for him, hunting for the murderer of an officer in the Federal Republic's air arm. It took no imagination to foresee what would happen next. The passengers would be questioned – including the salesman – and suddenly a newspaper would be in someone's hand, a photograph studied, the connection made. A crazed killer last seen in a back street in Brussels was not on his way to Paris or London or Moscow. He was on a train out of Bonn, passing through Köln, Essen, and Düsseldorf – he killed again in a town called Wesel.

Suddenly he heard the high-pitched wail of a horn. He looked up the small hill towards the tracks; a southbound train was gathering speed out of the station several thousand feet away. His *hat*. It was upturned half way down the hill. Joel crept out of tangling brush, staggered to his feet, and ran to it, refusing to listen to that part of his mind which told him he could barely walk. He grabbed the hat off the ground, and began running to his right. The southbound train passed; he raced up the hill and across the tracks, heading for an old building, apparently deserted. More of its windows were shattered than intact. He might rest there for a few moments but no longer; it was too obvious a hiding place. In ten or fifteen minutes, it would be surrounded, men with guns aimed at every exit, every window.

He tried desperately to remember. How had he done it before? How had he eluded the patrols in the jungles north of Phu Loc? . . . Vantage points! Get where you can see them but they can't see you! But there were tall trees then and he was younger and stronger and could climb them, concealing himself behind green screens of full branches on firm limbs. There was nothing like that here on the outskirts of a railroad yard . . . or maybe there was! To the right of the building was a landfill dump, tons of earth and debris piled high in several pyramids; it was his only choice.

His arms and legs aching, gasping, his wound inflamed, he ran towards the last of the pyramids. He reached it, propelled his way around the mass, and started climbing the rear side, his feet slipping into soft earth, and wood and cardboard and patches where garbage had been layered. The sickening smells were oddly distracting: they took his mind off the pain. He kept crawling, clawing with each slipping foot. If he had to, he could burrow himself into the stinking mess. There were no rules for survival, and if sinking himself into the putrid hill kept a spray of bullets from ending his life, so be it.

He reached the top and lay prone below the ridge, dirt and protruding debris all around him. Sweat rolled down his face, stinging the scrapes on his face, his legs and arms heavy with stabbing pain, his breathing erratic from the trembling caused by unused muscles and fear. He looked down at the outskirts of the railroad yard, then up ahead at the station. The train had stopped, its journey halted, the platform filled with people milling around, bewildered. Several uniformed men were shouting orders, trying to separate passengers – apparently those in the two cars flanking the scene of the killing or anyone else who knew anything. In the parking lot surrounding the station house was a blue and white striped police car, its red roof light spinning, the signal of emergency. There was a rapid clanging in the distance and seconds later a long white ambulance streaked into the lot, whipped into a horseshoe turn and plunged back, stopping close to the platform. As the rear doors opened, two attendants jumped out carrying a stretcher; a police officer above them on the steps shouted at them, gesturing with his arm. They ran up the metal staircase and followed him.

A second patrol car swerved into the lot, tyres screeching as it stopped next to the ambulance. Two police officers got out and walked up the steps: the previous officer joined them, two civilians, a man and woman beside him. The five talked and moments later the two patrolmen returned to their vehicle. The driver backed up and spun to his left, gunning the engine, heading for the south end of the parking lot, directly towards Converse. Again they stopped and got out, now with weapons drawn; they raced across the tracks and down the slope of gravel and tar into the wild grass. They would be coming back in minutes, thought Joel, absently clawing the ragged surface by his shoulders. They would stop and check out the deserted building, perhaps call for assistance, but sooner or later they would examine the huge mounds of landfill.

Converse looked behind him: there was a dirt road marked with the tracks of heavy trucks leading to a tall link fence, the gate held in place with a thick chain. A man running up that road and climbing that fence would be seen; he had to stay where he was, hidden in the putrid rubble.

Another sound interrupted his frantic calculations . . . a sound like one he had heard only moments before. On his right, in the parking lot. A third patrol car came speeding in, its klaxon howling, but instead of heading for the ambulance and the first police vehicle by the platform, it veered to its left, racing over to join the striped car at the south end of the lot. The two policemen in the field *had* radioed for assistance and Joel felt a numbing sense of despair. He was looking at his own executioners . . . Executioner. The newly-arrived patrol car contained only a driver . . . or did it? Did the policeman turn his head and speak? No, he was disengaging something, a seat belt probably.

A grey-haired uniformed man got out, looked around, then started walking rapidly towards the tracks. He crossed them and stood on the top of the slope, shouting down at the police officers in the brown, sun-drenched grass. Converse had no idea what the man was saying but the scene appeared strangely out of place.

The two policemen came racing into view, their guns no longer in their hands but holstered. There was a brief heated conversation. The older officer was pointing to a distant area south of the landfill; his words by their volume were commands. Joel looked back at his patrol car; on the panel of the front door was an insignia that was absent on the other car. The man held a superior rank to his young associates; he was issuing orders.

The younger policemen ran back across the tracks to their vehicle, their superior following, but not running. They swung back the doors, literally jumped in, and in the burst of an engine's roar, swerved to the right and sped out the parking lot. The older man reached his patrol car, but he made no movement to open the door or get inside. Instead, he spoke – at least his lips moved – and five seconds later the rear doors opened and two men emerged. One man Converse knew well. His gun was in Joel's pocket. It was Leifhelm's chauffeur, a taped bandage across his forehead, another on the ridge of his nose. He pulled out a gun and barked a command to the other man, in his voice the fury of an injured fanatic combat soldier.

Peter Stone left the hotel in Washington. He had told the young Navy lieutenant and the slightly older Army captain that he would contact them in the morning. *Children*, he thought. Idealistic amateurs were the worst because their righteousness was usually as valid as their actions were impractical. Their childish disdain for duplicity and deceit did not countenance the fact that to rip the maniacal bastards out frequently required greater malevolence and far more venal deception than they could imagine.

Stone got into a taxi – leaving his car in the basement parking area – and gave the driver the address of an apartment building on Nebraska Avenue. It was a lovely apartment but it did not belong to him: it was leased by an Albanian diplomat at the United Nations who was rarely there; naturally based in New York. But the former intelligence officer had worked hard and turned the Albanian several years ago, not merely with ideological pleas to a fine scholar's conscience, but also with photographs of this same scholar in all manner of sexual indulgences with very strange women. They were in their sixties and seventies, bag ladies off the streets, who, after carnal abuse, were subject to sheer physical abuse. He was a winner, the scholar-diplomat. A psychiatrist in Langley had said something about wish-fulfilling – sexually-repressed matricide. Stone did not need that nonsense: he had the photographs of a son of a bitch sadist. But it was the children that occupied his mind now, not the excesses of a fool that permitted him access to a luxury apartment far beyond his consultation fees.

The *children. Jesus!* They were so right, their sensibilities so correctly on target, but they did not understand that when they took on the George Marcus Delavanes of today's world it was war in all its shades of brutality, because that was the way these men fought. Righteousness had to join with a commitment to crawl in the gutter if it was necessary, no quarter sought for none would be given. This was the last fifth of the twentieth century and the generals were going for it all; the paranoia of their disgust and frustration had come to the end of endurance.

Stone had seen it coming for years and there were times when he had come close to applauding, throwing his hands up in frustration, willing to sell what was left of his soul. Strategies had been aborted – men *lost* – because of the maddening bureaucratic restraints that led back to laws and a constitution which were never written with anything like Moscow in mind. The 'Mad Marcuses' of this planet – this part of the planet – had a number of very plausible points. There were those in the Company years ago who were adamant and not squirrelly about it. They said: *Bomb* the nuclear plants in Tashkent and Tselinograd! Blow them the hell up in Chengdu and Shenyang! Don't let them begin! We are responsible and they are *not!*

Who knew? Would the world have been better off?

Then Peter would wake up in the morning and that part of his soul he had not sold would tell him, no, we cannot do that. There had to be another way, a way without confrontation and wholesale death. He still clung to that alternative, but he could not dismiss the Delavanes as megabomb off-the-wallers. Where were we heading now?

He knew where *he* was heading – had been heading for years. It was why he had joined the children. Their righteousness was justified, their indignation valid. He had seen it all before in too many places – always at the extremes of the political spectrum. The Delavanes of the planet would turn everyone into robots. In many ways, death was preferable.

Stone unlocked the door of the apartment, closed it, took off his jacket and made himself the only drink he would permit himself for the evening. He walked to the leather chair by the telephone and sat down, taking several swallows before putting the glass on the table beneath the floor lamp. He picked up the phone and dialled seven digits, then three more, and one more after that. A very faint dial tone replaced the original and he dialled again. Everything was in order. The call was being routed through a KGB diplomatic scrambler-cable on an island in the Cabot Strait south-west of Newfoundland. Only Dzerzhinsky Square would be confused. Peter had paid six negatives for the service. Five rings preceded the sound of a male voice in Bern, Switzerland.

'*Allo?*'

'This is your old friend from Bahrain, also the vendor in Lisbon and a buyer in the Dardanelles. Do I have to sing *Dixie?*'

'Well, *mah wuhd,*' said the man in Bern stretching out the phrase in a dialect bred in the American deep south, the French pretence dropped. 'You go back a long time, don't you, suh?'

'I do, sir.'

'I hear you're one of the bad guys now.'

'Unloved, mistrusted, but still appreciated,' said Stone. 'That's more accurate. The Company won't touch me but it's got its share of unfriendlies in town who throw me consultations pretty regularly. I wasn't as smart as you. No deposits from Uncle No-Name in Swiss accounts.'

'I was told you had a little juice problem.'

'A big one but it's over.'

'Never negotiate a release from people worse than you if you can't pass a Breathalyser test. You've got to scare them, not make 'em laugh.'

'I found that out. I hear you do some consulting yourself.'

'On a limited basis and only with clients who could pass Uncle No-Name's muster. That's the agreement and I stick to it. Either I do or some Boom Boom Botticelli is flown over and massa's in de cole, cole ground.'

'Where the threats don't do you any good,' completed the civilian.

'That's the stand-off, Pearlie May. It's our little *détente*.'

'Would I pass muster? I give you my word I'm working with good people. They're young and they're on to something and they haven't got an evil thought in their heads, which under the circumstances is no recommendation. But I can't tell you anything substantive. For your sake as well as mine and theirs. Is that good enough?'

'If the consultation doesn't take place in outer space it's more than enough, and you know it. You saved Johnny Reb's ass three times, only y'awl got the sequence backwards. In the Dardanelles and Lisbon you got me out before the guns came in. Over in Bahrain you rewrote a report about a little matter of missing contingency funds that probably kept me from five years in a Leavenworth stockade.'

'You were too valuable to lose over a minor indiscretion. Besides, you weren't the only one, you merely got caught – or nearly did.'

'Regardless, Johnny Reb owes. What is it?'

Stone reached for his glass and took a drink. He spoke, choosing his words carefully. 'One of our commanders is missing. It's a Navy problem, SAND PAC based, and the people I'm with want to keep it contained. No Washington input at this stage.'

'Which is part of what you can't tell me,' said the Southerner. 'Okay. SAND PAC – that's San Diego and points west and wet until the date-line, right?'

'Yes, but it's not relevant. He's the chief legal out there – maybe *was*, by now. If he's not past tense, *if* he's alive, he's nearer you than me. Also if I get on a plane, my passport ignites the computers and things can't go that way.'

'Which is also part of what you can't tell me.'

'Check.'

'What *can* you tell me?'

'You know the embassy in Bonn?'

'I know it's in trouble. Just like the security units in Brussels. That psycho's cutting one hell of a path. What about Bonn?'

'It's all related. Our commander was last seen there.'

'He's got something to do with this *Converse*?'

Stone paused. 'You can probably fill in more spaces than is good for any of us, but the bones of the scenario are as follows. Our commander was a very upset man. His brother-in-law – who, incidentally was his closest friend – was killed in Geneva . . .'

'Down the road from here,' interrupted the expatriate in Bonn. 'The American lawyer whose demise was engineered by Converse, at least that's what I've read.'

'That's what our commander believed. How or from whom he got the information no one knows, but apparently he found out that Converse was heading for Bonn. He went on leave to go after him.'

'Commendable but dumb,' said the Southerner. 'A one-man lynching mob?'

'Actually, no. By simple equations we can assume he went to the embassy, at least he met someone *from* the embassy to explain why he was there, perhaps to warn them, who knows? But the rest speaks for itself. This Converse struck and our commander disappeared. We'd like to find out whether he's alive or dead.'

It was the Southerner's turn to pause, his breathing, however, clearly heard on the line. Finally, 'Brer Rabbit, you've simply *got* to put a little flesh on those bones.'

'I'm about to, General Lee.'

'Much obliged, Yankee.'

'It's also related. If you were a lieutenant commander in the United States Navy and wanted to reach someone at the embassy in Bonn, someone who would accord you the attention your rank deserved, who would you call?'

'The military *chargé d'affaires*, who else?'

'That's the man, Uncle Remus. Among other things he's a liar, but I can't go into that. It's our thinking that the commander spoke with him and the *chargé* dismissed him as a fringe case, probably didn't even give him an appointment with Ambassador Peregrine. And when it happened, to save his ass and his career . . . well, people do strange things.'

'What you're suggesting is awful damned strange.'

'I won't back away from it,' said the civilian.

'Okay, what's his name?'

'Washburn. He's a . . .'

'*Norman* Washburn?! Major Norman Anthony Washburn, the Third, Fifth or Sixth?'

'That's the one.'

'*Don't* back away. You left the field too early. Washburn was in Beirut, then Athens and after that Madrid. He gave every Company flack in the territories the business! He'd nail his Park Avenue mama to a velvet wall for a good evaluation report. He figures by forty-five he'll be heading the Joint Chiefs – and he intends to.'

'By forty-five?'

'I've been out of touch for a couple of years, but he can't be any more than thirty-six, thirty-seven. The last I heard they were going to jump the light-colonel status and make him a full bird, then a brigadier soon after that. He is *loved*, Yankee!'

'He's a liar,' said the civilian in the dimly-lit apartment on Nebraska Avenue.

'Sure 'nuff,' agreed the man in Bern, 'but I never figured anything this radical. I mean, he's got to be scratchin' mule shit for oil to do something so far out.'

'I still won't back away,' repeated the civilian, drinking his bourbon.

'Which means you know.'

'Check.'

'And you can't talk about that, either.' A statement.

'Check again.'

'Are you firm?'

'No room for error. He knows where the commander is – if he's alive.'

'Holy *Jesus!* What *are* you Northern boys *into?*'

'Will you track? Starting yesterday?'

'With pleasure, Yankee. How do you want it?'

'In the twilight zone. Only words that come with needles – that's important. He has to wake up thinking he ate a bad piece of meat.'

'Women?'

'I don't know. You probably have a better fix on that than I do. Would he risk his image?'

'With two or three *Fräuleins* I've got in Bonn, Jesuits would risk the papacy, suh. The name of the commander, please?'

'Fitzpatrick, Lieutenant-Commander Connal Fitzpatrick . . . And, Uncle Remus, whatever you hear under the needles, give only to me. No one else. *No one.*'

'Which is the last part of what you can't tell me, right?'

'Check.'

'My blinders are in place. One objective only with only one target. No side trips and no curiosity, just a tape recorder in my head or my hand.'

Again Stone paused, filling the silence with a tentative whisper. '*Tape* . . . ?' Then he continued. 'The latter's not a bad idea. Mini-micro, of course.'

'Naturally. Those little mothers are so small you can hide them in the most embarrassing places. Where do I reach you? My quill is poised.'

'All right, the area code's eight-zero-four.' The former CIA man gave the expatriate in Bern a telephone number in Charlotte, North Carolina. 'A woman will answer. Tell her you're from the Tatiana family and leave a number.'

Their brief goodbyes concluded, Peter hung up the phone, got out of the chair and carried his drink to the window. It was a hot, still night in Washington, the air outside barely moving, the hint of a summer storm. If the rains came they would wash the streets and cleanse at least part of the pollution.

The former deep-cover agent wished there was some balm on earth or from the skies that could wash his hands and cleanse that part of his soul he had not put on the auction block – or for a disastrous period of time into a bottle of bourbon. Maybe all he had done was hammer another nail in Converse's coffin, one more scrap of credibility that labelled the lawyer something he was not. Stone realized that instead of casting reasonable doubts based on his own certain knowledge, he had compounded the fiction that Converse was the psychopathic killer the international media described. Worse, he had attributed that credibility to a responsible missing man, a naval officer who was most likely dead. There were two justifications for the lie, and only one was remotely feasible: the other, however, was probably the most productive move they could make. The first assumed that Fitzpatrick *might* be alive, a weak premise. But if he was dead, the missing commander provided the reason to call in an old debt and go after a *chargé d'affaires* named Washburn and do so without any connection to George Marcus Delavane. Even if 'Johnny Reb' was caught – and every man in a grey to black operation had to assume the possibility – no mention could be made of an international conspiracy of generals – Major Norman Washburn, IV, might or might not know the fate of Connal Fitzpatrick, but everything else he might say under the needles especially about the commander would be of value.

What surprised the civilian was Converse himself in the matter of the lying military attaché. If Converse was running and not under lock and key he certainly must have learned about the lie that had condemned him. If so, why hadn't the attorney done something about it? The major's lie was the chain's weakest link; it could be snapped with a minimum of effort – the man's a liar. I was here, or there, or anywhere except where he placed me when he placed me. Stone drank sparingly from the glass; he knew the futility of speculating because he knew the answer. It was why he did not feel that yet another part of his soul had been clipped away. Converse was not in a position to do anything. He was either trapped or taken, soon to be offered up as a sacrificial corpse by the generals. There was nothing anyone could do for him. He was a dead man, a sacrifice in the truest sense of the word – given up even by his own.

Peter walked back to the chair and sat down, loosening his tie and kicking off his shoes. He had learned years ago to cut losses in the field wherever possible. If it meant disowning pawns or plants or blinds, one took the statistical approach and let the executions follow. It was better than losing more. But what was even better was to make a significant progress with whatever the loss. He was doing that now with Converse's death and 'Johnny Reb' in Bern . . . and a liar named Washburn.

Oh, *Christ!* He was playing *God* again with charts and diagrams – pluses and minuses of human value! Yet the objective was worth more than anything he had ever faced before. Delavane and his legions had to be stopped, and they would not be stopped in Washington. There were too many watchful eyes, too many ears, too many men in unknown corners who believed in the myth; men who had nothing else. The children were right about that. And there would be no empty bottles of bourbon on the floor now, or blurred memories of nights past, or words passed. Despite advancing age, he was ready; he was primed.

It was odd, thought the civilian. He had not used the *Tatiana family* in years.

Joel watched from the ridge of the landfill as Leifhelm's chauffeur and his companion approached the deserted building. Both were experienced; one raced before the other, stopping behind displaced rocks from the fill and barrels used for early morning fires. Almost simultaneously they reached separate doors, each door off its hinges, angling into the dirt. The chauffeur gestured with his weapon and both men disappeared inside.

Converse again looked behind him. The fence was about two hundred yards away. Could he slide down the stinking hill, race to the interwoven wire and climb over the fence before his executioners came out of the decrepit building? Why *not*? He could *try!* He raised himself off his stomach, hands sinking into the debris, spun to his right, and plunged downward.

A distant crash came first and then a scream. He spun around again and scrambled up the ten odd feet his lunge had carried him. The chauffeur was racing out of his door, around the corner to where his companion had entered, his gun levelled, prepared to fire. He approached cautiously then, seeing something, exploded in disgust as he entered the shadows. Seconds later he emerged holding the other man; obviously a staircase or a floorboard had collapsed. The second man held his leg and limped.

Two piercing blasts came from the station; the platform was empty, the milling passengers back on board. The panic had subsided and the train would make a Teutonic effort to be on time. The last police car and the ambulance were gone.

Below, the chauffeur slapped his companion repeatedly in fury, shoving him backwards to the ground. The man got up, gesturing, pleading for no more, and the chauffeur relented, ordering his subordinate to a position between the building, the landfill and the fence and, when the man was in place, the chauffeur went back into the deserted building.

A half hour passed, the descending sun intercepted by low-flying clouds in the west, creating long, lateral shadows over the outskirts of the railroad yard. Finally the chauffeur came into view, emerging from an unseen exit on another side of the building. He stood for a moment and looked west across the tracks, to the expanse of wild grass and marshland beyond. Then he turned and stared at the mounds of landfill and made up his mind.

'*Rechts über Ihnen!*' he screamed at his companion, pointing to the second mound. '*Hinter Ihnen! Er schiept!*'

Joel crawled, racing down the debris like a panicked sand crab. Halfway to the bottom his left hand was snared; he yanked at the looping entrapment, pulled it free and was about to discard it when he saw it was a length of ordinary, electric cord. He bunched it up in his hand and frantically continued downward. When he was within six feet of the ground, he whipped his whole body into frenzy and clawed at the dirt and garbage. He stabbed his legs repeatedly into the rubbish and loose earth and he sank his body into the mass, pulling debris around his head. The stench was overpowering and he could feel the insects penetrating his clothes, crawling over his skin. But he was hidden, of that he was certain. He began to comprehend what his fragmented mind was trying to tell him. He was back in the jungle, about to spring on a scout from an unseen place.

Minutes passed and the shadows became longer, then permanent as the sun's trajectory dropped below the top of the landfill. Converse remained immobile, straining every muscle, grinding his teeth to stop himself from thrashing his arms and scratching his clothes and his exposed skin to rip away the maddening insects. But he knew he could not move. It would happen any moment, any second.

The prelude came. The limping man was in view, peering up at the hill of refuse and dirt, squinting against the residue of sunlight at the top, his gun held out, angled diagonally, prepared to fire. He side-stepped slowly, cautiously, apprehensive of what he could not see. He passed directly in front of Joel, the extended gun no more than three feet away from Converse's face. Another step and the line of contact would be clear.

Now! Joel lunged out, grabbing the barrel of the gun, instantly and violently twisting it clockwise and downward. As the German fell forward Converse crashed his knee up into the bridge of the man's nose, stunning him before he could scream. The weapon spiralled off into the debris. The man staggered, about to find his voice, and Joel lunged again, a section of the wire cord stretched out in both hands; he whipped it over the scout's head, pulling it taut around the scout's throat. The *scout* had to die because the *scout* would kill him! It was as simple as that! No, it was *not* that simple. This was a soldier of Aquitaine, *garbage* from Aquitaine. He killed on command – he followed *orders!* He would never kill again.

The man went limp, and Converse bent over the body, about to roll it into the base of the landfill and conceal it, but then he stopped. There had to be another way because there was another option, one he had taken a hundred years ago with another scout in a jungle. He looked around; there was a pile of carelessly dumped railroad ties thirty-odd yards away on his right – old ties, several broken . . . forming a low wall. A *wall.*

It was a risk. If Leifhelm's chauffeur finished his examination of the first mound of landfill and stepped out towards the second one at any three of the four angles, he would have a clear line of sight. The man had been sent to the Emmerich train for two reasons – one, he knew the quarry by sight, and, two, the quarry had disgraced him; Joel's corpse would be his redemption. Such a man was an expert with weapons . . . which the quarry was not. What was the point of thinking! Since Geneva, *everything* was a risk, a gamble against death when he did not know it.

He gripped the German's body under the armpits, and breathing hard – for some reason foolishly counting off *one, two, three* – he lurched backwards, hauling the dead man across a dead man's zone.

He reached the railroad ties and swung the corpse around them, the heels of its shoes digging an arc into the dirt as he dragged the dead German into the base of his wall. Then, without thinking, acting only on instinct, Converse did what he had been wanting to do for the last hour. Concealed by the ties, he ripped off his jacket and shirt and rolled on the ground, scattering the insects like an infested dog in a field, scratching them out of his hair, away from his face. It was all he could do for the moment. He crawled into the bank of railroad ties and found a space between two separated logs.

'*Werner! Wo sind Sie?*'

The shouts preceded the figure of Leifhelm's chauffeur. He appeared at the far end of the second mound, moving slowly, his gun raised, each step taken cautiously, his head shifting in all directions, a soldier experienced in combat patrol. Converse thought how much better off the world would be if he were an expert shot. He was not. In pilot training he had gone through the obligatory small arms course, and at twenty-five feet had rarely hit the target. This second soldier of Aquitaine had to be sucked in much closer.

'*Werner! Antworten Sie doch!*'

Silence.

The chauffeur was alarmed; he walked backwards, now crouching, scanning the hill of refuse, kicking away any object in his backward path, his head pivoting. Joel knew what he had to do; he had done it before. Divert the killer's attention, pulling him closer to the encounter, then move away.

'*Auughh* . . . !' Converse let the wail come out of his throat. Then added in clear English, 'Oh, my *God!*' Instantly he crawled to the far end of the wall of railroad ties. He peered around the side, his head in shadows.

'*Werner! Wo sind* . . . !' The German stood erect, his eyes following his line of hearing. Suddenly he broke into a run, his weapon thrust in front of him like a man cornering a hated object, an escaped sound in English leading him to that loathed enemy.

The chauffeur lunged prone across the railroad ties, his expression alert, his gun in front of him. He fired into the shadowed corpse below, a roar of vengeance accompanying the explosions.

Joel got to his knees, aimed his automatic, and pulled the trigger once. The German spun off the ties, a trickle of blood erupting in his chest.

'Some win,' whispered Converse rising to his feet, remembering the man on the train to Emmerich.

He was down in the marshlands, the clothes in his arms. He had scrambled across the railroad tracks, down through the wild grass into the swampy dampness of the marsh. It was water, and that was all he had to know. Water was cleansing, whether as an escape route or to bathe one's racking body – also lessons he had learned years ago. He sat naked on a sloping marsh bank, taking his inhibiting money belt off, wondering if the paper bills inside were soaked but not caring enough to examine them.

He did, however, examine every pocket of the clothes he had stripped from his would-be executioners. He was not sure what was of value and what was not. The money was irrelevant, except for the small bills; and the drivers' licences had photographs embedded in plastic – neither was worth the risk of scrutiny. There was an ominous-looking knife, the long blade released through the head by the touch of a button on the handle; he kept it. Also a cheap butane lighter and a comb and for the drinking man, two breath fresheners. The rest were personal effects – keys, a 4-leaf clover good luck charm . . . photographs in the wallets – he did not care to look at them. Death was death, enemy and friend fundamentally equalized. The only things he was interested in were the clothes. *They* were the option, the option he had used in the jungle a lifetime ago. He had crammed himself inside a scout's tattered uniform and twice across a narrow riverbank he had not been shot by the enemy who had spotted him. Instead, they had waved.

He selected the articles of clothing that fitted best and put them on; the rest he threw into the marsh. Whatever he looked like, there was little or no resemblance to the tweedy academic he had tried to be in Bonn. If anything, he could be mistaken for a man who worked on the Rhine, a rough-hewn mate or a foreman of a barge crew. He had chosen the chauffeur's coat, a dark, coarse-woven jacket cut to the hips, with the man's blue denim shirt underneath – both bullet holes washed clean of blood. The trousers were those of the subordinate executioner; brown creaseless corduroys, flared slightly at the ankles, which thankfully they reached. Neither man had worn a hat and his was somewhere in the landfill; he would find one or buy one or steal one. He had to; without a hat or a cap covering part of his face, he felt as naked, as exposed and as frightened as he felt without his clothes.

He lay back in the dry wild grass as the sun disappeared over an unseen horizon, and stared up at the sky.

24

'Well, *Ah'll be* . . . !' exclaimed the distinguished-looking man with the flowing mane of white hair, his full, nearly white eyebrows arched in astonishment. 'You're Molly Washburn's boy?'

'I beg your pardon?' said the Army officer at the adjacent table along the banquette in Bonn's *Am Tulpenfeld* restaurant. 'Have we met, sir?'

'Not so's you'd remember, Major . . . Please forgive my intruding.' The Southerner addressed the apology to the officer's companion across the table, a balding middle-aged man who had been speaking English with a pronounced German accent. 'But Molly would never forgive this poor old Georgia cracker if he didn't say hello to her son and insist on buyin' him a drink.'

'I'm afraid I'm at a loss,' said Washburn pleasantly but without enthusiasm.

'I would be, too, young fella. I know it sounds cornpone but you were just barely in long pants back then. The last time I saw you, you were in a blue blazer jacket and madder 'n hell at losing a soccer game. I think you blamed it on your left wing, which in my opinion then and now is a logical place to blame *anything*.'

The major and his companion laughed appreciatively. 'Good Lord, that does go back a long time – to when I was at Dalton.'

'And captain of the team, as I recall.'

'How did you ever recognize me?'

'I dropped in on your momma the other week at the house in Southampton. Proud girl that she is, there were a few real handsome photographs of you in the living room.'

'Of course, on the piano.'

'That's where they were, silver frames and all.'

'I'm afraid I've forgotten your name.'

'Thayer. Thomas Thayer, or just plain old "T.T." as your momma calls me.' The two shook hands.

'Good to see you again, sir,' said Washburn, gesturing at his companion.

'This is Herr Schindler. He handles a great deal of our press relations with the West German media.'

'How do you do, Mr Schindler.'

'A pleasure, Herr Thayer.'

'Speaking of the embassy and I assume you were, I promised Molly I'd ring you up over there when I got here. Mah word on it, I was going to do just that tomorrow – I'm fightin' jet lag today. One hell of a coincidence, isn't it? You bein' here and my bein' here, right *next* to each other!'

'Herr Major,' interrupted the German courteously. 'Two people who go back so many years must have a great deal to reminisce about. And since our business is fundamentally concluded, I think I shall press on.'

'Now hold on, Mr Schindler,' objected Thayer. 'Ah simply couldn't allow you to do that!'

'No, really, it's perfectly all right.' The German smiled. 'Truthfully, Major Washburn felt he should insist on taking me to dinner this evening after the terrible things we've had to deal with during the past few days – he far more than I – but to be quite honest, I'm exhausted. Also I am far older than my young friend and nowhere near as resilient. The bed cries out, Herr Thayer. Believe me when I tell you that.'

'Hey, Mr Schindler, Ah've got an idea. You're fanned out and I'm droppin' from the jet stream, so why don't we leave the young skunk here and *both* hit the pillows?'

'But *I* couldn't allow *you* to do that.' The German got up from the table and extended his hand to Thayer. They shook, and Schindler turned to Washburn, shaking his hand also. 'I'll call you in the morning, Norman.'

'All right, Gerhart . . . Why didn't you just say you were tired?'

'And conceivably offend one of my largest clients? Be reasonable, Norman. Good night, gentlemen.' The German smiled again, and walked away.

'Ah guess we're stuck with each other, young man,' said the Southerner. 'Why not move over here and let me save the embassy a couple of dollars?'

'All right,' replied Washburn, getting up with his drink and sidling between the tables to the chair opposite Thayer. He sat down. 'How is mother? I haven't called her in a couple of weeks.'

'Molly is always Molly, my boy. She came forth and they broke the mould, but I don't have to tell *you* that. She looks the same as she did twenty years ago. I swear I don't know how she *does* it!'

'And she's not going to tell you, either.'

Both men laughed as the Southerner raised his glass, pressing it forward for the touch. The glasses met, the gentle ring heard. It was the beginning.

Converse waited, watching from a dark storefront on the shabby street in Emmerich. Across the way were the dim lights of a cheap hotel, the entrance uninviting, sleazy. Yet with any luck he would have a bed there in the next few minutes. A bed with a basin in the corner of the room and, with even more luck, hot water with which he could bathe his wound and change the bandage again. During the last two nights he had learned that such places were his only stops of refuge. No questions were asked and a false name on a registration card was to be expected. But even the most sullen greeting was a menace for him. He opened his mouth and whatever came out identified him as an American who could not speak German.

He felt like a deaf-mute careening off walls of people in a labyrinth designed as a gauntlet. He was so helpless, so goddamned *helpless!* The killings in Bonn, Brussels and Wesel somehow made every American male over thirty and under fifty suspect. The melodramatic suspicions were compounded by speculations that the obsessed man was being aided, perhaps manipulated, by terrorist organizations – Baader Meinhof, the PLO, Libyan splinter groups, even KGB destabilization teams sent out by the dreaded *Voennaya*. He was being hunted everywhere and as of yesterday, the *International Herald Tribune* had printed further reports that the assassin was heading for Paris – which meant that the generals of Aquitaine wanted the concentration to be *on* Paris, not where they knew he was, where their soldiers could run him down, take him, kill him.

To get off the streets he had to move with the flotsam and jetsam, and a run-down hotel like the one across the street was more appealing than the Waldorf Astoria. And he *had* to get off the streets; there were too many traps outside. So on the first night in Wesel he remembered the student, Johann, and looked for ways to recreate vaguely similar circumstances. Young people were less prone to be suspicious, the promise of immediate reward quelling doubts for pockets and appetites more in need.

It was odd but that first night in Wesel was both the most difficult and the easiest. Difficult because he had no idea where to look, easy because it happened so rapidly, so logically. He had stopped at a drug store, buying gauze, adhesive tape, antiseptic and an inexpensive cap with a visor. Then he went to a café, to the men's room, where he had washed his face and stung the wound, binding it tight, skin joining skin, the bandage firmly in place. Suddenly, as he finished his ministrations, he heard the familiar words and emphatic melody, young raucous voices in song.

'*On Wisconsin . . . On Wisconsin . . . on to victoreee . . . we shall . . .*'

A group of students from the German Society at the University of Wisconsin were bicycling through the northern Rhineland. Casually approaching a young man getting more beers from the bar, and introducing himself as an exhausted and ashamed fellow American, he told an outrageous story of having been taken by a whore and rolled by her pimp – who stole his passport but never thought of a money belt. He was a respected businessman who had to sleep it off, gather his wits together, and reach his firm back in New York. However, he spoke no German; would the student consider the payment of a hundred dollars for helping him out?

He would and did. Down the block was a dingy hotel where no questions were asked; the young man paid for a room and brought Converse his receipt and his key outside.

All yesterday he had walked, following the roads in sight of the railroad tracks until he reached a town named Halden. It was smaller than Wesel, but there was a run-down, industrial section east of the railroad yards. The only 'hotel' he could find, however, was a large, shoddy house at the end of a row of shoddy houses with signs in two ground-floor windows and a larger one over the front door all proclaiming the same message. *Zimmer. 20 Mark.* It was a boarding house, and several doors beyond in the spill of the street lamps, a heated argument was taking place between an older woman and a young man. Above, a few neighbours sat in their windows, arms on the sills, obviously listening. Then Joel heard the words, shouted in heavily accented English.

'. . . "I hate it here!" *Das habe ich ihm gesagt.* "I do not care to stay, Onkel! I vill go back to Germany! Maybe join Baader-Meinhof!" *Das habe ich ihm gesagt.*'

'*Narr!*' screamed the woman, turning and going up the steps. '*Schweine-hund!*' she roared, as she opened the door, went inside and slammed it shut behind her.

The young man had looked up at his audience in the windows and shrugged. A few clapped, so he made an exaggerated, elaborate bow. Converse approached; there was no harm in trying, he thought, as he spoke.

'You speak very good English,' he said.

'Vye not?' replied the German. 'They spend bags of groceries for five years to give me lessons. I must go to her brother in America. I say *Nein!* They say *Ja!* I go. I *hate* it!'

'I'm sorry to hear that. I'm an American and I like the German people. Where were you?'

'In Yorktown.'

'Virginia?'

'*Nein!* The city of New York.'

'Oh, *that* Yorktown.'

'*Ja*, my uncle has two butcher shops in New York, in what they call Yorktown. *Shit*, as you say in America!'

'I'm sorry. Why?'

'The *Schwarzen* and the *Juden!* If you speak like me, the black people steal from you with knives, and the Jews steal from you with their cash registers. *Heinie*, they call me, and *Nazi*. I told a Jew he cheated me – I was nice, I was not impolite – and he told me to get out of his shop or he would call the "cops"! I was *shit*, he said! . . . You wear a good German suit and spend good German money, they don't say those things. You are a delivery boy trying to learn, they kick the shit out of you! What do *I* know! My father was too young to be anything but a fourteen-year-old soldier. *Shit!*'

'Again, I'm telling you I'm sorry. I mean it. It's not in our nature to blame children.'

'*Shit!*'

'Perhaps I can make up for a little of what you went through. I'm in trouble – because I was a *stupid* American. But I'll pay you a hundred American dollars . . .'

The young German happily got him a room at the boarding house. It was no better than the one in Wesel, but the water was hotter, the toilet nearer his door.

But tonight was different, thought Joel, as he looked across the street at the time-worn old hotel in Emmerich with no significance in its past. Tonight could lead to his passage into Holland. To Cort Thorbecke and a plane to Washington. The man he had recruited was somewhat older than the others. He was a merchant seaman out of Bremerhaven, in Emmerich to make a duty call on his family with whom he felt ill at ease. He had made the obligatory call, been soundly rebuked by his mother and father, and had returned to the environs and the people he loved best – a bar on the bend of the riverbank.

Again, as it had been in Wesel, it was a song and the lyrics of a song that caused Joel to stare at the young seaman standing at the bar, a guitar in his hands. What he played was no college football anthem, but the words were in English, albeit Germanically anglicized, and the melody was an odd, haunting mixture of slow biting rock and a sad madrigal.

'. . . *When you finally came down . . . when your feet hit the ground, did you know where you were? . . . When you finally were real, could you touch what you feel, were you there in the know? . . .*'

The men around the bar were caught up by the precise beat of the minor key music. When the seaman finished there was respectful applause, followed by fast talk and faster refilled mugs of beer. Minutes later Converse was standing next to the sea-going troubadour, the guitar now slung over his shoulder, held in place by a wide strap like a weapon. Joel wondered if the man really knew English or only lyrics. He would find out in seconds. The seaman laughed at a companion's remark; when the laughter subsided, Converse spoke.

'I'd like to buy you a drink,' he said. 'For reminding me of home. It was a nice song.'

The man looked at him quizzically. Joel stammered, thinking that the seaman had no idea what he was talking about; the German spoke only lyrics, not the language. Then, to Converse's relief, the man answered.

'*Danke.* It is a good song. Sad but good, like some of ours. You are *Amerikaner?*'

'Yes. And you speak English.'

'Okay. I don't read no good, *aber* I speak okay. I'm on merchant ship. We sail Boston, New York, Baltimore – sometimes ports, Florida.'

'What'll you have?'

'*Ein Bier,*' said the seaman, shrugging.

'Why not whisky?'

'*Ja?*'

'Certainly.'

'*Ja.*'

Minutes later they were at a table. Joel told his story about a non-existent whore and a fictional pimp. He told it slowly, not because he felt he had to pace the narrative to his listener's understanding, but because another option was coming sharply into focus. The guitar-playing merchant man was young but there was a patina about him that indicated he knew the docks and the waterfront and the various businesses that flourished in that very special world.

'You should go to the *Polizei,*' said the man when Converse had finished. 'They know the whores and they will not print your name.' The German smiled. 'We want you back to spend more money.'

'I can't take the chance. In spite of the way I look, I deal with a lot of important people – here and in America.'

'Which makes *you* important, *ja?*'

'And very stupid. If I could just get over into Holland, I could handle everything.'

'*Der Niederlande?* What is problem?'

'I told you, my passport was taken. And it's just my luck that every American crossing any border is looked at very carefully. You know, that crazy bastard who killed the ambassador in Bonn and the NATO commander.'

'*Ja*, and in Wesel two, three days ago,' completed the German. 'They say he goes to Paris.'

'I'm afraid that doesn't help me . . . Look, you know the river people, the men who have boats going out every day. I told you I'd pay you a hundred dollars for the hotel . . .'

'I agreed, *Mein Herr*. You are generous.'

'I'll pay you a great deal more if you can somehow get me over into Holland. You see my company has an office in Amsterdam. They can help me. Will *you* help me?'

The German grimaced and looked at his watch. 'Is too late for such arrangements tonight and I leave for Bremerhaven on the morning train. My ship sails at fifteen hundred.'

'That was the amount I had in mind. Fifteen hundred.'

'*Deutschmarks?*'

'Dollars.'

'You are more crazy than your *Landsmann* who kills soldiers. If you knew the language, it would cost no more than fifty.'

'I don't know the language. Fifteen hundred American dollars – for you if you can arrange it.'

The young man looked hard at Converse, then moved back his chair. 'Wait here. I will make a phone call.'

'Send over more whisky on your way.'

'*Danke.*'

The waiting was neither pleasant nor unpleasant; it was time spent in a vacuum of anxiety. Joel looked at the weathered guitar lying below across an extra chair. What were the words? '. . . *When you finally came down, when your feet hit the ground . . . did you know where you were? When . . . you were real, could you touch . . . what you feel, were you there in the know? . . .*'

'I will stop for you at five o'clock in the morning.' The announcement came from the merchant seaman who sat down with two glasses of whisky. 'The captain will accept two hundred dollars, *aber* only if there are no drugs. If there are drugs, you don't come on board.'

'I have no drugs,' said Converse, smiling, controlling his elation. 'That's done and you've earned your money. I'll pay you at the dock or pier or whatever it is.'

'*Natürlich.*'

It had all happened less than an hour ago, thought Joel, watching the hotel entrance across the street. Tonight *was* different. At five o'clock in the morning he would be on his way to Holland, to Amsterdam, to a man named Cort Thorbecke, Mattilon's broker of illegal passports. All the passenger manifests on all aircraft heading to the United States would be watched by Aquitaine, but a hundred years ago he had learned that there were ways to elude the watchers. He had done it before from a deep, cold shaft in the ground and a barbed wire fence in the darkness. He could do it again.

A figure emerged under the dimly-lit marquee of the hotel. It was the young merchant seaman. Grinning, he beckoned Converse to join him.

'Hell's fire and Jeesus *H*, what *is* it, Norman?' cried the Southerner, as Washburn suddenly began an erratic series of convulsions, his lips trembling as he gasped for air.

'I . . . don't . . . know.' The major's eyes grew wide, the pupils now dancing and out of control.

'Maybe it's that Heimlich thing!' said Thomas Thayer, rising from the banquette and quickly side-stepping his way between the table on the left and Washburn. 'Hell no, it *can't* be! Our food's not here; you haven't *eaten!*'

The couples on both sides expressed alarm, talking loudly, rapidly in German. At one of the diner's remarks, the Southerner turned and spoke to the man. '*Das glaube ich nicht,*' said Johnny Reb. '*Mein Wagen steht draussen. Ich kenne einen Arzt.*'

The *maître* came rushing over and, seeing that the commotion involved the Americans, addressed his concern in English. 'Is the major ill, *Mein Herr?* Shall I ask if there is . . .'

'No doctor I'm not familiar with, thanks,' interrupted Thayer, bent over the embassy's *chargé d'affaires*, who was now inhaling deeply, his eyes half-closed, his head swaying back and forth. 'This here is Molly Washburn's boy and I'll see he gets the best! My car's outside. Maybe if a couple of your waiters will give a hand we can put him in the limo and I'll take him right over to my man. He's a specialist. At my age you gotta have 'em everywhere.'

'*Bestimmt.* Certainly!' The *maître* snapped his fingers; three waiters responded instantly.

'The embassy . . . the *embassy!*' choked Washburn as the three men half carried the officer to the door of the restaurant.

'Don't you worry, Norman-boy!' said the Southerner, hearing the plea, walking behind with the *maître*. 'I'll phone 'em from the car, tell 'em to meet us at Rudi's place.' Thayer turned to the German beside him. 'You know what Ah think? Ah think this fine soldier is jest plumb wore out. He's been workin' from sunrise to sunrise with nary a break. I mean, can you imagine everything he's had to contend with these last couple of days? That crazy mongrel goin' around shootin' up a feud, killin' the ambassador then that honcho in Brussels! You know, Molly's boy here is the *char-jay d'affaires.*'

'Yes, the major is our guest frequently – an honoured guest.'

'Well, even the most honourable among us has a right and a time to say "the hell with it, I'll sit this one out".'

'I'm not sure I understand?'

'Ah have an idea this fine young man who I knew as a mere saplin' lad never learned about the quantitative effects of old demon whisky.'

'Ohh?' The *maître* looked at Johnny Reb as might a carrier of fashionable gossip hearing a new rumour.

'He had several mites too much, that's all – and *that's* jest between *us.*'

'He vas not in focus . . .'

'He started bustin' corks before the sun hit the roof of the west barn.'
They reached the front entrance, the unit of busboys manoeuvring Washburn out the door. 'Who was more entitled? That's what I say.' Thayer removed his wallet.

'*Ja*, I agree.'

'Here,' said the Southerner, removing bills. 'I haven't had time to convert, so there's a hundred American – that should cover the tab and plenty for the boys outside . . . And here's a hundred for you – for not talkin' too much, *verstehen?*'

'Completely, *Mein Herr!*' The German pocketed both hundred dollar bills, smiling and nodding his head obsequiously. 'I vill say absolutely nozzing!'

'Well, I wouldn't go that far. It might be a good thing for Molly's boy to learn that it ain't the end of the world if a few people know he's had a drink or two. Might loosen him up a bit, and in mah Georgia judgment, he needs a little loosenin'. Maybe you might wink at him when he next come in.'

'*Vink?*'

'Give him a friendly smile, like you know and it's okay. *Verstehen Sie?*'

'*Ja*, I agree! He vas entitled!'

Outside at the kerb, Johnny Reb instructed the waiters just how to place Major Norman Anthony Washburn, IV, into the back seat. Stretched out, facing up, supine. The Southerner gave each man a twenty-dollar American bill and dismissed them. He then spoke to the two men in front, pressing a button so they could hear his voice beyond the glass partition.

'Ah got the jump seats down,' he said, pulling the velvet backs out of the velvet wall. 'He's out. Come on and join me, Witch Doctor. And you, Klaus, you entertain us with a long drive in your beautiful countryside.'

Minutes later, as the limousine entered a back country road, the overhead light switched on, the doctor unbuckled Washburn's belt, slid the trousers down, and rolled the *chargé d'affaires* over and into the seat. He found the area he wanted at the base of the spine, the needle held above in his steady hand.

'Ready, chap?' asked the dark-skinned Palestinian, yanking down the elastic top of the unconscious man's shorts.

'You got it, Pookie,' answered Johnny Reb, holding a small recorder over the edge of the jump seat. 'Right where he won't find it for a week, if he ever does. Take him up, Arab. I want him to *fly*.'

The doctor inserted the long hypodermic needle, slowly pressing his thumb on the plunger. 'It will be quick,' said the Palestinian. 'It is a heavy dose and I've seen it happen when the patient began babbling before the interrogator was ready.'

'I'm ready.'

'Put him on track instantly. Ask direct questions, centre his concentration immediately.

'Oh, Ah will, indeed. This is a bad man, Pookie. A nasty little boy who tells tall tales that ain't got nothin' to do with a big catfish that broke off a hook.' The Southerner gripped the unconscious Washburn's left shoulder and yanked him forward, face up on the seat. 'All right, Molly's boy, let's you and me talk. How come you got the *audacity* to mess around with an officer of the United States Navy named Fitzpatrick? Connal Fitzpatrick, boy! Fitzpatrick, Fitzpatrick, *Fitzpatrick!* C'mon, baby, talk to daddy, 'cause you've got nobody else *but* daddy! Everyone you think you got is gone! They set you up, Molly's boy! They made you lie in print so the whole world *knows* you lied! But daddy can make it right. Daddy can straighten it all out and put you on top – right on the very *top!* The joint chiefs – the *big* chief! Daddy's your tit, boy! Grab it or suck air! Where'd you put Fitzpatrick? Fitzpatrick, *Fitzpatrick!*'

The whisper came, as Washburn's body writhed on the seat, his head whipping back and forth, saliva oozing out of the edges of his mouth. 'Scharhörn, the isle of Scharhörn . . . The Heligoland Bight.'

Caleb Dowling was not only angry, he was bewildered. Despite a thousand doubts he could not let it go; too many things did not make sense, not the least of which was the fact that for three days he had been unable to get an appointment with the acting-ambassador. The scheduling *attaché* claimed there was too much confusion resulting from Walter Peregrine's assassination to permit an audience at this time. Perhaps in a week . . . In short words, *actor get lost, we have important things to do and you're not one of them.* He was being checked, shoved into a corner, and given the lip service one gave to a well-known but insignificant person. His motives as well as his intelligence were undoubtedly questioned out loud by arrogant, harried diplomats. Or someone else.

Which was why he was sitting now at a back table in the dimly lit bar of the Königshof Hotel. He had learned the name of Peregrine's secretary, one Enid Heathley, and had sent the stunt man, Moose Rosenberg, to the embassy with a sealed letter purportedly from a close friend of Miss Heathley's in the States. Moose's instructions had been to deliver the envelope personally, and as Rosenberg's size was formidable, no one in the reception room had argued. Heathley had come down in person. The message was short and to the point.

Dear Miss Heathley:
I believe it to be of the utmost importance that we talk as soon as possible. I will be in the bar of the Königshof at 7.30 this evening. If it is convenient, please have a drink with me, but I urge you not to speak to anyone about our meeting. Please, no one.
Sincerely,
C. Dowling

It was 7.38 and Caleb was growing anxious. For the past several years he was used to people being on time for appointments and interviews; it was one of the minor perks of being Pa Ratchet. But there could be several reasons why the secretary might not wish to meet him. She knew he and Peregrine had become friends of sorts and there were actors and then there were actors – some were known to seek publicity from events they had nothing to do with, posturing with statesmen and politicians when they couldn't spell out a position on slavery. He hoped to hell . . .

There she *was*. The middle-aged woman had come through the door, squinting in the dim light. The *maître* approached her and moments later she was escorted to Dowling's table.

'Thank you for coming,' said Caleb, rising as Enid Heathley took her chair. 'I wouldn't have asked you if I didn't think it was important,' he added, sitting down again.

'I gathered that from your note,' said the pleasant-faced woman with signs of grey in her hair and very intelligent eyes. Her drink ordered, casual talk covered its arrival.

'I imagine it's been very difficult for you,' said Dowling.

'It hasn't been easy,' agreed Miss Heathley. 'I was Mr Peregrine's secretary for nearly twenty years. He used to call us a team, and Jane and I – Mrs Peregrine – are quite close. I should be with her now, but I told her I had some last minute things to do at the office.'

'How is she?'

'Still in shock, of course. But she'll make it. She's strong. Walter wanted the women around him strong. He thought they were worthwhile and they shouldn't hide their worth.'

'I like that kind of thinking, Miss Heathley.'

Her drink came, the waiter left, and the secretary looked quizzically at Caleb. 'Forgive me, Mr Dowling, I can't say I'm a devoted follower of your television show, but, of course, I've seen it a number of times. It seems that whenever I'm asked to dinner and the magic hour arrives, meals are suspended.'

'I'd suggest those people upgrade their kitchens.'

The woman smiled. 'You're too modest but that's not what I mean. You don't sound at all like the man on the television screen.'

'Because I'm not he, Miss Heathley,' said the former university professor, his expression serious, his intelligent eyes level with hers. 'I assume we share certain traits because I'm the physical instrument through which his fictions are filtered, but that's the extent of any similarity.'

'I see. That's very well put.'

'I've had practice saying it. But I didn't ask you here to expound on theories of acting. It's a subject with limited appeal.'

'Why did you ask me?'

'Because I don't know who else to go to. Well, I do but I can't get near him.'

'Who's that?'

'The acting-ambassador, the one who flew over from Washington.'

'He's up to his ears . . .'

'He should be told,' interrupted Caleb. 'Warned.'

'Warned?' The woman's eyes grew wide. 'An attempt on his *life?* Another killing – that maniac, *Converse?*'

'Miss Heathley,' began the actor, his posture rigid, his voice quiet. 'What I'm about to say may shock you, even offend you, but as I said, I don't know another person I can go to at the embassy. However, I *do* know there are people over there I *can't* go to.'

'What are you talking about?'

'I'm not convinced that Converse is either a maniac or that he killed Walter Peregrine.'

'*What?* You can't be serious! You've heard what they say about him, how unbalanced he is. He was the last person *with* Mr Peregrine. Major Washburn established that!'

'Major Washburn is one of those people I'd rather not see.'

'He's considered one of the finest officers in the United States Army,' objected the secretary.

'Then for an officer he has a strange concept of taking orders from a superior. Last week I brought Peregrine to meet someone. The man ran and Walter told the major to stop him. Instead, Washburn tried to kill him.'

'Oh, *now* I understand,' said Enid Heathley, her tone unpleasant. 'That was the night you arranged a meeting with Converse – it *was* you, I remember now! Mr Peregrine told me. What *is* this, Mr Dowling? A Hollywood actor protecting his image? Afraid he'll be held responsible and his ratings, or whatever they are, will plummet – that *is* the word, isn't it? This conversation is despicable.' The woman moved her chair back, prepared to leave.

'Walter Peregrine was a man of his word, Miss Heathley,' said Caleb, still immobile, staring at the secretary. 'I think you'll agree with that.'

'*And?*'

'He made a promise to me. He told me that if Converse reached him and asked to meet with him, I'd come along. *Me*, Miss Heathley. Specifically *not* Major Washburn, whose actions that night at the university were as bewildering to him as they were to me.'

The middle-aged woman held her place, her eyes narrowed, concerned. 'He *was* upset the next morning,' she said softly.

'Damned angry better describes him, I think. The man who ran away wasn't Converse – and he also wasn't crazy. He was deadly serious, with the speech of someone used to authority. There was – or is – some kind of confidential investigation going on involving the embassy. Peregrine didn't know what it was but he intended to find out. He mentioned that he was going to call Washington on a scrambler phone. I'm not up on the technology but I don't think a person places a call like that unless he's worried that someone might try to tap the line.'

'He *did* place a scrambler call. He told you that?'

'Yes, he did. And there's something else, Miss Heathley. As you correctly stated, I'm the one responsible for Walter Peregrine ever having heard of Converse, and I don't feel very good about it. But isn't it odd that in spite of the fact that it wasn't a secret – *you* knew, Washburn knew – nobody has come to question me since Walter was killed.'

'No one?' asked the woman incredulously. 'But I included your name in my report.'

'Who did you give it to?'

'Well, Norman was handling everything . . .' Enid Heathley stopped.

'Washburn?'

'Yes.'

'Didn't you speak to anyone else? Weren't you questioned?'

'Yes, of course. An inspector from the Bonn police. I'm sure I mentioned your name – I'm *positive* I did.'

'Was anybody else in the room?'

'Yes,' said the murdered ambassador's secretary. 'Norman,' she whispered.

'Strange behaviour for a police department, isn't it?' Caleb leaned forward, but only slightly. 'Let me re-emphasize something you said, Miss Heathley. You asked me if I was a Hollywood actor trying to protect his image. It's a logical question and if you ever saw the unemployment lines in Los Angeles you'd understand just how logical it is. Don't you think other people believe the same thing? I haven't been questioned because *specific* people here in Bonn think I'm shaking in Pa Ratchet's boots, keeping silent so as to protect that late-coming image and the ratings that make it possible. Oddly enough, that reasoning is my best physical protection. You don't kill off a Pa Ratchet unless you want the wrath of millions of viewers who, in my judgement, would latch on to the flimsiest connection to raise hysterical questions. *National Inquirer*, you are there.'

'But you're not keeping silent,' said Enid Heathley.

'I'm not talking loudly, either,' corrected the actor. 'But not for the reasons I've described. I owe Walter Peregrine – I know that better than anyone else. And I can't pay that debt if a man I think is innocent is hung for his murder. But here's where I step back into my own confusion. I can't be certain. I could be wrong.'

The woman returned Dowling's stare, then slowly frowned, keeping her eyes on him. 'I'm going to leave now but I'd like you to stay here for a while, if you wouldn't mind. I'm going to call someone I think you should see. You'll understand. He'll reach you here – no paging, of course. Do as he says, go where he wants you to go.'

'Can I trust him?'

'Mr Peregrine did,' said Enid Heathley, nodding. 'And he didn't like him.'

'That's trust,' said the actor.

The phone call came and Caleb wrote out the address. The doorman at the Königshof secured him a taxi, and eight minutes later he got out in front of an ornate Victorian house on the outskirts of Bonn. He walked up to the door and rang the bell.

Two minutes later he was ushered into a large room – once a library, perhaps – but now with shades covering the obvious bookshelves. Shades that were detailed maps of East and West Germany. A man wearing glasses got up from behind a desk. He nodded perfunctorily and spoke.

'Mr Dowling?'

'Yes.'

'I appreciate your coming out here, sir. My name is not important – why not call me George?'

'All right, George.'

'But for your own confidential information – and I must stress *confidential* – I am the Station Chief for the Central Intelligence Agency here in Bonn.'

'All right, George.'

'What do you do, Mr Dowling? What's your line of work?'

'*Ciao*, baby,' said the actor, shaking his head.

25

The first indefinite light of dawn crept up the lower wall of the eastern sky, and along the river pier boats bobbed in their slips, straining their lines, composing an eerie symphony of creaks and thumps. Joel walked beside the young merchant seaman, his right arm bent at the elbow, his hand unconsciously straying to his face, to the new soft hair that was the outgrowth of a stubble. He had not shaved in four days, since Bonn, and now he had the beginnings of a short, neat beard, not yet full but no longer a shabby bristle. One more day and he would have to begin clipping it, shaping it, another plane of removal from the photograph in the newspapers.

And in one more day he would have to decide whether or not to phone Val at Cape Ann. Actually, he had made his decision – negative. His instructions had been clear enough and the possibility that her telephone was tapped was more than he could handle. Yet he wanted so terribly to hear her voice, to hear the support he knew he would find in it. Negative. To hear it was to involve her. *Negative!*

'It is the last boat on the right,' said the seaman, slowing his pace. 'I must ask you again as I have given my word. You carry no drugs.'

'I carry no drugs.'

'He may care to search you.'

'I can't permit that,' broke in Converse, thinking of his money belt. What could be mistaken for a cache for narcotics would reveal many times the amount of money for which most of the dregs on the river front would kill.

'Perhaps he will want to know why. Drugs bring bad penalties, long prison terms.'

'I'll explain to him privately,' said Joel, thinking again. He would do so with his gun in one hand and an additonal five hundred dollar bill in the other. 'But I give you my word, no drugs.'

'It is not my boat.'

'But you made the arrangements, and you know enough about me to come after me if they come after you.'

'*Ja*, I remember. Connect-teecut – I been to visit friends in Bridge-*port*. A broker house, vice-president. I find you, if I have to.'

'I wouldn't want that. You're a nice fellow who's helping me out and I'm grateful. I won't get you in trouble.'

'*Ja*,' said the young German, nodding his head. 'I believe you. I believed you last night. You talk very good, very high class, but you were stupid. You did a stupid thing and your face is red. A red face costs more than you want to pay, so you pay much more to make it go away.'

'Your homilies are getting to me.'

'*Was ist?*'

'Nothing. You're right. It's the story of upper-level management. Here.'

Joel had the bills in his left-hand pocket; he pulled them out. 'I promised you fifteen hundred dollars. Count it, if you like.'

'*Vye?* If is not there I talk loud and you stay here. You are too afraid to risk that.'

'You're a natural born lawyer.'

'Come, I bring you to the captain. That is all he is to you, only "captain". You will be dropped off where he says . . . And a caution, *Mein Herr*. Watch the men on the boat. They will suspect you have money.'

'That's why I don't want to be searched,' admitted Converse.

'I know. I do my best for you.'

The seaman's best was not quite good enough. The captain of the filthy barge, a short hulk of a man with very poor teeth, brought Joel up to the wheelhouse where he told him in broken but perfectly clear English to remove his jacket.

'I explained to my friend on the dock that I can't do that.'

'Two hundred dollars, *Amerikaner*,' said the captain.

Converse had the money in his right-hand pocket. He reached down for it, his eyes briefly glancing at the port-side window where he saw two other men climb on board below in the dim light. They did not glance up; they had not seen him in the wheelhouse shadows.

The blow came suddenly, without warning, the impact such that Joel doubled over, expunging his breath, gripping his stomach. In front of him the surly bull of a captain was shaking his right hand, the grimace on his face indicating sharp pain. The German's fist had crashed into the gun lodged in Converse's belt. Joel staggered back into the bulkhead, leaned against it, and lowered himself to the floor as he reached under his jacket and took out the weapon. On his haunches, his legs bracing him against the wall, he aimed the automatic at the captain's huge chest.

'That was a rotten thing to do,' said Converse, breathing hard, still holding his stomach. 'Now, you bastard, *your* jacket!'

'*Was* . . . ?'

'You heard me! Take it off, hold it upside down, and shake the goddamned thing!'

The German slowly, reluctantly slid off his waist-length coat, twice darting his eyes to the left of Joel, towards the wheelhouse door. 'I look only for drugs.'

'I'm not carrying any, and if I were, I suspect whoever sold them to me would have a better way to get across the river than with you. Turn it upside down! *Shake* it!'

The captain held his coat by the bottom edge and let it fall away. A short, ugly revolver plummeted to the floor, clacking on the wood, followed by the lighter sound of a long knife encased in a flat bone handle, flared at the end. As it struck the deck, the blade shot out.

'This is the river,' said the German without elaboration.

'And I just want to cross it without any trouble – and trouble to someone as nervous as I am is anyone walking through that door.' Converse angled his head, gesturing at the wheelhouse entrance on his left. 'In my state of mind, I'd fire this gun. I'd probably kill you and whoever else came in here.

I'm not as strong as you, Captain, but I'm afraid, and that makes me much more dangerous. Can you understand that?'

'*Ja*. I not hurt you. I look only for drugs.'

'You hurt me plenty,' corrected Joel. 'And that frightens me.'

'*Nein. Bitte* . . . please.'

'When do you take the boat out?'

'When I say.'

'How many crew?'

'One man, that is all.'

'*Liar!*' whispered Converse sharply, the gun thrust forward.

'*Zwei*. Two men . . . *today*. We pick up heavy crates in Elten. On my word, is normal only one man. I can't pay more.'

'Start the engine,' ordered Joel. 'Or engines. I only know Chris Crafts and Bertrams, which is a silly fucking thing to say.'

'*Was?*'

'*Do* it!'

'*Die Mannschaft*. The . . . crew. I must give *Befehle*.'

'Wait!' Converse crawled sideways past the wheelhouse door, glancing above to his left at the thick wooden panelling of the pilot's window, his gun never once wavering from its line of fire into the German's chest. Again, he used the bulkhead and his braced legs to shinny himself up the wall; he was in shadows, with a clear view of the bow, and through both wheelhouse windows behind him, the stern of the boat. In sight were the fore and aft piles on both sides, the lines looped around the thick protrusions of weather-beaten logs. The two crewmen were sitting on a storage hatchway, smoking cigarettes, one drinking from a can of beer. 'All right,' said Joel, clicking the hammer back on the automatic – a weapon with which he was not sure he could be accurate within ten feet. 'Open that door and give your orders. And if either of those men down there does anything but free those ropes, I'll kill you. Can you understand that?'

'I understand . . . everything you say, but you do not understand me. I search you for drugs – not a *grosse Mann* – the *Polizei* do not go after such people, they leave them alone. They go after the *Kleine*, the small people who use the river boats. It makes them look good, you see. I would not hurt you, *Mein Herr*. I only protect myself. I want to believe what my *Neffe* – nephew – told me, but I must be sure.'

'Your *nephew?*'

'The seaman from Bremerhaven. How you think he got his job? *Ach, mein Bruder* sells flowers! It is his *Frau's* shop! He once sailed the oceans as I did. Now, he is a *Blumenhändler!*'

'I swear to Christ I don't understand anything,' said Joel, partially lowering his gun.

'Would it help to tell you that he offered to pay me one half of the fifteen hundred dollars you pay him?'

'Absolutely nothing. A consortium of thieves.'

'*Nein*, I not take. I tell him buy a new *Gitarre*.'

Converse sighed. 'I have no drugs. Do you believe me?'

'*Ja*, you are only a fool, he told me. Rich fools pay more. They cannot afford to admit their foolishness. The poor do not care.'

'Do those little bromides run in the family?'

'*Was?*'

'Forget it. Give the orders. Let's get out of here.'

'*Ja*. Watch through the windows, please. I would not want you to be more afraid. You are right. A man afraid is much more dangerous.'

Joel leaned back against the bulkhead as the captain shouted his orders. The engines started and the lines were released from their pilings. It was so contrary, he thought. Hostile, belligerent men who struck out in anger were not always his enemies, while pleasant, seemingly friendly people wanted to kill him. It was a world he knew nothing about, a long stretch from a courtroom or a boardroom, where courtesy and 'killing' could mean a variety of things. There were no such grey areas a hundred years ago in the camps and the jungles. One knew who the enemy was: the definitions were clear on all sides. But during the past four days he had learned that there were no defined lines for him now. He *was* in a labyrinth, a gauntlet, its deceptive walls lined with progressively more grotesque people he could not understand. Converse stared out the window, at the pockets of mist rising out of the water, a few spiralling up to catch the early light in their clouds of vapour. His mind went blank. He did not care to think for a while . . .

'Five, perhaps six minutes, *Mein Herr*,' said the captain, swinging the wheel to his left.

Joel blinked; he had been in a peaceful, rest-filled void, for how long he was not sure. 'What are the procedures?' he asked, conscious of the rising orange sun firing what was left of the river mists. 'I mean what do I do?'

'As little as you can,' answered the German. 'Just walk as if you walked the pier every morning and go through the repair yard to the street. You will be in the south section of the city of Lobith. You will be in *Die Niederlande* and we have never seen each other.'

'I understand that, but how?'

'You see that *Bootshafen*?' said the captain, pointing to a complex of docks with heavy winch machinery and hoisting devices across the water.

'It's a marina.'

'*Ja*, marina. My second petrol tank is empty – I say I test. I stall the engines three hundred metres off shore and go in. I yell at the Dutchman's price but I pay, for I do not buy from the *Deutsche* thief this far down river. You get off with one of my crew, have a cigarette and laugh at your stupid captain – then you walk away.'

'Just like that?'

'*Ja*.'

'It's so easy.'

'*Ja*. No one said it was difficult. You have only to keep your eyes clear.'

'For the police?'

'*Nein*,' said the captain, shrugging. 'If there is *Polizei* they come to the boat, you stay on board.'

'Then who am I looking for?'

'Men who may watch you, may see you walk away.'

'What men?'

'*Gesindel, Gauner* – what you call scum. They come each morning to the piers to look for work, most still drunk. Watch for such men. They will think you have drugs or money. They will break your head and steal.'

'Your nephew told me to watch the men on your own boat.'

'Only the new man, he is a *Gauner*. He chokes on his *Bier* hoping it will clear his head. He thinks he fools me but he does not. I keep him on board, tell him to scrape the rail, something. The other is no problem for you. He is loyal to me, an *Idiot* with a strong back and no head. The river boats do not hire him. I do. *Verstehen Sie?*'

'I think so. You're quite a guy, Captain.'

'I once sailed the oceans, not a stinking river. Fifteen years of age I ship out with *mein Bruder*. By twenty-three I am *Obermaat* – "petit" officer – good money, good life . . . Very happy.' The German lowered his voice as he throttled back the engines and spun the wheel to starboard; the boat skidded on the water. 'Why talk? It is over,' he added angrily.

'What happened?'

'It is not for you, *Amerikaner*.' The captain pushed the throttle forward; the engines coughed.

'I'm interested.'

'*Warum?* Why?'

'I don't know. Maybe it takes my mind off my own problems,' said Converse honestly.

The German looked briefly at him. 'You ask? Okay. We never see each other . . . I stole money, much money. It took the company purser nine months to find me. *Aber, ach*, he *find* me! It was many years ago. No more oceans, only the river.'

'But you said you were making good money. Why did you steal?'

'Why do most men steal, *Mein Herr?*'

'They need it – the money – or they want things they can't have normally, or they're just basically dishonest – which I don't think you are.'

'Go back. Adam stole the apple, *Amerikaner*.'

'Not exactly. You mean a woman?'

'Many years ago, *Mein Herr*. She was with child and she did not want her man on the seas and the ships. She wanted more.' The captain permitted himself the slightest glint in his eyes and a touch of a smile on his lips. 'She wanted a flower shop.'

From the core of his stomach, his pain momentarily forgotten, Joel laughed. 'You're *quite* a guy, Captain.'

'I never see you again.'

'Then your nephew . . .'

'Never *see* you again!' broke in the German, now laughing out loud himself, his eyes on the water as he headed into the Dutch marina.

Converse leaned against a pile smoking a cigarette, the visor of his cheap cap angled over his forehead, his eyes roaming up and down the pier and beyond to the repair yard in the Dutch marina. The men milling about the huge machinery were mechanically going about their tasks while those around the boats seemed more intent on inspecting than doing, shaking their heads over solemn pronouncements of disrepair. The captain argued with the dispenser of fuel, making obscene gestures at the rapidly climbing figures on the glass-encased face of the pump while his soft-headed deck hand grinned several feet away. On board, the *Gauner* alternately leaned over the railing, a large wire brush in his hands, abruptly turning back to his scraping whenever his employer glanced over at him.

The time was right, thought Joel as he pushed himself away from the piling. No one anywhere had the slightest interest in him; the despondent chores and the early morning dissatisfactions took precedence over the insignificant and unfamiliar.

He started walking up the pier, his pace casual to the point of being slovenly, his eyes, however, alert. He proceeded to the edge of the repair yard approaching a row of hulls in dry dock. Beyond the last elevated boat, no more than three hundred feet away, was an inordinately tall hurricane fence and an open gate. A uniformed guard sat on the left drinking coffee and reading a newspaper, his chair angled back into the criss-crossing wire mesh. Seeing him, Joel stopped, his breath suspended, an internal alarm going off – for no reason. Men passed back and forth through the gate, but the guard did not so much as glance at anyone, his eyes devouring only the tabloid angled on his lap.

Converse turned, a last look at the river. Suddenly, he was aware of the captain. The German had run to the base of the pier and was gesturing wildly, pressing his hands forward in short, rapid strokes. He was trying to warn his smuggled cargo. Then he shouted at the top of his lungs; men stared at him and turned away, none caring to be involved. They had seen too much in the early hours on the waterfront, slashing hooks too frequently the language of the docks.

'*Lauf! Run! Get out!*'

Joel was mystified; he looked around. Then he saw them. Two – no *three* – burly men were lurching up from the pier, their glassy eyes focused on him. The first man staggered forward to the left of the captain. The German grabbed his shoulder, swinging him around, stopping him, but only for seconds as the other two men crashed their fists into the captain's neck and spine. They were animals – *Gauner* – their nostrils inflamed by the scent of trapped fat quarry who might keep them in food and drink for days.

Converse dived under the row of dry-docked boats, smashing his head on several hulls as he scrambled towards the other side and the shafts of light beyond. He could see frantic legs pounding the earth behind him; they were gaining on him; they were running, he was crawling. He reached the end of the suspended row of hulls, sprang out and started for the gate. He pulled out his shirt, tore off the lower section and held it against the cuts on his head as he walked rapidly past the guard and through the gate. He looked around. The three men were arguing furiously, drunkenly among themselves, two crouching, peering unsteadily under the boats. Then the man standing saw him. He shouted to the others; they stood up and started after Joel. He ran faster, until he could see them no longer; the animals had given up.

He was in the Netherlands, the welcome less than gracious, but he was there, one step closer to Amsterdam. On the other hand he had no idea where he was right now except that the town was named Lobith. He had to catch his breath and think. He stepped into a deserted storefront where a dark shade behind the entrance served as a dim mirror; it was enough. He was a mess. Think. For God's sake, *think!*

Mattilon had told him to take the train from Arnhem to Amsterdam, he remembered that clearly. And the captain of the barge had said he had to take an 'omnibus' from Lobith to Arnhem; there was no train in Lobith. The first thing he had to do was reach the railroad station in Arnhem and clean himself up, then study the crowds and judge whether to risk becoming part of them. And relative to this consideration, his mind darted in several directions at once. The plain-lensed glasses had long since disappeared, undoubtedly during the insane events in Wesel; he would replace them with dark glasses. There was little he could do about the scrapes on his face but they would appear less menacing after soap and water, and certainly in or around a railroad station something could be done about his torn clothing . . . and a *map*. Goddamn it, he was a pilot! He could reach Point A from Point B – and he had to do so quickly. He had to reach Amsterdam and find a way to make contact with a man named Cort Thorbecke . . . and call Nathaniel Simon in New York. There was so much to *do!*

He walked out of the storefront suddenly aware of what was happening to him. It had happened before – a lifetime ago, in the jungle – when the fears of the night sounds had passed and he could watch the dawn and accurately plot his directions, his lines of march, his survival. He was thinking, his mind functioning again. All things considered, he was far less than what he had been, but he could be better than he was – he *had* to be. Every day that passed brought the generals of Aquitaine closer to whatever madness they were planning. Everywhere. He and they had to reverse roles. The hunted had to become the hunter. Delavane's disciples had convinced the world he was a psychopathic assassin and so they had to find him, take him, kill him and hold him up as one more example of the spreading insanity that could be contained only with *their* solutions. Aquitaine had to be exposed and destroyed before it was too late. The countdown was in progress, the commanders surely, inexorably, moving into their positions, consolidating their powers.

Move! shouted Converse silently to himself, as he walked faster down the pavement.

He sat in the last car of the train, still wary but satisfied by the progress he had made. He had done everything cautiously but without wasting motion, his concentration absolute, aware of a dozen possible malfunctions – eyes that stared at him, a man or a woman seen twice in too short a time, a clerk delaying him by being more helpful than the hour and the crowds would normally permit. These calculated possibilities were his read-outs, his dials, his gauges; without clearance he would abort all forward motion, take-off cancelled, the escape hatch sprung, safety found in the streets. His equipment was not an aircraft that was an extension of himself, it *was* himself, and he had never flown with such precision in his life.

English Spoke, had read the sign tacked to the roof of the busy corner newsstand in Lobith. He had asked directions to the 'omnibus' to Arnhem while buying a map and a newspaper, holding both close to his face. The owner was too preoccupied with customers to notice his appearance and shouted rapid instructions, useful in the pointed finger more than in the words. Joel found the bus stop some four blocks away. He sat in the crowded vehicle, his face buried in a newspaper he could not read, and forty-odd minutes later he got off at the railroad station in Arnhem.

First on his checklist was a trip to the farthest wash basin in the men's room where he cleaned himself up. He had brushed his clothes as best he could and looked in the mirror. He was still a mess but somehow he looked more like a man who had been injured than one who had been beaten; there was a difference. The checklist had continued.

Outside in the station he converted his Deutschmarks and five hundred American dollars into florin and guilder. He then bought a pair of wide-rimmed dark glasses at a pharmacy several doors from the currency exchange. As he got into the cashier's line, his hand casually covering the bruises on his face, his eyes fell on a cosmetics counter across the far side. It triggered a memory. He stepped out of the line and made his way around the cases to the display of creams and colognes, shampoos, and nail polish.

He had remembered. Shortly after they were married, in one of those maddening accidents that only happen at the most inopportune times, Valerie had slipped on a foyer rug and fell, hitting her head against the corner of an antique hallway table. By 7 o'clock that night she had what Joel had described as 'one hell of a mouse'. The black eye was an almost perfect oval, arcing from the bridge of her nose to the edge of her left temple, and at ten the next morning she was leading a bi-lingual presentation for agency clients from Stuttgart. She had sent him out to the drug store for a small bottle of liquid make-up which, except at close range, had covered the bruise remarkably well.

'I don't want people to think my brand new husband beat the hell out of me for not fulfilling his wildest sexual fantasies.'

'Which one did you miss?'

He recognized the bottle, chose a darker shade, and returned to the cashier's line.

A second trip to a wash basin had taken ten minutes but the results justified the time. He applied the make-up carefully; the scrapes and bruises faded. Unless someone stood very close to him, he was no longer a battered brawler but a man who had perhaps suffered a serious fall. Converse had congratulated himself in that men's room in the railroad station. Under other circumstances, he might not have dressed a client so well before a trial for assault and battery. The checklist continued.

It had taken him to where he was now, in the last car on the straight-through train from Arnhem to Amsterdam. After buying his ticket on what he inferred was a low-priced excursion train that made numerous stops, he had walked out on the platform prepared to run back at the slightest negative read-out, the first steady glance that held him in focus. Instead he saw a group of men and women, couples around his own age, talking and laughing together, friends more than likely off for a short summer's holiday, perhaps leaving the river for the sea. The men carried worn, dented suitcases, most held together with rope, while a number of the women held wicker baskets looped over their arms. Their luggage and their clothing denoted working class – factories for the men, home and children or the less-demanding clerical jobs for the women – all within that part of the spectrum that suited Joel's own appearance. He had walked behind them, laughing quietly when they laughed, climbing on board as though he were part of the group, sitting in an aisle seat across from a burly man with a slender woman who, despite her thin frame, proudly wore a pair of enormous breasts. Converse's eyes could hardly avoid them and the man grinned at Joel, no malice in his look as he had raised a bottle of beer to his lips.

Somewhere Converse had read or heard that in the northern countries people going on summer vacations – or on holiday, as was the term – gravitated to the last cars in the Trans-Europe-express. It was a custom that somehow signified their status, producing a general camaraderie, the working man's junket. Joel observed the none-too-subtle transformation. Men and women got out of their seats and walked up and down the aisle talking to friends and strangers alike, cans and bottles in their hands. From the front of the car a few people broke into a song, obviously a familiar country song; others took up the words and melody only to be drowned out by Converse's group who raised their voices in an entirely different chorus until both camps dwindled away in laughter. Conviviality, indeed, was the order of the morning in the last car on the train to Amsterdam. The stations went by, a few passengers getting off at each, more getting on, suitcases, baskets, and broad smiles accompanying the arrivals, boisterous greetings welcoming them on board. A number of men wore tee-shirts emblazoned with the names of town and district teams – soccer, assumed Converse. Catcalls and amiably derisive shouts were hurled at them by age-old competitors. The railroad car was turning into an odd Dutch version of a trainload of suddenly freed adults going off to a summer camp. The volume grew.

The towns were announced, the brief stops made as Joel remained in his seat, motionless and unobtrusive, now and then glancing at his adopted group, half-smiling or laughing softly when it seemed appropriate. Otherwise he looked like someone of limited intelligence poring over a map as a child might, equal parts wonderment and confusion. Neither was the case; he was studying the streets and canals of Amsterdam. There was a man who lived on the south-west corner of Utrechtsestraat and Kerkstraat, a man he had to identify by sight, isolate and make contact with . . . his springboard to Washington found as a 'member of the Tatiana family'. He had to pull Cort Thorbecke away from his base of operations without alerting the hunters of Aquitaine. He would pay an English-speaking intermediary to use a telephone, the words sufficiently plausible to draw the broker out to some other location, with no mention of the Tatiana connection or its source in Paris. Those words would have to be found; he would find them somehow, he *had* to. He was psychologically on his way back towards friendly fire – in terms of actual time less than seven hours from Washington – and men who would listen to him with Nathan Simon's help and an extraordinary file that would persuade them to hide him and protect him until the soldiers of Aquitaine were exposed. It was not the way envisioned by a man he had once known in Connecticut as Avery Fowler, hardly the legal tactics whose roots were in ridicule as prescribed by A. Preston Halliday in Geneva, but there was no time now. Time was running out for manipulated webs of legality.

The train slowed down, jerking as it did so, as if the engineer far up ahead was trying to send another kind of message to a rowdy car in the rear which felt the shocks most severely. If that was his intent, it, too, backfired. The pitching motion served only to accelerate the laughter and provoke insults shouted at an unseen incompetent.

'*Amstel!*' screamed a conductor, opening the forward door between the cars. '*Amsterdam! Amst . . . !*' The poor man did not finish, instead pulling the door shut to avoid a barrage of rolled-up newspapers thrown at him.

Summer camp in the Netherlands.

The train pulled into the station and a contingent of tee-shirted chests and breasts announced their entrance with shouts of recognition. Five or six people at the front of Joel's group rose as one to welcome their friends, again cans and bottles extended in the air, laughter bouncing off the narrow walls, nearly drowning out the whistles of departure outside. Bodies fell over bodies, hugs exchanged, breasts playfully grabbed at.

Beyond the new arrivals, walking unsteadily, was the illogically logical capstone for the juvenile antics taking place in front of Converse. An old woman, obviously drunk, made her way down the aisle, her flowing dishevelled clothes matching the large, tattered canvas bag she clutched in her left hand, while she steadied herself with her right on the edge of the seats as the train accelerated. Grinning, she accepted a bottle of beer, as another was thrown into her satchel, followed by several sandwiches wrapped in wax paper. Again, there were greetings of welcome as two men in the aisle bowed to the waist as if to a queen. A third slapped her behind and whistled. For several minutes the ritual continued, a new mechanical toy for the children off to summer camp. The old woman drank and danced a jig and made playfully suggestive gestures at men and women alike, sticking out her tongue and rolling it around, her ancient eyes bulging, rolling, her ragged shawl twirling in circles like some macabre Scheherazade. She amused everyone with her drunken antics as she accepted all that was dropped into her offering cloth, including coins. The Dutch vacationers were kind, thought Joel: they took care of someone less fortunate than themselves, someone who would be barred from another class of car on another train. The woman approached him, her canvas bag now held in front of her so as to accept alms from both sides. Converse reached into his pocket for a few guilder, letting them slip from his hand into the bag.

'*Goedemorgen,*' said the old woman, weaving. '*Dank U wel, beste man, erg, vriendelijk van U!*'

Joel nodded, returning to his map, but the bag lady remained.

'*Uw hoofd! Ach, heb je een ongeluk gehad, jongen?*'

Again Converse nodded, reaching again into his pocket and giving the inebriated old hag more money. He pointed to his map, waving her away, as yet another raucous chorus erupted from the front, now rolling back, the words picked up and sung with enormous enthusiasm by everyone around him.

'*Spreekt U Engels?!*' shouted the bag lady, leaning over unsteadily.

Joel shrugged, sinking back into the seat, his eyes riveted on the map.

'I think you *do*.' The old woman spoke hoarsely, clearly, soberly, her right hand no longer steadying herself on the edge of the seat, but instead in the canvas bag. 'We've been looking for you every day, on every train. Don't *move!* The gun is equipped with a silencer. With all this noise, if I pull the trigger no one would know the difference, including the man beside you who wants only to join the party and the big-breasted woman. I think we shall let him. We *have* you, *Mijnheer* Converse!'

There was no summer camp after all. Only death, minutes away from Amsterdam.

26

'*Mag ik u even lastig vallen?*' shouted the old woman, once more weaving unsteadily as she spoke to the passenger beside Converse. The man took his eyes off the raucous festivities in the aisle and glanced up at the harridan. She shouted again, her right hand still in the bag, her mass of grey, dishevelled hair springing back and forth as she nodded to her right, towards the front of the car. '*Zou ik op uw plaats mogen zitten?*'

'*Mij best!*' The man got up, grinning, as Joel instinctively moved his legs to let him pass. '*Dank U wel,*' the man added, heading for a single empty seat seen beyond a couple disco-ing in the aisle.

'Move over!' commanded the old woman harshly, swaying – not drunkenly – but with the rhythm of the racing train.

If it was going to happen, thought Converse, it was going to happen *now*. He started to rise, his eyes straight ahead, his right elbow inches from the bulging bag. Suddenly, his elbow slipped on the arm rest and he lashed out and downward, plunging his hand into the open canvas, gripping the fat wrist that held the unseen gun. Straining, pressing farther down, clutching flesh and metal, he swung violently to his left, yanking the old woman through the narrow space, twisting her, crashing her down into the seat next to the window. There was a sharp spit as the gun exploded, burning a hole in the heavy cloth, smoke billowing, the bullet embedding itself somewhere below. The hag's strength was maniacal, unlike anything he might have imagined. She fought viciously, clawing at his face until he pulled her arm above her head, twisting it, clamping it behind her, their two hands still struggling below in the bag. She would not let go of the weapon and he could not pry it loose, only hold it downward, his grip immobilizing her fingers, force against force, her contorted face telling him she would not surrender.

The mid-morning revels of the railroad car reached a crescendo; a cacophony of rising voices in countering melodies filled out the swelling echoes of laughter. And no one paid the slightest attention to the savage struggle that was literally one of life and death taking place in the narrow seat. Suddenly, within the panic of that struggle, within the violent impasse,

Joel was aware that the train was slowing down, if only imperceptibly. Once again his pilot's instincts told him a descent was imminent. He jammed his elbow into the old woman's right breast, trying to jolt her so to free the gun. Still she held on, bracing herself against the seat, her arm pinned, her fat legs stretched below, angled like thick pylons anchored beneath the forward seat, her obese body twisted, locking his own arm in place so he could not dislodge the weapon from her grip.

'Let go!' he whispered hoarsely. 'I won't hurt you – I won't kill you. Whatever you're being paid, I'll pay you more!'

'*Nee!* I would be found at the bottom of a canal! You can't escape, *Mijnheer!* They wait for you in Amsterdam, they wait for the *train!*' Grimacing, the old woman kicked out, briefly freeing her left arm. She swung her hand around, clawing his face, her nails sliding down his beard until he grabbed her wrist, pulling her arm across the seat and cracking it into her own knee, twisting her hand clockwise, forcing her to be still. It made no difference. Her right hand had the strength of an ageing lioness protecting its pride; she would not release the gun below.

'You're lying!' cried Converse. 'No one knows I'm on this train! *You* just got on twenty minutes ago!'

'Wrong, *Amerikaan!* I've been on since Arnhem – I start in the front, walk back. I found you out at Utrecht and a telephone call was made.'

'*Liar!*'

'You will see.'

'Who hired you?'

'Men.'

'*Who?*'

'You will see.'

'God*damn* you, you're not part of them! You *can't* be!'

'They pay. Up and down the railroad they pay. On the piers, in the airports. They say you speak nothing but English.'

'What else do they say?'

'Why should I tell you? You're caught. It is you who should let me go. It could be easier for you.'

'How? A quick bullet in the head instead of a Hanoi rack?'

'Whatever it is, the bullet could be better. You are too young to know, *Mijnheer.* You were never under occupation.'

'And you're too old to be so goddamned strong, I'll give you that.'

'*Ja*, I learn that, too.'

'Let *go!*'

The train was braking and the heavily-drinking crowd in the car roared its approval, as men grabbed suitcases from the upper racks. The passenger who had been sitting next to Joel hastily yanked his from above the seat, his stomach pressing into Converse's shoulder. Joel tried to appear as though he were in a deep conversation with his grimacing half-prisoner; the man fell back, suitcase in hand, laughing.

The old woman lurched forward, sinking her mouth in Converse's upper arm, millimetres from his wound. She bit him viciously, her yellow teeth penetrating his flesh, blood bursting out of his skin, trickling down the woman's grey chin.

He pulled back in pain. She freed her hand from his grip in the canvas bag; the gun was hers! She fired; the muted spit was accompanied by a splintering, shattering section of the floor in the aisle, missing Joel's feet by inches. He grabbed the unseen barrel, twisted it, pulled it, trying with all his strength to wrench it away. She fired again.

Her eyes grew wide as she arched back into the seat. They remained open as she slumped into the window, blood spreading quickly through the thin fabric of her dress in the upper section of her stomach. She was dead, and Joel felt ill, nauseous – so thoroughly sick he had to swallow air to keep from vomiting. Trembling, he wondered briefly who this old woman was, why she was – what had she lived through that made her become what she was. *You were too young to know . . . You were never under occupation.*

No time! She had wanted to kill him, that was all he had to know, and that men were waiting for him only minutes away. He had to think, *move!*

He twisted the gun from her rigid fingers inside the canvas bag, quickly lifting it up and shoving it beneath his coarse jacket, inserting it under his belt, feeling the weight of the other weapon in his pocket. He reached over and bunched the woman's dress in folds, layering her shawl over the blood stains, and pushing her mass of dishevelled grey hair over her right cheek, concealing the wide, dead eyes. Experience in the camps told him not to try to close the eyes; too often they would not respond. The action might only call attention to him – to her. The last thing he did was to pull a can of beer out of the bag, open it, and place it on her lap; the liquid spilled out, drenching her lap.

'*Amsterdam! De volgende halte is Amsterdam-Centraal!*'

A roar went up from the vacationing crowd as the line began to form towards the door. Oh, *Christ!* thought Converse. *How?* The old woman said a telephone call was made. *A* telephone call, which implied she had not made it herself. It was logical; there was too little time. She had undoubtedly paid one of her sister bag ladies who plied the trains at the station in Utrecht to make it. The information therefore would be minimal, simply because there *was* no time. She was a special employee, one who had been researched as only Aquitaine could research, an old woman who was strong and who could use a weapon and who would not shrink from taking a life – who would not say too much to anyone. She would merely give a telephone number and instruct the hired caller to repeat the time of the train's arrival. Again . . . therefore . . . he had a chance. Every male passenger would be scrutinized, every face matched against the face in the newspapers. But he was and he was *not* that face. And he did not speak any other language but English, that information had been spread with emphasis.

Think!

'*Ze is dronken!*' The words were shouted by the burly man with the enormously endowed wife at his side as he pointed to the dead woman. Both were laughing, and Joel did not need an interpreter to understand. They thought the woman had passed out. Converse nodded, grinning broadly as he shrugged. He had found his way out of the station in Amsterdam.

For Converse understood there was a universal language employed when the decibel of noise was such that one could neither hear nor be heard. It was also used when one was bored at cocktail parties, or when one watched football games on television with clowns who were convinced they knew a great deal more than coaches or quarterbacks, or when one was gathered and trapped into an evening in New York with the 'beautiful people' – most of whom qualified as neither in the most rudimentary sense, egos far outdistancing either talent or humanity, the ability to make a productive dollar very much in question. In such situations one nodded; one smiled; one occasionally placed a friendly hand on a shoulder, the touch signifying communication – but one said nothing.

Joel did all of these things as he got off the train with the burly man and the excessively-breasted wife. He became almost manic, playing the role as one who knew there was nothing left between death and survival but a certain kind of controlled madness. The lawyer in him provided the control; the child pilot tested the winds, knowing his aircraft would respond to the elemental pressures because it was sound and he was good and he enjoyed the craziness of a stall forced by a downdraught; he could easily pull out.

He had removed his dark glasses; his cap was now perched far over his forehead, his hand on the burly man's shoulder. They walked up the platform, the Dutchman laughing as he spoke, Joel nodding, slapping his companion's shoulder, laughing in return whenever there was a break in the man's monologue. Since the couple had been drinking, neither took much notice of his incomprehensible replies; he seemed like a nice person, and in their state nothing else really mattered.

As they walked along the platform towards the terminal Converse's constantly roving eyes were drawn to a man standing in a crowd of welcomers beyond the archway at the end of the ramp. Joe first noticed him because, unlike those around him – whose faces were lit up in varying degrees of anticipation – this man's expression was serious to the point of being solemn. He was aware; he studied the column of arrivals but he was not there to offer welcome. Then suddenly Converse knew there was another reason why this man caught his attention. He recognized the face, and the instant he realized the fact he also knew exactly where he had seen it. Walking rapidly down a path surrounded by thick foliage with another man, another guard. The man up ahead was one of the patrols from Erich Leifhelm's compound above the Rhine.

As they approached the arch, Joel laughed a little louder and made it a point to clap the burly Dutchman's shoulder a little harder, his cap still angled down over his forehead, the movements of his head fluid and precise. He followed several nods with a shrug or two, then a good-humoured negative; he shook his head, his brows furrowed, his lips constantly moving, obviously in fluent conversation. Through the squinting flesh of his eyelids Converse saw that Leifhelm's guard was staring at him; then the man looked away. They passed through the arch and in the corner of his vision Joel was abruptly aware of a head snapping, whipping around; then of a figure pushing other figures out of his path, remaining on the sidelines, as it were, but propelling himself forward. Converse turned, looking over the Dutchman's shoulder. It happened. His eyes locked with those of Leifhelm's guard. The moment of recognition was instant and for that instant the German panicked, turning his head back toward the ramp. He started to shout, then stopped. He reached under his jacket and moved forward.

Joel broke away from the couple and began racing, threading his way through succeeding walls of bodies, heading for a series of arch-like ascending exits through which sunlight streamed into the ornate terminal. Twice he looked behind him as he ran; the first time he could not see the man, the second time he did. Leifhelm's guard was screaming orders to someone across the way, rising on the balls of his feet to see and be seen, gesturing at the exit doors in the distance. Converse ran faster, pulling his way through the crowd towards the steps that led to the massive exit. He climbed the staircase swiftly but within the rhythm of the most hurried departing passengers, holding to the centre, trying to call as little attention to himself as possible.

He bolted through a door into the sunlight, into total confusion. Below was water and piers and glass-covered boats bobbing up and down, people rushing past them, others ushered on board under the watchful eyes of men in white and blue uniforms. He had come off a train only to emerge on some kind of strange waterfront. Then he remembered; the railroad station in Amsterdam was built on an island facing the centre of the city; thus it was know as the Central Station. Yet there was a street – two streets, *three* streets bridging the water towards other streets and trees and buildings . . . no *time!* He was out in the open and those streets in the distance were his caves of survival; they were the ravines and the thick, impenetrable acres of bush and swamp that would hide him from the enemy! He ran as fast as he could along the wide boulevard bordered by water reaching an even wider thoroughfare clogged with traffic, buses, trams and automobiles, all at their own starting gates, anxious for bells to release them. He saw a dwindling line at the door of an electric tramway, the final two passengers climbing on board; he raced ahead, stopping abruptly, turning before the door swung shut. He stepped up into the tram entrance and was the last fare.

He walked quickly to the back of the huge vehicle spotting an empty seat in the last row. He sat down, breathing hard, desperately, the sweat matting his hairline and his temples, rolling down his face, the shirt under his jacket drenched. It was the first moment he realized how exhausted he was, how loud and rapid the tattoo was in his chest, how blurred his vision and his thoughts. Fear and pain had combined into a form of hysteria. The desire to stay alive and the hatred of Aquitaine had kept him going. Pain? He was suddenly aware of the ache in his arm above his wound, an old woman's last act of vengeance – against what? For what? An enemy? Money? No time!

The tram started up and he turned in his seat to look out the rear window. He saw what he wanted to see. Leifhelm's guard racing across the intersection, a second man running to join him from the waterfront quay. They met and the words they exchanged were obviously shouted in near panic. Another joined them, from where Joel could not see; he was suddenly just there. The three men spoke rapidly, Leifhelm's guard apparently the leader; he pointed in several directions, issuing orders. One man ran down the street, below the kerb, and began checking the half-dozen or so taxis in the traffic jam; a second stayed on the pavement, slowly making his way around the tables of a sidewalk café, then going inside. Finally, Leifhelm's guard ran back across the intersection, dodging cars, reaching the kerb and signalling. A woman walked out of a store and met him at the corner.

No one had thought of the tram. It was his first cave of survival. He sat back and tried to collect his thoughts, knowing they would be difficult to face. Aquitaine would penetrate all of Amsterdam, canvass it, tear it apart until they found him. Was there conceivably a way to reach Thorbecke or had he been fooling himself, reaching into the past where too often accidents and misplaced arrogance led to success? No, he could not think for a while. He had to lie down in the cave and rest and, if sleep came, hope the nightmares did not come with it. He looked out the window and saw a sign. It read *Damrak*.

He remained on the tram for well over an hour. The lively streets, and the lovely architecture of the centuries-old buildings and the endless canals calmed him. His arm still ached from the old woman's teeth but not severely, and thoughts of cleansing it faded. She probably had been more hygienic than most lawyers in New York, whose teeth were whiter but whose grips paled beside the old hag's. He could not weep for the old woman but, as with certain, strange witnesses at a trial, he wished he knew her story.

Hotels were out. The foot soldiers of Aquitaine would scour them, offering large sums for any information about any American of his general description – which they now specifically had. Thorbecke would be watched, his telephone tapped, his every move and conversation scrutinized. Even the embassy, or consulate – which it was in Amsterdam – would have another military *chargé d'affaires* or his equivalent on the prowl for a signal that a non-assassin wanted to come in and start the process of rectification. If his perceptions were right, that left him with only one escape hatch. Nathan Simon.

Nathan-the-Wise, Joel had dubbed him once, only to be told that a gentile with his intelligence should certainly come up with something more original. Then after a particularly long session at the office in which Nate expounded in excruciating detail why they should not take on a client named Liebowitz, who in his opinion would put too great a burden on the obligation to respect a client's confidence, and during which Lawrence Talbot had dozed off, Converse suggested that he alter his soubriquet to Nathan, the Talmudic-pain-in-the-ass. Nate had roared, shocking Talbot awake, and proclaiming: 'I love it! And Sylvia will love it better!'

Joel had learned more about the law from Nathan Simon than from anyone else, but there was always a distance between them. It was as though Nate never really wanted them to be too close in spite of the obvious affection the older man had for the younger. Converse thought he understood; it was a question of loyalty. Simon had two sons who, in the properly guarded phrase 'were in business for themselves in California and Florida'. One sold insurance in Santa Barbara and the other ran a bar in Key West. Nate Simon was a tough act to follow, and Joel was given a hint of just how hard it was one late afternoon when Simon had offered to buy him a drink at '21' after a harrowing conference on Fifth Avenue.

'I like your father, Converse. I like Roger. He has minimal legal requirements, of course, but he's a good man.'

'He had *no* legal requirements, and I tried to stop him from coming to us.'

'You couldn't. It was the gesture he had to make. Put some business where the son is. Very touching.'

'With an unnecessary will that you much too generously charged him only two hundred dollars for, and some crazy disposition of his war medals to three different institutions – *for* which you refused to bill him on patriotic grounds?'

'We were in the same theatre of operations.'

'Where?'

'Europe.'

'Come on, Nate. He's my father and I love him but I also know he's off-the-wall. Take him out of a vintage prop and he's not sure where he is. Pan Am got their money's worth, not in any administrative sense, but because he was a pistol at conventions.'

Nathan Simon had gripped his glass that late afternoon at '21' and when he spoke, the quiet thunder of a deeply troubled man poured forth. 'You have respect for your father, do you hear me, Joel? My friend Roger offered a gesture to his son for it was all he had, all he could imagine. I had a great deal more and I didn't know how to make such gestures. I only gave commands . . . He said I could still do it. I'm going to take up flying.'

Simon would help him, but only if he were convinced there was substance to his case. But he would legally lean over backwards in the negative if he thought a relationship or personal sentimentality were being used to manipulate him. Of course, if an indictment followed, he would rush in for the defence after the fact. That was professional; those were his ethics. And by now Valerie would have sent him the envelope with the dossiers and their awesome implications. *They* were one substance Simon required. Knowing Val, she would have sent them down by car, the great American postal service having given rise to a score of competitors who eschewed the tax payer's dollar. Joel's decision was made. Since there was a five hour time difference, he would wait until early evening and then call Nathan Simon. He was functioning again.

The tram came to the last stop before its return run. At least he was the only one left on board; he walked up the aisle, got off and saw another. He got on. Sanctuary.

A hundred streets and a dozen criss-crossed canals later, he looked out the window, encouraged by the seedy neighbourhood he saw, washed clean on the surface, but with the promise of far more interesting bacteria below. There was a row of pornography shops, their wares in magnified displays in the storefronts. Above, in open windows, garishly painted girls stood provocatively, brassieres slipped on and off lethargically, faces bored but pelvises churning, disassociated from the feelings of their owners. The crowds in the streets were animated, some curious, some feigning shock, others interested in buying. There was a carnival atmosphere, one into which he could melt, thought Converse, as he got out of his seat and went to the door.

He wandered around the streets, quite frankly astonished, even embarrassed, as he always was when sex was paraded so publicly. He enjoyed sexual encounters and never lacked for them but the privacy of the acts was intrinsic to their fulfilment. He could no more walk into one of those neon-lighted doors up-to-heaven then he could have performed a bowel movement on the kerb.

There was a café across the street; it was above a canal, tables on the sidewalk, dark within. He crossed the crowded thoroughfare, wove his way between the tables and went inside. Sleep might be out of the question but he needed food. He had not eaten a real meal in nearly three days. He found a small empty table in the back of the room, annoyed that a television set, clamped above on the wall to his right, kept blaring its afternoon inanities. At least the language was Dutch; that helped but not much.

Straight whisky helped, too, but again not much. The anxiety of the hunted came back and he kept turning his head towards the entrance, at any moment expecting to see one of the foot soldiers of Aquitaine walk through the door, out of the sunlight and into the cave to find him. He went to the men's room at the rear of the café, removed his jacket, placed the gun with the silencer in the inside pocket, and tore the left sleeve of his shirt. He filled one of the two basins with cold water, and then he plunged his face into it, pouring the water through his hair over the back of his neck. He felt a vibration, a sound! He whipped his head up, gasping, frightened, his hand instinctively reaching for his coat on a hook to his left. A portly middle-aged man nodded and went to a urinal. Quickly, Joel looked at the teeth marks on his arm; they were like a dog bite. He drained the basin, turned on the hot water tap and, with a paper towel, squeezed and blotted the painful area until blood emerged from the broken skin. It was the best he could do; he had done much the same thing a lifetime ago when attacking water rats swam through the bars of his bamboo cage. Then, in another kind of panic, he learned that rats could be frightened. And killed. The man at the urinal turned and went out the door, glancing uncomfortably at Converse.

Joel layered a paper towel over the teeth marks, put on his coat and combed his hair. He opened the door and went back to his table, once again annoyed by the blaring television on the wall.

The menu was in four languages, the last Oriental, undoubtedly Japanese. He was tempted to go for the largest, rarest piece of meat he could find but here his pilot's control dictated otherwise. He'd had no solid sleep in days, oddly enough since his imprisonment at Leifhelm's compound, where the sleep itself had been greatly induced by the huge quantities of excellent food – the healing process for a defecting pawn. A heavy meal would make him drowsy and one did not fly a jet going 600 miles an hour in that condition. At the moment his air speed was approaching Mach I. He ordered fillet of sole and rice: he could always order twice. And one more whisky.

The voice! Oh, Christ. The *voice!* He was hallucinating! He was going mad! He was hearing a voice – an echo of a voice – he could not *possibly* be *hearing!*

'. . . Actually, I think it's a national disgrace, but like so many others I speak only English.'

'*Frau* Converse . . .'

'Miss . . . *Fräulein* . . . I think that's right . . . Charpentier, if you don't mind.'

'*Dammes en heren . . .*' a third voice broke in quietly, authoritatively, speaking Dutch.

Converse gasped for the air he could not find, gripping his wrist, closing his eyes with such intensity every muscle in his face was in pain, twisting his neck away from the source of the terrible, horrible hallucination.

'I'm in Berlin on business – I'm a consultant for a firm in New York . . .'

'*Mevrouw Converse, of Juffrouw Charpentier, zoals we . . .*'

Joel felt the madness complete – he *was* mad; he was *insane!* Hearing and listening . . . ! *Hearing! Listening!* He spun around and looked up. The television screen! It was *she!* It was *Valerie!* She was *there!*

'Whatever you say, *Fräulein* Charpentier, will be accurately translated, I can assure you.'

'*Zoals Juffrouw Charpentier zojuist zei . . .*' The third voice, the voice in Dutch.

'I haven't seen my former husband in several years – three or four, I'd say. Actually we're strangers. I can only express the shock my whole country feels . . .'

'*Juffrouw Charpentier, de vroegere Mevrouw Converse . . .*'

'. . . he was a deeply disturbed man, subject to extreme depressions, but I never imagined anything like this.'

'*Hij moet mentaal gestoord zijn . . .*'

'There's no connection between us and I'm surprised you learned I was flying to Berlin. But I appreciate the chance to clear the air, as we say.'

'*Mevrouw Converse gelooft . . .*'

'In spite of the dreadful circumstances over which, of course, I had no control, I'm delighted to be in your beautiful city. Half city, I guess, but yours is the beautiful part. And I hear the Bristol-Kempinski . . . I'm terribly sorry, that's what we call a "plug" and I shouldn't.'

'It is a landmark, *Fräulein* Charpentier. It is not *verboten* over here. Do you feel at all threatened?'

'*Mevrouw Converse, voelt u zich bedreigd?*'

'No, not really. We've had nothing to do with each other for so long.'

My *God!* Val had come over to *find* him! She was sending him a signal – signals! She spoke every bit as fluent German as the interviewer! They kept in touch every month; they had lunch together six weeks ago in Boston! Everything she was saying was a lie and in those lies was the code. *Their* code! *Reach me!*

PART III

Stunned, he tried to isolate the words, the phrases. The message was in them! The Bristol-Kempinski was a hotel in West Berlin, he knew that. It was something else she said, something that should trigger a memory – one of *their* memories. What *was* it?

I haven't seen my former husband in years . . . No, only one of the lies. *He was a deeply disturbed man* . . . Less a lie, but not what she was trying to tell him. *Actually we're strangers* . . . *There's no connection between us* . . . Another lie but hardly a fraudulent assertion in terms of interpretive context – *stop it!* What *was* it?! . . . Before, earlier . . . *I'm a consultant* . . . That was it!

'May I speak with Miss Charpentier, please? My name is Mr Whistletoe, Bruce Whistletoe. I'm the confidential consultant for Springtime Anti-perspirant for which your agency is doing some artwork, and it's urgent, *most* urgent!' *Con vibrato.*

Val's secretary had been a talker, a marvellous spreader of in-house gossip, and whenever Joel and Valerie had wanted an extra hour for lunch or even a day, he would make such a phone call. It never failed. If a demanding vice-president (of which there were dozens) wanted to know where she was the excitable secretary would tell of an urgent call from one of those outside watchdogs of a *very* large account. It was enough for any ulcer-prone executive, and Valerie's understated professionalism took care of the rest. She would say 'things' were under control and rarely did a relieved account man pursue what might give him an acid attack.

She was telling him to use the tactic in case the police were monitoring her calls. He would have done so in any event; she was simply reminding him, warning him.

The interview was over, the last few minutes obviously a recap in Dutch, the camera on a still frame of Valerie's face. *Still* frame! The interview was taped, not live! When had the tape been made! How long had she been in Berlin? *Goddamn* it, why couldn't he understand anything unless it was spoken in English? In the lie proclaiming her own inability to speak German, Val said it was a national disgrace. She was right, but she might have gone farther; it was a national disorder rooted in arrogance. He looked around the café for a telephone; there was one on the rear wall several feet from the door to the men's room and he hadn't the vaguest idea of how to use it! His frustrations grew, swirling up into circles of panic. It was only the beginning. Suddenly, he heard his name.

'De Amerikaanse moodenaar Converse is advocaat en was piloot en de Vietnam-orloog. Een andere advocaat Franz, een vriend van Converse . . .'

Joel looked up at the screen bewildered, at once shocked, then paralysed. There was a film clip, a hand-held camera entered an office door centring on a body slumped over a desk, streams of blood spreading out from the head like a hideous Medusa wig over the shiny wooden surface. Oh, *Christ!* It was René!

As the recognition came an insert appeared on the upper left of the screen. It was a photograph of Mattilon – then another photograph was suddenly, dramatically, inserted on the right. It was he, the *Amerikaanse moodenaar,* Joel Converse. Neither language nor diagrams were necessary. René had been killed and he had been named the killer. It answered the question; it was the reason Aquitaine had put out the word that an assassin was heading for Paris.

He was a giver of death; it was his gift to new and old friends. René Mattilon, Edward Beale . . . Avery Fowler. And to enemies he did not know, could not evaluate, either as enemies or as individuals – a man in a tan overcoat in a Paris cellar, a guard above a river bank on the Rhine, a pilot on a train, a memorably unmemorable face at the base of a landfill pyramid, a chauffeur moments later who had actually befriended him in a stone house with bars in the windows . . . an old woman who had played her role brilliantly in a raucous railway car. *Death.* He was either the distant observer or the executioner, all in the unholy name of Aquitaine. He *was* back, back in the camps and the jungles that he had sworn never to visit again. He could only survive and hope that someone better than himself would provide the solutions. But at that moment, death was his closest ally, and his most hostile adversary. He was not capable of accepting the responsibility of recognition; he was not equipped. He wanted to collapse into nothingness, let someone else take up the cause no one knew had been given him in Geneva.

Jesus! The tape! If it was even twelve or twenty-four hours old, Val could not – probably *had* not – received the envelope he had sent from Bonn! She could *not* have. She would not have flown to Europe if she *had!*

Oh, my God! thought Joel, swallowing the last of the whisky as he rubbed his forehead, his confusion complete. Without the envelope in Nathan Simon's hands, no plea to him made sense! No call to him would evoke anything but a demand that Joel turn himself in and a telephone trace would be put on the line. Nate would not disobey the law; he would fight violently for a client afterwards, but not before that client obeyed the law. It was his religion, far more important to him than his temple, for the law allowed mistakes: it was essentially human, not esoterically metaphysical. Converse's hands began to tremble; he *had* to find out!

'Your fillet of sole, *Mijnheer.*'

'*What?*'

'Your sole, sir,' repeated the waiter.

'You speak English?'

'But, of course,' said the gaunt, bald-headed man with detached courtesy. 'We spoke before, but you were very excited. This district can do that to a man, I understand.'

'Listen . . . to . . . me.' Joel brought his hand across his lips emphasizing each word. 'I will pay you a lot of money if you will place a phone call for me. I . . . I don't speak Dutch, or French, or German or anything but English. Can you understand that?'

'I understand, *Mijnheer.*'

'To West Berlin.'

'It is not difficult, sir.'

'Will you do it for me?'

'But, of course, *Mijnheer*. You have a telephone credit card.'

'Yes . . . no. I don't want to use it.'

'Of course.'

'I mean I don't . . . I don't want it recorded anywhere. I have money.'

'I understand. In a few minutes I shall be off my shift, *Mijnheer*. I shall come for you. We shall place your call and I shall know the amount from the operator. You shall pay.'

'Absolutely.'

'And "a lot of money", *ja?* Fifty guilder, *ja?*'

'You're on. Yes.'

Twenty minutes later Converse sat behind a small desk in a very small office. The waiter handed him the phone. 'They speak English, *Mijnheer*.'

'Miss Charpentier, please,' said Joel, his voice choking, overwhelmed by a kind of paralysis. If he heard her voice he was not sure he could handle his own reaction. For an instant he thought about slamming down the phone. He could not *involve* her!

'Hello?'

It was *she* and as a part of him died, another part came alive. A thousand pictures flashed across his mind, memories of happiness and anger, of love and of hate. He could not speak, but she was *there!*

'Hello? Who's this?'

'Oh . . . there you are. Sorry, it's a lousy connection. This is Jack Talbot from . . . Boston Graphics. How are you, Val?'

'Fine . . . Jack. How are you? It's been a couple of months. Since lunch at the Four Seasons, if I remember.'

'That's right. When did you get in?'

'Last night.'

'Staying long?'

'Just for the day. I've been in crisis meetings all morning with another one this afternoon. If I'm not too bushed I'll catch the plane back tonight. When did you get to Berlin?'

'Actually, I'm not. I saw you on a Belgian broadcast. I'm in . . . Antwerp, but I'm going to Amsterdam this afternoon. Christ, I'm sorry about all that crap you had to take. Would you ever have guessed it? About Joel, I mean.'

'I should have guessed it, Jack. It's all so horrible. He's so very sick. I hope they catch him quickly for everyone's sake. He needs help.'

'He needs a firing squad, if you don't mind my saying so.'

'I'd rather not discuss it.'

'Did you get the sketches I sent you when we lost the Gillette account? I figured it was a way to your sack.'

'Sketches? . . . No, Jack, I never got anything like that. But thanks for the thought, the sack notwithstanding.'

Christ! 'Oh? I thought you might have looked at your mail.'

'I did . . . until the day before yesterday. It doesn't matter – you'll be in Amsterdam?'

'For a week. I wondered if you were going to check any of the agency's accounts up there before heading back to New York.'

'I should, but I don't think so. There's no time. If I do, I'll be at the Amstel Hotel. If not, I'll see you back in New York. You can buy me lunch at Lutèce, and we'll swap trade secrets.'

'I've got more of them. You buy. Take care, youngster.'

'Take care . . . Jack.'

She was *magnificent*. And she had not received the envelope from Bonn.

He roamed the streets, afraid of walking too fast, frightened of staying in one place too long, knowing only that he had to keep moving, watching, finding the shadows and letting them envelop him. She would be in Amsterdam by evening; he knew that, it was in her voice, and she had told him to reach her at the Amstel Hotel. *Why?* Why had she come? What did she think she was *doing?* Suddenly, the face of René Mattilon came to him. It was in sharp focus, filling his inner eye, surrounded by sunlight, the face a mask – a death mask. René had been killed by Aquitaine for sending him to Amsterdam. Valerie would not be spared if the disciples of George Marcus Delavane thought she had flown over to find him, help him.

He would *not* reach her! He *could* not! It was signing another death warrant! *Her* death warrant. He had taken so much from her, giving so little. The last gift could not be the taking of her life. Yet . . . yet there was Aquitaine and he meant what he had said to Larry Talbot on the phone. He, one Joel Converse, was inconsequential where the gathering of the generals was concerned. So was A. Preston Halliday and Edward Beale and Connal Fitzpatrick. If Val could help he had no right to let his feelings stop her – the lawyer in him told him that, the outraged man confirmed it. And it was possible she *could* help, do the things he could not do himself. She could fly back, get the envelope and go to Nathan Simon herself, saying that she had seen him, talked to him, *believed* him.

It was 3.30; it would be dark by 8 o'clock or so. He had roughly five hours to remain unseen and stay alive. And somehow find a car.

He stopped on the pavement and looked up at an overly made-up, extremely bored whore in a window on the second floor of a colourful brick house. Their eyes made contact and she smiled a bored smile at him, the thumb and forefinger of her right hand meeting, the wrist motion leaving little to the imagination.

Why not? thought Converse. The only certain thing in a very uncertain world was the fact that there was a bed beyond that window.

The '*concierge*' was a clerk, a man in his middle fifties with the pink face of an ageing cherub, who explained in perfectly fluent English that payment was based on twenty-minute sessions, two sessions paid in advance, one to be refunded should the guest come downstairs during the final five minutes of the first period. It was a loan shark's dream, thought Converse, glancing at the various clocks on the counter – placed on numbered squares – as an elderly man walked down the staircase. The clerk grabbed one of the clocks hastily and pushed the second hand forward.

Joel calculated rapidly, converting guilder to dollars, the rate of acceleration based on roughly $30.00 per session. He gave the astonished '*concierge*' the equilavent of $275.00, accepted his number and headed for the staircase.

'She is a friend, sir?' asked the stunned custodian-of-revels, as Converse reached the first step. 'An old lover, perhaps?'

'She's a Dutch cousin I haven't seen in years,' replied Joel, sadly. 'We have to have a long talk.' With heavy shoulders, he continued up the staircase.

'*Slapen?*' exclaimed the woman with the spangled dark hair and heavily rouged cheeks. She was as astonished as her keeper below. 'You want *slapen?*'

'It doesn't translate well, but yes,' said Converse, removing his glasses and his cap and sitting on the bed. 'I'm very tired and sleep would be terrific, but I suspect I'll just rest. Read one of your magazines. I won't bother you.'

'What is the matter? You think I am not pretty? Not clean? You yourself are no fine picture, *Mijnheer*! Cuts on your face, a bruise here and there, red eyes. Perhaps it is you who are not clean!'

'I fell down. Come on, I think you're adorable and I love your deep-purple eye shadow but I really want to rest.'

'Why *here?*'

'I don't want to go back to the hotel. My wife's lover is there. He's my boss.'

'*Amerikaans!*'

'You speak our language very well,' Joel took off his shoes and stretched out on the bed.

'Ach, I start with *Amerikaanse* college boys. All talk, most are too afraid for nothing but talk. Those boys who get on the bed – *poof!* . . . is over. Then talk, too goddamn much talk. Then your soldiers and your sailors and your businessmen. Most drunk; they behave like giggle-children. All talk. Twelve years, *I* learn.'

'Don't write a book. They're probably all senators and congressmen and priests by now.' Converse placed his hands behind his head and stared at the ceiling. There was a glimmer of peace. He softly whistled the tune first, then found the words. '"Yankee Doodle" came to Holland/nothing in his pistol . . .'

'You are amusing, *Mijnheer*,' said the whore, laughing coarsely and picking up a thin blanket off a chair. She carried it to the bed and spread it over him. 'You don't tell the truth but you are amusing.'

'How do you know I'm not telling you the truth?'

'If your wife had a lover, you would kill him.'

'Not so.'

'Then she would not be your wife. I see many men, *Mijnheer*. It's in your face. You are a good man, perhaps, but you would kill.'

'I'll have to think about that,' said Joel, uncomfortably.

'Sleep, if you wish. You paid. I am here.' The woman walked to the chair against the wall and sat down with a magazine.

'What's your name?' asked Converse.

'Emma,' replied the whore.

'You're a nice person, Emma.'

'No, *Mijnheer*, I am not.'

He awoke, startled by the touch, bolting upright on the bed, his hand instinctively rushing to his waist to make sure his money belt was in place. He had been so deep in sleep that for a moment he had no idea where he was, then he saw the garishly made-up woman standing beside him, her hand on his shoulder as she spoke.

'*Mijnheer*, are you hiding from people?' she asked softly.

'What?'

'Word goes up and down the *Leidseplein*. Men are asking questions.'

'What?' Converse whipped the blanket off the bed and swung his legs to the floor. 'What men? Up and down *where*?'

'*Het Leidseplein* – This district. Men ask questions. They look for an American.'

'Why *here*?' Joel moved his right hand from the money belt up to the outline of the weapon above.

'People who wish not to be seen often come down to the Leidseplein.'

Why not? thought Converse. If he thought of it, why wouldn't the enemy?' 'Do they have a description?'

'It is you,' answered the whore frankly.

'*And*?' Joel looked into the woman's eyes.

'Nothing was said.'

'I can't believe our friend downstairs felt so charitable towards me. I'm sure they offered money.'

'It was given,' corrected the whore. 'More promised with additional information. A man remains behind down the street. In a café next to a telephone. He is to be called and will bring back the others. Our . . . friend downstairs thought you might want to match the funds.'

'I see. An auction. One head on the block.'

'I do not understand.'

'What are we talking about? How much?'

'A thousand guilder. Much more if you are taken.'

'Our friend still sounds too charitable. I'd think he'd grab it and close up shop.'

'He owns the building. Also, the man was German and spoke like a soldier giving orders, that's what our friend downstairs said.'

'He was right. The man is a soldier but not in any army Bonn knows about.'

'*Zo?*'

'Nothing. Find out if our friend will take American money.'

'Of course he will.'

'Then I'll match the offer and double it.'

The whore hesitated. 'Now it is my turn, *Mijnheer*.'

'I beg your pardon?'

'*En?* As you say . . . "*and*"?'

'Oh. You?'

'*Ja.*'

'I have something special for you. Can you drive a car, or do you know someone who can?'

'I do myself, *natuurlijk*. In bad weather I drive my children to school.'

'Oh, Jesus . . . I mean, that's good.'

'Without my face like *so*, of course.'

The stories. Oh, God, the stories! thought Converse. 'I want you to rent a car and bring it around here to the front door. Then get out and leave the keys inside. Can you do that?'

'*Ja*, but nothing is for nothing.'

'Three hundred dollars – eight hundred guilder, give or take.'

'Five hundred – fourteen hundred, take or give,' countered the woman. 'And the money to rent the automobile.'

Joel nodded as he unbuttoned his jacket and pulled out his shirt. The handle of the gun with the short barrel and the extended silencer was clearly visible beneath the wide canvas belt. The whore saw it, a short gasp emerging from her throat. 'It's not mine,' said Converse quickly. 'Whether you believe it or not doesn't matter to me, but I took it from someone who tried to kill me.'

The woman stared at him, her look partially one of fear, but it was not hostile, only curious. 'The man – this soldier from no German army – the others who ask questions in the street. They wish to kill you?'

'Yes.' Joel unzipped the belt and counted off the money with his thumb. He pulled out the bills and closed the pocket.

'You have done them much harm?'

'Not yet, but I hope to.' Converse held out the money. 'There's enough for our friend downstairs and the rest is for you. Just bring me the car along with one of those tourist maps of Amsterdam that show where all the major stores and hotels and restaurants are.'

'Perhaps I can tell you where it is you wish to go.'

'No, thank you.'

'*Ja*.' The whore nodded knowingly and took the money. 'These people are bad people?' she asked, counting out the bills.

'The pits, lady.'

'They do those things to your face?'

'Yes. Mostly.'

'Go to the *politie*.'

'The police? It's not practical. They wouldn't understand.'

'They want you also,' concluded the woman.

'Not for anything I did.'

The whore shrugged. 'It is no problem for me,' she said, going to the door. 'I will say the auto is stolen. There is a *Tromp* garage twelve blocks from here; they know me. I have rented there when my Peugeot has troubles and I must get home. *Ach, kinderen!* Recitals, dance classes! Be downstairs in twenty minutes.'

'Recitals?. . .'

'Don't look so, *Mijnheer*. I do my job and call it what it is. Most people do the same and call it something else. Twenty minutes.' The spangled-haired woman went out the door, closing it behind her.

Joel approached the sink against the wall without enthusiasm, then saw it was spotless, a can of cleanser and a bottle of bleach below on the floor next to a roll of paper towels. Naturally. Dance lessons and recitals were part of the whore's life, as well as a car that often gave her trouble, just like any other commuter. Converse looked in the mirror; the woman was right, he was 'no fine picture', but one had to be quite close to him to notice the severity of the bruises. He splashed water on his face, then blotted it, put on the dark glasses and made himself as presentable as possible.

It had happened. Val had come to find him, and despite the horrors surrounding their seeing each other again, a part of him wanted to sing – silently, or shout silently into the mists of his imagination. He wanted so much to look at her, to touch her, hear her voice close to him – and he knew it was for all the wrong reasons. He was the hunted and in pain and vulnerable, all the things he never was when they were together, and because he was what he had become, he permitted her to find him. It was hardly admirable. He did not care to be a hungry dog in a cold rain; it did not fit his part of their past dual image, the *de suite*, as René Mattilon had phrased it . . . René. A telephone call had signed the order for his execution. *Aquitaine.* How in God's name could he let Val even come near him? thought Joel, a terrible pain in his throat. The answer was the same: Aquitaine. And the fact that he thought he knew what he was doing. Every move he made in the streets, and on the trains, and in the cafés, was as carefully thought out as the steps he had taken in the jungle; in the routes he had chosen, in the rivers and streams he had forged and used as watery tunnels to bypass an enemy time and again. He would use an automobile in Amsterdam, and a map of Amsterdam.

He looked at his watch; it was almost five-thirty. He had roughly two and a half hours to find the Amstel Hotel and drive around again and again until he knew every foot of the area, every stop light, every side street and canal. And then the route to one other place – the American Embassy, or the consulate. It was part of his plan, the only protection he could give her – if she followed his instructions. And somewhere an airline schedule; that, too, was part of the plan.

Twelve minutes had passed and he wanted to be at the doorway when Emma, the honest commuter, drove up in front of the house on the crowded street. If there was no place to park at the kerb he would walk out on the pavement and signal her to leave the car, quickly replacing her behind the wheel so as not to hold up traffic. He left the small room, went to the staircase, and started down, aware of the feigned groans of ecstasy behind several closed doors. He wondered briefly if the girls had thought of using cassette recorders; they could push buttons while reading magazines. He reached the second landing; below in clear view was the cherub-faced middle-aged owner of the establishment behind his counter. He was on the telephone. Joel continued down the steps, in his hand a hundred dollar bill he had decided to give the man – an additional gratuity in exchange for his life.

As he set foot on the lobby floor, he suddenly was not at all sure he should let the '*concierge*' have anything but a cage in the Mekong River. The pink-faced man looked over at Converse, his eyes wide, staring in place, the blood draining from his cherubic cheeks. He trembled as he hung up the phone and pretended first a smile, then spoke in a high-pitched voice.

'Problems! There are always problems, *Mijnheer*. Scheduling is so difficult I should buy a computer.'

The *bastard* had done it! He had made the call to a man down the street in a café! 'Keep your hands on the counter!' shouted Joel.

The command did not come in time; the Dutchman raised a gun from below. Converse rushed forward, lunging to his right, his hand tearing at the buttons of his jacket, finding the handle of the gun in his belt. The *'concierge'* fired wildly as Joel crashed his left shoulder up into the flimsy counter; it collapsed and Converse saw the extended arm, the hand holding the gun. He swung the barrel of his own weapon into the Dutchman's wrist; the gun went flying, clattering over the lobby floor.

'You bastard!' cried Joel, grabbing the man by the front of his shirt, pulling him up. 'You *bastard! I paid you!*'

'Don't kill me! *Please!* I am a poor man in much debt! They said they only wished to talk to you! What harm is there in that? *Please!* Don't do this!'

'You're not worth the price – to me, you son of a bitch.' Converse crashed the barrel of the gun into the Dutchman's head and ran to the door. The street was crowded with traffic, then suddenly there was a break and the cars and buses and open tourist vans lurched forward. Where *was* she? Where was Emma-the-Practical?

'*Theodoor! Deze Kerel is onmogelijk! Hij wil . . . !*' The hysterical words came from a bare-breasted woman rushing down the staircase, a thin, short slip covering the essentials of her trade. She stopped on the next to last step, saw the carnage and the unconscious Theodoor and screamed. Joel ran to her, clamping his left hand over her mouth, his right – with the gun, pressing against her shoulder, pushing her into the railing.

'Be quiet!' whispered Converse – intending to whisper, instead shouting. 'Shut up!' He slammed his elbow into the prostitute's neck; it careened off her throat, the weapon now in front of her face. She screamed again and kicked viciously out at his groin, her two fingers in his nostrils, scratching, pushing him away. There was nothing else; he pummelled his fist with the handle of the gun into the base of her jaw. Her red lips parted and remained open; she went limp.

Doors crashed everywhere above, beyond the staircase, metal and wood smashing into walls. Shouts descended, angry, frightened, questioning. The words were incomprehensible to him, but not the alarms. A horn suddenly intruded, blaring from the street beyond the open front door. He ran to the doorframe, his right arm supporting him, the gun out of sight.

It was Emma-the-whore, the car in the middle of the street, unable to crawl into the kerb. He shoved the weapon under his jacket, under his belt, and ran outside. She understood his gestures and got out of the car; he raced around the hood, meeting her briefly.

'*Thank* you!' he said.

'It was stolen!' she replied shrugging. 'Good fortune, *Mijnheer*. I think you will need it, but it is not my problem.'

He jumped into the seat, behind the wheel, his eyes studying the panel as if he were approaching Mach I and had to understand the read-outs of every dial. He did; they were primitive; he pulled the gear into *D* and started up with the surrounding traffic.

Without warning, the figure of an immense man slammed into the window on his right. Joel lurched, slapping the lock on the window, taking advantage of another break in the traffic, spurting forward. The killer held on, as he yanked a gun from some unseen place in his body. Converse careened into the side of an automobile parked at the kerb, and still the man held on. Joel reached under his jacket as the killer, holding on to God-knew-what, brought his weapon up, levelling it into the glass, aiming at Converse. Joel ducked, smashing his head into the window frame as the explosion shattered the glass, fragments entering his skin above his eyes. But his gun was free; he pointed it at the figure hugging the window and pulled the trigger. Twice.

Two muted spits echoed in the darkness of the car as two holes appeared in the area of the glass that had not been shattered. Screaming, both hands covering his throat, the man fell away, rolling into the gutter between two trucks. Converse turned right into a wide, empty alleyway. *One man remains behind, down the street . . . He will bring back the others.* He was free again – for a while – thought Joel. A dead man could not identify an automobile. He parked the car in shadows and pulled out a cigarette, trying to steady his hand as he struck the match. Inhaling deeply, he felt his forehead, and slowly, carefully removed the particles of glass.

He now prowled the streets like a mechanized animal, with each hesitation, each stop, employing the eyes and nostrils of a primitive thing, knowing only it had to survive in a violently hostile environment. He had made the run four times from the Amstel Hotel on the Tulpplein, across the streets and over the canals to the American consulate on the city square called Museumplein. He had learned the alternate approaches; he knew the side streets that would bring him back to the main route without interruption. Lastly, he drove east and crossed the Schellingwouder Brug, the bridge over the I J River Sea-Canal and took the road along the coast until he found a stretch of deserted fields above the water. They would do; they were isolated. He turned around and headed back to Amsterdam.

It was 8.30; the sky dark; he was ready. He had studied the tourist map, which included a paragraph on the use of pay phones. He had once been a pilot; instructions were second nature. They were the difference between blowing an aircraft apart and landing it on a carrier. He parked the car across the street from the Amstel Hotel and walked into a booth.

'Miss Charpentier, please.'

'*Dank U,*' said the operator, shifting instantly to English. 'One moment please . . . Oh, yes, *Mejnffrouw* Charpentier arrive only an hour ago. I have her room now.'

'Thank you.'

'Hello?'

Oh God, should he speak? *Could* he speak? *Aquitaine.* 'Val, it's Jack Talbot. I took a chance you might fly in. Glad you did. How are you youngster?'

'Totally exhausted, you awful man. I talked to New York this afternoon and mentioned our accounts in Amsterdam – courtesy of one Jack Talbot.

The orders were for me to get to Canal City and spend tomorrow morning holding hands.'

'Why not hold mine?'

'They're too cold. You can, however, buy me dinner.'

'Be delighted, but first I need a favour. Can you grab a cab and pick me up at the consulate on Museumplein?'

'*What* . . . ?' The pause was filled with fear. 'Why, Jack?' The question was a whisper.

Converse lowered his voice. 'I've been here for a couple of hours taking too damn much abuse and I'm afraid I blew my cork.'

'What . . . happened?'

'It was dumb. My passport expired today and I needed a temporary extension. Instead I got a half dozen lectures and told to come back in the morning. I was very loud and not too benign.'

'And now it would be embarrassing for you to ask them to call you a cab, is that it?'

'That's it. If I knew this part of the city I'd walk and try to find one, but I've never been over here before.'

'I'll straighten my face and pick you up. Say in about twenty minutes?'

'Thanks, I'll be outside. If I'm not, wait in the cab; I'll only be a few minutes. You've got yourself a good dinner, youngster.' Joel hung up the phone, left the booth and went back to the rented car. The waiting had begun, the watching would soon follow.

Ten minutes later he saw her and the pounding in his chest accelerated. A mist clouded his eyes. She walked out the glass doors of the Amstel, carrying a large, dark cloth bag, her posture erect, her stride long and graceful, bespeaking the dancer she might have been, breaking the space in front of her, announcing her presence without pretence, telling anyone who watched her that she was herself; no artifices were necessary. He had once loved her so, as much for the person she appeared to be, as the woman she was. But he had not loved her enough; she had slipped away from him because he had not cared enough. There was not that much love or care in him. *Burn out!* she had shouted. *Emotional burn out!*

There had been nothing left to say; he could not dispute her. He had been running so fast, so furiously, wanting it all yet not wanting to remember the reasons why – wanting only to get even. He had concealed the intensity of his feelings with flippancy and a casualness that bordered on disdain, but he was not casual at all, and there was little room for the time consumed in being disdainful. There was also very little room for people, for Val. Being together demanded the responsibility that was part of any relationship and, as the months stretched into a year then two and three, he knew it was not in him to live up to that responsibility. As much as he profoundly disliked himself for it, he could not be dishonest – with either himself or Valerie. He had nothing left to give; he could only take. It was better to break clean.

The waiting was over; the watching began. The Amstel doorman hailed her a cab and she climbed in, immediately leaning forward in the seat giving instructions. Twenty tense seconds later, during which his eyes scanned the street and the pavements in every direction, he started the car and switched on the headlights. No automobile had crept out from the kerb after the taxi;

still, he had to be certain. Joel swung the wheel and drove into the street heading for the most direct route to the consulate. A minute later he saw Val's cab take the correct right turn over a canal. There were two cars behind her; he concentrated on their shapes and sizes; but instead of following, he continued straight ahead, pressing down on the accelerator, using an alternate route on the bare chance that he himself had been picked up by a hunter from Aquitaine. Three minutes later, after two right turns, and a left, he entered the Museumplein. The taxi was directly ahead, the two other automobiles no longer in sight. His strategy was working. The possibility that Val's phone was being tapped was real – René's had been, and his death was the result – so in Val's case he assumed the worst. If it was relayed that the Charpentier woman was heading over to the American consulate to pick up a business acquaintance, one Joel Converse would be ruled out. The consulate was no place for the fugitive assassin; he would not go near it. He was a killer of Americans.

The taxi pulled into the kerb in front of number 19 Museumplein, the stone building that was the consulate. Converse remained a half a block behind, waiting again, watching again. Several cars went by, none stopping or even slowing down. A lone cyclist pedalled down the street, an old man who braked and turned around and disappeared in the opposite direction. The tactic *had* worked. Val was alone in the cab sixty yards away and no one had followed her from the Amstel. He could make his final move to her, his hand under his coat, gripping the gun with the perforated silencer attached to the barrel.

He got out of the car and walked up the pavement, his gait slow, casual, a man taking a summer night's stroll. There were perhaps a dozen people – couples mainly – also walking, strolling in both directions. He studied them as a rigid but frenzied cat studies the new mounds of mole holes in a field; no one in the street had the slightest interest in the stationary taxi. He approached the rear door and knocked once on the window. She rolled it down.

They stared at each other for a brief moment, then Val brought her hand to her lips, stifling a gasp, 'Oh, my God,' she whispered.

'Pay him and walk back to a grey car about two hundred feet behind us. The last three numbers of the licence are one, three, six. I'll be there in a few minutes.' He tipped his hat, as if he had just answered a question from a bewildered tourist, and proceeded down the pavement. Thirty feet past the taxi, at the end of the block, he turned and crossed the Museumplein, reaching the other side with his head angled to the left, a pedestrian watching for traffic; in reality he was apprehensively watching a lone woman make her way down the sidewalk towards an automobile. He went swiftly into the shadows of a doorway and stood there watching, breathing erratically, peering into every pocket of darkness along the opposite pavement. Nothing. No one. He walked out of the doorway, suppressing a maddening desire to run, and ambled casually down the block until he was directly across from the rented car. Again he paused, now lighting a cigarette, the flame cupped in his hand, again waiting, watching . . . No one. He threw the cigarette to the kerb, and unable to contain himself any longer ran across the street, opened the door and climbed in behind the wheel.

She was inches from him, her long, dark hair framing her face in the dim light, that lovely face, taut, filled now with anxiety, her piercing wide eyes burning into his. '*Why*, Val? Why did you *do* it?' he asked, a cry in the question.

'I didn't have a choice,' she answered quietly, enigmatically. 'Drive away from here, please.'

28

They drove for several minutes. Neither of them spoke. Joel was concentrating on the streets, knowing the turns he wanted to make – knowing, too, he wanted to *shout*. It was all he could do to control himself, to keep from stopping the car and grabbing her, demanding to know why she had done what she did, furiously replying to whatever she said that she was a goddamned *fool!* Why had she come back into his life? He was *death!* . . . Above all he wanted to hold her in his arms, his face against hers, and thank her and tell her how sorry he was – for so much, for now.

'Do you know where you're going?' asked Val, breaking the silence.

'I've had the car since six o'clock. A map of the city came with it and I've spent the time driving around, learning what I thought I had to learn.'

'Yes, you'd do that. You were always methodical.'

'I thought I *should*,' he said defensively. 'I followed you from the hotel just in case anybody else did. Also I'm better off in a car than on the streets.'

'I wasn't insulting you.'

Converse glanced at her; she was studying him, her eyes roving over his face in the erratic progressions of light and shadow. 'Sorry. I guess I'm a little sensitive these days. Can't imagine why.'

'Neither can I. You're only wanted on two continents and in some eight countries. They say you're the most talented assassin since that maniac they call Carlos.'

'Do I have to tell you it's all a lie? All a huge lie with a very clear motive – purpose is better.'

'No,' replied Valerie simply. 'You don't have to tell me that because I know it. But you've got to tell me everything else. *Everything*.'

He looked at her again, searching her eyes in the flashes of light, trying to penetrate, trying to peel away the layers of clouded glass that held her thoughts, her reasons. Once he had been able to do that, in love and in anger. He could not do it now; what she felt was too deep inside her, but it was not love, he knew that. It was something else, and the lawyer in him was cautious, oblique. 'What made you think I'd see you on television? I almost missed you.'

'I didn't think about television, I was counting on the newspapers. I knew my face would be on the front pages all over Europe. I assumed your memory was not so dulled that you wouldn't recognize me, and reporters always pick up on hotels or addresses – it lends authenticity.'

'I can't read anything but English.'

'Your memory *is* dulled. I made three trips with you to Europe, two to Geneva and one to Paris. You wouldn't have coffee in the morning unless the *Herald Tribune* was on the room service table. Even when we went skiing in Chamonix – from Geneva – you made an awful fuss until the waiter brought the *Tribune*.'

'You were in the *Tribune?*'

'Class acts aside, it's their kind of story. With all the details. I assumed you'd pick one up and realize what I was doing.'

'Because we were strangers and hadn't seen each other in years, and, of course, you couldn't speak German or French or anything else.'

'Yes. It was an acceptable explanation for those who knew I did. A cover, I guess. A lot of people who speak several languages do it all the time. It's common practice; it cuts conversations short or at least keeps them to basic statements, and you always know if you're misquoted.'

'I forgot, that's your business in a way.'

'It's not where the idea came from. It came from Roger.'

'*Dad?*'

'Yes. He flew in from Hong Kong a few days ago and some hungry clerk alerted the newspapers that he was on the flight. When he got into Kennedy it was a media blitz. He hadn't read a newspaper or listened to a radio or seen a television screen in two days. He was in a panic and called me. I simply made sure the wire services in West Berlin knew I was flying in.'

'How *is* Dad? He can't handle this.'

'He's handling it. So's your sister – less so than your father but her husband stepped into the breach and took over. He's a better man than you thought, Converse.'

'What's happening to them. How *are* they taking it?'

'Confused, angry, bewildered. They've changed their telephone numbers. They speak through attorneys, supporting you, incidentally. You may not realize it but they love you very much, although I'm not sure you gave them much reason to.'

'I think we're closer to home,' said Joel quietly, as they approached the Schellingwouder Brug. 'Our once and former home.' They entered the dark span of the bridge, diaphanous lights above, speckled dots far below on the water. Valerie did not respond to his statement; it was not like her to avoid a provocation. He could not *stand* it. '*Why*, Val?' he cried. 'I asked you before, and I have to *know!* Why did you fly over?'

'I'm sorry, I was thinking,' she said, her eyes leaving his face, staring straight ahead through the windscreen. 'I guess it's better I say it now while you're driving and I don't have to look at you. You look awful, you're a mess, and your face tells me what you've gone through, and I don't *want* to look at you.'

'I'm hurt,' said Converse gently, trying genuinely to lessen the impact of his appearance. 'Helen Gurley Brown called and wants me for *Cosmopolitan*'s centrefold.'

'*Stop* that! It's not remotely funny and you know it – worse you don't even feel like saying it!'

'I retreat. There were times when you never read me right.'

'I *always* read you right, Joel!' Valerie continued to focus on the road and beams of the headlights; she did not move her head. 'Don't play the serious fool any longer. We haven't time for that; we haven't time for your flip remarks. It was always a little sad to watch you put people off who really wanted to talk to you, but it's finished now.'

'Glad to hear it. Then *talk!* Why the hell did you walk *into* this?'

Their eyes met in anger, in abrupt recognition, in a love once remembered, perhaps. She turned away as Converse steered the car into the right exit off the bridge, then peeled into the road that ran along the coastline.

'All right,' said Valerie, hesitant but in complete control. 'I'll spell it out as best I can. I say as best I can because I'm not entirely sure – there are too many complications to be absolutely sure ... You may be a rotten husband and careless beyond stoning where another person's feelings are concerned, but you're not what they say you are. You didn't kill those men.'

'I know that. You said you knew it, too. Why did you come *over* here?'

'Because I had to,' said Val, her voice firm, still staring straight ahead. 'The other night after the news – your picture was on every channel, so different from what it was years ago – I walked along the beach and thought about you. They weren't pleasant thoughts, but they were honest ones ... You put me through my own personal hell, Joel. You were driven by terrible things in your past, and I tried to understand because I knew what had happened to you. But you never tried to understand *me*. I, too, had things I wanted to do, but they faded, they weren't important ... Okay, I thought. Someday it'll pass and the nightmares will go away for him and he'll stop and look at me and say, "Hey, you're *you*." Well, the nightmares went away and it never happened.'

'I concede my adversary's logic,' said Converse painfully. 'I still don't understand.'

'I needed you, Joel, but you couldn't respond. You were amusing as hell, even when I knew you didn't feel like it, and you were terrific in bed, but your only real concerns were for you, always you.'

'Conceded again, learned counsellor. *And?*'

'I remembered something I said to myself that afternoon when you left the apartment, said it silently as I watched you leave. I promised myself that if ever a person I was close to needed me as much as I needed you then, I wouldn't walk away. Call it the one moral commitment I've ever made in my life. Only the irony is that that person turned out to be you. You're not a madman and you're not a killer but someone wants the world to think you are. And whoever it is, has done it very well. Even your friends who've known you for years believe what's being said about you. I don't, and I can't walk away.'

'Oh *Christ*, Val ...'

'No strings, Converse. No playing an old sweet song and hopping into bed. That's out. I came here to help you, not console you. And over here I can. My roots go back several generations. They may be withering underground but they *were* the underground – undergrounds – and they're willing to help. For once you need *me*, and that's a twist, isn't it, friend?'

'A veritable twist,' said Joel, understanding her last statement, but little else, speeding down the coast road towards the deserted fields. 'Only a few minutes,' he added. 'I can't be seen in the city and neither can you – and you wouldn't have a chance with me.'

'I wouldn't worry so much. We're being watched by friends.'

'*What?* What . . . "friends"?'

'Keep your eyes on the road. There were people in front of the Amstel, didn't you see them?'

'I suppose so. No one got in a car and went after you.'

'Why should they? There were others on the street and over the canals to the consulate.'

'What the hell are you talking about?'

'And an old man on a bicycle on the Museumplein.'

'I saw *him*. Was *he* . . . ?'

'Later,' said Valerie, shifting the large cloth bag at her feet into another position and stretching her long legs. 'They may follow us out here but they'll stay out of sight.'

'Who *are* you, lady?'

'The niece of Hermione Geyner, my mother's sister. You never knew my father, of course, but if you had he would have regaled you with tales of mom during the war, but he would have choked at the mention of my aunt. Even according to the French she went too far. The Dutch and German undergrounds worked together. I'll tell you all about it later.'

'You'll tell me *later! Following* us?'

'You're new at this. You won't see them.'

'*Shit!*'

'That's expressive.'

'All right, all right! . . . What about Dad?'

'He's weathering it. He's staying at my place.'

'Cape Ann?'

'Yes.'

'I sent the envelope there! The "sketches" I mentioned on the phone. It's everything! Everything about what's happened. It names the names, gives the reasons. Everything!'

'I left three days ago. It hadn't arrived by then. But Roger's there.' Valerie's face paled. 'Oh, my God!'

'What?'

'I've been trying to call him! Two days ago, then yesterday and again today!'

'*Goddamn it!*' In the distance there were the lights of a bay front café. Joel spoke rapidly, giving an order that could not be disobeyed. 'I don't care how you do it but you call Cape Ann! You come back here and tell me my father's all right, do you *understand?*'

'Yes. Because I want to hear it, too.'

Converse skidded to a stop in front of the café, knowing he should not have done so, but not caring, not seeing, really. Valerie rushed out of the car, her purse open, her telephone credit card in her hand. If there was a phone on the premises, she would use it; no one could stop her. Joel lighted a cigarette; the smoke was acrid, stinging his throat; it was no relief. He stared out at the dark water, at the lights spanning the bridge in the distance, trying not to think. It was no use. What had he *done?* His father knew his handwriting and the instant he recognized it he would rip open the envelope. He would be looking for exculpation for his son and he would find it. He would undoubtedly call Nathan Simon immediately – and therein was the horrible possibilty. Val would know enough from the material itself to say little or nothing on the phone, but not his father, not Roger. He would blurt out everything in a frenzy of anger and defence. And if others were listening on that line . . . Where was Val! She was taking too *long!*

Converse could not stop himself. He cracked the handle of the door and leaped out of the car, his feet hitting the ground, instantly propelling him around the hood. He raced towards the entrance of the café, stopping abruptly on the gravel. Valerie walked out, gesturing for him to back away. He could see the tears rolling down her cheeks.

'Get in the car,' she said, approaching him.

'No. Tell me what happened. *Now.*'

'Please, Joel, get back in the car. Two men in there kept watching me while I was on the phone. I spoke German but they knew I was placing a call to the States, and they saw I was upset. I think they recognized me. We have to get out of here.'

'Tell me what *happened!*'

'In the car.' Valerie tossed her head to the side, her dark hair flying over her shoulder as she brushed away several tears, and walked past Converse to the automobile. She opened the door and got in, sitting motionless in the seat.

'*Goddamn you!*' Trembling, Converse ran to the car, jumped in behind the wheel and started the engine, slamming the door shut as he pulled on the gearshift. Turning the wheel, he backed up, then shot forward into the road, the tyres spinning on the border of gravel. He kept his foot on the accelerator until the dark scenery outside was a racing blur.

'Slow down,' said Val, simply, without emphasis. 'You'll only call attention to us.'

He could barely hear her through his panic, but he heard the order. He eased his foot off the pedal. 'He's dead, isn't he?'

'Yes.'

'Oh, *Christ!* What happened? What did they tell you? Who did you talk to?'

'A neighbour, the name's not important. We have keys to each other's house. She volunteered to take in the newspaper and check the place until the police reached me. She happened to be there when I called. I asked her if there was a large envelope sent from Germany in the pile of mail. She said there wasn't.'

'Police? What *happened?*'

'You know my house is on the beach. There's a jetty of rocks about a hundred yards up-water. It's not large or long really, just some kind of marking from years ago . . .'

'Tell me!' shouted Joel, gripping the wheel.

'They say he must have gone for a walk last night, went out on the jetty and slipped on the wet rocks. There was a large bruise on his head. His body was washed up on shore and found this morning.'

'Lies! *Lies!* They heard him! They went after him!'

'My telephone? On the plane over here I thought about that.'

'You would, he *wouldn't!* I killed him. Goddamn it, I *killed* him!'

'No more than I did, Joel,' insisted ex-Mrs Converse, touching his arm, wincing at the sight of tears in his eyes. 'And I loved him very much. You and I left each other but he was still a very close friend, perhaps my closest.'

'He called you "Valley",' said Joel, choking, trying to push back the pain of his feelings. 'The bastards! *bastards!*'

'Do you want me to drive?'

'*No!*'

'The telephone. I have to ask you – I thought the police or the FBI or people like that might get a court order.'

'Of course they would! It's why I knew I couldn't call you. I was going to call Nate Simon.'

'But you're not talking about the police or the FBI. You're talking about someone else, some*thing* else.'

'Yes. No one knows who they are – where they are. But they're there. And they can do whatever they want to do. Jesus! Even *Dad!* That's what's so goddamn frightening.'

'And that's what you're going to tell me about, isn't it?' said Valerie, gripping his arm.

'Yes. A few minutes ago I was going to hold back and *not* tell you everything, instead try to persuade you to get Nate to fly over here so we could meet and he could see I wasn't crazy. But not now. There's no time now; they're cutting off every outlet. They've got the envelope – it was all I *had!*. . . I'm sorry, Val, but I *am* going to tell you everything. I wish to God I didn't have to – for your sake – but like you, I don't have a choice any more.'

'I didn't come over here to give you a choice.'

He drove into the field near the water's edge and stopped the car. The grass was high, the moon a bright crescent over the bay, the lights of Amsterdam in the distance. They got out and he led her to the darkest spot he could find, holding her hand, suddenly realizing that he had not held her hand in years – the touch, the grip, so comfortable, so much a part of them. He repelled the thought; he was a provider of death.

'Here, I guess,' he said, releasing her hand.

'All right.' She lowered herself gracefully, like a dancer and sat down on the soft grass, pushing the reeds aside. 'How do you feel?' she asked.

'Awful,' said Joel, looking up at the dark sky. 'I meant what I said. I killed him. All the years of trying – his trying, my trying – and I end up killing him. If I'd only let him alone, let him be himself, not someone I wanted him to be, he'd probably be drinking up a storm somewhere thousands of miles away, telling his crazy stories, making everyone laugh. But not in your house at Cape Ann yesterday.'

'You didn't force him to fly back from Hong Kong, Joel.'

'Oh, hell, not by pleading or giving him an order, if that's what you mean. But the order was there nevertheless. After mother died it was the unspoken words between us. "Grow up, Dad. Have your little trips but don't stay away so long, people worry. Be responsible, father mine." Christ, I was so *fucking* holier-than-thou! And I end up killing him.'

'You *didn't* kill him! *Others* did! Now tell me about them.'

Converse swallowed, brushing the tears from his eyes. 'Yes, you're right – there isn't time, even for old Roger.'

'There'll be time later.'

'If there's a later,' said Joel, breathing deeply, finding control. 'You know about René, don't you?'

'Yes, I read about it yesterday. I was sick . . . Larry Talbot told me that you saw him in Paris. How even René thought you were disturbed, as Larry did when you talked to him. And René was killed for seeing you. Larry must be going out of his mind.'

'That's not the reason René was killed. Let's talk about Larry. The first time I reached him I needed information without asking him directly. He was being used because of me, followed, and he didn't know it. If I'd told him, the jock in him would have reacted, and he'd have been shot down in the street. But the last time I spoke with him I walked into it. I'd broken away from the people who'd caught me – I was exhausted, still frightened, and I was open with him. I told him everything.'

'He mentioned it to me,' interrupted Val. 'He said you were reliving your experiences in North Vietnam. There was a psychiatric term for it.'

Converse shook his head, a short, derisive laugh emerging from his throat. 'Isn't there always? I suppose there were similarities and I'm sure I alluded to them, but that's all they were, similarities . . . Larry didn't hear what I was saying. He was listening for words that confirmed what others had said about me, what he believed was true. He pretended to be the friend I knew but he wasn't. He was a lawyer trying to convince a client that he was sick, that for everyone's safety the client should turn himself in. When I realized what he was doing and that I'd told him where I was, I knew he'd spread the word, thinking he was doing the right thing. I just wanted to get out of there, so I half-way agreed with him, hung up, and ran . . . I was lucky. Twenty minutes later I saw a car drive up in front of the hotel with two of my would-be executioners.'

'You're sure of that?'

Joel nodded. 'The next day one of them stated for the record that he'd seen me at the Adenauer Bridge with Walter Peregrine. I wasn't anywhere near that bridge, at least I don't think so. I don't know where it is.'

'I read that story in the *Times*. The man was an army officer, a major from the embassy named Washburn.'

'That's right.' Converse broke off a long blade of grass, twisting it, tearing it in his fingers. 'They're great at manipulating the media – newspapers, radio, television. Every word they put out is cleansed through channels, branded authentic, official. They take out lives as if people were pieces in a chess game, including their own. They don't care; they only want to win. And it's the biggest game in modern history. The terrifying thing is that they can win it.'

'Joel, do you know what you're *saying?* An American ambassador, the Supreme Commander of NATO, René, your father . . . *you*. Then killers in the embassy, a manipulated press, lies out of Washington, Paris, Bonn – all given official status. You're describing some kind of *Anschluss*, some demonic, political *take over!*'

Converse looked at her in the moonlight, the breezes off the water bending the tall grass. 'That's exactly what it is, conceived by one man and run by a handful of others, all completely sincere in their beliefs and as persuasive as any group of professionals I've ever heard. But the bottom line is that they're fanatics, killers in a quest they consider nothing less than holy. They've recruited – *are* recruiting – like-minded men everywhere, other frustrated professionals who think there's nowhere else to turn. They grab at the theories and the promises, accepting – accepting, hell, extolling – the myths of efficiency and discipline and self-sacrifice, because they know it leads to power. Power to replace the inefficient, the undisciplined, the corruptors and the corrupted. They're blind; they can't see beyond their own distorted image of themselves . . . If that sounds like a summation it probably is. I haven't slept much but I do a lot of thinking.'

'The jury's still in place, Joel,' said Valerie, her eyes alive, again levelled at his. 'I don't want a summation, I want it all. I think you should begin at the beginning – where it began for you.'

'Okay. It started in Geneva . . .'

'I *knew* it,' interrupted Val, whispering.

'What?'

'Nothing. Go on.'

'With a man I hadn't seen in twenty-three years. I knew him by one name then, but in Geneva he was using another. He explained it and it didn't matter. Except that it was a little eerie . . . I didn't know how eerie it was, or how much he didn't explain, or how many lies he told me in order to manipulate me. The hell of it is he did what he did for all the right reasons. I was the man they needed. *They*. And I don't know who they are, only that they're there, somewhere . . . As long as I live – however long I'm permitted – I'll never forget the words he used when he reached the core of why he had come to Geneva. "They're back," he said. "The generals are back".'

He told her everything, allowing his mind and his thoughts to wander, to include every detail he could recall. The countdown was in progress. In a matter of days, or at best a week or two there would be eruptions of violence everywhere – like what was taking place in Northern Ireland right now. 'Accumulations,' they said. 'Rapid acceleration!' Only no one knew who or what or where the targets were. George Marcus Delavane was the madman who conceived it all, and other powerful madmen were listening to him, following his orders, moving into positions from which they would leap for the controls. *Everywhere*.

Finally he was finished, a part of him in anguish, knowing that if she were caught by the soldiers of Aquitaine, the narcotics inserted in her body would reveal the information that would result in her death. He said as much when he had finished, wanting desperately to breach the space between them and hold her, telling her how much he hated himself for doing what he knew he had to do. But he made no move towards her; her eyes told him not to; she was evaluating, thinking things out for herself.

'Sometimes,' she said quietly, 'when the dreams would come, or you drank too much, you'd talk about this Delavane. You'd become so panicked you'd tremble and close your eyes and every now and then you'd scream. You hated that man so. You were also frightened to death of him.'

'He *caused* a lot of death, unnecessary death. Kids . . . children in grown-up uniforms who didn't know that *gung-ho* meant search-and-destroy and get blown apart.'

'There's no way you could be – what do they call it – transferring your emotions?'

'If you believe that, I'll drive you back to the Amstel and you can fly home in the morning and go back to your easels. I'm not crazy, Val. I'm here and it's happening.'

'All right, I had to ask. You didn't live through some of those nights, I did. You were either crashing into the bed or so scratched by a bottle you didn't know where you were.'

'It didn't happen often.'

'I'll grant you that, but when it did you were *there*. And hurting.'

'Which is exactly why I was reached in Geneva – recruited in Geneva.'

'And this Fowler, or Halliday, knew the exact words to use. Your own.'

'Fitzpatrick got it all for him. He thought he was doing the right thing, too.'

'Yes, I know, you told me. What do you think happened to him? Fitzpatrick, I mean.'

'For days I've tried to come up with a reason for them to keep him alive. I can't. He's more dangerous to them than I am. He's worked the streets they're undermining; he knows his way around Pentagon procurements and export clearances so well he could nail them with half the evidence. They've killed him.'

'You liked him, didn't you?'

'Yes, I did, and just as important I was almost in awe of that mind of his. He was quick and perceptive and had one hell of an imagination which he wasn't afraid to use.'

'He sounds like someone I was married to,' said Val gently.

Converse kept his eyes on her for a moment, then looked away at the water. 'If I get out of this alive – and I don't really think I will – I'm going hunting. I'm going to find out who did it, who pulled the trigger. There won't be any trail, no witnesses for the prosecution or the defence, no circumstances, mitigating or otherwise. Just me – and a gun.'

'Sorry to hear that, Joel. I always admired your principles. They were a constant, like your attraction – your reverence, I think – for the law. It wasn't all conceit and ambition, I knew that. It gave you the only real roots you ever had. You could look at the law and argue, as a child does with a parent, knowing the parent is some kind of absolute . . . Your father never gave you that – by his own admission, incidentally.'

'I think that's pretty tasteless.'

'I'm sorry. He brought it up once. I *am* sorry.'

'It's all right. We're talking. We didn't do much of that the last year or so together, did we?'

'I didn't think you wanted to.'

'You're on target. Forget it. There's now.'

'And there's so much you can deny! All they have is words against you! I said the same thing to Larry – they say you were here, you were there, you did this and you did that, but you *weren't* where they said you were and you *didn't* do what they say! You're the lawyer, Converse. For God's sake, stand up and defend yourself!'

'I'd never get near a courtroom, can't you understand that? Wherever and whenever I showed up someone would be there, someone ordered to kill me even if it meant losing his own life – considering the consequences, an insignificant sacrifice. My idea was to use the envelope – the dossiers and all the information they contained, the information that could only have come from government sources, which means I have partners somewhere in Washington. With all of that I could reach people I knew – the firm knew – and with Nathan's help get them to listen to me, see I wasn't crazy. Hear from *me* what I saw, what I heard, what I *learned*. But without that envelope, even Nate couldn't help. Besides, he'd insist I go by the book and come *in*, telling me he had guarantees of full protection. There *is* no protection, not from them. They're in embassies and naval stations and army bases; in the Pentagon, police departments, Interpol, and the Department of State. They're bag ladies on a train and commuters with attaché cases – you don't know who they are but they're there. And they can't afford to let me live. I've heard their almighty credo first hand.'

'Checkmate,' said Val, softly.

'Check,' agreed Converse.

'Then we have to find somebody else.'

'What?'

'Someone those people you want to reach would listen to. Someone whose presence might force those men in Washington who sent you out from Geneva to say who they are – to show themselves.'

'Who are you thinking of? John the Baptist?'

'Not John. Sam. Sam Abbott.'

'*Sam?* My God, I thought about him that night in Paris! How did you . . . ?'

'Like you, I've had a lot of time to think. In New York, on the plane, last night after I saw my aunt in Berlin.'

'Your aunt?'

'I'll get to that . . . I knew that if you were alive there had to be a reason why you stayed in hiding, why you didn't come out shooting, denying all those things they were saying about you. It didn't make sense; it wasn't *you*. And if you'd been killed or captured it would have been on the front pages everywhere, on all the broadcasts. Since there was no such story, I assumed you had to be alive. But why did you keep running, hiding? Then I thought, "my God, if Larry Talbot doesn't believe him, who will?" And if Larry didn't, it meant that the people around him, men like him, all your friends and your so-called contacts had been reached and convinced that you were the maniac everyone in Europe was talking about. No one would touch you and you needed someone. Not me, heaven knows. I'm your ex-wife and I don't carry any weight and you needed someone who did . . . So I thought about everyone you'd ever talked about, everyone we knew. One name kept on coming back to me. Sam Abbott. Brigadier-General Abbott now, according to the papers about six months ago.'

'"Sam the Man",' said Joel, shaking his head in approval. 'He was shot down three days after I was, and we were both shoved around from one camp to another. Once he was in the cell next to mine and we'd tap out Morse on the walls until they moved me. He stayed in the Air Force for all the right reasons. He knew he could be his best there.'

'He thought the world of you,' said Val, her voice a mixture of conviction and quiet enthusiasm. 'He said you did more for morale than anyone in the camps, that your last escape gave everyone hope.'

'That's a crock. I was a trouble-maker – that's what they called me – who could afford to take chances. Sam had the roughest job. He could have done what I did, but he was the ranking officer. He knew there'd be reprisals if he ever tried. He held everyone together, I didn't.'

'He said otherwise. I think he's the reason you never thought much of your sister's husband. Remember when Sam flew into New York and you tried to match him up with Ginny? We all had dinner at the restaurant we couldn't afford.'

'Ginny scared the hell out of him. He told me later that if she'd been drafted and put in charge of Command-Saigon it never would have fallen. He wasn't going to refight that war for the rest of his life.'

'And you lost a desirable brother-in-law.' Valerie smiled: then the smile faded and she leaned forward. 'I can reach him, Joel. I'll find him and talk to him, tell him everything you've told me. Above all that you're no more insane than I am, than *he* is. That you were manipulated by people you don't know, men who lied to you so you'd do the work they either couldn't do or were afraid to do.'

'That's unfair,' said Converse. 'If they started digging around State and the Pentagon, there could be a rash of accidents – very fatal and very dead . . . No, they were right. It had to start over here and be traced back. It was the only way.'

'If you can say that after all you've been through, you're saner than any of us. Sam will know that. He'll help.'

'He *could*,' said Joel slowly, pensively, breaking off another blade of grass. 'He'd have to be careful – none of the usual channels – but he could do it. Three or four years ago – after you and I broke up – he found out I was in Washington for a few days and called me. We had dinner and later too many drinks; he ended up spending the night on the sofa in my hotel room. We talked – both of us too much. Me about me – and you – and Sam about his newest monumental frustration.'

'Then you're still close. It wasn't that long ago.'

'That isn't my point. It's what he was doing. He'd worked his ass off to get into the NASA programme, but they turned him down. They said he was too valuable where he was. No one was in his class when it came to all-altitude, sub-mach manoeuvres. He designed more patterns in the sky than any designer on Seventh Avenue ever did on the ground. He could look at an aircraft – specs aside – and tell you what it could do.'

'I don't understand.'

'Oh, sorry. He'd been brought to Washington from wherever he was stationed as a consultant to the National Security Agency, cross-pollinating with the CIA. It was his job to evaluate the capabilities of the new Soviet and Chinese equipment.'

'What?'

'Airplanes, Val. He worked over at Langley and at a dozen different safe-houses in Virginia and Maryland, appraising photographs brought out by agents, questioning defectors – especially pilots, mechanics and technicians. He knows the people I have to reach, he's worked with them.'

'You're talking about the intelligence service, or services, I gather.'

'Not just services,' corrected Joel. 'Men who crawl around in the shadows of those paintings of yours. People trained to cut down bastards like Delavane and his tribe, cut them out silently by using methods and techniques you and I know nothing about – drugs and whores and little boys. They should have been brought in at the beginning. Not Geneva, not me. They kill when it's the pragmatic thing to do, and justify the killing because it's in the ultimate interest of the country. And Lord, how I railed against them, the righteous attorney in me demanding that they be held accountable. Well, Mr Naive has changed – been changed – because I've seen the enemy and he isn't us – not the us I think we are. If it takes a garrotte to choke off a cancer when legal medicine can't do it, hand me the wire, pal, and I'll read the manual.'

'I thought you loathed fanatics.'

'I do. I . . . do.'

'Sam,' persisted Valerie. 'I'll go home tomorrow and find him.'

'No,' said Converse. 'I want you to fly back tonight. You always carried your passport in your purse – still the same?'

'Of course. But I have . . .'

'I don't want you going back to the Amstel. You've got to get out of Amsterdam. There's a KLM night flight to New York at 11.45.'

'But my things . . .'

'They're not worth it. Call the hotel when you get back. Wire them money and say it was an emergency. They'll mail everything to you.'

'You're serious, aren't you?'

'Never more so in my life. I think you should know the truth about René. He wasn't killed because we met in Paris; nothing had happened then. I called him from Bonn four days ago and we talked. He believed me. He was shot to death because he sent me to Amsterdam, to reach a man who might have gotten me on a plane to Washington. That's out now and it doesn't matter. You do. You came here and you found me and the people who are looking for me all over the city will know it soon if they don't know it already.'

'I never said I was going to Amsterdam,' broke in Valerie. 'I specifically left word at the Kempinski that I was flying directly home, that if I got any calls to refer them to New York.'

'Did you have a reservation on the plane?'

'Naturally. I just never showed up.'

'Good, but not good enough. Delavane's people are efficient. Leifhelm has connections at every airport and immigration point in Germany. They'll find out otherwise. We might. We might have fooled them once tonight, not twice. My guess is there's a German waiting for you at the Amstel now, probably in your room. I want him to think you're coming back, that you're still here.'

'If someone like that goes to my room – *into* my room – he's in for a shock.'

'What do you mean?'

'Someone else is there. An old man with a long memory, who's been given instructions I'd rather not repeat.'

'Your aunt's doing?'

'She sees things in black and white, no greys. There *is* the enemy and there is *not* the enemy. And anyone who would harm her sister's daughter is very definitely the enemy. You don't know these people, Joel. They live in the past; they never forget. They're old now and not what they once were, but they remember what they were and why they did the things they did. It was so simple for them. Good and evil. They live with those memories – frankly, it's a little scary, *they're* a little scary, to tell you the truth. Nothing in their lives since has been so alive, so important to them. I honestly think they'd all prefer going back to those days, the horror and all.'

'What about your aunt, though? After everything that's been said about me in the newspapers and on television, she went along with you? She didn't ask any questions? The fact that you were her sister's daughter was *enough?*'

'Oh, no, she asked one very specific question and I answered it. *That* was enough. I must tell you, though. She's odd – very odd – but she can do what has to be done and that's all that matters.'

'Okay . . . You will go back tonight?'

'Yes,' said Val, nodding. 'It's reasonable and I can do more from New York in the morning than from here. From everything you've said, every hour's important.'

'Vital. Thanks . . . Also you may have trouble reaching Sam. I don't have any idea where he is and the services aren't cooperative when it comes to a woman trying to locate an officer – especially one with high rank. It's too complicated – an overseas love affair, a child the man never knew about, probably not his – they're very circumspect.'

'Then I won't ask them to tell me where he is. I'll say I'm a relative *he's* been trying to reach, that I travel a great deal and if he wishes to call me, I'll be at the so-and-so hotel for the next twenty-four hours. Certainly they have to relay that kind of message to a general.'

'Certainly,' agreed Joel. 'But if you leave your name, you're risking too much. For you *and* Sam.'

'I'll use a variation, one he'll recognize.' Valerie blinked, staring at the ground. 'Like Parquet only I'll feminize it – Parquette. A floor, wood – something associated with a Charpentier. Then I'll add Virginia – he'd remember Ginny because of you. Virginia Parquette, he'll figure it out.'

'He probably will. So might others. When you don't show up tonight, Leifhelm will have the airports checked. They could pick you up at Kennedy.'

'Then I'll lose them at LaGuardia. I'll go to a motel where I stay when I take the plane to Boston. I'll check in and get out without their knowing it.'

'You're very quick.'

'I told you, my roots go back; I've heard the stories . . . Now what about you?'

'I'll stay out of sight. I'm getting pretty good at it and I can pay for anything I need.'

'Your words, Converse: Not good enough. The more money you spread the more of a trail you leave. They'll find you. You have to get out of Amsterdam, too.'

'Well, I could slip across a few borders and head down to Paris for my old suite at the George V. Of course it might be a little obvious but then if I tipped high enough, they *are* French.'

'Don't try to be funny.'

'I don't feel remotely amusing. Also, I'd like a private toilet and a shower – even a second-hand bath. The rooms I find you *can't* find in the most esoteric travel guides.'

'You haven't had a shower in God knows how long, that much I can tell you in the open air.'

'Oh, beware the wife who's offended by her husband's hygiene. It's a sign of something.'

'Cut it out, Joel, I'm not your wife . . . I've got to be able to reach you.'

'Let me think, *I'm* also getting *very* inventive. I'll figure out something. I could . . .'

'I've already figured it out,' interrupted Val firmly. 'Before I flew over I talked with my aunt.'

'From your house?'

'From the mid-town hotel in New York where I registered under a different name.'

'You *were* thinking about your phone.'

'Not the way you were . . . I told her what I thought had happened, what I was going to try to do. She came to see me in Berlin last night. She talked up a storm – how she could do this, do that – but it all boiled down to the fact that she'll help. She'll hide you. So will others.'

'In *Germany?*'

'Yes. She lives in the countryside, on the outskirts of Osnabrück. It's the safest place you could go, the last place those people would think to look for you.'

'How do I get *back* into Germany? It was rough enough getting out! Delavane's people aside, every border's on the alert, my photograph on every wall.'

'I talked to Hermione this afternoon, after you called – from a pay phone; she was staying with a friend. She started making arrangements right away and when I flew in here a few hours ago, an old man met me at the airport, the same man you'll be staying with tonight. You don't know him but you've seen him, he was riding the bicycle in the Museumplein. I was taken to a house on the Lindengracht where I was to call my aunt; the phone was what they term *unaangeroerd*, clean, untouched.'

'My God, they are back in the 'forties.'

'Not much has changed, has it?'

'No, I guess not. What did she say?'

'Only your instructions. Late tomorrow afternoon, when the terminal's full, you're to go to the Central Station here in Amsterdam and walk around by the information booth. A woman will come up to you and say hello, saying she recognized you as someone she met in Los Angeles. Respond to her, and during the conversation she'll hand you an envelope. Inside will be a passport, a letter and a train ticket.'

'A passport? *How?*'

'All they needed was a photograph. I knew that much when I left your father in Cape Ann.'

'You *knew?*'

'I told you, I've heard stories all my life. How they got Jews and gypsies and all the men who parachuted down from the planes out of Germany and into neutral or occupied countries. The false papers, the photographs, they became an art form.'

'And you brought a photograph?'

'It seemed logical. Roger thought so, too. Remember, he was in that war.'

'Logical . . . a photograph.'

'Yes. I found one in an album. Do you remember when we went to the Virgin Islands and you scorched yourself that first day in the sun?'

'Sure. You made me wear a tie to dinner and my neck was killing me.'

'I was trying to teach you a lesson. That picture's a close-up. I wanted your sunburn in all its agony.'

'It's still my *face*, Val.'

'That photograph was taken eight years ago and the burn softened your features. It'll do.'

'Don't I have to *know* anything?'

'If you're detained for that kind of questioning, you'll probably be caught. My aunt doesn't think you will be.'

'Why is she so confident?'

'The letter. It spells out what you're doing.'

'Which is?'

'A pilgrimage to Bergen-Belsen, later to Auschwitz in Poland. It's written in German and you're to hand it to anyone who stops you because you speak only English.'

'But why would that . . . ?'

'You're a priest,' interrupted Valerie. 'The pilgrimage was financed by an organization in Los Angeles called The Coalition of Christians and Jews for World Peace and Repentance. Only a German very sure of himself will call attention to you. I've got a dark suit in your size in my tote bag, along with a black hat, shoes and a clerical collar. The instructions will be with your ticket. You'll take the northern express to Hanover where you're supposed to switch trains for Celle and be driven to Bergen-Belsen in the morning, but of course you won't. When you reach Osnabrück, get off. My aunt will be waiting for her priest. And by then I'll be back in New York getting in touch with Sam.'

Converse shook his head. 'Val, it's all very impressive but you weren't listening to me. Leifhelm's men have seen me – in that station, as a matter of fact. They know what I look like.'

'They saw a pale-faced man with a beard and a battered face. Shave off the beard tonight.'

'And apply for cosmetic surgery?'

'No, apply a generous amount of lotion called *Instant Sun* – it's in the clothes I bought you. It'll darken your face more like the photograph on the passport and also cover the bruises; they won't be that noticeable. The black hat and the clerical collar will take care of the rest.'

'Omens,' said Joel, touching his bruises on his face, noting that they were less painful to the touch. 'Do you remember when you fell and hit the table in the foyer, the black eye?'

'I was in panic; I had a presentation the next day. You went out and got the make-up for me.'

'I bought the same stuff this morning. It helped.'

'I'm glad.'

They looked at each other across the short distance between them in the moonlit field. 'I'm sorry about everything, Val. I wish you weren't part of this. If there was any other way I wouldn't let you be, you know that.'

'I know it, but it doesn't matter to me one way or the other. I came over here because of a promise I made to myself – a promise I meant. Not you. I'm *over* you, Joel, believe that.'

'The promise you made to yourself was provoked by me. As the offending party of the second part that should have cancelled it.'

'That's probably a rotten legal opinion,' said Val, shifting her legs and looking away. 'There's also the obvious. Everything you've told me terrifies me – not fact *A* and fact *B*, or who's conspiring with whom; I'm a landscape painter; I can't deal with such things. But I'm so terribly afraid because I can personalize. I can see how these people – this Aquitaine – *can* win, can take control of our lives, turning us all into complacent flocks of sheep. Good *God*, Joel, we'd *welcome* them!'

'I missed something.'

'Then you're blind. I don't think it's just women who live alone like me, I think it's most of the people walking around in the streets, trying to earn a living, trying to make the rent or a mortgage or a car payment, trying to *make* it through life. We're *sick* of everything around us! We're told one minute we may be blown up in a nuclear war unless we're taxed out of our houses to pay for bigger bombs, and that our water's contaminated, or that we can't buy this or that because it might be poisoned. Children disappear, and people are killed walking into a store for a quart of milk, and addicts and muggers with guns and knives cut people down on the streets. I live in a small town and I won't go there after dark, and if I'm in the city – any city – I look behind me in broad daylight, and I'll be damned if I'll get into an elevator unless it's crowded . . . I couldn't afford it but I put in a burglar alarm system in a house I don't own because there was a boat out in the water one day that stayed there overnight. In my mind I saw men crawling up the beach to my windows. We all see such things, whether out on the water, or down city blocks, or in a field like this. We're frightened; we're sick of the problems, sick of the *violence*. We want someone strong to *stop* it – and I'm not sure it even matters who they are. And if the men you're talking about push things any farther – believe me they know what they're doing. They can walk in and be crowned, no votes required . . . And in spite of everything I've said, that's even more frightening. Which is why you're going to take me to the airport.'

'Why did I ever let you go?' whispered Joel, more to himself than her.

'Cut it out, Converse. It's over. *We're* over.'

He watched from the darkest area of the parking lot at Amsterdam's Schiphol airport as the plane sped down the runway and lifted off into the night sky. He had driven up to a crowded platform where Val had got out, giving him the scrap of paper with the address that was to be his refuge for the night. So that he would know she had been able to get on the flight, she was to come out the glass doors, look at her watch and go back inside. If the plane was overbooked, she was to continue on the pedestrian walk to the temporary lot a hundred yards away from the entrance where he would be waiting for her. She had come outside, glanced at her watch and returned to the terminal. A part of him had felt relief, another part a quiet, hollow emptiness.

He watched the huge silver plane bank to the left and disappear, its fading lights a trajectory in the dark sky.

He stood naked in front of the mirror in the small bathroom in the house on the Lindengracht. The car was some twenty streets away. He had made the return journey cautiously on foot. The old man who owned the flat was pleasant and spoke in haltingly clear English, but his eyes were far away and never really made contact. His mind was in another place, another time.

Joel had shaved carefully, showered far longer than a guest should, and had finished applying the deep red lotion to his face, neck and hands. In moments his skin was bronzed. The result was far more authentic than he remembered the earlier products, when anyone who used them stood out with a mask of sickly brown, too smooth and cosmeticized to be anything but unnatural. The new colouring further concealed the bruises on his face: he looked almost normal. He would discard the tinted glasses: they would only call attention to him, especially from anyone who had seen him or had been given his description. He washed his hands repeatedly, kneading them together to remove the stains from his fingertips.

He gasped silently, his body stiffened. From somewhere beyond the door came the sound of an erratic bell. He quickly turned off the water and listened, his breathing suspended, his eyes on the gun he had placed on the narrow window sill. He heard the sound again; it stopped. Then he heard a single voice, a man on a telephone. He dried his hands and slipped on the short cotton bathrobe that had been left on the bed in his small, immaculate room. He put the gun in his pocket, went out the door and down the dark, narrow hallway that led to the old man's 'study', a former bedroom filled with old magazines, a few books, and tabloid newspapers on tables and chairs opened to the bloodiest sections, red crayon marks circling articles and pictures. On the walls were prints and photographs of long-past wartime accomplishments – including corpses in various poses of death. In an odd way it reminded Converse of *Les Étalons Blancs* in Paris, except that here there were no glories of war, only the ugliness of death. It was more honest, he thought, if nothing else.

'Ah, *Mijnheer*,' said the old man, sitting forward in a huge leather chair that engulfed his frail body, the telephone beside him. 'You are safe, *quite safe!* That was Kabel – code name, Kabel, *natuurlijk*. He has left the hotel and reports his progress.' Fragile, in his seventies, the Dutchman struggled out of the chair and stood erect, his thin shoulders back, his body rigid – a foolish old man playing soldier. 'Operation Osnabrück proceeds!' he said, as if reporting to a commanding officer. 'As contemplated by underground intelligence reports, the enemy infiltrated the area and has been compromised.'

'He's been what?'

'Executed, *Mijnheer*. A wire around the throat, taken from behind. The blood stays on the clothes as the neck is pulled back, thus there are no signs of combat and the enemy is removed from the place of compromise.'

'*What* did you say?'

'Kabel is strong for one of his age,' said the old man grinning, his weathered face a thousand creases, his posture now relaxed. 'He took the body from the room, dragging it to the fire exit and down into the alley. From there he gained access to the cellars and put the corpse back by the furnaces It is summer; the man may not be found for days – unless the stench becomes too much.'

Converse heard the words, but his concentration was only on one. *Compromise*. In this odd language of another time it meant . . . execution. Execution . . . murder . . . assassination!

What would you say to compromising certain powerful individuals in specific governments . . . ? Leifhelm's words.

It wouldn't work. His own.

You do not take into consideration the time element! Accumulation! Rapid acceleration! Chaim Abrahms.

My *God!* thought Joel. Was that what the generals of Aquitaine meant? *Assassinations?* Was it the reason for the glaring, disapproving looks directed at the Israeli and Abrahms' sudden retreat into qualification then voidance.

It's merely a point . . . I'm not sure it even applies.

Accumulation, rapid acceleration, one after another – national leaders cut down *everywhere*. Presidents and prime ministers, ministers of state and vice-presidents, powerful men and women from all shades of the narrow, acceptable political spectrum violently eliminated – governments in chaos. All to take place in a matter of hours, savagery erupting in the streets, fuelled by hysteria, victims and violators blurred until the commanders were summoned to restore order, not to leave until the controls were theirs. The climate was established, the day was coming. *Assassinations!*

He had to get back into Germany. He had to reach Osnabrück and be there when Val called. Sam Abbott had to be told.

29

His hands manacled and chained, his wounded right forearm encased in a filthy bandage, Connal Fitzpatrick gripped the ledge of the small window and peered out beyond the bars at the strange, violent activity taking place in the huge concrete parade ground. That it was a parade ground had been clear on the second morning of his capture when, along with the other prisoners, he was granted an hour's exercise outside the concrete barracks – and they *were* barracks, once part of an old refuelling station for the submarines was his guess. The slips along the water as well as the winching machinery were far too small and too obsolete for today's nuclear marauders – no Trident could fit in any space along the concrete and steel piers – but once, he judged, the base had served the German undersea navy well.

Now, however, it was being used to the great *disservice* of the Federal Republic of Germany and of free governments everywhere. It was Aquitaine's training ground, the place where strategies were being refined, manoeuvres perfected, and the final preparations made for the massive assaults that would propel Delavane's military commanders to power over paralysed civilian authorities. Everything was reduced to killing – swift and brutal, the shock of the acts themselves intrinsic to the wave of violence.

Beyond the window, units of four and five men raced separately, and in succession around and between a crowd of perhaps a hundred others, taking their turns at the sickening exercise they were perfecting. For at the end of the parade ground was a concrete platform, 7 feet high and perhaps 30 feet long, where mannequins were lined up in a row – some standing, others in chairs – their inanimate figures rigid, their lifeless glass eyes staring straight ahead. They were the targets. At the centre of each clothed chest, 'male' and 'female', was an encased circle of bullet-proof wire mesh; within each was a high-intensity orange light, seen clearly in the afternoon sun. At the discretion of the compound's trainer, it flashed on. It was the signal that this particular mannequin was the particular unit's specific target or, if more than one, targets. Hits were recorded electronically by other lights on the high stone wall above each figure on the platform. Red was a kill, blue merely a wound. Red was acceptable, blue was not.

The screaming admonitions over the loud speakers did not vary except in terms of numbers – of time. They were delivered in nine languages, four of which Connal understood. The words were the same.

Thirteen days to Ground Zero! Accuracy is uppermost! Escape is with the diversion of a kill! Otherwise there is only death!

Eleven days to Ground Zero! Accuracy is uppermost . . . !

Eight days to Ground Zero! Accuracy is . . . !

Individual members of the killer teams fired at their targets – exploding stuffed skulls and pulverizing chests and stomachs – sometimes by themselves, at other times in unison with their comrades. Each 'kill' was greeted with vocal exuberance, as the men raced through the crowd, melting into it, finally becoming part of it as their manoeuvre was completed. Another team was then instantly formed from within the ranks of the spectators; and another exercise in assassination was mounted, executed swiftly. And so it went on, hour after hour, the crowd reacting to the 'kills' with shouts of approval as weapons were reloaded for up-coming assaults against the eerily-marked mannequins. Every twenty minutes or so, as sections of the lifeless figures on the platform were progressively blown apart, they would be replaced with fresh heads and torsos. All that was missing were rivers of blood and mass hysteria.

In anger and frustration, Connal spread his manacled wrists apart, snapping the unbreakable chain, yanking with all his might, as the rusted, circular braces dug into his flesh, the scrapes red, his wrist bones bruised. There was nothing he could do, no way to get out! He knew the secret of Aquitaine! The enigma of its ultimate strategy was right there before his eyes! Assassinations! The mass killing of political figures in nine different nations – eight days away! Something was going to happen in eight days, something he knew nothing about, but widespread enough and provocative enough to demand the appearances of statesmen the world over. He did not know what it was, but others would – if he could *reach* them! What tore him apart was the simple truth: There was nothing he could do – *absolutely nothing!*

He turned away from the window, arms and wound aching, wrists stinging, and looked around at the barracks full of prisoners, forty-three men trying not to fail but failing fast. Many were lying listlessly on their beds, others stared forlornly out of various windows; a number talked quietly in small groups against the blank walls. All were manacled, as he was, all pathetic, as he was rapidly becoming pathetic, the abysmally short rations and the now-prolonged brutal periods of 'exercise' designed to weaken them swiftly in both body and mind. Whispering among themselves, when languages were understood, they had come to several conclusions, but their unique captivity eluded reason. They were part of a strategy none could understand, and only Connal understood who the strategists were. In unwatched corners he tried to explain, only to be met with blank stares and expressions of bewilderment.

Several points were established – for whatever they signified. To begin with, they were all military officers ranging in rank from the middle to the higher echelons. Secondly, all were bachelors or divorced, none with children or currently involved in serious relationships that demanded constant communication. Lastly, all were on 30- to 45-day leaves, only one other with emergency status like Connal, the rest on normal summer holidays. There was a pattern, but what did it mean?

There *was* a clue to that meaning only it, too, was beyond understanding. Every other day or so the prisoners were brought postcards from widely diverse locations – resort areas in Europe and North America – and instructed to write specific messages to specific individuals they all recognized as various fellow officers at the posts or bases from which they were on leave. The messages were always in the vein of *Having-wonderful-time;*

Wish-you-were-here; Off-to-(another location). To refuse to write these peripatetic greetings in their own hands was to be denied the scant food they were given and driven out to the parade ground where the objectors ran as fast as they could in laps, under guns, until they dropped.

They agreed among themselves that the reason behind the near-starvation level of daily rations had a purpose. They were all trained, competent officers. Such men in decent physical and mental condition were capable of attempting escapes or, at the least, creating serious disturbances. But that was all they could understand. All but Connal had been there for a minimum of twenty-two to a maximun of thirty-four days. With a specific regimen of repeated punishment and a disastrously insufficient diet, the times of imprisonment were sufficient to inflict severe physical and psychological damage rapidly. They were in a concentration camp somewhere on some undetermined coastline, not knowing their crimes, real or imagined by their captors.

'*Qué pasa?*' asked a prisoner named Enrique from Madrid.

'*Afuera en el campo de maniobras es lo mismo,*' replied Fitzpatrick, nodding his head at the window and continuing in Spanish. 'They're killing stuffed dummies out there, figuring each hit makes them heroes or martyrs or both.'

'It's crazy!' cried the Spaniard. 'It's crazy and it's sick in the head! What do they accomplish? Why this madness?'

'They're going to cut down a lot of important people eight days from now. They're going to kill them during some kind of international holiday or celebration or something like that. What the *hell* is happening eight days from now? Have you any idea?'

'I am only a major at the garrison at Zaragoza. I make my reports on the Basque provisionals, and read my books. What do I know of such things? Whatever it is, it would not reach Zaragoza – barbarous country, but I would wear corporal's stripes to return to it.'

'*Vite! Contre le mur!*'

'*Schnell! Gegen die Mauer!*'

'Move! Against the wall!'

'*Fa presto! Contro il muro.*'

Four guards burst through the barrack doors, others following, repeating the same order in different languages. It was a manacles-and-chain inspection, carried out at whim day and night, never less than once an hour during the daylight, as frequently as four times at night. The slightest evidence of any prisoner having attempted to break or weaken his chain or crack his manacles by filing against the concrete or smashing into rock was met with immediate punishment. The sentences were the the same for each prisoner: Running naked – preferably in the rain – until collapse, remaining in chains where he fell with no food or water for thirty-six hours. Of the forty-three men, twenty-nine of the strongest among them had been 'convicted', a number more than twice and three times until they had little strength left. Connal had run the gauntlet only once, thanks apparently to his bi-lingual guard, an Italian who seemed to appreciate the fact that his *americano* had taken the trouble to learn *italiano*. The man from Genoa was a bitter, cynical former paratrooper – and probably a convict – who referred to himself as a *rifiut* coming into his own, garbage soon to be rewarded. But like most men from his part of the world, there was an instinctive response to a foreigner's reference to *bella Italia, bellissima Roma.*

It was from their short, quiet yet staccato conversations that Fitzpatrick had learned as much as he had, his legal military mind operating on the level of addressing a malcontented military client. He pushed the buttons he had pushed so often before.

'What's in it for *you?* They *know* you're garbage!'

'They promise me. They pay me much money to teach what I know. Without people like me – many of us here – they will not accomplish.'

'Accomplish what?'

'That is for them to say. I am, as *you* say, employed.'

'To show them how to kill?'

'And to run and not be seen. That is our life – the lives of many of us here.'

'You could lose everything.'

'Most of us have nothing. We were used and discarded.'

'These men will do the same to you.'

'Then we will kill again. We are experienced, *Signore.*'

'Suppose their enemies find this place?'

'They will not. They cannot.'

'Why not?'

'It's an island no one thinks of.'

'They know that.'

'Impossible! No planes fly over, no boats approach. We would know if they did.'

'Why don't you think about what *was* here?'

'*Che cosa volete dire?*'

'Submarines. Surrounding your island.'

'If such were the case, *americano*, the – how you say? – the *custode* . . .'

'The warden.'

'He would explode everything away. Everything on this side of the island would be *fumo* – smoke, nothing. It is part of our *contratto*. We understand.'

'The warden – the *custode* – he's the big German with the short grey hair, isn't he?'

'Enough talk. Have your drink of water.'

'I have information for you,' whispered Connal, as the guard checked his manacles and chain. 'Information that will guarantee you a big reward and might possibly save my life.'

'What kind of information?'

'Not here. Not now. There isn't time. Come back tonight; everyone's so exhausted they're asleep before they reach their beds. I'll stay awake. Come and get me, but come alone. You don't want to share this.'

'My head is filled with *zucchini?* I come alone to a barracks filled with condemned men?'

'What can any of us do? What can *I* do? I'll stay by the door; you open it and I'll step out, your gun no doubt at my head. I don't want to die, that's why I'm talking to you!'

'You will die. May you go with God.'

'You're a fool, a *buffone!* You could have a fortune instead of a bullet in your chest.'

The Italian looked guardedly at Fitzpatrick, then around at the others; the inspections were nearly finished. 'For me to do such a thing, I need more than what you have told me.'

'Two of your guards are traitors,' whispered Connal.

'*Che cosa?*'

'That's all you get until tonight.'

Fitzpatrick lay in the darkness, waiting, listening for the sound of footsteps, the sweat of anxiety drenching his face. All around him were the sleep-induced moans of hungry, punished men. He pushed his own pains out of his mind; he had other things to think about. If he could reach the water the manacles would slow him down but not stop him; he could side-stroke nearly indefinitely – and somewhere down the coastline, away from 'this side of the island', there would be a beach or a dock, a place where he could crawl out of the sea. There was nothing else left; he had to try it. He also had to make sure his Italian guard could raise no alarms.

The bolt in the door was quietly sliding back! He had missed the footsteps; his thoughts had intruded. He got up silently and started up the aisle, each step on the balls of his feet, flexing his hands but keeping the chain taut. He could not make any noise whatsoever; several prisoners had begun to have nightmares, provoked by the slightest disturbance. He reached the door and somehow understood he was to push it open, not the other way around; the guard would stay back, his weapon aimed at the imformer.

It was so. The Italian gestured with his gun for Connal to move forward as he side-stepped to the door and secured the bolt. He then pointed with the barrel of his weapon, ordering Fitzpatrick to walk ahead. Moments later both men stood in the shadows in front of the barracks, the old refuelling station still visible in the darkness, the ocean waves lapping at the pilings.

'Now we talk, *Signore*,' said the guard. 'Who are these traitors and why should I believe you?'

'I want your word that you'll tell your superiors I turned them in. I don't say anything until I have your word!'

'My word, *americano?*' said the Italian, laughing softly. 'Very well, *amico*, you have my word.'

The guard's quiet, cynical laughter covered the seconds. Connal suddenly whipped out the chain, crashing it down on the man's weapon, grabbing the barrel of the gun with his right hand and wrenching it free; it fell to the grass beneath. He then raised the chain, as he kicked the guard in the groin, and slammed the heavy links into the man's face, smashing the manacles into the Italian's skull until the guard's eyes grew wide and then closed in unconsciousness. Fitzpatrick crouched, finding his bearings.

It was directly ahead – an old submarine slip, its long pier extending out to the middle water. He got up and ran, the air exhilarating, the breezes from the sea telling him to run faster, *faster!* Escape was seconds away!

He plunged over the dock into the water, knowing he would find the strength to do *anything*, swim *anywhere!* He was *free!*

Suddenly, he was blinded, the floodlights everywhere. Then a fusillade of bullets exploded from all sides, ripping up the water around him, cracking the air overhead, but none entering his body or blowing apart his head. And words over a loudspeaker filled the night.

'You are most fortunate, Prisoner Number Forty-three, that we still might have need of your handwriting or your voice over a telephone. Otherwise, your corpse would be food for the North Sea fishes.'

30

Joel walked out of the bright afternoon sun into Amsterdam's cavernous Central Station. The dark suit and hat fit comfortably; the clerical collar and the black shoes pinched but were bearable, and the small suitcase was an impediment he could discard at any time, although it was a correct accessory and held odd bits of clothing, none of which was likely to fit. His *déjà vu* being no illusion, he walked cautiously, every sudden movement – no matter how inconsequential – observed, studied, faces explored. He expected at any instant to see men rushing towards him, their eyes alert, filled with purpose, and the intent to kill.

None came, but even if they did he had done his best. He had written the most complete brief of his legal career, written it with painstakingly clear handwriting, organizing the material, pulling together the facts to support his judgments and conjectures. He had recalled the salient points of each dossier to lend credibility to his own conclusions. Regarding his own painful experiences and first-hand observations he weighed every statement, discarding those that might seem too emotional, reshaping the rest to reflect the cold objectivity of a trained, *sane*, legal mind. He had lain awake for hours during the night, allowing the organizational locks to fall into place, then started writing in the early morning, ending with a personal letter that dispelled any misconceptions of madness on his part. He was a pawn who had been manipulated by frightened, unseen men who had supplied the tools and knew exactly what they were doing. In spite of everything that had happened, he understood, and felt that perhaps there had not been any other way to do it. He had finished it all an hour ago and sealed the pages in a large envelope supplied by the old man who said he would send it on the Damrak after dropping Converse off. Joel had sent it to Nathan Simon.

'*Pastoor* Wilcrist! It is *you*, is it not?'

Converse spun round at the touch on his arm. He saw that the shrill greeting came from a gaunt, slightly bent woman in her late seventies. Her wizened face was dominated by intense eyes, her head framed by a nun's crown, her slender body encased in a black habit. 'Yes,' he said, startled, briefly looking around. 'Hello, Sister?'

'I can tell you don't remember me, *Pastoor*,' exclaimed the woman, her

English heavily – loudly – accented. 'No, don't fib, I can see you have no idea who I am!'

'I might if you'd keep your voice down, Sister.' Joel spoke softly, leaning down and trying to smile. 'You'll call attention to us, lady.'

'The religious always greet each other *zo*,' said the old woman confidentially, her eyes wide and direct, too direct. 'They wish to appear like normal people.'

'Shall we walk over here so we can talk quietly?' Converse took the woman by the arm and led her toward a crowded area of a gate. 'You have something for me?'

'Where are you from?'

'Where am I from? What do you mean?'

'You know the rules. I have to be certain.'

'Of what?'

'That you are the proper contact. There can be no substitutes, no deviations. We are not fools, *Mijnheer*. Now, where are you *from?* Quickly! Hesitation itself is a lie.'

'Wait a minute! You were told to meet me here; you were given a description. What more do you want?'

'To know where you're from.'

'*Christ*, how many sunburned priests did you expect to see at the information booth?'

'They are not *zo* un-normal. Some swim, I am told. Others play tennis. The Pope himself once skied in the mountain sun! You see I am a good Catholic, I know these things.'

'You were *given* a description! Am I that man?'

'You all look alike. The father last week at confession was not a good man. He told me I had too many sins for my age and he had others waiting. He was not a patient man of God.'

'Neither am I.'

'All alike.'

'*Please*,' said Joel, looking at the thick, narrow envelope in the woman's hands, knowing that if he took it forcibly from her she would scream. 'I have to reach Osnabrück, you know that!'

'You are from *Osnabrück?*' The 'nun' clutched the envelope to her chest, her body bent further, protecting a holy thing.

'No, not Osnabrück!' Converse tried to remember Val's words. He was a priest on a pilgrimage . . . to Auschwitz and Bergen-Belsen . . . from, from . . .'*Los Angeles!*' he whispered harshly.

'*Ja, goed.* What country?'

'Jesus!'

'*Wat?*'

'The United States of America.'

'*Goed!* Here you are, *Mijnheer*.' The old woman handed him the envelope, now smiling sweetly. 'We all must do our jobs, must we not? Go with God, my fellow servant of the Lord . . . I do like this costume. I was on the stage, you know. I don't think I'll give it back. Everyone smiles, and a gentleman who came out of one of those dirty houses, stopped and gave me fifty guilder.'

The old woman walked away, turning once and smiling again, discreetly showing him a pint of whisky she had taken from under her habit.

It might have been the same platform, he could not tell, but his fears were the same as when he arrived in Amsterdam twenty-four hours ago. He had come to the city as an innocuous-looking labourer with a beard and a pale, bruised face. He was leaving as a priest, erect, clean-shaven, sunburned, a properly-dressed man of the cloth on a pilgrimage of repentance and reaffirmation. Gone was the outraged lawyer in Geneva, the manipulating supplicant in Paris, the captured dupe in Bonn. What remained was the hunted, and to survive he had to be able to stalk the hunters before they stalked him; that meant spotting them before they spotted him. It was a lesson he had learned eighteen years ago when his eyes were sharper and his body more resilient. To compensate he had to use whatever talents he had developed; all were reduced to concentration — without appearing to concentrate. Which was how and why Joel saw the man.

He was standing by a concrete pillar up ahead on the platform, reading an unfolded train schedule in the dim light. Converse glanced at him — as, indeed, he glanced briefly at nearly everyone in sight — then seconds later he looked again. Something was odd, incongruous. There could be several reasons why a man remained outside a well-lighted railroad car to read a schedule — a last cigarette in the open air, waiting for someone — but that same man could hardly read the very small print while casually holding the schedule midway between his head and his waist without any evidence of a squint. It was like trying to read a page from a telephone directory in a car stuck in traffic in the Lincoln Tunnel; it took observable effort. The man showed none.

Converse continued down the platform, approaching the two open doors that signified the end of one railway car and the beginning of the next. He purposely let his suitcase catch on a protruding window ledge, pivoting as it did so, apologizing to a couple behind him. Courteously he let them pass and courteously, as each saw his collar, they smiled and nodded. But whilst his head remained facing them, his eyes strayed to the man diagonally to the left by the pillar. He clutched the schedule in his hand — another forgotten accessory. The man was concentrating now on Joel. It was enough.

Converse entered the second door, his gait casual again, but altered the instant he could no longer see the man by the pillar. He rushed ahead inside the railroad car and tripped, falling to the floor by the first seat, again apologizing to those behind him — a divine undone by profane luggage. He looked out the window, past the two passengers in the seat, both of whom paid attention to his collar before his face.

The man by the pillar had dropped the schedule and was now signalling with quick, short beckoning gestures, his right hand moving frantically. In seconds he was joined by another man; their conversation was rapid, each separating, one to the door at the front of the car, the other heading for the entrance Joel had just passed through.

They had found him. He was trapped.

* * *

Valerie paid the driver and climbed out of the cab, acknowledging the assistance of the doorman. It was the second hotel reservation she had made in the space of two hours, having left a dead end trail in case anyone was following her. She had taken a cab from Kennedy to LaGuardia, buying a ticket to Boston on a mid-morning shuttle, then registering at the airport motel, both under the name of Charpentier. She had left the motel thirty minutes later, having paid the cab driver to return for her at a side exit and calling the hotel in Manhattan to see if a reservation was possible at that hour. It was. The St Regis would welcome Mrs DePinna, who had flown in from Tulsa, Oklahoma, on a sudden emergency.

At the all-night Travellers Shop in Schiphol Airport, Val had purchased a carry-on bag, filling it with toiletries and whatever more subdued articles of clothing she could find on the all too colourful racks. It was still the height of the summer – the heat of the summer – and, depending upon the circumstances, such clothes might come in handy. Also she had something to show customs.

She registered at the hotel desk using a 'Cherrywood Lane' without a number she remembered from her childhood in St Louis. Indeed, the name DePinna came from those early days as well, a neighbour down the street, the face a blur now, only a memory of a sad, vituperative woman who loathed all things foreign, including Val's parents. 'Mrs R. DePinna'; she had no idea where the R came from – possibly Roger for balance.

In the room she turned on the radio to the all-news station, a habit she inherited from her marriage, and proceeded to unpack her clothing and toiletries. She undressed, took a shower, washed out her underthings, and slipped into the out-sized T-shirt. This last was another habit; 'T-sacks', as she called them, had replaced bathrobes and morning coats on her patio in Cape Ann although none had a sunburst emblazoned on the front with words above and below heralding: *Tot Ziens – Amsterdam!*

She resisted calling Room Service for a pot of tea; it would be calming but it was an unnecessary act that at 3 o'clock in the morning had to call even minor attention to the woman in *714*. She sat in the chair staring absently at the window wishing she hadn't given up cigarettes; it would give her something to do while thinking, and she had to think. She had to rest too, but first she had to think, organize herself. She looked around the room, her eyes centring on her purse which she had placed on a bedside table. She was rich, if nothing else. Joel had insisted she take the risk of getting through customs with more than the $5,000 legal limit. So she had rolled up an additional twenty five-hundred dollar bills and shoved them into her brassiere. He had been right; she could not use credit cards or anything that carried her name.

She lowered her gaze to the two telephone directories on the shelf of the table, got out of the chair and went to the bed. Sitting on the edge she removed both volumes. One read, *New York County, Business to Business*; the other, *Manhattan* – and in the upper left-hand corner, printed across a blue diagonal strip: *Government Listings. See Blue pages.* It was the place to start. She returned the Business directory to the shelf and carried the Manhattan book over to the desk. She sat down, opened to the blue pages and found her beginning. *Department of the Air Force . . . Command Post ARPC.* It was an

800 number, the address on York Street in Denver, Colorado. If it was not the number she needed, whoever she reached could supply the correct one. She wrote it down on a page of St Regis stationery.

Suddenly Val heard the words. Her head snapped around towards the television set, her eyes on the vertical radio dial.

'. . . And now the latest update on the search for the American attorney, Joel Converse, one of the most tragic stories of the decade. The former Navy pilot, once honoured for outstanding bravery in the Vietnam war, whose dramatic escape electrified the nation, and whose subsequent tactical reports shocked the military, leading, many believed, to basic changes in Washington's South-east Asian policies, is still at large, hunted not for the man he was, but for the homicidal killer he has become. Reports are that he may still be in Paris. Although not official, word has been leaked from unnamed but authoritative sources within the *Sûreté* that fingerprints found on the premises where the French lawyer, René Mattilon, was slain are definitely those of Converse, thus confirming what the authorities believed – that Converse killed his French acquaintance for cooperating with Interpol and the *Sûreté*. The manhunt is spreading out from Paris and this station will bring you . . .'

Valerie sprang from the chair and ran to the television set, furiously pushing several buttons until the radio was silent. She stood for a moment, trembling with anger – and fear. And something else she could not define – did not care to define. It tore her apart and she had to stay together.

She lay on the bed staring at the ceiling, seeing the reflections of light from moving things below in the street, hearing the sounds of the city. None of it was comforting, only abrasive intrusions that kept her mind alert, rejecting sleep. She had not slept on the plane; but had dozed intermittently, repeatedly jarred awake by half-formed nightmares, not helped by excessive turbulence over the North Atlantic. She needed sleep now . . . she needed Joel now. The first came; the latter was out of reach.

There was a shattering dissonance accompanied by a burst of sunlight that remained constant, blinding her as she shot up from the bed, kicking away the sheets, throwing her feet on the floor. It was the telephone. The telephone? She looked at her watch; it was 7.25, the sun streaming through the windows, the phone once again ringing, piercing the mists of sleep but not clearing them away. The telephone? How . . . ? *Why?* She reached over and picked it up, gripping it with all her strength, trying to find herself before speaking.

'Hello?'

'Mrs DePinna?' inquired a male voice.

'Yes.'

'We trust everything is satisfactory.'

'Are you in the habit of waking up your guests at seven o'clock in the morning to ask if they're comfortable?'

'I'm terribly sorry, but we were anxious for you. This *is* the Mrs DePinna from Tulsa, Oklahoma, isn't it?'

'Yes.'

'We've been looking for you all night . . . since the flight from Amsterdam arrived at one-thirty this morning.'

'Who are you?' asked Val, petrified, holding her wrist below the phone.

'Someone who wants to help you, Mrs Converse,' said the voice, now relaxed and friendly. 'You've given us quite a run around. We must have woken up a hundred and fifty women who checked in at hotels since two A.M. . . . the "plane from Amsterdam" did it; you didn't ask me what I was talking about. Believe me, we want to help, Mrs Converse. We're both after the same thing.'

'Who *are* you?'

'The United States Government covers it. Stay where you are. I'll be over in fifteen minutes.'

The hell United States Government covers it! thought Val shivering, as she hung up the phone. The United States Government had cleaner ways of identifying itself . . . She had to get *out!* What did the fifteen minutes mean? Was it a trap? Were men downstairs waiting for her now – waiting to see if she would run? She had no *choice!*

She ran to the bathroom, grabbing the carry-on case off a chair and throwing her things into it. She dressed in seconds, stuffing what clothes remained into the bag, snatching the room key off the bureau, and running to the door. She stopped. Oh, *Lord*, the stationery with the Air Force number! She raced back to the desk, picked up the page beside the open telephone book and shoved it into her purse. She glanced wildly about; was there anything *else?* No. She left the room and walked rapidly down the hall to the elevators.

Maddeningly, the elevator stopped at nearly every floor, men and women getting on, most of the men with puffed circles under their eyes, a few of the women looking drawn, sheepish. Several apparently knew one another, others nodded absently, gazes straying to lapels and upper blouses. Then Valerie understood; the majority of the passengers had plastic name plates affixed to the fronts of their jackets and dresses; it was some sort of convention.

The doors opened to a crowded bank of elevators; the ornate lobby to the right was swarming with people, voices raised in greetings, questions and instructions. Cautiously, Val approached the gilded arch that led to the lobby-proper, looking around in controlled panic to see if anyone was looking at her. A large gold-framed sign with block letters arranged in black felt under glass was on the wall; it explained the commotion.

Welcome: Micmac Distributors.

There followed a descending list of meetings and activities.

Buffet Breakfast 7.30–8.30 a.m.
Regional Conferences 8.45–10.00 a.m.
Advertising Symposium Q and A 10.15–11.00 a.m.
Mid-morning Break. Make reservations for city tours.

'Hey, sweet face,' said a burly, red-eyed man standing next to Val. 'That's a no-no.'

'I beg your pardon?'

'We are *marked*, princess!'

Valerie stopped breathing; she stared at the man, gripping the handles of her carry-on, prepared to smash it into his face and bolt for the glass doors thirty feet away. 'I have no idea what you mean?'

'The *name*, princess! Where's your Micmac spirit? How can I ask you to have breakfast with me if I don't know your name?'

'Oh . . . the name tag. I'm sorry.'

'What's your region, beautiful creature?'

'Region?' Again Valerie understood; she suddenly smiled. 'Actually, I'm new – just hired yesterday. They said my instructions would be at the desk, but it's so crowded I'll never get over there. Of course, with *your* shoulders I might make it before I'm fired.'

'Grab hold, princess! These shoulders used to play semi-pro ball.' The heavy-set salesman was an effective blocking back; they reached the counter and the man growled appropriately, a lion preening before its conquest. 'Hey, fella! This lady's been trying to get your attention. Need I say more, fella?' The salesman grinned at Val, holding in his stomach.

'No, sir – yes, mam?' said the perplexed clerk who was not at all busy. The activity was taking place in front of the counter, not *at* the counter.

Valerie leaned forward, ostensibly to be heard through the noise. She placed her key on the counter and opened her purse, taking out three fifty-dollar bills. 'This should cover the room. I've been here one night, and there are no charges. What's left is yours.'

'Thank *you*, mam.'

'I need a favour.'

'Of course!'

'My name is Mrs DePinna – but of course the key tells you that.'

'What, mam?'

'I'm visiting a friend who's just had an operation. Could you tell me where the . . . Lebanon Hospital is?'

'The Lebanon . . . ? It's in the Bronx, I think. Somewhere on the Grand Concourse. Any cab driver will know, mam.'

'Mrs DePinna's the name.'

'Yes, Mrs DePinna. *Thank* you.'

Valerie turned to the heavy-set, red-eyed salesman, again smiling. 'I'm sorry. Apparently I'm at the wrong hotel, the wrong company, can you imagine? It would have been nice. Thanks for your help.' She turned and quickly dodged her way through the crowd toward the revolving doors.

The street was only beginning to come alive. Valerie walked rapidly down the pavement, stopping almost immediately in front of a small, elegant bookstore; she decided to wait in the doorway. The stories she had heard all her life included not only tales of leaving false information, but lessons involving the necessity of knowing what the enemy looked like; it was often the difference.

A taxi drove up in front of the St Regis and, before it had come to a stop, the rear door opened. She could see the passenger clearly, his hand extended over the front seat paying the fare without thought of change. He climbed out swiftly and started running toward the glass doors. He was hatless, with unkempt, nearly blond hair, and dressed in a madras jacket and light-blue summer jeans. He was the enemy, Valerie knew that and accepted it. What she found hard to accept was his youth. He was in his twenties, hardly more than a boy. But the face was hard and set in anger, the eyes cold – distant flashes of steel in the sunlight. *Wie ein Hitlerjunge*, thought Val, walking out of the bookstore doorway.

A car streaked past her, heading west towards the hotel and within seconds she heard screeching tyres, expecting a crash to follow. She turned, as any pedestrian might turn, hearing the sudden, hysterical sound in the street. But the hysteria belonged to her. Fifty feet away, a brown sedan had come to a stop, on its door panels and trunk in clear black lettering: *US Army*. A uniformed officer got out quickly. He was staring at her.

She broke into a run.

Converse sat in an aisle seat roughly in the middle of the railway car. His palms perspired as he turned the pages of the small, black prayer book. It had been placed in the envelope along with his passport, the letter of pilgrimage and a typewritten sheet of instructions which included a few basic facts about Father William Wilcrist, should they be necessary. At the bottom of the page was a final order: *Commit to memory, tear up, flush down toilet before immigration at Oldenzaal*.

The instructions were unnecessary, even distracting. Quite simply, he was to get off at Osnabrück, coincidentally taking a stroll through the railway cars twenty minutes out of a station called Rheine, leaving the suitcase behind as if he intended to return to his seat. The details of his supposedly changing trains at Hanover for Celle and the subsequent morning drive north to Bergen-Belsen could have been said in one sentence rather than the complicated paragraphs entailing deep motivations and past successes. They were irrelevant. The facts about Father William Wilcrist, however, were succinct and he had memorized them after the second reading. Wilcrist was thirty-eight years old, a graduate of Fordham with theological degrees from Catholic University in Washington, and ordained at St Ignatius in New York. He was an 'activist priest' and currently assigned to the Church of the Blessed Sacrament in Los Angeles. In Valerie's words, if he was asked to recite more than that he was probably caught.

For all practical purposes he was caught now, thought Joel, gazing at the back of a man's head in the front of the car, the same man who had joined another standing by a pillar on the platform in Amsterdam. Undoubtedly that first man was now looking at the back of *his* head from a seat in the rear, mused Converse, turning another page in the prayer book. On the surface, the odds against him were overwhelming but there was a fact and a factor just below the surface. The fact was that he knew who his executioners were and they did not know he knew. The factor was a state of mind he had drawn upon in the past – he was desperate.

The train travelled north, then east; there were two stops before Oldenzaal, after which he presumed they would cross the Rhine into West Germany. They had pulled in and out of the Deventer station; that left one more, a city named Hengelo. The announcement came and Joel got out of his seat before any of the Hengelo commuters rose from theirs; he turned in the aisle and walked back to the rear of the car. As he passed the man who stood by the pillar, he saw that Aquitaine's hunter stared straight ahead, his body so rigid it barely moved with the movement of the train. Converse had seen such postures many times before, at trials and in boardrooms; they invariably belonged to insecure witnesses and unsure negotiators. The man was tense, frightened perhaps of failing an assignment or of the people who had sent him to Amsterdam – whatever it was, his anxiety was showing and Joel could use it. *He was crawling out of a deep shaft in the ground, one tenuous grasp of earth after another, the indentations pre-formed after nights of preparation. The wire fence was in the distance, the rain falling, the patrols concerned, anxious – frightened by every sound they could not quickly identify. He needed only one and he had it . . . he could reach the fence!*

Reach Osnabrück . . . alone.

The toilet was unoccupied; he opened the door, went inside, and took out the page of instructions. He folded it, tore it in shreds, and dropped the pieces into the bowl, pressing the foot button as he did so. They disappeared with the flush; he turned back to the door and waited.

A second announcement blared from the speakers outside as the train slowed down; the sound of gathering feet was inches away beyond the door. The train came to a stop; he could feel the vibration of moving bodies, determined commuters thinking of home and relief and undoubtedly the Dutch equivalent of a martini. The vibrations stopped; the sounds faded away. Converse opened the door no more than half an inch. The rigid hunter was not in his seat. *Now.*

Joel slid out of the door and stepped quickly into the open separation between cars, excusing himself between the stragglers getting off from the car behind, walking rapidly inside and down the aisle. As he approached the last rows he saw an empty seat – two seats, facing the platform – and swung in, sitting beside the window, his hand in front of his face, peering through his fingers.

Aquitaine's hunter raced back and forth, sufficiently aggressive to stop three men who were walking away, their backs to him; rapid apologies followed. The hunter turned to the train, the exiting possibilities exhausted. He got back on board, his face a creased map falling apart – valleys of anxiety.

More, thought Converse. *I want more, I want you stretched, as patrols before you were stretched. Until you can't stand it!*

Oldenzaal arrived, then was left behind. The train crossed the Rhine, the clattering of the bridge below like snares – hammering tympany, kettledrums to follow. The hunter had crashed the forward doors open, too panicked to do anything but quickly look around to his companion, or to a lone suitcase, perhaps. Joel's head was below the back of the seat in front of him. Minutes later the heavy drums came in the form of *Sonderpolizei* checking the border, scrutinizing every male of a vague description, dozens of uniformed men walking through the railway cars. They were courteous to be sure, but nevertheless they gave rise to ugly vestiges of a time past. Converse showed his passport and the letter written in German for the conscience of Germans. A policeman grimaced sadly, then nodded in acquiescence and went on to the next seat. The uniforms left; the minutes became quarter hours. He could see through the windows into the forward car; the two hunters met several rows behind where he had been sitting. Again they separated; one fore, one aft. *Now.*

Joel got up from his seat and side-stepped into the aisle, checking his schedule and bending down to look out of the darkened window, meaningless motions. But he would stay there for as long as he had to, until one of the hunters spotted him. It took less than ten seconds. As Converse pitched his head down supposedly to see a passing sign outside, he caught a glimpse of a figure moving into the upper panel of glass on the forward door. Joel stood up. The man behind the glass spun out of sight. It was the sign he was waiting for, the moment to move quickly.

He turned and walked to the rear of the car, went out the door and across the dark clattering space to the car behind. He went inside and swiftly made his way down the aisle, again to the rear and again into the next car, turning in the intervening darkness to see what he expected to see, what he wanted to see. The man was following him. *A guard was taking himself out of position in the downpour. Only seconds and he could reach the barbed wire.*

He ran through the third car aware that a number of passengers looked up at him, looked up at a running priest. Most turned in their seats to see if there was an emergency, and seeing none shook their heads in bewilderment. He reached the door, pulled it open and stepped into the shadows, suddenly startled by what he saw, by what he physically felt. In front of him, instead of another railroad car door, the upper part of a window, there was a solid panel of heavy wood, the word *FRACHT* printed across the midsection above a large steel knob. Then he heard the announcement over the loud speakers.

'*Bad Bentheim! Nächste Station, Bad Bentheim!*'

The train was slowing down, the first of the two stops before Osnabrück. Joel moved forward into the darkest area and inched his head in view of the window behind him, confident that he would not be seen by a man facing reflected light off a panel of glass. What he saw again startled him – not by the activity , but by the *inactivity*. The hunter made no move towards the door; instead, he sat down – sat *down* facing forward, a commuter finding a more comfortable seat, nothing else on his mind. The train came to a stop, those passengers getting off forming a line in front . . . in *front*.

There had been a sign above this last door but since he could not read it, he had simply gone outside. He looked now at the exit doors; there were no handles. Obviously that incomprehensible sign had informed any who approached the door that it was not an exit. If he had been facing a trap before, he was in a cage now, a steel cage that began moving again, as the wheels gathered speed against the tracks. A racing jail from which there was no escape. Converse reached into his shirt pocket and took out his cigarettes. *He was so close to the barbed wire; he had to think!*

A rattle? A key . . . a *bolt*. The door of heavy wood with the word *FRACHT* stencilled on it opened and the figure of a stout man emerged, preceded by his stomach.

'*Eine Zigarette für Sie, während ich zum Pinkeln gehe!*' said the railroad guard, laughing, as he crossed through the short, dark corridor to the door. '*Dann ein Whiskey, ja?*'

The German was going for a drink, and although he had pulled the door of his domain nearly shut, he had not closed it; he was an untroubled man, a guard with nothing he felt worth guarding. Joel pushed the heavy panel open and went inside, knowing what would happen; it *had* to happen the instant the guard walked by the hunter on his way to 'ein Whisky.'

There were half a dozen sealed crates and roughly ten cages holding animals – dogs mostly and several cats, cowering in corners, claws extended at the sound of growls and coughing barks. The only light came from a naked bulb swaying on a thick wire from the ceiling beyond another cage, this one built for man with wire mesh at the end of the freight car. Converse concealed himself behind a crate near the door. He reached under his priestly coat and pulled out the gun with the perforated cylinder, the silencer.

The door opened – cautiously, millimetre by millimetre – the weapon appeared before the hand or the arm. Finally there was the man, the hunter, the foot soldier from Aquitaine.

Joel fired twice, not trusting a single shot. The arm crashed back into the edge of the half-open door, the gun spinning out of the killer's hand, a single spurt of blood erupting near the executioner's wrist. Converse sprang from behind the crate – *the patrol was his, and so was the stretch of barbed wire fence! He could climb it and crawl over now! The rock had smashed the window in the barracks! The staccato barrage of machine gun fire was spraying where he was not! Seconds, and he was out!*

Joel pinned the man to the floor, gripping the hunter's throat, his knee pressed into the executioner's chest – one enormous plunge and the soldier from Aquitaine was dead. He held the barrel of the gun against the man's temple.

'You speak any *English?*'

'*Ja!*' coughed the German. '*Ich spreche Englisch!*'

'*What?*'

'I . . . speak English.'

'What were your orders?'

'Follow you. Only follow you. Don't shoot! I am *Angestellte!* I know not a thing!'

'A *what?*'

'A hired man!'

'*Aquitaine!*'

'*Was* . . . ?'

The man was not lying; there was too much panic in his eyes. Converse raised the gun and abruptly shoved it into the German's left eye, the perforated cylinder pressed deep into the socket.

'You tell me exactly what you were told to do! The truth – and I'll know a lie – and if you lie your skull will be all over this wall! Talk to me!'

'To follow you!'

'*And?*'

'If you left the train we were to phone the *Polizei*. Wherever. Then . . . we were to kill you before they came. But I would not *do* that! I swear by my *Christ* I would *never* do that! I am a good Christian. I even love the Jews! I am unemployed, *Mein Herr!*'

Joel crashed the weapon into the man's skull – *the patrol had been taken out!*

He could climb the fence now! He pulled the German behind a crate and waited. How long it was impossible to tell; his heartbeat was too rapid to consider time. The railway guard came back, somewhat more drunk than sober, and took refuge behind his wire meshed office with the single light bulb.

The other cages were not so serene. The smell of human blood and sweat was more than the dogs could take; they began to react, viciousness the cousin of fear. Within minutes the railway car labelled *FRACHT* became a madhouse, the animals were now incensed – the dogs snarling, barking, hurling themselves against their cages; the cats screeching, hissing, backs arched, fur extended, provoked by the dogs. The guard was perplexed and frightened, anchoring himself to the chair in his sanctuary of wire mesh, drinking whisky from a bottle. He stared at the cages, his eyes wide within the folds of puffed flesh. Twice he looked at a glass-encased lever on the wall inches above the desk, above his hand. He had only to lift the casing and pull it.

'*Rheine! Nächste Station, Rheine!*'

The last stop before Osnabrück. Before long the German would revive and unless Joel's eyes were on him at that instant the man would scream and an emergency lever would be pulled. Too, there was another man only cars behind who was also hired to follow him, to kill. To remain where he was any longer was to let the trap close. He had to get off.

The train stopped and Converse lunged for the door, his movement causing a dozen caged animals to vent their anger and confusion. He pushed back the bolt, opened the heavy door and raced into the forward car. He ran up the aisle – a priest perhaps on an errand of mercy – and excused himself past the departing passengers, intent only on getting off before an unconscious body was found, a lever pulled, an alarm sounded. He reached the exit and leaped from the second step to the platform; he looked around and ran into the shadows of the station. He would have to keep running.

He was free. He was alive. But he was miles away from an old woman waiting for her priest.

31

Valerie kept running, afraid to look behind, but she was not a fool. She did so and saw that the Army officer was arguing with the driver of the Army car. Seconds later she looked again as she reached the corner of Madison Avenue; she tried not to panic. The officer was now running after her, shortening the distance between them with each stride. She raced across the street as the light turned, the blaring of horns signifying the anger of several drivers.

Thirty feet away a taxi heading north pulled to the kerb and a grey-haired man lethargically stretched himself out to the pavement, tired, unwilling to accept the morning. Val ran back into the street, into the traffic, and raced to the cab's outer door; she opened it and climbed in as the startled grey-haired man was accepting change.

'Hey, lady, you *crazy?*' yelled the black driver. 'You're supposed to use the kerb! You'll get flattened by a bus!'

'I'm *sorry!*' cried Val, unable to control herself, sinking low and back on the seat. *What the hell?* 'My husband is running up the street after me and I *will* not be hit again! I *hurt*. He's . . . he's an Army officer.'

The grey-haired man sprang out of the cab like a decathlon contender, slamming the door behind him. The taxi driver turned around and looked at her, his large face suspicious, curious.

'You tellin' the truth?'

'I threw up all morning from the punches last night.'

'An officer? In the Army?'

'Yes! Will you please get *out* of here?' Val sank lower. 'He's at the corner now! He'll cross the street – he'll see me!'

'Fret not, mam,' said the driver, calmly reaching over the seat and pressing down the locks on the rear doors. 'Oh, you were right on! Here he comes runnin' across like a crazy man. And would you look at them ribbons! Would you believe that horseshit – excuse me, mam. He's kind'a skinny, ain't he? Most of the real bad characters were skinny. They compensated – that's a psychiatric term, you know.'

'Get out of here!'

'The law's precise, mam. It's the duty of every driver of a medallion vehicle to protect the well-being of his fare . . . And I was an infantry grunt, mam, and I've waited a hell of a long time for this particular opportunity. Having a real good reason and all that. I mean, you sure can't deny the words you said to me.' The driver climbed out of the cab; he matched his face; he was a very large man, indeed. Val watched in horrified astonishment as the black walked around the car to the kerb and shouted.

'Hey, Captain! Over here, on the sidewalk! You lookin' for a very pretty lady? Like maybe your wife?'

'*What?*' The officer ran up on the pavement to the black man.

'Well, Captain-baby, I'm afraid I can't salute 'cause my uniform's in the attic – if I had an attic – but I want you to know that this search-and-destroy has successfully been completed. Would you step over to my jeep, sir?'

The officer started to run toward the taxi, but he was suddenly grabbed by the driver who spun him around and punched him first in the stomach, then brought his knee crashing up into the army man's groin, and finally 'completed' the assignment by hammering a huge fist into the officer's mouth. Val gasped; blood spread over the captain's entire face as he fell to the pavement. The driver ran back to the cab, climbed in, shut the door and pulled the gear; the taxi shot forward in the traffic.

'Lawdy, *lawdy!*' said the driver in a caricatured dialect. 'That felt *real* good! Is there an address, mam? The meter's running.'

'I . . . I'm not sure.'

'Let's start with the basics. Where do you want to go?'

'To a telephone . . . Why did you *do that?*'

'That's my business, not yours.'

'You're *sick!* You could have been arrested!'

'For what? Protecting a fare from assault? That bad character was actually runnin' toward my cab and the vibes were not good, not good at all. Also there weren't no cops around.'

'I presume you were in Vietnam,' said Val, after a period of silence, looking at the large head of black hair in front of her.

'Oh, yes, I was accorded that privilege. Very scenic, mam.'

'What did you think of General Delavane? General George Marcus Delavane?'

The cab suddenly, violently swerved as the driver gripped the wheel and slammed his heavy foot on the brake, causing the taxi to bolt to a stop, throwing Val into the rim of the front seat. The huge black head whipped around, the coal-black eyes filled with fury and loathing and that deep unmistakable core of fear Valerie had seen so many times in Joel's eyes. The driver swallowed, his piercing stare somehow losing strength, turning inward, the fear taking over. He turned back to the wheel and answered simply. 'I didn't do much thinking about the General mam. What's the address, Mrs? The meter's running.'

'I don't know . . . A telephone, I have to get to a telephone. Will you wait?'

'Do you have the money? Or did the captain take it all? There are limits to my concern, lady. I don't get no compensation for good deeds.'

'I have money. You'll be well paid.'

'Show me a bill.'

Valerie reached into her purse and pulled out a hundred dollars. 'Will that do?' she asked.

'It's fine, but don't do that with every cab you want in a hurry. You could end up the Bed-Stuy a damn good lookin' corpse.'

'I don't want to believe that.'

'Oh, my, we have a liberal! Stick to it, mam, until they stick it to you. Me, I want 'em all to *fry!* Your kind don't really get it – *we* do. You only get the *periphery*, you *dig?* A couple of rapes in the classy suburbs – and some of *them* might be open to dispute – and a few heists of silver and jewellery – *hell*, you're covered by insurance! Where I come from we're covered by a gun under the pillow, and God help the son of a bitch who tries to take it from me.'

'A telephone, please.'

'Your meter, lady.'

They stopped at a booth on the corner of Madison and 78th Street. Valerie got out, opening her purse and removing the page of St Regis stationery with the Air Force telephone number. She inserted a coin, and dialled.

'Air Force, Recruit Command, Denver,' announced the female operator.

'I wondered if you could help me, miss,' said Val, her eyes darting about at the traffic, looking for a roving brown sedan with *US Army* printed across its doors. 'I'm trying to locate an officer, a relative, actually . . .'

'One minute, please. I'll transfer you.'

'Personnel, Denver Units,' came a second voice, now male. 'Sergeant Porter.'

'Sergeant, I'm trying to locate an officer,' repeated Valerie. 'A relative of mine who left word with an aunt he wanted to reach me.'

'Where in Colorado, mam?'

'Well, I'm not sure.'

'The Springs? The Academy? Lowery field or possibly Cheyenne Mountain?'

'I don't know that he *is* in Colorado, Sergeant.'

'Why did you call Denver then?'

'You were in the telephone book.'

'I see.' The Army man paused, then continued, his words spoken by rote. 'And this officer left word that he wanted to reach you?'

'Yes.'

'But he didn't leave an address or a telephone number.'

'If he did, my aunt lost it. She's quite elderly.'

'The procedure is as follows, miss. If you will write a letter to the MPC – Military Personnel Center – at the Randolph Air Force Base, San Antonio, Texas, stating your request and the officer's name and rank, the letter will be processed.'

'I don't have time, Sergeant! I travel a great deal . . . I'm calling from an airport now, as a matter of fact.'

'I'm sorry, miss, those are the regulations.'

'I'm not a "Miss" and my cousin's a general and he really does want to speak to me! I just want to know where he is, and if you can't tell me, certainly you can call him and give him my name. I'll call *you* back with a number where he can reach me. That's reasonable, isn't it, Sergeant. Frankly, this is an emergency.'

'A general, mam?'

'Yes, Sergeant Potter. A General Abbott.'

'Sam Abbott? I mean, Brigadier General Samuel Abbott?'

'That's the one, Sergeant Potter.'

'Porter, mam.'

'I'll remember that.'

'Well, I can't see any security breach here, miss – mam. Everybody knows where General Abbott is stationed. He's a popular officer and in the newspapers a lot.'

'Where is that, Sergeant? I'll personally tell him you've been most helpful – to us both.'

'Nellis Air Force Base in Nevada, mam, just outside Las Vegas. He commands the advanced tactical manoeuvre squadrons. All the squadron commanders get their final training at Nellis. He's the *man* . . . May I have your name, please?'

'Oh, good lord! There's the last boarding call for my plane! Thank you, Sergeant.' Valerie hung up the phone, her eyes still scanning the street, trying to decide what to do – whether to call Sam now or wait. Suddenly she realized she could *not* call; it would mean using a credit card, origin of call and destination listed. She went out of the booth and returned to the taxi.

'Lady, I'd just as soon get out of here, if you don't mind,' said the driver, a quiet urgency in his voice.

'What's the matter?'

'I keep a police scanner in my cab in case there's a problem in my neighbourhood, and I just heard the word. An army captain was clobbered on Fifty-fifth and Madison by a black driver of a taxi heading north. Lucky for me they didn't get the licence or the company, but the description's pretty good. "A big black son of a bitch with a size twelve fist", was the way those mothers put it.'

'Let's go,' said Val. 'I hate to say this, and I mean that, but I can't get involved.' The cab sped forward, the driver turning east on Eighty-first Street. 'Is ... my husband pressing charges?' she asked, suddenly bewildered.

'No, I'm off the hook there,' replied the driver. 'He must have punched you real bad. He just fled and had nuthin' to say. Bless his white heart. Where to?'

'Let me think.'

'It's your meter.'

She had to get to Las Vegas but the idea of going back to Kennedy or LaGuardia Airports frightened her. They seemed too logical, too easily anticipated. Then she remembered. About five or six years ago she and Joel were week-ending with friends in Short Hills, New Jersey, when Joel got a call from Nathan Simon, telling him he had to fly to Los Angeles on Sunday for a Monday morning meeting. All the legal papers would be sent to the Beverly Hills Hotel by air express. Joel had taken the plane from Newark Airport.

'Can you drive me to Newark?'

'I can drive you to Alaska, lady, but *Newark?*'

'The airport.'

'That's better. It's one of the best. I guess Newark's okay, too. I got a brother there and, hell, he's still alive. I'll swing through the Park at Sixty-sixth and head down to the Lincoln Tunnel. Do you mind if I turn on the scanner again?'

'No, go right ahead.'

The voices went in and out, then the driver pushed a button and the phrases were steady. *'Incident at Fifty-fifth and Madison is a negative. Precinct Ten has called it off as the victim refused assistance and did not identify himself. So patrols, onward and upward. We helps them what helps themselves. On, brothers.'*

'Oh, he's a *brother!*' shouted the driver in relief, as he turned off the radio. 'You catch that "incident is a negative?" They could'a used him in 'Nam, in those big body-count press conferences ... Come to think of it, he was probably there – not with the press, just one of the bodies. They never did get it right.'

Valerie leaned forward on the seat. 'I asked you about ...'Nam. About General Delavane. Would you tell me about him?'

It was nearly a minute before the black replied, and when he did so, his voice was soft, even mellifluous. And somewhere at the base of it was abject defeat. 'My driver's identification is lookin' at you, lady. I'm driving you to Newark Airport – that's what you're payin' for, and that's what you'll get.'

The rest of the ride was made in silence, an oppressive sense of fear pervading the cab. *After all these years*, thought Val. *Oh, God.*

They hit heavy traffic at the Tunnel and then on the Turnpike; it was the start of the weekend and vacationers were heading for the Jersey shore. The airport was worse; it was jammed, cars backed up for a quarter of a mile in the departure lanes. Finally, they edged up into a parking space and Valerie got out. She paid the driver a hundred dollars above the fare and thanked him. 'You've been much more than helpful, you know that. I'll never really know why but I'll think about it.'

'Like I said, it's my business. I got my reasons.'

'I wish I could say something, something that could help.'

'Don't try, lady. The green is enough.'

'No, it's not.'

'Sure it is until something better comes along, and that ain't gonna be in my lifetime . . . You take care, Mrs. I think you got bigger problems than most of us. You said too much, which I don't recall, of course.'

Valerie turned and went into the terminal. The lines in front of the counters were horrendous and before joining one she had to know which one. Twenty minutes later she was in the proper line and nearly an hour after that she had a ticket to Las Vegas on American's 12.35 flight, another hour before boarding. It was time to see it if all made sense. If Sam Abbott made sense, or whether she was grasping desperately at a man she once remembered who might not be that man any longer. She had exchanged $20.00 in bills for two $10.00 rolls of quarters. She hoped it would be enough. She took an escalator up to the first floor and went to a telephone at the far end of the wide corridor past the shops. Nevada information gave her the number of main switchboard at Nellis Air Force Base. She dialled and asked to be put through to General Samuel Abbott.

'I don't know if he's on the base yet,' said the operator.

'Oh?' She had forgotten. There was a three hour time difference.

'Just a minute, he's checked in. Early morning flight schedule.'

'General Abbott's office.'

'May I speak to the General, please. The name is Parquette, Mrs Virginia Parquette.'

'May I ask what this is in reference to?' asked the secretary. 'The general's extremely busy and is about to head down to the field.'

'I'm a cousin he hasn't seen in a long time, actually. There's been a tragedy in the family.'

'Oh, I'm terribly sorry.'

'Please tell him I'm on the line. He may not recall my name; it's been so many years. But you might remind him that in the old days we had some wonderful dinners in New York. It's really most urgent. I wish someone else were making this call, but I'm afraid I was elected.'

'Yes . . . yes, of course.'

The waiting put Valerie in the last circle of hell. Finally there was a click, followed by the voice she remembered.

'Virginia . . . Parquette?'

'Yes.'

'*Ginny* – from New York? *Dinner* in New York?'

'Yes.'

'You're the wife, not the sister.'

'*Yes!*'

'Give me a number. I'll call you back in ten minutes.'

'It's a pay phone.'

'*Stay* there. The number.'

She gave it to him and hung up, frightened, wondering what she had done, but knowing that she could not have done anything else. She sat in the plastic chair by the phone, watching the escalators, looking at the people going into and walking out of the various shops, the bar, the fast-food restaurant. She tried not to look at her watch; twelve minutes passed. The phone rang.

'Yes?'

'Valerie . . .'

'*Yes!*'

'I wanted to get out of the office – too many interruptions. Where are you? I know the area code's New Jersey.'

'Newark Airport. I'm on the twelve-thirty flight to Las Vegas. I've got to see you.'

'I tried to call *you*. Talbot's secretary gave me your number . . .'

'*When?*'

'Starting two days ago. I was in the Mojave on manoeuvres and too bushed to turn on a radio – we didn't have newspapers. A man answered and when he said you weren't there I hung up.'

'That was Roger, Joel's father. He's dead.'

'I know. They say it might have been suicide.'

'*No!* . . . I've seen him, Sam. I've seen Joel! It's all lies!'

'That's what we have to talk about,' said the general. 'Call me when you get in. Same name. I don't want to pick you up at the airport; too many people know me over there. I'll figure out a place where we can meet.'

'*Thank* you, Sam!' said Valerie. 'You're all we have left.'

'We?'

'For the time being, yes. I'm all *he* has left.'

Converse watched from the dark corner of the railroad station as the train for Osnabrück started up, its huge wheels pressing into the tracks, groaning for momentum. At any moment he expected whistles to pierce the quiet night and the train to stop, a bewildered half-drunken guard running from the freight car, screaming. None of it happened. Why? Was the man more than half drunk? Had the sounds of the enraged animals driven him further into the bottle, strengthening his resolve to remain in the safety of his cage? Had he seen only a blur racing to the door in the dim light, or perhaps nothing, an unconscious body subsequently not discovered? Then Joel saw that there was another possibility, a brutal one. He could see a figure running forward through the second to last car, twice lunging between the seats, his face pressed against the glass. Moments later the man was leaning out above the lower door of the first exit, the steps below blocked off by the heavy solid gate. In his hand was a gun, held laterally across his forehead as he squinted against the station lights, peering into the shadows.

Suddenly the killer made his decision. He gripped the metal rim and leaped over the guardrail, dropping to the ground, rolling over in the gravel away from the gathering speed of the train. The hunter from Aquitaine was in panic; he dared not lose the quarry, dared not fail to carry out his assignment.

Converse spun around the corner and raced along the dark side of the building to a parking area. The passengers who had got off the train were starting automobiles or climbing into them; two couples were chatting on the near platform, obviously waiting to be picked up. A car came curving in off the road beyond; the two men waved and in moments all four were inside, laughing as the car sped away. The parking area was deserted, the station shut down for the night. A single floodlight from the roof illuminated the emptiness, a border of tall trees beyond the wide expanse of coarse gravel gave the appearance of a huge impenetrable wall.

Staying as best he could in the shadows, Joel darted from one space of darkness to another, remaining in the last, a solid, indented arch at the end of the building, his back pressed into the brick. He waited, his hand gripping the gun at his side, wondering if he would have to use it, even perhaps if he would have a chance to use it. He had been lucky on the train and he knew it; he was no match for professional killers. And no matter how strongly he tried to convince himself, he was not in the jungle a lifetime ago, not the younger man he had been then. But when he thought about it – as he was thinking about it now – those memories were all he had to guide him. He ducked out of the shadowed arch and quickly dashed to the corner.

The explosion came, blowing out the stone to the left of his head! He lunged to his right, rolling on the gravel, rising, and running away from the spill of the floodlight. Three more shattering explosions tore up the rock and earth around his feet. He reached a dark row of foliage and dived into the bushes, suddenly, instinctively, knowing exactly what he had to do!

'*Augh! Aughhh . . .!*' His final scream ended in expelled agony.

He then crawled through the undergrowth as fast as he could penetrate the tangled nets of scraping greenery. He was at least ten feet away from where he had shouted; he stopped and pivoted on his knees, remaining still, facing the floodlit expanse beyond the bushes.

It happened, as it had happened before when three children in official pyjamas had killed another child indelicately in the jungle. Anxious men were drawn to the last sounds they heard – as this hunter from Aquitaine was drawn now. The man stalked out of the darkness of the railroad station's rear platform, his gun extended, held steady with both hands. He walked directly, cautiously to that small section in the overgrowth where the two screams had come from.

Converse scratched the ground silently until he found a rock larger than his fist. He gripped it, waiting, staring. In his throat he could feel the drumming in his chest. The killer was within eight feet of the border of greenery. Joel lobbed the rock, arcing it in the air to his right.

The crunching thud was loud and Aquitaine's soldier crouched, firing one round after another – *two, three, four!* Converse raised his weapon and pulled the trigger twice. The man spun to his left, gasping, the start of a roar aborted as he clutched his upper stomach and fell to the ground.

There was no time to think or feel or consider what had happened. Joel crawled out to the gravel, raced over to his would-be executioner, grabbng him by the arms and dragging him back into the bushes. Still, he had to find out. He knelt down and held his fingers against the base of the man's throat. He was dead, another scout taken out in the war of the modern Aquitaine, the military confederation of George Marcus Delavane.

There was no one around – if there had been the gunshots would have provoked screams and running feet; the police would have been summoned; they would have been there by now. How far away was Osnabrück? He had read the schedule and tried to figure out the times, but everything had happened so swiftly, so brutally, he had not absorbed what he read. It was less than an hour, that much he knew. Somehow he had to get the word to the station at Osnabrück. Christ, *how?*

He walked out on the platform, glancing up at the sign: *Rheine.* It was a start; he had only counted the stops, not the names. Then he saw it – a glow of light? There was something in the distance – above the ground, high above – with lights on the inside, a tower! He had seen them dozens of times in Switzerland and France . . . signal depots! They dotted the Eurorail landscape, controlling the trains that sped across their sectors. He started running along the tracks suddenly wondering what he looked like. His hat was gone, his clothes soiled, but his clerical collar was still in place – he was still a priest. He would *be* a priest.

He reached the base of the tower, brushed off his clothes, and tried to smooth his hair. He composed himself and began climbing the metal steps. At the top he saw that the steel door to the tower itself was bolted, the inch-thick bulletproof glass a sign of the terrorist times; speeding trains were vulnerable targets. He approached the door and rapped on the metal frame. Three men were inside, huddled over electronic consoles; an elderly man turned from the numerous screens and came to the door. He peered through the glass and crossed himself, but was not sufficiently religious to open the door. Instead, there was a sudden echoing sound projected into the air, and the man's voice emerged from a speaker.

'*Was ist, Hochwürden?*'

'I don't speak German. Do you speak English?'

'*Engländer?*'

'Yes – *ja.*'

The old man turned to his associates and shouted something. Both shook their heads, but one held up his hand, and came to the door.

'*Ich spreche* . . . a little, Mister *Engländer. Nicht* come enter here, *verstehen?*'

'I have to call Osnabrück! A woman is waiting for me . . . a *Frau!*'

'*Ohh? Hochwürden! Eine Frau?*'

'No, *no!* You don't understand! Can't anybody here speak *English?*'

'*Sie sprechen Deutsch?*'

'No!'

'*Warten Sie,*' said the third man from the console. There was a rapid exchange between the two men. The one who spoke 'a little' turned back to the door.

'*Eine Kirche,*' said the man groping for words. 'Church! *Ein Pfarrer* – priest! *Er spricht nur Englisch. Drie* . . . *t'ee strattes* . . . *there!*' The German pointed to his left; Joel looked down over his shoulder. There was a street in the distance. He understood; there was a church three blocks away, and a priest who spoke English, presumably a priest who had a telephone.

'The train to Osnabrück. *When?* When does it *get* there?' Converse pointed to his watch. 'When? *Osnabrück?*'

The man looked over at the console, seeing what, Converse could not tell. He turned back to Joel and smiled; why he smiled was beyond understanding. '*Zwölf Minuten, Hochwürden!*'

'How? *What?*'

'*Zwölf* . . . Tvelf.'

'*Twelve?*'

'*Ja!*'

Converse turned and clattered down the steps; on the ground he ran as fast as he could toward the street lamps in the distance. Once there, he raced in the middle of the street, clutching his chest, vowing for the five hundredth time to give up cigarettes. He had persuaded Val to throw them away; why hadn't he taken his own advice? He was invulnerable, that's why. Or did he simply care for her more than he cared for himself? *Enough!* Where was the goddamned *church?*

It was there, on the right. A small church with fake spires, a silly-looking church with what looked like a decorated Quonset hut for a rectory beside it. Joel ran up the short path to the door, a door with a hideously be-jewelled crucifix in the centre – a rhinestone Jesus; rock-along with Christ – and knocked. Moments later an overweight, cherubic-looking man with very little white hair – albeit perfectly groomed – opened the door.

'*Ah, Guten Tag, Herr Kollege.*'

'Forgive me,' said Converse, out of breath, 'I don't speak German. I was told you speak English.'

'Ah, yes, indeed, I should hope so. I spent my novitiate in the Mother Country – as opposed to the Fatherland – you understand the difference in gender, of course. Come in, come *in!* A visit from a fellow priest calls for a *Schnapps*. "A touch of wine" sounds better, doesn't it? Again the Mother Country – so soft, so understanding. My, you're an attractive young man!'

'Not so young, Father,' said Joel, stepping inside.

'That's relative, isn't it?' The German priest walked unsteadily into what was obviously his living room. Again there were jewelled figures on the walls, the cheap stones set in black velvet, the faces of the saints unmistakably feminine. 'What would you like? I have Sherry and Muscatel and for rare occasions a Port I've been saving for very special visitors . . . Who sent you? That wicked novice from Lengerich?'

'I need *help*, Father.'

'Great Jesus, who *doesn't?* Is this to be a confessional? If so, for God's sake give me until morning. I love the Lord my God with all my soul and all my strength – and if there are sins of the flesh – they are *Satan's*. Not I, but the *Archangel of Darkness!*'

The man was drunk; he fell over a hassock, tumbling to the floor. Converse ran to him and lifted him up, lowering him into a chair – a chair by the telephone in the room.

'Please understand me, Father. Or don't *mis*understand me. I have to reach a woman who's waiting for me at Osnabrück. It's *important!*'

'A woman? *Satan!* He is *Lucifer* with the eyes of fire! You think you're better than *me?*'

'Not at all. *Please*. I need *help!*'

It took ten minutes of pleading, but finally the priest calmed down and got on the telephone. He identified himself as a man of God and moments later Joel heard the words that allowed him to breathe steadily again.

'*Frau Geyner? Es tut mir leid . . .*' The old priest and the old woman talked for several minutes, the priest nodding for the last thirty seconds. He hung up and turned to Converse. 'She waited for you,' he said, frowning in bewilderment. 'She thought you might have got off in the freight yards . . . What freight yards?'

'I understand.'

'I do not. But she knows the way here and will pick you up in thirty minutes or so . . . You have sobered me, Father. Was I disgraceful?'

'Not at all,' said Joel. 'You welcomed a man in trouble, there's nothing wrong with that.'

'Let's have a drink. Forget *Schnapps* and "a glass of wine"; they're a bore, aren't they? I have some American bourbon in the refrigerator. You *are* American, are you not?'

'Yes, and a glass of bourbon would be just fine.'

'Good! Follow me into my humble kitchen. It's right through here, mind the sequinned curtain, dear boy. It *is* too much, isn't it? . . . Oh, well, for all of that – whatever it is – I'm a good man. I believe that. I give comfort.'

'I'm sure you do.'

'Where were you schooled, Father?' asked the priest.

'Catholic University in Washington,' replied Converse, pleased with himself that he remembered and answered so quickly.

'Good Lord, I was there *myself!*' exclaimed the German prelate. 'They shunted me around, you understand. Do you remember what's his name . . .'

Oh, my God! thought Joel.

Frau Hermione Geyner arrived and took Converse in tow – commandeered him, in fact. She was a small woman, far older than Joel had imagined, her face withered, reminding him of the woman in the Amsterdam station . . . dominated by wide, intense eyes that shot out bolts of electricity. He got into the car as she closed the door for him, pushing the lock in place. She climbed behind the wheel and sped up the street, reaching what had to be sixty miles an hour in a matter of seconds.

'I appreciate everything you're doing for me,' said Converse, bracing his feet against the floor.

'It is *nothing!*' exclaimed the old woman. 'I have myself taken out officers from airplanes that crashed in Bremerhaven and Stuttgart and Mannheim! I spat in soldiers' eyes, and crashed through barricades! I never failed! The pigs could not touch me!'

'I only meant that you're saving my life, and I want you to know I'm grateful. I'm aware that Valerie – your niece, and my . . . my former wife – told you I didn't do the things they said I did, and she was right. I didn't.'

'*Ach*, Valerie! A sweet child, but not very reliable, *ja?* You got rid of her, *ja?*'

'That's not exactly the way it happened.'

'How *could* she be?' continued Hermione Geyner, as if he had not spoken. 'She is an artist and we all know how unstable they are. And, of course, her father was a Frenchman. I ask you, *Mein Herr*, could she have a greater disadvantage? *Franzosen!* The worms of Europe! As untrustworthy as their wine, which is mostly in their stomachs. They're drunkards, you know. It's in their blood.'

'But you believed her where I was concerned. You're helping me, you *are* saving my life.'

'Because we *could, Mein Herr!* We *knew* we could!'

Stunned, Joel stared at the road ahead, at the rapidly oncoming curves, taken as the tyres screeched. Hermione Geyner was not at all what he expected, but then nothing was any more. She was so old and it was late at night and she had been through a great deal these last two days; it must have taken its toll on her. Old prejudices came to the surface when very old people were tired. Perhaps in the morning they could have a clear-headed conversation. The morning – it was the start of the second day and Valerie had promised to call him in Osnabrück with news of Sam Abbott and the progress she was making to reach the pilot. She *had* to make that call! Sam had to be told about the strange language Joel had heard from an old man in Amsterdam, where a word meaning one thing, also meant something else entirely. Assassination! *Val, call me. For God's sake, call me!*

Converse looked out of the window. The minutes passed, the countryside peaceful, the silence awkward.

'Here we are *Mein Herr!*' shouted Hermione Geyner, turning crazily into the drive that led to a large, old, three storey house set back off the country road. From what Converse could see, it was a house that once had a certain majesty, if only by its size and the proliferation of roofed windows and gables everywhere. In the moonlight now, the majesty was gone; like its owner, it was very old, its grandeur frayed and shabby.

They walked up the worn wooden steps of the huge porch and crossed to the door. Frau Geyner knocked rapidly, insistently; in seconds an old woman – another old woman – opened it, nodding solemnly as they went inside.

'It's very lovely,' began Joel. 'I want you to know . . .'

'Sshh!' Hermione Geyner dropped her car keys in a red-lacquered bowl on a hall table and held up her hand. '*Diese Richtung!*'

Converse followed her to a pair of double doors; she opened them and Joel walked in behind her. He stopped, confusion and astonishment coming together. For in front of them in the large Victorian room with the subdued lighting was a row of high-backed chairs and seated in each was an old woman – nine old women! Mesmerized, he looked closely at them. Some smiled weakly, several trembled with age and infirmity, obviously senile; a few wore stern, intense expressions, and one seemed to be humming to herself.

There was an eruption of fragile applause – hands thin and veined, others swollen with flesh, flesh striking flesh with obvious effort. Two chairs had been placed in front of the women; Valerie's aunt indicated that they were for Joel and herself. They sat down as the applause dwindled off to silence.

'*Meine Schwestern Soldaten,*' cried Hermione Geyner. Rising. '*Heute Nacht . . .*'

The old woman spoke for nearly ten minutes, interrupted occasionally by scattered applause and audible expressions of wonder and respect. Finally, she sat down, acknowledging the barely animated ovation. '*Nun. Fragen!*'

As if in reply, the women one after another began to speak – frail, halting voices for the most part, yet several were emphatic, almost hostile. And then Converse realized that most were looking at him. They were asking him questions, one or two crossing themselves as they spoke, as if the fugitive they had saved were actually a priest.

'Come, *Mein Herr!*' cried Hermione Geyner. 'Answer the ladies. They deserve the courtesy of your replies.'

'I can't answer what I can't understand,' protested Joel quietly.

Suddenly, without any indication or sign of warning, Valerie's aunt rose quickly out of the chair, turned to him and struck him across the face. 'Such evasive tactics will not serve you *here!*' she screamed, striking him again, the ring on her finger breaking his skin. 'We know you understand every word that's been spoken! Why do you Czechs and Poles always think you can fool us? You *collaborated!* We have *proof!*'

The old women began to shout, their lined, contorted faces filled with hate. Converse got to his feet; he understood. Hermione Geyner and everyone in that room was mad or senile or both. They were living in a violent time that was forty years in the past.

And then, as if on some demented cue, a door opened across the room and two men came out, one in a raincoat, his right hand in his pocket, some kind of package in his left. The second man held a topcoat over his arm, that arm extended, a weapon without doubt concealed under the fabric. And then a third man appeared and Joel closed his eyes, pressing them shut, the pain in his chest unbearable. The third man had a bandage across his forehead, his arm in a sling. Converse had caused those wounds; he had last seen the man in a freight car filled with incensed animals on a train.

The first man came up to him and held out the package. It was a thick manila envelope with no stamps on the cover. It was the brief he had sent to Nathan Simon in New York.

'General Leifhelm sends you his regards, even his respects,' said the man, pronouncing the word general with the hard German *G*.

32

Peter Stone watched as the CIA-approved doctor put the third and final stitch into the corner of the Army officer's mouth as the captain sat straining in the chair.

'The bridge will have to be repaired,' said the doctor. 'I have a man in the laboratory who'll do it in a few hours and a dentist on Seventy-second Street; he'll do the rest. I'll call you later when I've made the arrangements.'

'Son of a *bitch!*' roared the captain, as loud as he could with half his mouth novacained. 'He was a tank, a fucking black *tank!* He couldn't have been working for her, he was just a goddamned cab driver! Why the *hell?*'

'Maybe you triggered him,' said the civilian, walking away, reading several pages of notes. 'It happens.'

'*What* happens?' yelled the officer.

'Cut it out, captain. You'll break the stitches.' The doctor held up a hypodermic needle; it was a threat.

'Okay, okay.' The officer spoke in a softer voice. 'What does "trigger" mean in that esoteric language of yours?'

'It's perfectly clear English.' Stone turned to the doctor. 'You know I'm not employed any longer, so you'd better give me a bill.'

'When you're in town a dinner will do. The lab and the dentist are different, though. I'd suggest cash. And get him out of uniform.'

'Will do.'

'What does . . . ?' The captain stopped, seeing the civilian's hand held unobtrusively up in front of his chest.

The doctor put his instruments in the black bag and went to the door. 'By the way, Stone,' he said turning, addressing the former CIA agent, 'thanks for the Albanian. His wife is spending Moscow's roubles like mad for every ache I can find a name for.'

'The ache is her husband. He has an apartment in DC she doesn't know about and some very strange sex habits.'

'I'll never tell.'

The doctor left and Stone turned back to the captain, 'When you're with men like that, don't say any more than you have to and that includes questions. They don't want to hear and they don't want to know.'

'Sorry. What did you mean – *I* triggered that hulk?'

'Come on. An attractive woman being chased down the street by a be-ribboned Army officer. How many memories – black memories – do you think are out there with less than fondness for your ilk?'

'Ilk? I never thought of myself as an ilk, but I see what you mean . . . You were on the phone when I got here, and then there were two other calls. What is it? Any line on the Converse woman?'

'No.' Stone again looked down at his notes, shuffling the pages. 'We can assume she came back to reach someone – someone she and her ex-husband trust.'

'He knows his way around Washington. Maybe someone on the Hill, or even in the administration, or State.'

'I don't think so. If he knew anyone like that and thought his story would get out before his head was shot off, he would have surfaced days ago. Remember he's been tried, convicted, and condemned. Can you think of anyone in Washington who wouldn't play it – play *him* – strictly by the rules? He's contaminated. Too many "authoritative sources" have confirmed it, even diagnosed the disease.'

'And by now he's learned what we found out months ago. You don't know where they are or who you're talking to.'

'Or whom they've hired,' added Stone. 'Or whom they've blackmailed into doing what they want without giving away any trade secrets.' The civilian sat down opposite the Army officer. 'But a couple of other things have fallen into place. We're getting a pattern and a few additional names.

If we could pull Converse out and combine what he's learned with what we've got . . . it might just possibly be enough.'

'*What?*' The captain shot forward in the chair.

'Take it easy. I said just possibly. I've been calling in some old debts and if we could put it all together, there are one or two left I can trust.'

'That's why we called *you* in,' said the officer quietly. 'Because you know what to do, we don't . . . What have you got?'

'To begin with, have you ever heard of an actor named Caleb Dowling – actually, it's Calvin but that's not important except for the computers.'

'I know who he is. He plays the father on a television show called *Santa Fe*. Don't shout it from the rooftops, but my wife and I watch it now and then. What about him?'

Stone looked at his watch. 'He'll be here in a few minutes.'

'No kidding? I'm impressed.'

'You may be more impressed after we've talked to him.'

'Jesus, fill me in!'

'It's one of those odd breaks we all look for that seem to come out of left field but are perfectly logical. It's the timing that's not logical . . . Dowling was in Bonn filming a picture and struck up a friendship with Peregrine. American celebrity, *et cetera*. He also met Converse on a plane and got him a hotel room when they were tough to find. Most significant, Dowling was the initial contact between Peregrine and Converse – which didn't work out because Fitzpatrick stepped in.'

'So?'

'When Peregrine was killed, Dowling called the embassy a number of times trying to get an appointment with the acting-ambassador, but he was put on hold. Finally he sent a note to Peregrine's secretary saying he had to see her, that it was important. The secretary met with him and this Dowling dropped a clap of thunder in her lap. Apparently he and Peregrine had an agreement that if Converse called the embassy and contact was to be made, Dowling would go along. He didn't think Peregrine would go back on his word. Secondly, Peregrine told Dowling that something was rotten in the embassy ranks, some very odd behaviour. One incident Dowling witnessed himself. He said there were too many things that didn't make sense – from Converse's sane and lucid conversations to the fact that he, Dowling, hadn't been officially questioned, as if people were avoiding one of the last people to see Converse. The bottom line was that he didn't think Converse had anything to do with Peregrine's murder. The secretary damn near fainted but told him he would be contacted. She knew the Agency's Station Chief in Bonn and called him . . . So did I, two days ago, telling him I was brought in deep-down by State.'

'He confirmed all of this?'

'Yes. He called Dowling in, listened to him, and has begun digging himself. He's coming up with names, one of which we know but there'll be others. I was on the phone with him when you got here. Dowling flew in yesterday; he's at the Pierre and will be here by eleven-thirty.'

'That's movement,' said the captain, nodding. 'Anything else?'

'Two other things. You know how stymied we were when Judge Anstett caught it and how strong the case was made for a mob killing. Hell, we weren't even sure why Halliday used Anstett in the first place. Well, the computer boys at the Army data banks have come up with the answer. It goes back to October 1944. Anstett was a legal officer in Bradley's first Army, where Delavane held a battalion command. Delavane railroaded a sergeant who'd cracked through a court martial. The charge was desertion under fire, and Colonel Delavane wanted an example both for his own troops and the Germans, to let the first know they were being led by a ramrod, and the second that they were fighting one. The verdict was guilty, the sentence execution.'

'Oh, my God,' exclaimed the Army officer. 'Slovic all over again.'

'Exactly. Except that a lowly lieutenant named Anstett heard about it and came rolling in with all his legal barrels smoking. By using psychiatric evaluation reports he not only got the sergeant sent home for treatment, but literally turned the proceedings around and put Delavane himself on trial. Using the same kind of psychological evaluations – stress mainly – he called into question Delavane's fitness for command. It damned near ruined an illustrious military career, and would have if it hadn't been for the colonel's friends in the War Department. They buried the report so well it was under another Delavane's name and wasn't picked up until all the records were computerized in the 'sixties.'

'That's one hell of an explanation, Stone.'

'It's only part of it,' said the civilian, shaking his head. 'I didn't explain Anstett's killing itself. And make no mistake, it was the Mafia down to the man with the gun.' Stone paused and turned a page. 'So there had to be a connection somewhere, somehow a link, probably going back years. The boys with the discs looked farther and I think we've got it. Guess who was Colonel Delavane's chief aide in the First Army? No, don't bother, you couldn't. He was a Captain Parelli, Mario Alberto Parelli.'

'Good Christ! The senator?'

'The five-term senator, thirty years in that august body. Up-from-the-bootstraps Mario, with a slight push from the GI Bill, some early benefactors and a few lucrative legal retainers.'

'Wow . . .' said the captain softly, without enthusiasm as he leaned back in the chair. 'That's pretty heavy, isn't it?'

'It's there. It fits. And I don't mind telling now that in 'sixty-two and three, during the let's-get-Fidel days, Parelli was a frequent visitor at the White House, courtesy of both the Kennedy boys.'

'Even in the Senate. He's one of the biggest cannons on the Hill.'

'While you're staring, let me give you the last item. We've found Commander Fitzpatrick.'

'*What?*'

'At least we know where he is,' completed Stone. 'As to whether we can bring him out, or even want to try, that's another question.'

Valerie got in the cab at McCarran Airport in Las Vegas and gave the driver the address of a restaurant on Route 93, repeated twice by Sam Abbott over the phone. The driver looked at her in his rearview mirror, creases across his forehead. Val was used to men scrutinizing her; she was neither flattered nor annoyed any more. Frankly, she was just bored by the childishness of it all, by the fantasies of grown up children abusing themselves with their eyes.

'Are you sure, miss?' asked the driver.

'I beg your pardon?'

'That isn't a restaurant – like I mean a *restaurant*. It's a diner, a pit stop for trucks.'

'It's where I wish to go,' said Val coolly.

'Sure, okay, fine.' The taxi pulled out into the departing traffic.

The driver was right. A half acre of asphalt surrounded the long, low, L-shaped diner, housing a dozen huge trucks that dwarfed the cars, the latter parked at respectful distances from their mammoth cousins. Val paid the driver and went inside; she looked around and walked past the cashier's counter toward the L-shaped section. Sam had told her he would be in one of the booths in that area.

He was, at the rear of the second aisle. As Valerie approached she looked at the man she had not seen in nearly seven years. He had not changed much; the brown hair had a fringe of grey around the temples, but the strong relaxed face was not very different – perhaps the eyes were a little deeper, a few more lines at the sides and the cheekbones a touch more pronounced. It was a better face for a portrait now, she thought; the character beneath was emerging. Their eyes met and the brigadier general got out of the booth, his clothes denying his rank and profession. He was dressed in an open sports shirt, tan summer slacks and dark loafers. He was somewhat shorter than Joel, but not much. He was a welcome sight; it was in his grey eyes.

'*Val*.' Abbott held her briefly, obviously not wanting to call attention to them.

'You look well, Sam,' she said, sitting down across from him, putting the carry-on case beside her.

'You look merely outstanding, which is military for all those other adjectives.' Abbott smiled. 'It's funny, but I come out here a lot because no one pays any attention to me, so I thought, hell, it's the perfect place. I should have remembered – you walk through that arcade of gorillas and eggs get put in ears with coffee spoons.'

'Thanks. I could use some confidence.'

'I could probably use a strong alibi. If someone does recognize me, word will go back that the brigadier's pulling outside duty.'

'You're *married*, Sam?'

'Five years ago. Late but with all the fixings. A lovely bride and two beguiling daughters.'

'I'm so happy for you. I hope I get a chance to meet her, meet them – but not on this trip. Definitely not this trip.'

Abbott paused, looking into her eyes, a touch of sadness in his. 'Thank you for understanding,' he said.

'There's nothing to understand, or rather, there's everything to understand. The fact that you're willing to meet me after all that's happened is more than we had a right to expect. Both Joel and I know the risks you're taking – legally, as a general, all of it – and if there was any other way we wouldn't involve you. We just don't know one, and after you hear what I have to say, you'll understand why we can't wait any longer, why Joel agreed to let me try and find you ... You were my idea, Sam, but Joel wouldn't have heard of it unless he had to – not for himself; he doesn't expect to live. That's what he said and he believes it.'

A waitress brought coffee and Abbott thanked her. 'We'll order later,' he said, staring at Valerie. 'You'll have to trust my judgment, you understand that, don't you?'

'Yes. Because I trust you.'

'When I couldn't reach you I made a few phone calls to people I worked with a couple of years ago in Washington. They're men who're deep into these kind of things, who have answers long before most of us know the questions.'

'Those are the people Joel wants you to reach!' interrupted Val. 'You saw him then; you spent the night at his hotel, don't you remember? He said you both drank too much.'

'We did,' agreed Sam. 'And talked too much.'

'You were evaluating aircraft – "equipment", Joel called it – with specialists from various intelligence units.'

'That's right.'

'They're the ones he has to contact! He has to see them, talk to them, tell them everything he knows! I'm getting ahead of myself, Sam, but Joel thinks those people should have come in at the beginning – the beginning for him. He understands why he was chosen and, incredibly, he doesn't even now fault that decision! But *they* should have been there!'

'You're way ahead of yourself.'

'I'll go back.'

'Let me finish first. I talked to them, telling them I didn't believe what I was reading and hearing; it wasn't the Converse I knew, and to a man they told me to back off. It was hopeless and I could get badly tarnished. It *wasn't* the Converse I knew, they said. He'd psyched out; he was another person. There was too much evidence to support the blow out.'

'But you took *my* call. Why?'

'Two reasons. The first is obvious – I knew Joel; we went through a lot together and none of this makes sense to me, maybe I don't want it to make sense. The second reason is a lot less subjective. I know a lie when I hear one – when I know it can't be the truth – and a lie was fed to me just as it was fed to the people who delivered it.' Abbott sipped his coffee, as if telling himself to slow down and be clear. The leader of the squadron was in control; he had to be. 'I spoke to three men I knew, men I trust, and each checked with his own sources. They all came back to me, each telling me essentially the same thing but in different language, different viewpoints depending on their priorities – that's the way it works with these people. But one item didn't vary so much as a syllable and it was the lie. The label is drugs. Narcotics.'

'*Joel?*'

'Their words were practically identical. "Evidence is pouring in from New York, Geneva, Paris, that Converse was a heavy buyer." That was one phrase; the other was: "Medical opinion has it that the hypodermics finally blew him up and blew him back".'

'That's crazy! It's *insane!*' cried Valerie, as Abbott grabbed her hand, silencing her. 'I'm sorry, but it's such a *terrible* lie,' she whispered. 'You don't know . . .'

'Yes, Val, I do know. Joel was pumped five or six times in the camps with substances sent down from Hanoi and no one fought it harder or hated it more than he did. The only chemicals he'd allow in his body after that were tobacco and alcohol. I've seen us both with third degree hangovers and while I tore medicine cabinets apart for a Bromo or an aspirin, he wouldn't touch them.'

'Whenever his passport shots came up, he had to have four martinis before he went to the doctor,' said Valerie. 'Good God, who would spread a thing like that?'

'When I tried to find out I was told that even I couldn't have that information.'

The former Mrs Converse now stared at the brigadier-general. 'You *have* to find out, Sam, you know that, don't you?'

'Tell me why, Val. Put it together for me.'

'It began in Geneva, and for Joel the operative name – the *operative* name – was George Marcus Delavane.'

Abbott closed his eyes, pressing them shut, as his face became suddenly older.

The cry of the cat on a frozen lake became a scream as the man in the wheelchair fell to the floor, his two stumps that once were legs scissoring maniacally to no avail, his strong arms pushing his torso up from the rug.

'Adjutant! *Adjutant!*' roared General George Marcus Delavane, as the dark red telephone kept ringing on the desk below the fragmented map.

A large, muscular middle aged man in full uniform ran out of a door and rushed to his superior. 'Let me help you, sir,' he said emphatically, pulling the wheelchair towards them both.

'Not me!' yelled Delavane. 'The *phone!* Get the phone! Tell whoever it is I'll be right there!' The old soldier began crawling pathetically towards the desk.

'Just one minute, please,' said the adjutant into the phone. 'The general will be with you in a moment.' The lieutenant-colonel placed the red telephone on the desk and ran first to the chair and then to Delavane. 'Please, sir, let me *help* you.'

A look of loathing on his face, the half-man permitted himself to be manoeuvred back into the wheelchair. He propelled himself forward. 'Give me the phone!' he ordered. It was given. 'Palo Alto International. You're red! What is the day's code?'

'Charing Cross,' was the reply, spoken in a clipped British accent.

'What is it, England?'

'Radio relay from Osnabrück. We've got him.'

'*Kill him!*'

Chaim Abrahms sat in his kitchen, tapping his fingers on the table trying to take his eyes off the telephone and the clock on the wall. It was the fourth time span and still there was no word from New York. The orders had been clear: the calls were to be placed within thirty minute periods every six hours commencing twenty-four hours ago, the estimated arrival time of the plane from Amsterdam. Twenty-four hours and nothing! The first omission had not troubled him; transatlantic flights were rarely on schedule. The second he had rationalized; if the woman was in transit, travelling somewhere else either in a car or by plane, the surveillance might find itself in a difficult position to place an overseas call to Israel. The third omission was unacceptable, this fourth intolerable! It was nearly the end of the thirty-minute span, six minutes to go. When in the name of God would it *ring?*

It rang. Abrahms leaped from the chair and picked it up.

'Yes?'

'We lost her,' was the flat statement.

'You *what?*'

'She took a taxi to LaGuardia Airport and bought a ticket for a morning flight to Boston. Then she checked into a motel and must have left minutes later.'

'Where were our *people?*'

'One parked in a car outside, the other in a room down the hall. There was no reason to suspect she would leave. She had a ticket to Boston.'

'Idiots! *Garbage!*'

'They will be disciplined ... Our men in Boston have checked every flight, every train. She hasn't shown up.'

'What makes you think she *will?*'

'The ticket. There was nothing else.'

'*Imbeciles!*'

Valerie had finished; there was nothing more to say. She looked at Sam Abbott who seemed far older than he had been an hour ago.

'There are so many questions,' said the brigadier-general. 'So much I want to ask Joel. The lousy thing is I'm not qualified, but I know someone who is. I'll talk to him tonight and tomorrow the three of us will fly to Washington. Like today, I have an early A.M. squadron run but I'll finish by ten. I'll take the rest of the day off – one of the kids is sick, but nothing serious, nothing out of the ordinary. Alan will know whom we should go to, whom we can trust.'

'Can you trust *him?*'

'Metcalf? With my life.'

'Joel says you're to be careful. He warns that they can be anywhere – where you least expect them.'

'But somewhere there's got to be a list. *Somewhere.*'

'Delavane? San Francisco?'

'Probably not. It's too simple, too dangerous. It's the first place anyone would look; he'd consider that ... This countdown? Joel thinks it's tied into massive riots taking place in various cities?'

'On a vast scale, larger and more violent than anything we can imagine. Eruptions, total destabilization, spreading from one place to another, fuelled by the same people who are called in to restore order.'

Abbott shook his head. 'It doesn't sound right. It's too complicated and there are too many built-in controls. Police, troops from the National Guard; they have separate commands. The chain would break somewhere.'

'It's what he believes. He says he can't think of anything else, and they could do it. He's convinced they have warehouses everywhere stocked with weapons and explosives, even armoured vehicles and conceivably planes in out-of-the-way airfields.'

'Val, that's *crazy* – sorry, wrong word. The logistics are simply too overwhelming.'

'Newark, Watts, Miami. They were also overwhelming.'

'They were different. They were essentially racial and economic.'

'The cities burned, Sam. People were killed and order came with guns. Suppose there were more guns than either of us could count? On both sides. Just like what's happening in Northern Ireland right now.'

'Ireland? The slaughter in Belfast? It's a war no one can stop.'

'It's *their* war! *They* did it! Joel called it a test, a trial run!'

'It's *wild*,' said the pilot.

'"Accumulation, rapid acceleration". Those were the words Abrahms used in Bonn. Joel tried to figure them out. He couldn't buy Leifhelm's statement that they referred to blackmail or extortion. That wouldn't work, he said.'

'Extortion?' Abbott frowned. 'I don't remember your mentioning it.'

'I probably didn't because Joel discounted it. Leifhelm asked him what he thought about powerful figures in various governments being compromised, and Joel said it wouldn't work. The cleansing process was too certain, the reaction too quick.'

'Compromised . . . ?' Sam Abbott leaned forward in the booth. '*Compromised*, Val?'

'Yes.'

'Oh, my *God*.'

'What do you mean?'

'Mean?. . . Meaning, that's what I mean. "Compromised" has more than one meaning. Like "neutralize" and "take-out", and probably a dozen others I don't know about.'

'You're beyond me, Sam.'

'In one context, the word "compromise" means *killing*. Pure simple murder. Assassination.'

Valerie checked into the MGM-Grand Hotel giving the bewildered clerk three days' advance for the room in lieu of a credit card. Key in hand, she took the elevator up to the ninth floor and let herself into a pleasantly garish opulence found only in Las Vegas. She stood briefly out on the balcony, watching the setting orange sun, thinking about the insanity of everything. She would call Joel first thing in the morning – noon or thereabouts in Osnabrück, West Germany.

She ordered from room service, ate what she could, watched an hour or so of mind-numbing television, and finally lay down on the bed. She had been right about Sam Abbott. Dear Sam, straight-as-the-proverbial-arrow Sam, direct and uncomplicated. If anyone would know what to do Sam would, and if he did not know he would find out. For the first time in days,

Val felt a degree of relief. Sleep came and this time there were no horrible dreams.

She awoke to the sight of the early sun firing the mountains beyond the balcony doors in the distance. For a moment or two while she emerged through the layers of vanishing sleep she thought she was back at Cape Ann, the sunlight streaming into her bedroom from the balcony outside, a distant nightmare vaguely recalled. Then the bold floral drapes came into focus and the far away mountains and the slightly stale odour of thick hotel carpeting, and she knew the nightmare was very much with her.

She got out of the oversized bed and navigated to the bathroom, stopping on the way at the television set to switch on the radio. She reached the door and suddenly stopped, gripping the edge, bracing herself, her head detonating with a thousand explosions, her eyes and throat on fire.

She could only scream. And scream again and again as she fell to the floor.

Peter Stone turned up the radio in the New York apartment, then walked quickly to the table where there was an open telephone directory, the pages blue, the book itself having been taken from 'Mrs DePinna's' room in the St Regis Hotel. Stone listened to the news report as he scanned the opposing blue pages of government listings.

'. . . It has now been confirmed that the earlier reports of the crash of an F-18 jet fighter plane at Nellis Air Force Base in Nevada are accurate. The accident took place this morning at seven-forty-two, Pacific time, during first-light manoeuvres over the desert thirty-eight miles northwest of the Nellis field. The pilot, Brigadier-General Samuel Abbott, was Chief of Tactical Operations and considered one of the finest pilots in the Air Force as well as a superb aerial tactician. The press officer at Nellis said a full enquiry will be launched, but stated that according to the other pilots the lead plane of the squadron, flown by General Abbott, plunged to the ground after executing a relatively low altitude manoeuvre. The explosion could be heard as far away as Las Vegas. The press officer's remarks were charged with emotion as he described the downed pilot. "The death of General Abbott is a tragic loss for the Air Force and the nation," he told reporters. A few minutes ago the President . . .'

'That's it,' said Stone, turning to the Army Captain across the room. 'That's where she was heading . . . Shut that damn thing off, will you? I knew Abbott; worked with him out of Langley a couple of years ago.'

The Army officer stared at the civilian as he turned off the radio. 'Do you know what you're saying?' he asked.

'Here it is,' replied Stone, his right hand extended, his index finger pointing to the lower left hand corner of a page in the thick telephone directory. 'Blue thirteen, three pages from the end of the book. "United States Government offices." "Air Force, Department of the – "'

'There are dozens of other listings, too, including your former employer. "Central Intelligence – New York Field Office". Why not it? Them? It fits better.'

'He can't go that route and he knows it.'

'He didn't go,' corrected the captain. 'He sent her.'

'*That* doesn't fit – with everything we know about him. She'd be sent to Virginia and come out a basket case. No, she came back here to find a particular person, not a faceless department or a section or an agency. An individual they both knew and trusted. Abbott. She found him, told him everything Converse told her and he talked to others – the wrong others. *Goddamn it!*'

'How can you be sure?' pressed the Army man.

'*Christ*, Captain, what do you want, a *diagram*? Sam Abbott was shot down over the coast of the Tonkin Gulf. He was a POW and so was Converse. I have an idea that if we put it through the computers, we'd find out they knew each other. I'm so sure I won't use up another debt. *Fuck it!*'

'You know,' said the Army officer. 'I've never seen you lose your temper. The cold can get hot, can't it, Stone. I believe you.'

The former intelligence officer looked hard at the captain and when he spoke his voice was flat – and cold. 'Abbott was a good man – even an exceptional man for someone in uniform – but don't mistake me, Captain. He was killed – and he *was* killed – because whatever that woman told him was so conclusive he had to be compromised hours later.'

'Compromised?'

'Figure it out . . . I'm angry at Sam's death, yes, you're damned right. But I'm a lot angrier that we don't have the woman. Among other things, with us she has a chance, without us I judge very little and I don't want her on my conscience – what little I've got left. Also to get Converse out we have to find her, there's no other way.'

'But if you're right she's somewhere near Nellis, probably Las Vegas.'

'Undoubtedly Las Vegas, and by the time we reach anyone who could check around for us, she'll be on her way somewhere else . . . You know, I'd hate to be her now. The only avenue she had was neutralized. Whom can she turn to, where can she go? It's what Dowling said about Converse yesterday, what he didn't tell Peregrine's secretary. Our man was systematically isolated and more afraid of US Embassy personnel than anyone else. He would never have agreed to a meeting with Peregrine because he knew it'd be a trap, therefore he couldn't have killed him. He was set up, everywhere he looked another trap to keep him running and out of sight.' The civilian paused, then added firmly. 'The woman's finished, Captain. She's at the end of a bad road – their road. And that may be the best part of it for us. If she panics, we could find her. But we're going to have to take some risks. How's that neck of yours? Have you made out a will?'

Valerie wept quietly by the glass doors overlooking the gaudy strip of Las Vegas. Her tears were not only for Sam Abbott and his wife and children, but for herself and Joel. It was permitted under the circumstances and she could not lie to herself. She had no idea what to do next. No matter whom she went to the answer would be the same. *Tell him to come out of hiding and we'll listen to him.* And the minute he did, Joel would be dead, fulfilling his own prophecy. And if through a bureaucratic miracle she was granted a meeting with someone of power and influence, how strong would her case be? What words would she use?

I was married to this man for four years and I divorced him – let's call it incompatibility – but I know him! I know he couldn't have done what they say he did, he didn't kill those men . . . What proof? I just told you, I know him! . . . What does incompatibility mean? I'm not sure, we didn't get along – he was remote, distant. What difference does it make? What are you implying? Oh, God! You're so wrong! I have no interest in him in that way. Yes. He's successful but I don't need his money. I don't want it! . . . You see, he told me about this . . . this incredible plot to put the military establishments of the United States and the countries of Western Europe in virtual control of their governments, that they could do it by massive rioting in key cities, terrorism, destabilization everywhere. He's met them and talked with them; there's a plan already in progress! They see themselves as a dedicated international organization, as a strong alternative to the weak governments of the West who won't stand up to the Soviet bloc. But they're not a reasonable alternative, they're fanatics! They're killers; they want total control of all of us! . . . My former husband wrote it all up, everything he's learned, and sent it to me but it was stolen, his own father killed because he undoubtedly read it. No, it was not suicide! . . . He calls it a conspiracy of generals conceived by a general who'd been labelled a madman. General George Delavane – 'Mad Marcus' Delavane . . . Yes, I know what the police in Paris and Bonn and Brussels say, what Interpol says, what our own embassy has reported – finger-prints and ballistics and seeing him in this place and that place, and drugs, and meeting with Peregrine – but can't you understand, they're all lies! . . . Yes, I know what happened when he was a prisoner of war – what he went through, the things he said when he was discharged. None of that is relevant! His feelings aren't relevant! He told me that! He told me – he looks so terrible . . . he's been so hurt.

Who would believe her?

Tell him to come in. We'll listen.

He can't! He'll be killed!. . . You'll kill him!

The telephone rang, for a moment paralysing her. She stared at it, terrified but forcing herself to stay in control. Sam Abbott was dead and he told her only he would call – only he. My God, thought Val, they'd *found* her, just as they'd found her in New York. But they would not repeat the mistakes they had made in New York. She had to remain calm and think – and out-think. The ringing stopped and she approached the phone, lifting it up and pressing the button marked *O*.

'Operator, this is Room Nine-one-four. Please send the Security police up here right away. It's an emergency.'

She had to move quickly, be ready to leave the instant the security men arrived. She had to get out and find a telephone that was . . . *unberührt*. She had heard the stories; she knew what to do. She had to reach Joel in Osnabrück.

Colonel Alan Metcalf, Chief Intelligence Officer, Nellis Air Force Base, walked out of the telephone booth and looked around the shopping mall, his hand in the pocket of his sports jacket, gripping the small revolver inside. He glanced at his watch; his wife and children would be in Los Angeles soon, then reach Cleveland by late afternoon. The four of them would stay with her parents until he said otherwise. It was better this way – since he had no idea what the 'way' would be like.

He only knew that Sam Abbott had run that sub-mach manoeuvre a thousand times; he knew every stress point and PSI throughout the entire aircraft, and he never flew a jet that had not been scanned electronically. To ascribe that crash to pilot error was ludicrous; instead, someone had lied to that pilot, a circuit and back-up shorted. Sam was killed because his friend, Metcalf, had made a terrible mistake. After talking with Abbott for nearly five hours, Metcalf had called a man in Washington, telling him to prepare a conference the following afternoon with two ranking members each from the NSC, G-2, and Naval Intelligence. The reason-of-record: Brigadier-General Samuel Abbott had pertinent and startling information about the fugitive Joel Converse.

And if they could kill the man who had the information so readily, so efficiently, they might easily go after the messenger, the intelligence officer bringing him in. It was better this way, with Doris and the kids in Cleveland. He had a great deal to do and a terrible debt to repay.

The Converse woman! Oh, Christ, why had she *done* it, why had she run so quickly? He expected it, of course, but he had hoped against hope that he could reach her in time, but it was not possible. First there was Doris and the kids and plane reservations and the call to her folks; they had to get out; he could be next. Then racing to the field, his revolver beside him in the car, and ransacking Sam's office – as Nellis' intelligence officer, a particularly loathsome duty, but in this case vital – and questioning Abbott's distraught secretary. A name had emerged: Parquette.

'I'll pick her up,' Sam had said last night. 'She's staying at the Grand and I promised only I'd phone her. She's a cool lady but she had a close call in New York. She wants to hear a voice she knows and I can't blame her.'

Cool lady, thought Alan Metcalf, as he climbed into his car, *you made the biggest mistake of your shortened life. With me you had a chance to live – perhaps – but now as they say in this part of Nevada, the odds are heavily against.*

Nevertheless she would be on his conscience, reasoned the intelligence officer, now speeding into the cut-off toward Route 15 and points south.

Conscience. He wondered if those silent bastards in Washington had Joel Converse on their collective conscience. They had sent a man out and abandoned him, not even having the grace to make sure he was killed quickly, mercifully. The programmers of the kamikaze were saints beside such people.

Converse. Where *was* he?

33

Joel stood silently as Leifhelm's man removed his gun and turned to speak to the assembled row of senile old women in the high-backed chairs. He spoke for less than a minute, then grabbed Converse by the arm – his and their trophy – forcing Joel to face Hermione Geyner, whose true prisoner he was. It was a mystical ritual of triumph from a time long past.

'I have just told these brave women of the Underground,' said the German looking at Converse, 'that they have uncovered a traitor to our cause. Frau Geyner will confirm this, *ja, Meine Dame?*'

'*Ja!*' spat out the intense old woman, her face alive with arrogance and victory, 'Betrayal!' she screamed.

'The telephone calls have been made and our instructions received,' continued Leifhelm's soldier. 'We shall leave now, *Amerikaner*. There's nothing you can do, so let us go quietly.'

'If you had this whole thing so organized, why those two men on the train, including that one?' asked Joel, nodding at the man with his arm in the sling, instinctively stalling for time, an attorney allowing an adversary to compliment himself.

'Observed, not organized,' answered the German. 'We had to be sure you did everything expected of you. Everyone here agrees, *Stimmt das, Frau Geyner?*'

'*Ja!*' exploded Valerie's aunt.

'The other one is dead,' said Joel.

'A loss for the cause and we shall mourn him. Come!' The German bowed to the ladies, as did his two companions, and led Converse through the large double doors to the front entrance. Outside on the huge decrepit porch, Leifhelm's hunter gave the thick envelope to the man with the sling and issued orders. Both nodded and walked rapidly down the steps, the wounded man steadying himself on an unsteady railing. Below on the long circular drive they hurried to the right. Down at the far exit, near the country road, Joel could see the shape of a long sedan in the darkness.

The three prison guards led him out of the compound. It was the middle of the night and he was either being transferred to another camp or to his own execution, the killing ground somewhere in the dense jungle where his screams would be muted. The head guard barked a command to his two subordinates who bowed and began running down the road toward a captured American jeep several hundred yards away in the darkness. He was alone with the man, thought Converse, knowing the moment would not come again except as a corpse. If it was going to happen, it had to happen now. He moved his head slightly, lowering his gaze to the dark outline of the gun in the guard's hand . . .

The German's hand was steady, the weapon in it rigid, angled up at Joel's chest. Inside the timeworn house, the old women had broken into a song, frail voices growing louder in some pathetic victory anthem heard through the large casement windows open for the summer breezes. Converse inched his right foot around the floorboards at his side, testing several and finding one weaker than the others. He pressed down with his full weight; the resulting creak was loud and sharp. Startled, the German turned at the echo all around them.

Now. Joel grabbed the barrel of the gun, twisting hand and steel back and clockwise, hammering the man across the porch into the wall, gripping the weapon with all his strength, twisting farther, fuller, shoving it into the man's stomach . . . The gunshot was partially muffled by the cloth and flesh, by an engine starting and the sound of excited senile voices raised in song, louder now through the open windows. The German collapsed, his head snapping to the right, his eyes bulging, the stench of burnt fabric and intestines floating up; he was dead. Converse crouched, whipping around and looked down at the long U-shaped drive, half expecting to see the other two men racing toward him, guns extended. Instead, he saw the lights of the car in the distance; it was on the country road outside, now turning into the entrance gate on the left. It would be at the porch in moments.

Prying the weapon out of the German's hand, Joel dragged him across the floorboards into the shadows to the right of the steps. Seconds now.

Get the jeep. Use the jeep. The nearest vehicle check was five miles down the road – they had seen it on work details. Get the jeep! Cover the ground! The jeep!

The long sedan pulled up in front of the porch and the man with his arm in the sling got out of the right front door. Converse watched him from behind the thick corner pillar as the wounded German stood on the pavement, looking up into the shadows.

'Koenig?' he asked softly, questioning. *'Wo ist* Koenig?' He started up the steps, his left hand awkwardly, tentatively going inside his jacket.

Joel spun around the pillar, rushing down the old staircase and grabbing the wounded man by the sling. He jammed the pistol into the foot soldier's throat, turning him and rushing him back to the car, crashing his head into the roof, again crouching, thrusting the weapon through the open front window.

The astonished driver was quicker than the foot soldier; he was yanking his gun out of an unseen holster. He fired wildly, shattering the windscreen. Converse fired back, blowing the man's head half out of the window.

Take the bodies into the jungle! Don't leave them here near the compound! Every second counts, every minute!

Joel sprang up and pulled the wounded German away from the car as he opened the front door. 'You're going to help me, you good Christian!' he whispered, remembering the whining supplications of a killer in a freight car. 'You do as I tell you or you'll join your friends. *Capisce,* or is it *verstehen Sie?* Whatever the hell it is, you do as I say, do you understand me? I'm a panicked man, mister – on the *edge,* and I'll argue that position in front of the Supreme Court! . . . What the hell am I *saying?* I've got the gun and I've killed again – it gets easier when you don't want to be killed yourself. *Move!* That lousy son-of-Gestapo on the porch! Bring him down here! In the back!'

Perhaps a minute later, Joel would never know the time, the wounded man was behind the wheel, driving with difficulty, the two corpses in the back seat. A tableau of horror, and Converse thought he would vomit. Illness aside – and it was not easily surmounted – he watched every landmark in the countryside as he directed the driver to take this turn and that, pilotage indelibly imprinted on the mind for the flight back without a radio or a map or a means to obtain either. They reached what looked like a series of rocky pastures at the base of a mountain and Converse told the German to get off the road. They clambered over several hundred yards until there was a sharp decline, ending at a row of full-blown trees. He ordered the driver out.

He had given the last guard a chance. He was a kid in a mismatched uniform, his eyes intense but his face in question. How much was felt, how much indoctrinated? He had given the boy – the child – a simple exam, and a believer had failed the examination.

'Listen to me,' said Joel. 'You told me on the train that you were *hired* – I didn't understand the German word – but that you didn't want to kill anybody. You were just unemployed and needed a job, is that right?'

'Yes, *Mein Herr*! I kill *no one*! I only watched, followed!'

'All right. I'll put the gun away and I'm going to walk out of here. You go wherever you want to go, okay?'

'*Ich verstehe*! Yes, of course!'

Converse shoved the weapon in his belt and turned, his fingers still gripping the handle as he started up the slope. The *scratch*! The rocks displaced! He pivoted, dropping to his knees as the German lunged.

He fired once at the body above him. The footsoldier screamed as he arced in the air and rolled down the hill in silence. A *believer had failed the examination.*

Joel walked up the incline with the envelope addressed to Nathan Simon and across the rocky field to the road. He knew the landmarks; the pilot in him would make no mistakes. He knew what he had to do.

He was concealed far back in the bushes on the edge of Hermione Geyner's property, thirty yards from the decaying house, twenty from the U-shaped drive which was filled with ruts and bordered by brown, overgrown grass, dead from the heat and a lack of water. He had to stay awake, for if it was going to happen, it would happen soon. Human nature could take only so much anxiety; he had played upon the the truism too often as a lawyer. Answers had to be given to anxious men – panicked men. The sun was up, the birds foraging in the early light, myriad noises replacing the stillness of the night. But the house was silent, the large casement windows, through which only hours ago the voices of demented old women helped muffle gunshots, were closed, more panes cracked than clear. And through all the madness, the insanity of violent events, he still wore the clerical collar, still had his priestly passport and the letters of pilgrimage. The next few hours would tell him whether or not they were of any value.

The roar of an engine came first and then the sight of a black Mercedes swerving off the country road into the drive. It sped up to the porch, jolting to a stop; two men climbed out, the driver racing around the back to join his companion. They stood for a moment looking up at the porch and the windows of the house, then turned and scanned the grounds, walking over to Hermione Geyner's car and peering inside. The driver nodded and reached under his jacket, pulling out a gun; they went back to the steps, taking them rapidly, heading across the porch. Finding no bell, the man without a gun in his hand knocked harshly, repeatedly, finally pounding with a closed fist while twisting the knob to no avail.

Guttural shouts came from inside as the door swung back revealing an angry Frau Geyner dressed in a tattered bathrobe. Her voice was that of a shrewish teacher lambasting two students for cheating when in fact they had not. Each time one of the men tried to speak her voice rose to new, shrill heights; the man with the gun put it away. His companion, however, apparently moved by a far greater fear, suddenly grabbed Valerie's aunt by the shoulders and spoke harshly, directly, forcing her to listen.

Whatever change the man sought, it was minor. Hermione Geyner did listen but when she replied her answers were equally harsh, equally direct, and delivered with authority. She pointed down at the overgrown drive and apparently described what she had witnessed in the dark, early morning hours – what she herself had accomplished. The men looked at each other, their eyes questioning and afraid, but not questioning what the old woman had told them, only what she could not tell them. They raced across the porch and down the steps to their car. The driver started the engine with a vengeance so pronounced the ignition mechanism flew into a high-pitched, grinding scream. The Mercedes plunged forward, skirting past Frau Geyner's car and in a sudden attempt to avoid a hole in the overgrown pavement, the driver swung briefly to his left, then to his right, skidding on the surface, the tyres sliding on the crawling vine weeds until the side of the car careened into the disintegrating stone gate. Roars of abuse from both men filled the morning air as the Mercedes was straightened and raced through the exit. It swung left and sped down the country road, as Hermione Geyner slammed the door up on the porch.

There was nothing any longer without risk, thought Joel, as he crawled out of the foliage, but the risk for him now was one he faced with a degree of confidence. Aquitaine had used up Frau Geyner; there was nothing more to be learned. To return to a madwoman held a greater risk for them. Envelope in hand he walked across the ugly drive, up the creaking steps, and across the sagging porch to the door. He knocked and ten seconds later a screeching Hermione Geyner opened it. He then did something so totally unpredictable, so completely out of character, he did not believe it himself as he followed through with the sudden impulse.

He punched the old woman squarely in the centre of her lower jaw. It was the beginning of the longest eight hours of his life.

The bewildered Security Police from the MGM-Grand Hotel reluctantly refused Valerie's offer of a gratuity, especially as she had raised it from $50 to $100, thinking that the economy of Las Vegas was somewhat different from New York and certainly Cape Ann. They had driven around the streets of the old and the new city for nearly forty-five minutes, until both men, both professionals in their work, assured her that no one was following their car. And they would put a special patrol on the Ninth floor in an attempt to catch the man who had harassed her, who had attempted to gain entrance to the room. They were, of course, naturally chagrined that she took a room across the boulevard at Caesar's Palace.

Val tipped the bellman, took her small overnight bag from him, and closed the door. She ran to the phone on the table by the bed.

'I *haff* to go to the toilet!' shouted Hermione Geyner, holding an ice pack under her chin.

'Again?' asked Converse, his eyes barely open, sitting across from the old woman, the envelope and the gun in his lap.

'You make me nervous. You struck me.'

'You did the same and a hell of a lot more to me last night,' said Joel, getting up from the chair and shoving the gun under his belt, the envelope in his hand.

'I vill see you hanging from a rope! *Betrayer*! How many hours now? You think our operatives in the *Untergrundbewegung* will not *miss* me?'

'I think they're probably feeding pigeons in the park, cooing along with the best of them. Go on, I'll follow.'

The telephone rang, the hours suddenly meaningless. Converse grabbed the old woman by the back of her neck and propelled her to the antique desk and the phone. 'Just as we practised,' he whispered, holding her firmly. '*Do* it!'

'*Ja?*' said Hermione Geyner into the telephone, Joel's ear next to hers.

'*Tante! Ich bin's,* Valerie!'

'*Val!*' shouted Converse, pushing the old woman away. 'It's *me*! I'm not sure the phone's clean; she was set up, *I* was set up! Quickly! Tell Sam I was *wrong* – I *think* I was wrong! The countdown could be *assassinations* – all over the goddamned place!'

'He knew that!' shouted Valerie in reply. 'He's dead, Joel! He's *dead*! They *killed* him!'

'Oh, *Christ*! There's no time, Val, no *time*! The *phone*!'

'*Meet me!*' screamed the ex-Mrs Converse.

'Where? Tell me *where*?'

The pause was less than several seconds, an eternity for both. 'Where it began, my darling!' cried Valerie. 'Where it began but *not* where it began . . . The clouds, darling! The patch and the clouds!'

Where it began. Geneva. But not Geneva. Clouds, a patch. A patch!

'Yes, I *know*!'

'Tomorrow! The next day! I'll be there!'

'I have to get out of here . . . Val . . . I love you so much! *So* much!'

'The clouds, my darling – my only darling – oh, *God* stay alive!'

Joel ripped the telephone out of the wall, as Hermione Geyner came rushing at him, swinging a heavy brass-handled poker from the fireplace. The iron hook glanced off his cheek; he grabbed her arm and shouted.

'I haven't got time for you, you crazy *bitch*! My *client* doesn't have time!' He spun her around and pushed her forward, picking up the envelope from the table. 'You were on your way to the bathroom, remember?'

It was in the hall and Converse saw what he hoped he would see in the red-lacquered bowl on the wall table; the old woman had dropped them there last night – the keys to her car. The bathroom door pulled out; it was the solution. Once she was inside, Joel grabbed a heavy chair from against the wall, dragged it over and jammed the thick rim under the knob, kicking the legs in place, wedging them into the floor. Valerie's aunt heard the commotion and tried to open the door; it held. The harder she pressed, the firmer the legs were embedded.

'We convene again tonight!' she roared. 'We will send out our best people! The *best*!'

'God help Eisenhower when you meet,' muttered Converse, inwardly relieved. If Aquitaine did not have the phone covered, the old woman would be found in a few hours. He took the keys from the lacquered bowl, the envelope under his arm, and pulled the gun from his belt. He ran to the front door, opening it cautiously. There was no one, nothing, only Hermione Geyner's car parked on the weed-ridden drive. He went outside, pulling the door shut, leaving it unlocked, and raced down the steps to the stationary automobile. He started the engine; there was half a tank of gas, enough to get him far away from Osnabrück before refilling. Until he could get a map, he would go by the sun, heading south.

Valerie made arrangements at the travel office in Caesar's Palace, paying cash and using her mother's maiden name, hoping perhaps that some of the facile woman's wartime expertise might find its way to the daughter. The was a 6 P.M. Air France to Paris from Los Angeles. She would be on it, the hour's trip to LAX made on a chartered plane to which she would be chauffeured, thus avoiding the terminal at McCarran Airport. Such courtesies were always available, usually for celebrities and casino winners. There was no basic problem with a false name on the Air France passenger manifest – at worst only embarrassment, in her case easily explained; her former husband, now a stranger, was an infamous man, a hunted man; she preferred anonymity. She would not legally be required to produce her passport until she arrived at Immigration in Paris, and once through, she could travel anywhere she wished, under any name she gave, for she would not be leaving the borders of France. It was why she had thought of Chamonix.

She sat in the chair, looking out of the window, thinking of those days – in Chamonix. She had flown over with Joel to Geneva where he had three days of conferences with the promise of five days off to go skiing at Mont Blanc, a bonus from John Brooks, the brilliant international negotiator of Talbot, Brooks and Simon, who flatly refused to give up some reunion dinner for what he termed 'lizard-shit meetings between idiots – our boy can do it. He'll charm their asses off while emptying their corporate pockets.' It was the first time Joel really knew that he was on his way, yet oddly enough he was almost as excited about the skiing. They both enjoyed it so much. Together. Perhaps because they both were good.

But Joel had not enjoyed the skiing at Chamonix that trip. On the second day he had taken a terrible fall and sprained his ankle. The swelling was enormous, the pain as acute in his head as in his foot. She had knighted him 'Sir Grump'; he demanded his *Herald Tribune* in the morning, childishly refusing to have his breakfast before the paper arrived, and even more childishly playing the martyr as his wife went off to the slopes. When she had suggested that she really did not care to go without him, it was worse.

He had charged her with trying to be some kind of saint. He would be perfectly fine – he had things to read, which artists would not understand. Reading, that was.

Oh, what a little boy he had been, thought Val. But during the nights it was so different, he was so different. He became the man again, loving and tender, at once the generous lion and the sensitive lamb. They made love, it seemed for hours on end, the moonlight on the snow outside, finally the hint of the sun's earliest rays on the mountains until they fell – together – into exhausted sleep.

On their last day before heading back to Geneva for the night flight to New York, she had surprised him. Instead of going out for a few final hours of skiing, she went downstairs at the hotel and bought him a sweater, to which she had sewn a large patch on the sleeve. It read: *Downhill Racer – Chamonix*. She had presented it to him while a porter waited outside the door with a wheelchair – she had made arrangements through the influential manager of the hotel. They were taken to the centre of Chamonix, to the cable car that scaled 13,000 feet to the top of Mont Blanc – through the clouds to the top of the world, it seemed. When they reached the final apex, where the view was breathtaking, Joel had turned to her, that silly, oblique look in his eyes that belied everything he was and everything he had been through – again, as always, his way of thanking her.

'Enough of this foolish scenery,' he said. 'Take off your clothes. It's not really that cold.'

They had hot coffee, sitting on a bench outside, the magnificence of natural grandeur all around them. They held hands, and *Christ!* she had held back the tears of love she felt.

She felt them now and got out of the chair, rejecting the imposition. It was the wrong time for such reflections. Whatever clarity of mind she could summon, she needed it now. She had to travel halfway across the world avoiding God knew how many people who were looking for her.

He had said he loved her – *so much*. Was it love or was it need . . . support? She had replied with the words *my darling* – no, she had said more than that; she had been far more specific. She had said *my only darling*. Was it a response born of the panic?

Not knowing was the worst of it, thought Converse, studying the road signs in the wash of the headlights. He had been driving for nearly seven hours, having picked up a map in the city of Hagen while refilling the tank – seven hours and according to the map he was still a long way from the border crossing he had chosen. The reason lay in his ignorance, in not knowing whether Hermione Geyner's car had been the object of a search in the first few hours out of Osnabrück. It undoubtedly was now – officially by the police – but during those early hours he could have made better time on the highways he dared not use in case Aquitaine had raced to Geyner's house with Val's call. He had travelled circuitous back country roads, his pilot's eye on the sun, veering always south until he reached Hagen. Now the back roads were a necessity; whether they were before he would never know. Now, however, Hermione Geyner and her band of lunatics must have gone to the police to report her stolen car. Joel had no idea what they could possibly say that would convince the *Polizei* Valerie's aunt was an injured party, but a stolen car was a stolen car, whether driven by St Francis of Assisi or Jack the Ripper. He would stay on the back roads.

Lennestadt to Krentzel, crossing the Rhine at Bendorf and following the west bank of the river through Koblenz, Oberwessel and Bingen, then south to Neustadt and east to Speyer and the Rhine again. And again south through the border towns of Alsace-Lorraine, finally to the city of Kehl. It was where he would cross into France, a decision based on the fact that several years ago John Brooks had sent him to Strasbourg, the French city across the river border, to a terribly dull conference at which eight lawyers argued continuously with one another over minor aspects of language and translation to the point where nothing of substance was accomplished. As a result, Joel had walked the city and driven out to the countryside, awed by its beauty. He had taken several boat trips up and down the Rhine and remembered the ferries that shuttled back and forth between the piers of Germany and France. Above all, he remembered the crowds in Strasbourg – always the crowds, especially now.

It would take another three to four hours of driving, but somewhere he would have to stop and sleep for a while. He was exhausted; he had not slept for so long he could not accurately remember when. But there was Chamonix and Val ahead. He told her he loved her – he had *said* it. He had got it out after so many years, the relief was incredible – the response more incredible. *My darling – my only darling.* Did she mean it? Or was she supporting him again, the artist's emotions riding over the reason and experience?

Aquitaine! Push everything out of your mind and get into France!

The polar flight from Los Angeles to Paris was uneventful, the moonscapes of ice over the northernmost regions of the world hypnotically peaceful, suspending thought by the sheer expanse of their cold infinity. Nothing seemed to matter to Val as she looked down from the sub-stratosphere. But whatever tranquillity the flight produced, it came to an end in Paris.

'Are you in France on business or on holiday, Madame?' asked the Immigration official, taking Valerie's passport and typing her name into the computer.

'*Les deux.*'

'*Vous parlez français?*'

'*Je le préfère. Mes parents étaient de Paris,*' explained Val, continuing in French. 'I'm an artist and I'll be talking with several galleries. Naturally, I'll want to travel . . .' She stopped, seeing the official's eyes glance up from his screen, studying her. 'Is anything the matter?' she asked.

'Nothing of concern, Madame,' said the man, picking up his telephone and talking in a low voice, the words indistinguishable under the hum of the huge customs hall. 'There is someone who wishes to speak with you.'

'That's of considerable concern to *me*,' objected Valerie, suddenly fright- ened. 'I'm not travelling under my own name for a very good reason – which I suspect that machine of yours has told you, and I will *not* be subjected to interrogations or the indignity of the press! I've said all I have to say. Please reach the American Embassy for me.'

'There is no need for that, Madame,' said the man, replacing the phone. 'It is not an interrogation and no one of the press will know you are in Paris unless you tell them. Also, there is nothing in this machine but the name on your passport – and a request.'

A second uniformed official hurriedly entered the roped-off aisle from a nearby office. He bowed politely. 'If you will come with me, Madame,' he said quietly in English, obviously noticing the fear in her eyes, and assuming her objections. 'You may, of course, refuse, as this is in no way official, but I hope you will not. It is a favour between old friends.'

'Who are you?'

'Chief Inspector of Immigration, Madame.'

'And who wishes to speak with me?'

'It would be up to him to tell you that – his name does not appear on the request. However, I'm going to give you another name. Mattilon. He says you, too, were old friends and he respected him a great deal.'

'*Mattilon?*'

'If you will be so kind as to wait in my office, I will personally clear your luggage.'

'This is my luggage,' said Val, her thoughts on someone who would bring up René's name. 'I'll want a police officer nearby, one who can watch through a glass door.'

'*Pourquoi?* . . . Why, Madame?'

'*Sécurité,*' replied Valerie.

'*Oui, bien sûr, mais ce n'est pas nécessaire.*'

'*J'insiste, ou je pars tout de suite.*'

'*D'accord.*'

It was explained that the person who wished to speak with her was driving out to de Gaulle Airport from the centre of Paris; it would take thirty-five minutes, during which time she had coffee and a small glass of Calvados. The man walked through the door. He was late middle-aged and dressed in rumpled clothing, as if his appearance did not matter any longer. His face seemed lined as much from weariness as from age, and when he spoke his voice was tired but nevertheless precise.

'I will keep you but a few minutes, Madame. I'm sure you have places to go, people to see.'

'As I explained,' said Val, looking hard at the Frenchman, 'I'm in Paris to talk with several galleries . . .'

'That is no concern of mine,' interrupted the man, holding up his hands. 'Forgive me, I do not care to hear. I care to hear nothing unless Madame wishes to speak after I've spoken to her.'

'Why did you use the name of Mattilon?'

'An introduction. You were friends. May I go back before Monsieur Mattilon?'

'Go back by all means.'

'My name is Prudhomme. I am with the *Sûreté.* A man died in a hospital here in Paris several weeks ago. It is said your former husband, Monsieur Converse, was responsible.'

'I'm aware of that.'

'It was not possible,' said the Frenchman calmly, sitting down and taking out a cigarette. 'Have no fear, this office is not "tapped" or "bugged". The Chief Inspector and I go back to the *Résistance*.'

'The man died after a brutal fight with my former husband,' said Val cautiously. 'I read it in the newspapers, heard it on the radio. Yet you're telling me he wasn't responsible for his death. How can you say that?'

'The man did not *die* in the hospital, he was killed. Between 2.15 and 2.45 in the morning. Your husband was on a flight from Copenhagen to Hamburg during those hours. It has been established.'

'You *know* this?'

'Not officially, Madame. I was removed from the case. A subordinate, a man with little police experience but with the Army – later in the Foreign Legion, no less – was given the assignment while I was shifted to more "important" matters. I asked questions; I will not bore you with details but the man's lungs collapsed – a sudden trauma unrelated to his wounds. The man was suffocated. It was not in the report. It was removed.'

Valerie controlled herself, keeping her voice cool and distant despite her anxiety. 'Now,' she said, 'what about Mattilon? My *friend*, Mattilon.'

'Fingerprints,' replied the Frenchman, wearily. 'They suddenly are discovered twelve hours after the *arrondissement* police – who are *very* good – have examined that office? And yet there was a death in Wesel, West Germany, within the rising and the setting of the same sun. Your former husband's countenance was described, his identity all but confirmed. And an old woman on a train to Amsterdam – the same routing – who is found with a gun in her hand – again a description given. Has this Converse wings? Does he fly over borders by himself? Again it is not possible.'

'What are you trying to tell me, Monsieur Prudhomme?'

The man from the *Sûreté* inhaled on his cigarette as he tore off a page from his notepad and wrote something out on the edge of the table. 'I'm not certain, Madame, since I am no longer officially privileged in these matters. But if your former husband did not cause the man in Paris to die and could not have shot your old friend, Monsieur Mattilon . . . how many others did he *not* kill, including the American ambassador in Bonn and the Supreme Commander of NATO? And who are these people who can tell government sources to confirm this and confirm that, to change assignments of senior police personnel at will, to alter medical reports removing – suppressing – evidence?. . . There are things I do not understand, Madame, but I am certain those are the very things I am not *meant* to understand. And that is why I'm giving you this telephone number. It is not my office; it is my flat in Paris – my wife will know where to reach me. Simply remember, in an emergency say that you are from the *Tatiana* family.'

Stone sat at the desk, the ever-present telephone in his hand. He was alone – had been alone when the call came from Charlotte, North Carolina, from a woman he had once loved very dearly years ago in the field. She had left the 'terrible game', as she called it; he had stayed, their love not strong enough.

The connection was completed to Cuxhaven, West Germany, to a telephone the civilian was sure would be sterile. That certainty was one of the pleasures in dealing with Johnny Reb.

'Bobbie-Jo's Chicken Fry,' was the greeting over the line. 'We deliver.'

'I gather that. It's Stone.'

'*Mah wuhd*, the Tatiana re-route!' exclaimed the Southerner. 'Someday you must tell me about this here fascinating family of yours, Brer Rabbit.'

'Someday I will.'

'I seem to recollect having heard the name somewheres around the late 'sixties, but I didn't know what it meant.'

'Trust whoever used it.'

'Why should I do that?'

'Because whoever it was was trusted by the hangingest judges in the world.'

'Who might that be?'

'The enemy, Rebel.'

'If that's a parable, Yankee, you lost me.'

'Someday, Johnny, not now. What have you got?'

'Well, let me tell you. I saw the damnedest little island over here you ever did see. It's not twenty miles off the coast near the mouth of the Elbe, right where it's supposed to be. In the Heligoland Bight, they call it, which is a section of the North Sea.'

'Scharhörn,' said the civilian, making a statement. 'You found it.'

'It wasn't tough to find – everybody seems to know about it – but nobody goes near a certain south-west shoreline. It used to be a U-boat refuelling station in World War II. The security was so tight most of the German High Command didn't know about it, and the Allies never got a clue. The old concrete and steel structures are still there and it's supposed to be deserted except for a couple of caretakers, who, I'm told, wouldn't pick you out of the water if your boat crashed into one of the old submarine winches.' Johnny Reb paused, then continued softly. 'I went out there last night and saw lights, too many in too many places. There are people out there on that old base, not just a couple of watchmen, and you can bet a Yankee pot roast your lieutenant commander is one of them. Also around two o'clock in the morning after the lights went out, the tallest mother-lovin' antenna this side of Houston slid up like a bionic cornstalk, but there was no corn on the top. Instead, it bloomed like a regular flower. It was a disc, the kind they use for satellite transmissions . . . You want me to mount a team? I can do it; there's a lot of unemployment these days. Also the cost will be minimal, because the more I think about it, the more I appreciate your swinging me out of the Dardanelles before those guns got there. That was really more important than getting me off the hook with those contingency funds in Bahrain.'

'Thanks, but not yet. If you go in for him now, we show cards we can't show.'

'How long can you wait? Remember I taped that prick Washburn.'

'How much did you put together?'

'More than this old brain can absorb, if you want the truth. But not more than I can accept. It's been a long time coming, hasn't it? The eagles think they're gonna catch the goddamned sparrows after all, don't they? 'Cause they're gonna turn everyone *into* sparrows . . . You know, Stone, I shouldn't say this because in your old age you became a bit softer than I did in mine, but if they get it off the ground, a lot of people everywhere may just lie back in their hammocks, or go fishin', and say the hell with it – let the big, uniformed daddys do it. Let 'em straighten things out – get the pot-heads with their guns and switchblades off the streets and out of the parks. Show the Ruskies and the oil boys in bathrobes we don't take their crap any more. Let's show Jesus we're the good guys with a lot of clout. Those soldiers, they got the guts and the guns, the corporations and the conglomerates, so what does it mean to me? Where do *I* change, says the Joe in the hammock, except maybe for the better?'

'Not better,' said Stone icily. 'Those same people become robots. We all become robots, if we live. Don't you understand that?'

'Yeah, *I* do,' answered Johnny Reb. 'I guess I always have. I live on a hog-high in Bern while you scratch in DC. Yes, old buddy, I understand. Maybe better than you do . . . Forget it, I'm enlisted. But what in all-fire hell are you going to do about this Converse? I don't think he's going to get out.'

'He *has* to. We think he has the answers – the *first-hand* answers – that give us the proof.'

'In my opinion he's dead,' said the Southerner. 'Maybe not now but soon – soon's they find him.'

'We have to find him first. Can you help?'

'I started the night I needled Major Norman Anthony Washburn, the Fourth, Fifth, or Sixth – I keep losin' track of the numerals. You got the computers – the ones you have access to – and I've got the streets where they sell things you're not supposed to buy. So far, nothing.'

'Try to find something because you were right before – we don't have much time. And, Johnny, do you have the same feeling I have about that island, about Scharhörn?'

'Like Appomattox, way down deep in the stomach. I can taste the bile, Brer Rabbit, which is why I'm going to possum down here for a few days. We found ourselves a beehive, boy, and the drones are restless, I can sense it.'

34

Joel put the map and the thick envelope on the grass and began pulling branches down from the small tree in the field to cover Hermione Geyner's car. Every snap of wood, each yanking of a limb, filled him with pain, as much from fatigue as from the strain in his arms. Finally, he bunched together reeds of tall grass and threw them everywhere over the frame. The result in the moonlight was an immense mound of hay under an innocuous tree in an orchard. He picked up the map and the envelope and started walking toward the road two hundred yards away. According to the map, he was on the outskirts of a city or town called Appenweier, ten miles from the border at Kehl, directly across the Rhine from Strasbourg.

He walked along the road, running into the grass whenever he saw the headlights of a car in either direction. He had travelled perhaps five or six miles – there was no way to tell – and he knew that he could go no further.

In the jungles he had rested, knowing that rest was as much a weapon as a gun, the eyes and the mind far more lethal when alert than a dozen steel weapons strapped to his body.

He found a short ravine that bordered a country brook, the rocks his fortress, and fell asleep.

Valerie walked out of the Charles de Gaulle Airport on the arm of the *Sûreté*'s Prudhomme, having accepted the scrap of paper with his telephone number but volunteering nothing. They approached the cab stand on the platform and Prudhomme spoke.

'I will make myself clear, Madame. You may take a taxi here and I shall bid you *adieu*, or you may permit me to drive you wherever you like – perhaps to another taxi stand in the city, to go wherever you wish – and I will know if anyone is following you.'

'You would?'

'In thirty-two years, even a fool learns something. My wife keeps telling me she has no lovers only because I have learned the rudiments of my profession.'

'I accept your invitation,' interrupted Val, smiling. 'I'm terribly tired. A small hotel, perhaps. *Le Pont Royal*, I know it.'

'An excellent choice, but I must say that my wife would welcome you – without any questions.'

'My time must be my own, Monsieur,' said Valerie, climbing into the car. '*D'accord.*'

'*Why* are you doing this?' she asked, as Prudhomme got behind the wheel. 'My husband was a lawyer – *is* a lawyer. The rules can't be that different. Aren't you some kind of accessory – assuming what I know damned well you're assuming?'

'I only wish that you will call me, saying that you are from the Tatiana family. That is my risk and that is my reward.'

Converse looked at his watch – a watch taken from a collapsed body so long ago he could not remember – and saw that it was 5.45 in the morning, the sun abruptly illuminating his fortress-ravine. The stream was below and so he took care of his necessities – downstream – and he plunged his face into the flow of water – upstream. He had to move; he had five miles to walk to the border, as he remembered.

He remembered well. He reached Kehl and bought a razor reasoning that a priest would maintain his appearance as best he could even under the duress of poor travel accommodation. He shaved at the river depot then took the ferry across the scenic Rhine to Strasbourg. The customs officials were so deferential to his collar and his passport, as well as his somewhat shabby presence – undoubtedly taken for the vow of poverty – that he found himself blessing a number of men, and by extension their entire families, as he was passed through the building.

Out on the bustling streets he knew that the first thing he had to do was to get into a hotel room, shower off two days of fear and violence, and have his clothes cleaned or replaced. An impoverished-looking priest did not travel to the expensive wonders of Chamonix; it would be unseemly. A normally-dressed priest, however, was perfectly acceptable, even desirable, a figure of respectability among the crowds. And a priest he would remain, Converse had decided – the decision here again based on legal experience. Think out – anticipate – what your adversary expects you to do, then do not conform unless you retain the advantage. The hunters of Aquitaine would expect him to shed his priestly habit as it was his last known means of disguise; he would not do that; there were too many priests in France and too much advantage in being one.

He registered at the Sofitel on the Place St Pierre-le-Jeune and, without elaboration, explained to the *concierge* that he had been through a dreadful three days of travelling and would the kind man see to several items he needed rather desperately. He was from a very well-endowed parish in Los Angeles and – an American $100 bill took care of the rest. His suit was cleaned and pressed within the hour, his muddy shoes shined, and two new shirts with clerical collars purchased from a shop 'unfortunately quite a distance away on the Quai Kellermann', thus necessitating an additional charge. The gratuities, the expenses and the surcharges for *Rush* – all were a hotelman's dream. The sun-tanned priest with a blemish or two on his face, and odd demands based on time, certainly had to come from a 'well-endowed' parish. It was worth it. He had checked in at 8.30 in the morning and by 9.55 he was ready to make his final arrangements for Chamonix.

He could not risk taking a plane or going by rail; too much had happened to him at airports and on trains – they would be watched. And sooner or later Hermione Geyner's car would be found and his direction if not his destination would be known. Aquitaine's alarms would go out across the three borders of Germany, France and Switzerland; again the safest way was by automobile. The eagerly-accommodating *concierge* was summoned; a fine rental car was arranged for the youngish monsignor, and a route planned to Geneva, some 238 miles south.

Of course, he would not cross over into Geneva, but round the border roads and head for Chamonix, an hour-plus away. His estimated travel time was between five and six hours; he would reach the base of the majestic Mont Blanc by 4.30 in the afternoon, five o'clock at the latest. He wasted no time speeding out of Strasbourg on the Alpine Autoroute marked *83* on his map.

Valerie dressed as the first light silhouetted the irregular-shaped buildings of Paris outside her windows on the Boulevard Raspail. She had not slept nor had she made any attempt to; she had lain awake pondering the words of the strange Frenchman from the *Sûreté* who could not speak officially. She had been tempted to tell him the truth but knew she would not, not yet, perhaps not at all, for the possibility of a trap was considerable, revelations based in truth too easily employed to corner the one being hunted. Still, his plea had the ring of truth, his own truth, not someone else's . . . *Call and say you are from the Tatiana family. That is my wish and my reward.*

Joel would have an opinion. If the man was not simply bait put out by

Aquitaine, it was a crack in their strategy the generals knew nothing about. She hoped it was and he was not, but to trust such a man at this point was impossible.

She had read the domestic schedules provided by Air France on the plane from Los Angeles and knew the routing she would take to Chamonix. Touraine Air had four flights daily to Annecy, the nearest airport to Chamonix and Mont Blanc. She had hoped to make reservations on the 7.00 a.m. flight last night but the sudden, unnerving intrusion of Prudhomme had ruled it out, and by the time she called Touraine from the Pont Royal there were no seats – it was summer and Mont Blanc was a tourist attraction. Nevertheless, she was on standby for the 11 o'clock flight. It was better to be at Orly Airport, better to be in the crowds, as Joel insisted.

She took the open, brass-grilled elevator down to the lobby, paid her bill, and asked for a taxi.

'*A quelle heure, Madame?*'

'*Maintenant, s'il vous plaît.*'

'*Dans quelques minutes.*'

'*Merci.*'

The taxi arrived and Val went outside, greeted by a surly, sleepy-eyed driver through the window, who had no intention of getting out of the cab, only vaguely willing to accept her patronage.

'*Orly, s'il vous plaît.*'

The driver started up, reached the corner and swung his wheel to the left, making a rapid U-turn so as to head back into the Boulevard Raspail towards the expressway that led to the airport. The intersection appeared to be deserted. It was not.

The crash behind them was close by and sudden – metal crashing against metal as glass shattered and tyres screeched. The driver slammed on his brakes, screaming in shock and fear as the taxi veered into the kerb. Val was thrown against the front seat, her knees scraping the floor. Awkwardly, she started to get up as the driver leaped from the cab yelling at the offending parties behind.

Suddenly, the right rear door opened and the lined, weary face of Prudhomme was above her, a trickle of blood rolling down from a gash in his forehead. He spoke quietly.

'Go, Madame – wherever it is you go. No one will follow you now.'

'*You?* . . . You've been here all night! You were waiting for me, watching. It was you who crashed into that car!'

'There is no time. I will send your driver back. I must make out my tedious report while scattering a few items in the man's car, and you must leave. Now – before others learn.'

'That name!' cried Val. 'It was *Tatiana*?'

'Yes.'

'Thank you!'

'*Bonjour. Bonne chance.*' The man from the *Sûreté* ducked away, closing the door, and ran back to the two Frenchmen shouting at one another behind the taxi.

*   *   *

It was 3.20 in the afternoon when Converse saw the sign: *St Julien en Genevois* – 15 km. He had rounded the border of Switzerland, the autoroute to Chamonix directly ahead, east of Geneva, just south of Annemasse. He would reach Mont Blanc in something over an hour; he had done it! He had also driven as he had never driven in his life before, the powerful Citroën responding to his pilot's touch, his pilot's mind oblivious to everything but the sweep in front of him, the equipment around him – the feel of the hard road beneath as he took the Alpine curves. He had stopped to refuel once at Pontarlier, where he drank steaming hot tea from a vending machine. Since he had left the expressway for the shorter distance of the mountain roads, his speed depended on his every reaction being instantaneous and accurate. An hour now. *Be there, Val. Be there, my love*!

Furious, Valerie looked at her watch ready to scream – as she had wanted to scream since 6.30 in the morning at Orly Airport. It was 4.10 in the afternoon and the entire day had been filled with one crisis after another, from the crash in the Boulevard Raspail and Prudhomme's revelation that she was being followed to her arrival at Annecy on the 1 o'clock flight from Paris – itself delayed by a malfunctioning luggage door. Her nerves were stretched to the outer limits yet she knew above all – had known throughout the day – that she could not lose her control. Doing so would only rivet attention on her; it briefly had.

There were no seats on the 7 o'clock flight and the 11 o'clock plane had been overbooked. Only those with tickets in their hands were permitted through the gate. She had so angrily protested that people began staring at her. Then she retreated to the soft-spoken bribe which only served to irritate the clerk – not that he was morally offended, only that he could not accommodate her and accept the money. Again passengers behind and on both sides, in both lines, had looked over as the clerk admonished her with true Gallic *hauteur*. It was no way to get to Chamonix alive, thought Val, accepting a ticket on the 1 o'clock flight.

The plane landed at Annecy over a half-hour late, several minutes after 3.00, and the subsequent crush at the taxi platform caused her to behave in a way she generally tried to avoid. Being a relatively tall woman – tall in appearance, certainly – she knew the effect she provoked when she looked disdainfully down at those around her: A genetic preordination had made her privileged, didn't they know? Foolishly, too many people accepted the posturing as proof of some sort of preordained fact; the women were intimidated, the men both intimidated and sexually aroused. It had gained her a few forward places in the taxi line, but the line was still long. Then she had glanced to her right; at the far end of the platform were the limousines, several chauffeurs leaning against their glistening vehicles, smoking cigarettes, picking their teeth and chattering. *What in heaven's name was she doing*? She had broken away from the line, opening her purse as she ran.

Her final frustration now was the result of something she should have remembered. There was a point in the theatrical setting that was the wondrous 'village' of Chamonix where automobiles could not pass, only small official vehicles, and tourist minibuses. She got out of the limousine; she was on her own, as she walked rapidly down the wide, crowded boulevard. She could see the large red terminal of the cable car in the distance. Somewhere above, above the clouds, was Joel. Her Joel. She could not stop herself; she did not try to impose the control she had imposed all day. She began to run – faster, faster! *Be up there, my darling! Be alive, my darling – my only darling!*

It was ten minutes to five when Converse literally screeched into the parking lot, slamming on the brakes as he crashed himself out of the car. There had been traffic on the Mont Blanc autoroute, a holdover at the new construction over the vast gorge bridge. Every muscle in his right leg had been cramped with every anticipation, every opportunity seized to swing around the lethargic traffic. He was *here*! He was in Chamonix, the majestic splendour of the Alps in front of him, the village below. He started running, his breath gone, taking swallows of breath from the clear air of the clean mountains, forgetting the pain – welcoming it – for she *had* to be there! *Please, Val, make it! I love you so . . . Goddamn it, I need you so! Be there!*

She stood outside the cable lift, the clouds below on the mountains forming a barrier from the peaks beneath, a wall of mist from any concerns of the earth they knew. She shivered in the Alpine cold but she could not leave. She stood by the stone railing, by a thick mountain telescope through which tourists could observe the wonders of the Alpine world for a few francs. She was frightened to death he would not come – could not come. *Death.*

It was the last cable car, none were permitted after the sun descended over the western peaks – cables were suddenly frozen with shadows. Except for the bartender and several customers inside the glass doors of the bar, she was the only one outside. *Joel! I told you to stay alive! Please do what I said, my darling – my only darling! My only love!*

The cable car ground into a thousand grinding aberrations then screechingly came to a stop. There was no one *there*! It was empty, without people! *Death.*

And then he walked into view, a tall man in a clerical collar, and the top of the world made sense again. He stepped down out of the car and she ran to him as he ran to her. They embraced, both holding each other as they had never held each other as man and wife.

'I love you!' he whispered. 'Oh, *God*, I love you.'

She pulled back, holding his shoulders, tears filling her eyes. 'You're alive, you're here! You did what I asked you to do.'

'What I had to do,' he said. 'Because it was you.'

35

They slept naked, their bodies together, their arms around each other, for a while pushing out the world as they knew it to be, a world they would face in the morning. But for a time there had to be something for themselves, for each other, giving and receiving, precious hours alone, speaking in whispers, trying to understand what they had lost and why, each telling the other it would never be lost again.

When morning came, they both wanted to deny its arrival, yet not completely. There *was* the world as they knew it, and there was another world as the generals of Aquitaine would have it. They ordered Continental breakfast and an extra pot of coffee.

While Val combed her hair, Joel went to the window and looked down at the colourfully vibrant town of Chamonix. Hoses pouring out water were seemingly everywhere, as the streets were washed down. The storefronts were splashed until they glistened. Chamonix was preparing for the onslaught of summer tourists – thinking of which, mused Converse, they had been lucky to find rooms. They had gone to three hotels – the first was nearly a disaster before they reached the desk. 'For God's sake, get rid of that *collar!*' Valerie had whispered. None of the three had anything available, but the fourth, the *Croix Blanche Inn*, had just received a cancellation.

'I'll go out and get you some clothes later,' said Val, coming up behind him, placing her head on his shoulder.

'I've missed that,' he said, turning, putting his arms around her. 'I've missed you. So much.'

'We've found each other, darling. That's all that matters.' There was a knock on the door, the polite knock of a waiter. 'That'll be the coffee. Go use my toothbrush.'

They sat across from each other at the small marble table in front of the window. It was time and they both knew it. Joel placed a page of hotel stationery beside his coffee, a hotel pen on top.

'I still can't get over my aunt!' said Val, suddenly. 'How could I have *done* it?' How could I not have *known?*'

'A couple of times I asked myself the same question.' Converse smiled gently. 'About you, I mean.'

'God, I was *stupid!*'

'No, you were desperate,' corrected Joel. 'Just as she was desperate. You were clutching for possibilities, for help. She was desperately trying to go back to the only meaningful days of her life. A person can be terribly convincing feeling like that. She had the proper words, all those esoteric phrases you'd heard all your life. You believed her. I would have believed her, too.'

'You're devastating when you're kind, darling. Go easy, it's morning.'

'Tell me about Sam Abbott,' he said.

'Yes, of course, but before I do I want you to know we're not alone. There's a man in Paris, an inspector from the *Sûreté*, who knows you didn't kill René and you couldn't have killed the one they called a chauffeur at the George V.'

Startled, Joel leaned forward over his coffee. 'But I did kill that man. God knows I didn't mean to – I thought at first he was reaching for a gun, not a radio – but I fought him, I smashed his head into the wall; he died from a cranial something-or-other.'

'No, he didn't. He was killed in the hospital. He was suffocated; his lungs were collapsed by suffocation. It was unrelated to his injuries, that's what Prudhomme said. As he put it, if you didn't kill the driver and you didn't kill René, how many others didn't you kill? He thinks you've been set up; he doesn't know why any more than he can understand why evidence has been suppressed, or suddenly found when it would have been found earlier if it existed – in this case your fingerprints in Mattilon's office. He wants to help; he gave me a telephone number where we can reach him.'

'Can we trust him?' asked Joel, writing a note on the stationery.

'I think so. He did something remarkable this morning, but I'll get to that.'

'The man at the George V,' said Converse softly. 'Bertholdier's aide. It's where the running began. It's as though the moment was suddenly seized upon, someone recognizing a possible strategy, not wanting to let the opportunity slip away. "Brand him a killer now, maybe we can use it, build on it. All it cost is a life." *Jesus!*' Joel struck a hotel match and lit a cigarette. 'Go on,' he continued. 'Go back. What about Sam?'

She told him everything, starting with the madness at the St Regis in New York – the frightening telephone call that led to an intense young man racing up the steps and an Army officer running after her down the street.

'The odd thing here,' interrupted Converse, 'is that those men, that call, might have been legitimate.'

'*What?* How? The first one looked like a Hitler youth and the other was in uniform!'

'Most people in uniform would be the first ones to want the generals of Aquitaine cut loose in a typhoon. Remember Fitzpatrick said those four dossiers came from way down deep in official vaults and, judging from much of the material, Connal thought there was heavy military input. Maybe my silent partners in Washington are beginning to crawl out of their sewers. Sorry. Go on.'

She told him of meeting Sam at the diner in Las Vegas, the married Sam, Sam the father of two young girls. Wincing, Joel listened, all his antennae revolving, catching every turn of phrase, every meaning that might have more than one meaning, trying desperately to find a clue, a way – something, *anything* they might use or act upon. And then he held up his hand, only inches above the table but it was a signal for Val to stop.

'The *three* of you were going to Washington?'

'Yes.'

'You and Sam and this third person he was going to see, going to talk to – the one he said would know what to do.'

'Yes. The man who had Sam killed. He was the *only* one Sam talked to.'

'But Abbott said he trusted him. With "his life", I think you said.'

'Sam said,' corrected Valerie. 'He was wrong.'

'Not necessarily. Sam was easy-going but not easily conned. He chose his friends carefully; he didn't have too many because he knew his rank was vulnerable.'

'But he didn't talk with anyone else . . . .'

'I'm sure he didn't but this other man had to. I know something about crisis conferences in Washington – and that's exactly what Sam meant when he said you were going there. Those meetings don't just happen, some strong words are used to cut a path through the bureaucratic mess. Certainly Sam's name would be put forward first – he had the status and the rank – and just possibly my name, or yours, or even Delavane's, any of which would have been enough.' Converse picked up the pen. 'What was his name?'

'Oh, Lord,' said Val, closing her eyes, her fingers massaging her forehead. 'Let me think. . . .Alan, the first name was Alan. . . .Alan Metzger? Metland . . . ?'

'Was there a rank, a title of some kind?'

'No. *Metcalf!* Alan Metcalf, that was it.'

Joel wrote down the name. 'Okay, let's get to Paris, the man from the *Sûreté.*'

She began with the odd behaviour of the immigration officials which led to the strange meeting with the lined, weary, rumpled Prudhomme. She reached the end of the Frenchman's startling revelations, repeating herself but filling in all the details she had omitted previously. When she had finished Converse held up his palm for the second time, his mouth open in astonishment, his eyes wide and alive.

'The *Tatiana* family?' he asked incredulously. 'Are you certain?'

'Completely. I asked him again yesterday.'

'Yesterday? Yes, you said he did something remarkable yesterday. What happened?'

'He stayed up all night outside the hotel in his car and when I left in a taxi shortly after the sun was up he crashed – and I mean crashed – into the car behind us. I was being followed. He told me to hurry up and get out of there. That's when I asked him to repeat the name. It was Tatiana.'

'That was the name René told me to use with Cort Thorbecke in Amsterdam. "Say you're a member of the Tatiana family". Those were his instructions.'

'What does it mean?'

'René didn't go into it too deeply but I got the drift. Apparently it means some kind of trust, a litmus test that clears someone for a level of information that would be withheld from ninety-nine per cent of the people wanting it.'

'Why?'

'It sounds crazy but Mattilon said it was because whoever was part of Tatiana was trusted by the most suspicious people on earth – men who couldn't afford to make a mistake.'

'My God, *who?*'

'Russians. Commissars in the Kremlin who floated money out to brokers in the West who invested it.'

'You're right,' said Val. 'It's crazy.'

'But it works, don't you see? Decent men who for one reason or another found themselves in a world they probably hated, never knowing whom they could trust, figured out a code among themselves. To be a member of the Tatianas is some kind of clearance. It's not only a signal of emergency, it's more than that. It means that whoever sends that signal is all right – in spite of what he may have to do. I'll bet it's one hell of a small circle. René, this Prudhomme, they'd fit into it. And for us it's a key; we can trust it.'

'You're in court, aren't you?' said the now and former Mrs Converse, reaching across the table for his free hand.

'I don't know any other way to do it. Facts, names, tactics; somewhere there's a crack, a road we can take – we *have* to take. Quickly.'

'I'd start with Prudhomme,' said Val.

'We'll call in his hand but maybe not first. Let's take things in sequence. Are there two phones in here? A certain – ex-wife had me too preoccupied to notice last night.'

'She's probably pregnant.'

'Wouldn't that be *wonderful*?'

'Down, boy. Yes, there's another phone. It's in the bathroom.'

'I want you to call this Metcalf, Alan Metcalf in Las Vegas. We'll get the number from information. I'll listen.'

'What do I say?'

'What name did you and Sam use?'

'The one I told you. Parquette.'

'Say that's who's calling, nothing else. Let him make the first move. If it's wrong, I'll know – we'll both know – and I'll hang up. You'll hear me and you hang up, too.'

'Suppose he's not there? Suppose I get a wife or a girl friend or a child?'

'Leave your name quickly and say you'll call back in an hour.'

The civilian sat in the sofa, his feet up on the coffee table. Across, in two arm chairs, were the Army captain – out of uniform – and the young Navy lieutenant, also in street clothes.

'We agree, then,' said Stone. 'We try this Metcalf and hope for the best. If we're wrong – if *I'm* wrong – we could be traced and don't fool yourselves, you've been seen here, you could be identified. But as I told you before, there comes a time where you have to take a risk you'd rather not take. You're out of safe-territory and you hope to Christ you get through it fast. I can't promise that you will. This phone is tapped into another number, a hotel across town, so any trace would be delayed, but only delayed while everyone registered was checked, every room checked. Once that's over with, any experienced telephone repairman could go down in the cellars and find the intercept.'

'How much time would that give us?' asked the Army officer.

'It's one of the largest hotels in New York,' replied the civilian. 'With luck, twenty-four to thirty-six hours.'

'Go for it!' ordered the Navy man.

'Oh, for God's sake,' said the captain, running his hand through his hair. 'Yes, of course, try it, try *him*. But I'm still not sure *why*?'

'Scat-patterns. It was routine information and easy to get. Abbott wrote out his schedules every day and he was precise about them. There was a predominance of lunches alone with Metcalf, and dinners with both families at either the Abbott or the Metcalf homes. I think he trusted the man, and as a long-time intelligence officer Metcalf was the logical one to go to. Also, there's something else. Along with Converse, all three were prisoners of war in Vietnam.'

'Go for it!' cried the Navy lieutenant.

'For Christ's sake, find another phrase,' said the captain.

'It's an answering machine!' shouted Val, gripping the mouthpiece of the telephone.

Joel came out of the bathroom. 'One hour,' he whispered.

'One hour,' she said. 'Miss Parquette will call back in an hour.' She hung up.

'And every hour after that,' added Converse, staring down at the phone. 'I don't like this. It's one o'clock in the morning back there, and if there's a wife or children around, someone should have been there.'

'Sam didn't mention a wife or children, except his own.'

'No reason why he would.'

'There could be a dozen explanations, Joel.'

'I just hope it's not the one I keep thinking about.'

'Let me call Prudhomme,' said Valerie. 'Let's use this Tatiana family.'

'Not yet.'

'Why *not*?'

'We need something else – *he* needs something else.'

Suddenly, Converse's gaze fell on the thick envelope addressed to Nathan Simon. It was on the bureau, his false passport on top. 'My God, we may *have* it,' he said quietly. 'It's been right there all the time and I didn't see it.'

Val followed his eyes. 'The analysis you wrote for Nathan?'

'I called it the best brief I ever wrote, but of course it's not a brief at all. It doesn't address points of law except in the widest, most abstract sense, without acceptable evidence to support the accusations. What it does address is the perverted ambitions of powerful men who want to *change* the laws, altering governments, supplanting them with raw, military controls, all in the name of maintaining the *law* and preserving the *order* they themselves will be called upon to maintain and preserve. And if "compromise" means killing – if they intend mounting wholesale assassinations – they can do it.'

'What's your *point*, Joel?'

'If I'm going to build a case, I'd better do it the only way I know how – from premise to conclusion based on affidavits – depositions – starting with my own and ending with pre-trial examinations.'

'What the hell are you talking about?'

'The law, Mrs Converse,' said Joel, picking up the envelope. 'And what it's meant to do. I can use most of what's in here – just in a different form. Naturally, I'll want other corroborating depositions, the farther afield the better. That's when you'll call this Prudhomme and join the Tatiana family. Then hopefully we'll reach Sam's friend, Metcalf – goddamn it, he'll have *something* to give us . . . Finally, I'm going to want to examine at least two of the alleged defendants orally – Leifhelm, for one, and probably Abrahms, maybe Delavane himself.'

'You're *mad*!' cried Valerie.

'No, I'm not,' said Converse simply. 'I'll need help, I know that. But I've got enough money to hire a couple of squads of miscreants – and once Prudhomme understands, I have an idea he'll know where the union hall is. We've got a lot of work to do, Val. All courts like immaculate manuscripts.'

'For Christ's sake, Joel, speak English .'

'You're a romantic, Mrs Converse,' he said approaching her. 'These are the nuts and bolts you don't find in seascapes.'

'They *do* have to be sketched, my darling. And balanced or unbalanced, the colours deliberate . . . What *are* you talking about?'

'A stenographer – a legal secretary, if you can find one. Someone who's willing to stay here all day and half the night, if need be. Offer three times the going rate.'

'Say I find one,' said Val. 'What in heaven's name are you going to tell her? Or him?'

Joel frowned as he crossed aimlessly to the window. 'A novel,' he said, turning. 'We're writing a novel. The first twenty or thirty pages are to be read as an upcoming court case, a trial.'

'Based on real people, men everyone's read about?'

'It's a new kind of fiction, but it's only a novel. That's all it is.'

Morning came to New York and Stone was alone again. The Navy lieutenant and the Army captain back at their desks in Washington. It was better this way; they could not help him and the less they were seen around the apartment the more likely they might escape detection if the hammer came down. And the hammer could come down, Stone knew it. It was as clear as the fact that Colonel Alan Metcalf was the chord they needed to start the music. 'Without him,' as Johnny Reb might have said in the old days, 'the tune ain't gonna get out of the fiddle – no stompin' unless he shows up.' But could he show up? wondered the former operations officer for Central Intelligence. For all intents and purposes he had disappeared, that was the word from Nellis, and the investigating unit did not pretend to understand or appreciate his absence. That, too, was the word and it was delivered harshly.

But Stone understood. Metcalf now knew what he knew – what they knew – and the colonel would not play by any rules written in the regulations, not if he was any good. Not if he was alive. And the ex-agent also understood something else when it came to telephone answering machines and intelligence personnel. The equipment was adaptable and sophisticated, courtesy of the American taxpayer and one of the better investments he made considering the extraordinary waste. Metcalf would play it well – if he was alive and any good. He would use a remote, programming it and reprogramming it, hearing what he wanted to hear, erasing what he wanted to erase, and leaving in certain information, preferably misleading. There would also be a code, probably changed daily, that if not inserted accurately would melt the tape with a ten second burst of microwaves – all standard. If he was any good. If he was alive.

Stone counted on both – that the colonel was both good and that he was alive. There was no point in thinking otherwise; that only led to staying in Johnny Reb's hammock or 'goin' fishin'', doing whatever one did as a robot. Which was why Stone had left a message on Metcalf's machine an hour ago at 6.35. He had chosen a name Converse's wife – former wife – must have relayed to the dead Samuel Abbott. *Marcus Aurelius ascending. Respond and erase, please.* Then Stone had given the telephone number at the apartment, which, if traced, would lead the tracers to the Hilton Hotel on Fifty-Second Street.

There was only one other person in the world Stone wished he could reach, but that man was 'on holiday – we have no means of getting in touch'. The words were patently a lie, but to intrude on that lie would mean Peter would have to say more than he wanted to say. The man was Derek Belamy, Chief of Clandestine Operations for Britain's MI6 and one of the only real friends Stone ever had in all his years with the Central Intelligence Agency. Belamy was such a good friend that when Peter was Station Chief in London, the Englishman told him bluntly to get out for a while before the whisky took over altogether and his ass was nailed to an alcoholic cross.

I have a doctor who'll certify a minor breakdown, Peter. I've a guest cottage on the grounds in Kent. Stay there, get well, old boy.

Stone had refused, and it was the most destructive decision he had ever made. The rest was the drunken nightmare Belamy had predicted.

But it was not Derek's concerns for a friend that caused Peter to want to reach him. It was Belamy's brilliance, his perceptions quietly concealed behind a pleasant, even prosaic exterior. And the fact that Derek Belamy had the pulse of Europe in his head, he could smell out a Delavane operation given the most basic facts. And, in fact, thought Stone hopefully, he was smelling them out now in Ireland – certainly where he was now. Sooner or later – preferably sooner – Belamy would return his call. When he did, a munitions shipment from Beloit, Wisconsin, would be described in full. Derek Belamy loathed the Delavanes of this world. His old friend would become an ally against the generals.

The telephone rang; the civilian looked at it and let it ring again. *Metcalf?* He reached over and picked it up.

'Yes?'

'*Aurelius?*'

'Somehow I knew you'd come through, Colonel.'

'Who the hell *are* you?'

'The name's Stone and we're on the same side, at least I think we are. However, you wear a uniform and I don't, so I need a little more confidence in you. Can you understand that?'

'You're one of those *bastards* in DC who sent him out!'

'You're warmer, Colonel. I came on late, but yes, I am one of those bastards. What happened to General Abbott?'

'He was killed, you son of a bitch! . . . I assume this phone is clean.'

'For at least twenty-four hours. Then we all disappear, just like you disappeared.'

'No remorse? No conscience? Do you know what you've *done*?'

'We don't have time for that, Colonel. Perhaps later, if there's a later for us . . . Get *off* it, soldier! I've *lived* with this! *Now*. Where do we meet? Where are you?'

'Okay, okay,' said the obviously exhausted Air Force officer. 'I took a dozen different flights. I'm in – where the hell am I? – in Knoxville, Tennessee. I've got a flight to Washington in twenty minutes.'

'Why?'

'To blow this fucking thing out of the air, what *else*?'

'Forget it, you're a dead man. I'd think you'd have learned that by now. You set up something on the information Abbott gave you, right?'

'Yes.'

'And *he* was blown out of the air, right?'

'Goddamn you, shut up!'

'You should have learned. They're where you can't see them or find them. But the wrong word to the wrong person and they can find you.'

'I *know* that!' shouted Metcalf. 'But I've been in this business for twenty years. There's got to be *someone* I can trust!'

'Let's talk about it, Colonel. Scratch DC and fly up to New York. I'll get a room at the Algonquin – actually I've already reserved one.'

'What name?'

'What else? Marcus.'

'You're on, but since we're in this deep I should tell you. The woman's been trying to reach me since one o'clock this morning.'

'Converse's *wife*?'

'Yes.'

'We need her. We need *him*!'

'I'll re-program the machine. The Algonquin?'

'That's it.'

'He's from New York, isn't he? I mean he's a New Yorker.'

'Whatever that means, yes. He's lived here for years.'

'I hope he's bright – they're bright.'

'Neither of them would be alive now if they weren't very bright, Colonel.'

'See you in a few hours, Stone.'

The civilian hung up the phone, his hands shaking, his eyes on a bottle of bourbon across the room. *No!* There would be no drinks, he had *promised* himself! He got out of the chair and went to the bed where his small suitcase was open, a gaping mouth waiting to be filled. He filled it, leaving the bottle of whisky on the table, and went outside to the elevators down the hall.

I, Joel Harrison Converse, an attorney admitted to practise before the bar of the State of New York and employed by the firm of Talbot, Brooks and Simon, 666 Fifth Avenue, New York City, New York, arrived in Geneva, Switzerland, on 9 August for legal conferences on behalf of our client, the Comm Tech Corporation, for the purpose of finalizing a contemplated business association referred to hereafter as the Comm Tech-Bern merger. On the morning of 10 August, at approximately 8 o'clock, I was contacted by the chief counsel representing the Bern Group, Mr Avery Preston Halliday of San Francisco, California. As he was an American only recently retained by the Swiss companies, I agreed to meet with him to clarify the existing points of argument and our positions with respect to them. When I arrived at the café on the Quai du Mont Blanc, I recognized Mr Halliday as a student and close friend I had know years ago at The Taft School in Watertown, Connecticut. His name then was Avery P. Fowler. Mr Halliday readily confirmed this fact, explaining that his surname had been changed upon the death of his father and the remarriage of his mother to a John Halliday of San Francisco. The explanation was acceptable, the circumstances, however, were not. Mr Halliday had ample prior time and opportunity to apprise me of his identity – the identity with which I was familiar – but did not do so. There was a reason. On that morning of 10 August, Mr Halliday sought a confidential meeting with the undersigned regarding a matter totally unrelated to the Comm Tech-Bern merger. This meeting was the primary reason for his being in Geneva. It was the first of many disturbing revelations . . .

If the very proper and distant British stenographer had the slightest interest in the material she transcribed in segments from dictation to the typewritten page, she did not show it. Her thin lips pursed, her grey hair knotted into a forbidding bun on the top of her head, she performed like a machine, as if everything was accepted in rote and by rote. Valerie's somewhat guarded explanation that her husband was an American novelist intrigued by recent events in Europe was greeted with a cold stare and the gratuitous information that the legal secretary never watched television and rarely read the newspapers. She was a member of the Franco Italian Alpine Society, which took up all her time and efforts in defence of natural endowments being eroded by man – when not earning a living so as to remain in her beloved mountains. She was an automaton putting in her time; one could dictate the book of Genesis and Val doubted the woman would know what she was typing.

It was the seventh hour and still no answer at Alan Metcalf's telephone in Las Vegas. Only a machine. It was time for the eighth call.

'If we don't get him now,' said Converse grimly, under the quiet tapping of the typewriter across the room, 'go ahead and reach Prudhomme. I wanted to talk to this Metcalf first but it's possible – that it may not be possible.'

'What difference does it make? You need help quickly and he's willing to help.'

'The difference is I know where Prudhomme's coming from, you've told me. I've got an idea what he can do and what he can't do, but I don't know anything about Metcalf – except that Sam put him way up on a high priority. Whoever I call first I've got to make specific statements to him, accusations and observations that'll blow his mind. Those are commitments, Val, and I have to go with the strongest . . . Try Metcalf again.' Joel turned and headed for the telephone in the bathroom as Valerie dialled the international codes for Las Vegas, Nevada.

'Caller C, message received. Please re-identify yourself twice followed by a slow count to ten. Stay on the line.'

Joel put the phone down on the edge of the basin and rushed out to the bedroom-sitting room. He walked over to Val, holding up his hand as he reached for a pencil on the desk. He wrote out the words on a page of stationery.

Go ahead. Stay calm. PSE.

'This is Miss Parquette speaking,' said Valerie, frowning, bewildered. 'This is Miss Parquette speaking. One, two, three, four . . .'

Converse returned to the bathroom, picked up the telephone and listened. '. . . eight, nine, ten.'

Silence. Finally, there were two sharp clicks and the metallic voice came back on the line.

'Confirmed, thank you. This is the second tape and will be microed out when completed. Listen carefully. There is a place on an island well known for its tribal nights. The King will be in his chair. That's it. We are burning.'

Joel hung up the phone and studied the only half-legible words he had hastily scribbled in soap on the mirror above the basin. The door opened and Valerie walked in, the page of hotel stationery in her hand.

'I wrote it down,' she said, handing him the paper.

'I wrote it sideways – your way is better. Christ, a *riddle!*'

'No more than the one you gave me. What in heaven's name does PSE mean?'

'"Psychological Stress Evaluator",' answered Converse, leaning against the wall and reading the words of Metcalf's message. He looked at her. 'It's a voice scanner you can attach to a phone or a recording machine that supposedly tells you whether the person you're talking to is lying or not. Larry Talbot played around with one for a while but claimed he couldn't find anyone telling the truth including his ninety-two-year-old mother. He threw it away.'

'Does it work?'

'They say it's much more accurate than a lie detector and I suppose it is if you know how to read it or use it. It worked in your case. Your voice was matched against the other calls you made, which means this Metcalf is into pretty high-tech equipment. That scanner tripped the second tape and it was all done by remote, from another phone, otherwise he would have answered himself after you passed the test.'

'But if I passed, why the riddle? Why an island with tribal nights?'

'Because any machine like that can be beaten. It's why they're not admissible in court. Years ago Willie Sutton was wired into a lie detector and according to the results he never even broke into a piggy bank much less Chase Manhattan. Metcalf was willing to take a risk, but not all the way. He's running, too.' Converse returned to the page of stationery.

'An island.' Val spoke softly, reading the soaped words on the mirror. 'Tribes . . . The Carib tribes; they were all through the Antilles. Or Jamaica – tribal nights, obeah rituals, voodoo rites in Haiti. Even the Bahamas – the Lucayan Indians – they held puberty rituals, they all did.'

'You impress me,' said Joel, looking up from the paper. 'How come?'

'Art courses,' she replied. 'Those nuts and bolts you won't grant us that go into the make-up of a culture's visual work . . . And it doesn't fit. It's too loose.'

'Why? It could mean some place in the Caribbean, some resort that's advertised a lot. The King is an emperor and that has to mean Delavane –

Mad Marcus as in Aurelius ... All those television commercials, the newspaper ads – pictures of people doing the limbo under torches with costumed blacks smiling down benignly, counting the dollars. Which *one*?'

'Too loose,' repeated Val. 'Too abstract – blacks and geometric shapes without specifics – no representational images.'

'Now what the hell are *you* talking about,' objected Converse.

'It's too wide, Joel, too many places to choose from, places you might not know anything about. It has to be closer, more familiar to you or to me, something we can recognize. Like Bruegel or Vermeer, littered with specific detail.'

'They sound like dentists.'

Valerie took the paper from him. '*Manhattan's* an island,' she said softly, reading and frowning again.

'If there are torches and tribal puberty rites, it's not my part of town.'

'Not tribal rites, tribal nights,' corrected Val. 'Tribal – not black but red? "The King will be in his chair" – chair ... table. His *table*. Tribal ... nights. Nights! That's where we're misreading it. *Nights*!'

'How else can you read it?'

'Not nights but *knights*! With a *K*!'

'And a table,' broke in Converse. 'Knights of the Round Table.'

'But *not* the King Arthur legend, nor Camelot. Much nearer, much closer. Tribal – *American* natives. American *Indians*.'

'Algonquins. The Roundtable!'

'The Algonquin Hotel,' cried Valerie. 'That's it, that's what he meant!'

'We'll know in a few minutes,' said Joel. 'Go inside and place the call.'

The wait was both intolerable and interminable. Converse looked at his face in the mirror; perspiration began to drench his face, the salt stinging his scrapes and burning his eyes. Far more telling, his hand shook and his breath was short. The Algonquin switchboard answered and Val asked for a Mr Marcus. There was a stretch of silence and when the operator came back on the line, Joel thought he would smash the telephone into the mirror.

'There are two Marcuses registered, Mam. Which one did you wish to speak to?'

'*Already* it's a rotten day!' Val broke in suddenly over the phone, startling Converse with her words. 'My boss, the *clown*, told me to call Mr Marcus at the Algonquin right away and give him the time and place for lunch. Now the clown's disappeared to a meeting somewhere outside and I'm left holding it. Sorry, dear, I didn't mean to take it out on you.'

'It's okay, hon, we got a few like that around here.'

'Maybe you can help me. Which Marcus is which. Maybe I'll recognize the first name or a company.'

'Sure. Lemme plug into Big Reggie. We all gotta stick together when it comes to the clowns, right? ... Okay, here they are. Marcus, Myron. Sugarman's Original Replicas, Los Angeles. And Marcus, Peter ... not much help here, sweetie. Just says Georgetown, Washington, DC.'

'That's the one. Peter. I'm sure of it. Thanks, dear.'

'Glad to be of help, hon. I'll ring now.'

* * *

The folded *New York Times* resting on his knee, Stone inked in the last two words of the crossword puzzle and looked at his watch. It had taken him nine minutes, nine minutes of relief; he wished it had been longer. One of the joys of having been Station Chief in London was *The Times* crossword. He could always count on at least a half hour when he could forget problems in the search for words and meanings.

The telephone rang. Stone whipped his head around, staring at it, his pulse accelerating, his throat suddenly dry. No one knew he had checked into the Algonquin under the name of Marcus. *No* one! . . . Yes, there was someone but he was in the air, flying up from Knoxville, Tennessee. What had gone *wrong*? Or had he been wrong about Metcalf? Was the supposedly angry, sermonizing Air Force intelligence officer one of *them*? Had his own instincts, honed over a thousand years of sorting out garbage, deserted him because he so desperately sought an opening, an escape from a steel net that was dropping down on him, a hammer descending within it? He got out of his chair and walked slowly, in fear, to the bedside table. He picked up the insistently ringing phone.

'Yes?'

'Alan Metcalf?' said the soft, firm voice of a woman.

'*Who?*' Stone was so thrown by the name he could barely concentrate, barely think!

'I beg your pardon, I have the wrong room.'

'*Wait!* Don't hang up. Metcalf's on his way here.'

'I'm sorry.'

'Please! Oh Christ, *please*! I was tired, I was *asleep*. We've been up night and day . . . Metcalf. I talked with him two hours ago – he said he was going to reprogram his machine, that someone had been trying to reach him since one o'clock this morning. He had to get *out* of there. A man was killed, a pilot. It was *not* an *accident*! Am I making sense to you?'

'Why should I talk to you?' asked the woman. 'So you can trace the call?'

'*Listen* to me,' said Stone, his voice now in total control. 'Even if I wanted to – and I don't – this is a hotel, not a private line, and to do what you suggest would take at least three men on the trunk lines and another controlling the switchboard. And even with such a unit it would be at least four minutes before they could isolate the wire and send out a tracer signal – which, incidentally, would only give us an area location, not a specific phone. *And* if you were calling from overseas we'd have to have another man, an expert, *in* that specific location to narrow it down to *perhaps* a twenty miles radius, but only if you stayed on *your* phone for at least eight minutes . . . Now, for God's sake, give me at least *two*!'

'Go on. Quickly!'

'I'm going to assume something. Maybe I shouldn't, but you're a clever woman, Mrs DePinna, and you could do it.'

'*DePinna?*'

'Yes. You left a telephone book open to the blue pages, the government pages. When the *accident* happened in Nevada, I made a simple connection with a listing and two hours ago I learned I was right. Metcalf returned my call – from a pay phone at an airport. A pilot, a general, had talked to him at length. He's joining us . . . You ran from the wrong people, Mrs DePinna.'

But as for what I'm thinking, I think the man we want to find is listening on this phone.'

'There's no one else here!'

'Please don't interrupt me, I've got to use every second.' Stone's voice suddenly became stronger. '*Leifhelm, Bertholdier, van Headmer, Abrahms!* And a fifth man we can't identify, an Englishman who's down so deep he makes Burgess, Maclean and Blunt look like amateurs. We don't know who he is but he's there, using warehouses in Ireland and off-shore cargo ships, and long-forgotten airfields to transport materials that shouldn't be going out. The dossiers came from *us, Converse!* We sent them to you! You're a lawyer and you know that by using your name I'm incriminating myself *or* committing suicide if anyone's taping this. I'll go farther. We sent you out through Preston Halliday in Geneva. We sent you out to build a legal case – from left field – so we could abort this thing with a minimum of fallout, sending all those goddamned idiots back to reality. But we were wrong. They were much farther ahead than we ever suspected – *we* ever suspected – but not Beale on Mykonos. He was dead right and he's dead because he was right. Incidentally, he was the "man from San Francisco". It was his five hundred thousand dollars; he came from a rich family which, among other things, bequeathed him a conscience. Think back to Mykonos! To what he told you – what his life was all about. From celebrated soldier to a scholar – to a killing that must have killed a part of him to commit . . . He said you almost caught him up on a couple of things he didn't mean to say. He said you were a good lawyer, a good choice. Preston Halliday was a student of his at Berkeley, and when this broke a year and a half ago, when Halliday realized what Delavane was doing and how he was being used, he went to Beale who was about to retire. The rest you can figure out.'

The woman's voice interrupted. 'Say what I want to hear you say. *Say* it!'

'Of course I will. Converse didn't kill Peregrine and he didn't kill the commander of NATO. Both of them were marked by Delavane – George Marcus Delavane – because both those men would have taken him and his ilk to the mat! They were convenient, *very* convenient, targets. I don't know about the others – I don't know what you've been through – but we broke a liar in Bad Godesberg, the major from the embassy who put *you, Converse,* at the Adenauer Bridge! He doesn't know it, but we broke him, and we learned something. We think we know where Connal Fitzpatrick is. We think he's alive!'

A male voice intruded. 'You *bastards,*' said Joel Converse.

'Thank *God!*' said the civilian, sitting down on the hotel bed. 'Now we can talk. We have to talk. Tell me everything you can. This phone is clean.'

Twenty minutes later, his hands trembling, Peter Stone hung up the phone.

36

General Jacques Louis Bertholdier ceased the rushing pelvic thrusts of intercourse, withdrew himself from the moaning dark haired woman beneath him, and rolled over, grabbing the telephone.

'*Yes?*' he shouted angrily. And then he listened, his flushed face growing ashen as his organ collapsed. 'Where did it happen?' he whispered, not in confidence but in sudden fear. 'The Boulevard Raspail? The charges? . . . *Narcotics? Impossible!*'

Holding the phone, the general swung his legs over the side of the bed, listening carefully, concentrating as he stared at the wall. The naked woman rose to her knees and leaned into him, her breasts pressed into his back, her open mouth caressing his ear, her teeth gently biting his lobe.

Bertholdier suddenly, viciously, swung his arm back, cracking the phone into the woman's face, sending her reeling to the other side of the bed, blood erupting from her broken lower lip.

'Repeat that, please,' he said into the phone. 'It's obvious then, isn't it? The man cannot be questioned further, can he? There is always the larger strategy to consider, losses to be anticipated in the field, no? It is the hospital all over again, I'm afraid. See to it then, like the fine officer you are. The Legion's loss was our immense gain . . . Oh? What is it? The arresting officer was *Prudhomme?*' Bertholdier paused, his breathing steady and audible; then he spoke, rendering a command decision. 'A stubborn bureaucrat from the *Sûreté* will not let go, will he? . . . He is your second assignment, to be carried out with your usual expertise before the day is over. Call me when both are accomplished, and consider yourself the aide to General Jacques Bertholdier.'

The general hung up and turned to the dark-haired woman who was wiping her lips with a bed sheet, her eyes an admixture of anger, embarrassment and fear.

'Apologies, my dear,' he said courteously. 'But you must leave now. I have telephone calls to make, business to attend to.'

'I will not come back!' cried the woman defiantly.

'You will come back,' said the legend of France standing up, his body rigid in its nakedness. 'If you are asked.'

Erich Leifhelm walked rapidly into his study and directly over to the large desk, where he took the phone from a white-jacketed attendant, dismissing the man with the nod of his head. The instant the door was closed he spoke. 'What is it?'

'The Geyner car was found, Herr General.'

'Where?'

'Appenweier.'

'And what is *that?*'

'A town fifteen or eighteen kilometres from Kehl. In the Alsace.'

'*Strasbourg!* He crossed into France! He *was* a priest!'

'I don't understand, Herr . . .'

'We never *thought* . . . ! Never mind! Who have you got in the sector?'

'Only one man, *Mein Herr*. The man with the police.'

'Tell him to hire others. Send them into Strasbourg! Look for a priest!'

'Get *out* of here!' roared Chaim Abrahms, as his wife walked through the door into their kitchen. 'This is no place for you now!'

'The Testaments say otherwise, my husband – yet not my husband,' said the frail woman dressed in black, the circle of soft white hair framing her gentle features, her brown eyes dark, receding mirrors. 'Will you deny the Bible you employ so readily when it suits you? It is not all thunder and vengeance. Must I read it to you?'

'Read *nothing!* Say nothing! These are matters for men!'

'Men who kill? Men who use the primitive savagery of the scriptures to justify the spilling of children's blood? My *son's* blood? I wonder what the mothers of the Masada would have said had they been permitted to speak their hearts . . . Well, I speak now, *General*. You will not kill any more. You will not use this house to move your armies of death, to plot your tactics of death – always your holy tactics, Chaim, your holy vengeance.'

Abrahms slowly got out of the chair. 'What are you talking about?'

'You think I haven't heard you? Phone calls in the middle of the night, calls from men who sound like you, who speak of killing so easily . . .'

'You *listened!*'

'Several times. You were breathing so hard you heard nothing but the sound of your own voice, your own orders to kill. Whatever you're doing will be done without you now, my husband – yet not my husband. The killing is over for you. It lost its purpose years ago but you could not stop. You invented new reasons until there was no reason left in you.'

The Sabra's wife removed her right hand from the folds of her black dress. She was holding Abrahms' service automatic. The soldier slapped his holster in disbelief, then whipped to his right, suddenly lunging to his left, crashing into the woman he had lived with for thirty-eight years, grabbing her wrist, spinning her. She would not relent! She resisted him, clawing at his face as he crashed her back into the wall, twisting her hand, trying to disarm her.

The explosion filled the kitchen and the woman who had borne him four children, finally a son, fell to the floor at his feet. In horror, Chaim Abrahms looked down. Her dark brown eyes were wide, saying nothing, her black dress drenched with blood, half her chest torn away.

The telephone rang. Abrahms ran to the wall and grabbed it, screaming. 'The children of Abraham *will not be denied!* A blood bath will follow – we will have the land delivered to us by God! Judea, Samaria – they are *ours!*'

'*Stop* it!' roared the voice over the line. 'Stop it, *Jew!*'

'Who calls me *Jew* calls me *righteous!*' yelled Chaim Abrahms, the tears falling down his face as he stared at the dead woman with the wide brown eyes. 'I have sacrificed with *Abraham!* No one could ask *more!*'

'*I* ask more!' came the cry of the cat. 'I ask *always* more!'

'*Marcus?*' whispered the Sabra, closing his eyes and leaning, collapsing into the wall, turning away from the corpse below him. 'Is it you . . . my leader, my *conscience*? Is it you?'

'It is I, Chaim, my friend. We have to move fast. Are the units in place?'

'Yes. Scharhörn. Twelve units in place, all trained, prepared. Death is no consideration.'

'That's what I had to know,' said Delavane.

'They await your codes, my General.' Abrahms gasped, then wept uncontrollably.

'What is it, Chaim? Get hold of yourself!'

'She's dead. My wife lies dead at my *feet*!'

'My God, what *happened*?'

'She overheard, she listened . . . she tried to kill me. We fought and she's dead.'

'A terrible, terrible loss, my dear friend. You have my deepest affection and condolences in your bereavement.'

'Thank you, Marcus.'

'You know what you must do, don't you, Chaim?'

'Yes, Marcus. I know.'

There was a knock at the door. Stone got out of the chair and picked up his gun awkwardly from the table. In all the years of sorting out garbage, he had fired a weapon only once. He had blown the foot off a KGB informant in Istanbul for the simple reason that the man had been exposed while drunk and had lunged at him with a knife. That one incident was enough. Stone did not like guns.

'Yes?' he said, the automatic at his side.

'Aurelius,' replied the voice behind the door.

Stone opened it and greeted his visitor. 'Metcalf?'

'Yes. Stone?'

'Come in. And I think we'd better change the code.'

'I suppose I could use "Aquitaine",' said the intelligence officer, walking into the room.

'Somehow I'd rather you didn't.'

'Somehow I don't think I will. Do you have coffee?'

'I'll get some. You look exhausted.'

'I've looked better on a beach in Hawaii,' said the slender, muscular middle-aged Air Force man. He was dressed in summer slacks and a white Izod jacket and his thin face matched his short, thinning brown hair, the dark circles prominent under his clear authoritative eyes. 'At nine o'clock yesterday morning I drove south out of Las Vegas to Halloran and from there I began a series of cross-country flights a computer couldn't follow, hopping from airport to airport under more names than I can remember.'

'You're a frightened man,' said the civilian.

'If you're not, I'm talking to the wrong person.'

'I'm not only frightened, Colonel, I'm petrified.' Stone went to the phone, ordered coffee and before hanging up, turned to Metcalf. 'Would you like a drink?' he asked.

'I would. Canadian on the rocks, please.'

'I envy you.' The civilian gave the order and both men sat down, for several moments the sounds of the street outside the only intrusion. They looked at each other, neither concealing the fact that each was silently evaluating the man across the way.

'You know who and what I am,' said the Colonel, breaking the silence. 'Who are you? What?'

'CIA. Twenty-nine years. Station Chief in London, Athens, Istanbul and points east and north. A once-disciple of Angleton and coordinator of clandestine operations until I was fired. Anything else?'

'No.'

'Whatever you did to your answering machine, you did it right. The Converse woman called.'

Metcalf shot forward in the chair. '*And?*'

'It was touch and go for a while – I wasn't at my best – but he finally got on the line, or I should say he finally spoke. He was there all the time.'

'Your second best must have been pretty good.'

'All he wanted to hear was the truth. It wasn't hard.'

'Where is he? Where are *they?*'

'The Alps, that's all he'd say.'

'Goddamn it!'

'For now,' completed the civilian. 'He wants something from me first.'

'What?'

'Affidavits. You could call them depositions.'

'*What?*'

'You heard me. Affidavits from myself and the people I'm working with – working for, actually – stating what we know and what we did.'

'He's out to hang you and I don't blame him.'

'That's part of it and I don't blame him, either, but he says it's secondary and I believe that. He wants Aquitaine. He wants Delavane and his crowd of maniacs nailed to the wall before the whole damn thing erupts – before the killing begins.'

'That was Sam Abbott's judgment. The killing – multiple assassinations, here and throughout Europe, the quickest and surest way to international chaos.'

'The woman told him.'

'No, he pieced it together from things Converse told *her*. Converse didn't understand the words.'

'He does now,' said Stone. 'Did I say I was petrified? What's a stronger phrase?'

'Whatever it is it applies to both of us because we both know how simple it would be – so *simple*. We're not dealing with woolly-brained crazies or even your run-of-the-mill terrorists – we've got thirty years' experience and ninety per cent of them are in our computers. When the signals break out we know where they are and usually we can stop them. But here we're dealing with the roughest professionals in our own and in allied ranks, also with years of experience. They're walking around the Pentagon, and on Army and Navy bases – and at an Air Force base in Nevada. *Christ*, where *are* they? You open your mouth and you don't know whom you're talking to, who'll cut you down or program an aircraft to break apart in the sky. How can we stop what we can't see?'

'Perhaps Converse's way.'

'With *affidavits?*'

'Maybe. Incidentally, he wants one from you. Your meeting with Abbott, everything he told you, as well as your evaluation of his mental capacities and stability. That means you'll have to stay here tonight. Half an hour ago I reserved three other rooms – I said I'd give the front desk the names later.'

'Would you mind answering my question? What the hell are affidavits going to do? We're dealing with an army out there – how large and how wide-spread we don't know – but it *is* an *army!* At minimum, a couple of battalions, here and in Europe. Professional officers trained to carry out orders, believing in those orders and in the generals who are issuing them. Affidavits, depositions, for Christ's sake! Is this some kind of flaky legal handspring that doesn't mean anything? Do we have *time* for this?'

'You're not thinking anything I didn't think, Colonel. But then I'm not a lawyer and neither are you. Converse is, and I had a long conversation with him. He's taking the only route he knows. The legal route. Oddly enough, it's why we sent him out.'

'Give me an answer, Stone,' said Metcalf coldly.

'Protection,' replied Stone. 'What Converse wants is instant protection and for all of us to be taken seriously. Not as psychopaths or as cranks or as people with mental aberrations or diminished capacities – I think those were his words.'

'Aren't they nice? What in the name of sweet Jesus do they mean? How?'

'With formal legal documents. Responsible men setting forth what they know and in the case of depositions, under qualified examination. Through the courts, Colonel. *A* court – it only takes one, only one judge. On the basis of the affidavits a petition is made to the court – *a* court, *a* judge – that protection be given under seal.'

'Under what?'

'Under seal. It's completely confidential – no press, no divulging of information, simply an order from the court transmitted to the authorities most suited to carry out the order. In this case, all the branches of the Secret Service instructed by the court to provide *extraordinary* service.'

'Extraordinary . . . ? For whom?'

'The President of the United States, the Vice President, the Speaker of the House, the Secretary of Defense, the Secretary of State – right on down the line. The law, Colonel. That's what the law can do – also his words, I think.'

'*Jesus!*'

There was a rapping on the door, but this time Stone covered his automatic with the folded *New York Times.* He got up, crossed to the door, and admitted a waiter rolling in a table with a pot of coffee, two cups, a bottle of Canadian whisky, ice and glasses. He signed the bill and the man left.

'Coffee or a drink first?' asked Stone.

'My God, a drink. *Please.*'

'I envy you.'

'You're not going to join me?'

'Sorry, I can't. I allow myself one in the evening; I'll join you then. You live in Las Vegas, so you'll understand. I'm trying to beat the odds, Colonel. I intend to beat them. I was fired, remember?' Stone brought the Air Force officer a drink and sat down.

'You can't beat the odds, don't you know that?'

'I've beaten a few. I'm still here.'

'The courts,' said Metcalf, shaking his head. 'A court! It's an end run. He's using the law to go around the flanks of the government people he should reach but whom he can't trust. Can it *work*?'

'It buys time, a few days perhaps, it's hard to tell. "Under seal" lasts only so long. The law also calls for full disclosure. But what's most important is that it legitimately tightens the security around potential targets, hopefully screwing up whatever tactics Aquitaine is mounting, forcing the generals to regroup, rethink. Again time.'

'But that's only over here in the States.'

'Yes. That's why Converse wants the time.'

'What for?'

'He won't tell me and I'm in no position to make demands.'

'I see,' said the colonel, his drink to his lips. 'You said three rooms. Who are the others?'

'You'll meet them and you won't like them. They're two kids who stumbled into this along with a few others I don't know and they won't say who they are. After Halliday reached them – or one of them – they provided the dossiers for Converse. They're young but they're all right, Colonel. If I ever had a son, I'd like to think he'd be one of them.'

'I have a son and I expect he would be,' said Metcalf. 'Otherwise, I blew it. What are the procedures?'

Stone sat rigidly back in the chair and spoke slowly, his voice pitched in the static emphasis of a monotone. He was repeating instructions not of his own making and certainly not to his liking. 'At three o'clock this afternoon I'm to call an attorney named Simon, Nathan Simon, one of the senior partners of Converse's firm here in New York. Presumably by then Converse's wife will have reached him, telling him to expect a call from me and to please do as I ask – apparently they believe he will. To be brief about it, Simon will come over here to the hotel accompanied by a stenographer and take all our depositions, along with our credentials, ranks and current responsibilities. He'll stay until he's finished.'

'You were right on the phone,' interrupted the military man. 'We're dead.'

'I said as much to Converse and he asked me how it felt. He was inquiring, of course, from first-hand knowledge.'

'He wants all of you.'

'But not you,' said Stone. 'He'd like your testimony – and by extension Abbott's – but he won't insist on it. He knows he can't ask you to walk in on this.'

'I walked in when that plane went down. Also there's something else. If we can't stop Delavane and his generals, what the hell's left for people like us? . . . Converse wouldn't tell you what he was going to do?'

'Not in terms of what he calls the countdown, but yes, as far as tomorrow is concerned. He's sending over his own affidavit and, he expects, another from a man from the *Sûreté* who has information showing that most of the official reports out of Paris are lies ... And we're not dead yet, Colonel. Converse made it clear that Nathan Simon was the best attorney we could have – as long as he believes us.'

'What can a lawyer do?'

'I asked Converse the same thing and he gave me a strange answer. He said "he can use the law, because the law isn't men, it's the law".'

'That's beyond me,' said Metcalf, irritated. 'Not in a philosophical context but how it applies now – right goddamned *now*! ... Hell, it doesn't make any difference – *we* don't make any difference! Once those guns go off and the bodies fall in Washington and London, Paris or Bonn – wherever – they've got the controls and we won't get them back. I know that because I know how long so many people have wanted someone to *take* control. Stop the carnage, make things safe, piss on the Soviets. God help me, there were times I thought that way myself.'

'So did I,' said the civilian quietly.

'We were wrong.'

'I know that. It's why I'm here.'

Metcalf drank, holding the cold glass against his warm cheek. 'I keep thinking about what Sam said to me. "There's got to be a list", he said. "A master list of everyone in this Aquitaine". He ruled out all the obvious places – not in a vault, not on paper – probably electronically programmed, flashed on with codes, as his aerial tactics were frequently flashed on a screen inside a jet's cockpit. Someplace no one would ever think of, away from anything official or tied in with anyone remotely military. "A list. There *has* to be a list!" he kept saying. For a pilot, he had a hell of an imagination. I guess it's why he was so good at that tactical stuff at forty thousand feet in the air. Come out of the sun where they don't expect you, or from a dark horizon where the radar can't pick you up. He knew it all. He was a tactical genius.'

As Metcalf talked, Stone leaned forward in the chair, his eyes centring on the Air Force officer's face, his ears absorbing every word the man spoke.

'Scharhörn,' he said, barely above a whisper. 'It's *Scharhörn!*'

The twin engine Riems 406 circled the private airfield at St Gervais, fifteen miles east of Chamonix, the amber lights of the two runways throwing an orange glow up into the lower night sky. Inside, Prudhomme checked the straps of his seatbelt as the pilot on his left received clearance to make his final approach to the north-south strip.

Mon Dieu, what an incredible day! thought the man from the *Sûreté*, as he glanced at his right hand under the spill of the panel lights. The dark bruises on his fingers were at least less noticeable than the blood that had covered his entire hand only hours ago. *Formidable!* His ordained executioner had not even bothered to conceal his assignment, such was his arrogance – bred undoubtedly *as a Légionnaire!* And the sentence of death had been delivered right inside the car at the far end of the parking area in the Bois de Boulogne! The man had called him at the office and, in truth, it had entered Prudhomme's thoughts that this man might call him, and so it was less a surprise than it could have been – and certainly gave him cause to be prepared. The man had asked his recent superior to meet him at the Boulogne, in the parking lot; he had startling news. He would be driving his official Peugeot and, since he could not leave his radio phone, would the inspector mind joining him. Of course not.

But there had been no startling news other than the fundamental revelation. Only questions, asked very arrogantly.

Why did you do what you did this morning?

Shave? Go to the toilet? Eat breakfast? Kiss my wife goodbye? What are you talking about?

You know what I refer to! Earlier! The man on the Boulevard Raspail. You crashed into his car, stopping him. You threw narcotics inside. You arrested him falsely!

I didn't approve of what he was doing. Any more than I approve of this conversation. Prudhomme had awkwardly reached for the handle of the door with his left hand, his right having other business.

Stop! shouted his subordinate, grabbing his shoulder. *You were protecting the woman!*

Read my report. Let me go.

I'll let you go to hell! I'm going to kill you, meddler! Insignificant bureaucrat!

The former subordinate had yanked a gun from his jacket holster but he was too late. Prudhomme had fired twice, the small weapon under his coat gripped in his right hand. Unfortunately, it was a small calibre and the ex-colonel of the Legion was a very large man; he had lunged at Prudhomme in a final assault inside the automobile. However, the veteran of the *Résistance* had gone back to the old habit from the war – just in case. Along the lapels of his coat was threaded a long wire – a wire with two braided loops at each end. He had whipped it out, looping it over his subordinate's head, his wrists crossed, violently yanking it taut, until the flesh burst around his executioner's throat, drenching the condemned man's hands – condemned but very much alive.

'We're cleared for landing, Inspector,' said the pilot, grinning. 'I swear to Christ no one would *believe* this! Of course I have no intention of saying a thing, I swear on my mother's grave!'

'She's probably drinking brandy in Montmartre at this moment,' interjected Prudhomme dryly. 'Say nothing and you may have another six months flying in your foolish tobacco from Malta.'

'Nothing else! *Never* anything else, Inspector. I am a father!'

'You are to be commended. Six months and then get out, do you understand?'

'On my father's grave, I swear!'

'He's very much alive and in jail – he'll be out in sixty days. Tell him to stop his presses – government relief cheques, *really.*'

Joel and Valerie listened in silence as the man from the *Sûreté* told his story. He was finished now; there was nothing left to say. Interpol had been compromised, the *arrondissement* police manipulated, the *Sûreté* itself corrupted, and official government communiqués issued on the basis of lies – all lies. Why?

'I'll tell you because I want your help – much more help,' said Converse, getting out of the chair and going to the desk where the typewritten pages of his affidavit were in the centre of the green blotter. 'Better, you can read it yourself, but I'm afraid you'll have to read it here. In the morning I'll have copies made; until then I don't want it to leave this room. By the way, Val got you a reservation, a single – don't ask me how but a clerk downstairs will have a new wardrobe if not a new house by tomorrow.'

'*Merci*, Madame.'

'The name is French,' added Joel.

'Yes?'

'No, I mean the *name* is French.'

'*Oui.*'

'No, what I mean is . . .'

'*Pardon, mon vieux,*' interrupted Valerie. '*Le nom sur le registre est "Monsieur French", c'est un nom anglais, pas français. French. Arthur French.*'

'But I will have to sign, talk. Surely they will know.'

'You sign nothing and you say nothing,' said Val, taking a key off the bedside table and handing it to Prudhomme. 'The room is paid for – three days to be precise. After that – before, if possible, if you agree to help – the three of us will be someplace else.'

'*Formidable.* I must read.'

'*Mon ami – mon époux – est un avoué brillant.*'

'*Je comprends.*'

'There are some forty pages here,' said Converse, bringing the papers to Prudhomme. 'To absorb it will take you at least an hour. We'll go downstairs and grab a bite to eat and leave you alone.'

'*Bien.* There is much I wish to learn.'

'What about you?' asked Joel, standing above the Frenchman. 'I mean now. They'll find the body in the car.'

'Most certainly,' agreed Prudhomme. 'I left it where it was. But for the *Sûreté* there will be no connection to me.'

'Fingerprints? The fact that you were away from your office?'

'Another old habit from the war,' said the man from the *Sûreté* reaching into his pocket. He pulled out a pair of extremely thin rubberized gloves – surgical gloves – cut off above the fingers, before the wrist. 'I washed these out at the Boulogne. The German occupation forces had all our fingerprints in a thousand files. There was no point in asking for our own executions. As for my absence at my desk, it is quite simple. I explained to an assistant that I would be in Calais for several days on a contraband investigation and would call in. My years permit a certain latitude and flexibility.'

'That's the *Sûreté*, not the others. Not where the *Légionnaire* came from.'

'I am aware of that, Monsieur. So I must be careful. It will not be the first time.'

'Enjoy your reading,' said Converse, nodding at Val to join him. 'If you want anything, call room service.'

'*Bon appétit,*' said Prudhomme.

Chaim Abrahms lifted the stiffening wrist of his dead wife's hand, the weapon gripped fiercely in her white fingers, and angled the gun toward her chest, into the bloody cavern between her breasts.

The wide, brown eyes would not stay closed! They stared up at him, accusing – accusing!

'What do you *want* from me?!' he screamed. 'I have seen the dead. I have *lived* with the dead! Leave me be, woman! You couldn't *understand*!'

Yet she had, for so many years. She had cooked the meat – the desert chicken and the lamb – caught in the outlying marshes – and fed the units of the Irgun and the Haganah, never questioning death then. Fighting for a hope, a simple hope that was the beginning of a dream. The land was *theirs*, rightfully, biblically, *logically* theirs! They had fought and they had won! Two thousand years of being outcasts – despised, reviled, scorned and spat upon by the almighty gentiles until the tribes were burned and gassed and told to eliminate themselves from the face of the earth – and yet they had survived. Now the tribes were strong! They were the *conquerors*, not the conquered!

'It's what we fought for! What we prayed for! Why do you insult me with your eyes!' Chaim Abrahms roared as he pressed his forehead against the dead flesh of his wife's face.

Hitabdut was among the most heinous crimes committed against the laws of the Talmud. It was *Ebude Atzmo*, the taking of one's own life against the wishes of almighty God in whose image man was created. A Jew who consigned his or her earthly being to *hitabdut* was denied burial in the Hebrew cemetery. It would be so for Chaim Abrahms' wife, the most devout human being ever known.

'I have to do it!' he screamed, raising his eyes in supplication. 'It is for the best, can't you *understand*?'

Prudhomme poured himself a cup of coffee and returned to his chair. Valerie sat opposite him as Converse stood by the window looking over at the man from the *Sûreté*, listening.

'I cannot think of any other questions,' said the Frenchman, his troubled eyes darting about intensely above the cup in his hand, his lined face wearier than before. 'Although it's possible I'm still too deep in shock to think at all. To say it's incredible serves no purpose; also it would not be true. It's all *too* credible. The world is so frightened it cries out for stability, for a place to hide, for protection – from the skies, from the streets, from each other. I believe the time has come when it will settle for sheer, absolute strength, no matter the cost.'

'The operative word is absolute,' said Joel, 'as in controls and power. A confederation of military governments fuelling one another, interlocking policies and altering the laws all in the name of stability – until anyone who disagrees with them is declared unstable and silenced. And if too many disagree the chaos erupts again – stability wins, Aquitaine wins. All they need is that initial wave of terror, a *tidal* wave of killing and confusion. "Key figures" were the words they used. "Accumulation" . . . "rapid acceleration" . . . chaos. Powerful men cut down as riots break out in half a dozen capitals and the generals march in with their commanders. That's the scenario, right from their own words.'

'That also is the problem, Monsieur. They are only words, words you can pass along to very few people for they could be the wrong people. You could move up this countdown, as you call it, trigger this holocaust yourself.'

'The countdown's running out, make no mistake,' broke in Converse. 'But there *is* a way. "Accumulation" and "rapid acceleration" can be used in another manner, and you're right, it's only with words – *accumulated* words, *accelerated* words. I can't come out, not yet. I can't show myself. There's no protection any court or government agency or the police could provide that would stop them from killing me, and then once I'm dead, calling whatever I said the ravings of a psychopath. Don't misunderstand me, I have no death wish but my death in itself isn't important. What is important is that the truth goes down with me because I'm the only one who's talked directly to Delavane's four Caesars over here, and probably the fifth, the Englishman.'

'And these *declarations* – these affidavits you speak of can change that?'

'They can turn things around, maybe just enough.'

'Why?'

'Because that's a real world out there, a practical complicated world that has to be penetrated as fast as possible – people have to be reached who can be trusted, who can do something. Quickly. It's what I wanted to do a couple of weeks ago but I was going about it the wrong way. I wanted to get everything I knew to someone I knew. Nathan Simon, the best attorney I've ever met. I wrote it all out – twice – not realizing that I was only tying his hands, probably killing him.' Joel stepped away from the window, a lawyer in summation. 'Who could he go to without me, without the presence of an obviously sane man and not simply the words of a "psychopathic killer"? And if I did come out, as he would have rightfully insisted, we were both dead. Then Val told me about the man in New York who reached her on the phone and the other who chased her down the street and I guessed right. Those aren't the methods of people who want to kill you; they don't announce themselves. They were the men in Washington who had sent me out and were now trying to make contact with me. Then she described her meeting with Sam Abbott and his mentioning this Metcalf, a man he trusted and who had to be some kind of very-important-person for him to tell the story to . . . Finally, there was you in Paris – what you said, what you did, and how you offered to help, using the same code as René Mattilon – the Tatiana family. Tatiana, a name or a word I think means trust, even among sharks.'

'You are right, Monsieur.'

'That's when it all came together for me. If I could somehow establish lines of communication and reach all of you, there was a way. You people knew the truth; some of you knew all of it, others like yourself, knew only fragments, but regardless, you understood the immensity, the reality of the generals and their Aquitaine and what they could do – what they're *doing*. Even you, Prudhomme. What did you say? Interpol is compromised, the police manipulated, the *Sûreté* corrupted – official reports all lies? Added to these, Anstett in New York, Peregrine, the commander of NATO, Mattilon, Beale, Sam Abbott . . . Connal Fitzpatrick – the only question mark – and God knows how many others. All dead. The generals are marching – forget theories, they're *killing*! . . . If I could persuade all of you to write out affidavits – or have depositions taken – and get them to Nathan Simon, he'd have the ammunition he needs. I fed legal mumbo-jumbo to Stone in New York; some of it applies, most of it doesn't, but he'll do his part and force the others to join me – he has no choice. The main point, the *only* point, is to get this material to Simon. Once he has written testimony, a series of events and observations all sworn to be true by diverse men of experience, he has a *case*. Believe me, he'll treat them like the plans of a neutron bomb. He'll have it all tomorrow and he'll reach the right people if he has to walk into the Oval Office – which he could do, but may not choose to.' Joel paused and looked hard at the man from the *Sûreté*, nodding at the pages of his own affidavit on the table beside the Frenchman. 'I've made arrangements for that to be flown to New York tomorrow. I'd like one from you.'

'Certainly you may have it. But can you trust the courier?'

'The world could blow apart and she'd still be sitting in her house in the mountains and not know it. Or care. How's your English?'

'Adequate, I believe. We've talked for several hours.'

'I mean written English. It'd save time if you wrote it out tonight.'

'My spelling is probably no better than yours is in French.'

'Make that English,' corrected Valerie. 'I'll straighten it out and if you're not sure of something – *écrivez en français*.'

'*Merci*. Tonight?'

'The secretary will be here first thing in the morning,' explained Converse. 'She'll type it up. She's the one taking the flight from Geneva to New York tomorrow afternoon.'

'She agreed to do this?'

'She agreed to accept a large donation to a nature organization that apparently runs her life.'

'Very convenient.'

'There's something else,' said Joel, sitting on an arm of Valerie's chair and leaning forward. 'You know the truth now, and beyond the material that has to reach Simon, there's one last thing I have to do. I've got a lot of money and a banker in Mykonos who'll confirm I have access to a great deal more – but you've read all that. With time to find the personnel and the equipment I might be able to pull it off myself, but we don't have the time. I need your help, I need the resources you have.'

'For what, Monsieur?'

'The final depositions. The last part of the testimony. I want to kidnap three men.'

37

I, Peter Charles Stone, age 58, a resident of Washington, DC, was employed by the Central Intelligence Agency for twenty-nine years during which time I attained the rank of Station Chief in various European posts and ultimately 2nd Director of Clandestine Operations, Langley, Virginia. My record is on file at the Central Intelligence Agency and may be obtained pursuant to the regulations governing such procedures. Since separation from the CIA, I have worked as a consultant and analyst for numerous intelligence departments, the specifics therein withheld from this statement pending government clearances should they be deemed pertinent to this document.

On or about 15 March last, I was contacted by Captain Howard Packard, United States Army, who asked if he might come to my apartment to discuss a confidential matter. When he arrived, he stated at the outset that he was speaking for a small group of men from both the military services and the State Department, the number and identities of which he would not divulge. He stated further that they sought professional consultation from an experienced intelligence officer no longer associated (permanently) with any branch of the intelligence community. He said he had certain funds available he believed would be adequate and would I be interested. It should be noted here that Captain Packard and his associates had made a thorough if not exhaustive search of my background – warts and alcohol and all, as is said . . .

I, Captain Howard N.M.I. Packard, US Army, 507538, age 31, currently residing in Oxon Hill, Maryland, and assigned to Section 27, Department of Technological Controls, the Pentagon, Arlington, Virginia. In December of last year, Mr A. Preston Halliday, an attorney from San Francisco with whom I had struck up a friendship as a result of his numerous petitions to our section on behalf of clients (all successful and above reproach), asked me to have dinner with him at a small restaurant in Clinton, approximately ten miles from my house. He apologized for not asking my wife, explaining that what he had to say would only disturb her, as, indeed, it would disturb me, but in this case it was my responsibility to be disturbed. He added that there was no conceivable conflict in our meeting as he had no business pending, only business that should be investigated and stopped . . .

I, Lieutenant (J.G.) William Michael Landis, US Navy, a bachelor, age 28; current address, The Somerset Garden Apartments, Vienna, Virginia, am a computer programmer for the Department of the Navy, Sea-Armaments Procurements Division, stationed at the Pentagon, Arlington, Virginia. Actually, in all but rank (due within 60 days), I'm in command of most programming for Pentagon-Navy having received a doctorate in advanced computer technology from the University of Michigan, College of Engineering . . . I'm probably not saying this right, sir.

Go ahead, young man.

I state this because with the highly sophisticated equipment at my disposal as well as the classified micro-conversion codes available to me, I'm able to tap into a great many restricted computers with a tracing capacity that can circumvent – or penetrate, if you like – closures placed on extremely sensitive information.

Last February, Captain Howard Packard, US Army, and three other men – two from the Department of State, Office of Munitions Controls, and the third a Marine Corps officer I knew from the Amphibious Section, Navy Procurements – came out to see me on a Sunday morning. They said they were alarmed over a series of weapons and high-tech transfers that appeared to violate Department of Defense and State Department sanctions. They gave me the data they had concerning nine such incidents, impressing upon me the confidentiality of the inquiry.

The next afternoon I went to the maximum security computers and with the conversion codes inserted the data for the nine transfers. The initial entries were confirmed – those numbers never change so as to eliminate the possibility of duplication – but in each case, after confirmation, the remaining information was erased, wiped off the computer tapes. Six of those nine transfers were traced through the initial entries to a firm called Palo Alto International, owned by a retired Army general named Delavane. This was my first involvement, sir.

Who were the three other men, Lieutenant?

It wouldn't do any good to give their names, sir. It could only hurt their families.

I'm not sure I understand – can possibly understand.

They're dead. They went back and asked questions and they're dead sir. Two supposedly in automobile accidents involving trucks – on back roads they never took home – and the third indiscriminately shot by a deranged sniper while jogging in Rock Creek Park. All those joggers and he was the one who got it . . .

As an Army captain with full security clearance and frequently dealing in top-secret procedures, I was able to set up a sterile telephone (i.e.: constantly scanned for taps or intercepts) so Mr Halliday could reach me any time of day or night without fear of being overheard. Also in concert with Mr Stone and Lieutenant Landis, we pooled our sources and obtained in-depth intelligence dossiers on the well-known names Halliday found among General Delavane's notes. Specifically, Generals Bertholdier, Leifhelm, Abrahms and van Headmer. Using funds provided by Dr

Edward Beale, we secured the services of private firms in Paris, Bonn, Tel Aviv and Johannesburg to up-date the dossiers with all available current information about the subjects.

By now we had uncovered ninety-seven additional computer erasures directly related to export licensing and military transfers involving an estimated $45,000,000. A great many were initiated by Palo Alto International but without further data there was nothing to trace. It was like a series of blips disappearing from a radar screen . . .

My years in the CIA's Clandestine Operations taught me that the larger the pattern, the greater the numbers, and those areas with the heaviest concentration of activity invariably held the tightest and most ruthless security. Nothing terribly original here but the reverse application is frequently overlooked. Since Washington was the clearing house for illegal exports totalling millions upon millions in American merchandise and material, it stood to reason that there would be a range of safeguards, scores of Delavane's informants – both knowing and unknowing; that is ideologically involved or simply hired or threatened – in the government agencies and departments related to the activities of Palo Alto International. Without going into specifics, Captain Packard confirmed this judgment by telling me an incident had recently taken place that cost the lives of three men who tried to follow up on a number of computer erasures. We had moved from the realm of ideological extremists into one of fanatics and killers. Therefore it was my contention – and I hereby assume full responsibility for the decision – that safer and more rapid progress could be made by sending a man out into the peripheral sectors of Delavane's operation with enough information to trace connections back to Palo Alto International. By the nature of illegal export licensing itself there is more open territory at the receiving end. The obvious place to start was with the four generals whose names were found in Delavane's notes. I had no candidate with the expertise I felt was necessary for the assignment . . .

On or about 10 July, Mr Halliday called me on the sterile phone I'd set up for him and said he believed he'd found the proper candidate for the assignment as outlined by Mr Stone. An attorney whose field was international law, a man he had know years ago and a former prisoner of war in Vietnam who conceivably had the motivation to go after someone like General Delavane. His name was Joel Converse . . .

I, Alan Bruce Metcalf, age 48, am an officer in the US Air Force, holding the rank of Colonel and currently stationed at the Nellis Air Force Base, Clark County, Nevada, as Chief Intelligence officer. Thirty-six hours ago, as I dictate this statement, on 25 August at 4 o'clock in the afternoon, I received a telephone call from Brigadier General Samuel Abbott, Commanding Officer, Tactical Operations, Nellis Air Force Base. The general said it was urgent that we meet, preferably off-base, as soon as possible. He had new and extraordinary information regarding the recent assassinations of the Supreme Commander of NATO and the American Ambassador to Bonn, West Germany. He insisted that we be in civilian clothes and suggested the library at the University of Nevada, Las Vegas campus. We met at approximately 5. 30 p.m. and talked for five hours. I will be as accurate as possible and that will be very accurate as the conversation is still fresh in my mind, indelibly heightened by the tragic death of General Abbott, a close friend for many years and a man I admired greatly . . .

The above then are the events as told to General Abbott by the former Mrs Converse, and as he related them to me, and the subsequent actions I took to convene an emergency meeting of the highest level intelligence personnel in Washington. General Abbott believed what he had been told, based on his knowledge and perceptions of the individuals involved. He was a brilliant and stable man, not given to bias where judgments were concerned. In my opinion, he was deliberately murdered because he had 'new and extraordinary information' about a fellow prisoner of war, one Joel Converse.

Nathan Simon, tall, portly, sitting well back in his chair, removed the tortoiseshell glasses from his tired face and tugged at the small chin-beard that covered the scars of shrapnel embedded at Anzio years ago. His thick salt-and-pepper eyebrows were arched above his hazel eyes and sharp, straight nose. The only other person in the room was Peter Stone. The stenographer had been dismissed; Metcalf, exhausted, had retired to his room, and the other two officers, Packard and Landis, had opted to return to Washington – on separate planes. Simon carefully placed the typewritten affidavits on the table beside his chair.

'There was *no one* else, Mr Stone?' he asked, his deep voice gentle, far gentler than his eyes.

'No one I knew, Mr Simon,' replied the former intelligence officer. 'Everyone I've used since – what we call pulling-in-old-debts – was lower level with access to upper level equipment, not decisions. Please remember, three men were killed when this thing barely started.'

'Yes, I know.'

'Can you do what Converse said? Can you get something "under-seal" and move some mountains we can't move?'

'He told you that?'

'Yes. It's why I agreed to all of this.'

'He had his reasons. And I have to think.'

'There's no time to *think*. We have to act, we have to *do* something! Time's running out!'

'To be sure, but we cannot do the wrong thing, can we?'

'Converse said you had access to powerful people in Washington. I could trust you to reach them.'

'But you've just told me I don't know whom to trust, isn't that right?'

'Oh, *Christ!*'

'A lovely and inspired prophet.' Simon looked at his watch as he gathered up the papers and rose from the chair. 'It's two-thirty in the morning, Mr Stone, and this weary body has come to the end of its endurance. I'll be in touch with you later in the day. Don't try to reach me. I'll be in touch.'

'In *touch?* The package from Converse is on its way here. I'm picking it up at Kennedy Airport on the Geneva flight at 2.45 this afternoon. He wants you to have it right away. *I* want you to have it!'

'You'll be at the airport?' asked the lawyer.

'Yes, meeting our courier. I'll be back here by four or four-thirty depending on when the plane gets in and traffic, of course.'

'No, don't do that, Mr Stone, stay at the airport. I'll want everything Joel has compiled for us in my hands as soon as possible, of course. As there is a courier from Geneva, you may be the courier from New York.'

'Where are you going? Washington?'

'Perhaps, perhaps not. At this moment I'm going home to my apartment to think. Also I hope to sleep, which is doubtful. Give me a name I can use to have you paged at the airport.'

Johnny Reb sat low in the small boat, the motor idling, the waves slapping the sides of the shallow hull in the darkness. He was dressed in black trousers, a black turtleneck sweater and a black knit hat, and he was as close as he dared drift into the south-west coast of the island of Scharhörn. He had spotted the bobbing green glows of the series of buoys the first night; they were trip lights, beams intersecting each other above the water, ringing the approach to the old U-boat base. They formed an impenetrable, unseen wall – to penetrate it would set off alarms. This was the third night and he began to feel vindicated.

Trust the gut, trust the stomach and the bile that crept up into the mouth. The bellies of the old-time whores of the community knew when things were going to happen – partly out of dread, partly because a score was near that would enlarge an account in Bern. There was no account in the offing now, of course, only a succession of outlays to pay back a considerable debt, but there was a score to be made. Against the Delavanes and the Washburns, and those German and French and Jewish catfish who would sweep the ponds and make it impossible for gentlemen like Johnny Reb to make a high-hog living. He didn't know much about the South African, except that those nigger-haters had better-the-hell wise up. The coloureds were coming along just fine and that was fine by Johnny; his current girlfriend was a lovely black singer from Tallahassee, who just happened to be in Switzerland for silly reasons involving a little cocaine – and a good-sized account in Bern.

But the other catfish were *bad. Real* bad. Johnny Reb had it in for men who would make it jailhouse for people to think the way they wanted to. *No sir*, those people had to go!

Johnny Reb was very seriously committed to that proposition.

It was happening! He focused his infra-red binoculars on the old concrete piers of the sub base. It was also flat-out crazy! The seventy-foot motor launch had pulled into a dock, and moving out on the pier was a long, double line of men – 40, 60, 80 . . . nearly 100 – preparing to board. What was crazy was the way they were dressed. Dark suits and conservative summer jackets and ties; a number wore hats and every damned one of them carried luggage and a *briefcase*. They looked like a convention of bankers or a parade of lace-pants from the diplomatic corps. *Or*, thought The Rebel as he inched his binoculars backward along the line of passengers, ordinary businessmen, middle to upper-level management – nothing really out of the ordinary – men seen every day standing on railroad platforms and getting out of taxis and flying in planes. It was the very ordinariness of their collective appearance compared to the exotically macabre dark outlines of the old U-boat refuelling station that gnawed at Johnny's imagination. These men could go unnoticed almost anywhere yet they did not *come* from anywhere. They came from Scharhörn; they came from what was undoubtedly a highly sophisticated cell of this multinational military collusion that could put the goddamned catfish generals in the catbird seats. Ordinary people going wherever they were ordered to go – looking like everyone else, behaving like everyone else, their attaché cases open on planes and trains; reading company reports, sipping drinks but not too many, an occasional paperback novel permitted to ease the strain of business – *going wherever they were ordered to go*.

That was it, thought The Rebel, as he lowered the binoculars. *That was it!* These were the *hit teams!* The stomach never lied; the bile was sent up for a reason, its acrid sickening taste an ugly alarm that came to those privileged enough to have survived. Johnny Reb turned and fingered the motor, cautiously pushing the rudder to the right and inching the throttle forward. The small boat spun in the water and the rogue intelligence officer – former intelligence officer – headed back to his berth in Cuxhaven, accelerating the engine with each fifty feet of distance.

Twenty-five minutes later he pulled into the slip, lashed the lines to the cleats, grabbed his small waterproof case, and with effort climbed up onto the pier. He had to move quickly, but very, *very* cautiously. He knew vaguely the area of the Cuxhaven waterfront where the motor launch would return for he had watched the lights of the vessel as it bobbed its way out of the harbour toward the island. Once in the vicinity he could determine the specific dock as the boat headed into port, and then he would have only minutes to scout the area and get into position. Carrying his unmarked waterproof case, he hurried to the base of the pier and turned left, walking rapidly through the shadows toward the area from which he judged the launch had departed. He passed a huge warehouse and reached an open space beyond; there were five short piers, one after the other, extending no more than two hundred feet out into the water. It was dockage for small and medium-sized craft; several trawlers and a few antiquated pleasure boats, long past their primes, were lashed to the pilings on each of the piers except one. The fourth pier was empty. The Rebel knew it belonged to the launch; he could taste the bitterness in his mouth. He started out across the space; he would find a place to conceal himself.

'Halt – *Stehenbleiben!*' shot out the guttural command, as a man walked out of the darkness from around the hull of a trawler at the third pier. '*Was machen Sie hier? Wer sind Sie?*'

Johnny Reb knew when to use his age; he stooped his shoulders and extended his head slightly forward, lowering his neck. '*Passen Sie auf diese alten Kästen?*' he asked, continuing in German. 'I'm a fisherman on one of these relics and I lost my billfold this afternoon. Is it a crime to look for it?'

'Come back later, old man. You can't look for it now.'

'*Eh?* What?' The Rebel raised his right hand to his ear, twisting the ring on his middle finger as he did so and pressing a catch on the band. 'My hearing's not what it was, Mr Watchman. What did you say?'

The man stepped forward, first looking out at the water, as the sound of a powerful engine was heard in the distance. 'Get out of here!' he shouted, his lips close to Johnny's ear. '*Now!*'

'Good heavens, you're Hans!'

'Who?'

'*Hans!* It's so good to *see* you!' The Rebel slapped his hand around the German's neck, prelude to an affectionate embrace – and plunged the surface of his ring into the man's flesh, the needle firmly, deeply embedded.

'Get your hands off me, you stinking old man! My name's not Hans and I never saw you before. Get out of here or I'll put a . . . a bullet . . . in your . . . *head!*' The German's hand plunged inside his jacket but did not come out. Instead the man collapsed.

'You younger catfish really ought to have more respect for your elders,' mumbled Johnny, as he dragged the unconscious body into the shadows to the left of the trawler on the third pier. 'Cause you don't know the flies we use. Your daddys do, but you little pricks don't. And I *want* your daddys, those mind-suckers!'

The Rebel climbed aboard the trawler and dashed across the deck to the gunrail. The motor launch was heading directly into the fourth pier. He opened his waterproof case, into which he had snapped the binoculars in place, and adjusted his eyes to the dim light, studying the tools of his trade. He unlatched a camera and then a lens, a Zeiss Icon telescopic, developed by conscientious Germans during World War II for photographing Allied installations at night; it was the best. He inserted it into the lens mount, locking it into position, and switched on the camera's motor, noting with satisfaction that the battery was at full capacity, but then he knew it would be. He had been too long in the deadly game to make amateurish mistakes.

The huge motor launch slid into the pier like a mammoth black whale, a killer whale. The lines were secured, and as the passengers disembarked, Johnny Reb began taking pictures.

'Honeychile, this is Tatiana. I've got to reach my boy.'

'The Algonquin Hotel in New York City,' said the calm female voice. 'The number is Area Code two-one-two, eight-four-zero, six-eight-zero-zero. Ask for Peter Marcus.'

'Subtle son of a bitch, isn't he?' said Johnny Reb. 'Pardon my language, mam.'

'I've heard it before, Rebel. This is Anne.'

'*Goddamn*, little lady, why didn't you tell me *before!* How *are* you, sweet child?'

'Doing fine in my dotage, Johnny. I'm out, you know. This is just a courtesy for an old friend.'

'An old *friend*? Fair girl, if it wasn't for Petey, I'd have made one hell of a play for you!'

'You should have, Reb. I wasn't in his cards, his terribly important cards. And you were one of the nicest – a little more subterranean than most but a nice person. What was it? "Gentleman Johnny Reb"?'

'I've always tried to keep up appearances, Annie. May I request the privilege of calling you one day, if we ever get out of this mess?'

'I don't know what the mess is, Reb, but I do know you have my telephone number.'

'You give me heart, fair girl!'

'We're older now, Johnny, but I guess you wouldn't understand that.'

'Never, child. Never.'

'Stay well, Reb. You're too good to lose.'

The operator at the Algonquin Hotel was adamant. 'I'm sorry, sir. Mr Marcus is not in his room and does not answer the page.'

'I'll call back,' said The Rebel.

'Sorry sir. There's no answer from Mr Marcus' room and no response to the page.'

'I believe we spoke several hours ago, sir. There's still no answer from Mr Marcus' room so I took the liberty of calling the desk. He hasn't checked out and he didn't list an alternate number. Why not leave a message?'

'I believe I will. As follows, please. "Stay put until I reach you. Or you reach me. Imperative. Signed, Z. Tatiana." That's TATIA . . .'

'Yes, sir. Thank you, sir. "Z", sir?'

'As in zero, miss.' Johnny Reb hung up the phone in the flat in Cuxhaven. The taste in his mouth was overpoweringly sour.

Erich Leifhelm entertained his luncheon guests at his favourite table at the Ambassador restaurant on the eighteenth floor of the Steigenberger Hotel in Bonn. The huge, elegant room had a magnificent view of the city and the river and the mountains beyond, and this particular table was positioned to take advantage of that view. It was a clear, bright, cloudless afternoon and the natural wonders of the northern Rhineland were there for the fortunate to observe: none could help but be touched or awed or both.

'I never tire of it,' said the former field marshal, addressing the three men at his table, gesturing with masculine grace at the enormous window behind him. 'I wanted you to see it before returning to Buenos Aires – indeed, one of the most beautiful cities in the world, I must add.'

The *maître d'hôtel* intruded with deference, bowing as he spoke softly to Leifhelm. '*Herr General*, there is a telephone call for you.'

'An aide is dining at Table fifty-five,' said Leifhelm casually, in spite of his racing pulse. Perhaps there was word of a priest in Strasbourg! 'I'm sure he can take it for me.'

'The gentleman on the line specifically requested that I speak with you personally. He said to tell you he was calling from California.'

'I see. Very well.' Leifhelm got out of his chair, apologizing to his guests. 'No surcease from the vagaries of commerce, is there? Forgive me, I shall only be a moment or two. Please, more wine.'

The *maître* nodded, adding, 'I've had the call put through to my private office, *Herr General*. It's right inside the foyer.'

'That pleases me. Thank you.'

Erich Leifhelm casually, even subtly, shook his head as he passed Table fifty-five near the entrance. The lone diner acknowledged the dismissal with a nod of his head. In all the years of strategies and tactics, military and political, that dismissal was among the field marshal's gravest errors.

Two men stood in the foyer, one looking at his watch, the other looking annoyed. By their expensive clothes they belonged to the Ambassador's clientele and were obviously waiting for late luncheon companions, probably their wives as they had not gone to their table. A third man stood outside the glass doors in the corridor; he was dressed in the maintenance uniform of the hotel and watched the two men inside.

Leifhelm thanked the *maître*, as the latter held the door open for the general to enter his modest office. The restaurateur closed the door and returned to the dining room. The two men – swiftly, as one – raced inside after the old soldier, who was at that moment picking up the telephone.

'*Was geht hier vor? Wer ist . . .* !'

The first man lunged across the desk, gripping Leifhelm's head, clamping the general's mouth with very strong hands. The second man pulled a hypodermic needle from his pocket and removed the rubber shield as he tore at Leifhelm's jacket, then the collar of his shirt. He plunged the needle into the base of the general's throat, released the serum, pulled out the syringe and immediately began massaging the flesh as he restored the collar and pulled the jacket in place.

'He'll be mobile for about five minutes,' said the doctor in German. 'But he can neither speak nor reason. His motor controls are now mechanical and have to be guided.'

'And after five minutes?' asked the first man.

'He collapses, probably vomiting.'

'A nice picture. Hurry! Get him up, *guide* him, for God's sake! I'll check outside and knock once.'

Seconds later the knock came and the doctor, with Leifhelm firmly in his grip, propelled the general out of the office and through the glass doors into the hotel corridor.

'This way!' ordered the third man in the maintenance uniform, heading to the right.

'*Quickly!*' added the doctor.

Among the strollers in the plush hallway and the diners heading for the restaurant, a number recognized the legendary old soldier, not a few staring at his pale, comatose face with the lips trembling, trying to speak. Or scream.

'The great man has had terrible news,' said the doctor reverentially and repeatedly. 'It's terrible, simply terrible!'

They reached a service elevator, which was on *hold*, and went inside. A stretcher on wheels stood against the padded back wall. The third man took a key from his pocket, inserted it in the *hold* lock releasing the controls, as he pressed the nonstop switch for the basement. The other two lifted Leifhelm up on the stretcher covering him with a sheet – covering all of him.

'They'll start talking up there,' said the first man. 'His bulls will come running. They're never far away.'

'The ambulance is downstairs now by the elevator door,' said the man in the maintenance uniform. 'The plane is waiting at the airfield.'

The once great field marshal of the Third Reich threw up under the sheet.

Jacques Louis Bertholdier let himself into the apartment on the Boulevard Montaigne and removed his woven silk jacket, throwing it on a chair. He walked over to the mirrored bar against the wall, poured a vodka, threw in two cubes of ice from a sterling silver bucket, and strolled to the window beyond the elegantly upholstered couch. The tree-lined Montaigne was so peaceful at mid-afternoon, so spotlessly clean, and somehow so pastoral although very much part of the city. There were times when he thought it was the essence of the Paris he loved, the Paris of influence and wealth, whose inhabitants never had to soil their hands. It was why he had purchased the extravagant flat and installed his most extravagant and desirable mistress. He needed her now. My *God*, how he needed release!

The *Légionnaire* shot and garrotted in his own automobile! In the parking lot of the Bois de Boulogne! And Prudhomme, the filthy bureaucrat, supposedly in Calais! No fingerprints! *Nothing*! The once and foremost general of France needed an hour or so of tranquillity, of – release.

'*Elise*! Where *are* you? Come out, Egyptian! I trust you're wearing what I instructed you to wear. If you need reminding, it's the short black Givenchy, nothing underneath, you understand! Absolutely *nothing*.'

'Of course, my general,' came the words, strangely hesitant, from behind the bedroom door.

Bertholdier laughed silently to himself as he turned and walked back to the couch. *Le Grand Timon* was still an event to be reckoned with, even by highly sexual twenty-five year olds who loved money and fast cars and elegant apartments as much as they adored having their bodies penetrated. Well, he was too upset to disrobe, his nerves too frayed to go through any prolonged nonsense. He had something else in mind – release without effort.

The sound of the turning knob broke off his thoughts. The door opened and the raven-haired girl emerged, her elongated, perfectly proportioned face set in anticipation, her brown eyes wide in a distant wonder. Perhaps she had been smoking marijuana, thought Bertholdier. She was dressed in a short negligee of black lace, her breasts circled like diadems in grey, her hips revolving in sexual provocation as she approached the couch.

'Exquisite, you whore of the Nile. Sit down. It's been a dreadful day, a *horrible* day and it is not over. My driver will return in two hours and until then I need rest – and release. Give it to me, Egyptian.' Bertholdier zipped down the fly of his trousers and reached for the girl. 'Fondle it, as I will fondle you, and then do what you can do.' He grabbed her breasts, forcing her, pulling her head down into his groin. 'Now. *Now*. *Do* it!'

A blinding flash filled the room as two men walked out of the bedroom. The girl sprang back into the couch, as Bertholdier looked up in shock. The man in front put the camera in his pocket, as his companion, a short, middle-aged heavy-set man with a gun in his hand, walked slowly toward the legend of France.

'I admire your taste, General,' he said in a gruff voice. 'But then, I suppose I've always admired you, even when I disagreed with you. You don't remember me, but you court-martialled me in Algiers, sending me to the stockade for thirty-six months because I struck an officer. I was a sergeant-major and he had brutally abused my men with excessive penalties over minor offences. Three years for hitting a Paris-tailored pig. Three years in those filthy barracks for taking care of my men.'

'Sergeant-Major LeFevre,' said Bertholdier with authority, calmly replacing his pants and zipping up his fly. 'I remember. I never forget. You were guilty of treasonable conduct: assaulting an officer. I should have had you shot.'

'There were moments during those three years when I would have welcomed the execution, Monsieur. But I'm not here to discuss Algiers – it's when I knew you were all crazy. I'm here to tell you you're coming with me. You'll be returned unharmed to Paris in several days.'

'Preposterous!' spat out the general. 'You think your weapon frightens me?'

'No, it's merely to protect myself from you, from the last gesture of a brave and famous soldier. I know you too well to think that threats of bodily harm, or even death, could move you. I have another persuasion, however, one you've just made quite irresistible.' The ex-sergeant-major withdrew a second, odd-shaped gun from his pocket. 'This weapon does not hold bullets, instead it fires darts containing a chemical that accelerates the heart to bursting point. My thoughts were to threaten you with fielding the photograph after your death, showing that the great general died ignominiously at what he did best. Now, perhaps, there is another approach. The angle was advantageous for certain, expert brushwork – your position and the expression on your face would not be touched, of course – but your companion might easily become a *he* rather than a she, a little boy rather than a girl . . . There were rumours of your excesses once, and a hastily arranged marriage few could understand. Was this the secret *Le Grand Timon* ran from all his life? Was it the threat the great de Gaulle held over the head of his popular but all too ambitious and rebellious colonel? That the appetites of this pretender, this would-be successor, were so extensive they included anything he could get his hands on, his body on, the gender making no difference. Small boys when there were no women. The whispers of corrupted young lieutenants and captains, of rapes, conveniently called interrogations in your quarters . . .'

'*Enough!*' cried Bertholdier, shooting up from the couch. 'Further conversation is pointless. Regardless of how absurd and unfounded I will not permit my name to be dragged through filth! I want that film!'

'My God, it's true,' said the ex-infantry sergeant. 'All of it.'

'The *film!*' shouted the general. 'Give it to me!'

'You shall have it,' replied LeFevre. 'On the plane.'

Chaim Yakov Abrahms walked with a bowed head out of the *Ihud Shivat Zion* synagogue on the Ben Yehuda in Tel Aviv. The solemn crowds outside formed two deep flanks of devoted followers, men and women who wept openly at the terrible suffering this great man, this patriot-soldier of Israel, had been forced to endure at the hands of his wife. *Hitabdut*, they spoke in hushed voices. *Ebude Atzmo*, they said to one another, cupping mouths to ears, out of Chaim's hearing. The rabbis would not relent; the sins of a despicable woman were visited upon this son of Sabras, this fierce child of

Abraham, this biblical warrior who loved the land and the Talmud with equal fervour. The woman had been refused burial in a holy place; she was to remain outside the gates of the *beht Hakvahroht*, her soul left to struggle with the wrath of Almighty God, the pain of that knowledge an unbearable burden for the one left behind.

It was said she did it out of vengeance and a diseased mind. She had her daughters. It was the father's son – always the *father's* son – who had been slain on the father's battlefield. Who would weep more, who *could* weep more, or be in greater anguish than the father? And now this, the further agony of knowing that the woman he had given his life to had most heinously violated God's Talmud. The shame of it, the *shame*! Oh, Chaim, our brother, father, son and leader, we weep with you. For you! Tell us what to do and we will do it. You are our *king*! King of Eretz Israel, of Judea and Samaria, and all the lands you seek for your protection! Show us the way and we shall follow you, oh *King*!

'She's done more for him in death than she could ever do alive,' said a man on the outskirts of the crowd and not part of it.

'What do you think really happened?' asked the man's companion.

'An accident. Or worse, far worse. She came to our temple frequently and I can tell you this. She never would have considered *Hitabdut* . . . We must watch him carefully before these fools and thousands like them crown him emperor of the Mediterranean and he marches us to oblivion.'

An Army staff car, two flags of blue and white on either side of the hood, made its way up the street to the kerb in front of the synagogue. Abrahms, wearing his bereavement like a heavy mantle of sorrow only his strength could endure, bowing his lowered head to the crowds, his eyes opening and closing, his hands reaching out to touch and be touched, listened to the words of a young soldier at his side.

'Your car, General.'

'Thank you, my son,' said the legend of Israel, as he climbed inside and sank back in the seat, his eyes shut in anguish. Weeping faces pressed against the windows. The door closed and when he spoke, his eyes still closed, there was anything but anguish in his harsh voice. 'Get me *out* of here! Take me to my cottage in the country. We'll all have whisky and forget this *crap*. Holy rabbinical bastards! They had the temerity to *lecture* me! The next war, I'll call up the rabbis and put those Talmudic chicken-shits in the front lines! Let them lecture while the shrapnel flies up their asses!'

No one spoke as the car gathered speed and left the crowds behind. Moments later Chaim opened his eyes and pulled his thick back from the seat; he stretched his barrel-chested frame and reclined again in a more comfortable – less anguished – position. Then slowly, as if aware of the stares of the two soldiers beside him, he looked at both men, his head whipping back and forth.

'Who *are* you?!' he shouted. 'You're not my men, not my *aides*!'

'They'll wake up in an hour or so,' said the man in the front seat beside the driver. He turned facing Abrahms. 'Good afternoon, General.'

'You!'

'Yes, it is I, Chaim. Your goons couldn't stop me from testifying before the Lebanon Tribunal and nothing on earth could stop me from what I'm doing today. I told about the slaughter of women and children and quivering old men as they pleaded for their lives and watched you laugh. You call yourself a Jew? You can't begin to understand. You're just a man filled with hate, and I don't care for you to claim to be any part of what I am or what I believe. You're shit, Abrahms. But you'll be brought back to Tel Aviv in several days.'

One by one the planes landed, the propeller-driven aircraft from Bonn and Paris having flown at low altitudes, the jet from Israel, a Dassault-Bruguet Mystere 10/100, dropping swiftly from 28,000 feet to the private airfield at St Gervais. And as each taxied to a stop at the end of the runway, the same dark blue sedan waited to drive the 'guest' and his escort to an Alpine château fifteen miles east in the mountains. It had been rented for two weeks from a real estate firm in Chamonix.

The arrivals had been scheduled carefully, as none of the three visitors was to know the others were there. The planes from Bonn and Paris landed at 4.30 and 5.45 respectively, the jet from the Mediterranean nearly three hours later at 8.27. And to each stunned guest, Joel Converse said the identical words.

'As I was offered hospitality in Bonn, I offer you mine here. Your accommodation will be better than I was given, although I doubt the food will be as good. However, I know one thing – your departure will be far less dramatic than mine.'

But not your stay, thought Converse, as he spoke to each man. *Not your stay*. It was part of the plan.

38

The first light floated up into the dark sky above the trees in Central Park. Nathan Simon sat in his study and watched the new day's arrival from the large, soft leather chair facing the huge window. It was his thinking-seat, as he called it. Recently he had used it as much for dozing as for thought. But there were no brief interludes of sleep tonight – this morning. His mind was on fire; he had to explore and re-explore the options, stretching the limits of his perceptions of the dangers within each. To choose the wrong one would send out alarms that would force the generals to act immediately, and once underway, events would swiftly race out of control, the control of events solely in the hands of the generals – everywhere. Of course, they might start within hours quite by themselves but Nathan did not think so; the generals were not fools. All chaos had its visual beginnings, the initial turbulence that gave rise to the credibility of violence. If nothing else, confusion had to be established as the players moved into place without being seen. Abstractions, yes, but that was where ideas began, and the concept of military control over governments was a time-worn idea since the age of the Pharaohs. It bore early fruit in Peloponnisos and Sparta's conquest of

Athens, later with the Caesars, and later still, was capitalized on by the emperors of the Holy Roman Empire, then exercised by the Renaissance princes and finally brought to totality by the Soviets and the Germans in the twentieth century. Unrest preceded violence and violence preceded takeover, whether it was a revolution entailing hundreds of thousands of oppressed Russians or the strangling inequities of a Versailles Treaty.

Therein lay the weakness of the generals' strategy: The unrest had to exist before the violence erupted. The people – ordinary hordes of people – had to be worked into a frenzy, but for that to happen the hordes had to be there in the first place. That would be the sign, the prelude as it were, but where; *when*? And what could he do, what moves could he make that would escape the attention of Delavane's informers? He was an employer and friend of Joel Converse, the 'psychopathic assassin' the generals had created. He had to presume he was being watched – at the very least any overt action he took would be scrutinized and if he became suspect he would be thwarted. His life was immaterial. In a sense he was trapped, as he and frightened, frustrated multitudes like him had been trapped on the beaches of Anzio, realizing there was a degree of safety in the foxholes behind the dunes, knowing that to rise out of them was to face screaming, unending barrages of bullets. Yet knowing, too, nothing was accomplished if they remained where they were, only more and more lives lost with each burst of mortar fire.

Contrary to what he had told Peter Stone, Nathan knew precisely whom he had to see – not one man, but three. The President, the Speaker of the House, and the Attorney General. The apex of the Executive, the leader of the Legislative, and the nation's chief law enforcement officer. He would see no one less and it was far more advantageous to see them all together rather than individually. In either case, he had to see them and that was his dilemma; it was the trap. One did not simply pick up a telephone and make appointments with such men. There were procedures, formalities, and screening processes to ensure the validity of the requests; men with their responsibilities could not waste time. The trap. As soon as his name was mentioned, the word would go out. Delavane himself would know within a matter of hours, if not minutes.

Despite Joel's gratuitous and highly dubious statements to Peter Stone, it was not easy to reach powerful government figures, any more than it was logical to have a judge issue a court order under-seal that somehow miraculously, *legally*, guaranteed extraordinary protection for those same people without informing the entire security apparatus as to why the protection was deemed vital. Ridiculous! Such court orders were reasonable where intimidated witnesses were concerned before a criminal trial and even afterwards in terms of fabricated rehabilitation, but that process hardly applied to the White House, the Congress, or the Justice Department. Joel had taken a legal manoeuvre, ballooned it way out of probability, and scaled it up into orbit – for a reason, of course. Stone and his colleagues had provided depositions. And yet, thought Simon, there was an odd logic in Converse's misapplied exaggerations. Not in any way Joel had considered but as a means to reach these men. 'A court, a single judge . . .' Converse had said to Stone. That was the logic, the rest was nonsense. *The Supreme*

Court, a justice of that court. Not a request from one Nathan Simon who would have to be screened, if only in terms of content not character, but an urgent message to the President from a venerated justice of the *Supreme Court!* No one would dare question such a man if he pronounced his business to be between the President and himself. Presidents were far more solicitous of the Court than of Congress and with good reason. The latter was a political battleground, and the former an arena of moral judgment, and no one lived his life in a deep freeze, not even – perhaps especially – presidents. And Nathan Simon knew the man he could call *and* see, a Justice in his late seventies. The Court was not in session, October was a month away. He was somewhere in New England, his private number was at the office.

Nathan blinked, then brought his hand up to shield his eyes. For a brief moment, the fireball of the early sun had careened a blinding ray through a geometric maze of glass and steel across the park and entered his window before being blocked by a distant building. And suddenly, at that instant of blindness, he was given the answer to the terrifying question of *where* and *when* – the unrest that had to be the prelude for the eruption of violence. There was scheduled throughout Free Europe, Great Britain, Canada and the United States, an internationally coordinated week-long series of anti-nuclear protests. Millions of concerned, frightened people joining hands and snarling up traffic in the streets of the major cities and capitals, making their voices heard at the expense of normality. Rallies were to be held in the parks and in the squares and in front of government buildings. Politicians and statesmen, perceiving as always the power of ground swells, had promised to address huge crowds everywhere – in Paris and Bonn, Rome and Madrid, Brussels and London – Toronto, Ottawa, New York and Washington. And again, as always, these moulders and benefactors, these sincere advocates and posturing sycophants of the bodies politic would blame the lack of arms control progress on the intransigence of evil adversaries, never their own deficiencies. The genuine and the phony walked hand in hand across podiums, none sure of the other's stripes.

Crowds everywhere, espousing deeply-felt, deeply-divisive issues, pitting the believers of universal restraint against pockets of those who sincerely believed in the raw power of excessive strength, and the latter would surely be heard. No one thought the massive demonstrations would be without incidents . . . yet how far might these minor confrontations escalate if the incidents themselves were massive? Units of terrorist fanatics financed anonymously, persuaded to infiltrate and savagely disrupt so as to get their message across, messages of real and imagined grievances having nothing to do with the protests, creating chaos primarily because the crowds were not of their world or their fevers. The crowds – everywhere. *These* were the hordes of people who could be galvanized by sudden violence and worked into multiple frenzies! It was the prelude. Everywhere.

The demonstrations were scheduled to begin in three days.

Peter Stone walked down the wide dirt path toward the lake behind the A-frame house somewhere in lower New Hampshire – he did not know precisely where, only that it was twenty minutes from the airport. It was close to dusk, the end of a day filled with surprises and apparently it was not over – they were not over, the surprises. Ten hours ago, in his room at the Algonquin, he had called Swissair to see if the flight from Geneva was on schedule, only to be told it was thirty-four minutes ahead of schedule and, barring landing delays, was expected a half hour early. It was the first surprise and inconsequential; the second was not. He had arrived at Kennedy shortly before 2 o'clock and within a few minutes he heard the page over the public address system for a 'Mr Lackland', the name he had given Nathan Simon.

'Take Pilgrim Airlines to Manchester, New Hampshire,' the lawyer had said. 'There's a reservation for Mr Lackland on the 3.15 plane. Can you make it?'

'Easily. The flight from Geneva's early. I assume that's LaGuardia?'

'Yes. You'll be met in Manchester by a man with red hair. I've described you to him. See you around five-thirty.'

Manchester, New Hampshire? Stone had been so sure Simon would ask him to fly to Washington he had not even bothered to put a toothbrush in his pocket. Surprise number Two.

Surprise number Three was the courier from Geneva. A prim, gaunt Englishwoman with a face of pale granite and the most uncommunicative pair of eyes he had seen outside of Dzerzhinsky Square. As arranged, she had met him in front of the Swissair Lounge, a copy of *The Economist* in her left hand. After studying the wrong side of his out-of-date government identification, she had given him the attaché case and made the following statement – in British high dudgeon.

'I don't like New York, I never have. I don't like flying either, but everyone's been so lovely and it's better to get the whole whack-a-doo over all at once, righto? They've arranged for me to take the next plane back to Geneva. I miss my mountains. They need me and I do try to give them my *very* all, righto?'

With that obtuse information she smiled wanly and turned, somewhat oddly, and started back toward the escalator. It was then that Stone began to understand. The woman's eyes were not uncommunicative, the whole person was. She was drunk – or, perhaps, pickled – having overcome her fear of flying with liquid courage. Converse had a strange concept of couriers, Stone had thought, instantly changing his mind. Who could be less suspect?

The fourth surprise came at the Manchester airport. An ebullient, middle-aged red-headed man had greeted him as though they were long-lost fraternity brothers from some mid-western university in the late 'thirties when such fraternal ties were deemed far deeper than blood. He was positively effusive to the point where Stone was not only embarrassed by the display of camaraderie, but seriously concerned that unwarranted attention would be drawn to them. But once in the parking lot, the red-head had suddenly slammed him into the doorframe of the car and shoved the barrel of a gun into the back of his neck while the man's free hand stabbed his clothes for a weapon.

'I wouldn't take the risk of going through metal detectors with a gun, *damn* it!' protested the ex-CIA agent.

'Just making sure, spook. I've dealt with you assholes, you think you're something else. Me, I was Federal.'

'Which explains a great deal,' said Stone, meaning it.

'You drive.'

'Is that a question or an order?'

'An order. All spooks drive,' replied the red-head.

Surprise number Five came in the car, as Stone took the sudden turns commanded by the red-headed man who casually replaced the gun in his jacket holster.

'Sorry about the horseshit,' he said in a voice far less hostile than in the parking lot, but nowhere near the false ebullience in the terminal. 'I had to be careful, piss you off, see where you stood, you know what I mean? And I was never Federal – I hated those turkeys. They always wanted you to know they were better than you were just because they came from DC. I was a cop in Cleveland, name's Gary Frazier. How are you?'

'Somewhat more comfortable,' Stone had said. 'Where are we going?'

'Sorry, pal. If he wants you to know, he'll tell you.'

Surprise number Six awaited Stone when he drove the car up through the New Hampshire hills to an isloated house of wood and glass, surrounded by forests, the structure an inverted *V*, two narrowing storeys looking out in all directions on woods and water. Nathan Simon had walked down the stone steps from the front door.

'You've brought it?' he asked.

'Here it is,' said Stone, handing the attaché case to the lawyer through the open window. 'Where are we? Who are you seeing?'

'It's a very unlisted residence, but if everything is in order we'll call you. There are guest quarters attached to the boathouse down at the lake. Why not freshen up after your trip? The driver will point the way. If we need you for anything, we'll ring you on the phone. It's a separate number from the house, so just pick it up.'

And now Peter Stone was walking down the wide dirt path that led to the boathouse by the lake, aware that eyes were following him. Surprise number Seven: He had no idea where he was and Simon wasn't going to tell him unless 'everything was in order', whatever that meant.

The guest quarters alluded to by the attorney was a three-room cottage on the edge of the lake with an entrance to the adjacent boathouse, in which was berthed a small sleek motor boat and a nondescript catamaran that looked more like a raft with two canvas seats and fishing equipment for drift trawling. Stone wandered about trying to find some clue as to the owner's identity but there was nothing. Even the names on the boats were meaningless, but not lacking in humour. The cumbersome, raftlike sailcraft was named *Hawk*, while the aggressive-looking little speedboat was *Dove*.

The former deep cover intelligence officer sat on the porch and looked out at the peaceful waters of the lake and the rolling, darkening green hills of New Hampshire. Everything *was* peaceful. The cries of the loons were cushioned french horns proclaiming the permanence of tranquillity in this special place. But Stone's insides were not peaceful; his stomach churned and he remembered what Johnny Reb used to say in the field. 'Trust the

stomach, Br'er Rabbit, trust the bile. They never lie.' He wondered what
The Rebel was doing, what he was learning.

The phone rang, a strident, unnerving porch bell accompanying the softer
ring from inside the cottage. As if jolted by an electric prod, Stone sprang
from the chair, swung back the door and walked rapidly across the room to
the telephone.

'Come up to the house, please,' said Nathan Simon; adding, 'if you were
out on the porch, I apologize for not telling you about that damned bell.'

'I accept your apology. I was.'

'It's for guests who expect calls and may be out in one of the boats.'

'The loons are quiet. I'll be right there.'

Stone walked up the dirt path and saw the lawyer standing by a screen
door that was the lake entrance to the house; it was on a patio reached by
curving brick steps. He started climbing, prepared for surprise number
Eight.

Supreme Court Justice Andrew Wellfleet, his thinning unkempt white
hair falling in strands over his wide forehead, sat behind the large desk in
his library. Converse's thick affidavit was in front of him and a floor lamp
on his left threw light down on the pages. It was several moments before he
looked up and removed his steel-rimmed glasses; his eyes were not pleasant.
They were stern and disapproving, matching the nickname given him over
two decades ago when he was summoned to the Court. 'Irascible Andy' was
the sobriquet the clerks had assigned to him, but temperament notwithstanding, no one ever questioned his awesome intelligence, his fairness, or his
devotion to the law. All things considered, surprise number Eight was as
welcome a shock as Stone could imagine.

'Have you read this?' asked Wellfleet, offering neither his hand nor a
chair.

'Yes, sir,' replied Stone. 'On the plane. It's essentially what he told me
over the phone, in far greater detail of course. The affidavit from the
Frenchman, Prudhomme, was a bonus. It tells us how they operate – how
they're *capable* of operating.'

'And what in hell did you think you were going to do with all of this?' The
elderly Justice waved his hand over the desk on which were scattered the
other affidavits. 'Petition the courts here and in Europe to please, if they'd
be so kind, to issue injunctions restricting the activities of all military
personnel above a certain rank on the conceivable possibility that they may
be part of this?'

'I'm not a lawyer, sir, the courts never entered my mind. But I did think
that once we had Converse's own words – along with what we knew – they'd
be sufficient to reach the right people in the highest places who *could* do
something. Obviously Converse thought the same thing insofar as he called
in Mr Simon and, if you'll forgive me, Mr Justice, you're reading it all now.'

'It isn't enough,' said the Supreme Court Justice. 'And damn the courts,
I shouldn't have to tell you that, Mr Former CIA Man. You need names, a
lot more names, not just five generals, three of whom are retired and one of
them, the so-called instigator, a man who had an operation several months
ago that left him without legs.'

'Delavane?' asked Simon, stepping away from the window.

'That's right,' said Wellfleet. 'Kind of pathetic, huh? Not exactly the picture of a very imposing threat, is he?'

'It could drive him into being an extraordinary threat.'

'I'm not denying that, Nate. I'm just looking at the collection you've got here. Abrahms? As anyone worth his kosher salt in Israel will tell you, he's a strutting, bombastic hothead – a brilliant soldier but with ten screws loose. Besides, his only real concerns are for Israel. Van Headmer? He's a relic of the nineteenth century, pretty fast with a hangman's rope but his voice doesn't mean doodly-shit outside South Africa.'

'Mr Justice,' said Stone, speaking more firmly than he had before. 'Are you implying that we're wrong? Because if you are, there are other names – and I don't just mean a couple of attachés at the embassy in Bonn – names of men who have been killed because they tried to find answers.'

'You weren't listening!' snapped back Wellfleet. 'I just told Nate I wasn't denying anything. How in hell could I? Forty-five *million* in untraceable, *illegal* exports! An apparatus that can shape the news media here and in Europe, that can corrupt government agencies, and as Nate here puts it, "create a psychopathic assassin" so that they can find *you*, or make you back *down*. Oh, no, Mister, I'm not saying you're wrong. I'm saying you better damn well do what I'm told you're pretty good at, and you'd better do it quickly. Haul in this Washburn and any others you can find in Bonn; pick a cross section of those people at State and the Pentagon and fill 'em full of dope or whatever the hell you use and get *names*! And if you ever mention that I suggested such wanton measures that violate our most sacred human rights, I'll say you're full of shit. Talk to Nate here. You don't have time for niceties, Mister.'

'We don't have the resources, either,' said Stone. 'As I explained to Mr Simon, there are a few friends I can call upon for information but nothing like you suggest – like what you didn't suggest. I simply don't have the leverage, the men or the equipment. I'm not even employed by the government any longer.'

'I can help you there.' Wellfleet made a note. 'You'll get whatever you need.'

'There's the other problem,' continued Stone. 'No matter how careful we are, we'd send out alarms. These people are *believers*, not just mindless extremists. They're orchestrated; they have lines of fall-backs and know exactly what they're doing. It's a progression, a logical capitalizing on sequences until we're all forced to accept them – or accept the unacceptable, the continuation of violence, of wholesale rioting, of the killing.'

'Very nice, Mister. And what are *you* going to do? *Nothing*?'

'Of course not. Rightly or wrongly I believed Converse when he told me that with our affidavits – with all the evidence we provided him – Mr Simon could reach people we couldn't reach. Why shouldn't I have believed him? It was an extension of my own thinking *without* a Nathan Simon but with Converse himself. Only my way would take longer. The precautions would be far more elaborate, but it *could* be done. We'd reach the right people and start the counter attack.'

'Who'd you have in mind?' asked Wellfleet sharply.

'The President first, obviously. Then because we're dealing with half a dozen other countries, the Secretary of State. A maximum security screening process would be set up immediately – one undoubtedly using those chemicals you didn't speak of – until we had unblemished personnel, men and women we were certain beyond doubt had no connections to this Aquitaine. We create cells, command posts here and abroad. Incidentally, there's a man who can help us immeasurably in this, a man named Belamy in Britain's MI6. I've worked with him and he's the best – knows the best – and he's done this sort of thing before. Once our cells are in place and in deep cover we then pull in Washburn and at least two others we know of by description in Bonn. Prudhomme can furnish us with the names of those in the *Sûreté* who approve transfers, and who furnished evidence against Converse when it didn't exist. And as you know from my own affidavit, we've got the island of Scharhörn under surveillance now – we think it's a nerve centre or a communications relay. With the proper equipment we could tap in. The whole point is we widen the circles of information. Once you know a strategy you can mount a counter-strategy without setting off alarms.' Stone paused and looked at both men. 'Mr Justice, Mr Simon. I *know* it can be done.'

'I don't doubt you,' said Nathan Simon. 'How long would it take?'

'If Justice Wellfleet can get me the cooperation and the equipment I need, with the people I select – here and abroad – Derek Belamy and I can mount a crash programme. We'd be operational in eight to ten days.'

Simon looked at the Supreme Court Justice then back at Stone. 'We don't have eight or ten days,' he said. 'We have three – less than three days now.'

Peter Stone stared at the tall, portly attorney with the sad, penetrating eyes. He could feel the blood draining from his face.

The cry of the cat was muted in fury. General George Marcus Delavane slowly replaced the telephone on the console. His half body was propped into the wheelchair, his waist strapped to the steel poles, his arms as heavy as his breath was short, the veins in his neck protruding. He brought his hands together, entwining his fingers and pressing his knuckles against each other until the surrounding flesh was white. He raised his large head, his cold, angry eyes narrowing up at the uniformed aide standing in front of the desk.

'They've disappeared,' he said, his high-pitched voice icily controlled. 'Leifhelm was taken from a restaurant in Bonn. They say there was an ambulance that raced away, no one knows where. Abrahms' guards were drugged. Others took their places. He was driven off in his own staff car, picked up in front of a synagogue. Bertholdier did not come down from his apartment on the Montaigne so the driver went up to discreetly remind him of the time. The woman was bound naked on the bed, the word "whore" written in lipstick across her breasts. She said two men took him away at gunpoint. There was talk of a plane, she said.'

'What about van Headmer?' asked the aide.

'Nothing. Our charming and oblivious Afrikaner dines at the Johannesburg Military Club and says he will put himself under extra guard. He's not part of the orbit; he's too far away to matter.'

'What do you mean, General? What happened?'

'What happened? This *Converse* happened! We created our own most accomplished enemy, Colonel – and I can't say we weren't warned. Chaim said it, our man in the Mossad made it clear. The North Vietnamese created a hellhound – the Mossad's words – and we created a monster. He should have been killed in Paris, certainly in Bonn.'

'You couldn't have ordered it then,' said the aide, shaking his head. 'You had to know where he came from and if you couldn't find out, you had to isolate him, make him – what was it? A pariah – so no one would come forth to claim him. It was sound strategy, General. It still remains sound. No one's come forth – no one's *coming* forth. You held them back and now it's too late.'

Delavane's eyes widened as he appraised the colonel's face. 'You've always been the best of adjutants, Paul. You tactfully remind a superior that, regardless of immediate set-backs, his decisions were based on sound reasons, and that those reasons will prevail.'

'I've disagreed when I thought it was necessary, General, because whatever I learned, I learned from you, so I merely reminded you of yourself. Right now, at this moment, I'm right. *You* were right.'

'Yes, I was – I am. Nothing matters now. Everything's set in motion and nothing can stop it. This Converse – this bold, resourceful enemy – was also held in check by having to keep running. And now *he's* too late. In any event, the men he's taken were merely symbols, magnets to attract others. That's the beauty of clean strategy, Colonel. Once it's set in motion, it rolls like the ocean wave. The power underneath is unseen but relentlessly propels it forward. Events will dictate the only acceptable solutions. It's my legacy, Colonel.'

Nathan Simon had nearly finished his explanation. It had taken less than three minutes, during which time Peter Stone remained motionless, his eyes riveted on the older man, his face ashen, the taste in his mouth unbearable.

'You can see the pattern, can't you?' concluded the attorney. 'The protests begin in the Middle East and follow the sun and the time zones across the Mediterranean, up through Europe, and over the Atlantic, culminating in Canada and the United States. They start with the *Peace Now* movement in Jerusalem, then Beirut, Rome, Paris, Bonn, London, Toronto, Washington, New York, Chicago, *et cetera*. Gigantic rallies in the major cities and capitals covering every nation and government Delavane and his people have infiltrated. Confrontations occur – the initial unrest – growing into major disruptions with the infusion of terrorist units. Bombs wired into cars, or under the streets in sewers, or simply rolled into the crowds – the second wave of greater violence – all leading to the mass confusion and disorder they require to put their leading players in position. Or more precisely, once in position to exercise their assignments.'

'The final assaults,' broke in Stone quietly. 'Selected assassinations.'

'Chaos,' agreed Simon. 'Men of awesome responsibilities suddenly dead, the descending mantles of authority unclear, too many men protesting, fighting one another, screaming that *they* are in charge. Total chaos.'

'*Scharhörn!*' said the middle-aged, former intelligence officer. 'We have no

choice now. We have to go in! May I use your telephone, Mr Justice?'
Without waiting for a reply Stone walked to Wellfleet's desk as he removed
his billfold and pulled out the small piece of paper with a number in
Cuxhaven, West Germany, written on it. He turned the phone around under
the harsh gaze of the Supreme Court Justice, picked it up and dialled. The
sequence of trans-Atlantic relays was intolerable. It rang.

'Rebel?' The explosive invective over the line from half a world away
could be heard throughout the library. Stone broke it off. '*Stop* it, Johnny! I
haven't been near the hotel in hours and I haven't time for this! . . . You
what?' The CIA man listened, his eyes growing wide, his breathing stopped.
He covered the mouthpiece and turned to Nathan Simon. 'My God, there's
a break-through!' he whispered. 'Photographs. Infra-red, taken last night
and developed this morning – all clear. Ninety-seven men from Scharhörn
getting off a boat, heading for the airport and train station. He thinks they're
the hit teams.'

'Get those photographs to Brussels and flown to Washington on the fastest
goddamned military transport you can find!' ordered the venerated Justice
of the Supreme Court.

39

'*Preposterous!*' shouted General Jacques Louis Bertholdier from the brocaded
wing chair in the spacious study of the Alpine château. 'I don't believe you
for a minute!'

'That's a favourite word of yours, isn't it?' said Converse, standing by the
open cathedral window across the room, the mountain fields beyond. He
was dressed in a dark suit, white shirt and a regimental tie, all purchased in
Chamonix. 'The word "preposterous", I mean,' he continued. 'You used it
at least twice when we spoke in Paris, I think. It's as though whoever
presents you with information you don't like is preposterous – absurd,
unwarranted – the person as well as the information. Is that the way you
look at people who don't accommodate you?'

'Certainly not! It is the way I treat liars.' The legend of France began to
rise. 'And I see no reason . . .'

'*Stay in that chair!*' Joel's voice was a sudden, sharp command. 'Or only
your corpse will get back to Paris,' he added simply, without hostility,
merely a clarification. 'I told you, all I wanted was this conversation with
you. It won't take long and then you'll be free to go. That's more charity
than any of you showed me.'

'You were expendable. I apologize for being so blunt but it is the truth.'

'If I was so expendable, why didn't you just kill me? Why the elaborate
build-up, all that trouble to make me a killer, an assassin, a man hunted all
over Europe.'

'The Jew gave us that.'

'The Jew? Chaim Abrahms?'

'It makes no difference now,' said Bertholdier. 'Our man in the Mossad – incidentally, a brilliant analyst – made it clear that if we could not find where you came from – if you yourself did not know – then we had to put you in "forbidden territory", I believe was the expression. And that was not preposterous. No one claims you. You were – you *are* – indeed, untouchable.'

'Why doesn't it make any difference now – the fact that you've told me what you presume I already know?'

'You've lost, Monsieur Converse.'

'I have?'

'Yes, and if you have delusions of drugging me – as we drugged you – let me spare you and me the discomfort of such procedures. I do not have the information. Actually, no one does. Only a machine that is set in motion and issues commands.'

'To other machines?'

'Of course not. To men – men who will do what they have been trained to do, who believe in what they're doing. I have no idea who they are.'

'That's the killing, isn't it? They're the killers.'

'All war is reduced to killing, young man. And make no mistake. This *is* war. The world has had enough. We will put it to rights, as the English say. You will see; we will not be opposed. We are not only needed, we are wanted.'

'"Accumulation . . . rapid acceleration", those were the words, weren't they?'

'The Jew was precipitous. He talks too much.'

'He says you're the pompous asshole of creation. He told me that he and van Headmer were going to put you in a glass room with little boys and girls and watch you screw yourself into a coronary.'

'His conversations were always tasteless . . . But no, I *don't* believe you.'

'So we're back to my original statement.' Joel walked away from the window and sat down in an armchair diagonally across from Bertholdier. 'Why do you find it so difficult to believe? Because you didn't think of it?'

'No, Monsieur. Because it's unthinkable.'

Converse pointed to a telephone on the desk. 'You know their private numbers,' he said. 'Call them. Call Leifhelm in Bonn and Abrahms in Tel Aviv. Also van Headmer, if you like, although I'm told he's in the States, probably California.'

'California?'

'Ask each if he came to see me at that little stone house on Leifhelm's property. Ask them what we talked about. Go on, the phone's right over there.'

Bertholdier looked sharply at the telephone as Joel held his breath. Then the soldier turned back to Converse, reluctance winning out over inclination. 'What are you trying to do? What sort of trick is this?'

'What trick? There's the phone. I can't rig it, I can't make it dial numbers or hire people hundreds or thousands of miles away to impersonate those men.'

The Frenchman looked again at the telephone. 'What could I say?' he asked quietly, more to himself than Joel.

'Try the truth. You're very big on truth, as you see it, as it pertains to large global concepts and this is only a small matter of several minor omissions. *They're* omitting to tell you that each one of them came to see *me*. Or perhaps they weren't so minor.'

'How would I know they came to see you?'

'You weren't listening to me. I said try the truth. I had you kidnapped, no one else. I did it because I didn't understand, and if push-comes-to-shove, I want to save my life. There's a huge world out there, General. Large parts of it you'll leave intact and I could live very nicely as long as I didn't have to worry about someone coming out of a doorway to blow my head off.'

'You're not the man I thought you were – we thought you were.'

'We're all what circumstances make us. I've had my share of sweat. I'm bowing out of the crusading business, or the lid-blowing business, or whatever you want to call it. Would you like to know why?'

'Very much so,' said Bertholdier, staring at Joel, confusion and curiosity fighting each other in his eyes.

'Because I listened to you in Bonn. Maybe you're right, or maybe I just don't care anymore because I was left way out in the cold. Maybe the world really does need you arrogant bastards right now.'

'It *does*! There's no other *way*!'

'It's the year of the generals then, isn't it?'

'No, not simply the *generals*! We are the consolidators, the symbols of strength and discipline and lawful order. Surely what follows in the aggregate – in the international market places, in joint foreign policies, and yes, in the legal processes themselves – will reflect our leadership, our example, and out of it all will come what is most lacking in today's world. *Stability*, Monsieur Converse! No more madmen like the senile Khomeini or the hollow braggard Gaddafi, or the insane Palestinians. Such men and such nations and would-be nations will be pincered by truly international forces, crushed by the overwhelming might of like-minded governments. Retribution will be swift and total. I am a military strategist of some reputation, so let me assure you the Russians will stand aside, appalled, not daring to interfere – knowing at last they cannot divide us any longer. They cannot rattle their sabres, frightening one segment while appeasing others, for we are all one!'

'Aquitaine,' said Joel softly.

'An adequate codename, yes,' agreed Bertholdier.

'You're as convincing as you were in Bonn,' added Converse. 'And maybe it could all work, but not this way, not with you people.'

'I beg your pardon?'

'Nobody has to divide *you* – you're already oceans apart.'

'I don't understand.'

'Place those calls, General. Make it easy on yourself. Reach Leifhelm first. Tell him you just heard from Abrahms in Tel Aviv and you're appalled. Say Abrahms wants to meet with you because he has information about me, that he admitted he and van Headmer came to see me alone in Bonn. You could add that *I* told Abrahms he and his Afrikaner friend were my second and third visitors. Leifhelm was the first.'

'Why would I tell him this?'

'Because you're angry as hell. No one told you about these separate meetings with me and you consider them highly improper – which, if you don't you damn well should. A little while ago you said I was expendable. Well, you're in for a shock, General.'

'Explain that!'

'No. Use the phone. Listen to what he says, how he reacts, how they all react. You'll know. See if I'm telling you the truth.'

Bertholdier placed both his hands on the arms of the brocaded chair and started to rise, his eyes on the telephone. Converse sat motionless, watching the Frenchman closely, barely breathing, his pulse racing. Suddenly, the general pushed himself violently back into the chair, pressing his spine into the fabric, his fingers now gripping the arms. 'All *right*!' he shouted. 'What was *said*? What did they *say*?'

'I think you should use that phone first.'

'Pointless!' snapped Bertholdier. 'As you say, you cannot make it dial other numbers – well, I suppose you could, but to what end? Impostors? Ridiculous! I could ask any of several hundred questions and know they were merely play-actors.'

'All the more reason to call them,' said Joel calmly. 'You'd know I was telling the truth.'

'And give an advantage where none was shown to *me*.'

Converse breathed normally again. 'It's up to you, General. I'm just looking for a safe way out.'

'Then tell me what was said to you.'

'Each asked me the obvious – as if he didn't trust the drugs or the one who administered them or each other. Whom did I really represent?' Joel paused; he was about to fish with a witness, but knew he had to pull back instantly if the pond was barren. 'I guess I mentioned Beale on Mykonos,' he offered hesitantly.

'You did,' confirmed the general. 'He was reached several months ago but our contact never returned. You explained that also.'

'You thought he might be one of you, didn't you?'

'We thought he threw away a brilliant military career out of disgust. Apparently it was a different disgust, the very weakness we abhorred. But these are not the things I want to hear. You made reference to some aspect of expendability. That is what I want to hear. *Now*.'

'You want it straight. Without the frills?'

'No frills, Monsieur.'

'Leifhelm said you'll be out in a matter of months, if not sooner. You give too many orders; the others are sick of them – and you want too much for France.'

'*Leifhelm*? The hypocritical *weasel* who sold his very soul to deny everything he espoused?! Who betrayed his leaders in the dock at Nuremberg, furnishing the court with all manner of evidence so as to worm his way into the Allies' *bowels*! Everywhere, whatever our commitments, we cringed! He brought dishonour on the most honourable profession in this world. Let me tell you, Monsieur, it is not *I* who will be out, it is *he*!'

'Abrahms said you were a sexual embarrassment,' continued Converse, as though Bertholdier's response was irrelevant. 'That was the phrase he used, "a sexual embarrassment". He mentioned the fact that there was a record – one he obtained, in fact – that spelled out a string of rapes, female and male, that were covered up by the French army because you were damned good at what you did. But then he asked the question. Could a bisexual opportunist, one who ravaged women at will and who sodomized young men and boys, who corrupted the word "interrogation" as well as whole sections of the officer corps, be truly considered the French leader of codename Aquitaine? He *also* said you wanted too many controls centred in your own government. But by the time there were such controls, you'd be gone.'

'*Gone?*' cried the Frenchman, his eyes once more on fire as they had been weeks ago in Paris, his postured body trembling with rage. 'Convicted by a *barbarian*, a smelly, uneducated *Jew?*'

'Van Headmer didn't go that far. He said you were simply too vulnerable . . .'

'Forget van Headmer!' roared Bertholdier. 'He's a fossil! He was courted solely on the basis that he might deliver raw materials. He's of no consequence.'

'I didn't think he was,' agreed Joel truthfully.

'But the strutting, foul-mouth Israeli thinks he can move against *me*? Let me tell you, Monsieur, I have been threatened before – by a great man – and nothing ever came of those threats because, as you put it, I was "damned good" at what I did. I *still* am! And there is another record, one of outstanding and brilliant service, that dwarfs any compilation of filthy rumours and barrack gossip. My record is unmatched by any in codename Aquitaine, and that includes the legless egomaniac in San Francisco. He believes it was all *his* idea! *Preposterous!* I refined it! He merely gave it a name based on a far-fetched reading of history.'

'He also got the ball started by exporting one hell of a lot of hardware,' interrupted Converse.

'Because it was *there*, Monsieur! And there were profits to be made!' The general paused, not finished, leaning forward in the chair. 'I will be frank with you. As with any élite corps of leadership, one man rises above the others by the sheer strength of his character and his mind. Beside me the others – all the others – pale into mediocrity. Delavane is a deformed, hysterical caricature. Leifhelm is a Nazi and Abrahms is a bombastic polarizer; alone he could set off waves of anti-semitism, the worst sort of symbol of leadership. When the tribunals rise out of the confusion and the panic they will look to me. I shall be the true leader of codename Aquitaine.'

Joel got out of the chair and walked back to the cathedral window, staring out at the mountain fields, feeling the soft breezes on his face. 'This examination is finished, General,' he said.

As if on cue the door opened and a former sergeant-major in the French army based in Algiers stood there waiting to escort the bewildered legend of France out of the room.

Chaim Abrahms sprang out of the brocaded chair, his barrel chest pressed against the seams of his black safari jacket. 'He said those things about *me*? About *himself?*'

'I told you before we got into any of this to use the phone,' broke in Converse, sitting across from the Israeli, a pistol on the newly set table beside his chair. 'Don't take my word for it. I've heard it said you've got good gut instincts. Call Bertholdier. You don't have to say where you are – as a matter of fact, I'd put a bullet in your head if you tried. Just tell him one of Leifhelm's guards, a man you bought to keep his eyes open for you because of a certain innate mistrust you have of Germans, told you that he, Bertholdier, came to see me alone on two separate occasions. Since I haven't been found, you want to know why. It'll work. You'll hear enough to know whether I'm telling you the truth or not.'

Abrahms stared down at Joel. 'But why *do* you tell me this truth – if it is the truth? Why do you abduct me to tell me these things? *Why?*'

'I thought I made that clear. My money's running out and although I'm not wild about saltfish or blintzes, I'd be better off living in Israel under a protective cover than being hunted and ultimately killed running around Europe. You can do that for me, but I know I've got to deliver something to you first. I'm delivering it now. Bertholdier intends to take over what he calls codename Aquitaine. He said you're a foul-mouthed Jew, a destructive symbol, you'll have to go. He said the same about Leifhelm; the spectre of a Nazi couldn't be tolerated, and van Headmer was a "fossil", that was the word, "fossil".'

'I can hear him,' said Abrahms softly, his hands clasped behind his back, pacing toward the window. 'Are you sure our military *boulevardier* with the cock of steel did not say "smelly Jew"? I've heard our French hero use such words, always of course apologizing to me, saying I was exempt.'

'He used them.'

'But *why*? Why would he say such things to *you*? I don't deny part of his logic, for Christ's sake. Leifhelm will be shot once controls are established. A *Nazi* running the goddamned German government? Absurd! Even Delavane understands this, he will be eliminated. And poor old van Headmer is a relic, we all know that. Still there is gold in South Africa. He could deliver it. But why *you*? Why would Bertholdier come to *you*?'

'Ask him yourself. There's the phone. Use it.'

The Israeli stood motionless, his narrow eyes encased in swells of flesh riveted on Converse. 'I *will*,' he said quietly, emphatically. 'You are far too clever, Mr Lawyer. The fire inside you remains in your head – it has not reached your stomach. You think too much. You say you were manipulated? I say you manipulate.' Abrahms turned and strode like a bulky, compact Coriolanus to the phone. He stood for a moment, squinting, remembering, then picked up the phone and dialled the series of numbers long ago committed to memory.

Joel remained in the chair, every muscle in his body taut, his throat suddenly dry, as the pounding in his chest reached his temples. Slowly he inched his hand over the arm of the chair nearer the pistol. In seconds he might have to use it, his strategy – his *only* strategy – blown apart by a phone call he never thought would be made. *What was wrong with him? Where were his vaunted examining tactics taking him? Had he forgotten who he was dealing with?*

'Code Isaiah,' said Abrahms into the phone, his angry eyes again staring across the room at Converse. 'Patch me through to Verdun-sur-Meuse. *Quickly!*' The Israeli's massive chest heaved with every breath, but it was the only part of his stocky frame that moved. He spoke again, furiously. 'Yes, code *Isaiah*! I have no time to waste! Reach Verdun-sur-Meuse! *Now!*' Abrahms' eyes grew wide as he listened. He looked briefly away from Converse, then snapped his head back, his eyes filled with knowledge and loathing, Joel the object of both. '*Repeat* that!' he shouted. And then he slammed the telephone down with such force the desk shook. '*Liar!*' he screamed.

'You mean me?' asked Joel, his hand inches from the gun.

'They say he *disappeared*! They cannot *find him*!'

'*And?*' The dryness in Converse's throat was now a vacuum. He had lost.

'He *lies*! The cock of steel is no more than a whining coward! He's hiding – he *avoids* me! He will not *face* me!'

Joel swallowed repeatedly as he moved his hand away from the weapon. 'Force the issue,' he said, somehow managing to keep the tremor out of his voice. 'Track him down. Call Leifhelm, van Headmer. Say it's imperative you reach Bertholdier.'

'*Stop* it! And let him know I *know*? He had to give you a reason! Why did he come to see you in the first place?'

'I wanted to wait until you'd spoken to him,' said Converse, crossing his legs and picking up a pack of cigarettes next to the pistol. 'He might have told you himself – then again he might not. He has this idea I was sent out by Delavane to test all of you. To see who might betray him.'

'*Betray* him? Betray the legless one? *How*? Why? And if our French peacock believed that, again why would he say these things to you?'

'I'm an attorney. I provoked him. Once he understood how I felt about Delavane, what that bastard did to me, he knew I couldn't possibly have anything to do with him. His defences were down; the rest was easy. And as he talked I saw a way to save my own life.' Joel struck a match, lighting a cigarette. 'By reaching you,' he said.

'At the end you bank on the morality of a Jew then? His acknowledgment of a debt.'

'In part, yes, but not entirely, General. I know something about Leifhelm, about the way he's manoeuvred through the years. He'd have me shot, then send his men after the rest of you, leaving himself in the number one position.'

'That's exactly what he'd do,' agreed the Israeli.

'And I didn't think van Headmer had any real authority north of Pretoria.'

'Right again,' said Abrahms, walking back toward Converse. 'So the hellhound created in South-east Asia is a survivor.'

'Let's be more specific,' countered Joel. 'I was sent out by people I don't know who abandoned me without raising the slightest question as to my guilt or innocence. For all I know they joined in the hunt to kill me to save their own lives. Given these conditions I intend to survive.'

'What about the woman? Your woman?

'She goes with me.' Converse put down the cigarette and picked up the gun. 'What's your answer? I can kill you now, or leave that to Bertholdier, or Leifhelm, if he kills the Frenchman first ... Or I can bank on your morality, your acknowledgment of a debt. What's it going to be?'

'Put away the gun,' said Chaim Abrahms. 'You have the word of a Sabra.'

'What'll you do?' asked Joel, placing the weapon back on the table.

'*Do?*' shouted the Israeli in a sudden burst of anger. 'What I've always *intended* to do! You think I give a horse's fart for this abstraction, this Aquitaine's infrastructure? Do you think I care one whit for titles or labels or chains of command? Let them have it all! I only care that it works and for it to work *respectability* must come out of the chaos *along* with strength. Bertholdier was right. I am too divisive a figure – as well as a Jew – to be so visible on the Euro-American scene. So I will be *invisible* – except in Eretz Israel, where my word will be the law of this new order. I, myself, will help the French bull get whatever medals he wants. I will not fight him, I will *control* him.'

'How?'

'Because I can destroy his respectability.'

Converse sat forward, suppressing his astonishment. 'His *sex* life? Those buried scandals?'

'My God, no, you imbecile! You kick a man below his belt in public you ask for trouble. Half the people cry 'foul' thinking it could happen to them, and the other half applaud his courage to indulge himself – which they would very much like to do.'

'Then how, General? How can you do this, destroy his respectability?'

Abrahms sat down again in the brocaded chair, his thick body squeezed dangerously between the delicately carved mahogany arms. 'By exposing the role he played in "codename, Aquitaine". The roles we all played in this extraordinary adventure that forced the civilized world to summon us and the strengths of our professional leadership. It's entirely possible that all free Europe will turn to Bertholdier, as France nearly turned to him after de Gaulle. But one must understand a man like Bertholdier. He doesn't merely seek power, he seeks the *glory* of power – the trappings, the adulation, the mysticism. He would rather give up certain intrinsic authority than lose any part of the glory. *Me?* I don't give a shit about the glory. All I want is the power to get what I need, what I command. For the kingdom of Israel and its imprimatur in all of the Middle East.'

'You expose him, you expose yourself. How can you win that way?'

'Because he'll blink first. He'll think of the glory and submit. He'll do as I say, give me what I want.'

'I think he'll have you shot.'

'Not when he's told that if I die several hundred documents will be released describing every meeting we attended, every decision we made. Everything is scrupulously detailed, I assure you.'

'You intended this from the beginning?'

'From the beginning.'

'You play rough.'

'I'm a Sabra. I play for the advantage – without it we would have been massacred decades ago.'

'Among these documents is there a list of everyone in Aquitaine?'

'No. It has never been my intention to jeopardize the movement. Call it whatever you will, I believe truly in the concept. There *must* be a unified, international military-industrial complex. The world will not stay sane without it.'

'But there is such a list.'

'In a machine, a computer, but it must be programmed correctly, the proper codes used.'

'Could you do it?'

'Not without help.'

'What about Delavane?'

'You have certain perceptions yourself,' said the Israeli, nodding. 'What about him?'

Again Joel had to control his astonishment. The computer codes that released the master list of Aquitaine were with Delavane. At least the key symbols were. The remainder were provided by his spokes, the four leaders across the Atlantic. Converse shrugged. 'You haven't really mentioned him. You've talked about Bertholdier, about the elimination of Leifhelm, and the impotence of van Headmer who could, however, bring in raw materials . . .'

'I said gold,' corrected Abrahms.

'Bertholdier said raw materials . . . But what about George Marcus Delavane?'

'Marcus is finished,' said the Israeli flatly. 'He was coddled – we all coddled him – because he brought us the concept and he worked his end in the United States. We have equipment and *matériel* all over Europe, say nothing of the contraband we've shipped to insurgents, just to keep them occupied.'

'Clarification,' interrupted Joel. ' "Occupied" means killing?'

'All is killing. Disingenuous philosophers notwithstanding the ends *do* justify the means. Ask a man hunted by killers if he will jump into human excrement to conceal himself.'

'I've asked him,' said Converse. 'I'm he, remember? What about Delavane?'

'He's a madman, a maniac. Have you ever heard his voice? He speaks like a man with testicles in a vice. They cut off his legs, you know, amputated only months ago for diabetes. The great general felled from an excess of *sugar*! He's tried to keep it a secret. He sees no one and no longer goes to his impressive office filled with photographs and flags and a thousand decorations. He operates out of his home where the servants come only when he's hidden in a darkened bedroom. How he wished it could have been a mortar shell or a bayonet charge, but no. Only sugar. He's become worse, a raving fool, but even fools can have flashes of brilliance. He had it once.'

'What *about* him?'

'We have a man with him, an aide with the rank of colonel. When everything begins, when our commands are in place, the colonel will do as instructed. Marcus will be shot for the good of his own concept.'

It was Joel's turn to get out of his chair. Once again he walked to the cathedral window across the room and felt the cool mountain breezes on his face. 'This examination is finished, General,' he said.

'*What?*' roared Abrahms. 'You want your life. *I* want guarantees!'

'Finished,' repeated Converse, as the door opened and a captain in the Israeli army walked inside, his gun levelled at Chaim Abrahms.

'There will be no discussion between us, Herr Converse,' said Erich Leifhelm, standing by the door of the study, the doctor from Bonn having left, closing it behind him. 'You have your prisoner. Execute him. Over many years and in many ways I have been waiting for this moment. In truth, I'm weary of the morbidity.'

'Are you telling me you want to die?' asked Joel, by the table with the pistol on top.

'No one *wants* to die, least of all a soldier in the quiet of a strange room. Drums and sharp commands to a firing squad are preferable – there's a certain meaning in that. But I've seen too much death to go into hysterics. Pick up your pistol and get it over with. I would if I were you.'

Converse studied the German's face, his strange non-committal eyes that said nothing, accepting whatever was before him with only contempt. 'You mean it, don't you?'

'Shall I give orders myself? There was a newsreel years ago. A black man did that against a blood-stained wall in Castro's Cuba. I've always admired that soldier.' Leifhelm suddenly shouted. '*Achtung! Soldaten! Das Gewehr präsentieren! Vorbereiten . . .*'

'For Christ's sake, why not *talk*?' roared Joel, riding over the fanatical voice.

'Because I have nothing to say. My actions speak, my life has *spoken*! What is it, Herr Converse? You have no stomach for executions? You cannot give the order to yourself? A small, insignificant man's conscience will not permit him to kill? You are laughable!'

'I remind you, General, I've killed several people these past few weeks. Killed with less feeling than I ever thought possible.'

'The lowliest coward running for his life will kill in panic. There is no character in that, merely survival. No, Herr Converse, you *are* insignificant, an impediment even your own forces care nothing about. You abound in this world. There is an odd phrase you have in your country that so readily applies to you, a phrase our associate uses frequently. You are a "shit-kicker", Herr Converse, nothing more and probably less.'

'What did you say? What did you call me?'

'You heard me clearly. A shit-kicker. A little man who steps in waste. Shit-kicker, Herr Converse. *Shit-kicker!*'

He was back a lifetime ago, on the bridge of a carrier, the face in front of him contorted, obscene, the voice shrill. Shit-kicker! Shit-kicker, shit-kicker, shit-kicker! Then other explosions followed, and he was blown into the dark clouds, the wind and the rain buffeting him, hammering him as he swung down toward the earth. Down to the ground and four years of madness and death and dying children weeping. Madness! Shit-kicker . . . shit-kicker . . . shit-kicker!

Converse reached down for the pistol on the table. He picked it up and levelled it at Erich Leifhelm, his index finger around the trigger, slowly, slowly squeezing it.

And then a sudden shock went through him. *What was he doing? He needed all three men of Aquitaine. Not one, not two, but three! It was the basis, the spine of what he had to do! But still there was something else. He had to kill, he had to destroy the deadly human virus staring at him, wanting death. Oh, Jesus! Had Aquitaine won after all? Had he become one of them? If he had, he had lost.*

'Your kind of courage is cheap, Leifhelm,' he said softly, lowering the gun. 'Better a quick bullet than other alternatives.'

'I live by my code. I die by it gladly.'

'Cleanly, you mean. Swiftly. No Dachau, no Auschwitz.'

'You have the gun.'

'I thought you had so much to offer.'

'My successor has been chosen carefully. He will carry out details, every nuance of my agenda.'

The opening was there, a strategy suddenly revealed. Joel pushed the button.

'Your successor?'

'*Ja.*'

'You have no successor, Field Marshal.'

'What?'

'Any more than you have an agenda. You don't have anything without me. It's why I brought you here. Just you.'

'What are you saying?'

'Sit down, General. I've several things to tell you, and for your own sake you'd better be seated. Your own execution might be more preferable to you than what I've got to say.'

'*Liar!*' screamed Erich Leifhelm four minutes later, his hands gripping the arms of the brocaded chair. 'Liar, liar, *liar!*' he roared, his eyes furious.

'I didn't expect you to believe me,' said Joel calmly, standing halfway across the spacious, book-lined study. 'Call Bertholdier in Paris and tell him you just heard some disturbing news and you'd like a clarification. Say it outright; you've learned that while you were in Essen, Bertholdier and Abrahms came to see me at your place in Bonn.'

'How would I *know* that?'

'The truth. They paid a guard to open the door – I don't know which one, I didn't see him – but a guard did unlock the door and let them in.'

'Because they believed you were an *informer*, sent out by Delavane himself?'

'That's what they told me.'

'You were drugged! There were no such indications!'

'They were suspicious. They didn't know the doctor and they didn't trust the Englishman. I don't have to tell you they don't trust you. They thought the whole thing might be a hoax. They wanted to cover themselves.'

'*Incredible!*'

'Not when you think about it,' said Converse sitting down opposite the German. 'How did I really get the information I had? How did I know the exact people to reach – except through Delavane. That was their thinking.'

'That Delavane would do this – *could* do it?' began the perplexed, astonished Leifhelm.

'I know what that means now,' interrupted Joel quickly, centring in on the new opening presented him. 'Delavane's finished, they both admitted it when they understood he was the last person on earth I'd work for. Maybe they were throwing me a few crumbs before setting me up for my own execution.'

'That had to be done!' exclaimed the Third Reich's once youngest field marshal. 'Certainly you can understand. Who *were* you? Where did you come from? You yourself did not know. You spoke of inconsequential names and lists and a great deal of money but nothing that made sense. Who had penetrated us? Since we could not find out you had to be turned into a *fauliger Abfall*.'

'I beg your pardon?'

'Something rotten. A thing of rot no one would touch, the disease catching.'

'You did it very well.'

'For that I must take credit,' said Leifhelm, nodding. 'It was essentially my organization. Everything was mine.'

'I didn't bring you here to discuss your achievements. I brought you here to save my life. You can do that for me – the people who sent me out either can't or won't – but you can. All I have to do is give you a reason.'

'By implying Abrahms and Bertholdier conspire against me?'

'I won't imply anything, I'll give it to you straight in their own words. Remember, neither one of them thought I'd leave your place except as a corpse conveniently shot in the vicinity of some particularly gruesome assassination.' Suddenly Converse got out of the chair, shaking his had. '*No!*' he said emphatically. 'Call your trusted French and Israeli allies, your fellow *Aquitainians*. Say nothing if you like, just listen to their voices – you'll be able to tell. It takes an accomplished liar to spot other liars and you're the best.'

'I find that offensive.'

'Oddly enough I meant it as a compliment. It's why I reached you. I think you're going to be the winner over here and after what I've been through I want to go with a winner.'

'Why do you say that?'

'Oh, come on, let's be honest. Abrahms is hated; he's insulted everyone in Europe, the UK and the US who doesn't agree with his expansionist policies for Israel. Even his own countrymen can't shut him up. All they can do is censure him and he keeps on screaming. He'd never be tolerated in any kind of international federation.'

The Nazi quickly, repeatedly shook his head. '*Never!*' he shouted. 'He is the most loathsome, unattractive man to come out of the Middle East. And, of course, he's a Jew. But how is Bertholdier to be equated in this manner?'

Joel paused before answering. 'His manner,' he replied thoughtfully. 'I'm not trying to be cute, I mean it. He's imperious, arrogant. He sees himself not only as a great military figure and a history-making power-broker, but also as some sort of god, above other men. There's no room on his Olympus for mortals. Also he's French. The English and the Americans wouldn't give him spit; one de Gaulle for them in a century is enough.'

'There's clarity in your thoughts. He's the sort of abominable egotist only the French can suffer. He is, of course, a reflection of the entire country.'

'Van Headmer doesn't count except where he can bring South Africa around for raw materials.'

'Agreed,' said the German.

'But you, on the other hand,' went on Converse rapidly, again sitting down, 'worked with the Americans and the English in Berlin and Vienna. You helped implement occupation policies, and in good conscience you turned over evidence to both the US and the UK prosecution teams in Nuremberg. Finally you became Bonn's spokesman in NATO. Whatever you were in the past, they like you.' Again Joel paused, and when he continued there was a degree of simple deference in his voice. 'Therefore, General, you're the winner, and you can save my life. All you need is a reason.'

'Then give it to me.'

'Use the phone first.'

'Don't be an idiot and don't take *me* for one! You would not insist so unless you were sure of yourself, which means you are telling the truth. And if those *Schweinhunde* conspire against me, I will not inform them that I'm *aware* of it! What did they say?'

'You're to be killed. They can't risk the accusation that an old-line member of the Nazi Party has assumed vital controls in West Germany. Even under Aquitaine there'd be too many cries of "foul!", too much fuel for the inescapable dissenters. A younger man or someone who thinks like they do but with no Party affiliations in his past will take your place. But no one you recommend.'

Leifhelm was braced rigidly in the brocaded chair, his aged but still taut body immobile, his pallid face surrounding his piercing light-blue eyes like an alabaster mask. '*They* have made this most *holy* decision?' he said icily through lips that barely moved. 'The vulgar Jew and the depraved French prince of maggots *dare* to attempt such a move against me?'

'Not that it matters, but Delavane agrees.'

'Delavane! A raging, infantile clump of fantasies! The man we knew two years ago has disintegrated to a point beyond senility! He doesn't know it, but we give *him* orders, couched naturally as suggestions and beneficial possibilities. He has no more power of reason than Adolf Hitler had in his last years of madness.'

'I don't know about that,' said Converse. 'Abrahms and Bertholdier didn't go into it other than to say he was finished. They talked about you.'

'Really? Well, let *me* talk about *me*! Who do you think it was that made Aquitaine feasible throughout all Europe and the Mediterranean? Who fed the terrorists with weapons and millions of pounds of explosives – from the Baader-Meinhof to the Brigate Rosse to the Palestinians – priming them for their final, let's say their *finest*, hours? *Who*? It was *I, Mein Herr*! Why are all directives funnelled, ultimately *issued* through *me*? Let me explain. *I* have the organization! *I* have the manpower – dedicated men ready to do my bidding with a single order. *I* have the *money*! I created an advanced, highly sophisticated communications centre out of rubble; no one else in Europe could have done that . . . I've known it all along. Bertholdier has nothing to speak of in Paris other than influence and the aura that hovers about him – in true battle, meaningless. The Jew and the South African are a continent away. When the chaos comes, it is *I* who will be the voice of Aquitaine in

Europe. I never thought otherwise! My men will cut down Bertholdier and Abrahms at their toilets!'

'Scharhörn's the communications centre, isn't it?' asked Joel with no emphasis whatsoever.

'They told you that?'

'The name was dropped. The master list of Aquitaine's in a computer there, isn't it?'

'That, *also*?'

'It's not important. I don't care anymore. I was abandoned, remember? You must have figured out the computer, too – no one else could.'

'A considerable accomplishment,' admitted Leifhelm, his humility shining brightly on his waxen face. 'I even assumed the catastrophe of death. There are sixteen letters; we each carry different sets of four, the remaining twelve are with the legless maniac. He thinks no one can activate the codes without his primary set but in truth a *pre*-coded combination of two sequences doubled will do it.'

'That's ingenious,' said Converse. 'Do the others know?'

'Only my trusted French comrade,' answered the German coldly. 'The prince of traitors, Bertholdier. But, naturally, I never gave him the accurate combination, and an inaccurate insertion would erase everything.'

'That was a winner thinking.' Joel nodded approvingly, then frowned with concern. 'What would happen, though, if your centre was assaulted?'

'Like Hitler's plans for the bunker, it would go up in flames. There are explosives everywhere.'

'I see.'

'But since you speak of winners, and in my judgment such men are prophets,' continued Leifhelm, leaning forward in the brocaded chair, his eyes widening with enthusiasm. 'Let me tell you about the isle of Scharhörn. Years ago, in 1945, out of the ashes of defeat, it was to be the site of the most incredible creation designed by true believers the world has ever known, only to be aborted by cowards and traitors. It was called *Operation Sonnenkinder* – the children of the sun – infants biologically selected and sent out all over the world to people waiting for them, prepared to guide them through their lives to positions of power and wealth. As adults, the *Sonnerkinder* were to have but one mission across the globe. The rising of the Fourth Reich! You see now the symbolic choice of Scharhörn? From this inner complex of Aquitaine will come forth the *new order*! We will have *done* it!'

'Stow it,' said Converse, getting out of the chair and walking away from Erich Leifhelm. 'The examination's finished.'

'*Was?*'

'You heard me, get out of here. You make me sick.' The door opened and the young doctor from Bonn came in, his eyes on the once celebrated field marshal. 'Strip him,' ordered Converse. 'Search him.'

Joel entered the dimly lit room where Valerie and the *Sûreté*'s Prudhomme flanked a man behind a tripodded video camera, its thick lens inserted in the wall. Ten feet away was a television monitor, showing only the deserted study, the brocaded wing-back chair now in the centre of the screen.

'Everything go all right?' he asked.

'Beautifully,' said Valerie. 'The operator didn't understand a word, but he claimed the lighting was exquisite. He can make as many copies as you like; they'll take about thirty-five minutes each.'

'Ten and the original print will be enough,' said Converse, looking at his watch, then up at Prudhomme, as Val spoke quietly in French to the cameraman. 'You can take the first copy and still make the five o'clock flight to Washington.'

'With the greatest of enthusiasm, my friend. I assume one of these prints will be for Paris.'

'And every other head of government along with our affidavits. You'll bring back copies of the depositions Simon took in New York?'

'I'll go and make the arrangements,' said the Frenchman. 'It is best my name does not appear on the passenger manifest.' He turned and left the room, followed by the cameraman who headed for his duplicating equipment down the hall.

Valerie went to Joel, reaching for him, taking his face in both her hands and kissing him lightly on the lips. 'For a few minutes in there you had me in knots. I didn't think you were going to make it.'

'Neither did I.'

'But you did. That was some display, Mister. I'm so very proud of you, my darling.'

'A lot of lawyers'll cringe. It was the worst sort of entrapment. As an old, bewildering, but very bright law professor of mine would have put it, they were admissions elicted on the basis of false statements, those same admissions forming the basis of further entrapment.'

'Stow it, Converse. Let's go for a walk. We used to walk a lot and I'd like to get back in the habit. It's not much fun alone.'

Joel took her in his arms. They kissed, gently at first, feeling the warmth and the comfort that had come back to them. He pulled his head away, his hands sliding to her shoulders, and looked into her wide vibrant eyes, loving them so. 'Will you marry me, Mrs Converse?' he said.

'Good Lord, again? Well, why not? As you said once before I wouldn't even have to change the initials on my lingerie.'

'You never had initials on it.'

'You found that out long before you made the remark.'

'I didn't want you to think I stared.'

'Yes, my darling, I'll marry you. But first we have things to do. Even before our walk.'

'I know Peter Stone by way of the Tatiana family in Charlotte, North Carolina. He did terrible things to me but strange as it seems, I think I like him.'

'I don't,' said Valerie firmly. 'I want to kill him.'

40

It was the end of the second day in the countdown of three. The world-wide demonstrations against nuclear war were only ten hours away, to start at first light halfway across the world. The killings would begin, the chaos set in motion.

The group of eighteen men and fifteen women sat scattered about in the dark projection room in the underground strategy complex of the White House. Each had a small writing tray attached to his seat with a yellow pad lighted by a Tensor lamp. On the screen was flashed in thirty-second intervals one face after another, each with a number in the upper right hand corner. The instructions had been terse, in the language best understood by these people, and delivered by Peter Stone who had selected them. *Study the faces, make no audible comments, and mark down by number any you recognize, bearing in mind terminal-operations. At the end of the series the lights will be turned on and we'll talk. And, if need be, run the series again and again until we come up with something. Remember, we believe these men are killers. Concentrate on that.*

They were told nothing else. Except MI6's Derek Belamy, who had arrived within a half hour of the extraordinary session, looking haggard from his obviously exhausting journey. When Derek walked through the door, Peter had pulled him aside, their arms gripping each other, Stone never so happy or so relieved in his life to see a man. Whatever *he* might have missed or could miss, Belamy would find it. The British agent had a tenth sense above anyone else's sixth, including Peter's, denied of course with modesty by Derek.

'I need you, old friend,' said Peter, as their hands gripped each other's arms. 'I need you badly.'

'It's why I'm here, old friend,' replied Belamy, his warm eyes reassuring. 'Can you tell me anything?'

'There's no time now but I can give you a name. Delavane.'

'Mad Marcus?'

'The same. It's his crisis and it's real.'

'The *bastard*!' whispered the Englishman. 'There's no one I'd rather see at the end of a barbed wire rope. Talk to you later, Peter. You've got your socializing to do. Incidentally, from what I can see, you've got the best here tonight.'

'The best, Derek. We can't afford any less.'

Beyond the American military personnel who had initially approached Stone, as well as Colonel Alan Metcalf, Nathan Simon, Justice Andrew Wellfleet, and the Secretary of State, the remaining audience was composed of the most experienced and secure intelligence officers Peter Stone had known in a lifetime of clandestine operations. They had been flown over by military transport from France, Great Britain, West Germany, Israel, Spain and the Netherlands. Among them were, of course, the extraordinary Derek

Belamy, then François Villard, chief of France's highly secretive *Organisation Étrangère*; Yosef Behrens, the Mossad's leading authority on terrorism; Pablo Amandariaz, Madrid's specialist in KGB Mediterranean penetrations and Hans Vonmeer of the Netherlands' Secret State Police. The others, including the women, were equally respected in the caverns of deep-cover, beyond-salvage operations. They knew by name, face, or reputation the legions of killers-for-hire, killers-by-order, and killers-by-reason-of-ideology. Above all each was trusted, each a man or woman Stone had worked with; collectively they were the élite of the shadow world.

A face! He knew the face! It stayed on the screen and he wrote on his pad. *Dobbins, Number 27. Cecil or Cyril Dobbins. British Army. Transferred to British Intelligence . . . Personal aide to . . . Derek Belamy!*

Stone looked over at his friend across the aisle, fully expecting him to be writing on his yellow pad. Instead, the Englishman frowned and sat motionless in his chair, his pencil poised above the paper. The next face appeared on the screen. And the next, and the next, until the series was over. The lights came on and the first person to speak was the Mossad's Yosef Behrens.

'Number 17 is an artillery officer in the IDF recently transferred to the Security Branch, Jerusalem. His name is Arnold.'

'Number 38,' said François Villard, 'is a colonel in the French Army attached to the guard of *Les Invalides*. It is the face; the name I do not recall.'

'Number 26,' said the man from Bonn, 'is Oberleutnant Ernst Müller of the Federal Republic's Luftwaffe. He is a highly skilled pilot frequently assigned to fly ministers of state to conferences both within and without West Germany.'

'Number 44,' said a dark-skinned woman with a pronounced Hispanic accent, 'has no such credentials as your candidates. He is a drug dealer, suspected of many killings and operates out of Ibiza. He was once a paratrooper. Name, Orejo.'

'Son of a *gun*, I just don't believe it!' said the young lieutenant, William Landis, the computer expert from the Pentagon. 'I know Number 51, I'm almost positive! He's one of the adjutants in Middle East procurements. I've seen him a lot but I don't know his name.'

Six other men and two women volunteered twelve additional identities and positions, as everyone in the room silently looked for an emerging pattern. There was a preponderance of military personnel but by no means all, and the umbrella of the rest was puzzling. In the main they were ex-combat soldiers from high-casualty outfits who had drifted into crime – largely violent crime, the sort of men Peter Stone knew the generals of Aquitaine considered human garbage.

Finally Derek Belamy spoke in his hard, clipped distant voice. 'There are four or five faces I associate with dossiers, but I'm not making connections.' He looked over at Stone. 'You'll run them again, won't you, old boy?'

'Of course, Derek,' replied the former Station Chief in London. Then Stone, who had said nothing before, rose from his chair and addressed the gathering. 'Everything you've given us will be fed immediately into computers and we'll see if we come up with any correlations. And to repeat what I said previously, I want to thank you all and apologize again for not giving you the explanations you deserve, not only for your help but for the trouble we've caused you. Speaking personally, my consolation is that you've all been here before and I know you understand. We'll break for fifteen minutes and start again. There are coffee and sandwiches in the next room.' Stone nodded his thanks once more and started for the door. Derek Belamy intercepted him in the aisle.

'Peter, I'm dreadfully sorry it took me so long to get back to you. Truth is, the office had a devil of a time tracking me down. I was visiting friends in Scotland.'

'I thought you might be in Northern Ireland. It's a hell of a mess, isn't it?'

'You were always better than you thought you were. I was in Belfast, of course. But right now I promise to do better – I'm sure I will – but the fact is I'm bushed; it was a perfectly terrible trip and, of course, no sleep whatsoever. All those faces began to look alike – I either knew them all or I didn't know a damned one!'

'Running them again will help,' said Stone.

'Quite so,' agreed Belamy. 'And Peter, whatever this tangle is with that maniac, Delavane, I couldn't have been more delighted to see you in the control chair. We were all told you were out, rather firmly out.'

'I'm back in. Very firmly.'

'I can see that, old chap. That *is* your Secretary of State in the back row, isn't it?'

'Yes, it is.'

'*Congratulations*, old boy. Well, off for coffee, black and hot. See you in a few minutes.'

'Across the aisle, old friend.'

Stone walked out of the door and turned right in the white corridor. He could feel the rapid acceleration of his heartbeat; it was a cousin to Johnny Reb's claims of a churning stomach and an acid taste in his mouth – bile, The Rebel called it. He had to get to a telephone quickly. Converse's courier, the Sûreté's Prudhomme, would be arriving within the hour; a Secret Service escort was waiting for him at Dulles Airport with instructions to bring him directly to the White House. But it was not the Frenchman who concerned Stone now, it was Converse himself. He had to reach him before the session began again. He *had* to!

When the lawyer had contacted him through the Tatiana relay, Peter had been astonished by the sheer audacity of what Converse had done. *Kidnapping* the three generals – *video*-taping the interrogations or the 'oral examinations' or whatever the legal terminology was; it was insane! The only thing more insane was the fact that he had carried it off – due obviously to the resources of a very determined, very angry man from the Sûreté. The computer *was* in Scharhörn, the master list of Aquitaine buried somewhere in its intricate mechanism, only to be erased by inaccurate codes, the complex itself mined with explosives. *Jesus!*

And now the final insanity. The man no one could find, the source so deeply shrouded they frequently doubted his existence despite the fact that all logic insisted he was there. Aquitaine's man in England *had* to be, for there could be no Aquitaine without the British. Further, Stone knew he was the conduit, the primary communicator between Palo Alto and the generals overseas, for constant screenings of Delavane's telephone charges showed repeated calls to a number in the Hebrides, and such a relay device was all too familiar to the former intelligence agent. The calls disappeared at that number in the Scottish islands, just as the KGB calls processed through Canada's Prince Edward Island disappeared, and the Company's communications routed through Key West could not be traced.

Belamy! The man whose face never appeared in any publication – films were destroyed instantly by aides if he was even in the background of a photograph. The most guarded operations officer in England, with access to secrets culled over decades and scores of devices created by the best minds of MI6. And yet, was it *possible?* Derek Belamy, the quiet good-humoured chess player, the *friend* who gave good whisky and a fine ear to an American colleague who progressively had serious doubts about his calling in life. The *better* friend for having the wisdom and the courage to warn his colleague that he was drinking too much, that perhaps he should take a sabbatical and if money was a problem, surely some sort of quiet consultation agreement could be worked out with his own organization. *Was* it possible, this decent man, this *friend?*

Stone reached the door in the hallway marked simply by the number *14, Occupied*. He walked inside the small room and went to the desk and the telephone. He did not sit down; his anxiety would not permit it. He picked up the phone and dialled the White House switchboard, as he took out the slip of paper in his pocket with Converse's number somewhere in France. He gave it to the operator, adding simply, 'This should be scrambled. I'm talking from Strategy Fourteen, confirm by trace.'

'Trace confirmed, sir. Scrambler will be in operation. Shall I call you back?'

'No, thanks, I'll stay on the line.' Stone remained standing as he heard the hollow echo of numbers being punched and the faint hum of the scrambling machine. And then he heard an intruding sound, the sound of a door opening. He turned.

'Put the phone down, Peter,' said Derek Belamy quietly, as he shut the door. 'There's no point to this.'

'It *is* you, isn't it?' Stone slowly, awkwardly replaced the phone in its cradle.

'Yes, it is. And I want everything you want, my old friend. Neither of us could deny ourselves the parting shots, could we? I said I was visiting friends in Scotland and you said you thought I was in Ireland . . . We've learned over the years, haven't we? The eyes don't lie. Scotland – calls to the Hebrides; the glass fell over your eyes. And earlier, when that face came on the screen you looked across the aisle a bit too obviously, I think.'

'Dobbins. He worked for you.'

'You wrote frantically on your pad yet you said nothing.'

'I was waiting for you to say something.'

'Yes, of course, but I couldn't could I?'

'Why, Derek? For Christ's sake, *why?*'

'Because it's right and you know it.'

'I *don't* know it! You're a sane, reasonable man. They're *not!*'

'They'll be replaced, naturally. How often have you and I used drones we couldn't abide because their contributions were necessary to the objective?'

'*What* objective? An international totalitarian alliance? A military state without borders? All of us robots marching to the drums of fanatics?'

'Oh, come off it, Peter. Spare us both the liberal drivel. You left this business once, drinking yourself into a stupor because of the waste, the futility, the deceits we all practised – the *people* we killed – to maintain what we laughingly called the *status quo*. What *status quo*, old man? To be continuously harassed by our inferiors the world over? To be held hostage by screaming *mullahs* and hysterical fools who still live in the dark ages and would cut our throats over the price of a barrel of oil? To be manipulated at every turn by Soviet deceptions? No, Peter, there really *is* a better way. The means may be distasteful but the end result is not only desirable, it's also honourable.'

'Whose definition? George Marcus Delavane's? Erich Leifhelm's? Chaim . . .'

'They'll be *replaced*!' broke in Belamy angrily.

'They *can't* be!' shouted Stone. 'Once it starts, you can't stop it. The image becomes the reality. It's expected, *demanded*! To deviate is to be accused, to oppose is to be ostracized, penalized! It's lock-step and lock-jaw, and you damn well *know* that!'

The telephone rang.

'Let it ring,' ordered the man from MI6.

'It doesn't matter now. *You* were the Englishman at Leifhelm's house in Bonn. A brief description of you would have confirmed it for me.'

'That's *Converse*?' The phone rang again.

'Would you like to talk to him? I understand he's quite a lawyer, although he broke the fundamental rule – he took himself on as a client. He's coming out, Derek, and he's going after you, all of you. We all are – after all of you.'

'You won't!' cried Belamy. 'You *can't*! As you yourself put it, once it starts you can't *stop* it!'

Without the slightest indication that he was about to move, the Englishman suddenly lunged at Stone, the three middle fingers of his right hand rigid, zeroing in on the CIA man's throat like three steel projectiles. Stone took the agonizing blow, gasping for air as the room spiralled out of control, a thousand dazzling irregular spots of white light in his eyes. He could hear the door opening and closing, as the phone insistently rang again. But Peter could not see it; the white lights had turned into darkness. The ringing stopped as Stone wildly, blindly careened around the room, trying to trace the bell, trying to find the phone. The minutes passed in madness as he smashed into walls and fell over the desk. Then the door crashed open and Colonel Alan Metcalf shouted.

'Stone! What *happened*?' The Air Force officer raced to Peter, instantly recognizing the effects of the judo chop. He began massaging Stone's throat, pressing his knee into the CIA man's stomach to force up air. 'The switchboard reached us, saying that Room Fourteen had placed a scrambler call but didn't pick up. *Christ*, who *was* it?'

Vague images came back to Stone, but still he could not speak; he was capable only of gasping coughs. He writhed under Metcalf's strong hands, pointing to a notepad that had fallen from the desk. The colonel understood; he reached for it, yanking out a ballpoint pen from his pocket. He rolled Stone over, placing the pen in his hand, guiding the hand to the pad.

Struggling for control Peter wrote.

BELMY. STP. AQUTAIN.

'Oh, my *God*!' whispered Metcalf, reaching for the phone and dialling *zero*. 'Operator, this is an emergency. Give me Security . . . Security? Colonel Alan Metcalf talking from Strategy Fourteen. *Emergency*! There's an Englishman named Belamy who may still be on the premises trying to leave. Stop him! Hold him! Consider him dangerous. And get word to the infirmary. Send a doctor to Strategy Fourteen. *Quickly*!'

The White House staff doctor removed the oxygen mask from Stone's face, placing it on the desk next to the cylinder. He then gently moved Peter's head back in the chair, inserting a tongue depressor and peering into the CIA man's throat with a pencil light.

'It was a nasty shot,' he said, 'but you'll feel better in a couple of hours. I'll give you some pills for the pain.'

'What's in them?' asked Stone hoarsely.

'A mild analgesic with some codeine.'

'No thanks, Doctor,' said Peter, looking over at Metcalf. 'I don't think I like what I see on your face.'

'I don't either. Belamy got out. His pass was high priority and he told the East Gate he was needed urgently at the British Embassy.'

'*Goddamn* it!'

'Try not to strain your voice,' said the doctor.

'Yes, of course,' replied Stone. 'Thank you very much, and now if you'll excuse us.' He got out of the chair, as the doctor nodded, picking up his medical bag and heading for the door. 'I meant what I said, Doctor. Thanks very much.'

'Sure. I'll send someone back for the air.'

The telephone rang as the door closed. Metcalf picked it up. 'Yes? Yes it is; he's right here.' The colonel listened for several moments then turned to Stone. 'Breakthrough,' he said. 'All those military who were identified have two things in common. Each is on a minimum thirty-day summer leave and every request was made five months ago, nearly to the day.'

'Thus guaranteeing request-granted status because they were first in line,' added the CIA man with difficulty. 'And the plans for the anti-nuclear demonstrations were announced in Sweden *six* months ago.'

'Clockwork,' said Metcalf. 'To identify and neutralize the others we'll send out the word. Every officer in half a dozen armies and navies who returns from summer leave is to be restricted to quarters. There'll be errors but that's rough. We can send out the photographs and correct them.'

'It's time for Scharhörn.' Stone got out of the chair, massaging his throat. 'And I don't mind telling you it scares me to death. A wrong symbol and we erase Aquitaine's master list. Worse, a wrong move and that whole complex is blown away.' The CIA man went to the phone.

'Are you going to call The Rebel?' asked the colonel.

'Converse first. He's working on the codes.'

* * *

The three generals of Aquitaine sat stunned in their chairs, staring straight ahead, refusing to look at one another. The lights had been turned on, the large television screen turned off. Behind each soldier was a man with a gun and concise instructions. *If he gets up, kill him.*

'You know what I want,' said Converse, walking in front of the generals. 'And as you've just seen there's really no reason why any of you shouldn't give it to me. Four little numbers or letters each of you has memorized in sequence. Of course, if you refuse there's a doctor here who I'm told has a bag of magic – the same sort of magic you administered to me in Bonn. What'll it be, gentlemen?'

Silence.

'Four, three, L, one,' said Chaim Abrahms, looking down at the floor. 'They're *filth*,' he added quietly.

'Thank you, General.' Joel wrote in a small notepad. 'You're free to go now. You can get out of the chair.'

'Go?' said the Israeli, getting up. '*Where?*'

'Wherever you like,' replied Converse. 'I'm sure you'll have no trouble at the airport in Annecy. You'll be recognized.'

General Chaim Abrahms left the room accompanied by the Israeli Army captain.

'Two, M, zero, six,' said Erich Leifhelm. 'And, if you wish, I will submit to the drugs for verification. I will not be associated with such treacherous pigs.'

'I want the combination,' pressed Joel, writing. 'And I won't hesitate to send you up into space to get it.'

'Inversion,' said the German. 'Reverse the order of the symbols in the second sequence.'

'He's yours, Doctor.' Converse nodded to the man behind Leifhelm's chair. 'We can't take the chance blowing this one.'

General Erich Leifhelm, once the youngest field marshal of the Third Reich, got up and walked slowly out of the room, followed by the doctor from Bonn.

'You're all unworthy, all blind,' said General Jacques Louis Bertholdier with imperious calm. 'I prefer to be shot.'

'I'm sure you would, but no such luck,' answered Joel. 'I don't need you now, and I want to know you're back in Paris where everyone can see you. Take him to his room.'

'The room? I thought I was free to leave, or was that another lie?'

'Not at all. Just a matter of logistics – you know what logistics are, General. We're a little short of transportation and drivers here, so when the doctor's finished, I'm lending the three of you a car. You can draw straws for who drives.'

'*What?*'

'Get him out of here,' said Converse, addressing a former sergeant-major in the French army once stationed at Algiers.

'Move, *vache!*'

The door opened, only coincidentally for Bertholdier. It was Valerie and she looked at Joel. 'Stone's on the telephone. He says hurry.'

* * *

It was 2.05 a.m. when the Mystere jet dropped out of the night sky and landed at the airstrip eight miles from Cuxhaven, West Germany. It taxied to the north end of the runway where the stately, white-maned figure of Johnny Reb waited by a black Mercedes sedan.

The doors of the plane opened, the short steps swinging down in place, and Converse climbed out, taking Valerie's hand as she descended after him. Next came the former sergeant-major from Algiers, followed by a fourth passenger, a slender blond man in his mid-forties who wore tortoise-shell glasses. They walked away from the aircraft as the pilot retracted the steps and closed the automatic doors; the twin engines accelerated and the plane swerved around heading back toward the maintenance hangars. The Rebel came away from the car and met them, extending his hand to Joel.

'Ah've seen your picture here and there and it's a pleasure, sir. Frankly, I never thought I'd meet you, leastways not in this world.'

'There were a number of times I had my doubts just how long I'd be here. This is my wife, Valerie.'

'Ah'm enchanted, ma'am,' said the southerner, bringing Val's hand to his lips as he bowed gallantly. 'Your accomplishments have astonished some of the best minds in my former profession.'

'I hope not *too* former,' interjected Converse.

'Not at the moment, son.'

'This is Monsieur LeFevre and Dr Geoffrey Larson. Stone said you've been briefed.'

'A pleasure, sir,' exclaimed The Rebel, shaking the Frenchman's hand. 'My hat's off to you, to all of you for what you did with those three generals. Absolutely *remarkable!*'

'Such men have enemies,' said LeFevre simply. 'They are not hard to find and Inspector Prudhomme knew that. We are in many places with many memories. Let us hope they will be put to rest tonight.'

'Let's hope,' said The Rebel, turning to the fourth passenger. 'Dr Larson, so nice to meet you, sir. I understand you know just about everything there is to know about every computer ever made.'

'An exaggeration, I'm sure,' said the Englishman, shyly. 'But I suspect if it ticks I can make it hum. Actually, I was vacationing in Geneva.'

The *non-sequitur* momentarily threw Johnny Reb, who could only utter, 'Sorry about that,' as he looked at Joel.

It had been the most difficult decision Peter Stone had made in all his years of agonizing decisions. To make the wrong move – to telegraph the incursion into the complex at Scharhörn – would result in its destruction by the setting off of explosives all over the Communications centre. There would be nothing left of the old U-boat station but shattered concrete and twisted equipment. Stone had gone by instincts honed over a lifetime in the shadow world. There could be no élite commando units, no official special forces ordered up for an extraordinary assignment, for there was no telling who within the various government forces could be a member, an officer of Aquitaine. Such a man could make a telephone call and the complex at Scharhörn would be blown up. Therefore the incursion had to be made by rogue elements, men hired by outlaws who had no allegiance to anyone or anything but money and their immediate employers. Nothing was a secret any longer without the master list of Aquitaine. The President of the United States gave Stone twelve hours, after which he said he would convene an emergency session of the Security Council of the United Nations. Peter Stone could hardly believe he had replied to the most powerful man in the free world with the words: 'That's meaningless. It would be too late.'

The Rebel finished his briefing, his flashlight still shining on the map spread over the hood of the Mercedes. 'As I told you, this is the original layout we got from the Zoning Commission in Cuxhaven. Those Nazis sure were particular when it came to specifics – I figure everyone was justifyin' a salary or a rank. We get over the ocean radar and head to the old strip that was used for supplies, then do our number. Now mind you, there are still a lot of lights out there, still a lot of people, but a hell of a lot less than there were two days ago. There are some walls but we got grappling hooks and a few boys who know how to use them.'

'Who are they?' asked Converse.

'No one you'd ask into your mother's parlour, my friend, but five of the meanest hornets you could find. I tell you they have absolutely no redeeming social qualities. They're perfect.'

'What's the aircraft?'

'The best Petey could get, and it's *the* best. A Fairchild Scout. It holds nine people.'

'With a glide-ratio of nine to one at four thousand feet,' said Joel. 'I'm flying.'

41

Converse inched the half-wheel forward as he cut the engines and entered a left bank glide over the small airstrip 2,400 feet below. It was erratically visible through the tails of low-flying North Sea clouds, but Joel guessed it could be seen clearly at 500 feet. He would then start his final circle for the short approach, his touchdown heading away from the old U-boat base, minimizing whatever sound the outsized balloon tyres made while braking. The manoeuvre itself was the nearest thing to a carrier landing he could imagine, and he noted with satisfaction that his hands were as steady as his concentration. The fear he had anticipated did not materialize; it was strangely absent. The anxiety and the anger were another matter.

Valerie and LeFevre – over the Frenchman's strenuous objections – remained behind on a deserted pier in Cuxhaven where Johnny Reb had managed to install a primitive but functional relay station. It was Val's job to stay in radio contact with the team – either The Rebel or Converse operating the powerful handheld equipment on Scharhörn – and the former sergeant from Algiers was to stand guard, letting no one on that pier. The five 'recruits' Johnny Reb had hired for apparently large amounts of money were difficult to appraise for they said very little and wore dark woolknit caps pulled down above their eyes and black turtleneck sweaters pulled up around their throats. The same clothing was provided for Joel and the British computer expert, Geoffrey Larson; The Rebel had his in the Mercedes. Each man, except Larson, carried a pistol with an attached silencer that was held firmly in an extended holster strapped to his waist. On the left side of the black leather belt was a long-bladed hunting knife, and beside it a coil of thin wire. At the back, above the kidneys, and held in place by clips, were two canisters of a mace-like gas that rendered their victims helpless and silent. The fact that each, including the ageing Johnny Reb, wore his equipment with such casual authority made Converse feel out of place, but the degree of concentration they gave to the installation's plans and the curt suggestions they had for gaining entry and subsequent explorations also made him feel The Rebel had hired well.

Joel circled slowly, delicately into his final approach, silently gliding over the darkened U-boat base, his eyes on both the strip ahead and the instrument-guidance altimeter. He struck the flaps and dropped; the heavy tyres absorbed the jarring shock of contact. *Touchdown.*

'We're down,' said Johnny Reb into the radio. 'And with a little luck we'll stop, won't we, son?'

'We'll stop,' said Converse. They did, no more than forty feet from the end of the airstrip. Joel removed the knit hat, breathing deeply; his hairline and forehead were drenched with sweat.

'We're going out.' The Rebel snapped off the radio and pressed it into the front of his chest; it stayed in place. 'Oh,' he added seeing that Converse was watching him. 'I forgot to mention it. There's heavy-duty Velcro around the case and on your sweater.'

'You're full of surprises.'

'You had a fair share yourself during the past few weeks. Let's go catfishin', boy.' Johnny Reb opened his door; Joel did the same, both of them climbing out followed by Larson and the five men, three of them carrying rubberized grappling hooks attached to coils of rope. The second man who had said nothing during the strategy session stood in front of Converse and spoke quietly, startling Joel with his American accent.

'I'm a pilot, Mister, and that was supposed to be part of my job. I'm glad it wasn't. You're good, man.'

'Where did you fly? With whom?'

'Let's say a new kind of Peruvian airline. The scenic Florida run.'

'Come *on!*' The Rebel ordered, starting for the overgrown borders of the airstrip.

They approached the high walls of the old U-boat base all crouching in the tall grass, studying what was before them. Converse was struck by the sheer immensity of the unending, thick concrete. It was like a fortress with no fort inside, no treasured structure that warranted the protection of the impenetrable walls. The only break was over on the left, in a section that faced the airstrip. A pair of steel double doors layered with plates of bolted, reinforced iron stood ominously in the erratic moonlight. They were also impenetrable.

'This place has quite a history,' whispered Johnny Reb beside Joel. 'Half the German High Command had no idea it was here and the Allies never got a smell of it. It was Doenitz's private base. Some said he was going to use it as a threat if Hitler didn't turn things over to him.'

'It was also going to be used for something else,' said Converse, remembering Leifhelm's incredible story of the rising of the Fourth Reich a generation after the war. *Operation Sonnenkinder.*

One of the men with a grappling hook crawled over and spoke to The Rebel in German. The Southerner replied angrily, looking pained, but finally nodding as the man crawled away. He turned to Joel.

'Son of a no-account hound dog *bitch*!' he exclaimed under his breath. 'He stole me blind! He said he'd make the first assault on the east flank – which you know damn well that mother studied – if I guaranteed him an additional five thousand American!'

'And you'll pay, of course.'

'Of course. We're honourable men. If he's killed, every penny goes to his wife and children. I know the lad; we took a building once with the Meinhof inside. He scaled eight storeys, dropped down through an elevator shaft, kicked a door open and shot the bastards cold with his Uzi on rapid fire.'

'I don't *believe* all this,' whispered Converse.

'Believe,' said The Rebel softly, as he looked at Joel. 'We do it because no one else will. And somebody has to do it. We may be rogues, son, but there are times we're on the side of the angels – for a price.'

The muted sound of the rubberized grappling hook split the air, and took hold on top of the wall, the rope stretched taut. In seconds the black-clothed man could be seen climbing hand over hand, his feet bracing, racing up the dark concrete. He reached the ledge, his left hand disappearing over the top, his right leg swinging up as he vaulted into a prone position, his body level with the ledge of concrete. Suddenly, he held out his left arm, waving it back and forth twice, a signal. Then bracing himself, he reached for his holstered weapon with his right hand, pulling it out slowly.

A single spit was heard and once more there was silence as the man's left arm shot out for a second time. A second signal.

The two other men with grappling hooks raced out of the grass, flanking the first man, swinging their hooks in circles and heaving them up, each accurately as the ropes were yanked taut and the two figures began scaling the wall. Joel knew it was his turn; it was part of the plan if he was up to it and he was determined to be. He rose and walked out, joining the remaining two men hired by The Rebel; the American pilot who had spoken to him pointed to the centre rope. He gripped it and started the painful climb to the top of the wall.

Only in the last extremity were the elderly Johnny Reb and the slender, professional Geoffrey Larson expected to use the ropes. By his own admission the Southerner might not be capable, and the risk of injury to the computer expert was unacceptable.

Arms and legs aching, Converse was hauled up the final inches by his German companion. 'Pull up the rope!' ordered the man in a heavily accented whisper. 'Drop it slowly down the other side and reverse the hooks.'

Joel did as he was told, seeing for the first time the interior of the strange fortress – and a uniformed man below on the ground, dead, blood trickling down the centre of his forehead from the incredibly accurate shot. In the moonlit darkness he could make out a series of huge watery slips in the distance broken up by concrete piers on which there were giant winches, black wheels of immense machinery, long out of use, relics of a violent past. In a semi-circle facing the U-boat docks and the sea were five low, concrete one-storey buildings with small windows, the first two with dim lights on inside. The buildings were joined by cement walkways, wide steps where they were necessary as the central structures were higher off the ground, no doubt once the officers' quarters, commanders of the behemoths that prowled the deep waters of the Atlantic, killers for an abominable cause.

Directly below the wall where the three ropes now dangled were more wide steps that led up both sides of what appeared to be a concrete podium or platform, the area in front some kind of courtyard, perhaps 200 feet wide, that led to the rear of the buildings facing the U-boat slips. A parade ground, thought Converse, visualizing rows of submarine crews, standing at attention, receiving orders and listening to the exhortations of their officers as they prepared once more to enter the deep in search of tonnage and carnage.

'Follow me!' said the German, tapping Joel's shoulder and grabbing the rope as he slid over the wall and lowered himself to the concrete platform beneath. On both sides, the four men were on their way down, one after the other. Converse, less gingerly than the professionals, rolled over the ledge, his hands gripping the rope and slid to the ground.

The two men on Joel's left raced silently across the platform and down the steps toward the huge steel doors. The two men on his right, as if by instinct, ran down the opposing steps, returning below to crouch in front of the platform, their weapons drawn. Converse, following the German, swiftly joined the pair at the doors. Both men were studying the bolts and the layers of plating and the complicated lock with tiny flashlights.

'Fuse it and blow it,' said the American. 'There's no alarm.'

'Are you sure?' asked Joel. 'From what I gathered this whole place is wired.'

'The trips are down there,' explained the second pilot, pointing toward the concrete sides of the parade ground, a three-foot-high wall on both sides.

'Trips?'

'Trip lights. Intersecting beams.'

'Which means there are no animals,' said the German, nodding. '*Keine Hunde. Sehr gut!*'

The fourth man had finished stuffing wads of a soft, puttylike substance into the lock mechanism, using his knife to finish the job. He then took out a small circular device no larger than a 50-cent coin from his pocket, layered another mound of the substance directly over the lock and plunged the coin into it. 'Move back,' he ordered.

Converse watched, mesmerized. There was no explosion, no detonation whatsoever, but there was intense heat and a glowing blue-white flame that literally melted the steel. Then a series of clicks could be heard and, hearing them, the American quickly slid back the triple bolts. He pushed the right door open and blinked his flashlight outside. Moments later Johnny Reb and Geoffrey Larson walked through the door into the strange compound.

'Trips,' repeated the American to The Rebel. 'They're all along those two walls,' he said, pointing. 'See them?'

'I can,' replied the Southerner. 'And that means there'll be a few shooting straight up on top for tip-toeing feet. All right, boys, let's do a little crawling. Bellies down with knees and asses wiggling.' The six at the door joined the two crouched in front of the platform. Johnny whispered in German, then turned to Larson. 'My English friend, I want you to stay right here until us old timers give you the high sign to catch up with us.' He looked at Joel. 'Sure you want to come?'

'I won't bother to answer that. Let's go.'

One by one, with the German who was $5,000 richer in the lead, the seven men snaked their way across the old parade ground. Barely breathing, trousers torn, knees and hands scraped by the rough, cracked concrete. The German headed for the break between buildings 2 and 3, counting from the right. It was a connecting cement path with gradually rising steps on the left. He reached the open space and stood up.

Suddenly, he snapped his fingers once – not very loud but loud enough. Everyone froze where he was under the field of intersecting alarm beams. Converse angled his head on the ground to get what vision he could manage. The German was crouched in the shadows as a man came into view, a guard with a rifle slung over his shoulder. Aware of another presence, the guard whipped his head around; the German lunged out of the shadows, his long-bladed knife arcing in mid-air toward the man's head. Joel closed his eyes, the sound of savagely expelled air telling him more than he cared to know.

The movement began again, and again one by one each member of the unit reached the path. Converse was soaked with sweat. He looked at the row of U-boat slips beyond and the sea beyond them and wished to God he could fall into the water. His brief musings were interrupted by The Rebel touching his elbow, indicating that Joel should take out his gun as the Southerner had done. It was now Johnny Reb who took the lead; he crept out to the front of building 2 and turned right, crouching close to the ground, heading toward the lighted windows. His fingers snapped; all movement stopped, bodies now prone. Diagonally to the left, by the edge of a giant slip, were the glow of cigarettes and the sound of men talking quietly – three men, guards with rifles.

As if on a silent order, three of the five men hired by The Rebel – which ones Converse could not tell – broke away and started crawling in a wide arc toward the opposite side of the old U-boat berth. Approximately a minute and a half later – the longest ninety seconds Joel could remember – a barrage of muted reports punctured the night breezes off the sea. The subsequent sounds were minimal, as hands clutched at heads and bodies snapped falling to the concrete ground. The hired guns returned and Johnny Reb waved them forward, Converse forced to be the last as men grabbed his shoulders and passed him. They reached the only lighted window in building 2; The Rebel stood up, inching his way to the glass. He turned and shook his head; the unit proceeded.

They came to the open space between buildings 1 and 2. Cautiously each one ran across, crouching the instant he reached the opposite edge then racing ahead. It was Joel's turn; he got to his knees, then to his feet.

'*Horst? Bist du da?*' said a man harshly, walking out of a door and up the cement path.

Converse stood motionless. The rest of the unit was well past the edge of building 1 as the sounds of the North Sea crashing on the rocks in the distance blocked out the intruder's voice. Joel tried not to panic. He was alone and he alone could blow the operation apart, destroy the complex at Scharhörn, killing everyone including Connal Fitzpatrick, if, indeed, the young commander was there.

'*Ja*,' he heard himself saying as he turned away into the shadow, his right hand reaching across his waist for the hunting knife. He could not trust his gun in the darkness.

'*Warten Sie einen Augenblick! Sie sind nicht Horst!*'

Joel shrugged, and waited. The footsteps approached; a hand grabbed his shoulder. He spun round, gripping the handle of the knife with such force it nearly blocked out the terrible thing his mind told him he had to do. He grabbed the man's hair and brought the razor-sharp blade across the throat beneath.

Wanting to vomit, he pulled the man into the darker shadows; the head was all but severed from the body. He raced across the open space and caught up with the others. No one had missed him; each man was taking his turn peering into one of the four lighted windows in a row. Johnny Reb was beyond the first, gesturing as each man ducked away, pointing in successive directions firmly, rapidly, receiving nods of acceptance. Commands were being given, an assault planned for immediate execution. Converse raised himself to the edge of the last window and looked inside. Instantly he understood why The Rebel had to act quickly. There were ten guards in what could only be described as para-military uniforms belonging to no recognizable army. Each was either strapping on a weapon, looking at his watch, or crushing out a cigarette. Then, more ominously, they checked the ammunition clips in their rifles and automatics. Several laughed, raising their voices as if making demands or requests at the expense of the others. Joel could not understand the words. He ducked away from the window only to be confronted by Johnny Reb close to the ground.

'It's a patrol going out, isn't it?' whispered Converse.

'No, son,' replied the Southerner. 'It's a firing squad. They just got their orders.'

'My *God*!'

'We follow them, staying low and out of sight. You may find your old buddy Fitzpatrick after all.'

The next minutes were insanely out of Kafka, thought Joel. The ten men lined up and walked out of the door leading to building 2. Suddenly floodlights erupted throughout the parade ground, the trip lights obviously turned off as the squad walked out on the concrete. Two men with automatics in their hands ran over to building 4; they unlocked then unbolted the heavy door and raced inside shouting orders, as lights were turned on.

'*Aufwachen! Aufstehen! Raus antreten! Macht schnell! Eilt Euch!*'

Seconds later, gaunt, manacled figures began straggling out, blinking at the harsh lights in their ragged clothes, some barely able to walk, supported by others who were stronger. Ten, twenty, twenty-five, thirty-two, forty . . . forty-three. Forty-three prisoners of Aquitaine about to be executed! They were marched toward the concrete wall fronting the platform at the far end of the parade ground.

It happened with the hysterical force of a crowd gone mad! The condemned men suddenly bolted in all directions, those nearest the two guards with the automatics crashing the chains of their manacled hands into the stunned faces. Shots rang out, three prisoners fell, writhing on the ground. The firing squad raised its rifles.

'Now, you mother-lovin' catfish hunters!' shouted Johnny Reb, as the Scharhörn unit, as one, raced into the mêlée, pistols firing, muted spits mingling with the ear-shattering explosions of the unsilenced weapons.

It was over in less than twenty seconds. The ten men of Aquitaine lay on the ground. Six were dead, three wounded, one on his knees trembling in fear. Two men of the Scharhörn unit sustained minor wounds – the American pilot and one other.

'*Connal!*' roared Joel, racing about the scattered prisoners, relieved that most were moving. '*Fitzpatrick!* Where the hell *are* you?'

'Over here, Lieutenant,' said a weak voice on Converse's right. Joel threaded his way through the fallen bodies and knelt down beside the frail, bearded Navy lawyer. 'You took your sweet time getting here,' continued the commander. 'But then junior grade officers usually have deficiencies.'

'What *happened* back there?' asked Converse. 'You could all have been killed!'

'That was the point, wasn't it? It was made clear to us last night so we figured what the hell?'

'But why *you*! Why *all* of you?'

'We talked and we couldn't figure it out. Except one thing – we were all senior officers on thirty- to forty-day leaves, most of them summer leaves. What did it mean?'

'It was meant to throw people off if they began to see a pattern. There are ninety-seven men out in hit teams – all on summer leaves. Numerically you were nearly fifty per cent of that number, presumably above suspicion. You were a bonus and it saved your life.'

Suddenly, Connal whipped his head to the left. A man was running out of building 5, racing down the concrete path. 'That's the warden!' shouted Fitzpatrick as loud as he could. '*Stop him*! If he gets into the second barracks he'll blow the place up!'

Joel got to his feet and started after the racing figure as fast as his painful legs would carry him, his gun in his hand. The man had reached the mid-point of building 3; he had less than thirty yards to go to the door of 2. Converse fired; the bullet was way off its mark, ricocheting off a steel window frame. The man reached the door, smashing it open and slamming it shut. Joel raced into it crashing the full weight of his body into the heavy wood. It gave way, swinging violently back into the wall. The man was running to a metal-encased panel; Converse fired wildly, frantically, again and again. The man spun, wounded in the legs, the panel open. He reached up for a bank of switches. Joel lunged, gripping the man's hand, smashing his head into the stone floor.

Gasping for breath, Converse crawled away from the man, his hands covered with warm blood, his empty pistol on the floor. One of the Scharhörn team burst through the door.

'Are you fine?' he asked in an accent Joel could not place.

'Splendid,' said Converse, feeling weak and sick.

The hired man walked past Joel, glancing at the still figure on the floor on his way to the open panel. He studied it and reached into his pocket for some kind of small, multifaceted tool. In seconds, he was taking out screws and pulling off the interior metal plating. Moments later, with another part of the instrument, he was cutting wires far back into their receptacles, leaving nothing but stubs of copper.

'You are not to worry,' said the man, finished. 'I am best of Norwegian demolitions. Now we do not concern ourselves that a stray pig can do damage. Come, there is much work left to do.'

The team member stopped and stood above Converse. 'We owe you our lives. We will pay.'

'It's not necessary,' said Joel, getting up.

'It is the custom,' replied the man, heading for the door.

Out on the parade ground, Aquitaine's prisoners were sitting up against the wall – all but five whose bodies were covered with sheets, apparently obtained from one of the buildings. Converse went over to Fitzpatrick.

'We lost them,' said the naval officer, no strength in his voice, only sorrow.

'Look to the things you believe in, Connal,' said Joel. 'It may sound banal, but it's the only thing I can think of to say.'

'It's good enough.' Fitzpatrick looked up, a wan smile on his lips. 'Thanks for reminding me. Go on. They need you over there.'

'*Larson!*' shouted Johnny Reb, standing over the trembling, unhurt guard. 'Get in here!'

The professorial Englishman walked hesitantly through the steel door at the base of the airstrip into the floodlights. He came over to The Rebel, his eyes wandering about the parade ground, his expression one of awe and consternation. 'Good *God!*' he uttered.

'I guess that says it,' said the Southerner, as two members of the Scharhörn team came running out of building 5. 'What'd you *find?*' yelled Johnny Reb.

'Seven others!' shouted one of the men. 'They're in a toilet which is an appropriate place.'

'I *say!*' said Geoffrey Larson, raising his voice. 'Would any by chance be the computer chap?'

'We did not ask, *Mein Herr!*'

'Go *ask!*' ordered The Rebel. 'Time's run out!' He turned to Converse. 'I've been in touch with your lady. The word out of Israel and Rome is downright awful – some of the hit teams eluded Stone's men. The demonstrations began an hour ago and already twelve government people have been killed. In Jerusalem and Tel Aviv they're screaming for Abrahms to take over. In Rome the police can't handle the riots and the panic; the army's moved in.'

Joel felt the sharp, hollow pain in his lower chest and for the first time noticed the early light in the sky beyond the walls. The day had come, and so had the killing. Everywhere. 'Oh, *Jesus*,' he said, feeling helpless.

'The computer, *boy*!' roared Johnny Reb, his pistol jammed into the temple of the guard beneath him. 'You don't have any choices left, *catfish*!'

'*Baracke vier*!'

'*Danke*! It's in building 4. Come on, Brit, let's *go*! *Move*!'

The enormous, glistening machine stood in an air-filtered room, covering the length of the 15-foot wall. Larson spent nine agonizing minutes studying it, turning dials, punching the keyboard and flipping switches on the console, Joel's notepad in front of him. Finally he announced, 'There's a lock on the inner reels. They can't be released without an access code.'

'What in *goddamned catfish hell* are you talkin' about?!' screamed The Rebel.

'There's a pre-designed set of symbols that when inserted releases the springs that permit the locked reels to be activated. It's why I asked if there was a computer man about.'

Johnny Reb's radio hummed and Converse grabbed it, ripping it off the Southerner's velcroed chest.

'*Val*?'

'*Darling*! You're all right?'

'Yes. What's happening?'

'Radio-France. Bombs set off in the Elysée Palace. Two deputies were shot riding to the dawn rallies. The government's calling in the armed forces.'

'*Christ! Out!*'

A man was brought into the room by two members of the Scharhörn team, who were gripping him by the arms. 'He did not care to admit his function,' said the hired gun on the left. 'But when all were against the wall, the others were not so secretive.'

The Rebel went to the man, grabbing him by the throat, but Joel rushed forward, pushing the Southerner aside, the hunting knife in his hand.

'I've been through a lot because of you bastards,' he said, raising the bloodstained blade to the man's nose. 'And now it's the *end*!' He shoved the point into the man's nostrils; the computer expert screamed as blood erupted, streaming downward. Then Converse raised the blade again, the point now in the corner of the man's right eye. 'The codes, or it goes in!' he roared.

'*Zwei, eins, null, fünf*!' Again the technician screamed.

'Process it!' yelled Joel.

'They're *free*!' said the Englishman.

'Now the *symbols*!' cried Converse, shoving the man back into the hands of the Scharhörn hornets.

They all looked in astonishment at the green letters on the black television screen. Name after name, rank after rank, position after position. Larson had punched the print-out button and the curling, unending ream of paper spewed out with hundreds of identities.

'It won't do any good!' shouted Joel. 'We can't get them *out*!'

'Don't be so antediluvian, old chap,' said the Englishman, pointing to a strange-looking telephone recessed in the console. 'This is splendid equipment. There are those lovely satellites in the sky and I can send this to anyone anywhere with compatible machinery. This is the age of technology, no longer Aquarius.'

'Get it *out*,' said Converse, his back against the wall, sliding down to the floor in exhaustion.

The world watched, stunned by the eruption of widespread assassinations and random homicidal violence. Everywhere people cried out for protection, for leadership, for an end to the savagery that had turned whole cities into battlegrounds as panicked, polarized groups of citizens hurled rocks and gas and finally bullets at one another because bullets were being fired at them. Few could tell who their enemies were, therefore anyone who attacked was an enemy and the attackers were everywhere, the orders issued from unseen, unmarked command posts. The police were helpless; then militias and state troops appeared but it was soon evident that they and their leaders were inadequate. The chaos was out of control; stronger measures would have to be implemented. Martial law was pronounced. Everywhere. And military commanders would assume control. *Everywhere.*

In Palo Alto, California, former general of the army, George Marcus Delavane, sat strapped to his wheelchair, watching the recorded hysteria erupting from three television sets. The set on the left went blank, preceded by the screams of a mobile crew as their truck came under sudden attack, the entire unit blown up by grenades. On the centre screen, a woman newscaster was weeping, her barely controlled voice angry, tears of tragedy and outrage streaming down her face as she read the reports of wholesale destruction and wanton murder. The screen on the right showed a Marine colonel being interviewed on a barricaded street in New York's financial district. His .45 Marine issue Colt automatic was in his hand as he tried to answer questions while shouting orders to his subordinates. The screen on the left pulsated with new light, as a familiar anchorman came into focus, his voice numbed, his eyes glassy. He started to speak, but could not; he pivoted in his chair and vomited as the camera swung away to an unsuspecting newsroom editor screaming into a phone. 'Goddamned shit-*bastards*! What the fuck *happened?*' He, too, wept, as the woman in the centre screen was weeping; he pounded the desk with his fist, finally collapsing, his head in his arms, his body in spasms as the screen again went dark.

A slow smile emerged on Delavane's lips. Abruptly he reached for two remote controls, switching off the sets on the right and left, as he concentrated on the centre screen. A helmeted army lieutenant general was picked up by the camera as he strode into a press room somewhere in Washington. The soldier removed his helmet, went to a lectern, and spoke harshly into the microphone.

'We have sealed off all roads leading to Washington and my words are to serve as a warning to unauthorized personnel and civilians everywhere! Any attempts to cross the check points will be met by immediate force. My orders are brief and clear. Shoot to kill. My authority is derived by the emergency powers just granted to me by the Speaker of the House in the absence of the President and the Vice President who have been flown out of the capital for security purposes. The military is now in charge, the Army its spokesman, and martial law is in full effect until further notice.'

Delavane snapped off the set with a gesture of triumph. 'We *did* it, Paul!' he said, turning to his uniformed aide who stood next to the fragmented map on the wall. 'Not even the whining pacifists want that law reversed! And if they *do* . . .' The general of Aquitaine raised his right hand, his index finger extended, thumb upright, and mimed a series of pistol shots.

'Yes, it's done,' agreed the aide reaching down to Delavane's desk and opening a drawer.

'What are you doing?'

'I'm sorry, General. This also must be done.' The aide pulled out a .357 Magnum revolver.

Before he could raise it, however, Delavane's left hand shot up out of the inside cushion of the wheelchair. In it was a short-barrelled automatic. He shouted as he fired four times in rapid succession.

'You think I haven't been *waiting* for this? Scum! Coward! *Traitor!* You think I trust *any* of you? The way you *look at me!* The way you talk in whispers in the hallways! None of you can stand the fact that *without* legs I'm better than *all* of you! Now you know, scum! And soon the others will know because they'll be shot! Executed for treason against the founder of Aquitaine! . . . You think any of you are worth trusting? You've all tried to be what I am and you *can't do it!*'

The uniformed aide had crashed back into the wall, into the fragmented map. Gasping, blood flowing from his neck, his wide eyes stared at the raving general. From some inner core of strength he raised the powerful Magnum and fired once as he collapsed.

George Marcus Delavane was blown across the room, a massive haemorrhage in his chest, as the wheelchair spun and fell on its side, its strapped-in passenger dead.

No one knew when it started to happen, but gradually, miraculously, the gunfire slowly began to diminish. It was accompanied by squads of uniformed men, many units having broken away from their commanders, racing through the streets and buildings, confronting other men. It was soldier against soldier, the eyes of the interrogators filled with anger and disgust, staring at faces consumed with arrogance and defiance. The commanders of Aquitaine were adamant. They were *right!* Could not their inferiors *understand?* In many cases lives were lost by refusals to surrender and by biting into cyanide capsules.

In Palo Alto, California, a legless legend named George Marcus was found shot to death, but apparently not before he had been able to kill his assailant, an obscure army colonel. No one knew what had happened. In southern France, the bodies of two other legendary heroes were found in a mountain ravine; each of whom, upon leaving a château in the Alps, had been given a weapon with his clothing. Generals Bertholdier and Leifhelm had lost. General Chaim Abrahms disappeared. On military bases throughout the Middle East, all Europe, Great Britain, Canada and the United

States, officers of high rank and responsibilities were challenged by subordinates with levelled weapons. *Were they members of an organization called
Aquitaine? Their names were on a list! Answer!* In Norfolk, Virginia, an admiral
named Scanlon threw himself out of a sixth-storey window; and in San
Diego, California, another admiral named Hickman was ordered to arrest a
4-striper who lived in La Jolla – the charge: murder of a legal officer in the
hills above that elegant suburb. Colonel Alan Metcalf personally made the
call to the Chief Operations Officer of Nellis Air Force Base; the order was
blunt – throw into a maximum security cell the major who was in charge of
all aircraft maintenance. In Washington, a venerated senator of Italian
descent was called out of the cloakroom by a Captain Guardino of Army G-
2 and taken away; while over at State and the Pentagon, eleven men in
armaments controls and procurements were placed under guard.

In Tel Aviv, Israeli Army Intelligence rounded up twenty-three aides and
fellow officers of General Chaim Abrahms, as well as one of the Mossad's
most brilliant analysts. In Paris, thirty-one associates – military and non-
military – of General Jacques Louis Bertholdier, including deputy directors
of both the *Sûreté* and Interpol, were held in isolation, and in Bonn no fewer
than fifty-seven colleagues of General Erich Leifhelm, among them former
Wehrmacht commanders and current officers of the Federal Republic's Army
and its Luftwaffe, were seized. Also in Bonn, the Marine Corps Guard at
the American Embassy, on orders from the State Department, arrested four
attachés including the military *chargé d'affaires*, Major Norman Anthony
Washburn, IV.

And so it went on. Everywhere. The fever of madness that was Aquitaine
was broken by legions of the very military the Generals assumed would
carry them to absolute global power. By nightfall the guns were still and
people began to come out from behind their barricades – from cellars,
subways, boarded-up buildings, railroad yards, wherever sanctuary could
be found. They wandered out on the streets, numbed, bewildered, wondering
.what had happened, as trucks with loudspeakers roamed the cities everywhere telling the citizens that the crisis was over. In Tel Aviv, Rome, Paris,
Bonn, London, and across the Atlantic in Toronto, New York, Washington
and points west, the lights were turned on but certainly the world had not
returned to normal. A terrible force had struck in the midst of a universal
cry for peace. What was it? What had *happened*?

It would be explained on the following day, blared the sound trucks in a
dozen different languages, pleading for patience on the part of citizens
everywhere. The hour chosen was 3.00 p.m. Greenwich Mean Time; 10.00
a.m. Washington; 7.00 a.m. Los Angeles. Throughout the night and the
morning hours in all the time zones, heads of state conferred over telephones
until the texts of all the statements were essentially the same. At 10.03 a.m.
the President of the United States went on the air.

'Yesterday an unprecedented wave of violence swept through the Free
 World taking lives, paralysing governments, creating a climate of terror
 that very nearly cost free nations everywhere their freedom and might
 have led them to look for solutions where no solutions should be sought in
 democratic societies – namely turning ourselves into police-states, handing

over controls to men who would subjugate free people to their collective will. It was an organized conspiracy led by demented and deluded men who sought power for its own sake, willing even to sacrifice their own fellow conspirators to achieve it, and to deceive others who were seduced into believing it was the way of the future, the answer to the serious ills of the world. It is not, nor can it ever be.

'As the days and weeks go by – as this terrible thing is put behind us – the facts will be placed before you. For this has been our warning, the toll taken in blood and in the shaken confidence of our institutions. I remind you, however, that our institutions have prevailed. They will prevail.

'In an hour from now a series of meetings will start taking place involving the White House, the Departments of State and Defense, the majority and minority leaders of the House and the Senate, and the National Security Council. Beginning tomorrow, in concert with other governments, reports will be issued on a daily basis until all the facts are before you.

'The nightmare is over. Let the sunlight of truth guide us and clear away the darkness.'

On the following morning, Deputy Director Peter Stone of the Central Intelligence Agency, accompanied by Captain Howard Packard and Lieutenant William Landis, were brought to the Oval Office for a private ceremony. The specific honours awarded them were never made public as there was no reason to do so. Each man, with deep respect and gratitude – but with no regrets – declined to accept, each stating that whatever honours were involved belonged to a man not currently residing in the United States.

A week later, in Los Angeles, California, an actor named Caleb Dowling stunned the producers of a television show called *Santa Fe* by giving them his notice – effective before the start of the new season. He refused all inducements, claiming simply that there was not enough time to spend with his wife. They were going to travel. Alone. And if the residuals ever ran out, hell, she could always type and he could always teach. Together. *Ciao, friends.*

Epilogue

Geneva. City of bright reflections and inconstancy.

Joel and Valerie Converse sat at the table where it all began, by the glistening brass railing in the *Chat Botté*. The traffic on the lakeside Quai du Mont Blanc was disciplined, unhurried – purpose mixed with civility. As the pedestrians passed by, both were aware of the glances directed at Joel. *There he is*, the eyes were saying. *There is . . . the man*. It was rumoured he was living in Geneva, at least for a while.

By agreement, the second report issued across the Free World made a direct but – on Converse's insistence – brief reference to his role in the tragedy that was Aquitaine. He was exonerated of all charges. The labels were removed and refuted, the debt to him acknowledged without specifics on the basis of NATO security. He refused all interviews although the media dredged up his experiences in South-east Asia, speculating on correlations to the drama of the generals. He was consoled by the fact that as the interest in him had dwindled years ago, it would do so again – faster in Geneva, city of purpose.

They had leased a house on the lake, an artist's house with a studio built on the slope leading to the water, the skylight catching the sun from early morning to dusk. The beach house in Cape Ann was closed, the lease paid in full and returned to the realtor in Boston. Val's friend and neighbour had packed her clothes and all her paints, brushes and favourite easel, sending everything air freight to Geneva. Valerie worked for several hours each morning, happier than she had ever been in her life, permitting her husband to evaluate her progress daily. He judged it to be eminently acceptable, wondering out loud whether there was a market for 'lakescapes' as opposed to seascapes. It took him two days to remove the last dabs of paint from his hair.

Nor was Joel without employment; he was Talbot, Brooks and Simon's European branch all by himself. The income, itself, however, was not a vital factor, as Converse never remotely considered himself in the mould of those attorneys in films and on television who rarely if ever collected fees. Since his legal talents had been called upon for crucial evidence, he billed the major governments a reasonable $400,000 apiece; the minor ones, $250,000. No one argued. The total came to something over $2.5 million, safely deposited in an interest-bearing Swiss account.

'What are you thinking about?' asked Valerie, reaching for his hand.

'About Chaim Abrahms and Derek Belamy. They haven't been found – they're still out there and I wonder if they ever will be found. I hope so, because until they are it really isn't over.'

'It's over, Joel, you've got to believe it. But that's not what I meant. I meant you. How do you feel?'

'I'm not sure. I only knew I had to come here and find out.' He looked into her eyes, and at the cascading dark hair that fell to her shoulders, framing the face he loved so very much. 'Empty, I think. Except for you.'

'No anger? No resentment?'

'Not against Avery, or Stone or any of the others. That's past. They did what they had to do; there wasn't any other way.'

'You're far more generous than I am, my darling.'

'I'm more realistic, that's all. The evidence had to be obtained by penetrating the outside – by an outsider wanting to get inside. The core was too tight, too lethal.'

'I think they were bastards. And cowards.'

'I don't. I think they should all be canonized, immortalized, bronzed and with poems written about them for the ages.'

'That's absolute rubbish! How can you possibly say such a thing?'

Joel again looked into his wife's eyes. 'Because you're here. I'm here. And you're painting lakescapes, not seascapes. And I'm not in New York and you're not in Cape Ann. And I don't have to worry about you, hoping that you're worrying about me.'

'If only there'd been another woman or another man. It would have been easier, so much more logical, darling.'

'There was always you. Only you.'

'Try to get away from me again, Converse.'

'No way, Converse.'

Their hands gripped, unashamed tears in their eyes. The nightmare was over.